Further Praise for
The New Annotated H. P. Lovecraft

"*The New Annotated H. P. Lovecraft*, with its astonishingly informed and detailed notes and photographs, edited by Leslie S. Klinger, is a treasure trove for Lovecraft readers, for whom it will be an essential purchase. A pleasure to peruse, encyclopediac in its information, and deeply sympathetic with its subject."

—Joyce Carol Oates

"Erudite and informed, often playful, just as often dryly funny, Klinger's remarks open up a breathtaking, authoritative, affectionate vision of this cherished but often misunderstood genius of weird fiction."

—Peter Straub, author of *Ghost Story* and
A Dark Matter, and editor of *H. P. Lovecraft: Tales*

"Leslie Klinger's annotated take on Lovecraft scrupulously draws on earlier scholarship while adding new insights of his own. Existing fans will find plenty to savor in this up-to-date compendium, which also serves as a perfect starting point for curious newcomers."

—Peter Cannon, coeditor of
More Annotated H. P. Lovecraft

"A book I have profoundly hoped to see for ages, which gave me many very happy hours—thank you, thank you, thank you, Mr. Klinger and Liveright!"

—Gahan Wilson, author of *Gahan Wilson: Fifty Years of Playboy Cartoons*

"The ultimate guide for the Lovecraftian connoisseur—filled with eldritch lore and blasphemous knowledge you will not find in even the mad Arab's infamous tome."

—Stephen Jones, editor of *Necronomicon:
The Best Weird Tales of H. P. Lovecraft*

THE NEW ANNOTATED

H. P. LOVECRAFT

The New Annotated Dracula
by Bram Stoker, with an introduction by Neil Gaiman,
edited with a preface and notes by Leslie S. Klinger

The Annotated Wind in the Willows
by Kenneth Grahame, with an introduction by Brian Jacques,
edited with a preface and notes by Annie Gauger

The Annotated Peter Pan
by J. M. Barrie, edited with an introduction and notes by Maria Tatar

ALSO BY LESLIE S. KLINGER

⁂ ⁂ ⁂

*The Life and Times of Mr. Sherlock Holmes, John H. Watson, M.D.,
Sir Arthur Conan Doyle, and Other Notable Personages*

"The Date Being—?": A Compendium of Chronological Data
with Andrew Jay Peck

The Sherlock Holmes Reference Library
a ten-volume scholarly edition of the Sherlock Holmes stories

Baker Street Rambles

*Sherlock Holmes, Conan Doyle, & The Bookman: Pastiches, Parodies, Letters,
Columns, and Commentary from America's "Magazine of Literature and Life"
(1895–1933)*
with S. E. Dahlinger

The Grand Game: A Celebration of Sherlockian Scholarship
with Laurie R. King

A Study in Sherlock: Stories Inspired by the Holmes Canon
with Laurie R. King

In the Shadow of Sherlock Holmes: Classic Detective Fiction

In the Shadow of Dracula: Classic Vampire Fiction, 1819–1914
with Jeff Conner

The Annotated Sandman
with Neil Gaiman

Howard Phillips Lovecraft (1890–1937),
pictured here at age forty-four.

THE NEW ANNOTATED

H. P. LOVECRAFT

Howard Phillips Lovecraft

Edited with a Foreword and Notes by

LESLIE S. KLINGER

INTRODUCTION BY ALAN MOORE

Liveright Publishing Corporation

A Division of W. W. Norton & Company

New York London

For information about permission to reproduce selections from this book, write to Permissions, Liveright Publishing Corporation, a division of W. W. Norton & Company, Inc., 500 Fifth Avenue, New York, NY 10110

For information about special discounts for bulk purchases, please contact W. W. Norton Special Sales at specialsales@wwnorton.com or 800-233-4830

Manufacturing by Courier Kendallville
Book design by JAM Design
Production manager: Anna Oler

ISBN 978-0-87140-453-4

Liveright Publishing Corporation
500 Fifth Avenue, New York, N.Y. 10110
www.wwnorton.com

W. W. Norton & Company Ltd.
Castle House, 75/76 Wells Street, London W1T 3QT

1 2 3 4 5 6 7 8 9 0

TO HOWARD PHILLIPS LOVECRAFT

"I am Providence."

Contents

THE STORIES

ADDITIONAL MATERIAL

Introduction

by Alan Moore

With an increasing distance from the twentieth century and concomitant broadening of cultural perspective, the New England poet, author, essayist, and stunningly profuse epistoler Howard Phillips Lovecraft is beginning to emerge as one of that tumultuous period's most critically fascinating and yet enigmatic figures. Lovecraft is intriguing for not only the rich substrate of astonishing and sometimes prescient ideas that is the bedrock of his work, but for the sheer unlikelihood of his ascent into the ranks of the respected U.S. literary canon: Progeny of mentally ill parents and product of an estranging cloistered upbringing, he wrote a scant few dozen short tales and some longer pieces that were published only in sensational and stigmatized pulp magazines during his lifetime, if indeed they were published at all. After his 1937 death, the earliest mainstream response was typified by critic Edmund Wilson's withering dismissal, and even those parties most responsible for keeping Lovecraft's name alive would often only do so by (perhaps unwittingly) misrepresenting Lovecraft's fiction, his philosophy, and his essential nature as a human being. Furthermore, acceptance of his output as substantial literature has undeniably been hindered by his problematic stance on most contemporary issues, with his racism, alleged misogyny, class prejudice, dislike of homosexuality, and anti-Semitism needing to be both acknowledged and addressed before a serious appraisal of his work could be commenced. Such is the mesmerizing power of Lovecraft's language and imagination that despite these obstacles he is today revered to a degree comparable with that of his formative idol Edgar Allan Poe, a posthumous trajectory from pulp to academia that is perhaps unique in modern letters.

As for Lovecraft's status as enigma, while this is implied by the perpetually expanding sphere of critical attention that attempts to penetrate his complex worldview and unusual persona, surely the real mystery lies in our continuing capacity to find him and his work mysterious. He lived for only forty-six years during an unusually well-documented period of recent history and in addition saw fit to record his daily doings, thoughts, and observations for the greater part of that short lifespan in a multitude of letters, possibly a hundred thousand such, according to some estimates, some running to extraordinary lengths and a great many of them archived or preserved in print. With even the minutiae of his dreams available; with structuralist, poststructuralist, and psychological analyses of his most juvenile or marginal material proliferating by the day, how can there be a molecule of H. P. Lovecraft's world or circumstance or psyche that remains to be examined? What is the source of our enduring curiosity regarding this unworldly and aggressively old-fashioned individual?

Born in 1890, with his first great rush of literary productivity occurring in the roaring, emblematic year of 1920, Lovecraft came of age in an America yet to cohere as a society, much less as an emergent global superpower, and still beset by a wide plethora of terrors and anxieties. The twenty years since the beginning of the century had seen the largest influx of migrants and refugees that the immigrant-founded nation had heretofore experienced, bringing with them fears that the established European settler stock might soon be overwhelmed by sprawling foreign populations or diluted by pernicious interbreeding and miscegenation. On the streets of Harlem, Greenwich Village, Times Square, and the Bowery in New York, a novel populace of highly visible and unapologetically flamboyant homosexual men (and women, albeit less noticeably) were establishing themselves, much to the consternation of the city's moral arbiters. This was the year when women's suffrage would be finally achieved—a period of industrial unrest and widespread strikes that seemed all the more worrying in the wake of Russia's only recently concluded revolution. All of these prevailing fears, afflicting an extremely broad swath of conventional American society, would find expression in the writing and the ideology of H. P. Lovecraft. However, Lovecraft's intellect and omnivorous reading habits meant that he was capable of understanding and experiencing a still wider spectrum of unease than the beleaguered average citizen. Contemporaneous advances in humanity's expanding comprehension of the universe with its immeasurable distances and its indifferent random processes had redefined, dramatically, mankind's position in the cosmos. Far from being the whole point and purpose of creation, human life became a motiveless and accidental outbreak on a vanishingly tiny fleck of matter situated in the furthest corner of a stupefying swarm of stars, itself but one of many such swarms strewn in incoherent disarray across black vastness inconceivable. These possibly more rarefied yet more unsettling and fundamental phobias would also be articulated in the work of the Rhode Island visionary, as his pantheon of mindless or chaotic cosmic powers or in his much-loved everyday New England landscape altered and infected by conceptions from beyond.

In this light, it is possible to perceive Howard Lovecraft as an almost unbearably sensitive barometer of American dread. Far from outlandish eccentricities, the fears that generated Lovecraft's stories and opinions were precisely those of the white, middle-class, heterosexual, Protestant-descended males who were most threatened by the shifting power relationships and values of the modern world. Though he may have regarded himself, in accordance with the view held of him by his readership and even those that knew him personally, as an embodiment of his most emblematic fable, "The Outsider," in his frights and panics he reveals himself as that almost unheard-of fluke statistical phenomenon, the absolutely average man, an entrenched social *insider* unnerved by new and alien influences from without. This, it might be suggested, is the underlying reason for our ongoing absorption in his work, a fascination that seems only to increase as Lovecraft and his times recede into the past: In H. P. Lovecraft's tales, we are afforded an oblique and yet unsettlingly perceptive view into the haunted origins of the fraught modern world and its attendant mind-set that we presently inhabit. Coded in an alphabet of monsters, Lovecraft's writings offer a potential key to understanding our current dilemma, although crucial to this is that they are understood in the full context of the place and times from which they blossomed.

This, by a circuitous route, brings us to Leslie S. Klinger's *The New Annotated H. P. Lovecraft*. In the previously mentioned rapidly dilating sphere of Lovecraft scholarship, it would appear that Mr. Klinger has succeeded admirably in the unenviable effort of appending Lovecraft's oeuvre in a manner that is not redundant or repetitive, but rather complementary to the body of existing commentary. Even more notably, the welcome strategy of focusing upon the sociohistoric references in Lovecraft's narratives—casually mentioned items or events the full import of which might easily escape the reader of today—allows us to locate this hard-to-categorize author in the context of the era that engendered him, assisted by the text's profusion of illuminating photographic reference. If, as maintained above, an understanding of his fiction is not possible without consideration of the societal landscape that surrounded him, such an approach is surely necessary.

In addition to this careful referencing of the gentleman from Providence's times and circumstances, Mr. Klinger understands the need to study Lovecraft's work through the variety of fine-ground lenses that are now available to us by way of modern Lovecraft criticism. To this end, besides its clarifying commentary on the narratives included here, in *The New Annotated H. P. Lovecraft* we are offered a wide sampling of the latest literary theory as pertaining to the writer and his end-lessly engrossing world of fiction. In effect, the reader is permitted to explore even the most familiar story in a new way, the dense prose and myriad associations skilfully unpacked to conjure details of a bygone artifact or attitude, the differing critical perceptions proffering an opportunity to view the same tales and same words from multiple perspectives. Given the intensity of thought, originality, and effort behind even Lovecraft's simplest pieces, it is perhaps unsurprising that there turned out to be so much to unpack, and yet this only makes what Leslie Klinger has accomplished more impressive.

Painfully acute, Howard Phillips Lovecraft flourished in the two decades between world wars and wrote of his disquiet at what he saw as the most likely future, with the species overwhelmed by its own exponentially accumulating knowledge of itself and of the vast and alien universe about it, fleeing to the reas-suring shadow of a new Dark Ages. As our world increasingly comes to resemble Lovecraft's anxious speculations, the importance of this long-neglected pulp pur-veyor of the weird and the unnameable becomes more evident, more unmistak-able. In his attempts to ground the awesome realms of cosmic speculation in the soil and streets and gambrel roofs of his immediate locality, there may conceivably exist a key to many of our present psychosocial dilemmas, although finding this depends on our ability to view both the man and his environment in the round. In *The New Annotated H. P. Lovecraft*, Leslie Klinger has compiled what may be our best means to date of doing so. Acknowledging the exemplary biographical and critical advances made by Messrs. Joshi, Cannon, Waugh, and their confederates, this volume correlates their insights into its richly presented tapestry of Lovecraft's best New England stories and, perhaps even more importantly, into the almost-lost America of the last century, in which those stories were created. Whether for that lucky reader venturing into the tempting undergrowth of Lovecraft's prose for the first time or the more seasoned Elder God enthusiast, this necessary volume guar-antees new insights and a new experience of possibly the most important author of weird fiction that the world has ever seen. An eldritch triumph.

Foreword

by Leslie S. Klinger

. . . engulfed in the infinite immensity of spaces whereof I know nothing, and which know nothing of me, I am terrified. The eternal silence of these infinite spaces fills me with dread.

—BLAISE PASCAL[1]

It is man's relation to the cosmos—to the unknown—which alone arouses in me the spark of creative imagination. . . .

—H. P. LOVECRAFT[2]

The American author Joyce Carol Oates describes two writers as having "had an incalculable influence on succeeding generations of writers of horror fiction."[3] One is Edgar Allan Poe, who achieved only moderate success during his lifetime and died in 1849, virtually penniless, at age forty. The other is Howard Phillips Lovecraft (1890–1937), whose stories appeared primarily in the "pulp" magazines, known only to the cult of their readers, with only one published in book form before his death. Poe is now credited with inventing the detective tale as well as with perfecting the gothic story; Lovecraft fused the gothic story with science and a realism never before attempted. Yet Poe is renowned, read by virtually every schoolchild, while Lovecraft until recently was poorly known except to readers and students of the fantastic.

1. French mathematician and philosopher Blaise Pascal (1623–1662), from his *Pensées* (published posthumously in 1670). Pascal was speaking of the actual immensity of space, as discovered by contemporary astronomers, not merely mathematical infinities.

2. This is from the second part of the essay usually named "In Defense of Dagon," although this part of the essay, published separately, bore the title "The Defence Remains Open!"; written in April 1921, it was reprinted in *In Defense of Dagon*.

3. Joyce Carol Oates, "The King of Weird."

WHAT CAME BEFORE

HORROR HAS BEEN part of oral and recorded stories of humanity from the beginning.[4] Stories designed to elucidate the mysterious worlds of dreams, explain the supernatural, and assuage humans' fear of pain and death have a prominent place in literature. Homer's epic poem *The Odyssey*, for example, records Odysseus's confrontations with several witches, including Circe. Ancient Greek myths tell the story of Queen Lamia, who was turned by Zeus's wife, Hera, into a child-eating monster. In later versions, Greek writers depict various forms of vampires, chiefly the cunning and murderous lamiae. Phlegon of Tralles (ca. 117–138 CE) wrote in his *Book of Marvels* of Philinium, a woman who returns from the grave to sleep with a young man, Machates.[5] Originally a demigoddess, Empusa, reincarnated as a shape-shifting monster or specter, appears—in guises ranging from a bull to a beautiful young woman to a figure of indeterminate origin, one of whose legs is made of excrement—in Aristophanes' comic play *The Frogs* (ca. 405 BCE), set in Hades. Flavius Philostratus's *Life of Apollonius of Tyana* (ca. 200 CE) tells of a near-fatal relationship involving Menippus, a handsome youth who falls in love with the apparition of a "Phoenician woman." When challenged, the phantom confesses that she is a vampire.

Fascination with the supernatural can be found in Judeo-Christian sources as well as in pagan myths and literature. The Old Testament (1 Samuel 28:3–25) records Saul's consultation with the Witch of Endor, a medium who calls up a spirit

4. In his essay "Supernatural Horror in Literature," first published in 1927 in the amateur journal *The Recluse*, Lovecraft himself contributed an overview of the genre that so absorbed him. It was serialized in another amateur magazine, *The Fantasy Fan*, beginning in October 1933, with new material added. There were previous studies of the field—notably, Dorothy Scarborough's *The Supernatural in Modern English Fiction* (1917), Edith Birkhead's *The Tale of Terror** (1921) and, later, Eino Railo's *The Haunted Castle* (1927)—but these essentially ignored writers after Poe. Lovecraft took almost a year and a half to complete the essay. Since 1933, many, many other guides, studies, and encyclopedias have covered the field. S. T. Joshi has penned a two-volume study entitled *Unutterable Horror: A History of Supernatural Fiction* (2012). Joshi's useful bibliography surveys the similar work of others, such as Les Daniel's *Living in Fear: A History of Horror in the Mass Media* (1975), but not all of his judgments are approving—for example, he states, "I do not find much value" in David Punter's two-volume *The Literature of Terror* (1980, rev. 1996).

Lovecraft's library—books he is known to have possessed at some time in his life—is painstakingly catalogued in *Lovecraft's Library: A Catalogue* by S. T. Joshi (2002), and works or bodies of work mentioned here that are included there are marked in this foreword thus: *. The same symbol appears after the name of writers whose work Lovecraft collected.

5. See Augustine Calmet, *The Phantom World; or, the Philosophy of Spirits, Apparitions, &c.*, vol. 2, 22–23, 28.

whom Saul identifies as the prophet Samuel. The Roman satirist and philosopher Lucius Apuleius, in *The Golden Ass** (translated into English in 1566), tells of a narrator, absorbed by magic, who meets or learns of witches, sorcerers, and a vampiric creature. The Norse Eddas and early Anglo-Saxon works like *Beowulf* are filled with horrific tales of monsters and shape-shifting men (werebeasts). Chaucer and Shakespeare knew the prevailing traditions of the supernatural, and their works include tales of tregetours (illusionists), ghosts, fiends, enchantresses, and witches, as does Malory's *Morte d'Arthur* (still studied at universities) and the plays of Marlowe and Webster, both of whom gave major roles to the devil.

The Renaissance polymath Niccolò Machiavelli wrote a novel-length story about an archdemon called Belphagor (or Belfagor). In the late seventeenth century and early eighteenth century, the popular English writer Daniel Defoe, best known for *Robinson Crusoe*, penned a number of stories that are today classed as horror tales.

However, stories of horror as we know them emerged in the late eighteenth century. Horace Walpole's *Castle of Otranto** (1764) initiated the genre that became known as the gothic horror or gothic romance. Walpole sought to bring together medieval notions of the supernatural and the realism of the contemporary novel. Above all, he aimed to create an atmosphere of terror, a world in which the totally unexpected could happen: A giant helmet falls from the heavens, crushing Conrad, the infirm son of the book's villain, Manfred, on his wedding day; immense limbs appear within the castle itself; mysterious blood flows; and a hodgepodge of bogeymen wander in and out of the tale.

The immense success of Walpole's novel, which he wrote under a pseudonym and passed off as drawn from historical records, led to others exploring the genre. In 1777, Clara Reeve published an anonymous work originally titled *The Champion of Virtue;** it was retitled *The Old English Baron* in 1778. The author shamelessly termed it the "literary offspring" of *Otranto*, and the public embraced it with the same fervor as it had Walpole's melodrama. Although it was similar in style to *Otranto*, Reeve attempted to inject more realism, avoiding some of the absurdities of Walpole.

The work of the better-known Ann Radcliffe combined romantic descriptions of place, love stories, and inexplicable gothic terrors and was immensely popular through most of the nineteenth century. Radcliffe's six novels, most notably *The Mysteries of Udolpho** (1794)—parodied brilliantly by Jane Austen in *Northanger Abbey* (published in 1817, although likely written in the period from 1798 to 1799)—all focused on young heroines confronted with mysterious castles and even more mysterious nobles. Matthew Gregory Lewis's *The Monk** (1796), of which Coleridge famously remarked that "if a parent saw [it] in the hands of a son or daughter, he

Wm Cole 1765.

THE

CASTLE of OTRANTO,

A

STORY.

Translated by

WILLIAM MARSHAL, Gent.

From the Original ITALIAN of

ONUPHRIO MURALTO,

CANON of the Church of St. NICHOLAS
at OTRANTO.

wrote by the honble Horace Walpole Esqr.

LONDON:

Printed for THO. LOWNDS in Fleet-Street.
MDCCLXV.

Title page from *The Castle of Otranto* by Horace Walpole, showing the fictional author
Onuphrio Muralto and Walpole's pseudonym Walter Marshal.

might reasonably turn pale,"[6] is said to have provided, in the physical description of Ambrosio, the titular monk, the basis for Bram Stoker's Count Dracula. An admirer of the work of Ann Radcliffe, Sir Walter Scott* included many horrific folktales, notably the portion of *Redgauntlet* known as "Wandering Willie's Tale," or "The Feast of Redgauntlet" (1824), in his immense output in the early years of the nineteenth century.

Nor was the newly founded American nation a stranger to horror literature. Washington Irving penned tales focusing on regional supernatural phenomena,* among them "The Legend of Sleepy Hollow" and "Rip Van Winkle" (both appearing in 1820). Although his psychological tales of New England are the works that brought him fame, Nathaniel Hawthorne was also fascinated by strange stories, and among his numerous tales of the occult, both "Dr. Heidegger's Experiment"* (1837) and the posthumously published *Septimius Felton, or The Elixir of Life* (1871) reflect the author's fascination with the search for immortality.

The gothic novel, or romance, was not limited to English-speaking countries. The French *roman noir* (black novel) and the German *Schauerroman* (literally, "shudder-novel") thrived in their respective nations. The bizarre tales of German writer E. T. A. Hoffmann and Polish nobleman and occultist Jan Potocki were also a part of the tradition, reflected earlier in the horrific tales drawn from folklore collected by the Brothers Grimm and first published in 1812. In general, the work of these continental cousins was generally more violent than that of their English counterparts.

The first stages of the Romantic movement, born in the late years of the eighteenth century, produced twin icons of horror: the "scientific monster" and the vampire. Curiously, both emerged from a single night devoted to the telling of stories of horror. In 1816, Dr. John William Polidori accompanied his friend and patient Lord Byron on a trip to Italy and Switzerland. That summer, they stayed at the Villa Diodati, near Lake Geneva, where they were visited by poet Percy Bysshe Shelley, his wife, Mary, and her stepsister, Jane "Claire" Clairmont. When incessant rain kept the five friends indoors, they began reading aloud a book of ghost tales. According to Mary Shelley, Byron suggested that they each write a ghost story to rival those in the book. Her husband wrote nothing in response to the challenge; Byron started on a story but reportedly abandoned it.

Boris Karloff as the monster, in *Frankenstein* (Universal Studios, 1931).

Mary Shelley's effort became *Frankenstein,** published two years later. The tale of the scientist Victor Frankenstein and his misbegotten creature spawned a number of stage plays, a revised edition

6. Samuel Taylor Coleridge, review of *The Monk*.

in 1831, and eventually countless films, parodies, comic books, radio dramas, and advertising images. Called by some the first science-fiction novel, *Frankenstein* made icons of the mad scientist and the artificially created monster, who subsequently appeared, sometimes separately, sometimes together, in dozens, if not hundreds, of unrelated tales. Seemingly every schoolchild knows the meaning of a staggering walk with outstretched arms; every filmgoer knows the indelible image of a horrific creature sharing a flower with an innocent child. While Shelley's book was more a reverie on moral responsibility than a forecast of science gone wrong, generations read it as the ultimate horror tale, a stern warning about the arrogance of humankind.

Another fruit of that famous summer evening, depicted idiosyncratically in Ken Russell's 1986 film *Gothic*, was John William Polidori's *The Vampyre*, the first popular account of vampirism published in England, in April 1819. Originally heralded as a work of Byron—and then seen as a satire of Byron—the story

Dr. John Polidori, author of *The Vampyre*, by F. G. Gainsford.

recounts the activities of the vampire Lord Ruthven, a nobleman marked by his aloof manner and the "deadly hue of his face, which never gained a warmer tint."[7] As the tale begins, the enigmatic yet strangely compelling Ruthven befriends a gentleman named Aubrey, who finds that even Ruthven's death does not rid him of his deadly companion. When Ruthven returns from death, he rejoins Aubrey, to the latter's horror, and soon attacks and kills Ianthe, the object of Aubrey's affections. Plunged into a breakdown, Aubrey recovers only to find that his beloved sister has also become the victim of the creature, who then vanishes.

Polidori was no great writer, as is evident from the concluding lines of the book: "Lord Ruthven had disappeared, and Aubrey's sister had glutted the thirst of a VAMPYRE!" His is credited as the first of the great vampire tales, however, primarily for its depiction of a *gentleman* vampire—a far remove from the disgusting, blood-sucking corpses detailed in the accounts of vampires written by Calmet and other historians. It was immensely successful; within Polidori's lifetime (he died two years after publication), the work was translated into French, German, Spanish, and Swedish and adapted several times for the stage, playing to horror-struck audiences until the early 1850s.

*Melmoth the Wanderer*** (1820), an early Romantic work admired by Balzac, Baudelaire, and other prominent mid-nineteenth-century French writers, was written by Charles Robert Maturin, an Irish clergyman and the great-uncle of Oscar Wilde. Its protagonist, John Melmoth, has sold his soul to gain 150 extra years of life and wanders the earth searching for someone to take over this contract. The reader learns the scope and sorrow of his wanderings through the accounts of those whom Melmoth begs to relieve him of his pact. Although the book is convoluted, with numerous tales within tales, Melmoth has been compared to Molière's Don Juan, Goethe's Faust, and Byron's Manfred as a great allegorical figure. Lovecraft called the work "an enormous stride in the evolution of the horror-tale."

Title page of *Varney the Vampire,* ca. 1845.

Varney the Vampire, written by James Malcolm Rymer and serialized from 1845 to 1847 in 109 weekly installments in one-cent pulp publications known as "penny dreadfuls," was the first novel-length account of a vampire in English: "Her bosom heaves, and her limbs tremble, yet she cannot withdraw her eyes from that marble-looking face. . . . With a plunge he seizes her neck in his fang-like teeth—a

7. There are numerous texts of *The Vampyre*, which was printed at first without Polidori's involvement and subsequently revised by him several times. D. L. Macdonald and Kathleen Scherf, in *The Vampyre and Ernestus Berchtold; or, The Modern Oedipus: Collected Fiction of John William Polidori*, created a preferred text from Polidori's editing. In later editions, Polidori changed the vampire's name to Lord Strongmore, perhaps to avoid confusion with a real Lord Ruthven.

Edgar Allan Poe. (Edwin Manchester daguerreotype, 1848)

gush of blood, and a hideous sucking noise follows. The girl has swooned, and the vampire is at his hideous repast!" Despite its artistic shortcomings, *Varney* delivers a vivid, monstrous portrait of the undead. The vampire is Sir Francis Varney, born in the seventeenth century, frequently reborn from the dead: a "tall gaunt figure" whose face, similar to Ruthven's, is "perfectly white—perfectly bloodless," with eyes like "polished tin" and "fearful-looking teeth—projecting like those of some wild animal, hideously, glaringly white, and fang-like."

The tales of Edgar Allan Poe* were mid-nineteenth-century milestones on the trail of the horror story and would significantly influence Lovecraft. Beginning in 1835 with "Berenice," a dark tale of a man who becomes obsessed by his lover's teeth, Poe's stories covered the gamut of science fiction, mystery, and horror. In many of his works, Poe strove to create a "single effect" with a tale, focusing on an intense emotional experience. His narrators seem to seek to rejoin

Illustration from first publication of "Carmilla," *Dark Blue*, 1872. (artist: D. H. Friston)

humanity, having been ostracized by an intolerable or inexplicable existence. Poe was widely hailed in Europe, especially after Baudelaire translated his work into French (the translations were published in 1852, 1857, and 1865, after Poe's death), and achieved the dubious distinction of being one of the first American authors to be better regarded abroad than at home. One of his master poems, "The Raven" (1845), and "The Gold Bug" (1843), a puzzle-story, were immensely popular in America, but he earned little from his writing, and his reputation was unsavory; at his death, he was viewed as depraved, alcoholic, and drug-crazed, which indeed in many ways he was. Although Poe's writing had a very strong and early influence on him, Lovecraft later felt himself to be burdened by the weight of Poe's work and reputation, as much of his own early work was deemed Poesque by himself and his friends.[8]

Although Poe's work was the high-water mark of that century, others continued the horror tradition in subsequent years. Among the many fantasy tales written by the Irish writer Joseph Sheridan Le Fanu* is his highly sensitive "Carmilla"

8. Writing to Elizabeth Toldridge on March 15, 1929, he despaired of ever finding his own voice: "There are my 'Poe' pieces & my 'Dunsany' pieces—but alas—where are any *Lovecraft* pieces?" (This passage was mistakenly quoted as "my 'Lovecraft' pieces" in the original edition of *Selected Letters*, II, 315).

Cover of 1916
edition of *Dracula*
(London: William Rider
& Son).

(1872). Building on the works of Polidori and Rymer, it records the history of a female vampire. After a carriage accident, the charming and beautiful Carmilla is taken in by Laura, the narrator, a lonely young woman. Laura experiences terrifying dreams in which a mysterious woman visits her in bed and kisses her neck. Laura discovers that Carmilla is the Countess Mircalla, a vampire. Laura and a band of men exhume Countess Mircalla's body and destroy her by driving a stake through her heart. The work is important as lesbian literature but even more so for its influence on the vampire tale, focusing, as it does, on the emotions and feelings of the vampire as well as those of the victim.

The end of the nineteenth century saw an explosion of outlets for short stories as reading spread among the middle classes and production of magazines became cheaper. This *fin-de-siècle* period produced a number of writers fascinated by horror. Arthur Conan Doyle,* Rudyard Kipling,* Oscar Wilde,* Guy de Maupassant,* Henry James,* and Robert Louis Stevenson* all produced numerous stories in the genre. Lesser-known practitioners include E. F. Benson,* M. P. Shiel,* and—one of Lovecraft's favorites—William Hope Hodgson. The publication, in 1897, of *Dracula*,* however, was a defining event in horror literature as the century came to a close. Bram Stoker—a theater critic, business manager, and writer of romantic fiction and minor stories of fantasy and terror—created in *Dracula* a work so chilling that it set the standard for every subsequent story of creatures of the night. Stoker's later fantastic tales, including *The Jewel of Seven*

Stars (1903), *The Lady of the Shroud* (1909), and *The Lair of the White Worm* (1911), are still read, as are some of the works that benefited from the popularity of *Dracula*, including, for example, Richard Marsh's *The Beetle* (1917) and Sax Rohmer's *Brood of the Witch-Queen* (1918). All of these writers would have been known to Lovecraft, and he publicly expressed his admiration of many.

Among American writers, journalist Ambrose Bierce* (1842–1913), whose short stories Lovecraft called "grim and savage," is best remembered for "An Occurrence at Owl Creek Bridge" (1891)—one of his Civil War tales strangely echoed in Nikos Kazantzakis's novel *The Last Temptation of Christ* (1953) and Martin Scorsese's 1988 film of the novel—and for *The Devil's Dictionary* (1911). While less well known, Bierce's "The Moonlit Road" (1907) is a very powerful ghost story about pas-

Ambrose Bierce, ca. 1866.
(Painting by
J. H. E. Partington, 1893)

sion and revenge, and his visions of horror amid the ordinary had a great influence on Lovecraft.[9]

By the second half of the nineteenth century, the supernatural had become a common element of popular fiction. The following are only a few of the distinctive supernatural writers of the period. F. Marion Crawford* (1854–1909), son of American sculptor Thomas Crawford and brother of writer Anne Crawford (Baroness Erich von Rabe), was born and raised in Italy and wrote many romances, including mystical tales and ghost stories. He is well known for "The Upper Berth" (1885) and "For the Blood Is the Life" (1905), the latter a classic vampiress tale. Robert W. Chambers, before he took up writing romance novels, produced *The King in Yellow** (1895), a series of loosely connected stories about a suppressed book not unlike Lovecraft's *Necronomicon*. Chambers's tale "The Yellow Sign" made a powerful impression on writers like Robert

Robert W. Chambers, 1903.

E. Howard and Clark Ashton Smith, who borrowed from its mythology. Another writer noted by Lovecraft was Mary Eleanor Wilkins Freeman* (1852–1930), who was the product of a strict religious upbringing in Massachusetts. She began writing stories as a teenager to help support her family and quickly achieved success, eventually producing more than three dozen volumes of poetry and novels. She married at fifty, an age at which women were generally considered unmarriageable (in the 1920s, the median age for a woman's first marriage was twenty-one), and continued to work—eventually, at the end of her career, in 1926, becoming the first winner of the William Dean Howells Medal for Distinction in Fiction from the American Academy of Arts and Letters. Lovecraft singled out her story "The Shadows on the Wall" (1902) for praise, and its New England setting must have had a special appeal to him. Charlotte Perkins Gilman, who also published as Charlotte Gilman Stetson (1860–1935), was a prolific author of novels, short stories, and nonfiction, a leading feminist of the day, and the great-niece of Harriet Beecher Stowe, author of *Uncle Tom's Cabin*. She suffered postpartum depression following the birth of her only child, Katharine, which inspired her chilling semiautobiographical tale

9. See James Goho's "The Shape of Darkness: Origins for H. P. Lovecraft within the American Gothic Tradition" for a detailed study of Bierce's influence on Lovecraft.

Arthur Machen, ca. 1905.

Lord Dunsany, probably ca. 1920.

"The Yellow Wall Paper" (1892). A proponent of euthanasia for the terminally ill, Gilman apparently practiced what she preached and committed suicide at the age of seventy-five, three years after receiving a diagnosis of cancer and one year after the death of her second husband. While her outspoken nature and radical lifestyle gave her a special prominence among women, she—like Lovecraft—was ultimately out of step with the times. In particular, her views on sex, racial problems, and immigration, while they may have endeared her to Lovecraft, cost her favor.

It is evident from a review of Lovecraft's library that he read widely in many fields. Certainly, he was well aware of those who came before him, and he openly acknowledged Edgar Allan Poe in particular as his "God of Fiction."[10] Lovecraft's superb essay "Supernatural Horror in Literature"[11] was intended as an objective study of the field but clearly reveals the writers who exerted the greatest influence on his own writing. He named four "modern masters"—Arthur Machen,* Lord Dunsany,* Algernon Blackwood,* and M. R. James*—whose work he greatly admired.[12] Arthur Machen (1863–1947) was a prolific Welsh writer of novels and stories. His work suffered from the fallout surrounding the trial of Oscar Wilde; it was seen as part of the same school of decadent horror, and much of it was not widely published until long

10. Lovecraft to Reinhardt Kleiner, February 2, 1916, *Selected Letters*, II, 20. In a letter to Bernard Austin Dwyer dated March 3, 1927, Lovecraft described his introduction to Poe at the age of eight: "Then I struck EDGAR ALLAN POE!! It was my downfall, and at the age of eight I saw the blue firmament of Argos and Sicily darkened by the miasmal exhalations of the tomb" (*Selected Letters*, II, 109).

11. See note 4, above.

12. The four, plus Ambrose Bierce and Lovecraft himself, are the subjects of S. T. Joshi's fine book-length study *The Weird Tale* (1990).

after. Machen is probably best known for "The Great God Pan" (1890; 1894), which Stephen King called "one of the best horror stories ever written. Maybe the best in the English language."[13] Reminiscent of *Frankenstein* in telling of an experiment gone horribly wrong, the story mixes science and Roman folklore in an inimitable mystery. Lovecraft absorbed Machen's introduction of the supernatural amid the ordinary and the idea that old entities still exist amid humankind.

Another of Lovecraft's "modern masters" was Edward John Moreton Drax Plunkett, 18th Baron of Dunsany, who wrote as Lord Dunsany (1878–1957). Dunsany was a prolific Irish writer of fantastic stories, novels, and plays who published more than sixty books and hundreds of short stories. Today he is probably best remembered for his first collection, *The Gods of Pegāna* (1905)—which described a world unto itself, complete with geography and politics—and *The Book of Wonder* (1912). Dunsany's work, and in particular his inventive mythology, exotic visions, and "crystalline singing prose," in Lovecraft's words, had a profound influence on Lovecraft and on writers as diverse as Robert E. Howard, Clark Ashton Smith, J. R. R. Tolkien, Jorge Luis Borges, Arthur C. Clarke, Neil Gaiman, and Peter S. Beagle. Lovecraft aped Dunsany's style and idolized him to the point of writing embarrassingly unreadable poetry about him.[14]

A writer whose technical abilities dazzled Lovecraft was the English author Algernon Henry Blackwood (1869–1951). Blackwood wrote twelve novels for adults (he also wrote several for children) and more than one hundred weird stories. His most lasting influence is seen in "The Willows" (1907) and "The Wendigo" (1910), both about unseen spirits, and the 1908 *John Silence—Physician Extraordinary* volume, tales about a psychic detective. Lovecraft applauded his unmatched "skill, seriousness, and minute fidelity with which he records the overtones of strangeness in ordinary things and experiences. . . ."[15]

Algernon Blackwood.

Lovecraft also admired Montague Rhodes James (1862–1936), who published as M. R. James. James was an English medieval scholar and provost of Kings College, Cambridge, and is often cited as the greatest ghost-story-teller of the century. The qualities of James's writing that undoubtedly appealed to Lovecraft were his abandonment of the gothic trappings of his predecessors coupled with his free use of the fruits of his passion for antiquarian studies.

M. R. James, depicted on one of the "Britons of Distinction" postage stamps issued by the Royal Post in 2013.

13. Stephen King, "Self-Interview," 10:50 a.m., Sept. 4, 2008, http://stephenking.com/stephens_messages.html.

14. Dunsany's influence is considered in detail in "Lovecraft's Debt to Lord Dunsany," by Darrell Schweitzer.

15. Lovecraft, "Supernatural Horror in Literature."

James's best-known stories are "Count Magnus" and "Lost Hearts," both first published in his collection *Ghost Stories of an Antiquary* (1904); many of his tales have been broadcast on radio, televised, or filmed. James has been cited as influential by Clark Ashton Smith, John Bellairs, Sir John Betjeman, Stephen King, and contemporary horror writer Ramsey Campbell.

While the genre that Lovecraft labeled "supernatural horror" was fairly well established, science fiction or "scientifiction," as editor Hugo Gernsback dubbed it in 1926,[16] was in its infancy when Lovecraft began writing. Brian W. Aldiss, in his monumental *Trillion Year Spree: The History of Science Fiction* (1986), counts Shelley's *Frankenstein* and some of Poe's stories—for example, *The Narrative of Arthur Gordon Pym** (1836), well known to Lovecraft—as its progenitors. Aldiss labels as "honourable ancestors" Thomas More (*Utopia*, 1516); Cyrano de Bergerac (*L'Autre Monde: ou les États et Empires de la Lune* [The Other World: or the States and Empires of the Moon], 1657, and *Les États et Empires du Soleil* [The States and Empires of the Sun], 1662); Margaret Cavendish (*The Blazing World*, 1666); Jonathan Swift (*Gulliver's Travels,** 1726; the author's preferred edition appeared in 1735); and Voltaire* ("Micromégas," 1752).

The first commercial success in the new genre was achieved by Jules Verne* (1828–1905), who claimed that he invented science fiction (though he did not term it as such), and his successes (including, most famously, *Journey to the Center of the Earth*, 1864; *From the Earth to the Moon*, 1865; and *Twenty Thousand Leagues Under the Sea*, 1870) did not go unnoticed. Lovecraft certainly knew that speculative fiction had flourished in the years immediately before his birth, and that among the works that had exerted far-reaching influence were Bulwer-Lytton's *The Coming Race** (1871); *Erewhon*, by Samuel Butler (1872); *Flatland—A Romance of Many Dimensions*, by Edwin A. Abbott (1884); Robert Louis Stevenson's *The Strange Case of Dr. Jekyll and Mr. Hyde* (1886); *A Crystal Age*, by W. H. Hudson (1887); Albert Robida's *War in the Twentieth Century* (1887); and *The Great War in England in 1897* (1893), by William Le Queux. Lovecraft scholar T. R. Livesey[17] points out that several of Lovecraft's stories, notably "The Dunwich Horror" and "The Shadow over Innsmouth," fall squarely in the tradition of the genre of science-fictional accounts of invasions that began with *The Battle of Dorking* (1871), written by George Tomkyns Chesney, a former lieutenant colonel in the Bengal Engineers, and published anonymously.

16. Gernsback, founder and editor of *Amazing Stories*, for which Lovecraft eventually wrote, editorialized in April 1926: "By 'scientifiction' I mean the Jules Verne, H. G. Wells and Edgar Allan Poe type of story—a charming romance intermingled with scientific fact and prophetic vision."

17. Livesey, "Green Storm Rising: Lovecraft's Roots in Invasion Literature."

H. G. Wells, ca. 1920.

Lovecraft's efforts in the new field of science fiction owe a clear debt to Herbert George Wells (1866–1946), who wrote as H. G. Wells. Wells produced more than 120 books, and his first, the one that was to lift science fiction to the heights of literature, was *The Time Machine* (1895). In an age in love with the machine and progress, Wells shared a vision of the earth's future that was pessimistic to an extreme. In *The Time Machine*, the time traveler stands alone at the end of the world: ". . . the world was silent. Silent? It would be hard to convey the stillness of it. All the sounds of man, the bleating of sheep, the cries of birds, the hum of insects, the stir that makes the background of our lives—all that was over."

Wells is best remembered for his shocking *War of the Worlds* (1898); its infamous and convincing 1938 radio dramatization, narrated by Orson Welles, provoked mass hysteria. Wells posited that an ancient race of Martians in need of fresh territories mounted an invasion of Earth by means of ships shot from large guns: "Yet across the gulf of space, minds that are to our minds as ours are to those of the beasts that perish, intellects vast and cool and unsympathetic, regarded this earth with envious eyes, and slowly and surely drew their plans against us." The Martians subjugate the population with heat-rays, the "Black Smoke," and other weapons and roam the landscape at will, only to succumb to infections from bacteria indigenous to Earth. The story of a future war was not original, as mentioned above; nonetheless, the idea that the war would involve combat with extraterrestrial life was new.[18] "The Dunwich Horror" and "The Shadow over Innsmouth," as well as Lovecraft's "The Colour Out of Space" and *At the Mountains of Madness*, may be said to have built on this idea.

In addition to a number of ingenious and compelling short stories, Wells also produced in quick succession such important works as *The Island of Doctor Moreau* (1896), *The Invisible Man* (1897), *When the Sleeper Wakes* (1899), *The First Men in the Moon* (1901), and *The Food of the Gods* (1904). Lovecraft called *The War of the Worlds* a "semi-classic," and Wells's influence on him is readily apparent, particularly with respect to Lovecraft's "cosmicism," which we will explore later.

In his essay "Some Notes on Interplanetary Fiction,"[19] Lovecraft rails,

> Despite the current flood of stories dealing with other worlds and universes, and with intrepid flights to and from them through cosmic space, it is probably no exaggeration to say that not more than a half-dozen of these things, including the novels of H. G. Wells, have even the slightest shadow of a claim to artistic seriousness or literary rank. Insincerity, conventionality, tiredness, artificiality, false emotion, and puerile extravagance reign triumphant throughout this overcrowded genre, so that none but its rarest products can possibly claim a truly adult status.

An 1896 issue of *Argosy*.

For many writers in the dual genres of horror and science fiction, a primary American marketplace for their work was the so-called pulp magazines. Here, Lovecraft was no exception. It appears that he read widely and voraciously in the pulps, though he later concealed this,[20] and virtually all of his stories published during his lifetime that did not appear in amateur publications (and reprints of some that did) were printed in the pulp magazines. The first of these was Frank Munsey's revamped *Argosy Magazine* of 1896. Advances in printing technology had made "dime novels" widely available to readers, but prior to Munsey's *Argosy*,

18. In 1892, an obscure Australian clergyman named Robert Potter published a novel called *The Germ Growers* in London. It reports a secret invasion of Earth by aliens who take on the appearance of human beings and attempt to develop a disease that will wipe out Earth's population. The aliens' methodology is somewhat similar to Wells's "Red Weed," a biological weapon of the Martian invaders, but is ironically inverted in Wells's conclusion. For a brief discussion of some other early works featuring extraterritorial life, see "Beyond the Wall of Sleep," note 12, below.

19. First published in 1935.

20. S. T. Joshi, in his introduction to *H. P. Lovecraft in the Argosy: Collected Correspondence from the Munsey Magazines*, writes, "When we read, in Lovecraft's letter to the *All-Story* for 7 March 1914, that he had 'read every number of your magazine since its beginning in January, 1905,' we are taken aback both by the voluminous amount of early pulp fiction Lovecraft must have already absorbed and by the fact that in later years he would actually conceal this absorption."

no magazine had put affordable entertainment—low-cost, pulp-printed, flimsy magazines—in the hands of the working class. At its height in 1902, *Argosy* had achieved circulation of a half-million copies per issue. At ten cents per copy, these were comparable to such publications as the *Strand Magazine* in England, which sold for sixpence a copy.[21]

A milestone for the American pulps occurred in 1905, when Street & Smith, publishers of *Popular* magazine, acquired the rights to serialize *Ayesha*, by H. Rider Haggard, a sequel to his well-received novel *She*. In 1907 the cover price of *Popular* rose to 15 cents, but, with determined efforts to build a stable of popular authors, circulation began to near that of *Argosy*. With the innovation of genre-specific titles, focusing on detective stories, romance, and the like, the magazines flourished, and by the 1920s, at the peak of their popularity, successful pulps were selling up to 1 million copies per issue. Among the best-known genre-specific titles of this period were *Amazing Stories*, *Black Mask*, *Dime Detective*, *Flying Aces*, *Horror Stories*, *Love Story*, *Marvel Tales*, *Oriental Stories*, *Planet Stories*, *Spicy Detective*, *Startling Stories*, *Thrilling Wonder Stories*, *Unknown*, *Weird Tales*, and *Western Story*. While the magazines paid notoriously low fees, then little-known authors such as Sinclair Lewis, Upton Sinclair, F. Scott Fitzgerald, Sax Rohmer, Dashiell Hammett, Lovecraft, Robert E. Howard, and Clark Ashton Smith got their start in the pages of the pulp magazines. The influence on Lovecraft's work of many of these writers—and other pulp writers, including Edgar Rice Burroughs, Victor Rousseau, George Allan England, and A. Merritt—was enormous.[22] Specific Lovecraftian plot elements, such as lost cities and civilizations, Atlantis

Argosy by 1906.

The Popular Magazine, April 1915.

21. The exchange rate was about $4.87 per pound, a sixpence representing $\frac{1}{40}$ of a pound.

22. Many pulps lasted until the 1950s and continued to nurture writers such as Poul Anderson, Isaac Asimov, Ray Bradbury, Robert Bloch, Max Brand, Arthur C. Clarke, Raymond Chandler, C. S. Forester, Zane Grey, Robert E. Heinlein, Frank Herbert, Louis L'Amour, John D. MacDonald, Rafael Sabatini, Jim Thompson, Tennessee Williams, and Cornell Woolrich.

and other lost continents, mind-transfers, savagery, cannibalism, and vanished races, all can be found in the pulp magazines, though in Lovecraft's hands these became transformed into embodiments of his ideas about elitism and "cosmicism," discussed in "Lovecraft's Philosophy and the Cthulhu Mythos," below.[23]

LIFE OF H. P. LOVECRAFT

The Lovecraft family, 1892.

Howard Phillips
Lovecraft, ca. 1892.

THE EXTERNAL LIFE of Howard Phillips Lovecraft is simple enough to limn; details of his writing career will be considered separately.[24] Peter Cannon, in his essential *H. P. Lovecraft*, sums up the author's life's activities as follows: "contributing to amateur journals, composing eighteenth century verse, revising the works of talentless would-be authors, and on occasion publishing highly original horror fiction in pulp magazines like *Weird Tales*—all far removed from the literary mainstream." Indeed, much of Lovecraft's day-to-day life was itself far removed from the mainstream, as a matter of choice.[25]

Lovecraft was born of solid New England stock—his great-grandfather moved to Canada in 1827 and shortly thereafter to Rochester, New York; his mother's ancestors came to America in 1630, ten years after the arrival of the *Mayflower*. He lived virtually his entire life in Providence, Rhode Island. Born on August 20, 1890, to Winfield Scott Lovecraft and Sarah Susan Phillips Lovecraft, he lost his father, in a real sense, almost immediately, for when Howard was three, his

23. The influence of the Munsey magazines on Lovecraft is studied in detail in Gavin Callaghan's groundbreaking essay "A Reprehensible Habit: H. P. Lovecraft and the Munsey Magazines."

24. That is not to say that Lovecraft's life has not been thoroughly studied: S. T. Joshi has produced several biographical studies, culminating in the publication of his massive two-volume *I Am Providence: The Life and Times of H. P. Lovecraft*, and the pages of *Lovecraft Studies* and *Crypt of Cthulhu*, two journals devoted to the study of Lovecraft, as well as dozens of books, are filled with biographical studies, reminiscences, and dissections. As a result of Lovecraft's voluminous correspondence, far more has been published about his life than about his work. See text following note 64, below.

25. It is an incomplete and incorrect judgment on Lovecraft to term him a "recluse" (as did Peter Penzoldt—see note 66, below). One of Lovecraft's many correspondents, the hugely successful writer Robert Bloch, wrote: "During the four-year span of our association (1933–1937) the avowed 'recluse' sent me letters and postcards from all over the New England states, from Charleston, Richmond, Fredericksburg, Florida and Quebec." During this period, Lovecraft had many visitors at his home, and his far-ranging correspondence, Bloch observes, demonstrated his lively interest in contemporary politics and literary and scientific theory ("Out of the Ivory Tower").

father was confined to Butler Hospital for the Insane,[26] in Providence, where he remained until his death in 1898, almost certainly a victim of paresis caused by syphilis (though Lovecraft characterized it as "nervous exhaustion"). The young Lovecraft was raised by his mother, who was known as Susie, his two aunts, and his maternal grandfather.

Apparently a prodigy, mastering the alphabet at two, reading at three, and composing poetry by age seven,[27] Howard nonetheless seems to have had an active and sociable childhood. In 1904 the death of his grandfather brought severe financial hardship to Howard's family, and he and his mother moved into a modest apartment. Always a sickly child prone to nerves and fatigue, as a fourteen-year-

Lovecraft as a boy.

26. The hospital was founded in 1844 with seed money from Cyrus Butler, after whom it was named, and Nicholas Brown Jr., Rhode Island merchant-philanthropist, who also helped found Brown University. See *The Case of Charles Dexter Ward*, note 60, below.

Butler Hospital for the Insane, ca. 1878.

27. In a letter to Maurice W. Moe dated January 1, 1915 (*Selected Letters*, I, 7), Lovecraft claims that he began "versification" at the age of six. He produced his first published verse—eighty-eight lines and titled *The Young Folks'* Ulysses *or the* Odyssey *in plain Olden English Vers, an Epick Poem*—when he was seven. The work was self-published. Lovecraft composed hundreds of poems over his career, some appearing in amateur journals, some in *Weird Tales*. These may be found in the following: *Collected Poems*, which contains the *Fungi from Yuggoth* sonnet cycle; *A Winter Wish*; and *The Ancient Track: Complete Poetical Works*.

Lovecraft's official United Press Association photograph, 1915.

old he fell victim to illness, probably psychologically induced, and he dropped out of high school in 1908, after completing the eleventh grade. By then his health "completely gave way," according to his own account, and he abandoned thoughts of college. Under the strong influence of his mother, Lovecraft was declared unfit for the military and sat out the Great War.

For the next ten or eleven years, Lovecraft occupied himself with amateur journalism. Despite his avowed worship of Edgar Allan Poe, whose work he first read at the age of eight, his passions were chemistry, astronomy, and the Greek and Roman classics, and these interests are reflected in his sparse writings during this youthful period. In 1919, a major change occurred in the young man's life: After extended periods of depression and what was then termed hysteria, his mother, too, was confined to Butler Hospital, where she died in 1921. Lovecraft's biographers have expressed various judgments of Susie Lovecraft. S. T.

Joshi, for example, states that she "psychologically damaged Lovecraft at least to the point of declaring him physically hideous and perhaps in other ways that are now irrecoverable."[28] Kenneth W. Faig Jr., however, asserts that Lovecraft's "finely honed aesthetic sensibilities and seasoned artistic judgment" were the result of her influence, and he points out that she indulged the young man in developing interests in chemistry, astronomy, and various mythologies.[29] "My mother was, in all probability," wrote Lovecraft in 1921, shortly after her death, "the only person who thoroughly understood me, with the possible exception of Alfred Galpin."[30]

Lovecraft's initial response to his mother's death was predictable: "The death of my mother . . . gave me an extreme nervous shock, and I find concentration and continuous endeavour quite impossible."[31] Not long after, however, Lovecraft's health improved considerably, as he admitted, perhaps disingenuously, in a letter

28. Joshi, *I Am Providence*, 391.

29. Faig Jr., *The Parents of Howard Phillips Lovecraft*, 40.

30. Lovecraft to Mrs. Anne Tillery Renshaw, June 1, 1921, *Selected Letters*, I, 134. Galpin, an American writer and composer (1901–1963), met Lovecraft through the offices of his high school teacher, Lovecraft's friend Maurice Moe, who introduced Galpin to the amateur press association, and Lovecraft and Galpin corresponded regularly from 1917 to 1937.

31. This remark is from the same letter.

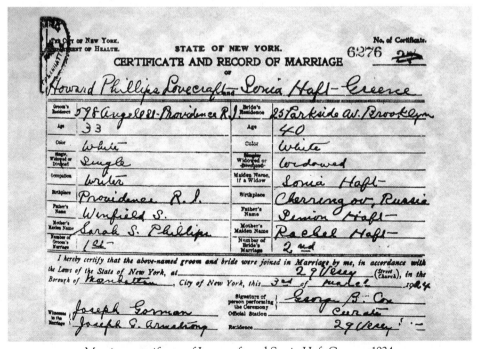

Marriage certificate of Lovecraft and Sonia Haft-Greene, 1924.

in 1931: "My health improved vastly and rapidly, though without any ascertainable cause, about 1920–21."[32] A few weeks after Susie died, he attended an amateur press convention in Boston, where he met Sonia Greene, a Ukrainian Jew seven years his elder, who had her own aspirations as a writer. At the time, Greene was an executive of a hat shop in New York. He said of her initially, "Mrs. G. has an acute, receptive, and well-stored mind. . . ." Others described her as "Junoesque" and very attractive, but Lovecraft expressed nothing more until, after an apparently persistent courtship press by Sonia, they married in 1924. The marriage engendered surprise, shock, and even alarm among their friends, and Lovecraft's description of the relationship may well explain those responses:

> [I]t began to be apparent that I was not alone in finding psychological solitude more or less of a handicap. A detailed intellectual and aesthetic acquaintance since 1921, and a three-months visit in 1922 wherein congeniality was tested and found perfect in an infinity of ways, furnished abundant proof not only that S.H.G. is the most inspiriting and encouraging influence which could possibly be brought to bear on me, but that she herself had begun to find me more congenial than anyone else, and had come to depend to a great extent on my correspondence and conversation for mental contentment and artistic and philosophical enjoyment.[33]

Lovecraft moved to New York, where he and Sonia took up residence at 259 Parkside Avenue in Brooklyn (now the Prospect Lefferts Gardens neighborhood of Flatbush). Brooklyn, with its farms and gardens, was viewed by many as a refuge from the bustle of the city, but the 1920s saw massive changes there, as roads were paved, sewers installed, and the Coney Island boardwalk opened, and as crowds of immigrants arrived to stay. Lovecraft remained in New York for two years. Greene, meanwhile, opened her own hat shop, which lasted for a brief period only; when she lost the shop, she found employment in Cincinnati (apparently through a want ad) and, at the beginning of 1925, after only ten months of cohabitation with Lovecraft, moved to Ohio to work.[34] She visited Lovecraft from time to time in Brooklyn and took care to send him money regularly, but after Sonia's departure, Lovecraft lived near the Red Hook neighbor-

---

32. Lovecraft to Maurice W. Moe, April 5, 1931, *Selected Letters*, III, 370.

33. Lovecraft to Mrs. F. C. Clark, March 9, 1924, *Selected Letters*, III, 320. Lovecraft wrote this letter six days after the wedding, and it took him numerous pages of similar preamble to work up to telling his aunt of his marriage.

34. Sonia soon left to take a job in Cleveland. She was also hospitalized for a portion of 1924 for gastric problems.

Sonia Greene Lovecraft.

hood of Brooklyn in a state of penury and near-starvation. Although he had had hopes of success in the New York literary world, he made only slight efforts to find employment and spent his time with friends he seemed to have little or no trouble acquiring and cultivating.

Lovecraft apparently hated the city: In a letter describing a brief trip to Philadelphia during this period, he contrasted New York and Philadelphia: "None of the crude, foreign hostility & underbreeding of New York—none of the vulgar trade spirit & plebeian hustle. A city of real American background—an integral & continuous outgrowth of a definite & aristocratic past instead of an Asiatic hell's huddle of the world's cowed, broken, inartistic, & unfit."[35] He despised the immi-

35. Lovecraft to Mrs. F. C. Clark, November 17–18, 1924, *Letters from New York*, 92–93.

The apartment Lovecraft occupied with Sonia Greene Lovecraft,
259 Parkside Avenue, Brooklyn, shown in 2010.
Photograph copyright © Donovan K. Loucks 2010, reprinted with permission

grant population. Sonia described his experiences walking in New York: "[W]hen-
ever he would meet crowds of people—in the subway, or, at the noon hour, on the
sidewalks in Broadway, or crowds, wherever he happened to find them, and these
were usually the workers of minority races—he would become livid with anger

Lovecraft's apartment at 169 Clinton Street, Brooklyn, shown in 2010.
Photograph copyright © Donovan K. Loucks 2010, reprinted with permission

and rage."[36] In a letter, she elaborates: "[H]e became *livid with rage* at the foreign elements he would see in large number, especially at noon-time, in the streets of New York City, and I would try to calm his outbursts by saying: 'You don't have to love them; but hating them so outrageously can't do any good.' It was then that he said: 'It is more important to know what to hate than it is to know what to love.'"[37]

Alienated from the city, unable to write, and separated from Greene, he capitulated and returned to Providence in the spring of 1926, where he remained for the rest of his life. "[I]n New York I could not live. Everything I saw became unreal & two-dimensional, & everything I thought & did became trivial & devoid of meaning through lack of any points of reference belonging to any fabric of which I could conceivably form a part. I was stifled—poisoned—imprisoned in a nightmare—& now not even the threat of damnation could induce me to dwell in the accursed place again."[38] Neither he nor

Sonia Greene Lovecraft, probably in 1921.

36. In Sonia H. [Greene] Davis, *The Private Life of H. P. Lovecraft.*

37. Sonia Davis to Winfield Townley Scott, September 24, 1948 (John Hay Library, Brown University). Lovecraft held Sonia out as an example of how Jews could fit in by assimilation. See note 35, above. He privately expressed support for the racial views of the Nazis, if not their methods. Joshi, in *I Am Providence* (941), repeats a story of a German-American friend of Lovecraft's who returned to Germany in 1936 and there learned of the Nazi treatment of the Jews. Although some have suggested that Lovecraft was incensed by this report, he never denounced the Nazis, though he did at least stop talking about the matter.

38. Letter to Donald Wandrei, February 10, 1927, *Mysteries of Time and Spirit: The Letters of H. P. Lovecraft and Donald Wandrei,* 35.

Sonia Greene Davis, ca. 1950.

Sonia said much about the failure of the marriage. Lovecraft spoke of the need for "the inviolate integrity" of his cerebral life. Sonia told one friend that Lovecraft's harping hatred of Jews was the primary reason for their estrangement and separation.[39] Whatever their private reasons, the couple's divorce was never finalized. Lovecraft traveled occasionally in the eastern United States, his farthest destination being a sightseeing trip to New Orleans, but appeared to prefer a frugal life at home. He lived alone until 1933, when he moved in with his aged aunt, Annie Gamwell, allowing the two to pool their meager resources. Three years later he developed cancer of the intestine. He died in 1937.

39. Sonia wrote, "Although [Howard] once said he loved New York and that henceforth it would be his 'adopted state,' I soon learned that he hated it and all its 'alien hordes.' When I protested that I too was one of them, he'd tell me I 'no longer belonged to these mongrels.' *'You are now Mrs. H. P. Lovecraft of 598 Angell St., Providence, Rhode Island'*" (Davis, *Private Life of H. P. Lovecraft*, 11).

Sonia Greene (Lovecraft) Davis, ca. 1949.

Lovecraft's aunt Annie Gamwell, outside the apartment they shared at
66 College Street in Providence, ca. 1933.

Lovecraft's gravestone in Swan Point Cemetery, Providence.
Photograph copyright © Donovan K. Loucks 2010, reprinted with permission

#37524

Know All Men:

I, Howard P. Lovecraft of the city of Providence in the State of Rhode Island, being of sound mind and memory, make, execute and declare this instrument as my last will, hereby revoking any and all former wills by me at any time heretofore made.

First: I direct that my executor pay out of my estate all my just debts and funeral expenses.

Second: All the rest, residue and remainder of my property and estate, real, personal and mixed, however described and wherever situated, of which I die seized and possessed, or in or to which at the time of my decease I have any right, title or interest, I give, devise and bequeath to my mother Sarah S. Lovecraft - To Have and To Hold the same unto and to the use of herself and her heirs and assigns forever.

Third: In case my said mother should not be living at the time of my decease, I give, devise and bequeath said rest, residue and remainder of my property and estate absolutely and in fee simple, two thirds thereof to my aunt Lillie D. Clark, wife of Franklin C. Clark, of said Providence, and the remaining one third thereof to my aunt Annie E. Gamwell, wife of Edward F. Gamwell of the city of Cambridge in the State of

Massachusetts, or in case either of my said aunts shall decease prior to my death without leaving any descendant living at the time of my death to take by representation such deceased's share in my residuary property and estate, I give, devise and bequeath such share to the other of them, or if she also shall have deceased prior to the time of my death, to the descendants of such other equally but per stirpes and not per capita.

Fourth: I hereby nominate, constitute and appoint my said mother Sarah S. Lovecraft sole executor of this my will, and if for any reason she should not serve or continue to serve my said aunt Lillie D. Clark, and if for any reason neither my said mother nor my said aunt shall serve or continue to serve Albert A. Baker of said Providence as sole executor hereof, and I hereby request and direct any and all courts taking probate hereof not to require any of said persons to furnish any surety on any bond, or to file any inventory or to return any account of my estate as such executor.

In Witness Whereof I have hereunto set my hand and seal and declared this to be my last will, in the presence of three witnesses, at Providence, Rhode Island, this Twelfth day of August, A. D., 1912.

Howard P. Lovecraft

Lovecraft's last will, executed in 1912 (at the age of twenty-two).

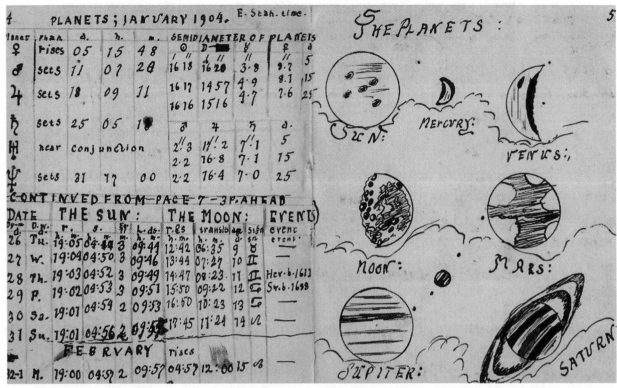

A page from Lovecraft's publication *Rhode Island Journal of Science and Astronomy*,
prepared when he was fourteen.

LOVECRAFT'S LITERARY CAREER

THIS BARE OUTLINE of Lovecraft's life reveals little of what must be deemed a
nearly incredible amount of writing. Early on, Lovecraft wrote a large quantity of
scientific material, principally focused on astronomy. His first published piece, a
criticism of the "science" of astrology, appeared in 1906 in the *Providence Sunday
Journal*. Later that year, he had a letter printed in *Scientific American* on trans-
Neptunian objects. He produced two periodicals of his own, the *Scientific Gazette*
and the *Rhode Island Journal of Astronomy*. His main outlet at this stage, however,
was a regular monthly column on astronomy for the *Providence Tribune*.

As a result of frequent appearances in the letters column of *Argosy*, one of the
most popular of the Munsey magazines,[40] he was recruited in 1914 by the United
Amateur Press Association, a group of correspondents who circulated among

40. See note 20, above.

A postcard from Lovecraft
to Clark Ashton Smith
dated December 14, 1933.

themselves in amateur journals criticism of their own poetry and prose. Lovecraft started his own journal in 1915 (the *Conservative*), which ran for thirteen issues, and engaged in the politics of the highly vocal organization, eventually serving as its president. He wrote numerous essays expressing his political views and philosophical beliefs as well as extensive criticism of amateur and commercial publications. Lovecraft even proposed a course of pedagogy to lift the standards of amateur journalism—to teach grammar, rhetoric, and versification to budding writers—and the creation of suggested reading lists. He attended conventions as far away as Boston and found himself with a growing circle of friends, many of them as amateurishly devoted to writing as he was.

These friends inspired Lovecraft's major written output, which took the form of letters and postcards. Peter Cannon, in *H. P. Lovecraft*, calls him "the Horace Walpole of this [twentieth] century, a compulsive communicator who generated in his abbreviated lifetime tens of thousands of missives, ranging from postcards to treatises forty, fifty, sixty, even seventy, closely handwritten pages long." Although five volumes of *Selected Letters* have been published, these comprise only 930 letters, a tiny fraction of Lovecraft's estimated epistolary output. S. T. Joshi, the leading Lovecraft scholar, has begun to issue a complete collection of Lovecraft's extant correspondence.[41] The letters that have been studied cover a remarkable range of subjects, from ancient Rome to views on ice-cream flavors, but also shed much light on Lovecraft's influences, sources, and philosophies. These biographical aspects are explored in depth in the volumes of annotated stories edited by Joshi; the present edition has made use of them outside this foreword only for purposes of interpretation of the texts of the stories.

Lovecraft's career as an author of weird tales can be dated to age fifteen, when he wrote "The Beast in the Cave." Of course, there may have been earlier efforts, but he shared this story with friends, and it was eventually published. His first published work, however, was "The Tomb," followed shortly thereafter by "Dagon"

41. While far from all have been published to date, since publication of *Selected Letters*, many volumes of Lovecraft's letters, collected by correspondent, have appeared. For example, Joshi recently published a two-volume collection of correspondence between Lovecraft and August Derleth. See note 78, below. A great many of Lovecraft's letters are to be found in the John Hay Library of Brown University, but hundreds, perhaps thousands, remain in private hands and many more are untraceable.

The cover of *Weird Tales* for October 1923. Note that Lovecraft did not
then (or ever) have an illustration of one of his stories appear on the cover,
although his name often appeared.

(page 3, below). These appeared in amateur journals in 1919, the year of his mother's commitment to Butler Hospital for the Insane, and over the next few years he wrote dozens of stories that circulated in the same manner. Later, virtually all of these were reprinted in *Weird Tales*, with his first appearance there being "Dagon," in October 1923. Lovecraft's earliest efforts have been classed as "Poe" stories (evocations of horror, cast in the form of confessions or narratives) or "Dunsany" stories (inventive of mythology and folklore), and Lovecraft admitted that he attempted to copy their styles.[42] While the early stories showed an emerging talent, they little reflect (perhaps with the exception of "Dagon") what would eventually become Lovecraft's own voice. In this volume, the first eight tales (concluding with "The Hound") were all written prior to 1922 and are often overlooked in assessing Lovecraft's achievements. Some—like "The Picture in the House" and "The Hound"—reveal Lovecraft beginning to work out how he could adapt the narrative and intense emotional style of Poe to fit his own themes, while others, such as "Dagon," "Nyarlathotep," and "The Nameless City," in particular, show Lovecraft playing with the creation of mythologies.

With the composition of "The Festival" in 1923, Lovecraft began to write tales set in the recognizable landscape of New England, yet modified to include invented locales: the seaport of Kingsport, the vaguely inland town of Arkham, and the regions of the Miskatonic River. While "The Picture in the House" is set in New England and "Herbert West: Reanimator" takes place in part in Arkham, the locations are poorly developed. With "The Festival," the town of Kingsport becomes an even more important "character" than the nameless narrator. But Lovecraft was not interested in mere local color or in establishing himself as a regional writer. His aims were much less mundane. He sought to show how commonplace, well-known neighborhoods could harbor and conceal the supernatural. The imaginative writer, wrote Lovecraft,

> devotes himself to art in its most essential sense. It is not his business to fashion a pretty trifle to please the children, to point a useful moral, to concoct superficial "uplift" stuff . . . or to rehash insolvable human problems didactically. He is the painter of moods and mind-pictures—a capturer and amplifier of elusive dreams and fancies—a voyager into those unheard of lands which are glimpsed through the veil of actuality but rarely, and only by the most sensitive.[43]

"Tales of ordinary characters would appeal to a larger class," Lovecraft admitted,

> but I have no wish to make such an appeal. The opinions of the masses are of no interest to me, for praise can truly gratify only when it comes from a mind sharing the author's perspective. There are probably seven persons, in all, who really like my work; and they are enough. I should write even if I were the only patient reader, for my aim is merely self-expression. I could not write about "ordinary people"

42. See note 14, above.

43. Lovecraft, "The Defence Reopens," January 1921. Quoted in *In Defense of Dagon*, note 2, above.

because I am not in the least interested in them. Without interest there can be no art. Man's relations to man do not captivate my fancy. It is man's relations to the cosmos—to the unknown—which alone arouses in me the spark of creative imagination.[44]

Lovecraft's stories circulated largely among his friends, and when he began selling them in 1923 to *Weird Tales*, the leading purveyor of similar fiction,[45] he was paid, in keeping with the standards of the day, poorly. That is, he worked for the lofty rate of 1 cent per word (the "top" writers got 1½ cents per word, a rate never achieved by Lovecraft). The fledgling magazine settled in for a long run (1924 to 1954, though it appeared earlier than 1924 and had shrunk considerably by the late 1930s), but it never achieved the success of the bigger pulps such as *Argosy*, and its circulation was estimated at less than 50,000 at its peak. S. T. Joshi states that in 1925, Lovecraft received $35 for "The Festival" and $25 for "The Unnamable."[46]

Lovecraft's time of experimentation with styles and imitation was over by 1926, when he returned to Providence, and in his remaining years, he produced his greatest stories. "The Call of Cthulhu," in many ways his signature tale, was written then, swiftly followed by his autobiographical *The Dream-Quest of Unknown Kadath* and his grand *The Case of Charles Dexter Ward* (1927), both unpublished during his lifetime. Lovecraft's own favorite,[47] "The Colour Out of Space," was also written in 1927.

---

44. *In Defense of Dagon*, note 2, above.

45. In 1923, J. C. Henneberger, a former journalist, created *Real Detective Tales and Mystery Stories* and *Weird Tales*, issued by a company he called Rural Publications, located in Indianapolis. Henneberger had a taste for ghoulish stories, and he wanted to provide, in *Weird Tales*, an outlet for some of his favorite writers. He hired Edwin Baird as the first editor of the monthly, assisted by Farnsworth Wright. The magazine sold poorly at first, amassing serious debt. After thirteen issues, Henneberger reorganized, selling off *Detective Tales* and giving controlling ownership of *Weird Tales* to his printer. Baird went with *Detective Tales*, and Henneberger, now in Chicago, needed a new editor. His first choice was Lovecraft, who had already had a number of stories published in the magazine, but Lovecraft—perhaps fearing the financial instability of the job and definitely disliking the idea of a move to the Midwest—turned the offer down. Henneberger then promoted Wright, who remained at the helm until 1940, when new owners let him go to cut costs.

46. See *I Am Providence*, 572. The former was about 3,700 words, the latter about 3,000 words. Lovecraft later got the top rate of 1½ cents per word for "The Dunwich Horror," $240 for that tale. Short story writers don't do much better today—*Ellery Queen's Mystery Magazine*, for example, probably the preeminent venue for mystery short stories, pays 5–8 cents per word, less than Lovecraft's 1 cent in today's dollars!

47. Lovecraft expressed this view in numerous letters and in the context of suggestions for anthologies.

To make ends meet, he began the work known as "revision," rewriting (and in many cases writing) more than thirty stories to be sold under the name of other authors. He published a formal schedule of fees for such work, and it became an important means of support for him. Clients came to him from his friends and correspondents and ranged from experienced writers to rank amateurs. The "revisions" are set forth in a table in Appendix 6. Some of the stories are almost pure Lovecraft (for example, Zealia Bishop's "The Mound," written in 1930, and "Through the Gates of the Silver Key," nominally cowritten with E. Hoffmann Price in 1933); others partake more of the original authors. All reflect Lovecraft's influence, for better or for worse.

Though the nation was still reeling from the effects of the stock market crash of 1929, the year 1931 brought forth two of Lovecraft's most famous stories, *At the Mountains of Madness* and "The Shadow over Innsmouth," written six years before his sudden death. *At the Mountains of Madness* demonstrated that the newly invented genre of scientific fiction could be used to explore deep themes, in particular Lovecraft's vision of the insignificant place of mankind in the universe. The story—the record of an expedition to the Antarctic leading to the discovery of a hitherto-unknown civilization populated by races other than humans—has been produced in radio and film as well as graphic form, and its Antarctic setting was reused (without the philosophical weight) in John W. Campbell's 1938 *Who Goes There?* and the 1951 and 1982 movie versions of *The Thing.* "The Shadow over Innsmouth," containing none of the science-fictional elements of *At the Mountains of Madness*, is Lovecraft's version of an "invasion" tale, cast in the form of a narrative by a young man making a rite-of-passage journey around New England. It reeks of an indescribable *genius loci* that hides dark secrets. "The Shadow over Innsmouth" was eventually his first published book, issued in 1936 in a very limited edition (two hundred copies were distributed) by a small press aptly named Visionary Publishing Co.

Lovecraft's remaining years produced a few more masterpieces of horror— "The Dreams in the Witch House" in 1932 and "The Thing on the Doorstep" in 1933—and two powerful and shocking evocations of alien beings among humankind, "The Shadow Out of Time" and "The Haunter of the Dark" in 1934 and 1935. By late 1935, however, he seemed to have lost his interest in writing fiction. Suffering from constant stomach pains, he produced a few revisions and nothing truly his own. By late 1936, he was composing "Instructions in Case of Decease," which expressed his wishes regarding control of and potential profits from his literary estate, also addressing potential exploitation of same, and no fiction. At the beginning of 1937, suffering lingering digestive problems, he was in intense pain; nonetheless, he began keeping a meticulous "death diary" of his last months of life, maintained until he was too weak to write.[48] By the end of February, his physician recollects, Lovecraft was told that he was terminally ill, suffering from intestinal cancer. He was heavily medicated with painkillers, and on March 10, he was hospitalized. He died five days later, before which his copious correspondence did not diminish; as late as the date of his death, a long, apparently half-finished letter was found at his desk, begun just prior to his hospitalization.

Several years before his death, in 1933, Lovecraft summarized his achievements:

> It is now clear to me that any actual literary merit I have is confined to tales of dream-life, strange shadow, and cosmic "outsideness", notwithstanding a keen interest in many other departments of life and a professional practice of general prose and verse revision. Why this is so, I have not the least idea. I have no illusions concerning the precarious status of my tales, and do not expect to become a serious competitor of my favourite weird authors—Poe, Arthur Machen, Dunsany, Algernon Blackwood, Walter de la Mare, and Montague Rhodes James. The only thing I can say in favour of my work is its sincerity. I refuse to follow the mechanical conventions of popular fiction or to fill my tales with stock characters and situ-

---

48. The journal is lost but portions remain, copied into various letters. Before the disappearance of the journal, a complete reprint was published; see R. Alain Everts, *The Death of a Gentleman: The Last Days of Howard Phillips Lovecraft, Including Lovecraft's Diary for 1937.* The following are condensed entries for March 1937:

> Mch 1—AEPG [Lovecraft's aunt Annie E. Phillips Gamwell] tel. [Dr. Cecil Calvert] Dustin [an internal medicine doctor] about specialist—enormous abdominal distension—feet again swollen—intense pain—drowse
>
> 2—pain—drowse—intense pain—rest—great pain
>
> 3—pain—callers—Brobst—pain—pain
>
> 4—pain worse—[Lovecraft's friend Harry] Brobst call—read—pain worse—bad night, frequent immersions [in hot tub]
>
> 5—pain intense
>
> Sat 6—Dr. [William Lessel] Leet [internal medicine specialist] call while in bath—bad day—hideous pain—read paper—bad night
>
> 7—hideous pain
>
> 8—weak—pain less—pain

The following are full entries:

> 9—pain—do very little—AEPG tel Dr. Leet—pain—nourishment difficult—very bad night
>
> 10—pain & weakness—Brobst call—Dr. Leet call—recommend hospital, prepare—off with AEPG to J[ane]. Brown [Memorial Hospital]—wait—finally get room—AEPG stay for dinner—ho—Leet call—very bad nigh—regurg.
>
> 11—pain—Dr. Jones take blood—bath—pain—elec. pad—AEPG call.

Lovecraft wrote nothing further and died on the morning of the fifteenth.

ations, but insist on reproducing real moods and impressions in the best way I can command. The result may be poor, but I had rather keep aiming at serious literary expression than accept the artificial standards of cheap romance.

It was not only his chosen subjects that worried Lovecraft; he also thought little of his own craftsmanship:

I have tried to improve and subtilise my tales with the passing of years, but have not made the progress I wish. Some of my efforts have been cited in the O'Brien and O. Henry annuals, and a few have enjoyed reprinting in anthologies; but all proposals for a published collection have come to nothing. It is possible that one or two short tales may be issued as separate brochures before long. I never write when I cannot be spontaneous—expressing a mood already existing and demanding crystallisation. Some of my tales involve actual dreams I have experienced. My speed and manner of writing vary widely in different cases, but I always work best at night. Of my products, my favourites are "The Colour out of Space" and "The Music of Erich Zann," in the order named. I doubt if I could ever succeed well in the ordinary kind of science fiction.

Summing up what he saw as the future of the genre, and in typical fashion revealing his own sense of alienation from the world of commercial and popular tastes, he wrote:

I believe that weird writing offers a serious field not unworthy of the best literary artists; though it is at most a very limited one, reflecting only a small section of man's infinitely composite moods. Spectral fiction should be realistic and atmospheric—confining its departure from Nature to the one supernatural channel chosen, and remembering that scene, and phenomena are more important in conveying what is to be conveyed than are characters and plot. The "punch" of a truly weird tale is simply some violation or transcending of fixed cosmic law—an imaginative escape from palling reality—hence phenomena rather than persons are the logical "heroes." Horrors, I believe, should be original—the use of common myths and legends being a weakening influence. Current magazine fiction, with its incurable leanings toward conventional sentimental perspectives, brisk, cheerful style, and artificial "action" plots, does not rank high.[49]

49. This and the previous quotation are from Lovecraft's essay "Some Notes on a Nonentity," written in November 1933 for William L. Crawford, who requested it for *Unusual Stories*; later reprinted in *Beyond the Wall of Sleep*.

Like the posthumous enshrinement of figures such as Janis Joplin and Jimi Hendrix some three and a half decades later, death brought Lovecraft attention from the wider public that he never achieved in life. The *Providence Evening Bulletin* ran an error-filled obituary on March 15, 1937, but made note of Lovecraft's "death diary," and on March 16, the *New York Times* ran an obituary headed "Writer Charts Fatal Malady." A small funeral service was held a few days later. In the communities of weird writing and the amateur press, mourning was widespread and numerous tributes were published. More significantly, within two weeks of his death, two of Lovecraft's friends, August Derleth and Donald Wandrei, with what David E. Schultz called "breath taking swiftness,"[50] were communicating with other friends and undertaking to build a monument to Lovecraft's literary reputation by collecting his stories and papers for the first time.

Derleth was then only twenty-eight but already a veteran short story writer; his stories had begun to appear in *Weird Tales* when he was seventeen. He never met Lovecraft, but their correspondence, which began in 1926, was extensive and intimate. Wandrei, a poet and short story writer, also had begun his association with Lovecraft in 1926. He and Lovecraft saw and wrote to each other sporadically until Lovecraft's death. Wandrei was only a year older than Derleth, and after Lovecraft introduced them to each other, the two became close friends. Deeply moved by the death of a fellow writer and friend whose literary output and personal ministrations they had come to cherish, the two younger men decided to form Arkham House Publishers, and in 1939 they put out an edition of 1,268 copies of *The Outsider and Others*.[51] It received far-flung attention, discussed below, and encouraged the publishers to compile a second collection, *Beyond the Wall of Sleep*, in 1943, followed by collections of Lovecraft's writings edited by Derleth that Arkham House entitled *Marginalia* (1944) and *Something About Cats and Other Pieces* (1949). *The Dunwich Horror and Others* was published in 1963 and *At the Mountains of Madness and Other Novels* in 1964. In 1965, the first volume of *Selected Letters* appeared from Arkham House, also edited by Derleth and Wandrei, who began repackaging some of Lovecraft's stories in additional collections. The first major single-volume collection of selected works, edited by Joyce Carol Oates and titled *Tales of H. P. Lovecraft*, appeared in 1997 from Ecco Press, a division of HarperCollins. S. T. Joshi, Lovecraft's leading biographer, has published a number of annotated editions of Lovecraft's work, both in the form of collections and single stories (all listed in the bibliography). In 2005 the Library

50. David E. Schultz, "Who Needs the 'Cthulhu Mythos'?"

51. A "spectacular copy" of the book was offered for sale in 2013 for $15,000.

of America released *Tales*, a collection of twenty-two of Lovecraft's best stories, edited and with notes by modern horror master Peter Straub. In 2013, Oxford University Press published a small collection of Lovecraft stories, annotated by Roger Luckhurst.

CRITICAL RECEPTION OF LOVECRAFT'S WORK

IT IS EVIDENT from Lovecraft's letters that he freely shared his stories with his friends during the process of composition and sought their comments and suggestions. The first unbiased comments, however, were those of the readers of the *Weird Tales* magazines in which the stories first appeared. Published in "The Eyrie," the letters column of the magazine, these were apparently nearly uniformly fulsome ("surely [Lovecraft] is as great a writer as has ever lived"),[52] though the editors—especially Farnsworth Wright, according to Robert Weinberg, the preeminent historian of *Weird Tales*—were "not loath to praise a story highly in The Eyrie."[53]

Outside the hard-core group of readers, however, few were enthusiastic. In fact, until 1945, virtually no one outside of the pulp fandom had paid any attention to Lovecraft (or for that matter, many other pulp writers), negative or positive. In 1924, "The Picture in the House" had received a one-star ranking in the *O. Henry Memorial Award Prize Stories*, and "Pickman's Model" was similarly recognized in the category of "Stories Ranking Third" in the 1928 volume, while Lovecraft's story "The Colour Out of Space" was listed on the Roll of Honor of the 1928 volume of Edward J. O'Brien's *Best Short Stories*. In 1930, William Bolitho's article "Pulp Magazines" in the January 4 issue of *New York World* noted Lovecraft's work, "[which] I am sure I would rather read than many fashionable lady novelists they give teas to; and poets too."

It was left to the cadre of readers of weird fiction to bring Lovecraft into the light. Derleth, writing shortly after Lovecraft's death, called him "the outstanding American exponent of the macabre tale" and expressed the cautious hope that while "[n]either his prose nor his poetry will ever attain the status of world recognition . . . his genius will be recognized. . . ."[54] W. Paul Cook, an early fan and publisher, warned in 1945 of overwrought treatment of the writer: "Irreparable harm is being done to Lovecraft by indiscriminate and even unintelligent praise, by lack of

52. Quoted in Robert E. Weinberg's *The* Weird Tales *Story*, 121.

53. Ibid., 120.

54. "H. P. Lovecraft, Outsider," *In Defense of Dagon*.

unbiased and intelligent criticism, and by a warped sense of what is due him in the way of publication of his works. . . ."[55]

Certainly, the harshest critical assessment came from Lovecraft himself. In 1931, he said of his own work, "It is excessively extravagant & melodramatic, & lacks depth and subtlety. . . . My style is bad, too—full of obvious rhetorical devices & hackneyed word & rhythm patterns. It comes a long way from the stark, objective simplicity which is my goal."[56] Possibly this was false modesty—the pose of what he felt was the essence of the gentleman amateur—but several of what Lovecraft regarded as his best works had been rejected by editors in 1931, and he struggled to make ends meet. In fact, many reviewers and booksellers were simply unaware of his work until *The Outsider and Others*, the first collection of Lovecraft's stories ever published, appeared in December 1939. For example, *Publishers Weekly*, the primary organ of the bookselling community, which today reviews thousands of books annually (though it handled fewer in 1939), noted, "We had never heard of author or publisher. . . ."[57]

The publication of *The Outsider and Others* led to the first review of Lovecraft's work by an academician, Thomas Ollive Mabbott (1898–1968), professor of English at Northwestern, Brown, and, later, Hunter College. Mabbott was well known as a Poe scholar, and his three-volume critical edition of Poe appeared posthumously between 1969 and 1978. Mabbott called Lovecraft's stories "striking and original. . . . Time will tell if his place be very high in our literary history; that he has a place seems certain."[58] He also commented favorably on Lovecraft's essay "Supernatural Horror in Literature," included in the volume, calling its discussions of Poe, Hawthorne, and Bierce "so penetrating, sympathetic, and imaginatively keen that scholars will not want to miss them."

In 1943, Peter De Vries, an acclaimed author of satirical fiction and frequent contributor to *The New Yorker*, reviewed *Beyond the Wall of Sleep* (the second Arkham House collection) for the *Chicago Sun*: "There are moments when he strikes fire, achieving exquisite eerie details, but on the whole his somewhat dated context, his languid and pearly style, adds up at best to a competently wrought anachronism rather than the creative individuality his publishers claim

55. "A Plea for Lovecraft."

56. Lovecraft to J. Vernon Shea, December 9, 1931, *Selected Letters*, III, 441, quoted with apparent agreement by humorist and critic Will Cuppy in his review of *The Outsider and Others*. Cuppy (see note 60, below) did call Lovecraft a "modest genius," however.

57. *Publishers Weekly*, February 24, 1940, 890–91.

58. Thomas Ollive Mabbott, review of *The Outsider and Others*.

for him—a knick-knack on the whatnot of Neo-Romanticism."[59] Will Cuppy, writing for the *New York Herald Tribune*, also had guardedly positive comments: "We confess that we are knocked silly by the mass of mania, nightmare, and such in these Lovecraft collections, both of which should be possessed, or at least perused, by any citizen who goes for hideous dream states, demons from the vast abyss, humans doomed and damned, things unnamable and so forth in truly astonishing variety. . . . Heartily recommended to all that way inclined."[60]

The most damaging review of Lovecraft's work, ultimately reflecting the view of the prevailing literary establishment, appeared in 1945. "Tales of the Marvellous and the Ridiculous," written by Edmund Wilson for *The New Yorker*,[61] had an enormous impact because of the stature of

Edmund Wilson, at *The New Yorker*.
(Photograph by Henri Cartier-Bresson)

its author. Often called the dean of American critics, Wilson (1895–1972) notoriously had little regard for speculative fiction; eleven years hence, in a review of *The Fellowship of the Ring*, he expressed his unfettered disdain for J. R. R. Tolkien, suggesting to readers that, if they "must read about imaginary kingdoms," they instead choose Poictesme—an invented French province in the fictional series *Biography of the Life of Manuel*, by James Branch Cabell, whose work has largely been forgotten.[62] At the time, Wilson's own defining achievement was *To the Finland Station* (1940), a history of socialism and a study of European political thought from Michelet through the Russian Revolution. In the case of Lovecraft, having familiarized himself with the material published by Arkham House, Wilson declared, "I regret that, after examining these books, I am no more enthusiastic than before. . . . [T]he truth is that these stories were hack-work contributed to such publications as *Weird Tales* and *Amazing Stories*, where, in my opinion, they ought to have been left. The only real horror in most of these fictions is the horror of bad taste and bad art." Wilson went on: "Lovecraft was not a good writer. The fact that

59. Peter De Vries, review of *Beyond the Wall of Sleep*.

60. Will Cuppy, review of *Beyond the Wall of Sleep*.

61. Edmund Wilson, *The New Yorker*, November 24, 1945.

62. Edmund Wilson, "Oo, Those Awful Orcs."

his verbose and undistinguished style has been compared to Poe's is only one of the many sad signs that almost nobody any more pays real attention to writing." Wilson found it "terrifying" that a critic as respected as Thomas Ollive Mabott had contributed a Lovecraft tribute to one of the Arkham House volumes. "One of Lovecraft's worst faults is his incessant effort to work up the expectations of the reader by sprinkling his stories with such adjectives as 'horrible,' 'terrible,' 'frightful,' 'awesome,' 'eerie,' 'weird,' 'forbidden,' 'unhallowed,' 'unholy,' 'blasphemous,' 'hellish' and 'infernal.' Surely one of the primary rules for writing an effective tale of horror is never to use any of these words—especially if you are going, at the end, to produce an invisible whistling octopus."[63] Reflecting a profound literary bias, Wilson concluded his essay with these hostile words: "[T]he Lovecraft cult, I fear, is on an even more infantile level than the Baker Street Irregulars and the cult of Sherlock Holmes."[64]

Prior to 1990, Lovecraft gained little attention from any but devoted fans and

---

63. Wilson was not alone in deploring Lovecraft's use of adjectives; similar views were expressed by Colin Wilson and L. Sprague de Camp.

64. In "Mr. Holmes, They Were the Footprints of a Gigantic Hound!," he had similar faint praise for the Sherlock Holmes stories of Arthur Conan Doyle, preferring writers like Henry James. While Doyle's stories were enjoyable, Wilson admitted, these were "literature on a humble but not ignoble level." He added: "The writing, of course, is full of clichés, but these clichés are dealt out with a ring which gives them a kind of value, while the author makes speed and saves space so effectively that we are rarely in danger of getting bogged down in anything boring. . . . [O]ver the whole epic there hangs an air of irresponsible comedy, like that of some father's rigmarole for his children. . . ."

The Baker Street Irregulars, the object of Wilson's scorn, was founded in 1934 by bookman Christopher Morley as a literary society dedicated to the study of Sherlock Holmes. Not surprisingly, there is a fair amount of crossover between fans of Lovecraft and the Holmes fans. In fact, August Derleth was a lifelong Sherlockian, though he did not become a member of the Baker Street Irregulars until 1971, the year of his death. Beginning in 1929—at the age of twenty—he wrote a long series of highly regarded stories about a Holmes-like detective, Solar Pons. (Lovecraft himself appears as a character in the Pons case "The Adventure of the Six Silver Spiders.") These were first published in the pulps but later collected and published by Derleth under the Mycroft & Moran imprint. Vincent Starrett, who wrote a generous appreciation of Lovecraft in his "Books Alive!" column in the *Chicago Sun-Times* in 1944, was an early member of the Baker Street Irregulars as well. Peter Cannon wrote several Holmes/Lovecraft-related articles, for the *Baker Street Journal*, the quarterly journal of Sherlockian scholarship published by the Baker Street Irregulars, *Nyctalops*, and *Lovecraft Studies*, as well as a book-length Holmes-Lovecraft mash-up, *Pulptime*. Phillip A. Shreffler, author of the *Lovecraft Companion*, has been a member of the Baker Street Irregulars since 1974. There is a fine overview and detailed analysis of the influence of the Holmes stories on Lovecraft's work in "Elementary, My Dear Lovecraft: H. P. Lovecraft and Sherlock Holmes" by Gavin Callaghan. See also Robert H. Waugh's "Lovecraft's Rats and Doyle's Hound: A Study in Reason and Madness."

Lovecraft himself was a devotee of the Great Detective. In a May 27, 1918, letter to Alfred Galpin (*Selected Letters*, I, 66–68), Lovecraft wrote, "As to 'Sherlock Holmes'—I used to be infatuated with him! I read every Sherlock Holmes story published, and even organised a *detective agency* when I was thirteen, arrogating to myself the proud pseudonym of S. H." Joshi states, in *I Am Providence*, that he suspects that after high school Lovecraft read no more detective fiction.

specialists. Fritz Leiber Jr., a correspondent of Lovecraft's late in the latter's life, published a general critical essay entitled "A Literary Copernicus," extolling the writer's achievements.[65] Peter Penzoldt's *The Supernatural in Fiction* (1952),[66] a study of the field, included a large section on Lovecraft. Yet for all the attention he lavishes on Lovecraft, Penzoldt appears unsure of whether his attention is justified. "Lovecraft's work has both great merits and great defects. He was an exceedingly cultivated and well-read man. . . . Yet Lovecraft's greatest merit was also his greatest fault. He was too well read. . . . [H]e was influenced by so many authors that one is often at a loss to decide what is really Lovecraft and what some half-conscious memory of the books he has read." Another influential early scholar was Barton L. St. Armand, a Brown University professor who published two important critical works in the 1970s, *The Roots of Horror in the Fiction of H. P. Lovecraft* (1977) and an earlier piece appearing in the journal *Rhode Island History*. Paperback editions of Lovecraft's tales from Lancer and Ballantine in the 1960s and early 1970s and publicaton of 1975 of *Lovecraft: A Biography*, by fantasy writer L. Sprague de Camp, focused further interest on Lovecraft's writings.

Eric Hoefler, in his dissertation on the growth of Lovecraft-related scholarship,[67] essentially dismisses the period prior to 1990. His primary reason for doing so is that virtually all of the serious scholarship during that period appeared outside what he calls "established" journals—journals that are not devoted exclusively to genre fiction or that are little-recognized in the academic community. In 1979, Necronomicon Press, founded in 1976 by Marc Michaud, then an undergraduate at Brown University, began publishing *Lovecraft Studies*, edited by S. T. Joshi, who served many years as editorial director for the press. This contained many excellent scholarly articles and lasted for forty-three issues (1979–2005), but it had a tiny circulation. With only a year's hiatus, it was succeeded by the *Lovecraft Annual*, also superbly edited by Joshi, which began in 2007 and continues today. Shortly after the launch of *Lovecraft Studies*, in 1981, *Crypt of Cthulhu*, a charming

65. The essay first appeared in *Something About Cats and Other Pieces*, a highly specialized book edited by August Derleth. Though Leiber (1910–1992) achieved a reputation as a fine writer of horror and science fiction, the essay cannot be said to have had any significant impact at the time.

66. In his survey of the literature, Penzoldt remarked, "Indeed, during the last decade Lovecraft has been praised and over-praised. It was as if critics were trying to compensate for past neglect. In so doing they exaggerated more than a little." By 1952, Lovecraft was surely not suffering from overpraise, except from his devoted fans; perhaps Penzoldt was not aware that the "critics" who were praising Lovecraft so highly were his protégés, such as Leiber and Derleth (see below for a discussion of Lovecraft's circle of friends).

67. Eric Hoefler, "Lovecraft Rising: Tracing the Growth of Scholarship on Howard Phillips Lovecraft, 1990–2004." Hoefler amassed a detailed bibliography of Lovecraft criticism published between 1990 and 2004, available here: http://erichoefler.com/resources/genre/lovecraft/.

On our cover are featured some of the contributors and behind-the-scenes people who have made the past ten years of Lovecraft Studies such a success:

1. H. P. Lovecraft
2. Marc A. Michaud
3. Marie-Marthe Michaud
4. Alfred S. Michaud
5. Donald R. Burleson
6. S. T. Joshi
7. Susan Michaud
8. Steven Mariconda
9. Will Murray
10. Robert M. Price
11. Peter Cannon
12. Kenneth W. Faig, Jr.
13. J. Vernon Shea
14. David E. Schultz
15. Jason Eckhardt
16. Victoria Szatkowska

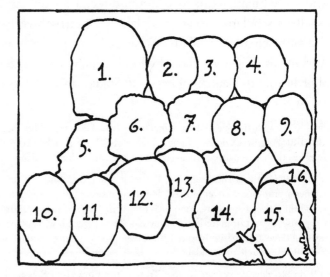

Lovecraft Studies, 19/20 (Fall 1989), cover by Jason C. Eckhardt, depicting frequent contributors.

mixture of Lovecraft criticism, original fiction, and lively correspondence among Lovecraftians, edited by Robert M. Price, began publication (ceasing only in 2002, after 107 issues). The magazine began as Price's contribution to the Esoteric Order of Dagon, an amateur press organization formed by a group of Lovecraft devotees in 1973. A large fanzine, *Nyctalops*, with copious original artwork as well as criticism and original fiction, first appeared in May 1970; edited initially by Harry O. Morris and later Edward Berglund, it ran for nineteen issues until 1991. This body of fan-created criticism led Peter Cannon, by then one of the foremost Lovecraft scholars, to observe in 1990, "We have attracted little notice in the academy, apart from Brown University. The audience of *Lovecraft Studies* consists almost entirely of horror fiction fans; only a handful of college libraries carry the premier journal in the field. Serious Lovecraft criticism has rarely appeared in print outside the science-fiction horror-fantasy realm."[68]

By 1990, the dam was effectively broken, no doubt helped by publication of Peter Cannon's *H. P. Lovecraft* the previous year. Cannon addressed this critical introduction to "the believers and the skeptics" with the hope of persuading the latter that "Lovecraft is more than a mere horror writer." S. T. Joshi's *H. P. Lovecraft: The Decline of the West*, the first full-length philosophical study of Lovecraft's work, was published in 1990, and explored the evolution of Lovecraft's view that the current phase of Western civilization was declining and ending. In the same year, the University Press of Kentucky published Donald Burleson's *Lovecraft: Disturbing the Universe*, a work of criticism founded in the deconstructionist school and the first to approach Lovecraft's fiction without leaning heavily on biographical detail or Lovecraft's correspondence or essays. While Burleson has been almost exclusively associated with criticism of horror fiction,[69] this marked the first serious, in-depth examination of Lovecraft's literature by "literary" standards.

Many surveys of horror writing and book-length works of Lovecraft scholarship have been published since; the majority are listed in this volume's bibliography. In Hoefler's words: "Lovecraft scholarship has begun its rise to visibility in the larger academic community, moving from the relatively closed circle of scholarship in the 1980s. . . . After 2000, scholarship was advanced by articles

---

68. "Some Thoughts on the Current State of Lovecraft Studies." Hoefler, note 67, above, lists only three essays on Lovecraft that appeared in what he terms "established" periodicals: an article by Donald R. Burleson in *Extrapolation* (published by Kent State University) in 1981, a 1984 piece in the *Baker Street Journal* by Peter Cannon, and an essay by Robert M. Price for the Starmont Studies in Literary Criticism volume on Stephen King, published in 1985. It can be argued that, while these may indeed be said to be established academic journals, they are not widely known, and all of the authors were regular contributors to *Lovecraft Studies* and *Crypt of Cthulhu*.

69. Burleson's Ph.D. thesis was on Lovecraft. Today he is the author of over twenty books, ranging from textbooks on statistics and precalculus to novels and many short stories.

that, though few in number to date, received wider recognition and contributed substantially to the field rather than merely recapitulating previous work, connecting Lovecraft to larger trends in Western intellectual history and new schools of analysis."[70] This is confirmed by Joshi's 2009 bibliography,[71] listing 112 books and pamphlets about Lovecraft and numerous items of criticism in books and periodicals (371 general studies, 310 biographies and memoirs, and 244 studies of individual stories). Certainly, the crowning achievement of this period was S. T. Joshi's massive two-volume biography of Lovecraft, *I Am Providence*, released by Hippocampus Press, now the leading publisher of Lovecraftian scholarship. The monumental work considers in detail Lovecraft's correspondence and the writing of each and every story.

LOVECRAFT'S PHILOSOPHY AND THE CTHULHU MYTHOS

"HOWARD PHILLIPS LOVECRAFT was not a theoretician," declares Michel Houellebecq.[72] But "philosophy," meaning a worldview and statements of ethical principles, is found throughout Lovecraft's stories and letters, and scholars have explored Lovecraft's "philosophy" in detail.[73] In a review of a book on the subject, Graham Harman's *Weird Realism: Lovecraft and Philosophy*,[74] Brian Kim Stefans explains:

> Even if Lovecraft were not writing philosophy proper, much of the coherence of his "cosmicism" results not in the noncontradictory material or technological universes typical of most science fiction—think of the droids and lightsabers that populate the world of *Star Wars*—but in a singularly fraught metaphysical universe. In Lovecraft's version of reality, laws seem to function in ways that make our foundational certainties—Euclidean geometry, the private experience of dreams, the inviolable divisions between human, animal, plant, and the nonliving, etc.—merely contingent: just the way things appear to us, rather than absolute necessities.[75]

70. Eric Hoefler, "Lovecraft Rising," 17.

71. S. T. Joshi, *H. P. Lovecraft: A Comprehensive Bibliography*.

72. In *H. P. Lovecraft: Against the World, Against Life*.

73. See S. T. Joshi's *A Subtler Magick: The Writings and Philosophy of H. P. Lovecraft* and Timo Airaksinen's *The Philosophy of H. P. Lovecraft: The Route to Horror*.

74. Harman is a professor of philosophy at the American University in Cairo.

75. "Let's Get Weird: On Graham Harman's H. P. Lovecraft."

In other words, one may search in vain in Lovecraft's writing for a detailed cosmogony of the "Lovecraft universe." Lovecraft's essential view was that much of the cosmos is in fact without rules, at least rules intelligible to humans, and that it is not only inaccurate but *inartistic* to depict alien beings and worlds in human terms. Lovecraft was not J. R. R. Tolkien, in that his stories were not based on some carefully thought-out tapestry of language and mythology, nor even a consistent backstory. Although some have claimed that Lovecraft penned a Cthulhu Mythos, no such coherent mythology can be found in his writings. Such mythology as may have grown up was the later invention of the circle of friends and admirers who surrounded him and the writers who aped his stories.[76]

Clark Ashton Smith,
probably in his forties.

Although the biographical details of Lovecraft's life suggest a man uncomfortable with humanity and fundamentally unable to have a relationship with a wife or companion, this ignores his very real connections with dozens of friends, colleagues, and acquaintances. Lovecraft corresponded with hundreds of individuals, ranging from family members to readers, like Clark Ashton Smith, Donald Wandrei, August Derleth, Bernard Austin Dwyer, and, later, Robert Bloch, as well as his "clients"—the writers who engaged his services for revisions, such as Zealia Bishop. He also devoted much time to visiting, traveling with, and entertaining friends. He enjoyed forming "clubs" or "unions" of these colleagues. The "Gallomo" (Albert Galpin, Lovecraft, and Maurice Moe) was one of the earliest groups, formed in 1919, with whom he shared his dreams. In New York, the men who loosely formed the Kalem Club (Reinhardt Kleiner, James F. Morton, Frank Belknap Long, Arthur Leeds, Everett McNeil, George Kirk) were his primary source of intellectual sustenance.

In his letters, Lovecraft often discussed his work. The phrase Cthulhu Mythos never appears in any of his known correspondence. He mentions the term "Arkham cycle" in a letter to Clark Ashton Smith[77] without specifying to which stories he

76. That is not to say that Lovecraft did not think about the genealogy of some of his creations. In a letter to James F. Morton (April 27, 1933, *Selected Letters*, IV, 183; reproduced as Appendix 4, below), Lovecraft laid out how his creations might be related.

77. Lovecraft to Clark Ashton Smith, August 31, 1928, *Selected Letters*, II, 246–47.

HP Lovecraft *Frank B. Long, jr.*

Lovecraft and Frank Belknap Long, 1931.

refers, but he never spoke seriously about any mythology or pseudomythology. In 1931, August Derleth, then thirty, suggested that the label "the Mythology of Hastur" (referencing Chambers's *The King in Yellow*) be applied to the litany of folklore referenced by Lovecraft in "The Whisperer in Darkness" (1930). Lovecraft wrote, "It's not a bad idea to call this Cthulhuism & Yog-Sothothery of mine 'The Mythology of Hastur'—although it was really from Machen & Dunsany & others rather than through the Bierce-Chambers line, that I picked up my gradually developing hash of theogony—or daimonogeny."[78] Lovecraft actually suggested that Derleth make reference to this quasi-mythology in his story "The Horror from the Lake" and was incensed when *Weird Tales* editor Farnsworth Wright rejected the piece:[79]

78. Lovecraft to August Derleth, May 16, 1931, *Essential Solitude: The Letters of H. P. Lovecraft and August Derleth*, 336.

79. What follows is from a letter from Lovecraft to August Derleth, August 3, 1931, *Essential Solitude*, 353.

Of all Boeotion[80] blundering & irrelevancy! And what pointless censure of the introduction of Cthulhu & Yog-Sothoth—as if their use constituted any "infringement" on my stuff! Hades! The more these synthetic daemons are mutually written up by different authors, the better they become as general background- material. I *like* to have others use my Azathoths & Nyarlathoteps—& in return I shall use Klarkash-Ton's Tsathoggua,[81] your monk Clithanus, & Howard's Bran.[82]

Derleth failed to understand that Lovecraft did not intend to create a permanent or unchanging pantheon. Lovecraft's views were different from those of his role model Lord Dunsany, who said of his Pegāna cosmosgony that his inability to master Greek "left me with a curious longing for the mighty lore of the Greeks, of which I had had glimpses like a child seeing wonderful flowers through the shut gates of a garden; and it may have been the retirement of the Greek gods from my vision after I left Eton that eventually drove me to satisfy some such longing by making gods unto myself, as I did in my first two books."[83] In contrast, Lovecraft viewed his creations as part of an "open source" universe, to be visited by those whom it interested.

Nonetheless, in "H. P. Lovecraft: Outsider,"[84] Derleth asserted that Lovecraft intended to create a fixed framework:

> After a time there became apparent in his tales a curious coherence, a myth-pattern so convincing that after its early appearance the readers of Lovecraft's stories began to explore libraries and museums for certain imaginary tales of Lovecraft's own creation, so powerful that many another writer, with Lovecraft's permission, availed himself of facets of the mythos for his own use. Bit by bit it grew, and finally its outlines became distinct, and it was given a name [by Derleth!]: the Cthulhu Mythology. . . .

Derleth goes on to quote—he says—Lovecraft: ". . . all my stories, unconnected as they may be, are based on the fundamental lore or legend that this world was

---

80. A pejorative apparently coined by the Athenians and repeated by Pindar (from the proverbial "Boeotian swine"), meaning stupid or dull. Its continued existence proves that every culture creates someone to look down on.

81. See "The Whisperer in Darkness," note 29, below.

82. Ibid., note 38, below.

83. Dunsany, *Patches of Sunlight*, 30.

84. Written with Donald Wandrei, it appeared as the introduction to *The Outsider and Others* (1939).

inhabited at one time by another race outside ever ready to take possession of this earth again. . . ." In fact, the quotation from Lovecraft now appears to be spurious, having been fabricated, in all innocence, by a mutual friend, Harold S. Farnese. Farnese had written Derleth a letter, "quoting" Lovecraft as follows (emphasis added to highlight the only part of the original construction that Derleth left out):

> . . . all my stories, unconnected as they may be, are based on the fundamental lore or legend that this world was inhabited at one time by another race *who in practicing black magic lost their foothold and were expelled, yet live on* outside ever ready to take possession of this earth again. . . .

Derleth's view of Lovecraft's intentions took firm hold: As the esteemed scholar and critic George T. Wetzel, writing in 1955, asserted, "[w]hen the body of Lovecraft's prose is studied, it is at once seen that there is a varied and elaborate repetition of certain concepts and supernatural actors to which the phrase 'The Cthulhu Mythos' has justifiably been given."[85]

Derleth called the Cthulhu Mythos "basically similar to the Christian mythos," yet there is no evidence whatsoever that Lovecraft modeled his mythology, such as it was, on the monotheistic Christian religion. In fact, Lovecraft rejected Christianity, labeling himself a "sceptic," an adherent of "cynical materialism."[86] Schultz summarizes: "Derleth's 'Cthulhu Mythos' is, at best, an artificial, rigid grouping of Lovecraft's stories based upon a misinterpretation by someone not attuned to Lovecraft's philosophical outlook. . . . Lovecraft's stories were founded on his own philosophical outlook, whereas Derleth's interpretation is founded on his."[87] Richard L. Tierney has suggested abandoning the Cthulhu Mythos as a descriptor, calling it nothing more than Derleth's incorrect and earthbound interpretation of Lovecraft's cosmic vision.[88] Dirk W. Mosig reached a similar conclusion, proposing the term "Yog-Sothoth Cycle of Myth," though this seems hardly less didactic.[89]

---

85. George T. Wetzel, "The Cthulhu Mythos: A Study," 18–27.

86. In an essay called "A Confession of Unfaith" (first published in *The Liberal* in February 1922), Lovecraft wrote, "I am by nature a sceptic and analyst, hence settled early into my present general attitude of cynical materialism, subsequently changing in regard to details and degree rather than to basic ideals." He copied much of the essay in an autobiographical letter to Edwin Baird dated February 3, 1924 (*Selected Letters*, I, 299–303), and there is nothing in his writing to suggest that he ever changed this view.

87. See note 50, above.

88. "The Derleth Mythos."

89. "H. P. Lovecraft: Myth-Maker."

Lovecraft did not see life as a struggle between good and evil or light and dark forces. Rather, like Blaise Pascal,[90] he perceived the universe as frightening because of its indifference. "I am . . . an *indifferentist*," he wrote. "I do not make the mistake of thinking that the resultant of the natural forces surrounding and governing organic life will have any connexion with the wishes or tastes of any part of that organic life-process. . . . [The cosmos] doesn't give a damn one way or the other about the especial wants and ultimate welfare of mosquitoes, rats, lice, dogs, men, horses, pterodactyls, trees, fungi, dodos, or other forms of biological energy."[91]

It would be a mistake to say that the Cthulhu Mythos does not exist. It does; it is merely not Lovecraft's invention. Instead, it is the product of Derleth (who wrote numerous stories consistent with what he perceived to be the mythology) and numerous other acolytes who have carried on the tradition.[92] Of course, the influence of Lovecraft extends far beyond those writers who are identified as authors of Cthulhu-mythologic tales. Stephen King suggests the following (incomplete) pantheon of those writers "touched" by Lovecraft and his dreams: Clark Ashton Smith, Robert E. Howard, Robert Bloch, William Hope Hodgson, Fritz Leiber Jr., Harlan Ellison, Jonathan Kellerman, Peter Straub, Charles Willeford, Poppy Z. Brite, James Crumley, John D. MacDonald, Michael Chabon, Ramsey Campbell, Joyce Carol Oates, Kingsley Amis, Neil Gaiman, Flannery O'Connor, and Tennessee Williams.[93] "This is just where the list *starts*, mind you," says King.[94]

THE LEGACY OF H. P. LOVECRAFT

A CASUAL INTERNET search reveals dozens of "complete," "definitive," "collected" volumes of his stories, along with many books exploring the "mythos" and "worlds" of Lovecraft. T-shirts depicting Lovecraft and Cthulhu in various forms

90. See note 1, above.

91. Lovecraft to James F. Morton, October 30, 1929, *Selected Letters*, III, 39–40.

92. These include Donald Wandrei, Fred Chappell, Robert Bloch, Fritz Leiber Jr., Manly Wade Wellman, Robert A. W. Lowndes, C. Hall Thompson, Ramsey Campbell, Colin Wilson, Lin Carter, Brian Lumley, Thomas Ligotti, and Basil Copper. For a detailed study of the literature, S. T. Joshi's *The Rise and Fall of the Cthulhu Mythos* is essential.

93. At sixteen, Williams published "The Vengeance of Nitocris" (*Weird Tales*, August 1928), described by biographer Donald Spoto, in *The Kindness of Strangers: The Life of Tennessee Williams*, 24, as a "surprisingly lurid" tale of murder in ancient Egypt. Lovecraft did not appear in the issue, but work by his friends Donald Wandrei and Frank Belknap Long Jr. did, and it is likely that Williams, who began writing at fourteen, was already a regular reader of the magazine.

94. Stephen King, "Lovecraft's Pillow," 17.

NecronomiCon, Providence, 2013.

abound. A convention (the NecronomiCon), not held since 1999, was relaunched in Providence, Rhode Island, in August 2013. MythosCon is another convention focused on Lovecraft, while the H. P. Lovecraft Film Festival takes place annually in Portland, Oregon, and in Los Angeles. The year 2015 marks Lovecraft's 125th birthday, with attendant celebrations and tributes. How can one explain the continuing interest in Howard Phillips Lovecraft and his writing?

"[It] isn't so much literary merit—oh, such a slippery term—as his brute staying power," concludes Stephen King.[95] Lovecraft's stories are *pulp* fiction, and, worse, *genre* fiction—meaning, to too many critics, not worthy of attention and surely doomed to evanescence. Yet despite Lovecraft's commercial failure during his lifetime, his death finally focused attention on his work, and his stories have never since been out of print. The academic community and tastemakers have slowly but perceptibly come to terms with him. Popularity is no touchstone for quality, but *increasing* popularity more than seventy-five years after the author's death? There must be something *there* there, to explain how such an "infantile" cult can last.

Despite his increasing popularity, Lovecraft's racism and xenophobic views cannot be whitewashed. In the words of Lovecraft scholar Bruce Lord, "Lovecraft's racism is blunt, ugly, and unavoidable."[96] Although his attitudes may be dismissed as products of the times, his words do not display casual racism, merely reflecting the racist society in which he lived (as may be said, for example, of a few racial slurs in the Sherlock Holmes stories of Conan Doyle). Nor can Lovecraft's views be defended on the grounds that other great writers, such as Charles Dickens, Ezra Pound, T. S. Eliot, Theodore Dreiser, and Ernest Hemingway, were anti-Semitic or racist. It seems that Lovecraft's peculiar upbringing, combined with his family's tenuous social position in Rhode Island society, grafted onto his consciousness a hostility to virtually all who were not white New Englanders. He was able to tolerate a Jewish friend like the writer Samuel Loveman or a Jewish wife because, in his view, they had essentially given up their alienness, assimilating into the white population. Blacks, of course, could not readily do this, and so seem to have earned his permanent censure. Although the times changed, and the "scientific" bases for racism and the eugenics that he embraced eroded over his lifetime, Lovecraft remained static and unbending. Worst of all, his beliefs may be seen as essential to

95. Ibid., 15.

96. "The Genetics of Horror: Sex and Racism in H. P. Lovecraft's Fiction."

several of his stories, such as "The Shadow over Innsmouth," which imagines the horror of interspecies breeding.[97]

In the end, though one may despise his outmoded and pernicious social views, Lovecraft's vision of the place of mankind in the cosmos—his "cosmicism"—is more important than those views. His work speaks to the outsider in many readers, that sense that we stand outside the stream of humanity looking on, that deep-rooted feeling that one is "a stranger in this century."[98] Fundamentally, Lovecraft believed that we must make our own place in a cosmos that has no answers to give us. Humans desire to reinterpret or reshape life into a more coherent and manageable pattern than is apparent on its chaotic surface. Some great literature does that for us, by offering examples of ordered worlds, indications of our place in the universe, and philosophies that we can apply to our own lives. Lovecraft's fiction presents no simple coherent worldview or philosophy; rather, he showed, in the context of richly detailed and realistic frameworks, that we must find our own way. Until all such speculations have been put to rest, readers will continue to turn to Lovecraft's stories to be frightened, to be perpetually reminded that there is more than one way to look at the universe.

> *That is not dead which can eternal lie,*
> *And with strange æons even death may die.*[99]

---

97. In fact, hereditary degeneration is a theme in many of Lovecraft's stories, including "The Facts Concerning the Late Arthur Jermyn and His Family," "The Rats in the Walls," "Beyond the Wall of Sleep," "The Outsider," "The Dunwich Horror," and even *At the Mountains of Madness*, with the degraded Shoggoths. Lovecraft spoke little of his parents' insanity, but it must have weighed on his mind—witness, for example, the frequent appearance of hospitals or asylums for the insane in stories like "Beyond the Wall of Sleep," "Herbert West: Reanimator," "The Call of Cthulhu," *The Case of Charles Dexter Ward*, "The Colour Out of Space," "The Shadow over Innsmouth," and "The Thing on the Doorstep." It may well be that Lovecraft's racism, his hatred of what he viewed as degenerate beings, was the product of self-loathing and fear regarding his own genetic disposition to insanity and degradation.

98. Lovecraft, "The Outsider."

99. Lovecraft, "The Nameless City."

Editor's Note

Presenting a collection of the fiction of Howard Phillips Lovecraft is a matter of selection. First, Lovecraft wrote seventy stories under his own name (some mere fragments, admittedly), three of short-novel length. They are of uneven quality, and some were never published. Including all of the stories would make this collection unwieldy and, as a practical matter, inaccessible to a wide audience. Therefore, I have selected twenty-two stories for this volume, which are presented in the order written. I do not characterize these as the "best" of Lovecraft or the "most important"; rather, I have selected stories that I believe exemplify the best of the author's "Arkham cycle," his term for those stories, set in or around the fictional town of Arkham, Massachusetts, that are central to the mythology he created. I have included seminal references to its geography and its meaning. Had space permitted, I would have liked to include "The Terrible Old Man," "The Other Gods," "The Strange High House in the Mist," and *The Dream-Quest of Unknown Kadath*, and study of those is recommended. Other fine stories include "The Tomb," "The Outsider," "The Rats in the Wall," "The Music of Erich Zann," "Pickman's Model," and "The Shunned House," all readily accessible on the Internet.

The second problem for the editor is the choice of text. Because none of the stories received Lovecraft's careful attention in the publishing process (and some were published posthumously), the first-published text of the stories is far from reliable. Fortunately for the scholarly community, the estimable S. T. Joshi has undertaken to prepare and publish definitive texts for Lovecraft's work, drawing upon Lovecraft's notes, manuscripts, journals, and letters, and he very kindly provided them to me. Of course, "definitive" is a subjective matter, and in some cases I have noted errors in Joshi's work or expressed a different opinion about the "best" text. Notwithstanding the diligent proofreading by my very supportive wife (who had no idea what to expect from her first reading of Lovecraft's work), errors remaining in the text are my own.

In adding notes to the selected stories, I have focused on three areas. First, Lovecraft is determinedly an antiquarian, and he deliberately chose archaic and in many cases obsolete words when a modern term might have been more familiar to his readers. Therefore, many of the notes serve the function of glossary. Second, I have added historical and cultural background, explaining many of Lovecraft's references to contemporary and historical personages and events for the modern reader. Third, I have treated the stories as Lovecraft meant them to be regarded— as "hoaxes." That is, Lovecraft insisted that "a tale should be plausible—even a bizarre tale *except for the single element where supernaturalism is involved.*"[1] Therefore, I have attempted to verify Lovecraft's assertions of fact and circumstance down to the smallest details and pointed out occasional errors. I have not tried to replicate the work of S. T. Joshi, whose selected annotated texts focus more on the sources of Lovecraft's ideas and inspirations and the biographical events the stories reflect; and the reader who seeks that kind of scholarship should consult the editions set forth in the bibliography. I have also stayed away from literary criticism of the sort so ably applied by Donald Burleson, Robert H. Waugh, and others to Lovecraft's stories.

My intentions in assembling this book are simple: I want to share the pleasures of reading Lovecraft with a wider readership than he has historically enjoyed. Unlike with my previous editions of the stories of Sherlock Holmes and *Dracula*, I have found myself many times answering the question "Who is Lovecraft?" when my listener learned that I was preparing this text. But it is an important question, and one that I hope this work answers—if not fully, then at least sufficiently to make clear why Lovecraft should be added to the pantheon of great original minds of the twentieth century.

—LESLIE S. KLINGER

1. Lovecraft to Myrta Alice Little, May 17, 1921; the letter was first published in its entirety in *Lovecraft Studies* 26 (Spring 1992), 28.

THE
STORIES

Dagon[1]

"Dagon" is not only one of Lovecraft's earliest tales, it is the earliest to contain any elements of what eventually became known as the Cthulhu Mythos. Indeed, the name Dagon itself will reappear in future works. Part confession, part suicide note, part self-justification, the tale introduces some of Lovecraft's stories' signature features: truly ancient beings, experiences and sensations that cannot be processed by human brains, and a deep sense of doom.

I am writing this under an appreciable mental strain, since by tonight I shall be no more. Penniless, and at the end of my supply of the drug which alone makes life endurable, I can bear the torture no longer; and shall cast myself from this garret window into the squalid street below. Do not think from my slavery to morphine that I am a weakling or a degenerate. When you have read these hastily scrawled pages you may guess, though never fully realise, why it is that I must have forgetfulness or death.

It was in one of the most open and least frequented parts of the broad Pacific that the packet of which I was supercargo fell a victim to the German sea-raider. The great war[2] was then at its very beginning, and the ocean forces of the Hun[3] had not completely sunk to their later degradation;[4] so that our vessel was made legitimate prize, whilst we of her crew were treated with all the fairness and consideration due us as naval prisoners. So liberal, indeed, was the discipline of our captors, that five days after we were taken I managed to escape alone in a small boat with water and provisions for a good length of time.

When I finally found myself adrift and free, I had but little idea of my surroundings. Never a competent navigator, I could only guess vaguely by the sun and stars that I was somewhat south of the equator. Of the longitude I knew nothing, and no island or

1. Written in the summer of 1917, it first appeared in *The Vagrant* 11 (November 1919), 23–29. It subsequently appeared in *Weird Tales* 2, no. 3 (October 1923), 23–25.

2. Now commonly referred to as World War I, the Great War began on June 28, 1914, with the assassination of Archduke Franz Ferdinand of Austria, and ended with the signing of the Treaty of Versailles on June 28, 1919, exactly five years later. The nations at war included the German Empire, the Austro-Hungarian Empire, the Ottoman Empire, the Russian Empire, the British Empire, France, and Italy.

3. In the version published in *The Vagrant*, the narrator refers to the forces of the "Kaiser," not the Hun. In a speech reported in *Die Weser-Zeitung* on July 28, 1900, Kaiser Wilhelm II of Germany made the following remarks concerning rebels in China (with regard to suppressing what became known as the Boxer Rebellion): "Mercy will not be shown, prisoners will not be taken. Just as a thou-

sand years ago, the Huns under Attila won a reputation of might that lives on in legends, so may the name of Germany in China, such that no Chinese will ever again dare so much as to look askance at a German." The term "Huns," with a push from Allied propaganda, came to be applied broadly to the militant Germans in the Great War.

4. The narrator here refers to the shift in German policy regarding attacks by submarine, or *Unterseeboot* (U-boat). Initially, German commanders observed the historical "prize rules" governing the capture of enemy civilian ships and their crew and passengers, internationally agreed-upon protocol dating from the previous century. However, on October 20, 1914, the German *U-17* sank the SS *Glitra*, a merchant ship, off Norway, and on February 4, 1915, the kaiser declared the waters surrounding England and Ireland to be a war zone. Thereafter, U-boat captains were permitted to sink merchant ships, even potentially neutral ones, without warning.

". . . I finally found myself adrift and free . . ."
Weird Tales 2, no. 3 (October 1923) (artist: William F. Heitman)

coast-line was in sight. The weather kept fair, and for uncounted days I drifted aimlessly beneath the scorching sun; waiting either for some passing ship, or to be cast on the shores of some habitable land. But neither ship nor land appeared, and I began to despair in my solitude upon the heaving vastnesses of unbroken blue.

The change happened whilst I slept. Its details I shall never know; for my slumber, though troubled and dream-infested, was continuous. When at last I awaked, it was to discover myself half sucked into a slimy expanse of hellish black mire which extended about me in monotonous undulations as far as I could see, and in which my boat lay grounded some distance away.

Though one might well imagine that my first sensation would be of wonder at so prodigious and unexpected a transformation of scenery, I was in reality more horrified than astonished; for there was in the air and in the rotting soil a sinister quality which chilled me to the very core. The region was putrid with the carcasses of decaying fish, and of other less describable things which I saw protruding from the nasty mud of the unending plain. Perhaps I should not hope to convey in mere words the unutterable hideousness that can dwell in absolute silence and barren immensity. There was nothing within hearing, and nothing in sight save a vast reach of black slime; yet the very completeness of the stillness and homogeneity of the landscape oppressed me with a nauseating fear.

The sun was blazing down from a sky which seemed to me almost black in its cloudless cruelty; as though reflecting the inky marsh beneath my feet. As I crawled into the stranded boat I realised that only one theory could explain my position. Through some unprecedented volcanic upheaval,[5] a portion of the ocean floor must have been thrown to the surface, exposing regions which for innumerable millions of years had lain hidden under unfathomable watery depths. So great was the extent of the new land which had risen beneath me, that I could not detect the faintest noise of the surging ocean, strain my ears as I might. Nor were there any sea-fowl to prey upon the dead things.

For several hours I sat thinking or brooding in the boat, which lay upon its side and afforded a slight shade as the sun moved across the heavens. As the day progressed, the ground lost some of its stickiness, and seemed likely to dry sufficiently for travelling purposes in a short time. That night I slept but little, and the next day I made for myself a pack containing food and water, preparatory to an overland journey in search of the vanished sea and possible rescue.

On the third morning I found the soil dry enough to walk upon with ease. The odour of the fish was maddening; but I was too much concerned with graver things to mind so slight an evil, and set out boldly for an unknown goal. All day I forged steadily westward, guided by a far-away hummock which rose higher than any other elevation on the rolling desert. That night I encamped, and on the following day still travelled toward the hummock, though that object seemed scarcely nearer than when I had first espied it. By the fourth evening I attained the base of the mound, which turned out to be much higher than it had appeared from a distance; an intervening valley setting it out in sharper relief from the general surface. Too weary to ascend, I slept in the shadow of the hill.

I know not why my dreams were so wild that night; but ere

5. No land-based volcanic eruption was recorded in 1914 or 1915 in the Pacific. Records of submarine volcanic activity are poor to nonexistent. In September 1909, George R. Putnam, whom President William Taft the following year appointed the first commissioner of lighthouses (Putnam would go on to serve six presidents), wrote, in "The Hidden Perils of the Deep" (*National Geographic*), "Volcanic action in well authenticated cases has caused islands to rise or disappear. In the present location of Bogoslof Island, in [the] Bering Sea, the early voyagers described a 'sail rock.' In this position in 1796 there arose a high island. In 1883 another island appeared near it. In 1906 a high cone arose between the two, and a continuous island was formed. . . ." Earlier in 1909, a piece in *National Geographic* by Captain F. M. Munger referred to Bogoslof Island as a "jack in the box" and reported "the appearance and disappearance of peaks on the island. . . ."

6. More than half full. T. R. Livesey, in "Dispatches from the Providence Observatory: Astronomical Motifs and Sources in the Writings of H. P. Lovecraft," points out that full moons rise at sunset and quarter moons rise at noon or midnight; so only a gibbous moon could rise after sunset and be "near the zenith." That is, this and other data in the story regarding the moon are accurate.

7. In John Milton's epic poem *Paradise Lost* (1667), a treatment of the biblical Fall of Man, Satan rebels against God and climbs from Tartarus, to which he has fallen, to the material world. In Greek mythology, Tartarus is both a primordial deity and a place situated in the bowels of the underworld. The word is derived from Τάρταρος, the grime (or tartar) on the inside surface of a cask.

8. "Stygian" refers to the river Styx in a dark and gloomy region of the underworld.

9. The scene compares to the discovery of the monolith, first by apes and then by human visitors to Earth's moon, in Stanley Kubrick's epic film *2001: A Space Odyssey* (1968).

the waning and fantastically gibbous[6] moon had risen far above the eastern plain, I was awake in a cold perspiration, determined to sleep no more. Such visions as I had experienced were too much for me to endure again. And in the glow of the moon I saw how unwise I had been to travel by day. Without the glare of the parching sun, my journey would have cost me less energy; indeed, I now felt quite able to perform the ascent which had deterred me at sunset. Picking up my pack, I started for the crest of the eminence.

I have said that the unbroken monotony of the rolling plain was a source of vague horror to me; but I think my horror was greater when I gained the summit of the mound and looked down the other side into an immeasurable pit or canyon, whose black recesses the moon had not yet soared high enough to illuminate. I felt myself on the edge of the world; peering over the rim into a fathomless chaos of eternal night. Through my terror ran curious reminiscences of *Paradise Lost*, and of Satan's hideous climb through the unfashioned realms of darkness.[7]

As the moon climbed higher in the sky, I began to see that the slopes of the valley were not quite so perpendicular as I had imagined. Ledges and outcroppings of rock afforded fairly easy foot-holds for a descent, whilst after a drop of a few hundred feet, the declivity became very gradual. Urged on by an impulse which I cannot definitely analyse, I scrambled with difficulty down the rocks and stood on the gentler slope beneath, gazing into the Stygian deeps[8] where no light had yet penetrated.

All at once my attention was captured by a vast and singular object on the opposite slope, which rose steeply about an hundred yards ahead of me; an object that gleamed whitely in the newly bestowed rays of the ascending moon. That it was merely a gigantic piece of stone, I soon assured myself; but I was conscious of a distinct impression that its contour and position were not altogether the work of Nature. A closer scrutiny filled me with sensations I cannot express; for despite its enormous magnitude, and its position in an abyss which had yawned at the bottom of the sea since the world was young, I perceived beyond a doubt that the strange object was a well-shaped monolith whose massive bulk had known the workmanship and perhaps the worship of living and thinking creatures.[9]

Dazed and frightened, yet not without a certain thrill of the scientist's[10] or archæologist's delight, I examined my surroundings more closely. The moon, now near the zenith, shone weirdly and vividly above the towering steeps that hemmed in the chasm, and revealed the fact that a far-flung body of water flowed at the bottom, winding out of sight in both directions, and almost lapping my feet as I stood on the slope. Across the chasm, the wavelets washed the base of the Cyclopean monolith;[11] on whose surface I could now trace both inscriptions and crude sculptures. The writing was in a system of hieroglyphics[12] unknown to me, and unlike anything I had ever seen in books; consisting for the most part of conventionalised aquatic symbols such as fishes, eels, octopi, crustaceans, molluscs, whales, and the like. Several characters obviously represented marine things which are unknown to the modern world, but whose decomposing forms I had observed on the ocean-risen plain.[13]

It was the pictorial carving, however, that did most to hold me spellbound. Plainly visible across the intervening water on account of their enormous size, were an array of bas-reliefs whose subjects would have excited the envy of a Doré.[14] I think that these things were supposed to depict men—at least, a certain sort of men; though the creatures were shewn disporting like fishes in the waters of some marine grotto, or paying homage at some monolithic shrine which appeared to be under the waves as well. Of their faces and forms I dare not speak in detail; for the mere remembrance makes me grow faint. Grotesque beyond the imagination of a Poe or a Bulwer,[15] they were damnably human in general outline despite webbed hands and feet, shockingly wide and flabby lips, glassy, bulging eyes, and other features less pleasant to recall. Curiously enough, they seemed to have been chiselled badly out of proportion with their scenic background; for one of the creatures was shewn in the act of killing a whale represented as but little larger than himself. I remarked, as I say, their grotesqueness and strange size, but in a moment decided that they were merely the imaginary gods of some primitive fishing or seafaring tribe; some tribe whose last descendant had perished eras before the first ancestor of the Piltdown[16] or Neanderthal Man[17] was born. Awestruck at this unexpected glimpse into a past beyond the conception of the most daring anthropologist, I

10. It is hard to recall today that "scientist" was a relatively new term, first used in 1840, according to the *Oxford English Dictionary*.

11. "Huge, massive, like the Cyclops of classic mythology" (E. Cobham Brewer, *Dictionary of Phrase and Fable* [hereinafter "Brewer"], 322). The Pelasgic ruins of Greece, Asia Minor, and Italy, such as the Gallery of Tiryns, the Gate of Lyons, the Treasury of Athens, and the Tombs of Phoroneus and Danaos, are examples of so-called Cyclopean masonry. Cyclopean architecture is mentioned in numerous other stories below. Whatever else may be said definitely about the Elder Gods and their followers, they liked large buildings.

Mycenaean wall.

12. The earliest evidence of symbolic writing is cuneiform, highly stylized wedge-shaped writing found in Sumerian texts dating from about 3300 BCE. While cuneiform may have originated as pictures, the pictorial element became lost and the shapes arbitrary. Hieroglyphic or pictographic writing with recognizable pictures may be traced as far back as the Egyptian writing that flourished a few hundred years after the Sumerians, as well as that of Cretan and Minoan civilizations of the Bronze Age (more than 2,000 years before the common era). Hieroglyphic writing remained static in Egypt for more than 3,000 years and flourished in many later cultures, including several in the New World. Egyptyian hieroglyphics were largely decoded in the early nineteenth century, after the dis-

covery of the Rosetta Stone in 1799, but Cretan hieroglyphs, although compiled in 1909, have resisted definitive decipherment. Recently, crowdsourcing the decipherment has been propounded as a means to address the formidable task. .

13. It has long been speculated that forms of sea life unknown to contemporary science exist at great depths. See, for example, Jules Verne's *Twenty Thousand Leagues Under the Sea* (1869), in which giant cuttlefish attack. For a menagerie of real-life horrors discovered in the deep, see http://www.oddee.com/item_79915.aspx.

14. Paul Gustave Doré (1832–1883) was a French artist, engraver, and sculptor best remembered for his nightmarish *London: A Pilgrimage* (1872), a collection of 180 engravings depicting some of the worst slums of London.

"Turn him out!—Ratcliff" by Gustave Doré, 1872.

15. Edward George Earle Lytton Bulwer-Lytton, 1st Baron Lytton (1803–1873), was an immensely popular writer of his day, primarily of novels. Bulwer-Lytton

stood musing whilst the moon cast queer reflections on the silent channel before me.

Then suddenly I saw it. With only a slight churning to mark its rise to the surface, the thing slid into view above the dark waters. Vast, Polyphemus-like,[18] and loathsome, it darted like a stupendous monster of nightmares to the monolith, about which it flung its gigantic scaly arms, the while it bowed its hideous head and gave vent to certain measured sounds.[19] I think I went mad then.

Of my frantic ascent of the slope and cliff, and of my delirious journey back to the stranded boat, I remember little. I believe I sang a great deal, and laughed oddly when I was unable to sing. I have indistinct recollections of a great storm some time after I reached the boat; at any rate, I know that I heard peals of thunder and other tones which Nature utters only in her wildest moods.

When I came out of the shadows I was in a San Francisco hospital; brought thither by the captain of the American ship which had picked up my boat in mid-ocean. In my delirium I had said much, but found that my words had been given scant attention. Of any land upheaval in the Pacific, my rescuers knew nothing; nor did I deem it necessary to insist upon a thing which I knew they could not believe. Once I sought out a celebrated enthnologist, and amused him with peculiar questions regarding the ancient Philistine legend of Dagon, the Fish-God;[20] but soon perceiving that he was hopelessly conventional, I did not press my inquiries.

It is at night, especially when the moon is gibbous and waning, that I see the thing. I tried morphine; but the drug has given only transient surcease, and has drawn me into its clutches as a hopeless slave. So now I am to end it all, having written a full account for the information or the contemptuous amusement of my fellow-men. Often I ask myself if it could not all have been a pure phantasm—a mere freak of fever as I lay sun-stricken and raving in the open boat after my escape from the German man-of-war. This I ask myself, but ever does there come before me a hideously vivid vision in reply. I cannot think of the deep sea without shuddering at the nameless things that may at this very moment be crawling and floundering on its slimy bed, worshipping their ancient stone idols and carving their own detestable likenesses on submarine obelisks of water-soaked granite. I dream of a day when they may rise above the billows to drag down in their reeking talons the remnants of puny, war-exhausted mankind—of a day when the land shall sink, and the dark ocean floor shall ascend amidst universal pandemonium.

The end is near. I hear a noise at the door, as of some immense slippery body lumbering against it. It shall not find me. God, *that hand*! The window! The window![21]

Cover from *The Worlds of H. P. Lovecraft: Dagon*, no. 1.
Caliber Press, 1993
(artist: Sergio Cariello)

Poster from *Dagon* (Castelao Producciones, 2001), directed by Stuart Gordon.

Cover of *The Worlds of H. P. Lovecraft: Dagon*, no. 2.
Caliber Press, 1993
(artist: Sergio Cariello)

Cover from *H. P. Lovecraft's Dagon* by Mark Rudolph. (CVBooks4, 2011)

coined many phrases but will always be remembered for the purple prose that opens his 1830 novel *Paul Clifford*: "It was a dark and stormy night; the rain fell in torrents—except at occasional intervals, when it was checked by a violent gust of wind which swept up the streets (for it is in London that our scene lies), rattling along the housetops, and fiercely agitating the scanty flame of the lamps that struggled against the darkness." In this context, however, the narrator is thinking of Bulwer-Lytton's horror/science-fiction stories, such as "The Haunted and the Haunters; or, the House and the Brain" (1859) or *The Coming Race*, published later as *Vril: The Power of the Coming Race* (1871), which tells of a subterranean race waiting to reclaim the surface of the earth (a theme with obvious resonance here).

16. In 1912, amateur archaeologist Charles Dawson claimed to have reconstructed from fragments discovered at Piltdown (in East Sussex, England) a skull of a prehistoric man predating the then earliest-known specimens. The "Piltdown Man," as the discovery became known, was immediately challenged, and as early as 1923, a complete refutation was made by anatomist and physical anthropologist Franz Weidenreich. However, it was not until 1953 that the discovery was exposed as a forgery, made by an unknown hoaxer.

17. Neanderthals—*Homo neanderthalensis* or *Homo sapiens neanderthalensis*—were first identified in 1829 by Philippe-Charles Schmerling. They are generally believed to have first appeared, in fully developed form, about 130,000 years ago.

18. Polypheme, a son of Poseidon, the sea god, was "[o]ne of the Cyclops, who lived in Sicily. He was an enormous giant, with

only one eye, and that in the middle of his forehead. When Ulyssses landed on the island, this monster made him and twelve of his crew captives; six of them he ate, and then Ulysses contrived to blind him, and make good his escape with the rest of the crew" (Brewer, 995).

19. S. T. Joshi, in *The Rise and Fall of the Cthulhu Mythos* (27), points out that the creature is *worshipping* at the monolith, as are the creatures depicted on it. "Polyphemus-like," then, appears to refer to the creature's size, not to the number of its eyes. Note that the beings depicted on the monolith are also quite large, and so we may conclude that the creature is one of that race of beings.

20. Brewer mentions Dagon as "the idol of the Philistines; half woman and half fish" (325). Milton's *Paradise Lost* (Book I, lines 462–65) refers to this god as well:

> Dagon his name; sea-monster, upward
> man
> And downward fish; yet had his temple
> high;
> Rear'd in Azotus, dreaded through the
> coast
> Of Palestine, in Gath and Ascalon,
> And Accaron and Gaza's frontier
> bounds.

The Bible also speaks of the worship of Dagon (Hebrew for "little fish") in the temple of Azotus, an ancient Philistine city now identified with modern Gaza or Ashdod in southern Israel (1 Samuel 5:1–7). Later, Dagon was conflated with an agricultural god and worshipped as a national god by the Philistines. However, the *Encyclopædia Britannica* (9th ed.) suggests that the notion of the half-human part of the idol is mistaken and that "only his fish part was left to him." Lovecraft is likely to have known of this reading.

The Philistines were an identifiable Middle Eastern population from about 1500 BCE until conquered by David and subsequent kings of Israel. As a result of these conquests, they began to be assimilated into neighboring populations and by 500 BCE had lost their identity as a nation.

21. Most scholars agree that the reader is intended to conclude that the narrator is hallucinating, but according to S. T. Joshi (in *I Am Providence*, 251), "some readers" evidently believe that Dagon (or whatever the creature is that the narrator saw) did indeed follow him to San Francisco. The "hand" witnessed by the narrator must have been webbed or else grotesquely large to evoke such a reaction.

Cover of Dagon and Other Macabre Tales.
Arkham House Publishers, 1965
(artist: Raymond Bayless)

The Statement of Randolph Carter[1]

Weird Tales 5, no. 2 (February 1925) (artist: Andrew Brosnatch)

One of several stories based on a dream of Lovecraft's, "The Statement of Randolph Carter" introduces the persona of Carter, generally regarded as autobiographical. Once again, the story is cast as self-justification, a narrative designed to explain the bizarre behavior of the narrator. The geographical details of the story are confused, as perhaps befits a dreamscape, but the juxtaposition of modern technology—telephone gear—and exploration of an unknown crypt makes for a powerful scare.

repeat to you, gentlemen, that your inquisition is fruitless.[2] Detain me here forever if you will; confine or execute me if you must have a victim to propitiate the illusion you call justice;[3] but I can say no more than I have said already. Everything that I can remember, I have told with perfect candour. Nothing has been distorted or concealed, and if anything remains vague, it is only because of the dark cloud which has come over my mind—that cloud and the nebulous nature of the horrors which brought it upon me.

Again I say, I do not know what has become of Harley

1. Written in 1919, the story first appeared in *The Vagrant* 13 (May 1920), 41–48. It subsequently appeared in *Weird Tales* 5, no. 2 (February 1925), 149–53, and again in *Weird Tales* 30, no. 2 (August 1937), 242–46.

2. Randolph Carter appears in several other stories by Lovecraft, including as the protagonist of *The Dream-Quest of Unknown Kadath*, in which the character is in his twenties; "The Unnamable" (pp.

114–22 below), likely set shortly after the events recounted here; and "The Silver Key" (pp. 158–70 below), when he is age fifty-four. Carter is also briefly mentioned in *The Case of Charles Dexter Ward* (pp. 171–309, below) as a friend of Dr. Willett. Some suggest that Carter is Lovecraft's alter ego, a melancholy, commercially unsuccessful writer. More of Carter's history is given in "Through the Gates of the Silver Key," written by Lovecraft and E. Hoffmann Price between October 1932 and April 1933 and first published in July 1934 in *Weird Tales* 24, no. 1, 60–85. However, this tale is thought to be largely the work of Price and must be regarded as an unreliable source of information. Carter also appears, under one of his known aliases, in "Out of the Aeons," by Lovecraft and Hazel Heald, another "revision" story, probably written in 1933, and which first appeared in *Weird Tales*, 25, no. 4 (April 1935), 478–96. The alter ego aspect of Carter is strongest in this tale, which mirrors in many respects a dream of Lovecraft's, recorded in a letter to the "Gallomo" (Alfred Galpin, Lovecraft, and Maurice Moe [December 11, 1919, *Selected Letters*, vol. 1, 94–97]). Robert M. Price goes so far, in "You Fool! Loveman Is Dead!" (16), to call Lovecraft's transcript of his dream a "first draft" of the tale.

3. Friedrich Nietzsche explored the idea of the sources of justice in his *On the Genealogy of Morals* (1887). American theologian Henry Sylvester Nash, in his *Genesis of the Social Conscience* (1902), wrote, "The State derives its stability from the reality or the illusion of justice. It has no power to permanently bind men's wills, to master their imagination, and to levy taxes upon their property except in so far as it is or is thought to be an institution of right either human or divine or both" (280).

Warren, though I think—almost hope—that he is in peaceful oblivion, if there be anywhere so blessed a thing. It is true that I have for five years been his closest friend, and a partial sharer of his terrible researches into the unknown. I will not deny, though my memory is uncertain and indistinct, that this witness of yours may have seen us together as he says, on the Gainesville pike, walking toward Big Cypress Swamp,[4] at half past eleven on that awful night. That we bore electric lanterns, spades, and a curious coil of wire with attached instruments, I will even affirm; for these things all played a part in the single hideous scene which remains burned into my shaken recollection. But of what followed, and of the reason I was found alone and dazed on the edge of the swamp next morning, I must insist that I know nothing save what I have told you over and over again. You say to me that there is nothing in the swamp or near it which could form the setting of that frightful episode. I reply that I know nothing beyond what I saw. Vision or nightmare it may have been—vision or nightmare I fervently hope it was—yet it is all that my mind retains of what took place in those shocking hours after we left the sight of men. And why Harley Warren did not return, he or his shade—or some nameless *thing* I cannot describe—alone can tell.

As I have said before, the weird studies of Harley Warren were well known to me, and to some extent shared by me. Of his vast collection of strange, rare books on forbidden subjects I have read all that are written in the languages of which I am master; but these are few as compared with those in languages I cannot understand. Most, I believe, are in Arabic; and the fiend-inspired book which brought on the end—the book which he carried in his pocket out of the world—was written in characters whose like I never saw elsewhere.[5] Warren would never tell me just what was in that book. As to the nature of our studies—must I say again that I no longer retain full comprehension? It seems to me rather merciful that I do not, for they were terrible studies, which I pursued more through reluctant fascination than through actual inclination. Warren always dominated me, and sometimes I feared him. I remember how I shuddered at his facial expression on the night before the awful happening, when he talked so incessantly of his theory, *why certain corpses never* decay, *but rest firm and fat in their tombs for a thousand years*. But I do not fear him now, for I suspect that he has known horrors beyond my ken. Now I fear *for* him.

Once more I say that I have no clear idea of our object on that night. Certainly, it had much to do with something in the book which Warren carried with him—that ancient book in undecipherable characters which had come to him from India a month before—but I swear I do not know what it was that we expected to find. Your witness says he saw us at half past eleven on the Gainesville pike, headed for Big Cypress Swamp. This is probably true, but I have no distinct memory of it. The picture seared into my soul is of one scene only, and the hour must have been long after midnight; for a waning crescent moon was high in the vaporous heavens.

The place was an ancient cemetery; so ancient that I trembled at the manifold signs of immemorial years. It was in a deep, damp hollow, overgrown with rank grass, moss, and curious creeping weeds, and filled with a vague stench which my idle fancy associated absurdly with rotting stone. On every hand were the signs of neglect and decrepitude, and I seemed haunted by the notion that Warren and I were the first living creatures to invade a lethal silence of centuries. Over the valley's rim a wan, waning crescent moon peered through the noisome vapours that seemed to emanate from unheard-of catacombs, and by its feeble, wavering beams I could distinguish a repellent array of antique slabs, urns, cenotaphs,[6] and mausolean facades; all crumbling, moss-grown, and moisture-stained, and partly concealed by the gross luxuriance of the unhealthy vegetation. My first vivid impression of my own presence in this terrible necropolis concerns the act of pausing with Warren before a certain half-obliterated sepulchre, and of throwing down some burdens which we seemed to have been carrying. I now observed that I had with me an electric lantern and two spades, whilst my companion was supplied with a similar lantern and a portable telephone outfit.[7] No word was uttered, for the spot and the task seemed known to us; and without delay we seized our spades and commenced to clear away the grass, weeds, and drifted earth from the flat, archaic mortuary. After uncovering the entire surface, which consisted of three immense granite slabs, we stepped back some distance to survey

4. There is a "Big Cypress Swamp" in Florida and a town named Gainesville (places with those names also exist in Georgia), but in both cases, they are quite a distance apart. Harley Warren is described in "The Silver Key" (pp. 158–70, below) as "a man in the South." There is also a Gainesville, Virginia, and plentiful cypress swamps there. We must conclude that the Big Cypress Swamp was not an official place-name but only a description, and it is impossible to determine which of these three southern locations—in Virginia, Georgia, or Florida—is referred to here. Perhaps it is just as well.

5. S. T. Joshi concludes, in *The Call of Cthulhu and Other Weird Stories* (364, n.4), that this is not the *Necronomicon*, a work invented by Lovecraft and available, according to Lovecraft's history (see Appendix 3), only in Arabic, and in Greek, Latin, and English translation. However, the book could have been a hitherto unknown translation or transcription of the *Necronomicon* or a hand-encrypted, annotated version of the text (cf. the diary of Wilbur Whateley, described in "The Dunwich Horror," pp. 343–87, below).

6. A monument for a person who is buried elsewhere or whose body is lost (for example, lost at sea).

7. The nature of this "portable telephone outfit" is unclear. Frederick F. Strong filed a patent application as early as 1905 for a portable telephone apparatus that required a wired connection between two instruments, and commercial portable telephones were marketed for the deaf and others who needed direct instantaneous communications. Film footage recently discovered by British Pathé shows a demonstration of a portable *wireless* telephone in 1922. See http://www.telegraph.co.uk/technology/mobile-phones/7764405/Footage-shows-worlds-first-mobile-phone.html.

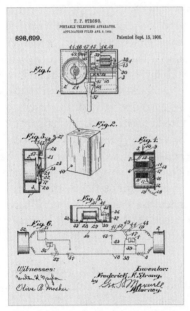

Shown is the diagram from a 1908 patent application for a portable wireless telephone —requiring a matched pair, however.

The early-twentieth-century advertisement explains the product.

the charnel scene; and Warren appeared to make some mental calculations. Then he returned to the sepulchre, and using his spade as a lever, sought to pry up the slab lying nearest to a stony ruin which may have been a monument in its day. He did not succeed, and motioned to me to come to his assistance. Finally our combined strength loosened the stone, which we raised and tipped to one side.

The removal of the slab revealed a black aperture, from which rushed an effluence of miasmal gases so nauseous that we started back in horror. After an interval, however, we approached the pit again, and found the exhalations less unbearable. Our lanterns disclosed the top of a flight of stone steps, dripping with some detestable ichor of the inner earth, and bordered by moist walls encrusted with nitre. And now for the first time my memory records verbal discourse, Warren addressing me at length in his mellow tenor voice; a voice singularly unperturbed by our awesome surroundings.

"I'm sorry to have to ask you to stay on the surface," he said, "but it would be a crime to let anyone with your frail nerves go down there. You can't imagine, even from what you have read and from what I've told you, the things I shall have to see and do. It's fiendish work, Carter, and I doubt if any man without ironclad sensibilities could ever see it through and come up alive and sane. I don't wish to offend you, and heaven knows I'd be glad enough to have you with me; but the responsibility is in a certain sense mine, and I couldn't drag a bundle of nerves like you down to probable death or madness. I tell you, you can't imagine what the thing is really like! But I promise to keep you informed over the telephone of every move—you see I've enough wire here to reach to the centre of the earth and back!"

I can still hear, in memory, those coolly spoken words; and I can still remember my remonstrances. I seemed desperately anxious to accompany my friend into those sepulchral depths, yet he proved inflexibly obdurate. At one time he threatened to abandon the expedition if I remained insistent; a threat which proved effective, since he alone held the key to the *thing*. All this I can still remember, though I no longer know what manner of *thing* we sought. After he had secured my reluctant acquiescence in his design, Warren picked up the reel of wire and adjusted the instruments. At his nod I took one of the latter and seated myself upon an aged, discoloured gravestone close by the newly uncovered aperture. Then he shook my hand, shouldered the coil of wire, and disappeared within that indescribable ossuary.[8]

For a moment I kept sight of the glow of his lantern, and heard the rustle of the wire as he laid it down after him; but the glow soon disappeared abruptly, as if a turn in the stone staircase had been encountered, and the sound died away almost as quickly. I was alone, yet bound to the unknown depths by those magic strands whose insulated surface lay green beneath the struggling beams of that waning crescent moon.

In the lone silence of that hoary and deserted city of the dead, my mind conceived the most ghastly phantasies and illusions; and the grotesque shrines and monoliths seemed to assume a hideous personality—a half-sentience. Amorphous shadows seemed to lurk in the darker recesses of the weed-choked hollow and to flit as in some blasphemous ceremonial procession past the portals of the mouldering tombs in the hillside; shadows which could not have been cast by that pallid, peering crescent moon. I constantly consulted my watch by the light of my electric lantern, and listened with feverish anxiety at the receiver of the telephone; but for more than a quarter of an hour heard nothing. Then a faint clicking came from the instrument, and I called down to my friend in a tense voice. Apprehensive as I was, I was nevertheless unprepared for the words which came up from that uncanny vault in accents more alarmed and quivering than any I had heard before from Harley Warren. He who had so calmly left me a little while previously, now called from below in a shaky whisper more portentous than the loudest shriek:

"God! If you could see what I am seeing!"

I could not answer. Speechless, I could only wait. Then came the frenzied tones again:

"Carter, it's terrible—monstrous—unbelievable!"

This time my voice did not fail me, and I poured into the transmitter a flood of excited questions. Terrified, I continued to repeat, "Warren, what is it? What is it?"

Once more came the voice of my friend, still hoarse with fear, and now apparently tinged with despair:

"I can't tell you, Carter! It's too utterly beyond thought—I dare

8. A burial site.

9. The slang phrase "Beat it!" (meaning to depart quickly) is quite a bit older than Warren's schooldays; Luciana utters the phrase in Shakespeare's *Comedy of Errors* (act 2, scene 1): "Self-harming jealousy, fie, beat it hence."

not tell you—no man could know it and live—Great God! I never dreamed of THIS!"

Stillness again, save for my now incoherent torrent of shuddering inquiry. Then the voice of Warren in a pitch of wilder consternation:

"Carter! for the love of God, put back the slab and get out of this if you can! Quick!—leave everything else and make for the outside—it's your only chance! Do as I say, and don't ask me to explain!"

I heard, yet was able only to repeat my frantic questions. Around me were the tombs and the darkness and the shadows; below me, some peril beyond the radius of the human imagination. But my friend was in greater danger than I, and through my fear I felt a vague resentment that he should deem me capable of deserting him under such circumstances. More clicking, and after a pause a piteous cry from Warren:

"Beat it! For God's sake, put back the slab and beat it, Carter!"

Something in the boyish slang of my evidently stricken companion unleashed my faculties.[9] I formed and shouted a resolution, "Warren, brace up! I'm coming down!" But at this offer the tone of my auditor changed to a scream of utter despair:

"Don't! You can't understand! It's too late—and my own fault. Put back the slab and run—there's nothing else you or anyone can do now!" The tone changed again, this time acquiring a softer quality, as of hopeless resignation. Yet it remained tense through anxiety for me.

"Quick—before it's too late!" I tried not to heed him; tried to break through the paralysis which held me, and to fulfil my vow to rush down to his aid. But his next whisper found me still held inert in the chains of stark horror.

"Carter—hurry! It's no use—you must go—better one than two—the slab—" A pause, more clicking, then the faint voice of Warren:

"Nearly over now—don't make it harder—cover up those damned steps and run for your life—you're losing time—So long, Carter—won't see you again." Here Warren's whisper swelled into a cry; a cry that gradually rose to a shriek fraught with all the horror of the ages—

"Curse these hellish things—legions—My God! Beat it! Beat it! Beat it!"

After that was silence. I know not how many interminable

æons I sat stupefied; whispering, muttering, calling, screaming into that telephone. Over and over again through those æons I whispered and muttered, called, shouted, and screamed, "Warren! Warren! Answer me—are you there?"

And then there came to me the crowning horror of all—the unbelievable, unthinkable, almost unmentionable thing. I have said that æons seemed to elapse after Warren shrieked forth his last despairing warning, and that only my own cries now broke the hideous silence. But after a while there was a further clicking in the receiver, and I strained my ears to listen. Again I called down, "Warren, are you there?," and in answer heard the *thing* which has brought this cloud over my mind. I do not try, gentlemen, to account for that *thing*—that voice—nor can I venture to describe it in detail, since the first words took away my consciousness and created a mental blank which reaches to the time of my awakening in the hospital. Shall I say that the voice was deep; hollow; gelatinous; remote; unearthly; inhuman; disembodied? What shall I say? It was the end of my experience, and is the end of my story. I heard it, and knew no more. Heard it as I sat petrified in that unknown cemetery in the hollow, amidst the crumbling stones and the falling tombs, the rank vegetation and the miasmal vapours. Heard it well up from the innermost depths of that damnable open sepulchre as I watched amorphous, necrophagous[10] shadows dance beneath an accursed waning moon. And this is what it said:

"*YOU FOOL, WARREN IS DEAD!*"

10. "Necrophagous," a wonderfully creepy-sounding word, literally means "feeding on carrion or corpses"!

Poster from *The Unnamable II: The Statement of Randolph Carter.* The Unnamable Productions Co. and Yankee Classic Pictures, 1993

Beyond the Wall of Sleep[1]

"Beyond the Wall of Sleep" is one of the very earliest stories of Lovecraft's to be published. It is pure science fiction—written before the genre existed—with a technological explanation for the transfer of brain waves and the recording of an event verifiable with astronomical data. At the same time, it is the first instance of Lovecraft's exploration of the idea of "brain transference," explored in much greater depth in "The Whisperer in Darkness" and "The Shadow Out of Time"—an idea that opened the door to travel through time and space in ways never imagined previously. The story is also revelatory of Lovecraft's deep-rooted antipathy to those not of pure New England stock.

"I have an exposition of sleep come upon me."
—SHAKESPEARE[2]

1. Written in the spring of 1919, it first appeared in *Pine Cones* (October 1919), an amateur journal edited by John Clinton Pryor. It also appeared in *Weird Tales* 31, no. 3 (March 1938), 331–38, where it included the following reading line: "What strange, splendid yet terrible experiences came to the poor mountaineer in the hours of sleep?—a story of a supernal being from Algol, the Demon-star."

2. *A Midsummer Night's Dream*, act 4, scene 1.

3. The narrator refers here to the sexual interpretations placed on many dreams by Freud. This phrase did not appear in the first publication of the story; it was added when the story was reprinted in *Fantasy Fan* in October 1934 and also

have frequently wondered if the majority of mankind ever pause to reflect upon the occasionally titanic significance of dreams, and of the obscure world to which they belong. Whilst the greater number of our nocturnal visions are perhaps no more than faint and fantastic reflections of our waking experiences—Freud to the contrary with his puerile symbolism[3]—there are still a certain remainder whose immundane[4] and ethereal character permits of no ordinary interpretation, and whose vaguely exciting and disquieting effect suggests possible minute glimpses into a sphere of mental existence no less important than physical life, yet separated from that life by an all but impassable barrier. From my experience I cannot doubt but that man, when lost to terrestrial consciousness, is indeed sojourning in another and uncorporeal life of far different nature from the life we know; and of which only the slightest and most indistinct memories linger after waking. From those blurred and fragmentary memories we may infer much, yet prove little. We may guess that in dreams life, matter, and vitality, as the earth knows such things, are not necessarily constant; and that time and space do not exist as our waking selves comprehend them. Sometimes I believe that this less material life is our truer life, and that our vain presence on the terraqueous globe is itself the secondary or merely virtual phenomenon.

It was from a youthful reverie filled with speculations of this sort that I arose one afternoon in the winter of 1900–1901, when to the state psychopathic institution in which I served as an interne was brought the man whose case has ever since haunted me so unceasingly. His name, as given on the records, was Joe Slater, or Slaader, and his appearance was that of the typical denizen of the Catskill Mountain region; one of those strange, repellent scions of a primitive colonial peasant stock whose isolation for nearly three centuries in the hilly fastnesses of a little-travelled countryside has caused them to sink to a kind of barbaric degeneracy, rather than advance with their more fortunately placed brethren of the thickly settled districts. Among these odd folk, who correspond exactly to the decadent element of "white trash" in the South, law and morals are non-existent; and their general mental status is probably below that of any other section of native American people.[5]

Joe Slater, who came to the institution in the vigilant custody of four state policemen, and who was described as a highly dangerous character, certainly presented no evidence of his perilous disposition when I first beheld him. Though well above the middle stature, and of somewhat brawny frame, he was given an absurd appearance of harmless stupidity by the pale, sleepy blueness of his small watery eyes, the scantiness of his neglected and never-shaven growth of yellow beard, and the listless drooping of his heavy nether lip. His age was unknown, since among his kind neither family records nor permanent family ties exist; but from the baldness of his head in front, and from the decayed condition of his teeth, the head surgeon wrote him down as a man of about forty.

From the medical and court documents we learned all that could be gathered of his case. This man, a vagabond, hunter, and trapper, had always been strange in the eyes of his primitive associates. He had habitually slept at night beyond the ordinary

appears in the *Weird Tales* reprint of March 1938.

4. "Immundane" does not appear in the *Oxford English Dictionary* but is found in various theological publications of the nineteenth century. Literally, it means something like "not of this world," the opposite of mundane, and hence is paired here with "ethereal" as descriptive of the stuff of dreams.

5. An article in the *Catskill Mountain News* in 1913 recounted the tale of two locals who were fined for trapping and shooting a fox that had threatened local chickens. The paper concluded, "Owners of chickens would best take out hunting licenses at once for if a skunk, weasel, mink, fox or other fur-bearing animal gets into your chicken coop, he may carry your choicest bird to the line fence or the neighbor's yard and sit there and eat it with impunity for it will cost you from $25 to $100 to touch a hair on his head. If it's some poor white trash or a col'ed gent you may shoot or club or kill them but not the skunk."

In a similar vein, a 1927 article about New York State troopers described the area as follows: "the Catskills and their outlying spurs, whose depths shelter a people as lawless and decadent as any in the southern highlands, and the Adirondacks, whose natives have held for years a hearty contempt for all man-made law." Describing Polly Hollow, a Catskills village populated by a number of families named Slater (pronounced Slah-ter), the article points out that none of the residents can read or write and terms them "degenerate."

However, the presence of "white trash" in rural New York appears to have been more myth than fact: According to 1910 census data, only 1.6 percent of the native white rural population was illiterate (although this was four times the rate of illiteracy in the native white urban population), and school attendance among fifteen-to-twenty-year-olds was actually higher in the rural population (41.3 percent) than in the urban population (34 percent).

time, and upon waking would often talk of unknown things in a manner so bizarre as to inspire fear even in the hearts of an unimaginative populace. Not that his form of language was at all unusual, for he never spoke save in the debased patois of his environment; but the tone and tenor of his utterances were of such mysterious wildness, that none might listen without apprehension. He himself was generally as terrified and baffled as his auditors, and within an hour after awakening would forget all that he had said, or at least all that had caused him to say what he did; relapsing into a bovine, half-amiable normality like that of the other hill-dwellers.

As Slater grew older, it appeared, his matutinal aberrations had gradually increased in frequency and violence; till about a month before his arrival at the institution had occurred the shocking tragedy which caused his arrest by the authorities. One day near noon, after a profound sleep begun in a whiskey debauch at about five of the previous afternoon, the man had roused himself most suddenly; with ululations so horrible and unearthly that they brought several neighbours to his cabin—a filthy sty where he dwelt with a family as indescribable as himself. Rushing out into the snow, he had flung his arms aloft and commenced a series of leaps directly upward in the air; the while shouting his determination to reach some "big, big cabin with brightness in the roof and walls and floor, and the loud queer music far away." As two men of moderate size sought to restrain him, he had struggled with maniacal force and fury, screaming of his desire and need to find and kill a certain "thing that shines and shakes and laughs." At length, after temporarily felling one of his detainers with a sudden blow, he had flung himself upon the other in a dæmoniac ecstasy of bloodthirstiness, shrieking fiendishly that he would "jump high in the air and burn his way through anything that stopped him." Family and neighbours had now fled in a panic, and when the more courageous of them returned, Slater was gone, leaving behind an unrecognisable pulp-like thing that had been a living man but an hour before. None of the mountaineers had dared to pursue him, and it is likely that they would have welcomed his death from the cold; but when several mornings later they heard his screams from a distant ravine they realised that he had somehow managed to survive, and that his removal in one way or another would be necessary. Then had followed an armed searching party, whose purpose (whatever it may have been originally) became that of a sheriff's posse after one of the seldom popular state troopers had by accident observed, then questioned, and finally joined the seekers.

On the third day Slater was found unconscious in the hollow of a tree, and taken to the nearest gaol; where alienists[6] from Albany examined him as soon as his senses returned. To them he told a simple story. He had, he said, gone to sleep one afternoon about sundown after drinking much liquor. He had awaked to find himself standing bloody-handed in the snow before his cabin, the mangled corpse of his neighbour Peter Slader at his feet. Horrified, he had taken to the woods in a vague effort to escape from the scene of what must have been his crime. Beyond these things he seemed to know nothing, nor could the expert questioning of his interrogators bring out a single additional fact.

That night Slater slept quietly, and the next morning he wakened with no singular feature save a certain alteration of expression. Dr. Barnard, who had been watching the patient, thought he noticed in the pale blue eyes a certain gleam of peculiar quality; and in the flaccid lips an all but imperceptible tightening, as if of intelligent determination. But when questioned, Slater relapsed into the habitual vacancy of the mountaineer, and only reiterated what he had said on the preceding day.

On the third morning occurred the first of the man's mental attacks. After some show of uneasiness in sleep, he burst forth into a frenzy so powerful that the combined efforts of four men were needed to bind him in a strait-jacket. The alienists listened with keen attention to his words, since their curiosity had been aroused to a high pitch by the suggestive yet mostly conflicting and incoherent stories of his family and neighbours. Slater raved for upward of fifteen minutes, babbling in his backwoods dialect of great edifices of light, oceans of space, strange music, and shadowy mountains and valleys. But most of all did he dwell upon some mysterious blazing entity that shook and laughed and mocked at him. This vast, vague personality seemed to have done him a terrible wrong, and to kill it in triumphant revenge was his paramount desire. In order to reach it, he said, he would soar through abysses of emptiness, *burning* every obstacle that stood

6. Historically, an alienist was a "mad-doctor" who treated mental disease—mental "alienation"—usually in an asylum. By 1919, when this story was written, alienists were no longer confined to asylums, and a survey of the early journals of the Alienists and Neurologists of America (founded in 1911) reveals that the self-image of the profession was changing from that of custodians of the insane to healers focused on insanity and mental and nervous diseases.

Alienists have often found their way into fiction, especially as the public's interest in psychology grew. Arthur Conan Doyle, a practicing physician himself, frequently wrote stories about the medical profession. In "A Medical Document," written in 1894, three doctors are swapping experiences—"talking shop," as one puts it. The alienist comments about a patient: "A disease of the body is bad enough, but this seems to be a disease of the soul. Is it not a shocking thing—a thing to drive a reasoning man into absolute Materialism—to think that you may have a fine, noble fellow with every divine instinct and that some little vascular change, the dropping, we will say, of a minute spicule of bone from the inner table of his skull on to the surface of his brain may have the effect of changing him to a filthy and pitiable creature with every low and debasing tendency? What a satire an asylum is upon the majesty of man, and no less upon the ethereal nature of the soul." At the beginning of Joseph Conrad's *Heart of Darkness* (1899), Marlow meets a doctor who questions Marlow's motives for journeying to Africa, and Marlow immediately asks whether the doctor is an alienist. "Every doctor should be—a little," is the answer.

The alienist as detective is also a popular trope—witness Nicholas Meyer's *The Seven-Per-Cent Solution* (1974), in which no less than Sigmund Freud joins forces with Sherlock Holmes, and Caleb Carr's popular 1994 mystery *The Alienist* and its sequel, *The Angel of Darkness* (1997), set in late Victorian New York.

in his way. Thus ran his discourse, until with the greatest suddenness he ceased. The fire of madness died from his eyes, and in dull wonder he looked at his questioners and asked why he was bound. Dr. Barnard unbuckled the leathern harness and did not restore it till night, when he succeeded in persuading Slater to don it of his own volition, for his own good. The man had now admitted that he sometimes talked queerly, though he knew not why.

Within a week two more attacks appeared, but from them the doctors learned little. On the *source* of Slater's visions they speculated at length, for since he could neither read nor write, and had apparently never heard a legend or fairy tale, his gorgeous imagery was quite inexplicable. That it could not come from any known myth or romance was made especially clear by the fact that the unfortunate lunatic expressed himself only in his own simple manner. He raved of things he did not understand and could not interpret; things which he claimed to have experienced, but which he could not have learned through any normal or connected narration. The alienists soon agreed that abnormal dreams were the foundation of the trouble; dreams whose vividness could for a time completely dominate the waking mind of this basically inferior man. With due formality Slater was tried for murder, acquitted on the ground of insanity, and committed to the institution wherein I held so humble a post.

I have said that I am a constant speculator concerning dream life, and from this you may judge of the eagerness with which I applied myself to the study of the new patient as soon as I had fully ascertained the facts of his case. He seemed to sense a certain friendliness in me, born no doubt of the interest I could not conceal, and the gentle manner in which I questioned him. Not that he ever recognised me during his attacks, when I hung breathlessly upon his chaotic but cosmic word-pictures; but he knew me in his quiet hours, when he would sit by his barred window weaving baskets of straw and willow, and perhaps pining for the mountain freedom he could never enjoy again. His family never called to see him; probably it had found another temporary head, after the manner of decadent mountain folk.

By degrees I commenced to feel an overwhelming wonder at the mad and fantastic conceptions of Joe Slater. The man himself was pitiably inferior in mentality and language alike; but his glowing, titanic visions, though described in a barbarous and disjointed jargon, were assuredly things which only a superior or even exceptional brain could conceive. How, I often asked myself, could the stolid imagination of a Catskill degenerate conjure up sights whose very possession argued a lurking spark of genius? How could any backwoods dullard have gained so much as an idea of those glittering realms of supernal radiance and space about which Slater ranted in his furious delirium? More and more I inclined to the belief that in the pitiful personality who cringed before me lay the disordered nucleus of something beyond my comprehension; something infinitely beyond the comprehension of my more experienced but less imaginative medical and scientific colleagues.

And yet I could extract nothing definite from the man. The sum of all my investigation was, that in a kind of semi-uncorporeal dream life Slater wandered or floated through resplendent and prodigious valleys, meadows, gardens, cities, and palaces of light; in a region unbounded and unknown to man. That there he was no peasant or degenerate, but a creature of importance and vivid life; moving proudly and dominantly, and checked only by a certain deadly enemy, who seemed to be a being of visible yet ethereal structure, and who did not appear to be of human shape, since Slater never referred to it as a *man*, or as aught save a *thing*. This *thing* had done Slater some hideous but unnamed wrong, which the maniac (if maniac he were) yearned to avenge.

From the manner in which Slater alluded to their dealings, I judged that he and the luminous *thing* had met on equal terms; that in his dream existence the man was himself a luminous *thing* of the same race as his enemy. This impression was sustained by his frequent references to *flying through space* and *burning* all that impeded his progress. Yet these conceptions were formulated in rustic words wholly inadequate to convey them, a circumstance which drove me to the conclusion that if a true dream world indeed existed, oral language was not its medium for the transmission of thought. Could it be that the dream-soul inhabiting this inferior body was desperately struggling to speak things which the simple and halting tongue of dulness could not utter? Could it be that I was face to face with intellectual emanations which would explain the mystery if I could but learn to discover

7. The "ether" (also spelled "æther") was conceived by ancient scientists as a substance that filled the space between the planets and the stars, thought by later scientists to be necessary for the transmission of electromagnetic or gravitational waves; the term "luminiferous aether" came to be thought of as the medium through which light was transmitted. Einstein's 1905 theory of special relativity demonstrated that the perceived effects long thought to require the existence of the ether could be explained without it. However, many scientists refused to let go of the notion and ignored or denied Einstein's explanations. The *Enyclopædia Britannica* (11th ed.), for example, published in 1911, has a detailed explanation of the æther or ether by the physicist Sir Oliver Lodge (1851–1940). In 1929, cosmologist Sir James Hopwood Jeans wrote, "The ether has dropped out of science, not because scientists as a whole have formed a reasoned judgment that no such thing exists, but because they find they can describe all the phenomena of nature quite perfectly without it. It merely cumbers the picture, so they leave it out. If at some future time they find they need it, they will put it back again" (*The Universe Around Us*, 339). That time has not yet come.

8. In 1901, when these events occurred, little was known of electrical activity in the brain, or "brain waves" such as described here. In 1875, based on experiments with animals, electrophysiologist Richard Caton (1842–1926) reported to the British Medical Association that he had measured electrical changes in the brain, varying in location and direction but probably related to function. Others, including Adolf Beck (1863–1942) and Ernst Fleischl von Marxov (1846–1892), were among the first to demonstrate cortical localization with electophysiological methods. By 1890, Beck had discovered

and read them? I did not tell the older physicians of these things, for middle age is sceptical, cynical, and disinclined to accept new ideas. Besides, the head of the institution had but lately warned me in his paternal way that I was overworking; that my mind needed a rest.

It had long been my belief that human thought consists basically of atomic or molecular motion, convertible into ether[7] waves of radiant energy like heat, light and electricity.[8] This belief had early led me to contemplate the possibility of telepathy or mental communication by means of suitable apparatus,[9] and I had in my college days prepared a set of transmitting and receiving instruments somewhat similar to the cumbrous devices employed in wireless telegraphy at that crude, pre-radio period. These I had tested with a fellow-student, but achieving no result, had soon packed them away with other scientific odds and ends for possible future use.

Now, in my intense desire to probe into the dream-life of Joe Slater, I sought these instruments again, and spent several days in repairing them for action. When they were complete once more I missed no opportunity for their trial. At each outburst of Slater's violence, I would fit the transmitter to his forehead and the receiver to my own, constantly making delicate adjustments for various hypothetical wave-lengths of intellectual energy. I had but little notion of how the thought-impressions would, if successfully conveyed, arouse an intelligent response in my brain, but I felt certain that I could detect and interpret them. Accordingly I continued my experiments, though informing no one of their nature.

It was on the twenty-first of February, 1901, that the thing finally occurred. As I look back across the years I realise how unreal it seems, and sometimes half wonder if old Dr. Fenton was not right when he charged it all to my excited imagination. I recall that he listened with great kindness and patience when I told him, but afterward gave me a nerve-powder[10] and arranged for the half-year's vacation on which I departed the next week.

That fateful night I was wildly agitated and perturbed, for despite the excellent care he had received, Joe Slater was unmistakably dying. Perhaps it was his mountain freedom that he missed, or perhaps the turmoil in his brain had grown too acute for his rather sluggish physique; but at all events the flame of vitality flickered low in the decadent body. He was drowsy near the end, and as darkness fell he dropped off into a troubled sleep.

I did not strap on the strait-jacket as was customary when he slept, since I saw that he was too feeble to be dangerous, even if he woke in mental disorder once more before passing away. But I did place upon his head and mine the two ends of my cosmic "radio"; hoping against hope for a first and last message from the dream-world in the brief time remaining. In the cell with us was one nurse, a mediocre fellow who did not understand the purpose of the apparatus, or think to inquire into my course. As the hours wore on I saw his head droop awkwardly in sleep, but I did not disturb him. I myself, lulled by the rhythmical breathing of the healthy and the dying man, must have nodded a little later.

The sound of weird lyric melody was what aroused me. Chords, vibrations, and harmonic ecstasies echoed passionately on every hand; while on my ravished sight burst the stupendous spectacle of ultimate beauty. Walls, columns, and architraves[11] of living fire blazed effulgently around the spot where I seemed to float in air, extending upward to an infinitely high vaulted dome of indescribable splendour. Blending with this display of palatial magnificence, or rather, supplanting it at times in kaleidoscopic rotation, were glimpses of wide plains and graceful valleys, high mountains and inviting grottoes; covered with every lovely attribute of scenery which my delighted eye could conceive of, yet formed wholly of some glowing, ethereal, plastic entity, which in consistency partook as much of spirit as of matter. As I gazed, I perceived that my own brain held the key to these enchanting metamorphoses; for each vista which appeared to me, was the one my changing mind most wished to behold. Amidst this elysian realm I dwelt not as a stranger, for each sight and sound was familiar to me; just as it had been for uncounted æons of eternity before, and would be for like eternities to come.

Then the resplendent aura of my brother of light drew near and held colloquy with me, soul to soul, with silent and perfect interchange of thought. The hour was one of approaching triumph, for was not my fellow-being escaping at last from a degrading periodic bondage; escaping forever, and preparing to follow the accursed oppressor even unto the uttermost fields of ether,

patterns of oscillation in animal brain activity. It was not until 1929, however, that Hans Berger (1873–1941) published his electroencephalograph work on humans, and serious study began. *Radio* waves (to which the narrator analogizes the "brain waves" he receives) were predicted as early as 1865 by mathematician James Clerk Maxwell and demonstrated in the laboratory by Heinrich Hertz in 1887.

9. Compare the views of Thomas Alva Edison, who, according to a 1920 interview with B. C. Forbes for *American Magazine*, "Edison Working on How to Communicate with the Next World," said, "'If our personality survives, then it is strictly logical and scientific to assume that it retains memory, intellect, and other faculties and knowledge that we acquire on earth. . . . I am inclined to believe that our personality hereafter will be able to affect matter. If this reasoning be correct, then, if we can evolve an instrument so delicate as to be affected, moved, or manipulated . . . by our personality as it survives in the next life, such an instrument, when made available, ought to record something.'" See also Edison's interview with Austin C. Lescarboura in *Scientific American Monthly* for October 1920.

10. According to vol. 58 (1911) of the *American Druggist and Pharmaceutical Record*, a "semi-monthly illustrated journal of practical pharmacy," popular products of the sort included Young's Kidney and Nerve Powder and Adamson's Head Ache and Nerve Powder. Tonics, "cures," and "plasters" were also sold to treat nerves: Spiegel's Blood and Nerve Tonic; Adironda (Wheeler's Heart and Nerve) Cure; Brod's Stomach, Nerve and Asthma Plaster. Other proprietary (that is, nonprescription) products included "nerve invigorators," "nerve foods," and

nerve beans, nerve seeds, and nerve gum. *Merck's 1899 Manual of the Materia Medica* lists over twenty-five drugs to be prescribed by physicians for "nervous affections," including arsenic and cocaine!

11. An architectural term of several meanings—here, probably, ornamental moldings around the exterior of an arch.

that upon it might be wrought a flaming cosmic vengeance which would shake the spheres? We floated thus for a little time, when I perceived a slight blurring and fading of the objects around us, as though some force were recalling me to earth—where I least wished to go. The form near me seemed to feel a change also, for it gradually brought its discourse toward a conclusion, and itself prepared to quit the scene; fading from my sight at a rate somewhat less rapid than that of the other objects. A few more thoughts were exchanged, and I knew that the luminous one and I were being recalled to bondage, though for my brother of light it would be the last time. The sorry planet-shell being well-nigh spent, in less than an hour my fellow would be free to pursue the oppressor along the Milky Way and past the hither stars to the very confines of infinity.

A well-defined shock separates my final impression of the fading scene of light from my sudden and somewhat shamefaced awakening and straightening up in my chair as I saw the dying figure on the couch move hesitantly. Joe Slater was indeed awaking, though probably for the last time. As I looked more closely, I saw that in the sallow cheeks shone spots of colour which had never before been present. The lips, too, seemed unusual, being tightly compressed, as if by the force of a stronger character than had been Slater's. The whole face finally began to grow tense, and the head turned restlessly with closed eyes.

I did not arouse the sleeping nurse, but readjusted the slightly disarranged head-bands of my telepathic "radio," intent to catch any parting message the dreamer might have to deliver. All at once the head turned sharply in my direction and the eyes fell open, causing me to stare in blank amazement at what I beheld. The man who had been Joe Slater, the Catskill decadent, was now gazing at me with a pair of luminous, expanded eyes whose blue seemed subtly to have deepened. Neither mania nor degeneracy was visible in that gaze, and I felt beyond a doubt that I was viewing a face behind which lay an active mind of high order.

At this juncture my brain became aware of a steady external influence operating upon it. I closed my eyes to concentrate my thoughts more profoundly, and was rewarded by the positive knowledge that *my long-sought mental message had come at last.* Each transmitted idea formed rapidly in my mind, and though no actual language was employed, my habitual association of conception and expression was so great that I seemed to be receiving the message in ordinary English.

"Joe Slater is dead," came the soul-petrifying voice or agency from beyond the wall of sleep. My opened eyes sought the couch of pain in curious horror, but the blue eyes were still calmly gazing, and the countenance was still intelligently animated. "He is better dead, for he was unfit to bear the active intellect of cosmic entity. His gross body could not undergo the needed adjustments between ethereal life and planet life. He was too much of an animal, too little a man; yet it is through his deficiency that you have come to discover me, for the cosmic and planet souls rightly should never meet. He has been my torment and diurnal prison for forty-two of your terrestrial years.

"I am an entity like that which you yourself become in the freedom of dreamless sleep. I am your brother of light, and have floated with you in the effulgent valleys. It is not permitted me to tell your waking earth-self of your real self, but we are all roamers of vast spaces and travellers in many ages. Next year I may be dwelling in the dark Egypt which you call ancient, or in the cruel empire of Tsan-Chan which is to come three thousand years hence. You and I have drifted to the worlds that reel about the red Arcturus, and dwelt in the bodies of the insect-philosophers that crawl proudly over the fourth moon of Jupiter.[12] How little does the earth-self know life and its extent! How little, indeed, ought it to know for its own tranquility!

"Of the oppressor I cannot speak. You on earth have unwittingly felt its distant presence—you who without knowing idly gave to its blinking beacon the name of *Algol, the Dæmon-Star*.[13] It is to meet and conquer the oppressor that I have vainly striven for æons, held back by bodily encumbrances. Tonight I go as a Nemesis bearing just and blazingly cataclysmic vengeance. *Watch me in the sky close by the Dæmon-Star.*

"I cannot speak longer, for the body of Joe Slater grows cold and rigid, and the coarse brains are ceasing to vibrate as I wish. You have been my friend in the cosmos; you have been my only friend on this planet—the only soul to sense and seek for me within the repellent form which lies on this couch. We shall meet again—perhaps in the shining mists of Orion's Sword,[14]

12. Jupiter has sixty-one moons. Four were discovered by Galileo in 1610; a fifth moon was discovered in 1892, and several others were found over the next few decades. The bulk were not discovered until the twenty-first century. In 1901, if the speaker were up on his astronomy (as Lovecraft undoubtedly was), the "fourth" moon, in terms of distance from the planet, was actually Ganymede. The speaker was probably not conversant with the latest discoveries, however, and meant the four Gallilean moons, Io, Europa, Ganymede, and Callisto, and Callisto was the fourth most distant of those moons from the planet's surface.

The idea that life exists beyond Earth was first suggested in ancient literature. The Jewish Talmud speaks of 18,000 worlds, and the Qu'ran and Hindu mythology assume that life exists on other worlds. In the late nineteenth century, after the observations by Schiaparelli in 1878 of *canali* on the surface of the planet Mars, intense speculation began regarding life there, including French astronomer Camille Flammarion's 1892 book *Le planète Mars* and the subsequent writings of American astronomer Percival Lowell: *Mars* (1895); *Mars and Its Canals* (1906); and *Mars as the Abode of Life* (1908). Life on other worlds was also a popular topic of fiction, including such early works as *Across the Zodiac* (1880) by Percy Greg; *Journey to Mars* (1894) by Gustavus W. Pope, an adventure story that may have influenced Edgar Rice Burroughs's later books; and of course *The War of the Worlds* (1898) by H. G. Wells. Lovecraft may also have read *Edison's Conquest of Mars* (1898) by Garrett P. Serviss (see note 15, below). In this "Edisonade" (a popular genre of fictional adventures of inventor Thomas A. Edison, and a precursor to the "Tom Swift" stories that first appeared in 1910), and essentially a sequel to Wells's popular book, Earthmen respond to an attack from Mars with a successful genocide of the Martian race.

13. Beta Persei, a bright star in the constellation of Perseus. It is a binary star and its brightness varies markedly. Richard H. Allen, in his invaluable 1899 work *Star Names: Their Lore and Meaning*, writes: "Algol, the Demon, the Demon Star, and the Blinking Demon, from the Arabians' Ra's al Ghul, the Demon's Head, is said to have been thus called from its rapid and wonderful variations; but I find no evidence of this, and that people probably took the title from Ptolemy. Al Ghul literally signifies a Mischief-maker, and the name still appears in the Ghoul of the Arabian Nights and of our day. Its name derives from *ras al-ghul*, Arabic for head of the ghoul. . . . Astrologers of course said that it was the most unfortunate, violent, and dangerous star in the heavens, and it certainly has been one of the best observed, as the most noteworthy variable in the northern sky." Ra's al Ghul is a nemesis of Batman and head of the Demon, an international crime cartel, in the DC Comics Universe.

14. The middle "star" of the three forming the "sword" depending from the belt of the constellation Orion is the Orion Nebula.

perhaps on a bleak plateau in prehistoric Asia. Perhaps in unremembered dreams tonight; perhaps in some other form an æon hence, when the solar system shall have been swept away."

At this point the thought-waves abruptly ceased, and the pale eyes of the dreamer—or can I say dead man?—commenced to glaze fishily. In a half-stupor I crossed over to the couch and felt of his wrist, but found it cold, stiff, and pulseless. The sallow cheeks paled again, and the thick lips fell open, disclosing the repulsively rotten fangs of the degenerate Joe Slater. I shivered, pulled a blanket over the hideous face, and awakened the nurse. Then I left the cell and went silently to my room. I had an insistent and unaccountable craving for a sleep whose dreams I should not remember.

The climax? What plain tale of science can boast of such a rhetorical effect? I have merely set down certain things appealing to me as facts, allowing you to construe them as you will. As I have already admitted, my superior, old Dr. Fenton, denies the

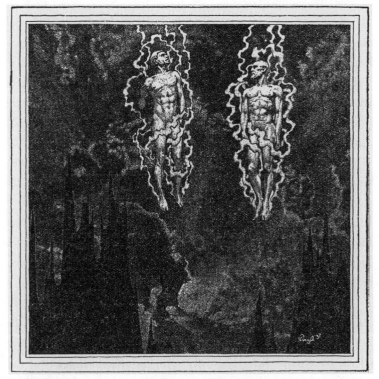

"We shall meet again, perhaps in the shining mists of Orion's Sword."
Weird Tales 31, no. 3 (March 1938) (artist: Virgil Finlay)

reality of everything I have related. He vows that I was broken down with nervous strain, and badly in need of the long vacation on full pay which he so generously gave me. He assures me on his professional honour that Joe Slater was but a low-grade paranoiac, whose fantastic notions must have come from the crude hereditary folk-tales which circulate in even the most decadent of communities. All this he tells me—yet I cannot forget what I saw in the sky on the night after Slater died. Lest you think me a biassed witness, another's pen must add this final testimony, which may perhaps supply the climax you expect. I will quote the following account of the star *Nova Persei* verbatim from the pages of that eminent astronomical authority, Prof. Garrett P. Serviss:[15]

"On February 22, 1901, a marvellous new star was discovered by Dr. Anderson of Edinburgh, *not very far from Algol*. No star had been visible at that point before. Within twenty-four hours the stranger had become so bright that it outshone Capella. In a week or two it had visibly faded, and in the course of a few months it was hardly discernible with the naked eye."

15. Serviss (1851–1929) was an astronomer, a popularizer of astronomy, and an early science fiction writer. The quotation is from his *Astronomy with the Naked Eye* (1908). Of course, if the nova was first visible in 1901, it did not *occur* in 1901; Algol is approximately 93 light-years from Earth, and so the nova would have occurred in 1808. Perhaps the thought-transmission from the "brother of light" also traveled at the speed of light (rather than instantaneously), making it appear contemporary although it was actually almost a century old. This does not explain, however, how the "brother" was able to tell that, ninety-three years in the future, Slater would die.

The following appeared in the *Providence Manufacturers and Farmers Journal* for February 28, 1901: "[A] tremendous phenomenon was plainly visible [last night] to the unaided eye, provided one was somewhat informed about what was going on in space. Briefly told, the thing that has aroused a lively interest, and even a sensation among astronomers in all the Northern Hemisphere[,] is a new star, discovered last Thursday by a Scotch student of the heavens, Dr. T. D. Anderson, at Edinburgh. . . . This new star discovered by Dr. Anderson . . . is something quite out of the range of known laws of the science of astronomy, although it would hardly have been so promptly observed without the close watch of the movements of the heavenly bodies which makes possible the accurate knowledge just referred to. Neither Dr. Anderson nor any other man is able to tell why a star that is now one of the most brilliant in the sky at night, should have suddenly burst forth at a point where a short time ago absolutely nothing was visible, even to the most powerful telescope. The scientist can do nothing more than speculate concerning it and tell us that something of awful and stupendous character is the cause." It is unlikely that the eleven-year-old Lovecraft would have read the article.

Nyarlathotep[1]

Like "The Statement of Randolph Carter," "Nyarlathotep" is a record of a dream of Lovecraft's. A vision of the downfall of civilization, its powerful images are impossible to pin down—disturbing in the way that dreams disturb us. The persona of "Nyarlathotep" returns in future versions of the Cthulhu Mythos, yet never in more dramatic fashion than here.

Nyarlathotep . . . the crawling chaos. . . . I am the last . . . I will tell the audient void. . . .[2]

1. Written in December 1920, the tale first appeared in the *United Amateur* (dated November 1920 but published no earlier than January 1921).

2. Will Murray, in "Behind the Mask of Nyarlathotep," points out that not only is this Lovecraft's first fictitious god, but it is the first to appear in more than one Lovecraft story. Nyarlathotep appears as a character in six of Lovecraft's works, "The Rats in the Walls" (1924), as a faceless god in the caverns of the center of the Earth; *The Dream-Quest of Unknown Kadath* (1926–27), unpublished during Lovecraft's lifetime; the twenty-first sonnet of the thirty-six-poem cycle "Fungi from Yuggoth" (1929–30); and the stories "The Dreams in the Witch House" (1933) and "The Haunter of the Dark" (1936). The name, according to David Haden, in *Walking with Cthulhu: H. P. Lovecraft as Psychogeographer, New York City, 1924–26*, may be roughly translated as "the message (messenger) that is

I do not recall distinctly when it began, but it was months ago.[3] The general tension was horrible. To a season of political and social upheaval was added a strange and brooding apprehension of hideous physical danger; a danger widespread and all-embracing, such a danger as may be imagined only in the most terrible phantasms of the night. I recall that the people went about with pale and worried faces, and whispered warnings and prophecies which no one dared consciously repeat or acknowledge to himself that he had heard. A sense of monstrous guilt was upon the land, and out of the abysses between the stars swept chill currents that made men shiver in dark and lonely places. There was a dæmoniac alteration in the sequence of the seasons—the autumn heat lingered fearsomely, and everyone felt that the world and perhaps the universe had passed from the control of known gods or forces to that of gods or forces which were unknown.

And it was then that Nyarlathotep came out of Egypt. Who he was, none could tell, but he was of the old native blood and looked like a Pharaoh. The fellahin[4] knelt when they saw him, yet could not say why. He said he had risen up out of the blackness of twenty-seven centuries,[5] and that he had heard messages from places not on this planet. Into the lands of civilisation came Nyarlathotep, swarthy, slender, and sinister, always buying strange instruments of glass and metal and combining them into instruments yet stranger. He spoke much of the sciences—of electricity and psychology—and gave exhibitions of power which sent his spectators away speechless, yet which swelled his fame to exceeding magnitude.[6] Men advised one another to see Nyarlathotep, and shuddered. And where Nyarlathotep went, rest vanished; for the small hours were rent with the screams of nightmare. Never before had the screams of nightmare been such a public problem; now the wise men almost wished they could forbid sleep in the small hours, that the shrieks of cities might less horribly disturb the pale, pitying moon as it glimmered on green waters gliding under bridges, and old steeples crumbling against a sickly sky.

I remember when Nyarlathotep came to my city—the great, the old, the terrible city of unnumbered crimes. My friend had told me of him,[7] and of the impelling fascination and allurement of his revelations, and I burned with eagerness to explore his uttermost mysteries. My friend said they were horrible and impressive beyond my most fevered imaginings; that what was thrown on a screen in the darkened room[8] prophesied things none but Nyarlathotep dared prophesy, and that in the sputter of his sparks there was taken from men that which had never been taken before yet which shewed only in the eyes. And I heard it hinted abroad that those who knew Nyarlathotep looked on sights which others saw not.

It was in the hot autumn that I went through the night with the restless crowds to see Nyarlathotep; through the stifling night and up the endless stairs into the choking room. And shadowed on a screen, I saw hooded forms amidst ruins, and yellow evil faces[9] peering from behind fallen monuments. And I saw the world battling against blackness; against the waves of destruction from ultimate space; whirling, churning, struggling around the dimming, cooling sun.[10] Then the sparks played amazingly around the heads of the spectators, and hair stood up on end whilst shadows more grotesque than I can tell came out and squatted on the heads. And when I, who was colder and more scientific than the rest, mumbled a trembling protest about "imposture" and "static electricity," Nyarlathotep drave us all out, down

trusted of (by) the gods." In "Cthulhu's Scald: Lovecraft and the Nordic Tradition," Jason C. Eckhardt points out similarities between Nyarlathotep and the Norse mythological figures of Loki (a devious, mysterious shape-shifter) and Surt (Lord of Muspelheim, land of fire, who, it is suggested, will figure prominently in the end of the world).

3. David Haden, in *Walking with Cthulhu*, argues that the "season" is late 1919. The world was still recovering from the mortal and psychic consequences of the Great War, a worldwide influenza epidemic killed over 25 million worldwide, the scientific world was in upheaval due to the theories of Einstein, and a terrible heat wave in New England and New York took almost 600 lives.

4. The rural people of the Middle East.

5. S. T. Joshi, in *The Call of Cthulhu and Other Weird Stories* (370, n. 1), interprets this ambiguous phrase to mean that Nyarlathotep was born twenty-seven centuries previous, approximately 820 BCE. This would place his rise in the 22nd Dynasty of Egypt, which lasted from 943 BCE to 730 BCE, the so-called Middle Intermediate Period. However, it is equally possible that Nyarlathotep meant that his birth occurred in Egypt at some unknown date, perhaps even earlier than the founding of the first dynasty in 3100 BCE, after twenty-seven centuries of "blackness." In other words, the "rising up" need not refer to the present day; it is clear from other references to Nyarlathotep that he appeared at various times other than the present (see note 2, above). Elsewhere, in his biography of Lovecraft (*I Am Providence*, 370), Joshi states that Nyarlathotep arose at the end of the 4th Dynasty of the Old Kingdom, "either in the reign of Khufu (Cheops) in

2590–68 BCE or in that of Khafre (Chephren) in 2559–35 BCE," and suggests that Lovecraft was implying a connection between Nyarlathotep and the Sphinx (Khafre was the builder of the Sphinx). In a footnote to this work (554, n. 18), he calls George Wetzel's analysis, in "The Cthulhu Mythos: A Study," "wildly erroneous" in tying Nyarlathotep to the Ethiopian invasion of Europe that took place from 760 to 650 BCE. Something is plainly wrong with Joshi's arithmetic: 1920 CE less 2,700 years is about 780 BCE. There is no basis for the view that the "rising up" of Nyarlathotep occurred at the opening of the Common Era.

6. Nikola Tesla (1856–1943), best known as an electrical engineer, inventor, and rival of Thomas Edison, was called by one friend a poet, philosopher, and connoisseur of fine music and art. He presented his discoveries to the public in great showman-like demonstrations, often with his Tesla coil pumping electricity through the room, terrifying the audience. There is no evidence that Lovecraft met Tesla or even read firsthand accounts of his presentations. However, Will Murray, in "Behind the Mask of Nyarlathotep," argues that Tesla made "a profound impression" on Lovecraft, sufficient to shape the description of Nyarlathotep.

7. In 1920, Lovecraft wrote his friend Reinhardt Kleiner of a dream that he had had, in which his friend Samuel Loveman had written him: "Don't fail to see Nyarlathotep if he comes to Providence. He is horrible—horrible beyond anything you can imagine—but wonderful. He haunts one for hours afterward. I am still shuddering at what he showed." (The letter is dated December 14, 1920; *Selected Letters*, I, 161, misdates it to December 14, 1921.)

the dizzy stairs into the damp, hot, deserted midnight streets. I screamed aloud that I was *not* afraid; that I never could be afraid; and others screamed with me for solace. We sware to one another that the city was exactly the same, and still alive; and when the electric lights began to fade we cursed the company over and over again, and laughed at the queer faces we made.

I believe we felt something coming down from the greenish moon, for when we began to depend on its light we drifted into curious involuntary formations and seemed to know our destinations though we dared not think of them. Once we looked at the pavement and found the blocks loose and displaced by grass, with scarce a line of rusted metal to shew where the tramways had run. And again we saw a tram-car, lone, windowless, dilapidated, and almost on its side. When we gazed around the horizon, we could not find the third tower by the river, and noticed that the silhouette of the second tower was ragged at the top.[11] Then we split up into narrow columns, each of which seemed drawn in a different direction. One disappeared in a narrow alley to the left, leaving only the echo of a shocking moan. Another filed down a weed-choked subway entrance, howling with a laughter that was mad. My own column was sucked toward the open country, and presently I felt a chill which was not of the hot autumn; for as we stalked out on the dark moor, we beheld around us the hellish moon-glitter of evil snows. Trackless, inexplicable snows, swept asunder in one direction only, where lay a gulf all the blacker for its glittering walls. The column seemed very thin indeed as it plodded dreamily into the gulf. I lingered behind, for the black rift in the green-litten snow was frightful, and I thought I had heard the reverberations of a disquieting wail as my companions vanished; but my power to linger was slight. As if beckoned by those who had gone before, I half-floated between the titanic snowdrifts, quivering and afraid, into the sightless vortex of the unimaginable.

Screamingly sentient, dumbly delirious, only the gods that were can tell. A sickened, sensitive shadow writhing in hands that are not hands, and whirled blindly past ghastly midnights of rotting creation, corpses of dead worlds with sores that were cities, charnel winds that brush the pallid stars and make them flicker low. Beyond the worlds vague ghosts of monstrous things;

half-seen columns of unsanctified temples that rest on nameless rocks beneath space and reach up to dizzy vacua above the spheres of light and darkness. And through this revolting graveyard of the universe the muffled, maddening beating of drums, and thin, monotonous whine of blasphemous flutes from inconceivable, unlighted chambers beyond Time; the detestable pounding and piping whereunto dance slowly, awkwardly, and absurdly the gigantic, tenebrous[12] ultimate gods—the blind, voiceless, mindless gargoyles whose soul is Nyarlathotep.[13]

"Völker Europas, wahrt eure heiligsten Güter!"
(Peoples of Europe, Protect Your Holiest Possessions!)
by Wilhelm II, ca. 1895.

8. The year 1920 was a fine one for the silent screen (sound films did not appear until 1927). John Barrymore starred in *Dr. Jekyll and Mr. Hyde*, and two other versions of the same story appeared. *The Cabinet of Dr. Caligari*, a classic horror tale, was released. Most significantly for this purpose, however, was the release of the film *Algol*, starring Emil Jannings. In it, an alien from the planet Algol attempts to conquer Earth. See "Beyond the Wall of Sleep," above.

9. "Yellow peril," the stereotype of the threatening Asian, gained political currency when the epithet was popularized by Kaiser Wilhelm II during the Sino-Japanese war of 1894–95. The kaiser sent Tsar Nicholas II a scurrilously allegorical drawing, *"Völker Europas, wahrt eure heiligsten Güter!"* (Peoples of Europe, Protect Your Holiest Possessions!), showing persons representing the European powers against a backdrop of storm clouds atop which rode a fiery image of the Buddha. He had mentally "developed" the image himself and then commissioned "a first class draughtsman," the painter Hermann Knackfuss, to render it, as he explained to the tsar: "and after it was finished [I] had it engraved for public use. It shows the powers of Europe represented by their respective Genii called together by the Arch-Angel Michael,—sent from Heaven,—to *unite* in resisting the inroad of Buddhism, heathenism and barbarism for the Defence of the Cross" (Kaiser Wilhelm II to Tsar Nicholas II, September 26, 1895, in John C. G. Röhl's *Wilhelm II: The Kaiser's Personal Monarchy, 1888–1900*, 909, citing Walter Goetz and Max Theodor Behrmann, *Briefe Wilhelms II. an den Zaren* [Berlin: Ulstein & Co., 1920], 294–96).

Fomented in part by the Hearst newspapers and the stories of Dr. Fu Manchu by the British-born Irish-Catholic novelist Sax Rohmer (1883–1959), the stereotype of "yellow evil faces" soon seized the public imagination.

In a letter to his friends Alfred Galpin and Maurice W. Moe (part of the "Gallomo"—Galpin, Lovecraft, Moe—cycle) dated September 30, 1919 (*Selected Letters*, I, 89–90), Lovecraft wrote: "Orientals must be kept in their native East till the fall of the white race. Sooner or later a great Japanese war will take place, during which I think the virtual destruction of Japan will have to be effected in the interests of European safety. The more numerous Chinese are a menace of the still more distant future. They will probably be the exterminators of Caucasian civilisation, for their numbers are amazing. But all that is too far ahead for consideration today. . . ."

10. No specific film with these images can be identified. The scene described is reminiscent of the end of H. G. Wells's *The Time Machine* (1898) and of William Hope Hodgson's *The Night Land* (1912), neither of which had yet been filmed. Are the "yellow evil faces" Asian? Or the result of baleful light on the planet's surface? (There are several yellow beasts described in *The Night Land*.) A color film would likely have been hand-tinted at this early stage of filmmaking; color stencils were also used occasionally. Technicolor was not introduced until 1922.

11. That is, the audience has now traveled into the future, when the city has passed into ruins.

12. Shadowy or obscure.

13. Commercial radio broadcasts of music (mostly live, including church choirs), election returns, and the like began in the United States in 1920, with the appearance, in August, of a Detroit station, WWJ, operated under an amateur license by teenage radio buff Michael DeLisle Lyons, who was supported in the effort by the Scripps family, owners of the *Detroit News*, and, in November, of KDKA, which sent its signal from the roof of a Westinghouse Electric Company building in Turtle Creek, Pennsylvania, near Pittsburgh. Both stations used 100-watt transmitters.

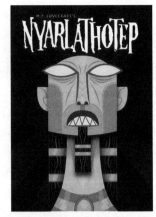

Cover of *H. P. Lovecraft's Nyarlathotep.*
Boom! Studios, 2008
(artist: Chuck BB)

The Picture in the House[1]

Poesque in its evocation of horror, the tale explores how an appreciation of terror can lead one to the edge—to a test of character and of whether, as an "epicure in the terrible," one is as horrifying and pitiful as the grim spectacle one takes pleasure in observing. It is also important as the first story to be sited in Lovecraft's fictional geography of the valley of the Miskatonic River and the neighborhood of the town of Arkham.

1. The story was written in December 1920. It first appeared in *National Amateur* 41, no. 6 (dated July 1919 but not published until the spring of 1921), 246–49. It also appeared twice in *Weird Tales*, in 3, no. 1 (January 1924), 400–442, and in 29, no. 3 (March 1937), 370–73.

2. Although there are several possible sources, this is probably a reference to the ancient Egyptian city of Crocodilopolis, called Shedet during the time of the pharaohs. Located on the western bank of the Nile, between the river and Lake Moeris, southwest of Memphis, it was the center of worship for Sobek, the crocodile-god, who was also known as Lord of Faiyum—Crocodilopolis being within the Faiyum Governorate, some sixty miles southwest of present-day Cairo. When the rule of Egypt passed to the Ptolemies, the name of the city was changed (probably around 330 BCE) to Ptolemais Euergetis. It went through several subsequent name changes—for a time it was called Arsinoe, after the second wife (and sister) of Ptolemy II Philadelphus (his first wife was also

Searchers after horror haunt strange, far places. For them are the catacombs of Ptolemais,[2] and the carven mausolea of the nightmare countries.[3] They climb to the moonlit towers of ruined Rhine castles, and falter down black cobwebbed steps beneath the scattered stones of forgotten cities in Asia. The haunted wood and the desolate mountain are their shrines, and they linger around the sinister monoliths on uninhabited islands. But the true epicure in the terrible, to whom a new thrill of unutterable ghastliness is the chief end and justification of existence, esteems most of all the ancient, lonely farmhouses of backwoods New England; for there the dark elements of strength, solitude, grotesqueness, and ignorance combine to form the perfection of the hideous.

Most horrible of all sights are the little unpainted wooden houses remote from travelled ways, usually squatted upon some damp grassy slope or leaning against some gigantic outcropping of rock.[4] Two hundred years and more they have leaned or squatted there, while the vines have crawled and the trees have swelled and spread. They are almost hidden now in lawless luxuriances of green and guardian shrouds of shadow; but the small-paned windows still stare shockingly, as if blinking through a lethal stupor which wards off madness by dulling the memory of unutterable things.

named Arsinoe). There was a celebrated necropolis and labyrinth there.

3. Lord Dunsany, in his 1918 *Tales of War*, wrote, in a chapter titled "Nightmare Countries": "There are certain lands in the darker dreams of poetry that stand out in the memory of generations. There is for instance Poe's 'Dark tarn of Auber, the ghoul-haunted region of Weir'; there are some queer twists in the river Alph as imagined by Coleridge; two lines of Swinburne:

By the tideless dolorous inland sea
In a land of sand and ruin and gold

are as haunting as any. There are in literature certain regions of gloom, so splendid that whenever you come on them they leave in the mind a sort of nightmare country which one's thoughts revisit on hearing the lines quoted" (73).

4. Compare, as Peter Cannon observes, in "The Return of Sherlock Holmes and H. P. Lovecraft," Holmes's statement to Dr. Watson in "The Copper Beeches": "You look at these scattered houses, and you are impressed by their beauty. I look at them, and the only thought which comes to me is a feeling of their isolation and of the impunity with which crime may be committed there. . . . But look at these lonely houses, each in its own fields, filled for the most part with poor ignorant folk who know little of the law. Think of the deeds of hellish cruelty, the hidden wickedness which may go on, year in, year out, in such places, and none the wiser." There are ad ditional parallels between this tale and "The Copper Beeches," examined in depth by Cannon in "Parallel Passages in 'The Adventure of the Copper Beeches' and 'The Picture in the House.'" Note that "The Copper Beeches" first appeared in America in

In such houses have dwelt generations of strange people, whose like the world has never seen. Seized with a gloomy and fanatical belief which exiled them from their kind, their ancestors sought the wilderness for freedom. There the scions of a conquering race indeed flourished free from the restrictions of their fellows, but cowered in an appalling slavery to the dismal phantasms of their own minds. Divorced from the enlightenment of civilisation, the strength of these Puritans turned into singular channels; and in their isolation, morbid self-repression, and struggle for life with relentless Nature, there came to them dark furtive traits from the prehistoric depths of their cold Northern heritage. By necessity practical and by philosophy stern, these folk were not beautiful in their sins. Erring as all mortals must, they were forced by their rigid code to seek concealment above all else; so that they came to use less and less taste in what they concealed. Only the silent, sleepy, staring houses in the backwoods can tell all that has lain hidden since the early days; and they are not communicative, being loath to shake off the drowsiness which helps them forget. Sometimes one feels that it would be merciful to tear down these houses, for they must often dream.[5]

It was to a time-battered edifice of this description that I was driven one afternoon in November, 1896, by a rain of such chilling copiousness that any shelter was preferable to exposure. I had been travelling for some time amongst the people of the Miskatonic Valley[6] in quest of certain genealogical data; and from the remote, devious, and problematical nature of my course, had deemed it convenient to employ a bicycle despite the lateness of the season. Now I found myself upon an apparently abandoned road which I had chosen as the shortest cut to Arkham;[7] overtaken by the storm at a point far from any town, and confronted with no refuge save the antique and repellent wooden building which blinked with bleared windows from between two huge leafless elms near the foot of a rocky hill. Distant though it was from the remnant of a road, the house none the less impressed me unfavourably the very moment I espied it. Honest, wholesome structures do not stare at travellers so slyly and hauntingly, and in my genealogical researches I had encountered legends of a century before which biassed me against places of this kind. Yet the force of the elements was such as to overcome my scruples, and I did not hesitate to wheel my machine up the weedy rise to the closed door which seemed at once so suggestive and secretive.

I had somehow taken it for granted that the house was abandoned, yet as I approached it I was not so sure; for though the walks were indeed overgrown with weeds, they seemed to retain their nature a little too well to argue complete desertion. Therefore instead of trying the door I knocked, feeling as I did so a trepidation I could scarcely explain. As I waited on the rough, mossy rock which served as a doorstep, I glanced at the neighbouring windows and the panes of the transom above me, and noticed that although old, rattling, and almost opaque with dirt, they were not broken. The building, then, must still be inhabited, despite its isolation and general neglect. However, my rapping evoked no response, so after repeating the summons I tried the rusty latch and found the door unfastened. Inside was a little vestibule with walls from which the plaster was falling, and through the doorway came a faint but peculiarly hateful odour. I entered, carrying my bicycle, and closed the door behind me. Ahead rose a narrow staircase, flanked by a small door probably leading to the cellar, while to the left and right were closed doors leading to rooms on the ground floor.

Illustration for "Bilden i huset" ("Pictures in the House"), *Mannen i svart*, edited by Torsten Jungstedt. Simrishamn, Sweden: Rabén & Sjögren, 1990 (artist: Hans Arnold)

Map of the watercourse of the Miskatonic River and the approximate locations of other sites. (artist: Hoodinski)

June 1892 in various newspapers and in various American book editions later that year; the narrator may have come across the story soon after its publication.

5. The view of the narrator—that the Puritans were warped by their fanatical beliefs—was a popular one, shared by Lovecraft himself. In a letter to Elizabeth Toldridge, he wrote, "An abnormal Puritan psychology led to all kinds of repression, furtiveness, & grotesque hidden crime, while the long winters & backwoods isolation fostered monstrous secrets which never came to light" (October 9, 1931, *Selected Letters*, III, 423). For a more thoughtful study of the Puritans and the consequences of their rigid moral code, see Charles Lloyd Cohen's *God's Caress: The Psychology of Puritan Religious Experience*. Cohen, director of the Lubar Institute for the Study of Abrahamic Religions and a professor of history and religious studies at the University of Wisconsin–Madison, writes: "To friends they seemed militant soldiers in the army of the Lord; to foes, officious busybodies disrupting village camaraderie, but on at least one point all observers could agree: to be a Puritan meant living a life distinctively ardent" (4).

6. The Miskatonic River is first named in this story. It may be seen to follow an easterly course across Massachusetts and, as will become clear later, it originates in the hills west of Dunwich. It runs eastward past Dunwich, turns southeast, and flows through the town of Arkham. The river empties into the sea two miles to the south near Kingsport, which lies just to the northeast. A detailed "History of the Miskatonic Valley, Part One" by Peter Rawlik (alas, with no supporting notes and covering only the Indians and early colonists) appeared in *Crypt of Cthulhu* in 2000.

7. This is the first mention of the town of Arkham, which (as will be seen) is the seat of Miskatonic University. Arkham figures prominently in a number of stories, including "The Dunwich Horror," "Herbert West: Reanimator," "The Thing on the Doorstep," and "The Dreams in the Witch House" and is mentioned in many more. Although this editor will point out correspondences between Kingsport, Arkham, and other Massachusetts towns, Lovecraft wrote to August Derleth on November 6, 1931:

> About "Arkham" and "Kingsport"— bless my soul! but I thought I'd told you all about them years ago! They are typical but imaginary places— like the river "Miskatonic," whose name is simply a jumble of Algonquin roots. Vaguely, "Arkham" corresponds to Salem (though Salem has no college), while "Kingsport" corresponds to Marblehead. Similarly, there is no "Dunwich"—the place being a vague echo of the decadent Massachusetts countryside around Springfield—say Wilbraham, Monson, and Hampden (*Selected Letters*, III, 432).

Although numerous scholars continue to delve into the *real* locations of incidents described in Lovecraft's works, Peter Cannon, in *H. P. Lovecraft*, calls Arkham the "quintessential, cosmically haunted New England town. As befits such status, Arkham transcends any one spot on the map." Even Will Murray, who has expended more energy on identifying the locations than any other Lovecraftian scholar and who names Oakham, Massachusetts, as the *real* Arkham (in "In Search of Arkham Country"), admits: "It is clear . . . that Lovecraft is not consistent with his placement of locales. . . .

Leaning my cycle against the wall I opened the door at the left, and crossed into a small low-ceiled chamber but dimly lighted by its two dusty windows and furnished in the barest and most primitive possible way. It appeared to be a kind of sitting-room, for it had a table and several chairs, and an immense fireplace above which ticked an antique clock on a mantel. Books and papers were very few, and in the prevailing gloom I could not readily discern the titles. What interested me was the uniform air of archaism as displayed in every visible detail. Most of the houses in this region I had found rich in relics of the past, but here the antiquity was curiously complete; for in all the room I could not discover a single article of definitely post-revolutionary date. Had the furnishings been less humble, the place would have been a collector's paradise.

As I surveyed this quaint apartment, I felt an increase in that aversion first excited by the bleak exterior of the house. Just what it was that I feared or loathed, I could by no means define; but something in the whole atmosphere seemed redolent of unhallowed age, of unpleasant crudeness, and of secrets which should be forgotten. I felt disinclined to sit down, and wandered about examining the various articles which I had noticed. The first object of my curiosity was a book of medium size lying upon the table and presenting such an antediluvian aspect that I marvelled at beholding it outside a museum or library. It was bound in leather with metal fittings, and was in an excellent state of preservation; being altogether an unusual sort of volume to encounter in an abode so lowly. When I opened it to the title page my wonder grew even greater, for it proved to be nothing less rare than Pigafetta's account of the Congo region, written in Latin from the notes of the sailor Lopez and printed at Frankfort in 1598.[8] I had often heard of this work, with its curious illustrations by the brothers De Bry, hence for a moment forgot my uneasiness in my desire to turn the pages before me. The engravings were indeed interesting, drawn wholly from imagination and careless descriptions, and represented negroes with white skins and Caucasian features;[9] nor would I soon have closed the book had not an exceedingly trivial circumstance upset my tired nerves and revived my sensation of disquiet. What annoyed me

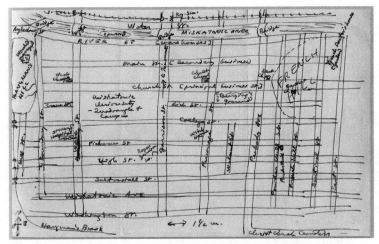

Map of Arkham drawn by Lovecraft in 1934.

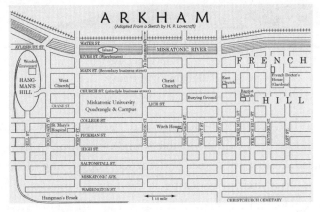

Lovecraft's map. Adapted by Joseph Morales and copyright ©
Joseph Morales 2006, reprinted with permission

None of Lovecraft's conceptions are intrinsically fixed. Rather, they are fluid and protean as befits fantasy creations" (66–67). But not even Murray can resist: In "In Search of Arkham Country Revisited," he reverses his field and concludes that Arkham is a combination of Greenwich and New Salem.

This edition will adopt a less dogmatic approach. While similarities between specific locations and the names given to the locales of the stories may be observed, this editor believes that it is futile to attempt to pin down a specific location on conventional maps of New England as the place where a specific series of events occurred. Like Dr. Watson in his chronicles of Sherlock Holmes, Lovecraft's narrators deftly conceal the names and places of their tales.

In 1934, Lovecraft drew a map of Arkham, which he mentioned in a March 28 letter to Donald Wandrei, a writer, friend, and protégé: "One thing I did lately was to construct a Map of Arkham, so that allusions in any future tale I may write may be consistent." It was first published, as "Map of Arkham," in *The Acolyte* 1, no. 1 (Fall 1942), 26, and is reproduced here, along with a 2006 adaptation.

8. *Report of the Kingdom of Congo*, "Drawn Out of the Writings and Discourses of the Portuguese, Duarte Lopez" (or Lopes), by Filippo Pigafetta (1591), reprinted in English (London: John Murray, 1881). The work first appeared in Italian in 1591; there were subsequent editions in German (1597, with the De Bry plates) and Latin (1598, under the title *Regnum Congo*).

9. Johannes Theodorus and Johannes Israel De Bry, born in Liège, were the sons of the German-Flemish engraver,

was merely the persistent way in which the volume tended to fall open of itself at Plate XII, which represented in gruesome detail a butcher's shop of the cannibal Anziques.[10] I experienced some shame at my susceptibility to so slight a thing, but the drawing nevertheless disturbed me, especially in connexion with some adjacent passages descriptive of Anzique gastronomy.

I had turned to a neighbouring shelf and was examining its meagre literary contents—an eighteenth-century Bible, a *Pilgrim's Progress* of like period, illustrated with grotesque woodcuts and printed by the almanack-maker Isaiah Thomas,[11] the rotting bulk of Cotton Mather's *Magnalia Christi Americana*,[12] and goldsmith, printer, and bookseller Dirk De Bry, whose popular, sometimes fanciful illustrations of French and British colonization of North America gave generations of Europeans slightly erroneous notions of the New World. The brothers' work, too, was in part inaccurate, largely because they drew their illustrations based on secondhand accounts and pictures—as did their father—rather than from actual observation. (None of the De Brys crossed the Atlantic.) However, the black-and-white illustrations make it difficult to determine whether the natives' skin is white or black, and their features in some of the illustrations do appear different from those of the Caucasian visitor. S. T. Joshi, in *The Call of Cthulhu and Other Weird Stories* (370), ascribes the description to Lovecraft's deriving his knowledge of Pigafetta from Thomas Henry Huxley's *Man's Place in Nature and Other Anthropological Essays* (1894), which contained redrawn versions of the De Bry illustrations, but in fact the description is close to the truth and may simply be ascribed to a hasty viewing of the book.

10. The Anziques were a distinct tribe or nation of people living in the Congo. The picture mentioned is here:

11. Isaiah Thomas, a Worcester writer and printer, and the founder of the American Society of Antiquaries (now the American Antiquarian Society), published John Bunyan's *Pilgrim's Progress* in 1791, only the second American illustrated edition. His first almanac appeared in 1802.

12. *The Glorious Works of Jesus Christ in America*, subtitled, in English, *The Ecclesiastical History of New-England* (only the book's title was in Latin). Nearly seven hundred pages long, and described by

Argumentum XII, "De Regnis Coangani incolis & Anziquis, de quibus sap. s. primi libri fit mentio" (from *Vera Descriptio Regni Africani* by Phillipum Pigafettam).

a few other books of evidently equal age—when my attention was aroused by the unmistakable sound of walking in the room overhead. At first astonished and startled, considering the lack of response to my recent knocking at the door, I immediately afterward concluded that the walker had just awakened from a sound sleep; and listened with less surprise as the footsteps sounded on the creaking stairs. The tread was heavy, yet seemed to contain a curious quality of cautiousness; a quality which I disliked the more because the tread was heavy. When I had entered the room I had shut the door behind me. Now, after a moment of silence during which the walker may have been inspecting my bicycle in the hall, I heard a fumbling at the latch and saw the panelled portal swing open again.

In the doorway stood a person of such singular appearance that I should have exclaimed aloud but for the restraints of good breeding. Old, white-bearded, and ragged, my host possessed a countenance and physique which inspired equal wonder and respect. His height could not have been less than six feet, and despite a general air of age and poverty he was stout and powerful in proportion. His face, almost hidden by a long beard which grew high on the cheeks, seemed abnormally ruddy and less wrinkled than one might expect; while over a high forehead fell a shock of white hair little thinned by the years. His blue eyes, though a trifle bloodshot, seemed inexplicably keen and burning. But for his horrible unkemptness the man would have been as distinguished-looking as he was impressive. This unkemptness, however, made him offensive despite his face and figure. Of what his clothing consisted I could hardly tell, for it seemed to me no more than a mass of tatters surmounting a pair of high, heavy boots; and his lack of cleanliness surpassed description.[13]

The appearance of this man, and the instinctive fear he inspired, prepared me for something like enmity; so that I almost shuddered through surprise and a sense of uncanny incongruity when he motioned me to a chair and addressed me in a thin, weak voice full of fawning respect and ingratiating hospitality. His speech was very curious, an extreme form of Yankee dialect I had thought long extinct; and I studied it closely as he sat down opposite me for conversation.

"Ketched in the rain, be ye?" he greeted. "Glad ye was nigh the haouse en' hed the sense ta come right in. I calc'late I was asleep, else I'd a heerd ye—I ain't as young as I uster be, an' I need a paowerful sight o' naps naowadays. Trav'lin' fur? I hain't seed many folks 'long this rud sence they tuk off the Arkham stage."

I replied that I was going to Arkham, and apologised for my rude entry into his domicile, whereupon he continued.

"Glad ta see ye, young Sir—new faces is scurce araount here, an' I hain't got much ta cheer me up these days. Guess yew hail from Bosting, don't ye? I never ben thar, but I kin tell a taown man when I see 'im—we hed one fer deestrick schoolmaster in 'eighty-four, but he quit suddent an' no one never heerd on 'im sence—" Here the old man lapsed into a kind of chuckle, and made no explanation when I questioned him. He seemed to be in an aboundingly good humour, yet to possess those eccentricities which one might guess from his grooming. For some time he rambled on with an almost feverish geniality, when it struck me to ask him how he came by so rare a book as Pigafetta's *Regnum Congo*. The effect of this volume had not left me, and I felt a certain hesitancy in speaking of it, but curiosity overmastered all the vague fears which had steadily accumulated since my first glimpse

one critic as "a chaotick mass of history, biography, obsolete creeds, witchcraft, and Indian wars, interspersed with bad puns, and numerous quotations in Latin, Greek, and Hebrew which rise up like so many decayed, hideous stumps to arrest the eye and deform the surface" (William Tudor, *North American Review*, January 1818, 255–72), it was published in 1702. Lovecraft's library contained a first edition of this ornate, heavily allusive work, an inheritance. A sweeping, often brilliant, treatise on the culture of the New England colonies, it detailed, among other events, the Salem Witch Trials of 1692, of which Mather, an eminent Puritan minister, is judged to have been both one of the architects and, later, a critic. He is on record as having supported the admission in court of so-called spectral evidence—the visions and dreams of the defendants—although he is also said to have been conflicted about the consequences of its having been made admissible.

13. In the first appearance of the story, the following sentence came after the description of the character's clothing and hygiene: "On a beard which might have been patriarchal were unsightly stains, some of them disgustingly suggestive of blood." It was later removed.

14. The American Civil War was long over by 1868, so Holt could not have been killed in that war. Therefore, he presumably was killed in the War of 1812 (and may well have acquired his captaincy in the Revolutionary War), and he traded the book to the man in *1768*, making him well over 130 years old.

15. A cargo ship out of Salem, Massachusetts. They thrived before the War of 1812, when many sailors were impressed into the American navy.

16. Perhaps the old man means the palmetto-like trees in the third illustration.

"Argumentum III. Edicti Regii, de quo cap. 3. fecundi libri agitur, executio" (from *Vera Descriptio Regni Africani* by Phillipum Pigafettam).

of the house. To my relief, the question did not seem an awkward one; for the old man answered freely and volubly.

"Oh, thet Afriky book? Cap'n Ebenezer Holt traded me thet in 'sixty-eight—him as was kilt in the war."[14] Something about the name of Ebenezer Holt caused me to look up sharply. I had encountered it in my genealogical work, but not in any record since the Revolution. I wondered if my host could help me in the task at which I was labouring, and resolved to ask him about it later on. He continued.

"Ebenezer was on a Salem merchantman[15] for years, an' picked up a sight o' queer stuff in every port. He got this in London, I guess—he uster like ter buy things at the shops. I was up ta his haouse onct, on the hill, tradin' hosses, when I see this book. I relished the picters, so he give it in on a swap. 'Tis a queer book—here, leave me git on my spectacles—" The old man fumbled among his rags, producing a pair of dirty and amazingly antique glasses with small octagonal lenses and steel bows. Donning these, he reached for the volume on the table and turned the pages lovingly.

"Ebenezer cud read a leetle o' this—'tis Latin—but I can't. I hed two er three schoolmasters read me a bit, and Passon Clark, him they say got draownded in the pond—kin yew make anything outen it?" I told him that I could, and translated for his benefit a paragraph near the beginning. If I erred, he was not scholar enough to correct me; for he seemed childishly pleased at my English version. His proximity was becoming rather obnoxious, yet I saw no way to escape without offending him. I was amused at the childish fondness of this ignorant old man for the pictures in a book he could not read, and wondered how much better he could read the few books in English which adorned the room. This revelation of simplicity removed much of the ill-defined apprehension I had felt, and I smiled as my host rambled on:

"Queer haow picters kin set a body thinkin'. Take this un here near the front. Hev yew ever seed trees like thet, with big leaves a-floppin' over an' daown?[16] And them men—them can't be niggers—they dew beat all. Kinder like Injuns, I guess, even ef they be in Afriky. Some o' these here critters looks like monkeys, or half monkeys an' half men, but I never heerd o' nothing like this un." Here he pointed to a fabulous creature of the artist, which one might describe as a sort of dragon with the head of an alligator.[17]

"But naow I'll shew ye the best un—over here nigh the middle—" The old man's speech grew a trifle thicker and his eyes assumed a brighter glow; but his fumbling hands, though seemingly clumsier than before, were entirely adequate to their mission. The book fell open, almost of its own accord and as if from frequent consultation at this place, to the repellent twelfth plate shewing a butcher's shop amongst the Anzique cannibals. My sense of restlessness returned, though I did not exhibit it. The especially bizarre thing was that the artist had made his Africans look like white men—the limbs and quarters hanging about the walls of the shop were ghastly, while the butcher with his axe was hideously incongruous. But my host seemed to relish the view as much as I disliked it.

"What d'ye think o' this—ain't never see the like hereabouts, eh? When I see this I told Eb Holt, 'Thar's suthin' ta stir ye up an' make yer blood tickle.' When I read in Scripter about slayin'—like them Midianites was slew—I kinder think things, but I ain't got no picter of it. Here a body kin see all they is to it—I s'pose 'tis sinful, but ain't we all born an' livin' in sin?—Thet feller bein' chopped up gives me a tickle every time I look at 'im—I hev ta keep lookin' at 'im—see whar the butcher cut off his feet? Thar's his head on thet bench, with one arm side of it, an' t'other arm's on the graound side o' the meat block."

As the man mumbled on in his shocking ecstasy the expression on his hairy, spectacled face became indescribable, but his voice sank rather than mounted. My own sensations can scarcely be recorded. All the terror I had dimly felt before rushed upon me actively and vividly, and I knew that I loathed the ancient and abhorrent creature so near me with an infinite intensity. His madness, or at least his partial perversion, seemed beyond dispute. He was almost whispering now, with a huskiness more terrible than a scream, and I trembled as I listened.

"As I says, 'tis queer haow picters sets ye thinkin'. D'ye know, young Sir, I'm right sot on this un here. Arter I got the book off Eb I uster look at it a lot, especial when I'd heerd Passon Clark rant o' Sundays in his big wig. Onct I tried suthin' funny—here,

17. Some strange creatures are depicted in the De Bry illustrations, but none that matches this description (none appears in the plates of the Huxley version of the book, either, but such a creature is described there—see note 9, above).

18. P. S. Owens points out, in "The Mirror in the House: Looking at the Horror of Looking at the Horror," that this means that the corpse on which the old man has been dining—for we are led to the conclusion that he is a cannibal—is in his bedroom, not the kitchen or another convenient storage place, making the bedroom "a scene of violent, animalistic, unnatural acts" and adding, in Owens's phrase "a carnality to the carnivorousness." The narrator's mind is "saved" because he stops *enjoying* the perverse and horrible revelations.

young Sir, don't git skeert—all I done was ter look at the picter afore I kilt the sheep for market—killin' sheep was kinder more fun arter lookin' at it—" The tone of the old man now sank very low, sometimes becoming so faint that his words were hardly audible. I listened to the rain, and to the rattling of the bleared, small-paned windows, and marked a rumbling of approaching thunder quite unusual for the season. Once a terrific flash and peal shook the frail house to its foundations, but the whisperer seemed not to notice it.

"Killin' sheep was kinder more fun—but d'ye know, 'twan't quite *satisfyin'*. Queer haow a *cravin'* gits a holt on ye—As ye love the Almighty, young man, don't tell nobody, but I swar ter Gawd thet picter begun ta make me *hungry fer victuals I couldn't raise nor buy*—here, set still, what's ailin' ye?—I didn't do nothin', only I wondered haow 'twud be ef I *did*—They say meat makes blood an' flesh, an' gives ye new life, so I wondered ef 'twudn't make a man live longer an' longer ef 'twas *more the same*—" But the whisperer never continued. The interruption was not produced by my fright, nor by the rapidly increasing storm amidst whose fury I was presently to open my eyes on a smoky solitude of blackened ruins. It was produced by a very simple though somewhat unusual happening.

The open book lay flat between us, with the picture staring repulsively upward. As the old man whispered the words "*more the same*" a tiny spattering impact was heard, and something shewed on the yellowed paper of the upturned volume. I thought of the rain and of a leaky roof, but rain is not red. On the butcher's shop of the Anzique cannibals a small red spattering glistened picturesquely, lending vividness to the horror of the engraving. The old man saw it, and stopped whispering even before my expression of horror made it necessary; saw it and glanced quickly toward the floor of the room he had left an hour before. I followed his glance, and beheld just above us on the loose plaster of the ancient ceiling a large irregular spot of wet crimson which seemed to spread even as I viewed it.[18] I did not shriek or move, but merely shut my eyes. A moment later came the titanic thunderbolt of thunderbolts; blasting that accursed house of unutterable secrets and bringing the oblivion which alone saved my mind.

Herbert West: Reanimator

Lovecraft reportedly despised the story as "hack" work, having little literary merit, and he may have even intended it as parody. It is seminal, however, as the first great zombie story, written with Lovecraft's usual meticulous scientific background. Firmly set in Arkham, it confirms that town and its university as the epicenter of the weird. The Herbert West saga has been retold in a series of films from the 1980s to the 2000s starring Jeffrey Combs as West and has even manifested itself as a porn film (Re-Penetrator).

"To be dead, to be truly dead, must be glorious. There are far worse things awaiting man than death."

—COUNT DRACULA[1]

PART I: FROM THE DARK[2]

OF HERBERT WEST, who was my friend in college and in after life, I can speak only with extreme terror. This terror is not due altogether to the sinister manner of his recent disappearance, but was engendered by the whole nature of his life-work, and first gained its acute form more than seventeen years ago,[3] when we were in the third year of our course at the Miskatonic University Medical School in Arkham.[4] While he was with me, the wonder and diabolism of his experiments fascinated me utterly, and I was his closest companion. Now that he is gone and the spell is broken, the actual fear is greater. Memories and possibilities are ever more hideous than realities.

The first horrible incident of our acquaintance was the greatest shock I ever experienced, and it is only with reluctance that I repeat it. As I have said, it happened when we were in the medical school, where West had already made himself notorious through his wild theories on the nature of death and the possibility of

1. This is not from Bram Stoker's 1897 novel *Dracula*; rather, it is a slight variation on the following dialogue from the 1931 Tod Browning film, whose script is credited to Garrett Ford:

> DRACULA: To die . . . to be really dead . . . that must be glorious.
>
> MINA: Why, Count Dracula!
>
> DRACULA: There are far worse things . . . awaiting man . . . than death.

The quotation is omitted from many published versions of this story.

2. The six parts of the story were written in 1921–22. The first part was published in February 1922, in *Home Brew* 1, no.

1, 19–25, and reprinted after Lovecraft's death in *Weird Tales* 36, no. 4 (March 1942), 84–88. Because Lovecraft knew that the story would be serialized, in each part he deftly recapitulates key elements that first appeared earlier.

3. Later references confirm that this is probably October or November 1903 (in the third school year, "many weeks" after the start of the experiments, which may have started at the beginning of the fall term, but evidently before the cold of winter had set in, because it is later revealed that a drowning took place in a pond that had not yet frozen over). In the fourth West tale, below, set in July 1910, the narrator states that he and West were medical students "seven years ago." This confirms the 1903 date.

4. This is the first mention of the famed university. Its library holdings figure significantly in "The Dunwich Horror." Fritz Leiber Jr., in "A Literary Copernicus," traces the known history of this institution from 1882, when the meteor described in "The Colour Out of Space" fell, to the Australian expedition of 1935 detailed in "The Shadow Out of Time." "Certainly the Miskatonic faculty," remarked Leiber, "constitutes a kind of Lovecraftian utopia of highly intelligent, aesthetically sensitive, yet tradition-minded scholars" (303). A partial roster of the faculty is presented in Appendix 2.

5. In short, West seeks to reanimate the dead. The idea of scientific resurrection is not original to West, of course; his most famous predecessor is Dr. Victor Frankenstein, whose experiments are reported in Mary Shelley's 1818 *Frankenstein, or The Modern Prometheus*. Prior to Frankenstein's work, from 1801 to 1804, natural philosopher and physicist Giovanni Aldini (1762–1834) reportedly made many attempts, using galvanic

overcoming it artificially. His views, which were widely ridiculed by the faculty and his fellow-students, hinged on the essentially mechanistic nature of life; and concerned means for operating the organic machinery of mankind by calculated chemical action after the failure of natural processes.[5] In his experiments with various animating solutions he had killed and treated immense numbers of rabbits, guinea-pigs, cats, dogs, and monkeys, till he had become the prime nuisance of the college. Several times he had actually obtained signs of life in animals supposedly dead; in many cases violent signs; but he soon saw that the perfection of this process, if indeed possible, would necessarily involve a lifetime of research. It likewise became clear that, since the same solution never worked alike on different organic species, he would require human subjects for further and more specialised progress. It was here that he first came into conflict with the college authorities, and was debarred from future experiments by no less a dignitary than the dean of the medical school himself—the learned and benevolent Dr. Allan Halsey,[6] whose work in behalf of the stricken is recalled by every old resident of Arkham.

I had always been exceptionally tolerant of West's pursuits, and we frequently discussed his theories, whose ramifications and corollaries were almost infinite. Holding with Hæckel[7] that all life is a chemical and physical process, and that the so-called "soul" is a myth, my friend believed that artificial reanimation of the dead can depend only on the condition of the tissues; and that unless actual decomposition has set in, a corpse fully equipped with organs may with suitable measures be set going again in the peculiar fashion known as life. That the psychic or intellectual life might be impaired by the slight deterioration of sensitive brain-cells which even a short period of death would be apt to cause,[8] West fully realised. It had at first been his hope to find a reagent which would restore vitality before the actual advent of death, and only repeated failures on animals had shewn him that the natural and artificial life-motions were incompatible. He then sought extreme freshness in his specimens, injecting his solutions into the blood immediately after the extinction of life. It was this circumstance which made the professors so carelessly sceptical, for they felt that true death had not occurred in any case. They did not stop to view the matter closely and reasoningly.

It was not long after the faculty had interdicted his work that West confided to me his resolution to get fresh human bodies in some manner, and continue in secret the experiments he could no longer perform openly.[9] To hear him discussing ways and means was rather ghastly, for at the college we had never procured anatomical specimens ourselves. Whenever the morgue proved inadequate, two local negroes attended to this matter, and they were seldom questioned.[10] West was then a small, slender, spectacled youth with delicate features, yellow hair, pale blue eyes, and a soft voice, and it was uncanny to hear him dwelling on the relative merits of Christchurch Cemetery and the potter's field. We finally decided on the potter's field, because practically every body in Christchurch was embalmed; a thing of course ruinous to West's researches.

I was by this time his active and enthralled assistant, and helped him make all his decisions, not only concerning the source of bodies but concerning a suitable place for our loathsome work. It was I who thought of the deserted Chapman farmhouse beyond Meadow Hill,[11] where we fitted up on the ground floor an operating room and a laboratory, each with dark curtains to conceal our midnight doings. The place was far from any road, and in sight of no other house, yet precautions were none the less necessary; since rumours of strange lights, started by chance nocturnal roamers, would soon bring disaster on our enterprise. It was agreed to call the whole thing a chemical laboratory if discovery should occur. Gradually we equipped our sinister haunt of science with materials either purchased in Boston or quietly borrowed from the college—materials carefully made unrecognisable save to expert eyes—and provided spades and picks for the many burials we should have to make in the cellar. At the college we used an incinerator, but the apparatus was too costly for our unauthorised laboratory. Bodies were always a nuisance—even the small guinea-pig bodies from the slight clandestine experiments in West's room at the boarding-house.

We followed the local death-notices like ghouls, for our specimens demanded particular qualities. What we wanted were corpses interred soon after death and without artificial preservation; preferably free from malforming disease, and certainly with all organs present. Accident victims were our best hope. Not for

forces, to achieve human reanimation. Like Herbert West, German naturalist Johann Konrad Dippel (1673–1734) experimented with chemical means to extend the life span of humans. Dippel reported discovering the "elixir of life," but there is no evidence of its effects; though rumors spread that he engaged in what was called "soul-transference" with cadavers, this has not been verified. Curiously, Dippel was born in Castle Frankenstein, in central-southern Germany.

6. Note that Charles Dexter Ward (see *The Case of Charles Dexter Ward*, pp. 171–309, below) lived in "the old Halsey mansion" in Providence.

7. Ernst Heinrich Philipp August Haeckel (1834–1919) was an eminent German biologist, naturalist, philosopher, physician, professor, and artist. A popular lecturer and supporter of Darwin's theories, he coined the terms "ontogeny" (the growth of an organism) and "phylogeny" (the interrelatedness of species) and famously dogmatized that "ontogeny recapitulates phylogeny." Most important for purposes of this story, Haeckel theorized about *Urschleim*, primordial slime from which life evolved. He rejected the idea that there was some special vital force, arguing that biology was merely a branch of physics and that living matter was subject to the same laws as inorganic or dead substances.

8. One hundred years ago, little was known of brain death; today, the subject still remains shrouded in mystery. Studies in 2002 provided evidence that brain cells could be kept alive for weeks after the death of the body. However, there is no evidence that intellectual activity continues. Scientists have recorded a "wave of death" passing through the brain, a burst of brain cell activity, about one minute after clinical death, and

many speculate that this signals the loss of membrane potential and irreversible brain death, a "point of no return." Others, however, remain unconvinced, pointing to experiments in which electrical activity returned to reoxygenated brain cells after fifteen minutes of oxygen deprivation.

9. West follows in the tradition of medical researchers in the early nineteenth century who had difficulty finding the cadavers they required. The scarcity was the combined result of the expansion of medical training, the decrease of capital punishment, and the lack of refrigeration. As a result, "body-snatchers" or "resurrectionists" stole corpses from graveyards. In the notorious case of the Edinburgh serial killers William Burke and William Hare (1827–28) and the copycat London Burkers (1831), the sellers provided fresh corpses by murdering their wares. The plan was mooted by the passage of the Anatomical Act of 1832 in England, widening the pool of corpses available to supply the market.

10. Compare this with the activities of two medical students and an African-American cemetery worker, Jess, who exhume the body of a man named Henry Armstrong in Ambrose Bierce's "One Summer Night" (1906). Upon discovering that Armstrong is not dead, the three flee; but Jess returns and clubs Armstrong with a spade, and thus the students procure the fresh corpse they needed.

11. No Meadow Hill is found in Marblehead or Salem. The location is also mentioned in "The Unnamable," "The Colour Out of Space," and "The Dreams in the Witch House," below.

12. A dark lantern was a modification of an ordinary gas or kerosene hand lantern that could be darkened while lit, by a

many weeks did we hear of anything suitable; though we talked with morgue and hospital authorities, ostensibly in the college's interest, as often as we could without exciting suspicion. We found that the college had first choice in every case, so that it might be necessary to remain in Arkham during the summer, when only the limited summer-school classes were held. In the end, though, luck favoured us; for one day we heard of an almost ideal case in the potter's field; a brawny young workman drowned only the morning before in Sumner's Pond, and buried at the town's expense without delay or embalming. That afternoon we found the new grave, and determined to begin work soon after midnight.

It was a repulsive task that we undertook in the black small hours, even though we lacked at that time the special horror of graveyards which later experiences brought to us. We carried spades and oil dark lanterns,[12] for although electric torches were then manufactured, they were not as satisfactory as the tungsten contrivances of today.[13] The process of unearthing was slow and sordid—it might have been gruesomely poetical if we had been artists instead of scientists—and we were glad when our spades struck wood. When the pine box was fully uncovered West scrambled down and removed the lid, dragging out and propping up the contents. I reached down and hauled the contents out of the grave, and then both toiled hard to restore the spot to its former appearance. The affair made us rather nervous, especially the stiff form and vacant face of our first trophy, but we managed to remove all traces of our visit. When we had patted down the last shovelful of earth, we put the specimen in a canvas sack and set out for the old Chapman place beyond Meadow Hill.

On an improvised dissecting-table in the old farmhouse, by the light of a powerful acetylene lamp,[14] the specimen was not very spectral looking. It had been a sturdy and apparently unimaginative youth of wholesome plebeian type—large-framed, grey-eyed, and brown-haired—a sound animal without psychological subtleties, and probably having vital processes of the simplest and healthiest sort. Now, with the eyes closed, it looked more asleep than dead; though the expert test of my friend soon left no doubt on that score. We had at last what West had always longed for—a real dead man of the ideal kind, ready for the solution as prepared according to the most careful calculations and theories for human use. The tension on our part became very great. We knew that there was scarcely a chance for anything like complete success, and could not avoid hideous fears at possible grotesque results of partial animation. Especially were we apprehensive concerning the mind and impulses of the creature, since in the space following death some of the more delicate cerebral cells might well have suffered deterioration. I, myself, still held some curious notions about the traditional "soul" of man, and felt an awe at the secrets that might be told by one returning from the dead.[15] I wondered what sights this placid youth might have seen in inaccessible spheres, and what he could relate if fully restored to life. But my wonder was not overwhelming, since for the most part I shared the materialism of my friend. He was calmer than I as he forced a large quantity of his fluid into a vein of the body's arm, immediately binding the incision securely.

The waiting was gruesome, but West never faltered. Every now and then he applied his stethoscope to the specimen, and bore the negative results philosophically. After about three-quarters of an hour without the least sign of life he disappointedly pronounced the solution inadequate, but determined to make the most of his opportunity and try one change in the formula before disposing of his ghastly prize. We had that afternoon dug a grave in the cellar, and would have to fill it by dawn—for although we had fixed a lock on the house, we wished to shun even the remotest risk of a ghoulish discovery. Besides, the body would not be even approximately fresh the next night. So taking the solitary acetylene lamp into the adjacent laboratory, we left our silent guest on the slab in the dark, and bent every energy to the mixing of a new solution; the weighing and measuring supervised by West with an almost fanatical care.

The awful event was very sudden, and wholly unexpected. I was pouring something from one test-tube to another, and West was busy over the alcohol blast-lamp[16] which had to answer for a Bunsen burner in this gasless edifice, when from the pitch-black room we had left there burst the most appalling and dæmoniac succession of cries that either of us had ever heard. Not more unutterable could have been the chaos of hellish sound if the pit itself had opened to release the agony of the damned, for in one inconceivable cacophony was centred all the supernal terror

sliding shield that covered the light without extinguishing the flame.

13. The electric torch, or flashlight, was first patented in 1899. The torch ran on zinc-carbon batteries and carbon-filament bulbs that required frequent rest periods to recharge. The light was best used in brief intervals, or "flashes."

14. Known as carbide lamps, these burned acetylene gas and provided a bright light for lighthouses, also serving as headlamps for cars and bicycles.

15. Near-death experiences (previous to West, these were limited to persons who died and were resuscitated by medical means or spontaneously revived) came to public attention with the book *Life After Life*, by Raymond Moody Jr., published in 1975. Numerous scientific studies of near-death experiences have produced little consensus among subjects or researchers, and much controversy over the definition of "death."

16. These were used to produce a high heat. The flame of a small portion of the alcohol was made to heat the reservoir containing the remainder, thereby vaporizing it. The escaping vapor issued with considerable force and burned with a smokeless flame.

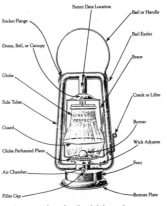

A simple alcohol blast lamp.

17. Vessels or chambers in which substances are distilled or decomposed by heat.

"We laid the specimen on an improvised dissecting table
in the old farm house. Then we set to work . . ."
Weird Tales 36, no. 4 (March 1942) (artist: G. Roller)

and unnatural despair of animate nature. Human it could not have been—it is not in man to make such sounds—and without a thought of our late employment or its possible discovery both West and I leaped to the nearest window like stricken animals; overturning tubes, lamp, and retorts,[17] and vaulting madly into the starred abyss of the rural night. I think we screamed ourselves as we stumbled frantically toward the town, though as we reached the outskirts we put on a semblance of restraint—just enough to seem like belated revellers staggering home from a debauch.

We did not separate, but managed to get to West's room, where we whispered with the gas up until dawn. By then we had calmed ourselves a little with rational theories and plans for investigation, so that we could sleep through the day—classes being disregarded. But that evening two items in the paper, wholly unrelated, made it again impossible for us to sleep. The old deserted Chapman house had inexplicably burned to an amorphous heap of ashes; that we could understand because of the upset lamp.[18] Also, an attempt had been made to disturb a new grave in the potter's field, as if by futile and spadeless clawing at the earth. That we could not understand, for we had patted down the mould very carefully.[19]

And for seventeen years after that West would look frequently over his shoulder, and complain of fancied footsteps behind him. Now he has disappeared.

PART II: THE PLAGUE-DÆMON[20]

Weird Tales 36, no. 5 (July 1942) (artist: G. Roller)

I SHALL NEVER forget that hideous summer sixteen years ago,[21] when like a noxious afrite from the halls of Eblis[22] typhoid[23] stalked leeringly through Arkham. It is by that satanic scourge that most recall the year, for truly terror brooded with bat-wings over the piles of coffins in the tombs of Christchurch Cemetery;

18. Coincidentally, another Chapman house burned in 1920. Lovecraft recorded that "the large Chapman house . . . two lawns to the north of #598 Angell" (where Lovecraft lived prior to 1924) was destroyed in "a titanic pillar of roaring, living flame" (Lovecraft to R. Kleiner, February 10, 1920, *Selected Letters*, I, 108).

19. Are we to understand that the reanimated corpse sought to return to its grave? Why?

20. First published in *Home Brew* 1, no. 2 (March 1922), and reprinted in *Weird Tales* 36, no. 5 (July 1942), 86–90.

21. Likely August 1905. Part VI, "The Tomb-Legions," is definitely set in 1921 (see note 62, below), and the events described here are referred to there as "sixteen years ago."

22. In Arabic and Persian lore, Eblis (Iblis) is the equivalent of Satan. When Adam was created, God ordered all the angels to reverence him, but Eblis refused, and God turned Eblis into a devil, the father of all evil devils.

23. Epidemic typhoid is caused by the spread of the *Rickettsia prowazekii* bacterium, usually through lice, and, prior to the discovery of vaccines, had a high fatality rate. While a major typhoid epidemic occurred in 1885 in Plymouth, Pennsylvania, and in 1903 in Ithaca, New York, the Arkham epidemic is not otherwise recorded, and no other took place subsequently in the United States until 1915, when typhoid broke out in New York, and the next year, when a typhoid epidemic was reported in Illinois. However, in 1918, Rhode Island, and Providence in particular, was devastated by influenza, with almost 33,000

deaths from influenza reported in Rhode Island in a two-month period. In May 1921, when the narrator was recording these tales, *Providence Magazine* reported a talk by the health commissioner of New York in which he warned about the influx of contagion from immigrants bringing typhus, cholera, and bubonic plague from Europe, where diseases raged in the years after World War I.

Worcester Lunatic Asylum, later known as Worcester State Hospital, shown in 2008.

24. A fictitious asylum in a fictitious town, described later (in Part VI, "The Tomb-Legions") as fifty miles from West's home in Boston. It is possibly based on Worcester State Insane Hospital, about forty miles from Boston, in Worcester, Massachusetts, near *Grafton*, Massachusetts, which may have suggested the name. Its significance is explained later in the story.

yet for me there is a greater horror in that time—a horror known to me alone now that Herbert West has disappeared.

West and I were doing post-graduate work in summer classes at the medical school of Miskatonic University, and my friend had attained a wide notoriety because of his experiments leading toward the revivification of the dead. After the scientific slaughter of uncounted small animals the freakish work had ostensibly stopped by order of our sceptical dean, Dr. Allan Halsey; though West had continued to perform certain secret tests in his dingy boarding-house room, and had on one terrible and unforgettable occasion taken a human body from its grave in the potter's field to a deserted farmhouse beyond Meadow Hill.

I was with him on that odious occasion, and saw him inject into the still veins the elixir which he thought would to some extent restore life's chemical and physical processes. It had ended horribly—in a delirium of fear which we gradually came to attribute to our own overwrought nerves—and West had never afterward been able to shake off a maddening sensation of being haunted and hunted. The body had not been quite fresh enough; it is obvious that to restore normal mental attributes a body must be very fresh indeed; and a burning of the old house had prevented us from burying the thing. It would have been better if we could have known it was underground.

After that experience West had dropped his researches for some time; but as the zeal of the born scientist slowly returned, he again became importunate with the college faculty, pleading for the use of the dissecting-room and of fresh human specimens for the work he regarded as so overwhelmingly important. His pleas, however, were wholly in vain; for the decision of Dr. Halsey was inflexible, and the other professors all endorsed the verdict of their leader. In the radical theory of reanimation they saw nothing but the immature vagaries of a youthful enthusiast whose slight form, yellow hair, spectacled blue eyes, and soft voice gave no hint of the supernormal—almost diabolical—power of the cold brain within. I can see him now as he was then—and I shiver. He grew sterner of face, but never elderly. And now Sefton Asylum[24] has had the mishap and West has vanished.

West clashed disagreeably with Dr. Halsey near the end of our

HERBERT WEST: REANIMATOR

last undergraduate term in a wordy dispute that did less credit to him than to the kindly dean in point of courtesy. He felt that he was needlessly and irrationally retarded in a supremely great work; a work which he could of course conduct to suit himself in later years, but which he wished to begin while still possessed of the exceptional facilities of the university. That the tradition-bound elders should ignore his singular results on animals, and persist in their denial of the possibility of reanimation, was inexpressibly disgusting and almost incomprehensible to a youth of West's logical temperament. Only greater maturity could help him understand the chronic mental limitations of the "professor-doctor" type—the product of generations of pathetic Puritanism; kindly, conscientious, and sometimes gentle and amiable, yet always narrow, intolerant, custom-ridden, and lacking in perspective. Age has more charity for these incomplete yet high-souled characters, whose worst real vice is timidity, and who are ultimately punished by general ridicule for their intellectual sins—sins like Ptolemaism,[25] Calvinism,[26] anti-Darwinism,[27] anti-Nietzscheism,[28] and every sort of Sabbatarianism[29] and sumptuary legislation. West, young despite his marvellous scientific acquirements, had scant patience with good Dr. Halsey and his erudite colleagues; and nursed an increasing resentment, coupled with a desire to prove his theories to these obtuse worthies in some striking and dramatic fashion. Like most youths, he indulged in elaborate day-dreams of revenge, triumph, and final magnanimous forgiveness.

And then had come the scourge, grinning and lethal, from the nightmare caverns of Tartarus.[30] West and I had graduated about the time of its beginning, but had remained for additional work at the summer school, so that we were in Arkham when it broke with full dæmoniac fury upon the town. Though not as yet licenced physicians, we now had our degrees, and were pressed frantically into public service as the numbers of the stricken grew. The situation was almost past management, and deaths ensued too frequently for the local undertakers fully to handle. Burials without embalming were made in rapid succession, and even the Christchurch Cemetery receiving tomb was crammed with coffins of the unembalmed dead. This circumstance was not without

25. The belief, propounded by Ptolemy, second-century geologer and astronomer, that the sun, planets, and stars revolve around the earth.

26. The doctrines of the Reformed church, first espoused by French theologian John Calvin (1509–1564), and in particular, predestination.

27. Darwinism, a term coined upon the publication, in 1859, of naturalist Charles Darwin's *On the Origin of Species*, is the biological theory that humans were evolved from an unknown species lower on the ladder of development; its most well-known precept is the "survival of the fittest." The anti-Darwinists rejected evolution and embraced Creationism, the notion that God created man in the image of God, without earlier experiments.

28. As wide-ranging and indefinite as the philosophy of Friedrich Nietzsche (1844–1900) may be seen to be—including, as it does, such statements as "God is dead"—there can be no precise definition of a school of anti-Nietzscheanism, unless it perhaps refers to an embrace of traditional philosophies.

29. Sabbatarianism required strict observance of the Sabbath, producing the "blue laws" in many states that forbade the operation of businesses on Sundays. Sumputary laws regulated consumption of certain goods, such as alcoholic beverages, and conduct, such as dog fighting or horse racing.

30. In Greek mythology Tartarus was a region beneath Hades, into which originally only those who were a threat to the gods were cast. Other mythologies made it synonymous with Hades.

effect on West, who thought often of the irony of the situation—so many fresh specimens, yet none for his persecuted researches! We were frightfully overworked, and the terrific mental and nervous strain made my friend brood morbidly.

But West's gentle enemies were no less harassed with prostrating duties. College had all but closed, and every doctor of the medical faculty was helping to fight the typhoid plague. Dr. Halsey in particular had distinguished himself in sacrificing service, applying his extreme skill with whole-hearted energy to cases which many others shunned because of danger or apparent hopelessness. Before a month was over the fearless dean had become a popular hero, though he seemed unconscious of his fame as he struggled to keep from collapsing with physical fatigue and nervous exhaustion. West could not withhold admiration for the fortitude of his foe, but because of this was even more determined to prove to him the truth of his amazing doctrines. Taking advantage of the disorganisation of both college work and municipal health regulations, he managed to get a recently deceased body smuggled into the university dissecting-room one night, and in my presence injected a new modification of his solution. The thing actually opened its eyes, but only stared at the ceiling with a look of soul-petrifying horror before collapsing into an inertness from which nothing could rouse it. West said it was not fresh enough—the hot summer air does not favour corpses. That time we were almost caught before we incinerated the thing, and West doubted the advisability of repeating his daring misuse of the college laboratory.

The peak of the epidemic was reached in August. West and I were almost dead, and Dr. Halsey did die on the 14th. The students all attended the hasty funeral on the 15th, and bought an impressive wreath, though the latter was quite overshadowed by the tributes sent by wealthy Arkham citizens and by the municipality itself. It was almost a public affair, for the dean had surely been a public benefactor. After the entombment we were all somewhat depressed, and spent the afternoon at the bar of the Commercial House; where West, though shaken by the death of his chief opponent, chilled the rest of us with references to his notorious theories. Most of the students went home, or to various duties, as the evening advanced; but West persuaded me to aid him in "making a night of it." West's landlady saw us arrive at his room about two in the morning, with a third man between us; and told her husband that we had all evidently dined and wined rather well.

Apparently this acidulous matron was right; for about 3 a.m. the whole house was aroused by cries coming from West's room, where when they broke down the door they found the two of us unconscious on the blood-stained carpet, beaten, scratched, and mauled, and with the broken remnants of West's bottles and instruments around us. Only an open window told what had become of our assailant, and many wondered how he himself had fared after the terrific leap from the second story to the lawn which he must have made. There were some strange garments in the room, but West upon regaining consciousness said they did not belong to the stranger, but were specimens collected for bacteriological analysis in the course of investigations on the transmission of germ diseases. He ordered them burnt as soon as possible in the capacious fireplace. To the police we both declared ignorance of our late companion's identity. He was, West nervously said, a congenial stranger whom we had met at some downtown bar of uncertain location. We had all been rather jovial, and West and I did not wish to have our pugnacious companion hunted down.

That same night saw the beginning of the second Arkham horror—the horror that to me eclipsed the plague itself. Christchurch Cemetery was the scene of a terrible killing; a watchman having been clawed to death in a manner not only too hideous for description, but raising a doubt as to the human agency of the deed. The victim had been seen alive considerably after midnight—the dawn revealed the unutterable thing. The manager of a circus at the neighbouring town of Bolton[31] was questioned, but he swore that no beast had at any time escaped from its cage. Those who found the body noted a trail of blood leading to the receiving tomb,[32] where a small pool of red lay on the concrete just outside the gate. A fainter trail led away toward the woods, but it soon gave out.

The next night devils danced on the roofs of Arkham, and

31. Bolton is a small town in Worcester County, Massachusetts, bordered by the towns of Harvard to the north, Stow to the east, Hudson and Berlin to the south, Clinton to the southwest, and Lancaster to the northwest. S. T. Joshi, in *The Annotated H. P. Lovecraft*, suggests that the mention of Bolton is confirmation that Arkham is in central Massachusetts, not on the eastern coast. Bolton, forty-three miles from Boston and fifty-six miles from Providence, lies on the Still River. The Still is not the Miskatonic; the former empties south into Long Island Sound, while the latter ends in Kingsport. As will be seen below, the village of Bolton also lacks the industry it is described as having. This must be rejected as a spurious clue regarding the location of Arkham.

32. This presumably refers to the structure where cadavers and coffins are delivered to the cemetery.

33. The only Crane Street in Massachusetts is in Danvers, far from any possible location of Arkham. Nathaniel Wingate Peaslee ("The Shadow Out of Time," pp. 711–78, below) lives at 27 Crane Street.

34. In modern English, "nauseating eyes."

unnatural madness howled in the wind. Through the fevered town had crept a curse which some said was greater than the plague, and which some whispered was the embodied dæmon-soul of the plague itself. Eight houses were entered by a nameless thing which strewed red death in its wake—in all, seventeen maimed and shapeless remnants of bodies were left behind by the voiceless, sadistic monster that crept abroad. A few persons had half seen it in the dark, and said it was white and like a malformed ape or anthropomorphic fiend. It had not left behind quite all that it had attacked, for sometimes it had been hungry. The number it had killed was fourteen; three of the bodies had been in stricken homes and had not been alive.

On the third night frantic bands of searchers, led by the police, captured it in a house on Crane Street[33] near the Miskatonic campus. They had organised the quest with care, keeping in touch by means of volunteer telephone stations, and when someone in the college district had reported hearing a scratching at a shuttered window, the net was quickly spread. On account of the general alarm and precautions, there were only two more victims, and the capture was effected without major casualties. The thing was finally stopped by a bullet, though not a fatal one, and was rushed to the local hospital amidst universal excitement and loathing.

For it had been a man. This much was clear despite the nauseous eyes,[34] the voiceless simianism, and the dæmoniac savagery. They dressed its wound and carted it to the asylum at Sefton, where it beat its head against the walls of a padded cell for sixteen years—until the recent mishap, when it escaped under circumstances that few like to mention. What had most disgusted the searchers of Arkham was the thing they noticed when the monster's face was cleaned—the mocking, unbelievable resemblance to a learned and self-sacrificing martyr who had been entombed but three days before—the late Dr. Allan Halsey, public benefactor and dean of the medical school of Miskatonic University.

To the vanished Herbert West and to me the disgust and horror were supreme. I shudder tonight as I think of it; shudder even more than I did that morning when West muttered through his bandages, "Damn it, it wasn't *quite* fresh enough!"

PART III: SIX SHOTS BY MIDNIGHT[35]

35. Published April 1922 in *Home Brew* 1, no. 3, 21–26, and reprinted in *Weird Tales* 36, no. 7 (September 1942), 75–78.

Cover of *Re-Animator*, no. 1.
Adventure Comics, October 1991 (artist: Dave Dorman)

IT IS UNCOMMON to fire all six shots of a revolver with great suddenness when one would probably be sufficient, but many things in the life of Herbert West were uncommon. It is, for instance, not often that a young physician leaving college is obliged to conceal the principles which guide his selection of a home and office, yet that was the case with Herbert West. When he and I obtained our degrees at the medical school of Miskatonic University, and sought to relieve our poverty by setting up as general practitioners, we took great care not to say that we chose our house because it was fairly well isolated, and as near as possible to the potter's field.

Reticence such as this is seldom without a cause, nor indeed was ours; for our requirements were those resulting from a life-work distinctly unpopular. Outwardly we were doctors only, but beneath the surface were aims of far greater and more terrible moment—for the essence of Herbert West's existence was a quest amid black and forbidden realms of the unknown, in which he hoped to uncover the secret of life and restore to perpetual animation the graveyard's cold clay. Such a quest demands strange materials, among them fresh human bodies; and in order to keep supplied with these indispensable things one must live quietly and not far from a place of informal interment.

West and I had met in college, and I had been the only one to sympathise with his hideous experiments. Gradually I had come

36. Curiously, there was a Worsted Mills in Bolton, England, the namesake of Bolton, Massachusetts, but the latter was a small agricultural hamlet. More likely, this is the Wood Worsted Mills in Lawrence, Massachusetts, twenty miles from Salem (the possible site of Arkham), completed in 1906 and reported to be, at 1,490 feet long, the largest mill in the world "under one roof."

37. There is a Pond Street in Lawrence, Massachusetts, near a densely wooded area and close by the aptly named World End Pond.

to be his inseparable assistant, and now that we were out of college we had to keep together. It was not easy to find a good opening for two doctors in company, but finally the influence of the university secured us a practice in Bolton—a factory town near Arkham, the seat of the college. The Bolton Worsted Mills[36] are the largest in the Miskatonic Valley, and their polyglot employees are never popular as patients with the local physicians. We chose our house with the greatest care, seizing at last on a rather run-down cottage near the end of Pond Street;[37] five numbers from the closest neighbour, and separated from the local potter's field by only a stretch of meadow land, bisected by a narrow neck of the rather dense forest which lies to the north. The distance was greater than we wished, but we could get no nearer house without going on the other side of the field, wholly out of the factory district. We were not much displeased, however, since there were no people between us and our sinister source of supplies. The walk was a trifle long, but we could haul our silent specimens undisturbed.

Our practice was surprisingly large from the very first—large enough to please most young doctors, and large enough to prove a bore and a burden to students whose real interest lay elsewhere. The mill-hands were of somewhat turbulent inclinations; and besides their many natural needs, their frequent clashes and stabbing affrays gave us plenty to do. But what actually absorbed our minds was the secret laboratory we had fitted up in the cellar—the laboratory with the long table under the electric lights, where in the small hours of the morning we often injected West's various solutions into the veins of the things we dragged from the potter's field. West was experimenting madly to find something which would start man's vital motions anew after they had been stopped by the thing we call death, but had encountered the most ghastly obstacles. The solution had to be differently compounded for different types—what would serve for guinea-pigs would not serve for human beings, and different human specimens required large modifications.

The bodies had to be exceedingly fresh, or the slight decomposition of brain tissue would render perfect reanimation impossible. Indeed, the greatest problem was to get them fresh enough—West had had horrible experiences during his secret college researches with corpses of doubtful vintage. The results of partial or imperfect animation were much more hideous than were the total failures, and we both held fearsome recollections of such things. Ever since our first dæmoniac session in the deserted farmhouse on Meadow Hill in Arkham, we had felt a brooding menace; and West, though a calm, blond, blue-eyed scientific automaton in most respects, often confessed to a shuddering sensation of stealthy pursuit. He half felt that he was followed—a psychological delusion of shaken nerves, enhanced by the undeniably disturbing fact that at least one of our reanimated specimens was still alive—a frightful carnivorous thing in a padded cell at Sefton. Then there was another—our first—whose exact fate we had never learned.

We had fair luck with specimens in Bolton—much better than in Arkham. We had not been settled a week before we got an accident victim on the very night of burial, and made it open its eyes with an amazingly rational expression before the solu-

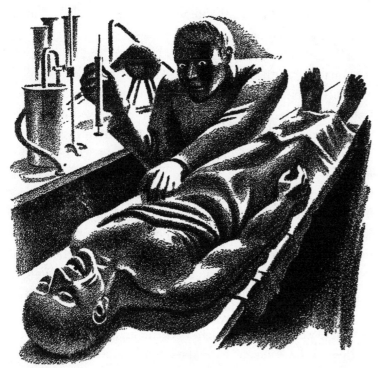

"Madly, ceaselessly, West experimented to find something that would start man's vital motions anew after they had been stopped by . . . Death!" *Weird Tales* 36, no. 7 (September 1942) (artist: Correll)

38. In fact, public boxing matches were illegal throughout Massachusetts from 1895 until October 30, 1920. There is no way to date the "March night" in question beyond placing it sometime after 1906, when the mill was completed and West and the narrator established their practice (in "The Plague-Daemon," they are "post-graduate" students in the autumn of 1905), and earlier than 1920.

39. Awkward and stupid; the noun is "lubber."

40. Lovecraft suggests a Jewish heritage that stands in contrast to the boxer's Irish moniker. He created another Jewish-Irish hybrid in Bridget Goldstein, mentioned in his story "Sweet Ermengarde" (not published until 1943), and Gavin Callaghan, in *H. P. Lovecraft's Dark Arcadia*, calls this "emblematic . . . of Lovecraft's collectivized view of America's various ethnicities . . . into a single, loathsome mass" (7).

41. Kid O'Brien was an actual boxer in the 1930s; Buck Robinson a boxer in the 1980s. Neither appears to have been aware of his predecessors, and one suspects that the names in the story are aliases.

42. Lovecraft had a deep-seated abhorrence of blacks, Jews, southern Italians, Portuguese, Poles, Mexicans, French Canadians, and virtually every other race that was not "light-skinned Nordic." In a letter to Lillian D. Clark (January 11, 1926, quoted in S. T. Joshi and David E. Schultz, eds., *Lord of a Visible World: An Autobiography in Letters—H. P. Lovecraft*, 181), he wrote, "In general, America has made a fine mess of its population, and will pay for it in tears amidst a premature rottenness unless something is done extremely soon."

tion failed. It had lost an arm—if it had been a perfect body we might have succeeded better. Between then and the next January we secured three more; one total failure, one case of marked muscular motion, and one rather shivery thing—it rose of itself and uttered a sound. Then came a period when luck was poor; interments fell off, and those that did occur were of specimens either too diseased or too maimed for use. We kept track of all the deaths and their circumstances with systematic care.

One March night, however, we unexpectedly obtained a specimen which did not come from the potter's field. In Bolton the prevailing spirit of Puritanism had outlawed the sport of boxing—with the usual result.[38] Surreptitious and ill-conducted bouts among the mill-workers were common, and occasionally professional talent of low grade was imported. This late winter night there had been such a match; evidently with disastrous results, since two timorous Poles had come to us with incoherently whispered entreaties to attend to a very secret and desperate case. We followed them to an abandoned barn, where the remnants of a crowd of frightened foreigners were watching a silent black form on the floor.

The match had been between Kid O'Brien—a lubberly[39] and now quaking youth with a most un-Hibernian hooked nose[40]—and Buck Robinson, "The Harlem Smoke."[41] The negro had been knocked out, and a moment's examination shewed us that he would permanently remain so. He was a loathsome, gorilla-like thing, with abnormally long arms which I could not help calling fore legs, and a face that conjured up thoughts of unspeakable Congo secrets and tom-tom poundings under an eerie moon.[42] The body must have looked even worse in life—but the world holds many ugly things. Fear was upon the whole pitiful crowd, for they did not know what the law would exact of them if the affair were not hushed up; and they were grateful when West, in spite of my involuntary shudders, offered to get rid of the thing quietly—for a purpose I knew too well.

There was bright moonlight over the snowless landscape, but we dressed the thing and carried it home between us through the deserted streets and meadows, as we had carried a similar thing one horrible night in Arkham. We approached the house from the field in the rear, took the specimen in the back door and down the cellar stairs, and prepared it for the usual experiment. Our fear of the police was absurdly great, though we had timed our trip to avoid the solitary patrolman of that section.

The result was wearily anticlimactic. Ghastly as our prize appeared, it was wholly unresponsive to every solution we injected in its black arm; solutions prepared from experience with white specimens only.[43] So as the hour grew dangerously near to dawn, we did as we had done with the others—dragged the thing across the meadows to the neck of the woods near the potter's field, and buried it there in the best sort of grave the frozen ground would furnish. The grave was not very deep, but fully as good as that of the previous specimen—the thing which had risen of itself and uttered a sound. In the light of our dark lanterns we carefully covered it with leaves and dead vines, fairly certain that the police would never find it in a forest so dim and dense.

The next day I was increasingly apprehensive about the police, for a patient brought rumours of a suspected fight and death. West had still another source of worry, for he had been called in the afternoon to a case which ended very threateningly. An Italian woman had become hysterical over her missing child—a lad of five who had strayed off early in the morning and failed to appear for dinner—and had developed symptoms highly alarming in view of an always weak heart. It was a very foolish hysteria, for the boy had often run away before; but Italian peasants are exceedingly superstitious, and this woman seemed as much harassed by omens as by facts. About seven o'clock in the evening she had died, and her frantic husband had made a frightful scene in his efforts to kill West, whom he wildly blamed for not saving her life. Friends had held him when he drew a stiletto,[44] but West departed amidst his inhuman shrieks, curses and oaths of vengeance. In his latest affliction the fellow seemed to have forgotten his child, who was still missing as the night advanced. There was some talk of searching the woods, but most of the family's friends were busy with the dead woman and the screaming man. Altogether, the nervous strain upon West must have been tremendous. Thoughts of the police and of the mad Italian both weighed heavily.

We retired about eleven, but I did not sleep well. Bolton had a surprisingly good police force for so small a town, and I could

43. This racist sentiment turns out to be unjustified, for the solution indeed does work on the African American.

44. A slender, narrow, but thick-bladed stabbing knife, not the bayonet-style or later switchblade versions popularized in the world wars and the postwar era.

not help fearing the mess which would ensue if the affair of the night before were ever tracked down. It might mean the end of all our local work—and perhaps prison for both West and me. I did not like those rumours of a fight which were floating about. After the clock had struck three the moon shone in my eyes, but I turned over without rising to pull down the shade. Then came the steady rattling at the back door.

I lay still and somewhat dazed, but before long heard West's rap on my door. He was clad in dressing-gown and slippers, and had in his hands a revolver and an electric flashlight. From the revolver I knew that he was thinking more of the crazed Italian than of the police.

"We'd better both go," he whispered. "It wouldn't do not to answer it anyway, and it may be a patient—it would be like one of those fools to try the back door."

So we both went down the stairs on tiptoe, with a fear partly justified and partly that which comes only from the soul of the weird small hours. The rattling continued, growing somewhat louder. When we reached the door I cautiously unbolted it and threw it open, and as the moon streamed revealingly down on the form silhouetted there, West did a peculiar thing. Despite the obvious danger of attracting notice and bringing down on our heads the dreaded police investigation—a thing which after all was mercifully averted by the relative isolation of our cottage—my friend suddenly, excitedly, and unnecessarily emptied all six chambers of his revolver into the nocturnal visitor.

For that visitor was neither Italian nor policeman. Looming hideously against the spectral moon was a gigantic misshapen thing not to be imagined save in nightmares—a glassy-eyed, ink-black apparition nearly on all fours, covered with bits of mould, leaves, and vines, foul with caked blood, and having between its glistening teeth a snow-white, terrible, cylindrical object terminating in a tiny hand.

PART IV: THE SCREAM OF THE DEAD[45]

Weird Tales 36, no. 8 (November 1942) (artist: Damon Knight)

45. Published in May 1922 in *Home Brew* 1, no. 4, 53–58, and reprinted in *Weird Tales* 36, no. 8 (November 1942), 96–99.

THE SCREAM OF a dead man gave to me that acute and added horror of Dr. Herbert West which harassed the latter years of our companionship. It is natural that such a thing as a dead man's scream should give horror, for it is obviously not a pleasing or ordinary occurrence; but I was used to similar experiences, hence suffered on this occasion only because of a particular circumstance. And, as I have implied, it was not of the dead man himself that I became afraid.

Herbert West, whose associate and assistant I was, possessed scientific interests far beyond the usual routine of a village physician. That was why, when establishing his practice in Bolton, he had chosen an isolated house near the potter's field. Briefly and brutally stated, West's sole absorbing interest was a secret study of the phenomena of life and its cessation, leading toward the reanimation of the dead through injections of an excitant solution. For this ghastly experimenting it was necessary to have a constant

46. Seven years before 1910—that is, in 1903. This confirms the dating of the first West tale in autumn 1903.

supply of very fresh human bodies; very fresh because even the least decay hopelessly damaged the brain structure, and human because we found that the solution had to be compounded differently for different types of organisms. Scores of rabbits and guinea-pigs had been killed and treated, but their trail was a blind one. West had never fully succeeded because he had never been able to secure a corpse sufficiently fresh. What he wanted were bodies from which vitality had only just departed; bodies with every cell intact and capable of receiving again the impulse toward that mode of motion called life. There was hope that this second and artificial life might be made perpetual by repetitions of the injection, but we had learned that an ordinary natural life would not respond to the action. To establish the artificial motion, natural life must be extinct—the specimens must be very fresh, but genuinely dead.

The awesome quest had begun when West and I were students at the Miskatonic University Medical School in Arkham, vividly conscious for the first time of the thoroughly mechanical nature of life. That was seven years before,[46] but West looked scarcely a day older now—he was small, blond, clean-shaven, soft-voiced, and spectacled, with only an occasional flash of a cold blue eye to tell of the hardening and growing fanaticism of his character under the pressure of his terrible investigations. Our experiences had often been hideous in the extreme; the results of defective reanimation, when lumps of graveyard clay had been galvanised into morbid, unnatural, and brainless motion by various modifications of the vital solution.

One thing had uttered a nerve-shattering scream; another had risen violently, beaten us both to unconsciousness, and run amuck in a shocking way before it could be placed behind asylum bars; still another, a loathsome African monstrosity, had clawed out of its shallow grave and done a deed—West had had to shoot that object. We could not get bodies fresh enough to shew any trace of reason when reanimated, so had perforce created nameless horrors. It was disturbing to think that one, perhaps two, of our monsters still lived—that thought haunted us shadowingly, till finally West disappeared under frightful circumstances. But at the time of the scream in the cellar laboratory of the isolated Bolton cottage, our fears were subordinate to our anxiety for extremely fresh specimens. West was more avid than I, so that it almost seemed to me that he looked half-covetously at any very healthy living physique.

It was in July, 1910, that the bad luck regarding specimens began to turn. I had been on a long visit to my parents in Illinois, and upon my return found West in a state of singular elation. He had, he told me excitedly, in all likelihood solved the problem of freshness through an approach from an entirely new angle—that of artificial preservation. I had known that he was working on a new and highly unusual embalming compound,[47] and was not surprised that it had turned out well; but until he explained the details I was rather puzzled as to how such a compound could help in our work, since the objectionable staleness of the specimens was largely due to delay occurring before we secured them. This, I now saw, West had clearly recognised; creating his embalming compound for future rather than immediate use, and trusting to fate to supply again some very recent and unburied corpse, as it had years before when we obtained the negro killed in the Bolton prize-fight. At last fate had been kind, so that on this occasion there lay in the secret cellar laboratory a corpse whose decay could not by any possibility have begun. What would happen on reanimation, and whether we could hope for a revival of mind and reason, West did not venture to predict. The experiment would be a landmark in our studies, and he had saved the new body for my return, so that both might share the spectacle in accustomed fashion.

West told me how he had obtained the specimen. It had been a vigorous man; a well-dressed stranger just off the train on his way to transact some business with the Bolton Worsted Mills. The walk through the town had been long, and by the time the traveller paused at our cottage to ask the way to the factories his heart had become greatly overtaxed. He had refused a stimulant, and had suddenly dropped dead only a moment later. The body, as might be expected, seemed to West a heaven-sent gift. In his brief conversation the stranger had made it clear that he was unknown in Bolton, and a search of his pockets subsequently revealed him to be one Robert Leavitt of St. Louis, apparently without a family to make instant inquiries about his disappearance. If this man could not be restored to life, no one would

47. Great strides had been made during the nineteenth century (especially during the American Civil War) in the practice of embalming; by the early twentieth century, the techniques had become well established. In fact, two different embalming compounds or fluids were often used, one (often Formalin, formaldehyde mixed with water) injected arterially and the other (Formalin mixed with alcohols, emulsifiers, and other substances) introduced into body cavities. Only recently have "green" techniques not involving harsh carcinogens won acceptance.

know of our experiment. We buried our materials in a dense strip of woods between the house and the potter's field. If, on the other hand, he could be restored, our fame would be brilliantly and perpetually established. So without delay West had injected into the body's wrist the compound which would hold it fresh for use after my arrival. The matter of the presumably weak heart, which to my mind imperiled the success of our experiment, did not appear to trouble West extensively. He hoped at last to obtain what he had never obtained before—a rekindled spark of reason and perhaps a normal, living creature.

So on the night of July 18, 1910, Herbert West and I stood in the cellar laboratory and gazed at a white, silent figure beneath the dazzling arc-light. The embalming compound had worked uncannily well, for as I stared fascinatedly at the sturdy frame which had lain two weeks without stiffening I was moved to seek West's assurance that the thing was really dead. This assurance he gave readily enough; reminding me that the reanimating solution was never used without careful tests as to life; since it could have no effect if any of the original vitality were present. As West proceeded to take preliminary steps, I was impressed by the vast intricacy of the new experiment; an intricacy so vast that he could trust no hand less delicate than his own. Forbidding me to touch the body, he first injected a drug in the wrist just beside the place his needle had punctured when injecting the embalming compound. This, he said, was to neutralise the compound and release the system to a normal relaxation so that the reanimating solution might freely work when injected. Slightly later, when a change and a gentle tremor seemed to affect the dead limbs, West stuffed a pillow-like object violently over the twitching face, not withdrawing it until the corpse appeared quiet and ready for our attempt at reanimation. The pale enthusiast now applied some last perfunctory tests for absolute lifelessness, withdrew satisfied, and finally injected into the left arm an accurately measured amount of the vital elixir, prepared during the afternoon with a greater care than we had used since college days, when our feats were new and groping. I cannot express the wild, breathless suspense with which we waited for results on this first really fresh specimen—the first we could reasonably expect to open its lips in rational speech, perhaps to tell of what it had seen beyond the unfathomable abyss.

West was a materialist, believing in no soul and attributing all the working of consciousness to bodily phenomena; consequently he looked for no revelation of hideous secrets from gulfs and caverns beyond death's barrier. I did not wholly disagree with him theoretically, yet held vague instinctive remnants of the primitive faith of my forefathers; so that I could not help eyeing the corpse with a certain amount of awe and terrible expectation. Besides—I could not extract from my memory that hideous, inhuman shriek we heard on the night we tried our first experiment in the deserted farmhouse at Arkham.

Very little time had elapsed before I saw the attempt was not to be a total failure. A touch of colour came to cheeks hitherto chalk-white, and spread out under the curiously ample stubble of sandy beard. West, who had his hand on the pulse of the left wrist, suddenly nodded significantly; and almost simultaneously a mist appeared on the mirror inclined above the body's mouth. There followed a few spasmodic muscular motions, and then an audible breathing and visible motion of the chest. I looked at the closed eyelids, and thought I detected a quivering. Then the lids opened, shewing eyes which were grey, calm, and alive, but still unintelligent and not even curious.

In a moment of fantastic whim I whispered questions to the reddening ears; questions of other worlds of which the memory might still be present. Subsequent terror drove them from my mind, but I think the last one, which I repeated, was: "Where have you been?" I do not yet know whether I was answered or not, for no sound came from the well-shaped mouth; but I do know that at that moment I firmly thought the thin lips moved silently, forming syllables I would have vocalised as "only now" if that phrase had possessed any sense or relevancy. At that moment, as I say, I was elated with the conviction that the one great goal had been attained; and that for the first time a reanimated corpse had uttered distinct words impelled by actual reason. In the next moment there was no doubt about the triumph; no doubt that the solution had truly accomplished, at least temporarily, its full mission of restoring rational and articu-

48. That is, Leavitt did not "drop dead"—West killed him with an injection.

49. Published June 1922 in *Home Brew* 1, no. 5, 45–50, and reprinted in *Weird Tales* 37, no. 1 (September 1943), 88–91.

late life to the dead. But in that triumph there came to me the greatest of all horrors—not horror of the thing that spoke, but of the deed that I had witnessed and of the man with whom my professional fortunes were joined.

For that very fresh body, at last writhing into full and terrifying consciousness with eyes dilated at the memory of its last scene on earth, threw out its frantic hands in a life and death struggle with the air; and suddenly collapsing into a second and final dissolution from which there could be no return, screamed out the cry that will ring eternally in my aching brain:

"Help! Keep off, you cursed little tow-head fiend—keep that damned needle away from me!"[48]

PART V: THE HORROR FROM THE SHADOWS[49]

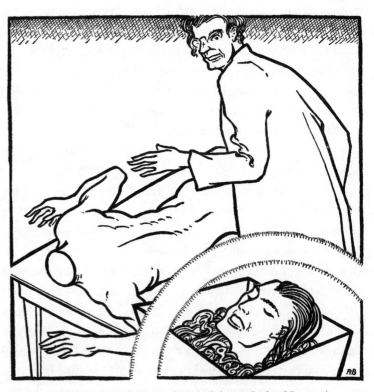

Weird Tales 37, no. 1 (September 1943) (artist: Richard Bennett)

MANY MEN HAVE related hideous things, not mentioned in print, which happened on the battlefields of the Great War. Some of these things have made me faint, others have convulsed me with devastating nausea, while still others have made me tremble and look behind me in the dark; yet despite the worst of them I believe I can myself relate the most hideous thing of all—the shocking, the unnatural, the unbelievable horror from the shadows.

In 1915 I was a physician with the rank of First Lieutenant in a Canadian regiment in Flanders, one of many Americans to precede the government itself into the gigantic struggle.[50] I had not entered the army on my own initiative, but rather as a natural result of the enlistment of the man whose indispensable assistant I was—the celebrated Boston surgical specialist, Dr. Herbert West.[51] Dr. West had been avid for a chance to serve as surgeon in a great war, and when the chance had come he carried me with him almost against my will. There were reasons why I would have been glad to let the war separate us; reasons why I found the practice of medicine and the companionship of West more and more irritating; but when he had gone to Ottawa and through a colleague's influence secured a medical commission as Major, I could not resist the imperious persuasion of one determined that I should accompany him in my usual capacity.[52]

When I say that Dr. West was avid to serve in battle, I do not mean to imply that he was either naturally warlike or anxious for the safety of civilisation. Always an ice-cold intellectual machine; slight, blond, blue-eyed, and spectacled; I think he secretly sneered at my occasional martial enthusiasms and censures of supine neutrality. There was, however, something he wanted in embattled Flanders; and in order to secure it he had to assume a military exterior. What he wanted was not a thing which many persons want, but something connected with the peculiar branch of medical science which he had chosen quite clandestinely to follow, and in which he had achieved amazing and occasionally hideous results. It was, in fact, nothing more or less than an abundant supply of freshly killed men in every stage of dismemberment.

Herbert West needed fresh bodies because his life-work was the reanimation of the dead. This work was not known to the fashionable clientele who had so swiftly built up his fame after his arrival in Boston; but was only too well known to me, who had been his closest friend and sole assistant since the old days

50. The hostilities of World War I commenced in late July 1914; the United States did not officially declare war on Germany until April 1917, and American troops did not enter the trenches in Europe until a year later. Many Americans did enlist in the Canadian forces, and in 1925, Canadian prime minister Mackenzie King proposed that a "Cross of Sacrifice" be presented to honor those volunteers. The monument was erected in 1927 in the National Cemetery in Arlington, Virginia.

51. This is five years after the murder of Robert Leavitt, about twelve years after the narrator and West commenced their experimentation.

52. The narrator has now sunk into depravity. He knew perfectly well that West killed Robert Leavitt in the pursuit of his experiments but decided to carry on as his colleague.

53. The events recounted here evidently took place earlier than 1919, when, as has been shown, Dr. Halsey escaped from the Sefton Asylum.

in Miskatonic University Medical School at Arkham. It was in those college days that he had begun his terrible experiments, first on small animals and then on human bodies shockingly obtained. There was a solution which he injected into the veins of dead things, and if they were fresh enough they responded in strange ways. He had had much trouble in discovering the proper formula, for each type of organism was found to need a stimulus especially adapted to it. Terror stalked him when he reflected on his partial failures; nameless things resulting from imperfect solutions or from bodies insufficiently fresh. A certain number of these failures had remained alive—one was in an asylum[53] while others had vanished—and as he thought of conceivable yet virtually impossible eventualities he often shivered beneath his usual stolidity.

West had soon learned that absolute freshness was the prime requisite for useful specimens, and had accordingly resorted to frightful and unnatural expedients in body-snatching. In college, and during our early practice together in the factory town of Bolton, my attitude toward him had been largely one of fascinated admiration; but as his boldness in methods grew, I began to develop a gnawing fear. I did not like the way he looked at healthy living bodies; and then there came a nightmarish session in the cellar laboratory when I learned that a certain specimen had been a living body when he secured it. That was the first time he had ever been able to revive the quality of rational thought in a corpse; and his success, obtained at such a loathsome cost, had completely hardened him.

Of his methods in the intervening five years I dare not speak. I was held to him by sheer force of fear, and witnessed sights that no human tongue could repeat. Gradually I came to find Herbert West himself more horrible than anything he did—that was when it dawned on me that his once normal scientific zeal for prolonging life had subtly degenerated into a mere morbid and ghoulish curiosity and secret sense of charnel picturesqueness. His interest became a hellish and perverse addiction to the repellently and fiendishly abnormal; he gloated calmly over artificial monstrosities which would make most healthy men drop dead from fright and disgust; he became, behind his pallid intellectuality, a fastidious Baudelaire[54] of physical experiment—a languid Elagabalus[55] of the tombs.

Dangers he met unflinchingly; crimes he committed unmoved. I think the climax came when he had proved his point that rational life can be restored, and had sought new worlds to conquer by experimenting on the reanimation of detached parts of bodies. He had wild and original ideas on the independent vital properties of organic cells and nerve-tissue separated from natural physiological systems; and achieved some hideous preliminary results in the form of never-dying, artificially nourished tissue obtained from the nearly hatched eggs of an indescribable tropical reptile. Two biological points he was exceedingly anxious to settle—first, whether any amount of consciousness and rational action may be possible without the brain, proceeding from the spinal cord and various nerve-centres; and second, whether any kind of ethereal, intangible relation distinct from the material cells may exist to link the surgically separated parts of what has previously been a single living organism. All this research work required a prodigious supply of freshly slaughtered human flesh—and that was why Herbert West had entered the Great War.

The phantasmal, unmentionable thing occurred one midnight late in March, 1915, in a field hospital behind the lines at St. Eloi.[56] I wonder even now if it could have been other than a dæmoniac dream of delirium. West had a private laboratory in an east room of the barn-like temporary edifice, assigned him on his plea that he was devising new and radical methods for the treatment of hitherto hopeless cases of maiming. There he worked like a butcher in the midst of his gory wares—I could never get used to the levity with which he handled and classified certain things. At times he actually did perform marvels of surgery for the soldiers; but his chief delights were of a less public and philanthropic kind, requiring many explanations of sounds which seemed peculiar even amidst that babel of the damned. Among these sounds were frequent revolver-shots—surely not uncommon on a battlefield, but distinctly uncommon in an hospital. Dr. West's reanimated specimens were not meant for long existence or a large audience. Besides human tissue, West employed much of the reptile embryo tissue which he had culti-

54. The poetry of the towering French modernist Charles Baudelaire (1821–1867) is much admired today but was decried at the time of publication for themes of sexuality and the corruption of the city. The only son of François Baudelaire, a civil servant and former priest (he resigned from the priesthood during the Reign of Terror), and Caroline Dufayis, an orphan, who were sixty-two and twenty-eight years old, respectively, when he was born, Baudelaire cultivated a reputation as a free spender, a rake, and a sensualist. A masterful prose stylist in his own right, he notably translated the work of Edgar Allan Poe, also publishing several studies of Poe's life and work. Baudelaire's own life was marked by artistic and political contradictions, among them his support of the overthrow of the French monarchy in the revolution of 1848—for Baudelaire, a short-lived period of support for political liberalism that he later described, in his *Journaux Intimes* (Intimate Journals, 1909), as "*Mon Ivresse*" (My Frenzy). Perhaps his best-known work is *Les Fleurs du Mal* (1857), a publishing undertaking that saw Baudelaire, an exacting proofreader, leasing a room close to the typesetting and printing operations so that he could oversee production. (His sympathetic publisher later was sent to debtor's prison; Baudelaire went to court to defend the volume.) Among the many acts of eccentricity (or depravity) that Baudelaire was said to have committed—many cannot be verified—was inviting a group of acquaintances to look at a pair of riding breeches reputed to have been fabricated from the hind quarters of his deceased stepfather, Jacques Aupick, with whom he had endured periods of decidedly hostile relations.

55. Elagabalus, also known as Heliogabalus (Latin: Marcus Aurelius Antoni-

nus Augustus; ca. 203–222 CE) was the emperor of Rome from 218 to 222. He was known for his decadence and sexual depravity. Edward Gibbon, in volume 1 of *The History of the Decline and Fall of the Roman Empire*, describes him as having "abandoned himself to the grossest pleasures with ungoverned fury. . . . It may seem probable, the vices and follies of Elagabalus have been adorned by fancy, and blackened by prejudice. Yet, confining ourselves to the public scenes displayed before the Roman people, and attested by grave and contemporary historians, their inexpressible infamy surpasses that of any other age or country" (172). Lovecraft had two editions of Gibbon in his personal library.

56. The village of St. Eloi, on the Western Front, later gained notoriety for its devastation by underground mines during the war. Thirty or more mines were detonated there by the British and German forces. Six were exploded by the British in March 1916; eighteen more were set off by British and Canadian forces to mark the start of the Battle of Messines on June 7, 1917.

57. The Distinguished Service Order is a military decoration established in 1886 by Queen Victoria for British officers serving meritoriously. Prior to 1917, the medal was frequently awarded to senior administrative officers as well as combatants; after 1916, it was limited to those serving under actual fire.

vated with such singular results. It was better than human material for maintaining life in organless fragments, and that was now my friend's chief activity. In a dark corner of the laboratory, over a queer incubating burner, he kept a large covered vat full of this reptilian cell-matter; which multiplied and grew puffily and hideously.

On the night of which I speak we had a splendid new specimen—a man at once physically powerful and of such high mentality that a sensitive nervous system was assured. It was rather ironic, for he was the officer who had helped West to his commission, and who was now to have been our associate. Moreover, he had in the past secretly studied the theory of reanimation to some extent under West. Major Sir Eric Moreland Clapham-Lee, D.S.O.,[57] was the greatest surgeon in our division, and had been hastily assigned to the St. Eloi sector when news of the heavy fighting reached headquarters. He had come in an aëroplane piloted by the intrepid Lieut. Ronald Hill, only to be shot down when directly over his destination. The fall had been spectacular and awful; Hill was unrecognisable afterward, but the wreck yielded up the great surgeon in a nearly decapitated but otherwise intact condition. West had greedily seized the lifeless thing which had once been his friend and fellow-scholar; and I shuddered when he finished severing the head, placed it in his hellish vat of pulpy reptile-tissue to preserve it for future experiments, and proceeded to treat the decapitated body on the operating table. He injected new blood, joined certain veins, arteries, and nerves at the headless neck, and closed the ghastly aperture with engrafted skin from an unidentified specimen which had borne an officer's uniform. I knew what he wanted—to see if this highly organised body could exhibit, without its head, any of the signs of mental life which had distinguished Sir Eric Moreland Clapham-Lee. Once a student of reanimation, this silent trunk was now gruesomely called upon to exemplify it.

I can still see Herbert West under the sinister electric light as he injected his reanimating solution into the arm of the headless body. The scene I cannot describe—I should faint if I tried it, for there is madness in a room full of classified charnel things, with blood and lesser human debris almost ankle-deep on the slimy floor, and with hideous reptilian abnormalities sprouting, bubbling, and baking over a winking bluish-green spectre of dim flame in a far corner of black shadows.

The specimen, as West repeatedly observed, had a splendid nervous system. Much was expected of it; and as a few twitching motions began to appear, I could see the feverish interest on West's face. He was ready, I think, to see proof of his increasingly strong opinion that consciousness, reason, and personality can exist independently of the brain—that man has no central connective spirit, but is merely a machine of nervous matter, each section more or less complete in itself. In one triumphant demonstration West was about to relegate the mystery of life to the category of myth. The body now twitched more vigorously, and beneath our avid eyes commenced to heave in a frightful way. The arms stirred disquietingly, the legs drew up, and various muscles contracted in a repulsive kind of writhing. Then the headless thing threw out its arms in a gesture which was unmistakably one of desperation—an intelligent desperation apparently sufficient to prove every theory of Herbert West. Certainly, the nerves were recalling the man's last act in life; the struggle to get free of the falling aëroplane.

What followed, I shall never positively know. It may have been wholly an hallucination from the shock caused at that instant by the sudden and complete destruction of the building in a cataclysm of German shell-fire—who can gainsay it, since West and I were the only proved survivors? West liked to think that before his recent disappearance, but there were times when he could not; for it was queer that we both had the same hallucination. The hideous occurrence itself was very simple, notable only for what it implied.

The body on the table had risen with a blind and terrible groping, and we had heard a sound. I should not call that sound a voice, for it was too awful. And yet its timbre was not the most awful thing about it. Neither was its message—it had merely screamed, "Jump, Ronald, for God's sake, jump!" The awful thing was its source.

For it had come from the large covered vat in that ghoulish corner of crawling black shadows.

58. Published July 1922 in *Home Brew* 1, no. 6, 57–62, and reprinted in *Weird Tales* 37, no. 2 (November 1943), 101–7.

PART VI: THE TOMB-LEGIONS[58]

Weird Tales 37, no. 2 (November 1943) (artist: Richard Bennett)

WHEN DR. HERBERT West disappeared a year ago, the Boston police questioned me closely. They suspected that I was holding something back, and perhaps suspected graver things; but I could not tell them the truth because they would not have believed it. They knew, indeed, that West had been connected with activities beyond the credence of ordinary men; for his hideous experiments in the reanimation of dead bodies had long been too extensive to admit of perfect secrecy; but the final soul-shattering catastrophe held elements of dæmoniac phantasy which make even me doubt the reality of what I saw.

I was West's closest friend and only confidential assistant. We had met years before, in medical school, and from the first I had shared his terrible researches. He had slowly tried to perfect a solution which, injected into the veins of the newly deceased, would restore life; a labour demanding an abundance of fresh corpses and therefore involving the most unnatural actions. Still more shocking were the products of some of the experiments— grisly masses of flesh that had been dead, but that West waked to a blind, brainless, nauseous animation. These were the usual results, for in order to reawaken the mind it was necessary to have specimens so absolutely fresh that no decay could possibly affect the delicate brain-cells.

This need for very fresh corpses had been West's moral undoing. They were hard to get, and one awful day he had secured his specimen while it was still alive and vigorous. A struggle, a needle, and a powerful alkaloid had transformed it to a very fresh corpse, and the experiment had succeeded for a brief and memorable moment; but West had emerged with a soul calloused and seared, and a hardened eye which sometimes glanced with a kind of hideous and calculating appraisal at men of especially sensitive brain and especially vigorous physique. Toward the last I became acutely afraid of West, for he began to look at me that way. People did not seem to notice his glances, but they noticed my fear; and after his disappearance used that as a basis for some absurd suspicions.

West, in reality, was more afraid than I; for his abominable pursuits entailed a life of furtiveness and dread of every shadow. Partly it was the police he feared; but sometimes his nervousness was deeper and more nebulous, touching on certain indescribable things into which he had injected a morbid life, and from which he had not seen that life depart. He usually finished his experiments with a revolver, but a few times he had not been quick enough. There was that first specimen on whose rifled grave marks of clawing were later seen. There was also that Arkham professor's body which had done cannibal things before it had been captured and thrust unidentified into a madhouse cell at Sefton, where it beat the walls for sixteen years. Most of the other possibly surviving results were things less easy to speak of—for in later years West's scientific zeal had degenerated to an unhealthy and fantastic mania, and he had spent his chief skill in vitalising not entire human bodies but isolated parts of bodies, or parts joined to organic matter other than human. It had become fiendishly disgusting by the time he disappeared; many of the experiments could not even be hinted at in print. The Great War,

59. Possibly the Granary Burying Ground, founded in 1660. Located on Tremont Street, it is the burial place of Paul Revere, three signatories to the Declaration of Independence, and the five victims of the 1770 Boston Massacre. Copp's Hill Burying Ground, near the North End of Boston, established in 1659, is the resting place of Cotton, Increase, and Samuel Mather. We may rule out the King's Chapel Burying Ground, where John Winthrop, the first governor of Massachusetts, is buried, because it is clearly the *oldest*, founded in 1630, not "one of the oldest."

Cover of *Re-Animator*, no. 3. Adventure Comics, April 1992 (artist: Lurene Haines)

through which both of us served as surgeons, had intensified this side of West.

In saying that West's fear of his specimens was nebulous, I have in mind particularly its complex nature. Part of it came merely from knowing of the existence of such nameless monsters, while another part arose from apprehension of the bodily harm they might under certain circumstances do him. Their disappearance added horror to the situation—of them all, West knew the whereabouts of only one, the pitiful asylum thing. Then there was a more subtle fear—a very fantastic sensation resulting from a curious experiment in the Canadian army in 1915. West, in the midst of a severe battle, had reanimated Major Sir Eric Moreland Clapham-Lee, D.S.O., a fellow-physician who knew about his experiments and could have duplicated them. The head had been removed, so that the possibilities of quasi-intelligent life in the trunk might be investigated. Just as the building was wiped out by a German shell, there had been a success. The trunk had moved intelligently; and, unbelievable to relate, we were both sickeningly sure that articulate sounds had come from the detached head as it lay in a shadowy corner of the laboratory. The shell had been merciful, in a way—but West could never feel as certain as he wished, that we two were the only survivors. He used to make shuddering conjectures about the possible actions of a headless physician with the power of reanimating the dead.

West's last quarters were in a venerable house of much elegance, overlooking one of the oldest burying-grounds in Boston.[59] He had chosen the place for purely symbolic and fantastically æsthetic reasons, since most of the interments were of the colonial period and therefore of little use to a scientist seeking very fresh bodies. The laboratory was in a sub-cellar secretly constructed by imported workmen, and contained a huge incinerator for the quiet and complete disposal of such bodies, or fragments and synthetic mockeries of bodies, as might remain from the morbid experiments and unhallowed amusements of the owner. During the excavation of this cellar the workmen had struck some exceedingly ancient masonry; undoubtedly connected with the old burying-ground, yet far too deep to correspond with any known sepulchre therein. After a number of calculations West decided that it represented some secret chamber beneath the tomb of the Averills,[60] where the last interment had been made in 1768. I was with him when he studied the nitrous, dripping walls laid bare by the spades and mattocks of the men, and was prepared for the gruesome thrill which would attend the uncovering of centuried grave-secrets; but for the first time West's new timidity conquered his natural curiosity, and he betrayed his degenerating fibre by ordering the masonry left intact and plastered over. Thus it remained till that final hellish night; part of the walls of the secret laboratory. I speak of West's decadence, but must add that it was a purely mental and intangible thing. Outwardly he was the same to the last—calm, cold, slight, and yellow-haired, with spectacled blue eyes and a general aspect of youth which years and fears seemed never to change. He seemed calm even when he thought of that clawed grave and looked over his shoulder; even when he thought of the carnivorous thing that gnawed and pawed at Sefton bars.

The end of Herbert West began one evening in our joint study when he was dividing his curious glance between the newspaper and me. A strange headline item had struck at him from the crumpled pages, and a nameless titan claw had seemed to reach down through sixteen years. Something fearsome and incredible had happened at Sefton Asylum fifty miles away, stunning the neighbourhood and baffling the police. In the small hours of the morning a body of silent men had entered the grounds, and their leader had aroused the attendants. He was a menacing military figure who talked without moving his lips and whose voice seemed almost ventriloquially connected with an immense black case he carried. His expressionless face was handsome to the point of radiant beauty, but had shocked the superintendent when the hall light fell on it—for it was a wax face with eyes of painted glass. Some nameless accident had befallen this man. A larger man guided his steps; a repellent hulk whose bluish face seemed half eaten away by some unknown malady.[61] The speaker had asked for the custody of the cannibal monster committed from Arkham sixteen years before; and upon being refused, gave a signal which precipitated a shocking riot. The fiends had beaten, trampled, and bitten every attendant who did not flee; killing four and finally succeeding in the liberation of the monster. Those victims who could recall the event without hysteria swore

60. The Averill/Averell/Averhill genealogy reveals numerous residents of Boston in colonial times and later. See http://averillproject.com/documents/william1william2job3.pdf.

61. This is presumably Buck Robinson, the Harlem Smoke, from "Six Shots by Moonlight."

A less tasteful poster from *Re-Animator* (Empire Pictures, 1985), directed by Stuart Gordon.

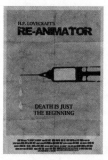

A more tasteful poster from *Re-Animator* (Empire Pictures, 1985), directed by Stuart Gordon.

62. That is, in 1915. The date is given there in very precise fashion. Therefore, these events took place in the spring of 1921 (slightly more than a year before publication). That would place the interment of Dr. Halsey in Sefton Asylum in 1905, sixteen years earlier.

The French poster from *Re-Animator* (Empire Pictures, 1985), directed by Stuart Gordon.

Another poster from *Re-Animator* (Empire Pictures, 1985), directed by Stuart Gordon.

Cover of *Re-Animator*, no. 2. Adventure Comics, April 1992 (artist: Tony Harris)

that the creatures had acted less like men than like unthinkable automata guided by the wax-faced leader. By the time help could be summoned, every trace of the men and of their mad charge had vanished.

From the hour of reading this item until midnight, West sat almost paralysed. At midnight the doorbell rang, startling him fearfully. All the servants were asleep in the attic, so I answered the bell. As I have told the police, there was no wagon in the street; but only a group of strange-looking figures bearing a large square box which they deposited in the hallway after one of them had grunted in a highly unnatural voice, "Express—prepaid." They filed out of the house with a jerky tread, and as I watched them go I had an odd idea that they were turning toward the ancient cemetery on which the back of the house abutted. When I slammed the door after them West came downstairs and looked at the box. It was about two feet square, and bore West's correct name and present address. It also bore the inscription, "From Eric Moreland Clapham-Lee, St. Eloi, Flanders." Six years before,[62] in Flanders, a shelled hospital had fallen upon the headless reanimated trunk of Dr. Clapham-Lee, and upon the detached head which—perhaps—had uttered articulate sounds.

West was not even excited now. His condition was more ghastly. Quickly he said, "It's the finish—but let's incinerate—this." We carried the thing down to the laboratory—listening. I do not remember many particulars—you can imagine my state of mind—but it is a vicious lie to say it was Herbert West's body which I put into the incinerator. We both inserted the whole unopened wooden box, closed the door, and started the electricity. Nor did any sound come from the box, after all.

It was West who first noticed the falling plaster on that part of the wall where the ancient tomb masonry had been covered up. I was going to run, but he stopped me. Then I saw a small black aperture, felt a ghoulish wind of ice, and smelled the charnel bowels of a putrescent earth. There was no sound, but just then the electric lights went out and I saw outlined against some phosphorescence of the nether world a horde of silent toiling things which only insanity—or worse—could create. Their outlines were human, semi-human, fractionally human, and not human at all—the horde was grotesquely heterogeneous. They were removing the stones quietly, one by one, from the centuried wall. And then, as the breach became large enough, they came out into the laboratory in single file; led by a stalking thing with a beautiful head made of wax. A sort of mad-eyed monstrosity behind the leader seized on Herbert West. West did not resist or utter a sound. Then they all sprang at him and tore him to pieces before my eyes, bearing the fragments away into that subterranean vault of fabulous abominations. West's head was carried off by the wax-headed leader, who wore a Canadian officer's uniform. As it disappeared I saw that the blue eyes behind the spectacles were hideously blazing with their first touch of frantic, visible emotion.

Servants found me unconscious in the morning. West was gone. The incinerator contained only unidentifiable ashes. Detectives have questioned me, but what can I say? The Sefton tragedy they will not connect with West; not that, nor the men with the box, whose existence they deny. I told them of the vault, and they pointed to the unbroken plaster wall and laughed. So I told them no more. They imply that I am a madman or a murderer—probably I am mad. But I might not be mad if those accursed tomb-legions had not been so silent.

Cover of *The Chronicles of Dr. Herbert West*, no. 1. Zenescope, September 2008 (artist: Jason Craig)

Cover from *Re-Animator*, no. 0. Dynamite Entertainment, 2005 (artist: Jim Charalampidis)

The Nameless City[1]

The story is the first in which Lovecraft squarely addresses the mythology he was to explain later. He not only describes the existence of an elder race and a civilization predating humans but specifically mentions the Necronomicon (though not by name) and its author as a central plot point. Later tales will further elucidate his vision of elder races, but here, in a truly terrifying tale, the experience of a naïve explorer who discovers the existence of such beings is recorded.

1. Written in January 1921, the story first appeared later that year in *Wolverine* 11 (November 1921), 3–15. It later appeared in *Weird Tales* 32, no. 5 (November 1938), 617–26, with this reading line: "It lay silent and dead under the cold desert moonlight, but what strange race inhabited the abyss under those cyclopean ruins?"

2. Presumably the biblical Flood described in *Genesis*, the date of which has been calculated to be 1,656 years after the date of Creation.

3. If the Egyptian pyramids are meant here, the eldest was probably constructed between 2600 and 2300 BCE.

4. Probably around 3000 BCE.

5. Most likely a small town by 3000 BCE.

6. A female parent of a person with offspring; that is, a grandmother.

7. This is the first mention of Abdul Alhazred, the prophet said to be the

When I drew nigh the nameless city I knew it was accursed. I was travelling in a parched and terrible valley under the moon, and afar I saw it protruding uncannily above the sands as parts of a corpse may protrude from an ill-made grave. Fear spoke from the age-worn stones of this hoary survivor of the deluge,[2] this great-grandmother of the eldest pyramid;[3] and a viewless aura repelled me and bade me retreat from antique and sinister secrets that no man should see, and no man else had ever dared to see.

Remote in the desert of Araby lies the nameless city, crumbling and inarticulate, its low walls nearly hidden by the sands of uncounted ages. It must have been thus before the first stones of Memphis were laid,[4] and while the bricks of Babylon[5] were yet unbaked. There is no legend so old as to give it a name, or to recall that it was ever alive; but it is told of in whispers around campfires and muttered about by grandams[6] in the tents of sheiks, so that all the tribes shun it without wholly knowing why. It was of this place that Abdul Alhazred[7] the mad poet dreamed on the night before he sang his unexplainable couplet:

> *That is not dead which can eternal lie,*
> *And with strange æons even[8] death may die.*[9]

"When I drew nigh the Nameless city, I knew it was accursed."
Weird Tales 32, no. 5 (November 1938) (artist: Joseph Doolin)

I should have known that the Arabs had good reason for shunning the nameless city, the city told of in strange tales but seen by no living man, yet I defied them and went into the untrodden waste with my camel. I alone have seen it, and that is why no other face bears such hideous lines of fear as mine; why no other man shivers so horribly when the night-wind rattles the windows. When I came upon it in the ghastly stillness of unending sleep it looked at me, chilly from the rays of a cold moon amidst the desert's heat. And as I returned its look I forgot my triumph at finding it, and stopped still with my camel to wait for the dawn.

For hours I waited, till the east grew grey and the stars faded, and the grey turned to roseal light edged with gold. I heard a moaning and saw a storm of sand stirring among the antique stones though the sky was clear and the vast reaches of the desert still. Then suddenly above the desert's far rim came the blazing edge of the sun, seen through the tiny sandstorm which was passing away, and in my fevered state I fancied that from some remote

author of the *Necronomicon*. S. T. Joshi has noted that the name is highly unusual in the use of the doubled "ul" and "Al," each an Arabic article. In the introduction to the book *Al Azif*, L. Sprague de Camp points out that this form of the name is "a corruption of a lost original, which passed through several languages before it reached its present form." De Camp hypothesizes that the original form may have been Abdallah Zahr-ad-Din (Servant of God, Flower of the Faith). Robert M. Price, in "A Critical Commentary on the *Necronomicon*," concludes that De Camp's hypothesis "is about as close to the truth as anyone is likely to come" (8).

8. In the first published version, the word "even" is omitted, but it appears in the manuscript and subsequent published versions.

Aions (or aeons) are the emanations of God in the Gnostic system, the equivalent of the "Old Ones" of the Cthulhu cultists. It is no accident that the term "aeon" also means a span of time, or an age; and, according to Robert M. Price, in "The Old Ones' Promise of Eternal Life," Alhazred made knowing use of the pun. He concludes from both the form and content of the lines that the couplet is not Alhazred's own work. "Rather," Price asserts, "it is revealed as an ancient piece of traditional lore stemming from the Gnostic cult of the *Aions*" (10).

9. Cf. John Donne's "Holy Sonnets," X, lines 13–14:

One short sleep past, we wake eternally,
And Death shall be no more; Death, thou shalt die.

Did Donne read the *Necronomicon*? In "Song," lines 10–15, he hints of an interest in the occult:

If thou be'st born to strange sights,
Things invisible to see,
Ride ten thousand days and nights,
Till age snow white hairs on thee,
Thou, when thou return'st, wilt tell
    me,
All strange wonders that befell thee.

10. Twin colossi were built in Thebes around the fourteenth century BCE by the Egyptian pharaoh Amenhotep III, bearing his own image; these eventually formed part of his own memorial temple. The Greeks later claimed that the colossi were depictions of the Hellenic hero Memnon, described by Homer in *The Iliad* as the son of Tithonus and the dawn (Eos). In 28 BCE, the statues were partially destroyed by an earthquake. Subsequently, the eastern colossus was reported to emit a singing sound at dawn. (The effect was probably the result of the evaporation of dew in the porous stone and ceased to be reported after reconstruction of the statues in the late second or early third century CE.) The colossus was thereafter known as the Vocal Statue of Memnon and became associated with a myth that the statue depicted Memnon singing a daily greeting to his mother.

The Colossi of Memnon.

11. The ancient capital of the Meroitic kingdom, which began in Egypt with the 25th Dynasty around 800 BCE; the city flourished until ca. 350 CE.

depth there came a crash of musical metal to hail the fiery disc as Memnon[10] hails it from the banks of the Nile. My ears rang and my imagination seethed as I led my camel slowly across the sand to that unvocal stone place; that place too old for Egypt and Meroë[11] to remember; that place which I alone of living men had seen.

In and out amongst the shapeless foundations of houses and palaces I wandered, finding never a carving or inscription to tell of those men, if men they were, who built the city and dwelt therein so long ago. The antiquity of the spot was unwholesome, and I longed to encounter some sign or device to prove that the city was indeed fashioned by mankind.[12] There were certain *proportions* and *dimensions* in the ruins which I did not like. I had with me many tools, and dug much within the walls of the obliterated edifices; but progress was slow, and nothing significant was revealed. When night and the moon returned I felt a chill wind which brought new fear, so that I did not dare to remain in the city. And as I went outside the antique walls to sleep, a small sighing sandstorm gathered behind me, blowing over the grey stones though the moon was bright and most of the desert still.

I awaked just at dawn from a pageant of horrible dreams, my ears ringing as from some metallic peal. I saw the sun peering redly through the last gusts of a little sandstorm that hovered over the nameless city, and marked the quietness of the rest of the landscape. Once more I ventured within those brooding ruins that swelled beneath the sand like an ogre under a coverlet, and again dug vainly for relics of the forgotten race. At noon I rested, and in the afternoon I spent much time tracing the walls, and the bygone streets, and the outlines of the nearly vanished buildings. I saw that the city had been mighty indeed, and wondered at the sources of its greatness. To myself I pictured all the splendours of an age so distant that Chaldæa[13] could not recall it, and thought of Sarnath the Doomed, that stood in the land of Mnar when mankind was young, and of Ib, that was carven of grey stone before mankind existed.[14]

All at once I came upon a place where the bed-rock rose stark through the sand and formed a low cliff; and here I saw with joy what seemed to promise further traces of the antediluvian people. Hewn rudely on the face of the cliff were the unmistakable facades of several small, squat rock houses or temples; whose interiors might preserve many secrets of ages too remote for calculation, though sandstorms had long since effaced any carvings which may have been outside.

Very low and sand-choked were all of the dark apertures near me, but I cleared one with my spade and crawled through it, carrying a torch to reveal whatever mysteries it might hold. When I was inside I saw that the cavern was indeed a temple, and beheld plain signs of the race that had lived and worshipped before the desert was a desert. Primitive altars, pillars, and niches, all curiously low, were not absent; and though I saw no sculptures nor frescoes, there were many singular stones clearly shaped into symbols by artificial means. The lowness of the chiselled chamber was very strange, for I could hardly more than kneel upright; but the area was so great that my torch shewed only part at a time. I shuddered oddly in some of the far corners; for certain altars and stones suggested forgotten rites of terrible, revolting, and inexplicable nature and made me wonder what manner of men could have made and frequented such a temple. When I had seen all that the place contained, I crawled out again, avid to find what the other temples might yield.

Night had now approached, yet the tangible things I had seen made curiosity stronger than fear, so that I did not flee from the long moon-cast shadows that had daunted me when first I saw the nameless city. In the twilight I cleared another aperture and with a new torch crawled into it, finding more vague stones and symbols, though nothing more definite than the other temple had contained. The room was just as low, but much less broad, ending in a very narrow passage crowded with obscure and cryptical shrines. About these shrines I was prying when the noise of a wind and my camel outside broke through the stillness and drew me forth to see what could have frightened the beast.

The moon was gleaming vividly over the primeval ruins, lighting a dense cloud of sand that seemed blown by a strong but decreasing wind from some point along the cliff ahead of me. I knew it was this chilly, sandy wind which had disturbed the camel, and was about to lead him to a place of better shelter when I chanced to glance up and saw that there was no wind atop the cliff. This astonished me and made me fearful again, but I imme-

12. A rare explorer to imagine that there were builders before humankind!

13. A land near modern Iraq; at some point in its history, it probably ruled Babylon, approximately 600 BCE. The Chaldeans are not an old civilization compared to some of the others mentioned earlier.

14. These places feature in the story "The Doom That Came to Sarnath," written by Lovecraft and first published in 1920. The tale tells of the destruction of the metropolis of Sarnath more than 10,000 years ago by the vengeance of the people of Ib, whom Sarnath had exterminated, and their lizard-god Bokrug. Mnar and Ib are also mentioned in *At the Mountains of Madness* (pp. 457–572, below).

diately recalled the sudden local winds I had seen and heard before at sunrise and sunset, and judged it was a normal thing. I decided that it came from some rock fissure leading to a cave, and watched the troubled sand to trace it to its source; soon perceiving that it came from the black orifice of a temple a long distance south of me, almost out of sight. Against the choking sand-cloud I plodded toward this temple, which as I neared it loomed larger than the rest, and shewed a doorway far less clogged with caked sand. I would have entered had not the terrific force of the icy wind almost quenched my torch. It poured madly out of the dark door, sighing uncannily as it ruffled the sand and spread about the weird ruins. Soon it grew fainter and the sand grew more and more still, till finally all was at rest again; but a presence seemed stalking among the spectral stones of the city, and when I glanced at the moon it seemed to quiver as though mirrored in unquiet waters. I was more afraid than I could explain, but not enough to dull my thirst for wonder; so as soon as the wind was quite gone I crossed into the dark chamber from which it had come.

This temple, as I had fancied from the outside, was larger than either of those I had visited before; and was presumably a natural cavern, since it bore winds from some region beyond. Here I could stand quite upright, but saw that the stones and altars were as low as those in the other temples. On the walls and roof I beheld for the first time some traces of the pictorial art of the ancient race, curious curling streaks of paint that had almost faded or crumbled away; and on two of the altars I saw with rising excitement a maze of well-fashioned curvilinear carvings. As I held my torch aloft it seemed to me that the shape of the roof was too regular to be natural, and I wondered what the prehistoric cutters of stone had first worked upon. Their engineering skill must have been vast.

Then a brighter flare of the fantastic flame shewed me that for which I had been seeking, the opening to those remoter abysses whence the sudden wind had blown; and I grew faint when I saw that it was a small and plainly *artificial* door chiselled in the solid rock. I thrust my torch within, beholding a black tunnel with the roof arching low over a rough flight of very small, numerous, and steeply descending steps. I shall always see those steps in my dreams, for I came to learn what they meant. At the time I hardly knew whether to call them steps or mere foot-holds in a precip-itous descent. My mind was whirling with mad thoughts, and the words and warnings of Arab prophets seemed to float across the desert from the lands that men know to the nameless city that men dare not know. Yet I hesitated only a moment before advancing through the portal and commencing to climb cau-tiously down the steep passage, feet first, as though on a ladder.

It is only in the terrible phantasms of drugs or delirium that any other man can have had such a descent as mine. The narrow passage led infinitely down like some hideous haunted well, and the torch I held above my head could not light the unknown depths toward which I was crawling. I lost track of the hours and forgot to consult my watch, though I was frightened when I thought of the distance I must be traversing. There were changes of direction and of steepness, and once I came to a long, low, level passage where I had to wriggle feet first along the rocky floor, holding my torch at arm's length beyond my head. The place was not high enough for kneeling. After that were more of the steep steps, and I was still scrambling down interminably when my failing torch died out. I do not think I noticed it at the time, for when I did notice it I was still holding it high above me as if it were ablaze. I was quite unbalanced with that instinct for the strange and the unknown which has made me a wanderer upon earth and a haunter of far, ancient, and forbidden places.

In the darkness there flashed before my mind fragments of my cherished treasury of dæmonic lore; sentences from Alhaz-red the mad Arab, paragraphs from the apocryphal nightmares of Damascius,[15] and infamous lines from the delirious *Image du Monde* of Gauthier de Metz.[16] I repeated queer extracts, and mut-tered of Afrasiab[17] and the dæmons that floated with him down the Oxus;[18] later chanting over and over again a phrase from one of Lord Dunsany's tales[19]—"the unreverberate blackness of the abyss." Once when the descent grew amazingly steep I recited something in sing-song from Thomas Moore[20] until I feared to recite more:

> *A reservoir of darkness, black*
> *As witches' cauldrons are, when fill'd*
> *With moon-drugs in th' eclipse distill'd*

15. A pagan scholar (ca. 458–538 CE), best known for his commentaries on Plato and Aristotle. What his "apocry-phal nightmares" might be is unknown.

16. French priest and poet. His name is more often spelled without the *h*. The book was published around 1246 CE and mixes poetry, cosmology, astrology, and depictions of a spherical earth (a concept not yet universally acknowledged). It was widely translated during the Middle Ages. Sabine Baring-Gould, in *Curi-ous Myths of the Middle Ages* (1866), a copy of which was in Lovecraft's library, mentions that Gautier "places the ter-restrial Paradise in an unapproachable region of Asia, surrounded by flames, and having an armed angel to guard the only gate" (253), though, as Baring-Gould points out, many other medieval writers expressed similar views, and so it is hard to see how such a description could be described as "infamous."

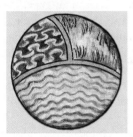

Detail from a portrait of John Gower, ca. 1400, depicting a spherical world, with compartments representing earth, wind, and water.

17. The mythical king of central Asia, named in the *Shahnameh* (*Book of Kings*) by the Persian poet Ferdowsi around 1000 CE. Afrasiab reportedly wandered over central Asia, hounded by the king of Iran, Kay Khosrow.

18. The Greek name of the river Amu Dar'ya in central Asia.

19. The tale "Probable Adventure of the Three Literary Men," first published in *Sketch*, February 8, 1911.

20. A poet and balladeer, Moore (1779–1852) is as closely identified with Ireland as Robert Burns is with Scotland. He was close friends with Lord Byron; charged by Byron with publication of the Romantic poet's memoirs after his death, Moore famously destroyed them, thinking them too honest to be read. Moore wrote a novel in 1827 entitled *The Epicurean*, about a Greek named Alciphron who experiences the rites of the Epicurean sect as well as initiation into Christianity at a monastery. The conceit of the book is that it is a translation of a manuscript found in Egypt at the dawn of the nineteenth century. In 1839, Moore published an epic poem, *Alciphron*, from which this quotation is drawn. Alciphron travels from Greece to Egypt to explore mysteries; he discovers a huge well far beneath a pyramid and has many experiences similar to those that befall the narrator of "The Nameless City," including entering a small chapel and encountering clanging metallic gates.

21. The word should be "all."

22. The Paleozoic era extended from 542 million years ago to 251 million years ago. According to fossil evidence, large sophisticated reptiles were the highest form of life. Having not yet seen anything reptilian, the narrator has no reason to guess that the ruin is actually that old. Possibly he simply means that it is really, really old.

Leaning to look if foot might pass
Down thro' that chasm, I saw, beneath,
As far as vision could explore,
The jetty sides as[21] smooth as glass,
Looking as if just varnish'd o'er
With that dark pitch the Sea of Death
Throws out upon its slimy shore.

Time had quite ceased to exist when my feet again felt a level floor, and I found myself in a place slightly higher than the rooms in the two smaller temples now so incalculably far above my head. I could not quite stand, but could kneel upright, and in the dark I shuffled and crept hither and thither at random. I soon knew that I was in a narrow passage whose walls were lined with cases of wood having glass fronts. As in that Palæozoic[22] and abysmal place I felt of such things as polished wood and glass I shuddered at the possible implications. The cases were apparently ranged along each side of the passage at regular intervals, and were oblong and horizontal, hideously like coffins in shape and size. When I tried to move two or three for further examination, I found they were firmly fastened.

I saw that the passage was a long one, so floundered ahead rapidly in a creeping run that would have seemed horrible had any eye watched me in the blackness; crossing from side to side occasionally to feel of my surroundings and be sure the walls and rows of cases still stretched on. Man is so used to thinking visually that I almost forgot the darkness and pictured the endless corridor of wood and glass in its low-studded monotony as though I saw it. And then in a moment of indescribable emotion I did see it.

Just when my fancy merged into real sight I cannot tell; but there came a gradual glow ahead, and all at once I knew that I saw the dim outlines of the corridor and the cases, revealed by some unknown subterranean phosphorescence. For a little while all was exactly as I had imagined it, since the glow was very faint; but as I mechanically kept on stumbling ahead into the stronger light I realised that my fancy had been but feeble. This hall was no relic of crudity like the temples in the city above, but a monument of the most magnificent and exotic art. Rich, vivid, and daringly fantastic designs and pictures formed a continuous scheme of mural painting whose lines and colours were beyond description. The cases were of a strange golden wood, with fronts of exquisite glass, and contained the mummified forms of creatures outreaching in grotesqueness the most chaotic dreams of man.

To convey any idea of these monstrosities is impossible. They were of the reptile kind, with body lines suggesting sometimes the crocodile, sometimes the seal, but more often nothing of which either the naturalist or the palæontologist ever heard. In size they approximated a small man, and their fore-legs bore delicate and evidently flexbile feet curiously like human hands and fingers. But strangest of all were their heads, which presented a contour violating all known biological principles. To nothing can such things be well compared—in one flash I thought of comparisons as varied as the cat, the bulldog, the mythic Satyr, and the human being. Not Jove himself had so colossal and protuberant a forehead, yet the horns and the noselessness and the alligator-like jaw placed the things outside all established categories. I debated for a time on the reality of the mummies, half suspecting they were artificial idols; but soon decided they were indeed some palæogean[23] species which had lived when the nameless city was alive. To crown their grotesqueness, most of them were gorgeously enrobed in the costliest of fabrics, and lavishly laden with ornaments of gold, jewels, and unknown shining metals.

The importance of these crawling creatures must have been vast, for they held first place among the wild designs on the frescoed walls and ceiling. With matchless skill had the artist drawn them in a world of their own, wherein they had cities and gardens fashioned to suit their dimensions; and I could not but think that their pictured history was allegorical, perhaps shewing the progress of the race that worshipped them. These creatures, I said to myself, were to the men of the nameless city what the she-wolf was to Rome, or some totem-beast is to a tribe of Indians.

Holding this view, I thought I could trace roughly a wonderful epic of the nameless city; the tale of a mighty sea-coast metropolis that ruled the world before Africa rose out of the waves, and of its struggles as the sea shrank away, and the desert crept into the fertile valley that held it. I saw its wars and triumphs, its

23. The Paleogene period was from 65 million years ago to about 25 million years ago. Mammals appeared during this period, and indeed primates appeared at its end, just as South America and Africa separated and the Atlantic Ocean grew. Africa did not rise "out of the waves"; it was part of the supercontinent popularly called Pangaea and its position did not change. The Sahara Desert has seen at least two fertile spells, one prior to the last Ice Age and one after the end of the last Ice Age, beginning around 10,500 BCE and ending around 5000 BCE.

troubles and defeats, and afterward its terrible fight against the desert when thousands of its people—here represented in allegory by the grotesque reptiles—were driven to chisel their way down through the rocks in some marvellous manner to another world whereof their prophets had told them. It was all vividly weird and realistic, and its connexion with the awesome descent I had made was unmistakable. I even recognised the passages.

As I crept along the corridor toward the brighter light I saw later stages of the painted epic—the leave-taking of the race that had dwelt in the nameless city and the valley around for ten million years; the race whose souls shrank from quitting scenes their bodies had known so long, where they had settled as nomads in the earth's youth, hewing in the virgin rock those primal shrines at which they had never ceased to worship. Now that the light was better I studied the pictures more closely and, remembering that the strange reptiles must represent the unknown men, pondered upon the customs of the nameless city. Many things were peculiar and inexplicable. The civilisation, which included a written alphabet, had seemingly risen to a higher order than those immeasurably later civilisations of Egypt and Chaldæa, yet there were curious omissions. I could, for example, find no pictures to represent deaths or funeral customs, save such as were related to wars, violence, and plagues; and I wondered at the reticence shewn concerning natural death. It was as though an ideal of earthly immortality had been fostered as a cheering illusion.

Still nearer the end of the passage were painted scenes of the utmost picturesqueness and extravagance; contrasted views of the nameless city in its desertion and growing ruin, and of the strange new realm for paradise to which the race had hewed its way through the stone. In these views the city and the desert valley were shewn always by moonlight, a golden nimbus hovering over the fallen walls, and half-revealing the splendid perfection of former times, shewn spectrally and elusively by the artist. The paradisal scenes were almost too extravagant to be believed; portraying a hidden world of eternal day filled with glorious cities and ethereal hills and valleys. At the very last I thought I saw signs of an artistic anti-climax. The paintings were less skilful, and much more bizarre than even the wildest of the earlier scenes. They seemed to record a slow decadence of the ancient stock, coupled with a growing ferocity toward the outside world from which it was driven by the desert. The forms of the people—always represented by the sacred reptiles—appeared to be gradually wasting away, though their spirit as shewn hovering about the ruins by moonlight gained in proportion. Emaciated priests, displayed as reptiles in ornate robes, cursed the upper air and all who breathed it; and one terrible final scene shewed a primitive-looking man, perhaps a pioneer of ancient Irem, the City of Pillars,[24] torn to pieces by members of the elder race. I remembered how the Arabs fear the nameless city, and was glad that beyond this place the grey walls and ceiling were bare.

As I viewed the pageant of mural history I had approached very closely the end of the low-ceiled hall and was aware of a great gate through which came all of the illuminating phosphorescence. Creeping up to it, I cried aloud in transcendent amazement at what lay beyond; for instead of other and brighter chambers there was only an illimitable void of uniform radiance, such as one might fancy when gazing down from the peak of Mount Everest upon a sea of sunlit mist. Behind me was a passage so cramped that I could not stand upright in it; before me was an infinity of subterranean effulgence.

Reaching down from the passage into the abyss was the head of a steep flight of steps—small numerous steps like those of the black passages I had traversed—but after a few feet the glowing vapours concealed everything. Swung back open against the left-hand wall of the passage was a massive door of brass, incredibly thick and decorated with fantastic bas-reliefs, which could if closed shut the whole inner world of light away from the vaults and passages of rock. I looked at the steps, and for the nonce dared not try them. I touched the open brass door, and could not move it. Then I sank prone to the stone floor, my mind aflame with prodigious reflections which not even a death-like exhaustion could banish.

As I lay still with closed eyes, free to ponder, many things I had lightly noted in the frescoes came back to me with new and terrible significance—scenes representing the nameless city in its heyday, the vegetation of the valley around it, and the distant lands with which its merchants traded. The allegory of the crawling creatures puzzled me by its universal prominence, and I

24. Irem or Iram, the City of a Thousand Pillars, is a "lost" city of the Arabian Peninsula, mentioned in the Quran: "Have you not considered how your Lord dealt with Aad / With Irem of lofty pillars / the like of which has never been seen in the Land?" (Q'uran, chap. 89, 6–14). Excavations of the city of Ebla in Syria in 1973 produced records showing that, 4,500 years ago, Ebla had traded with Iram. It is unclear whether this "Iram" is the same city.

According to the *Encyclopædia Britannica* (9th ed.), "Very gorgeous are the descriptions given [by Arab chroniclers] of 'Irem,' the 'city of pillars,' as the Koran styles it, supposed to have been erected by Shadad, the latest despot of 'Ad in the Regions of Hadramant'; and which yet, after the annihilation of its tenants, remains entire, so Arabs say, invisible to ordinary eyes, but occasionally, and at rare intervals, revealed to some heaven-favoured traveller" (II, 255b).

wondered that it should be so closely followed in a pictured history of such importance. In the frescoes the nameless city had been shewn in proportions fitted to the reptiles. I wondered what its real proportions and magnificence had been, and reflected a moment on certain oddities I had noticed in the ruins. I thought curiously of the lowness of the primal temples and of the underground corridor, which were doubtless hewn thus out of deference to the reptile deities there honoured; though it perforce reduced the worshippers to crawling. Perhaps the very rites had involved a crawling in imitation of the creatures. No religious theory, however, could easily explain why the level passage in that awesome descent should be as low as the temples—or lower, since one could not even kneel in it. As I thought of the crawling creatures, whose hideous mummified forms were so close to me, I felt a new throb of fear. Mental associations are curious, and I shrank from the idea that except for the poor primitive man torn to pieces in the last painting, mine was the only human form amidst the many relics and symbols of primordial life.

But as always in my strange and roving existence, wonder soon drove out fear; for the luminous abyss and what it might contain presented a problem worthy of the greatest explorer. That a weird world of mystery lay far down that flight of peculiarly small steps I could not doubt, and I hoped to find there those human memorials which the painted corridor had failed to give. The frescoes had pictured unbelievable cities, hills, and valleys in this lower realm, and my fancy dwelt on the rich and colossal ruins that awaited me.

My fears, indeed, concerned the past rather than the future. Not even the physical horror of my position in that cramped corridor of dead reptiles and antediluvian frescoes, miles below the world I knew and faced by another world of eerie light and mist, could match the lethal dread I felt at the abysmal antiquity of the scene and its soul. An ancientness so vast that measurement is feeble seemed to leer down from the primal stones and rock-hewn temples in the nameless city, while the very latest of the astounding maps in the frescoes shewed oceans and continents that man has forgotten, with only here and there some vaguely familiar outline. Of what could have happened in the geological æons since the paintings ceased and the death-hating race resentfully succumbed to decay, no man might say. Life had once teemed in these caverns and in the luminous realm beyond; now I was alone with vivid relics, and I trembled to think of the countless ages through which these relics had kept a silent and deserted vigil.

Suddenly there came another burst of that acute fear which had intermittently seized me ever since I first saw the terrible valley and the nameless city under a cold moon, and despite my exhaustion I found myself starting frantically to a sitting posture and gazing back along the black corridor toward the tunnels that rose to the outer world. My sensations were much like those which had made me shun the nameless city at night, and were as inexplicable as they were poignant. In another moment, however, I received a still greater shock in the form of a definite sound— the first which had broken the utter silence of these tomb-like depths. It was a deep, low moaning, as of a distant throng of condemned spirits, and came from the direction in which I was staring. Its volume rapidly grew, till soon it reverberated frightfully through the low passage, and at the same time I became conscious of an increasing draught of cold air, likewise flowing from the tunnels and the city above. The touch of this air seemed to restore my balance, for I instantly recalled the sudden gusts which had risen around the mouth of the abyss each sunset and sunrise, one of which had indeed served to reveal the hidden tunnels to me. I looked at my watch and saw that sunrise was near, so braced myself to resist the gale which was sweeping down to its cavern home as it had swept forth at evening. My fear again waned low, since a natural phenomenon tends to dispel broodings over the unknown.

More and more madly poured the shrieking, moaning night wind into that gulf of the inner earth. I dropped prone again and clutched vainly at the floor for fear of being swept bodily through the open gate into the phosphorescent abyss. Such fury I had not expected, and as I grew aware of an actual slipping of my form toward the abyss I was beset by a thousand new terrors of apprehension and imagination. The malignancy of the blast awakened incredible fancies; once more I compared myself shudderingly to the only other human image in that frightful corridor, the man who was torn to pieces by the nameless race, for in the fiendish

25. This couplet also occurs in "The Call of Cthulhu." See text accompanying note 52 in that story.

26. The narrator's meaning here is unclear. Abaddon was originally a place-name, a region of the underworld and in particular, a realm of the cursed sacrificial grounds of Gehenna. Some scholars treat Abaddon as the angel of death and destruction (the name is derived from the Hebrew אבד, which means "to perish"); others contend that he is a good angel, holding the key to the bottomless pit. The primary source for information about Abbadon is Revelation 9:1–11, which characterizes him as the "king" of the pit:

And the fifth angel sounded, and I saw a star fall from heaven unto the earth: and to him was given the key of the bottomless pit.

And he opened the bottomless pit; and there arose a smoke out of the pit, as the smoke of a great furnace; and the sun and the air were darkened by reason of the smoke of the pit.

And there came out of the smoke locusts upon the earth: and unto them was given power, as the scorpions of the earth have power.

And it was commanded them that they should not hurt the grass of the earth, neither any green thing, neither any tree; but only those men which have not the seal of God in their foreheads.

And to them it was given that they should not kill them, but that they should be tormented five months: and their torment was as the torment of a scorpion, when he striketh a man.

And in those days shall men seek death, and shall not find it; and shall

clawing of the swirling currents there seemed to abide a vindictive rage all the stronger because it was largely impotent. I think I screamed frantically near the last—I was almost mad—but if I did so, my cries were lost in the hell-born babel of the howling wind-wraiths. I tried to crawl against the murderous invisible torrent, but I could not even hold my own as I was pushed slowly and inexorably toward the unknown world. Finally reason must have wholly snapped, for I fell to babbling over and over that unexplainable couplet of the mad Arab Alhazred, who dreamed of the nameless city:

That is not dead which can eternal lie,
And with strange æons even death may die.[25]

Only the grim brooding desert gods know what really took place—what indescribable struggles and scrambles in the dark I endured or what Abaddon[26] guided me back to life, where I must always remember and shiver in the night-wind till oblivion—or worse—claims me. Monstrous, unnatural, colossal, was the thing—too far beyond all the ideas of man to be believed except in the silent damnable small hours when one cannot sleep.

I have said that the fury of the rushing blast was infernal—cacodæmoniacal[27]—and that its voices were hideous with the pent-up viciousness of desolate eternities. Presently those voices, while still chaotic before me, seemed to my beating brain to take articulate form behind me; and down there in the grave of unnumbered æon-dead antiquities, leagues below the dawn-lit world of men, I heard the ghastly cursing and snarling of strange-tongued fiends. Turning, I saw outlined against the luminous æther of the abyss what could not be seen against the dusk of the corridor—a nightmare horde of rushing devils; hate-distorted, grotesquely panoplied, half-transparent devils of a race no man might mistake—the crawling reptiles of the nameless city.

And as the wind died away I was plunged into the ghoul-peopled blackness of earth's bowels; for behind the last of the creatures the great brazen door clanged shut with a deafening peal of metallic music whose reverberations swelled out to the distant world to hail the rising sun as Memnon hails it from the banks of the Nile.

desire to die, and death shall flee from them.

And the shapes of the locusts were like unto horses prepared unto battle; and on their heads were as it were crowns like gold, and their faces were as the faces of men.

And they had hair as the hair of women, and their teeth were as the teeth of lions.

And they had breastplates, as it were breastplates of iron; and the sound of their wings was as the sound of chariots of many horses running to battle.

And they had tails like unto scorpions, and there were stings in their tails: and their power was to hurt men five months.

And they had a king over them, which is the angel of the bottomless pit, whose name in the Hebrew tongue is Abaddon, but in the Greek tongue hath his name Apollyon. (King James Version)

27. This great word just means a bad demon, from the Greek *kakos* (bad) and *daimon* (divinity or spirit).

The Hound[1]

In many ways the most Poe-like of all Lovecraft's stories, and the first to appear in Weird Tales, *with which Lovecraft would be indelibly linked, "The Hound" combines elements of classic horror fiction from a variety of literary progenitors. It also includes the first mention by name of Alhazred's Necronomicon. While S. T. Joshi calls the story "roundly abused for being wildly overwritten," he sees it as a deliberate parody. Its "adjectivitis" mocks the prose of Poe and other writers whom Lovecraft admired, including Ambrose Bierce and Joris-Karl Huysmans. Lovecraft again casts the tale as a suicide note. Unlike in the case of the "epicure of the terrible" who relates "The Picture in the House," however, it is too late for this narrator to be saved!*

1. The story first appeared in *Weird Tales* 2 (February 1924), 50–52, 78; it was probably written, however, in September 1922.

2. Weird, fantastic. Clark Ashton Smith (1893–1961), many of whose works appeared alongside Lovecraft's in *Weird Tales* and elsewhere, wrote a poem in 1912 entitled "The Eldritch Dark":

> Now as the twilight's doubtful interval
> Closes with night's accomplished certainty,
> A wizard wind goes crying eerily,
> And on the wold misshapen shadows crawl,
> Miming the trees, whose voices climb and fall,
> Imploring, in Sabbatic ecstacy,
> The sky where vapor-mounted phantoms flee
> From the scythed moon impendent over all.

I.

In my tortured ears there sounds unceasingly a nightmare whirring and flapping, and a faint distant baying as of some gigantic hound. It is not dream—it is not, I fear, even madness—for too much has already happened to give me these merciful doubts.

St. John is a mangled corpse; I alone know why, and such is my knowledge that I am about to blow out my brains for fear I shall be mangled in the same way. Down unlit and illimitable corridors of eldritch[2] phantasy sweeps the black, shapeless Nemesis that drives me to self-annihilation.

May heaven forgive the folly and morbidity which led us both to so monstrous a fate! Wearied with the commonplaces of a prosaic world; where even the joys of romance and adventure soon grow stale, St. John and I had followed enthusiastically every æsthetic and intellectual movement which promised respite from our devastating ennui. The enigmas of the Symbolists[3] and the ecstasies of the pre-Raphælites[4] all were ours in their time, but each new mood was drained too soon, of its diverting novelty and appeal.

Only the sombre philosophy of the Decadents[5] could hold us, and this we found potent only by increasing gradually the depth and diabolism of our penetrations. Baudelaire and Huysmans were soon exhausted of thrills, till finally there remained for us only the more direct stimuli of unnatural personal experiences and adventures. It was this frightful emotional need which led us eventually to that detestable course which even in my present fear I mention with shame and timidity—that hideous extremity of human outrage, the abhorred practice of grave-robing.[6]

I cannot reveal the details of our shocking expeditions, or catalogue even partly the worst of the trophies adorning the nameless museum we prepared in the great stone house where we jointly dwelt, alone and servantless. Our museum was a blasphemous, unthinkable place, where with the satanic taste of neurotic virtuosi we had assembled an universe of terror and decay to excite our jaded sensibilities. It was a secret room, far, far underground; where huge winged dæmons carven of basalt and onyx vomited from wide grinning mouths weird green and orange light, and hidden pneumatic pipes ruffled into kaleidoscopic dances of death the lines of red charnel things hand in hand woven in voluminous black hangings. Through these pipes came at will the odours our moods most craved; sometimes the scent of pale funeral lilies; sometimes the narcotic incense of imagined Eastern shrines of the kingly dead, and sometimes—how I shudder to recall it!—the frightful, soul-upheaving stenches of the uncovered grave.

Around the walls of this repellent chamber were cases of antique mummies alternating with comely, life-like bodies perfectly stuffed and cured by the taxidermist's art, and with headstones snatched from the oldest churchyards of the world. Niches here and there contained skulls of all shapes, and heads preserved in various stages of dissolution. There one might find the rotting, bald pates of famous noblemen, and the fresh and radiantly golden heads of new-buried children.

Statues and paintings there were, all of fiendish subjects and some executed by St. John and myself. A locked portfolio, bound

Twin veils of covering cloud and
    silence, thrown
Across the movement and the sound
    of things,
Make blank the night, till in the
    broken west
The moon's ensanguined blade awhile
    is shown. . . .
The night grows whole again. . . . The
    shadows rest,
Gathered beneath a greater shadow's
    wings.

3. The *fin-de-siècle* French poets Charles Baudelaire, Stéphane Mallarmé, Paul Verlaine, and Arthur Rimbaud, whose emotional, intuitive structures and—especially in the case of Verlaine—classical form and musicality changed the course of nineteenth-century letters. The group is frequently also said to have included Paul Valéry.

4. English poets, painters, and critics of the late nineteenth century who styled themselves (at first secretly) the "Pre-Raphaelite Brotherhood" and, largely rejecting the academic styles then prevalent, embraced the influence of late medieval and early Renaissance European art before the time of Raphael (1483–1520). Their works were characterized by noble subject matter and a luminous, bright palette achieved by the use of tempera paint. The most prominent member was Dante Gabriel Rossetti; others included William Holman Hunt, John Everett Millais, William Michael Rossetti, James Collinson, Frederic George Stephens, and Thomas Woolner.

5. A late-nineteenth-century artistic movement that grew out of symbolism and included Baudelaire (who was viewed as leading the symbolist movement), Théophile Gautier, Joris-Karl Huysmans, and, in England, Oscar Wilde. *Là-Bas* (*The Damned*) (1891), a best-selling novel by

Huysmans, which treated, among other subjects, Satanism, was seen as the Bible of the movement; the Huysmans novel *À Rebours* (*Against Nature*) (1884), still widely read today, features an antihero based both on Huysmans himself and on Robert de Montesquiou, the French dandy who also served as inspiration for Baron de Charlus in Marcel Proust's *À la Recherche du Temps Perdu* (1871–1922).

6. Grave-robbing certainly did not begin as "thrill-seeking"; rather, it was conducted for profit. See "Herbert West: Reanimator," note 9, above.

7. Francisco José de Goya y Lucientes (1746–1828), who is considered the most important and influential Spanish artist of the late eighteenth and early nine-

Goya's most famous work in the "Black Paintings" series, *Saturn Devouring His Son* (1819–23).

in tanned human skin, held certain unknown and unnamable drawings which it was rumoured Goya[7] had perpetrated but dared not acknowledge. There were nauseous musical instruments, stringed, brass, and wood-wind,[8] on which St. John and I sometimes produced dissonances of exquisite morbidity and cacodæmoniacal ghastliness; whilst in a multitude of inlaid ebony cabinets reposed the most incredible and unimaginable variety of tomb-loot ever assembled by human madness and perversity. It is of this loot in particular that I must not speak—thank God I had the courage to destroy it long before I thought of destroying myself.

The predatory excursions on which we collected our unmentionable treasures were always artistically memorable events. We were no vulgar ghouls, but worked only under certain conditions of mood, landscape, environment, weather, season, and moonlight. These pastimes were to us the most exquisite form of æsthetic expression, and we gave their details a fastidious technical care. An inappropriate hour, a jarring lighting effect, or a clumsy manipulation of the damp sod, would almost totally destroy for us that ecstatic titillation which followed the exhumation of some ominous, grinning secret of the earth. Our quest for novel scenes and piquant conditions was feverish and insatiate— St. John was always the leader, and he it was who led the way at last to that mocking, that accursed spot which brought us our hideous and inevitable doom.

By what malign fatality were we lured to that terrible Holland churchyard? I think it was the dark rumour and legendry, the tales of one buried for five centuries, who had himself been a ghoul in his time and had stolen a potent thing from a mighty sepulchre. I can recall the scene in these final moments—the pale autumnal moon over the graves, casting long horrible shadows; the grotesque trees, drooping sullenly to meet the neglected grass and the crumbling slabs; the vast legions of strangely colossal bats that flew against the moon; the antique ivied church pointing a huge spectral finger at the livid sky; the phosphorescent insects that danced like death-fires under the yews in a distant corner; the odours of mould, vegetation, and less explicable things that mingled feebly with the night-wind from over far swamps and seas; and worst of all, the faint deep-toned baying of some gigantic hound which we could neither see nor definitely place. As we heard this suggestion of baying we shuddered, remembering the tales of the peasantry; for he whom we sought had centuries before been found in this selfsame spot, torn and mangled by the claws and teeth of some unspeakable beast.[9]

I remembered how we delved in this ghoul's grave with our spades, and how we thrilled at the picture of ourselves, the grave, the pale watching moon, the horrible shadows, the grotesque trees, the titanic bats, the antique church, the dancing death-fires, the sickening odours, the gently moaning night-wind, and the strange, half-heard directionless baying of whose objective existence we could scarcely be sure.

Then we struck a substance harder than the damp mould, and beheld a rotting oblong box crusted with mineral deposits from the long-undisturbed ground. It was incredibly tough and thick, but so old that we finally pried it open and feasted our eyes on what it held.

Much—amazingly much—was left of the object despite the lapse of five hundred years. The skeleton, though crushed in places by the jaws of the thing that had killed it, held together with surprising firmness, and we gloated over the clean white skull and its long, firm teeth and its eyeless sockets that once had glowed with a charnel fever like our own. In the coffin lay an amulet of curious and exotic design, which had apparently been worn around the sleeper's neck. It was the oddly conventional-ised figure of a crouching winged hound, or sphinx with a semi-canine face,[10] and was exquisitely carved in antique Oriental fashion from a small piece of green jade.[11] The expression on its features was repellent in the extreme, savouring at once of death, bestiality and malevolence. Around the base was an inscription in characters which neither St. John nor I could identify; and on the bottom, like a maker's seal, was graven a grotesque and formidable skull.

Immediately upon beholding this amulet we knew that we must possess it; that this treasure alone was our logical pelf from the centuried grave. Even had its outlines been unfamiliar we would have desired it, but as we looked more closely we saw that it was not wholly unfamiliar. Alien it indeed was to all art and literature which sane and balanced readers know, but we recog-

teenth centuries, and whose work made the transition from classical to modern. Toward the end of his life, isolated and lacking royal commissions, Goya conceived the Black Paintings, fourteen works in fresco done on the walls of his country house, which depicted dark supernatural themes. The drawings mentioned here might be sketches for those paintings.

According to S. T. Joshi (in *I Am Providence*, 433), the original typescript described the skinbound portfolio as containing "the unknown and unnamable drawings of Clark Ashton Smith."

8. The narrator is exaggerating here: The instruments could hardly be at fault, only the sounds that St. John and he made on them.

9. Such tales have a long history in many countries. Arthur Conan Doyle's *The Hound of the Baskervilles* (1902), hailed by many as the greatest mystery of the twentieth century, tells of the death of Hugo Baskerville, a man of ill repute who hunted a local girl for sport, by the ravages of a spectral hound. "Mr. Holmes, they were the footprints of a gigantic hound!" (echoed in the opening sentence of this narration and below) is the most famous line of that famous story. Robert H. Waugh's essay "The Hounds of Hell, the Hounds of Heaven, and the Hounds of Earth," notes a number of similarities between the two tales, and there is no doubt that Lovecraft was very familiar with Doyle's masterwork.

10. The Great Sphinx of Egypt has the body of a lion and the head of a Pharaoh; however, in Greek mythology, the sphinx had the body of a lion, the head and breasts of a woman, and the wings of an eagle. In *Oedipus Tyrannus* by Sophocles, the Sphinx who poses riddles to Oedipus is referred to as "dog-faced."

11. Carved jade has been a part of Chinese culture for more than six thousand years.

12. Alhazred has been mentioned in a previous tale (see "The Nameless City," note 7), but this is the first time that the *Necronomicon* has been referred to by name.

Lovecraft wrote an outline for a history of the book, only published after his death, set forth in Appendix 3, below. In 1937, in a letter to Harry O. Fischer, he revealed that the name came to him in a dream (late February 1937, *Selected Letters*, V, 418), and he understood the translation to be "An Image (or Picture) of the Law of the Dead." However, there is great controversy over the correct translation of the Greek. Alexandre Bouchard and Louis-Pierre Smith Lacroix examine the competing theories in some detail in "*Necronomicon*: A Note" and offer four versions, for which they claim equal merit: *Eaters of the Dead*, *Chants of the Dead*, *Book of the Districts/Habitations Hiding/Enclosing the Dead*, and *Law of the Dead*. There is also controversy over the *contents* of the book. Here, as in other tales (for example, in "The Statement of Randolph Carter," pp. 11–17, above), it seems to be a demonology, a scholarly work studying various supernatural entities, and indeed here, Alhazred is described as a demonologist. Elsewhere, it seems to be a grimoire, a book providing spells and incantations to be used to summon those entities. See, for example, *The Case of Charles Dexter Ward* (pp. 171–309, below). In "History of the *Necronomicon*," Alhazred is described as worshipping the entities, not studying them.

13. Leng, like other lands mentioned in Lovecraft's work, is "inaccessible" and hence unknown. It is mentioned again in "The Whisperer in Darkness" and *At the Mountains of Madness*, where it is

nised it as the thing hinted of in the forbidden *Necronomicon* of the mad Arab Abdul Alhazred;[12] the ghastly soul-symbol of the corpse-eating cult of inaccessible Leng,[13] in Central Asia. All too well did we trace the sinister lineaments described by the old Arab dæmonologist; lineaments, he wrote, drawn from some obscure supernatural manifestation of the souls of those who vexed and gnawed at the dead.

Seizing the green jade object, we gave a last glance at the bleached and cavern-eyed face of its owner and closed up the grave as we found it. As we hastened from that abhorrent spot, the stolen amulet in St. John's pocket, we thought we saw the bats descend in a body to the earth we had so lately rifled, as if seeking for some cursed and unholy nourishment. But the autumn moon shone weak and pale, and we could not be sure. So, too, as we sailed the next day away from Holland to our home, we thought we heard the faint distant baying of some gigantic hound in the background. But the autumn wind moaned sad and wan, and we could not be sure.

II.

LESS THAN A week after our return to England, strange things began to happen. We lived as recluses; devoid of friends, alone, and without servants in a few rooms of an ancient manor-house on a bleak and unfrequented moor;[14] so that our doors were seldom disturbed by the knock of the visitor. Now, however, we were troubled by what seemed to be frequent fumblings in the night, not only around the doors but around the windows also, upper as well as lower. Once we fancied that a large, opaque body darkened the library window when the moon was shining against it, and another time we thought we heard a whirring or flapping sound not far off. On each occasion investigation revealed nothing, and we began to ascribe the occurrences to imagination alone—that same curiously disturbed imagination which still prolonged in our ears the faint far baying we thought we had heard in the Holland churchyard. The jade amulet now reposed in a niche in our museum, and sometimes we burned strangely scented candles before it. We read much in Alhazred's *Necro-*

nomicon about its properties, and about the relation of ghouls' souls to the objects it symbolised; and were disturbed by what we read. Then terror came.

On the night of September 24, 19—, I heard a knock at my chamber door. Fancying it St. John's, I bade the knocker enter, but was answered only by a shrill laugh. There was no one in the corridor. When I aroused St. John from his sleep, he professed entire ignorance of the event, and became as worried as I. It was that night that the faint, distant baying over the moor became to us a certain and dreaded reality. Four days later, whilst we were both in the hidden museum, there came a low, cautious scratching at the single door which led to the secret library staircase. Our alarm was now divided, for besides our fear of the unknown, we had always entertained a dread that our grisly collection might be discovered. Extinguishing all lights, we proceeded to the door and threw it suddenly open; whereupon we felt an unaccountable rush of air, and heard as if receding far away a queer combination of rustling, tittering, and articulate chatter. Whether we were mad, dreaming, or in our senses, we did not try to determine. We only realised, with the blackest of apprehensions, that the apparently disembodied chatter was beyond a doubt *in the Dutch language*.

After that we lived in growing horror and fascination. Mostly we held to the theory that we were jointly going mad from our life of unnatural excitements, but sometimes it pleased us more to dramatise ourselves as the victims of some creeping and appalling doom. Bizarre manifestations were now too frequent to count. Our lonely house was seemingly alive with the presence of some malign being whose nature we could not guess, and every night that dæmoniac baying rolled over the windswept moor, always louder and louder. On October 29 we found in the soft earth underneath the library window a series of footprints utterly impossible to describe.[15] They were as baffling as the hordes of great bats which haunted the old manor-house in unprecedented and increasing numbers.

The horror reached a culmination on November 18, when St. John, walking home after dark from the distant railway station, was seized by some frightful carnivorous thing and torn to ribbons. His screams had reached the house, and I had hastened to

described as bordering the region known as the Cold Wastes. The name had its origin in Tibetan legend and is described in H. A. Jäschke's *A Tibetan-English Dictionary* (1881) as "one of the four imaginary parts of the earth, as taught by the geographers of Tibet" (80). See Marco Frenschkowski's "The Secret of Leng" for a further discussion.

14. Again, the narrator rings the same chimes as Conan Doyle; *The Hound of the Baskervilles* takes place almost wholly in Dartmoor. "Avoid the moor in those hours of darkness when the powers of evil are exalted."

15. See note 9, above.

". . . St. John, walking home after dark . . ." *Weird Tales* 3, no. 2 (February 1924) (artist: William F. Heitman)

16. Cf. Ambrose Bierce's 1893 story "The Damned Thing," about an object of a color outside the spectrum of human vision and, by extension, things that humans cannot expect to understand. Lovecraft owned several collections of Bierce's works, one including this tale.

17. So, who killed St. John? The same being as the skeleton in the grave? A winged hound in England? The ambiguities of the tale are explored, complete with a table with sixteen different alternatives, in "Who Killed St. John?" by Peter F. Jeffery.

the terrible scene in time to hear a whir of wings and see a vague black cloudy thing silhouetted against the rising moon.

My friend was dying when I spoke to him, and he could not answer coherently. All he could do was to whisper, "The amulet—that damned thing—."[16] Then he collapsed, an inert mass of mangled flesh.[17]

I buried him the next midnight in one of our neglected gardens, and mumbled over his body one of the devilish rituals he had loved in life. And as I pronounced the last dæmoniac sentence I heard afar on the moor the faint baying of some gigantic hound. The moon was up, but I dared not look at it. And when I saw on the dim-litten moor a wide nebulous shadow sweeping from mound to mound, I shut my eyes and threw myself face down upon the ground. When I arose trembling, I know not how much later, I staggered into the house and made shocking obeisances before the enshrined amulet of green jade.

Being now afraid to live alone in the ancient house on the moor, I departed on the following day for London, taking with me the amulet after destroying by fire and burial the rest of the impious collection in the museum. But after three nights I heard the baying again, and before a week was over felt strange eyes upon me whenever it was dark. One evening as I strolled on Victoria Embankment[18] for some needed air, I saw a black shape obscure one of the reflections of the lamps in the water. A wind stronger than the night-wind rushed by, and I knew that what had befallen St. John must soon befall me.

The next day I carefully wrapped the green jade amulet and sailed for Holland. What mercy I might gain by returning the thing to its silent, sleeping owner I knew not; but I felt that I must at least try any step conceivably logical. What the hound was, and why it pursued me, were questions still vague; but I had first heard the baying in that ancient churchyard, and every subsequent event including St. John's dying whisper had served to connect the curse with the stealing of the amulet. Accordingly I sank into the nethermost abysses of despair when, at an inn in Rotterdam, I discovered that thieves had despoiled me of this sole means of salvation.

The baying was loud that evening, and in the morning I read of a nameless deed in the vilest quarter of the city. The rabble were in terror, for upon an evil tenement had fallen a red death[19] beyond the foulest previous crime of the neighbourhood. In a squalid thieves' den an entire family had been torn to shreds by an unknown thing which left no trace, and those around had heard all night above the usual clamour of drunken voices a faint, deep, insistent note as of a gigantic hound.

So at last I stood again in that unwholesome churchyard where a pale winter moon cast hideous shadows, and leafless trees drooped sullenly to meet the withered, frosty grass and cracking slabs, and the ivied church pointed a jeering finger at the unfriendly sky, and the night-wind howled maniacally from over frozen swamps and frigid seas. The baying was very faint now, and it ceased altogether as I approached the ancient grave I had

18. A walkway along the north bank of the Thames, built in 1865.

The Thames Embankment, late nineteenth century, showing a reproduction of the Sphinx statue which "guards" Cleopatra's Needle.

19. A phrase perhaps borrowed from Edgar Allan Poe's 1845 story "The Masque of the Red Death," in which death is inexorably brought about by plague.

20. Generally a synonym for Satan. Belial is referred to in 2 Corinthians 6:15 (King James Version): "And what concord hath Christ with Belial? or what part hath he that believeth with an infidel?"

once violated, and frightened away an abnormally large horde of bats which had been hovering curiously around it.

I know not why I went thither unless to pray, or gibber out insane pleas and apologies to the calm white thing that lay within; but, whatever my reason, I attacked the half-frozen sod with a desperation partly mine and partly that of a dominating will outside myself. Excavation was much easier than I expected, though at one point I encountered a queer interruption; when a lean vulture darted down out of the cold sky and pecked frantically at the grave-earth until I killed him with a blow of my spade. Finally I reached the rotting oblong box and removed the damp nitrous cover. This is the last rational act I ever performed.

For crouched within that centuried coffin, embraced by a close-packed nightmare retinue of huge, sinewy, sleeping bats, was the bony thing my friend and I had robbed; not clean and placid as we had seen it then, but covered with caked blood and shreds of alien flesh and hair, and leering sentiently at me with phosphorescent sockets and sharp ensanguined fangs yawning twistedly in mockery of my inevitable doom. And when it gave from those grinning jaws a deep, sardonic bay as of some gigantic hound, and I saw that it held in its gory filthy claw the lost and fateful amulet of green jade, I merely screamed and ran away idiotically, my screams soon dissolving into peals of hysterical laughter.

Madness rides the star-wind . . . claws and teeth sharpened on centuries of corpses . . . dripping death astride a bacchanale of bats from night-black ruins of buried temples of Belial[20] . . . Now, as the baying of that dead, fleshless monstrosity grows louder and louder, and the stealthy whirring and flapping of those accursed web-wings circles closer and closer, I shall seek with my revolver the oblivion which is my only refuge from the unnamed and unnamable.

The Festival[1]

*Kingsport is also the locale of "The Terrible Old Man," but there it was mere
backdrop. In "The Festival," the town reflects Lovecraft's fascination with
places such as Marblehead and Salem, Massachusetts, and their evocations of
antiquity. The religion described in this tale long predates the founding of those
towns and indeed predates Christianity. In that way, the story revisits the true
horror of "Dagon"—the narrator's discovery that there are things still present
on this planet that began before human history.*

Weird Tales 5, no. 1 (January 1925) (artist: Andrew Brosnatch)

*Efficiunt Dæmones, ut quæ non sunt, sic tamen
quasi sint, conspicienda hominibus exhibeant.*
—LACTANTIUS[2]

I was far from home, and the spell of the eastern sea was upon
me. In the twilight I heard it pounding on the rocks, and I
knew it lay just over the hill where the twisting willows
writhed against the clearing sky and the first stars of evening.
And because my fathers had called me to the old town beyond, I
pushed on through the shallow, new-fallen snow along the road

1. Probably written in October 1923, the
story first appeared in *Weird Tales* 5, no.
1 (January 1925), 169–74.

2. The writer and poet Lucius Caecilius
Firmianus Lacantius, or Lactantius (ca.
245–325 CE), presumed to have been

born in Numidia, North Africa (then a Libyan kingdom, it now straddles Algeria and Tunisia), taught rhetoric and Latin in both Nicomedia, Greece, where he was raised, and, later, in Trier, Germany. He was a convert from paganism to Christianity, and his life was marked by penury. The sentence is translated by Cotton Mather in his *Magnalia Christi Americana; or, The Ecclesiastical History of New-England* (1702; see "The Picture in the House," note 12): "It is one of the chief arts of evil spirits, to make things which have no reality seem real to those who witness them." Cotton Mather borrowed this from *Cases of Conscience Concerning Evil Spirits Personating Men* (1693), a work by his father, Increase Mather. However, Dennis Quinn, in "Endless Bacchanal: Rome, Livy, and Lovecraft's Cthulhu Cult," casts doubt on the Lactantian source: "[It] may be more correct to say that it is a quotation from Increase Mather misquoting Lactantius. . . .'"

3. Aldebaran, or Alpha Tauri, is the brightest star in the constellation Taurus (the Bull) and one of the brighter stars in the northern sky. Orange-yellow in color, it is a "red giant" in age. According to Richard Hinkley Allen (*Star Names: Their Lore and Meaning*, 1899), the name means "the follower." "Aldebaran was the divine star in the worship of the tribe Misām, who thought that it brought rain, and that its heliacal rising unattended by showers portended a barren year."

4. The winter solstice, the day on which the earth's axis tilts farthest away from the Sun (and hence the shortest day of the year), occurs in the Northern Hemisphere on December 21 or 22, and adherents of pagan religions may have celebrated the day. Certainly, the Yule or Yuletide is associated with pagan Scandinavians and is mentioned in the *Prose Edda*; however, its antiquity is uncertain.

that soared lonely up to where Aldebaran[3] twinkled among the trees; on toward the very ancient town I had never seen but often dreamed of.

It was the Yuletide, that men call Christmas though they know in their hearts it is older than Bethlehem and Babylon, older than Memphis and mankind.[4] It was the Yuletide, and I had come at last to the ancient sea town where my people had dwelt and kept festival in the elder time when festival was forbidden; where also they had commanded their sons to keep festival once every century, that the memory of primal secrets might not be forgotten. Mine were an old people, and were old even when this land was settled three hundred years before. And they were strange, because they had come as dark furtive folk from opiate southern gardens of orchids,[5] and spoken another tongue before they learnt the tongue of the blue-eyed fishers.[6] And now they were scattered, and shared only the rituals of mysteries that none living could understand. I was the only one who came back that night to the old fishing town as legend bade, for only the poor and the lonely remember.

Then beyond the hill's crest I saw Kingsport[7] outspread frostily in the gloaming; snowy Kingsport with its ancient vanes and steeples, ridgepoles and chimney-pots, wharves and small bridges, willow-trees and graveyards; endless labyrinths of steep, narrow, crooked streets, and dizzy church-crowned central peak[8] that time durst not touch; ceaseless mazes of colonial houses piled and scattered at all angles and levels like a child's disordered blocks; antiquity hovering on grey wings over winter-whitened gables and gambrel roofs; fanlights and small-paned windows one by one gleaming out in the cold dusk to join Orion and the archaic stars. And against the rotting wharves the sea pounded; the secretive, immemorial sea out of which the people had come in the elder time.[9]

Beside the road at its crest a still higher summit rose, bleak and windswept, and I saw that it was a burying-ground where black gravestones stuck ghoulishly through the snow like the decayed fingernails of a gigantic corpse.[10] The printless road was very lonely, and sometimes I thought I heard a distant horrible creaking as of a gibbet in the wind. They had hanged four kinsmen of mine for witchcraft in 1692, but I did not know just where.[11]

As the road wound down the seaward slope I listened for the merry sounds of a village at evening, but did not hear them. Then I thought of the season, and felt that these old Puritan folk might well have Christmas customs strange to me,[12] and full of silent hearthside prayer. So after that I did not listen for merriment or look for wayfarers, but kept on down past the hushed lighted farmhouses and shadowy stone walls to where the signs of ancient shops and sea-taverns creaked in the salt breeze, and the grotesque knockers of pillared doorways glistened along deserted, unpaved lanes in the light of little, curtained windows.

I had seen maps of the town, and knew where to find the home of my people.[13] It was told that I should be known and welcomed, for village legend lives long; so I hastened through Back Street to Circle Court,[14] and across the fresh snow on the one full flagstone pavement in the town, to where Green Lane leads off behind the Market house. The old maps still held good, and I had no trouble; though at Arkham they must have lied when they said the trolleys ran to this place, since I saw not a wire overhead. Snow would have hid the rails in any case. I was glad I had chosen to walk, for the white village had seemed very beautiful from the hill; and now I was eager to knock at the door of my people, the seventh house on the left in Green Lane, with an ancient peaked roof and jutting second story, all built before 1650.

There were lights inside the house when I came upon it, and I saw from the diamond window-panes that it must have been kept very close to its antique state. The upper part overhung the narrow grass-grown street and nearly met the overhanging part of the house opposite, so that I was almost in a tunnel, with the low stone doorstep wholly free from snow. There was no sidewalk, but many houses had high doors reached by double flights of steps with iron railings. It was an odd scene, and because I was strange to New England I had never known its like before. Though it pleased me, I would have relished it better if there had been footprints in the snow, and people in the streets, and a few windows without drawn curtains.

When I sounded the archaic iron knocker I was half afraid. Some fear had been gathering in me, perhaps because of the strangeness of my heritage, and the bleakness of the evening, and

5. The phrase is not very helpful in determining the origin of these "dark furtive folk": Orchids are found worldwide, although most species originate in the tropics.

6. The first settlers of New England were English Protestants; these were followed by Canadians, Irish, Italian, and East European immigrants.

7. Many scholars, including S. T. Joshi, identify Kingsport as Marblehead, Massachusetts, and Lovecraft himself noted the identification. See "The Picture in the House," note 7, above. First settled by British colonists in the early seventeenth century, Marblehead has been a fishing port and a launching point for privateers and clipper ships and claims the title of birthplace of the American navy. For a good overview of the points of identification, see Donovan K. Loucks's "Antique Dreams: Marblehead and Lovecraft's Kingsport." However, Salem, Massachusetts, also shares some of the traits of Kingsport (see note 11, below).

8. There is no "peak" in Marblehead; its highest elevation is 42 meters (138 feet) above sea level.

9. As we shall see, the narrator doesn't mean that "the people" arrived in Marblehead by sea; he means that the people originally lived *under* the sea.

10. Almost certainly Old Burial Hill in Marblehead, at the intersection of Orne and Pond streets, founded around 1638.

11. The Salem witch trials of 1692 resulted in nineteen hangings, fourteen women and five men (one additional man, who refused to speak at his trial, was executed by the medieval method of *peine forte et dure*, pressing with heavy rocks). Surprisingly, the exact location of the hangings

is controversial. The official Gallows Hill Park in Salem, at the location which Rev. Charles Upham named as the site of the hangings in his 1867 book *Salem Witchcraft*, has been rejected by many historians as an incorrect identification. The most likely site, credibly asserted by historian Sidney Perley in his 1921 *History of Salem, Massachusetts*, appears to be a hill at the junction of Boston, Bridge, and Proctor streets in Salem. See http://www.boudillion.com/gallowshill/gallowshill.htm for additional photographs. The historical records agree that the hangings did not take place on a gallows; rather, the convicted were hanged from the branches of trees. Note that there were no witch trials in Marblehead, although one victim, Wilmot Redd, is buried there.

The highest point in Marblehead, Massachusetts, is Abbot Hall, atop Windmill Hill, shown here in 2013. Photograph copyright © Donovan K. Loucks 2013, reprinted with permission

12. S. T. Joshi explains, "The Christian holiday is a mere veneer for a much older

the queerness of the silence in that aged town of curious customs. And when my knock was answered I was fully afraid, because I had not heard any footsteps before the door creaked open. But I was not afraid long, for the gowned, slippered old man in the doorway had a bland face that reassured me; and though he made signs that he was dumb, he wrote a quaint and ancient welcome with the stylus and wax tablet he carried.

He beckoned me into a low, candle-lit room with massive exposed rafters and dark, stiff, sparse furniture of the seventeenth century. The past was vivid there, for not an attribute was missing. There was a cavernous fireplace and a spinning-wheel at which a bent old woman in loose wrapper and deep poke-bonnet[15] sat back toward me, silently spinning despite the festive season. An indefinite dampness seemed upon the place, and I marvelled that no fire should be blazing. The high-backed settle[16] faced the row of curtained windows at the left, and seemed to be occupied, though I was not sure. I did not like everything about what I saw, and felt again the fear I had had. This fear grew stronger from what had before lessened it, for the more I looked at the old man's bland face the more its very blandness terrified me. The eyes never moved, and the skin was too like wax. Finally I was sure it was not a face at all, but a fiendishly cunning mask. But the flabby hands, curiously gloved, wrote genially on the tablet and told me I must wait a while before I could be led to the place of festival.

Pointing to a chair, table, and pile of books, the old man now left the room; and when I sat down to read I saw that the books were hoary and mouldy, and that they included old Morryster's wild *Marvells of Science*,[17] the terrible *Saducismus Triumphatus* of Joseph Glanvill, published in 1681,[18] the shocking *Dæmonolatreia* of Remigius,[19] printed in 1595 at Lyons, and worst of all, the unmentionable *Necronomicon* of the mad Arab Abdul Alhazred, in Olaus Wormius' forbidden Latin translation;[20] a book which I had never seen, but of which I had heard monstrous things whispered. No one spoke to me, but I could hear the creaking of signs in the wind outside, and the whir of the wheel as the bonneted old woman continued her silent spinning, spinning. I thought the room and the books and the people very morbid and disquieting, but because an old tradition of my fathers had summoned me to strange feastings, I resolved to expect queer things. So I tried to read, and soon became tremblingly absorbed by something I found in that accursed *Necronomicon*; a thought and a legend too hideous for sanity or consciousness. But I disliked it when I fancied I heard the closing of one of the windows that the settle faced, as if it had been stealthily opened. It had seemed to follow a whirring that was not of the old woman's spinning-wheel. This was not much, though, for the old woman was spinning very hard, and the aged clock had been striking. After that I lost the feeling that there were persons on the settle, and was reading intently and shudderingly when the old man came back booted and dressed in a loose antique costume, and sat down on that very bench, so that I could not see him. It was certainly nervous waiting, and the blasphemous book in my hands made it doubly so. When eleven struck, however, the old man stood up, glided to a massive carved chest in a corner, and got two hooded cloaks; one of which he donned, and the other of which he draped round the old woman, who was ceasing her monotonous spinning. Then they both started for the outer door; the woman lamely creeping, and the old man, after picking up the very book I had been reading, beckoning me as he drew his hood over that unmoving face or mask.

We went out into the moonless and tortuous network of that incredibly ancient town; went out as the lights in the curtained windows disappeared one by one, and the Dog Star[21] leered at the throng of cowled, cloaked figures that poured silently from every doorway and formed monstrous processions up this street and that, past the creaking signs and antediluvian gables, the thatched roofs and diamond-paned windows; threading precipitous lanes where decaying houses overlapped and crumbled together, gliding across open courts and churchyards where the bobbing lanthorns[22] made eldritch drunken constellations.

Amid these hushed throngs I followed my voiceless guides; jostled by elbows that seemed preternaturally soft, and pressed by chests and stomachs that seemed abnormally pulpy; but seeing never a face and hearing never a word. Up, up, up the eerie columns slithered, and I saw that all the travellers were converging as they flowed near a sort of focus of crazy alleys at the top of a high hill in the centre of the town, where perched a great white

festival that reaches back to the agricultural rhythms of primitive man—the winter solstice, whose passing foretells the eventual reawakening of the earth in spring" (*I Am Providence*, 462).

13. Philip A. Shreffler, in *The H. P. Lovecraft Companion* (67), suggests that this is the William Waters/Nathan Bowen house (1695), at 1 Mugsford Street, but the evidence is thin, and several points of description fail to match.

14. There is no Back Street or Circle Court; however, *Front* Street and Circle *Street* meet in Marblehead, and there is a Green Street, but not nearby. There is also no building known as the "Market House"; however, not far from the intersection of Front and Circle streets is Market Square, near Town House Square, where the Old Town House stands; its first story was used as a market.

15. A woman's hood-shaped bonnet with a projecting rim.

16. A long high-backed wooden bench, usually with storage beneath the seat.

17. First mentioned in Ambrose Bierce's "The Man and the Snake" (which first appeared in the *San Francisco Examiner*, June 29, 1890): "'It is of veritabyll report, and attested of so many that there be nowe of wyse and learned none to gaynsaye it, that ye serpente hys eye hath a magnetick propertie that whosoe falleth into its svasion is drawn forwards in despyte of his wille, and perisheth miserabyll by ye creature hys byte.'

"Stretched at ease upon a sofa, in gown and slippers, Harker Brayton smiled as he read the foregoing sentence in old Morryster's 'Marvells of Science': 'The only marvel in the matter,' he said to himself, 'is that the wise and learned in Morryster's day should have believed such nonsense as is rejected by most of even the ignorant in ours.'"

18. A book on witchcraft, adducing evidence of its reality. Glanvill (1636–1680) was a clergyman and, although not a scientist himself, an apologist for the natural philosophers of the day; this work was published posthumously. Cotton Mather's *Wonders of the Invisible World* (1693), an account of the Salem witch trials, evidences familiarity with the book and in particular its account of earlier Swedish witch trials.

19. French magistrate Nicolas Remy (1530–1616), also known as Remigius, wrote *Dæmonolatreiæ Libri Tres* (Demonolatry in Three Books), a manual for witch-hunters that eventually replaced the *Malleus Maleficarum*

church.[23] I had seen it from the road's crest when I looked at Kingsport in the new dusk, and it had made me shiver because Aldebaran had seemed to balance itself a moment on the ghostly spire.

There was an open space around the church; partly a churchyard with spectral shafts, and partly a half-paved square swept nearly bare of snow by the wind, and lined with unwholesomely archaic houses having peaked roofs and overhanging gables. Death-fires[24] danced over the tombs, revealing gruesome vistas, though queerly failing to cast any shadows. Past the churchyard, where there were no houses, I could see over the hill's summit and watch the glimmer of stars on the harbour, though the town was invisible in the dark. Only once in a while a lanthorn bobbed horribly through serpentine alleys on its way to overtake the throng that was now slipping speechlessly into the church. I waited till the crowd had oozed into the black doorway, and till all the stragglers had followed. The old man was pulling at my

Old Burial Hill in Marblehead, Massachusetts, in 2013, the probable model for the Kingsport cemetery.
Photograph copyright © Donovan K. Loucks 2013, reprinted with permission

St. Michael's Church in Marblehead, Massachusetts. Artist: Jason C. Eckhardt, copyright © Jason C. Eckhardt 2013, reprinted with permission

sleeve, but I was determined to be the last. Then I finally went, the sinister man and the old spinning woman before me. Crossing the threshold into that swarming temple of unknown darkness, I turned once to look at the outside world as the churchyard phosphorescence cast a sickly glow on the hill-top pavement. And as I did so I shuddered. For though the wind had not left much snow, a few patches did remain on the path near the door; and in that fleeting backward look it seemed to my troubled eyes that they bore no mark of passing feet, not even mine.[25]

The church was scarce lighted by all the lanthorns that had entered it, for most of the throng had already vanished. They had streamed up the aisle between the high white pews to the trapdoor of the vaults which yawned loathsomely open just before the pulpit, and were now squirming noiselessly in. I followed dumbly down the footworn steps and into the dank, suffocating crypt. The tail of that sinuous line of night-marchers seemed very horrible, and as I saw them wriggling into a venerable tomb they seemed more horrible still. Then I noticed that the tomb's floor had an aperture down which the throng was sliding, and

as the standard work. The Demonolatry included accounts of the capital trials of some nine hundred individuals in Lorraine, France, who, over a fifteen-year period, received the death penalty for commission of the crime of witchcraft.

20. Ole Worm (1588–1655), a Danish physician and scholar, used the Latinized name Olaus Wormius. He was an early embryologist. In "The Dunwich Horror" (pp. 343–87, below), it is recorded that Worm's translation was printed in Spain in the seventeenth century.

21. Sirius, the Dog Star, also known as Al Shira and Canicula, is among the nearest stars to Earth and the brightest in the sky. Technically, Alpha Canis Majoris is a double star, part of the Canis Major constellation, the large dog following Orion the hunter (and near the constellation of Orion). The name σειρίους, given by the early Greek authors, meant "bright and sparkly" and, according to Allen's *Star Names*, was applied to any bright and sparkling heavenly object but eventually became a proper name for this star. Sirius has long been the subject of worship and is found identified in Chaldean, Babylonian, and Egyptian records. However, it is not associated with the Yuletide or winter solstice.

T. R. Livesey, in "Dispatches from the Providence Observatory" (43–44), notes that the astronomical data regarding the time of sunset, the absence of the moon, and the elevation of Sirius is consistent with a date of December 17, 1922 (the new moon occurred only a few minutes later, at 12:20).

22. An archaic form of the word "lanterns." This is the only story in this volume in which the word appears in that form, and by using it, the narrator has nicely evoked the age of Kingsport

(or perhaps revealed something about his own age).

23. Identified by Philip A. Shreffler (in his *The H. P. Lovecraft Companion*, 67) as St. Michael's Episcopal Church (1714), at 13 Summer Street in Marblehead; however, St. Michael's, while it has the requisite crypt, lacks a clock tower and a "half-paved square." This may well have been the First Meeting House (1648, on Old Burial Hill) or the Second Congregational Church on Mugford Street (1715). Donovan Loucks, in "Antique Dreams: Marblehead and Lovecraft's Kingsport," argues for one of the Congregational churches in Marblehead.

Das Irrlicht by Arnold Böcklin (1862), depicting a will-o'-the-wisp.

24. Presumably will-o'-the-wisps, also known as corpse candles, corpse lights, and by countless other names. Coleridge describes death-fires in Part III of "The Rime of the Ancient Mariner" (1798).

25. This makes no sense. We're prepared for the lack of others' footprints (no

in a moment we were all descending an ominous staircase of rough-hewn stone; a narrow spiral staircase damp and peculiarly odorous, that wound endlessly down into the bowels of the hill past monotonous walls of dripping stone blocks and crumbling mortar. It was a silent, shocking descent, and I observed after a horrible interval that the walls and steps were changing in nature, as if chiselled out of the solid rock. What mainly troubled me was that the myriad footfalls made no sound and set up no echoes. After more æons of descent I saw some side passages or burrows leading from unknown recesses of blackness to this shaft of nighted mystery. Soon they became excessively numerous, like impious catacombs of nameless menace; and their pungent odour of decay grew quite unbearable. I knew we must have passed down through the mountain and beneath the earth of Kingsport itself, and I shivered that a town should be so aged and maggoty with subterraneous evil.

Then I saw the lurid shimmering of pale light, and heard the insidious lapping of sunless waters. Again I shivered, for I did not like the things that the night had brought, and wished bitterly that no forefather had summoned me to this primal rite. As the steps and the passage grew broader, I heard another sound, the thin, whining mockery of a feeble flute; and suddenly there spread out before me the boundless vista of an inner world—a vast fungous[26] shore litten by a belching column of sick greenish flame and washed by a wide oily river that flowed from abysses frightful and unsuspected to join the blackest gulfs of immemorial ocean.

Fainting and gasping, I looked at that unhallowed Erebus[27] of titan toadstools, leprous fire,[28] and slimy water, and saw the cloaked throngs forming a semicircle around the blazing pillar. It was the Yule-rite, older than man and fated to survive him; the primal rite of the solstice and of spring's promise beyond the snows; the rite of fire and evergreen, light and music. And in the Stygian grotto I saw them do the rite, and adore the sick pillar of flame, and throw into the water handfuls gouged out of the viscous vegetation which glittered green[29] in the chlorotic[30] glare. I saw this, and I saw something amorphously squatted far away from the light, piping noisomely on a flute; and as the thing piped I thought I heard noxious muffled flutterings in the fœtid darkness where I could not see. But what frightened me most was that flaming column; spouting volcanically from depths profound and inconceivable, casting no shadows as healthy flame should, and coating the nitrous stone above with a nasty, venomous verdigris. For in all that seething combustion no warmth lay, but only the clamminess of death and corruption.

The man who had brought me now squirmed to a point directly beside the hideous flame, and made stiff ceremonial motions to the semicircle he faced. At certain stages of the ritual they did grovelling obeisance, especially when he held above his head that abhorrent *Necronomicon* he had taken with him; and I shared all the obeisances because I had been summoned to this festival by the writings of my forefathers. Then the old man made a signal to the half-seen flute-player in the darkness, which player thereupon changed its feeble drone to a scarce louder drone in another key; precipitating as it did so a horror unthinkable and unexpected. At this horror I sank nearly to the lichened earth, transfixed with a dread not of this nor any world, but only of the mad spaces between the stars.

Out of the unimaginable blackness beyond the gangrenous glare of that cold flame, out of the Tartarean leagues through which that oily river rolled uncanny, unheard, and unsuspected, there flopped rhythmically a horde of tame, trained, hybrid winged things that no sound eye could ever wholly grasp, or sound brain ever wholly remember. They were not altogether crows, nor moles, nor buzzards, nor ants, nor vampire bats, nor decomposed human beings; but something I cannot and must not recall. They flopped limply along, half with their webbed feet and half with their membraneous wings; and as they reached the throng of celebrants the cowled figures seized and mounted them, and rode off one by one along the reaches of that unlighted river, into pits and galleries of panic where poison springs feed frightful and undiscoverable cataracts.[31]

The old spinning woman had gone with the throng, and the old man remained only because I had refused when he motioned me to seize an animal and ride like the rest. I saw when I staggered to my feet that the amorphous flute-player had rolled out of sight, but that two of the beasts were patiently standing by. As I hung back, the old man produced his stylus and tablet and

sounds as the old man approaches the door of his own house, no footprints in the snow outside the houses), but why would the narrator's own footprints not show? Later, we learn more about the kinship of the narrator and the villagers, but it seems reasonable to expect that the narrator would have noticed earlier that he himself leaves no footprints.

26. The narrator apparently means the word literally—covered with fungi—rather than employing its figurative meaning of "appearing suddenly like mushrooms." See the sentence following. The geography described here is startling: The narrator ascends the highest hill in Kingsport and then descends a very long staircase, only to come out on a vast ocean shore fed by a wide river that derives from underground sources. This suggests that the town of Kingsport—which is on the edge of the sea—is essentially an enormous thin dome over ocean waters.

27. Brewer describes Erebus as "[t]he gloomy cavern underground through which the Shades had to walk in their passage to Hades" (424).

28. The narrator uses the term "leprous" in a very loose fashion, probably meaning "unnatural," apparently to emphasize the "sick greenish" color of the flames; there is certainly nothing in the symptoms of leprosy that could be characteristic of a fire.

29. The glittering green "viscous" vegetation, a form of lichen, apparently grows on the shore, amid the mushrooms. Lichen are composite organisms of fungi and algæ and thrive on virtually any surface.

30. Another great word for a sickly green color.

31. So the river comes up out of the depths, and these creatures come out of the same opening. The participants in the festivities mount them and go down into the depths.

32. There is no "Orange Point" in Marblehead or Salem, but there is a "Peach Point" in the former.

33. Whose prints? See note 25, above.

34. In contrast to the narrator's earlier observation of Kingsport as a sea of ancient structures, with no sign of automobiles or any modern transport.

35. Also mentioned in "The Unnamable," at note 16, below.

36. This is the first indication that a copy of the *Necronomicon* is among the university's holdings. This copy will be central to the story of "The Dunwich Horror," (pp. 343–87, below).

wrote that he was the true deputy of my fathers who had founded the Yule worship in this ancient place; that it had been decreed I should come back, and that the most secret mysteries were yet to be performed. He wrote this in a very ancient hand, and when I still hesitated he pulled from his loose robe a seal ring and a watch, both with my family arms, to prove that he was what he said. But it was a hideous proof, because I knew from old papers that that watch had been buried with my great-great-great-great-grandfather in 1698.

Presently the old man drew back his hood and pointed to the family resemblance in his face, but I only shuddered, because I was sure that the face was merely a devilish waxen mask. The flopping animals were now scratching restlessly at the lichens, and I saw that the old man was nearly as restless himself. When one of the things began to waddle and edge away, he turned quickly to stop it; so that the suddenness of his motion dislodged the waxen mask from what should have been his head. And then, because that nightmare's position barred me from the stone staircase down which we had come, I flung myself into the oily underground river that bubbled somewhere to the caves of the sea; flung myself into that putrescent juice of earth's inner horrors before the madness of my screams could bring down upon me all the charnel legions these pest-gulfs might conceal.

At the hospital they told me I had been found half frozen in Kingsport Harbour at dawn, clinging to the drifting spar that accident sent to save me. They told me I had taken the wrong fork of the hill road the night before, and fallen over the cliffs at Orange Point;[32] a thing they deduced from prints found in the snow.[33] There was nothing I could say, because everything was wrong. Everything was wrong, with the broad window shewing a sea of roofs in which only about one in five was ancient, and the sound of trolleys and motors in the streets below.[34] They insisted that this was Kingsport, and I could not deny it. When I went delirious at hearing that the hospital stood near the old churchyard on Central Hill, they sent me to St. Mary's Hospital in Arkham,[35] where I could have better care. I liked it there, for the doctors were broad-minded, and even lent me their influence in obtaining the carefully sheltered copy of Alhazred's objectionable *Necronomicon* from the library of Miskatonic University.[36]

They said something about a "psychosis," and agreed I had better get any harassing obsessions off my mind.

So I read again that hideous chapter, and shuddered doubly because it was indeed not new to me. I had seen it before, let footprints tell what they might; and where it was I had seen it were best forgotten. There was no one—in waking hours—who could remind me of it; but my dreams are filled with terror, because of phrases I dare not quote. I dare quote only one paragraph, put into such English as I can make from the awkward Low Latin.

"The nethermost caverns," wrote the mad Arab, "are not for the fathoming of eyes that see; for their marvels are strange and terrific. Cursed the ground where dead thoughts live new and oddly bodied, and evil the mind that is held by no head. Wisely did Ibn Schacabao[37] say, that happy is the tomb where no wizard hath lain, and happy the town at night whose wizards are all ashes. For it is of old rumour that the soul of the devil-bought hastes not from his charnel clay, but fats and instructs *the very worm that gnaws*; till out of corruption horrid life springs, and the dull scavengers of earth wax crafty to vex it and swell monstrous to plague it. Great holes secretly are digged where earth's pores ought to suffice, and things have learnt to walk that ought to crawl."

37. The name "Ibn Schacabao" is mentioned again in *The Case of Charles Dexter Ward*, note 135, below. "Schacabao" is not a proper Arabic name, and the suggestion has been made that it is a corruption of *Ibn Shayk Abol* (Son of the Sheik Abol) or *Ibn Mushacab* (Son of the Dweller; *shacab* means to sit or dwell). It may also be derived from the Hebrew *shakhabh* (a sexual term connoting homosexuality or bestiality); or it may be a corruption of the Arabic name Schacabac—a poor man who appears in the tale "The Barmecide's Feast" recorded in *The Arabian Nights*.

The Unnamable[1]

"The Unnamable" reads more like a treatise on Lovecraft's view of supernaturalism and its literature than a story. Setting the tale firmly in New England, however, and much like a great winemaker, Lovecraft creates typicity—the evocation of a specific location, in this case perhaps a real cemetery. The story also features Carter, probably the same person as Randolph Carter, so often identified with Lovecraft himself. This Carter, however, is of quite a different temperament than the bold chronicler of "The Statement" and nothing like the dreamy narrator of "The Silver Key." The better view is probably that Lovecraft used the name Carter from time to time to speak of certain aspects of his mind and—like most of us—never quite grasped his own contradictions.

1. The story first appeared in *Weird Tales* 6, no. 1 (July 1925), 78–82, and was written in September 1923.

Poster from *The Unnamable* (1988).

We were sitting on a dilapidated seventeenth-century tomb in the late afternoon of an autumn day at the old burying-ground in Arkham, and speculating about the unnamable. Looking toward the giant willow in the centre of the cemetery, whose trunk has nearly engulfed an ancient, illegible slab, I had made a fantastic remark about the spectral and unmentionable nourishment which the colossal roots must be sucking in from that hoary, charnel earth; when my friend chided me for such nonsense and told me that since no interments had occurred there for over a century, nothing could possibly exist to nourish the tree in other than an ordinary manner. Besides, he added, my constant talk about "unnamable" and "unmentionable" things was a very puerile device, quite in keeping with my lowly standing as an author. I was too fond of ending my stories with sights or sounds which paralysed my heroes' faculties and left them without courage, words, or associations to tell what they had experienced. We know things, he said, only through our five senses or our religious intuitions; wherefore it is quite impossible to refer to any object or spectacle which cannot be clearly depicted by the solid definitions of fact or the correct doctrines of theology—preferably those of the Congregationalists, with whatever modifications tradition and Sir Arthur Conan Doyle may supply.[2]

With this friend, Joel Manton, I had often languidly disputed. He was principal of the East High School, born and bred in Boston and sharing New England's self-satisfied deafness to the delicate overtones of life. It was his view that only our normal, objective experiences possess any æsthetic significance, and that it is the province of the artist not so much to rouse strong emotion by action, ecstasy, and astonishment, as to maintain a placid interest and appreciation by accurate, detailed transcripts of every-day affairs. Especially did he object to my preoccupation with the mystical and the unexplained; for although believing in the supernatural much more fully than I, he would not admit that it is sufficiently commonplace for literary treatment. That a mind can find its greatest pleasure in escapes from the daily treadmill, and in original and dramatic recombinations of images usually thrown by habit and fatigue into the hackneyed patterns of actual existence, was something virtually incredible to his clear, practical, and logical intellect. With him all things and feelings had fixed dimensions, properties, causes, and effects; and although he vaguely knew that the mind sometimes holds visions and sensations of far less geometrical, classifiable, and workable nature, he believed himself justified in drawing an arbitrary line and ruling out of court all that cannot be experienced and understood by the average citizen. Besides, he was almost sure that nothing can be really "unnamable." It didn't sound sensible to him.

Though I well realised the futility of imaginative and metaphysical arguments against the complacency of an orthodox sun-dweller, something in the scene of this afternoon colloquy moved me to more than usual contentiousness. The crumbling slate slabs, the patriarchal trees, and the centuried gambrel roofs of the witch-haunted old town[3] that stretched around, all combined to rouse my spirit in defence of my work; and I was soon carrying my thrusts into the enemy's own country. It was not, indeed, difficult to begin a counter-attack, for I knew that

2. This presumably refers to Conan Doyle's public embrace of Spiritualism, which occurred in 1887. Spiritualism, although greatly misunderstood today, was a serious effort to put religion, and all matters regarded as pertaining to the afterlife, within the framework of science rather than faith. Congregationalism is a body of independent churches (independent, that is, from the Protestant, Episcopalian, Baptist, and Catholic churches).

3. The town is not named but may be Marblehead, Massachusetts. In "The Silver Key" (pp. 158–70, below), Carter is to be found in Kingsport, which S. T. Joshi identifies as Marblehead (see "The Festival," note 7, above). However, "witch-haunted" Salem seems equally likely, and in a letter in 1927, Lovecraft pointed out "an ancient slab half engulfed by a giant willow in the middle of the Charles St. Burying Ground in Salem" (Lovecraft to Bernard Austin Dwyer, June 1927, *Selected Letters*, II, 139).

4. In the same 1927 letter (see note 3, above), Lovecraft reported that the "genuine old New England superstition . . . —that one about the faces of past generations becoming fixed on windows was told to me *and believed* by a highly intelligent old lady who has a successful novel and other important literary work to her credit."

Charter Burial Ground, Salem, Massachusetts, in 2013. Photograph copyright © Donovan K. Loucks 2013, reprinted with permission

Joel Manton actually half clung to many old-wives' superstitions which sophisticated people had long outgrown; beliefs in the appearance of dying persons at distant places, and in the impressions left by old faces on the windows through which they had gazed all their lives.[4] To credit these whisperings of rural grandmothers, I now insisted, argued a faith in the existence of spectral substances on the earth apart from and subsequent to their material counterparts. It argued a capability of believing in phenomena beyond all normal notions; for if a dead man can transmit his visible or tangible image half across the world, or down the stretch of the centuries, how can it be absurd to suppose that deserted houses are full of queer sentient things, or that old graveyards teem with the terrible, unbodied intelligence of generations? And since spirit, in order to cause all the manifestations attributed to it, cannot be limited by any of the laws of matter; why is it extravagant to imagine psychically living dead things in shapes—or absences of shapes—which must for human spectators be utterly and appallingly "unnamable"? "Common sense" in reflecting on these subjects, I assured my friend with some warmth, is merely a stupid absence of imagination and mental flexibility.

Twilight had now approached, but neither of us felt any wish to cease speaking. Manton seemed unimpressed by my arguments, and eager to refute them, having that confidence in his own opinions which had doubtless caused his success as a teacher; whilst I was too sure of my ground to fear defeat. The dusk fell, and lights faintly gleamed in some of the distant windows, but we did not move. Our seat on the tomb was very comfortable, and I knew that my prosaic friend would not mind the cavernous rift in the ancient, root-disturbed brickwork close behind us, or the utter blackness of the spot brought by the intervention of a tottering, deserted seventeenth-century house between us and the nearest lighted road. There in the dark, upon that riven tomb by the deserted house, we talked on about the "unnamable" and after my friend had finished his scoffing I told him of the awful evidence behind the story at which he had scoffed the most.

My tale had been called "The Attic Window," and appeared in the January, 1922, issue of *Whispers*.[5] In a good many places, especially the South and the Pacific coast, they took the magazines off the stands at the complaints of silly milksops;[6] but New England didn't get the thrill and merely shrugged its shoulders at my extravagance. The thing, it was averred, was biologically impossible to start with; merely another of those crazy country mutterings which Cotton Mather had been gullible enough to dump into his chaotic *Magnalia Christi Americana*,[7] and so poorly authenticated that even he had not ventured to name the locality where the horror occurred. And as to the way I amplified the bare jotting of the old mystic—that was quite impossible, and characteristic of a flighty and notional scribbler! Mather had indeed told of the thing as being born, but nobody but a cheap sensationalist would think of having it grow up, look into people's houses at night, and be hidden in the attic of a house, in flesh and in spirit, till someone saw it at the window centuries later and couldn't describe what it was that turned his hair grey. All this was flagrant trashiness, and my friend Manton was not slow to insist on that fact. Then I told him what I had found in an old diary kept between 1706 and 1723, unearthed among family papers not a mile from where we were sitting; that, and the certain reality of the scars on my ancestor's chest and back which the diary described. I told him, too, of the fears of others in that region, and how they were whispered down for generations; and how no mythical madness came to the boy who in

5. Life imitates art: *Whispers* began its life as a magazine in the 1970s, named after this suggestion.

6. Carter's work share the fate of C. M. Eddy's story "The Loved Dead," which appeared in the May–June–July issue of *Weird Tales* and suffered similar suppression.

7. Published in 1702; see "The Picture in the House," note 12, above.

8. See "The Hound," note 2, above.

9. The sixth book of Mather's *Magnalia Christi Americana* is "Remarkables of the Divine Providence, Among the People of New-England," and the relevant chapter is "Thaumatographia Pneumatica" (Wonders of the Spirit World), with this subtitle "Relating the Wonders of the Invisible World in Preternatural Occurrences."

10. That is, a denunciation.

11. Traditionally, the Jewish prophets are Abraham, Moses, Miriam, Isaiah, Samuel, Ezekiel, Malachi, and Job, as well as the later seers Haggai, Zechariah, and Malachi. Daniel is not termed a prophet. Modern scholar Abraham Joshua Heschel, in *The Prophets*, argues that "[p]rophecy is the voice that God has lent to the silent agony, a voice to the plundered poor, to the profane riches of the world. It is a form of living, a crossing point of God and man. God is raging in the prophet's words (5–6)."

12. The split or cloven hoof is a physical characteristic of deer and goats but is also traditionally associated with the devil.

1793 entered an abandoned house to examine certain traces suspected to be there.

It had been an eldritch[8] thing—no wonder sensitive students shudder at the Puritan age in Massachusetts. So little is known of what went on beneath the surface—so little, yet such a ghastly festering as it bubbles up putrescently in occasional ghoulish glimpses. The witchcraft terror is a horrible ray of light on what was stewing in men's crushed brains, but even that is a trifle. There was no beauty; no freedom—we can see that from the architectural and household remains, and the poisonous sermons of the cramped divines. And inside that rusted iron strait-jacket lurked gibbering hideousness, perversion, and diabolism. Here, truly, was the apotheosis of the unnamable.

Cotton Mather, in that dæmoniac sixth book which no one should read after dark,[9] minced no words as he flung forth his anathema.[10] Stern as a Jewish prophet,[11] and laconically unamazed as none since his day could be, he told of the beast that had brought forth what was more than beast but less than man—the thing with the blemished eye—and of the screaming drunken wretch that they hanged for having such an eye. This much he baldly told, yet without a hint of what came after. Perhaps he did not know, or perhaps he knew and did not dare to tell. Others knew, but did not dare to tell—there is no public hint of why they whispered about the lock on the door to the attic stairs in the house of a childless, broken, embittered old man who had put up a blank slate slab by an avoided grave, although one may trace enough evasive legends to curdle the thinnest blood.

It is all in that ancestral diary I found; all the hushed innuendoes and furtive tales of things with a blemished eye seen at windows in the night or in deserted meadows near the woods. Something had caught my ancestor on a dark valley road, leaving him with marks of horns on his chest and of ape-like claws on his back; and when they looked for prints in the trampled dust they found the mixed marks of split hooves[12] and vaguely anthropoid paws. Once a post-rider said he saw an old man chasing and calling to a frightful loping, nameless thing on Meadow Hill in the thinly moonlit hours before dawn, and many believed him. Certainly, there was strange talk one night in 1710 when the childless, broken old man was buried in the crypt behind his own house in sight of the blank slate slab. They never unlocked that attic door, but left the whole house as it was, dreaded and deserted. When noises came from it, they whispered and shivered; and hoped that the lock on that attic door was strong. Then they stopped hoping when the horror occurred at the parsonage, leaving not a soul alive or in one piece. With the years the legends take on a spectral character—I suppose the thing, if it was a living thing, must have died. The memory had lingered hideously—all the more hideous because it was so secret.

During this narration my friend Manton had become very silent, and I saw that my words had impressed him. He did not laugh as I paused, but asked quite seriously about the boy who went mad in 1793, and who had presumably been the hero of my fiction. I told him why the boy had gone to that shunned, deserted house, and remarked that he ought to be interested, since he believed that windows retained latent images of those who had sat at them. The boy had gone to look at the windows of that horrible attic, because of tales of things seen behind them, and had come back screaming maniacally.

Manton remained thoughtful as I said this, but gradually reverted to his analytical mood. He granted for the sake of argument that some unnatural monster had really existed, but reminded me that even the most morbid perversion of Nature need not be *unnamable* or scientifically indescribable. I admired his clearness and persistence, and added some further revelations I had collected among the old people. Those later spectral legends, I made plain, related to monstrous apparitions more frightful than anything organic could be; apparitions of gigantic bestial forms sometimes visible and sometimes only tangible, which floated about on moonless nights and haunted the old house, the crypt behind it, and the grave where a sapling had sprouted beside an illegible slab. Whether or not such apparitions had ever gored or smothered people to death, as told in uncorroborated traditions, they had produced a strong and consistent impression; and were yet darkly feared by very aged natives, though largely forgotten by the last two generations—perhaps dying for lack of being thought about. Moreover, so far as æsthetic theory was involved, if the psychic emanations of human creatures be grotesque distortions, what coherent representation could express or

13. See "Dagon," note 6, above.

14. Note that the narrator is "Carter," likely Randolph Carter, who appears in several other tales in this volume. See "The Statement of Randolph Carter," note 2, above. However, the skepticism of *this* Carter contradicts the experiences of Randolph Carter.

15. Carter means that the neighboring house, described earlier as "a tottering, deserted seventeenth-century house," is the very house featured in the story he has related.

portray so gibbous[13] and infamous a nebulosity as the spectre of a malign, chaotic perversion, itself a morbid blasphemy against Nature? Moulded by the dead brain of a hybrid nightmare, would not such a vaporous terror constitute in all loathsome truth the exquisitely, the shriekingly *unnamable*?

The hour must now have grown very late. A singularly noiseless bat brushed by me, and I believe it touched Manton also, for although I could not see him I felt him raise his arm. Presently he spoke.

"But is that house with the attic window still standing and deserted?"

"Yes," I answered. "I have seen it."

"And did you find anything there—in the attic or anywhere else?"

"There were some bones up under the eaves. They may have been what that boy saw—if he was sensitive he wouldn't have needed anything in the window-glass to unhinge him. If they all came from the same object it must have been an hysterical, delirious monstrosity. It would have been blasphemous to leave such bones in the world, so I went back with a sack and took them to the tomb behind the house. There was an opening where I could dump them in. Don't think I was a fool—you ought to have seen that skull. It had four-inch horns, but a face and jaw something like yours and mine."

At last I could feel a real shiver run through Manton, who had moved very near. But his curiosity was undeterred.

"And what about the window-panes?"

"They were all gone. One window had lost its entire frame, and in the other there was not a trace of glass in the little diamond apertures. They were that kind—the old lattice windows that went out of use before 1700. I don't believe they've had any glass for an hundred years or more—maybe the boy broke 'em if he got that far; the legend doesn't say."

Manton was reflecting again.

"I'd like to see that house, Carter.[14] Where is it? Glass or no glass, I must explore it a little. And the tomb where you put those bones, and the other grave without an inscription—the whole thing must be a bit terrible."

"You did see it—until it got dark."[15]

My friend was more wrought upon than I had suspected, for at this touch of harmless theatricalism he started neurotically away from me and actually cried out with a sort of gulping gasp which released a strain of previous repression. It was an odd cry, and all the more terrible because it was answered. For as it was still echoing, I heard a creaking sound through the pitchy blackness, and knew that a lattice window was opening in that accursed old house beside us. And because all the other frames were long since fallen, I knew that it was the grisly glassless frame of that dæmoniac attic window.

Then came a noxious rush of noisome, frigid air from that same dreaded direction, followed by a piercing shriek just beside me on that shocking rifted tomb of man and monster. In another instant I was knocked from my gruesome bench by the devilish threshing of some unseen entity of titanic size but undetermined nature; knocked sprawling on the root-clutched mould of that abhorrent graveyard, while from the tomb came such a stifled uproar of gasping and whirring that my fancy peopled the rayless gloom with Miltonic legions of the misshapen damned. There was a vortex of withering, ice-cold wind, and then the rattle of loose bricks and plaster; but I had mercifully fainted before I could learn what it meant.

Manton, though smaller than I, is more resilient; for we opened our eyes at almost the same instant, despite his greater injuries. Our couches were side by side, and we knew in a few seconds that we were in St. Mary's Hospital.[16] Attendants were grouped about in tense curiosity, eager to aid our memory by telling us how we came there, and we soon heard of the farmer who had found us at noon in a lonely field beyond Meadow Hill, a mile from the old burying ground, on a spot where an ancient slaughterhouse is reputed to have stood. Manton had two malignant wounds in the chest, and some less severe cuts or gougings in the back. I was not so seriously hurt, but was covered with welts and contusions of the most bewildering character, including the print of a split hoof. It was plain that Manton knew more than I, but he told nothing to the puzzled and interested physicians till he had learned what our injuries were. Then he said we were the victims of a vicious bull—though the animal was a difficult thing to place and account for.[17]

16. The closest "St. Mary's Hospital" was in Dorchester, a southern suburb of Boston, about twenty miles from Marblehead and farther from Salem. It is likely that this is a concealment of Mary A. Alley Hospital, a small emergency hospital donated in 1904 to the town of Marblehead by Mary Alley, a teacher, nurse, and founder of the Soldiers Aid Society during the Civil War. The hospital opened in 1921 and continued until 1953; it was subsequently sold as condominiums.

Mary Alley, founder of the Mary A. Alley Hospital, renamed "St. Mary's."

17. Of course, no bull has a split hoof.

18. James Arthur Anderson, in *Out of the Shadows: A Structuralist Approach to Understanding the Fiction of H. P. Lovecraft*, points out that the essence of the "unnamable" is that because it cannot be named, it cannot be catalogued, controlled, or defeated (96). While the clever *S. Petersen's Field Guide to Cthulhu Monsters* in fact illustrates, classifies, and describes Lovecraft's creations in detail, not even that volume describes or illustrates the "unnamable."

19. The Maelstrom is a large whirlpool off the coast of Norway, the Moskstraumen, a tidal current in the Lofoten islands; its name has been appropriated for any large vortex. Note that Manton falls back on Edgar Allan Poe's titles for various terrors to describe the unnamable: "The Pit and the Pendulum" and "A Descent into the Maelström."

After the doctors and nurses had left, I whispered an awe-struck question:

"Good God, Manton, *but what was it?* Those scars—*was it like that?*"

And I was too dazed to exult when he whispered back a thing I had half expected—

"*No—it wasn't that way at all.* It was everywhere—a gelatin—a slime—yet it had shapes, a thousand shapes of horror beyond all memory.[18] There were eyes—and a blemish. It was the pit—the maelstrom[19]—the ultimate abomination. Carter, *it was the unnamable!*"

The Call of Cthulhu[1]

Weird Tales 11, no. 2 (February 1928) (artist: Hugh Rankin)

"The Call of Cthulhu" is a monumental achievement. Although some term it a mere expansion of "Dagon," it is much more. It is Lovecraft's first mature work, with carefully crafted narrative within narrative within narrative, dubious narrators, and a tone that builds from calm reflection of the enormity of the primary narrator's task to a fevered expression of the ultimate horror he discovers. It is also the first comprehensive view of Lovecraft's cosmicism. As Fritz Leiber observed, here for the first time Lovecraft moves horror from the realm of Earth to the stars. This story is founded on his "anti-mythology," in the phrase of David Schultz. Unlike mythology, which, in the words of Joseph Campbell, "reconcile[s] waking consciousness to the mysterium tremendum

et fascinans [fearful and fascinating mystery] of this universe,"[2] Lovecraft's anti-mythology informs humankind of the impossibility of an understanding of the universe. As we have seen, his followers, rather than Lovecraft himself, gave a name to his cosmogony: the Cthulhu Mythos. His own intentions were rediscovered by modern critics through careful readings of his letters.

[Found Among the Papers of the Late Francis Wayland Thurston,[3] of Boston]

Of such great powers or beings there may be conceivably a survival . . . a survival of a hugely remote period when . . . consciousness was manifested, perhaps, in shapes and forms long since withdrawn before the tide of advancing humanity . . . forms of which poetry and legend alone have caught a flying memory and called them gods, monsters, mythical beings of all sorts and kinds. . . .

—ALGERNON BLACKWOOD[4]

I. THE HORROR IN CLAY

1. The story first appeared in *Weird Tales* 11, no. 2 (February 1928), 159–78, 287, but it was likely written in August or September 1926, based on earlier outlining. It was rejected by *Weird Stories* in its initial form, rewritten in July 1927, and subsequently published.

2. Joseph Campbell, *The Masks of God*, vol. 4: *Creative Mythology* (New York: Penguin, 1991), 4.

3. Francis Wayland (1796–1865) was president of Brown University from 1827 to 1855 and was a well-known Providence resident. Howard Thurston (1869–1936) was the most famous stage magician in the world. Peter Cannon, in his shrewd and succinct biographical assessment of Thurston ("The Late Francis Wayland Thurston, of Boston: Lovecraft's Last Dilettante"), concludes, "Probably only an educated and cultured person, possessed of unlimited wealth and time, and

THE MOST MERCIFUL thing in the world, I think, is the inability of the human mind to correlate all its contents. We live on a placid island of ignorance in the midst of black seas of infinity, and it was not meant that we should voyage far. The sciences, each straining in its own direction, have hitherto harmed us little; but some day the piecing together of dissociated knowledge will open up such terrifying vistas of reality, and of our frightful position therein, that we shall either go mad from the revelation or flee from the deadly light into the peace and safety of a new dark age.

Theosophists[5] have guessed at the awesome grandeur of the cosmic cycle wherein our world and human race form transient incidents. They have hinted at strange survivals in terms which would freeze the blood if not masked by a bland optimism. But it is not from them that there came the single glimpse of forbidden æons which chills me when I think of it and maddens me when I dream of it. That glimpse, like all dread glimpses of truth, flashed out from an accidental piecing together of separated things—in this case an old newspaper item and the notes of a dead professor. I hope that no one else will accomplish this piecing out; certainly, if I live, I shall never knowingly supply a link in so hideous a chain. I think that the professor, too, intended to keep silent regarding the part he knew, and that he would have destroyed his notes had not sudden death seized him.

My knowledge of the thing began in the winter of 1926–27 with the death of my grand-uncle, George Gammell Angell, Professor Emeritus of Semitic Languages in Brown University, Providence, Rhode Island.[6] Professor Angell was widely known as an authority on ancient inscriptions, and had frequently been resorted to by the heads of prominent museums; so that his passing at the age of ninety-two may be recalled by many. Locally, interest was intensified by the obscurity of the cause of death. The professor had been stricken whilst returning from the Newport boat;[7] falling suddenly, as witnesses said, after having been jostled by a nautical-looking negro who had come from one of the queer dark courts on the precipitous hillside[8] which formed a short cut from the waterfront to the deceased's home in Williams Street. Physicians were unable to find any visible disorder, but concluded after perplexed debate that some obscure lesion of the heart, induced by the brisk ascent of so steep a hill by so elderly a man, was responsible for the end. At the time I saw no reason to dissent from this dictum, but latterly I am inclined to wonder—and more than wonder.

As my grand-uncle's heir and executor, for he died a childless widower, I was expected to go over his papers with some thoroughness; and for that purpose moved his entire set of files and boxes to my quarters in Boston. Much of the material which I correlated will be later published by the American Archæological Society,[9] but there was one box which I found exceedingly puzzling, and which I felt much averse from shewing to other eyes. It had been locked, and I did not find the key till it occurred to me to examine the personal ring which the professor carried always in his pocket. Then indeed I succeeded in opening it, but when I did so seemed only to be confronted by a greater and more closely locked barrier. For what could be the meaning of the queer clay bas-relief[10] and the disjointed jottings, ramblings, and cuttings which I found? Had my uncle, in his latter years, become credulous of the most superficial impostures? I resolved to search out the eccentric sculptor responsible for this apparent disturbance of an old man's peace of mind.

free of emotional encumbrances, could have cracked the global Cthulhu conspiracy." (39)

4. From his novel *The Centaur*, published in 1911. Lovecraft regarded Blackwood's "The Willows" as the finest weird tale in literature—see Lovecraft's "Supernatural Horror in Literature." Lovecraft slightly misquotes the original, which uses the phrase "her Consciousness," not "consciousness," in referring to what Blackwood calls the "Being of the Earth." This misquotation is pointed out in a letter by Thomas G. Cockcroft to the editor of *Nyctalops*.

5. Those who speculate about the nature of the soul; in particular, those who espouse the system of beliefs and teachings of the Theosophical Society, founded in New York City in 1875, incorporating aspects of Buddhism and Brahmanism, especially the belief in reincarnation and spiritual evolution. See the discussion of its central text, the Book of Dzyan, in "The Haunter of the Dark," note 14, below.

6. Founded in 1764, it is the seventh oldest educational institution in America. It is sited on College Hill, on the east side of Providence. As a prominent feature of Providence, it is mentioned in several other stories set there or in the vicinity, including *The Case of Charles Dexter Ward* and "The Haunter of the Dark," below.

7. A regular boat service between Providence and Newport, Rhode Island, along Narragansett Bay.

8. College Hill. Henry L. P. Beckwith Jr., in *Lovecraft's Providence & Adjacent Parts*, contends that the intersection of Williams Street and the former Well Street is "almost certainly" the scene of the death of Professor Angell (65).

9. The Archaeological Institute of America was founded in 1879, and a local society in Boston in 1884, but the institute disclaims all knowledge of Professor Angell's papers (private communication with the editor).

10. A bas-relief is a fixed sculptural form, usually molded to the face of a building with slightly raised figures or images.

11. Cubism originated with paintings produced by Georges Braque and Pablo Picasso in 1907–9 that, to the French art critic Louis Vauxcelles, seemed to consist of *"bizarre cubiques"* and "little cubes"; the first public Cubist exhibition, which included neither Picasso nor Braque, occurred in 1911, at the Salon des Indépendants in Paris. Among the artists represented were Fernand Léger, Robert Delaunay, Henri Le Fauconnier, Jean Metzinger, and Albert Gleizes. Cubism (along with a lesser-known idiom, Divisionism) influenced Futurism, a literary and artistic movement that originated in Italy in 1908–10 and which glorified speed and machinery, rejecting the past. Its precepts were explained by the writer and editor Filippo Tommaso Marinetti in "The Founding and Manifesto of Futurism," a lengthy piece printed on the front page of *Le Figaro* (February 20, 1909), the French newspaper: "We affirm that the world's magnificence has been enriched by a new beauty: the beauty of speed. A racing car whose hood is adorned with great pipes, like serpents of explosive breath—a roaring car that seems to ride on grapeshot is more beautiful than the [190 BCE Greek sculpture] *Victory of Samothrace*" (R. W. Flint, ed., *Let's Murder the Moonshine: Selected Writings/F. T. Marinetti*, 47–52). Futurism influenced Art Deco, Surrealism, and Dada, among other artistic schools.

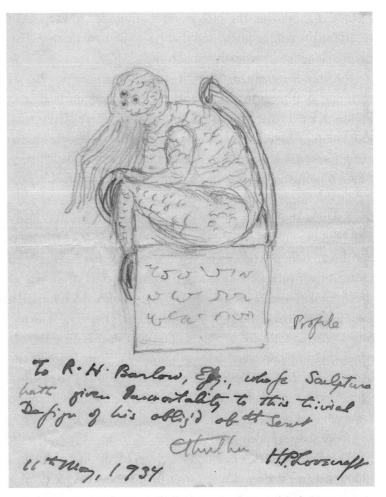

Lovecraft's drawing of the Wilcox sculpture, dated 1934.

The bas-relief was a rough rectangle less than an inch thick and about five by six inches in area; obviously of modern origin. Its designs, however, were far from modern in atmosphere and suggestion; for although the vagaries of cubism and futurism[11] are many and wild, they do not often reproduce that cryptic regularity which lurks in prehistoric writing. And writing of some kind the bulk of these designs seemed certainly to be; though my memory, despite much familiarity with the papers and collections of my uncle, failed in any way to identify this particular species, or even to hint at its remotest affiliations.

Above these apparent hieroglyphics was a figure of evidently pictorial intent, though its impressionistic execution forbade a very clear idea of its nature. It seemed to be a sort of monster, or symbol representing a monster, of a form which only a diseased fancy could conceive. If I say that my somewhat extravagant imagination yielded simultaneous pictures of an octopus, a dragon, and a human caricature, I shall not be unfaithful to the spirit of the thing.[12] A pulpy, tentacled head surmounted a grotesque and scaly body with rudimentary wings; but it was the *general outline* of the whole which made it most shockingly frightful. Behind the figure was a vague suggestion of a Cyclopean architectural background.

The writing accompanying this oddity was, aside from a stack of press cuttings, in Professor Angell's most recent hand; and made no pretence to literary style. What seemed to be the main document was headed "CTHULHU[13] CULT" in characters painstakingly printed to avoid the erroneous reading of a word so unheard-of. The manuscript was divided into two sections, the first of which was headed "1925—Dream and Dream Work of H. A. Wilcox, 7 Thomas St., Providence, R. I.,"[14] and the second, "Narrative of Inspector John R. Legrasse, 121 Bienville St., New Orleans, La.,[15] at 1908 A. A. S. Mtg.—Notes on Same, & Prof. Webb's Acct." The other manuscript papers were all brief notes, some of them accounts of the queer dreams of different persons, some of them citations from theosophical books and magazines (notably W. Scott-Elliot's *Atlantis and the Lost Lemuria*),[16] and the rest comments on long-surviving secret societies and hidden cults, with references to passages in such mythological and anthropological source-books as Frazer's *Golden Bough*[17] and Miss Murray's *Witch-Cult in Western Europe*.[18] The cuttings largely alluded to outré mental illnesses and outbreaks of group folly or mania in the spring of 1925.

The first half of the principal manuscript told a very peculiar tale. It appears that on March 1st, 1925, a thin, dark young man of neurotic and excited aspect had called upon Professor Angell bearing the singular clay bas-relief, which was then exceedingly damp and fresh. His card bore the name of Henry Anthony Wilcox, and my uncle had recognised him as the youngest son of an excellent family slightly known to him, who had latterly been studying sculpture at the Rhode Island School of Design[19] and living alone at the Fleur-de-Lys Building near that institution.[20] Wilcox was a precocious youth of known genius but great

Umberto Boccioni's *The City Rises* (1910), a fine example of Futurist painting.

Pablo Picasso's *Figure dans un Fauteuil (Figure in an Armchair)* (1909–10), an early Cubist work.

12. In "The Dunwich Chimera and Others: Correlating the Cthulhu Mythos," Will Murray argues that there is only one creature in folklore that resembles Cthulhu, the Kraken, the gigantic sea creature first described in Erik Ludvigsen Pontoppidan's *The Natural History of Norway* (1755): "'It is called the Kraken, Kraxen, or some name it Krabben, that word being applied by way of eminences to this creature. This last name seems indeed best to agree with the description of this creature, which is round, flat, and full of arms, or branches.'" According to legend, there were only two such creatures, nearly immortal and said to rise with the apocalypse. Alfred Lord Tennyson's 1830 poem "The Kraken," describing the creature and its legend,

says Murray, must have been familiar to Lovecraft.

13. Lovecraft gave directions for the pronunciation of the name: " . . . the word is supposed to represent a fumbling human attempt to catch the phonetics of an *absolutely non-human* word. The name of the hellish entity was invented by beings whose vocal organs were not like man's, hence it has no relation to the human speech equipment. The syllables were determined by a physiological equipment wholly unlike ours, *hence could never be uttered perfectly by human throats.* . . . Up to the time of the story, when Prof. Angell became interested in the matter, there had never been any attempt to render the name of the hellish *R'lyeh* monster in our alphabet—, although Abdul Alhazred made an attempt in Arabic letters, which was repeated in Greek by the Byzantine translator. The Latin translator merely copied the Greek. The letters CTHULHU were merely what Prof. Angell devised to represent (roughly and imperfectly, of course) the dream-name orally mouthed to him by the young artist Wilcox. The actual sound—as near as human organs could imitate it or human letters record it—may be taken as something like *Khlûl'-hloo*, with the first syllable pronounced gutturally and very thickly. The *u* is about like that in *full*; and the first syllable is not unlike *klul* in sound, hence the *h* represents the guttural thickness" (Lovecraft to Duane Rimel, July 23, 1934, *Selected Letters*, V, 10–11). Of course, how could Lovecraft know?

Note that this is the first name ascribed by Lovecraft to a supernatural being. While earlier tales describe Earth gods, "other" gods, elder gods, and so forth, none has been hitherto named. See Appendix 4 for a detailed genealogy of the named beings.

eccentricity, and had from childhood excited attention through the strange stories and odd dreams he was in the habit of relating. He called himself "psychically hypersensitive," but the staid folk of the ancient commercial city dismissed him as merely "queer." Never mingling much with his kind, he had dropped gradually from social visibility, and was now known only to a small group of æsthetes from other towns. Even the Providence Art Club,[21] anxious to preserve its conservatism, had found him quite hopeless.

On the occasion of the visit, ran the professor's manuscript, the sculptor abruptly asked for the benefit of his host's archeological knowledge in identifying the hieroglyphics of the bas-relief. He spoke in a dreamy, stilted manner which suggested pose and alienated sympathy; and my uncle shewed some sharpness in replying, for the conspicuous freshness of the tablet implied kinship with anything but archeology. Young Wilcox's rejoinder, which impressed my uncle enough to make him recall and record it verbatim, was of a fantastically poetic cast which must have typified his whole conversation, and which I have since found highly characteristic of him. He said, "It is new, indeed, for I made it last night in a dream of strange cities; and dreams are older than brooding Tyre,[22] or the contemplative Sphinx, or garden-girdled[23] Babylon."

It was then that he began that rambling tale which suddenly played upon a sleeping memory and won the fevered interest of my uncle. There had been a slight earthquake tremor the night before, the most considerable felt in New England for some years;[24] and Wilcox's imagination had been keenly affected. Upon retiring, he had had an unprecedented dream of great Cyclopean cities of titan blocks and sky-flung monoliths, all dripping with green ooze and sinister with latent horror. Hieroglyphics had covered the walls and pillars, and from some undetermined point below had come a voice that was not a voice; a chaotic sensation which only fancy could transmute into sound, but which he attempted to render by the almost unpronounceable jumble of letters: "*Cthulhu fhtagn.*"

This verbal jumble was the key to the recollection which excited and disturbed Professor Angell. He questioned the sculptor with scientific minuteness; and studied with almost frantic

The Fleur-de-Lys House in which Wilcox had his studio. Artist: Jason C. Eckhardt, copyright © Jason C. Eckhardt 2013, reprinted with permission

Fleur de Lys House, in 2006. Photograph copyright © Donovan K. Loucks 2006, reprinted with permission

14. This is a real address, and the house there, Fleur de Lys, is exceedingly strange in appearance, its exterior covered with bas-reliefs. It is described by the Providence Art Club (see note 21, below) as having a "Norman, half-timbered facade." Erected in 1885 by Sydney Richmond Burleigh, Fleur de Lys now serves as an art studio—having been deeded to the art club in 1939 by Burleigh's wife—and is listed in the National Register of Historic Places. Curiously, Thomas Street is the continuation of Angell Street in Providence, suggesting a source for the disguised name of the narrator's great-uncle. Lovecraft himself was born at 454 Angell Street and lived there until he was eleven. He lived at 598 Angell Street for an additional twenty years, from 1904 to 1924.

intensity the bas-relief on which the youth had found himself working, chilled and clad only in his night-clothes, when waking had stolen bewilderingly over him. My uncle blamed his old age, Wilcox afterward said, for his slowness in recognising both hieroglyphics and pictorial design. Many of his questions seemed highly out of place to his visitor, especially those which tried to connect the latter with strange cults or societies; and Wilcox could not understand the repeated promises of silence which he was offered in exchange for an admission of membership in some widespread mystical or paganly religious body. When Professor

598 Angell Street, in 2003. Photograph copyright © Donovan K. Loucks 2003, reprinted with permission

15. This is a fictitious address.

16. William Scott-Elliot's *The Story of Atlantis* was published in 1896, *The Lost Lemuria* in 1904. A combined edition first appeared in 1925. All three works were published by the Theosophical Publishing Society. Scott-Elliot was an investment banker and an amateur anthropologist who joined the London Lodge of the Theosophical Society before 1893. Professor Angell would also have consulted the Minnesota politician Ignatius Donnelly's popular *Atlantis: The Antediluvian World* (1882), which propounded the idea that the legendary island, first described in a Socratic dialogue by Plato in 360 BCE, was an actual place, the font of many ancient civilizations.

17. Sir James George Frazer's *The Golden Bough: A Study in Magic and Religion*, a wide-ranging work on comparative religion and mythology, first appeared in 1890 in two volumes and then from 1906 to 1915 in twelve volumes. Frazer (1845–1941), a Scottish anthropologist, took a dispassionate, rather than a theological, approach, viewing religion as a cultural phenomenon.

18. Margaret Alice Murray's 1921 book espoused the controversial view that an

Angell became convinced that the sculptor was indeed ignorant of any cult or system of cryptic lore, he besieged his visitor with demands for future reports of dreams. This bore regular fruit, for after the first interview the manuscript records daily calls of the young man, during which he related startling fragments of nocturnal imagery whose burden was always some terrible Cyclopean vista of dark and dripping stone, with a subterrene voice or intelligence shouting monotonously in enigmatical sense-impacts uninscribable save as gibberish. The two sounds most frequently repeated are those rendered by the letters "Cthulhu" and "R'lyeh."

On March 23d, the manuscript continued, Wilcox failed to appear; and inquiries at his quarters revealed that he had been stricken with an obscure sort of fever and taken to the home of his family in Waterman Street.[25] He had cried out in the night, arousing several other artists in the building, and had manifested since then only alternations of unconsciousness and delirium. My uncle at once telephoned the family, and from that time forward kept close watch of the case; calling often at the Thayer Street[26] office of Dr. Tobey, whom he learned to be in charge. The youth's febrile mind, apparently, was dwelling on strange things; and the doctor shuddered now and then as he spoke of them. They included not only a repetition of what he had formerly dreamed, but touched wildly on a gigantic thing "miles high" which walked or lumbered about.

He at no time fully described this object, but occasional frantic words, as repeated by Dr. Tobey, convinced the professor that it must be identical with the nameless monstrosity he had sought to depict in his dream-sculpture. Reference to this object, the doctor added, was invariably a prelude to the young man's subsidence into lethargy. His temperature, oddly enough, was not greatly above normal; but the whole condition was otherwise such as to suggest true fever rather than mental disorder.

On April 2nd at about 3 p.m. every trace of Wilcox's malady suddenly ceased. He sat upright in bed, astonished to find himself at home and completely ignorant of what had happened in dream or reality since the night of March 22. Pronounced well by his physician, he returned to his quarters in three days; but to Professor Angell he was of no further assistance. All traces of strange dreaming had vanished with his recovery, and my uncle

Home of the Providence Art Club, 10-11 Thomas Street, in 1990. Photograph courtesy of Will Hart

kept no record of his night-thoughts after a week of pointless and irrelevant accounts of thoroughly usual visions.

Here the first part of the manuscript ended, but references to certain of the scattered notes gave me much material for thought—so much, in fact, that only the ingrained scepticism then forming my philosophy can account for my continued distrust of the artist. The notes in question were those descriptive of the dreams of various persons covering the same period as that in which young Wilcox had had his strange visitations. My uncle, it seems, had quickly instituted a prodigiously far-flung body of inquiries amongst nearly all the friends whom he could question without impertinence, asking for nightly reports of their dreams, and the dates of any notable visions for some time past. The reception of his request seems to have been varied; but he must, at the very least, have received more responses than any ordinary man could have handled without a secretary. This origi-

underground pagan religion flourished until overlaid by Christianity. Her views were also reflected in *Encyclopædia Britannica* entries (1929–1968) on witchcraft. Modern Wicca claims to embody that historical cult.

19. Headquartered in Providence and founded in March 1877 by the Rhode Island Women's Centennial Commission, which discovered a $1,675 surplus after mounting the state's art exhibition at the 1876 World's Fair, the school offers a broad curriculum of studies in art and design. It is a few blocks from the Fleur de Lys House on Thomas Street and adjacent to Brown University.

20. See note 14, above.

21. A professional association in continuous existence since 1880, it serves to promote the visual arts. It is headquartered two doors away from the Fleur de Lys House on Thomas Street.

22. Now located in modern Lebanon, the city of Tyre was founded in Phoenicia at the start of the third millennium BCE.

23. The Hanging Gardens of Babylon, one of the seven wonders of the ancient world, have come to be regarded as more likely legendary than real, although in *The Mystery of the Hanging Garden of Babylon: An Elusive World Wonder Traced*, Stephanie Dalley, an authority on cuneiform texts, challenges the existing theory. The gardens are traditionally credited to King Nebuchadnessar II (around 600 BCE), but Dalley provides evidence of their having been built by the Assyrian ruler Sennacherib (705–681 BCE), perhaps in Nineveh—considered the "New Babylon" after 689 BCE, when Babylon was conquered by Assyria.

24. In fact, a magnitude 7 shock occurred on February 28, 1925, in the region, with an epicenter in the St. Lawrence River region. Intensity V–level effects were felt in Providence, the first of that level since 1883.

25. This is very close to the Fleur de Lys House, where Wilcox resided.

26. Another College Hill neighborhood address.

27. It is tempting to identify this architect as the prominent Dutch Theosophist architect Karel de Bazel, but he died in 1923, not 1925. Many architects were drawn to Theosophy, a popularized esoteric philosophy based on a study of the relations between the world, humanity, and the divine. In 1875, Helena Blavatsky

nal correspondence was not preserved, but his notes formed a thorough and really significant digest. Average people in society and business—New England's traditional "salt of the earth"—gave an almost completely negative result, though scattered cases of uneasy but formless nocturnal impressions appear here and there, always between March 23d and April 2nd—the period of young Wilcox's delirium. Scientific men were little more affected, though four cases of vague description suggest fugitive glimpses of strange landscapes, and in one case there is mentioned a dread of something abnormal.

It was from the artists and poets that the pertinent answers came, and I know that panic would have broken loose had they been able to compare notes. As it was, lacking their original letters, I half suspected the compiler of having asked leading questions, or of having edited the correspondence in corroboration of what he had latently resolved to see. That is why I continued to feel that Wilcox, somehow cognisant of the old data which my uncle had possessed, had been imposing on the veteran scientist. These responses from æsthetes told a disturbing tale. From February 28th to April 2nd a large proportion of them had dreamed very bizarre things, the intensity of the dreams being immeasurably the stronger during the period of the sculptor's delirium. Over a fourth of those who reported anything, reported scenes and half-sounds not unlike those which Wilcox had described; and some of the dreamers confessed acute fear of the gigantic nameless thing visible toward the last. One case, which the note describes with emphasis, was very sad. The subject, a widely known architect with leanings toward theosophy and occultism,[27] went violently insane on the date of young Wilcox's seizure, and expired several months later after incessant screamings to be saved from some escaped denizen of hell. Had my uncle referred to these cases by name instead of merely by number, I should have attempted some corroboration and personal investigation; but as it was, I succeeded in tracing down only a few. All of these, however, bore out the notes in full. I have often wondered if all the objects of the professor's questioning felt as puzzled as did this fraction. It is well that no explanation shall ever reach them.

The press cuttings, as I have intimated, touched on cases of panic, mania, and eccentricity during the given period. Professor

Angell must have employed a cutting bureau, for the number of extracts was tremendous, and the sources scattered throughout the globe. Here was a nocturnal suicide in London, where a lone sleeper had leaped from a window after a shocking cry. Here likewise a rambling letter to the editor of a paper in South America, where a fanatic deduces a dire future from visions he has seen. A despatch from California describes a theosophist colony as donning white robes en masse for some "glorious fulfilment" which never arrives, whilst items from India speak guardedly of serious native unrest toward the end of March.[28] Voodoo orgies multiply in Hayti,[29] and African outposts report ominous mutterings. American officers in the Philippines find certain tribes bothersome about this time,[30] and New York policemen are mobbed by hysterical Levantines on the night of March 22–23.[31] The west of Ireland, too, is full of wild rumour and legendry, and a fantastic painter named Ardois-Bonnot hangs a blasphemous "Dream Landscape" in the Paris spring salon of 1926.[32] And so numerous are the recorded troubles in insane asylums, that only a miracle can have stopped the medical fraternity from noting strange parallelisms and drawing mystified conclusions. A weird bunch of cuttings, all told; and I can at this date scarcely envisage the callous rationalism with which I set them aside. But I was then convinced that young Wilcox had known of the older matters mentioned by the professor.

II. THE TALE OF INSPECTOR LEGRASSE

THE OLDER MATTERS which had made the sculptor's dream and bas-relief so significant to my uncle formed the subject of the second half of his long manuscript. Once before, it appears, Professor Angell had seen the hellish outlines of the nameless monstrosity, puzzled over the unknown hieroglyphics, and heard the ominous syllables which can be rendered only as "Cthulhu"; and all this in so stirring and horrible a connexion that it is small wonder he pursued young Wilcox with queries and demands for data.

The earlier experience had come in 1908, seventeen years before, when the American Archæological Society held its

(1831–1891) and others founded the Theosophical Society, embracing mystical eastern esotericism and purporting to be based on Blavatsky's studies in Tibet. See "The Haunter of the Dark," note 14, below, for more on these studies. See also Susan R. Henderson's "Architecture and Theosophy: An Introduction." Henderson observes that at the beginning of the century, many architects strove to base their work on esoteric philosophies rather than mere functionalism.

28. Between February 28 and March 23, two other earthquakes with magnitudes of 7.0 or greater occurred, one in China and the other in the Vanuatu Islands (about 1,100 miles north-northeast of Australia). Quakes also rocked central Italy during this interval.

29. Voodoo (properly, Vadou or Vodou) is a religion originating in Haiti fostering worship of gods subservient to Bondye, the unknowable creator. Rituals involve trancelike states in which worshippers are possessed by the *loa*, or lesser gods (also called *orishas*); these have often been mistakenly referred to as orgies.

30. There was virtually no time during the United States' occupation of the Philippines that the natives were *not* considered to have been bothersome by the officers of the occupying force. The history of the American "pacification" of the population after occupation in 1898 is long and sad. See especially Marcial P. Lichauco and Moorfield Storey, *The Conquest of the Philippines by the United States, 1898–1925.*

31. March 23 saw "the biggest round-up of crooks and criminals ever ordered in New York City since the days of Police Chief Devery," according to the *New York Times.* The effort commenced on

the evening of the twenty-third, when all patrolmen and detectives throughout the city received confidential orders to arrest all known thieves and criminals and bring them to the lineup at police headquarters at 9 A.M. on the twenty-fourth. There is no record in the newspaper of discontent among the Semitic population.

32. By 1926, the "Paris spring salon" was no longer a single venue. From about the mid-eighteenth century, the Salon (always thus designated), sponsored by the national Académie des Beaux-Arts, was the official exhibition of French art, held biannually. (Predating this was the late-seventeenth-century Salon, held in the Cour Carrée of the Louvre.) In 1880, the French government turned over administration of the Salon to a private group, the Société des Artistes Français. However, discontent grew with both the selection process and the manner of exhibition of selected works, and in 1890, after contention regarding the status of medals that had been awarded at the 1889 World's Fair, a group led by prominent Salon artist Ernest Meissonier split off. The Société Nationale des Beaux-Arts was formed and began to conduct its own spring salon, with a new approach to the exhibitions. In 1903, led by art patron Frantz Jourdain and painters Georges Rouault, André Derain, and Henri Matisse, still another group of artists arranged their own salon, which they named the Salon d'Automne, to distinguish it from the two spring salons. The first exhibition featured works of Bonnard and Matisse, plus a retrospective of the work of Gauguin (who died in 1903). Later the Salone d'Automne featured the works of the Fauvists and eventually the Cubists. See Michelle C. Montgomery's "The Modernization of the Salon of the

annual meeting in St. Louis.[33] Professor Angell, as befitted one of his authority and attainments, had had a prominent part in all the deliberations; and was one of the first to be approached by the several outsiders who took advantage of the convocation to offer questions for correct answering and problems for expert solution.

The chief of these outsiders, and in a short time the focus of interest for the entire meeting, was a commonplace-looking middle-aged man who had travelled all the way from New Orleans for certain special information unobtainable from any local source. His name was John Raymond Legrasse, and he was by profession an Inspector of Police.[34] With him he bore the subject of his visit, a grotesque, repulsive, and apparently very ancient stone statuette whose origin he was at a loss to determine. It must not be fancied that Inspector Legrasse had the least interest in archæology. On the contrary, his wish for enlightenment was prompted by purely professional considerations. The statuette, idol, fetish, or whatever it was, had been captured some months before in the wooded swamps south of New Orleans during a raid on a supposed voodoo meeting; and so singular and hideous were the rites connected with it, that the police could not but realise that they had stumbled on a dark cult totally unknown to them, and infinitely more diabolic than even the blackest of the African voodoo circles.[35] Of its origin, apart from the erratic and unbelievable tales extorted from the captured members, absolutely nothing was to be discovered; hence the anxiety of the police for any antiquarian lore which might help them to place the frightful symbol, and through it track down the cult to its fountain-head.

Inspector Legrasse was scarcely prepared for the sensation which his offering created. One sight of the thing had been enough to throw the assembled men of science into a state of tense excitement, and they lost no time in crowding around him to gaze at the diminutive figure whose utter strangeness and air of genuinely abysmal antiquity hinted so potently at unopened and archaic vistas. No recognised school of sculpture had animated this terrible object, yet centuries and even thousands of years seemed recorded in its dim and greenish surface of unplaceable stone.

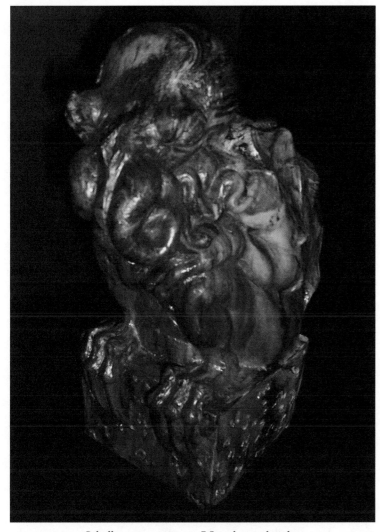

Cthulhu statue, approx. 7.5 inches in height,
no. 142 of 500 copies. Copyright © 2007 Corinne Crowe
(photograph reprinted with permission of the artist)

The figure, which was finally passed slowly from man to man for close and careful study, was between seven and eight inches in height, and of exquisitely artistic workmanship. It represented a monster of vaguely anthropoid outline, but with an octopus-like head whose face was a mass of feelers, a scaly, rubbery-looking body, prodigious claws on hind and fore feet, and long, narrow wings behind. This thing, which seemed instinct with a fearsome and unnatural malignancy, was of a somewhat bloated cor-

Société Nationale" and Norbert Wolf's *The Art of the Salon: The Triumph of 19th-Century Painting* for a brief history of the earlier Salons and a stunning collection of representative works.

33. In fact, the Archaeological Institute of America held its tenth general meeting in late December 1908 in Toronto. Although the Boston society was well represented, no Brown University representatives are recorded in the Proceedings.

34. In New Orleans, the inspector of police was the head of the force, selected by the mayor. E. S. Whitaker served as inspector of police until January 2, 1908. It is possible that after leaving office he traveled to Toronto for the conference. The subsequent holder of the title, William J. O'Connor, served from the day Whitaker surrendered the office until his death on November 29, 1910, and so could not have been interviewed by the narrator in 1925. It is more probable that the narrator confused the officer's title—that the latter was likely a mere junior official of the NOPD given the task of the strange raid described following.

35. Louisiana or New Orleans voodoo, a religious-cultural movement that emphasizes intervention with divine will through charms, potions, and saint and ancestor worship. It derived from West African origins and came to New Orleans and then spread through Louisiana as a product of the African slave trade.

36. Professors Allan Marquand and Andrew Fleming West, both of Princeton University, attended the 10th General Meeting. Marquand specialized in Hellenistic archaeology, while West was deeply involved in Roman archaeology. West retained the Giger Professorship of Latin until 1929. Allan Marquand, however, died in 1924, but in 1860, "forty-eight years before," Marquand would have been only seven years old and hence not engaged in this capacity in a tour of Greenland and Iceland. Charles R. Morey, an art historian, also attended, but he lacks all of the identifying characteristics of "Professor Webb."

37. Alphabets dating from 150 CE used for the Germanic languages before the adoption of the Latin alphabet.

38. The Eskimos (an obsolete term) of western Greenland are the Kalaallit, a part of the Inuit people; Lalaallit Nunaat, the Greenlandic name for the island, simply means "land of the Greenlanders." More than 80 percent of Greenland's population are Kalaallit. They are regarded as descended from the Dorset people, a culture that dates from 500 BCE. Both archaeological records (see Robert McGhee, *The Last Imaginary Place: A Human History of the Arctic World*) and Inuit mythology suggest displacement, by the Dorset—who thrived until 1500 CE in the region—of the Tuniit or Sivullirmiut, or First Inhabitants; the latter also peopled Arctic Canada. The First Inhabitants probably arrived in Greenland around 3000 BCE. The Inuit invaded the Arctic around 1100 or 1200 CE, pushing out the Tuniit—who were not vanquished, however, until 1902 CE, when illness wiped out their last settlement.

pulence, and squatted evilly on a rectangular block or pedestal covered with undecipherable characters. The tips of the wings touched the back edge of the block, the seat occupied the centre, whilst the long, curved claws of the doubled-up, crouching hind legs gripped the front edge and extended a quarter of the way down toward the bottom of the pedestal. The cephalopod head was bent forward, so that the ends of the facial feelers brushed the backs of huge fore paws which clasped the croucher's elevated knees. The aspect of the whole was abnormally life-like, and the more subtly fearful because its source was so totally unknown. Its vast, awesome, and incalculable age was unmistakable; yet not one link did it shew with any known type of art belonging to civilisation's youth—or indeed to any other time. Totally separate and apart, its very material was a mystery; for the soapy, greenish-black stone with its golden or iridescent flecks and striations resembled nothing familiar to geology or mineralogy. The characters along the base were equally baffling; and no member present, despite a representation of half the world's expert learning in this field, could form the least notion of even their remotest linguistic kinship. They, like the subject and material, belonged to something horribly remote and distinct from mankind as we know it, something frightfully suggestive of old and unhallowed cycles of life in which our world and our conceptions have no part.

And yet, as the members severally shook their heads and confessed defeat at the Inspector's problem, there was one man in that gathering who suspected a touch of bizarre familiarity in the monstrous shape and writing, and who presently told with some diffidence of the odd trifle he knew. This person was the late William Channing Webb, Professor of Anthropology in Princeton University, and an explorer of no slight note.[36] Professor Webb had been engaged, forty-eight years before, in a tour of Greenland and Iceland in search of some Runic[37] inscriptions which he failed to unearth; and whilst high up on the West Greenland coast had encountered a singular tribe or cult of degenerate Esquimaux[38] whose religion, a curious form of devil-worship, chilled him with its deliberate bloodthirstiness and repulsiveness. It was a faith of which other Esquimaux knew little, and which they mentioned only with shudders, saying that it had come down from horribly ancient æons before ever the world was made. Besides nameless rites and human sacrifices there were certain queer hereditary rituals addressed to a supreme elder devil or *tornasuk*;[39] and of this Professor Webb had taken a careful phonetic copy from an aged *angekok* or wizard-priest, expressing the sounds in Roman letters as best he knew how. But just now of prime significance was the fetish which this cult had cherished, and around which they danced when the aurora leaped high over the ice cliffs. It was, the professor stated, a very crude bas-relief of stone, comprising a hideous picture and some cryptic writing. And so far as he could tell, it was a rough parallel in all essential features of the bestial thing now lying before the meeting.

This data, received with suspense and astonishment by the assembled members, proved doubly exciting to Inspector Legrasse; and he began at once to ply his informant with questions. Having noted and copied an oral ritual among the swamp cult-worshippers his men had arrested, he besought the professor to remember as best he might the syllables taken down amongst the diabolist Esquimaux. There then followed an exhaustive comparison of details, and a moment of really awed silence when both detective and scientist agreed on the virtual identity of the phrase common to two hellish rituals so many worlds of distance apart. What, in substance, both the Esquimaux wizards and the Louisiana swamp-priests had chanted to their kindred idols was something very like this—the word-divisions being guessed at from traditional breaks in the phrase as chanted aloud:

"Ph'nglui mglw'nafh Cthulhu R'lyeh wgah'nagl fhtagn."

Legrasse had one point in advance of Professor Webb, for several among his mongrel prisoners had repeated to him what older celebrants had told them the words meant. This text, as given, ran something like this:

"In his house at R'lyeh dead Cthulhu waits dreaming."

And now, in response to a general and urgent demand, Inspector Legrasse related as fully as possible his experience with the swamp worshippers; telling a story to which I could see my uncle attached profound significance. It savoured of the wildest dreams of myth-maker and theosophist, and disclosed an astonishing degree of cosmic imagination among such half-castes and pariahs as might be at least expected to possess it.

39. In *Tales and Traditions of the Eskimo, with a Sketch of Their Habits, Religion, Language, and other Peculiarities*, by Henry Rink (1875), the Tornasuk is translated as "'the supreme helper,' who only revealed himself to the *angakoks*, or wise men, that is to the priests."

40. Jean Lafitte (ca. 1776–ca. 1823) was a French buccaneer who, in exchange for a pardon, helped General Andrew Jackson defend New Orleans against the British in 1815.

41. There are dozens of small lakes south of New Orleans, and it is impossible to identify this lake from the scanty directions (at the end of a passable road, reached after a traverse of "miles" through the swamps).

42. Clearly this is not Cthulhu, for Cthulhu is described as a "green immensity." Is it one of the Great Old Ones?

43. Pierre Le Moyne d'Iberville (1661–1702 or 1706) was a Canadian trader, soldier, and colonial administrator credited with founding the New French colony of Louisiana.

44. Robert de La Salle (1643–1687) was a French explorer who claimed the Mississippi delta for France in 1682, naming it La Louisiane for the king, Louis XIV.

On November 1st, 1907, there had come to the New Orleans police a frantic summons from the swamp and lagoon country to the south. The squatters there, mostly primitive but good-natured descendants of Lafitte's men,[40] were in the grip of stark terror from an unknown thing which had stolen upon them in the night. It was voodoo, apparently, but voodoo of a more terrible sort than they had ever known; and some of their women and children had disappeared since the malevolent tom-tom had begun its incessant beating far within the black haunted woods where no dweller ventured. There were insane shouts and harrowing screams, soul-chilling chants and dancing devil-flames; and, the frightened messenger added, the people could stand it no more.

So a body of twenty police, filling two carriages and an automobile, had set out in the late afternoon with the shivering squatter as a guide. At the end of the passable road they alighted, and for miles splashed on in silence through the terrible cypress woods where day never came. Ugly roots and malignant hanging nooses of Spanish moss beset them, and now and then a pile of dank stones or fragment of a rotting wall intensified by its hint of morbid habitation a depression which every malformed tree and every fungous islet combined to create. At length the squatter settlement, a miserable huddle of huts, hove in sight; and hysterical dwellers ran out to cluster around the group of bobbing lanterns. The muffled beat of tom-toms was now faintly audible far, far ahead; and a curdling shriek came at infrequent intervals when the wind shifted. A reddish glare, too, seemed to filter through the pale undergrowth beyond endless avenues of forest night. Reluctant even to be left alone again, each one of the cowed squatters refused point-blank to advance another inch toward the scene of unholy worship, so Inspector Legrasse and his nineteen colleagues plunged on unguided into black arcades of horror that none of them had ever trod before.

The region now entered by the police was one of traditionally evil repute, substantially unknown and untraversed by white men. There were legends of a hidden lake[41] unglimpsed by mortal sight, in which dwelt a huge, formless white polypous thing with luminous eyes;[42] and squatters whispered that bat-winged devils flew up out of caverns in inner earth to worship it at midnight.

They said it had been there before D'Iberville,[43] before La Salle,[44] before the Indians, and before even the wholesome beasts and birds of the woods. It was nightmare itself, and to see it was to die. But it made men dream, and so they knew enough to keep away. The present voodoo orgy was, indeed, on the merest fringe of this abhorred area, but that location was bad enough; hence perhaps the very place of the worship had terrified the squatters more than the shocking sounds and incidents.

Only poetry or madness could do justice to the noises heard by Legrasse's men as they ploughed on through the black morass toward the red glare and muffled tom-toms. There are vocal qualities peculiar to men, and vocal qualities peculiar to beasts; and it is terrible to hear the one when the source should yield the other. Animal fury and orgiastic licence here whipped themselves to dæmoniac heights by howls and squawking ecstasies that tore and reverberated through those nighted woods like pestilential tempests from the gulfs of hell. Now and then the less organised ululation would cease, and from what seemed a well-drilled chorus of hoarse voices would rise in sing-song chant that hideous phrase or ritual:

"Ph'nglui mglw'nafh Cthulhu R'lyeh wgah'nagl fhtagn."

Then the men, having reached a spot where the trees were thinner, came suddenly in sight of the spectacle itself. Four of them reeled, one fainted, and two were shaken into a frantic cry which the mad cacophony of the orgy fortunately deadened. Legrasse dashed swamp water on the face of the fainting man, and all stood trembling and nearly hypnotised with horror.

In a natural glade of the swamp stood a grassy island of perhaps an acre's extent, clear of trees and tolerably dry. On this now leaped and twisted a more indescribable horde of human abnormality than any but a Sime[45] or an Angarola[46] could paint. Void of clothing, this hybrid spawn were braying, bellowing, and writhing about a monstrous ring-shaped bonfire; in the centre of which, revealed by occasional rifts in the curtain of flame, stood a great granite monolith some eight feet in height; on top of which, incongruous with its diminutiveness, rested the noxious carven statuette. From a wide circle of ten scaffolds set up at regular intervals with the flame-girt monolith as a centre hung, head downward, the oddly marred bodies of the helpless squat-

45. Sidney Sime (1864 or 1867–1941) was an English painter, born into poverty, who began working in the late Victorian period and whose patrons eventually included William Randolph Hearst. The newspaper magnate is said to have referred to Sime as "the Greatest Living Imaginative Artist." Sime's work often included weird, fantastic images, and he illustrated many stories for Lord Dunsany. Lovecraft mentioned his work again in "Pickman's Model."

"Romance Comes Down Out of Hilly Woodlands," 1910 illustration for Lord Dunsany's *A Dreamer's Tale*.

Self-portrait of Sidney Sime, ca. 1900.

46. Anthony Angarola (1893–1929), an American artist whose pictures often celebrated immigrants, is also mentioned by Lovecraft in "Pickman's Model." Angarola illustrated his fellow Chicagoan Ben Hecht's fantasy novel *The Kingdom of Evil* in 1924.

The Kingdom of Evil (1924).

47. The most southerly of the Cape Verde Islands, Brava is a volcano, or stratovolcano, like Mount Fuji.

ters who had disappeared. It was inside this circle that the ring of worshippers jumped and roared, the general direction of the mass motion being from left to right in endless Bacchanal between the ring of bodies and the ring of fire.

It may have been only imagination and it may have been only echoes which induced one of the men, an excitable Spaniard, to fancy he heard antiphonal responses to the ritual from some far and unillumined spot deeper within the wood of ancient legendry and horror. This man, Joseph D. Galvez, I later met and questioned; and he proved distractingly imaginative. He indeed went so far as to hint of the faint beating of great wings, and of a glimpse of shining eyes and a mountainous white bulk beyond the remotest trees—but I suppose he had been hearing too much native superstition.

Actually, the horrified pause of the men was of comparatively brief duration. Duty came first; and although there must have been nearly a hundred mongrel celebrants in the throng, the police relied on their firearms and plunged determinedly into the nauseous rout. For five minutes the resultant din and chaos were beyond description. Wild blows were struck, shots were fired, and escapes were made; but in the end Legrasse was able to count some forty-seven sullen prisoners, whom he forced to dress in haste and fall into line between two rows of policemen. Five of the worshippers lay dead, and two severely wounded ones were carried away on improvised stretchers by their fellow-prisoners. The image on the monolith, of course, was carefully removed and carried back by Legrasse.

Examined at headquarters after a trip of intense strain and weariness, the prisoners all proved to be men of a very low, mixed-blooded, and mentally aberrant type. Most were seamen, and a sprinkling of negroes and mulattoes, largely West Indians or Brava Portuguese from the Cape Verde Islands,[47] gave a colouring of voodooism to the heterogeneous cult. But before many questions were asked, it became manifest that something far deeper and older than negro fetichism was involved. Degraded and ignorant as they were, the creatures held with surprising consistency to the central idea of their loathsome faith.

They worshipped, so they said, the Great Old Ones who lived ages before there were any men, and who came to the young world out of the sky. Those Old Ones were gone now, inside the earth and under the sea; but their dead bodies had told their secrets in dreams to the first men, who formed a cult which had never died. This was that cult, and the prisoners said it had always existed and always would exist, hidden in distant wastes and dark places all over the world until the time when the great priest Cthulhu, from his dark house in the mighty city of R'lyeh under the waters, should rise and bring the earth again beneath his sway. Some day he would call, when the stars were ready, and the secret cult would always be waiting to liberate him.

Meanwhile no more must be told. There was a secret which even torture could not extract. Mankind was not absolutely alone among the conscious things of earth, for shapes came out of the dark to visit the faithful few. But these were not the Great Old Ones. No man had ever seen the Old Ones. The carven idol was great Cthulhu, but none might say whether or not the others were precisely like him. No one could read the old writing now, but things were told by word of mouth. The chanted ritual was not the secret—that was never spoken aloud, only whispered. The chant meant only this: "In his house at R'lyeh dead Cthulhu waits dreaming."

Only two of the prisoners were found sane enough to be hanged, and the rest were committed to various institutions. All denied a part in the ritual murders, and averred that the killing had been done by Black Winged Ones which had come to them from their immemorial meeting-place in the haunted wood. But of those mysterious allies no coherent account could ever be gained. What the police did extract, came mainly from an immensely aged mestizo[48] named Castro, who claimed to have sailed to strange ports and talked with undying leaders of the cult in the mountains of China.[49]

Old Castro remembered bits of hideous legend that paled the speculations of theosophists and made man and the world seem recent and transient indeed. There had been æons when other Things ruled on the earth, and They had had great cities. Remains of Them, he said the deathless Chinamen had told him, were still to be found as Cyclopean stones on islands in the Pacific. They all died vast epochs of time before men came, but there were arts which could revive Them when the stars had

48. That is, a person of mixed European and native descent.

49. This likely refers to visits to the monasteries of Tibet, the Himalayan region that become formally independent of China only in 1913. The Theosophists (see note 5, above) maintained that their teachings were based on those of Tibetan mahatmas.

50. According to Castro, the rise and fall of R'lyeh were predicted by the stars, and Richard L. Tierney, in "When the Stars Are Right," has worked out the precise star charts for the rise and fall of the cult-city.

51. Cf. Friedrich Nietzsche's *Beyond Good and Evil* (1886), an essay of intense interest to Lovecraft.

come round again to the right positions in the cycle of eternity.[50] They had, indeed, come themselves from the stars, and brought Their images with Them.

These Great Old Ones, Castro continued, were not composed altogether of flesh and blood. They had shape—for did not this star-fashioned image prove it?—but that shape was not made of matter. When the stars were right, They could plunge from world to world through the sky; but when the stars were wrong, They could not live. But although They no longer lived, They would never really die. They all lay in stone houses in Their great city of R'lyeh, preserved by the spells of mighty Cthulhu for a glorious resurrection when the stars and the earth might once more be ready for Them. But at that time some force from outside must serve to liberate Their bodies. The spells that preserved Them intact likewise prevented Them from making an initial move, and They could only lie awake in the dark and think whilst uncounted millions of years rolled by. They knew all that was occurring in the universe, but Their mode of speech was transmitted thought. Even now They talked in Their tombs. When, after infinities of chaos, the first men came, the Great Old Ones spoke to the sensitive among them by moulding their dreams; for only thus could Their language reach the fleshly minds of mammals.

Then, whispered Castro, those first men formed the cult around small idols which the Great Ones shewed them; idols brought in dim æras from dark stars. That cult would never die till the stars came right again, and the secret priests would take great Cthulhu from His tomb to revive His subjects and resume His rule of earth. The time would be easy to know, for then mankind would have become as the Great Old Ones; free and wild and beyond good and evil, with laws and morals thrown aside and all men shouting and killing and revelling in joy.[51] Then the liberated Old Ones would teach them new ways to shout and kill and revel and enjoy themselves, and all the earth would flame with a holocaust of ecstasy and freedom. Meanwhile the cult, by appropriate rites, must keep alive the memory of those ancient ways and shadow forth the prophecy of their return.

In the elder time chosen men had talked with the entombed Old Ones in dreams, but then something had happened. The great stone city R'lyeh, with its monoliths and sepulchres, had sunk beneath the waves; and the deep waters, full of the one primal mystery through which not even thought can pass, had cut off the spectral intercourse. But memory never died, and high-priests said that the city would rise again when the stars were right. Then came out of the earth the black spirits of earth, mouldy and shadowy, and full of dim rumours picked up in caverns beneath forgotten sea-bottoms. But of them old Castro dared not speak much. He cut himself off hurriedly, and no amount of persuasion or subtlety could elicit more in this direction. The *size* of the Old Ones, too, he curiously declined to mention. Of the cult, he said that he thought the centre lay amid the pathless deserts of Arabia, where Irem, the City of Pillars,[52] dreams hidden and untouched. It was not allied to the European witch-cult, and was virtually unknown beyond its members. No book had ever really hinted of it, though the deathless Chinamen said that there were double meanings in the *Necronomicon* of the mad Arab Abdul Alhazred which the initiated might read as they chose, especially the much-discussed couplet:

> *"That is not dead which can eternal lie,*
> *And with strange æons even death may die."*

Legrasse, deeply impressed and not a little bewildered, had inquired in vain concerning the historic affiliations of the cult. Castro, apparently, had told the truth when he said that it was wholly secret. The authorities at Tulane University could shed no light upon either cult or image, and now the detective had come to the highest authorities in the country and met with no more than the Greenland tale of Professor Webb.

The feverish interest aroused at the meeting by Legrasse's tale, corroborated as it was by the statuette, is echoed in the subsequent correspondence of those who attended; although scant mention occurs in the formal publications of the society. Caution is the first care of those accustomed to face occasional charlatanry and imposture. Legrasse for some time lent the image to Professor Webb, but at the latter's death it was returned to him and remains in his possession, where I viewed it not long ago. It is truly a terrible thing, and unmistakably akin to the dream-sculpture of young Wilcox.

52. See "The Nameless City," note 24, above.

53. This likely refers to the First Baptist Church in America, 75 North Main Street, finished in 1775 and actually the third house of worship erected there— the burgeoning congregation outgrew the two previous buildings. Lovecraft appreciated its architecture.

First Baptist Church, in 2010. Photograph copyright © Donovan K. Loucks 2010, reprinted with permission

54. A Welshman, Machen (1863–1947) was a prolific author of supernatural and horror fiction. He was regarded by Lovecraft as one of the four "modern masters" of supernatural literature (the others being Algernon Blackwood, M. R. James, and Lord Dunsany), and Machen's writing was important in Lovecraft's development of the Cthulhu Mythos. Stephen King said of Machen's novella *The Great God Pan* "[It is] as close as the horror genre comes to a

That my uncle was excited by the tale of the sculptor I did not wonder, for what thoughts must arise upon hearing, after a knowledge of what Legrasse had learned of the cult, of a sensitive young man who had dreamed not only the figure and exact hieroglyphics of the swamp-found image and the Greenland devil tablet, but had come in his dreams upon at least three of the precise words of the formula uttered alike by Esquimaux diabolists and mongrel Louisianans? Professor Angell's instant start on an investigation of the utmost thoroughness was eminently natural; though privately I suspected young Wilcox of having heard of the cult in some indirect way, and of having invented a series of dreams to heighten and continue the mystery at my uncle's expense. The dream-narratives and cuttings collected by the professor were, of course, strong corroboration; but the rationalism of my mind and the extravagance of the whole subject led me to adopt what I thought the most sensible conclusions. So, after thoroughly studying the manuscript again and correlating the theosophical and anthropological notes with the cult narrative of Legrasse, I made a trip to Providence to see the sculptor and give him the rebuke I thought proper for so boldly imposing upon a learned and aged man.

Wilcox still lived alone in the Fleur-de-Lys Building in Thomas Street, a hideous Victorian imitation of seventeenth century Breton architecture which flaunts its stuccoed front amidst the lovely colonial houses on the ancient hill, and under the very shadow of the finest Georgian steeple in America.[53] I found him at work in his rooms, and at once conceded from the specimens scattered about that his genius is indeed profound and authentic. He will, I believe, some time be heard from as one of the great decadents; for he has crystallised in clay and will one day mirror in marble those nightmares and phantasies which Arthur Machen[54] evokes in prose, and Clark Ashton Smith[55] makes visible in verse and in painting.

Dark, frail, and somewhat unkempt in aspect, he turned languidly at my knock and asked me my business without rising. When I told him who I was, he displayed some interest; for my uncle had excited his curiosity in probing his strange dreams, yet had never explained the reason for the study. I did not enlarge his knowledge in this regard, but sought with some subtlety to draw him out. In a short time I became convinced of his absolute sincerity, for he spoke of the dreams in a manner none could mistake. They and their subconscious residuum had influenced his art profoundly, and he shewed me a morbid statue whose contours almost made me shake with the potency of its black suggestion. He could not recall having seen the original of this thing except in his own dream bas-relief, but the outlines had formed themselves insensibly under his hands. It was, no doubt, the giant shape he had raved of in delirium. That he really knew nothing of the hidden cult, save from what my uncle's relentless catechism had let fall, he soon made clear; and again I strove to think of some way in which he could possibly have received the weird impressions.

He talked of his dreams in a strangely poetic fashion; making me see with terrible vividness the damp Cyclopean city of slimy green stone—whose *geometry*, he oddly said, was *all wrong*—and hear with frightened expectancy the ceaseless, half-mental calling from underground: "*Cthulhu fhtagn*," "*Cthulhu fhtagn*." These words had formed part of that dread ritual which told of dead Cthulhu's dream-vigil in his stone vault at R'lyeh, and I felt deeply moved despite my rational beliefs. Wilcox, I was sure, had heard of the cult in some casual way, and had soon forgotten it amidst the mass of his equally weird reading and imagining. Later, by virtue of its sheer impressiveness, it had found subconscious expression in dreams, in the bas-relief, and in the terrible statue I now beheld; so that his imposture upon my uncle had been a very innocent one. The youth was of a type, at once slightly affected and slightly ill-mannered, which I could never like; but I was willing enough now to admit both his genius and his honesty. I took leave of him amicably, and wish him all the success his talent promises.

The matter of the cult still remained to fascinate me, and at times I had visions of personal fame from researches into its origin and connexions. I visited New Orleans, talked with Legrasse and others of that old-time raiding-party, saw the frightful image, and even questioned such of the mongrel prisoners as still survived. Old Castro, unfortunately, had been dead for some years. What I now heard so graphically at first-hand, though it was really no more than a detailed confirmation of what my uncle had written,

great white whale. . . . sooner or later every writer who takes the form seriously must try to tackle its theme: that reality is thin, and the *true* reality behind is a limitless abyss filled with monsters" (*Just After Sunset*, 364).

55. Smith (1893–1961) wrote over a hundred stories of dark fantasy and was as popular as Lovecraft in magazines like *Weird Tales*. Though they never met, Smith and Lovecraft conducted an extensive correspondence over a period of fifteen years, and each freely used the cosmogony of the other in his own work. Smith, Lovecraft, and Robert E. Howard (who created the character Conan the Barbarian, among others) were the "Big Three" authors among *Weird Tales* readers.

56. See part III, below.

57. The *Bulletin* thrived as a Sydney weekly from 1880 to 2008. Originally a journal of political and business commentary, its literary influence grew, and it quickly became the launching place for many prominent Australian writers. However, the date given is wrong; April 18 was a Saturday in 1925, and the *Bulletin* appeared on Wednesdays.

excited me afresh; for I felt sure that I was on the track of a very real, very secret, and very ancient religion whose discovery would make me an anthropologist of note. My attitude was still one of absolute materialism, as I wish it still were, and I discounted with almost inexplicable perversity the coincidence of the dream notes and odd cuttings collected by Professor Angell.

One thing I began to suspect, and which I now fear I know, is that my uncle's death was far from natural. He fell on a narrow hill street leading up from an ancient waterfront swarming with foreign mongrels, after a careless push from a negro sailor. I did not forget the mixed blood and marine pursuits of the cult-members in Louisiana, and would not be surprised to learn of secret methods and poison needles as ruthless and as anciently known as the cryptic rites and beliefs. Legrasse and his men, it is true, have been let alone; but in Norway a certain seaman who saw things is dead.[56] Might not the deeper inquiries of my uncle after encountering the sculptor's data have come to sinister ears? I think Professor Angell died because he knew too much, or because he was likely to learn too much. Whether I shall go as he did remains to be seen, for I have learned much now.

III. THE MADNESS FROM THE SEA

IF HEAVEN EVER wishes to grant me a boon, it will be a total effacing of the results of a mere chance which fixed my eye on a certain stray piece of shelf-paper. It was nothing on which I would naturally have stumbled in the course of my daily round, for it was an old number of an Australian journal, the *Sydney Bulletin*[57] for April 18, 1925. It had escaped even the cutting bureau which had at the time of its issuance been avidly collecting material for my uncle's research.

I had largely given over my inquiries into what Professor Angell called the "Cthulhu Cult," and was visiting a learned friend in Paterson, New Jersey; the curator of a local museum and a mineralogist of note. Examining one day the reserve specimens roughly set on the storage shelves in a rear room of the museum, my eye was caught by an odd picture in one of the old papers spread beneath the stones. It was the *Sydney Bulletin* I have mentioned, for my friend has wide affiliations in all conceivable foreign parts; and the picture was a half-tone cut of a hideous stone image almost identical with that which Legrasse had found in the swamp.

Eagerly clearing the sheet of its precious contents, I scanned the item in detail; and was disappointed to find it of only moderate length. What it suggested, however, was of portentous significance to my flagging quest; and I carefully tore it out for immediate action. It read as follows:

MYSTERY DERELICT FOUND AT SEA

Vigilant Arrives With Helpless Armed New Zealand Yacht in Tow. One Survivor and Dead Man Found Aboard. Tale

The *Alert* is attacked. Artist: Jason C. Eckhardt, copyright © Jason C. Eckhardt 2013, reprinted with permission

58. Over 1,800 miles east-northeast of Wellington, New Zealand, and over 1,000 miles from the nearest inhabited islands.

59. The University of Sydney, the oldest in Australia, was founded in 1850.

60. The Royal Society describes itself as "the oldest learned society in the Southern Hemisphere, tracing its origin to the Philosophical Society of Australasia, founded in Sydney in 1821." In 1866, it lengthened its name to the Royal Society of New South Wales, and in 1881 it was incorporated by an act of the NSW Parliament.

61. The Colonial, or Sydney, Museum, as it was first known, was founded in 1827. In 1836, it became the Australian Museum. It has been sited on College Street in Sydney since its inception.

62. A port in Peru.

63. Almost 1,000 miles due south of the wreck and perhaps 500 miles south of the direct course of the *Emma* to Callao from Auckland.

64. "Kanaka" was originally a term for native Hawaiians, subsequently extended to all Pacific Islanders, who were frequently imported as workers in British and Australian colonies and parts of the United States. Now the term is largely regarded as offensive.

of Desperate Battle and Deaths at Sea. Rescued Seaman Refuses Particulars of Strange Experience. Odd Idol Found in His Possession. Inquiry to Follow.

The Morrison Co.'s freighter *Vigilant*, bound from Valparaiso, arrived this morning at its wharf in Darling Harbour, having in tow the battled and disabled but heavily armed steam yacht *Alert* of Dunedin, N.Z., which was sighted April 12th in S. Latitude 34°21', W. Longitude 152°17',[58] with one living and one dead man aboard.

The *Vigilant* left Valparaiso March 25th, and on April 2nd was driven considerably south of her course by exceptionally heavy storms and monster waves. On April 12th the derelict was sighted; and though apparently deserted, was found upon boarding to contain one survivor in a half-delirious condition and one man who had evidently been dead for more than a week. The living man was clutching a horrible stone idol of unknown origin, about a foot in height, regarding whose nature authorities at Sydney University,[59] the Royal Society,[60] and the Museum in College Street[61] all profess complete bafflement, and which the survivor says he found in the cabin of the yacht, in a small carved shrine of common pattern.

This man, after recovering his senses, told an exceedingly strange story of piracy and slaughter. He is Gustaf Johansen, a Norwegian of some intelligence, and had been second mate of the two-masted schooner *Emma* of Auckland, which sailed for Callao[62] February 20th with a complement of eleven men. The *Emma*, he says, was delayed and thrown widely south of her course by the great storm of March 1st, and on March 22nd, in S. Latitude 49°51' W. Longitude 128°34',[63] encountered the *Alert*, manned by a queer and evil-looking crew of Kanakas[64] and half-castes. Being ordered peremptorily to turn back, Capt. Collins refused; whereupon the strange crew began to fire savagely and without warning upon the schooner with a peculiarly heavy battery of brass cannon forming part of the yacht's equipment. The *Emma*'s men shewed fight, says the survivor, and though the schooner began to sink from shots beneath the waterline they managed to heave alongside their enemy and board her, grappling with the savage crew on the yacht's deck, and being forced to kill them all, the number being slightly superior, because of their particularly abhorrent and desperate though rather clumsy mode of fighting.

Three of the *Emma*'s men, including Capt. Collins and First Mate Green, were killed; and the remaining eight under Second Mate Johansen proceeded to navigate the captured yacht, going ahead in their original direction to see if any reason for their ordering back had existed. The next day, it appears, they raised and landed on a small island, although none is known to exist in that part of the ocean; and six of the men somehow died ashore, though Johansen is queerly reticent about this part of his story, and speaks only of their falling into a rock chasm. Later, it seems, he and one companion boarded the yacht and tried to manage her, but were beaten about by the storm of April 2nd. From that time till his rescue on the 12th the man remembers little, and he does not even recall when William Briden, his companion, died. Briden's death reveals no apparent cause, and was probably due to excitement or exposure. Cable advices from Dunedin report that the *Alert* was well known there as an island trader, and bore an evil reputation along the waterfront. It was owned by a curious group of half-castes whose frequent meetings and night trips to the woods attracted no little curiosity; and it had set sail in great haste just after the storm and earth tremors of March 1st. Our Auckland correspondent gives the *Emma* and her crew an excellent reputation, and Johansen is described as a sober and worthy man. The admiralty will institute an inquiry on the whole matter beginning tomorrow, at which every effort will be made to induce Johansen to speak more freely than he has done hitherto.

This was all, together with the picture of the hellish image; but what a train of ideas it started in my mind! Here were new treasuries of data on the Cthulhu Cult, and evidence that it had strange interests at sea as well as on land. What motive prompted the hybrid crew to order back the *Emma* as they sailed about with

65. Could this be the same island described in "Dagon"? Johansen is not the narrator of "Dagon"; the latter landed in San Francisco, not Sydney.

66. This is wishful thinking, notes Justin Taylor, in "'A Mountain Walked or Stumbled': Madness, Apocalypse, and H. P. Lovecraft's 'The Call of Cthulhu.'" "Did not Legrasse and his men find murdered bodies at the worship-site in Louisiana? Did not Wilcox's dreams have him carving sculpture?" Furthermore, Taylor points out, the newspaper article makes it clear that the cultists aboard the *Alert* were going *somewhere*, intent on doing *something*. (36) There is no reason to think that the actions set in motion would cease with the dreams, and Professor Angell's subsequent death should have by itself dissuaded Thurston from the comforting view that the horrors were "of the mind alone."

their hideous idol? What was the unknown island on which six of the *Emma*'s crew had died, and about which the mate Johansen was so secretive?[65] What had the vice-admiralty's investigation brought out, and what was known of the noxious cult in Dunedin? And most marvellous of all, what deep and more than natural linkage of dates was this which gave a malign and now undeniable significance to the various turns of events so carefully noted by my uncle?

March 1st—our February 28th according to the International Date Line—the earthquake and storm had come. From Dunedin the *Alert* and her noisome crew had darted eagerly forth as if imperiously summoned, and on the other side of the earth poets and artists had begun to dream of a strange, dank Cyclopean city whilst a young sculptor had moulded in his sleep the form of the dreaded Cthulhu. March 23d the crew of the *Emma* landed on an unknown island and left six men dead; and on that date the dreams of sensitive men assumed a heightened vividness and darkened with dread of a giant monster's malign pursuit, whilst an architect had gone mad and a sculptor had lapsed suddenly into delirium! And what of this storm of April 2nd—the date on which all dreams of the dank city ceased, and Wilcox emerged unharmed from the bondage of strange fever? What of all this—and of those hints of old Castro about the sunken, star-born Old Ones and their coming reign; their faithful cult *and their mastery of dreams*? Was I tottering on the brink of cosmic horrors beyond man's power to bear? If so, they must be horrors of the mind alone, for in some way the second of April had put a stop to whatever monstrous menace had begun its siege of mankind's soul.[66]

That evening, after a day of hurried cabling and arranging, I bade my host adieu and took a train for San Francisco. In less than a month I was in Dunedin; where, however, I found that little was known of the strange cult-members who had lingered in the old sea-taverns. Waterfront scum was far too common for special mention; though there was vague talk about one inland trip these mongrels had made, during which faint drumming and red flame were noted on the distant hills. In Auckland I learned that Johansen had returned *with yellow hair turned white* after a perfunctory and inconclusive questioning at Sydney, and had thereafter sold his cottage in West Street and sailed with his wife to his old home in Oslo. Of his stirring experience he would tell his friends no more than he had told the admiralty officials, and all they could do was to give me his Oslo address.

After that I went to Sydney and talked profitlessly with seamen and members of the vice-admiralty court. I saw the *Alert*, now sold and in commercial use, at Circular Quay in Sydney Cove, but gained nothing from its non-committal bulk. The crouching image with its cuttlefish head, dragon body, scaly wings, and hieroglyphed pedestal, was preserved in the Museum at Hyde Park; and I studied it long and well, finding it a thing of balefully exquisite workmanship, and with the same utter mystery, terrible antiquity, and unearthly strangeness of material which I had noted in Legrasse's smaller specimen. Geologists, the curator told me, had found it a monstrous puzzle; for they vowed that the world held no rock like it. Then I thought with a shudder of what old Castro had told Legrasse about the primal Great Ones: "They had come from the stars, and had brought Their images with Them."

Shaken with such a mental revolution as I had never before known, I now resolved to visit Mate Johansen in Oslo. Sailing for London, I reembarked at once for the Norwegian capital; and one autumn day landed at the trim wharves in the shadow of the Egeberg.[67] Johansen's address, I discovered, lay in the Old Town of King Harold Haardrada, which kept alive the name of Oslo during all the centuries that the greater city masqueraded as "Christiana."[68] I made the brief trip by taxicab, and knocked with palpitant heart at the door of a neat and ancient building with plastered front. A sad-faced woman in black answered my summons, and I was stung with disappointment when she told me in halting English that Gustaf Johansen was no more.

He had not survived his return, said his wife, for the doings at sea in 1925 had broken him. He had told her no more than he had told the public, but had left a long manuscript—of "technical matters" as he said—written in English, evidently in order to safeguard her from the peril of casual perusal. During a walk through a narrow lane near the Gothenburg dock,[69] a bundle of papers falling from an attic window had knocked him down. Two Lascar[70] sailors at once helped him to his feet, but before the ambulance could reach him he was dead. Physicians found no adequate cause for the end, and laid it to heart trouble and

67. A mountain to the east of Oslo.

68. Oslo was the original town founded by King Haardrada. After it was destroyed in a fire, the capital was rebuilt in 1624 under the name of Christiania (Lovecraft left out the final *i*), after the king of Norway, Christian IV. It took back the name of Oslo in 1925.

69. The "Gothenburg dock" is in Sweden, 180 miles from Oslo (the distance in nautical miles is about 140). What was Johansen doing there? The widow's account makes it seem that Johansen had retired from the sea. Was he conducting his own investigation into the matter?

70. An archaic Anglo-Persian term, which formerly meant a noncombatant but later came to mean any extra personnel on shipboard and especially "native" (that is, nonwhite) sailors who supplemented the crews of European vessels in Eastern waters. The large steamship companies especially favored them, reportedly on account of their docility, temperance, and obedience to orders.

71. About 1,700 miles southeast of the shipwreck, and 1,500 miles from the nearest inhabited land (the Pitcairn Islands).

a weakened constitution. I now felt gnawing at my vitals that dark terror which will never leave me till I, too, am at rest; "accidentally" or otherwise. Persuading the widow that my connexion with her husband's "technical matters" was sufficient to entitle me to his manuscript, I bore the document away and began to read it on the London boat.

It was a simple, rambling thing—a naive sailor's effort at a post-facto diary—and strove to recall day by day that last awful voyage. I cannot attempt to transcribe it verbatim in all its cloudiness and redundance, but I will tell its gist enough to shew why the sound of the water against the vessel's sides became so unendurable to me that I stopped my ears with cotton.

Johansen, thank God, did not know quite all, even though he saw the city and the Thing, but I shall never sleep calmly again when I think of the horrors that lurk ceaselessly behind life in time and in space, and of those unhallowed blasphemies from elder stars which dream beneath the sea, known and favoured by a nightmare cult ready and eager to loose them on the world whenever another earthquake shall heave their monstrous stone city again to the sun and air.

Johansen's voyage had begun just as he told it to the vice-admiralty. The *Emma*, in ballast, had cleared Auckland on February 20th, and had felt the full force of that earthquake-born tempest which must have heaved up from the sea-bottom the horrors that filled men's dreams. Once more under control, the ship was making good progress when held up by the *Alert* on March 22nd, and I could feel the mate's regret as he wrote of her bombardment and sinking. Of the swarthy cult-fiends on the *Alert* he speaks with significant horror. There was some peculiarly abominable quality about them which made their destruction seem almost a duty, and Johansen shews ingenuous wonder at the charge of ruthlessness brought against his party during the proceedings of the court of inquiry. Then, driven ahead by curiosity in their captured yacht under Johansen's command, the men sight a great stone pillar sticking out of the sea, and in S. Latitude 47°9', W. Longitude 126°43'[71] come upon a coast-line of mingled mud, ooze, and weedy Cyclopean masonry which can be nothing less than the tangible substance of earth's supreme terror—the nightmare corpse-city of R'lyeh, that was built in measureless æons behind history by the vast, loathsome shapes that seeped down from the dark stars. There lay great Cthulhu and his hordes, hidden in green slimy vaults and sending out at last, after cycles incalculable, the thoughts that spread fear to the dreams of the sensitive and called imperiously to the faithful to come on a pilgrimage of liberation and restoration. All this Johansen did not suspect, but God knows he soon saw enough!

I suppose that only a single mountain-top, the hideous monolith-crowned citadel whereon great Cthulhu was buried, actually emerged from the waters. When I think of the extent of all that may be brooding down there I almost wish to kill myself forthwith. Johansen and his men were awed by the cosmic majesty of this dripping Babylon of elder dæmons, and must have guessed without guidance that it was nothing of this or of any sane planet. Awe at the unbelievable size of the greenish stone blocks, at the dizzying height of the great carven monolith, and at the stupefying identity of the colossal statues and bas-reliefs with the queer image found in the shrine on the *Alert*, is poignantly visible in every line of the mate's frightened description.

Without knowing what futurism is like, Johansen achieved something very close to it when he spoke of the city; for instead of describing any definite structure or building, he dwells only on broad impressions of vast angles and stone surfaces—surfaces too great to belong to any thing right or proper for this earth, and impious with horrible images and hieroglyphs. I mention his talk about *angles* because it suggests something Wilcox had told me of his awful dreams. He had said that the *geometry* of the dream-place he saw was abnormal, non-Euclidean, and loathsomely redolent of spheres and dimensions apart from ours. Now an unlettered seaman felt the same thing whilst gazing at the terrible reality.

Johansen and his men landed at a sloping mud-bank on this monstrous Acropolis, and clambered slipperily up over titan oozy blocks which could have been no mortal staircase. The very sun of heaven seemed distorted when viewed through the polarising miasma welling out from this sea-soaked perversion, and twisted menace and suspense lurked leeringly in those crazily elusive angles of carven rock where a second glance shewed concavity after the first shewed convexity.

72. Johansen borrows this phrase from Edgar Allan Poe's "The Fall of the House of Usher": "darkness, as if an inherent positive quality, poured forth . . ."

Something very like fright had come over all the explorers before anything more definite than rock and ooze and weed was seen. Each would have fled had he not feared the scorn of the others, and it was only half-heartedly that they searched—vainly, as it proved—for some portable souvenir to bear away.

It was Rodriguez the Portuguese who climbed up the foot of the monolith and shouted of what he had found. The rest followed him, and looked curiously at the immense carved door with the now familiar squid-dragon bas-relief. It was, Johansen said, like a great barn-door; and they all felt that it was a door because of the ornate lintel, threshold, and jambs around it, though they could not decide whether it lay flat like a trap-door or slantwise like an outside cellar-door. As Wilcox would have said, the geometry of the place was all wrong. One could not be sure that the sea and the ground were horizontal, hence the relative position of everything else seemed phantasmally variable.

Briden pushed at the stone in several places without result. Then Donovan felt over it delicately around the edge, pressing each point separately as he went. He climbed interminably along the grotesque stone moulding—that is, one would call it climbing if the thing was not after all horizontal—and the men wondered how any door in the universe could be so vast. Then, very softly and slowly, the acre-great panel began to give inward at the top; and they saw that it was balanced.

Donovan slid or somehow propelled himself down or along the jamb and rejoined his fellows, and everyone watched the queer recession of the monstrously carven portal. In this phantasy of prismatic distortion it moved anomalously in a diagonal way, so that all the rules of matter and perspective seemed upset.

The aperture was black with a darkness almost material. That tenebrousness was indeed a positive quality;[72] for it obscured such parts of the inner walls as ought to have been revealed, and actually burst forth like smoke from its æon-long imprisonment, visibly darkening the sun as it slunk away into the shrunken and gibbous sky on flapping membraneous wings. The odour arising from the newly opened depths was intolerable, and at length the quick-eared Hawkins thought he heard a nasty, slopping sound down there. Everyone listened, and everyone was listening still when It lumbered slobberingly into sight and gropingly squeezed

Its gelatinous green immensity through the black doorway into the tainted outside air of that poison city of madness.

Poor Johansen's handwriting almost gave out when he wrote of this. Of the six men who never reached the ship, he thinks two perished of pure fright in that accursed instant. The Thing cannot be described—there is no language for such abysms of shrieking and immemorial lunacy, such eldritch contradictions of all matter, force, and cosmic order. A mountain walked or stumbled. God! What wonder that across the earth a great architect went mad, and poor Wilcox raved with fever in that telepathic instant? The Thing of the idols, the green, sticky spawn of the stars, had awaked to claim his own. The stars were right again, and what an age-old cult had failed to do by design, a band of innocent sailors had done by accident. After vigintillions[73] of years great Cthulhu was loose again, and ravening for delight.

Three men were swept up by the flabby claws before anybody turned. God rest them, if there be any rest in the universe. They were Donovan, Guerrera, and Ångstrom. Parker slipped as the other three were plunging frenziedly over endless vistas of green-crusted rock to the boat, and Johansen swears he was swallowed up by an angle of masonry which shouldn't have been there; an angle which was acute, but behaved as if it were obtuse. So only Briden and Johansen reached the boat, and pulled desperately for the *Alert* as the mountainous monstrosity flopped down the slimy stones and hesitated floundering at the edge of the water.

Steam had not been suffered to go down entirely, despite the departure of all hands for the shore; and it was the work of only a few moments of feverish rushing up and down between wheel and engines to get the *Alert* under way. Slowly, amidst the distorted horrors of that indescribable scene, she began to churn the lethal waters; whilst on the masonry of that charnel shore that was not of earth the titan Thing from the stars slavered and gibbered like Polypheme cursing the fleeing ship of Odysseus. Then, bolder than the storied Cyclops, great Cthulhu slid greasily into the water and began to pursue with vast wave-raising strokes of cosmic potency. Briden looked back and went mad, laughing shrilly as he kept on laughing at intervals till death found him one night in the cabin whilst Johansen was wandering deliriously.

But Johansen had not given out yet. Knowing that the Thing

73. A really, really big number: in American numeration, 1 followed by 63 zeros—twenty (*vingt*) sets of 3 zeros plus one more set); in British numeration, an even bigger number: 1 followed by 120 zeros. Current estimates of the age of the cosmos—the time since the Big Bang—is much smaller, a mere 13.75 billion years. Just as a reminder, the Earth is believed to be only about a third that old, and *Homo sapiens* about 500,000 years (that is, about 1/9,000 of the age of the Earth). The only larger number is a centillion, 10^{600}. This is of course an exaggeration, for Cthulhu could not have been confined in an earthly prison for longer than the age of the planet.

74. To cachinnate is to laugh convulsively.

could surely overtake the *Alert* until steam was fully up, he resolved on a desperate chance; and, setting the engine for full speed, ran lightning-like on deck and reversed the wheel. There was a mighty eddying and foaming in the noisome brine, and as the steam mounted higher and higher the brave Norwegian drove his vessel head on against the pursuing jelly which rose above the unclean froth like the stern of a dæmon galleon. The awful squid-head with writhing feelers came nearly up to the bowsprit of the sturdy yacht, but Johansen drove on relentlessly. There was a bursting as of an exploding bladder, a slushy nastiness as of a cloven sunfish, a stench as of a thousand opened graves, and a sound that the chronicler would not put on paper. For an instant the ship was befouled by an acrid and blinding green cloud, and then there was only a venomous seething astern; where—God in heaven!—the scattered plasticity of that nameless sky-spawn was nebulously *recombining* in its hateful original form, whilst its distance widened every second as the *Alert* gained impetus from its mounting steam.

That was all. After that Johansen only brooded over the idol in the cabin and attended to a few matters of food for himself and the laughing maniac by his side. He did not try to navigate after the first bold flight, for the reaction had taken something out of his soul. Then came the storm of April 2nd, and a gathering of the clouds about his consciousness. There is a sense of spectral whirling through liquid gulfs of infinity, of dizzying rides through reeling universes on a comet's tail, and of hysterical plunges from the pit to the moon and from the moon back again to the pit, all livened by a cachinnating[74] chorus of the distorted, hilarious elder gods and the green, bat-winged mocking imps of Tartarus.

Out of that dream came rescue—the *Vigilant*, the vice-admiralty court, the streets of Dunedin, and the long voyage back home to the old house by the Egeberg. He could not tell—they would think him mad. He would write of what he knew before death came, but his wife must not guess. Death would be a boon if only it could blot out the memories.

That was the document I read, and now I have placed it in the tin box beside the bas-relief and the papers of Professor Angell. With it shall go this record of mine—this test of my own sanity, wherein is pieced together that which I hope may never be pieced together again. I have looked upon all that the universe has to hold of horror, and even the skies of spring and the flowers of summer must ever afterward be poison to me. But I do not think my life will be long. As my uncle went, as poor Johansen went, so I shall go. I know too much, and the cult still lives.

Cthulhu still lives, too, I suppose, again in that chasm of stone which has shielded him since the sun was young. His accursed city is sunken once more, for the *Vigilant* sailed over the spot after the April storm; but his ministers on earth still bellow and prance and slay around idol-capped monoliths in lonely places. He must have been trapped by the sinking whilst within his black abyss, or else the world would by now be screaming with fright and frenzy. Who knows the end? What has risen may sink, and what has sunk may rise. Loathsomeness waits and dreams in the deep, and decay spreads over the tottering cities of men. A time will come—but I must not and cannot think! Let me pray that, if I do not survive this manuscript, my executors may put caution before audacity and see that it meets no other eye.

Poster from *The Call of Cthulhu*.
H. P. Lovecraft Historical Society, 2005

The Silver Key[1]

Here is another tale of Randolph Carter, at age fifty-four, in which the narrator suffers a crisis of faith. It expresses a literary philosophy not unlike that laid out, in the form of a Socratic dialogue, in "The Unnamable." The story—which will undoubtedly remind some readers of an early Twilight Zone episode called "Kick the Can"—likely represents Lovecraft's personal need to reaffirm his ancestry and the constant inspiration he draws from his New England roots. S. T. Joshi records, in his Lovecraft biography I Am Providence, that the readers of Weird Tales expressed a violent dislike for the story. It also provides a thorough survey of the dreamscape Lovecraft had so far invented.

1. Written in the fall of 1926, it first appeared in *Weird Tales* 13, no. 1 (January 1929), 41–49, 144.

2. See "The Statement of Randolph Carter," note 2, above, for reference to the other adventures of Randolph Carter, often viewed as Lovecraft's alter ego. The autobiographical aspects of this story and its setting are explored in great detail in Kenneth W. Faig Jr.'s "'The Silver Key' and Lovecraft's Childhood."

3. Classical writers claim that there are *two* gates of dream, the Gates of Horn and Ivory, first described in Homer's *Odyssey*, as follows: "Stranger, dreams verily are baffling and unclear of meaning, and in no wise do they find fulfilment in all things for men. For two are the gates of shadowy dreams, and one is fashioned of horn and one of ivory. Those dreams that pass through the gate of sawn ivory deceive men, bringing

When Randolph Carter[2] was thirty he lost the key of the gate of dreams.[3] Prior to that time he had made up for the prosiness of life by nightly excursions to strange and ancient cities beyond space, and lovely, unbelievable garden lands across ethereal seas; but as middle age hardened upon him he felt these liberties slipping away little by little, until at last he was cut off altogether. No more could his galleys sail up the river Oukranos[4] past the gilded spires of Thran,[5] or his elephant caravans tramp through perfumed jungles in Kled, where forgotten palaces with veined ivory columns sleep lovely and unbroken under the moon.

He had read much of things as they are, and talked with too many people. Well-meaning philosophers had taught him to look into the logical relations of things, and analyse the processes which shaped his thoughts and fancies. Wonder had gone away, and he had forgotten that all life is only a set of pictures in the brain, among which there is no difference betwixt those born of real things and those born of inward dreamings, and no cause to value the one above the other. Custom had dinned into his ears a superstitious reverence for that which tangibly and physically

Weird Tales 13, no. 1 (January 1929) (artist: Hugh Rankin)

words that find no fulfilment. But those that come forth through the gate of polished horn bring true issues to pass, when any mortal sees them" (vol. 2, book 19). Virgil's *Aeneid* describes Aeneas's return from the underworld after visiting his father, Anchises: "Two gates the silent house of Sleep adorn; / Of polish'd ivory this, that of transparent horn: / True visions thro' transparent horn arise; / Thro' polish'd ivory pass deluding lies. / Of various things discoursing as he pass'd, / Anchises hither bends his steps at last. / Then, thro' the gate of iv'ry, he dismiss'd / His valiant offspring and divining guest" (John Dryden translation, 1697).

4. Mentioned in Lovecraft's *The Dream-Quest of Unknown Kadath.*

5. A great city on the river, also mentioned in *The Dream-Quest of Unknown Kadath,* as is the region of Kled.

exists, and had made him secretly ashamed to dwell in visions. Wise men told him his simple fancies were inane and childish, and he believed it because he could see that they might easily be so. What he failed to recall was that the deeds of reality are just as inane and childish, and even more absurd because their actors persist in fancying them full of meaning and purpose as the blind cosmos grinds aimlessly on from nothing to something and from something back to nothing again, neither heeding nor knowing the wishes or existence of the minds that flicker for a second now and then in the darkness.

They had chained him down to things that are, and had then explained the workings of those things till mystery had gone out of the world. When he complained, and longed to escape into twilight realms where magic moulded all the little vivid fragments and prized associations of his mind into vistas of breathless expectancy and unquenchable delight, they turned him instead toward the new-found prodigies of science, bidding him find wonder in the atom's vortex and mystery in the sky's dimensions. And when he had failed to find these boons in things whose laws

6. A town in southwestern India, but with none of the attributes described here. Uncharacteristically, Narath is not mentioned elsewhere by Lovecraft.

7. A translucent variety of quartz or agate.

are known and measurable, they told him he lacked imagination, and was immature because he preferred dream-illusions to the illusions of our physical creation.

So Carter had tried to do as others did, and pretended that the common events and emotions of earthy minds were more important than the fantasies of rare and delicate souls. He did not dissent when they told him that the animal pain of a stuck pig or dyspeptic ploughman in real life is a greater thing than the peerless beauty of Narath[6] with its hundred carven gates and domes of chalcedony,[7] which he dimly remembered from his dreams; and under their guidance he cultivated a painstaking sense of pity and tragedy.

Once in a while, though, he could not help seeing how shallow, fickle, and meaningless all human aspirations are, and how emptily our real impulses contrast with those pompous ideals we profess to hold. Then he would have recourse to the polite laughter they had taught him to use against the extravagance and artificiality of dreams; for he saw that the daily life of our world is every inch as extravagant and artificial, and far less worthy of respect because of its poverty in beauty and its silly reluctance to admit its own lack of reason and purpose. In this way he became a kind of humorist, for he did not see that even humour is empty in a mindless universe devoid of any true standard of consistency or inconsistency.

In the first days of his bondage he had turned to the gentle churchly faith endeared to him by the naive trust of his fathers, for thence stretched mystic avenues which seemed to promise escape from life. Only on closer view did he mark the starved fancy and beauty, the stale and prosy triteness, and the owlish gravity and grotesque claims of solid truth which reigned boresomely and overwhelmingly among most of its professors; or feel to the full the awkwardness with which it sought to keep alive as literal fact the outgrown fears and guesses of a primal race confronting the unknown. It wearied Carter to see how solemnly people tried to make earthly reality out of old myths which every step of their boasted science confuted, and this misplaced seriousness killed the attachment he might have kept for the ancient creeds had they been content to offer the sonorous rites and emotional outlets in their true guise of ethereal fantasy.

But when he came to study those who had thrown off the old myths, he found them even more ugly than those who had not. They did not know that beauty lies in harmony, and that loveliness of life has no standard amidst an aimless cosmos save only its harmony with the dreams and the feelings which have gone before and blindly moulded our little spheres out of the rest of chaos. They did not see that good and evil and beauty and ugliness are only ornamental fruits of perspective, whose sole value lies in their linkage to what chance made our fathers think and feel, and whose finer details are different for every race and culture. Instead, they either denied these things altogether or transferred them to the crude, vague instincts which they shared with the beasts and peasants; so that their lives were dragged malodorously out in pain, ugliness, and disproportion, yet filled with a ludicrous pride at having escaped from something no more unsound than that which still held them. They had traded the false gods of fear and blind piety for those of licence and anarchy.

Carter did not taste deeply of these modern freedoms; for their cheapness and squalor sickened a spirit loving beauty alone, while his reason rebelled at the flimsy logic with which their champions tried to gild brute impulse with a sacredness stripped from the idols they had discarded. He saw that most of them, in common with their cast-off priestcraft, could not escape from the delusion that life has a meaning apart from that which men dream into it; and could not lay aside the crude notion of ethics and obligations beyond those of beauty, even when all Nature shrieked of its unconsciousness and impersonal unmorality in the light of their scientific discoveries. Warped and bigoted with preconceived illusions of justice, freedom, and consistency, they cast off the old lore and the old ways with the old beliefs; nor ever stopped to think that that lore and those ways were the sole makers of their present thoughts and judgments, and the sole guides and standards in a meaningless universe without fixed aims or stable points of reference. Having lost these artificial settings, their lives grew void of direction and dramatic interest; till at length they strove to drown their ennui in bustle and pretended usefulness, noise and excitement, barbaric display and animal sensation. When these things palled, disappointed,

8. The Foreign Legion was created by King Louis Philippe in 1831 to permit foreigners (that is, non-French persons) to serve in France's army. It saw extensive service on the Western Front in World War I, and many Americans and other foreign nationals enlisted in it at the outset of the Great War, serving with the Legion until their own countries entered the battle.

9. This is viewed by some scholars as Lovecraft's criticism of the later work of Lord Dunsany, much of which is considered self-parody.

or grew nauseous through revulsion, they cultivated irony and bitterness, and found fault with the social order. Never could they realise that their brute foundations were as shifting and contradictory as the gods of their elders, and that the satisfaction of one moment is the bane of the next. Calm, lasting beauty comes only in dream, and this solace the world had thrown away when in its worship of the real it threw away the secrets of childhood and innocence.

Amidst this chaos of hollowness and unrest Carter tried to live as befitted a man of keen thought and good heritage. With his dreams fading under the ridicule of the age he could not believe in anything, but the love of harmony kept him close to the ways of his race and station. He walked impassive through the cities of men, and sighed because no vista seemed fully real; because every flash of yellow sunlight on tall roofs and every glimpse of balustraded plazas in the first lamps of evening served only to remind him of dreams he had once known, and to make him homesick for ethereal lands he no longer knew how to find. Travel was only a mockery; and even the Great War stirred him but little, though he served from the first in the Foreign Legion of France.[8] For a while he sought friends, but soon grew weary of the crudeness of their emotions, and the sameness and earthiness of their visions. He felt vaguely glad that all his relatives were distant and out of touch with him, for they could not have understood his mental life. That is, none but his grandfather and great-uncle Christopher could, and they were long dead.

Then he began once more the writing of books, which he had left off when dreams first failed him. But here, too, was there no satisfaction or fulfilment; for the touch of earth was upon his mind, and he could not think of lovely things as he had done of yore. Ironic humour dragged down all the twilight minarets he reared, and the earthy fear of improbability blasted all the delicate and amazing flowers in his færy gardens.[9] The convention of assumed pity spilt mawkishness on his characters, while the myth of an important reality and significant human events and emotions debased all his high fantasy into thin-veiled allegory and cheap social satire. His new novels were successful as his old ones had never been; and because he knew how empty they must be to please an empty herd, he burned them and ceased his writing.

They were very graceful novels, in which he urbanely laughed at the dreams he lightly sketched; but he saw that their sophistication had sapped all their life away.

It was after this that he cultivated deliberate illusion, and dabbled in the notions of the bizarre and the eccentric as an antidote for the commonplace. Most of these, however, soon shewed their poverty and barrenness; and he saw that the popular doctrines of occultism are as dry and inflexible as those of science, yet without even the slender palliative of truth to redeem them. Gross stupidity, falsehood, and muddled thinking are not dream; and form no escape from life to a mind trained above their level. So Carter bought stranger books and sought out deeper and more terrible men of fantastic erudition; delving into arcana of consciousness that few have trod, and learning things about the secret pits of life, legend, and immemorial antiquity which disturbed him ever afterward. He decided to live on a rarer plane, and furnished his Boston home to suit his changing moods; one room for each, hung in appropriate colours, furnished with befitting books and objects, and provided with sources of the proper sensations of light, heat, sound, taste, and odour.

Once he heard of a man in the South who was shunned and feared for the blasphemous things he read in prehistoric books and clay tablets smuggled from India and Arabia. Him he visited, living with him and sharing his studies for seven years, till horror overtook them one midnight in an unknown and archaic graveyard, and only one emerged where two had entered.[10] Then he went back to Arkham, the terrible witch-haunted old town of his forefathers in New England, and had experiences in the dark, amidst the hoary willows and tottering gambrel roofs, which made him seal forever certain pages in the diary of a wild-minded ancestor.[11] But these horrors took him only to the edge of reality, and were not of the true dream country he had known in youth; so that at fifty he despaired of any rest or contentment in a world grown too busy for beauty and too shrewd for dream.

Having perceived at last the hollowness and futility of real things, Carter spent his days in retirement, and in wistful disjointed memories of his dream-filled youth. He thought it rather silly that he bothered to keep on living at all, and got from a South American acquaintance a very curious liquid to take him

10. This tale is told in "The Statement of Randolph Carter" (pp. 11–17, above).

11. The events are recounted in *The Case of Charles Dexter Ward* (pp. 171–309, below). This story was not written until January–March 1927 but evidently was in Lovecraft's mind earlier.

12. Originally, "Saracen" referred only to those non-Arabic people who lived in the desert areas around the Roman province of Arabia; later, the term came to be synonymous with "Muslim."

to oblivion without suffering. Inertia and force of habit, however, caused him to defer action; and he lingered indecisively among thoughts of old times, taking down the strange hangings from his walls and refitting the house as it was in his early boyhood—purple panes, Victorian furniture, and all.

With the passage of time he became almost glad he had lingered, for his relics of youth and his cleavage from the world made life and sophistication seem very distant and unreal; so much so that a touch of magic and expectancy stole back into his nightly slumbers. For years those slumbers had known only such twisted reflections of every-day things as the commonest slumbers know, but now there returned a flicker of something stranger and wilder; something of vaguely awesome immanence which took the form of tensely clear pictures from his childhood days, and made him think of little inconsequential things he had long forgotten. He would often awake calling for his mother and grandfather, both in their graves a quarter of a century.

Then one night his grandfather reminded him of a key. The grey old scholar, as vivid as in life, spoke long and earnestly of their ancient line, and of the strange visions of the delicate and sensitive men who composed it. He spoke of the flame-eyed Crusader who learnt wild secrets of the Saracens[12] that held him captive; and of the first Sir Randolph Carter who studied magic when Elizabeth was queen. He spoke, too, of that Edmund Carter who had just escaped hanging in the Salem witchcraft, and who had placed in an antique box a great silver key handed down from his ancestors. Before Carter awaked, the gentle visitant had told him where to find that box; that carved oak box of archaic wonder whose grotesque lid no hand had raised for two centuries.

In the dust and shadows of the great attic he found it, remote and forgotten at the back of a drawer in a tall chest. It was about a foot square, and its Gothic carvings were so fearful that he did not marvel no person since Edmund Carter had dared to open it. It gave forth no noise when shaken, but was mystic with the scent of unremembered spices. That it held a key was indeed only a dim legend, and Randolph Carter's father had never known such a box existed. It was bound in rusty iron, and no means was provided for working the formidable lock. Carter vaguely understood that he would find within it some key to the lost gate of dreams, but of where and how to use it his grandfather had told him nothing.

An old servant forced the carven lid, shaking as he did so at the hideous faces leering from the blackened wood, and at some unplaced familiarity. Inside, wrapped in a discoloured parchment, was a huge key of tarnished silver covered with cryptical arabesques; but of any legible explanation there was none. The parchment was voluminous, and held only the strange hieroglyphs of an unknown tongue written with an antique reed. Carter recognised the characters as those he had seen on a certain papyrus scroll belonging to that terrible scholar of the South who had vanished one midnight in a nameless cemetery. The man had always shivered when he read this scroll, and Carter shivered now.

But he cleaned the key, and kept it by him nightly in its aromatic box of ancient oak. His dreams were meanwhile increasing in vividness, and though shewing him none of the strange cities and incredible gardens of the old days, were assuming a definite cast whose purpose could not be mistaken. They were calling him back along the years, and with the mingled wills of all his fathers were pulling him toward some hidden and ancestral source. Then he knew he must go into the past and merge himself with old things, and day after day he thought of the hills to the north where haunted Arkham and the rushing Miskatonic and the lonely rustic homestead of his people lay.

In the brooding fire of autumn Carter took the old remembered way past graceful lines of rolling hill and stone-walled meadow, distant vale and hanging woodland, curving road and nestling farmstead, and the crystal windings of the Miskatonic, crossed here and there by rustic bridges of wood or stone. At one bend he saw the group of giant elms among which an ancestor had oddly vanished a century and a half before, and shuddered as the wind blew meaningly through them. Then there was the crumbling farmhouse of old Goody Fowler the witch, with its little evil windows and great roof sloping nearly to the ground on the north side. He speeded up his car as he passed it, and did not slacken till he had mounted the hill where his mother and her fathers before her were born, and where the old white house still

13. This occurred neither in Marblehead nor Salem and is no help in pinning down the identity of Carter's Kingsport.

14. These are described in "The Festival" (pp. 103–13, above).

looked proudly across the road at the breathlessly lovely panorama of rocky slope and verdant valley, with the distant spires of Kingsport on the horizon, and hints of the archaic, dream-laden sea in the farthest background.

Then came the steeper slope that held the old Carter place he had not seen in over forty years. Afternoon was far gone when he reached the foot, and at the bend half way up he paused to scan the outspread countryside golden and glorified in the slanting floods of magic poured out by a western sun. All the strangeness and expectancy of his recent dreams seemed present in this hushed and unearthly landscape, and he thought of the unknown solitudes of other planets as his eyes traced out the velvet and deserted lawns shining undulant between their tumbled walls, the clumps of færy forest setting off far lines of purple hills beyond hills, and the spectral wooded valley dipping down in shadow to dank hollows where trickling waters crooned and gurgled among swollen and distorted roots.

Something made him feel that motors did not belong in the realm he was seeking, so he left his car at the edge of the forest, and putting the great key in his coat pocket walked on up the hill. Woods now engulfed him utterly, though he knew the house was on a high knoll that cleared the trees except to the north. He wondered how it would look, for it had been left vacant and untended through his neglect since the death of his strange great-uncle Christopher thirty years before. In his boyhood he had revelled through long visits there, and had found weird marvels in the woods beyond the orchard.

Shadows thickened around him, for the night was near. Once a gap in the trees opened up to the right, so that he saw off across leagues of twilight meadow and spied the old Congregational steeple on Central Hill in Kingsport; pink with the last flush of day, the panes of the little round windows blazing with reflected fire. Then, when he was in deep shadow again, he recalled with a start that the glimpse must have come from childish memory alone, since the old white church had long been torn down to make room for the Congregational Hospital.[13] He had read of it with interest, for the paper had told about some strange burrows or passages found in the rocky hill beneath.[14]

Through his puzzlement a voice piped, and he started again

at its familiarity after long years. Old Benijah Corey had been his Uncle Christopher's hired man, and was aged even in those far-off times of his boyhood visits. Now he must be well over a hundred, but that piping voice could come from no one else. He could distinguish no words, yet the tone was haunting and unmistakable. To think that "Old Benijy" should still be alive!

"Mister Randy! Mister Randy! Whar be ye? D'ye want to skeer yer Aunt Marthy plumb to death? Hain't she tuld ye to keep nigh the place in the arternoon an' git back afur dark? Randy! Ran . . . dee! . . . He's the beatin'est boy fer runnin' off in the woods I ever see; haff the time a-settin' moonin' raound that snake-den in the upper timber-lot! . . . Hey, yew, Ran . . . dee!"

Randolph Carter stopped in the pitch darkness and rubbed his hand across his eyes. Something was queer. He had been somewhere he ought not to be; had strayed very far away to places where he had not belonged, and was now inexcusably late. He had not noticed the time on the Kingsport steeple, though he could easily have made it out with his pocket telescope; but he knew his lateness was something very strange and unprecedented. He was not sure he had his little telescope with him, and put his hand in his blouse pocket to see. No, it was not there, but there was the big silver key he had found in a box somewhere. Uncle Chris had told him something odd once about an old unopened box with a key in it, but Aunt Martha had stopped the story abruptly, saying it was no kind of thing to tell a child whose head was already too full of queer fancies. He tried to recall just where he had found the key, but something seemed very confused. He guessed it was in the attic at home in Boston, and dimly remembered bribing Parks with half his week's allowance to help him open the box and keep quiet about it; but when he remembered this, the face of Parks came up very strangely, as if the wrinkles of long years had fallen upon the brisk little Cockney.

"Ran . . . dee! Ran . . . dee! Hi! Hi! Randy!"

A swaying lantern came around the black bend, and old Benijah pounced on the silent and bewildered form of the pilgrim.

"Durn ye, boy, so thar ye be! Ain't ye got a tongue in yer head, that ye can't answer a body? I ben callin' this haff hour, an' ye must a heerd me long ago! Dun't ye know yer Aunt Mar-

15. Carter thinks nothing of the presence of his Aunt Martha and Uncle Chris, though the latter has been dead for more than thirty years. Carter has slipped back in time to his boyhood and, as will been seen shortly, has become a boy again.

16. Aegipan is Pan in goat form; hence aegipans are satyrs.

thy's all a-fidget over yer bein' off arter dark? Wait till I tell yer Uncle Chris when he gits hum! Ye'd orta know these here woods ain't no fitten place to be traipsin' this hour! They's things abroad what dun't do nobody no good, as my gran'sir' knowed afur me. Come, Mister Randy, or Hannah wun't keep supper no longer!"

So Randolph Carter was marched up the road where wondering stars glimmered through high autumn boughs. And dogs barked as the yellow light of small-paned windows shone out at the farther turn, and the Pleiades twinkled across the open knoll where a great gambrel roof stood black against the dim west. Aunt Martha was in the doorway, and did not scold too hard when Benijah shoved the truant in. She knew Uncle Chris well enough to expect such things of the Carter blood. Randolph did not shew his key, but ate his supper in silence and protested only when bedtime came. He sometimes dreamed better when awake, and he wanted to use that key.[15]

In the morning Randolph was up early, and would have run off to the upper timber-lot if Uncle Chris had not caught him and forced him into his chair by the breakfast table. He looked impatiently around the low-pitched room with the rag carpet and exposed beams and corner-posts, and smiled only when the orchard boughs scratched at the leaded panes of the rear window. The trees and the hills were close to him, and formed the gates of that timeless realm which was his true country.

Then, when he was free, he felt in his blouse pocket for the key; and being reassured, skipped off across the orchard to the rise beyond, where the wooded hill climbed again to heights above even the treeless knoll. The floor of the forest was mossy and mysterious, and great lichened rocks rose vaguely here and there in the dim light like Druid monoliths among the swollen and twisted trunks of a sacred grove. Once in his ascent Randolph crossed a rushing stream whose falls a little way off sang runic incantations to the lurking fauns and ægipans[16] and dryads.

Then he came to the strange cave in the forest slope, the dreaded "snake-den" which country folk shunned, and away from which Benijah had warned him again and again. It was deep; far deeper than anyone but Randolph suspected, for the boy had found a fissure in the farthermost black corner that led to a loftier grotto beyond—a haunting sepulchral place whose granite walls held a curious illusion of conscious artifice. On this occasion he crawled in as usual, lighting his way with matches filched from the sitting-room match-safe, and edging through the final crevice with an eagerness hard to explain even to himself. He could not tell why he approached the farther wall so confidently, or why he instinctively drew forth the great silver key as he did so. But on he went, and when he danced back to the house that night he offered no excuses for his lateness, nor heeded in the least the reproofs he gained for ignoring the noontide dinner-horn altogether.

Now it is agreed by all the distant relatives of Randolph Carter that something occurred to heighten his imagination in his tenth year. His cousin, Ernest B. Aspinwall, Esq., of Chicago, is fully ten years his senior; and distinctly recalls a change in the boy after the autumn of 1883.[17] Randolph had looked on scenes of fantasy that few others can ever have beheld, and stranger still were some of the qualities which he shewed in relation to very mundane things. He seemed, in fine, to have picked up an odd gift of prophecy; and reacted unusually to things which, though at the time without meaning, were later found to justify the singular impressions. In subsequent decades as new inventions, new names, and new events appeared one by one in the book of history, people would now and then recall wonderingly how Carter had years before let fall some careless word of undoubted connexion with what was then far in the future. He did not himself understand these words, or know why certain things made him feel certain emotions; but fancied that some unremembered dream must be responsible. It was as early as 1897 that he turned pale when some traveller mentioned the French town of Belloy-en-Santerre,[18] and friends remembered it when he was almost mortally wounded there in 1916, while serving with the Foreign Legion in the Great War.

Carter's relatives talk much of these things because he has lately disappeared. His little old servant Parks, who for years bore patiently with his vagaries, last saw him on the morning he drove off alone in his car with a key he had recently found. Parks had helped him get the key from the old box containing it, and had felt strangely affected by the grotesque carvings on the box, and by some other odd quality he could not name. When Carter left,

17. Carter has not been to his great-uncle's home for "more than 40 years," placing the events described here in the mid-1920s.

18. A commune in Picardie, in the north of France. The American poet Alan Seeger (the folksinger Pete Seeger's uncle) died there in 1916 after being mortally wounded in the Battle of the Somme.

19. Who is this narrator? In Lovecraft and Edgar Hoffmann Price's "Through the Gates of the Silver Key," which purports to trace the whereabouts of the Randolph Carter of Lovecraft's earlier story "The Silver Key," the narrator of the latter is identified as Ward Phillips, an "elderly eccentric of Providence, Rhode Island, who had enjoyed a long and close correspondence with Carter." Curiously, according to S. T. Joshi, Lovecraft used "Ward Phillips" as a pseudonym in connection with poetry published prior to 1922 (*I Am Providence*, 209). Why would the narrator have any standing to oppose a probate administration?

20. First mentioned in "The Cats of Ulthar" (1920) and featured in "The Other Gods" (1933).

he had said he was going to visit his old ancestral country around Arkham.

Half way up Elm Mountain, on the way to the ruins of the old Carter place, they found his motor set carefully by the roadside; and in it was a box of fragrant wood with carvings that frightened the countrymen who stumbled on it. The box held only a queer parchment whose characters no linguist or palæographer has been able to decipher or identify. Rain had long effaced any possible footprints, though Boston investigators had something to say about evidences of disturbances among the fallen timbers of the Carter place. It was, they averred, as though someone had groped about the ruins at no distant period. A common white handkerchief found among forest rocks on the hillside beyond cannot be identified as belonging to the missing man.

There is talk of apportioning Randolph Carter's estate among his heirs, but I shall stand firmly against this course because I do not believe he is dead.[19] There are twists of time and space, of vision and reality, which only a dreamer can divine; and from what I know of Carter I think he has merely found a way to traverse these mazes. Whether or not he will ever come back, I cannot say. He wanted the lands of dream he had lost, and yearned for the days of his childhood. Then he found a key, and I somehow believe he was able to use it to strange advantage.

I shall ask him when I see him, for I expect to meet him shortly in a certain dream-city we both used to haunt. It is rumoured in Ulthar, beyond the river Skai,[20] that a new king reigns on the opal throne in Ilek-Vad, that fabulous town of turrets atop the hollow cliffs of glass overlooking the twilight sea wherein the bearded and finny Gnorri build their singular labyrinths, and I believe I know how to interpret this rumour. Certainly, I look forward impatiently to the sight of that great silver key, for in its cryptical arabesques there may stand symbolised all the aims and mysteries of a blindly impersonal cosmos.

The Case of Charles Dexter Ward[1]

One of Lovecraft's two long published tales (the third, The Dream-Quest of Unknown Kadath, was issued posthumously), this began as a short story. Lovecraft soon realized that he had more to say, but the work was speedily written. Meticulously researched and a virtual showcase for Lovecraft's antiquarian interests, the story combines his frequent theme—that the unknown is often best left unknown—with a demonstration that New England was truly witch-haunted by its dark past. While he conveyed the same disturbing sense of deep-rooted local madness in "The Picture in the House," here its impact is much wider than on one isolated old man.

The essential Saltes of Animals may be so prepared and preserved, that an ingenious Man may have the whole Ark of Noah in his own Studie, and raise the fine Shape of an Animal out of its Ashes at his Pleasure; and by the lyke Method from the essential Saltes of humane Dust, a Philosopher may, without any criminal Necromancy, call up the Shape of any dead Ancestour from the Dust whereinto his Bodie has been incinerated.

—BORELLUS[2]

I. A RESULT AND A PROLOGUE

1.

From a private hospital for the insane near Providence, Rhode Island,[3] there recently disappeared an exceedingly singular person. He bore the name of Charles Dexter Ward, and was placed under restraint most reluctantly by the grieving father who had watched his aberration grow from a mere eccentricity to a dark mania involving both a possibility of murderous tendencies and a profound and peculiar change in the apparent contents of his mind. Doctors confess themselves quite

1. Written January–March 1927, the story first appeared (posthumously) in *Weird Tales* 35, no. 9 (May 1941), 8–40, and 35, no. 10 (July 1941), 84–121.

2. This is actually a description of Borellus's view taken from Cotton Mather's *Magnalia Christi Americana*, book I (see "The Picture in the House," note 12,

above), first identified in print by Barton Levi St. Armand in "The Source for Lovecraft's Knowledge of Borellus in *The Case of Charles Dexter Ward*." "Borellus" is Pierre Borel (1620–1689), a French physician who was a member of the Academy of Sciences and studied broadly in chemistry, biology, and related fields, probably including alchemy. Mather paraphrases Borel in the context of discussing the problems of biography and how much easier the task of research would be if the dead could be raised!

However, Mather's characterization of Borellus's work may be unfair. A more limited view is found in Antoine Augustine Calmet's treatise on vampires and revenants, usually titled *The Phantom World*, first published in 1746 and translated by the Rev. Henry Christmas in 1850:

> David Vanderbroch affirms that the blood of animals contains the idea of their species as well as their seed; he relates on this subject the experiment of M. Borelli, who asserts that the human blood, when warm, is still full of its spirits or sulphurs, acid and volatile, and that, being excited in cemeteries and in places where great battles are fought by some heat in the ground, the phantoms or ideas of the persons who are there interred are seen to rise; that we should see them as well by day as by night, were it not for the excess of light which prevents us even from seeing the stars. He adds that by this means we might behold the idea, and represent by a lawful and natural necromancy the figure or phantom of all the great men of antiquity, our friends and our ancestors, provided we possess their ashes.

This is quite different from the conclusions ascribed to Borellus by Mather. For a detailed discussion of Borellus's

Lead-in to *The Case of Charles Dexter Ward*, part 1. *Weird Tales* 35, no. 9 (May 1941) (artist: Harry Furman)

baffled by his case, since it presented oddities of a general physiological as well as psychological character.

In the first place, the patient seemed oddly older than his twenty-six years would warrant.[4] Mental disturbance, it is true, will age one rapidly; but the face of this young man had taken on a subtle cast which only the very aged normally acquire. In the second place, his organic processes shewed a certain queerness of proportion which nothing in medical experience can parallel. Respiration and heart action had a baffling lack of symmetry; the voice was lost, so that no sounds above a whisper were possible; digestion was incredibly prolonged and minimised, and neural reactions to standard stimuli bore no relation at all to anything heretofore recorded, either normal or pathological. The skin had a morbid chill and dryness, and the cellular structure of the

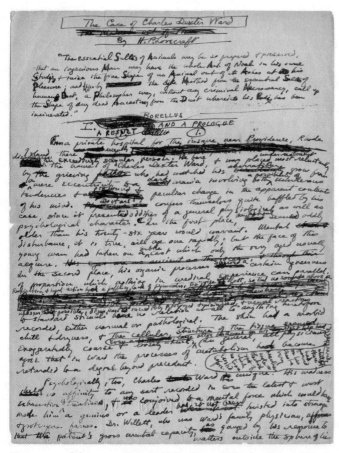

First page of the manuscript of *The Case of Charles Dexter Ward*,
now in the collection of the John Hay Library.

scientific work and writings, see Roger Bryant's "The Alchemist and the Scientist," in which Bryant incorrectly states that the narrator made up the passage from Mather.

3. The hospital is later described as sited on Conanicut Island, thirty-five miles south of Providence. Butler Hospital for the Insane, the first hospital in Rhode Island exclusively for mentally ill patients, was founded in 1847, as a result of a report by American health-care crusader Dorothea Dix. However, Butler Hospital, a few blocks east of College Hill in Providence, never had a facility on Conanicut Island.

4. Ward was born in 1902; this is consistent with Dr. Willett's later description of "the horrible and uncanny alienation of 1928."

tissue seemed exaggeratedly coarse and loosely knit. Even a large olive birthmark on the right hip had disappeared, whilst there had formed on the chest a very peculiar mole or blackish spot of which no trace existed before. In general, all physicians agree that in Ward the processes of metabolism had become retarded to a degree beyond precedent.

Psychologically, too, Charles Ward was unique. His madness held no affinity to any sort recorded in even the latest and most exhaustive of treatises, and was conjoined to a mental force which would have made him a genius or a leader had it not been twisted into strange and grotesque forms. Dr. Willett, who was Ward's family physician, affirms that the patient's gross mental capacity, as gauged by his response to matters outside the sphere of his insanity, had actually increased since the seizure. Ward, it is true, was always a scholar and an antiquarian; but even his most brilliant early work did not shew the prodigious grasp and insight displayed during his last examinations by the alienists. It was, indeed, a difficult matter to obtain a legal commitment to the hospital, so powerful and lucid did the youth's mind seem; and only on the evidence of others, and on the strength of many abnormal gaps in his stock of information as distinguished from his intelligence, was he finally placed in confinement. To the very moment of his vanishment he was an omnivorous reader and as great a conversationalist as his poor voice permitted; and shrewd observers, failing to foresee his escape, freely predicted that he would not be long in gaining his discharge from custody.

Only Dr. Willett, who brought Charles Ward into the world and had watched his growth of body and mind ever since, seemed frightened at the thought of his future freedom. He had had a terrible experience and had made a terrible discovery which he dared not reveal to his sceptical colleagues. Willett, indeed, presents a minor mystery all his own in his connexion with the case. He was the last to see the patient before his flight, and emerged from that final conversation in a state of mixed horror and relief which several recalled when Ward's escape became known three hours later. That escape itself is one of the unsolved wonders of Dr. Waite's hospital. A window open above a sheer drop of sixty feet could hardly explain it, yet after that talk with Willett the youth was undeniably gone. Willett himself has no public explanations to offer, though he seems strangely easier in mind than before the escape. Many, indeed, feel that he would like to say more if he thought any considerable number would believe him. He had found Ward in his room, but shortly after his departure the attendants knocked in vain. When they opened the door the patient was not there, and all they found was the open window with a chill April breeze blowing in a cloud of fine bluish-grey dust that almost choked them. True, the dogs howled some time before; but that was while Willett was still present, and they had caught nothing and shewn no disturbance later on. Ward's father was told at once over the telephone, but he seemed more saddened than surprised. By the time Dr. Waite called in person, Dr. Willett had been talking with him, and both disavowed any knowledge or complicity in the escape. Only from certain closely

The Prospect Street mansion of the Wards. Artist: Jason C. Eckhardt,
copyright © Jason C. Eckhardt 2013, reprinted with permission

5. College Hill—that is, the epicenter of much described in "The Call of Cthulhu," above.

confidential friends of Willett and the senior Ward have any clues been gained, and even these are too wildly fantastic for general credence. The one fact which remains is that up to the present time no trace of the missing madman has been unearthed.

Charles Ward was an antiquarian from infancy, no doubt gaining his taste from the venerable town around him, and from the relics of the past which filled every corner of his parents' old mansion in Prospect Street on the crest of the hill.[5] With the years his devotion to ancient things increased; so that history, genealogy, and the study of colonial architecture, furniture, and craftsmanship at length crowded everything else from his sphere of interests. These tastes are important to remember in considering his madness; for although they do not form its absolute nucleus, they play a prominent part in its superficial form. The gaps of information which the alienists noticed were all related to modern matters, and were invariably offset by a correspondingly excessive though outwardly concealed knowledge of bygone matters as brought out by adroit questioning; so that one would have fancied the patient literally transferred to a former age through some obscure sort of auto-hypnosis. The odd thing was that Ward seemed no longer interested in the antiquities he knew so well. He had, it appears, lost his regard for them through sheer familiarity; and all his final efforts were obviously bent toward master-

6. A Quaker day school in Providence, founded in 1784 and, until 1926, coeducational (it returned to admitting girls in 1976).

7. According to the *Collections of the Rhode Island Historical Society*, "It has been handed down by tradition [that,] soon after the settlement of Providence[,] a body of Indians approached the town in a hostile manner. Some of the townsmen by running and stamping on this hill induced them to believe that there was a large number of men stationed there to oppose them, upon which they relinquished their design and retired. From this circumstance the hill was always called Stampers hill or more generally the Stampers. Stampers street passes along the brow of this Hill."

ing those common facts of the modern world which had been so totally and unmistakably expunged from his brain. That this wholesale deletion had occurred, he did his best to hide; but it was clear to all who watched him that his whole programme of reading and conversation was determined by a frantic wish to imbibe such knowledge of his own life and of the ordinary practical and cultural background of the twentieth century as ought to have been his by virtue of his birth in 1902 and his education in the schools of our own time. Alienists are now wondering how, in view of his vitally impaired range of data, the escaped patient manages to cope with the complicated world of today; the dominant opinion being that he is "lying low" in some humble and unexacting position till his stock of modern information can be brought up to the normal.

The beginning of Ward's madness is a matter of dispute among alienists. Dr. Lyman, the eminent Boston authority, places it in 1919 or 1920, during the boy's last year at the Moses Brown School,[6] when he suddenly turned from the study of the past to the study of the occult, and refused to qualify for college on the ground that he had individual researches of much greater importance to make. This is certainly borne out by Ward's altered habits at the time, especially by his continual search through town records and among old burying-grounds for a certain grave dug in 1771; the grave of an ancestor named Joseph Curwen, some of whose papers he professed to have found behind the panelling of a very old house in Olney Court, on Stampers' Hill,[7] which Curwen was known to have built and occupied. It is, broadly speaking, undeniable that the winter of 1919–20 saw a great change in Ward; whereby he abruptly stopped his general antiquarian pursuits and embarked on a desperate delving into occult subjects both at home and abroad, varied only by this strangely persistent search for his forefather's grave.

From this opinion, however, Dr. Willett substantially dissents; basing his verdict on his close and continuous knowledge of the patient, and on certain frightful investigations and discoveries which he made toward the last. Those investigations and discoveries have left their mark upon him; so that his voice trembles when he tells them, and his hand trembles when he tries to write of them. Willett admits that the change of 1919–20 would

ordinarily appear to mark the beginning of a progressive decadence which culminated in the horrible and uncanny alienation
of 1928; but believes from personal observation that a finer distinction must be made. Granting freely that the boy was always
ill-balanced temperamentally, and prone to be unduly susceptible
and enthusiastic in his responses to phenomena around him, he
refuses to concede that the early alteration marked the actual
passage from sanity to madness; crediting instead Ward's own
statement that he had discovered or rediscovered something
whose effect on human thought was likely to be marvellous and
profound. The true madness, he is certain, came with a later
change; after the Curwen portrait and the ancient papers had
been unearthed; after a trip to strange foreign places had been
made, and some terrible invocations chanted under strange and
secret circumstances; after certain *answers* to these invocations
had been plainly indicated, and a frantic letter penned under
agonising and inexplicable conditions; after the wave of vampirism and the ominous Pawtuxet gossip; and after the patient's
memory commenced to exclude contemporary images whilst his
voice failed and his physical aspect underwent the subtle modification so many subsequently noticed.

It was only about this time, Willett points out with much
acuteness, that the nightmare qualities became indubitably
linked with Ward; and the doctor feels shudderingly sure that
enough solid evidence exists to sustain the youth's claim regarding his crucial discovery. In the first place, two workmen of high
intelligence saw Joseph Curwen's ancient papers found. Secondly,
the boy once shewed Dr. Willett those papers and a page of the
Curwen diary, and each of the documents had every appearance
of genuineness. The hole where Ward claimed to have found them
was long a visible reality, and Willett had a very convincing final
glimpse of them in surroundings which can scarcely be believed
and can never perhaps be proved. Then there were the mysteries
and coincidences of the Orne and Hutchinson letters, and the
problem of the Curwen penmanship and of what the detectives
brought to light about Dr. Allen; these things, and the terrible
message in mediæval minuscules[8] found in Willett's pocket when
he gained consciousness after his shocking experience.

And most conclusive of all, there are the two hideous *results*

8. Ancient and medieval manuscripts
in Latin and Greek were written in a
cursive script or handwriting known as
"minuscule," and the term has come to
mean books written in the script.

An example from the Freising
Manuscripts, ca. tenth century CE.

9. The school is at 250 Lloyd Avenue, a few blocks east of Prospect Street.

Moses Brown School, in 2013. Photograph copyright © Donovan K. Loucks 2013, reprinted with permission

10. A private membership library, located at 251 Benefit Street, near College Hill, since 1836. Henry L. P. Beckwith Jr. recounts, in *Lovecraft's Providence & Adjacent Parts*, that until the late 1980s, the Athenæum maintained a locked "scruple" room, in which were kept books "of questionable redeeming social merits, such as *Studs Lonigan* and the works of Erskine Caldwell." Newly acquired works that seemed destined for the "scruple" room were "kept temporarily in a drawer, known to the staff as 'The Sewer,' at the circulation desk" (35).

Providence Athenæum, in 2010. Photograph copyright © Donovan K. Loucks 2010, reprinted with permission

11. The Rhode Island Historical Society is currently at 110 Benevolent Street, also near College Hill; it previously occupied 68 Benefit Street, a structure now taken over by Brown University's Population Studies and Training Center.

which the doctor obtained from a certain pair of formulæ during his final investigations; results which virtually proved the authenticity of the papers and of their monstrous implications at the same time that those papers were borne forever from human knowledge.

2.

One must look back at Charles Ward's earlier life as at something belonging as much to the past as the antiquities he loved so keenly. In the autumn of 1918, and with a considerable show of zest in the military training of the period, he had begun his junior year at the Moses Brown School, which lies very near his home.[9] The old main building, erected in 1819, had always charmed his youthful antiquarian sense; and the spacious park in which the academy is set appealed to his sharp eye for landscape. His social activities were few; and his hours were spent mainly at home, in rambling walks, in his classes and drills, and in pursuit of antiquarian and genealogical data at the City Hall, the State House, the Public Library, the Athenæum,[10] the Historical Society,[11] the John Carter Brown and John Hay Libraries of Brown University,[12] and the newly opened Shepley Library in Benefit Street.[13] One may picture him yet as he was in those days; tall, slim, and blond, with studious eyes and a slight stoop, dressed

Providence City Hall, in 2010. Photograph copyright © Donovan K. Loucks 2010, reprinted with permission

The Rhode Island State House, in 2010. Photograph copyright © Donovan K. Loucks 2010, reprinted with permission

Rhode Island Historical Society, in a building now belonging to Brown University, in 2010. Photograph copyright © Donovan K. Loucks 2010, reprinted with permission

somewhat carelessly, and giving a dominant impression of harmless awkwardness rather than attractiveness.

His walks were always adventures in antiquity, during which he managed to recapture from the myriad relics of a glamorous old city a vivid and connected picture of the centuries before. His home was a great Georgian mansion[14] atop the well-nigh precipitous hill that rises just east of the river; and from the rear windows of its rambling wings he could look dizzily out over all the clustered spires, domes, roofs, and skyscraper summits of the

12. Lovecraft's own papers and manuscripts now reside at the latter library.

13. Colonel George Leander Shepley established the Shepley Library, said in 1937 to hold over 30,000 historical items, in a one-story stucco and limestone structure at 292 Benefit Street, near the Athenæum, in 1921; it was subsequently maintained by his daughter Mrs. Ernest T. H. Metcalf. It closed in 1938, and its considerable holdings—letters, maps, bound volumes, and so forth—were transferred to the Rhode Island Historical Society.

14. Although the address is not given, most scholars identify the Halsey House, at 140 Prospect Street, built in 1801, as the residence of the Ward family.

The Jenckes-Pratt House (ca. 1775), 133 North Prospect Street at Barnes Street, the north end of the "Little White Farmhouse," in 1990. Photograph courtesy of Will Hart

The Halsey House at 140 Prospect Street, in 2010. Photograph copyright © Donovan K. Loucks 2010, reprinted with permission

lower town to the purple hills of the countryside beyond. Here he was born, and from the lovely classic porch of the double-bayed brick facade his nurse had first wheeled him in his carriage; past the little white farmhouse of two hundred years before that the town had long ago overtaken, and on toward the stately colleges along the shady, sumptuous street, whose old square brick mansions and smaller wooden houses with narrow, heavy-columned Doric porches dreamed solid and exclusive amidst their generous yards and gardens.

He had been wheeled, too, along sleepy Congdon Street, one tier lower down on the steep hill, and with all its eastern homes on high terraces. The small wooden houses averaged a greater age here, for it was up this hill that the growing town had climbed; and in these rides he had imbibed something of the colour of a quaint colonial village. The nurse used to stop and sit on the benches of Prospect Terrace to chat with policemen; and one of the child's first memories was of the great westward sea of hazy roofs and domes and steeples and far hills which he saw one winter afternoon from that great railed embankment, all violet and mystic against a fevered, apocalyptic sunset of reds and golds and purples and curious greens. The vast marble dome of the State House stood out in massive silhouette, its crowning statue haloed fantastically by a break in one of the tinted stratus clouds that barred the flaming sky.

The view of Congdon Street from 75 Prospect Terrace, in 1990.
Photograph courtesy of Will Hart

Prospect Terrace, in 2010. Photograph copyright © Donovan K. Loucks 2010, reprinted with permission

15. Thomas Durfee (1826–1901) was a prominent Rhode Island jurist, serving as chief justice of the Rhode Island Supreme Court from 1875 to 1891. He and his wife lived at 49 Benefit Street.

49 Benefit Street, home of Thomas Durfee, in 2010. Photograph copyright © Donovan K. Loucks 2010, reprinted with permission

When he was larger his famous walks began; first with his impatiently dragged nurse, and then alone in dreamy meditation. Farther and farther down that almost perpendicular hill he would venture, each time reaching older and quainter levels of the ancient city. He would hesitate gingerly down vertical Jenckes Street with its bank walls and colonial gables to the shady Benefit Street corner, where before him was a wooden antique with an Ionic-pilastered pair of doorways, and beside him a prehistoric gambrel-roofer with a bit of primal farmyard remaining, and the great Judge Durfee[15] house with its fallen vestiges of Georgian grandeur. It was getting to be a slum here; but the titan elms cast a restoring shadow over the place, and the boy used to stroll south past the long lines of the pre-Revolutionary homes with their great central chimneys and classic portals. On the eastern side they were set high over basements with railed double flights of stone steps, and the young Charles could picture them as they were when the street was new, and red heels and periwigs[16] set off the painted pediments whose signs of wear were now becoming so visible.

Westward the hill dropped almost as steeply as above, down to the old "Town Street" that the founders had laid out at the river's edge in 1636. Here ran innumerable little lanes with leaning, huddled houses of immense antiquity; and fascinated though he

16. In the early eighteenth century, when the street was new, "pre-Revolutionary" wigs were obligatory items of fashion for men. (Women rarely wore wigs but

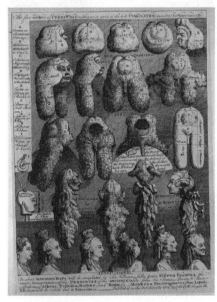

The Five Orders of Perriwigs as They Were Worn at the Late Coronation Measured Architectonically by William Hogarth (1761).

supplemented their natural hair with artificial strands, twists, and rolls, and used cork, horsehair padding, and pomade to build towering styles.) The fashion for men's wigs began in seventeenth-century France but, with the colonization of America, spread to England and across the Atlantic. It was satirized by William Hogarth in 1761, who depicted "five orders" of wigs worn to the coronation of King George III.

17. The church itself, properly the Cathedral of St. John's Episcopal, is at 271 North Main Street. There is also a St. John's Roman Catholic Church in Providence, but it was at 352 Atwells Avenue, not in this neighborhood.

St. John's Church, in 2010. Photograph copyright © Donovan K. Loucks 2010, reprinted with permission

18. The so-called Old Colony House, on Washington Square, essentially unaltered since its construction in 1760–62, and originally home to the colonial legislature and later the Rhode Island State

was, it was long before he dared to thread their archaic verticality for fear they would turn out a dream or a gateway to unknown terrors. He found it much less formidable to continue along Benefit Street past the iron fence of St. John's hidden churchyard[17] and the rear of the 1761 Colony House[18] and the mouldering bulk of the Golden Ball Inn[19] where Washington stopped. At Meeting Street—the successive Gaol Lane and King Street of other periods—he would look upward to the east and see the arched flight of steps to which the highway had to resort in climbing the slope, and downward to the west, glimpsing the old brick colonial schoolhouse that smiles across the road at the ancient Sign of Shakespear's Head where the *Providence Gazette and Country-Journal* was printed before the Revolution.[20] Then came the exquisite First Baptist Church of 1775,[21] luxurious with its matchless Gibbs[22] steeple, and the Georgian roofs and cupolas hovering by. Here and to the southward the neighbourhood became better, flowering at last into a marvellous group of early mansions; but still the little ancient lanes led off down the precipice to the west, spectral in their many-gabled archaism and dipping to a riot of iridescent decay where the wicked old waterfront recalls its proud East India days amidst polyglot vice and squalor, rotting wharves, and blear-eyed ship-chandleries, with such surviving alley names as Packet, Bullion, Gold, Silver, Coin, Doubloon, Sovereign, Guilder, Dollar, Dime, and Cent.

Sometimes, as he grew taller and more adventurous, young Ward would venture down into this mælstrom of tottering houses, broken transoms, tumbling steps, twisted balustrades, swarthy faces, and nameless odours; winding from South Main to South Water, searching out the docks where the bay and sound steamers still touched, and returning northward at this lower level past the steep-roofed 1816 warehouses and the broad square at the Great Bridge, where the 1773 Market House[23] still stands firm on its ancient arches. In that square he would pause to drink in the bewildering beauty of the old town as it rises on its eastward bluff, decked with its two Georgian spires and crowned by the vast new Christian Science dome[24] as London is crowned by St. Paul's. He liked mostly to reach this point in the late afternoon, when the slanting sunlight touches the Market House and the ancient hill roofs and belfries with gold, and throws magic around the dream-

Brick colonial schoolhouse at 24 Meeting Street, across from the Sign of Shakespeare's Head, in 2010. Photograph copyright © Donovan K. Loucks 2010, reprinted with permission

Legislature. A contemporary picture of the structure is at p. 192, above.

The Old Colony House, also known as the Old State House, shown here in 1891, is at 150 Benefit Street in Providence.

19. At 159 Benefit Street, since demolished.

20. Bookseller John Carter, who printed the *Gazette* and later was its publisher, owned a home and shop at 21 Meeting Street, built in 1772. He placed a sign depicting a bust of Shakespeare outside his shop, and the building retained the name.

ing wharves where Providence Indiamen used to ride at anchor. After a long look he would grow almost dizzy with a poet's love for the sight, and then he would scale the slope homeward in the dusk past the old white church and up the narrow precipitous ways where yellow gleams would begin to peep out in small-paned windows and through fanlights set high over double flights of steps with curious wrought-iron railings.

At other times, and in later years, he would seek for vivid contrasts; spending half a walk in the crumbling colonial regions northwest of his home, where the hill drops to the lower eminence of Stampers' Hill with its ghetto and negro quarter clustering round the place where the Boston stage coach used to start before the Revolution,[25] and the other half in the gracious southerly realm about George, Benevolent, Power, and Williams Streets, where the old slope holds unchanged the fine estates and bits of walled garden and steep green lane in which so many fragrant memories linger. These rambles, together with the diligent studies which accompanied them, certainly account for a large amount of the antiquarian lore which at last crowded the modern

Sign of Shakespeare's Head, 21 Meeting St., Providence, in 2010. Photograph copyright © Donovan K. Loucks 2010, reprinted with permission

21. Housing the oldest Baptist congregation in America (organized by Roger

Williams in 1638), the church was built in 1775.

22. James Gibbs (1682–1754), a prominent English architect, did not design the church; the narrator here refers to Gibbs's innovation of placing the steeple in the middle of the structure, rather than adjacent, as was the style of Christopher Wren's contemporary churches.

23. In Market Square, on South Main Street.

Market House, in 2010. Photograph copyright © Donovan K. Loucks 2010, reprinted with permission

24. First Church of Christ, Scientist, on the corner of Prospect and Meeting streets.

The First Church of Christ, Scientist, at 71 Prospect Street, in 1990. Photograph courtesy of Will Hart

world from Charles Ward's mind; and illustrate the mental soil upon which fell, in that fateful winter of 1919–20, the seeds that came to such strange and terrible fruition.

Dr. Willett is certain that, up to this ill-omened winter of first change, Charles Ward's antiquarianism was free from every trace of the morbid. Graveyards held for him no particular attraction beyond their quaintness and historic value, and of anything like violence or savage instinct he was utterly devoid. Then, by insidious degrees, there appeared to develop a curious sequel to one of his genealogical triumphs of the year before; when he had discovered among his maternal ancestors a certain very long-lived man named Joseph Curwen, who had come from Salem in March of 1692, and about whom a whispered series of highly peculiar and disquieting stories clustered.

Ward's great-great-grandfather Welcome Potter had in 1785 married a certain "Ann Tillinghast, daughter of Mrs. Eliza, daughter to Capt. James Tillinghast," of whose paternity the family had preserved no trace. Late in 1918, whilst examining a volume of original town records in manuscript, the young genealogist encountered an entry describing a legal change of name, by which in 1772 a Mrs. Eliza Curwen, widow of Joseph Curwen, resumed, along with her seven-year-old daughter Ann, her maiden name of Tillinghast; on the ground "that her Husband's name was become a publick Reproach by Reason of what was knowne after his Decease; the which confirming an antient common Rumour, tho' not to be credited by a loyall Wife till so proven as to be wholly past Doubting." This entry came to light upon the accidental separation of two leaves which had been carefully pasted together and treated as one by a laboured revision of the page numbers.

It was at once clear to Charles Ward that he had indeed discovered a hitherto unknown great-great-great-grandfather. The discovery doubly excited him because he had already heard vague reports and seen scattered allusions relating to this person; about whom there remained so few publicly available records, aside from those becoming public only in modern times, that it almost seemed as if a conspiracy had existed to blot him from memory. What did appear, moreover, was of such a singular and provocative nature that one could not fail to imagine curiously what it was that the colonial recorders were so anxious to conceal and forget; or to suspect that the deletion had reasons all too valid.

Before this, Ward had been content to let his romancing about old Joseph Curwen remain in the idle stage; but having discovered his own relationship to this apparently "hushed-up" character, he proceeded to hunt out as systematically as possible whatever he might find concerning him. In this excited quest he eventually succeeded beyond his highest expectations; for old letters, diaries, and sheaves of unpublished memoirs in cobwebbed Providence garrets and elsewhere yielded many illuminating passages which their writers had not thought it worth their while to destroy. One important sidelight came from a point as remote as New York, where some Rhode Island colonial correspondence was stored in the Museum at Fraunces' Tavern.[26] The really crucial thing, though, and what in Dr. Willett's opinion formed the definite source of Ward's undoing, was the matter found in August 1919 behind the panelling of the crumbling house in Olney Court. It was that, beyond a doubt, which opened up those black vistas whose end was deeper than the pit.

II. AN ANTECEDENT AND A HORROR

1.

JOSEPH CURWEN, AS revealed by the rambling legends embodied in what Ward heard and unearthed, was a very astonishing, enigmatic, and obscurely horrible individual. He had fled from Salem to Providence—that universal haven of the odd, the free, and the dissenting—at the beginning of the great witchcraft panic; being in fear of accusation because of his solitary ways and queer chemical or alchemical experiments. He was a colourless-looking man of about thirty, and was soon found qualified to become a freeman of Providence; thereafter buying a home lot just north of Gregory Dexter's at about the foot of Olney Street.[27] His house was built on Stampers' Hill west of the Town Street, in what later became Olney Court; and in 1761 he replaced this with a larger one, on the same site, which is still standing.[28]

Now the first odd thing about Joseph Curwen was that he did not seem to grow much older than he had been on his arrival. He

25. According to Welcome Arnold Greene's *The Providence Plantations for Two Hundred and Fifty Years: An Historical Review of the Foundation, Rise, and Progress of the City of Providence* (128), the Boston stage line was initiated in 1767. Lovecraft had a copy of Greene's book in his library.

26. A tavern and museum at 54 Pearl Street in New York City, seriously compromised by several nineteenth-century fires and then irrevocably damaged, in 1975, by a bombing that killed four and injured more than fifty people, now housed in a reconstructed building based on conjecture as to its original appearance. The original was host to pre-Revolution meetings of the Sons of Liberty.

27. According to Gertrude S. Kimball's *Providence in Colonial Times* (hereinafter "Kimball"), Dexter, formerly a London stationer and printer, had been given a lot on Towne Street (Kimball's spelling), at the extreme north end, in 1640. He became town clerk and a leader of the Fenner-Dexter faction (78).

28. The street doesn't exist, and Kenneth Faig Jr., in his 2013 monograph *The Site of Joseph Curwen's Home in H. P. Lovecraft's* The Case of Charles Dexter Ward, proposes that the house was actually at 6 Olney Street, razed in the 1930s. Curiously, the house later was the address of Mrs. Delilah Townsend, a housekeeper for Lovecraft.

29. A small rural village in Bristol County, Massachusetts, only eleven miles east of Providence.

engaged in shipping enterprises, purchased wharfage near Mile-End Cove, helped rebuild the Great Bridge in 1713, and in 1723 was one of the founders of the Congregational Church on the hill; but always did he retain the nondescript aspect of a man not greatly over thirty or thirty-five. As decades mounted up, this singular quality began to excite wide notice; but Curwen always explained it by saying that he came of hardy forefathers, and practiced a simplicity of living which did not wear him out. How such simplicity could be reconciled with the inexplicable comings and goings of the secretive merchant, and with the queer gleaming of his windows at all hours of night, was not very clear to the townsfolk; and they were prone to assign other reasons for his continued youth and longevity. It was held, for the most part, that Curwen's incessant mixings and boilings of chemicals had much to do with his condition. Gossip spoke of the strange substances he brought from London and the Indies on his ships or purchased in Newport, Boston, and New York; and when old Dr. Jabez Bowen came from Rehoboth[29] and opened his apothecary shop across the Great Bridge at the Sign of the Unicorn and Mortar, there was ceaseless talk of the drugs, acids, and metals that the taciturn recluse incessantly bought or ordered from him. Acting on the assumption that Curwen possessed a wondrous and secret medical skill, many sufferers of various sorts applied to him for aid; but though he appeared to encourage their belief in a non-committal way, and always gave them odd-coloured potions in response to their requests, it was observed that his ministrations to others seldom proved of benefit. At length, when over fifty years had passed since the stranger's advent, and without producing more than five years' apparent change in his face and physique, the people began to whisper more darkly; and to meet more than half way that desire for isolation which he had always shewn.

Private letters and diaries of the period reveal, too, a multitude of other reasons why Joseph Curwen was marvelled at, feared, and finally shunned like a plague. His passion for graveyards, in which he was glimpsed at all hours, and under all conditions, was notorious; though no one had witnessed any deed on his part which could actually be termed ghoulish. On the Pawtuxet Road he had a farm, at which he generally lived during the summer, and to which he would frequently be seen riding at various odd times of the day or night. Here his only visible servants, farmers, and caretakers were a sullen pair of aged Narragansett Indians;[30] the husband dumb and curiously scarred, and the wife of a very repulsive cast of countenance, probably due to a mixture of negro blood. In the lean-to of this house was the laboratory where most of the chemical experiments were conducted. Curious porters and teamers who delivered bottles, bags, or boxes at the small rear door would exchange accounts of the fantastic flasks, crucibles, alembics, and furnaces they saw in the low shelved room; and prophesied in whispers that the close-mouthed "chymist"—by which they meant *alchemist*—would not be long in finding the Philosopher's Stone. The nearest neighbours to this farm—the Fenners, a quarter of a mile away[31]—had still queerer things to tell of certain sounds which they insisted came from the Curwen place in the night. There were cries, they said, and sustained howlings; and they did not like the large number of livestock which thronged the pastures, for no such amount was needed to keep a lone old man and a very few servants in meat, milk, and wool. The identity of the stock seemed to change from week to week as new droves were purchased from the Kingstown farmers. Then, too, there was something very obnoxious about a certain great stone outbuilding with only high narrow slits for windows.

Great Bridge idlers likewise had much to say of Curwen's town house in Olney Court; not so much the fine new one built in 1761, when the man must have been nearly a century old, but the first low gambrel-roofed one with the windowless attic and shingled sides, whose timbers he took the peculiar precaution of burning after its demolition. Here there was less mystery, it is true; but the hours at which lights were seen, the secretiveness of the two swarthy foreigners who comprised the only menservants, the hideous indistinct mumbling of the incredibly aged French housekeeper, the large amounts of food seen to enter a door within which only four persons lived, and the *quality* of certain voices often heard in muffled conversation at highly unseasonable times, all combined with what was known of the Pawtuxet[32] farm to give the place a bad name.

In choicer circles, too, the Curwen home was by no means undiscussed; for as the newcomer had gradually worked into

30. A Native American tribe from the area, part of the Algonquin Nation.

31. According to Kimball, Arthur Fenner and two brothers came to Providence in 1647. Arthur built a "farm in the woods," probably in 1655, on the west side of the Great Salt River, in the present suburb of Cranston (80).

32. A village—actually, a section of the townships of Warwick and Cranston, Rhode Island, at the intersection of the Pawtuxet and Providence rivers. In the late nineteenth century, the Rhodes family, local merchants, developed a casino and dance hall there (known as Rhodes-on-the-Pawtuxet) that became

The Pawtuxet River, in 2009. Photograph copyright © Donovan K. Loucks 2010, reprinted with permission

Rhodes-on-the-Pawtuxet, in 2001. Photograph copyright © Donovan K. Loucks 2010, reprinted with permission

a popular tourist attraction—one could also rent canoes—which drew large numbers of visitors by trolley from Providence.

33. The Rev. John Checkley (1680–1754) was a well-known New England cleric, remembered in *John Checkley; or, The Evolution of Religious Tolerance in Massachusetts Bay* by the Rev. Edmund F. Slafter. Slafter's book reprints Checkley's *A Modest Proof of Church Government . . .* , a defence of episcopacy, which was the focus of Checkley's libel trial in 1724. Checkley is also described at some length in Kimball. She mentions his "racy humour and inexhaustible fund of anecdote," though she omits the incident of the meeting with Curwen (170).

34. The description of John Merritt is confirmed in Kimball. (178) Again, Kimball does not mention Curwen.

35. The Pawtuxet Neck is a cape in Providence County, just east of Pawtuxet.

the church and trading life of the town, he had naturally made acquaintances of the better sort, whose company and conversation he was well fitted by education to enjoy. His birth was known to be good, since the Curwens or Corwins of Salem needed no introduction in New England. It developed that Joseph Curwen had travelled much in very early life, living for a time in England and making at least two voyages to the Orient; and his speech, when he deigned to use it, was that of a learned and cultivated Englishman. But for some reason or other Curwen did not care for society. Whilst never actually rebuffing a visitor, he always reared such a wall of reserve that few could think of anything to say to him which would not sound inane.

There seemed to lurk in his bearing some cryptic, sardonic arrogance, as if he had come to find all human beings dull through having moved among stranger and more potent entities. When Dr. Checkley the famous wit came from Boston in 1738 to be rector of King's Church,[33] he did not neglect calling on one of whom he soon heard so much; but left in a very short while because of some sinister undercurrent he detected in his host's discourse. Charles Ward told his father, when they discussed Curwen one winter evening, that he would give much to learn what the mysterious old man had said to the sprightly cleric, but that all diarists agree concerning Dr. Checkley's reluctance to repeat anything he had heard. The good man had been hideously shocked, and could never recall Joseph Curwen without a visible loss of the gay urbanity for which he was famed.

More definite, however, was the reason why another man of taste and breeding avoided the haughty hermit. In 1746 Mr. John Merritt,[34] an elderly English gentleman of literary and scientific leanings, came from Newport to the town which was so rapidly overtaking it in standing, and built a fine country seat on the Neck[35] in what is now the heart of the best residence section. He lived in considerable style and comfort, keeping the first coach and liveried servants in town, and taking great pride in his telescope, his microscope, and his well-chosen library of English and Latin books. Hearing of Curwen as the owner of the best library in Providence, Mr. Merritt early paid him a call, and was more cordially received than most other callers at the house had been. His admiration for his host's ample shelves, which besides the Greek, Latin, and English classics were equipped with a remarkable battery of philosophical, mathematical, and scientific works[36] including Paracelsus,[37] Agricola,[38] Van Helmont,[39] Sylvius,[40] Glauber,[41] Boyle,[42] Boerhaave,[43] Becher,[44] and Stahl,[45] led Curwen to suggest a visit to the farmhouse and laboratory whither he had never invited anyone before; and the two drove out at once in Mr. Merritt's coach.

Mr. Merritt always confessed to seeing nothing really horrible at the farmhouse, but maintained that the titles of the books in the special library of thaumaturgical, alchemical, and theological subjects which Curwen kept in a front room were alone sufficient to inspire him with a lasting loathing. Perhaps, however, the facial expression of the owner in exhibiting them contributed much of the prejudice. The bizarre collection, besides a host of standard works which Mr. Merritt was not too alarmed to envy, embraced nearly all the cabbalists, dæmonologists, and magicians known to man; and was a treasure-house of lore in the doubtful realms of alchemy and astrology. Hermes Trismegistus in Mesnard's edition,[46] the *Turba Philosophorum*,[47] Geber's *Liber Investigationis*,[48] and Artephius's *Key of Wisdom*[49] all were there; with the cabbalistic *Zohar*,[50] Peter Jammy's set of Albertus Magnus,[51] Raymond Lully's *Ars Magna et Ultima* in Zetsner's edition,[52] Roger Bacon's *Thesaurus Chemicus*,[53] Fludd's *Clavis Alchimiæ*,[54] and Trithemius's *De Lapide Philosophico*[55] crowding them close.[56] Mediæval Jews and Arabs were represented in profusion, and Mr. Merritt turned pale when, upon taking down a fine volume conspicuously labelled as the *Qanoon-e-Islam*,[57] he found it was in truth the forbidden *Necronomicon* of the mad Arab Abdul Alhazred, of which he had heard such monstrous things whispered some years previously after the exposure of nameless rites at the strange little fishing village of Kingsport,[58] in the Province of the Massachusetts-Bay.

But oddly enough, the worthy gentleman owned himself most impalpably disquieted by a mere minor detail. On the huge mahogany table there lay face downward a badly worn copy of Borellus,[59] bearing many cryptical marginalia and interlineations in Curwen's hand. The book was open at about its middle, and one paragraph displayed such thick and tremulous pen-strokes beneath the lines of mystic black-letter that the visitor could not resist scanning it

36. As will be seen, the works include some by crackpots and some by respected scientists, but of course in the early days of modern science, it was difficult to tell one from the other. Note that all but one of the cited works is German or Dutch.

37. Philip von Hohenheim (1493–1541) was a German-Swiss alchemist and philosopher who took the name Theophrastus Philippus Aureolus Bombastus von Hohenheim and later the title Paracelsus ("greater than Celsus," a Roman physician and medical historian).

38. Georgius Agricola (the Latin version of his name), or Georg Bauer (1494–1555), was a German scholar and scientist known as the father of mineralogy. He was perhaps the first scholar to found a natural science upon observation, as opposed to speculation.

39. Jan Baptist van Helmont (1579–1644), a Flemish chemist, physiologist, and physician, was a successor to Paracelsus.

40. Franciscus Sylvius (1614–1672), born Franz de le Boë, another Dutch physician and scientist. Sylvius was an early champion of the work of Descartes, van Helmont, and William Harvey, and in particular Harvey's theories on anatomy and the circulation of blood, and he described an important deep sulcus—a crease—on the brain's lateral surface, called the Sylvian fissure.

41. Johann Rudolf Glauber (ca. 1604–1670), a German-Dutch alchemist and chemist and colleague of Sylvius's who studied chemical engineering.

42. Robert Boyle (1627–1691), a Fellow of the Royal Society, was an English natural philosopher, physicist, and inventor, the first modern chemist and the discoverer of Boyle's law, relating to the relation-

ship between pressure and volume of a gas. His 1661 masterwork, *The Sceptical Cymist: or, Cymico-Physical Doubts & Paradoxes*, was noted for the breadth and detail of its experiments, its classification of the science, its suggestion that there were more elements than previously believed, and, perhaps surprisingly for a book considered to be the first text in this newly codified discipline, its self-deprecating humor. Boyle's fears that "so maim'd and imperfect" a treatise would result not only in "somewhat numerous *Errata*" in future editions but the discovery of "grosser mistakes" were not realized, and the book remains a seminal work in the history of science.

43. Herman Boerhaave (1668–1738), a Dutch botanist, humanist, and physician, is often credited as the founder of clinical teaching and of the modern academic hospital. Referred to as the "Teacher of All Europe," his lectures at the University of Leiden were always full to capacity.

44. Johann Joachim Becher (1635–ca. 1682), a German chemist and physician whose theories of combustion influenced Georg Stahl's phlogiston theory, which was superseded by the theory of oxidation.

45. Georg Ernst Stahl (1659–1734), a German chemist and physician, postulated the existence of a flammable element that he called "phlogiston," contained within combustible bodies and released during combustion. Once the phlogiston was released or consumed, the substance would no longer burn.

46. Hermes Trismegistus ("thrice-great") is an unknown person whose body of Hermetic writing was studied in the Renaissance and after. Renaissance

through. Whether it was the nature of the passage underscored, or the feverish heaviness of the strokes which formed the underscoring, he could not tell; but something in that combination affected him very badly and very peculiarly. He recalled it to the end of his days, writing it down from memory in his diary and once trying to recite it to his close friend Dr. Checkley till he saw how greatly it disturbed the urbane rector. It read:

"The essential Saltes of Animals may be so prepared and preserved, that an ingenious Man may have the whole Ark of Noah in his own Studie, and raise the fine Shape of an Animal out of its Ashes at his Pleasure; and by the lyke Method from the essential Saltes of humane Dust, a Philosopher may, without any criminal Necromancy, call up the Shape of any dead Ancestour from the Dust whereinto his Bodie has been incinerated."

It was near the docks along the southerly part of the Town Street, however, that the worst things were muttered about Joseph Curwen. Sailors are superstitious folk; and the seasoned salts who manned the infinite rum, slave, and molasses sloops, the rakish privateers, and the great brigs of the Browns,[60] Crawfords,[61] and Tillinghasts,[62] all made strange furtive signs of protection when they saw the slim, deceptively young-looking figure with its yellow hair and slight stoop entering the Curwen warehouse in Doubloon Street or talking with captains and supercargoes on the long quay where the Curwen ships rode restlessly. Curwen's own clerks and captains hated and feared him, and all his sailors were mongrel riff-raff from Martinique, St. Eustatius,[63] Havana, or Port Royal. It was, in a way, the frequency with which these sailors were replaced which inspired the acutest and most tangible part of the fear in which the old man was held. A crew would be turned loose in the town on shore leave, some of its members perhaps charged with this errand or that; and when reassembled it would be almost sure to lack one or more men. That many of the errands had concerned the farm of Pawtuxet Road, and that few of the sailors had ever been seen to return from that place, was not forgotten; so that in time it became exceedingly difficult for Curwen to keep his oddly assorted hands. Almost invariably several would desert soon after hearing the gossip of the Providence wharves, and their replacement in the West Indies became an increasingly great problem to the merchant.

In 1760 Joseph Curwen was virtually an outcast, suspected of vague horrors and dæmoniac alliances which seemed all the more menacing because they could not be named, understood, or even proved to exist. The last straw may have come from the affair of the missing soldiers in 1758, for in March and April of that year two Royal regiments on their way to New France[64] were quartered in Providence, and depleted by an inexplicable process far beyond the average rate of desertion. Rumour dwelt on the frequency with which Curwen was wont to be seen talking with the red-coated strangers; and as several of them began to be missed, people thought of the odd conditions among his own seamen. What would have happened if the regiments had not been ordered on, no one can tell.

Meanwhile the merchant's worldly affairs were prospering. He had a virtual monopoly of the town's trade in saltpetre, black pepper, and cinnamon, and easily led any other one shipping establishment save the Browns in his importation of brassware, indigo, cotton, woollens, salt, rigging, iron, paper, and English goods of every kind. Such shopkeepers as James Green, at the Sign of the Elephant in Cheapside,[65] the Russells, at the Sign of the Golden Eagle across the Bridge, or Clark and Nightingale at the Frying-Pan and Fish near the New Coffee-House,[66] depended almost wholly upon him for their stock; and his arrangements with the local distillers, the Narragansett[67] dairymen and horse-breeders, and the Newport candle-makers,[68] made him one of the prime exporters of the Colony.

Ostracised though he was, he did not lack for civic spirit of a sort. When the Colony House burned down, he subscribed handsomely to the lotteries by which the new brick one—still standing at the head of its parade in the old main street—was built in 1761. In that same year, too, he helped rebuild the Great Bridge after the October gale. He replaced many of the books of the public library consumed in the Colony House fire, and bought heavily in the lottery that gave the muddy Market Parade and deep-rutted Town Street their pavement of great round stones with a brick footwalk or "causey" in the middle. About this time, also, he built the plain but excellent new house whose doorway is still such a triumph of carving. When the Whitefield[69] adherents broke off from Dr. Cotton's hill church in 1743[70] and

scholars thought that the author was a contemporary of Moses; later scholars, however, place the body of writing in the second or third century CE. The reference here should probably be to Louis Ménard, *Étude sur l'origine des livres hermetiques et translations d'Hermès Trismegistus* (Paris, 1866). Louis-Nicolas Ménard (1822–1901) was an artist, chemist, historian, and man of letters who wrote poetry, essays, *Du polythéisme hellénique* (1863), and two academic theses, *De sacra poesi graecorum* and *De la morale avant les philosophes* (1860).

47. The *Turba Philosophorum* (Assembly of the Alchemical Philosophers) is one of the earliest Latin alchemical texts, probably dating from the twelfth century. It introduced many of the key themes of the alchemical tradition and was often quoted in later writings.

48. Properly, *Liber Investigationis Magisterii Ejusdem*, published in Strasbourg in 1598. Geber probably flourished in the eighth century. He has been identified variously as an Arab and a Westerner. His alchemical theories regarding metals and elements were followed by chemists until the sixteenth century.

49. *Clavis Majoris Sapientiæ* (The Key to Higher Wisdom), by Artephius (who flourished around 1150 and was probably an Arab), was first published in Latin in 1609; a German translation was published in 1717.

50. A book, not a person; first published in the thirteenth century, it consisted of mystical commentary on the Bible. Its historical origins and authorship have been controversial from the first. The most likely author appears to be its "discoverer," a Spanish Jew named Moses de Léon (ca. 1250–1305).

51. Magnus's *Opera Omnia* was published in Lyon in a twenty-one-volume edition in 1651 edited by Father Peter Jammy, O.P. Albertus Magnus (ca. 1193–1280), also known as Albert the Great and Albert of Cologne, was a German Dominican friar and a bishop who achieved secular fame for his comprehensive knowledge of science. In 1931 he was made a saint by Pope Pius XI; ten years later, Pope Pius XII recognized him as the patron saint of the natural sciences.

52. Ramon Llull (ca. 1232–ca. 1315) (Anglicized Raymond Lully, Raymond Lull, in Latin Raimundus or Raymundus Lullus or Lullius) was a Majorcan writer, philosopher, and logician. His *Ars Generalis Ultima*, or *Ars Magna* (The Ultimate General Art), published in 1305, was a book on analytic thinking—essentially, an early computational tool—that influenced such thinkers as Gottfried Leibniz (1646–1716). Curwen owned a one-volume Latin edition of several of Lully's works, published by Lazarus Zetzner in Strasbourg in 1598. The Zetzner edition includes related works by the Italian friar, philosopher, and occultist Giordano Bruno (1548–1600) and the German magician-alchemist and philosopher Heinrich Cornelius Agrippa von Nettesheim (1486–1535; see note 119, below) on modes of thought.

53. Some scholars attribute the book to Roger Bacon (ca. 1214–1294). For example, the *Cabinet Portrait Gallery of British Worthies* (London: Charles Knight & Co., 1845) listed, among Bacon's writing, "*Thesaurus chemicus*, Franckfort [sic], 1603 and 1620, 8v (?) contains the *Specula mathematica*, the *Speculum alchymice*, and some other tracts, which Tanner puts down altogether as *Scripta sanioris medecince in arte chemicc*." Similar credit is given in the *Dictionary of National Biography*. However, although Bacon

The Old State House, 150 Benefit Street, in 2010.
Photograph copyright © Donovan K. Loucks 2010,
reprinted with permission

founded Deacon Snow's church across the Bridge,[71] Curwen had gone with them; though his zeal and attendance soon abated. Now, however, he cultivated piety once more; as if to dispel the shadow which had thrown him into isolation and would soon begin to wreck his business fortunes if not sharply checked.

2.

The sight of this strange, pallid man, hardly middle-aged in aspect yet certainly not less than a full century old, seeking at last to emerge from a cloud of fright and detestation too vague to pin down or analyse, was at once a pathetic, a dramatic, and a contemptible thing. Such is the power of wealth and of surface gestures, however, that there came indeed a slight abatement in the visible aversion displayed toward him; especially after the rapid disappearances of his sailors abruptly ceased. He must likewise have begun to practice an extreme care and secrecy in his graveyard expeditions, for he was never again caught at such wanderings; whilst the rumours of uncanny sounds and manoeuvres at his Pawtuxet farm diminished in proportion. His rate of food consumption and cattle replacement remained abnormally high; but not until modern times, when Charles Ward examined a set of his accounts and invoices in the Shepley Library, did it occur to any person—save one embittered youth, perhaps—to make dark comparisons between the large number of Guinea blacks he imported until 1766, and the disturbingly small number for whom he could produce bona fide bills of sale either to slave-dealers at the Great Bridge or to the planters of the Narragansett Country. Certainly, the cunning and ingenuity of this abhorred character were uncannily profound, once the necessity for their exercise had become impressed upon him.

But of course the effect of all this belated mending was necessarily slight. Curwen continued to be avoided and distrusted, as indeed the one fact of his continued air of youth at a great age would have been enough to warrant; and he could see that in the end his fortunes would be likely to suffer. His elaborate studies and experiments, whatever they may have been, apparently required a heavy income for their maintenance; and since a change of environment would deprive him of the trading advantages he had gained, it would not have profited him to begin anew in a different region just then. Judgment demanded that he patch up his relations with the townsfolk of Providence, so that his presence might no longer be a signal for hushed conversation, transparent excuses of errands elsewhere, and a general atmosphere of constraint and uneasiness. His clerks, being now reduced to the shiftless and impecunious residue whom no one else would employ, were giving him much worry; and he held to his sea-captains and mates only by shrewdness in gaining some kind of ascendancy over them—a mortgage, a promissory note, or a bit of information very pertinent to their welfare. In many cases, diarists have recorded with some awe, Curwen shewed almost the power of a wizard in unearthing family secrets for

was a prolific, indeed encylopedic, writer, other scholars doubt whether Bacon in fact wrote this work (see, for example, Dorothea Waley Singer, "Alchemical Writings Attributed to Roger Bacon," *Speculum* 7, no. 1 [January 1932]). Bacon's high profile as an alchemist of the day led to many alchemical tracts of the period being attributed to him, some plainly authored by others.

54. Robert Fludd, or Robertus de Fluctibus, a physician of Welsh descent (1574–1637), studied astrology and alchemy and employed so-called sympathetic cures (for example, the idea that a blade could draw the infection from a wound caused by that blade). He adopted the idea that diseases were an invasion of the body by the spirits of demons, set forth in his *Pathologia daemoniaca*. The work for which he is best known is *Utriusque Cosmi Maioris Utriusque Cosmi, Maioris Scilicet et Minoris, Metaphysica, Physica, Atque Technica Historia*, a "technical history of the two worlds, the greater and the lesser" (1617–1619), but he wrote numerous minor works, some of which remain unpublished, including *Clavis Philosophiæ et Alchimiæ Fluddanæ* (Frankfurt, 1633). He is best known, however, as an ardent English supporter of the Rosicrucian movement, though he is said not to have been a member.

55. Johannes Trimethius (1462–1516) was a German abbot, cryptographer, historian, and occultist who wrote several banned works on religion and cryptography, or steganography; his best-known work is *Steganographia*, which spent a full *three hundred years* on the Catholic Church's *Index Librorum Prohibitorum* (the ban was finally lifted in 1900). Nevertheless, he wrote nothing about the philosopher's stone, and this is more likely to be a work by Isaac Hollandus and Johan Isaac Hollandus, *Mineralia Opera Sue de*

Lapide Philosophico. These Dutch adepts probably lived around 1600, but virtually nothing is known of their lives or even their family name (Hollandus merely designates their nationality). *Isaaci et J. I. Hollandi Opera Universalia et Vegetabilia, Sive de Lapide Philosophorum* (The Universal and Vegetable Works of Isaac and J. I. Hollandus; or, On the Philosopher's Stone) was printed in Arnhem in 1617.

56. Many of these works, complete with inaccuracies (such as Mesnard instead of Ménard), are listed in the 1902 (10th edition) of the *Encylopædia Britannica.*

57. *Qanoon-e-Islam; or, The Customs of the Moosulmans of India,* by Ja'far Sharīf, treats the culture, religious rites, ceremonies, and clothing of Indian Muslims in the nineteenth century. (Of the "Rufaee, or Goorz-mar" tribe of "Fuqeers," for instance, Ja'far Sharīf writes: "Sometimes they sear their tongues with a red-hot iron, put a living scorpion into their mouths, make a chain red-hot, and pouring oil over it they draw their hands along it, when a sudden blaze is produced. I have heard it said, that they even cut a living human being into two, and unite the parts by means of spittle. They also eat arsenic, glass, and poisons. . . ." [London, 1879], 291–92.) However, that book was written in 1832, translated by Gerhard Andreas Herklots (whom the author acknowledges in his introduction), and published in that year, so it is not possible that Mr. Merritt saw the title in 1746; this must be another, unknown volume.

58. The story is told in "The Festival" (pp. 103–13, above).

59. See note 2, above.

60. Best known many years later was the industrialist Nicholas Brown Jr.

questionable use. During the final five years of his life it seemed as though only direct talks with the long-dead could possibly have furnished some of the data which he had so glibly at his tongue's end.

About this time the crafty scholar hit upon a last desperate expedient to regain his footing in the community. Hitherto a complete hermit, he now determined to contract an advantageous marriage; securing as a bride some lady whose unquestioned position would make all ostracism of his home impossible. It may be that he also had deeper reasons for wishing an alliance; reasons so far outside the known cosmic sphere that only papers found a century and a half after his death caused anyone to suspect them; but of this nothing certain can ever be learned. Naturally he was aware of the horror and indignation with which any ordinary courtship of his would be received, hence he looked about for some likely candidate upon whose parents he might exert a suitable pressure. Such candidates, he found, were not at all easy to discover; since he had very particular requirements in the way of beauty, accomplishments, and social security. At length his survey narrowed down to the household of one of his best and oldest ship-captains, a widower of high birth and unblemished standing named Dutee Tillinghast,[72] whose only daughter Eliza seemed dowered with every conceivable advantage save prospects as an heiress. Capt. Tillinghast was completely under the domination of Curwen; and consented, after a terrible interview in his cupolaed house on Power's Lane hill,[73] to sanction the blasphemous alliance.

Eliza Tillinghast was at that time eighteen years of age, and had been reared as gently as the reduced circumstances of her father permitted. She had attended Stephen Jackson's school[74] opposite the Court-House Parade; and had been diligently instructed by her mother, before the latter's death of smallpox in 1757, in all the arts and refinements of domestic life. A sampler of hers, worked in 1753 at the age of nine, may still be found in the rooms of the Rhode Island Historical Society.[75] After her mother's death she had kept the house, aided only by one old black woman. Her arguments with her father concerning the proposed Curwen marriage must have been painful indeed; but of these we have no record. Certain it is that her engagement to young Ezra

Weeden, second mate of the Crawford packet *Enterprise*,[76] was dutifully broken off, and that her union with Joseph Curwen took place on the seventh of March, 1763, in the Baptist church, in the presence of one of the most distinguished assemblages which the town could boast; the ceremony being performed by the younger Samuel Winsor.[77] *The Gazette*[78] mentioned the event very briefly, and in most surviving copies the item in question seems to be cut or torn out. Ward found a single intact copy after much search in the archives of a private collector of note, observing with amusement the meaningless urbanity of the language:

"Monday evening last, Mr. Joseph Curwen, of this Town, Merchant, was married to Miss Eliza Tillinghast, Daughter of Capt. Dutee Tillinghast, a young Lady who has real Merit, added to a beautiful Person, to grace the connubial State and perpetuate its Felicity."

The collection of Durfee-Arnold letters, discovered by Charles Ward shortly before his first reputed madness in the private collection of Melville F. Peters, Esq., of George St.,[79] and covering this and a somewhat antecedent period, throws vivid light on the outrage done to public sentiment by this ill-assorted match. The social influence of the Tillinghasts, however, was not to be denied; and once more Joseph Curwen found his house frequented by persons whom he could never otherwise have induced to cross his threshold. His acceptance was by no means complete, and his bride was socially the sufferer through her forced venture; but at all events the wall of utter ostracism was somewhat worn down. In his treatment of his wife the strange bridegroom astonished both her and the community by displaying an extreme graciousness and consideration. The new house in Olney Court was now wholly free from disturbing manifestations, and although Curwen was much absent at the Pawtuxet farm which his wife never visited, he seemed more like a normal citizen than at any other time in his long years of residence. Only one person remained in open enmity with him, this being the youthful ship's officer whose engagement to Eliza Tillinghast had been so abruptly broken. Ezra Weeden had frankly vowed vengeance; and though of a quiet and ordinarily mild disposition, was

(1769–1841), great-grandson of Pardon Tillinghast (see note 62, below) and descended from the well-known Baptist minister Chad Brown. Brown University, cofounded by his father, bears his name.

61. The descendants of Gideon Crawford, who (according to Kimball) came to Providence in 1687 and set himself up as a merchant; with the guidance of Gideon's widow, his sons John and William went on to own ships, warehouses, and wharves (150).

62. Captain Joseph Tillinghast (1734–1816) built a house on a site that had been claimed by his great-grandfather Pardon Tillinghast in 1645. Captain Tillinghast is remembered as the commander of one of the American boats involved in the burning of the schooner HMS *Gaspée* in 1772. The *Gaspée* was enforcing the customs laws when it ran aground in Narragansett Bay. A group of the Sons of Liberty rowed out to the ship and attacked the crew, wounding the commander, and burned the ship. The incident is celebrated as the first blood spilled in the American Revolution.

The house site was also the location of the first wharf and warehouse in Providence.

63. Sint Eustatius is part of the Leeward Islands in the Caribbean; it lies northwest of Saint Kitts. It was an important supplier of munitions to the Revolutionary army in the late 1700s.

64. In 1758, the French and Indian War (also known as the Seven Years' War) was raging on the North American continent, as British and French troops fought for control of the extensive holdings of these countries there. The troops Lovecraft makes reference to were probably part of the buildup for the Siege of Louisburg, the British attack on the

key French fort of Louisburg that controlled the St. Lawrence River and kept the British forces from reaching Quebec. The siege ended in July 1758 with the capitulation of the French commander. The British moved on to Quebec, and by 1763, in the Treaty of Paris, the French ceded the whole of Canada to the British.

65. According to Kimball, Green sold "'A Large and Compleat Assortment of Braziery, English Piece Goods, Rum, Flax, Indigo, and Tea'" (326).

66. "Sign of the Frying-Pan and Fish" adjoined the northwest corner of the Court-House lot, and according to Kimball, the proprietors, Clark and Nightingale, offered "a large Assortment of English and India Piece Goods; Likewise Stationary and Hard Ware . . ." (321).

67. Twenty-five miles south of Providence, Narragansett was still a small village then, dependent on farming and fishing out of Narragansett Bay.

68. By 1760, there were perhaps as many as seven candlemakers in Newport, all using whale products (head matter, sperm oil, and whale oil) as key ingredients. The process was new to America, having been introduced (most scholars believe) by a Sephardic Jew living in Newport named Jacob Rodrigues Rivera, who emigrated from Portugal. Others credit Benjamin Crabb, of Rehoboth, while yet another school of thought on the subject (see Patty Jo Rice's "Beginning with Candle Making: A History of the Whaling Museum") says most advances came about through the so-called Spermaceti Trust, established by manufacturers (twelve by 1763, according to Rice) whose price fixing—to control the escalating price of head matter—gave them a monopoly.

now gaining a hate-bred, dogged purpose which boded no good to the usurping husband.

On the seventh of May, 1765, Curwen's only child Ann was born; and was christened by the Rev. John Graves of King's Church,[80] of which both husband and wife had become communicants shortly after their marriage, in order to compromise between their respective Congregational and Baptist affiliations.[81] The record of this birth, as well as that of the marriage two years before, was stricken from most copies of the church and town annals where it ought to appear; and Charles Ward located both with the greatest difficulty after his discovery of the widow's change of name had apprised him of his own relationship, and engendered the feverish interest which culminated in his madness. The birth entry, indeed, was found very curiously through correspondence with the heirs of the loyalist Dr. Graves, who had taken with him a duplicate set of records when he left his pastorate at the outbreak of the Revolution. Ward had tried this source because he knew that his great-great-grandmother Ann Tillinghast Potter had been an Episcopalian.

Shortly after the birth of his daughter, an event he seemed to welcome with a fervour greatly out of keeping with his usual coldness, Curwen resolved to sit for a portrait. This he had painted by a very gifted Scotsman named Cosmo Alexander, then a resident of Newport, and since famous as the early teacher of Gilbert Stuart.[82] The likeness was said to have been executed on a wall-panel of the library of the house in Olney Court, but neither of the two old diaries mentioning it gave any hint of its ultimate disposition. At this period the erratic scholar shewed signs of unusual abstraction, and spent as much time as he possibly could at his farm on the Pawtuxet Road. He seemed, it was stated, in a condition of suppressed excitement or suspense; as if expecting some phenomenal thing or on the brink of some strange discovery. Chemistry or alchemy would appear to have played a great part, for he took from his house to the farm the greater number of his volumes on that subject.

His affectation of civic interest did not diminish, and he lost no opportunities for helping such leaders as Stephen Hopkins,[83] Joseph Brown,[84] and Benjamin West[85] in their efforts to raise the cultural tone of the town, which was then much below the level of Newport in its patronage of the liberal arts. He had helped Daniel Jenckes found his bookshop in 1763,[86] and was thereafter his best customer; extending aid likewise to the struggling *Gazette* that appeared each Wednesday at the Sign of Shakespear's Head. In politics he ardently supported Governor Hopkins against the Ward[87] party whose prime strength was in Newport, and his really eloquent speech at Hacker's Hall[88] in 1765 against the setting off of North Providence as a separate town with a pro-Ward vote in the General Assembly did more than any other one thing to wear down the prejudice against him. But Ezra Weeden, who watched him closely, sneered cynically at all this outward activity; and freely swore it was no more than a mask for some nameless traffick with the blackest gulfs of Tartarus. The revengeful youth began a systematic study of the man and his doings whenever he was in port; spending hours at night by the wharves with a dory in readiness when he saw lights in the Curwen warehouses, and following the small boat which would sometimes steal quietly off and down the bay. He also kept as close a watch as possible on the Pawtuxet farm, and was once severely bitten by the dogs the old Indian couple loosed upon him.

3.

In 1766 came the final change in Joseph Curwen. It was very sudden, and gained wide notice amongst the curious townsfolk; for the air of suspense and expectancy dropped like an old cloak, giving instant place to an ill-concealed exaltation of perfect triumph. Curwen seemed to have difficulty in restraining himself from public harangues on what he had found or learned or made; but apparently the need of secrecy was greater than the longing to share his rejoicing, for no explanation was ever offered by him. It was after this transition, which appears to have come early in July, that the sinister scholar began to astonish people by his possession of information which only their long-dead ancestors would seem to be able to impart.

But Curwen's feverish secret activities by no means ceased with this change. On the contrary, they tended rather to increase; so that more and more of his shipping business was handled by the captains whom he now bound to him by ties of fear as potent

69. George Whitefield (1714–1770) was a Methodist open-air preacher who converted many to Calvinsim in his campaigns throughout America. He was one of the first of the Methodist clergy to preach to the enslaved.

70. The Rev. Josiah Cotton was called in 1728 to serve in the place of worship established in 1723 by the Congregationalists (now the First Unitarian Church of Providence) at what is now the corner of College and Benefit streets in Providence.

The Congregationalist Church, now the First Unitarian Church, 301 Benefit Street, in 2010. Photograph copyright © Donovan K. Loucks 2010, reprinted with permission

71. William Read Staples's *Annals of the Town of Providence* records, "During the time that Josiah Cotton had the pastoral charge of the First Congregational Society, a part of his church and congregation seceded from his watch and care. The seceders deemed his preaching destitute of sound evangelical principles. They accused their pastor of preaching 'damnable good works'" (449). In 1743, Deacon Joseph Snow and a group

of adherents left and established a new church in a private house.

72. There is no record of Dutee Tillinghast in the records of the Tillinghast family, which was of some prominence (see note 62, above).

73. Probably now Hope Street—most of Power's Lane was subsumed under this name.

324 Hope Street, Hope High School in 1990 (across the street from the site of the school that HPL attended), possible site of Powers Lane Hill. Photograph courtesy of Will Hart

74. The schoolhouse between 1747 and 1758 was indeed across the street from the parade of the old Colony House, according to Kimball. It was on the west side of North Main Street. The town ceased to conduct a public school in 1754, but the building was leased to Stephen Jackson, who probably occupied it until 1763. Elijah Tillinghast, a likely relation, was on the Providence school committee in 1754. See Welcome Greene's *Providence Plantations*.

75. Unfortunately, the extensive catalogue of the RIHS fails to list this item; neither did it appear in Betty Ring's *Let Virtue Be a Guide to Thee*, catalogue of the comprehensive sampler show mounted at the RIHS in 1983.

as those of bankruptcy had been. He altogether abandoned the slave trade, alleging that its profits were constantly decreasing. Every possible moment was spent at the Pawtuxet farm; though there were rumours now and then of his presence in places which, though not actually near graveyards, were yet so situated in relation to graveyards that thoughtful people wondered just how thorough the old merchant's change of habits really was. Ezra Weeden, though his periods of espionage were necessarily brief and intermittent on account of his sea voyaging, had a vindictive persistence which the bulk of the practical townsfolk and farmers lacked; and subjected Curwen's affairs to a scrutiny such as they had never had before.

Many of the odd manoeuvres of the strange merchant's vessels had been taken for granted on account of the unrest of the times, when every colonist seemed determined to resist the provisions of the Sugar Act which hampered a prominent traffick. Smuggling and evasion were the rule in Narragansett Bay, and nocturnal landings of illicit cargoes were continuous commonplaces. But Weeden, night after night following the lighters or small sloops which he saw steal off from the Curwen warehouses at the Town Street docks, soon felt assured that it was not merely His Majesty's armed ships which the sinister skulker was anxious to avoid. Prior to the change in 1766 these boats had for the most part contained chained negroes, who were carried down and across the bay and landed at an obscure point on the shore just north of Pawtuxet; being afterward driven up the bluff and across country to the Curwen farm, where they were locked in that enormous stone outbuilding which had only high narrow slits for windows. After that change, however, the whole programme was altered. Importation of slaves ceased at once, and for a time Curwen abandoned his midnight sailings. Then, about the spring of 1767, a new policy appeared. Once more the lighters grew wont to put out from the black, silent docks, and this time they would go down the bay some distance, perhaps as far as Namquit Point, where they would meet and receive cargo from strange ships of considerable size and widely varied appearance. Curwen's sailors would then deposit this cargo at the usual point on the shore, and transport it overland to the farm; locking it in the same cryptical stone building which had formerly received the negroes. The cargo consisted almost wholly of boxes and cases, of which a large proportion were oblong and heavy and disturbingly suggestive of coffins.

Weeden always watched the farm with unremitting assiduity; visiting it each night for long periods, and seldom letting a week go by without a sight except when the ground bore a footprint-revealing snow. Even then he would often walk as close as possible in the travelled road or on the ice of the neighbouring river to see what tracks others might have left. Finding his own vigils interrupted by nautical duties, he hired a tavern companion named Eleazar Smith to continue the survey during his absences; and between them the two could have set in motion some extraordinary rumours. That they did not do so was only because they knew the effect of publicity would be to warn their quarry and make further progress impossible. Instead, they wished to learn something definite before taking any action. What they did learn must have been startling indeed, and Charles Ward spoke many times to his parents of his regret at Weeden's later burning of his notebooks. All that can be told of their discoveries is what Eleazar Smith jotted down in a none too coherent diary, and what other diarists and letter-writers have timidly repeated from the statements which they finally made—and according to which the farm was only the outer shell of some vast and revolting menace, of a scope and depth too profound and intangible for more than shadowy comprehension.

It is gathered that Weeden and Smith became early convinced that a great series of tunnels and catacombs, inhabited by a very sizeable staff of persons besides the old Indian and his wife, underlay the farm. The house was an old peaked relic of the middle seventeenth century with enormous stack chimney and diamond-paned lattice windows, the laboratory being in a lean-to toward the north, where the roof came nearly to the ground. This building stood clear of any other; yet judging by the different voices heard at odd times within, it must have been accessible through secret passages beneath. These voices, before 1766, were mere mumblings and negro whisperings and frenzied screams, coupled with curious chants or invocations. After that date, however, they assumed a very singular and terrible cast as they ran the gamut betwixt dronings of dull acquiescence and explosions of frantic pain or fury, rumblings of conversation and

76. Nothing is known of the *Enterprise*, other than its existence.

77. Samuel Winsor III (1722–1803), whose father was also a pastor at the First Baptist Church, must be the clergyman in question. In 1770 and 1771, a controversy within the church caused him to form a new Baptist church in Johnston, Rhode Island.

78. *The Providence Gazette and Country Journal* was first published in 1762. Coincidentally, Joseph Tillinghast, the great-great-grandson of Pardon Tillinghast (not the sea captain), was the publisher of the *Gazette* in 1809; later, he became a U.S. representative.

79. There are no records of this individual.

80. The American Revolution caused much dissension in New England churches, as many pastors refused to omit prayers for the king and the royal family. The Rev. John Graves, rector of King's Church in Providence from 1755 to 1781, was among that group, and his church was closed. Feeling against him remained so strong that he was unable to resume his parish duties after the Revolution. Graves's presence in Providence is recorded in Kimball, who reports that a broadside announced a sermon for December 10, 1772, by Dr. Graves at King's Church.

81. King's Church was funded by the Society for the Propagation of the Gospel, the missionary arm of the Anglican Church.

82. Cosmo Alexander (ca. 1724–1772) was a Scottish painter descended from several other well-known Scottish artists, including his father, John Alexander. A firm Jacobite, he fled Scotland after the

1745 uprising and went to Rome, where he painted many exiled Catholic leaders. From there, he moved to London and then the Netherlands, sailing for America in 1766. According to William Dunlap's 1834 *History of the Rise and Progress of the Arts of Design in the United States*, in 1769, when Alexander was visiting Newport, Rhode Island, he met Gilbert Stuart, one of whose later portrait subjects was, famously, George Washington. The portrait, begun in 1796 and never completed, formed the basis for the image on the U.S. dollar bill. One of Alexander's patrons, Dr. William Hunter, apparently facilitated the introduction to Stuart, then a teenager. Alexander gave the younger artist lessons and employed him as an assistant. In 1770, Stuart accompanied Alexander on a painting tour that included stops in Philadelphia, Delaware, and Virginia before their voyage to Edinburgh. Alexander died unexpectedly on August 25, 1772, leaving the seventeen-year-old Stuart stranded in Edinburgh. He went on to do portraits of the five men who succeeded Washington in the presidency, as well as of some one thousand other subjects. (I, 167, 197–98)

83. Nine times the governor of Rhode Island, Hopkins was a signatory to the Declaration of Independence and instrumental in the founding of Brown University.

Home of Stephen Hopkins, in 2010.
Photograph copyright © Donovan K. Loucks
2010, reprinted with permission

whines of entreaty, pantings of eagerness and shouts of protest. They appeared to be in different languages, all known to Curwen, whose rasping accents were frequently distinguishable in reply, reproof, or threatening. Sometimes it seemed that several persons must be in the house; Curwen, certain captives, and the guards of those captives. There were voices of a sort that neither Weeden nor Smith had ever heard before despite their wide knowledge of foreign parts, and many that they did seem to place as belonging to this or that nationality. The nature of the conversations seemed always a kind of catechism, as if Curwen were extorting some sort of information from terrified or rebellious prisoners.

Weeden had many verbatim reports of overheard scraps in his notebook, for English, French, and Spanish, which he knew, were frequently used; but of these nothing has survived. He did, however, say that besides a few ghoulish dialogues in which the past affairs of Providence families were concerned, most of the questions and answers he could understand were historical or scientific; occasionally pertaining to very remote places and ages. Once, for example, an alternately raging and sullen figure was questioned in French about the Black Prince's massacre at Limoges in 1370,[89] as if there were some hidden reason which he ought to know. Curwen asked the prisoner—if prisoner it were—whether the order to slay was given because of the Sign of the Goat[90] found on the altar in the ancient Roman crypt beneath the Cathedral, or whether the Dark Man of the Haute Vienne[91] Coven had spoken the Three Words. Failing to obtain replies, the inquisitor had seemingly resorted to extreme means; for there was a terrific shriek followed by silence and muttering and a bumping sound.

None of these colloquies were ever ocularly witnessed, since the windows were always heavily draped. Once, though, during a discourse in an unknown tongue, a shadow was seen on the curtain which startled Weeden exceedingly; reminding him of one of the puppets in a show he had seen in the autumn of 1764 in Hacker's Hall, when a man from Germantown, Pennsylvania, had given a clever mechanical spectacle advertised as a

View of the Famous City of Jerusalem, in which are represented Jerusalem, the Temple of Solomon, his Royal Throne, the noted Towers, and Hills, likewise the Sufferings of Our Saviour from the Garden of Gethsemane to the Cross on the Hill of Golgotha; an artful piece of Statuary, Worthy to be seen by the Curious.[92]

It was on this occasion that the listener, who had crept close to the window of the front room whence the speaking proceeded, gave a start which roused the old Indian pair and caused them to loose the dogs on him. After that no more conversations were ever heard in the house, and Weeden and Smith concluded that Curwen had transferred his field of action to regions below.

That such regions in truth existed, seemed amply clear from many things. Faint cries and groans unmistakably came up now and then from what appeared to be the solid earth in places far from any structure; whilst hidden in the bushes along the river-bank in the rear, where the high ground sloped steeply down to the valley of the Pawtuxet, there was found an arched oaken door in a frame of heavy masonry, which was obviously an entrance to caverns within the hill. When or how these catacombs could have been constructed, Weeden was unable to say; but he frequently pointed out how easily the place might have been reached by bands of unseen workmen from the river. Joseph Curwen put his mongrel seamen to diverse uses indeed! During the heavy spring rains of 1769 the two watchers kept a sharp eye on the steep river-bank to see if any subterrene secrets might be washed to light, and were rewarded by the sight of a profusion of both human and animal bones in places where deep gullies had been worn in the banks. Naturally there might be many explanations of such things in the rear of a stock farm, and in a locality where old Indian burying-grounds were common, but Weeden and Smith drew their own inferences.

It was in January 1770, whilst Weeden and Smith were still debating vainly on what, if anything, to think or do about the whole bewildering business, that the incident of the *Fortaleza* occurred. Exasperated by the burning of the revenue sloop *Liberty* at Newport during the previous summer,[93] the customs fleet under Admiral Wallace[94] had adopted an increased vigilance concerning strange vessels; and on this occasion His Majesty's armed schooner *Cygnet*,[95] under Capt. Charles Leslie, captured

84. One of the four Brown brothers; they included John, Nicholas Jr., and Moses. Joseph (1733–1785) was active in the brothers' commercial enterprises as well as in an important political role, serving as a state representative and state senator for Providence.

85. West (1730–1813) moved to Providence at age twenty-three, where he began as a bookseller. In 1770, he received an honorary Degree of Letters from Brown University. He published an almanac from 1765 to 1793. In 1769, West erected a temporary observatory in Providence, just off Benefit Street, and, along with Joseph Brown and Governor Stephen Hopkins, spent the day of June 3 observing the transit of Venus across the sun. West subsequently published *An Account of the Observation of Venus upon the Sun, the Third Day of June, 1769, at Providence, in New-England: With some Account of the Use of Those Observations.* West's telescope is on display at the John Hay Library. In 1781, West became a fellow of the American Academy of Arts and Sciences.

86. According to Edward Field's *State of Rhode Island and Providence Plantations at the End of the Century* (vol. 2, 640, n. 1), this was the first bookseller in Providence. Daniel Jenckes was the Chief Justice of the Inferior Court of Common Pleas for Providence County. Judge Jenckes was also the father of Rhoda Jenckes, who was the first wife of Nicholas Brown Jr.

87. Samuel Ward (1725–1776), who entered politics on the side of hard currency, opposing the faction of Stephen Hopkins, who favored paper money. Hard currency in colonial America, also known as specie, represented a promise to pay whatever was understood to be used as exchange—which could mean,

variously, silver, tobacco, sugar, and other commodities. Of course, British hard currency was gold or silver, and the value of the currency approximated the value of the metal. Paper currency meant actual pieces of paper used as tokens of money or exchange; it had no intrinsic value, only that assigned by the colony. Ward and Hopkins alternated as governors of Rhode Island, and Ward was another of the founders of Brown University.

88. Hackers Hall was destroyed by fire in 1801 and rebuilt.

89. Edward, known as the Black Prince, Prince of Wales (1330–1376), one of the heroic figures of the Hundred Years' War, whose reputation was sullied only by his siege of Limoges in 1370, in which the town's 3,000 inhabitants (men, women, and children) were slaughtered.

90. The upside-down pentagram, a sign of black magic, representing the goat of lust (with its cloven hooves) attacking the heavens.

91. The Haute-Vienne is the department (the French equivalent of a county) in which Limoges is located. However, the prisoner must have been confused by Curwen's question, for the *département* Haute-Vienne was not created until after the French Revolution. It certainly did not exist in 1370. While the upper Vienne ("haute Vienne") flows through the district around Limoges, the prisoner probably would have recognized only the names Limoges or Limousin, the traditional name for the region. See Anthony Pearsall's *The Lovecraft Lexicon*.

92. The spectacle was described in the *Gazette* in March 1864 as "an Entertainment for the Curious"—further

after a short pursuit one early morning the scow *Fortaleza* of Barcelona, Spain, under Capt. Manuel Arruda, bound according to its log from Grand Cairo, Egypt, to Providence. When searched for contraband material, this ship revealed the astonishing fact that its cargo consisted exclusively of Egyptian mummies, consigned to "Sailor A. B. C.," who would come to remove his goods in a lighter just off Namquit Point and whose identity Capt. Arruda felt himself in honour bound not to reveal. The Vice-Admiralty Court at Newport, at a loss what to do in view of the non-contraband nature of the cargo on the one hand and of the unlawful secrecy of the entry on the other hand, compromised on Collector Robinson's[96] recommendation by freeing the ship but forbidding it a port in Rhode Island waters. There were later rumours of its having been seen in Boston Harbour, though it never openly entered the Port of Boston.

This extraordinary incident did not fail of wide remark in Providence, and there were not many who doubted the existence of some connexion between the cargo of mummies and the sinister Joseph Curwen. His exotic studies and his curious chemical importations being common knowledge, and his fondness for graveyards being common suspicion; it did not take much imagination to link him with a freakish importation which could not conceivably have been destined for anyone else in the town. As if conscious of this natural belief, Curwen took care to speak casually on several occasions of the chemical value of the balsams found in mummies;[97] thinking perhaps that he might make the affair seem less unnatural, yet stopping just short of admitting his participation. Weeden and Smith, of course, felt no doubt whatsoever of the significance of the thing; and indulged in the wildest theories concerning Curwen and his monstrous labours.

The following spring, like that of the year before, had heavy rains; and the watchers kept careful track of the river-bank behind the Curwen farm. Large sections were washed away, and a certain number of bones discovered; but no glimpse was afforded of any actual subterranean chambers or burrows. Something was rumoured, however, at the village of Pawtuxet about a mile below, where the river flows in falls over a rocky terrace to join the placid landlocked cove. There, where quaint old cottages climbed the hill from the rustic bridge, and fishing-smacks[98] lay anchored at their sleepy docks, a vague report went round of things that were floating down the river and flashing into sight for a minute as they went over the falls. Of course the Pawtuxet is a long river which winds through many settled regions abounding in graveyards, and of course the spring rains had been very heavy; but the fisherfolk about the bridge did not like the wild way that one of the things stared as it shot down to the still water below, or the way that another half cried out although its condition had greatly departed from that of objects which normally cry out. That rumour sent Smith—for Weeden was just then at sea—in haste to the river-bank behind the farm; where surely enough there remained the evidences of an extensive cave-in. There was, however, no trace of a passage into the steep bank; for the miniature avalanche had left behind a solid wall of mixed earth and shrubbery from aloft. Smith went to the extent of some experimental digging, but was deterred by lack of success—or perhaps by fear of possible success. It is interesting to speculate on what the persistent and revengeful Weeden would have done had he been ashore at the time.

4.

By the autumn of 1770 Weeden decided that the time was ripe to tell others of his discoveries; for he had a large number of facts to link together, and a second eye-witness to refute the possible charge that jealousy and vindictiveness had spurred his fancy. As his first confidant he selected Capt. James Mathewson[99] of the *Enterprise*, who on the one hand knew him well enough not to doubt his veracity, and on the other hand was sufficiently influential in the town to be heard in turn with respect. The colloquy took place in an upper room of Sabin's Tavern[100] near the docks, with Smith present to corroborate virtually every statement; and it could be seen that Capt. Mathewson was tremendously impressed. Like nearly everyone else in the town, he had had black suspicions of his own anent Joseph Curwen; hence it needed only this confirmation and enlargement of data to convince him absolutely. At the end of the conference he was very grave, and enjoined strict silence upon the two younger men. He would, he said, transmit the information separately to some ten or so of the most learned and prominent citizens of Providence; ascertaining

explained, somewhat ambiguously, as "a work of seven years, done at German-town, in Pennsylvania" (reported by Kimball [310] and quoted in the October 1916 issue of *Providence Magazine*).

93. In 1769, the British armed sloop *Liberty* had seized a brig and accused its captain and crew of evading the customs laws. When the men of the *Liberty* came ashore to explain their actions, a group of locals seized the sloop and dismantled and scuttled her onshore. Although a substantial reward was offered by the Crown for arrest and conviction of those responsible, no arrests were ever made. A few days later, the ship floated to nearby Goat Island, where a violent thunder-storm destroyed it.

94. This is probably a reference to Sir James Wallace (1731–1803), who was twice posted to the North American station in his career, in 1763 and again in 1774, though he was but a captain at this time.

95. A fictitious ship; the real HMS *Cygnet* was an eighteen-gun sloop captured from the French by the British in 1758 and sold in 1768.

96. John Robinson, a customs collector employed by His Majesty's government. In this immediately pre-Revolutionary period, the Sugar Act and, shortly after-ward, the Stamp Act caused wealthy local merchants to align with common criminals to evade the royal customs officials. Robinson, while attempting to bring in to justice an illegal importer of molasses, was himself arrested for theft of the cargo by a sheriff sympathetic to the revolutionaries.

97. In popular opinion, mummies were an excellent source of many remedies,

including tinctures, treacles, elixirs, and balsams. Paracelsus and many others published recipes for these that drew on sources from as far back as the ninth century CE, which themselves purported to repeat formulae developed by the Egyptians who performed the mummification. Of course, mummies were only one source of such remedies; many other components of human remains—brains, bones (skulls in particular), blood, hair, and urine all formed part of the ancient pharmacopoeia.

98. A "smack" is a small boat, usually equipped with a well in which to keep the captured fish alive.

99. Nothing is known of Captain Mathewson beyond the information recorded in this tale.

100. The plotters of the *Gaspée* incident (see note 62, above) reportedly met in 1772 at Sabin's Tavern, where reportedly a written account of the affair later hung for many years on a wall, "engrossed by the hand of" the daughter of Colonel Ephraim Bowen, "the last survivor of the party" (Edward Field, *Manual of the Rhode Island Society of the Sons of the American Revolution*, 288).

101. See note 85, above.

102. Manning (1738–1791) was the first president of Brown University; however, at this time, he was the president of Rhode Island College. He had earlier opened a Latin school in Warren, Rhode Island, and in 1770 moved the college into which the school had grown to Providence. While the president's house was being built, he lived with Benjamin Bowen.

their views and following whatever advice they might have to offer. Secrecy would probably be essential in any case, for this was no matter that the town constables or militia could cope with; and above all else the excitable crowd must be kept in ignorance, lest there be enacted in these already troublous times a repetition of that frightful Salem panic of less than a century before which had first brought Curwen hither.

The right persons to tell, he believed, would be Dr. Benjamin West, whose pamphlet on the late transit of Venus proved him a scholar and keen thinker;[101] Rev. James Manning,[102] President of the College which had just moved up from Warren and was temporarily housed in the new King Street schoolhouse awaiting the completion of its building on the hill above Presbyterian-Lane; ex-Governor Stephen Hopkins, who had been a member of the Philosophical Society at Newport, and was a man of very broad perceptions; John Carter, publisher of the *Gazette*; all four of the Brown brothers, John, Joseph, Nicholas, and Moses, who formed the recognised local magnates, and of whom Joseph was an amateur scientist of parts; old Dr. Jabez Bowen,[103] whose erudition was considerable, and who had much first-hand knowledge of Curwen's odd purchases; and Capt. Abraham Whipple,[104] a privateersman of phenomenal boldness and energy who could be counted on to lead in any active measures needed. These men, if favourable, might eventually be brought together for collective deliberation; and with them would rest the responsibility of deciding whether or not to inform the Governor of the Colony, Joseph Wanton of Newport,[105] before taking action.

The mission of Capt. Mathewson prospered beyond his highest expectations; for whilst he found one or two of the chosen confidants somewhat sceptical of the possible ghastly side of Weeden's tale, there was not one who did not think it necessary to take some sort of secret and coördinated action. Curwen, it was clear, formed a vague potential menace to the welfare of the town and Colony; and must be eliminated at any cost. Late in December 1770 a group of eminent townsmen met at the home of Stephen Hopkins and debated tentative measures. Weeden's notes, which he had given to Capt. Mathewson, were carefully read; and he and Smith were summoned to give testimony anent details. Something very like fear seized the whole assemblage before the meeting was over, though there ran through that fear a grim determination which Capt. Whipple's bluff and resonant profanity best expressed. They would not notify the Governor, because a more than legal course seemed necessary. With hidden powers of uncertain extent apparently at his disposal, Curwen was not a man who could safely be warned to leave town. Nameless reprisals might ensue, and even if the sinister creature complied, the removal would be no more than the shifting of an unclean burden to another place. The times were lawless, and men who had flouted the King's revenue forces for years were not the ones to balk at sterner things when duty impelled. Curwen must be surprised at his Pawtuxet farm by a large raiding-party of seasoned privateersmen and given one decisive chance to explain himself. If he proved a madman, amusing himself with shrieks and imaginary conversations in different voices, he would be properly confined. If something graver appeared, and if the underground horrors indeed turned out to be real, he and all with him must die. It could be done quietly, and even the widow and her father need not be told how it came about.

While these serious steps were under discussion there occurred in the town an incident so terrible and inexplicable that for a time little else was mentioned for miles around. In the middle of a moonlight January night with heavy snow underfoot there resounded over the river and up the hill a shocking series of cries which brought sleepy heads to every window; and people around Weybosset Point[106] saw a great white thing plunging frantically along the badly cleared space in front of the Turk's Head.[107] There was a baying of dogs in the distance, but this subsided as soon as the clamour of the awakened town became audible. Parties of men with lanterns and muskets hurried out to see what was happening, but nothing rewarded their search. The next morning, however, a giant, muscular body, stark naked, was found on the jams of ice around the southern piers of the Great Bridge, where the Long Dock stretched out beside Abbott's distil-house,[108] and the identity of this object became a theme for endless speculation and whispering. It was not so much the younger as the older folk who whispered, for only in the patriarchs did that rigid face with horror-bulging eyes strike any chord of memory. They, shaking as they did so, exchanged furtive murmurs of wonder and fear; for

103. Jabez Bowen (1739–1815) served as the deputy governor of Rhode Island and the chief justice of the Rhode Island Supreme Court. However, "old Dr. Jabez" probably refers to his great-uncle Jabez Bowen (1696–1770), who was a Providence physician. Dr. Jabez Bowen was the father of Benjamin Bowen (see note 102, above).

104. Whipple (1733–1819) was later an American naval officer in the Revolutionary War and commanded one of the ships involved in the *Gaspée* incident (see note 62, above).

105. Wanton (1705–1780), governor from 1769 to 1775, remained neutral during the Revolution, although he was important in thwarting the Crown, which was endeavoring to discover who had been involved in the *Gaspée* incident (see note 62, above).

106. According to Henry R. Chace's *Owners and Occupants of the Lots, Houses, and Shops in the Town of Providence Rhode Island in 1798*, "At right angles to the Town Street and across the Great Bridge, was Weybosset Point. It had been called that since 1638, and had been used for a hundred years as a landing-place for cattle when fording the river in going to and from the village to the farms west and south in the country" (i).

107. Kimball (292–294) recounts that the Turk's Head was a local landmark, originally the figurehead of the ship *Sultan*. It served Jacob Whitman for many years as a signpost for his blacksmith's shop in the southern part of Providence, near the Tillinghast neighborhood, until it was swept away in a gale in 1815.

108. Daniel Abbott was the son of Daniel Abbott, "who played so prominent a part

North Burying Ground, 5 Branch Avenue, Providence, in 2001.
Photograph copyright © Donovan K. Loucks 2001, reprinted with permission

as town-clerk in the years immediately following King Philip's War," according to Kimball, and owned a distillery by the Parade, just in front of the Great Bridge.

in those stiff, hideous features lay a resemblance so marvellous as to be almost an identity—and that identity was with a man who had died full fifty years before.

Ezra Weeden was present at the finding; and remembering the baying of the night before, set out along Weybosset Street and across Muddy Dock Bridge whence the sound had come. He had a curious expectancy, and was not surprised when, reaching the edge of the settled district where the street merged into the Paw-tuxet Road, he came upon some very curious tracks in the snow. The naked giant had been pursued by dogs and many booted men, and the returning tracks of the hounds and their masters could be easily traced. They had given up the chase upon coming too near the town. Weeden smiled grimly, and as a perfunctory detail traced the footprints back to their source. It was the Paw-tuxet farm of Joseph Curwen, as he well knew it would be; and he would have given much had the yard been less confusingly trampled. As it was, he dared not seem too interested in full daylight. Dr. Bowen, to whom Weeden went at once with his report, performed an autopsy on the strange corpse, and discovered peculiarities which baffled him utterly. The digestive tracts of the huge man seemed never to have been in use, whilst the whole skin had a coarse, loosely knit texture impossible to account for. Impressed by what the old men whispered of this body's likeness to the long-dead blacksmith Daniel Green, whose great-grandson Aaron Hoppin was a supercargo in Curwen's employ, Weeden asked casual questions till he found where Green was buried. That night a party of ten visited the old North Burying Ground opposite Herrenden's Lane and opened a grave. They found it vacant, precisely as they had expected.

"They found the grave vacant—precisely as they had expected."
Weird Tales 35, no. 9 (May 1941) (artist: Harry Furman)

Meanwhile arrangements had been made with the post riders to intercept Joseph Curwen's mail, and shortly before the incident of the naked body there was found a letter from one Jedediah Orne of Salem which made the coöperating citizens think deeply. Parts of it, copied and preserved in the private archives of the Smith family where Charles Ward found it, ran as follows:

109. Ann Hibbins, convicted of witchcraft in 1656 in a precursor to the mass witchcraft trials in 1692, named as one of her executors Lieutenant Edward Hutchinson, described by Charles W. Upham, in his 1867 *Salem Witchcraft*, as one of a group of "leading citizens." (284) In a letter dated 1928, Hutchinson states that he has had 150 more years than Curwen to study occult matters, so it may well be that Hutchinson had lived in Salem for many years prior to this period of Curwen's life. However, one Joseph Hutchinson Sr., a mill operator, was a complainant in the Salem Witch Trials, and there were several other Hutchinson households in Salem by 1692.

110. Zariatnatmik is one of the names of God, according to the *Grand Grimoire* (a work that claims to be written in 1522 but probably dates from after the eighteenth century), and Ben Zariatnatmik means "Son of God."

111. A deity worshipped in northern Britain, identified with the Roman gods Mars, the god of war, and Sylvanus, the god of the forest.

I delight that you continue in ye Gett'g at Olde Matters in your Way, and doe not think better was done at Mr. Hutchinson's in Salem-Village.[109] *Certainely, there was Noth'g butt ye liveliest Awfulness in that which H. rais'd upp from What he cou'd gather onlie a part of. What you sente, did not Worke, whether because of Any Thing miss'g, or because ye Wordes were not Righte from my Speak'g or y^r Copy'g. I alone am at a Loss. I have not ye Chymicall art to followe Borellus, and owne my Self confounded by ye VII. Booke of ye Necronomicon that you recommende. But I wou'd have you Observe what was tolde to us aboute tak'g Care whom to calle up, for you are Sensible what Mr. Mather writ in ye Magnalia of—, and can judge how truely that Horrendous thing is reported. I say to you againe, doe not call up Any that you can not put downe; by the Which I meane, Any that can in Turne call up somewhat against you, whereby your Powerfullest Devices may not be of use. Ask of the Lesser, lest the Greater shall not wish to Answer, and shall commande more than you. I was frighted when I read of your know'g what Ben Zariatnatmik*[110] *hadde in his ebony Boxe, for I was conscious who must have tolde you. And againe I ask that you shalle write me as Jedediah and not Simon. In this Community a Man may not live too long, and you knowe my Plan by which I came back as my Son. I am desirous you will Acquaint me with what ye Blacke Man learnt from Sylvanus Cocidius*[111] *in ye Vault, under ye Roman Wall, and will be oblig'd for ye Lend'g of ye MS. you speak of.*

Another and unsigned letter from Philadelphia provoked equal thought, especially for the following passage:

I will observe what you say respecting the sending of Accounts only by y^r Vessels, but can not always be certain when to expect them. In the Matter spoke of, I require onlie one more thing; but wish to be sure I apprehend you exactly. You inform me, that no Part must be missing if the finest Effects are to be had, but you can not but know how hard it is to be sure. It seems a great Hazard and Burthen to take away the whole Box, and in Town (i.e. St. Peter's, St. Paul's, St. Mary's, or Christ Church) it can scarce be done at all. But I know what Imperfections were in the one I rais'd *up October last, and how many live Specimens you were forc'd to imploy before you hit upon the right Mode in the year 1766; so will be guided by you in all Matters. I am impatient for y' Brig, and inquire daily at Mr. Biddle's Wharf.*

A third suspicious letter was in an unknown tongue and even an unknown alphabet. In the Smith diary found by Charles Ward a single oft-repeated combination of characters is clumsily copied; and authorities at Brown University have pronounced the alphabet Amharic[112] or Abyssinian, although they do not recognise the word. None of these epistles was ever delivered to Curwen, though the disappearance of Jedediah Orne from Salem as recorded shortly afterward shewed that the Providence men took certain quiet steps. The Pennsylvania Historical Society also has some curious letters received by Dr. Shippen[113] regarding the presence of an unwholesome character in Philadelphia. But more decisive steps were in the air, and it is in the secret assemblages of sworn and tested sailors and faithful old privateersmen in the Brown warehouses by night that we must look for the main fruits of Weeden's disclosures. Slowly and surely a plan of campaign was under development which would leave no trace of Joseph Curwen's noxious mysteries.

Curwen, despite all precautions, apparently felt that something was in the wind; for he was now remarked to wear an unusually worried look. His coach was seen at all hours in the town and on the Pawtuxet Road, and he dropped little by little the air of forced geniality with which he had latterly sought to combat the town's prejudice. The nearest neighbours to his farm, the Fenners, one night remarked a great shaft of light shooting into the sky from some aperture in the roof of that cryptical stone building with the high, excessively narrow windows; an event which they quickly communicated to John Brown[114] in Providence. Mr. Brown had become the executive leader of the select group bent on Curwen's extirpation, and had informed the Fenners that some action was about to be taken. This he deemed needful because of the impossibility of their not witnessing the final raid; and he explained his course by saying that Curwen was known to be a spy of the customs officers at Newport, against whom the hand

112. A language of Ethiopia, the second-most-spoken Semitic language world-wide after Arabic.

113. Presumably William Shippen Sr. (1712–1801), a Philadelphia physician who represented Pennsylvania at the Continental Congress. His son William Shippen Jr. (1736–1808) was also a prominent physician; he served as surgeon general to the Continental Army and in 1765 founded the first maternity hospital in America, a lying-in ward and school for midwives in Philadelphia.

114. Brown (1736–1803) was another of the Brown brothers, successful in farming and shipping. He was one of the organizers of the *Gaspée* incident (see note 62, above). Brown was elected to the U.S. House of Representatives in 1798. He was also a slave trader and was the first person prosecuted under the federal slave importation laws in 1796.

115. A detail verified by Kimball, as were many other anecdotes in the story.

116. Esek Hopkins (1718–1802), a merchant and privateer captain, served as commander in chief of the Continental Navy during the Revolutionary War.

of every Providence shipper, merchant, and farmer was openly or clandestinely raised. Whether the ruse was wholly believed by neighbours who had seen so many queer things is not certain; but at any rate the Fenners were willing to connect any evil with a man of such queer ways. To them Mr. Brown had entrusted the duty of watching the Curwen farmhouse, and of regularly reporting every incident which took place there.

5.

The probability that Curwen was on guard and attempting unusual things, as suggested by the odd shaft of light, precipitated at last the action so carefully devised by the band of serious citizens. According to the Smith diary a company of about 100 men met at 10 P.M. on Friday, April 12th, 1771, in the great room of Thurston's Tavern at the Sign of the Golden Lion on Weybosset Point across the Bridge. Of the guiding group of prominent men in addition to the leader John Brown there were present Dr. Bowen, with his case of surgical instruments, President Manning without the great periwig (the largest in the Colonies) for which he was noted,[115] Governor Hopkins, wrapped in his dark cloak and accompanied by his seafaring brother Esek,[116] whom he had initiated at the last moment with the permission of the rest, John Carter, Capt. Mathewson, and Capt. Whipple, who was to lead the actual raiding party. These chiefs conferred apart in a rear chamber, after which Capt. Whipple emerged to the great room and gave the gathered seamen their last oaths and instructions. Eleazar Smith was with the leaders as they sat in the rear apartment awaiting the arrival of Ezra Weeden, whose duty was to keep track of Curwen and report the departure of his coach for the farm.

About 10:30 a heavy rumble was heard on the Great Bridge, followed by the sound of a coach in the street outside; and at that hour there was no need of waiting for Weeden in order to know that the doomed man had set out for his last night of unhallowed wizardry. A moment later, as the receding coach clattered faintly over the Muddy Dock Bridge, Weeden appeared; and the raiders fell silently into military order in the street, shouldering the firelocks, fowling-pieces, or whaling harpoons which they had

Great Bridge, in 2010. Photograph copyright © Donovan K. Loucks 2010, reprinted with permission

117. Also called Wega ("falling" in Arabic), Alpha Lyrae is the brightest star in the constellation Lyra (shaped like a lyre, according to the Greeks, or a falling vulture, per the Arabs). It is the second-brightest star in the Northern Hemisphere and was the polestar 12,000 years ago (and will be again in another 12,000 years).

with them. Weeden and Smith were with the party, and of the deliberating citizens there were present for active service Capt. Whipple, the leader, Capt. Esek Hopkins, John Carter, President Manning, Capt. Mathewson, and Dr. Bowen; together with Moses Brown, who had come up at the eleventh hour though absent from the preliminary session in the tavern. All these freemen and their hundred sailors began the long march without delay, grim and a trifle apprehensive as they left the Muddy Dock behind and mounted the gentle rise of Broad Street toward the Pawtuxet Road. Just beyond Elder Snow's church some of the men turned back to take a parting look at Providence lying outspread under the early spring stars. Steeples and gables rose dark and shapely, and salt breezes swept up gently from the cove north of the Bridge. Vega[117] was climbing above the great hill across the water, whose crest of trees was broken by the roof-line of the unfinished College edifice. At the foot of that hill, and along the narrow mounting lanes of its side, the old town dreamed; Old Providence, for whose safety and sanity so monstrous and colossal a blasphemy was about to be wiped out.

An hour and a quarter later the raiders arrived, as previously agreed, at the Fenner farmhouse; where they heard a final report on their intended victim. He had reached his farm over half an hour before, and the strange light had soon afterward shot once into the sky, but there were no lights in any visible windows. This was always the case of late. Even as this news was given another great glare arose toward the south, and the party realised that they had indeed come close to the scene of awesome and unnatural wonders. Capt. Whipple now ordered his force to separate into three divisions; one of twenty men under Eleazar Smith to strike across to the shore and guard the landing-place against possible reinforcements for Curwen until summoned by a messenger for desperate service, a second of twenty men under Capt. Esek Hopkins to steal down into the river valley behind the Curwen farm and demolish with axes or gunpowder the oaken door in the high, steep bank, and the third to close in on the house and adjacent buildings themselves. Of this division one third was to be led by Capt. Mathewson to the cryptical stone edifice with high narrow windows, another third to follow Capt. Whipple himself to the main farmhouse, and the remaining third to preserve a circle around the whole group of buildings until summoned by a final emergency signal.

The river party would break down the hillside door at the sound of a single whistle-blast, then waiting and capturing anything which might issue from the regions within. At the sound of two whistle-blasts it would advance through the aperture to oppose the enemy or join the rest of the raiding contingent. The party at the stone building would accept these respective signals in an analogous manner; forcing an entrance at the first, and at the second descending whatever passage into the ground might be discovered, and joining the general or focal warfare expected to take place within the caverns. A third or emergency signal of three blasts would summon the immediate reserve from its general guard duty; its twenty men dividing equally and entering the unknown depths through both farmhouse and stone building. Capt. Whipple's belief in the existence of catacombs was absolute, and he took no alternative into consideration when making his plans. He had with him a whistle of great power and shrillness, and did not fear any upsetting or misunderstanding of signals. The final reserve at the landing, of course, was nearly out of the whistle's range; hence would require a special messenger if needed for help. Moses Brown and John Carter went with Capt. Hopkins to the river-bank, while President Manning was detailed with Capt. Mathewson to the stone building. Dr. Bowen, with Ezra Weeden, remained in Capt. Whipple's party which was to storm the farmhouse itself. The attack was to begin as soon as a messenger from Capt. Hopkins had joined Capt. Whipple to notify him of the river party's readiness. The leader would then deliver the loud single blast, and the various advance parties would commence their simultaneous attack on three points. Shortly before 1 a.m. the three divisions left the Fenner farmhouse; one to guard the landing, another to seek the river valley and the hillside door, and the third to subdivide and attend to the actual buildings of the Curwen farm.

Eleazar Smith, who accompanied the shore-guarding party, records in his diary an uneventful march and a long wait on the bluff by the bay; broken once by what seemed to be the distant sound of the signal whistle and again by a peculiar muffled blend of roaring and crying and a powder blast which seemed to come from the same direction. Later on one man thought he caught some distant gunshots, and still later Smith himself felt the throb of titanic and thunderous words resounding in upper air. It was just before dawn that a single haggard messenger with wild eyes and a hideous unknown odour about his clothing appeared and told the detachment to disperse quietly to their homes and never again think or speak of the night's doings or of him who had been Joseph Curwen. Something about the bearing of the messenger carried a conviction which his mere words could never have conveyed; for though he was a seaman well known to many of them, there was something obscurely lost or gained in his soul which set him for evermore apart. It was the same later on when they met other old companions who had gone into that zone of horror. Most of them had lost or gained something imponderable and indescribable. They had seen or heard or felt something which was not for human creatures, and could not forget it. From them there was never any gossip, for to even the commonest of mortal instincts there are terrible boundaries. And from that single messenger the party at the shore caught a nameless awe which almost sealed their own lips. Very few are the rumours which ever came from any of them, and Eleazar Smith's diary is the only written record which has survived from that whole expedition which set forth from the Sign of the Golden Lion under the stars.

Charles Ward, however, discovered another vague sidelight in some Fenner correspondence which he found in New London, where he knew another branch of the family had lived. It seems that the Fenners, from whose house the doomed farm was distantly visible, had watched the departing columns of raiders; and had heard very clearly the angry barking of the Curwen dogs, followed by the first shrill blast which precipitated the attack. This blast had been followed by a repetition of the great shaft of light from the stone building, and in another moment, after a quick sounding of the second signal ordering a general invasion, there had come a subdued prattle of musketry followed by a horrible roaring cry which the correspondent Luke Fenner had represented in his epistle by the characters "Waaaahrrrrr-R'waaahrrr."

This cry, however, had possessed a quality which no mere writing could convey, and the correspondent mentions that his mother fainted completely at the sound. It was later repeated less loudly, and further but more muffled evidences of gunfire ensued; together with a loud explosion of powder from the direction of the river. About an hour afterward all the dogs began to bark frightfully, and there were vague ground rumblings so marked that the candlesticks tottered on the mantelpiece. A strong smell of sulphur was noted; and Luke Fenner's father declared that he heard the third or emergency whistle signal, though the others failed to detect it. Muffled musketry sounded again, followed by a deep scream less piercing but even more horrible than those which had preceded it; a kind of throaty, nastily plastic cough or gurgle whose quality as a scream must have come more from its continuity and psychological import than from its actual acoustic value.

Then the flaming thing burst into sight at a point where the Curwen farm ought to lie, and the human cries of desperate and frightened men were heard. Muskets flashed and cracked, and the flaming thing fell to the ground. A second flaming thing appeared, and a shriek of human origin was plainly distinguished. Fenner wrote that he could even gather a few words belched in frenzy: Almighty, protect thy lamb! Then there were more shots, and the second flaming thing fell. After that came silence for about three-quarters of an hour; at the end of which time little Arthur Fenner, Luke's brother, exclaimed that he saw "a red fog" going up to the stars from the accursed farm in the distance. No one but the child can testify to this, but Luke admits the significant coincidence implied by the panic of almost convulsive fright which at the same moment arched the backs and stiffened the fur of the three cats then within the room.

Five minutes later a chill wind blew up, and the air became suffused with such an intolerable stench that only the strong freshness of the sea could have prevented its being noticed by the shore party or by any wakeful souls in Pawtuxet village. This stench was nothing which any of the Fenners had ever encountered before, and produced a kind of clutching, amorphous fear beyond that of the tomb or the charnel-house. Close upon it came the awful voice which no hapless hearer will ever be able to forget. It thundered out of the sky like a doom, and windows rattled as its echoes died away. It was deep and musical; powerful as a bass organ, but evil as the forbidden books of the Arabs. What it said no man can tell, for it spoke in an unknown tongue, but this is the writing Luke Fenner set down to portray the dæmoniac intonations: "DEESMEES—JESHET—BONE DOSEFE DUVEMA—ENITEMOSS."[118] Not till the year 1919 did any soul link this crude transcript with anything else in mortal knowledge, but Charles Ward paled as he recognised what Mirandola[119] had denounced in shudders as the ultimate horror among black magic's incantations.

An unmistakably human shout or deep chorused scream seemed to answer this malign wonder from the Curwen farm, after which the unknown stench grew complex with an added odour equally intolerable. A wailing distinctly different from the scream now burst out, and was protracted ululantly in rising and falling paroxysms. At times it became almost articulate, though no auditor could trace any definite words; and at one point it seemed to verge toward the confines of diabolic and hysterical laughter. Then a yell of utter, ultimate fright and stark madness

118. Eliphas Levi's writings, collected in *The Mysteries of Magic*, instruct:

The formulae of evocation found in the magical elements of Peter d'Apono or in the Grimoires, whether printed or in manuscript, may then be recited. Those in the Great Grimoire, repeated in the common Red Dragon, have been wilfully altered in printing, and should read as follows:—

Per Adonai Elohim, Adonai Jehova, Adonai Sabaoth, Metraton On Agla Adonai Mathon, verbum pythonicum, mysterium salamandrae, conventus sylvorum, antra gnomorum, daemonia Coeli Gad, Almousin, Gibor, Jehosua, Evam, Zariatnatmik, veni, veni, veni.

The great invocation of Agrippa consists only in these words:—"DIES MIES JESCHET BOENEDOESEF DOUVEMA ENITEMAUS." We do not pretend to understand what they mean, they have possibly no meaning, and can certainly have none which is rational, since they are of efficacy in conjuring up the devil, who is supreme senselessness. Doubtless in the same opinion, Mirandola affirms that the most barbarous and absolutely unintelligible words are the best and most powerful in black magic. Ridiculous practices and imbecile evocations induce hallucination better than rites which are calculated to keep the understanding vigilant. Dupotet [Baron Dupotet de Sennevoy, a leading 19th-century mesmerist] affirms that he has tried the power of certain signs over ecstatics, and those in his "Magic Unveiled" are analogous if not absolutely identical with the diabolical signatures found in old editions of the "Great Grimoire." The same causes will always produce the same effects, and there is nothing new under the moon of the sorcerers any more than beneath the sun of the sages.

The conjurations should be repeated in a raised tone, accompanied by imprecations and menaces till the spirit responds. The spirit is usually preceded by a violent wind which seems to howl through the whole country. Domestic animals tremble at it, and seek a hiding place; the assistants feel a breath upon their faces, and their hair, damp with cold sweat, stands up on their heads (162).

Waite translated Lévi's invocation in another work, *The Ritual of Transcendental Magic* (1892), as "By Adonai Eloim, Adonai Jehova, Adonai Sabaoth, Metraton on Agla Mathon, the Pythonic word, the Mystery of the Salamander, the Assembly of Sylphs, the Grotto of Gnomes, the demons of the heaven of Gad, Almousin, Gibor, Jehosua, Evan, Zariatnatmik: Come, come, come!"

Lévi was the pseudonym of the French occultist Alphonse-Louis Constant (1810–1875), author of numerous works on spiritualism and magic.

119. Giovanni Pico della Mirandola (1463–1494) was an Italian scholar and philosopher, who, among many other interests, wrote on the topic of magic. However, the incantation set down here is properly attributed to Cornelius Agrippa (see note 52, above), who recorded it after Mirandola's death in his book on ritual magic, *De Occulta Philosophia Libri III* (Three Books of Occult Philosophy), written in 1509 or 1510 and published in 1533.

wrenched from scores of human throats—a yell which came strong and clear despite the depth from which it must have burst; after which darkness and silence ruled all things. Spirals of acrid smoke ascended to blot out the stars, though no flames appeared and no buildings were observed to be gone or injured on the following day.

Toward dawn two frightened messengers with monstrous and unplaceable odours saturating their clothing knocked at the Fenner door and requested a keg of rum, for which they paid very well indeed. One of them told the family that the affair of Joseph Curwen was over, and that the events of the night were not to be mentioned again. Arrogant as the order seemed, the aspect of him who gave it took away all resentment and lent it a fearsome authority; so that only these furtive letters of Luke Fenner, which he urged his Connecticut relative to destroy, remain to tell what was seen and heard. The non-compliance of that relative, whereby the letters were saved after all, has alone kept the matter from a merciful oblivion. Charles Ward had one detail to add as a result of a long canvass of Pawtuxet residents for ancestral traditions. Old Charles Slocum of that village said that there was known to his grandfather a queer rumour concerning a charred, distorted body found in the fields a week after the death of Joseph Curwen was announced. What kept the talk alive was the notion that this body, so far as could be seen in its burnt and twisted condition, was neither thoroughly human nor wholly allied to any animal which Pawtuxet folk had ever seen or read about.

6.

Not one man who participated in that terrible raid could ever be induced to say a word concerning it, and every fragment of the vague data which survives comes from those outside the final fighting party. There is something frightful in the care with which these actual raiders destroyed each scrap which bore the least allusion to the matter. Eight sailors had been killed, but although their bodies were not produced their families were satisfied with the statement that a clash with customs officers had occurred. The same statement also covered the numerous cases of wounds, all of which were extensively bandaged and treated only by Dr. Jabez Bowen, who had accompanied the party. Hardest to explain was the nameless odour clinging to all the raiders, a thing which was discussed for weeks. Of the citizen leaders, Capt. Whipple and Moses Brown were most severely hurt, and letters of their wives testify the bewilderment which their reticence and close guarding of their bandages produced. Psychologically every participant was aged, sobered, and shaken. It is fortunate that they were all strong men of action and simple, orthodox religionists, for with more subtle introspectiveness and mental complexity they would have fared ill indeed. President Manning was the most disturbed; but even he outgrew the darkest shadow, and smothered memories in prayers. Every man of those leaders had a stirring part to play in later years, and it is perhaps fortunate that this is so. Little more than a twelvemonth afterward Capt. Whipple led the mob who burnt the revenue ship *Gaspée*, and in this bold act we may trace one step in the blotting out of unwholesome images.

There was delivered to the widow of Joseph Curwen a sealed leaden coffin of curious design, obviously found ready on the spot when needed, in which she was told her husband's body lay. He had, it was explained, been killed in a customs battle about which it was not politic to give details. More than this no tongue ever uttered of Joseph Curwen's end, and Charles Ward had only a single hint wherewith to construct a theory. This hint was the merest thread—a shaky underscoring of a passage in Jedediah Orne's confiscated letter to Curwen, as partly copied in Ezra Weeden's handwriting. The copy was found in the possession of Smith's descendants; and we are left to decide whether Weeden gave it to his companion after the end, as a mute clue to the abnormality which had occurred, or whether, as is more probable, Smith had it before, and added the underscoring himself from what he had managed to extract from his friend by shrewd guessing and adroit cross-questioning. The underlined passage is merely this:

I say to you againe, doe not call up Any that you can not put downe; by the Which I meane, Any that can in Turne call up somewhat against you, whereby your Powerfullest Devices may

120. Wilde was convicted in 1895 of gross indecency and incarcerated in Pentonville Prison and then Wandsworth Prison, where he carried out his sentence of hard labor. He was released from prison in 1897; he died in exile, in Paris, three years later. Although memoirs of Wilde appeared shortly after his death, the first biography, written by his friend Frank Harris, did not appear until 1916. Wilde's reflections on his life, written in prison, were partially published under the title *De Profundis* in 1905, a decade after the criminal trial ended.

121. Lord Dunsany's tale, "The King That Was Not," was first published in 1905 in his collection *Time and the Gods*. Lovecraft had many collections of Dunsany's work in his library, and at least one of them included it. In the story, the king made images of the gods with faces of men (indeed, his own face). This so displeased the gods that they caused him to be erased: "passing suddenly out of . . . remembrance . . . [he] became no longer a thing that was or had ever been," his robe puddled on the floor near his throne and his crown beside it.

not be of use. Ask of the Lesser, lest the Greater shall not wish to Answer, and shall commande more than you.

In the light of this passage, and reflecting on what last unmentionable allies a beaten man might try to summon in his direst extremity, Charles Ward may well have wondered whether any citizen of Providence killed Joseph Curwen.

The deliberate effacement of every memory of the dead man from Providence life and annals was vastly aided by the influence of the raiding leaders. They had not at first meant to be so thorough, and had allowed the widow and her father and child to remain in ignorance of the true conditions; but Capt. Tillinghast was an astute man, and soon uncovered enough rumours to whet his horror and cause him to demand that his daughter and granddaughter change their name, burn the library and all remaining papers, and chisel the inscription from the slate slab above Joseph Curwen's grave. He knew Capt. Whipple well, and probably extracted more hints from that bluff mariner than anyone else ever gained respecting the end of the accused sorcerer.

From that time on the obliteration of Curwen's memory became increasingly rigid, extending at last by common consent even to the town records and files of the *Gazette*. It can be compared in spirit only to the hush that lay on Oscar Wilde's name for a decade after his disgrace,[120] and in extent only to the fate of that sinful King of Runazar in Lord Dunsany's tale,[121] whom the Gods decided must not only cease to be, but must cease ever to have been.

Mrs. Tillinghast, as the widow became known after 1772, sold the house in Olney Court and resided with her father in Power's Lane till her death in 1817. The farm at Pawtuxet, shunned by every living soul, remained to moulder through the years; and seemed to decay with unaccountable rapidity. By 1780 only the stone and brickwork were standing, and by 1800 even these had fallen to shapeless heaps. None ventured to pierce the tangled shrubbery on the river-bank behind which the hillside door may have lain, nor did any try to frame a definite image of the scenes amidst which Joseph Curwen departed from the horrors he had wrought.

Only robust old Capt. Whipple was heard by alert listeners to mutter once in a while to himself, "Pox on that ——, but he had no business to laugh while he screamed. 'Twas as though the damn'd —— had some'at up his sleeve. For half a crown I'd burn his —— house."

III. A SEARCH AND AN EVOCATION

1.

CHARLES WARD, AS we have seen, first learned in 1918 of his descent from Joseph Curwen. That he at once took an intense interest in everything pertaining to the bygone mystery is not to be wondered at; for every vague rumour that he had heard of Curwen now became something vital to himself, in whom flowed Curwen's blood. No spirited and imaginative genealogist could have done otherwise than begin forthwith an avid and systematic collection of Curwen data.

In his first delvings there was not the slightest attempt at secrecy; so that even Dr. Lyman hesitates to date the youth's madness from any period before the close of 1919. He talked freely with his family—though his mother was not particularly pleased to own an ancestor like Curwen—and with the officials of the various museums and libraries he visited. In applying to private families for records thought to be in their possession he made no concealment of his object, and shared the somewhat amused scepticism with which the accounts of the old diarists and letter-writers were regarded. He often expressed a keen wonder as to what really had taken place a century and a half before at that Pawtuxet farmhouse whose site he vainly tried to find, and what Joseph Curwen really had been.

When he came across the Smith diary and archives and encountered the letter from Jedediah Orne he decided to visit Salem and look up Curwen's early activities and connexions there, which he did during the Easter vacation of 1919. At the Essex Institute,[122] which was well known to him from former sojourns in the glamorous old town of crumbling Puritan gables and clustered gambrel roofs, he was very kindly received, and

122. A historic museum, now part of the Peabody Essex Museum in Salem.

The Essex Institute (now part of the Peabody Essex Museum), in 2013. Photograph copyright © Donovan K. Loucks 2010, reprinted with permission

123. That is, per the Gregorian calendar; the Julian calendar was not implemented in the English colonies until 1752. There were ten "missing days" in the switchover, so that the eighteenth of February would be February 28 under the Julian calendar.

124. See note 109, above, for a possible identification of this individual. Curwen's construction of a fraternity of like-minded alchemical scholars is paralleled by the efforts of John Winthrop, Jr. (later governor of colonial Massachusetts) to found a colony of alchemists in New London, Connecticut, in the mid seventeenth century. See Walter W. Woodward's *Prospero in America: John Winthrop, Jr., Alchemy, and the Creation of New England Culture (1606–1676)*.

125. Records reflect that one John Orne bought property in Salem in 1652; this is undoubtedly a family member.

unearthed there a considerable amount of Curwen data. He found that his ancestor was born in Salem-Village, now Danvers, seven miles from town, on the eighteenth of February (O.S.)[123] 1662–3; and that he had run away to sea at the age of fifteen, not appearing again for nine years, when he returned with the speech, dress, and manners of a native Englishman and settled in Salem proper. At that time he had little to do with his family, but spent most of his hours with the curious books he had brought from Europe, and the strange chemicals which came for him on ships from England, France, and Holland. Certain trips of his into the country were the objects of much local inquisitiveness, and were whisperingly associated with vague rumours of fires on the hills at night.

Curwen's only close friends had been one Edward Hutchinson of Salem-Village[124] and one Simon Orne of Salem.[125] With these men he was often seen in conference about the Common, and visits among them were by no means infrequent. Hutchinson had a house well out toward the woods, and it was not altogether liked by sensitive people because of the sounds heard there at night. He was said to entertain strange visitors, and the lights seen from his windows were not always of the same colour. The knowledge he displayed concerning long-dead persons and long-forgotten events was considered distinctly unwholesome, and he disappeared about the time the witchcraft panic began, never to be heard from again. At that time Joseph Curwen also departed, but his settlement in Providence was soon learned of. Simon Orne lived in Salem until 1720, when his failure to grow visibly old began to excite attention. He thereafter disappeared, though thirty years later his precise counterpart and self-styled son turned up to claim his property. The claim was allowed on the strength of documents in Simon Orne's known hand, and Jedediah Orne continued to dwell in Salem till 1771, when certain letters from Providence citizens to the Rev. Thomas Barnard and others brought about his quiet removal to parts unknown.

Certain documents by and about all of these strange characters were available at the Essex Institute, the Court House, and the Registry of Deeds, and included both harmless commonplaces such as land titles and bills of sale, and furtive fragments of a more provocative nature. There were four or five unmistakable allusions to them on the witchcraft trial records; as when one Hepzibah Lawson[126] swore on July 10, 1692, at the Court of Oyer and Terminer[127] under Judge Hathorne,[128] that "fortie Witches and the Blacke Man[129] were wont to meete in the Woodes behind Mr. Hutchinson's house," and one Amity How[130] declared at a session of August 8th before Judge Gedney[131] that "Mr. G. B. (Rev. George Burroughs) on that Nighte putt ye Divell his Marke upon Bridget S., Jonathan A., *Simon O.*, Deliverance W., *Joseph C.*, Susan P., Mehitable C., and Deborah B."[132]

Then there was a catalogue of Hutchinson's uncanny library as found after his disappearance, and an unfinished manuscript in his handwriting, couched in a cipher none could read. Ward had a photostatic[133] copy of this manuscript made, and began to work casually on the cipher as soon as it was delivered to him. After the following August his labours on the cipher became intense and feverish, and there is reason to believe from his speech and conduct that he hit upon the key before October or November. He never stated, though, whether or not he had succeeded.

But of the greatest immediate interest was the Orne material. It took Ward only a short time to prove from identity of penmanship a thing he had already considered established from the text of the letter to Curwen; namely, that Simon Orne and his supposed son were one and the same person. As Orne had said to his correspondent, it was hardly safe to live too long in Salem, hence he resorted to a thirty-year sojourn abroad, and did not return to claim his lands except as a representative of a new generation. Orne had apparently been careful to destroy most of his correspondence, but the citizens who took action in 1771 found and preserved a few letters and papers which excited their wonder. There were cryptic formulæ and diagrams in his and other hands which Ward now either copied with care or had photographed, and one extremely mysterious letter in a chirography[134] that the searcher recognised from items in the Registry of Deeds as positively Joseph Curwen's.

This Curwen letter, though undated as to the year, was evidently not the one in answer to which Orne had written the confiscated missive; and from internal evidence Ward placed it not much later than 1750. It may not be amiss to give the text in full, as a sample of the style of one whose history was so dark

126. A fictitious name.

127. "Oyer and Terminer" means "to hear and determine." This was a special court created for the express purpose of the witchcraft trials.

128. John Hathorne was an executor (like a magistrate) in the Salem Witch Trials and displayed no compassion for the accused.

129. The "black man" is mentioned by many of the witnesses in the trials as whispering in the ear of that victim or another and appears to be either Satan or a lesser devil.

130. Her name does not appear in Upham's expansive history of the trials or the transcript of the witchcraft trials papers.

131. Bartholomew Gedney served on the panel of judges along with Hathorne.

132. Burroughs was reportedly a man without guile and incapable of appreciating the wickedness of the witnesses. According to Upham, "He tried, in simplicity and ingenuousness, to explain what was brought against him; and this, probably, was all the 'twisting and turning' he exhibited." On April 30, 1692, two complainants, Jonathan Walcott and Thomas Putnam, swore before Hathorne and Jonathan Corwin that "high Suspition of Sundry acts of Witchcraft [having been] done or Committed by [Burroughs] Upon the Bodys of Mary Walcot Marcy Lewis Abigail Williams Ann putnam and Eliz Hubert and Susanah Sheldon (Viz) Upon Som: or all of them, of Salem Village or farm[es] whereby great hurt and dammage benne donn[e] to the Bodys of s'd persons above named therefore [the complainants] Craved Justice." Many gave testimony

against Burroughs, but no Amity How was among the witnesses. Burroughs was executed on August 19, 1692.

133. The Photostat machine was a device invented around 1907 for photographic copying of documents (its principal competitor was the Rectigraph). The machines were very popular, and "photostat" became the generic name for the photographic copy. The devices were supplanted by copying machines that used electrophotography (called *xerography*) in the 1940s, the technique still used today in common photocopiers.

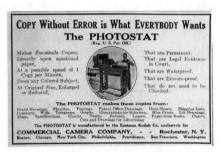

An advertisement for the "Photostat" device by the Commercial Camera Company, July 1920.

134. Handwriting.

135. See "The Festival," note 37, above. S. T. Joshi, in *The Rise and Fall of the Cthulhu Mythos*, argues that references to Yog-Sothoth and later references to the *Necronomicon* by Curwen and his associates suggest that they "were involved in more cosmic activity than merely the resurrection of dead human bodies" (59).

136. A volume of unknown provenance.

137. The "key." In arcane texts, usually the Greater or Lesser Key of Solomon.

138. Holy Rood Day, or Roodmas, is May 3, the Feast of the Cross, and is often identified with May Day or Walpurgis;

and terrible. The recipient is addressed as "Simon," but a line (whether drawn by Curwen or Orne Ward could not tell) is run through the word.

Providence, 1. May

Brother:—

My honour'd Antient ffriende, due Respects and earnest Wishes to Him whom we serve for y^r eternall Power. I am just come upon That which you ought to knowe, concern'g the Matter of the Laste Extremitie and what to doe regard'g yt. I am not dispos'd to fol-lowe you in go'g Away on acct. of my Yeares, for Prouidence hath not ye Sharpeness of ye Bay in hunt'g oute uncommon Things and bringinge to Tryall. I am ty'd up in Shippes and Goodes, and cou'd not doe as you did, besides the Whiche my ffarme at Patuxet hath under it What you Knowe, that wou'd not waite for my com'g Backe as an Other.

But I am not unreadie for harde ffortunes, as I haue tolde you, and haue longe work'd upon ye Way of get'g Backe after ye Laste. I laste Night strucke on ye Wordes that bringe up YOGGE-SOTHOTHE, and sawe for ye firste Time that fface spoke of by Ibn Schacabao[135] *in y^e ——. And IT said, that ye III Psalme in ye Liber-Damnatus*[136] *holdes ye Clauicle.*[137] *With Sunne in V House, Saturne in Trine, drawe ye Pentagram of Fire, and saye ye ninth Uerse thrice. This Uerse repeate eache Roodemas*[138] *and Hallow's Eue; and ye Thing will breede in ye Outside Spheres.*

And of ye Seede of Olde shal One be borne who shal looke Backe, tho' know'g not what he seekes.

Yett will this availe Nothing if there be no Heir, and if the Saltes, or the Way to make the Saltes, bee not Readie for his Hande; and here I will owne, I haue not taken needed Stepps nor founde Much. Y^e Process is plaguy harde to come neare; and it uses up such a Store of Specimens, I am harde putte to it to get Enough, notwithstand'g the Sailors I have from ye Indies. Y^e People aboute are become curious, but I can stande them off. Y^e Gentry are worse than the Populace, be'g more Circumstantiall in their Accts. and more believ'd in what they tell. That Parson and Mr. Merritt have talk'd some, I am fearfull, but no Thing soe far is Danger-

ous. Yᵉ Chymical substances are easie of get'g, there be'g II. goode Chymists in Towne, Dr. Bowen and Sam: Carew.[139] I am foll'g oute what Borellus saith, and haue Helpe in Abdool Al-Hazred his VII. Booke. Whatever I gette, you shal haue. And in yᵉ meane while, do not neglect to make use of yᵉ Wordes I haue here giuen. I haue them Righte, but if you Desire to see HIM, imploy the Writings on yᵉ Piece of — that I am putt'g in this Packet. Saye yᵉ Uerses every Roodmas and Hallow's Eue; and if yʳ Line runn out not, one shall bee in yeares to come that shal looke backe and use what Saltes or Stuff for Saltes you shal leaue him. Job XIV. XIV.

I rejoice you are again at Salem, and hope I may see you not longe hence. I have a goode Stallion, and am think'g of get'g a Coach, there be'g one (Mr. Merritt's) in Prouidence already, tho' yᵉ Roades are bad. If you are dispos'd to Travel, doe not pass me bye. From Boston take yᵉ Post Rd. thro' Dedham, Wrentham, and Attleborough, goode Taverns be'g at all these Townes. Stop at Mr. Bolcom's in Wrentham, where yᵉ Beddes are finer than Mr. Hatch's, but eate at yᵉ other House for their Cooke is better. Turne into Prou. by Patucket ffalls, and yᵉ Rd. past Mr. Sayles's Tavern.[140] My House opp. Mr. Epenetus Olney's Tavern[141] off yᵉ Towne Street, 1st on yᵉ N. side of Olney's Court. Distance from Boston Stone[142] abt. XLIV Miles.

Sir, I am yʳ olde and true ffriend and Servt. in

Almousin-Metraton.[143]

Josephus C.

To Mr. Simon Orne,
William's-Lane, in Salem.

This letter, oddly enough, was what first gave Ward the exact location of Curwen's Providence home; for none of the records encountered up to that time had been at all specific. The discovery was doubly striking because it indicated as the newer Curwen house, built in 1761 on the site of the old, a dilapidated building still standing in Olney Court and well known to Ward in his antiquarian rambles over Stampers' Hill. The place was indeed only a few squares from his own home on the great hill's higher ground, and was now the abode of a negro family much esteemed for occasional washing, housecleaning, and furnace-tending ser-

these fall exactly six months before All Hallows' Day (and Walpurgisnacht, associated with sorcerers and witches, is the eve of Walpurgis, just as Halloween or All Hallows' Eve is the night before All Hallows' Day).

139. Dr. Samuel Carew owned property in Providence in 1798, according to the official records.

140. According to Welcome Greene's *The Providence Plantations*, "The old Sayles place lay near by [in Pawtucket], where in later days Jeremiah Sayles kept a tavern" (377).

141. Epenetus Olney was the son of Epenetus and Mary (Whipple) Olney, born January 18, 1675, at Providence; he died there on September 17, 1740. According to the American Historical Society, he owned a large tract of land, which comprised a part of the sites of the present Glocester and Burrillville, and was a well-known man in the community. He married Mary Williams, granddaughter of Roger Williams, and they were the parents of the following children: James, Charles, Joseph, Anthony, Mary, Amey, Anna, Martha, and Freeborn. He may have owned a tavern that bore his name, but he was likely deceased by the time of this letter.

142. The Boston Stone, imported from England and once said to have been used as a millstone to grind pigments for paint, was embedded in 1737 in the wall of the building on Marshall Street that sits across from the Ebenezer Hancock House in Boston (built by John Hancock). Some believe that the stone was used for many years by surveyors to measure distances. It never had any official status as a milestone, and eventually the prominent Boston central point became the dome of the new State House.

143. Incorrectly "Almonsin" in early Arkham editions. Almousin or Almouzin is another name for God, drawn from the *Grand Grimoire*, described in note 110, above. In the cosmogony of the *Grand Grimoire*, Metratron (or Metatron or Metaraon) is the chief of the ten archangels, called the king of angels. He has been identified with various biblical angels, such as the angel who wrestled with Jacob (Genesis 32) or the watchman ("Watchman, what of the night?") in Isaiah 21, or the angel sent to guide the Israelites in Exodus 23:20.

144. Molding that projects in front of the face of the framing panel to cover a joint.

vices. To find, in distant Salem, such sudden proof of the significance of this familiar rookery in his own family history, was a highly impressive thing to Ward; and he resolved to explore the place immediately upon his return. The more mystical phases of the letter, which he took to be some extravagant kind of symbolism, frankly baffled him; though he noted with a thrill of curiosity that the Biblical passage referred to—*Job 14,14*—was the familiar verse, "If a man die, shall he live again? All the days of my appointed time will I wait, till my change come."

2.

Young Ward came home in a state of pleasant excitement, and spent the following Saturday in a long and exhaustive study of the house in Olney Court. The place, now crumbling with age, had never been a mansion; but was a modest two-and-a-half story wooden town house of the familiar Providence colonial type, with plain peaked roof, large central chimney, and artistically carved doorway with rayed fanlight, triangular pediment, and trim Doric pilasters. It had suffered but little alteration externally, and Ward felt he was gazing on something very close to the sinister matters of his quest.

The present negro inhabitants were known to him, and he was very courteously shewn about the interior by old Asa and his stout wife Hannah. Here there was more change than the outside indicated, and Ward saw with regret that fully half of the fine scroll-and-urn overmantels and shell-carved cupboard linings were gone, whilst much of the fine wainscotting and bolection moulding[144] was marked, hacked, and gouged, or covered up altogether with cheap wall-paper. In general, the survey did not yield as much as Ward had somehow expected; but it was at least exciting to stand within the ancestral walls which had housed such a man of horror as Joseph Curwen. He saw with a thrill that a monogram had been very carefully effaced from the ancient brass knocker.

From then until after the close of school Ward spent his time on the photostatic copy of the Hutchinson cipher and the accumulation of local Curwen data. The former still proved unyielding; but of the latter he obtained so much, and so many clues to similar data elsewhere, that he was ready by July to make a trip to New London and New York to consult old letters whose presence in those places was indicated. This trip was very fruitful, for it brought him the Fenner letters with their terrible description of the Pawtuxet farmhouse raid, and the Nightingale-Talbot[145] letters in which he learned of the portrait painted on a panel of the Curwen library. This matter of the portrait interested him particularly, since he would have given much to know just what Joseph Curwen looked like; and he decided to make a second search of the house in Olney Court to see if there might not be some trace of the ancient features beneath peeling coats of later paint or layers of mouldy wall-paper.

Early in August that search took place, and Ward went carefully over the walls of every room sizeable enough to have been by any possibility the library of the evil builder. He paid especial attention to the large panels of such overmantels as still remained; and was keenly excited after about an hour, when on a broad area above the fireplace in a spacious ground-floor room he became certain that the surface brought out by the peeling of several coats of paint was sensibly darker than any ordinary interior paint or the wood beneath it was likely to have been. A few more careful tests with a thin knife, and he knew that he had come upon an oil portrait of great extent. With truly scholarly restraint the youth did not risk the damage which an immediate attempt to uncover the hidden picture with the knife might have done, but just retired from the scene of his discovery to enlist expert help. In three days he returned with an artist of long experience, Mr. Walter C. Dwight,[146] whose studio is near the foot of College Hill; and that accomplished restorer of paintings set to work at once with proper methods and chemical substances. Old Asa and his wife were duly excited over their strange visitors, and were properly reimbursed for this invasion of their domestic hearth.

As day by day the work of restoration progressed, Charles Ward looked on with growing interest at the lines and shades gradually unveiled after their long oblivion. Dwight had begun at the bottom; hence since the picture was a three-quarter-length one, the face did not come out for some time. It was meanwhile seen that the subject was a spare, well-shaped man with dark-blue

145. Silas Talbot (1751–1813) was commander of the USS *Constitution* and later a congressman from the state of New York; and there are some papers referring to one "Nightingale" as well as "Curwen" among the family correspondence collected in the G. W. Blunt White Library at the Mystic Seaport Museum, about ten miles east of New London, Connecticut. These may well be the letters Ward consulted, although there is no evident connection between Talbot and Providence.

146. There is no record of Mr. Dwight.

147. A popular colonial style, after the Earl of Albemarle.

Portrait of Arnold Joost van Keppel, 1st Earl of Albemarle (1669–1718), by Sir Godfrey Kneller (ca. 1700).

148. In the town of West Warwick. There were two mills there, the Valley Queen and the Royal; both subsequently were destroyed in fires and not rebuilt.

coat, embroidered waistcoat, black satin small-clothes, and white silk stockings, seated in a carved chair against the background of a window with wharves and ships beyond. When the head came out it was observed to bear a neat Albemarle wig,[147] and to possess a thin, calm, undistinguished face which seemed somehow familiar to both Ward and the artist. Only at the very last, though, did the restorer and his client begin to gasp with astonishment at the details of that lean, pallid visage, and to recognise with a touch of awe the dramatic trick which heredity had played. For it took the final bath of oil and the final stroke of the delicate scraper to bring out fully the expression which centuries had hidden; and to confront the bewildered Charles Dexter Ward, dweller in the past, with his own living features in the countenance of his horrible great-great-great-grandfather.

Ward brought his parents to see the marvel he had uncovered, and his father at once determined to purchase the picture despite its execution on stationary panelling. The resemblance to the boy, despite an appearance of rather greater age, was marvellous; and it could be seen that through some trick of atavism the physical contours of Joseph Curwen had found precise duplication after a century and a half. Mrs. Ward's resemblance to her ancestor was not at all marked, though she could recall relatives who had some of the facial characteristics shared by her son and by the bygone Curwen. She did not relish the discovery, and told her husband that he had better burn the picture instead of bringing it home. There was, she averred, something unwholesome about it; not only intrinsically, but in its very resemblance to Charles. Mr. Ward, however, was a practical man of power and affairs—a cotton manufacturer with extensive mills at Riverpoint[148] in the Pawtuxet Valley—and not one to listen to feminine scruples. The picture impressed him mightily with its likeness to his son, and he believed the boy deserved it as a present. In this opinion, it is needless to say, Charles most heartily concurred; and a few days later Mr. Ward located the owner of the house—a small rodent-featured person with a guttural accent—and obtained the whole mantel and overmantel bearing the picture at a curtly fixed price which cut short the impending torrent of unctuous haggling.

It now remained to take off the panelling and remove it to the Ward home, where provisions were made for its thorough restoration and installation with an electric mock-fireplace in Charles's third-floor study or library. To Charles was left the task of superintending this removal, and on the twenty-eighth of August he accompanied two expert workmen from the Crooker decorating firm[149] to the house in Olney Court, where the mantel and portrait-bearing overmantel were detached with great care and precision for transportation in the company's motor truck. There was left a space of exposed brickwork marking the chimney's course, and in this young Ward observed a cubical recess about a foot square, which must have lain directly behind the head of the portrait. Curious as to what such a space might mean or contain, the youth approached and looked within; finding beneath the deep coatings of dust and soot some loose yellowed papers, a crude, thick copybook, and a few mouldering textile shreds which may have formed the ribbon binding the rest together. Blowing away the bulk of the dirt and cinders, he took up the book and looked at the bold inscription on its cover. It was in a hand which he had learned to recognise at the Essex Institute, and proclaimed the volume as the "*Journall and Notes of Jos: Curwen, Gent., of Providence-Plantations, Late of Salem.*"

Excited beyond measure by his discovery, Ward shewed the book to the two curious workmen beside him. Their testimony is absolute as to the nature and genuineness of the finding, and Dr. Willett relies on them to help establish his theory that the youth was not mad when he began his major eccentricities. All the other papers were likewise in Curwen's handwriting, and one of them seemed especially portentous because of its inscription: "*To Him Who Shal Come After, & How He May Gett Beyonde Time & yᵉ Spheres.*"

Another was in a cipher; the same, Ward hoped, as the Hutchinson cipher which had hitherto baffled him. A third, and here the searcher rejoiced, seemed to be a key to the cipher; whilst the fourth and fifth were addressed respectively to "Edw: Hutchinson, Armiger"[150] and "Jedediah Orne, Esq." "or Their Heir or Heirs, or Those Represent'g Them." The sixth and last

149. Alfred L. Crooker & Co., a manufacturer of wood mantels, is listed in the Providence Directory for 1889.

Advertisement for A. L. Crooker & Co., appearing in the 1889 Providence Directory (Providence: Sampson, Murdock & Co.).

150. "Armiger" is an honorific, like "Esquire"; it means someone entitled to bear arms.

was inscribed: "*Joseph Curwen his Life and Travells Bet'n ye yeares 1678 and 1687: Of Whither He Voyag'd, Where He Stay'd, Whom He Sawe, and What He Learnt.*"

3.

We have now reached the point from which the more academic school of alienists date Charles Ward's madness. Upon his discovery the youth had looked immediately at a few of the inner pages of the book and manuscripts, and had evidently seen something which impressed him tremendously. Indeed, in shewing the titles to the workmen, he appeared to guard the text itself with peculiar care, and to labour under a perturbation for which even the antiquarian and genealogical significance of the find could hardly account. Upon returning home he broke the news with an almost embarrassed air, as if he wished to convey an idea of its supreme importance without having to exhibit the evidence itself. He did not even shew the titles to his parents, but simply told them that he had found some documents in Joseph Curwen's handwriting, "mostly in cipher," which would have to be studied very carefully before yielding up their true meaning. It is unlikely that he would have shewn what he did to the workmen, had it not been for their unconcealed curiosity. As it was he doubtless wished to avoid any display of peculiar reticence which would increase their discussion of the matter.

That night Charles Ward sat up in his room reading the new-found book and papers, and when day came he did not desist. His meals, on his urgent request when his mother called to see what was amiss, were sent up to him; and in the afternoon he appeared only briefly when the men came to install the Curwen picture and mantelpiece in his study. The next night he slept in snatches in his clothes, meanwhile wrestling feverishly with the unravelling of the cipher manuscript. In the morning his mother saw that he was at work on the photostatic copy of the Hutchinson cipher, which he had frequently shewn her before; but in response to her query he said that the Curwen key could not be applied to it. That afternoon he abandoned his work and watched the men fascinatedly as they finished their installation of the picture with its woodwork above a cleverly realistic electric log, setting the mock-fireplace and overmantel a little out from the north wall as if a chimney existed, and boxing in the sides with panelling to match the room's. The front panel holding the picture was sawn and hinged to allow cupboard space behind it. After the workmen went he moved his work into the study and sat down before it with his eyes half on the cipher and half on the portrait which stared back at him like a year-adding and century-recalling mirror.

His parents, subsequently recalling his conduct at this period, give interesting details anent the policy of concealment which he practiced. Before servants he seldom hid any paper which he might be studying, since he rightly assumed that Curwen's intricate and archaic chirography would be too much for them. With his parents, however, he was more circumspect; and unless the manuscript in question were a cipher, or a mere mass of cryptic symbols and unknown ideographs (as that entitled "*To Him Who Shal Come After etc.*" seemed to be), he would cover it with some convenient paper until his caller had departed. At night he kept the papers under lock and key in an antique cabinet of his, where he also placed them whenever he left the room. He soon resumed fairly regular hours and habits, except that his long walks and other outside interests seemed to cease. The opening of school, where he now began his senior year, seemed a great bore to him; and he frequently asserted his determination never to bother with college. He had, he said, important special investigations to make, which would provide him with more avenues toward knowledge and the humanities than any university which the world could boast.

Naturally, only one who had always been more or less studious, eccentric, and solitary could have pursued this course for many days without attracting notice. Ward, however, was constitutionally a scholar and a hermit; hence his parents were less surprised than regretful at the close confinement and secrecy he adopted. At the same time, both his father and mother thought it odd that he would shew them no scrap of his treasure-trove, nor give any connected account of such data as he had deciphered. This reticence he explained away as due to a wish to wait until he might announce some connected revelation, but as the weeks passed without further disclosures there began to grow up

151. Subsequently moved to Newton and now closed, the library consisted of a collection of books on the Bible and the history of the Christian church. A catalogue of its collection was published in 1924.

between the youth and his family a kind of constraint; intensified in his mother's case by her manifest disapproval of all Curwen delvings.

During October Ward began visiting the libraries again, but no longer for the antiquarian matter of his former days. Witch-craft and magic, occultism and dæmonology, were what he sought now; and when Providence sources proved unfruitful he would take the train for Boston and tap the wealth of the great library in Copley Square, the Widener Library at Harvard, or the Zion Research Library in Brookline,[151] where certain rare works on Biblical subjects are available. He bought extensively, and fitted up a whole additional set of shelves in his study for newly acquired works on uncanny subjects; while during the Christmas holidays he made a round of out-of-town trips including one to Salem to consult certain records at the Essex Institute.

About the middle of January, 1920, there entered Ward's bearing an element of triumph which he did not explain, and he was no more found at work upon the Hutchinson cipher. Instead, he inaugurated a dual policy of chemical research and record-scanning; fitting up for the one a laboratory in the unused attic

The Harry Elkins Widener Memorial Library, in 1990.
Photograph courtesy of Will Hart

of the house, and for the latter haunting all the sources of vital statistics in Providence. Local dealers in drugs and scientific supplies, later questioned, gave astonishingly queer and meaningless catalogues of the substances and instruments he purchased; but clerks at the State House, the City Hall, and the various libraries agree as to the definite object of his second interest. He was searching intensely and feverishly for the grave of Joseph Curwen, from whose slate slab an older generation had so wisely blotted the name.

Little by little there grew upon the Ward family the conviction that something was wrong. Charles had had freaks and changes of minor interests before, but this growing secrecy and absorption in strange pursuits was unlike even him. His school work was the merest pretence; and although he failed in no test, it could be seen that the old application had all vanished. He had other concernments now; and when not in his new laboratory with a score of obsolete alchemical books, could be found either poring over old burial records down town or glued to his volumes of occult lore in his study, where the startlingly—one almost fancied increasingly—similar features of Joseph Curwen stared blandly at him from the great overmantel on the north wall.

Late in March Ward added to his archive-searching a ghoulish series of rambles about the various ancient cemeteries of the city. The cause appeared later, when it was learned from City Hall clerks that he had probably found an important clue. His quest had suddenly shifted from the grave of Joseph Curwen to that of one Naphthali Field; and this shift was explained when, upon going over the files that he had been over, the investigators actually found a fragmentary record of Curwen's burial which had escaped the general obliteration, and which stated that the curious leaden coffin had been interred "10 ft. S. and 5 ft. W. of Naphthali Field's grave in y^e ———." The lack of a specified burying-ground in the surviving entry greatly complicated the search, and Naphthali Field's grave seemed as elusive as that of Curwen; but here no systematic effacement had existed, and one might reasonably be expected to stumble on the stone itself even if its record had perished. Hence the rambles—from which St. John's (the former King's) Churchyard and the ancient Congre-

152. The gravestone of Howard Phillips Lovecraft is located in this cemetery.

153. "He died."

gational burying-ground in the midst of Swan Point Cemetery[152] were excluded, since other statistics had shewn that the only Naphthali Field (obiit[153] 1729) whose grave could have been meant had been a Baptist.

4.

It was toward May when Dr. Willett, at the request of the senior Ward, and fortified with all the Curwen data which the family had gleaned from Charles in his non-secretive days, talked with the young man. The interview was of little value or conclusiveness, for Willett felt at every moment that Charles was thoroughly master of himself and in touch with matters of real importance; but it at least forced the secretive youth to offer some rational explanation of his recent demeanour. Of a pallid, impassive type not easily shewing embarrassment, Ward seemed quite ready to discuss his pursuits, though not to reveal their object. He stated that the papers of his ancestor had contained some remarkable secrets of early scientific knowledge, for the most part in cipher, of an apparent scope comparable only to the discoveries of Friar Bacon and perhaps surpassing even those. They were, however, meaningless except when correlated with a body of learning now wholly obsolete; so that their immediate presentation to a world equipped only with modern science would rob them of all impressiveness and dramatic significance. To take their vivid place in the history of human thought they must first be correlated by one familiar with the background out of which they evolved, and to this task of correlation Ward was now devoting himself. He was seeking to acquire as fast as possible those neglected arts of old which a true interpreter of the Curwen data must possess, and hoped in time to make a full announcement and presentation of the utmost interest to mankind and to the world of thought. Not even Einstein, he declared, could more profoundly revolutionise the current conception of things.

As to his graveyard search, whose object he freely admitted, but the details of whose progress he did not relate, he said he had reason to think that Joseph Curwen's mutilated headstone bore certain mystic symbols—carved from directions in his will and ignorantly spared by those who had effaced the name—

which were absolutely essential to the final solution of his cryptic system. Curwen, he believed, had wished to guard his secret with care; and had consequently distributed the data in an exceedingly curious fashion. When Dr. Willett asked to see the mystic documents, Ward displayed much reluctance and tried to put him off with such things as photostatic copies of the Hutchinson cipher and Orne formulæ and diagrams; but finally shewed him the exteriors of some of the real Curwen finds—the *"Journall and Notes,"* the cipher (title in cipher also), and the formula-filled message *"To Him Who Shal Come After"*—and let him glance inside such as were in obscure characters.

He also opened the diary at a page carefully selected for its innocuousness and gave Willett a glimpse of Curwen's connected handwriting in English. The doctor noted very closely the crabbed and complicated letters, and the general aura of the seventeenth century which clung round both penmanship and style despite the writer's survival into the eighteenth century, and became quickly certain that the document was genuine. The text itself was relatively trivial, and Willett recalled only a fragment:

"Wedn. 16 Octr. 1754. My Sloope the *Wakeful* this Day putt in from London with XX newe Men pick'd up in yᵉ Indies, Spaniards from Martineco and 2 Dutch Men from Surinam. Yᵉ Dutch Men are like to Desert from have'g hearde Somewhat ill of these Ventures, but I will see to ye Inducing of them to Staye ffor Mr. Knight Dexter of yᵉ Boy and Book[154] 120 Pieces Camblets, 100 Pieces Assrtd. Cambleteens,[155] 20 Pieces blue Duffles, 100 Pieces Shalloons, 50 Pieces Calamancoes, 300 Pieces each, Shendsoy and Humhums. ffor Mr. Green at yᵉ Elephant 50 Gallon Cyttles, 20 Warm'g Pannes, 15 Bake Cyttles, 10 pr. Smoke'g Tonges. ffor Mr. Perrigo 1 Sett of Awles.[156] ffor Mr. Nightingale 50 Reames prime Foolscap. Say'd yᵉ SABAOTH[157] thrice last Nighte but None appear'd. I must heare more from Mr. H. in Transylvania,[158] tho' it is Harde reach'g him and exceeding strange he can not give me the Use of what he hath so well us'd these hundred yeares. Simon hath not Writ these V. Weekes, but I expecte soon hear'g from him."

154. Kimball notes that the shop known as the "Sign of the Boy and Book," of which Knight Dexter was the proprietor, sold a well-selected assortment of dry goods "whose very names have become obsolete. There were 'Shalloons, Tammies, Sagathees, Thicksetts, Taffaties and Persians; Allopeens, Callimancoes, red and blue Duffils, [and] black and blue Everlastings'" (325).

155. Camblet and cambleteen are materials, wool and silk woven with hair (usually goat hair). Shalloon is also a fabric, as are calamanco, shendsoy, and humhums (sometimes called hammam or hamoene), the last a cotton cloth woven in Bengal and often used to make towels.

156. According to Kimball, Robert Perrigo, "Cordwainer" [cobbler], operated at the Sign of the Boot. Awls would of course be an appropriate purchase for Perrigo (320).

157. "Sabaoth" means literally "an army" or "host"; God is frequently referred to in various texts as the "Lord of Hosts," "Adonai Sabaoth."

158. This is the first mention of Curwen's friend Mr. H. in Transylvania, and it is remarkable that it occurs as early as 1754. One wonders how they came in contact with each other, for Transylvania was virtually unvisited by persons from western Europe. The earliest English-language account of Transylvania's history and peoples was William Wilkinson's *An Account of the Principalities of Wallachia and Moldavia* (1820), and the connection between Transylvania and matters supernatural did not appear in literature until a tale by Alexandre Dumas père was published in 1849. The Dumas story is called, variously, "La Dame Pâle" ("The Pale Lady")

and "Mounts Krapach" ("The Carpath-
ian Mountains") and was issued in his
collection *Les Mille et un Fantômes*.

159. Sir Henry Raeburn (1756–1823), a
renowned portraitist. Of course, Alexander painted *before* Raeburn.

160. Although Ward would have been a
member of the Class of 1920, Henry L. P.
Beckwith Jr., in *Lovecraft's Providence &
Adjacent Parts*, assures us that "school
records appear to be incomplete on this
point . . ." (70).

When upon reaching this point Dr. Willett turned the leaf
he was quickly checked by Ward, who almost snatched the
book from his grasp. All that the doctor had a chance to see on
the newly opened page was a brief pair of sentences; but these,
strangely enough, lingered tenaciously in his memory. They ran:
"Y^e Verse from Liber-Damnatus be'g spoke V Roodmasses and
IV Hallows-Eves, I am Hopeful ye Thing is breed'g Outside y^e
Spheres. It will drawe One who is to Come, if I can make sure he
shal bee, and he shal think on Past thinges and look back thro'
all ye yeares, against ye which I must have ready ye Saltes or That
to make 'em with."

Willett saw no more, but somehow this small glimpse gave a
new and vague terror to the painted features of Joseph Curwen
which stared blandly down from the overmantel. Ever after that
he entertained the odd fancy—which his medical skill of course
assured him was only a fancy—that the eyes of the portrait had
a sort of wish, if not an actual tendency, to follow young Charles
Ward as he moved about the room. He stopped before leaving to
study the picture closely, marvelling at its resemblance to Charles
and memorising every minute detail of the cryptical, colourless
face, even down to a slight scar or pit in the smooth brow above
the right eye. Cosmo Alexander, he decided, was a painter worthy
of the Scotland that produced Ræburn,[159] and a teacher worthy
of his illustrious pupil Gilbert Stuart.

Assured by the doctor that Charles's mental health was in no
danger, but that on the other hand he was engaged in researches
which might prove of real importance, the Wards were more
lenient than they might otherwise have been when during the
following June the youth made positive his refusal to attend college. He had, he declared, studies of much more vital importance
to pursue; and intimated a wish to go abroad the following year
in order to avail himself of certain sources of data not existing
in America. The senior Ward, while denying this latter wish as
absurd for a boy of only eighteen, acquiesced regarding the university; so that after a none too brilliant graduation from the Moses
Brown School[160] there ensued for Charles a three-year period of
intensive occult study and graveyard searching. He became recognised as an eccentric, and dropped even more completely from
the sight of his family's friends than he had been before; keeping

close to his work and only occasionally making trips to other cities to consult obscure records. Once he went south to talk with a strange old mulatto who dwelt in a swamp[161] and about whom a newspaper had printed a curious article. Again he sought a small village in the Adirondacks whence reports of certain odd ceremonial practices had come. But still his parents forbade him the trip to the Old World which he desired.

Coming of age in April, 1923, and having previously inherited a small competence from his maternal grandfather, Ward determined at last to take the European trip hitherto denied him. Of his proposed itinerary he would say nothing save that the needs of his studies would carry him to many places, but he promised to write his parents fully and faithfully. When they saw he could not be dissuaded, they ceased all opposition and helped as best they could; so that in June the young man sailed for Liverpool with the farewell blessings of his father and mother, who accompanied him to Boston and waved him out of sight from the White Star pier in Charlestown. Letters soon told of his safe arrival, and of his securing good quarters in Great Russell Street, London; where he proposed to stay, shunning all family friends, till he had exhausted the resources of the British Museum in a certain direction. Of his daily life he wrote but little, for there was little to write. Study and experiment consumed all his time, and he mentioned a laboratory which he had established in one of his rooms. That he said nothing of antiquarian rambles in the glamorous old city with its luring skyline of ancient domes and steeples and its tangles of roads and alleys whose mystic convolutions and sudden vistas alternately beckon and surprise, was taken by his parents as a good index of the degree to which his new interests had engrossed his mind.

In June, 1924, a brief note told of his departure for Paris, to which he had before made one or two flying trips for material in the Bibliothèque Nationale. For three months thereafter he sent only postal cards, giving an address in the Rue St. Jacques and referring to a special search among rare manuscripts in the library of an unnamed private collector. He avoided acquaintances, and no tourists brought back reports of having seen him. Then came a silence, and in October the Wards received a picture card from Prague, Czecho-Slovakia, stating that Charles was

161. Presumably one of those discovered by Inspector Legrasse, as recounted in "The Call of Cthulhu" (pp. 123–57, above).

162. Now Cluj-Napoca, commonly known as Cluj, the second-most-populous city in Romania today, roughly equidistant from Budapest and Bucharest.

163. This must mean Rákos, or Racu, a small village northeast of Klausenburg, in the Harghita Mountains (part of the Carpathians).

164. Ward's visit sounds uncannily like that of *Dracula*'s Jonathan Harker, an English solicitor who had a similar experience with a Transylvanian *voivode* in his castle near Bistrita, about seventy-five miles west of Racu. Like Harker's client, the baron lives in a secluded castle, is unpopular with the neighbors, and is elderly. Dracula sends his carriage to meet Harker, just as the Baron sends his to meet Ward. Bram Stoker's account of Harker's visit had been published in 1897.

165. Ward was of course gone only a little more than three years, from April 1923 to May 1926, but the point is made: He missed Providence.

in that ancient town for the purpose of conferring with a certain very aged man supposed to be the last living possessor of some very curious mediæval information. He gave an address in the Neustadt, and announced no move till the following January; when he dropped several cards from Vienna telling of his passage through that city on the way toward a more easterly region whither one of his correspondents and fellow-delvers into the occult had invited him.

The next card was from Klausenburg[162] in Transylvania, and told of Ward's progress toward his destination. He was going to visit a Baron Ferenczy, whose estate lay in the mountains east of Rakus;[163] and was to be addressed at Rakus in the care of that nobleman. Another card from Rakus a week later, saying that his host's carriage had met him and that he was leaving the village for the mountains, was his last message for a considerable time; indeed, he did not reply to his parents' frequent letters until May, when he wrote to discourage the plan of his mother for a meeting in London, Paris, or Rome during the summer, when the elder Wards were planning to travel in Europe. His researches, he said, were such that he could not leave his present quarters; while the situation of Baron Ferenczy's castle did not favour visits. It was on a crag in the dark wooded mountains, and the region was so shunned by the country folk that normal people could not help feeling ill at ease. Moreover, the Baron was not a person likely to appeal to correct and conservative New England gentlefolk. His aspect and manners had idiosyncrasies, and his age was so great as to be disquieting.[164] It would be better, Charles said, if his parents would wait for his return to Providence; which could scarcely be far distant.

That return did not, however, take place until May 1926, when after a few heralding cards the young wanderer quietly slipped into New York on the *Homeric* and traversed the long miles to Providence by motor-coach, eagerly drinking in the green rolling hills, the fragrant, blossoming orchards, and the white steepled towns of vernal Connecticut; his first taste of ancient New England in nearly four years.[165] When the coach crossed the Pawcatuck and entered Rhode Island amidst the færy goldenness of a late spring afternoon his heart beat with quickened force, and the entry to Providence along Reservoir and Elmwood avenues was a breathless and wonderful thing despite the depths of forbidden lore to which he had delved. At the high square where Broad, Weybosset, and Empire Streets join, he saw before and below him in the fire of sunset the pleasant, remembered houses and domes and steeples of the old town; and his head swam curiously as the vehicle rolled down to the terminal behind the Biltmore,[166] bringing into view the great dome and soft, roof-pierced greenery of the ancient hill across the river, and the tall colonial spire of the First Baptist Church limned pink in the magic evening light against the fresh springtime verdure of its precipitous background.

Old Providence! It was this place and the mysterious forces of its long, continuous history which had brought him into being, and which had drawn him back toward marvels and secrets whose boundaries no prophet might fix. Here lay the arcana, wondrous or dreadful as the case might be, for which all his years of travel and application had been preparing him. A taxicab whirled him through Post Office Square with its glimpse of the river, the old Market House, and the head of the bay, and up the steep curved slope of Waterman Street to Prospect, where the vast gleaming dome and sunset-flushed Ionic columns of the Christian Science Church beckoned northward. Then eight squares past the fine old estates his childish eyes had known, and the quaint brick sidewalks so often trodden by his youthful feet. And at last the little white overtaken farmhouse on the right, on the left the classic Adam porch and stately bayed facade of the great brick house where he was born. It was twilight, and Charles Dexter Ward had come home.

5.

A school of alienists slightly less academic than Dr. Lyman's assign to Ward's European trip the beginning of his true madness. Admitting that he was sane when he started, they believe that his conduct upon returning implies a disastrous change. But even to this claim Dr. Willett refuses to accede. There was, he insists, something later; and the queernesses of the youth at this stage he attributes to the practice of rituals learned abroad—odd enough things, to be sure, but by no means implying mental aber-

166. The Biltmore Hotel stands at 11 Dorrance Street in Providence and opened in 1922; it was closed in 1974 for five years' worth of renovation and continues in operation today.

The Providence Biltmore Hotel, in 1990.
Photograph courtesy of Will Hart

167. Undoubtedly short for "Nigger," revelatory of the attitudes of the household and Lovecraft himself.

ration on the part of their celebrant. Ward himself, though visibly aged and hardened, was still normal in his general reactions; and in several talks with Willett displayed a balance which no madman—even an incipient one—could feign continuously for long. What elicited the notion of insanity at this period were the *sounds* heard at all hours from Ward's attic laboratory, in which he kept himself most of the time. There were chantings and repetitions, and thunderous declamations in uncanny rhythms; and although these sounds were always in Ward's own voice, there was something in the quality of that voice, and in the accents of the formulæ it pronounced, which could not but chill the blood of every hearer. It was noticed that Nig,[167] the venerable and beloved black cat of the household, bristled and arched his back perceptibly when certain of the tones were heard.

The odours occasionally wafted from the laboratory were likewise exceedingly strange. Sometimes they were very noxious, but more often they were aromatic, with a haunting, elusive quality which seemed to have the power of inducing fantastic images. People who smelled them had a tendency to glimpse momentary mirages of enormous vistas, with strange hills or endless avenues of sphinxes and hippogriffs stretching off into infinite distance. Ward did not resume his old-time rambles, but applied himself diligently to the strange books he had brought home, and to equally strange delvings within his quarters; explaining that European sources had greatly enlarged the possibilities of his work, and promising great revelations in the years to come. His older aspect increased to a startling degree his resemblance to the Curwen portrait in his library; and Dr. Willett would often pause by the latter after a call, marvelling at the virtual identity, and reflecting that only the small pit above the picture's right eye now remained to differentiate the long-dead wizard from the living youth. These calls of Willett's, undertaken at the request of the senior Wards, were curious affairs. Ward at no time repulsed the doctor, but the latter saw that he could never reach the young man's inner psychology. Frequently he noted peculiar things about; little wax images of grotesque design on the shelves or tables, and the half-erased remnants of circles, triangles, and pentagrams in chalk or charcoal on the cleared central space of the large room. And always in the night those rhythms and incantations thundered, till it became very difficult to keep servants or suppress furtive talk of Charles's madness.

In January, 1927, a peculiar incident occurred. One night about midnight, as Charles was chanting a ritual whose weird cadence echoed unpleasantly through the house below, there came a sudden gust of chill wind from the bay, and a faint, obscure trembling of the earth which everyone in the neighbourhood noted. At the same time the cat exhibited phenomenal traces of fright, while dogs bayed for as much as a mile around. This was the prelude to a sharp thunderstorm, anomalous for the season, which brought with it such a crash that Mr. and Mrs. Ward believed the house had been struck. They rushed upstairs to see what damage had been done, but Charles met them at the door to the attic; pale, resolute, and portentous, with an almost fearsome combination of triumph and seriousness on his face. He assured them that the house had not really been struck, and that the storm would soon be over. They paused, and looking through a window saw that he was indeed right; for the lightning flashed farther and farther off, whilst the trees ceased to bend in the strange frigid gust from the water. The thunder sank to a sort of dull mumbling chuckle and finally died away. Stars came out, and the stamp of triumph on Charles Ward's face crystallised into a very singular expression.

For two months or more after this incident Ward was less confined than usual to his laboratory. He exhibited a curious interest in the weather, and made odd inquiries about the date of the spring thawing of the ground. One night late in March he left the house after midnight, and did not return till almost morning; when his mother, being wakeful, heard a rumbling motor draw up to the carriage entrance. Muffled oaths could be distinguished, and Mrs. Ward, rising and going to the window, saw four dark figures removing a long, heavy box from a truck at Charles's direction and carrying it within by the side door. She heard laboured breathing and ponderous footfalls on the stairs, and finally a dull thumping in the attic; after which the footfalls descended again, and the four men reappeared outside and drove off in their truck.

The next day Charles resumed his strict attic seclusion, drawing down the dark shades of his laboratory windows and appearing to be working on some metal substance. He would open

168. The *Providence Journal*, that is, the leading newspaper of Providence, first published in 1820 as a semiweekly called the *Manufacturers' and Farmers' Journal, Providence and Pawtucket Advertiser*. It became a daily in 1829 as the *Daily Journal*; in 1920 the "Daily" was dropped from the name. The *Journal* is the oldest continuously published daily in America.

The offices of the *Providence Journal* in 2010. Photograph copyright © Donovan K. Loucks 2010, reprinted with permission

the door to no one, and steadfastly refused all proffered food. About noon a wrenching sound followed by a terrible cry and a fall were heard, but when Mrs. Ward rapped at the door her son at length answered faintly, and told her that nothing had gone amiss. The hideous and indescribable stench now welling out was absolutely harmless and unfortunately necessary. Solitude was the one prime essential, and he would appear later for dinner. That afternoon, after the conclusion of some odd hissing sounds which came from behind the locked portal, he did finally appear; wearing an extremely haggard aspect and forbidding anyone to enter the laboratory upon any pretext. This, indeed, proved the beginning of a new policy of secrecy; for never afterward was any other person permitted to visit either the mysterious garret workroom or the adjacent storeroom which he cleaned out, furnished roughly, and added to his inviolably private domain as a sleeping apartment. Here he lived, with books brought up from his library beneath, till the time he purchased the Pawtuxet bungalow and moved to it all his scientific effects.

In the evening Charles secured the paper before the rest of the family and damaged part of it through an apparent accident. Later on Dr. Willett, having fixed the date from statements by various members of the household, looked up an intact copy at the *Journal*[168] office and found that in the destroyed section the following small item had occurred:

NOCTURNAL DIGGERS SURPRISED IN NORTH BURIAL GROUND

Robert Hart, night watchman at the North Burial Ground, this morning discovered a party of several men with a motor truck in the oldest part of the cemetery, but apparently frightened them off before they had accomplished whatever their object may have been.

The discovery took place at about four o'clock, when Hart's attention was attracted by the sound of a motor outside his shelter. Investigating, he saw a large truck on the main drive several rods away; but could not reach it before the sound of his feet on the gravel had revealed his approach. The men hastily placed a large box in the truck and drove away toward the street before they could be overtaken; and since no known grave was disturbed, Hart believes that this box was an object which they wished to bury.

The diggers must have been at work for a long while before detection, for Hart found an enormous hole dug at a considerable distance back from the roadway in the lot of Amasa Field, where most of the old stones have long ago disappeared. The hole, a place as large and deep as a grave, was empty; and did not coincide with any interment mentioned in the cemetery records.

Sergt. Riley of the Second Station viewed the spot and gave the opinion that the hole was dug by bootleggers rather gruesomely and ingeniously seeking a safe cache for liquor in a place not likely to be disturbed. In reply to questions Hart said he thought the escaping truck had headed up Rochambeau Avenue, though he could not be sure.

During the next few days Ward was seldom seen by his family. Having added sleeping quarters to his attic realm, he kept closely to himself there, ordering food brought to the door and not taking it in until after the servant had gone away. The droning of monotonous formulæ and the chanting of bizarre rhythms recurred at intervals, while at other times occasional listeners could detect the sound of tinkling glass, hissing chemicals, running water, or roaring gas flames. Odours of the most unplaceable quality, wholly unlike any before noted, hung at times around the door; and the air of tension observable in the young recluse whenever he did venture briefly forth was such as to excite the keenest speculation. Once he made a hasty trip to the Athenæum for a book he required, and again he hired a messenger to fetch him a highly obscure volume from Boston. Suspense was written portentously over the whole situation, and both the family and Dr. Willett confessed themselves wholly at a loss what to do or think about it.

6.

Then on the fifteenth of April a strange development occurred. While nothing appeared to grow different in kind, there was certainly a very terrible difference in degree; and Dr. Willett somehow attaches great significance to the change. The day was Good Friday, a circumstance of which the servants made much, but which others quite naturally dismiss as an irrelevant coincidence. Late in the afternoon young Ward began repeating a certain formula in a singularly loud voice, at the same time burning some substance so pungent that its fumes escaped over the entire house. The formula was so plainly audible in the hall outside the locked door that Mrs. Ward could not help memorising it as she waited and listened anxiously, and later on she was able to write it down at Dr. Willett's request. It ran as follows, and experts have told Dr. Willett that its very close analogue can be found in the mystic writings of "Eliphas Levi," that cryptic soul who crept through a crack in the forbidden door and glimpsed the frightful vistas of the void beyond:

> *Per Adonai Eloim, Adonai Jehova,*
> *Adonai Sabaoth, Metraton On Agla Mathon,*
> *verbum pythonicum, mysterium salamandræ,*
> *conventus sylvorum, antra gnomorum,*
> *dæmonia Coeli Gad, Almousin, Gibor, Jehosua,*
> *Evam, Zariatnatmik, veni, veni, veni.*[169]

This had been going on for two hours without change or intermission when over all the neighbourhood a pandæmoniac howling of dogs set in. The extent of this howling can be judged from the space it received in the papers the next day, but to those in the Ward household it was overshadowed by the odour which instantly followed it; a hideous, all-pervasive odour which none of them had ever smelt before or have ever smelt since. In the midst of this mephitic flood there came a very perceptible flash like that of lightning, which would have been blinding and impressive but for the daylight around; and then was heard *the voice* that no listener can ever forget because of its thunderous remoteness, its incredible depth, and its eldritch dissimilarity to Charles Ward's voice. It shook the house, and was clearly heard by at least two neighbours above the howling of the dogs. Mrs. Ward, who had been listening in despair outside her son's locked laboratory, shivered as she recognised its hellish import; for Charles had told her of its evil fame in dark books, and of the manner in which it had thundered, according to the Fenner letters, above the doomed Pawtuxet farmhouse on the night of Joseph Curwen's annihilation. There was no mistaking that nightmare phrase, for Charles had described it too vividly in the old days when he had talked frankly of his Curwen investigations. And yet it was only this fragment of an archaic and forgotten language: "DIES MIES JESCHET BOENE DOESEF DOUVEMA ENITEMAUS."

Close upon this thundering there came a momentary darkening of the daylight, though sunset was still an hour distant, and then a puff of added odour different from the first but equally unknown and intolerable. Charles was chanting again now and his mother could hear syllables that sounded like "Yi-nash-Yog-Sothoth-he-lgeb-fi-throdog"—ending in a "Yah!" whose maniacal force mounted in an ear-splitting crescendo. A second later all previous memories were effaced by the wailing scream which burst out with frantic explosiveness and gradually changed form to a paroxysm of diabolic and hysterical laughter. Mrs. Ward, with the mingled fear and blind courage of maternity, advanced and knocked affrightedly at the concealing panels, but obtained no sign of recognition. She knocked again, but paused nervelessly as a second shriek arose, this one unmistakably in the familiar voice of her son, *and sounding concurrently with the still bursting cachinnations of that other voice.* Presently she fainted, although she is still unable to recall the precise and immediate cause. Memory sometimes makes merciful deletions.

Mr. Ward returned from the business section at about quarter past six; and not finding his wife downstairs, was told by the frightened servants that she was probably watching at Charles's door, from which the sounds had been far stranger than ever before. Mounting the stairs at once, he saw Mrs. Ward stretched at full length on the floor of the corridor outside the laboratory; and realising that she had fainted, hastened to fetch a glass of water from a set bowl in a neighbouring alcove. Dashing the cold fluid in her face, he was heartened to observe an immediate response on her part, and was watching the bewildered opening of her eyes when a chill shot through him and threatened to reduce him to the very state from which she was emerging. For the seemingly silent laboratory was not as silent as it had appeared to be, but held the murmurs of a tense, muffled conversation in tones too low for comprehension, yet of a quality profoundly disturbing to the soul.

It was not, of course, new for Charles to mutter formulæ; but this muttering was definitely different. It was so palpably a dialogue, or imitation of a dialogue, with the regular alteration of inflections suggesting question and answer, statement and response. One voice was undisguisedly that of Charles, but the other had a depth and hollowness which the youth's best powers of ceremonial mimicry had scarcely approached before. There was something hideous, blasphemous, and abnormal about it, and but for a cry from his recovering wife which cleared his mind by arousing his protective instincts it is not likely that Theodore Howland Ward could have maintained for nearly a year more his old boast that he had never fainted. As it was, he seized his wife in his arms and bore her quickly downstairs before she could notice the voices which had so horribly disturbed him. Even so, however, he was not quick enough to escape catching something himself which caused him to stagger dangerously with his burden. For Mrs. Ward's cry had evidently been heard by others than he, and there had come from behind the locked door the first distinguishable words which that masked and terrible colloquy had yielded. They were merely an excited caution in Charles's own voice, but somehow their implications held a nameless fright for the father who overheard them. The phrase was just this: "*Sshh!—write!*"

Mr. and Mrs. Ward conferred at some length after dinner, and the former resolved to have a firm and serious talk with Charles that very night. No matter how important the object, such conduct could no longer be permitted; for these latest developments transcended every limit of sanity and formed a menace to the order and nervous well-being of the entire household. The youth must indeed have taken complete leave of his senses, since only downright madness could have prompted the wild screams and imaginary conversations in assumed voices which the present day had brought forth. All this must be stopped, or Mrs. Ward would be made ill and the keeping of servants become an impossibility.

Mr. Ward rose at the close of the meal and started upstairs for Charles's laboratory. On the third floor, however, he paused at the sounds which he heard proceeding from the now disused library of his son. Books were apparently being flung about and papers wildly rustled, and upon stepping to the door Mr. Ward beheld the youth within, excitedly assembling a vast armful of literary matter of every size and shape. Charles's aspect was very drawn and haggard, and he dropped his entire load with a start at the sound of his father's voice. At the elder man's command he sat down, and for some time listened to the admonitions he had so long deserved. There was no scene. At the end of the lecture he agreed that his father was right, and that his noises, mutterings, incantations, and chemical odours were indeed inexcusable nuisances. He agreed to a policy of greater quiet, though insisting on a prolongation of his extreme privacy. Much of his future work, he said, was in any case purely book research; and he could obtain quarters elsewhere for any such vocal rituals as might be necessary at a later stage. For the fright and fainting of his mother he expressed the keenest contrition, and explained that the conversation later heard was part of an elaborate symbolism designed to create a certain mental atmosphere. His use of abstruse technical terms somewhat bewildered Mr. Ward, but the parting impression was one of undeniable sanity and poise despite a mysterious tension of the utmost gravity. The interview was really quite inconclusive, and as Charles picked up his armful and left the room Mr. Ward hardly knew what to make of the entire business. It was as mysterious as the death of poor old Nig, whose stiffening form had been found an hour before in the basement, with staring eyes and fear-distorted mouth.

Driven by some vague detective instinct, the bewildered parent now glanced curiously at the vacant shelves to see what his son had taken up to the attic. The youth's library was plainly and rigidly classified, so that one might tell at a glance the books or at least the kind of books which had been withdrawn. On this occasion Mr. Ward was astonished to find that nothing of the occult or the antiquarian, beyond what had been previously removed, was missing. These new withdrawals were all modern items; histories, scientific treatises, geographies, manuals of literature, philosophic works, and certain contemporary newspapers and magazines. It was a very curious shift from Charles Ward's recent run of reading, and the father paused in a growing vortex of perplexity and an engulfing sense of strangeness. The

170. This concluded the first part of two in the *Weird Tales* publication and was followed by this teaser: "What Happens 'To Him Who Shall Come After . . . ?' What is the outcome of Charles Ward's frantic delving into the life and secrets of his terrible ancestor? Read in the next issue of the horrors beyond Hell which a young man brings upon himself by his curiosity—the ghastly, incredible events that come to pass in the second and final installment of Lovecraft's enthralling novel."

171. The balance of the story appeared as the "second part of two" in its *Weird Tales* publication, where it was preceded by the following summary:

> Quite recently there disappeared—from a private mental hospital near Providence, Rhode Island—a certain rather unusual young man. His name is (or perhaps, more correctly, was) Charles Dexter Ward. Only twenty-six years of age, the patient seemed strangely older, and displayed a number of physical characteristics which left medical science completely baffled.
>
> Charles Ward's madness was of a most unusual type. An antiquarian since infancy, his knowledge of the 18th century had become simply stupendous, and of a kind possible only to someone who had in actual fact *lived* in those times; which was, of course, impossible, for Charles was born in 1902.
>
> This unwholesome insight into the 18th century he took great pains to conceal, and seemed to have wholly lost his taste for antiquarian delving. Instead he showed an avid interest in ordinary 20th century matters, absorbing greedily all the contemporary knowledge upon which he could lay his hands.

strangeness was a very poignant sensation, and almost clawed at his chest as he strove to see just what was wrong around him. Something was indeed wrong, and tangibly as well as spiritually so. Ever since he had been in this room he had known that something was amiss, and at last it dawned upon him what it was.

On the north wall rose still the ancient carved overmantel from the house in Olney Court, but to the cracked and precariously restored oils of the large Curwen portrait disaster had come. Time and unequal heating had done their work at last, and at some time since the room's last cleaning the worst had happened. Peeling clear of the wood, curling tighter and tighter, and finally crumbling into small bits with what must have been malignly silent suddenness, the portrait of Joseph Curwen had resigned forever its staring surveillance of the youth it so strangely resembled, and now lay scattered on the floor as a thin coating of fine bluish-grey dust.[170]

IV. A MUTATION AND A MADNESS[171]

1.

IN THE WEEK following that memorable Good Friday Charles Ward was seen more often than usual, and was continually carrying books between his library and the attic laboratory. His actions were quiet and rational, but he had a furtive, hunted look which his mother did not like, and developed an incredibly ravenous appetite as gauged by his demands upon the cook. Dr. Willett had been told of those Friday noises and happenings, and on the following Tuesday had a long conversation with the youth in the library where the picture stared no more. The interview was, as always, inconclusive; but Willett is still ready to swear that the youth was sane and himself at the time. He held out promises of an early revelation, and spoke of the need of securing a laboratory elsewhere. At the loss of the portrait he grieved singularly little considering his first enthusiasm over it, but seemed to find something of positive humour in its sudden crumbling.

About the second week Charles began to be absent from the house for long periods, and one day when good old black Hannah came to help with the spring cleaning she mentioned his frequent visits to the old house in Olney Court, where he would come with a large valise and perform curious delvings in the cellar. He was always very liberal to her and to old Asa, but seemed more worried than he used to be; which grieved her very much, since she had watched him grow up from birth. Another report of his doings came from Pawtuxet, where some friends of the family saw him at a distance a surprising number of times. He seemed to haunt the resort and canoe-house of Rhodes-on-the-Pawtuxet, and subsequent inquiries by Dr. Willett at that place brought out the fact that his purpose was always to secure access to the rather hedged-in river-bank, along which he would walk toward the north, usually not reappearing for a very long while.

Late in May came a momentary revival of ritualistic sounds in the attic laboratory which brought a stern reproof from Mr. Ward and a somewhat distracted promise of amendment from Charles. It occurred one morning, and seemed to form a resumption of the imaginary conversation noted on that turbulent Good Friday. The youth was arguing or remonstrating hotly with himself, for there suddenly burst forth a perfectly distinguishable series of clashing shouts in differentiated tones like alternate demands and denials which caused Mrs. Ward to run upstairs and listen at the door. She could hear no more than a fragment whose only plain words were "must have it red for three months," and upon her knocking all sounds ceased at once. When Charles was later questioned by his father he said that there were certain conflicts of spheres of consciousness which only great skill could avoid, but which he would try to transfer to other realms.

About the middle of June a queer nocturnal incident occurred. In the early evening there had been some noise and thumping in the laboratory upstairs, and Mr. Ward was on the point of investigating when it suddenly quieted down. That midnight, after the family had retired, the butler was nightlocking the front door when according to his statement Charles appeared somewhat blunderingly and uncertainly at the foot of the stairs with a large suitcase and made signs that he wished egress. The youth spoke no word, but the worthy Yorkshireman caught one sight of his fevered eyes and trembled causelessly. He opened the door and young Ward went out, but in the morning he presented his resignation to Mrs. Ward. There was, he said, something unholy in

His escape from Dr. Waite's hospital was itself practically a miracle—certainly an almost insoluble mystery. Charles disappeared immediately after a conversation with his family doctor; and he has never been seen since. His window opened onto a sheer drop of sixty feet—an ascent which the most accomplished cat burglar would give up as a bad job, and which even a fly would hesitate to climb. And yet the window was the only possible exit. Those who came to look for him found a cloud of fine bluish-gray dust—and nothing more.

Charles' troubles began when he discovered through old documents and letters that a certain unsavory gentleman of the 18th century (and if the truth be told, also of the 17th)—one Joseph Curwen—was his ancestor. Curwen's neighbors whispered that he would never die, and at an age which must have been well over a hundred, he married an eighteen year old girl. To this blasphemous alliance Charles owed his descent.

In the vast grim catacombs that lay deep beneath his lonely farmhouse on the moors beyond Providence, Curwen conducted unspeakably horrible experiments and rites of nameless and inconceivable obscenity, fast becoming a scandal and a terror to the entire district. A few influential men kept him under observation, and planned to rid the world of the unutterably frightful old man. One night they raided his farmhouse. The venture was apparently successful, for Curwen disappeared.

So, for a time at least, the earth was free of Joseph Curwen. But had the raiders only driven him into another world, and would men be able to keep him there? What is the next thing to happen after the portrait of the horrible old man is found scattered on the floor—in a thin coating of "fine bluish-gray dust"? The answers are waiting for you in this final instalment.

the glance Charles had fixed on him. It was no way for a young gentleman to look at an honest person, and he could not possibly stay another night. Mrs. Ward allowed the man to depart, but she did not value his statement highly. To fancy Charles in a savage state that night was quite ridiculous, for as long as she had remained awake she had heard faint sounds from the laboratory above; sounds as if of sobbing and pacing, and of a sighing which told only of despair's profoundest depths. Mrs. Ward had grown used to listening for sounds in the night, for the mystery of her son was fast driving all else from her mind.

The next evening, much as on another evening nearly three months before, Charles Ward seized the newspaper very early and accidentally lost the main section. The matter was not recalled till later, when Dr. Willett began checking up loose ends and searching out missing links here and there. In the *Journal* office he found the section which Charles had lost, and marked two items as of possible significance. They were as follows:

MORE CEMETERY DELVING

It was this morning discovered by Robert Hart, night watchman at the North Burial Ground, that ghouls were again at work in the ancient portion of the cemetery. The grave of Ezra Weeden, who was born in 1740 and died in 1824 according to his uprooted and savagely splintered slate headstone, was found excavated and rifled, the work being evidently done with a spade stolen from an adjacent tool-shed.

Whatever the contents may have been after more than a century of burial, all was gone except a few slivers of decayed wood. There were no wheel tracks, but the police have measured a single set of footprints which they found in the vicinity, and which indicate the boots of a man of refinement.

Hart is inclined to link this incident with the digging discovered last March, when a party in a motor truck were frightened away after making a deep excavation; but Sergt. Riley of the Second Station discounts this theory and points to vital differences in the two cases. In March the digging had been in a spot where no grave was known; but this time a well-marked and cared-for grave had been rifled with every evidence of deliberate purpose, and with a conscious malignity expressed in the splintering of the slab which had been intact up to the day before.

Members of the Weeden family, notified of the happening, expressed their astonishment and regret; and were wholly unable to think of any enemy who would care to violate the grave of their ancestor. Hazard Weeden of 598 Angell Street[172] recalls a family legend according to which Ezra Weeden was involved in some very peculiar circumstances, not dishonourable to himself, shortly before the Revolution; but of any modern feud or mystery he is frankly ignorant. Inspector Cunningham has been assigned to the case, and hopes to uncover some valuable clues in the near future.

DOGS NOISY IN PAWTUXET

Residents of Pawtuxet were aroused about 3 a.m. today by a phenomenal baying of dogs which seemed to centre near the river just north of Rhodes-on-the-Pawtuxet. The volume and quality of the howling were unusually odd, according to most who heard it; and Fred Lemdin, night watchman at Rhodes, declares it was mixed with something very like the shrieks of a man in mortal terror and agony. A sharp and very brief thunderstorm, which seemed to strike somewhere near the bank of the river, put an end to the disturbance. Strange and unpleasant odours, probably from the oil tanks along the bay, are popularly linked with this incident; and may have had their share in exciting the dogs.

The aspect of Charles now became very haggard and hunted, and all agreed in retrospect that he may have wished at this period to make some statement or confession from which sheer terror withheld him. The morbid listening of his mother in the night brought out the fact that he made frequent sallies abroad under cover of darkness, and most of the more academic alienists unite at present in charging him with the revolting cases of vampirism which the press so sensationally reported about this time, but which have not yet been definitely traced to any known per-

172. Coincidentally, the very residence of Howard Phillips Lovecraft prior to his departure for New York in 1924.

"These cases of Vampirism involved victims of every age and type."
Weird Tales 35, no. 9 (May 1941) (artist: Harry Furman)

petrator. These cases, too recent and celebrated to need detailed mention, involved victims of every age and type and seemed to cluster around two distinct localities; the residential hill and the North End, near the Ward home, and the suburban districts across the Cranston line near Pawtuxet. Both late wayfarers and sleepers with open windows were attacked, and those who lived to tell the tale spoke unanimously of a lean, lithe, leaping monster with burning eyes which fastened its teeth in the throat or upper arm and feasted ravenously.

Dr. Willett, who refuses to date the madness of Charles Ward as far back as even this, is cautious in attempting to explain these horrors. He has, he declares, certain theories of his own; and limits his positive statements to a peculiar kind of negation. "I will not," he says, "state who or what I believe perpetrated these attacks and murders, but I will declare that Charles Ward was innocent of them. I have reason to be sure he was ignorant of the taste of blood, as indeed his continued anæmic decline and increasing pallor prove better than any verbal argument. Ward meddled with terrible things, but he has paid for it, and he was never a monster or a villain. As for now—I don't like to think. A change came, and I'm content to believe that the old Charles Ward died with it. His soul did, anyhow, for that mad flesh that vanished from Waite's hospital had another."

Willett speaks with authority, for he was often at the Ward home attending Mrs. Ward, whose nerves had begun to snap under the strain. Her nocturnal listening had bred some morbid hallucinations which she confided to the doctor with hesitancy, and which he ridiculed in talking to her, although they made him ponder deeply when alone. These delusions always concerned the faint sounds which she fancied she heard in the attic laboratory and bedroom, and emphasised the occurrence of muffled sighs and sobbings at the most impossible times. Early in July Willett ordered Mrs. Ward to Atlantic City for an indefinite recuperative sojourn, and cautioned both Mr. Ward and the haggard and elusive Charles to write her only cheering letters. It is probably to this enforced and reluctant escape that she owes her life and continued sanity.

2.

Not long after his mother's departure Charles Ward began negotiating for the Pawtuxet bungalow. It was a squalid little wooden edifice with a concrete garage, perched high on the sparsely settled bank of the river slightly above Rhodes, but for some odd reason the youth would have nothing else. He gave the real-estate agencies no peace till one of them secured it for him at an exorbitant price from a somewhat reluctant owner, and as soon as it was vacant he took possession under cover of darkness, transporting in a great closed van the entire contents of his attic laboratory, including the books both weird and modern which he had borrowed from his study. He had this van loaded in the black small hours, and his father recalls only a drowsy realisation of stifled oaths and stamping feet on the night the goods were taken away. After that Charles moved back to his own old quarters on the third floor, and never haunted the attic again.

To the Pawtuxet bungalow Charles transferred all the secrecy with which he had surrounded his attic realm, save that he now appeared to have two sharers of his mysteries; a villainous-looking Portuguese half-caste from the South Main St. waterfront who acted as a servant, and a thin, scholarly stranger with dark glasses and a stubbly full beard of dyed aspect whose status was evidently that of a colleague. Neighbours vainly tried to engage these odd persons in conversation. The mulatto Gomes spoke very little English, and the bearded man, who gave his name as Dr. Allen, voluntarily followed his example. Ward himself tried to be more affable, but succeeded only in provoking curiosity with his rambling accounts of chemical research. Before long queer tales began to circulate regarding the all-night burning of lights; and somewhat later, after this burning had suddenly ceased, there rose still queerer tales of disproportionate orders of meat from the butcher's and of the muffled shouting, declamation, rhythmic chanting, and screaming supposed to come from some very deep cellar below the place. Most distinctly the new and strange household was bitterly disliked by the honest bourgeoisie of the vicinity, and it is not remarkable that dark hints were advanced connecting the hated establishment with the current epidemic of vampiristic attacks and murders; especially since the radius of that plague seemed now confined wholly to Pawtuxet and the adjacent streets of Edgewood.

Ward spent most of his time at the bungalow, but slept occasionally at home and was still reckoned a dweller beneath his father's roof. Twice he was absent from the city on week-long trips, whose destinations have not yet been discovered. He grew steadily paler and more emaciated even than before, and lacked some of his former assurance when repeating to Dr. Willett his old, old story of vital research and future revelations. Willett often waylaid him at his father's house, for the elder Ward was deeply worried and perplexed, and wished his son to get as much sound oversight as could be managed in the case of so secretive and independent an adult. The doctor still insists that the youth was sane even as late as this, and adduces many a conversation to prove his point.

About September the vampirism declined, but in the following January Ward almost became involved in serious trouble. For some time the nocturnal arrival and departure of motor trucks at the Pawtuxet bungalow had been commented upon, and at this juncture an unforeseen hitch exposed the nature of at least one item of their contents. In a lonely spot near Hope Valley had occurred one of the frequent sordid waylayings of trucks by "hijackers"[173] in quest of liquor shipments,[174] but this time the robbers had been destined to receive the greater shock. For the long cases they seized proved upon opening to contain some exceedingly gruesome things; so gruesome, in fact, that the matter could not be kept quiet amongst the denizens of the underworld. The thieves had hastily buried what they discovered, but when the State Police got wind of the matter a careful search was made. A recently arrested vagrant, under promise of immunity from prosecution on any additional charge, at last consented to guide a party of troopers to the spot; and there was found in that hasty cache a very hideous and shameful thing. It would not be well for the national—or even the international—sense of decorum if the public were ever to know what was uncovered by that awestruck party. There was no mistaking it, even by these far from studious officers; and telegrams to Washington ensued with feverish rapidity.

The cases were addressed to Charles Ward at his Pawtuxet bungalow, and State and Federal officials at once paid him a very forceful and serious call. They found him pallid and worried with his two odd companions, and received from him what seemed to be a valid explanation and evidence of innocence. He had needed certain anatomical specimens as part of a programme of research whose depth and genuineness anyone who had known him in the last decade could prove, and had ordered the required kind and number from agencies which he had thought as rea-

173. A new word in 1924, referring specifically to seizing illicit liquor for profit.

174. A not infrequent occurrence during the era of Prohibition, 1920–1933, when the United States, in the so-called noble experiment, banned the sale, manufacture, and transportation of alcohol. See "The Shadow over Innsmouth," note 3, below.

175. A popular psychiatric diagnosis at the time, also termed "delusional insanity" or "adolescent insanity"; the diagnosis is today essentially supplanted by differing forms of schizophrenia.

sonably legitimate as such things can be. Of the *identity* of the specimens he had known absolutely nothing, and was properly shocked when the inspectors hinted at the monstrous effect on public sentiment and national dignity which a knowledge of the matter would produce. In this statement he was firmly sustained by his bearded colleague Dr. Allen, whose oddly hollow voice carried even more conviction than his own nervous tones; so that in the end the officials took no action, but carefully set down the New York name and address which Ward gave them as a basis for a search which came to nothing. It is only fair to add that the specimens were quickly and quietly restored to their proper places, and that the general public will never know of their blasphemous disturbance.

On February 9, 1928, Dr. Willett received a letter from Charles Ward which he considers of extraordinary importance, and about which he has frequently quarrelled with Dr. Lyman. Lyman believes that this note contains positive proof of a well-developed case of *dementia præcox*,[175] but Willett on the other hand regards it as the last perfectly sane utterance of the hapless youth. He calls especial attention to the normal character of the penmanship; which though shewing traces of shattered nerves, is nevertheless distinctly Ward's own. The text in full is as follows:

100 Prospect St.
Providence, R.I.,
February 8, 1928.

Dear Dr. Willett:—

I feel that at last the time has come for me to make the disclosures which I have so long promised you, and for which you have pressed me so often. The patience you have shewn in waiting, and the confidence you have shewn in my mind and integrity, are things I shall never cease to appreciate.

And now that I am ready to speak, I must own with humiliation that no triumph such as I dreamed of can ever be mine. Instead of triumph I have found terror, and my talk with you will not be a boast of victory but a plea for help and advice in saving both myself and the world from a horror beyond all human conception or cal-

culation. You recall what those Fenner letters said of the old raiding party at Pawtuxet. That must all be done again, and quickly. Upon us depends more than can be put into words—all civilisation, all natural law, perhaps even the fate of the solar system and the universe. I have brought to light a monstrous abnormality, but I did it for the sake of knowledge. Now for the sake of all life and Nature you must help me thrust it back into the dark again.

I have left that Pawtuxet place forever, and we must extirpate everything existing there, alive or dead. I shall not go there again, and you must not believe it if you ever hear that I am there. I will tell you why I say this when I see you. I have come home for good, and wish you would call on me at the very first moment that you can spare five or six hours continuously to hear what I have to say. It will take that long—and believe me when I tell you that you never had a more genuine professional duty than this. My life and reason are the very least things which hang in the balance.

I dare not tell my father, for he could not grasp the whole thing. But I have told him of my danger, and he has four men from a detective agency watching the house. I don't know how much good they can do, for they have against them forces which even you could scarcely envisage or acknowledge. So come quickly if you wish to see me alive and hear how you may help to save the cosmos from stark hell.

Any time will do—I shall not be out of the house. Don't telephone ahead, for there is no telling who or what may try to intercept you. And let us pray to whatever gods there be that nothing may prevent this meeting.

In utmost gravity and desperation,
Charles Dexter Ward.

P.S. Shoot Dr. Allen on sight and dissolve his body in acid. *Don't burn it.*

Dr. Willett received this note about 10:30 A.M., and immediately arranged to spare the whole late afternoon and evening for the momentous talk, letting it extend on into the night as long as might be necessary. He planned to arrive about four o'clock, and through all the intervening hours was so engulfed in every sort of wild speculation that most of his tasks were very mechanically performed. Maniacal as the letter would have sounded to a stranger, Willett had seen too much of Charles Ward's oddities to dismiss it as sheer raving. That something very subtle, ancient, and horrible was hovering about he felt quite sure, and the reference to Dr. Allen could almost be comprehended in view of what Pawtuxet gossip said of Ward's enigmatical colleague. Willett had never seen the man, but had heard much of his aspect and bearing, and could not but wonder what sort of eyes those much-discussed dark glasses might conceal.

Promptly at four Dr. Willett presented himself at the Ward residence, but found to his annoyance that Charles had not adhered to his determination to remain indoors. The guards were there, but said that the young man seemed to have lost part of his timidity. He had that morning done much apparently frightened arguing and protesting over the telephone, one of the detectives said, replying to some unknown voice with phrases such as "I am very tired and must rest a while," "I can't receive anyone for some time," "you'll have to excuse me," "Please postpone decisive action till we can arrange some sort of compromise," or "I am very sorry, but I must take a complete vacation from everything; I'll talk with you later." Then, apparently gaining boldness through meditation, he had slipped out so quietly that no one had seen him depart or knew that he had gone until he returned about one o'clock and entered the house without a word. He had gone upstairs, where a bit of his fear must have surged back; for he was heard to cry out in a highly terrified fashion upon entering his library, afterward trailing off into a kind of choking gasp. When, however, the butler had gone to inquire what the trouble was, he had appeared at the door with a great show of boldness, and had silently gestured the man away in a manner that terrified him unaccountably. Then he had evidently done some rearranging of his shelves, for a great clattering and thumping and creaking ensued; after which he had reappeared and left at once. Willett inquired whether or not any message had been left, but was told that there was none. The butler seemed queerly disturbed about something in Charles's appearance and manner, and asked solicitously if there was much hope for a cure of his disordered nerves.

For almost two hours Dr. Willett waited vainly in Charles Ward's library, watching the dusty shelves with their wide gaps where books had been removed, and smiling grimly at the panelled overmantel on the north wall, whence a year before the suave features of old Joseph Curwen had looked mildly down. After a time the shadows began to gather, and the sunset cheer gave place to a vague growing terror which flew shadow-like before the night. Mr. Ward finally arrived, and shewed much surprise and anger at his son's absence after all the pains which had been taken to guard him. He had not known of Charles's appointment, and promised to notify Willett when the youth returned. In bidding the doctor goodnight he expressed his utter perplexity at his son's condition, and urged his caller to do all he could to restore the boy to normal poise. Willett was glad to escape from that library, for something frightful and unholy seemed to haunt it; as if the vanished picture had left behind a legacy of evil. He had never liked that picture; and even now, strong-nerved though he was, there lurked a quality in its vacant panel which made him feel an urgent need to get out into the pure air as soon as possible.

3.

The next morning Willett received a message from the senior Ward, saying that Charles was still absent. Mr. Ward mentioned that Dr. Allen had telephoned him to say that Charles would remain at Pawtuxet for some time, and that he must not be disturbed. This was necessary because Allen himself was suddenly called away for an indefinite period, leaving the researches in need of Charles's constant oversight. Charles sent his best wishes, and regretted any bother his abrupt change of plans might have caused. In listening to this message Mr. Ward heard Dr. Allen's voice for the first time, and it seemed to excite some vague and elusive memory which could not be actually placed, but which was disturbing to the point of fearfulness.

Faced by these baffling and contradictory reports, Dr. Willett was frankly at a loss what to do. The frantic earnestness of Charles's note was not to be denied, yet what could one think of its writer's immediate violation of his own expressed policy? Young Ward had written that his delvings had become blasphemous and menacing, that they and his bearded colleague must be extirpated at any cost, and that he himself would never return to their final scene; yet according to latest advices he had forgotten all this and was back in the thick of the mystery. Common sense bade one leave the youth alone with his freakishness, yet some deeper instinct would not permit the impression of that frenzied letter to subside. Willett read it over again, and could not make its essence sound as empty and insane as both its bombastic verbiage and its lack of fulfilment would seem to imply. Its terror was too profound and real, and in conjunction with what the doctor already knew evoked too vivid hints of monstrosities from beyond time and space to permit of any cynical explanation. There were nameless horrors abroad; and no matter how little one might be able to get at them, one ought to stand prepared for any sort of action at any time.

For over a week Dr. Willett pondered on the dilemma which seemed thrust upon him, and became more and more inclined to pay Charles a call at the Pawtuxet bungalow. No friend of the youth had ever ventured to storm this forbidden retreat, and even his father knew of its interior only from such descriptions as he chose to give; but Willett felt that some direct conversation with his patient was necessary. Mr. Ward had been receiving brief and non-committal typed notes from his son, and said that Mrs. Ward in her Atlantic City retirement had had no better word. So at length the doctor resolved to act; and despite a curious sensation inspired by old legends of Joseph Curwen, and by more recent revelations and warnings from Charles Ward, set boldly out for the bungalow on the bluff above the river.

Willett had visited the spot before through sheer curiosity, though of course never entering the house or proclaiming his presence; hence knew exactly the route to take. Driving out Broad Street one early afternoon toward the end of February in his small motor, he thought oddly of the grim party which had taken that selfsame road an hundred and fifty-seven years before on a terrible errand which none might ever comprehend.

The ride through the city's decaying fringe was short, and trim Edgewood and sleepy Pawtuxet presently spread out ahead. Willett turned to the right down Lockwood Street and drove his car as far along that rural road as he could, then alighted and walked north to where the bluff towered above the lovely bends of the river and the sweep of misty downlands beyond. Houses were still few here, and there was no mistaking the isolated bungalow with its concrete garage on a high point of land at his left. Stepping briskly up the neglected gravel walk he rapped at the door with a firm hand, and spoke without a tremor to the evil Portuguese mulatto who opened it to the width of a crack.

He must, he said, see Charles Ward at once on vitally important business. No excuse would be accepted, and a repulse would mean only a full report of the matter to the elder Ward. The mulatto still hesitated, and pushed against the door when Willett attempted to open it; but the doctor merely raised his voice and renewed his demands. Then there came from the dark interior a husky whisper which somehow chilled the hearer through and through though he did not know why he feared it. "Let him in, Tony," it said, "we may as well talk now as ever." But disturbing as was the whisper, the greater fear was that which immediately followed. The floor creaked and the speaker hove in sight—and the owner of those strange and resonant tones was seen to be no other than Charles Dexter Ward.

The minuteness with which Dr. Willett recalled and recorded his conversation of that afternoon is due to the importance he assigns to this particular period. For at last he concedes a vital change in Charles Dexter Ward's mentality, and believes that the youth now spoke from a brain hopelessly alien to the brain whose growth he had watched for six and twenty years. Controversy with Dr. Lyman has compelled him to be very specific, and he definitely dates the madness of Charles Ward from the time the typewritten notes began to reach his parents. Those notes are not in Ward's normal style; not even in the style of that last frantic letter to Willett. Instead, they are strange and archaic, as if the snapping of the writer's mind had released a flood of tendencies and impressions picked up unconsciously through boyhood antiquarianism. There is an obvious effort to be modern, but the spirit and occasionally the language are those of the past.

The past, too, was evident in Ward's every tone and gesture as he received the doctor in that shadowy bungalow. He bowed, motioned Willett to a seat, and began to speak abruptly in that strange whisper which he sought to explain at the very outset.

176. That is, suffering from phthisis; an antiquated word for consumptive or tubercular.

"I am grown phthisical,"[176] he began, "from this cursed river air. You must excuse my speech. I suppose you are come from my father to see what ails me, and I hope you will say nothing to alarm him."

Willett was studying these scraping tones with extreme care, but studying even more closely the face of the speaker. Something, he felt, was wrong; and he thought of what the family had told him about the fright of that Yorkshire butler one night. He wished it were not so dark, but did not request that any blind be opened. Instead, he merely asked Ward why he had so belied the frantic note of little more than a week before.

"I was coming to that," the host replied. "You must know, I am in a very bad state of nerves, and do and say queer things I cannot account for. As I have told you often, I am on the edge of great matters; and the bigness of them has a way of making me light-headed. Any man might well be frighted of what I have found, but I am not to be put off for long. I was a dunce to have that guard and stick at home; for having gone this far, my place is here. I am not well spoke of by my prying neighbours, and perhaps I was led by weakness to believe myself what they say of me. There is no evil to any in what I do, so long as I do it rightly. Have the goodness to wait six months, and I'll shew you what will pay your patience well.

"You may as well know I have a way of learning old matters from things surer than books, and I'll leave you to judge the importance of what I can give to history, philosophy, and the arts by reason of the doors I have access to. My ancestor had all this when those witless peeping Toms came and murdered him. I now have it again, or am coming very imperfectly to have a part of it. This time nothing must happen, and least of all through any idiot fears of my own. Pray forget all I writ you, Sir, and have no fear of this place or any in it. Dr. Allen is a man of fine parts, and I owe him an apology for anything ill I have said of him. I wish I had no need to spare him, but there were things he had to do elsewhere. His zeal is equal to mine in all those matters, and I suppose that when I feared the work I feared him too as my greatest helper in it."

Ward paused, and the doctor hardly knew what to say or think. He felt almost foolish in the face of this calm repudiation of the letter; and yet there clung to him the fact that while the present discourse was strange and alien and indubitably mad, the note itself had been tragic in its naturalness and likeness to the Charles Ward he knew. Willett now tried to turn the talk on early matters, and recall to the youth some past events which would restore a familiar mood; but in this process he obtained only the most grotesque results. It was the same with all the alienists later on. Important sections of Charles Ward's store of mental images, mainly those touching modern times and his own personal life, had been unaccountably expunged; whilst all the massed antiquarianism of his youth had welled up from some profound subconsciousness to engulf the contemporary and the individual. The youth's intimate knowledge of elder things was abnormal and unholy, and he tried his best to hide it. When Willett would mention some favourite object of his boyhood archaistic studies he often shed by pure accident such a light as no normal mortal could conceivably be expected to possess, and the doctor shuddered as the glib allusion glided by.

It was not wholesome to know so much about the way the fat sheriff's wig fell off as he leaned over at the play in Mr. Douglass' Histrionick Academy in King Street on the eleventh of February, 1762, which fell on a Thursday;[177] or about how the actors cut the text of Steele's *Conscious Lovers*[178] so badly that one was almost glad the Baptist-ridden legislature closed the theatre a fortnight later. That Thomas Sabin's Boston coach[179] was "damn'd uncomfortable" old letters may well have told; but what healthy antiquarian could recall how the creaking of Epenetus Olney's new signboard (the gaudy crown he set up after he took to calling his tavern the Crown Coffee House)[180] was exactly like the first few notes of the new jazz piece all the radios in Pawtuxet were playing?

Ward, however, would not be quizzed long in this vein. Modern and personal topics he waved aside quite summarily, whilst regarding antique affairs he soon shewed the plainest boredom. What he wished clearly enough was only to satisfy his visitor enough to make him depart without the intention of returning. To this end he offered to shew Willett the entire house, and at once proceeded to lead the doctor through every room from cellar to attic. Willett looked sharply, but noted that the visible books were far too few and trivial ever to have filled

177. The Histrionick Academy came to Providence in 1762, but, according to Kimball, the season did not open until July, with a work entitled *Moro Castle Taken by Storm*, which presumably treated the British attack, earlier in the year, on Morro Castle, in Havana, Cuba, a Spanish overseas possession (306). Part of a larger offensive intended as retaliation for Spain's entry into the Seven Years' War on France's side the previous year, the episode was one of the last naval battles of the conflict. David Douglass was the head of the troupe of actors who arrived from New York to perform the piece. On August 24, 1762, the legislature, bowing to public opinion, passed a bill to forbid plays and playhouses, and the troupe was thus summarily warned out of Providence. Kimball reports that the sheriff attended the final performance of the academy with the legislation in his pocket; only at the close of the show did he read the proclamation to the audience (308).

The Capture of Havana, 1762: The Morro Castle and the Boom Defence Before the Attack by Dominic Serres, 1770.

178. A five-act comedy written by Richard Steele in 1722, previously entitled *The Unfashionable Lovers*. It is based on *Andria*, by Terence (ca. 195–159 BCE), the Roman playwright and former slave; *Andria* itself was adapted from a work by Menander (ca. 341–290 BCE). Others who have treated the material in one form or another—the play is a story of marriage, social class, and mistaken

identity—include Niccolò Machiavelli (1469–1527) and, in his bestselling 1930 novel *The Woman of Andros*, Thornton Wilder (1897–1975).

179. Kimball reports that from the tavern of Richard Olney, "the stage-coach was advertised to set out every Thursday morning for Boston. This public accommodation was due to the enterprise of Thomas Sabin." She says nothing about its comfort (325).

180. Actually, according to Kimball, the owner was Richard Olney, not Epenetus (325).

the wide gaps on Ward's shelves at home, and that the meagre so-called "laboratory" was the flimsiest sort of a blind. Clearly, there were a library and a laboratory elsewhere; but just where, it was impossible to say. Essentially defeated in his quest for something he could not name, Willett returned to town before evening and told the senior Ward everything which had occurred. They agreed that the youth must be definitely out of his mind, but decided that nothing drastic need be done just then. Above all, Mrs. Ward must be kept in as complete an ignorance as her son's own strange typed notes would permit.

Mr. Ward now determined to call in person upon his son, making it wholly a surprise visit. Dr. Willett took him in his car one evening, guiding him to within sight of the bungalow and waiting patiently for his return. The session was a long one, and the father emerged in a very saddened and perplexed state. His reception had developed much like Willett's, save that Charles had been an excessively long time in appearing after the visitor had forced his way into the hall and sent the Portuguese away with an imperative demand; and in the bearing of the altered son there was no trace of filial affection. The lights had been dim, yet even so the youth had complained that they dazzled him outrageously. He had not spoken out loud at all, averring that his throat was in very poor condition; but in his hoarse whisper there was a quality so vaguely disturbing that Mr. Ward could not banish it from his mind.

Now definitely leagued together to do all they could toward the youth's mental salvation, Mr. Ward and Dr. Willett set about collecting every scrap of data which the case might afford. Pawtuxet gossip was the first item they studied, and this was relatively easy to glean since both had friends in that region. Dr. Willett obtained the most rumours because people talked more frankly to him than to a parent of the central figure, and from all he heard he could tell that young Ward's life had become indeed a strange one. Common tongues would not dissociate his household from the vampirism of the previous summer, while the nocturnal comings and goings of the motor trucks provided their share of dark speculation. Local tradesmen spoke of the queerness of the orders brought them by the evil-looking mulatto, and in particular of the inordinate amounts of meat and fresh blood secured from the two butcher shops in the immediate neighbourhood. For a household of only three, these quantities were quite absurd.

Then there was the matter of the sounds beneath the earth. Reports of these things were harder to pin down, but all the vague hints tallied in certain basic essentials. Noises of a ritual nature positively existed, and at times when the bungalow was dark. They might, of course, have come from the known cellar; but rumour insisted that there were deeper and more spreading crypts. Recalling the ancient tales of Joseph Curwen's catacombs, and assuming for granted that the present bungalow had been selected because of its situation on the old Curwen site as revealed in one or another of the documents found behind the picture, Willett and Mr. Ward gave this phase of the gossip much attention; and searched many times without success for the door in the river-bank which old manuscripts mentioned. As to popular opinions of the bungalow's various inhabitants, it was soon plain that the Brava Portuguese was loathed, the bearded and spectacled Dr. Allen feared, and the pallid young scholar disliked to a profound extent. During the last week or two Ward had obviously changed much, abandoning his attempts at affability and speaking only in hoarse but oddly repellent whispers on the few occasions that he ventured forth.

Such were the shreds and fragments gathered here and there; and over these Mr. Ward and Dr. Willett held many long and serious conferences. They strove to exercise deduction, induction, and constructive imagination to their utmost extent; and to correlate every known fact of Charles's later life, including the frantic letter which the doctor now shewed the father, with the meagre documentary evidence available concerning old Joseph Curwen. They would have given much for a glimpse of the papers Charles had found, for very clearly the key to the youth's madness lay in what he had learned of the ancient wizard and his doings.

4.

And yet, after all, it was from no step of Mr. Ward's or Dr. Willett's that the next move in this singular case proceeded. The father and the physician, rebuffed and confused by a shadow too shapeless and intangible to combat, had rested uneasily on their oars while the typed notes of young Ward to his parents grew fewer and fewer. Then came the first of the month with its customary financial adjustments, and the clerks at certain banks began a peculiar shaking of heads and telephoning from one to the other. Officials who knew Charles Ward by sight went down to the bungalow to ask why every cheque of his appearing at this juncture was a clumsy forgery, and were reassured less than they ought to have been when the youth hoarsely explained that his hand had lately been so much affected by a nervous shock as to make normal writing impossible. He could, he said, form no written characters at all except with great difficulty; and could prove it by the fact that he had been forced to type all his recent letters, even those to his father and mother, who would bear out the assertion.

What made the investigators pause in confusion was not this circumstance alone, for that was nothing unprecedented or fundamentally suspicious; nor even the Pawtuxet gossip, of which one or two of them had caught echoes. It was the muddled discourse of the young man which nonplussed them, implying as it did a virtually total loss of memory concerning important monetary matters which he had had at his fingertips only a month or two before. Something was wrong; for despite the apparent coherence and rationality of his speech, there could be no normal reason for this ill-concealed blankness on vital points. Moreover, although none of these men knew Ward well, they could not help observing the change in his language and manner. They had heard he was an antiquarian, but even the most hopeless antiquarians do not make daily use of obsolete phraseology and gestures. Altogether, this combination of hoarseness, palsied hands, bad memory, and altered speech and bearing must represent some disturbance or malady of genuine gravity, which no doubt formed the basis of the prevailing odd rumours; and after their departure the party of officials decided that a talk with the senior Ward was imperative.

So on the sixth of March, 1928, there was a long and serious conference in Mr. Ward's office, after which the utterly bewildered father summoned Dr. Willett in a kind of helpless resignation. Willett looked over the strained and awkward signatures of the cheques, and compared them in his mind with the penmanship of that last frantic note. Certainly, the change was radical and profound, and yet there was something damnably familiar about the new writing. It had crabbed and archaic tendencies of a very curious sort, and seemed to result from a type of stroke utterly different from that which the youth had always used. It was strange—but where had he seen it before? On the whole, it was obvious that Charles was insane. Of that there could be no doubt. And since it appeared unlikely that he could handle his property or continue to deal with the outside world much longer, something must quickly be done toward his oversight and possible cure. It was then that the alienists were called in, Drs. Peck and Waite of Providence and Dr. Lyman of Boston, to whom Mr. Ward and Dr. Willett gave the most exhaustive possible history of the case, and who conferred at length in the now unused library of their young patient, examining what books and papers of his were left in order to gain some further notion of his habitual mental cast. After scanning this material and examining the ominous note to Willett they all agreed that Charles Ward's studies had been enough to unseat or at least to warp any ordinary intellect, and wished most heartily that they could see his more intimate volumes and documents; but this latter they knew they could do, if at all, only after a scene at the bungalow itself. Willett now reviewed the whole case with febrile energy; it being at this time that he obtained the statements of the workmen who had seen Charles find the Curwen documents, and that he collated the incidents of the destroyed newspaper items, looking up the latter at the *Journal* office.

On Thursday, the eighth of March, Drs. Willett, Peck, Lyman, and Waite, accompanied by Mr. Ward, paid the youth their momentous call; making no concealment of their object and questioning the now acknowledged patient with extreme minuteness. Charles, though he was inordinately long in answering the summons and was still redolent of strange and noxious laboratory odours when he did finally make his agitated appearance, proved a far from recalcitrant subject; and admitted freely that his memory and balance had suffered somewhat from close application to abstruse studies. He offered no resistance when

181. There are and were no hospitals on Conanicut Island, but in the summer of 1906, a ward was established by the Rhode Island Hospital in an old hotel, refurbished for the purpose, for the treatment of tuberculosis. Waite's facility may have been such a small, temporary facility. In 1906, the island was indeed an island; today, however, bridges connect it to Newport and the west shore of the bay.

his removal to other quarters was insisted upon; and seemed, indeed, to display a high degree of intelligence as apart from mere memory. His conduct would have sent his interviewers away in bafflement had not the persistently archaic trend of his speech and unmistakable replacement of modern by ancient ideas in his consciousness marked him out as one definitely removed from the normal. Of his work he would say no more to the group of doctors than he had formerly said to his family and to Dr. Willett, and his frantic note of the previous month he dismissed as mere nerves and hysteria. He insisted that this shadowy bungalow possessed no library or laboratory beyond the visible ones, and waxed abstruse in explaining the absence from the house of such odours as now saturated all his clothing. Neighbourhood gossip he attributed to nothing more than the cheap inventiveness of baffled curiosity. Of the whereabouts of Dr. Allen he said he did not feel at liberty to speak definitely, but assured his inquisitors that the bearded and spectacled man would return when needed. In paying off the stolid Brava who resisted all questioning by the visitors, and in closing the bungalow which still seemed to hold such nighted secrets, Ward shewed no sign of nervousness save a barely noticed tendency to pause as though listening for something very faint. He was apparently animated by a calmly philosophic resignation, as if his removal were the merest transient incident which would cause the least trouble if facilitated and disposed of once and for all. It was clear that he trusted to his obviously unimpaired keenness of absolute mentality to overcome all the embarrassments into which his twisted memory, his lost voice and handwriting, and his secretive and eccentric behaviour had led him. His mother, it was agreed, was not to be told of the change; his father supplying typed notes in his name. Ward was taken to the restfully and picturesquely situated private hospital maintained by Dr. Waite on Conanicut Island in the bay,[181] and subjected to the closest scrutiny and questioning by all the physicians connected with the case. It was then that the physical oddities were noticed; the slackened metabolism, the altered skin, and the disproportionate neural reactions. Dr. Willett was the most perturbed of the various examiners, for he had attended Ward all his life and could appreciate with terrible keenness the extent of his physical disorganisation. Even the familiar olive mark on his hip was gone, while on his chest was a great black mole or cicatrice which had never been there before, and which made Willett wonder whether the youth had ever submitted to any of the witch markings reputed to be inflicted at certain unwholesome nocturnal meetings in wild and lonely places. The doctor could not keep his mind off a certain transcribed witch-trial record from Salem which Charles had shewn him in the old non-secretive days, and which read: 'Mr. G. B. on that Nighte putt ye Divell his Marke upon Bridget S., Jonathan A., Simon O., Deliverance W., Joseph C., Susan P., Mehitable C., and Deborah B." Ward's face, too, troubled him horribly, till at length he suddenly discovered why he was horrified. For above the young man's right eye was something which he had never previously noticed—a small scar or pit precisely like that in the crumbled painting of old Joseph Curwen, and perhaps attesting some hideous ritualistic inoculation to which both had submitted at a certain stage of their occult careers.

While Ward himself was puzzling all the doctors at the hospital a very strict watch was kept on all mail addressed either to him or to Dr. Allen, which Mr. Ward had ordered delivered at the family home. Willett had predicted that very little would be found, since any communications of a vital nature would probably have been exchanged by messenger; but in the latter part of March there did come a letter from Prague for Dr. Allen which gave both the doctor and the father deep thought. It was in a very crabbed and archaic hand; and though clearly not the effort of a foreigner, shewed almost as singular a departure from modern English as the speech of young Ward himself. It read:

Kleinstrasse 11,
Altstadt, Prague,
11th Feby. 1928.

Brother in Almousin-Metraton:—

I this day receiv'd y^r mention of what came up from the Salts I sent you. It was wrong, and meanes clearly that ye Headstones had been chang'd when Barnabas gott me the Specimen. It is often so, as you must be sensible of from the Thing you gott from ye Kings

182. At the end of the Great War, Hungary and Romania went to war. The Treaty of Versailles, ratified in July 1919, resolved the political situation, ceding Transylvania to the Romanians. Ironically, in August 1940, the northern half of Transylvania was reannexed to Hungary; it was returned to Romania at the end of World War II by the 1947 Treaty of Paris.

183. "B. F." and a source in Philadelphia surely suggest that *Benjamin Franklin's* was the desired cadaver.

Chapell ground in 1769 and what H. gott from Olde Bury'g Point in 1690, that was like to ende him. I gott such a Thing in Ægypt 75 yeares gone, from the which came that Scar ye Boy saw on me here in 1924. As I told you longe ago, do not calle up That which you can not put downe; either from dead Saltes or out of ye Spheres beyond. Have ye Wordes for laying at all times readie, and stopp not to be sure when there is any Doubte of Whom you have. Stones are all chang'd now in Nine groundes out of 10. You are never sure till you question. I this day heard from H., who has had Trouble with the Soldiers. He is like to be sorry Transylvania is pass'd from Hungary to Roumania,[182] and wou'd change his Seat if the Castel weren't so fulle of What we Knowe. But of this he hath doubtless writ you. In my next Send'g there will be Somewhat from a Hill tomb from ye East that will delight you greatly. Meanwhile forget not I am desirous of B. F.[183] if you can possibly get him for me. You know G. in Philada. better than I. Have him up firste if you will, but doe not use him soe hard he will be Difficult, for I must speake to him in ye End.

Yogg-Sothoth Neblod Zin
Simon O.

To Mr. J. C. in
Providence.

Mr. Ward and Dr. Willett paused in utter chaos before this apparent bit of unrelieved insanity. Only by degrees did they absorb what it seemed to imply. So the absent Dr. Allen, and not Charles Ward, had come to be the leading spirit at Pawtuxet? That must explain the wild reference and denunciation in the youth's last frantic letter. And what of this addressing of the bearded and spectacled stranger as "Mr. J. C."? There was no escaping the inference, but there are limits to possible monstrosity. Who was "Simon O."; the old man Ward had visited in Prague four years previously? Perhaps, but in the centuries behind there had been another Simon O.—Simon Orne, alias Jedediah, of Salem, who vanished in 1771, *and whose peculiar handwriting Dr. Willett now unmistakably recognised from the photostatic copies of the Orne formulæ which Charles had once shewn him. What hor-*

rors and mysteries, what contradictions and contraventions of Nature, had come back after a century and a half to harass Old Providence with her clustered spires and domes?

The father and the old physician, virtually at a loss what to do or think, went to see Charles at the hospital and questioned him as delicately as they could about Dr. Allen, about the Prague visit, and about what he had learned of Simon or Jedediah Orne of Salem. To all these inquiries the youth was politely non-committal, merely barking in his hoarse whisper that he had found Dr. Allen to have a remarkable spiritual rapport with certain souls from the past, and that any correspondent the bearded man might have in Prague would probably be similarly gifted. When they left, Mr. Ward and Dr. Willett realised to their chagrin that they had really been the ones under catechism; and that without imparting anything vital himself, the confined youth had adroitly pumped them of everything the Prague letter had contained.

Drs. Peck, Waite, and Lyman were not inclined to attach much importance to the strange correspondence of young Ward's companion; for they knew the tendency of kindred eccentrics and monomaniacs to band together, and believed that Charles or Allen had merely unearthed an expatriated counterpart—perhaps one who had seen Orne's handwriting and copied it in an attempt to pose as the bygone character's reincarnation. Allen himself was perhaps a similar case, and may have persuaded the youth into accepting him as an avatar of the long-dead Curwen. Such things had been known before, and on the same basis the hard-headed doctors disposed of Willett's growing disquiet about Charles Ward's present handwriting, as studied from unpremeditated specimens obtained by various ruses. Willett thought he had placed its odd familiarity at last, and that what it vaguely resembled was the bygone penmanship of old Joseph Curwen himself; but this the other physicians regarded as a phase of imitativeness only to be expected in a mania of this sort, and refused to grant it any importance either favourable or unfavourable. Recognising this prosaic attitude in his colleagues, Willett advised Mr. Ward to keep to himself the letter which arrived for Dr. Allen on the second of April from Rakus, Transylvania, in a handwriting so intensely and fundamentally like that of the

184. In other words, Ward is not a mortal being such as those called up from the "essential Saltes," and sorcery may have been involved in his birth, points out Donald R. Burleson, in *H. P. Lovecraft: A Critical Study.*

Hutchinson cipher that both father and physician paused in awe before breaking the seal. This read as follows:

Castle Ferenczy
7 March 1928.

Dear C.:—

Hadd a Squad of 20 Militia up to talk about what the Country Folk say. Must digg deeper and have less Hearde. These Roumanians plague me damnably, being officious and particular where you cou'd buy a Magyar off with a Drinke and ffood. Last monthe M. got me yᵉ Sarcophagus of yᵉ Five Sphinxes from yᵉ Acropolis where He whome I call'd up say'd it wou'd be, and I have hadde 3 Talkes with What was therein inhum'd. It will go to S. O. in Prague directly, and thence to you. It is stubborn but you know yᵉ Way with Such. You shew Wisdom in having lesse about than Before; for there was no Neede to keep the Guards in Shape and eat'g off their Heads, and it made Much to be founde in Case of Trouble, as you too welle know. You can now move and worke elsewhere with no Kill'g Trouble if needful, tho' I hope no Thing will soon force you to so Bothersome a Course. I rejoice that you traffick not so much with Those Outside; for there was ever a Mortall Peril in it, and you are sensible what it did when you ask'd Protection of One not dispos'd to give it. You excel me in gett'g yᵉ fformulæ so another may saye them with Success, but Borellus fancy'd it wou'd be so if just yᵉ right Wordes were hadd. Does yᵉ Boy use 'em often? I regret that he growes squeamish, as I fear'd he wou'd when I hadde him here nigh 15 Monthes, but am sensible you knowe how to deal with him. You can't saye him down with yᵉ fformula, for that will Worke only upon such as yᵉ other fformula hath call'd up from Saltes; but you still have strong Handes and Knife and Pistol, and Graves are not harde to digg, nor Acids loth to burne.[184] O. sayes you have promis'd him B. F. I must have him after. B. goes to you soone, and may he give you what you wishe of that Darke Thing belowe Memphis. Imploy care in what you calle up, and beware of yᵉ Boy. It will be ripe in a yeare's time to have up yᵉ Legions from Underneath, and then there are no Boundes to what shal be oures. Have Confidence in what I saye, for you knowe O. and I have hadd these 150 yeares more than you to consulte these Matters in.

Nephren-Ka nai Hadoth[185]

Edw.:H.

For J Curwen, Esq.
Providence.

But if Willett and Mr. Ward refrained from shewing this letter to the alienists, they did not refrain from acting upon it themselves. No amount of learned sophistry could controvert the fact that the strangely bearded and spectacled Dr. Allen, of whom Charles's frantic letter had spoken as such a monstrous menace, was in close and sinister correspondence with two inexplicable creatures whom Ward had visited in his travels and who plainly claimed to be survivals or avatars of Curwen's old Salem colleagues; that he was regarding himself as the reincarnation of Joseph Curwen, and that he entertained—or was at least advised to entertain—murderous designs against a "boy" who could scarcely be other than Charles Ward. There was organised horror afoot; and no matter who had started it, the missing Allen was by this time at the bottom of it. Therefore, thanking heaven that Charles was now safe in the hospital, Mr. Ward lost no time in engaging detectives to learn all they could of the cryptic, bearded doctor; finding whence he had come and what Pawtuxet knew of him, and if possible discovering his current whereabouts. Supplying the men with one of the bungalow keys which Charles yielded up, he urged them to explore Allen's vacant room which had been identified when the patient's belongings had been packed; obtaining what clues they could from any effects he might have left about. Mr. Ward talked with the detectives in his son's old library, and they felt a marked relief when they left it at last; for there seemed to hover about the place a vague aura of evil. Perhaps it was what they had heard of the infamous old wizard whose picture had once stared from the panelled overmantel, and perhaps it was something different and irrelevant; but in any case they all half sensed an intangible miasma which centred in that carven vestige of an older dwelling and which at times almost rose to the intensity of a material emanation.

185. Lovecraft's tale "The Outsider" (1921) refers to "the catacombs of Nephren-Ka in the sealed and unknown valley of Haddoth by the Nile." Nephren-Ka is identified as a pharaoh in "The Haunter of the Dark," text accompanying note 20, below. Why his name should serve as a benediction is unknown.

V. A NIGHTMARE AND A CATACLYSM

1.

AND NOW SWIFTLY followed that hideous experience which has left its indelible mark of fear on the soul of Marinus Bicknell Willett, and has added a decade to the visible age of one whose youth was even then far behind. Dr. Willett had conferred at length with Mr. Ward, and had come to an agreement with him on several points which both felt the alienists would ridicule. There was, they conceded, a terrible movement alive in the world, whose direct connexion with a necromancy even older than the Salem witchcraft could not be doubted. That at least two living men—and one other of whom they dared not think—were in absolute possession of minds or personalities which had functioned as early as 1690 or before was likewise almost unassailably proved even in the face of all known natural laws. What these horrible creatures—and Charles Ward as well—were doing or trying to do seemed fairly clear from their letters and from every bit of light both old and new which had filtered in upon the case. They were robbing the tombs of all the ages, including those of the world's wisest and greatest men, in the hope of recovering from the bygone ashes some vestige of the consciousness and lore which had once animated and informed them.

A hideous traffick was going on among these nightmare ghouls, whereby illustrious bones were bartered with the calm calculativeness of schoolboys swapping books; and from what was extorted from this centuried dust there was anticipated a power and a wisdom beyond anything which the cosmos had ever seen concentrated in one man or group. They had found unholy ways to keep their brains alive, either in the same body or different bodies; and had evidently achieved a way of tapping the consciousness of the dead whom they gathered together. There had, it seems, been some truth in chimerical old Borellus when he wrote of preparing from even the most antique remains certain "Essential Saltes" from which the shade of a long-dead living thing might be raised up. There was a formula for evoking such a shade, and another for putting it down; and it had now been so perfected that it could be taught successfully. One must be careful about evocations, for the markers of old graves are not always accurate.

Willett and Mr. Ward shivered as they passed from conclusion to conclusion. Things—presences or voices of some sort—could be drawn down from unknown places as well as from the grave, and in this process also one must be careful. Joseph Curwen had indubitably evoked many forbidden things, and as for Charles— what might one think of him? What forces "outside the spheres" had reached him from Joseph Curwen's day and turned his mind on forgotten things? He had been led to find certain directions, and he had used them. He had talked with the man of horror in Prague and stayed long with the creature in the mountains of Transylvania. And he must have found the grave of Joseph Curwen at last. That newspaper item and what his mother had heard in the night were too significant to overlook. Then he had summoned something, and it must have come. That mighty voice aloft on Good Friday, and those *different* tones in the locked attic laboratory. What were they like, with their depth and hollowness? Was there not here some awful foreshadowing of the dreaded stranger Dr. Allen with his spectral bass? Yes, *that* was what Mr. Ward had felt with vague horror in his single talk with the man—if man it were—over the telephone!

What hellish consciousness or voice, what morbid shade or presence, had come to answer Charles Ward's secret rites behind that locked door? Those voices heard in argument—"must have it red for three months"—

Good God! Was not that just before the vampirism broke out? The rifling of Ezra Weeden's ancient grave, and the cries later at Pawtuxet—whose mind had planned the vengeance and rediscovered the shunned seat of elder blasphemies? And then the bungalow and the bearded stranger, and the gossip, and the fear. The final madness of Charles neither father nor doctor could attempt to explain, but they did feel sure that the mind of Joseph Curwen had come to earth again and was following its ancient morbidities. Was dæmoniac possession in truth a possibility? Allen had something to do with it, and the detectives must find out more about one whose existence menaced the young man's life. In the meantime, since the existence of some vast crypt beneath the bungalow seemed virtually beyond dispute, some effort must be

Cover of *Os Mortos Podem Voltar* (*The Dead Can Return*) (Brazil: Colleçao Vampiro, n.d.). Translated by Silas Cerquiera. American title: *The Case of Charles Dexter Ward*.

[273]

made to find it. Willett and Mr. Ward, conscious of the sceptical attitude of the alienists, resolved during their final conference to undertake a joint secret exploration of unparalleled thoroughness; and agreed to meet at the bungalow on the following morning with valises and with certain tools and accessories suited to architectural search and underground exploration.

The morning of April 6th dawned clear, and both explorers were at the bungalow by ten o'clock. Mr. Ward had the key, and an entry and cursory survey were made. From the disordered condition of Dr. Allen's room it was obvious that the detectives had been there before, and the later searchers hoped that they had found some clue which might prove of value. Of course the main business lay in the cellar; so thither they descended without much delay, again making the circuit which each had vainly made before in the presence of the mad young owner. For a time everything seemed baffling, each inch of the earthen floor and stone walls having so solid and innocuous an aspect that the thought of a yawning aperture was scarcely to be entertained. Willett reflected that since the original cellar was dug without knowledge of any catacombs beneath, the beginning of the passage would represent the strictly modern delving of young Ward and his associates, where they had probed for the ancient vaults whose rumour could have reached them by no wholesome means.

The doctor tried to put himself in Charles's place to see how a delver would be likely to start, but could not gain much inspiration from this method. Then he decided on elimination as a policy, and went carefully over the whole subterranean surface both vertical and horizontal, trying to account for every inch separately. He was soon substantially narrowed down, and at last had nothing left but the small platform before the washtubs, which he had tried once before in vain. Now experimenting in every possible way, and exerting a double strength, he finally found that the top did indeed turn and slide horizontally on a corner pivot. Beneath it lay a trim concrete surface with an iron manhole, to which Mr. Ward at once rushed with excited zeal. The cover was not hard to lift, and the father had quite removed it when Willett noticed the queerness of his aspect. He was swaying and nodding dizzily, and in the gust of noxious air which swept up from the black pit beneath the doctor soon recognised ample cause.

In a moment Dr. Willett had his fainting companion on the floor above and was reviving him with cold water. Mr. Ward responded feebly, but it could be seen that the mephitic blast from the crypt had in some way gravely sickened him. Wishing to take no chances, Willett hastened out to Broad Street for a taxicab and had soon dispatched the sufferer home despite his weak-voiced protests; after which he produced an electric torch, covered his nostrils with a band of sterile gauze, and descended once more to peer into the new-found depths. The foul air had now slightly abated, and Willett was able to send a beam of light down the Stygian hole. For about ten feet, he saw, it was a sheer cylindrical drop with concrete walls and an iron ladder; after which the hole appeared to strike a flight of old stone steps which must originally have emerged to earth somewhat southwest of the present building.

Cover of *The Case of Charles Dexter Ward* (London: Panther Books, 1963).

2.

Willett freely admits that for a moment the memory of the old Curwen legends kept him from climbing down alone into that malodorous gulf. He could not help thinking of what Luke Fenner had reported on that last monstrous night. Then duty asserted itself and he made the plunge, carrying a great valise for the removal of whatever papers might prove of supreme importance. Slowly, as befitted one of his years, he descended the ladder and reached the slimy steps below. This was ancient masonry, his torch told him; and upon the dripping walls he saw the unwholesome moss of centuries. Down, down, ran the steps; not spirally, but in three abrupt turns; and with such narrowness that two men could have passed only with difficulty. He had counted about thirty when a sound reached him very faintly; and after that he did not feel disposed to count any more.

It was a godless sound; one of those low-keyed, insidious outrages of Nature which are not meant to be. To call it a dull wail, a doom-dragged whine, or a hopeless howl of chorused anguish and stricken flesh without mind would be to miss its most quintessential loathsomeness and soul-sickening overtones. Was it for this that Ward had seemed to listen on that day he was removed? It was the most shocking thing that Willett had ever heard, and it continued from no determinate point as the doctor reached the bottom of the steps and cast his torchlight around on lofty corridor walls surmounted by Cyclopean vaulting and pierced by numberless black archways. The hall in which he stood was perhaps fourteen feet high in the middle of the vaulting and ten or twelve feet broad. Its pavement was of large chipped flagstones, and its walls and roof were of dressed masonry. Its length he could not imagine, for it stretched ahead indefinitely into the blackness. Of the archways, some had doors of the old six-panelled colonial type, whilst others had none.

Overcoming the dread induced by the smell and the howling, Willett began to explore these archways one by one; finding beyond them rooms with groined stone ceilings, each of medium size and apparently of bizarre uses. Most of them had fireplaces, the upper courses of whose chimneys would have formed an interesting study in engineering. Never before or since had he seen such instruments or suggestions of instruments as here loomed up on every hand through the burying dust and cobwebs of a century and a half, in many cases evidently shattered as if by the ancient raiders. For many of the chambers seemed wholly untrodden by modern feet, and must have represented the earliest and most obsolete phases of Joseph Curwen's experimentation. Finally there came a room of obvious modernity, or at least of recent occupancy. There were oil heaters, bookshelves and tables, chairs and cabinets, and a desk piled high with papers of varying antiquity and contemporaneousness. Candlesticks and oil lamps stood about in several places; and finding a match-safe handy, Willett lighted such as were ready for use.

In the fuller gleam it appeared that this apartment was nothing less than the latest study or library of Charles Ward. Of the books the doctor had seen many before, and a good part of the furniture had plainly come from the Prospect Street mansion. Here and there was a piece well known to Willett, and the sense of familiarity became so great that he half forgot the noisomeness and the wailing, both of which were plainer here than they had been at the foot of the steps. His first duty, as planned long ahead, was to find and seize any papers which might seem of vital importance; especially those portentous documents found by Charles so long ago behind the picture in Olney Court. As he searched he perceived how stupendous a task the final unravelling would be; for file on file was stuffed with papers in curious hands and bearing curious designs, so that months or even years might be needed for a thorough deciphering and editing. Once he found large packets of letters with Prague and Rakus postmarks, and in writing clearly recognisable as Orne's and Hutchinson's; all of which he took with him as part of the bundle to be removed in his valise.

At last, in a locked mahogany cabinet once gracing the Ward home, Willett found the batch of old Curwen papers; recognising them from the reluctant glimpse Charles had granted him so many years ago. The youth had evidently kept them together very much as they had been when first he found them, since all the titles recalled by the workmen were present except the papers addressed to Orne and Hutchinson, and the cipher with its key. Willett placed the entire lot in his valise and continued his examination of the files. Since young Ward's immediate condition was the greatest matter at stake, the closest searching was done among the most obviously recent matter; and in this abundance of contemporary manuscript one very baffling oddity was noted. The oddity was the slight amount in Charles's normal writing, which indeed included nothing more recent than two months before. On the other hand, there were literally reams of symbols and formulæ, historical notes and philosophical comment, in a crabbed penmanship absolutely identical with the ancient script of Joseph Curwen, though of undeniably modern dating. Plainly, a part of the latter-day programme had been a sedulous imitation of the old wizard's writing, which Charles seemed to have carried to a marvellous state of perfection. Of any third hand which might have been Allen's there was not a trace. If he had indeed come to be the leader, he must have forced young Ward to act as his amanuensis.

In this new material one mystic formula, or rather pair of formulæ, recurred so often that Willett had it by heart before he had half finished his quest. It consisted of two parallel columns, the left-hand one surmounted by the archaic symbol called "Dragon's Head" and used in almanacks to indicate the ascending node, and the right-hand one headed by a corresponding sign of "Dragon's Tail" or descending node. The appearance of the whole was

"The Dragon's Head and Tail," from Guido Bonatti *Liber Astronomiae* (1550). The ascending mode is Ω and the descending mode is ℧.

something like this, and almost unconsciously the doctor realised that the second half was no more than the first written syllabically backward with the exception of the final monosyllables and of the odd name *Yog-Sothoth*, which he had come to recognise under various spellings from other things he had seen in connexion with this horrible matter. The formulæ were as follows— *exactly* so, as Willett is abundantly able to testify—and the first one struck an odd note of uncomfortable latent memory in his brain, which he recognised later when reviewing the events of that horrible Good Friday of the previous year.

Ω

Y'AI 'NG'NGAH,
YOG-SOTHOTH
H'EE-L'GEB
F'AI THRODOG
UAAAH

℧

OGTHROD AI'F
GEB'L-EE'H
YOG-SOTHOTH
'NGAH'NG AI'Y
ZHRO

So haunting were these formulæ, and so frequently did he come upon them, that before the doctor knew it he was repeating them under his breath. Eventually, however, he felt he had secured all the papers he could digest to advantage for the present; hence resolved to examine no more till he could bring the sceptical alienists en masse for an ampler and more systematic raid. He had still to find the hidden laboratory, so leaving his valise in the lighted room he emerged again into the black noisome corridor whose vaulting echoed ceaselessly with that dull and hideous whine.

The next few rooms he tried were all abandoned, or filled only with crumbling boxes and ominous-looking leaden coffins; but impressed him deeply with the magnitude of Joseph Curwen's original operations. He thought of the slaves and seamen who had disappeared, of the graves which had been violated in every part of the world, and of what that final raiding party must have seen; and then he decided it was better not to think any more. Once a great stone staircase mounted at his right, and he deduced that this must have reached to one of the Curwen outbuildings—perhaps the famous stone edifice with the high slit-like windows—provided the steps he had descended had led from the steep-roofed farmhouse. Suddenly the walls seemed to fall away ahead, and the stench and the wailing grew stronger. Willett saw that he had come upon a vast open space, so great that his torchlight would not carry across it; and as he advanced he encountered occasional stout pillars supporting the arches of the roof.

After a time he reached a circle of pillars grouped like the monoliths of Stonehenge, with a large carved altar on a base of three steps in the centre; and so curious were the carvings on that altar that he approached to study them with his electric light. But when he saw what they were he shrank away shuddering, and did not stop to investigate the dark stains which discoloured the upper surface and had spread down the sides in occasional thin lines. Instead, he found the distant wall and traced it as it swept round in a gigantic circle perforated by occasional black doorways and indented by a myriad of shallow cells with iron gratings and wrist and ankle bonds on chains fastened to the stone of the concave rear masonry. These cells were empty, but still the horrible odour and the dismal moaning continued, more insistent now than ever, and seemingly varied at times by a sort of slippery thumping.

186. An offensive smell or odor, spelled "fetor" in American usage.

3.

From that frightful smell and that uncanny noise Willett's attention could no longer be diverted. Both were plainer and more hideous in the great pillared hall than anywhere else, and carried a vague impression of being far below, even in this dark nether world of subterrene mystery. Before trying any of the black archways for steps leading further down, the doctor cast his beam of light about the stone-flagged floor. It was very loosely paved, and at irregular intervals there would occur a slab curiously pierced by small holes in no definite arrangement, while at one point there lay a very long ladder carelessly flung down. To this ladder, singularly enough, appeared to cling a particularly large amount of the frightful odour which encompassed everything. As he walked slowly about it suddenly occurred to Willett that both the noise and the odour seemed strongest directly above the oddly pierced slabs, as if they might be crude trap-doors leading down to some still deeper region of horror. Kneeling by one, he worked at it with his hands, and found that with extreme difficulty he could budge it. At his touch the moaning beneath ascended to a louder key, and only with vast trepidation did he persevere in the lifting of the heavy stone. A stench unnamable now rose up from below, and the doctor's head reeled dizzily as he laid back the slab and turned his torch upon the exposed square yard of gaping blackness.

If he had expected a flight of steps to some wide gulf of ultimate abomination, Willett was destined to be disappointed; for amidst that fœtor[186] and cracked whining he discerned only the brick-faced top of a cylindrical well perhaps a yard and a half in diameter and devoid of any ladder or other means of descent. As the light shone down, the wailing changed suddenly to a series of horrible yelps; in conjunction with which there came again that sound of blind, futile scrambling and slippery thumping. The explorer trembled, unwilling even to imagine what noxious thing might be lurking in that abyss, but in a moment mustered up the courage to peer over the rough-hewn brink; lying at full length and holding the torch downward at arm's length to see what might lie below. For a second he could distinguish nothing but the slimy, moss-grown brick walls sinking illimitably into that half-tangible miasma of murk and foulness and anguished frenzy; and then he saw that something dark was leaping clumsily and frantically up and down at the bottom of the narrow shaft, which must have been from twenty to twenty-five feet below the stone floor where he lay. The torch shook in his hand, but he looked again to see what manner of living creature might be immured there in the darkness of that unnatural well; left starving by young Ward through all the long month since the doctors had taken him away, and clearly only one of a vast number prisoned in the kindred wells whose pierced stone covers so thickly studded the floor of the great vaulted cavern. Whatever the things were, they could not lie down in their cramped spaces; but must have crouched and whined and waited and feebly leaped all those hideous weeks since their master had abandoned them unheeded.

But Marinus Bicknell Willett was sorry that he looked again; for surgeon and veteran of the dissecting-room though he was, he has not been the same since. It is hard to explain just how a single sight of a tangible object with measureable dimensions could so shake and change a man; and we may only say that there is about certain outlines and entities a power of symbolism and suggestion which acts frightfully on a sensitive thinker's perspective and whispers terrible hints of obscure cosmic relationships and unnamable realities behind the protective illusions of common vision. In that second look Willett saw such an outline or entity, for during the next few instants he was undoubtedly as stark raving mad as any inmate of Dr. Waite's private hospital. He dropped the electric torch from a hand drained of muscular power or nervous coördination, nor heeded the sound of crunching teeth which told of its fate at the bottom of the pit. He screamed and screamed and screamed in a voice whose falsetto panic no acquaintance of his would ever have recognised; and though he could not rise to his feet he crawled and rolled desperately away over the damp pavement where dozens of Tartarean wells poured forth their exhausted whining and yelping to answer his own insane cries. He tore his hands on the rough, loose stones, and many times bruised his head against the frequent pillars, but still he kept on. Then at last he slowly came to himself in the utter blackness and stench, and stopped his ears

Poster from *The Haunted Palace* (American International Pictures, 1963). Although billed as "Edgar Allan Poe's *The Haunted Palace*," the film is based on *The Case of Charles Dexter Ward*.

against the droning wail into which the burst of yelping had subsided. He was drenched with perspiration and without means of producing a light; stricken and unnerved in the abysmal blackness and horror, and crushed with a memory he never could efface. Beneath him dozens of those things still lived, and from one of the shafts the cover was removed. He knew that what he had seen could never climb up the slippery walls, yet shuddered at the thought that some obscure foot-hold might exist.

What the thing was, he would never tell. It was like some of the carvings on the hellish altar, but it was alive. Nature had never made it in this form, for it was too palpably *unfinished*. The deficiencies were of the most surprising sort, and the abnormalities of proportion could not be described. Willett consents only to say that this type of thing must have represented entities which Ward called up from *imperfect salts*, and which he kept for servile or ritualistic purposes. If it had not had a certain significance, its image would not have been carved on that damnable stone. It was not the worst thing depicted on that stone—but Willett never opened the other pits. At the time, the first connected idea in his mind was an idle paragraph from some of the old Curwen data he had digested long before; a phrase used by Simon or Jedediah Orne in that portentous confiscated letter to the bygone sorcerer:

> "Certainely, there was Noth'g but ye liveliest Awfulness in that which H. rais'd upp from What he cou'd gather onlie a part of."

Then, horribly supplementing rather than displacing this image, there came a recollection of those ancient lingering rumours anent the burned, twisted thing found in the fields a week after the Curwen raid. Charles Ward had once told the doctor what old Slocum said of that object; that it was neither thoroughly human, nor wholly allied to any animal which Pawtuxet folk had ever seen or read about.

These words hummed in the doctor's mind as he rocked to and fro, squatting on the nitrous stone floor. He tried to drive them out, and repeated the Lord's Prayer to himself; eventually trailing off into a mnemonic hodge-podge like the modernistic *Waste Land* of Mr. T. S. Eliot,[187] and finally reverting to the oft-repeated dual formula he had lately found in Ward's underground library: "*Y'ai 'ng'ngah, Yog-Sothoth*" and so on till the final underlined "*Zhro.*"

It seemed to soothe him, and he staggered to his feet after a time; lamenting bitterly his fright-lost torch and looking wildly about for any gleam of light in the clutching inkiness of the chilly air. Think he would not; but he strained his eyes in every direction for some faint glint or reflection of the bright illumination he had left in the library. After a while he thought he detected a suspicion of a glow infinitely far away, and toward this he crawled in agonised caution on hands and knees amidst the stench and howling, always feeling ahead lest he collide with the numerous great pillars or stumble into the abominable pit he had uncovered.

Once his shaking fingers touched something which he knew must be the steps leading to the hellish altar, and from this spot he recoiled in loathing. At another time he encountered the pierced slab he had removed, and here his caution became almost pitiful. But he did not come upon the dread aperture after all, nor did anything issue from that aperture to detain him. What had been down there made no sound nor stir. Evidently its crunching of the fallen electric torch had not been good for it. Each time Willett's fingers felt a perforated slab he trembled. His passage over it would sometimes increase the groaning below, but generally it would produce no effect at all, since he moved very noiselessly. Several times during his progress the glow ahead diminished perceptibly, and he realised that the various candles and lamps he had left must be expiring one by one. The thought of being lost in utter darkness without matches amidst this underground world of nightmare labyrinths impelled him to rise to his feet and run, which he could safely do now that he had passed the open pit; for he knew that once the light failed, his only hope of rescue and survival would lie in whatever relief party Mr. Ward might send after missing him for a sufficient period. Presently, however, he emerged from the open space into the narrower corridor and definitely located the glow as coming from a door on his right. In a moment he had reached it and was standing once more in young Ward's secret library, trembling with relief, and watching the sputterings of that last lamp which had brought him to safety.

187. Eliot (1888–1965) published this masterpiece of modern poetry in 1922, only six years prior to the incidents recorded here. The poem ends with a recitation of jumbled phrases:

> London Bridge is falling down falling
>   down falling down
> *Poi s'ascose nel foco che gli affina*
> *Quando fiam ceu chelidon*—O
>   swallow swallow
> *Le Prince d'Aquitaine à la tour abolie*
> These fragments I have shored against
>   my ruins
> Why then Ile fit you. Hieronymo's mad
>   againe.
> Datta. Dayadhvam. Damyata.
>
> Shantih shantih shantih

The poem did not meet with unalloyed praise, especially a mere six years after publication, and the narrator of this tale is evidently a modernist to evince such familiarity with it.

4.

In another moment he was hastily filling the burned-out lamps from an oil supply he had previously noticed, and when the room was bright again he looked about to see if he might find a lantern for further exploration. For racked though he was with horror, his sense of grim purpose was still uppermost; and he was firmly determined to leave no stone unturned in his search for the hideous facts behind Charles Ward's bizarre madness. Failing to find a lantern, he chose the smallest of the lamps to carry; also filling his pockets with candles and matches, and taking with him a gallon can of oil, which he proposed to keep for reserve use in whatever hidden laboratory he might uncover beyond the terrible open space with its unclean altar and nameless covered wells. To traverse that space again would require his utmost fortitude, but he knew it must be done. Fortunately neither the frightful altar nor the opened shaft was near the vast cell-indented wall which bounded the cavern area, and whose black mysterious archways would form the next goals of a logical search.

So Willett went back to that great pillared hall of stench and anguished howling; turning down his lamp to avoid any distant glimpse of the hellish altar, or of the uncovered pit with the pierced stone slab beside it. Most of the black doorways led merely to small chambers, some vacant and some evidently used as storerooms; and in several of the latter he saw some very curious accumulations of various objects. One was packed with rotting and dust-draped bales of spare clothing, and the explorer thrilled when he saw that it was unmistakably the clothing of a century and a half before. In another room he found numerous odds and ends of modern clothing, as if gradual provisions were being made to equip a large body of men. But what he disliked most of all were the huge copper vats which occasionally appeared; these, and the sinister incrustations upon them. He liked them even less than the weirdly figured leaden bowls whose rims retained such obnoxious deposits and around which clung repellent odours perceptible above even the general noisomeness of the crypt. When he had completed about half the entire circuit of the wall he found another corridor like that from which he had come, and out of which many doors opened. This he proceeded to investigate; and after entering three rooms of medium size and of no significant contents, he came at last to a large oblong apartment whose business-like tanks and tables, furnaces and modern instruments, occasional books and endless shelves of jars and bottles proclaimed it indeed the long-sought laboratory of Charles Ward—and no doubt of old Joseph Curwen before him.

After lighting the three lamps which he found filled and ready, Dr. Willett examined the place and all its appurtenances with the keenest interest; noting from the relative quantities of various reagents on the shelves that young Ward's dominant concern must have been with some branch of organic chemistry. On the whole, little could be learned from the scientific ensemble, which included a gruesome-looking dissecting-table; so that the room was really rather a disappointment. Among the books was a tattered old copy of Borellus in black-letter, and it was weirdly interesting to note that Ward had underlined the same passage whose marking had so perturbed good Mr. Merritt at Curwen's farmhouse more than a century and a half before. That older copy, of course, must have perished along with the rest of Curwen's occult library in the final raid. Three archways opened off the laboratory, and these the doctor proceeded to sample in turn. From his cursory survey he saw that two led merely to small storerooms; but these he canvassed with care, remarking the piles of coffins in various stages of damage and shuddering violently at two or three of the few coffin-plates he could decipher. There was much clothing also stored in these rooms, and several new and tightly nailed boxes which he did not stop to investigate. Most interesting of all, perhaps, were some odd bits which he judged to be fragments of old Joseph Curwen's laboratory appliances. These had suffered damage at the hands of the raiders, but were still partly recognisable as the chemical paraphernalia of the Georgian period.

The third archway led to a very sizeable chamber entirely lined with shelves and having in the centre a table bearing two lamps. These lamps Willett lighted, and in their brilliant glow studied the endless shelving which surrounded him. Some of the upper levels were wholly vacant, but most of the space was

188. A one-handled jug or cup, in the style found in the tombs at Phaleron, near Athens.

This lekythos depicts Theseus and is Eritrean, ca. 500 BCE.

filled with small odd-looking leaden jars of two general types; one tall and without handles like a Grecian lekythos or oil-jug, and the other with a single handle and proportioned like a Phaleron jug.[188] All had metal stoppers, and were covered with peculiar-looking symbols moulded in low relief. In a moment the doctor noticed that these jugs were classified with great rigidity; all the lekythoi being on one side of the room with a large wooden sign reading "Custodes" above them, and all the Phalerons on the other, correspondingly labelled with a sign reading "Materia."

Each of the jars or jugs, except some on the upper shelves that turned out to be vacant, bore a cardboard tag with a number apparently referring to a catalogue; and Willett resolved to look for the latter presently. For the moment, however, he was more interested in the nature of the array as a whole; and experimentally opened several of the lekythoi and Phalerons at random with a view to a rough generalisation. The result was invariable. Both types of jar contained a small quantity of a single kind of substance; a fine dusty powder of very light weight and of many shades of dull, neutral colour. To the colours which formed the only point of variation there was no apparent method of disposal; and no distinction between what occurred in the lekythoi and what occurred in the Phalerons. A bluish-grey powder might be by the side of a pinkish-white one, and any one in a Phaleron might have its exact counterpart in a lekythos. The most individual feature about the powders was their non-adhesiveness. Willett would pour one into his hand, and upon returning it to its jug would find that no residue whatever remained on his palm.

The meaning of the two signs puzzled him, and he wondered why this battery of chemicals was separated so radically from those in glass jars on the shelves of the laboratory proper. "Custodes," "Materia"; that was the Latin for "Guards" and "Materials," respectively—and then there came a flash of memory as to where he had seen that word "Guards" before in connexion with this dreadful mystery. It was, of course, in the recent letter to Dr. Allen purporting to be from old Edwin Hutchinson; and the phrase had read: "There was no Neede to keep the Guards in Shape and eat'g off their Heads, and it made Much to be founde in Case of Trouble, as you too welle knowe." What did this signify? But wait—was there not still *another* reference to "guards"

in this matter which he had failed wholly to recall when reading
the Hutchinson letter? Back in the old non-secretive days Ward
had told him of the Eleazar Smith diary recording the spying of
Smith and Weeden on the Curwen farm, and in that dreadful
chronicle there had been a mention of conversations overheard
before the old wizard betook himself wholly beneath the earth.
There had been, Smith and Weeden insisted, terrible colloquies
wherein figured Curwen, certain captives of his, *and the guards
of those captives.* Those guards, according to Hutchinson or his
avatar, had "eaten their heads off," so that now Dr. Allen did not
keep them in *shape.* And if not *in shape,* how save as the "salts"
to which it appears this wizard band was engaged in reducing as
many human bodies or skeletons as they could?

So *that* was what these lekythoi contained; the monstrous
fruit of unhallowed rites and deeds, presumably won or cowed
to such submission as to help, when called up by some hellish
incantation, in the defence of their blasphemous master or the
questioning of those who were not so willing? Willett shuddered
at the thought of what he had been pouring in and out of his
hands, and for a moment felt an impulse to flee in panic from that
cavern of hideous shelves with their silent and perhaps watching sentinels. Then he thought of the "Materia"—in the myriad
Phaleron jugs on the other side of the room. Salts too—and if
not the salts of "guards," then the salts of what? God! Could it be
possible that here lay the mortal relics of half the titan thinkers
of all the ages; snatched by supreme ghouls from crypts where
the world thought them safe, and subject to the beck and call
of madmen who sought to drain their knowledge for some still
wilder end whose ultimate effect would concern, as poor Charles
had hinted in his frantic note, "all civilisation, all natural law,
perhaps even the fate of the solar system and the universe"? And
Marinus Bicknell Willett had sifted their dust through his hands!

Then he noticed a small door at the farther end of the room,
and calmed himself enough to approach it and examine the
crude sign chiselled above. It was only a symbol, but it filled him
with vague spiritual dread; for a morbid, dreaming friend of his
had once drawn it on paper and told him a few of the things it
means in the dark abyss of sleep. It was the sign of Koth, that
dreamers see fixed above the archway of a certain black tower

189. A powerful image, later adopted by J. R. R. Tolkien and Stephen King. "Koth" is unidentifiable.

190. This is the first indication that Willett and Carter are acquainted.

191. An oil lamp, patented in 1784 but made obsolete by kerosene lanterns; it was named after its inventor, the Swiss physicist and chemist Aimé Argand (1750–1803), and burned whale oil. Argand's lamp was a considerable technical improvement over earlier sources of illumination—it modernized wick construction, enclosed the improved flame in glass to achieve a steady burn, enabled the wick to be raised and lowered so that the oil supply and the intensity of the light could be controlled, was virtually odorless, and didn't produce smoke—as well as an aesthetic marvel. Argand also ran distilleries in Languedoc and is said to have worked informally with his friends the Montgolfier brothers on the design of their hot-air balloon.

A kylix from Capua, ca. 500 BCE.

standing alone in twilight[189]—and Willett did not like what his friend Randolph Carter had said of its powers.[190] But a moment later he forgot the sign as he recognised a new acrid odour in the stench-filled air. This was a chemical rather than animal smell, and came clearly from the room beyond the door. And it was, unmistakably, the same odour which had saturated Charles Ward's clothing on the day the doctors had taken him away. So it was here that the youth had been interrupted by the final summons? He was wiser than old Joseph Curwen, for he had not resisted. Willett, boldly determined to penetrate every wonder and nightmare this nether realm might contain, seized the small lamp and crossed the threshold. A wave of nameless fright rolled out to meet him, but he yielded to no whim and deferred to no intuition. There was nothing alive here to harm him, and he would not be stayed in his piercing of the eldritch cloud which engulfed his patient.

The room beyond the door was of medium size, and had no furniture save a table, a single chair, and two groups of curious machines with clamps and wheels, which Willett recognised after a moment as mediæval instruments of torture. On one side of the door stood a rack of savage whips, above which were some shelves bearing empty rows of shallow pedestalled cups of lead shaped like Grecian kylikes. On the other side was the table; with a powerful Argand lamp,[191] a pad and pencil, and two of the stoppered lekythoi from the shelves outside set down at irregular places as if temporarily or in haste. Willett lighted the lamp and looked carefully at the pad, to see what notes young Ward might have been jotting down when interrupted; but found nothing more intelligible than the following disjointed fragments in that crabbed Curwen chirography, which shed no light on the case as a whole:

"B. dy'd not. Escap'd into walls and founde Place below.'
'Saw olde V. saye yᵉ Sabaoth and learnt yᵉ Way."
"Rais'd Yog-Sothoth thrice and was yᵉ nexte Day deliver'd."
"F. soughte to wipe out all know'g howe to raise Those from Outside."

As the strong Argand blaze lit up the entire chamber the doctor saw that the wall opposite the door, between the two groups of torturing appliances in the corners, was covered with pegs from which hung a set of shapeless-looking robes of a rather dismal yellowish-white. But far more interesting were the two vacant walls, both of which were thickly covered with mystic symbols and formulæ roughly chiselled in the smooth dressed stone. The damp floor also bore marks of carving; and with but little difficulty Willett deciphered a huge pentagram in the centre, with a plain circle about three feet wide half way between this and each corner. In one of these four circles, near where a yellowish robe had been flung carelessly down, there stood a shallow kylix of the sort found on the shelves above the whip-rack; and just outside the periphery was one of the Phaleron jugs from the shelves in the other room, its tag numbered 118. This was unstopped, and proved upon inspection to be empty; but the explorer saw with a shiver that the kylix was not. Within its shallow area, and saved from scattering only by the absence of wind in this sequestered cavern, lay a small amount of a dry, dull-greenish efflorescent powder which must have belonged in the jug; and Willett almost reeled at the implications that came sweeping over him as he correlated little by little the several elements and antecedents of the scene. The whips and the instruments of torture, the dust or salts from the jug of "Materia," the two lekythoi from the "Custodes" shelf, the robes, the formulæ on the walls, the notes on the pad, the hints from letters and legends, and the thousand glimpses, doubts, and suppositions which had come to torment the friends and parents of Charles Ward—all these engulfed the doctor in a tidal wave of horror as he looked at that dry greenish powder outspread in the pedestalled leaden kylix on the floor.

With an effort, however, Willett pulled himself together and began studying the formulæ chiselled on the walls. From the stained and incrusted letters it was obvious that they were carved in Joseph Curwen's time, and their text was such as to be vaguely familiar to one who had read much Curwen material or delved extensively into the history of magic. One the doctor clearly recognised as what Mrs. Ward heard her son chanting on that ominous Good Friday a year before, and what an authority had told him was a very terrible invocation addressed to secret gods outside the normal spheres. It was not spelled here exactly as Mrs. Ward had set it down from memory, nor yet as the authority had shewn it to him in the forbidden pages of "Eliphas Levi"; but its identity was unmistakable, and such words as *Sabaoth, Metraton, Almousin,* and *Zariatnatmik* sent a shudder of fright through the searcher who had seen and felt so much of cosmic abomination just around the corner.

This was on the left-hand wall as one entered the room. The right-hand wall was no less thickly inscribed, and Willett felt a start of recognition as he came upon the pair of formulæ so frequently occurring in the recent notes in the library. They were, roughly speaking, the same; with the ancient symbols of "Dragon's Head" and "Dragon's Tail" heading them as in Ward's scribblings. But the spelling differed quite widely from that of the modern versions, as if old Curwen had had a different way of recording sound, or as if later study had evolved more powerful and perfected variants of the invocations in question. The doctor tried to reconcile the chiselled version with the one which still ran persistently in his head, and found it hard to do. Where the script he had memorised began *"Y'ai 'ng'ngah, Yog-Sothoth,"* this epigraph started out as *"Aye, engengah, Yogge-Sothotha"*; which to his mind would seriously interfere with the syllabification of the second word.

Ground as the later text was into his consciousness, the discrepancy disturbed him; and he found himself chanting the first of the formulæ aloud in an effort to square the sound he conceived with the letters he found carved. Weird and menacing in that abyss of antique blasphemy rang his voice; its accents keyed to a droning sing-song either through the spell of the past and the unknown, or through the hellish example of that dull, godless wail from the pits whose inhuman cadences rose and fell rhythmically in the distance through the stench and the darkness.

> Y'AI 'NG'NGAH,
> YOG-SOTHOTH
> H'EE-L'GEB
> F'AI THRODOG
> UAAAH!

But what was this cold wind which had sprung into life at the very outset of the chant? The lamps were sputtering woefully, and the gloom grew so dense that the letters on the wall nearly faded from sight. There was smoke, too, and an acrid odour which quite drowned out the stench from the far-away wells; an odour like that he had smelt before, yet infinitely stronger and more pungent. He turned from the inscriptions to face the room with its bizarre contents, and saw that the kylix on the floor, in which the ominous efflorescent powder had lain, was giving forth a cloud of thick, greenish-black vapour of surprising volume and opacity. That powder—Great God! it had come from the shelf of "Materia"—what was it doing now, and what had started it? The formula he had been chanting—the first of the pair—Dragon's Head, *ascending node*—Blessed Saviour, could it be . . .

The doctor reeled, and through his head raced wildly disjointed scraps from all he had seen, heard, and read of the frightful case of Joseph Curwen and Charles Dexter Ward. "I say to you againe, doe not call up Any that you can not put downe . . . Have y^e Wordes for laying at all times readie, and stopp not to be sure when there is any Doubte of *Whom* you have . . . Three Talkes with *What* was therein inhum'd . . ." *Mercy of Heaven, what is that shape behind the parting smoke?*

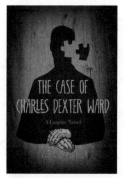

Cover of *The Case of Charles Dexter Ward: A Graphic Novel*, adapted by I. N. J. Culbard (London: SelfMadeHero, 2012).

5.

Marinus Bicknell Willett has no hope that any part of his tale will be believed except by certain sympathetic friends, hence he has made no attempt to tell it beyond his most intimate circle. Only a few outsiders have ever heard it repeated, and of these the majority laugh and remark that the doctor surely is getting old. He has been advised to take a long vacation and to shun future cases dealing with mental disturbance. But Mr. Ward knows that the veteran physician speaks only a horrible truth. Did not he himself see the noisome aperture in the bungalow cellar? Did not Willett send him home overcome and ill at eleven o'clock that portentous morning? Did he not telephone the doctor in vain that evening, and again the next day, and had he not driven to the bungalow itself on that following noon, finding his friend unconscious but unharmed on one of the beds upstairs? Willett had been breathing stertorously, and opened his eyes slowly when Mr. Ward gave him some brandy fetched from the car.

Then he shuddered and screamed, crying out, "*That beard . . . those eyes. . . . God, who are you?*" A very strange thing to say to a trim, blue-eyed, clean-shaven gentleman whom he had known from the latter's boyhood.

In the bright noon sunlight the bungalow was unchanged since the previous morning. Willett's clothing bore no disarrangement beyond certain smudges and worn places at the knees, and only a faint acrid odour reminded Mr. Ward of what he had smelt on his son that day he was taken to the hospital. The doctor's flashlight was missing, but his valise was safely there, as empty as when he had brought it. Before indulging in any explanations, and obviously with great moral effort, Willett staggered dizzily down to the cellar and tried the fateful platform before the tubs. It was unyielding. Crossing to where he had left his yet unused tool satchel the day before, he obtained a chisel and began to pry up the stubborn planks one by one. Underneath the smooth concrete was still visible, but of any opening or perforation there was no longer a trace. Nothing yawned this time to sicken the mystified father who had followed the doctor downstairs; only the smooth concrete underneath the planks—no noisome well, no world of subterrene horrors, no secret library, no Curwen papers, no nightmare pits of stench and howling, no laboratory or shelves or chiselled formulæ, no . . . Dr. Willett turned pale, and clutched at the younger man. "Yesterday," he asked softly, "did you see it here . . . and smell it?" And when Mr. Ward, himself transfixed with dread and wonder, found strength to nod an affirmative, the physician gave a sound half a sigh and half a gasp, and nodded in turn. "Then I will tell you," he said.

So for an hour, in the sunniest room they could find upstairs, the physician whispered his frightful tale to the wondering father. There was nothing to relate beyond the looming up of that form when the greenish-black vapour from the kylix parted, and Willett was too tired to ask himself what had really occurred. There were futile, bewildered head-shakings from both men, and once Mr. Ward ventured a hushed suggestion, "Do you suppose it would be of any use to dig?" The doctor was silent, for it seemed hardly fitting for any human brain to answer when powers of unknown spheres had so vitally encroached on this side of the Great Abyss. Again Mr. Ward asked, "But where did it go? It brought you here, you know, and it sealed up the hole somehow." And Willett again let silence answer for him.

But after all, this was not the final phase of the matter. Reaching for his handkerchief before rising to leave, Dr. Willett's fingers closed upon a piece of paper in his pocket which had not been there before, and which was companioned by the candles and matches he had seized in the vanished vault. It was a common sheet, torn obviously from the cheap pad in that fabulous room of horror somewhere underground, and the writing upon it was that of an ordinary lead pencil—doubtless the one which had lain beside the pad. It was folded very carelessly, and beyond the faint acrid scent of the cryptic chamber bore no print or mark of any world but this. But in the text itself it did indeed reek with wonder; for here was no script of any wholesome age, but the laboured strokes of mediæval darkness, scarcely legible to the laymen who now strained over it, yet having combinations of symbols which seemed vaguely familiar. The briefly scrawled message was this, and its mystery lent purpose to the shaken pair, who forthwith walked steadily out to the Ward car and gave orders to be driven first to a quiet dining place and then to the John Hay Library on the hill.

At the library it was easy to find good manuals of palæography, and over these the two men puzzled till the lights of evening shone out from the great chandelier. In the end they found what

John Hay Library, in 2010. Photograph copyright © Donovan K. Loucks 2010, reprinted with permission

192. A mixture of nitric acid and water, used to dissolve silver and other alchemical metals.

was needed. The letters were indeed no fantastic invention, but the normal script of a very dark period. They were the pointed Saxon minuscules of the eighth or ninth century A.D., and brought with them memories of an uncouth time when under a fresh Christian veneer ancient faiths and ancient rites stirred stealthily, and the pale moon of Britain looked sometimes on strange deeds in the Roman ruins of Cærleon and Hexham, and by the towers along Hadrian's crumbling wall. The words were in such Latin as a barbarous age might remember—"*Corvinus necandus est. Cadaver aq(ua) forti dissolvendum, nec aliq(ui)d retinendum. Tace ut potes.*"—which may roughly be translated, "Curwen must be killed. The body must be dissolved in aqua fortis,[192] nor must anything be retained. Keep silence as best you are able."

Willett and Mr. Ward were mute and baffled. They had met the unknown, and found that they lacked emotions to respond to it as they vaguely believed they ought. With Willett, especially, the capacity for receiving fresh impressions of awe was well-nigh exhausted; and both men sat still and helpless till the closing of the library forced them to leave. Then they drove listlessly to the Ward mansion in Prospect Street, and talked to no purpose into the night. The doctor rested toward morning, but did not go home. And he was still there Sunday noon when a telephone message came from the detectives who had been assigned to look up Dr. Allen.

Mr. Ward, who was pacing nervously about in a dressing-gown, answered the call in person; and told the men to come up early the next day when he heard their report was almost ready. Both Willett and he were glad that this phase of the matter was taking form, for whatever the origin of the strange minuscule message, it seemed certain that the "Curwen" who must be destroyed could be no other than the bearded and spectacled stranger. Charles had feared this man, and had said in the frantic note that he must be killed and dissolved in acid. Allen, moreover, had been receiving letters from the strange wizards in Europe under the name of Curwen, and palpably regarded himself as an avatar of the bygone necromancer. And now from a fresh and unknown source had come a message saying that "Curwen" must be killed and dissolved in acid. The linkage was too unmistakable to be factitious; and besides, was not Allen planning to murder young Ward upon the advice of the creature called Hutchinson? Of course, the letter they had seen had never reached the bearded stranger; but from its text they could see that Allen had already formed plans for dealing with the youth if he grew too "squeamish." Without doubt, Allen must be apprehended; and even if the most drastic directions were not carried out, he must be placed where he could inflict no harm upon Charles Ward.

That afternoon, hoping against hope to extract some gleam of information anent the inmost mysteries from the only available one capable of giving it, the father and the doctor went down the bay and called on young Charles at the hospital. Simply and gravely Willett told him all he had found, and noticed how pale he turned as each description made certain the truth of the discovery. The physician employed as much dramatic effect as he could, and watched for a wincing on Charles's part when he approached the matter of the covered pits and the nameless hybrids within. But Ward did not wince. Willett paused, and his voice grew indignant as he spoke of how the things were starving. He taxed the youth with shocking inhumanity, and shivered when only a sardonic laugh came in reply. For Charles, having dropped as useless his pretence that the crypt did not exist, seemed to see some ghastly jest in this affair; and chuckled hoarsely at something which amused him. Then he whispered, in accents doubly terrible because of the cracked voice he used, "Damn 'em, they *do* eat, but they *don't need to!* That's the rare part! A month, you say, without food? Lud, Sir, you be modest! D'ye know, that was the joke on poor old Whipple with his virtuous bluster! Kill everything off, would he? Why, damme, he was half-deaf with the noise from Outside and never saw or heard aught from the wells! He never dreamed they were there at all! Devil take ye, *those cursed things have been howling down there ever since Curwen was done for a hundred and fifty-seven years gone!*"

But no more than this could Willett get from the youth. Horrified, yet almost convinced against his will, he went on with his tale in the hope that some incident might startle his auditor out of the mad composure he maintained. Looking at the youth's face, the doctor could not but feel a kind of terror at the changes which recent months had wrought. Truly, the boy had drawn down nameless horrors from the skies. When the room with the formulæ and the greenish dust was mentioned, Charles shewed his first sign of animation. A quizzical look overspread his face as he heard what Willett had read on the pad, and he ventured the mild statement that those notes were old ones, of no possible significance to anyone not deeply initiated in the history of magic. "But," he added, "had you but known the words to bring up that which I had out in the cup, you had not been here to tell me this. 'Twas Number 118, and I conceive you would have shook had you looked it up in my list in t'other room. 'Twas never raised by me, but I meant to have it up that day you came to invite me hither."

Then Willett told of the formula he had spoken and of the greenish-black smoke which had arisen; and as he did so he saw true fear dawn for the first time on Charles Ward's face. "It *came* and you be here alive?" As Ward croaked the words his voice seemed almost to burst free of its trammels and sink to cavernous abysses of uncanny resonance. Willett, gifted with a flash of inspiration, believed he saw the situation, and wove into his reply a caution from a letter he remembered. "No. 118, you say? But don't forget that *stones are all changed now in nine grounds out of ten. You are never sure till you question!*" And then, without warning, he drew forth the minuscule message and flashed it before the patient's eyes. He could have wished no stronger result, for Charles Ward fainted forthwith.

All this conversation, of course, had been conducted with the greatest secrecy lest the resident alienists accuse the father and the physician of encouraging a madman in his delusions. Unaided, too, Dr. Willett and Mr. Ward picked up the stricken youth and placed him on the couch. In reviving, the patient mumbled many times of some word which he must get to Orne and Hutchinson at once; so when his consciousness seemed fully back the doctor told him that of those strange creatures at least one was his bitter enemy, and had given Dr. Allen advice for his assassination. This revelation produced no visible effect, and before it was made the visitors could see that their host had already the look of a hunted man. After that he would converse no more, so Willett and the father departed presently; leaving behind a caution against the bearded Allen, to which the youth only replied that this individual was very safely taken care of, and could do no one any harm even if he wished. This was said with an almost evil chuckle very painful to hear. They did not worry about any communications Charles might indite to that monstrous pair in Europe, since they knew that the hospital authorities seized all outgoing mail for censorship and would pass no wild or outré-looking missive.

There is, however, a curious sequel to the matter of Orne and Hutchinson, if such indeed the exiled wizards were. Moved by some vague presentiment amidst the horrors of that period, Willett arranged with an international press-cutting bureau for accounts of notable current crimes and accidents in Prague and in eastern Transylvania; and after six months believed that he had found two very significant things amongst the multifarious items he received and had translated. One was the total wrecking of a house by night in the oldest quarter of Prague, and the disappearance of the evil old man called Josef Nadek, who had dwelt in it alone ever since anyone could remember. The other was a titan explosion in the Transylvanian mountains east of Rakus, and the utter extirpation with all its inmates of the ill-regarded Castle Ferenczy, whose master was so badly spoken of by peasants and soldiery alike that he would shortly have been summoned to Bucharest for serious questioning had not this incident cut off a career already so long as to antedate all common memory. Willett maintains that the hand which wrote those minuscules was able to wield stronger weapons as well; and that while Curwen was left to him to dispose of, the writer felt able to find and deal with Orne and Hutchinson itself. Of what their fate may have been the doctor strives sedulously not to think.

6.

The following morning Dr. Willett hastened to the Ward home to be present when the detectives arrived. Allen's destruction or imprisonment—or Curwen's if one might regard the tacit claim to reincarnation as valid—he felt must be accomplished at any cost, and he communicated this conviction to Mr. Ward as they sat waiting for the men to come. They were downstairs this time, for the upper parts of the house were beginning to be shunned because of a peculiar nauseousness which hung indefinitely about; a nauseousness which the older servants connected with some curse left by the vanished Curwen portrait.

At nine o'clock the three detectives presented themselves and immediately delivered all that they had to say. They had not, regrettably enough, located the Brava Tony Gomes as they had wished, nor had they found the least trace of Dr. Allen's source or present whereabouts; but they had managed to unearth a considerable number of local impressions and facts concerning the reticent stranger. Allen had struck Pawtuxet people as a vaguely unnatural being, and there was a universal belief that his thick sandy beard was either dyed or false—a belief conclusively upheld by the finding of such a false beard, together with a pair of dark glasses, in his room at the fateful bungalow. His voice, Mr. Ward could well testify from his one telephone conversation, had a depth and hollowness that could not be forgotten; and his glance seemed malign even through his smoked and horn-rimmed glasses. One shopkeeper, in the course of negotiations, had seen a specimen of his handwriting and declared it was very queer and crabbed; this being confirmed by pencilled notes of no clear meaning found in his room and identified by the merchant. In connexion with the vampirism rumours of the preceding summer, a majority of the gossips believed that Allen rather than Ward was the actual vampire. Statements were also obtained from the officials who had visited the bungalow after the unpleasant incident of the motor truck robbery. They had felt less of the sinister in Dr. Allen, but had recognised him as the dominant figure in the queer shadowy cottage. The place had been too dark for them to observe him clearly, but they would know him again if they saw him. His beard had looked odd, and they thought he had some slight scar above his dark spectacled right eye. As for the detectives' search of Allen's room, it yielded nothing definite save the beard and glasses, and several pencilled notes in a crabbed writing which Willett at once saw was identical with that shared by the old Curwen manuscripts and by the voluminous recent notes of young Ward found in the vanished catacombs of horror.

Dr. Willett and Mr. Ward caught something of a profound, subtle, and insidious cosmic fear from this data as it was gradually unfolded, and almost trembled in following up the vague, mad thought which had simultaneously reached their minds. The false beard and glasses—the crabbed Curwen penmanship—the old portrait and its tiny scar—*and the altered youth in the hospital with such a scar*—that deep, hollow voice on the telephone—was it not of this that Mr. Ward was reminded when his son barked forth those pitiable tones to which he now claimed to be reduced? Who had ever seen Charles and Allen together? Yes, the officials had once, but who later on? Was it not when Allen left that Charles suddenly lost his growing fright and began to live wholly at the bungalow? Curwen—Allen—Ward—in what blasphemous and abominable fusion had two ages and two persons become involved? That damnable resemblance of the picture to Charles—had it not used to stare and stare, and follow the boy around the room with its eyes? Why, too, did both Allen and Charles copy Joseph Curwen's handwriting, even when alone and off guard? And then the frightful work of those people—the lost crypt of horrors that had aged the doctor overnight; the starved monsters in the noisome pits; the awful formula which had yielded such nameless results; the message in minuscules found in Willett's pocket; the papers and the letters and all the talk of graves and "salts" and discoveries—whither did everything lead? In the end Mr. Ward did the most sensible thing. Steeling himself against any realisation of why he did it, he gave the detectives an article to be shewn to such Pawtuxet shopkeepers as had seen the portentous Dr. Allen. That article was a photograph of his luckless son, on which he now carefully drew in ink the pair of heavy glasses and the black pointed beard which the men had brought from Allen's room.

For two hours he waited with the doctor in the oppressive house where fear and miasma were slowly gathering as the empty panel in the upstairs library leered and leered and leered. Then the men returned. Yes. *The altered photograph was a very passable likeness of Dr. Allen.* Mr. Ward turned pale, and Willett wiped a suddenly dampened brow with his handkerchief. Allen—Ward—Curwen—it was becoming too hideous for coherent thought. What had the boy called out of the void, and what had it done to him? What, really, had happened from first to last? Who was this Allen who sought to kill Charles as too "squeamish," and why had his destined victim said in the postscript to that frantic letter that he must be so completely obliterated in acid? Why, too, had the minuscule message, of whose origin no one dared think, said that "Curwen" must be likewise obliterated? What was the *change*, and when had the final stage occurred? That day when his frantic note was received—he had been nervous all the morning, then there was an alteration. He had slipped out unseen and swaggered boldly in past the men hired to guard him. That was the time, when he was out. But no—had he not cried out in terror as he entered his study—this very room? What had he found there? Or wait—*what had found him?* That simulacrum which brushed boldly in without having been seen to go—was that an alien shadow and a horror forcing itself upon a trembling figure which had never gone out at all? Had not the butler spoken of queer noises?

Willett rang for the man and asked him some low-toned questions. It had, surely enough, been a bad business. There had been noises—a cry, a gasp, a choking, and a sort of clattering or creaking or thumping, or all of these. And Mr. Charles was not the same when he stalked out without a word. The butler shivered as he spoke, and sniffed at the heavy air that blew down from some open window upstairs. Terror had settled definitely upon the house, and only the business-like detectives failed to imbibe a full measure of it. Even they were restless, for this case had held vague elements in the background which pleased them not at all. Dr. Willett was thinking deeply and rapidly, and his thoughts were terrible ones. Now and then he would almost break into muttering as he ran over in his head a new, appalling, and increasingly conclusive chain of nightmare happenings.

Then Mr. Ward made a sign that the conference was over, and everyone save him and the doctor left the room. It was noon now, but shadows as of coming night seemed to engulf the phantom-haunted mansion. Willett began talking very seriously to his host, and urged that he leave a great deal of the future investigation to him. There would be, he predicted, certain obnoxious elements which a friend could bear better than a relative. As family physician he must have a free hand, and the first thing he required was a period alone and undisturbed in the abandoned library upstairs, where the ancient overmantel had gathered about itself an aura of noisome horror more intense than when Joseph Curwen's features themselves glanced slyly down from the painted panel.

Mr. Ward, dazed by the flood of grotesque morbidities and unthinkably maddening suggestions that poured in upon him from every side, could only acquiesce; and half an hour later the doctor was locked in the shunned room with the panelling from Olney Court. The father, listening outside, heard fumbling sounds of moving and rummaging as the moments passed; and finally a wrench and a creak, as if a tight cupboard door were being opened. Then there was a muffled cry, a kind of snorting choke, and a hasty slamming of whatever had been opened. Almost at once the key rattled and Willett appeared in the hall, haggard and ghastly, and demanding wood for the real fireplace on the south wall of the room. The furnace was not enough, he said; and the electric log had little practical use. Longing yet not daring to ask questions, Mr. Ward gave the requisite orders and a man brought some stout pine logs, shuddering as he entered the tainted air of the library to place them in the grate. Willett meanwhile had gone up to the dismantled laboratory and brought down a few odds and ends not included in the moving of the July before. They were in a covered basket, and Mr. Ward never saw what they were.

Then the doctor locked himself in the library once more, and by the clouds of smoke which rolled down past the windows from the chimney it was known that he had lighted the fire. Later, after a great rustling of newspapers, that odd wrench and creaking were heard again; followed by a thumping which none of the eavesdroppers liked. Thereafter two suppressed cries of Willett's were heard, and hard upon these came a swishing rustle of indefinable hatefulness. Finally the smoke that the wind beat down from the chimney grew very dark and acrid, and everyone wished that the weather had spared them this choking and venomous inundation of peculiar fumes. Mr. Ward's head reeled, and the servants all clustered together in a knot to watch the horrible black smoke swoop down. After an age of waiting the vapours seemed to lighten, and half-formless sounds of scraping, sweeping, and other minor operations were heard behind the bolted door. And at last, after the slamming of some cupboard within, Willett made his appearance—sad, pale, and haggard, and bearing the cloth-draped basket he had taken from the upstairs laboratory. He had left the window open, and into that once accursed room was pouring a wealth of pure, wholesome air to mix with a queer new smell of disinfectants. The ancient overmantel still lingered; but it seemed robbed of malignity now, and rose as calm and stately in its white panelling as if it had never borne the picture of Joseph Curwen. Night was coming on, yet this time its shadows held no latent fright, but only a gentle melancholy. Of what he had done the doctor would never speak. To Mr. Ward he said, "I can answer no questions, but I will say that there are different kinds of magic. I have made a great purgation, and those in this house will sleep the better for it."

7.

That Dr. Willett's "purgation" had been an ordeal almost as nerve-racking in its way as his hideous wandering in the vanished crypt is shewn by the fact that the elderly physician gave out completely as soon as he reached home that evening. For three days he rested constantly in his room, though servants later muttered something about having heard him after midnight on Wednesday, when the outer door softly opened and closed with phenomenal softness. Servants' imaginations, fortunately, are limited, else comment might have been excited by an item in Thursday's *Evening Bulletin* which ran as follows:

NORTH END GHOULS ACTIVE AGAIN

After a lull of ten months since the dastardly vandalism in the Weeden lot at the North Burial Ground, a nocturnal prowler was glimpsed early this morning in the same cemetery by Robert Hart, the night watchman. Happening to glance for a moment from his shelter at about 2 A.M., Hart observed the glow of a lantern or pocket torch not far to the northwest, and upon opening the door detected the figure of a man with a trowel very plainly silhouetted against a nearby electric light. At once starting in pursuit, he saw the figure dart hurriedly toward the main entrance, gaining the street and losing himself among the shadows before approach or capture was possible.

Like the first of the ghouls active during the past year, this intruder had done no real damage before detection. A vacant part of the Ward lot shewed signs of a little superficial digging, but nothing even nearly the size of a grave had been attempted, and no previous grave had been disturbed.

Hart, who cannot describe the prowler except as a small man probably having a full beard, inclines to the view that all three of the digging incidents have a common source; but police from the Second Station think otherwise on account of the savage nature of the second incident, where an ancient coffin was removed and its headstone violently shattered.

The first of the incidents, in which it is thought an attempt to bury something was frustrated, occurred a year ago last March, and has been attributed to bootleggers seeking a cache. It is possible, says Sergt. Riley, that this third affair is of similar nature. Officers at the Second Station are taking especial pains to capture the gang of miscreants responsible for these repeated outrages.

All day Thursday Dr. Willett rested as if recuperating from something past or nerving himself for something to come. In the evening he wrote a note to Mr. Ward, which was delivered the next morning and which caused the half-dazed parent to ponder long and deeply. Mr. Ward had not been able to go down to business since the shock of Monday with its baffling reports and its sinister "purgation," but he found something calming about the doctor's letter in spite of the despair it seemed to promise and the fresh mysteries it seemed to evoke.

10 Barnes St.
Providence, R. I.
April 12, 1928.

Dear Theodore:—

I feel that I must say a word to you before doing what I am going to do tomorrow. It will conclude the terrible business we have been going through (for I feel that no spade is ever likely to reach that

10 Barnes Street, in 2010. Photograph copyright © Donovan K. Loucks 2010, reprinted with permission

monstrous place we know of), but I'm afraid it won't set your mind at rest unless I expressly assure you how very conclusive it is.

You have known me ever since you were a small boy, so I think you will not distrust me when I hint that some matters are best left undecided and unexplored. It is better that you attempt no further speculation as to Charles's case, and almost imperative that you tell his mother nothing more than she already suspects. When I call on you tomorrow Charles will have escaped. That is all which need remain in anyone's mind. He was mad, and he escaped. You can tell his mother gently and gradually about the mad part when you stop sending the typed notes in his name. I'd advise you to join her in Atlantic City and take a rest yourself. God knows you need one after this shock, as I do myself. I am going South for a while to calm down and brace up.

So don't ask me any questions when I call. It may be that some-thing will go wrong, but I'll tell you if it does. I don't think it will. There will be nothing more to worry about, for Charles will be very, very safe. He is now—safer than you dream. You need hold no fears about Allen, and who or what he is. He forms as much a part of the past as Joseph Curwen's picture, and when I ring your doorbell you may feel certain that there is no such person. And what wrote that minuscule message will never trouble you or yours.

But you must steel yourself to melancholy, and prepare your wife to do the same. I must tell you frankly that Charles's escape will not mean his restoration to you. He has been afflicted with a peculiar disease, as you must realise from the subtle physical as well as mental changes in him, and you must not hope to see him again. Have only this consolation—that he was never a fiend or even truly a madman, but only an eager, studious, and curious boy whose love of mystery and of the past was his undoing. He stumbled on things no mortal ought ever to know, and reached back through the years as no one ever should reach; and something came out of those years to engulf him.

And now comes the matter in which I must ask you to trust me most of all. For there will be, indeed, no uncertainty about Charles's fate. In about a year, say, you can if you wish devise a suitable account of the end; for the boy will be no more. You can put up a stone in your lot at the North Burial Ground exactly ten feet west of your father's and facing the same way, and that will mark the true resting-place of your son. Nor need you fear that it will mark any abnormality or changeling. The ashes in that grave will be those of your own unaltered bone and sinew—of the real Charles Dexter Ward whose mind you watched from infancy—the real Charles with the olive-mark on his hip and without the black witch-mark on his chest or the pit on his forehead. The Charles who never did actual evil, and who will have paid with his life for his "squeamishness."

That is all. Charles will have escaped, and a year from now you can put up his stone. Do not question me tomorrow. And believe that the honour of your ancient family remains untainted now, as it has been at all times in the past.

With profoundest sympathy, and exhortations to fortitude, calmness, and resignation, I am ever

Sincerely your friend,
Marinus B. Willett.

So on the morning of Friday, April 13, 1928, Marinus Bicknell Willett visited the room of Charles Dexter Ward at Dr. Waite's private hospital on Conanicut Island. The youth, though making no attempt to evade his caller, was in a sullen mood; and seemed disinclined to open the conversation which Willett obviously desired. The doctor's discovery of the crypt and his monstrous experience therein had of course created a new source of embarrassment, so that both hesitated perceptibly after the interchange of a few strained formalities. Then a new element of constraint crept in, as Ward seemed to read behind the doctor's mask-like face a terrible purpose which had never been there before. The patient quailed, conscious that since the last visit there had been a change whereby the solicitous family physician had given place to the ruthless and implacable avenger.

Ward actually turned pale, and the doctor was the first to speak. "More," he said, "has been found out, and I must warn you fairly that a reckoning is due."

"Digging again, and coming upon more poor starving pets?" was the ironic reply. It was evident that the youth meant to shew bravado to the last.

"No," Willett slowly rejoined, "this time I did not have to dig. We have had men looking up Dr. Allen, and they found the false beard and spectacles in the bungalow."

"Excellent," commented the disquieted host in an effort to be wittily insulting, "and I trust they proved more becoming than the beard and glasses you now have on!"

"They would become you very well," came the even and studied response, "*as indeed they seem to have done.*"

As Willett said this, it almost seemed as though a cloud passed over the sun; though there was no change in the shadows on the floor. Then Ward ventured:

"And is this what asks so hotly for a reckoning? Suppose a man does find it now and then useful to be twofold?"

"No," said Willett gravely, "again you are wrong. It is no business of mine if any man seeks duality; *provided he has any right to exist at all, and provided he does not destroy what called him out of space.*"

Ward now started violently. "Well, Sir, what *have* ye found, and what d'ye want with me?"

The doctor let a little time elapse before replying, as if choosing his words for an effective answer.

"I have found," he finally intoned, "something in a cupboard behind an ancient overmantel where a picture once was, and I have burned it and buried the ashes where the grave of Charles Dexter Ward ought to be."

The madman choked and sprang from the chair in which he had been sitting: "Damn ye, who did ye tell—and who'll believe it was he after these full two months, with me alive? What d'ye mean to do?"

Willett, though a small man, actually took on a kind of judicial majesty as he calmed the patient with a gesture.

"I have told no one. This is no common case—it is a madness out of time and a horror from beyond the spheres which no police or lawyers or courts or alienists could ever fathom or grapple with. Thank God some chance has left inside me the spark of imagination, that I might not go astray in thinking out this thing. *You cannot deceive me, Joseph Curwen, for I know that your accursed magic is true!*

"I know how you wove the spell that brooded outside the years and fastened on your double and descendant; I know how you drew him into the past and got him to raise you up from your detestable grave; I know how he kept you hidden in his laboratory while you studied modern things and roved abroad as a vampire by night, and how you later shewed yourself in beard and glasses that no one might wonder at your godless likeness to him; I know what you resolved to do when he balked at your monstrous rifling of the world's tombs, *and at what you planned afterward*, and I know how you did it.

"You left off your beard and glasses and fooled the guards around the house. They thought it was he who went in, and they thought it was he who came out when you had strangled and hidden him. But you hadn't reckoned on the different contents of two minds. You were a fool, Curwen, to fancy that a mere visual identity would be enough. Why didn't you think of the speech and the voice and the handwriting? It hasn't worked, you see, after all. You know better than I who or what wrote that message in minuscules, but I will warn you it was not written in vain. There are abominations and blasphemies which must be stamped out, and I believe that the writer of those words will attend to Orne and Hutchinson. One of those creatures wrote you once, 'do not call up any that you can not put down.' You were undone once before, perhaps in that very way, and it may be that your own evil magic will undo you all again. Curwen, a man can't tamper with Nature beyond certain limits, and every horror you have woven will rise up to wipe you out."

But here the doctor was cut short by a convulsive cry from the creature before him. Hopelessly at bay, weaponless, and knowing that any show of physical violence would bring a score of attendants to the doctor's rescue, Joseph Curwen had recourse to his one ancient ally, and began a series of cabbalistic motions with his forefingers as his deep, hollow voice, now unconcealed by feigned hoarseness, bellowed out the opening words of a terrible formula.

"PER ADONAI ELOIM, ADONAI JEHOVA, ADONAI SABAOTH, METRATON . . ."

But Willett was too quick for him. Even as the dogs in the yard outside began to howl, and even as a chill wind sprang suddenly up from the bay, the doctor commenced the solemn and measured intonation of that which he had meant all along to recite. An eye for an eye—magic for magic—let the outcome shew how well the lesson of the abyss had been learned! So in a clear voice Marinus Bicknell Willett began the *second* of that pair of formulæ whose first had raised the writer of those minuscules—the cryptic invocation whose heading was the Dragon's Tail, sign of the *descending node*—

"OGTHROD AI'F GEB'L-EE'H YOG-SOTHOTH 'NGAH'NG AI'Y ZHRO!"

At the very first word from Willett's mouth the previously commenced formula of the patient stopped short. Unable to speak, the monster made wild motions with his arms until they too were arrested. When the awful name of *Yog-Sothoth* was uttered, the hideous change began. It was not merely a *dissolution*, but rather a *transformation* or *recapitulation*; and Willett shut his eyes lest he faint before the rest of the incantation could be pronounced.

But he did not faint, and that man of unholy centuries and forbidden secrets never troubled the world again. The madness out of time had subsided, and the case of Charles Dexter Ward was closed. Opening his eyes before staggering out of that room of horror, Dr. Willett saw that what he had kept in memory had not been kept amiss. There had, as he had predicted, been no need for acids. For like his accursed picture a year before, Joseph Curwen now lay scattered on the floor as a thin coating of fine bluish-grey dust.

The Colour Out of Space[1]

This, Lovecraft's favorite story, is the first major tale of his to combine classic science fiction (before the genre even existed) and horror. "The Call of Cthulhu" may have suggested that terror could come from the stars, but here the fear is concrete and localized in New England. The banal depictions of the fruitless scientific investigations contrast starkly with the inexplicable, gradual destruction of the Gardner family. Preceding the famous Orson Welles broadcast of War of the Worlds *by more than ten years, the story brought home the fear of alien invasion.*

1. Written in March 1927, the tale first appeared in *Amazing Stories* 2, no. 6 (September 1927), 557–67.

From *The Night Side: Masterpieces of the Strange and Terrible.* New York: Rinehart & Co., 1947 (artist: Lee Brown Coye)

West of Arkham the hills rise wild, and there are valleys with deep woods that no axe has ever cut. There are dark narrow glens where the trees slope fantastically, and where thin brooklets trickle without ever having caught the glint of sunlight. On the gentler slopes there are farms, ancient and rocky, with squat, moss-coated cottages brooding eternally over old New England secrets in the lee of great ledges; but these are all vacant now, the wide chimneys crumbling and the shingled sides bulging perilously beneath low gambrel roofs.

The old folk have gone away, and foreigners do not like to live there. French-Canadians have tried it, Italians have tried it, and the Poles have come and departed. It is not because of anything that can be seen or heard or handled, but because of something that is imagined. The place is not good for the imagination, and does not bring restful dreams at night. It must be this which keeps the foreigners away, for old Ammi Pierce has never told them of anything he recalls from the strange days. Ammi, whose head has been a little queer for years, is the only one who still remains, or who ever talks of the strange days; and he dares to do this because his house is so near the open fields and the travelled roads around Arkham.

There was once a road over the hills and through the valleys, that ran straight where the blasted heath is now; but people ceased to use it and a new road was laid curving far toward the south. Traces of the old one can still be found amidst the weeds of a returning wilderness, and some of them will doubtless linger even when half the hollows are flooded for the new reservoir.[2] Then the dark woods will be cut down and the blasted heath will slumber far below blue waters whose surface will mirror the sky and ripple in the sun. And the secrets of the strange days will be one with the deep's secrets; one with the hidden lore of old ocean, and all the mystery of primal earth.

When I went into the hills and vales to survey for the new reservoir they told me the place was evil. They told me this in Arkham, and because that is a very old town full of witch legends I thought the evil must be something which grandams had whispered to children through centuries. The name "blasted heath" seemed to me very odd and theatrical, and I wondered how it had come into the folklore of a Puritan people. Then I saw that dark westward tangle of glens and slopes for myself, and ceased to wonder at anything besides its own elder mystery. It was morning when I saw it, but shadow lurked always there. The trees grew too thickly, and their trunks were too big for any healthy New England wood.[3] There was too much silence in the dim alleys

2. It is likely that the narrator speaks of the intended Quabbin Reservoir, for which surveys began in 1922 (although construction was delayed until 1939). Lovecraft denied that the Quabbin Reservoir was the subject of the tale; rather, he said in a letter, it was the Scituate Reservoir in Rhode Island, built in 1926 (Lovecraft to Richard Ely Morse, October 13, 1935, described in *I Am Providence*). However, Joshi does not trust Lovecraft's judgment on the source of the narrator's tale and believes that he was "also" thinking of the Quabbin Reservoir.

3. This characteristic—the alteration of the environment where darker powers rule—can be seen in "The Dunwich Horror": "The trees of the frequent forest belt seem too large. . . ." The quality was first noted by Bill Wallace in "The Untravelled Roads 'Round Arkham."

The Scituate Reservoir, shown in 2013. Photograph copyright © Donovan K. Loucks 2013, reprinted with permission

The Quabbin Reservoir in 2009.

4. An Italian Baroque painter of fantastic landscapes, he was born in 1615 and died in 1673.

5. The "blasted heath" is a phrase from Milton's *Paradise Lost* as well as Shakespeare's *Macbeth*. Which writer the narrator is indebted to is a matter of debate. Robert H. Waugh, in his essay "The Blasted Heath in 'The Colour Out of Space,'" argues that both poets were in the narrator's mind, and elements from both works appear throughout the tale.

between them, and the floor was too soft with the dank moss and mattings of infinite years of decay.

In the open spaces, mostly along the line of the old road, there were little hillside farms; sometimes with all the buildings standing, sometimes with only one or two, and sometimes with only a lone chimney or fast-filling cellar. Weeds and briers reigned, and furtive wild things rustled in the undergrowth. Upon everything was a haze of restlessness and oppression; a touch of the unreal and the grotesque, as if some vital element of perspective or chiaroscuro were awry. I did not wonder that the foreigners would not stay, for this was no region to sleep in. It was too much like a landscape of Salvator Rosa;[4] too much like some forbidden woodcut in a tale of terror.

But even all this was not so bad as the blasted heath. I knew it the moment I came upon it at the bottom of a spacious valley; for no other name could fit such a thing, or any other thing fit such a name. It was as if the poet had coined the phrase from having seen this one particular region.[5] It must, I thought as I viewed it, be the outcome of a fire; but why had nothing new ever grown over those five acres of grey desolation that sprawled open to the sky like a great spot eaten by acid in the woods and fields? It lay largely to the north of the ancient road line, but encroached a little on the other side. I felt an odd reluctance about approaching, and did so at last only because my business took me through and past it. There was no vegetation of any kind on that broad expanse, but only a fine grey dust or ash which no wind seemed ever to blow about. The trees near it were sickly and stunted, and many dead trunks stood or lay rotting at the rim. As I walked hurriedly by I saw the tumbled bricks and stones of an old chimney and cellar on my right, and the yawning black maw of an abandoned well whose stagnant vapours played strange tricks with the hues of the sunlight. Even the long, dark woodland climb beyond seemed welcome in contrast, and I marvelled no more at the frightened whispers of Arkham people. There had been no house or ruin near; even in the old days the place must have been lonely and remote. And at twilight, dreading to repass that ominous spot, I walked circuitously back to the town by the curving road on the south. I vaguely wished some clouds would gather, for an odd timidity about the deep skyey voids above had crept into my soul.

In the evening I asked old people in Arkham about the blasted heath, and what was meant by that phrase "strange days" which so many evasively muttered. I could not, however, get any good

Landscape with Tobit and the Angel by Salvator Rosa (ca. 1670).

answers except that all the mystery was much more recent than I had dreamed. It was not a matter of old legendry at all, but something within the lifetime of those who spoke. It had happened in the 'eighties, and a family had disappeared or was killed. Speakers would not be exact; and because they all told me to pay no attention to old Ammi Pierce's crazy tales, I sought him out the next morning, having heard that he lived alone in the ancient tottering cottage where the trees first begin to get very thick. It was a fearsomely archaic place, and had begun to exude the faint miasmal odour which clings about houses that have stood too long. Only with persistent knocking could I rouse the aged man, and when he shuffled timidly to the door I could tell he was not glad to see me. He was not so feeble as I had expected; but his eyes drooped in a curious way, and his unkempt clothing and white beard made him seem very worn and dismal. Not knowing just how he could best be launched on his tales, I feigned a matter of business; told him of my surveying, and asked vague questions about the district. He was far brighter and more educated than I had been led to think, and before I knew it had grasped quite as much of the subject as any man I had talked with in Arkham. He was not like other rustics I had known in the sections where reservoirs were to be. From him there were no protests at the miles of old wood and farmland to be blotted out, though perhaps there would have been had not his home lain outside the bounds of the future lake. Relief was all that he shewed; relief at the doom of the dark ancient valleys through which he had roamed all his life. They were better under water now—better under water since the strange days. And with this opening his husky voice sank low, while his body leaned forward and his right forefinger began to point shakily and impressively.

It was then that I heard the story, and as the rambling voice scraped and whispered on I shivered again and again despite the summer day. Often I had to recall the speaker from ramblings, piece out scientific points which he knew only by a fading parrot memory of professors' talk, or bridge over gaps where his sense of logic and continuity broke down. When he was done I did not wonder that his mind had snapped a trifle, or that the folk of Arkham would not speak much of the blasted heath. I hurried back before sunset to my hotel, unwilling to have the stars come out above me in the open; and the next day returned to Boston to give up my position. I could not go into that dim chaos of old forest and slope again, or face another time that grey blasted heath where the black well yawned deep beside the tumbled bricks and stones. The reservoir will soon be built now, and all those elder secrets will be safe forever under watery fathoms. But even then I do not believe I would like to visit that country by night—at least, not when the sinister stars are out; and nothing could bribe me to drink the new city water of Arkham.

It all began, old Ammi said, with the meteorite. Before that time there had been no wild legends at all since the witch trials,[6] and even then these western woods were not feared half so much as the small island in the Miskatonic where the devil held court beside a curious stone altar older than the Indians. These were not haunted woods, and their fantastic dusk was never terrible till the strange days. Then there had come that white noontide cloud, that string of explosions in the air, and that pillar of smoke from the valley far in the wood. And by night all Arkham had heard of the great rock that fell out of the sky and bedded itself in the ground beside the well at the Nahum Gardner place. That was the house which had stood where the blasted heath was to come—the trim white Nahum Gardner house amidst its fertile gardens and orchards.

Nahum had come to town to tell people about the stone, and had dropped in at Ammi Pierce's on the way. Ammi was forty then, and all the queer things were fixed very strongly in his mind. He and his wife had gone with the three professors from Miskatonic University who hastened out the next morning to see the weird visitor from unknown stellar space, and had wondered why Nahum had called it so large the day before. It had shrunk, Nahum said as he pointed out the big brownish mound above the ripped earth and charred grass near the archaic well-sweep[7] in his front yard; but the wise men answered that stones do not shrink. Its heat lingered persistently, and Nahum declared it had glowed faintly in the night. The professors tried it with a geologist's hammer and found it was oddly soft. It was, in truth, so soft as to be almost plastic; and they gouged rather than chipped a specimen to take back to the college for testing. They took it in an old pail borrowed from Nahum's kitchen, for even the small piece refused to grow cool. On the trip back they stopped at Ammi's

6. The Salem Witch Trials, that is. See "The Festival," note 11, above.

7. A device for raising and lowering buckets into a well.

A well-sweep.

8. Gases embedded in minerals, released in the process of heating metal or dissolving crystals or occasionally simply by cracking the structure. Such gases are a problem to be dealt with in mining, where they can be poisonous or explosive.

9. A test developed by the Swedish chemist Jöns Jacob Berzelius in 1812 to check for the presence of certain metals in substances.

10. A device invented in 1813 by American chemist Robert Hare and British mineralogist Edward Daniel Clarke to produce a high-temperature flame, used for chemical analysis—now superseded by the oxyacetylene blowpipe.

11. A scientific instrument permitting the analysis of the components of metals by study of the spectrum of colors displayed upon heating the metal to incandescence. German oculist Joseph von Fraunhofer (1787–1826) first understood that the lines of the spectrum displayed by materials revealed their composition, but his work depended on a simple prism to diffract the light source to a separate viewing scope, and detailed measurements were difficult to perform. It was not until 1859 that two scientists, Robert Bunsen and Gustav Kirchoff, working on an older experiment of passing sunlight through a strong sodium flame, developed the first spectroscope. The spectroscope that Bunsen and Kirchoff developed had an integrated slit, prism, and collimator.

12. A new element, protactinium, had been discovered in 1913; the next element to be discovered, technetium, was not found until 1937.

13. A mixture of nitric acid and hydrochloric acid, so-called because it dissolves the "royal" metals of gold and platinum.

to rest, and seemed thoughtful when Mrs. Pierce remarked that the fragment was growing smaller and burning the bottom of the pail. Truly, it was not large, but perhaps they had taken less than they thought.

The day after that—all this was in June of '82—the professors had trooped out again in a great excitement. As they passed Ammi's they told him what queer things the specimen had done, and how it had faded wholly away when they put it in a glass beaker. The beaker had gone, too, and the wise men talked of the strange stone's affinity for silicon. It had acted quite unbelievably in that well-ordered laboratory; doing nothing at all and shewing no occluded gases[8] when heated on charcoal, being wholly negative in the borax bead,[9] and soon proving itself absolutely non-volatile at any producible temperature, including that of the oxy-hydrogen blowpipe.[10] On an anvil it appeared highly malleable, and in the dark its luminosity was very marked. Stubbornly refusing to grow cool, it soon had the college in a state of real excitement; and when upon heating before the spectroscope[11] it displayed shining bands unlike any known colours of the normal spectrum there was much breathless talk of new elements,[12] bizarre optical properties, and other things which puzzled men of science are wont to say when faced by the unknown.

Hot as it was, they tested it in a crucible with all the proper reagents. Water did nothing. Hydrochloric acid was the same. Nitric acid and even aqua regia[13] merely hissed and spattered against its torrid invulnerability. Ammi had difficulty in recalling all these things, but recognised some solvents as I mentioned them in the usual order of use. There were ammonia and caustic soda, alcohol and ether, nauseous carbon disulphide[14] and a dozen others; but although the weight grew steadily less as time passed, and the fragment seemed to be slightly cooling, there was no change in the solvents to shew that they had attacked the substance at all. It was a metal, though, beyond a doubt. It was magnetic, for one thing; and after its immersion in the acid solvents there seemed to be faint traces of the Widmannstätten figures found on meteoric iron.[15] When the cooling had grown very considerable, the testing was carried on in glass; and it was in a glass beaker that they left all the chips made of the original fragment during the work. The next morning both chips and beaker were gone without trace, and only a charred spot marked the place on the wooden shelf where they had been.

All this the professors told Ammi as they paused at his door, and once more he went with them to see the stony messenger from the stars, though this time his wife did not accompany him. It had now most certainly shrunk, and even the sober professors could not doubt the truth of what they saw. All around the dwindling brown lump near the well was a vacant space, except where the earth had caved in; and whereas it had been a good seven feet across the day before, it was now scarcely five. It was still hot, and the sages studied its surface curiously as they detached another and larger piece with hammer and chisel. They gouged deeply this time, and as they pried away the smaller mass they saw that the core of the thing was not quite homogeneous.

They had uncovered what seemed to be the side of a large coloured globule imbedded in the substance. The colour, which resembled some of the bands in the meteor's strange spectrum, was almost impossible to describe; and it was only by analogy that they called it colour at all.[16] Its texture was glossy, and upon tapping it appeared to promise both brittleness and hollowness. One of the professors gave it a smart blow with a hammer, and it burst with a nervous little pop. Nothing was emitted, and all trace of the thing vanished with the puncturing. It left behind a hollow spherical space about three inches across, and all thought it probable that others would be discovered as the enclosing substance wasted away.

Conjecture was vain; so after a futile attempt to find additional globules by drilling, the seekers left again with their new specimen—which proved, however, as baffling in the laboratory as its predecessor had been. Aside from being almost plastic, having heat, magnetism, and slight luminosity, cooling slightly in powerful acids, possessing an unknown spectrum, wasting away in air, and attacking silicon compounds with mutual destruction as a result, it presented no identifying features whatsoever; and at the end of the tests the college scientists were forced to own that they could not place it. It was nothing of this earth, but a piece of the great outside; and as such dowered with outside properties and obedient to outside laws.[17]

That night there was a thunderstorm, and when the profes-

14. Carbon disulphide inhalation does indeed cause nausea, but many other solvents do as well.

15. The scientist Count Alois von Beckh Widmanstätten (1753–1849), born in Styria, in southeast Austria, learned the printing trade from his father as a boy and subsequently held jobs ranging from Emperor Franz Joseph I's technology officer to submanager of the Cotton Spinning and Weaving Mills of Pottendorf, a small market town situated twenty-one miles south of Vienna. The first such mill in Austria, established in 1801, it was, according to Joseph Arenstein's *Austria at the International Exhibition of 1862*, already a substantial operation in 1804, the year of Widmanstätten's employ there, with "18,000 mules and 430 throstle spindles a-going, furnishing about 12,000 knots of yarn (5 lb. Engl[ish] each) annually" (65). Widmanstätten is wrongly credited with discovering magnetic patterns in iron meteors in 1808. The discovery actually occurred sometime before 1804, when an English geologist, known only as G. Thomson, published a description of the patterns in the *Bibliothèque Britannique*. "Widmanstätten figures" are latticeworks of nickel-iron crystals, revealed by application of nitric acid.

16. Cf. Ambrose Bierce's "The Damned Thing," mentioned in "The Hound," note 16, above:

> At each end of the solar spectrum the chemist can detect the presence of what are known as "actinic" rays. They represent colors—integral colors in the composition of light—which we are unable to discern. The human eye is an imperfect instrument; its range is but a few octaves of the real "chromatic scale." I am not mad; there are colors that we cannot see.

And, God help me! the Damned
Thing is of such a color!

17. There is a long folkloric association of
gelatinous masses associated with mete-
orites, stretching back to fourteenth-
century Latin texts, according to David
Haden ("Some Notes on the Origins of
Lovecraft's 'The Colour Out of Space'" in
his *Lovecraft in Historical Context: Further
Essays and Notes*). See generally Hilary
Belcher and Erica Swale's "To Catch a
Falling Star." For example, in reporting
on a meteorite landing near Lowville,
New York, in 1846, *Scientific American*
wrote, "It [the meteor] appeared larger
than the sun, illumined the hemisphere
nearly as light as day. A large company
of the citizens immediately repaired to
the spot [of the meteorite's landing] and
found a body of fetid jelly, four feet in
diameter."

18. The stone here appears to have the
characteristics of the "thunderstones"
described by Charles Fort, in *The Book
of the Damned* (1919), supposed to have
fallen "in or with lightning"—that is,
fallen from the sky. Fort concluded that
while the stones' existence was irrefutable, the connection with lightning was
a myth and the stones were already present before lightning struck the spot (103).
See "The Whisperer in Darkness," note
10, below, for more about Fort.

sors went out to Nahum's the next day they met with a bitter
disappointment. The stone, magnetic as it had been, must have
had some peculiar electrical property; for it had "drawn the lightning," as Nahum said, with a singular persistence.[18] Six times
within an hour the farmer saw the lightning strike the furrow in
the front yard, and when the storm was over nothing remained
but a ragged pit by the ancient well-sweep, half-choked with
caved-in earth. Digging had borne no fruit, and the scientists
verified the fact of the utter vanishment. The failure was total; so
that nothing was left to do but go back to the laboratory and test
again the disappearing fragment left carefully encased in lead.
That fragment lasted a week, at the end of which nothing of
value had been learned of it. When it had gone, no residue was
left behind, and in time the professors felt scarcely sure they had
indeed seen with waking eyes that cryptic vestige of the fathomless gulfs outside; that lone, weird message from other universes
and other realms of matter, force, and entity.

As was natural, the Arkham papers made much of the incident with its collegiate sponsoring, and sent reporters to talk
with Nahum Gardner and his family. At least one Boston daily
also sent a scribe, and Nahum quickly became a kind of local
celebrity. He was a lean, genial person of about fifty, living with
his wife and three sons on the pleasant farmstead in the valley.
He and Ammi exchanged visits frequently, as did their wives; and
Ammi had nothing but praise for him after all these years. He
seemed slightly proud of the notice his place had attracted, and
talked often of the meteorite in the succeeding weeks. That July
and August were hot, and Nahum worked hard at his haying in
the ten-acre pasture across Chapman's Brook; his rattling wain
wearing deep ruts in the shadowy lanes between. The labour
tired him more than it had in other years, and he felt that age
was beginning to tell on him.

Then fell the time of fruit and harvest. The pears and apples
slowly ripened, and Nahum vowed that his orchards were prospering as never before. The fruit was growing to phenomenal size
and unwonted gloss, and in such abundance that extra barrels
were ordered to handle the future crop. But with the ripening
came sore disappointment; for of all that gorgeous array of spe-
cious lusciousness not one single jot was fit to eat. Into the fine

flavour of the pears and apples had crept a stealthy bitterness and sickishness, so that even the smallest of bites induced a lasting disgust. It was the same with the melons and tomatoes, and Nahum sadly saw that his entire crop was lost. Quick to connect events, he declared that the meteorite had poisoned the soil, and thanked Heaven that most of the other crops were in the upland lot along the road.

Winter came early, and it was very cold. Ammi saw Nahum less often than usual, and observed that he had begun to look worried. The rest of his family, too, seemed to have grown taciturn; and were far from steady in their church-going or their attendance at the various social events of the countryside. For this reserve or melancholy no cause could be found, though all the household confessed now and then to poorer health and a feeling of vague disquiet. Nahum himself gave the most definite statement of anyone when he said he was disturbed about certain footprints in the snow. They were the usual winter prints of red squirrels, white rabbits, and foxes, but the brooding farmer professed to see something not quite right about their nature and arrangement. He was never specific, but appeared to think that they were not as characteristic of the anatomy and habits of squirrels and rabbits and foxes as they ought to be. Ammi listened without interest to this talk until one night when he drove past Nahum's house in his sleigh on the way back from Clark's Corners. There had been a moon, and a rabbit had run across the road, and the leaps of that rabbit were longer than either Ammi or his horse liked. The latter, indeed, had almost run away when brought up by a firm rein. Thereafter Ammi gave Nahum's tales more respect, and wondered why the Gardner dogs seemed so cowed and quivering every morning. They had, it developed, nearly lost the spirit to bark.

In February the McGregor boys from Meadow Hill were out shooting woodchucks, and not far from the Gardner place bagged a very peculiar specimen. The proportions of its body seemed slightly altered in a queer way impossible to describe, while its face had taken on an expression which no one ever saw in a woodchuck before. The boys were genuinely frightened, and threw the thing away at once, so that only their grotesque tales of it ever reached the people of the countryside. But the shying away of the horses near Nahum's house had now become an acknowledged thing, and all the basis for a cycle of whispered legend was fast taking form.

People vowed that the snow melted faster around Nahum's than it did anywhere else, and early in March there was an awed discussion in Potter's general store at Clark's Corners. Stephen Rice had driven past Gardner's in the morning, and had noticed the skunk-cabbages coming up through the mud by the woods across the road. Never were things of such size seen before, and they held strange colours that could not be put into any words. Their shapes were monstrous, and the horse had snorted at an odour which struck Stephen as wholly unprecedented. That afternoon several persons drove past to see the abnormal growth, and all agreed that plants of that kind ought never to sprout in a healthy world. The bad fruit of the fall before was freely mentioned, and it went from mouth to mouth that there was poison in Nahum's ground. Of course it was the meteorite; and remembering how strange the men from the college had found that stone to be, several farmers spoke about the matter to them.

One day they paid Nahum a visit; but having no love of wild tales and folklore were very conservative in what they inferred. The plants were certainly odd, but all skunk-cabbages are more or less odd in shape and odour and hue. Perhaps some mineral element from the stone had entered the soil, but it would soon be washed away. And as for the footprints and frightened horses—of course this was mere country talk which such a phenomenon as the aërolite would be certain to start. There was really nothing for serious men to do in cases of wild gossip, for superstitious rustics will say and believe anything. And so all through the strange days the professors stayed away in contempt. Only one of them, when given two phials of dust for analysis in a police job over a year and a half later, recalled that the queer colour of that skunk-cabbage had been very like one of the anomalous bands of light shewn by the meteor fragment in the college spectroscope, and like the brittle globule found imbedded in the stone from the abyss. The samples in this analysis case gave the same odd bands at first, though later they lost the property.

The trees budded prematurely around Nahum's, and at night they swayed ominously in the wind. Nahum's second son Thaddeus, a lad of fifteen, swore that they swayed also when there was no wind; but even the gossips would not credit this. Certainly, however, restlessness was in the air. The entire Gardner family developed the habit of stealthy listening, though not for any sound which they could consciously name. The listening was, indeed, rather a product of moments when consciousness seemed half to slip away. Unfortunately such moments increased week by week, till it became common speech that "something was wrong with all Nahum's folks." When the early saxifrage came out it had another strange colour; not quite like that of the skunk-cabbage, but plainly related and equally unknown to anyone who saw it. Nahum took some blossoms to Arkham and shewed them to the editor of the *Gazette*, but that dignitary did no more than write a humorous article about them, in which the dark fears of rustics were held up to polite ridicule. It was a mistake of Nahum's to tell a stolid city man about the way the great, overgrown mourning-cloak butterflies behaved in connexion with these saxifrages.

April brought a kind of madness to the country folk, and began that disuse of the road past Nahum's which led to its ultimate abandonment. It was the vegetation. All the orchard trees blossomed forth in strange colours, and through the stony soil of the yard and adjacent pasturage there sprang up a bizarre growth which only a botanist could connect with the proper flora of the region. No sane wholesome colours were anywhere to be seen except in the green grass and leafage; but everywhere those hectic and prismatic variants of some diseased, underlying primary tone without a place among the known tints of earth. The Dutchman's breeches[19] became a thing of sinister menace, and the bloodroots[20] grew insolent in their chromatic perversion. Ammi and the Gardners thought that most of the colours had a sort of haunting familiarity, and decided that they reminded one of the brittle globule in the meteor. Nahum ploughed and sowed the ten-acre pasture and the upland lot, but did nothing with the land around the house. He knew it would be of no use, and hoped that the summer's strange growths would draw all the poison from the soil. He was prepared for almost anything now, and had grown used to the sense of something near him waiting to be heard. The shunning of his house by neighbours told on him, of course; but it told on his wife more. The boys were

19. A common wildflower, *Dicentra cucullaria*.

Dutchman's breeches.

20. Another pervasive wildflower, *Sanguinaria canadensis*.

Bloodroot.

better off, being at school each day; but they could not help being frightened by the gossip. Thaddeus, an especially sensitive youth, suffered the most.

In May the insects came, and Nahum's place became a nightmare of buzzing and crawling. Most of the creatures seemed not quite usual in their aspects and motions, and their nocturnal habits contradicted all former experience. The Gardners took to watching at night—watching in all directions at random for something . . . they could not tell what. It was then that they all owned that Thaddeus had been right about the trees. Mrs. Gardner was the next to see it from the window as she watched the swollen boughs of a maple against a moonlit sky. The boughs surely moved, and there was no wind. It must be the sap. Strangeness had come into everything growing now. Yet it was none of Nahum's family at all who made the next discovery. Familiarity had dulled them, and what they could not see was glimpsed by a timid windmill salesman from Bolton who drove by one night in ignorance of the country legends. What he told in Arkham was given a short paragraph in the *Gazette*; and it was there that all the farmers, Nahum included, saw it first. The night had been dark and the buggy-lamps faint, but around a farm in the valley which everyone knew from the account must be Nahum's, the darkness had been less thick. A dim though distinct luminosity seemed to inhere in all the vegetation, grass, leaves, and blossoms alike, while at one moment a detached piece of the phosphorescence appeared to stir furtively in the yard near the barn.

The grass had so far seemed untouched, and the cows were freely pastured in the lot near the house, but toward the end of May the milk began to be bad. Then Nahum had the cows driven to the uplands, after which the trouble ceased. Not long after this the change in grass and leaves became apparent to the eye. All the verdure was going grey, and was developing a highly singular quality of brittleness. Ammi was now the only person who ever visited the place, and his visits were becoming fewer and fewer. When school closed the Gardners were virtually cut off from the world, and sometimes let Ammi do their errands in town. They were failing curiously both physically and mentally, and no one was surprised when the news of Mrs. Gardner's madness stole around.

It happened in June, about the anniversary of the meteor's fall, and the poor woman screamed about things in the air which she could not describe. In her raving there was not a single specific noun, but only verbs and pronouns. Things moved and changed and fluttered, and ears tingled to impulses which were not wholly sounds. Something was taken away—she was being drained of something—something was fastening itself on her that ought not to be—someone must make it keep off—nothing was ever still in the night—the walls and windows shifted. Nahum did not send her to the county asylum, but let her wander about the house as long as she was harmless to herself and others. Even when her expression changed he did nothing. But when the boys grew afraid of her, and Thaddeus nearly fainted at the way she made faces at him, he decided to keep her locked in the attic. By July she had ceased to speak and crawled on all fours, and before that month was over Nahum got the mad notion that she was slightly luminous in the dark, as he now clearly saw was the case with the nearby vegetation.

It was a little before this that the horses had stampeded. Something had aroused them in the night, and their neighing and kicking in their stalls had been terrible. There seemed virtually nothing to do to calm them, and when Nahum opened the stable door they all bolted out like frightened woodland deer. It took a week to track all four, and when found they were seen to be quite useless and unmanageable. Something had snapped in their brains, and each one had to be shot for its own good. Nahum borrowed a horse from Ammi for his haying, but found it would not approach the barn. It shied, balked, and whinnied, and in the end he could do nothing but drive it into the yard while the men used their own strength to get the heavy wagon near enough the hayloft for convenient pitching. And all the while the vegetation was turning grey and brittle. Even the flowers whose hue had been so strange were greying now, and the fruit was coming out grey and dwarfed and tasteless. The asters and goldenrod bloomed grey and distorted, and the roses and zinneas and hollyhocks in the front yard were such blasphemous-looking things that Nahum's oldest boy Zenas cut them down. The strangely puffed insects died about that time, even the bees that had left their hives and taken to the woods.

By September all the vegetation was fast crumbling to a greyish powder, and Nahum feared that the trees would die before the poison was out of the soil. His wife now had spells of terrific screaming, and he and the boys were in a constant state of nervous tension. They shunned people now, and when school opened the boys did not go. But it was Ammi, on one of his rare visits, who first realised that the well water was no longer good. It had an evil taste that was not exactly fœtid nor exactly salty, and Ammi advised his friend to dig another well on higher ground to use till the soil was good again. Nahum, however, ignored the warning, for he had by that time become calloused to strange and unpleasant things. He and the boys continued to use the tainted supply, drinking it as listlessly and mechanically as they ate their meagre and ill-cooked meals and did their thankless and monotonous chores through the aimless days. There was something of stolid resignation about them all, as if they walked half in another world between lines of nameless guards to a certain and familiar doom.

Thaddeus went mad in September after a visit to the well. He had gone with a pail and had come back empty-handed, shrieking and waving his arms, and sometimes lapsing into an inane titter or a whisper about "the moving colours down there." Two in one family was pretty bad, but Nahum was very brave about it. He let the boy run about for a week until he began stumbling and hurting himself, and then he shut him in an attic room across the hall from his mother's. The way they screamed at each other from behind their locked doors was very terrible, especially to little Merwin, who fancied they talked in some terrible language that was not of earth. Merwin was getting frightfully imaginative, and his restlessness was worse after the shutting away of the brother who had been his greatest playmate.

Almost at the same time the mortality among the livestock commenced. Poultry turned greyish and died very quickly, their meat being found dry and noisome upon cutting. Hogs grew inordinately fat, then suddenly began to undergo loathsome changes which no one could explain. Their meat was of course useless, and Nahum was at his wit's end. No rural veterinary would approach his place, and the city veterinary from Arkham was openly baffled. The swine began growing grey and brittle and falling to pieces before they died, and their eyes and muzzles developed singular alterations. It was very inexplicable, for they had never been fed from the tainted vegetation. Then something struck the cows. Certain areas or sometimes the whole body would be uncannily shrivelled or compressed, and atrocious collapses or disintegrations were common. In the last stages—and death was always the result—there would be a greying and turning brittle like that which beset the hogs. There could be no question of poison, for all the cases occurred in a locked and undisturbed barn. No bites of prowling things could have brought the virus, for what live beast of earth can pass through solid obstacles? It must be only natural disease—yet what disease could wreak such results was beyond any mind's guessing. When the harvest came there was not an animal surviving on the place, for the stock and poultry were dead and the dogs had run away. These dogs, three in number, had all vanished one night and were never heard of again. The five cats had left some time before, but their going was scarcely noticed since there now seemed to be no mice, and only Mrs. Gardner had made pets of the graceful felines.

On the nineteenth of October Nahum staggered into Ammi's house with hideous news. The death had come to poor Thaddeus in his attic room, and it had come in a way which could not be told. Nahum had dug a grave in the railed family plot behind the farm, and had put therein what he found. There could have been nothing from outside, for the small barred window and locked door were intact; but it was much as it had been in the barn. Ammi and his wife consoled the stricken man as best they could, but shuddered as they did so. Stark terror seemed to cling round the Gardners and all they touched, and the very presence of one in the house was a breath from regions unnamed and unnamable. Ammi accompanied Nahum home with the greatest reluctance, and did what he might to calm the hysterical sobbing of little Merwin. Zenas needed no calming. He had come of late to do nothing but stare into space and obey what his father told him; and Ammi thought that his fate was very merciful. Now and then Merwin's screams were answered faintly from the attic, and in response to an inquiring look Nahum said that his wife was getting very feeble. When night approached, Ammi managed to get away; for not even friendship could make him stay in that spot when the faint glow of the vegetation began and the trees may or may not have swayed without wind. It was really lucky for Ammi that he was not more imaginative. Even as things were, his mind was bent ever so slightly; but had he been able to connect and reflect upon all the portents around him he must inevitably have turned a total maniac. In the twilight he hastened home, the screams of the mad woman and the nervous child ringing horribly in his ears.

Three days later Nahum lurched into Ammi's kitchen in the early morning, and in the absence of his host stammered out a desperate tale once more, while Mrs. Pierce listened in a clutching fright. It was little Merwin this time. He was gone. He had gone out late at night with a lantern and pail for water, and had never come back. He'd been going to pieces for days, and hardly knew what he was about. Screamed at everything. There had been a frantic shriek from the yard then, but before the father could get to the door the boy was gone. There was no glow from the lantern he had taken, and of the child himself no trace. At the time Nahum thought the lantern and pail were gone too; but when dawn came, and the man had plodded back from his all-night search of the woods and fields, he had found some very curious things near the well. There was a crushed and apparently somewhat melted mass of iron which had certainly been the lantern; while a bent bail and twisted iron hoops beside it, both half-fused, seemed to hint at the remnants of the pail. That was all. Nahum was past imagining, Mrs. Pierce was blank, and Ammi, when he had reached home and heard the tale, could give no guess. Merwin was gone, and there would be no use in telling the people around, who shunned all Gardners now. No use, either, in telling the city people at Arkham who laughed at everything. Thad was gone, and now Mernie was gone. Something was creeping and creeping and waiting to be seen and felt and heard. Nahum would go soon, and he wanted Ammi to look after his wife and Zenas if they survived him. It must all be a judgment of some sort; though he could not fancy what for, since he had always walked uprightly in the Lord's ways so far as he knew.

For over two weeks Ammi saw nothing of Nahum; and then, worried about what might have happened, he overcame his fears and paid the Gardner place a visit. There was no smoke from the great chimney, and for a moment the visitor was apprehensive of the worst. The aspect of the whole farm was shocking—greyish withered grass and leaves on the ground, vines falling in brittle wreckage from archaic walls and gables, and great bare trees clawing up at the grey November sky with a studied malevolence which Ammi could not but feel had come from some subtle change in the tilt of the branches. But Nahum was alive, after all. He was weak, and lying on a couch in the low-ceiled kitchen, but perfectly conscious and able to give simple orders to Zenas. The room was deadly cold; and as Ammi visibly shivered, the host shouted huskily to Zenas for more wood. Wood, indeed, was sorely needed; since the cavernous fireplace was unlit and empty, with a cloud of soot blowing about in the chill wind that came down the chimney. Presently Nahum asked him if the extra wood had made him any more comfortable, and then Ammi saw what had happened. The stoutest cord had broken at last, and the hapless farmer's mind was proof against more sorrow.

Questioning tactfully, Ammi could get no clear data at all about the missing Zenas. "In the well—he lives in the well—" was all that the clouded father would say. Then there flashed across the visitor's mind a sudden thought of the mad wife, and he changed his line of inquiry. "Nabby? Why, here she is!" was the surprised response of poor Nahum, and Ammi soon saw that he must search for himself. Leaving the harmless babbler on the couch, he took the keys from their nail beside the door and climbed the creaking stairs to the attic. It was very close and noisome up there, and no sound could be heard from any direction. Of the four doors in sight, only one was locked, and on this he tried various keys on the ring he had taken. The third key proved the right one, and after some fumbling Ammi threw open the low white door.

It was quite dark inside, for the window was small and half-obscured by the crude wooden bars; and Ammi could see nothing at all on the wide-planked floor. The stench was beyond enduring, and before proceeding further he had to retreat to another room and return with his lungs filled with breathable air. When he did enter he saw something dark in the corner, and upon seeing it more clearly he screamed outright. While he screamed he thought a momentary cloud eclipsed the window,

21. We are led to believe that Ammi beat or smashed the disintegrating wife to death, but no murder weapon is mentioned. There is no firewood in the house; perhaps he found a walking stick or broom or used a bedpost.

and a second later he felt himself brushed as if by some hateful current of vapour. Strange colours danced before his eyes; and had not a present horror numbed him he would have thought of the globule in the meteor that the geologist's hammer had shattered, and of the morbid vegetation that had sprouted in the spring. As it was he thought only of the blasphemous monstrosity which confronted him, and which all too clearly had shared the nameless fate of young Thaddeus and the livestock. But the terrible thing about this horror was that it very slowly and perceptibly moved as it continued to crumble.

Ammi would give me no added particulars to this scene, but the shape in the corner does not reappear in his tale as a moving object. There are things which cannot be mentioned, and what is done in common humanity is sometimes cruelly judged by the law. I gathered that no moving thing was left in that attic room,[21] and that to leave anything capable of motion there would have been a deed so monstrous as to damn any accountable being to eternal torment. Anyone but a stolid farmer would have fainted or gone mad, but Ammi walked conscious through that low doorway and locked the accursed secret behind him. There would be Nahum to deal with now; he must be fed and tended, and removed to some place where he could be cared for.

Commencing his descent of the dark stairs. Ammi heard a thud below him. He even thought a scream had been suddenly choked off, and recalled nervously the clammy vapour which had brushed by him in that frightful room above. What presence had his cry and entry started up? Halted by some vague fear, he heard still further sounds below. Indubitably there was a sort of heavy dragging, and a most detestably sticky noise as of some fiendish and unclean species of suction. With an associative sense goaded to feverish heights, he thought unaccountably of what he had seen upstairs. Good God! What eldritch dream-world was this into which he had blundered? He dared move neither backward nor forward, but stood there trembling at the black curve of the boxed-in staircase. Every trifle of the scene burned itself into his brain. The sounds, the sense of dread expectancy, the darkness, the steepness of the narrow steps—and merciful heaven! . . . the faint but unmistakable luminosity of all the woodwork in sight; steps, sides, exposed laths, and beams alike!

Then there burst forth a frantic whinny from Ammi's horse outside, followed at once by a clatter which told of a frenzied runaway. In another moment horse and buggy had gone beyond earshot, leaving the frightened man on the dark stairs to guess what had sent them. But that was not all. There had been another sound out there. A sort of liquid splash—water—it must have been the well. He had left Hero untied near it, and a buggy-wheel must have brushed the coping and knocked in a stone. And still the pale phosphorescence glowed in that detestably ancient woodwork. God! how old the house was! Most of it built before 1670, and the gambrel roof not later than 1730.

A feeble scratching on the floor downstairs now sounded distinctly, and Ammi's grip tightened on a heavy stick he had picked up in the attic for some purpose. Slowly nerving himself, he finished his descent and walked boldly toward the kitchen. But he did not complete the walk, because what he sought was no longer there. It had come to meet him, and it was still alive after a fashion. Whether it had crawled or whether it had been dragged by any external force, Ammi could not say; but the death had been at it. Everything had happened in the last half-hour, but collapse, greying, and disintegration were already far advanced. There was a horrible brittleness, and dry fragments were scaling off. Ammi could not touch it, but looked horrifiedly into the distorted parody that had been a face. "What was it, Nahum—what was it?" he whispered, and the cleft, bulging lips were just able to crackle out a final answer.

"Nothin' . . . nothin' . . . the colour . . . it burns . . . cold an' wet . . . but it burns . . . it lived in the well . . . I seen it . . . a kind o' smoke . . . jest like the flowers last spring . . . the well shone at night . . . Thad an' Mernie an' Zenas . . . everything alive . . . suckin' the life out of everything . . . in that stone . . . it must a' come in that stone . . . pizened the whole place . . . dun't know what it wants . . . that round thing them men from the college dug outen the stone . . . they smashed it . . . it was that same colour . . . jest the same, like the flowers an' plants . . . must a' ben more of 'em . . . seeds . . . seeds . . . they growed . . . I seen it the fust time this week . . . must a' got strong on Zenas . . . he was a big boy, full o' life . . . it beats down your mind an' then gits ye . . . burns ye up . . . in the well water . . . you was right about that

22. A flatbed wagon with two or more seats.

. . . evil water . . . Zenas never come back from the well . . . can't git away . . . draws ye . . . ye know summ'at's comin' but 'tain't no use . . . I seen it time an' agin sent Zenas was took . . . whar's Nabby, Ammi? . . . my head's no good . . . dun't know how long sent I fed her . . . it'll git her ef we ain't keerful . . . jest a colour . . . her face is gettin' to hev that colour sometimes towards night . . . an' it burns an' sucks . . . it come from some place whar things ain't as they is here . . . one o' them professors said so . . . he was right . . . look out, Ammi, it'll do suthin' more . . . sucks the life out . . ."

But that was all. That which spoke could speak no more because it had completely caved in. Ammi laid a red checked tablecloth over what was left and reeled out the back door into the fields. He climbed the slope to the ten-acre pasture and stumbled home by the north road and the woods. He could not pass that well from which his horse had run away. He had looked at it through the window, and had seen that no stone was missing from the rim. Then the lurching buggy had not dislodged anything after all—the splash had been something else—something which went into the well after it had done with poor Nahum . . .

When Ammi reached his house the horse and buggy had arrived before him and thrown his wife into fits of anxiety. Reassuring her without explanations, he set out at once for Arkham and notified the authorities that the Gardner family was no more. He indulged in no details, but merely told of the deaths of Nahum and Nabby, that of Thaddeus being already known, and mentioned that the cause seemed to be the same strange ailment which had killed the livestock. He also stated that Merwin and Zenas had disappeared. There was considerable questioning at the police station, and in the end Ammi was compelled to take three officers to the Gardner farm, together with the coroner, the medical examiner, and the veterinary who had treated the diseased animals. He went much against his will, for the afternoon was advancing and he feared the fall of night over that accursed place, but it was some comfort to have so many people with him.

The six men drove out in a democrat-wagon,[22] following Ammi's buggy, and arrived at the pest-ridden farmhouse about four o'clock. Used as the officers were to gruesome experiences, not one remained unmoved at what was found in the attic and under the red checked tablecloth on the floor below. The whole aspect of the farm with its grey desolation was terrible enough, but those two crumbling objects were beyond all bounds. No one could look long at them, and even the medical examiner admitted that there was very little to examine. Specimens could be analysed, of course, so he busied himself in obtaining them—and here it develops that a very puzzling aftermath occurred at the college laboratory where the two phials of dust were finally taken. Under the spectroscope both samples gave off an unknown spectrum, in which many of the baffling bands were precisely like those which the strange meteor had yielded in the previous year. The property of emitting this spectrum vanished in a month, the dust thereafter consisting mainly of alkaline phosphates and carbonates.

Ammi would not have told the men about the well if he had thought they meant to do anything then and there. It was getting toward sunset, and he was anxious to be away. But he could not help glancing nervously at the stony curb by the great sweep, and when a detective questioned him he admitted that Nahum had feared something down there—so much so that he had never even thought of searching it for Merwin or Zenas. After that nothing would do but that they empty and explore the well immediately, so Ammi had to wait trembling while pail after pail of rank water was hauled up and splashed on the soaking ground outside. The men sniffed in disgust at the fluid, and toward the last held their noses against the fœtor they were uncovering. It was not so long a job as they had feared it would be, since the water was phenomenally low. There is no need to speak too exactly of what they found. Merwin and Zenas were both there, in part, though the vestiges were mainly skeletal. There were also a small deer and a large dog in about the same state, and a number of bones of smaller animals. The ooze and slime at the bottom seemed inexplicably porous and bubbling, and a man who descended on hand-holds with a long pole found that he could sink the wooden shaft to any depth in the mud of the floor without meeting any solid obstruction.

Twilight had now fallen, and lanterns were brought from the house. Then, when it was seen that nothing further could be gained from the well, everyone went indoors and conferred in the ancient sitting-room while the intermittent light of a spectral half-moon played wanly on the grey desolation outside. The men were frankly nonplussed by the entire case, and could find no convincing common element to link the strange vegetable conditions, the unknown disease of livestock and humans, and the unaccountable deaths of Merwin and Zenas in the tainted well. They had heard the common country talk, it is true; but could not believe that anything contrary to natural law had occurred. No doubt the meteor had poisoned the soil, but the illness of persons and animals who had eaten nothing grown in that soil was another matter. Was it the well water? Very possibly. It might be a good idea to analyse it. But what peculiar madness could have made both boys jump into the well? Their deeds were so similar—and the fragments shewed that they had both suffered from the grey brittle death. Why was everything so grey and brittle?

It was the coroner, seated near a window overlooking the yard, who first noticed the glow about the well. Night had fully set in, and all the abhorrent grounds seemed faintly luminous with more than the fitful moonbeams; but this new glow was something definite and distinct, and appeared to shoot up from the black pit like a softened ray from a searchlight, giving dull reflections in the little ground pools where the water had been emptied. It had a very queer colour, and as all the men clustered round the window Ammi gave a violent start. For this strange beam of ghastly miasma was to him of no unfamiliar hue. He had seen that colour before, and feared to think what it might mean. He had seen it in the nasty brittle globule in that aërolite two summers ago, had seen it in the crazy vegetation of the springtime, and had thought he had seen it for an instant that very morning against the small barred window of that terrible attic room where nameless things had happened. It had flashed there a second, and a clammy and hateful current of vapour had brushed past him—and then poor Nahum had been taken by something of that colour. He had said so at the last—said it was the globule and the plants. After that had come the runaway in the yard and the splash in the well—and now that well was belching forth to the night a pale insidious beam of the same dæmoniac tint.

It does credit to the alertness of Ammi's mind that he puzzled even at that tense moment over a point which was essentially scientific. He could not but wonder at his gleaning of the same impression from a vapour glimpsed in the daytime, against a window opening on the morning sky, and from a nocturnal exhalation seen as a phosphorescent mist against the black and blasted landscape. It wasn't right—it was against Nature—and he thought of those terrible last words of his stricken friend, "It come from some place whar things ain't as they is here . . . one o' them professors said so . . ."

All three horses outside, tied to a pair of shrivelled saplings by the road, were now neighing and pawing frantically. The wagon driver started for the door to do something, but Ammi laid a shaky hand on his shoulder. "Dun't go out thar," he whispered. "They's more to this nor what we know. Nahum said somethin' lived in the well that sucks your life out. He said it must be some'at growed from a round ball like one we all seen in the meteor stone that fell a year ago June. Sucks an' burns, he said, an' is jest a cloud of colour like that light out thar now, that ye can hardly see an' can't tell what it is. Nahum thought it feeds on everything livin' an' gits stronger all the time. He said he seen it this last week. It must be somethin' from away off in the sky like the men from the college last year says the meteor stone was. The way it's made an' the way it works ain't like no way o' God's world. It's some'at from beyond."

So the men paused indecisively as the light from the well grew stronger and the hitched horses pawed and whinnied in increasing frenzy. It was truly an awful moment; with terror in that ancient and accursed house itself, four monstrous sets of fragments—two from the house and two from the well—in the woodshed behind, and that shaft of unknown and unholy iridescence from the slimy depths in front. Ammi had restrained the driver on impulse, forgetting how uninjured he himself was after the clammy brushing of that coloured vapour in the attic room, but perhaps it is just as well that he acted as he did. No one will ever know what was abroad that night; and though the blasphemy from beyond had not so far hurt any human of unweakened mind, there is no telling what it might not have done at that last moment, and with its seemingly increased strength and the special signs of purpose it was soon to display beneath the half-clouded moonlit sky.

23. Pliny the Elder recorded this phenomenon in his *Naturalis Historia* (published ca. 77–79 CE):

> Over and besides, there be fires seene suddainely to arise, both in waters and also about the bodies of men. Valerius Antias reporteth, That the lake Thrasymenus once burned all over: also that Servius Tullius in his childhood, as hee lay asleepe, had a light fire shone out of his head: likewise, as L. Martius made an Oration in open audience to the armie, after the two Scipios were slaine in Spain, and exhorted his souldiors to revenge their death, his head was on a flaming fire in the same sort. More of this argument, and in better order, will we write soone hereafter. For now we exhibit and shew the mervailes of all things huddled and intermingled together. But in the meane while, my mind being passed beyond the interpretation of Nature, hasteneth to lead as it were by the hand the minds also of the readers, throughout the whole world.

It is explained by the fact that a coronal discharge of a grounded object in an electrical field, usually a thunderstorm, causes luminous plasma to appear. Observed (as a purplish glowing flame) by sailors on the masts of ships, it was attributed to St. Erasmus or St. Ermo (corrupted to St. Elmo), the patron saint of Mediterranean sailors.

24. In Christianity, Pentecost is observed fifty days after Easter:

> And when the day of Pentecost was fully come, they were all with one accord in one place.
> And suddenly there came a sound from heaven as of a rushing mighty wind, and it filled all the house where they were sitting.

All at once one of the detectives at the window gave a short, sharp gasp. The others looked at him, and then quickly followed his own gaze upward to the point at which its idle straying had been suddenly arrested. There was no need for words. What had been disputed in country gossip was disputable no longer, and it is because of the thing which every man of that party agreed in whispering later on that the strange days are never talked about in Arkham. It is necessary to premise that there was no wind at that hour of the evening. One did arise not long afterward, but there was absolutely none then. Even the dry tips of the lingering hedge-mustard, grey and blighted, and the fringe on the roof of the standing democrat-wagon were unstirred. And yet amid that tense godless calm the high bare boughs of all the trees in the yard were moving. They were twitching morbidly and spasmodically, clawing in convulsive and epileptic madness at the moonlit clouds; scratching impotently in the noxious air as if jerked by some alien and bodiless line of linkage with subterrene horrors writhing and struggling below the black roots.

Not a man breathed for several seconds. Then a cloud of darker depth passed over the moon, and the silhouette of clutching branches faded out momentarily. At this there was a general cry; muffled with awe, but husky and almost identical from every throat. For the terror had not faded with the silhouette, and in a fearsome instant of deeper darkness the watchers saw wriggling at that treetop height a thousand tiny points of faint and unhallowed radiance, tipping each bough like the fire of St. Elmo[23] or the flames that came down on the apostles' heads at Pentecost.[24] It was a monstrous constellation of unnatural light, like a glutted swarm of corpse-fed fireflies dancing hellish sarabands[25] over an accursed marsh; and its colour was that same nameless intrusion which Ammi had come to recognise and dread. All the while the shaft of phosphorescence from the well was getting brighter and brighter, bringing to the minds of the huddled men a sense of doom and abnormality which far outraced any image their conscious minds could form. It was no longer *shining* out, it was *pouring* out; and as the shapeless stream of unplaceable colour left the well it seemed to flow directly into the sky.

The veterinary shivered, and walked to the front door to drop the heavy extra bar across it. Ammi shook no less, and had to tug

"... and in the fearsome instant of deeper darkness, the watchers saw wriggling at that treetop height, a thousand tiny points ..." *Amazing Stories* 2, no. 6 (September 1927) (artist: J. M. De Aragón)

And there appeared unto them cloven tongues like as of fire, and it sat upon each of them.

And they were all filled with the Holy Ghost, and began to speak with other tongues, as the Spirit gave them utterance (Acts 2:1–4, King James Version).

25. A rapid, erotic Latin dance of the sixteenth century, often performed to the accompaniment of castanets and seen as risqué. By the seventeenth and eighteenth centuries, it had evolved, in France and Spain, into a slower dance form that the authorities of both countries found relatively unobjectionable.

and point for lack of a controllable voice when he wished to draw notice to the growing luminosity of the trees. The neighing and stamping of the horses had become utterly frightful, but not a soul of that group in the old house would have ventured forth for any earthly reward. With the moments the shining of the trees increased, while their restless branches seemed to strain more and more toward verticality. The wood of the well-sweep was shining now, and presently a policeman dumbly pointed to some wooden sheds and bee-hives near the stone wall on the west. They were commencing to shine, too, though the tethered vehicles of the visitors seemed so far unaffected. Then there was a wild commotion and clopping in the road, and as Ammi quenched the lamp for better seeing they realised that the span of frantic greys had broke their sapling and run off with the democrat-wagon.

The shock served to loosen several tongues, and embarrassed whispers were exchanged. "It spreads on everything organic that's been around here," muttered the medical examiner. No one replied, but the man who had been in the well gave a hint that his long pole must have stirred up something intangible. "It was awful," he added. "There was no bottom at all. Just ooze and bubbles and the feeling of something lurking under there." Ammi's horse still pawed and screamed deafeningly in the road outside, and nearly drowned its owner's faint quaver as he mumbled his formless reflections. "It come from that stone . . . it growed down thar . . . it got everything livin' . . . it fed itself on 'em, mind and body . . . Thad an' Mernie, Zenas an' Nabby . . . Nahum was the last . . . they all drunk the water . . . it got strong on 'em . . . it come from beyond, whar things ain't like they be here . . . now it's goin' home . . ."

At this point, as the column of unknown colour flared suddenly stronger and began to weave itself into fantastic suggestions of shape which each spectator later described differently, there came from poor tethered Hero such a sound as no man before or since ever heard from a horse. Every person in that low-pitched sitting room stopped his ears, and Ammi turned away from the window in horror and nausea. Words could not convey it—when Ammi looked out again the hapless beast lay huddled inert on the moonlit ground between the splintered shafts of the buggy. That was the last of Hero till they buried him next day. But the present was no time to mourn, for almost at this instant a detective silently called attention to something terrible in the very room with them. In the absence of the lamplight it was clear that a faint phosphorescence had begun to pervade the entire apartment. It glowed on the broad-planked floor and the fragment of rag carpet, and shimmered over the sashes of the small-paned windows. It ran up and down the exposed corner-posts, coruscated about the shelf and mantel, and infected the very doors and furniture. Each minute saw it strengthen, and at last it was very plain that healthy living things must leave that house.

Ammi shewed them the back door and the path up through the fields to the ten-acre pasture. They walked and stumbled as

Famous Fantastic Mysteries 3, no. 4 (October 1941) (artist: Virgil Finlay)

in a dream, and did not dare look back till they were far away on the high ground. They were glad of the path, for they could not have gone the front way, by that well. It was bad enough passing the glowing barn and sheds, and those shining orchard trees with their gnarled, fiendish contours; but thank heaven the branches did their worst twisting high up. The moon went under some very black clouds as they crossed the rustic bridge over Chapman's Brook, and it was blind groping from there to the open meadows.

26. Henry Fuseli, born Füssli (1741–1825), Swiss painter of fantastic visions who spent his adult life in England. His most famous painting is *The Nightmare* (1781).

27. The Swan, also known by other bird names, a constellation lying in the plane of the Milky Way, of unusual density with over 145 visible stars. The most prominent, *Alpha Cygni*, or Deneb, a brilliant white star, the nineteenth-brightest in the sky. Its name is derived from the Arabic *Al Dhanab al Dajājah*, the hen's tail.

When they looked back toward the valley and the distant Gardner place at the bottom they saw a fearsome sight. All the farm was shining with the hideous unknown blend of colour; trees, buildings, and even such grass and herbage as had not been wholly changed to lethal grey brittleness. The boughs were all straining skyward, tipped with tongues of foul flame, and lambent tricklings of the same monstrous fire were creeping about the ridgepoles of the house, barn and sheds. It was a scene from a vision of Fuseli,[26] and over all the rest reigned that riot of luminous amorphousness, that alien and undimensioned rainbow of cryptic poison from the well—seething, feeling, lapping, reaching, scintillating, straining, and malignly bubbling in its cosmic and unrecognisable chromaticism.

Then without warning the hideous thing shot vertically up toward the sky like a rocket or meteor, leaving behind no trail and disappearing through a round and curiously regular hole in the clouds before any man could gasp or cry out. No watcher can ever forget that sight, and Ammi stared blankly at the stars of Cygnus,[27] Deneb twinkling above the others, where the unknown colour had melted into the Milky Way. But his gaze was the next moment called swiftly to earth by the crackling in the valley. It

The Nightmare by John Henry Fuseli (1781).

was just that. Only a wooden ripping and crackling, and not an explosion, as so many others of the party vowed. Yet the outcome was the same, for in one feverish kaleidoscopic instant there burst up from that doomed and accursed farm a gleamingly eruptive cataclysm of unnatural sparks and substance; blurring the glance of the few who saw it, and sending forth to the zenith a bombarding cloudburst of such coloured and fantastic fragments as our universe must needs disown. Through quickly closing vapours they followed the great morbidity that had vanished, and in another second they had vanished too. Behind and below was only a darkness to which the men dared not return, and all about was a mounting wind which seemed to sweep down in black, frore[28] gusts from interstellar space. It shrieked and howled, and lashed the fields and distorted woods in a mad cosmic frenzy, till soon the trembling party realised it would be no use waiting for the moon to shew what was left down there at Nahum's.

Too awed even to hint theories, the seven shaking men trudged back toward Arkham by the north road. Ammi was worse than his fellows, and begged them to see him inside his own kitchen, instead of keeping straight on to town. He did not wish to cross the nighted, wind-whipped woods alone to his home on the main road. For he had had an added shock that the others were spared, and was crushed forever with a brooding fear he dared not even mention for many years to come. As the rest of the watchers on that tempestuous hill had stolidly set their faces toward the road, Ammi had looked back an instant at the shadowed valley of desolation so lately sheltering his ill-starred friend. And from that stricken, far-away spot he had seen something feebly rise, only to sink down again upon the place from which the great shapeless horror had shot into the sky. It was just a colour—but not any colour of our earth or heavens. And because Ammi recognised that colour, and knew that this last faint remnant must still lurk down there in the well, he has never been quite right since.

Ammi would never go near the place again. It is forty-four years now[29] since the horror happened, but he has never been there, and will be glad when the new reservoir blots it out. I shall be glad, too, for I do not like the way the sunlight changed colour around the mouth of that abandoned well I passed. I hope the water will always be very deep—but even so, I shall never

28. An obsolete word meaning very cold, frozen.

29. "Over half a century now" in later publications.

30. Unmentionable, unspeakable.

drink it. I do not think I shall visit the Arkham country hereafter. Three of the men who had been with Ammi returned the next morning to see the ruins by daylight, but there were not any real ruins. Only the bricks of the chimney, the stones of the cellar, some mineral and metallic litter here and there, and the rim of that nefandous[30] well. Save for Ammi's dead horse, which they towed away and buried, and the buggy which they shortly returned to him, everything that had ever been living had gone. Five eldritch acres of dusty grey desert remained, nor has anything ever grown there since. To this day it sprawls open to the sky like a great spot eaten by acid in the woods and fields, and the few who have ever dared glimpse it in spite of the rural tales have named it "the blasted heath."

The "blasted heath," drawn by Lovecraft
(from a letter to F. Lee Baldwin, dated March 27, 1934).

The rural tales are queer. They might be even queerer if city men and college chemists could be interested enough to analyse the water from that disused well, or the grey dust that no wind seems ever to disperse. Botanists, too, ought to study the stunted flora on the borders of that spot, for they might shed light on the country notion that the blight is spreading—little by little, perhaps an inch a year. People say the colour of the neighbouring herbage is not quite right in the spring, and that wild things leave queer prints in the light winter snow. Snow never seems quite so heavy on the blasted heath as it is elsewhere. Horses—the few that are left in this motor age—grow skittish in the silent valley; and hunters cannot depend on their dogs too near the splotch of greyish dust.

They say the mental influences are very bad, too. Numbers went queer in the years after Nahum's taking, and always they lacked the power to get away. Then the stronger-minded folk all left the region, and only the foreigners tried to live in the crumbling old homesteads. They could not stay, though; and one sometimes wonders what insight beyond ours their wild, weird stores of whispered magic have given them. Their dreams at night, they protest, are very horrible in that grotesque country; and surely the very look of the dark realm is enough to stir a morbid fancy. No traveller has ever escaped a sense of strangeness in those deep ravines, and artists shiver as they paint thick woods whose mystery is as much of the spirit as of the eye. I myself am curious about the sensation I derived from my one lone walk before Ammi told me his tale. When twilight came I had vaguely wished some clouds would gather, for an odd timidity about the deep skyey voids above had crept into my soul.

Do not ask me for my opinion. I do not know—that is all. There was no one but Ammi to question; for Arkham people will not talk about the strange days, and all three professors who saw the aërolite and its coloured globule are dead. There were other globules—depend upon that. One must have fed itself and escaped, and probably there was another which was too late. No doubt it is still down the well—I know there was something wrong with the sunlight I saw above the miasmal brink. The rustics say the blight creeps an inch a year, so perhaps there is a kind of growth or nourishment even now. But whatever demon

Poster from *Colour from the Dark* (Studio Interzona, 2008).

Poster from *Die, Monster, Die!* (American International Pictures, 1965), loosely based on "The Colour Out of Space."

hatchling is there, it must be tethered to something or else it would quickly spread. Is it fastened to the roots of those trees that claw the air? One of the current Arkham tales is about fat oaks that shine and move as they ought not to do at night.

What it is, only God knows. In terms of matter I suppose the thing Ammi described would be called a gas, but this gas obeyed laws that are not of our cosmos. This was no fruit of such worlds and suns as shine on the telescopes and photographic plates of our observatories. This was no breath from the skies whose motions and dimensions our astronomers measure or deem too vast to measure. It was just a colour out of space—a frightful messenger from unformed realms of infinity beyond all Nature as we know it; from realms whose mere existence stuns the brain and numbs us with the black extra-cosmic gulfs it throws open before our frenzied eyes.

I doubt very much if Ammi consciously lied to me, and I do not think his tale was all a freak of madness as the townfolk had forewarned. Something terrible came to the hills and valleys on that meteor, and something terrible—though I know not in what proportion—still remains. I shall be glad to see the water come. Meanwhile I hope nothing will happen to Ammi. He saw so much of the thing—and its influence was so insidious. Why has he never been able to move away? How clearly he recalled those dying words of Nahum's—"can't git away . . . draws ye . . . ye know summ'at's comin', but 'tain't no use . . ." Ammi is such a good old man—when the reservoir gang gets to work I must write the chief engineer to keep a sharp watch on him. I would hate to think of him as the grey, twisted, brittle monstrosity which persists more and more in troubling my sleep.

The Dunwich Horror[1]

"The Dunwich Horror" has been viewed as biblical parody, and it clearly borrows elements from Arthur Machen's "Great God Pan," Guy de Maupassant's "The Horla," Fitz-James O'Brien's "What Was It?" and Ambrose Bierce's "The Wendigo." Despite the familiarity of the ideas, it was a great hit with the Weird Tales readership and remains one of Lovecraft's most popular and frequently reprinted tales. Building on "The Call of Cthulhu," it fits neatly into what Lovecraft called his Arkham cycle—stories set in his fictionalized backwoods of New England and the hallowed halls of Miskatonic University. This is also the only story with an extended excerpt from the Necronomicon.

Weird Tales 13, no. 4 (April 1929) (artist: Hugh Rankin)

Gorgons and Hydras, and Chimæras[2]—dire stories of Celæno[3] and the Harpies—may reproduce themselves in the brain of *superstition*—*but they were there before*. They are transcripts, types—the archetypes are in us, and eternal. How else should the recital of that which we know in a waking sense to be false come to affect us at all? . . . Is it that we naturally conceive terror from such objects, considered in their capacity of being able to inflict upon us bodily injury? O, least of all! *These terrors are of older standing. They date beyond body*— or without the body, they would have been the same . . . That the kind of fear here treated is purely spiritual—that it is strong in proportion as it is objectless on earth, that it predominates in the period of our sinless infancy—are difficulties the solution of which might afford some probable insight into our antemundane condition, and a peep at least into the shadowland of pre-existence.

—CHARLES LAMB, *Witches, and Other Night-Fears*[4]

1. The story was written in September 1928 and first appeared in *Weird Tales* 13, no. 4 (April 1929), 481–508.

2. The opening echoes Milton's *Paradise Lost*, book 1, lines 624–628: "Where all life dies, death lives, and Nature breeds, / Perverse, all monstrous, all prodigious things, / Abominable, inutterable, and worse / Then Fables yet have feign'd, or fear conceiv'd, / Gorgons and Hydras and Chimæras dire." In Greek mythology, the Gorgons are the three sisters Stethno, Euryale, and Medusa, the daughters of Phorcys and Ceto. Medusa was mortal. They were said to have serpents in place of hair, golden wings, claws of bronze, and glaring eyes. Most importantly, it was believed that looking at them made the observer turn to stone. Equally terrible to behold, the Hydra has many heads; slain by Hercules, it produced two more heads for each one lopped off. According to Homer, a Chimæra is "nothing human, all lion in front, all snake behind, all goat between" (*Iliad*, 201).

3. One of the Harpies, mentioned in Virgil's *Aeneid* as prophesying to Aeneas.

I.

When a traveller in north central Massachusetts takes the wrong fork at the junction of the Aylesbury pike[5] just beyond Dean's Corners[6] he comes upon a lonely and curious country. The ground gets higher, and the brier-bordered stone walls press closer and closer against the ruts of the dusty, curving road. The trees of the frequent forest belts seem too large, and the wild weeds, brambles and grasses attain a luxuriance not often found in settled regions. At the same time the planted fields appear singularly few and barren; while the sparsely scattered houses wear a surprisingly uniform aspect of age, squalor, and dilapidation. Without knowing why, one hesitates to ask directions from the gnarled solitary figures spied now and then on crumbling doorsteps or on the sloping, rock-strown meadows. Those figures are so silent and furtive that one feels somehow confronted by forbidden things, with which it would be better to have nothing to do. When a rise in the road brings the mountains in view above the deep woods, the feeling of strange uneasiness is increased. The summits are too rounded and symmetrical to give a sense of comfort and naturalness, and sometimes the sky silhouettes with especial clearness the queer circles of tall stone pillars with which most of them are crowned.

Gorges and ravines of problematical depth intersect the way, and the crude wooden bridges always seem of dubious safety. When the road dips again there are stretches of marshland that one instinctively dislikes, and indeed almost fears at evening when unseen whippoorwills chatter and the fireflies come out in abnormal profusion to dance to the raucous, creepily insistent rhythms of stridently piping bull-frogs. The thin, shining line of the Miskatonic's upper reaches has an oddly serpent-like suggestion as it winds close to the feet of the domed hills among which it rises.

As the hills draw nearer, one heeds their wooded sides more than their stone-crowned tops. Those sides loom up so darkly and precipitously that one wishes they would keep their distance, but there is no road by which to escape them. Across a covered bridge one sees a small village huddled between the stream and the vertical slope of Round Mountain,[7] and wonders at the cluster of rotting gambrel roofs bespeaking an earlier architectural period than that of the neighbouring region. It is not reassuring to see, on a closer glance, that most of the houses are deserted and falling to ruin, and that the broken-steepled church now harbours the one slovenly mercantile establishment of the hamlet. One dreads to trust the tenebrous tunnel of the bridge, yet there is no way to avoid it. Once across, it is hard to prevent the impression of a faint, malign odour about the village street, as of the massed mould and decay of centuries. It is always a relief to get clear of the place, and to follow the narrow road around the base of the hills and across the level country beyond till it rejoins the Aylesbury pike. Afterward one sometimes learns that one has been through Dunwich.

Outsiders visit Dunwich as seldom as possible, and since a certain season of horror all the signboards pointing toward it have been taken down. The scenery, judged by any ordinary æsthetic canon, is more than commonly beautiful; yet there is no influx of artists or summer tourists. Two centuries ago, when talk of witch-blood, Satan-worship, and strange forest presences was not laughed at, it was the custom to give reasons for avoiding the locality. In our sensible age—since the Dunwich horror of 1928 was hushed up by those who had the town's and the world's welfare at heart—people shun it without knowing exactly why.

4. An essay that first appeared in the *London Magazine* in 1821 and later was published in book form in 1823 in a collection entitled *Essays of Elia*. The italics were added by Lovecraft.

5. Robert D. Marten, in "Arkham Country: In Rescue of the Lost Searchers," suggests that this is the old Springfield Pike, Route 20. This would identify Aylesbury with Springfield, with which it shares some characteristics.

6. Dean's Corners will not be found on a regular map.

7. This is a real mountain, on the border of southwest Massachusetts and northwest Connecticut, lying partly in the towns of Mount Washington, Massachusetts, and Salisbury, Connecticut. One searches in vain, however, for the village of Dunwich.

8. Mentioned in Leviticus 16:10. Azazel is discussed in some detail in the *Book of Enoch*, of pre-Christian origin, where it is assigned the role of one of the chiefs of the fallen angels; in the *Sefer Hekhalot* (Book of Palaces), a mystical Hebrew text probably written between 200 and 500 CE, Azazel is identified as an angel who married a human woman. Beelzebub ("the lord of the flies") and Belial (another fallen angel, though possibly another name for Beelzebub) are also mentioned in the Bible. Beelzebub and Azazel appear in Neil Gaiman's *Sandman* comics.

9. An unknown demon; perhaps a corruption of Bezrial, one of the angelic guards of the 3rd Heaven, as reported in the *Pirkei Hekhalot* (Great Palaces), also known as the *Hekhalot Rabbati* (Rabbi's Palaces), a Hebrew text of mysticism probably written in the first millennium CE and part of the tradition of the Kabbalah. Muslim and kabbalist texts describe seven spherical heavens, one within the other. Within the heavens dwell God and the angels.

Lovecraft was no occultist—"I am, indeed, an absolute materialist so far as actual belief goes; with not a shred of credence in any form of supernaturalism—religion, spiritualism, transcendentalism, metempsychosis, or immortality," he wrote in an October 9, 1925, letter to Clark Ashton Smith (*Selected Letters*, II, 27)—but he made frequent references to occultism and occultists in his work. For example, the Esoteric Order of Dagon, mentioned in "The Call of Cthulhu" (pp. 123–57, above), is a parody of the late-nineteenth-century Hermetic Order of the Golden Dawn, a prominent English occult group.

Perhaps one reason—though it cannot apply to uninformed strangers—is that the natives are now repellently decadent, having gone far along that path of retrogression so common in many New England backwaters. They have come to form a race by themselves, with the well-defined mental and physical stigmata of degeneracy and inbreeding. The average of their intelligence is woefully low, whilst their annals reek of overt viciousness and of half-hidden murders, incests, and deeds of almost unnamable violence and perversity. The old gentry, representing the two or three armigerous families which came from Salem in 1692, have kept somewhat above the general level of decay; though many branches are sunk into the sordid populace so deeply that only their names remain as a key to the origin they disgrace. Some of the Whateleys and Bishops still send their eldest sons to Harvard and Miskatonic, though those sons seldom return to the mouldering gambrel roofs under which they and their ancestors were born.

No one, even those who have the facts concerning the recent horror, can say just what is the matter with Dunwich; though old legends speak of unhallowed rites and conclaves of the Indians, amidst which they called forbidden shapes of shadow out of the great rounded hills, and made wild orgiastic prayers that were answered by loud crackings and rumblings from the ground below. In 1747 the Reverend Abijah Hoadley, newly come to the Congregational Church at Dunwich Village, preached a memorable sermon on the close presence of Satan and his imps; in which he said:

"It must be allow'd, that these Blasphemies of an infernall Train of Dæmons are Matters of too common Knowledge to be deny'd; the cursed Voices of Azazel[8] and Buzræl,[9] of Beelzebub and Belial, being heard now from under Ground by above a Score of credible Witnesses now living. I my self did not more than a Fortnight ago catch a very plain Discourse of evil Powers in the Hill behind my House; wherein there were a Rattling and Rolling, Groaning, Screeching, and Hissing, such as no Things of this Earth cou'd raise up, and which must needs have come from those Caves that only black Magick can discover, and only the Divell unlock."

Mr. Hoadley disappeared soon after delivering this sermon;

but the text, printed in Springfield, is still extant. Noises in the hills continued to be reported from year to year, and still form a puzzle to geologists and physiographers.[10]

Other traditions tell of foul odours near the hill-crowning circles of stone pillars, and of rushing airy presences to be heard faintly at certain hours from stated points at the bottom of the great ravines; while still others try to explain the Devil's Hop Yard—a bleak, blasted hillside where no tree, shrub, or grass-blade will grow. Then too, the natives are mortally afraid of the numerous whippoorwills which grow vocal on warm nights. It is vowed that the birds are psychopomps[11] lying in wait for the souls of the dying, and that they time their eerie cries in unison with the sufferer's struggling breath. If they can catch the fleeing soul when it leaves the body, they instantly flutter away chittering in dæmoniac laughter; but if they fail, they subside gradually into a disappointed silence.[12]

These tales, of course, are obsolete and ridiculous; because they come down from very old times. Dunwich is indeed ridiculously old—older by far than any of the communities within thirty miles of it. South of the village one may still spy the cellar walls and chimney of the ancient Bishop house, which was built before 1700; whilst the ruins of the mill at the falls, built in 1806, form the most modern piece of architecture to be seen. Industry did not flourish here, and the nineteenth-century factory movement[13] proved short-lived. Oldest of all are the great rings of rough-hewn stone columns on the hill-tops, but these are more generally attributed to the Indians than to the settlers. Deposits of skulls and bones, found within these circles and around the sizeable table-like rock on Sentinel Hill,[14] sustain the popular belief that such spots were once the burial-places of the Pocumtucks;[15] even though many ethnologists, disregarding the absurd improbability of such a theory, persist in believing the remains Caucasian.

II.

IT WAS IN the township of Dunwich, in a large and partly inhabited farmhouse set against a hillside four miles from the vil-

10. The town of Moodus, Connecticut, has long been associated with spooky noises such as those described for Dunwich. It is thought that several Native American cults focused on Moodus as a place where a god, Hobomock (an evil deity), was actually present. The Algonquins named it Machimoodus, the place of bad noises. Scientists attribute the noises to microearthquakes (the region has a long history of quakes).

11. Conductors of souls to the underworld.

12. Dunwich was not the only locale to experience such a phenomenon. In the Wilbraham, Massachusetts, area, similar tales were told of a residence referred to by Lovecraft as "the old Randolph Beebe house," a structure with a lineage traceable to about 1790, where, it was said, whippoorwills clustered abnormally and were feared by locals. These were mentioned in an essay by Lovecraft in "Mrs. Miniter: Estimates and Recollections" (1934), reprinted in *Miscellaneous Writings*. There is much about Wilbraham to suggest Dunwich, as discussed in Robert D. Marten's "In Search of Arkham Country: In Rescue of the Lost Searchers."

13. The end of the nineteenth century in America saw the growth of large-scale factories—steel and other major milling operations. However, earlier in the century, the "factory movement" (as the narrator calls it) was already having a great impact on the South, with the mechanization and reorganization of southern cotton-growing plantations. These strides made possible the cotton-milling factories of the North, many of which were situated in New England.

14. There is a Sentinel Elm Farm in Athol, Massachusetts, in the "north central" part of the state, and Donald

Burleson argues in *H. P. Lovecraft: A Critical Study* that Athol is just as much a part of the "true" Dunwich as is Wilbraham (see note 12, above). Burleson also points out, in "Humour Beneath Horror: Some Sources for 'The Dunwich Horror' and 'The Whisperer in Darkness,'" that many of the names of local farmers are drawn from Athol history.

15. Also spelled "Pocumtuc." An Indian nation native to the Connecticut River valley of western Massachussetts that likely achieved a population of about 5,000 by 1600, it was subsequently destroyed in wars, absorbed into other nations, and dispersed.

16. The Feast of the Presentation of Jesus at the Temple, also known as the Feast of the Purification of the Virgin and the Meeting of the Lord, celebrated as Candelaria in Spanish-speaking countries. Traditionally, the eve of Candlemas was the occasion of the removal of all Christmas decorations, to assure that the ill omens of berries and hollies (associated with funerals as well as Christmas) were no longer present in the home.

17. Also Groundhog Day in the United States. This unofficial holiday is based on folklore that holds that the weather that would be observed by a groundhog emerging from his or her burrow is predictive of a late or early spring. The eponymous 1993 film, starring Bill Murray as a weatherman sent to observe the holiday in a small town in Pennsylvania, is a clever story of a man given repeated chances to relive a single day to change his ill-tempered behavior.

lage and a mile and a half from any other dwelling, that Wilbur Whateley was born at 5 A.M. on Sunday, the second of February, 1913. This date was recalled because it was Candlemas,[16] which people in Dunwich curiously observe under another name;[17] and because the noises in the hills had sounded, and all the dogs of the countryside had barked persistently, throughout the night before. Less worthy of notice was the fact that the mother was one of the decadent Whateleys, a somewhat deformed, unattractive albino woman of thirty-five, living with an aged and half-insane father about whom the most frightful tales of wizardry had been whispered in his youth. Lavinia Whateley had no known husband, but according to the custom of the region made no attempt to disavow the child; concerning the other side of whose ancestry the country folk might—and did—speculate as widely as they chose. On the contrary, she seemed strangely proud of the dark, goatish-looking infant who formed such a contrast to her own sickly and pink-eyed albinism, and was heard to mutter many curious prophecies about its unusual powers and tremendous future.

Lavinia was one who would be apt to mutter such things, for she was a lone creature given to wandering amidst thunderstorms in the hills and trying to read the great odorous books which her father had inherited through two centuries of Whateleys, and which were fast falling to pieces with age and worm-holes. She had never been to school, but was filled with disjointed scraps of ancient lore that Old Whateley had taught her. The remote farmhouse had always been feared because of Old Whateley's reputation for black magic, and the unexplained death by violence of Mrs. Whateley when Lavinia was twelve years old had not helped to make the place popular. Isolated among strange influences, Lavinia was fond of wild and grandiose day-dreams and singular occupations; nor was her leisure much taken up by household cares in a home from which all standards of order and cleanliness had long since disappeared.

There was a hideous screaming which echoed above even the hill noises and the dogs' barking on the night Wilbur was born, but no known doctor or midwife presided at his coming. Neighbours knew nothing of him till a week afterward, when Old Whateley drove his sleigh through the snow into Dunwich

Village and discoursed incoherently to the group of loungers at Osborn's general store. There seemed to be a change in the old man—an added element of furtiveness in the clouded brain which subtly transformed him from an object to a subject of fear—though he was not one to be perturbed by any common family event. Amidst it all he shewed some trace of the pride later noticed in his daughter, and what he said of the child's paternity was remembered by many of his hearers years afterward.

"I dun't keer what folks think—ef Lavinny's boy looked like his pa, he wouldn't look like nothin' ye expeck. Ye needn't think the only folks is the folks hereabaouts. Lavinny's read some, an' has seed some things the most o' ye only tell abaout. I calc'late her man is as good a husban' as ye kin find this side of Aylesbury; an' ef ye knowed as much abaout the hills as I dew, ye wouldn't ast no better church weddin' nor her'n. Let me tell ye suthin'—some day yew folks'll hear a child o' Lavinny's a-callin' its father's name on the top o' Sentinel Hill!"

The only persons who saw Wilbur during the first month of his life were old Zechariah Whateley, of the undecayed Whateleys, and Earl Sawyer's common-law wife, Mamie Bishop. Mamie's visit was frankly one of curiosity, and her subsequent tales did justice to her observations; but Zechariah came to lead a pair of Alderney cows[18] which Old Whateley had bought of his son Curtis. This marked the beginning of a course of cattle-buying on the part of small Wilbur's family which ended only in 1928, when the Dunwich horror came and went; yet at no time did the ramshackle Whateley barn seem overcrowded with livestock. There came a period when people were curious enough to steal up and count the herd that grazed precariously on the steep hillside above the old farmhouse, and they could never find more than ten or twelve anæmic, bloodless-looking specimens. Evidently some blight or distemper, perhaps sprung from the unwholesome pasturage or the diseased fungi and timbers of the filthy barn, caused a heavy mortality amongst the Whateley animals. Odd wounds or sores, having something of the aspect of incisions, seemed to inflict the visible cattle; and once or twice during the earlier months certain callers fancied they could discern similar sores about the throats of the grey, unshaven old man and his slatternly, crinkly-haired albino daughter.

18. A small, docile breed from Alderney, one of the British Channel Islands. There are no longer any purebred Alderney cows.

19. This is somewhat early, but in fact, many children are "cruising" (walking with assistance) at nine months and walking unassisted by twelve months.

In the spring after Wilbur's birth Lavinia resumed her customary rambles in the hills, bearing in her misproportioned arms the swarthy child. Public interest in the Whateleys subsided after most of the country folk had seen the baby, and no one bothered to comment on the swift development which that newcomer seemed every day to exhibit. Wilbur's growth was indeed phenomenal, for within three months of his birth he had attained a size and muscular power not usually found in infants under a full year of age. His motions and even his vocal sounds shewed a restraint and deliberateness highly peculiar in an infant, and no one was really unprepared when, at seven months, he began to walk unassisted, with falterings which another month was sufficient to remove.[19]

It was somewhat after this time—on Hallowe'en—that a great blaze was seen at midnight on the top of Sentinel Hill where the old table-like stone stands amidst its tumulus of ancient bones. Considerable talk was started when Silas Bishop—of the undecayed Bishops—mentioned having seen the boy running sturdily up that hill ahead of his mother about an hour before the blaze was remarked. Silas was rounding up a stray heifer, but he nearly forgot his mission when he fleetingly spied the two figures in the dim light of his lantern. They darted almost noiselessly through the underbrush, and the astonished watcher seemed to think they were entirely unclothed. Afterward he could not be sure about the boy, who may have had some kind of a fringed belt and a pair of dark trunks or trousers on. Wilbur was never subsequently seen alive and conscious without complete and tightly buttoned attire, the disarrangement or threatened disarrangement of which always seemed to fill him with anger and alarm. His contrast with his squalid mother and grandfather in this respect was thought very notable until the horror of 1928 suggested the most valid of reasons.

The next January gossips were mildly interested in the fact that "Lavinny's black brat" had commenced to talk, and at the age of only eleven months. His speech was somewhat remarkable both because of its difference from the ordinary accents of the region, and because it displayed a freedom from infantile lisping of which many children of three or four might well be proud. The boy was not talkative, yet when he spoke he seemed to reflect some elusive element wholly unpossessed by Dunwich and its denizens. The strangeness did not reside in what he said, or even in the simple idioms he used; but seemed vaguely linked with his intonation or with the internal organs that produced the spoken sounds. His facial aspect, too, was remarkable for its maturity; for though he shared his mother's and grandfather's chinlessness, his firm and precociously shaped nose united with the expression of his large, dark, almost Latin eyes to give him an air of quasi-adulthood and well-nigh preternatural intelligence. He was, how-ever, exceedingly ugly despite his appearance of brilliancy; there being something almost goatish or animalistic about his thick lips, large-pored, yellowish skin, coarse crinkly hair, and oddly elongated ears. He was soon disliked even more decidedly than his mother and grandsire, and all conjectures about him were spiced with references to the bygone magic of Old Whateley, and how the hills once shook when he shrieked the dreadful name of *Yog-Sothoth* in the midst of a circle of stones with a great book open in his arms before him. Dogs abhorred the boy, and he was always obliged to take various defensive measures against their barking menace.

III.

MEANWHILE OLD WHATELEY continued to buy cattle without measurably increasing the size of his herd. He also cut timber and began to repair the unused parts of his house—a spacious, peaked-roofed affair whose rear end was buried entirely in the rocky hillside, and whose three least-ruined ground-floor rooms had always been sufficient for himself and his daughter.

There must have been prodigious reserves of strength in the old man to enable him to accomplish so much hard labour; and though he still babbled dementedly at times, his carpentry seemed to shew the effects of sound calculation. It had already begun as soon as Wilbur was born, when one of the many tool sheds had been put suddenly in order, clapboarded, and fitted with a stout fresh lock. Now, in restoring the abandoned upper story of the house, he was a no less thorough craftsman. His mania shewed itself only in his tight boarding-up of all the windows in the reclaimed section—though many declared that it was a crazy thing to bother with the reclamation at all.

Less inexplicable was his fitting up of another downstairs room for his new grandson—a room which several callers saw, though no one was ever admitted to the closely-boarded upper story. This chamber he lined with tall, firm shelving; along which he began gradually to arrange, in apparently careful order, all the rotting ancient books and parts of books which during his own day had been heaped promiscuously in odd corners of the various rooms.

"I made some use of 'em," he would say as he tried to mend a torn black-letter page with paste prepared on the rusty kitchen stove, "but the boy's fitten to make better use of 'em. He'd orter hev 'em as well sot as he kin, for they're goin' to be all of his larnin'."

When Wilbur was a year and seven months old—in September of 1914—his size and accomplishments were almost alarming. He had grown as large as a child of four, and was a fluent and incredibly intelligent talker. He ran freely about the fields and hills, and accompanied his mother on all her wanderings. At home he would pore diligently over the queer pictures and charts in his grandfather's books, while Old Whateley would instruct and catechise him through long, hushed afternoons. By this time the restoration of the house was finished, and those who watched it wondered why one of the upper windows had been made into a solid plank door. It was a window in the rear of the east gable end, close against the hill; and no one could imagine why a cleated wooden runway was built up to it from the ground. About the period of this work's completion people noticed that the old tool-house, tightly locked and windowlessly clapboarded since Wilbur's birth, had been abandoned again. The door swung listlessly open, and when Earl Sawyer once stepped within after a cattle-selling call on Old Whateley he was quite discomposed by the singular odour he encountered —such a stench, he averred, as he had never before smelt in all his life except near the Indian circles on the hills, and which could not come from anything sane or of this earth. But then, the homes and sheds of Dunwich folk have never been remarkable for olfactory immaculateness.

The following months were void of visible events, save that

everyone swore to a slow but steady increase in the mysterious hill noises. On May-Eve of 1915 there were tremors which even the Aylesbury people felt, whilst the following Hallowe'en produced an underground rumbling queerly synchronised with bursts of flame—"them witch Whateleys' doin's"—from the summit of Sentinel Hill. Wilbur was growing up uncannily, so that he looked like a boy of ten as he entered his fourth year. He read avidly by himself now; but talked much less than formerly. A settled taciturnity was absorbing him, and for the first time people began to speak specifically of the dawning look of evil in his goatish face. He would sometimes mutter an unfamiliar jargon, and chant in bizarre rhythms which chilled the listener with a sense of unexplainable terror. The aversion displayed toward him by dogs had now become a matter of wide remark, and he was obliged to carry a pistol in order to traverse the countryside in safety. His occasional use of the weapon did not enhance his popularity amongst the owners of canine guardians.

The few callers at the house would often find Lavinia alone on the ground floor, while odd cries and footsteps resounded in the boarded-up second story. She would never tell what her father and the boy were doing up there, though once she turned pale and displayed an abnormal degree of fear when a jocose fish-peddler tried the locked door leading to the stairway. That peddler told the store loungers at Dunwich Village that he thought he heard a horse stamping on that floor above. The loungers reflected, thinking of the door and runway, and of the cattle that so swiftly disappeared. Then they shuddered as they recalled tales of Old Whateley's youth, and of the strange things that are called out of the earth when a bullock is sacrificed at the proper time to certain heathen gods. It had for some time been noticed that dogs had begun to hate and fear the whole Whateley place as violently as they hated and feared young Wilbur personally.

In 1917 the war came, and Squire Sawyer Whateley, as chairman of the local draft board, had hard work finding a quota of young Dunwich men fit even to be sent to development camp. The government, alarmed at such signs of wholesale regional decadence, sent several officers and medical experts to investigate; conducting a survey which New England newspaper readers may still recall. It was the publicity attending this investigation which set reporters on the track of the Whateleys, and caused the *Boston Globe* and *Arkham Advertiser* to print flamboyant Sunday stories of young Wilbur's precociousness, Old Whateley's black magic, the shelves of strange books, the sealed second story of the ancient farmhouse, and the weirdness of the whole region and its hill noises. Wilbur was four and a half then, and looked like a lad of fifteen. His lips and cheeks were fuzzy with a coarse dark down, and his voice had begun to break.

Earl Sawyer went out to the Whateley place with both sets of reporters and camera men, and called their attention to the queer stench which now seemed to trickle down from the sealed upper spaces. It was, he said, exactly like a smell he had found in the tool-shed abandoned when the house was finally repaired; and like the faint odours which he sometimes thought he caught near the stone circles on the mountains. Dunwich folk read the stories when they appeared, and grinned over the obvious mistakes. They wondered, too, why the writers made so much of the fact that Old Whateley always paid for his cattle in gold pieces of extremely ancient date. The Whateleys had received their visitors with ill-concealed distaste, though they did not dare court further publicity by a violent resistance or refusal to talk.

IV.

FOR A DECADE the annals of the Whateleys sink indistinguishably into the general life of a morbid community used to their queer ways and hardened to their May-Eve and All-Hallows orgies. Twice a year they would light fires on the top of Sentinel Hill, at which times the mountain rumblings would recur with greater and greater violence; while at all seasons there were strange and portentous doings at the lonely farmhouse. In the course of time callers professed to hear sounds in the sealed upper story even when all the family were downstairs, and they wondered how swiftly or how lingeringly a cow or bullock was usually sacrificed. There was talk of a complaint to the Society for the Prevention of Cruelty to Animals; but nothing ever came of it, since Dunwich folk are never anxious to call the outside world's attention to themselves.

About 1923, when Wilbur was a boy of ten whose mind, voice, stature, and bearded face gave all the impressions of maturity, a second great siege of carpentry went on at the old house. It was all inside the sealed upper part, and from bits of discarded lumber people concluded that the youth and his grandfather had knocked out all the partitions and even removed the attic floor, leaving only one vast open void between the ground story and the peaked roof. They had torn down the great central chimney, too, and fitted the rusty range with a flimsy outside tin stovepipe.

In the spring after this event Old Whateley noticed the growing number of whippoorwills that would come out of Cold Spring Glen to chirp under his window at night. He seemed to regard the circumstance as one of great significance, and told the loungers at Osborn's that he thought his time had almost come.

"They whistle jest in tune with my breathin' naow," he said, "an' I guess they're gittin' ready to ketch my soul. They know it's a-goin' aout, an' dun't calc'late to miss it. Yew'll know, boys, arter I'm gone, whether they git me er not. Ef they dew, they'll keep up a-singin' an' laffin' till break o' day. Ef they dun't they'll kinder quiet daown like. I expeck them an' the souls they hunts fer hev some pretty tough tussles sometimes."

On Lammas Night, 1924,[20] Dr. Houghton of Aylesbury was hastily summoned by Wilbur Whateley, who had lashed his one remaining horse through the darkness and telephoned from Osborn's in the village. He found Old Whateley in a very grave state, with a cardiac action and stertorous breathing that told of an end not far off. The shapeless albino daughter and oddly bearded grandson stood by the bedside, whilst from the vacant abyss overhead there came a disquieting suggestion of rhythmical surging or lapping, as of the waves on some level beach. The doctor, though, was chiefly disturbed by the chattering night birds outside; a seemingly limitless legion of whippoorwills that cried their endless message in repetitions timed diabolically to the wheezing gasps of the dying man. It was uncanny and unnatural—too much, thought Dr. Houghton, like the whole of the region he had entered so reluctantly in response to the urgent call.

Toward one o'clock Old Whateley gained consciousness, and interrupted his wheezing to choke out a few words to his grandson.

20. The night of August 1. Lammas Day, also known as the Feast of First Fruits, is a pagan festival celebrating the wheat harvest.

21. That is, All Hallows' Day (the day after Halloween).

"More space, Willy, more space soon. Yew grows—an' *that* grows faster. It'll be ready to sarve ye soon, boy. Open up the gates to Yog-Sothoth with the long chant that ye'll find on page 751 *of the complete edition*, an' *then* put a match to the prison. Fire from airth can't burn it nohaow."

He was obviously quite mad. After a pause, during which the flock of whippoorwills outside adjusted their cries to the altered tempo while some indications of the strange hill noises came from afar off, he added another sentence or two.

"Feed it reg'lar, Willy, an' mind the quantity; but dun't let it grow too fast fer the place, fer ef it busts quarters or gits aout afore ye opens to Yog-Sothoth, it's all over an' no use. Only them from beyont kin make it multiply an' work. . . . Only them, the old uns as wants to come back. . . ."

But speech gave place to gasps again, and Lavinia screamed at the way the whippoorwills followed the change. It was the same for more than an hour, when the final throaty rattle came. Dr. Houghton drew shrunken lids over the glazing grey eyes as the tumult of birds faded imperceptibly to silence. Lavinia sobbed, but Wilbur only chuckled whilst the hill noises rumbled faintly.

"They didn't git him," he muttered in his heavy bass voice.

Wilbur was by this time a scholar of really tremendous erudition in his one-sided way, and was quietly known by correspondence to many librarians in distant places where rare and forbidden books of old days are kept. He was more and more hated and dreaded around Dunwich because of certain youthful disappearances which suspicion laid vaguely at his door; but was always able to silence inquiry through fear or through use of that fund of old-time gold which still, as in his grandfather's time, went forth regularly and increasingly for cattle-buying. He was now tremendously mature of aspect, and his height, having reached the normal adult limit, seemed inclined to wax beyond that figure. In 1925, when a scholarly correspondent from Miskatonic University called upon him one day and departed pale and puzzled, he was fully six and three-quarters feet tall.

Through all the years Wilbur had treated his half-deformed albino mother with a growing contempt, finally forbidding her to go to the hills with him on May-Eve and Hallowmass;[21] and in 1926 the poor creature complained to Mamie Bishop of being afraid of him.

"They's more abaout him as I knows than I kin tell ye, Mamie," she said, "an' naowadays they's more nor what I know myself. I vaow afur Gawd, I dun't know what he wants nor what he's a-tryin' to dew."

That Hallowe'en the hill noises sounded louder than ever, and fire burned on Sentinel Hill as usual; but people paid more attention to the rhythmical screaming of vast flocks of unnaturally belated whippoorwills which seemed to be assembled near the unlighted Whateley farmhouse. After midnight their shrill notes burst into a kind of pandæmoniac cachinnation which filled all the countryside, and not until dawn did they finally quiet down. Then they vanished, hurrying southward where they were fully a month overdue. What this meant, no one could quite be certain till later. None of the country folk seemed to have died—but poor Lavinia Whateley, the twisted albino, was never seen again.

In the summer of 1927 Wilbur repaired two sheds in the farmyard and began moving his books and effects out to them. Soon afterward Earl Sawyer told the loungers at Osborn's that more carpentry was going on in the Whateley farmhouse. Wilbur was closing all the doors and windows on the ground floor, and seemed to be taking out partitions as he and his grandfather had done upstairs four years before. He was living in one of the sheds, and Sawyer thought he seemed unusually worried and tremulous. People generally suspected him of knowing something about his mother's disappearance, and very few ever approached his neighbourhood now. His height had increased to more than seven feet, and shewed no signs of ceasing its development.

V.

THE FOLLOWING WINTER brought an event no less strange than Wilbur's first trip outside the Dunwich region. Correspondence with the Widener Library at Harvard, the Bibliothèque Nationale in Paris, the British Museum, the University of Buenos

22. Why a copy was to be found in Argentina remains a mystery.

23. That the Arkham-based library is "nearest to him geographically" evidences that Arkham is in central Massachusetts. Dunwich is in north-central Massachusetts, and if Arkham were in the eastern part of Massachusetts, the Miskatonic Library would be no nearer Dunwich than the Widener Library in Cambridge.

24. See "The Festival," note 20, above.

25. Presumably Dr. John Dee (1527–1608 or 1609), an English mathematician also trained in geography, astronomy, and astrology (in which capacity he served the court of Queen Elizabeth I, for whom he cast horoscopes). He was fascinated by occult philosophy, and in 1582 he undertook the study of alchemy, which would become a consuming interest. Dee became an enormously important figure in the history of the subject, probably the most learned man of his time, and he has featured prominently in many works of contemporary fiction, including John Crowley's brilliant *Ægypt* quartet. The Dee translation is first mentioned in Frank Belknap Long's Cthulhu Mythos story "The Space-Eaters," appearing in *Weird Tales* in July 1928. Long (1901–1994) met Lovecraft when Long was nineteen, and for many years, Lovecraft was his close friend and mentor.

26. Armitage shares a name with the Derbyshire countryman "of some education and character" who hunts "The Terror of Blue John Gap," in Arthur Conan Doyle's story of the same name (first published in the *Strand Magazine* in 1911). The creature described in Doyle's story and the Whateley twins bear remarkable similarities, considered in Marc A. Beherec's "The Devil, the Terror, and the Horror:

Ayres,[22] and the Library of Miskatonic University of Arkham had failed to get him the loan of a book he desperately wanted; so at length he set out in person, shabby, dirty, bearded, and uncouth of dialect, to consult the copy at Miskatonic, which was the nearest to him geographically.[23] Almost eight feet tall, and carrying a cheap new valise from Osborn's general store, this dark and goatish gargoyle appeared one day in Arkham in quest of the dreaded volume kept under lock and key at the college library— the hideous *Necronomicon* of the mad Arab Abdul Alhazred in Olaus Wormius' Latin version,[24] as printed in Spain in the seventeenth century. He had never seen a city before, but had no thought save to find his way to the university grounds; where indeed, he passed heedlessly by the great white-fanged watchdog that barked with unnatural fury and enmity, and tugged frantically at its stout chain.

Wilbur had with him the priceless but imperfect copy of Dr. Dee's English version[25] which his grandfather had bequeathed him, and upon receiving access to the Latin copy he at once began to collate the two texts with the aim of discovering a certain passage which would have come on the 751st page of his own defective volume. This much he could not civilly refrain from telling the librarian—the same erudite Henry Armitage (A.M. Miskatonic, Ph.D. Princeton, Litt.D. Johns Hopkins)[26] who had once called at the farm, and who now politely plied him with questions. He was looking, he had to admit, for a kind of formula or incantation containing the frightful name *Yog-Sothoth*, and it puzzled him to find discrepancies, duplications, and ambiguities which made the matter of determination far from easy. As he copied the formula he finally chose, Dr. Armitage looked involuntarily over his shoulder at the open pages; the left-hand one of which, in the Latin version, contained such monstrous threats to the peace and sanity of the world.

"Nor is it to be thought," ran the text as Armitage mentally translated it, "that man is either the oldest or the last of earth's masters, or that the common bulk of life and substance walks alone. The Old Ones were, the Old Ones are, and the Old Ones shall be. Not in the spaces we know, but *between* them, They walk serene and primal, undimensioned and to us unseen. *Yog-Sothoth* knows the gate. *Yog-Sothoth* is the gate. *Yog-Sothoth* is the key and guardian of the gate. Past, present, future, all are one in *Yog-Sothoth*. He knows where the Old Ones broke through of old, and where They shall break through again. He knows where They have trod earth's fields, and where They still tread them, and why no one can behold Them as They tread. By Their smell can men sometimes know Them near, but of Their semblance can no man know, *saving only in the features of those They have begotten on mankind*; and of those are there many sorts, differing in likeness from man's truest eidolon[27] to that shape without sight or substance which is *Them*. They walk unseen and foul in lonely places where the Words have been spoken and the Rites howled through at their Seasons. The wind gibbers with Their voices, and the earth mutters with Their consciousness. They bend the forest and crush the city, yet may not forest or city behold the hand that smites. Kadath[28] in the cold waste hath known Them, and what man knows Kadath? The ice desert of the South and the sunken isles of Ocean hold stones whereon Their seal is engraven, but who hath seen the deep frozen city or the sealed tower long garlanded with seaweed and barnacles? Great Cthulhu is Their cousin, yet can he spy Them only dimly. *Iä! Shub-Niggurath!*[29] As a foulness shall ye know Them. Their hand is at your throats, yet ye see Them not; and Their habitation is even one with your guarded threshold. *Yog-Sothoth* is the key to the gate, whereby the spheres meet. Man rules now where They ruled once; They shall soon rule where man rules now. After summer is winter, and after winter summer. They wait patient and potent, for here shall They reign again."

Dr. Armitage, associating what he was reading with what he had heard of Dunwich and its brooding presences, and of Wilbur Whateley and his dim, hideous aura that stretched from a dubious birth to a cloud of probable matricide, felt a wave of fright as tangible as a draught of the tomb's cold clamminess. The bent, goatish giant before him seemed like the spawn of another planet or dimension; like something only partly of mankind, and linked to black gulfs of essence and entity that stretch like titan phantasms beyond all spheres of force and matter, space and time. Presently Wilbur raised his head and began speaking in that strange, resonant fashion which hinted at sound-producing organs unlike the run of mankind's.

The Whateley Twins' Further Debts to Folklore and Fiction."

27. An archaic word for "image."

28. Kadath is considered at some length in *The Dream-Quest of Unknown Kadath*. The tale depicts Kadath as a gigantic castle atop an enormous mountain range in the "cold waste." Cf. Lovecraft's description of the region of the South Pole in *At the Mountains of Madness* (pp. 457–572, below).

29. Shub-Niggurath is a "cloud-like entity," according to Lovecraft (Lovecraft to Willis Conover, September 1, 1936, *Selected Letters*, V, 303), a fertility goddess symbolized as the "black Goat of the Woods" or the "Goat with a Thousand Young." Shub-Niggurath, Lovecraft informed Conover, was Yog-Sothoth's wife, and "[b]y her he has two monstrous offspring—the evil twins Nug and Yeb" (see "Genealogy of the Elder Races," Appendix 4, below). That the Hellenes were her early worshippers is indicated by the cry "Iä!," identified with the Bacchantes, according to Robert M. Price, in "Lovecraft's 'Artificial Mythology.'" However, the "Black Goat" is a separate entity from Shub-Niggurath; instead, the Goat is somehow sacred to Shub-Niggurath. See "The Question of Shub-Niggurath," by Rodolfo A. Ferraresi.

30. Machen's story *The Great God Pan*, published in 1894, tells of the offspring of the mating of a mortal woman and the god Pan. Lovecraft thought very highly of Machen's work and this story in particular, addressing the topics in some detail in his seminal 1927 essay "Supernatural Horror in Literature."

"Mr. Armitage," he said, "I calc'late I've got to take that book home. They's things in it I've got to try under sarten conditions that I can't git here, an' it 'ud be a mortal sin to let a red-tape rule hold me up. Let me take it along, Sir, an' I'll swar they wun't nobody know the difference. I dun't need to tell ye I'll take good keer of it. It wa'n't me that put this Dee copy in the shape it is. . . ."

He stopped as he saw firm denial on the librarian's face, and his own goatish features grew crafty. Armitage, half-ready to tell him he might make a copy of what parts he needed, thought suddenly of the possible consequences and checked himself. There was too much responsibility in giving such a being the key to such blasphemous outer spheres. Whateley saw how things stood, and tried to answer lightly.

"Wal, all right, ef ye feel that way abaout it. Maybe Harvard wun't be so fussy as yew be." And without saying more he rose and strode out of the building, stooping at each doorway.

Armitage heard the savage yelping of the great watchdog, and studied Whateley's gorilla-like lope as he crossed the bit of campus visible from the window. He thought of the wild tales he had heard, and recalled the old Sunday stories in the *Advertiser*; these things, and the lore he had picked up from Dunwich rustics and villagers during his one visit there. Unseen things not of earth—or at least not of tri-dimensional earth—rushed foetid and horrible through New England's glens, and brooded obscenely on the mountain tops. Of this he had long felt certain. Now he seemed to sense the close presence of some terrible part of the intruding horror, and to glimpse a hellish advance in the black dominion of the ancient and once passive nightmare. He locked away the *Necronomicon* with a shudder of disgust, but the room still reeked with an unholy and unidentifiable stench. "As a foulness shall ye know them," he quoted. Yes—the odour was the same as that which had sickened him at the Whateley farmhouse less than three years before. He thought of Wilbur, goatish and ominous, once again, and laughed mockingly at the village rumours of his parentage.

"Inbreeding?" Armitage muttered half-aloud to himself. "Great God, what simpletons! Shew them Arthur Machen's Great God Pan[30] and they'll think it a common Dunwich scandal! But what thing—what cursed shapeless influence on or off this three-dimensional earth—was Wilbur Whateley's father? Born on Candlemas—nine months after May-Eve of 1912, when the talk about the queer earth noises reached clear to Arkham—What walked on the mountains that May-Night? What Rood-mas[31] horror fastened itself on the world in half-human flesh and blood?"

During the ensuing weeks Dr. Armitage set about to collect all possible data on Wilbur Whateley and the formless presences around Dunwich. He got in communication with Dr. Houghton of Aylesbury, who had attended Old Whateley in his last illness, and found much to ponder over in the grandfather's last words as quoted by the physician. A visit to Dunwich Village failed to bring out much that was new; but a close survey of the *Necronom-icon*, in those parts which Wilbur had sought so avidly, seemed to supply new and terrible clues to the nature, methods, and desires of the strange evil so vaguely threatening this planet. Talks with several students of archaic lore in Boston, and letters to many others elsewhere, gave him a growing amazement which passed slowly through varied degrees of alarm to a state of really acute spiritual fear. As the summer drew on he felt dimly that some-thing ought to be done about the lurking terrors of the upper Miskatonic valley, and about the monstrous being known to the human world as Wilbur Whateley.

VI.

THE DUNWICH HORROR itself came between Lammas and the equinox[32] in 1928, and Dr. Armitage was among those who witnessed its monstrous prologue. He had heard, meanwhile, of Whateley's grotesque trip to Cambridge, and of his frantic efforts to borrow or copy from the *Necronomicon* at the Widener Library. Those efforts had been in vain, since Armitage had issued warn-ings of the keenest intensity to all librarians having charge of the dreaded volume. Wilbur had been shockingly nervous at Cam-bridge; anxious for the book, yet almost equally anxious to get home again, as if he feared the results of being away long.

Early in August the half-expected outcome developed, and in the small hours of the 3d Dr. Armitage was awakened suddenly by

31. See *The Case of Charles Dexter Ward*, note 138, above.

32. That is, September 23, 1928.

33. The fluid that ran in the veins of the gods. It is mentioned in Homer's *Iliad* as well as in the works of Alexander Pope and Lord Byron.

the wild, fierce cries of the savage watchdog on the college campus. Deep and terrible, the snarling, half-mad growls and barks continued; always in mounting volume, but with hideously significant pauses. Then there rang out a scream from a wholly different throat—such a scream as roused half the sleepers of Arkham and haunted their dreams ever afterward—such a scream as could come from no being born of earth, or wholly of earth.

Armitage, hastening into some clothing and rushing across the street and lawn to the college buildings, saw that others were ahead of him; and heard the echoes of a burglar-alarm still shrilling from the library. An open window shewed black and gaping in the moonlight. What had come had indeed completed its entrance; for the barking and the screaming, now fast fading into a mixed growling and moaning, proceeded unmistakably from within. Some instinct warned Armitage that what was taking place was not a thing for unfortified eyes to see, so he brushed back the crowd with authority as he unlocked the vestibule door. Among the others he saw Professor Warren Rice and Dr. Francis Morgan, men to whom he had told some of his conjectures and misgivings; and these two he motioned to accompany him inside. The inward sounds, except for a watchful, droning whine from the dog, had by this time quite subsided; but Armitage now perceived with a sudden start that a loud chorus of whippoorwills among the shrubbery had commenced a damnably rhythmical piping, as if in unison with the last breaths of a dying man.

The building was full of a frightful stench which Dr. Armitage knew too well, and the three men rushed across the hall to the small genealogical reading-room whence the low whining came. For a second nobody dared to turn on the light, then Armitage summoned up his courage and snapped the switch. One of the three—it is not certain which—shrieked aloud at what sprawled before them among disordered tables and overturned chairs. Professor Rice declares that he wholly lost consciousness for an instant, though he did not stumble or fall.

The thing that lay half-bent on its side in a foetid pool of greenish-yellow ichor[33] and tarry stickiness was almost nine feet tall, and the dog had torn off all the clothing and some of the skin. It was not quite dead, but twitched silently and spasmodically while its chest heaved in monstrous unison with the mad piping of the expectant whippoorwills outside. Bits of shoe-leather and fragments of apparel were scattered about the room, and just inside the window an empty canvas sack lay where it had evidently been thrown. Near the central desk a revolver had fallen, a dented but undischarged cartridge later explaining why it had not been fired. The thing itself, however, crowded out all other images at the time. It would be trite and not wholly accurate to say that no human pen could describe it, but one may properly say that it could not be vividly visualised by anyone whose ideas of aspect and contour are too closely bound up with the common life-forms of this planet and of the three known dimensions. It was partly human, beyond a doubt, with very man-like hands and head, and the goatish, chinless face had the stamp of the Whateleys upon it. But the torso and lower parts of the body were teratologically[34] fabulous, so that only generous clothing could ever have enabled it to walk on earth unchallenged or uneradicated.

Above the waist it was semi-anthropomorphic; though its chest, where the dog's rending paws still rested watchfully, had the leathery, reticulated[35] hide of a crocodile or alligator. The back was piebald with yellow and black, and dimly suggested the squamous[36] covering of certain snakes. Below the waist, though, it was the worst; for here all human resemblance left off and sheer phantasy began. The skin was thickly covered with coarse black fur, and from the abdomen a score of long greenish-grey tentacles with red sucking mouths protruded limply. Their arrangement was odd, and seemed to follow the symmetries of some cosmic geometry unknown to earth or the solar system. On each of the hips, deep set in a kind of pinkish, ciliated[37] orbit, was what seemed to be a rudimentary eye; whilst in lieu of a tail there depended a kind of trunk or feeler with purple annular[38] markings, and with many evidences of being an undeveloped mouth or throat. The limbs, save for their black fur, roughly resembled the hind legs of prehistoric earth's giant saurians; and terminated in ridgy-veined pads that were neither hooves nor claws. When the thing breathed, its tail and tentacles rhythmically changed colour, as if from some circulatory cause normal to the non-human side of its ancestry. In the tentacles this was observable as a deepening of the greenish tinge, whilst in the tail it was

34. Teratology is the study of physiological abnormalities, from the Greek *teras*, monster.

35. Cross-hatched.

36. Scaly.

37. With long, thin hairs, like eyelashes.

38. Ringed.

manifest as a yellowish appearance which alternated with a sickly greyish-white in the spaces between the purple rings. Of genuine blood there was none; only the fœtid greenish-yellow ichor which trickled along the painted floor beyond the radius of the stickiness, and left a curious discolouration behind it.

As the presence of the three men seemed to rouse the dying thing, it began to mumble without turning or raising its head. Dr. Armitage made no written record of its mouthings, but asserts confidently that nothing in English was uttered. At first the syllables defied all correlation with any speech of earth, but toward the last there came some disjointed fragments evidently taken from the *Necronomicon*, that monstrous blasphemy in quest of which the thing had perished. These fragments, as Armitage recalls them, ran something like "*N'gai, n'gha'ghaa, bugg-shoggog, y'hah: Yog-Sothoth, Yog-Sothoth* . . ." They trailed off into nothingness as the whippoorwills shrieked in rhythmical crescendoes of unholy anticipation.

Then came a halt in the gasping, and the dog raised its head in a long, lugubrious howl. A change came over the yellow, goatish face of the prostrate thing, and the great black eyes fell in appallingly. Outside the window the shrilling of the whippoorwills had suddenly ceased, and above the murmurs of the gathering crowd there came the sound of a panic-struck whirring and fluttering. Against the moon vast clouds of feathery watchers rose and raced from sight, frantic at that which they had sought for prey.

All at once the dog started up abruptly, gave a frightened bark, and leaped nervously out of the window by which it had entered. A cry rose from the crowd, and Dr. Armitage shouted to the men outside that no one must be admitted till the police or medical examiner came. He was thankful that the windows were just too high to permit of peering in, and drew the dark curtains carefully down over each one. By this time two policemen had arrived; and Dr. Morgan, meeting them in the vestibule, was urging them for their own sakes to postpone entrance to the stench-filled reading-room till the examiner came and the prostrate thing could be covered up.

Meanwhile frightful changes were taking place on the floor. One need not describe the *kind* and *rate* of shrinkage and disintegration that occurred before the eyes of Dr. Armitage and Professor Rice; but it is permissible to say that, aside from the external appearance of face and hands, the really human element in Wilbur Whateley must have been very small. When the medical examiner came, there was only a sticky whitish mass on the painted boards, and the monstrous odour had nearly disappeared. Apparently Whateley had had no skull or bony skeleton; at least, in any true or stable sense. He had taken somewhat after his unknown father.

VII.

YET ALL THIS was only the prologue of the actual Dunwich horror. Formalities were gone through by bewildered officials, abnormal details were duly kept from press and public, and men were sent to Dunwich and Aylesbury to look up property and notify any who might be heirs of the late Wilbur Whateley. They found the countryside in great agitation, both because of the growing rumblings beneath the domed hills, and because of the unwonted stench and the surging, lapping sounds which came increasingly from the great empty shell formed by Whateley's boarded-up farmhouse. Earl Sawyer, who tended the horse and cattle during Wilbur's absence, had developed a woefully acute case of nerves. The officials devised excuses not to enter the noisome boarded place; and were glad to confine their survey of the deceased's living quarters, the newly mended sheds, to a single visit. They filed a ponderous report at the court-house in Aylesbury,[39] and litigations concerning heirship are said to be still in progress amongst the innumerable Whateleys, decayed and undecayed, of the upper Miskatonic valley.

An almost interminable manuscript in strange characters, written in a huge ledger and adjudged a sort of diary because of the spacing and the variations in ink and penmanship, presented a baffling puzzle to those who found it on the old bureau which served as its owner's desk. After a week of debate it was sent to Miskatonic University, together with the deceased's collection of strange books, for study and possible translation; but even the best linguists soon saw that it was not likely to be unriddled with

39. As Robert D. Marten points out, in "Arkham Country: In Rescue of the Lost Searchers," it may be inferred that Aylesbury is the county seat of the county in which Dunwich is located.

ease. No trace of the ancient gold with which Wilbur and Old Whateley always paid their debts has yet been discovered.

It was in the dark of September 9th that the horror broke loose. The hill noises had been very pronounced during the evening, and dogs barked frantically all night. Early risers on the 10th noticed a peculiar stench in the air. About seven o'clock Luther Brown, the hired boy at George Corey's, between Cold Spring Glen and the village, rushed frenziedly back from his morning trip to Ten-Acre Meadow with the cows. He was almost convulsed with fright as he stumbled into the kitchen; and in the yard outside the no less frightened herd were pawing and lowing pitifully, having followed the boy back in the panic they shared with him. Between gasps Luther tried to stammer out his tale to Mrs. Corey.

"Up thar in the rud beyont the glen, Mis' Corey—they's suthin' ben thar! It smells like thunder, an' all the bushes an' little trees is pushed back from the rud like they'd a haouse ben moved along of it. An' that ain't the wust, nuther. They's *prints* in the rud, Mis' Corey—great raound prints as big as barrel-heads, all sunk daown deep like a elephant had ben along, *only they's a sight more nor four feet could make!* I looked at one or two afore I run, an' I see every one was covered with lines spreadin' aout from one place, like as if big palm-leaf fans—twict or three times as big as any they is—hed of ben paounded daown into the rud. An' the smell was awful, like what it is araound Wizard Whateley's ol' haouse . . ."

Here he faltered, and seemed to shiver afresh with the fright that had sent him flying home. Mrs. Corey, unable to extract more information, began telephoning the neighbours; thus starting on its round the overture of panic that heralded the major terrors. When she got Sally Sawyer, housekeeper at Seth Bishop's, the nearest place to Whateley's, it became her turn to listen instead of transmit; for Sally's boy Chauncey, who slept poorly, had been up on the hill toward Whateley's, and had dashed back in terror after one look at the place, and at the pasturage where Mr. Bishop's cows had been left out all night.

"Yes, Mis' Corey," came Sally's tremulous voice over the party wire, "Cha'ncey he just come back a-postin', and couldn't haff talk fer bein' scairt! He says Ol' Whateley's haouse is all blowed up, with timbers scattered raound like they'd ben dynamite inside; only the bottom floor ain't through, but is all covered with a kind o' tar-like stuff that smells awful an' drips daown offen the aidges onto the graoun' whar the side timbers is blown away. An' they's awful kinder marks in the yard, tew—great raound marks bigger raound than a hogshead, an' all sticky with stuff like is on the blowed-up haouse. Cha'ncey he says they leads off into the medders, whar a great swath wider'n a barn is matted daown, an' all the stun walls tumbled every whichway wherever it goes.

"An' he says, says he, Mis' Corey, as haow he sot to look fer Seth's caows, frighted ez he was; an' faound 'em in the upper pasture nigh the Devil's Hop Yard in an awful shape. Haff on 'em's clean gone, an' nigh haff o' them that's left is sucked most dry o' blood, with sores on 'em like they's ben on Whateley's cattle ever senct Lavinny's black brat was born. Seth he's gone aout naow to look at 'em, though I'll vaow he wun't keer ter git very nigh Wizard Whateley's! Cha'ncey didn't look keerful ter see whar the big matted-daown swath led arter it leff the pasturage, but he says he thinks it p'inted towards the glen rud to the village.

"I tell ye, Mis' Corey, they's suthin' abroad as hadn't orter be abroad, an' I for one think that black Wilbur Whateley, as come to the bad eend he desarved, is at the bottom of the breedin' of it. He wa'n't all human hisself, I allus says to everybody; an' I think he an' Ol' Whateley must a raised suthin' in that there nailed-up haouse as ain't even so human as he was. They's allus ben unseen things araound Dunwich—livin' things—as ain't human an' ain't good fer human folks.

"The graoun' was a-talkin' lass night, an' towards mornin' Cha'ncey he heerd the whippoorwills so laoud in Col' Spring Glen he couldn't sleep nun. Then he thought he heerd another faint-like saound over towards Wizard Whateley's—a kinder rippin' or tearin' o' wood, like some big box er crate was bein' opened fur off. What with this an' that, he didn't git to sleep at all till sunup, an' no sooner was he up this mornin', but he's got to go over to Whateley's an' see what's the matter. He see enough I tell ye, Mis' Corey! This dun't mean no good, an' I think as all the men-folks ought to git up a party an' do suthin'. I know suthin' awful's abaout, an' feel my time is nigh, though only Gawd knows jest what it is.

40. Donald R. Burleson, in "Humour Beneath Horror," notes that Lovecraft visited the site—which Burleson describes as a deep rocky ravine with curious fissures in a place he calls North New Salem (actually, southwest of Athol, Massachusetts)—with H. Warner Munn in late June 1928.

"Did your Luther take accaount o' whar them big tracks led tew? No? Wal, Mis' Corey, ef they was on the glen rud this side o' the glen, an' ain't got to your haouse yet, I calc'late they must go into the glen itself. They would do that. I allus says Col' Spring Glen ain't no healthy nor decent place. The whippoorwills an' fireflies there never did act like they was creaters o' Gawd, an' they's them as says ye kin hear strange things a-rushin' an' a-talkin' in the air daown thar ef ye stand in the right place, atween the rock falls an' Bear's Den."[40]

By that noon fully three-quarters of the men and boys of Dunwich were trooping over the roads and meadows between the new-made Whateley ruins and Cold Spring Glen, examining in horror the vast, monstrous prints, the maimed Bishop cattle, the strange noisome wreck of the farmhouse, and the bruised, matted vegetation of the fields and roadsides. Whatever had burst loose upon the world had assuredly gone down into the great sinister ravine; for all the trees on the banks were bent and broken, and a great avenue had been gouged in the precipice-hanging underbrush. It was as though a house, launched by an avalanche, had slid down through the tangled growths of the almost vertical slope. From below no sound came, but only a distant, undefinable fœtor; and it is not to be wondered at that the men preferred to stay on the edge and argue, rather than descend and beard the unknown Cyclopean horror in its lair. Three dogs that were with the party had barked furiously at first, but seemed cowed and reluctant when near the glen. Someone telephoned the news to the *Aylesbury Transcript*; but the editor, accustomed to wild tales from Dunwich, did no more than concoct a humorous paragraph about it; an item soon afterward reproduced by the Associated Press.

That night everyone went home, and every house and barn was barricaded as stoutly as possible. Needless to say, no cattle were allowed to remain in open pasturage. About two in the morning a frightful stench and the savage barking of the dogs awakened the household at Elmer Frye's, on the eastern edge of Cold Spring Glen, and all agreed that they could hear a sort of muffled swishing or lapping sound from somewhere outside. Mrs. Frye proposed telephoning the neighbours, and Elmer was about to agree when the noise of splintering wood burst in upon their deliberations. It came, apparently, from the barn; and was quickly followed by a hideous screaming and stamping amongst the cattle. The dogs slavered and crouched close to the feet of the fear-numbed family. Frye lit a lantern through force of habit, but knew it would be death to go out into that black farmyard. The children and the womenfolk whimpered, kept from screaming by some obscure, vestigial instinct of defence which told them their lives depended on silence. At last the noise of the cattle subsided to a pitiful moaning, and a great snapping, crashing, and crackling ensued. The Fryes, huddled together in the sitting-room, did not dare to move until the last echoes died away far down in Cold Spring Glen. Then, amidst the dismal moans from the stable and the dæmoniac piping of late whippoorwills in the glen, Selina Frye tottered to the telephone and spread what news she could of the second phase of the horror.

The next day all the countryside was in a panic; and cowed, uncommunicative groups came and went where the fiendish thing had occurred. Two titan swaths of destruction stretched from the glen to the Frye farmyard, monstrous prints covered the bare patches of ground, and one side of the old red barn had completely caved in. Of the cattle, only a quarter could be found and identified. Some of these were in curious fragments, and all that survived had to be shot. Earl Sawyer suggested that help be asked from Aylesbury or Arkham, but others maintained it would be of no use. Old Zebulon Whateley, of a branch that hovered about half way between soundness and decadence, made darkly wild suggestions about rites that ought to be practiced on the hill-tops. He came of a line where tradition ran strong, and his memories of chantings in the great stone circles were not altogether connected with Wilbur and his grandfather.

Darkness fell upon a stricken countryside too passive to organise for real defence. In a few cases closely related families would band together and watch in the gloom under one roof; but in general there was only a repetition of the barricading of the night before, and a futile, ineffective gesture of loading muskets and setting pitchforks handily about. Nothing, however, occurred except some hill noises; and when the day came there were many who hoped that the new horror had gone as swiftly as it had come. There were even bold souls who proposed an offen-

41. Although it may be hard to credit, in the 1920s, telephones were found in less than 20 percent of American households, and of course there were fewer in rural areas. Prior to World War II, most American residential telephones were on "party lines," multiparty shared telephone lines, though some cities, such as New York and Washington, had all but eliminated them. Operators would distinguish the intended caller by distinctive ringing patterns. Party-line customers could of course listen to other customers' calls. This editor recalls an early telephone company instructional film emphasizing courtesy on party lines, desisting from improperly listening to others' calls, and keeping the length of one's calls to a minimum (to keep the party line open for other users).

sive expedition down in the glen, though they did not venture to set an actual example to the still reluctant majority.

When night came again the barricading was repeated, though there was less huddling together of families. In the morning both the Frye and the Seth Bishop households reported excitement among the dogs and vague sounds and stenches from afar, while early explorers noted with horror a fresh set of the monstrous tracks in the road skirting Sentinel Hill. As before, the sides of the road shewed a bruising indicative of the blasphemously stupendous bulk of the horror; whilst the conformation of the tracks seemed to argue a passage in two directions, as if the moving mountain had come from Cold Spring Glen and returned to it along the same path. At the base of the hill a thirty-foot swath of crushed shrubbery saplings led steeply upward, and the seekers gasped when they saw that even the most perpendicular places did not deflect the inexorable trail. Whatever the horror was, it could scale a sheer stony cliff of almost complete verticality; and as the investigators climbed around to the hill's summit by safer routes they saw that the trail ended—or rather, reversed—there.

It was here that the Whateleys used to build their hellish fires and chant their hellish rituals by the table-like stone on May-Eve and Hallowmass. Now that very stone formed the centre of a vast space thrashed around by the mountainous horror, whilst upon its slightly concave surface was a thick and fœtid deposit of the same tarry stickiness observed on the floor of the ruined Whateley farmhouse when the horror escaped. Men looked at one another and muttered. Then they looked down the hill. Apparently the horror had descended by a route much the same as that of its ascent. To speculate was futile. Reason, logic, and normal ideas of motivation stood confounded. Only old Zebulon, who was not with the group, could have done justice to the situation or suggested a plausible explanation.

Thursday night began much like the others, but it ended less happily. The whippoorwills in the glen had screamed with such unusual persistence that many could not sleep, and about 3 A.M. all the party telephones[41] rang tremulously. Those who took down their receivers heard a fright-mad voice shriek out, "Help, oh, my Gawd! . . ." and some thought a crashing sound followed the breaking off of the exclamation. There was nothing more. No one dared do anything, and no one knew till morning whence the call came. Then those who had heard it called everyone on the line, and found that only the Fryes did not reply. The truth appeared an hour later, when a hastily assembled group of armed men trudged out to the Frye place at the head of the glen. It was horrible, yet hardly a surprise. There were more swaths and monstrous prints, but there was no longer any house. It had caved in like an egg-shell, and amongst the ruins nothing living or dead could be discovered. Only a stench and a tarry stickiness. The Elmer Fryes had been erased from Dunwich.

VIII.

IN THE MEANTIME a quieter yet even more spiritually poignant phase of the horror had been blackly unwinding itself behind the closed door of a shelf-lined room in Arkham. The curious manuscript record or diary of Wilbur Whateley, delivered to Miskatonic University for translation had caused much worry and bafflement among the experts in languages both ancient and modern; its very alphabet, notwithstanding a general resemblance to the heavily shaded Arabic used in Mesopotamia,[42] being absolutely unknown to any available authority. The final conclusion of the linguists was that the text represented an artificial alphabet, giving the effect of a cipher; though none of the usual methods of cryptographic solution seemed to furnish any clue, even when applied on the basis of every tongue the writer might conceivably have used. The ancient books taken from Whateley's quarters, while absorbingly interesting and in several cases promising to open up new and terrible lines of research among philosophers and men of science, were of no assistance whatever in this matter. One of them, a heavy tome with an iron clasp, was in another unknown alphabet—this one of a very different cast, and resembling Sanscrit more than anything else. The old ledger was at length given wholly into the charge of Dr. Armitage, both because of his peculiar interest in the Whateley matter, and because of his wide linguistic learning and skill in the mystical formulæ of antiquity and the Middle Ages.

Armitage had an idea that the alphabet might be something

42. S. T. Joshi suggests that this may refer to Kufic script, used from the eighth century to the twelfth century in countries where Arabic was spoken. The script is named after Kufa, Iraq, but it was first found in Mesopotamia.

43. These works are all described in the Cryptography article of the *Encyclopædia Britannica* (9th ed.). John Trithemius, the abbot of Sponheim, was the first important writer on cryptography, and his *Poligraphia*, published in 1500, has been reprinted in many editions and is the foundation stone of most later work. Porta's book appeared in 1563; De Vigenère's in 1587. Falconer's book appeared in 1685, Davys's in 1737, and Thicknesse's in 1772. Blair's work, a comprehensive article on ciphers for Rees's *Cyclopædia*, appeared forty-seven years later, in 1819; von Marten's book appeared in 1801. According to the *Britannica*, the "best modern work" on the subject is J. L. Klüber's *Kryptographik*, published in 1809. The survey of the field was unchanged in the 11th edition of the *Britannica*. Of course, cryptanalysis (the deciphering of codes) would have been more relevant to Dr. Armitage, and it is surprising that he did not consult the important work *Die Geheimschriften und die Dechiffrierkunst*, by Friedrich W. Kasiski (1863), which described for the first time the solution of the Vigenère cipher, previously regarded as a problem that was not solvable.

esoterically used by certain forbidden cults which have come down from old times, and which have inherited many forms and traditions from the wizards of the Saracenic world. That question, however, he did not deem vital; since it would be unnecessary to know the origin of the symbols if, as he suspected, they were used as a cipher in a modern language. It was his belief that, considering the great amount of text involved, the writer would scarcely have wished the trouble of using another speech than his own, save perhaps in certain special formulæ and incantations. Accordingly he attacked the manuscript with the preliminary assumption that the bulk of it was in English.

Dr. Armitage knew, from the repeated failures of his colleagues, that the riddle was a deep and complex one; and that no simple mode of solution could merit even a trial. All through late August he fortified himself with the massed lore of cryptography; drawing upon the fullest resources of his own library, and wading night after night amidst the arcana of Trithemius' *Poligraphia*, Giambattista Porta's *De Furtivis Literarum Notis*, De Vigenère's *Traité des Chiffres*, Falconer's *Cryptomenysis Patefacta*, Davys' and Thicknesse's eighteenth-century treatises, and such fairly modern authorities as Blair, von Marten, and Klüber's *Kryptographik*.[43] He interspersed his study of the books with attacks on the manuscript itself, and in time became convinced that he had to deal with one of those subtlest and most ingenious of cryptograms, in which many separate lists of corresponding letters are arranged like the multiplication table, and the message built up with arbitrary key-words known only to the initiated. The older authorities seemed rather more helpful than the newer ones, and Armitage concluded that the code of the manuscript was one of great antiquity, no doubt handed down through a long line of mystical experimenters. Several times he seemed near daylight, only to be set back by some unforeseen obstacle. Then, as September approached, the clouds began to clear. Certain letters, as used in certain parts of the manuscript, emerged definitely and unmistakably; and it became obvious that the text was indeed in English.

On the evening of September 2nd the last major barrier gave way, and Dr. Armitage read for the first time a continuous passage of Wilbur Whateley's annals. It was in truth a diary, as all had thought; and it was couched in a style clearly shewing the mixed occult erudition and general illiteracy of the strange being who wrote it. Almost the first long passage that Armitage deciphered, an entry dated November 26, 1916, proved highly startling and disquieting. It was written, he remembered, by a child of three and a half who looked like a lad of twelve or thirteen.

Today learned the Aklo[44] for the Sabaoth[45] (it ran), which did not like, it being answerable from the hill and not from the air. That upstairs more ahead of me than I had thought it would be, and is not like to have much earth brain. Shot Elam Hutchins' collie Jack when he went to bite me, and Elam says he would kill me if he dast. I guess he won't. Grandfather kept me saying the Dho formula last night, and I think I saw the inner city at the 2 magnetic poles. I shall go to those poles when the earth is cleared off, if I can't break through with the Dho-Hna formula when I commit it. They from the air told me at Sabbat that it will be years before I can clear off the earth, and I guess grandfather will be dead then, so I shall have to learn all the angles of the planes and all the formulas between the Yr and the Nhhngr. They from outside will help, but they cannot take body without human blood. That upstairs looks it will have the right cast. I can see it a little when I make the Voorish[46] sign or blow the powder of Ibn Ghazi at it, and it is near like them at May-Eve on the Hill. The other face may wear off some. I wonder how I shall look when the earth is cleared and there are no earth beings on it. He that came with the Aklo Sabaoth said I may be transfigured, there being much of outside to work on.

Morning found Dr. Armitage in a cold sweat of terror and a frenzy of wakeful concentration. He had not left the manuscript all night, but sat at his table under the electric light turning page after page with shaking hands as fast as he could decipher the cryptic text. He had nervously telephoned his wife he would not be home, and when she brought him a breakfast from the house he could scarcely dispose of a mouthful. All that day he read on, now and then halted maddeningly as a reapplication of the complex key became necessary. Lunch and dinner were brought him,

44. A secret language first mentioned by Arthur Machen, in his 1899 short story "The White People," a tale greatly admired by Lovecraft (see note 30, above).

45. "Sabaoth" is a Hebrew word for "hosts" or "armies," usually used in the phrase "Lord of Hosts." See *The Case of Charles Dexter Ward*, note 157, above.

46. Another word drawn from Machen's "The White People." Machen refers to a voor as something drawn over the hills.

but he ate only the smallest fraction of either. Toward the middle of the next night he drowsed off in his chair, but soon woke out of a tangle of nightmares almost as hideous as the truths and menaces to man's existence that he had uncovered.

On the morning of September 4th Professor Rice and Dr. Morgan insisted on seeing him for a while, and departed trembling and ashen-grey. That evening he went to bed, but slept only fitfully. Wednesday—the next day—he was back at the manuscript, and began to take copious notes both from the current sections and from those he had already deciphered. In the small hours of that night he slept a little in an easy-chair in his office, but was at the manuscript again before dawn. Some time before noon his physician, Dr. Hartwell, called to see him and insisted that he cease work. He refused; intimating that it was of the most vital importance for him to complete the reading of the diary and promising an explanation in due course of time. That evening, just as twilight fell, he finished his terrible perusal and sank back exhausted. His wife, bringing his dinner, found him in a half-comatose state; but he was conscious enough to warn her off with a sharp cry when he saw her eyes wander toward the notes he had taken. Weakly rising, he gathered up the scribbled papers and sealed them all in a great envelope, which he immediately placed in his inside coat pocket. He had sufficient strength to get home, but was so clearly in need of medical aid that Dr. Hartwell was summoned at once. As the doctor put him to bed he could only mutter over and over again, "But what, in God's name, can we do?"

Dr. Armitage slept, but was partly delirious the next day. He made no explanations to Hartwell, but in his calmer moments spoke of the imperative need of a long conference with Rice and Morgan. His wilder wanderings were very startling indeed, including frantic appeals that something in a boarded-up farmhouse be destroyed, and fantastic references to some plan for the extirpation of the entire human race and all animal and vegetable life from the earth by some terrible elder race of beings from another dimension. He would shout that the world was in danger, since the Elder Things wished to strip it and drag it away from the solar system and cosmos of matter into some other plane or phase of entity from which it had once fallen, vigintillions of æons ago. At other times he would call for the dreaded *Necronomicon* and the *Dæmonolatreia* of Remigius,[47] in which he seemed hopeful of finding some formula to check the peril he conjured up.

47. See "The Festival," note 19, above.

"Stop them, stop them!" he would shout. "Those Whateleys meant to let them in, and the worst of all is left! Tell Rice and Morgan we must do something—it's a blind business, but I know how to make the powder. . . . It hasn't been fed since the second of August, when Wilbur came here to his death, and at that rate. . . ."

But Armitage had a sound physique despite his seventy-three years, and slept off his disorder that night without developing any real fever. He woke late Friday, clear of head, though sober with a gnawing fear and tremendous sense of responsibility. Saturday afternoon he felt able to go over to the library and summon Rice and Morgan for a conference, and the rest of that day and evening the three men tortured their brains in the wildest speculation and the most desperate debate. Strange and terrible books were drawn voluminously from the stack shelves and from secure places of storage; and diagrams and formulæ were copied with feverish haste and in bewildering abundance. Of scepticism there was none. All three had seen the body of Wilbur Whateley as it lay on the floor in a room of that very building, and after that not one of them could feel even slightly inclined to treat the diary as a madman's raving.

Opinions were divided as to notifying the Massachusetts State Police, and the negative finally won. There were things involved which simply could not be believed by those who had not seen a sample, as indeed was made clear during certain subsequent investigations. Late at night the conference disbanded without having developed a definite plan, but all day Sunday Armitage was busy comparing formulæ and mixing chemicals obtained from the college laboratory. The more he reflected on the hellish diary, the more he was inclined to doubt the efficacy of any material agent in stamping out the entity which Wilbur Whateley had left behind him—the earth-threatening entity which, unknown to him, was to burst forth in a few hours and become the memorable Dunwich horror.

Monday was a repetition of Sunday with Dr. Armitage, for the task in hand required an infinity of research and experiment. Further consultations of the monstrous diary brought about various changes of plan, and he knew that even in the end a large amount of uncertainty must remain. By Tuesday he had a definite line of action mapped out, and believed he would try a trip to Dunwich within a week. Then, on Wednesday, the great shock came. Tucked obscurely away in a corner of the *Arkham Advertiser* was a facetious little item from the Associated Press, telling what a record-breaking monster the bootleg whiskey of Dunwich had raised up. Armitage, half stunned, could only telephone for Rice and Morgan. Far into the night they discussed, and the next day was a whirlwind of preparation on the part of them all. Armitage knew he would be meddling with terrible powers, yet saw that there was no other way to annul the deeper and more malign meddling which others had done before him.

IX.

FRIDAY MORNING ARMITAGE, Rice, and Morgan set out by motor for Dunwich, arriving at the village about one in the afternoon. The day was pleasant, but even in the brightest sunlight a kind of quiet dread and portent seemed to hover about the strangely domed hills and the deep, shadowy ravines of the stricken region. Now and then on some mountain-top a gaunt circle of stones could be glimpsed against the sky. From the air of hushed fright at Osborn's store they knew something hideous had happened, and soon learned of the annihilation of the Elmer Frye house and family. Throughout that afternoon they rode around Dunwich, questioning the natives concerning all that had occurred, and seeing for themselves with rising pangs of horror the drear Frye ruins with their lingering traces of the tarry stickiness, the blasphemous tracks in the Frye yard, the wounded Seth Bishop cattle, and the enormous swaths of disturbed vegetation in various places. The trail up and down Sentinel Hill seemed to Armitage of almost cataclysmic significance, and he looked long at the sinister altar-like stone on the summit.

At length the visitors, apprised of a party of State Police which had come from Aylesbury that morning in response to the first telephone reports of the Frye tragedy, decided to seek out the officers and compare notes as far as practicable. This, however, they found more easily planned than performed; since no sign of the party could be found in any direction. There had been five of them in a car, but now the car stood empty near the ruins in the Frye yard. The natives, all of whom had talked with the policemen, seemed at first as perplexed as Armitage and his companions. Then old Sam Hutchins thought of something and turned pale, nudging Fred Farr and pointing to the dank, deep hollow that yawned close by.

"Gawd," he gasped, "I told 'em not ter go daown into the glen, an' I never thought nobody'd dew it with them tracks an' that smell an' the whippoorwills a-screechin' daown thar in the dark o' noonday. . . ."

A cold shudder ran through natives and visitors alike, and every ear seemed strained in a kind of instinctive, unconscious listening. Armitage, now that he had actually come upon the horror and its monstrous work, trembled with the responsibility he felt to be his. Night would soon fall, and it was then that the mountainous blasphemy lumbered upon its eldritch course. *Negotium perambulans in tenebris. . . .*[48] The old librarian rehearsed the formulæ he had memorised, and clutched the paper containing the alternative one he had not memorised. He saw that his electric flashlight was in working order. Rice, beside him, took from a valise a metal sprayer of the sort used in combating insects; whilst Morgan uncased the big-game rifle on which he relied despite his colleague's warnings that no material weapon would be of help.

Armitage, having read the hideous diary, knew painfully well what kind of a manifestation to expect; but he did not add to the fright of the Dunwich people by giving any hints or clues. He hoped that it might be conquered without any revelation to the world of the monstrous thing it had escaped. As the shadows gathered, the natives commenced to disperse homeward, anxious to bar themselves indoors despite the present evidence that all human locks and bolts were useless before a force that could bend trees and crush houses when it chose. They shook their heads at the visitors' plan to stand guard at the Frye ruins near the glen; and, as they left, had little expectancy of ever seeing the watchers again.

There were rumblings under the hills that night, and the whippoorwills piped threateningly. Once in a while a wind,

48. Roughly, "The business that passes through in the dark. . . ." Verses 5 and 6 of the 91st Psalm (King James Version) read, "Thou shalt not be afraid for the terror by night; nor for the arrow that flieth by day; / Nor for the pestilence that walketh in darkness; nor for the destruction that wasteth at noonday."

sweeping up out of Cold Spring Glen, would bring a touch of ineffable fœtor to the heavy night air; such a fœtor as all three of the watchers had smelled once before, when they stood above a dying thing that had passed for fifteen years and a half as a human being. But the looked-for terror did not appear. Whatever was down there in the glen was biding its time, and Armitage told his colleagues it would be suicidal to try to attack it in the dark.

Morning came wanly, and the night-sounds ceased. It was a grey, bleak day, with now and then a drizzle of rain; and heavier and heavier clouds seemed to be piling themselves up beyond the hills to the northwest. The men from Arkham were undecided what to do. Seeking shelter from the increasing rainfall beneath one of the few undestroyed Frye outbuildings, they debated the wisdom of waiting, or of taking the aggressive and going down into the glen in quest of their nameless, monstrous quarry. The downpour waxed in heaviness, and distant peals of thunder sounded from far horizons. Sheet lightning shimmered, and then a forky bolt flashed near at hand, as if descending into the accursed glen itself. The sky grew very dark, and the watchers hoped that the storm would prove a short, sharp one followed by clear weather.

It was still gruesomely dark when, not much over an hour later, a confused babel of voices sounded down the road. Another moment brought to view a frightened group of more than a dozen men, running, shouting, and even whimpering hysterically. Someone in the lead began sobbing out words, and the Arkham men started violently when those words developed a coherent form.

"Oh, my Gawd, my Gawd," the voice choked out. "It's a-goin' agin, *an' this time by day!* It's aout—it's aout an' a-movin' this very minute, an' only the Lord knows when it'll be on us all!"

The speaker panted into silence, but another took up his message.

"Nigh on a haour ago Zeb Whateley here heerd the 'phone a-ringin', an' it was Mis' Corey, George's wife, that lives daown by the junction. She says the hired boy Luther was aout drivin' in the caows from the storm arter the big bolt, when he see all the trees a-bendin' at the maouth o' the glen—opposite side ter this—an' smelt the same awful smell like he smelt when he faound the big tracks las' Monday mornin'. An' she says he says they was a swishin' lappin' saound, more nor what the bendin' trees an' bushes could make, an' all on a suddent the trees along the rud begun ter git pushed one side, an' they was a awful stompin' an' splashin' in the mud. But mind ye, Luther he didn't see nothin' at all, only just the bendin' trees an' underbrush.

"Then fur ahead where Bishop's Brook goes under the rud he heerd a awful creakin' an' strainin' on the bridge, an' says he could tell the saound o' wood a-startin' to crack an' split. An' all the whiles he never see a thing, only them trees an' bushes a-bendin'. An' when the swishin' saound got very fur off—on the rud towards Wizard Whateley's an' Sentinel Hill—Luther he had the guts ter step up whar he'd heerd it furst an' look at the graound. It was all mud an' water, an' the sky was dark, an' the rain was wipin' aout all tracks abaout as fast as could be; but beginnin' at the glen maouth, whar the trees had moved, they was still some o' them awful prints big as bar'ls like he seen Monday."

At this point the first excited speaker interrupted.

"But *that* ain't the trouble naow—that was only the start. Zeb here was callin' folks up an' everybody was a-listenin' in when a call from Seth Bishop's cut in. His haousekeeper Sally was carryin' on fit ter kill—she'd jest seed the trees a-bendin' beside the rud, an' says they was a kind o' mushy saound, like a elephant puffin' an' treadin', a-headin' fer the haouse. Then she up an' spoke sud-dent of a fearful smell, an' says her boy Cha'ncey was a-screamin' as haow it was jest like what he smelt up to the Whateley rewins Monday mornin'. An' the dogs was all barkin' an' whinin' awful.

"An' then she let aout a turrible yell, an' says the shed daown the rud had jest caved in like the storm hed blowed it over, only the wind wa'n't strong enough to dew that. Everybody was a-listenin', an' we could hear lots o' folks on the wire a-gaspin'. All to onct Sally she yelled agin, an' says the front yard picket fence hed just crumbled up, though they wa'n't no sign o' what done it. Then everybody on the line could hear Cha'ncey an' ol' Seth Bishop a-yellin' tew, an' Sally was shriekin' aout that suthin' heavy hed struck the haouse—not lightnin' nor nothin', but suthin' heavy agin the front, that kep' a-launchin' itself agin an' agin, though ye couldn't see nothin' aout the front winders. An' then . . . an' then . . ."

Lines of fright deepened on every face; and Armitage, shaken as he was, had barely poise enough to prompt the speaker.

"An' then . . . Sally she yelled aout, 'O help, the haouse is a-cavin' in' . . . an' on the wire we could hear a turrible crashin' an' a hull flock o' screamin' . . . jest like when Elmer Frye's place was took, only wuss. . . .'"

The man paused, and another of the crowd spoke.

"That's all—not a saound nor squeak over the 'phone arter that. Jest still-like. We that heerd it got aout Fords an' wagons an' raounded up as many able-bodied menfolks as we could git, at Corey's place, an' come up here ter see what yew thought best ter dew. Not but what I think it's the Lord's jedgment fer our iniquities, that no mortal kin ever set aside."

Armitage saw that the time for positive action had come, and spoke decisively to the faltering group of frightened rustics.

"We must follow it, boys." He made his voice as reassuring as possible. "I believe there's a chance of putting it out of business. You men know that those Whateleys were wizards—well, this thing is a thing of *wizardry*, and must be put down by the same means. I've seen Wilbur Whateley's diary and read some of the strange old books he used to read; and I think I know the right kind of spell to recite to make the thing fade away. Of course, one can't be sure, but we can always take a chance. It's invisible—I knew it would be—but there's a powder in this long-distance sprayer that might make it shew up for a second. Later on we'll try it. It's a frightful thing to have alive, but it isn't as bad as what Wilbur would have let in if he'd lived longer. You'll never know what the world has escaped. Now we've only this one thing to fight, and it can't multiply. It can, though, do a lot of harm; so we mustn't hesitate to rid the community of it.

"We must follow it—and the way to begin is to go to the place that has just been wrecked. Let somebody lead the way—I don't know your roads very well, but I've an idea there might be a shorter cut across lots. How about it?"

The men shuffled about a moment, and then Earl Sawyer spoke softly, pointing with a grimy finger through the steadily lessening rain.

"I guess ye kin git to Seth Bishop's quickest by cuttin' acrost the lower medder here, wadin' the brook at the low place, an' climbin' through Carrier's mowin' and the timber-lot beyont. That comes aout on the upper rud mighty nigh Seth's—a leetle t'other side."

Armitage, with Rice and Morgan, started to walk in the direction indicated; and most of the natives followed slowly. The sky was growing lighter, and there were signs that the storm had worn itself away. When Armitage inadvertently took a wrong direction, Joe Osborn warned him and walked ahead to shew the right one. Courage and confidence were mounting; though the twilight of the almost perpendicular wooded hill which lay toward the end of their short cut, and among whose fantastic ancient trees they had to scramble as if up a ladder, put these qualities to a severe test.

At length they emerged on a muddy road to find the sun coming out. They were a little beyond the Seth Bishop place, but bent trees and hideously unmistakable tracks shewed what had passed by. Only a few moments were consumed in surveying the ruins just around the bend. It was the Frye incident all over again, and nothing dead or living was found in either of the collapsed shells which had been the Bishop house and barn. No one cared to remain there amidst the stench and tarry stickiness, but all turned instinctively to the line of horrible prints leading on toward the wrecked Whateley farmhouse and the altar-crowned slopes of Sentinel Hill.

As the men passed the site of Wilbur Whateley's abode they shuddered visibly, and seemed again to mix hesitancy with their zeal. It was no joke tracking down something as big as a house that one could not see, but that had all the vicious malevolence of a dæmon. Opposite the base of Sentinel Hill the tracks left the road, and there was a fresh bending and matting visible along the broad swath marking the monster's former route to and from the summit.

Armitage produced a pocket telescope of considerable power and scanned the steep green side of the hill. Then he handed the instrument to Morgan, whose sight was keener. After a moment of gazing Morgan cried out sharply, passing the glass to Earl Sawyer and indicating a certain spot on the slope with his finger. Sawyer, as clumsy as most non-users of optical devices are, fumbled a while; but eventually focussed the lenses with Armitage's aid. When he did so his cry was less restrained than Morgan's had been.

"Gawd almighty, the grass an' bushes is a-movin'! It's a-goin' up—slow-like—creepin'—up ter the top this minute, heaven only knows what fur!"

Then the germ of panic seemed to spread among the seekers. It was one thing to chase the nameless entity, but quite another to find it. Spells might be all right—but suppose they weren't? Voices began questioning Armitage about what he knew of the thing, and no reply seemed quite to satisfy. Everyone seemed to feel himself in close proximity to phases of Nature and of being utterly forbidden and wholly outside the sane experience of mankind.

X.

IN THE END the three men from Arkham—old, white-bearded Dr. Armitage, stocky, iron-grey Professor Rice, and lean, youngish Dr. Morgan—ascended the mountain alone. After much patient instruction regarding its focussing and use, they left the telescope with the frightened group that remained in the road; and as they climbed they were watched closely by those among whom the glass was passed around. It was hard going, and Armitage had to be helped more than once. High above the toiling group the great swath trembled as its hellish maker re-passed with snail-like deliberateness. Then it was obvious that the pursuers were gaining.

Curtis Whateley—of the undecayed branch—was holding the telescope when the Arkham party detoured radically from the swath. He told the crowd that the men were evidently trying to get to a subordinate peak which overlooked the swath at a point considerably ahead of where the shrubbery was now bending. This, indeed, proved to be true; and the party were seen to gain the minor elevation only a short time after the invisible blasphemy had passed it.

Then Wesley Corey, who had taken the glass, cried out that Armitage was adjusting the sprayer which Rice held, and that something must be about to happen. The crowd stirred uneasily, recalling that this sprayer was expected to give the unseen horror a moment of visibility. Two or three men shut their eyes, but Curtis Whateley snatched back the telescope and strained his vision to the utmost. He saw that Rice, from the party's point of vantage above and behind the entity, had an excellent chance of spreading the potent powder with marvellous effect.

Those without the telescope saw only an instant's flash of grey cloud—a cloud about the size of a moderately large building—near the top of the mountain. Curtis, who had held the instrument, dropped it with a piercing shriek into the ankle-deep mud of the road. He reeled, and would have crumpled to the ground had not two or three others seized and steadied him. All he could do was moan half-inaudibly.

"Oh, oh, great Gawd . . . *that* . . . *that* . . ."

There was a pandemonium of questioning, and only Henry Wheeler thought to rescue the fallen telescope and wipe it clean of mud. Curtis was past all coherence, and even isolated replies were almost too much for him.

"Bigger'n a barn . . . all made o' squirmin' ropes . . . hull thing sort o' shaped like a hen's egg bigger'n anything with dozens o' legs like hogsheads that haff shut up when they step . . . nothin' solid abaout it—all like jelly, an' made o' sep'rit wrigglin' ropes pushed clost together . . . great bulgin' eyes all over it . . . ten or twenty maouths or trunks a-stickin' aout all along the sides, big as stovepipes an' all a-tossin' an' openin' an' shuttin' . . . all grey, with kinder blue or purple rings . . . *an' Gawd in heaven—that haff face on top!* . . ."

This final memory, whatever it was, proved too much for poor Curtis; and he collapsed completely before he could say more. Fred Farr and Will Hutchins carried him to the roadside and laid him on the damp grass. Henry Wheeler, trembling, turned the rescued telescope on the mountain to see what he might. Through the lenses were discernible three tiny figures, apparently running toward the summit as fast as the steep incline allowed. Only these—nothing more. Then everyone noticed a strangely unseasonable noise in the deep valley behind, and even in the underbrush of Sentinel Hill itself. It was the piping of unnumbered whippoorwills, and in their shrill chorus there seemed to lurk a note of tense and evil expectancy.

Earl Sawyer now took the telescope and reported the three

figures as standing on the topmost ridge, virtually level with the altar-stone but at a considerable distance from it. One figure, he said, seemed to be raising its hands above its head at rhythmic intervals; and as Sawyer mentioned the circumstance the crowd seemed to hear a faint, half-musical sound from the distance, as if a loud chant were accompanying the gestures. The weird silhouette on that remote peak must have been a spectacle of infinite grotesqueness and impressiveness, but no observer was in a mood for æsthetic appreciation. "I guess he's sayin' the spell," whispered Wheeler as he snatched back the telescope. The whippoorwills were piping wildly, and in a singularly curious irregular rhythm quite unlike that of the visible ritual.

Suddenly the sunshine seemed to lessen without the intervention of any discernible cloud. It was a very peculiar phenomenon, and was plainly marked by all. A rumbling sound seemed brewing beneath the hills, mixed strangely with a concordant rumbling which clearly came from the sky. Lightning flashed aloft, and the wondering crowd looked in vain for the portents of storm. The chanting of the men from Arkham now became unmistakable, and Wheeler saw through the glass that they were all raising their arms in the rhythmic incantation. From some farmhouse far away came the frantic barking of dogs.

The change in the quality of the daylight increased, and the crowd gazed about the horizon in wonder. A purplish darkness, born of nothing more than a spectral deepening of the sky's blue, pressed down upon the rumbling hills. Then the lightning flashed again, somewhat brighter than before, and the crowd fancied that it had shewed a certain mistiness around the altar-stone on the distant height. No one, however, had been using the telescope at that instant. The whippoorwills continued their irregular pulsation, and the men of Dunwich braced themselves tensely against some imponderable menace with which the atmosphere seemed surcharged.

Without warning came those deep, cracked, raucous vocal sounds which will never leave the memory of the stricken group who heard them. Not from any human throat were they born, for the organs of man can yield no such acoustic perversions. Rather would one have said they came from the pit itself, had not their source been so unmistakably the altar-stone on the peak. It is almost erroneous to call them *sounds* at all, since so much of their ghastly, infra-bass timbre spoke to dim seats of consciousness and terror far subtler than the ear; yet one must do so, since their form was indisputably though vaguely that of half-articulate *words*. They were loud—loud as the rumblings and the thunder above which they echoed—yet did they come from no visible being. And because imagination might suggest a conjectural source in the world of non-visible beings, the huddled crowd at the mountain's base huddled still closer, and winced as if in expectation of a blow.

"*Ygnaih . . . ygnaiih . . . thflthkh'ngha . . . Yog-Sothoth . . .*" rang the hideous croaking out of space. "*Y'bthnk . . . h'ehye—n'grkdl'lh. . . .*"

The speaking impulse seemed to falter here, as if some frightful psychic struggle were going on. Henry Wheeler strained his eye at the telescope, but saw only the three grotesquely silhouetted human figures on the peak, all moving their arms furiously in strange gestures as their incantation drew near its culmination. From what black wells of Acherontic[49] fear or feeling, from what unplumbed gulfs of extra-cosmic consciousness or obscure, long-latent heredity, were those half-articulate thunder-croakings drawn? Presently they began to gather renewed force and coherence as they grew in stark, utter, ultimate frenzy.

"*Eh-ya-ya-ya-yahaah—e'yayayaaaa . . . ngh'aaaaa . . . ngh'aaa . . . h'yuh . . . h'yuh . . .* HELP! HELP! . . . ff—ff—ff—FATHER! FATHER! YOG-SOTHOTH! . . ."

But that was all. The pallid group in the road, still reeling at the *indisputably English* syllables that had poured thickly and thunderously down from the frantic vacancy beside that shocking altar-stone, were never to hear such syllables again. Instead, they jumped violently at the terrific report which seemed to rend the hills; the deafening, cataclysmic peal whose source, be it inner earth or sky, no hearer was ever able to place. A single lightning-bolt shot from the purple zenith to the altar-stone, and a great tidal wave of viewless force and indescribable stench swept down from the hill to all the countryside. Trees, grass, and underbrush were whipped into a fury; and the frightened crowd at the mountain's base, weakened by the lethal fœtor that seemed about to asphyxiate them, were almost hurled off their feet. Dogs

49. The Acheron was one of the five rivers of the Greek underworld.

howled from the distance, green grass and foliage wilted to a curious, sickly yellow-grey, and over field and forest were scattered the bodies of dead whippoorwills.

The stench left quickly, but the vegetation never came right again. To this day there is something queer and unholy about the growths on and around that fearsome hill. Curtis Whateley was only just regaining consciousness when the Arkham men came slowly down the mountain in the beams of a sunlight once more brilliant and untainted. They were grave and quiet, and seemed shaken by memories and reflections even more terrible than those which had reduced the group of natives to a state of cowed quivering. In reply to a jumble of questions they only shook their heads and reaffirmed one vital fact.

"The thing has gone forever," Armitage said. "It has been split up into what it was originally made of, and can never exist again. It was an impossibility in a normal world. Only the least fraction was really matter in any sense we know. It was like its father— and most of it has gone back to him in some vague realm or dimension outside our material universe; some vague abyss out of which only the most accursed rites of human blasphemy could ever have called him for a moment on the hills."

There was a brief silence, and in that pause the scattered senses of poor Curtis Whateley began to knit back into a sort of continuity; so that he put his hands to his head with a moan. Memory seemed to pick itself up where it had left off, and the horror of the sight that had prostrated him burst in upon him again.

"Oh, oh, my Gawd, that haff face—that haff face on top of it . . . that face with the red eyes an' crinkly albino hair, an' no chin, like the Whateleys . . . It was a octopus, centipede, spider kind o' thing, but they was a haff-shaped man's face on top of it, an' it looked like Wizard Whateley's, only it was yards an' yards acrost. . . ."

He paused exhausted, as the whole group of natives stared in a bewilderment not quite crystallised into fresh terror. Only old Zebulon Whateley, who wanderingly remembered ancient things but who had been silent heretofore, spoke aloud.

"Fifteen year' gone," he rambled, "I heerd Ol' Whateley say as haow some day we'd hear a child o' Lavinny's a-callin' its father's name on the top o' Sentinel Hill . . ."

But Joe Osborn interrupted him to question the Arkham men anew.

"*What was it, anyhaow, an' haowever did young Wizard Whateley call it aout o' the air it come from?*"

Armitage chose his words very carefully.

"It was—well, it was mostly a kind of force that doesn't belong in our part of space; a kind of force that acts and grows and shapes itself by other laws than those of our sort of Nature. We have no business calling in such things from outside, and only very wicked people and very wicked cults ever try to. There was some of it in Wilbur Whateley himself—enough to make a devil and a precocious monster of him, and to make his passing out a pretty terrible sight. I'm going to burn his accursed diary, and if you men are wise you'll dynamite that altar-stone up there, and pull down all the rings of standing stones on the other hills. Things like that brought down the beings those Whateleys were so fond of—the beings they were going to let in tangibly to wipe out the human race and drag the earth off to some nameless place for some nameless purpose.

"But as to this thing we've just sent back—the Whateleys raised it for a terrible part in the doings that were to come. It grew fast and big from the same reason that Wilbur grew fast and big—but it beat him because it had a greater share of the outsideness in it. You needn't ask how Wilbur called it out of the air. He didn't call it out. *It was his twin brother, but it looked more like the father than he did.*"

Still from *The Dunwich Horror* starring Dean Stockwell and Sandra Dee, shown here (American International Pictures, 1970).

Poster from *The Dunwich Horror* (American International Pictures, 1970).

The Whisperer in Darkness[1]

This story may be seen as a more mature version of "Beyond the Wall of Sleep," achieving much greater depth by providing a detailed provenance for an alien race known as the Outer Ones instead of the vague history implied in the prior tale. Lovecraft here expands the panoply of beings of which humans form only a small part, and the story's documentary style, despite the narrator's almost unbelievable naïvete, gives it the ring of credibility and enhances its shocking final revelation.

1. Written between February and September 1930, the story first appeared in *Weird Tales* 18, no. 1 (August 1931), 32–73, with this reading line: "Wild horror stalked the Vermont hills—a story of weird fungi from the newly discovered ninth planet." Steven J. Mariconda has described in some detail Lovecraft's composition and revision of the tale in "Tightening the Coil: The Revision of 'The Whisperer in Darkness.'" Robert M. Price has reconstructed an ur-version of the tale and published it as "The Vermont Horror."

I.

Bear in mind closely that I did not see any actual visual horror at the end. To say that a mental shock was the cause of what I inferred—that last straw which sent me racing out of the lonely Akeley farmhouse and through the wild domed hills of Vermont in a commandeered motor at night—is to ignore the plainest facts of my final experience. Notwithstanding the deep extent to which I shared the information and speculations of Henry Akeley, the things I saw and heard, and the admitted vividness of the impression produced on me by these things, I cannot prove even now whether I was right or wrong in my hideous inference. For after all, Akeley's disappearance establishes nothing. People found nothing amiss in his house despite the bullet-marks on the outside and inside. It was just as though he had walked out casually for a ramble in the hills and failed to return. There was not even a sign that a guest had been there, or that those horrible cylinders and machines had been stored in the study. That he had mortally feared the crowded green hills and endless trickle of brooks among which he had been born and reared, means nothing at all, either; for thousands are subject to just such morbid fears. Eccentricity, moreover, could easily account for his strange acts and apprehensions toward the last.

The whole matter began, so far as I am concerned, with the historic and unprecedented Vermont floods of November 3, 1927.[2] I was then, as now, an instructor of literature at Miskatonic University in Arkham, Massachusetts, and an enthusiastic amateur student of New England folklore. Shortly after the flood, amidst the varied reports of hardship, suffering, and organised relief which filled the press, there appeared certain odd stories of things found floating in some of the swollen rivers; so that many of my friends embarked on curious discussions and appealed to me to shed what light I could on the subject. I felt flattered at having my folklore study taken so seriously, and did what I could to belittle the wild, vague tales which seemed so clearly an outgrowth of old rustic superstitions. It amused me to find several persons of education who insisted that some stratum of obscure, distorted fact might underlie the rumours.

The tales thus brought to my notice came mostly through newspaper cuttings; though one yarn had an oral source and was repeated to a friend of mine in a letter from his mother in Hardwick, Vermont. The type of thing described was essentially the same in all cases, though there seemed to be three separate instances involved—one connected with the Winooski River near Montpelier, another attached to the West River in Windham County beyond Newfane, and a third centring in the Passumpsic in Caledonia County above Lyndonville.[3] Of course many of the stray items mentioned other instances, but on analysis they all seemed to boil down to these three. In each case country folk reported seeing one or more very bizarre and disturbing objects in the surging waters that poured down from the unfrequented hills, and there was a widespread tendency to connect these sights with a primitive, half-forgotten cycle of whispered legend which old people resurrected for the occasion.

What people thought they saw were organic shapes not quite like any they had ever seen before. Naturally, there were many human bodies washed along by the streams in that tragic period; but those who described these strange shapes felt quite sure that they were not human, despite some superficial resemblances in

Springfield, Vermont, in November 1927.

2. Called by many Vermont's "greatest natural disaster," the flood wrought ruin on many parts of Vermont. The Vermont Historical Society wrote, "It had already been a wet October and rivers were swollen and the ground saturated. Nine inches of rain fell in a thirty-six hour period and horrendous flooding began. Though all of New England was affected, Vermont was devastated. The state flooded from Newport to Bennington, with the Winooski River Valley the hardest hit. Eighty-five people died and 9,000 were left homeless" (http://freedomandunity.org/1800s/natural_disaster.html). President Calvin Coolidge, traveling to Vermont a year after the flood, on September 21, 1928, in a speech thereafter known as the "Brave Little State of Vermont," expressed his admiration for the self-reliance of Vermonters in recovering from the disaster: "I love Vermont because of her hills and valleys, her scenery and invigorating climate, but most of all because of her indomitable people. They are a race of pioneers who have almost beggared themselves to serve others. If the spirit of liberty should vanish in other parts of the Union, and support of our institutions should languish, it could all be replenished from the generous store held by the people of this brave little state of Vermont" (http://en.wikipedia.org/wiki/Brave_Little_State_of_Vermont_speech). The speech is also inscribed at the President Calvin Coolidge Homestead in Plymouth Notch, Vermont.

3. All are within ninety miles of each other, certainly within the range of a central water source.

size and general outline. Nor, said the witnesses, could they have been any kind of animal known to Vermont. They were pinkish things about five feet long; with crustaceous bodies bearing vast pairs of dorsal fins or membraneous wings and several sets of articulated limbs, and with a sort of convoluted ellipsoid, covered with multitudes of very short antennæ, where a head would ordinarily be. It was really remarkable how closely the reports from different sources tended to coincide; though the wonder was lessened by the fact that the old legends, shared at one time throughout the hill country, furnished a morbidly vivid picture which might well have coloured the imaginations of all the witnesses concerned. It was my conclusion that such witnesses—in every case naive and simple backwoods folk—had glimpsed the battered and bloated bodies of human beings or farm animals in the whirling currents; and had allowed the half-remembered folklore to invest these pitiful objects with fantastic attributes.

The ancient folklore, while cloudy, evasive, and largely forgotten by the present generation, was of a highly singular character, and obviously reflected the influence of still earlier Indian tales. I knew it well, though I had never been in Vermont, through the exceedingly rare monograph of Eli Davenport, which embraces material orally obtained prior to 1839 among the oldest people of the state. This material, moreover, closely coincided with tales which I had personally heard from elderly rustics in the mountains of New Hampshire. Briefly summarised, it hinted at a hidden race of monstrous beings which lurked somewhere among the remoter hills—in the deep woods of the highest peaks, and the dark valleys where streams trickle from unknown sources. These beings were seldom glimpsed, but evidences of their presence were reported by those who had ventured farther than usual up the slopes of certain mountains or into certain deep, steep-sided gorges that even the wolves shunned.

There were queer footprints or claw-prints in the mud of brook-margins and barren patches, and curious circles of stones, with the grass around them worn away, which did not seem to have been placed or entirely shaped by Nature. There were, too, certain caves of problematical depth in the sides of the hills; with mouths closed by boulders in a manner scarcely accidental, and with more than an average quota of the queer prints leading both toward and away from them—if indeed the direction of these prints could be justly estimated. And worst of all, there were the things which adventurous people had seen very rarely in the twilight of the remotest valleys and the dense perpendicular woods above the limits of normal hill-climbing.

It would have been less uncomfortable if the stray accounts of these things had not agreed so well. As it was, nearly all the rumours had several points in common; averring that the creatures were a sort of huge, light-red crab with many pairs of legs and with two great bat-like wings in the middle of the back.[4] They sometimes walked on all their legs, and sometimes on the hindmost pair only, using the others to convey large objects of indeterminate nature. On one occasion they were spied in considerable numbers, a detachment of them wading along a shallow woodland watercourse three abreast in evidently disciplined formation. Once a specimen was seen flying—launching itself from the top of a bald, lonely hill at night and vanishing in the sky after its great flapping wings had been silhouetted an instant against the full moon.

These things seemed content, on the whole, to let mankind alone; though they were at times held responsible for the disappearance of venturesome individuals—especially persons who built houses too close to certain valleys or too high up on certain mountains. Many localities came to be known as inadvisable to settle in, the feeling persisting long after the cause was forgotten. People would look up at some of the neighbouring mountain-precipices with a shudder, even when not recalling how many settlers had been lost, and how many farmhouses burnt to ashes, on the lower slopes of those grim, green sentinels.

But while according to the earliest legends the creatures would appear to have harmed only those trespassing on their privacy; there were later accounts of their curiosity respecting men, and of their attempts to establish secret outposts in the human world. There were tales of the queer claw-prints seen around farmhouse windows in the morning, and of occasional disappearances in regions outside the obviously haunted areas. Tales, besides, of buzzing voices in imitation of human speech which made surprising offers to lone travellers on roads and cart-paths in the deep woods, and of children frightened out of their wits by things

4. Something like John Tenniel's Mock Turtle and Gryphon combined! In any case, such a creature would have eight legs (including two front legs like the turtle), a shell, and wings.

John Tenniel's 1865 illustration for Lewis Carroll's *Alice in Wonderland* shows Alice sitting between the Gryphon and the Mock Turtle.

5. Vermont was not one of the original thirteen colonies, and from 1777 to 1791, it existed as the Vermont Republic; the colonies of New York and New Hampshire sought the land. Benning Wentworth (1696–1770), the royal governor of New Hampshire, made extensive land grants west of the Connecticut River in defiance of the ruling of the English privy council that the land belonged to New York. In 1791, Vermont became the fourteenth state of the Union.

6. In Ireland, ráths (Anglicized as "raths") are enclosed circular fortifications, or ringforts, also called rounds, that are surrounded by stone walls. Most were built during the Iron Age.

7. The Pennacooks, or western Abnakis (also spelled Abenakis; the name means People of the Dawn Land), have a legend of a flying creature named the bmola (also P-mol-a, Pamola, and Pomola), or "wind bird," which "takes prisoners to *Alom-kik*, near *Mt. Katahdin*" (http://www .princeton.edu/~achaney/tmve/wiki100k/ docs/Abenaki_mythology.html), Maine's highest mountain (elevation 5,268 feet), and freezes the wind of the north. For a description of the terrain and the mood of Mt. Katahdin, see Henry David Thoreau's "Ktaadn," in *The Maine Woods*, 1–111.

seen or heard where the primal forest pressed close upon their dooryards. In the final layer of legends—the layer just preceding the decline of superstition and the abandonment of close contact with the dreaded places—there are shocked references to hermits and remote farmers who at some period of life appeared to have undergone a repellent mental change, and who were shunned and whispered about as mortals who had sold themselves to the strange beings. In one of the northeastern counties it seemed to be a fashion about 1800 to accuse eccentric and unpopular recluses of being allies or representatives of the abhorred things.

As to what the things were—explanations naturally varied. The common name applied to them was "those ones," or "the old ones," though other terms had a local and transient use. Perhaps the bulk of the Puritan settlers set them down bluntly as familiars of the devil, and made them a basis of awed theological speculation. Those with Celtic legendry in their heritage—mainly the Scotch-Irish element of New Hampshire, and their kindred who had settled in Vermont on Governor Wentworth's colonial grants[5]—linked them vaguely with the malign fairies and "little people" of the bogs and raths,[6] and protected themselves with scraps of incantation handed down through many generations. But the Indians had the most fantastic theories of all. While different tribal legends differed, there was a marked consensus of belief in certain vital particulars; it being unanimously agreed that the creatures were not native to this earth.

The Pennacook myths, which were the most consistent and picturesque, taught that the Winged Ones came from the Great Bear in the sky, and had mines in our earthly hills whence they took a kind of stone they could not get on any other world.[7] They did not live here, said the myths, but merely maintained outposts and flew back with vast cargoes of stone to their own stars in the north. They harmed only those earth-people who got too near them or spied upon them. Animals shunned them through instinctive hatred, not because of being hunted. They could not eat the things and animals of earth, but brought their own food from the stars. It was bad to get near them, and sometimes young hunters who went into their hills never came back. It was not good, either, to listen to what they whispered at night in the forest with voices like a bee's that tried to be like the voices of men. They knew the speech of all kinds of men—Pennacooks, Hurons, men of the Five Nations—but did not seem to have or need any speech of their own. They talked with their heads, which changed colour in different ways to mean different things.

All the legendry, of course, white and Indian alike, died down during the nineteenth century, except for occasional atavistical flareups. The ways of the Vermonters became settled; and once their habitual paths and dwellings were established according to a certain fixed plan, they remembered less and less what fears and avoidances had determined that plan, and even that there had been any fears or avoidances. Most people simply knew that certain hilly regions were considered as highly unhealthy, unprofitable, and generally unlucky to live in, and that the farther one kept from them the better off one usually was. In time the ruts of custom and economic interest became so deeply cut in approved places that there was no longer any reason for going outside them, and the haunted hills were left deserted by accident rather than by design. Save during infrequent local scares, only wonder-loving grandmothers and retrospective nonagenarians ever whispered of beings dwelling in those hills; and even such whisperers admitted that there was not much to fear from those things now that they were used to the presence of houses and settlements, and now that human beings let their chosen territory severely alone.

All this I had known from my reading, and from certain folk tales picked up in New Hampshire; hence when the flood-time rumours began to appear, I could easily guess what imaginative background had evolved them. I took great pains to explain this to my friends, and was correspondingly amused when several contentious souls continued to insist on a possible element of truth in the reports. Such persons tried to point out that the early legends had a significant persistence and uniformity, and that the virtually unexplored nature of the Vermont hills made it unwise to be dogmatic about what might or might not dwell among them; nor could they be silenced by my assurance that all the myths were of a well-known pattern common to most of mankind and determined by early phases of imaginative experience which always produced the same type of delusion.

It was of no use to demonstrate to such opponents that the

8. There is little in the way of consistent Greek legendry about the kallikantzaroi or kallikanzari, any more than there is consistent Western folklore about goblins or Irish tales of leprechauns, fairies, boggles, and the like. In *Ecstasies: Deciphering the Witches' Sabbath*, Carlo Ginzburg describes kallikantzoroi (spellings vary) as "groups of young men masquerading as animals" (see part 2, chap. 3). However, Leo Allatius in his influential 1645 treatise *De Græcorum hodie quorundam opinationibus* (one of the earliest documents to assert that vampires were creatures of the devil), names kallikantzoroi as vampires active only during the period from Christmas Day to Twelfth Night, with manic behavior and long fingernails or talons that enabled them to tear their victims to pieces.

9. "Mi-go" means "man-wild" (or wild man) in Tibetan. It is possible that the narrator encountered the word "mi-gou," another Tibetan name for the yeti or "Abominable Snowman" of the Himalayas. The term Abominable Snowman did not appear in print until 1922, when Lieutenant Colonel Charles K. Howard-Bury published his account *Mount Everest: The Reconnaissance, 1921* and reported seeing footprints that his coolies concluded were those of "'The Wild Man of the Snows,' to which they gave the name of Metohkangmi, 'the abominable snow man'" (141). The Mi-Go are mentioned again in *At the Mountains of Madness* (pp. 457–572, below), and in Lovecraft's sonnet cycle *Fungi from Yuggoth*.

10. Charles Fort (1874–1932), regarded by some as the father of paranormal studies, was an American writer who took notes on anomalous phenomena. It is difficult to say whether he believed many of the stories he researched on topics such as teleportation, alien abductions, uniden-

Vermont myths differed but little in essence from those universal legends of natural personification which filled the ancient world with fauns and dryads and satyrs, suggested the *kallikanzari*[8] of modern Greece, and gave to wild Wales and Ireland their dark hints of strange, small, and terrible hidden races of troglodytes and burrowers. No use, either, to point out the even more startlingly similar belief of the Nepalese hill tribes in the dreaded *Mi-Go*[9] or "Abominable Snow-Men" who lurk hideously amidst the ice and rock pinnacles of the Himalayan summits. When I brought up this evidence, my opponents turned it against me by claiming that it must imply some actual historicity for the ancient tales; that it must argue the real existence of some queer elder earth-race, driven to hiding after the advent and dominance of mankind, which might very conceivably have survived in reduced numbers to relatively recent times—or even to the present.

The more I laughed at such theories, the more these stubborn friends asseverated them; adding that even without the heritage of legend the recent reports were too clear, consistent, detailed, and sanely prosaic in manner of telling, to be completely ignored. Two or three fanatical extremists went so far as to hint at possible meanings in the ancient Indian tales which gave the hidden beings a non-terrestrial origin; citing the extravagant books of Charles Fort[10] with their claims that voyagers from other worlds and outer space have often visited the earth. Most of my foes, however, were merely romanticists who insisted on trying to transfer to real life the fantastic lore of lurking "little people" made popular by the magnificent horror-fiction of Arthur Machen.[11]

II.

AS WAS ONLY natural under the circumstances, this piquant debating finally got into print in the form of letters to the *Arkham Advertiser*; some of which were copied in the press of those Vermont regions whence the flood-stories came. The *Rutland Herald* gave half a page of extracts from the letters on both sides, while the *Brattleboro Reformer*[12] reprinted one of my long historical and mythological summaries in full, with some accompanying comments in "The Pendrifter's" thoughtful column[13] which supported and applauded my sceptical conclusions. By the spring of 1928 I was almost a well-known figure in Vermont, notwithstanding the fact that I had never set foot in the state. Then came the challenging letters from Henry Akeley which impressed me so profoundly, and which took me for the first and last time to that fascinating realm of crowded green precipices and muttering forest streams.

Most of what I now know of Henry Wentworth Akeley was gathered by correspondence with his neighbours, and with his only son in California, after my experience in his lonely farmhouse. He was, I discovered, the last representative on his home soil of a long, locally distinguished line of jurists, administrators, and gentlemen-agriculturists. In him, however, the family mentally had veered away from practical affairs to pure scholarship; so that he had been a notable student of mathematics, astronomy, biology, anthropology, and folklore at the University of Vermont. I had never previously heard of him, and he did not give many autobiographical details in his communications; but from the first I saw he was a man of character, education, and intelligence, albeit a recluse with very little worldly sophistication.

Despite the incredible nature of what he claimed, I could not help at once taking Akeley more seriously than I had taken any of the other challengers of my views. For one thing, he was really close to the actual phenomena—visible and tangible—that he speculated so grotesquely about; and for another thing, he was amazingly willing to leave his conclusions in a tentative state like a true man of science. He had no personal preferences to advance, and was always guided by what he took to be solid evidence. Of course I began by considering him mistaken, but gave him credit for being intelligently mistaken; and at no time did I emulate some of his friends in attributing his ideas, and his fear of the lonely green hills, to insanity. I could see that there was a great deal to the man, and knew that what he reported must surely come from strange circumstances deserving investigation, however little it might have to do with the fantastic causes he assigned. Later on I received from him certain material proofs which placed the matter on a somewhat different and bewilderingly bizarre basis.

tified flying objects, spontaneous fires, and strange objects or creatures falling from the skies. Fort collected his data from hundreds of newspapers, scientific journals, magazines, and other published sources found in his beloved New York Public Library and in London at the British Museum, and he particularly focused on phenomena that were either on the borders of science and "pseudoscience" or that were subject to multiple interpretations. The author of four books, *The Book of the Damned* (1919), *New Lands* (1923), *Lo!* (1931), and *Wild Talents* (1932), his work spawned international Fortean societies and led to a widening of the boundaries of "proper" scientific investigation. In *The Book of the Damned*, Fort expressed his views on alien contact cautiously: "If other worlds have ever in the past had relations with this earth, they were attempted positivizations: to extend themselves, by colonies, upon this earth; to convert, or assimilate, indigenous inhabitants of this earth" (172). In *New Lands*, sounding a slightly less sceptical note, he seemed to endorse the existentially cleansing effects of alien visitation: "If there be nearby lands in the sky and beings from foreign worlds that visit this earth, that is a great subject, and the trash that is clogging an epoch must be cleared away" (321).

11. See "The Dunwich Horror," note 30, above.

12. The *Herald* and the *Reformer* have, respectively, the second- and third-largest circulations of Vermont newspapers and commenced publication in 1794 and 1876. In the 1920s, the *Reformer's* circulation was probably around 2,500 copies daily; it grew to three times that by the 1950s and today is at about 6,700 print copies daily. The *Herald*, with a current print circulation of around 11,000 copies daily, went through a similar cycle. For

comparison, the largest circulation today is that of the *Burlington Free Press*, about 28,500 daily.

13. Charles Edward Crane wrote the Pendrift column for the *Brattleboro Reformer* for many years. By 1931, when a collection of some forty columns was published under the title *Pen-drift: Amenities of Column Conducting*, by the Pendrifter, Crane had written over 1,200 columns, all signed "by tf." The signature was indicative of Crane's sense of humor; in newspaper shorthand, "tf" ("'til forbidden") appeared at the bottom of advertisements that were to be printed until the advertiser ordered them discontinued.

14. Townshend, chartered in 1753, is seventeen miles north of Brattleboro, Vermont. It has about 1,200 residents.

I cannot do better than transcribe in full, so far as is possible, the long letter in which Akeley introduced himself, and which formed such an important landmark in my own intellectual history. It is no longer in my possession, but my memory holds almost every word of its portentous message; and again I affirm my confidence in the sanity of the man who wrote it. Here is the text—a text which reached me in the cramped, archaic-looking scrawl of one who had obviously not mingled much with the world during his sedate, scholarly life.

R.F.D. #2,
Townshend, Windham Co., Vermont.[14]
May 5, 1928

Albert N. Wilmarth, Esq.,
118 Saltonstall St.,
Arkham, Mass.

My dear Sir:

I have read with great interest the Brattleboro Reformer's *reprint (Apr. 23, '28) of your letter on the recent stories of strange bodies*

The Townshend, Vermont, post office, where Akeley's mail would have been picked up.

seen floating in our flooded streams last fall, and on the curious folklore they so well agree with. It is easy to see why an outlander would take the position you take, and even why "Pendrifter" agrees with you. That is the attitude generally taken by educated persons both in and out of Vermont, and was my own attitude as a young man (I am now 57) before my studies, both general and in Davenport's book, led me to do some exploring in parts of the hills hereabouts not usually visited.

I was directed toward such studies by the queer old tales I used to hear from elderly farmers of the more ignorant sort, but now I wish I had let the whole matter alone. I might say, with all proper modesty, that the subject of anthropology and folklore is by no means strange to me. I took a good deal of it at college, and am familiar with most of the standard authorities such as Tylor,[15] Lubbock,[16] Frazer,[17] Quatrefages,[18] Murray,[19] Osborn,[20] Keith,[21] Boule,[22] G. Elliot Smith,[23] and so on.[24] It is no news to me that tales of hidden races are as old as all mankind. I have seen the reprints of letters from you, and those arguing with you, in the Rutland Herald, *and guess I know about where your controversy stands at the present time.*

What I desire to say now is, that I am afraid your adversaries are nearer right than yourself, even though all reason seems to be on your side. They are nearer right than they realise themselves— for of course they go only by theory, and cannot know what I know. If I knew as little of the matter as they, I would not feel justified in believing as they do. I would be wholly on your side.

You can see that I am having a hard time getting to the point, probably because I really dread getting to the point; but the upshot of the matter is that I have certain evidence that monstrous things do indeed live in the woods on the high hills which nobody visits.

I have not seen any of the things floating in the rivers, as reported, but I have seen things like them under circumstances I dread to repeat. *I have seen footprints, and of late have seen them nearer my own home (I live in the old Akeley place south of Townshend Village, on the side of Dark Mountain)[25] than I dare tell you now. And I have overheard voices in the woods at certain points that I will not even begin to describe on paper.*

At one place I heard them so much that I took a phonograph

15. Sir Edward Burnett Tylor (1832–1917), English anthropologist, best known for his two-volume work *Primitive Culture* (1871) and for his enduring definition of the concept of culture.

16. Probably John Lubbock, 1st Baron Avebury (1834–1913), who in 1865 published the influential *Pre-historic Times, as Illustrated by Ancient Remains, and the Manners and Customs of Modern Savages,* the leading archaeology text-book for half a century. He was a friend and correspondent—and pallbearer—of Darwin's. A banker and a Liberal MP, the legislation he is chiefly remembered for sponsoring is the 1871 act that created bank holidays, informally known, at their inception, as St. Lubbock's Days.

17. Undoubtedly Sir James Frazer (1854–1941), author of the celebrated *The Golden Bough* (1890).

18. Jean Louis Armand de Quatrefages de Bréau (1810–1892), a French naturalist and head of the department of anthropology and ethnology at the Museum of Natural History in Paris. He wrote, among other works, *The Pygmies* (http://archive .org/stream/pygmiesquatr00quatrich/ pygmiesquatr00quatrich_djvu.txt), a history of "the small black races" (vii)—copiously illustrated with photographs of skulls and bodies and attendant detailed measurements—from the time of Aristotle through the Hottentots and Bushmen.

19. Margaret Alice Murray (1863–1963), a highly popular anthropologist-folklorist who received little esteem from the scientific community. Two of her areas of study were Egyptology and Wicca. See "The Call of Cthulhu," note 18, above.

20. Probably Henry Fairfield Osborn (1857–1935), nephew of J. P. Morgan and

son of the founder of the Illinois Central Railroad, an American geologist, paleontologist, and eugenicist, and the president of the American Museum of Natural History for twenty-five years. His selection as president marked the first time that a scientist had held the position. Prior to his tenure at the Museum of Natural History, he was vertebrate paleontologist for the U.S. Geological Survey. Osborn was a highly controversial figure. He opposed Darwin's theories regarding the descent of man, holding that humans had originated in Asia, not Africa; espoused radical views regarding eugenics; and urged immigration restrictions to maintain racial purity. Although he was enlisted by the defense team for the controversial Scopes Monkey Trial in 1925 (Scopes was eventually convicted of teaching evolution contrary to Tennessee law), Osborn's views were not unequivocally supportive of Scopes's position, as Osborn attempted to explain how he believed evolution was the working out of God's plans for creation. Lovecraft, who rejected traditional theism, criticized Osborn for what he called his "shoddy emotionalism and irresponsible irrationality" in trying to "capitalise the new uncertainty of everything in the interest of historical mythology" (Lovecraft to Frank Belknap Long Jr., November 22, 1930 [Lovecraft sardonically dates it "1730"], *Selected Letters*, III, 225).

21. Sir Arthur Keith (1866–1955), a Scottish anatomist and anthropologist. Like Grafton Elliot Smith, he supported the view that humans were of European, not African, descent.

22. Likely Pierre-Marcellin Boule (1861–1942), French geologist, paleontologist, and physical anthropologist who made extensive studies of human fossils from Europe, North Africa, and the Middle

there—with a dictaphone attachment and wax blank[26]—and I shall try to arrange to have you hear the record I got. I have run it on the machine for some of the old people up here, and one of the voices had nearly scared them paralysed by reason of its likeness to a certain voice (that buzzing voice in the woods which Davenport mentions) that their grandmothers have told about and mimicked for them. I know what most people think of a man who tells about "hearing voices"—but before you draw conclusions just listen to this record and ask some of the older backwoods people what they think of it. If you can account for it normally, very well; but there must be something behind it. Ex nihilo nihil fit,[27] you know.

Now my object in writing you is not to start an argument, but to give you information which I think a man of your tastes will find deeply interesting. This is private. Publicly I am on your side, for certain things shew me that it does not do for people to know too much about these matters. My own studies are now wholly private, and I would not think of saying anything to attract people's attention and cause them to visit the places I have explored. It is true—terribly true—that there are non-human creatures watching us all the time; with spies among us gathering information. It is from a wretched man who, if he

Early Dictaphone

was sane (as I think he was) was one of those spies, that I got a large part of my clues to the matter. He later killed himself, but I have reason to think there are others now.

The things come from another planet, being able to live in interstellar space and fly through it *on clumsy, powerful wings which have a way of resisting the æther but which are too poor at steering to be of much use in helping them about on earth. I will tell you about this later if you do not dismiss me at once as a madman. They come here to get metals from mines that go deep under the hills, and I think I know where they come from. They will not hurt us if we let them alone, but no one can say what will happen if we get too curious about them. Of course a good army of men could wipe out their mining colony. That is what they are afraid of. But if that happened, more would come from outside—any number of them. They could easily conquer the earth, but have not tried so far because they have not needed to. They would rather leave things as they are to save bother.*

I think they mean to get rid of me because of what I have discovered. There is a great black stone with unknown hieroglyphics half worn away which I found in the woods on Round Hill, east of here; and after I took it home everything became different. If they think I suspect too much they will either kill me or take me off the

Early Dictaphone

East and reconstructed the first more or less complete Neanderthal skeleton (1908), from La Chapelle-aux-Saints, France. His best-known work, published in 1921, is *Les Hommes Fossiles* (*Fossil Men*).

23. Sir Grafton Elliot Smith (1871–1937) was an Australian-British anatomist and the leading specialist of his day on the evolution of the brain.

24. The list seems a little too extensive to be true. Some of the scholars were little known at the time Akeley was in school (which must have been thirty to forty years earlier—that is, in the late nineteenth century). It sounds like he was seeking to impress Wilmarth with his up-to-dateness.

25. Presumably Black Mountain, in Windham County. Why would Akeley (or Wilmarth) conceal the name but record its proximity to Townshend?

26. The first recording machines came into use shortly after the phonograph, as early as 1881. In 1907, the Columbia Graphophone Company trademarked the name Dictaphone. Although music recordings soon evolved into flat discs, the wax cylinder (originally used for music as well) became the medium of choice for voice recording. In 1923, the Dictaphone Company Ltd. was formed to sell the devices exclusively.

27. "Out of nothing comes nothing," a phrase associated first with ancient Greek cosmology and today echoed in the laws of conservation of mass and energy. Here Akeley really means something folksier, like "Where there's smoke, there's fire."

earth to where they come from. *They like to take away men of learning once in a while, to keep informed on the state of things in the human world.*

This leads me to my secondary purpose in addressing you— namely, to urge you to hush up the present debate rather than give it more publicity. People must be kept away from these hills, and in order to effect this, their curiosity ought not to be aroused any further. Heaven knows there is peril enough anyway, with promoters and real estate men flooding Vermont with herds of summer people to overrun the wild places and cover the hills with cheap bungalows.

I shall welcome further communication with you, and shall try to send you that phonograph record and black stone (which is so worn that photographs don't shew much) by express if you are willing. I say "try" because I think those creatures have a way of tampering with things around here. There is a sullen furtive fellow named Brown, on a farm near the village, who I think is their spy. Little by little they are trying to cut me off from our world because I know too much about their world.

They have the most amazing way of finding out what I do. You may not even get this letter. I think I shall have to leave this part of the country and go live with my son in San Diego, Cal., if things get any worse, but it is not easy to give up the place you were born in, and where your family has lived for six generations. Also, I would hardly dare sell this house to anybody now that the creatures have taken notice of it. They seem to be trying to get the black stone back and destroy the phonograph record, but I shall not let them if I can help it. My great police dogs always hold them back, for there are very few here as yet, and they are clumsy in getting about. As I have said, their wings are not much use for short flights on earth. I am on the very brink of decipher- ing that stone—in a very terrible way—and with your knowledge of folklore you may be able to supply missing links enough to help me. I suppose you know all about the fearful myths antedating the coming of man to the earth—the Yog-Sothoth and Cthulhu cycles—which are hinted at in the Necronomicon. I had access to a copy of that once, and hear that you have one in your college library under lock and key.

To conclude, Mr. Wilmarth, I think that with our respective studies we can be very useful to each other. I don't wish to put you in any peril, and suppose I ought to warn you that possession of the stone and the record won't be very safe; but I think you will find any risks worth running for the sake of knowledge. I will drive down to Newfane or Brattleboro to send whatever you authorise me to send, for the express offices there are more to be trusted. I might say that I live quite alone now, since I can't keep hired help any more. They won't stay because of the things that try to get near the house at night, and that keep the dogs barking continually. I am glad I didn't get as deep as this into the business while my wife was alive, for it would have driven her mad.

Hoping that I am not bothering you unduly, and that you will decide to get in touch with me rather than throw this letter into the waste basket as a madman's raving, I am

Yrs. very truly, HENRY W. AKELEY

P.S. I am making some extra prints of certain photographs taken by me, which I think will help to prove a number of the points I have touched on. The old people think they are monstrously true. I shall send you these very soon if you are interested.

H. W. A.

It would be difficult to describe my sentiments upon reading this strange document for the first time. By all ordinary rules, I ought to have laughed more loudly at these extravagances than at the far milder theories which had previously moved me to mirth; yet something in the tone of the letter made me take it with paradoxical seriousness. Not that I believed for a moment in the hidden race from the stars which my correspondent spoke of; but that, after some grave preliminary doubts, I grew to feel oddly sure of his sanity and sincerity, and of his confrontation by some genuine though singular and abnormal phenomenon which he could not explain except in this imaginative way. It could not be as he thought it, I reflected, yet on the other hand it could not be otherwise than worthy of investigation. The man seemed unduly excited and alarmed about something, but it was hard to think that all cause was lacking. He was so specific and logical in certain ways—and after all, his yarn did fit in so perplexingly well with some of the old myths—even the wildest Indian legends.

That he had really overheard disturbing voices in the hills, and had really found the black stone he spoke about, was wholly possible despite the crazy inferences he had made—inferences probably suggested by the man who had claimed to be a spy of the outer beings and had later killed himself. It was easy to deduce that this man must have been wholly insane, but that he probably had a streak of perverse outward logic which made the naive Akeley—already prepared for such things by his folklore studies—believe his tale. As for the latest developments—it appeared from his inability to keep hired help that Akeley's humbler rustic neighbours were as convinced as he that his house was besieged by uncanny things at night. The dogs really barked, too.

And then the matter of that phonograph record, which I could not but believe he had obtained in the way he said. It must mean something; whether animal noises deceptively like human speech, or the speech of some hidden, night-haunting human being decayed to a state not much above that of lower animals. From this my thoughts went back to the black hieroglyphed stone, and to speculations upon what it might mean. Then, too, what of the photographs which Akeley said he was about to send, and which the old people had found so convincingly terrible?

As I re-read the cramped handwriting I felt as never before that my credulous opponents might have more on their side than I had conceded. After all, there might be some queer and perhaps hereditarily misshapen outcasts in those shunned hills, even though no such race of star-born monsters as folklore claimed. And if there were, then the presence of strange bodies in the flooded streams would not be wholly beyond belief. Was it too presumptuous to suppose that both the old legends and the recent reports had this much of reality behind them? But even as I harboured these doubts I felt ashamed that so fantastic a piece of bizarrerie as Henry Akeley's wild letter had brought them up.

In the end I answered Akeley's letter, adopting a tone of friendly interest and soliciting further particulars. His reply came almost by return mail; and contained, true to promise, a number of kodak views of scenes and objects illustrating what he had to tell. Glancing at these pictures as I took them from the envelope, I felt a curious sense of fright and nearness to forbidden things; for in spite of the vagueness of most of them, they had a damnably suggestive power which was intensified by the fact of their being genuine photographs—actual optical links with what they portrayed, and the product of an impersonal transmitting process without prejudice, fallibility, or mendacity.

The more I looked at them, the more I saw that my serious estimate of Akeley and his story had not been unjustified. Certainly, these pictures carried conclusive evidence of something in the Vermont hills which was at least vastly outside the radius of our common knowledge and belief. The worst thing of all was the footprint—a view taken where the sun shone on a mud patch somewhere in a deserted upland. This was no cheaply counterfeited thing, I could see at a glance; for the sharply defined pebbles and grass-blades in the field of vision gave a clear index of scale and left no possibility of a tricky double exposure. I have called the thing a "footprint," but "claw-print" would be a better term. Even now I can scarcely describe it save to say that it was hideously crab-like, and that there seemed to be some ambiguity about its direction. It was not a very deep or fresh print, but seemed to be about the size of an average man's foot. From a central pad, pairs of saw-toothed nippers projected in opposite directions—quite baffling as to function, if indeed the whole object were exclusively an organ of locomotion.

Another photograph—evidently a time-exposure taken in deep shadow—was of the mouth of a woodland cave, with a boulder of rounded regularity choking the aperture. On the bare ground in front of it, one could just discern a dense network of curious tracks, and when I studied the picture with a magnifier I felt uneasily sure that the tracks were like the one in the other view. A third picture shewed a druid-like circle of standing stones on the summit of a wild hill. Around the cryptic circle the grass was very much beaten down and worn away, though I could not detect any footprints even with the glass. The extreme remoteness of the place was apparent from the veritable sea of tenantless mountains which formed the background and stretched away toward a misty horizon.

But if the most disturbing of all the views was that of the footprint, the most curiously suggestive was that of the great black stone found in the Round Hill woods. Akeley had photographed it on what was evidently his study table, for I could see rows of books and a bust of Milton in the background. The thing, as nearly as one might guess, had faced the camera vertically with a somewhat irregularly curved surface of one by two feet; but to say anything definite about that surface, or about the general shape of the whole mass, almost defies the power of language. What outlandish geometrical principles had guided its cutting—for artificially cut it surely was—I could not even begin to guess; and never before had I seen anything which struck me as so strangely and unmistakably alien to this world. Of the hieroglyphics on the surface I could discern very few, but one or two that I did see gave me rather a shock. Of course they might be fraudulent, for others besides myself had read the monstrous and abhorred *Necronomicon* of the mad Arab Abdul Alhazred; but it nevertheless made me shiver to recognise certain ideographs which study had taught me to link with the most blood-curdling and blasphemous whispers of things that had had a kind of mad half-existence before the earth and the other inner worlds of the solar system were made.

Of the five remaining pictures, three were of swamp and hill scenes which seemed to bear traces of hidden and unwholesome tenancy. Another was of a queer mark in the ground very near Akeley's house, which he said he had photographed the morning after a night on which the dogs had barked more violently than usual. It was very blurred, and one could really draw no certain conclusions from it; but it did seem fiendishly like that other mark or claw-print photographed on the deserted upland. The final picture was of the Akeley place itself; a trim white house of two stories and attic, about a century and a quarter old, and with a well-kept lawn and stone-bordered path leading up to a tastefully carved Georgian doorway. There were several huge police dogs on the lawn, squatting near a pleasant-faced man with a close-cropped grey beard whom I took to be Akeley himself—his own photographer, one might infer from the tube-connected bulb in his right hand.

From the pictures I turned to the bulky, closely written letter itself; and for the next three hours was immersed in a gulf of unutterable horror. Where Akeley had given only outlines before, he now entered into minute details; presenting long transcripts of words overheard in the woods at night, long accounts of monstrous pinkish forms spied in thickets at twilight on the hills, and a terrible cosmic narrative derived from the application of profound and varied scholarship to the endless bygone discourses of the mad self-styled spy who had killed himself. I found myself faced by names and terms that I had heard elsewhere in the most hideous of connexions—Yuggoth,[28] Great Cthulhu, Tsathoggua,[29] Yog-Sothoth, R'lyeh, Nyarlathotep, Azathoth,[30] Hastur,[31] Yian,[32] Leng,[33] the Lake of Hali,[34] Bethmoora,[35] the Yellow Sign,[36] L'mur-Kathulos,[37] Bran,[38] and the Magnum Innominandum[39]—and was drawn back through nameless æons and inconceivable dimensions to worlds of elder, outer entity at which the crazed author of the *Necronomicon* had only guessed in the vaguest way. I was told of the pits of primal life, and of the streams that had trickled down therefrom; and finally, of the tiny rivulet from one of those streams which had become entangled with the destinies of our own earth.

My brain whirled; and where before I had attempted to explain things away, I now began to believe in the most abnormal and incredible wonders. The array of vital evidence was damnably vast and overwhelming; and the cool, scientific attitude of Akeley—an attitude removed as far as imaginable from the demented, the fanatical, the hysterical, or even the extravagantly speculative—had a tremendous effect on my thought and judgment. By the time I laid the frightful letter aside I could understand the fears he had come to entertain, and was ready to do anything in my power to keep people away from those wild, haunted hills. Even now, when time has dulled the impression and made me half question my own experience and horrible doubts, there are things in that letter of Akeley's which I would not quote, or even form into words on paper. I am almost glad that the letter and record and photographs are gone now—and I wish, for reasons I shall soon make clear, that the new planet beyond Neptune had not been discovered.[40]

With the reading of that letter my public debating about the Vermont horror permanently ended. Arguments from opponents remained unanswered or put off with promises, and eventually the controversy petered out into oblivion. During late May and

28. Later identified as the planet Pluto, Yuggoth was also named in Lovecraft's poetry cycle *Fungi from Yuggoth* (1929–1930). In a letter to Duane Rimel (February 14, 1934, *Selected Letters*, IV, 385–388), Lovecraft wrote, "'Yuggoth' has a sort of Arabic or Hebraic cast, to suggest certain words passed down from antiquity in the magical formulæ contained in Moorish and Jewish manuscripts. . . . 'Nug' and 'Yeb' suggest the dark and mysterious tone of Tartar or Thibetan folklore. . . . I try to represent the different variants under which different races refer to the same thing as remembered from primitive times. . . . Thus, I have had *Yog-Sothoth* occur . . . as *Yog-Sototl* among the Aztecs. . . ."

29. An "amorphous, toad-like god-creature," according to a description later in the tale.

30. The "monstrous nuclear chaos" personified, as described below in this story.

31. Hastur is a person, not a place, first mentioned by Ambrose Bierce in his 1891 story "Haita the Shepherd" as a god of the shepherds. Robert W. Chambers also mentions Hastur, in *The King in Yellow* (see note 36, below), and lists the name among constellations as well: ". . . the Hyades, Hastur, and Aldeberan. . . ."

32. Yian is first mentioned in Robert Chambers's *The Maker of Moons* (1896): "'Where is Yian, Ysonde?' I asked with deadly calmness. 'Yian? I don't know. . . . It is across seven oceans and the great river which is longer than from the earth to the moon.'"

33. See "The Hound," note 13, above.

34. The city of Carcosa, which figures in Ambrose Bierce's "An Inhabitant of Carcosa" (1891) and Robert Chambers's *The King in Yellow* (1895) (see note 36,

below), is said to be found on the shore of Lake Hali. Marco Frenschkowski, in "Hali," devotes enormous energy to identifying Arabian scholars and mystics named Hali and wonders why it is a lake. However, the *Encyclopædia Britannica* (11th ed.), undoubtedly familiar to Lovecraft, lists Hali as a town shown on a map of Arabia. It is southeast of Mecca, in the mountains west of the Dahna Desert. Neither the map nor Google Earth reveals whether there is a lake nearby, but Wadi Hali ("wadi" means a riverbed or water basin that is dry except when rain falls) is not distant.

35. A fabled city mentioned in a 1908 story of the same name by Lord Dunsany.

36. From a story of the same name by Robert Chambers. The story first appeared in *The King in Yellow*. The king is an evil figure who exercises mind control over his victims, who are identified by their association with the Yellow Sign (which in itself may control the victim). August Derleth, who developed the Cthulhu Mythos far beyond Lovecraft's plan, identified Hastur as the Yellow King and the Yellow Sign as a mark of his followers. Lovecraft had several collections of Chambers's work in his library, including this book.

37. Kathulos was a wizard who appeared in some of Robert E. Howard's tales. Howard was a friend of Lovecraft's and the creator of Conan the Barbarian. "L'mur" as a prefix may connect Kathulos to Lemuria.

38. This appears to be a reference to Bran Mak Morn, an ancient Scottish warrior whose accounts were compiled by Robert E. Howard. Bran was also an ancient British-Celtic-Welsh giant who possessed a magic cauldron with the power to restore life to dead soldiers.

June I was in constant correspondence with Akeley; though once in a while a letter would be lost, so that we would have to retrace our ground and perform considerable laborious copying. What we were trying to do, as a whole, was to compare notes in matters of obscure mythological scholarship and arrive at a clearer correlation of the Vermont horrors with the general body of primitive world legend.

For one thing, we virtually decided that these morbidities and the hellish Himalayan *Mi-Go* were one and the same order of incarnated nightmare. There were also absorbing zoölogical conjectures, which I would have referred to Professor Dexter in my own college but for Akeley's imperative command to tell no one of the matter before us. If I seem to disobey that command now, it is only because I think that at this stage a warning about those farther Vermont hills—and about those Himalayan peaks which bold explorers are more and more determined to ascend[41]—is more conducive to public safety than silence would be. One specific thing we were leading up to was a deciphering of the hieroglyphics on that infamous black stone—a deciphering which might well place us in possession of secrets deeper and more dizzying than any formerly known to man.

III.

TOWARD THE END of June the phonograph record came—shipped from Brattleboro, since Akeley was unwilling to trust conditions on the branch line north of there. He had begun to feel an increased sense of espionage, aggravated by the loss of some of our letters; and said much about the insidious deeds of certain men whom he considered tools and agents of the hidden beings. Most of all he suspected the surly farmer Walter Brown, who lived alone on a run-down hillside place near the deep woods, and who was often seen loafing around corners in Brattleboro, Bellows Falls,[42] Newfane,[43] and South Londonderry[44] in the most inexplicable and seemingly unmotivated way. Brown's voice, he felt convinced, was one of those he had overheard on a certain occasion in a very terrible conversation; and he had once found a footprint or claw-print near Brown's house which

Clyde Tombaugh as a boy on the family farm, in the early 1920s.

39. Latin for "The Great One Who Is Not to Be Named."

40. The search for a planet beyond Neptune began with the theories of astronomer Percival Lowell, who argued that, based on his study of the motions of Uranus and Neptune, such a body existed. Lowell funded three searches for "Planet X" and set up the Lowell Observatory, in Flagstaff, Arizona. While the first two searches turned up nothing, in 1929, a young man named Clyde Tombaugh was engaged to assist in the endeavor. Tombaugh has been described as a "farm boy," and indeed his family had seen its share of successes and setbacks on their farm in Burdett, Kansas, including a hailstorm in the mid-1920s that wiped out their crops, subsequent financial losses preventing Tombaugh from attending college as planned. He had built a nine-inch telescope by the age of twenty-two, for which he himself ground the mirrors. His sketches of Jupiter and Mars, drawn on the basis of images captured through the use of this homemade telescope, brought him to Lowell, where, using two specialized instruments, a thirteen-inch astrograph and a blink comparator, he surveyed the skies by taking photographs at intervals of one to two weeks and looked for the shifting of objects against the star fields. On February 18, 1930, after nearly a year of searching,

the 24-year-old Tombaugh was gazing into the eyepiece of a Zeiss Blink microscope at photographic images of a star field, examining a pair of plates taken in mid-January. Suddenly the monotony was broken when his attention was caught by one of the millions of minute specks of lights whose image had moved slightly between one photograph and the next. He checked and rechecked his photo-

might possess the most ominous significance. It had been curiously near some of Brown's own footprints—footprints that faced toward it.

So the record was shipped from Brattleboro, whither Akeley drove in his Ford car along the lonely Vermont back roads. He confessed in an accompanying note that he was beginning to be afraid of those roads, and that he would not even go into Townshend for supplies now except in broad daylight. It did not pay, he repeated again and again, to know too much unless one were very remote from those silent and problematical hills. He would be going to California pretty soon to live with his son, though it was hard to leave a place where all one's memories and ancestral feelings centred.[45]

Before trying the record on the commercial machine which I borrowed from the college administration building I carefully went over all the explanatory matter in Akeley's various letters. This record, he had said, was obtained about 1 A.M. on the first of May, 1915, near the closed mouth of a cave where the wooded west graphs for 45 minutes before calling his supervisors. He knew he had found Planet X (Kansas Historical Society, http://www.kshs.org/kansapedia/clyde-tombaugh/12222).

A few weeks later, after an international hunt for an appropriate name, Pluto was christened by the Lowell Observatory. Note that Lovecraft worked on "The Whisperer in Darkness" between February and September 1930.

In 2006, the International Astronomical Union established new criteria for planets and downgraded Pluto to the status of "dwarf planet," distinguished from "regular" planets. After much public outcry and debate, the category was revised to "plutoid" but still distinguished from other solar planets. Nonetheless, the states of New Mexico and Illinois, proud of the Lowell Observatory and Illini Tombaugh, respectively, declared that Pluto would remain a planet when in the skies of those states.

41. While Himalayan peaks in India and the former USSR were scaled in the 1930s by Westerners, the principal Himalayan mountains were not ascended until the mid-1950s. Wilmarth's concern was undoubtedly fueled by exploratory missions such as the Everest reconnaissance expedition reported in Howard-Bury's book (note 9, above).

42. A town in southern Vermont bounded by the upper Connecticut River.

Newfane, Vermont, ca. 1909.

slope of Dark Mountain rises out of Lee's Swamp. The place had always been unusually plagued with strange voices, this being the reason he had brought the phonograph, dictaphone, and blank in expectation of results. Former experience had told him that May-Eve—the hideous Sabbat-night of underground European legend—would probably be more fruitful than any other date, and he was not disappointed. It was noteworthy, though, that he never again heard voices at that particular spot.

Unlike most of the overheard forest voices, the substance of the record was quasi-ritualistic, and included one palpably human voice which Akeley had never been able to place. It was not Brown's, but seemed to be that of a man of greater cultivation. The second voice, however, was the real crux of the thing—for this was the accursed *buzzing* which had no likeness to humanity despite the human words which it uttered in good English grammar and a scholarly accent.

The recording phonograph and dictaphone had not worked uniformly well, and had of course been at a great disadvantage because of the remote and muffled nature of the overheard ritual; so that the actual speech secured was very fragmentary. Akeley had given me a transcript of what he believed the spoken words to be, and I glanced through this again as I prepared the machine for action. The text was darkly mysterious rather than openly horrible, though a knowledge of its origin and manner of gathering gave it all the associative horror which any words could well possess. I will present it here in full as I remember it—and I am fairly confident that I know it correctly by heart, not only from reading the transcript, but from playing the record itself over and over again. It is not a thing which one might readily forget!

(INDISTINGUISHABLE SOUNDS)
(A CULTIVATED MALE HUMAN VOICE)
. . . is the Lord of the Woods, even to . . . and the gifts of the men of Leng . . . so from the wells of night to the gulfs of space, and from the gulfs of space to the wells of night, ever the praises of Great Cthulhu, of Tsathoggua, and of Him Who is not to be Named. Ever Their praises, and abundance to the Black Goat of the Woods. Iä! Shub-Niggurath! The Goat with a Thousand Young!

(A BUZZING IMITATION OF HUMAN SPEECH)

Iä! Shub-Niggurath! The Black Goat of the Woods with a Thousand Young!

(HUMAN VOICE)

And it has come to pass that the Lord of the Woods, being . . . seven and nine, down the onyx steps . . . (tri)butes to Him in the Gulf, Azathoth, He of Whom Thou hast taught us marv(els) . . . on the wings of night out beyond space, out beyond th . . . to That whereof Yuggoth is the youngest child, rolling alone in black æther at the rim . . .

(BUZZING VOICE)

. . . go out among men and find the ways thereof, that He in the Gulf may know. To Nyarlathotep, Mighty Messenger, must all things be told. And He shall put on the semblance of men, the waxen mask and the robe that hides, and come down from the world of Seven Suns to mock . . .[46]

(HUMAN VOICE)

. . . (Nyarl)athotep, Great Messenger, bringer of strange joy to Yuggoth through the void, Father of the Million Favoured Ones, Stalker among . . .

(SPEECH CUT OFF BY END OF RECORD)

Such were the words for which I was to listen when I started the phonograph. It was with a trace of genuine dread and reluctance that I pressed the lever and heard the preliminary scratching of the sapphire point, and I was glad that the first faint, fragmentary words were in a human voice—a mellow, educated voice which seemed vaguely Bostonian in accent, and which was certainly not that of any native of the Vermont hills. As I listened to the tantalisingly feeble rendering, I seemed to find the speech identical with Akeley's carefully prepared transcript. On it chanted, in that mellow Bostonian voice . . . "Iä! Shub-Niggurath! The Goat with a Thousand Young! . . ."

And then I heard *the other voice*. To this hour I shudder retrospectively when I think of how it struck me, prepared though I was by Akeley's accounts. Those to whom I have since described the record profess to find nothing but cheap imposture or madness in it; but *could they have heard the accursed thing itself*, or read the bulk of Akeley's correspondence, (especially that terrible and

43. About fifteen miles northwest of Brattleboro.

44. Part of Londonderry, a small village about thirty miles northwest of Brattleboro. Why the narrator did not mention Putney or Jamaica, closer to Townshend than Londonderry, is unclear.

45. Robert H. Waugh, in "The Ecstasies of 'The Thing on the Doorstep' . . . and Other Erotic Studies," from his collection *A Monster of Voices: Speaking for H. P. Lovecraft*, points out, "For a New Englander that might as well be across the universe" (10A).

46. The reference to the "waxen mask and the robe that hides" may refer to the garments found by Wilmarth in the study during his escape. See note 77, below.

encyclopædic second letter), I know they would think differently. It is, after all, a tremendous pity that I did not disobey Akeley and play the record for others—a tremendous pity, too, that all of his letters were lost. To me, with my first-hand impression of the actual sounds, and with my knowledge of the background and surrounding circumstances, the voice was a monstrous thing. It swiftly followed the human voice in ritualistic response, but in my imagination it was a morbid echo winging its way across unimaginable abysses from unimaginable outer hells. It is more than two years now since I last ran off that blasphemous waxen cylinder; but at this moment, and at all other moments, I can still hear that feeble, fiendish buzzing as it reached me for the first time.

"*Iä! Shub-Niggurath! The Black Goat of the Woods with a Thousand Young!*"

But though that voice is always in my ears, I have not even yet been able to analyse it well enough for a graphic description. It was like the drone of some loathsome, gigantic insect ponderously shaped into the articulate speech of an alien species, and I am perfectly certain that the organs producing it can have no resemblance to the vocal organs of man, or indeed to those of any of the mammalia. There were singularities in timbre, range, and overtones which placed this phenomenon wholly outside the sphere of humanity and earth-life. Its sudden advent that first time almost stunned me, and I heard the rest of the record through in a sort of abstracted daze. When the longer passage of buzzing came, there was a sharp intensification of that feeling of blasphemous infinity which had struck me during the shorter and earlier passage. At last the record ended abruptly, during an unusually clear speech of the human and Bostonian voice; but I sat stupidly staring long after the machine had automatically stopped.

I hardly need say that I gave that shocking record many another playing, and that I made exhaustive attempts at analysis and comment in comparing notes with Akeley. It would be both useless and disturbing to repeat here all that we concluded; but I may hint that we agreed in believing we had secured a clue to the source of some of the most repulsive primordial customs in the cryptic elder religions of mankind. It seemed plain to us, also, that there were ancient and elaborate alliances; between the hidden outer creatures and certain members of the human race. How extensive these alliances were, and how their state today might compare with their state in earlier ages, we had no means of guessing; yet at best there was room for a limitless amount of horrified speculation. There seemed to be an awful, immemorial linkage in several definite stages betwixt man and nameless infinity. The blasphemies which appeared on earth, it was hinted, came from the dark planet Yuggoth, at the rim of the solar system; but this was itself merely the populous outpost of a frightful interstellar race whose ultimate source must lie far outside even the Einsteinian space-time continuum or greatest known cosmos.

Meanwhile we continued to discuss the black stone and the best way of getting it to Arkham—Akeley deeming it inadvisable to have me visit him at the scene of his nightmare studies. For some reason or other, Akeley was afraid to trust the thing to any ordinary or expected transportation route. His final idea was to take it across county to Bellows Falls and ship it on the Boston and Maine system through Keene and Winchendon and Fitchburg, even though this would necessitate his driving along somewhat lonelier and more forest-traversing hill roads than the main highway to Brattleboro. He said he had noticed a man around the express office at Brattleboro when he had sent the phonograph record, whose actions and expression had been far from reassuring. This man had seemed too anxious to talk with the clerks, and had taken the train on which the record was shipped. Akeley confessed that he had not felt strictly at ease about that record until he heard from me of its safe receipt.

About this time—the second week in July—another letter of mine went astray, as I learned through an anxious communication from Akeley. After that he told me to address him no more at Townshend, but to send all mail in care of the General Delivery at Brattleboro; whither he would make frequent trips either in his car or on the motor-coach line which had lately replaced passenger service on the lagging branch railway. I could see that he was getting more and more anxious, for he went into much detail about the increased barking of the dogs on moonless nights, and about the fresh claw-prints he sometimes found in the

47. In 1888, the Eastman Dry Plate & Film Company, headquartered in Rochester, New York, introduced its first camera, known simply as the Kodak Camera. (Kodak, despite its Slavic echoes, was a trade name invented by George Eastman.) Its marketing slogan was "You press the button—we do the rest." To make good this boast, the camera was preloaded with enough film for one hundred exposures. When the film was exposed, the entire camera had to be sent back to the manufacturer, which then developed the pictures and reloaded the camera.

The price of the first camera was $25, and the cost to develop the film was $10. In modern purchasing power, this was over $1,700 for the camera and $680 for development of the pictures. However, by 1891, Eastman had introduced less expensive models (costing as little as $6), and, with the introduction of a pocket model in 1895 for $5, the cameras began to be affordable for the masses. The price of a Kodak "Brownie" camera, made mostly of cardboard, was only $1 in 1900. By the early 1920s, Kodak was offering more sophisticated cameras as well; the "autographic" series, which allowed the user to write on the negative, sold for $20 and up. In 1923, Kodak made amateur motion pictures practicable as well, and Kodak processing laboratories proliferated.

48. The new moon occurred on July 17, 1928, so that a "moonless night" in the second week of July is accurate.

road and in the mud at the back of his farmyard when morning came. Once he told about a veritable army of prints drawn up in a line facing an equally thick and resolute line of dog-tracks, and sent a loathsomely disturbing kodak[47] picture to prove it. That was after a night on which the dogs had outdone themselves in barking and howling.[48]

On the morning of Wednesday, July 18, I received a telegram from Bellows Falls, in which Akeley said he was expressing the black stone over the B. & M. on Train No. 5508, leaving Bellows Falls at 12:15 P.M., standard time, and due at the North Station in Boston at 4:12 P.M. It ought, I calculated, to get up to Arkham at least by the next noon; and accordingly I stayed in all Thursday morning to receive it. But noon came and went without its advent, and when I telephoned down to the express office I was informed that no shipment for me had arrived. My next act, performed amidst a growing alarm, was to give a long-distance call to the express agent at the Boston North Station; and I was scarcely surprised to learn that my consignment had not appeared. Train No. 5508 had pulled in only 35 minutes late on the day before, but had contained no box addressed to me. The agent promised, however, to institute a searching inquiry; and I ended the day by sending Akeley a night-letter outlining the situation.

With commendable promptness a report came from the Boston office on the following afternoon, the agent telephoning as soon as he learned the facts. It seemed that the railway express clerk on No. 5508 had been able to recall an incident which might have much bearing on my loss—an argument with a very curious-voiced man, lean, sandy, and rustic-looking, when the train was waiting at Keene, N.H., shortly after one o'clock standard time. The man, he said, was greatly excited about a heavy box which he claimed to expect, but which was neither on the train nor entered on the company's books. He had given the name of Stanley Adams, and had had such a queerly thick droning voice, that it made the clerk abnormally dizzy and sleepy to listen to him. The clerk could not remember quite how the conversation had ended, but recalled starting into a fuller awakening when the train began to move. The Boston agent added that this clerk was a young man of wholly unquestioned veracity and reliability, of known antecedents and long with the company.

That evening I went to Boston to interview the clerk in person, having obtained his name and address from the office. He was a frank, prepossessing fellow, but I saw that he could add nothing to his original account. Oddly, he was scarcely sure that he could even recognise the strange inquirer again. Realising that he had no more to tell, I returned to Arkham and sat up till morning writing letters to Akeley, to the express company and to the police department and station agent in Keene. I felt that the strange-voiced man who had so queerly affected the clerk must have a pivotal place in the ominous business, and hoped that Keene station employees and telegraph-office records might tell something about him and about how he happened to make his inquiry when and where he did.

I must admit, however, that all my investigations came to nothing. The queer-voiced man had indeed been noticed around the Keene station in the early afternoon of July 18, and one lounger seemed to couple him vaguely with a heavy box; but he was altogether unknown, and had not been seen before or since. He had not visited the telegraph office or received any message so far as could be learned, nor had any message which might justly be considered a notice of the black stone's presence on No. 5508 come through the office for anyone. Naturally Akeley joined with me in conducting these inquiries, and even made a personal trip to Keene to question the people around the station; but his attitude toward the matter was more fatalistic than mine. He seemed to find the loss of the box a portentous and menacing fulfilment of inevitable tendencies, and had no real hope at all of its recovery. He spoke of the undoubted telepathic and hypnotic powers of the hill creatures and their agents, and in one letter hinted that he did not believe the stone was on this earth any longer. For my part, I was duly enraged, for I had felt there was at least a chance of learning profound and astonishing things from the old, blurred hieroglyphs. The matter would have rankled bitterly in my mind had not Akeley's immediate subsequent letters brought up a new phase of the whole horrible hill problem which at once seized all my attention.

IV.

THE UNKNOWN THINGS, Akeley wrote in a script grown pitifully tremulous, had begun to close in on him with a wholly new degree of determination. The nocturnal barking of the dogs whenever the moon was dim or absent was hideous now, and there had been attempts to molest him on the lonely roads he had to traverse by day. On the second of August, while bound for the village in his car, he had found a tree-trunk laid in his path at a point where the highway ran through a deep patch of woods; while the savage barking of the two great dogs he had with him told all too well of the things which must have been lurking near. What would have happened had the dogs not been there, he did not dare guess—but he never went out now without at least two of his faithful and powerful pack. Other road experiences had occurred on August 5th and 6th; a shot grazing his car on one occasion, and the barking of the dogs telling of unholy woodland presences on the other.

On August 15th I received a frantic letter which disturbed me greatly, and which made me wish Akeley could put aside his lonely reticence and call in the aid of the law. There had been frightful happenings on the night of the 12–13th, bullets flying outside the farmhouse, and three of the twelve great dogs being found shot dead in the morning. There were myriads of claw-prints in the road, with the human prints of Walter Brown among them. Akeley had started to telephone to Brattleboro for more dogs, but the wire had gone dead before he had a chance to say much. Later he went to Brattleboro in his car, and learned there that linemen had found the main telephone cable neatly cut at a point where it ran through the deserted hills north of Newfane. But he was about to start home with four fine new dogs, and several cases of ammunition for his big-game repeating rifle. The letter was written at the post office in Brattleboro, and came through to me without delay.

My attitude toward the matter was by this time quickly slipping from a scientific to an alarmedly personal one. I was afraid for Akeley in his remote, lonely farmhouse, and half afraid for myself because of my now definite connexion with the strange hill problem. The thing was *reaching out* so. Would it suck me in and engulf me? In replying to his letter I urged him to seek help, and hinted that I might take action myself if he did not. I spoke of visiting Vermont in person in spite of his wishes, and of helping him explain the situation to the proper authorities. In return, however, I received only a telegram from Bellows Falls which read thus:

APPRECIATE YOUR POSITION BUT CAN DO NOTHING TAKE NO ACTION YOURSELF FOR IT COULD ONLY HARM BOTH. WAIT FOR EXPLANATION

HENRY AKELY

But the affair was steadily deepening. Upon my replying to the telegram I received a shaky note from Akeley with the astonishing news that he had not only never sent the wire, but had not received the letter from me to which it was an obvious reply. Hasty inquiries by him at Bellows Falls had brought out that the message was deposited by a strange sandy-haired man with a curiously thick, droning voice, though more than this he could not learn. The clerk shewed him the original text as scrawled in pencil by the sender, but the handwriting was wholly unfamiliar. It was noticeable that the signature was misspelled—A-K-E-L-Y, without the second "E." Certain conjectures were inevitable, but amidst the obvious crisis he did not stop to elaborate upon them.

He spoke of the death of more dogs and the purchase of still others, and of the exchange of gunfire which had become a settled feature each moonless night. Brown's prints, and the prints of at least one or two more shod human figures, were now found regularly among the claw-prints in the road, and at the back of the farmyard. It was, Akeley admitted, a pretty bad business; and before long he would probably have to go to live with his California son whether or not he could sell the old place. But it was not easy to leave the only spot one could really think of as home. He must try to hang on a little longer; perhaps he could scare off the intruders—especially if he openly gave up all further attempts to penetrate their secrets.

Writing Akeley at once, I renewed my offers of aid, and spoke again of visiting him and helping him convince the authorities

49. The moon was indeed full on August 31, 1928.

of his dire peril. In his reply he seemed less set against that plan than his past attitude would have led one to predict, but said he would like to hold off a little while longer—long enough to get his things in order and reconcile himself to the idea of leaving an almost morbidly cherished birthplace. People looked askance at his studies and speculations, and it would be better to get quietly off without setting the countryside in a turmoil and creating widespread doubts of his own sanity. He had had enough, he admitted, but he wanted to make a dignified exit if he could.

This letter reached me on the twenty-eighth of August, and I prepared and mailed as encouraging a reply as I could. Apparently the encouragement had effect, for Akeley had fewer terrors to report when he acknowledged my note. He was not very optimistic, though, and expressed the belief that it was only the full moon season which was holding the creatures off.[49] He hoped there would not be many densely cloudy nights, and talked vaguely of boarding in Brattleboro when the moon waned. Again I wrote him encouragingly but on September 5th there came a fresh communication which had obviously crossed my letter in the mails; and to this I could not give any such hopeful response. In view of its importance I believe I had better give it in full—as best I can do from memory of the shaky script. It ran substantially as follows:

Monday

Dear Wilmarth

A rather discouraging P. S. to my last. Last night was thickly cloudy—though no rain—and not a bit of moonlight got through. Things were pretty bad, and I think the end is getting near, in spite of all we have hoped. After midnight something landed on the roof of the house, and the dogs all rushed up to see what it was. I could hear them snapping and tearing around, and then one managed to get on the roof by jumping from the low ell. There was a terrible fight up there, and I heard a frightful buzzing which I'll never forget. And then there was a shocking smell. About the same time bullets came through the window and nearly grazed me. I think the main line of the hill creatures had got close to the house when the dogs divided because of the roof business. What was up there I don't know yet, but I'm afraid the creatures are learning to steer better with their space wings. I put out the light and used the windows for loopholes, and raked all around the house with rifle fire aimed just high enough not to hit the dogs. That seemed to end the business, but in the morning I found great pools of blood in the yard, beside pools of a green sticky stuff that had the worst odour I have ever smelled. I climbed up on the roof and found more of the sticky stuff there. Five of the dogs were killed—I'm afraid I hit one myself by aiming too low, for he was shot in the back. Now I am setting the panes the shots broke, and am going to Brattleboro for more dogs. I guess the men at the kennels think I am crazy. Will drop another note later. Suppose I'll be ready for moving in a week or two, though it nearly kills me to think of it.

Hastily—AKELEY

But this was not the only letter from Akeley to cross mine. On the next morning—September 6th—still another came; this time a frantic scrawl which utterly unnerved me and put me at a loss what to say or do next. Again I cannot do better than quote the text as faithfully as memory will let me.

Tuesday

Clouds didn't break, so no moon again—and going into the wane anyhow. I'd have the house wired for electricity and put in a searchlight if I didn't know they'd cut the cables as fast as they could be mended.

I think I am going crazy. It may be that all I have ever written you is a dream or madness. It was bad enough before, but this time it is too much. They talked to me last night—talked in that cursed buzzing voice and told me things that I dare not repeat to you. I heard them plainly over the barking of the dogs, and once when they were drowned out a human voice helped them. Keep out of this, Wilmarth—it is worse than either you or I ever suspected. They don't mean to let me get to California now—they want to take me off alive, or what theoretically and mentally amounts to alive—not only to Yuggoth, but beyond that—away outside the galaxy and possibly beyond the last curved rim of

50. "Rural Free Delivery" was the extension of the postal system in 1891, providing for delivery of letters to addresses even in remote rural areas, replacing the system that required the addressee to pick up the letters at an often distant post office.

space. *I told them I wouldn't go where they wish, or in the terrible way they propose to take me, but I'm afraid it will be no use. My place is so far out that they may come by day as well as by night before long. Six more dogs killed, and I felt presences all along the wooded parts of the road when I drove to Brattleboro today. It was a mistake for me to try to send you that phonograph record and black stone. Better smash the record before it's too late. Will drop you another line tomorrow if I'm still here. Wish I could arrange to get my books and things to Brattleboro and board there. I would run off without anything if I could but something inside my mind holds me back. I can slip out to Brattleboro, where I ought to be safe, but I feel just as much a prisoner there as at the house. And I seem to know that I couldn't get much farther even if I dropped everything and tried. It is horrible—don't get mixed up in this.*

Yrs—AKELEY

I did not sleep at all the night after receiving this terrible thing, and was utterly baffled as to Akeley's remaining degree of sanity. The substance of the note was wholly insane, yet the manner of expression—in view of all that had gone before—had a grimly potent quality of convincingness. I made no attempt to answer it, thinking it better to wait until Akeley might have time to reply to my latest communication. Such a reply indeed came on the following day, though the fresh material in it quite overshadowed any of the points brought up by the letter nominally answered. Here is what I recall of the text, scrawled and blotted as it was in the course of a plainly frantic and hurried composition.

Wednesday

W—

Yr. letter came, but it's no use to discuss anything any more. I am fully resigned. Wonder that I have even enough will power left to fight them off. Can't escape even if I were willing to give up everything and run. They'll get me.

Had a letter from them yesterday—R.F.D.[50] *man brought it while I was at Brattleboro. Typed and postmarked Bellows Falls.*

Tells what they want to do with me—I can't repeat it. Look out for yourself, too! Smash that record. Cloudy nights keep up, and moon waning all the time. Wish I dared to get help—it might brace up my will power—but everyone who would dare to come at all would call me crazy unless there happened to be some proof. Couldn't ask people to come for no reason at all—am all out of touch with everybody and have been for years.

But I haven't told you the worst, Wilmarth. Brace up to read this, for it will give you a shock. I am telling the truth, though. It is this—I have seen and touched one of the things, or part of one of the things. *God, man, but it's awful! It was dead, of course. One of the dogs had it, and I found it near the kennel this morning. I tried to save it in the woodshed to convince people of the whole thing, but it all evaporated in a few hours. Nothing left. You know, all those things in the rivers were seen only on the first morning after the flood. And here's the worst. I tried to photograph it for you, but when I developed the film there wasn't anything visible except the woodshed. What can the thing have been made of? I saw it and felt it, and they all leave footprints. It was surely made of matter—but what kind of matter? The shape can't be described. It was a great crab with a lot of pyramided fleshy rings or knots of thick, ropy stuff covered with feelers where a man's head would be. That green sticky stuff is its blood or juice. And there are more of them due on earth any minute.*

Walter Brown is missing—hasn't been seen loafing around any of his usual corners in the villages hereabouts. I must have got him with one of my shots, though the creatures always seem to try to take their dead and wounded away.

Got into town this afternoon without any trouble, but am afraid they're beginning to hold off because they're sure of me. Am writing this in Brattleboro P. O. This may be goodbye—if it is, write my son George Goodenough Akeley, 176 Pleasant St., San Diego, Cal.,[51] *but don't come up here. Write the boy if you don't hear from me in a week, and watch the papers for news.*

I'm going to play my last two cards now—if I have the will power left. First to try poison gas on the things (I've got the right chemicals and have fixed up masks for myself and the dogs) and then if that doesn't work, tell the sheriff. They can lock me in a madhouse if they want to—it'll be better than what the other

51. Not surprisingly, a fictitious address in San Diego.

creatures *would do. Perhaps I can get them to pay attention to the prints around the house —they are faint, but I can find them every morning. Suppose, though, police would say I faked them somehow; for they all think I'm a queer character.*

Must try to have a state policeman spend a night here and see for himself—though it would be just like the creatures to learn about it and hold off that night. They cut my wires whenever I try to telephone in the night—the linemen think it is very queer, and may testify for me if they don't go and imagine I cut them myself. I haven't tried to keep them repaired for over a week now.

I could get some of the ignorant people to testify for me about the reality of the horrors, but everybody laughs at what they say, and anyway, they have shunned my place for so long that they don't know any of the new events. You couldn't get one of those run-down farmers to come within a mile of my house for love or money. The mail-carrier hears what they say and jokes me about it—God! If I only dared tell him how real it is! I think I'll try to get him to notice the prints, but he comes in the afternoon and they're usually about gone by that time. If I kept one by setting a box or pan over it, he'd think surely it was a fake or joke.

Wish I hadn't gotten to be such a hermit, so folks don't drop around as they used to. I've never dared shew the black stone or the kodak pictures, or play that record, to anybody but the ignorant people. The others would say I faked the whole business and do nothing but laugh. But I may yet try shewing the pictures. They give those claw-prints clearly, even if the things that made them can't be photographed. What a shame nobody else saw that thing this morning before it went to nothing!

But I don't know as I care. After what I've been through, a madhouse is as good a place as any. The doctors can help me make up my mind to get away from this house, and that is all that will save me.

Write my son George if you don't hear soon. Goodbye, smash that record, and don't mix up in this.

Yrs—AKELEY

The letter frankly plunged me into the blackest of terror. I did not know what to say in answer, but scratched off some incoherent words of advice and encouragement and sent them by registered mail. I recall urging Akeley to move to Brattleboro at once, and place himself under the protection of the authorities; adding that I would come to that town with the phonograph record and help convince the courts of his sanity. It was time, too, I think I wrote, to alarm the people generally against this thing in their midst. It will be observed that at this moment of stress my own belief in all Akeley had told and claimed was virtually complete, though I did think his failure to get a picture of the dead monster was due not to any freak of Nature but to some excited slip of his own.

52. This is a significant clue in "A Case of Identity," an early Sherlock Holmes tale well known to Lovecraft (but apparently not to Wilmarth).

V.

THEN, APPARENTLY CROSSING my incoherent note and reaching me Saturday afternoon, September 8th, came that curiously different and calming letter neatly typed on a new machine; that strange letter of reassurance and invitation which must have marked so prodigious a transition in the whole nightmare drama of the lonely hills. Again I will quote from memory—seeking for special reasons to preserve as much of the flavour of the style as I can. It was postmarked Bellows Falls, and the signature as well as the body of the letter was typed[52]—as is frequent with beginners in typing. The text, though, was marvellously accurate for a tyro's work; and I concluded that Akeley must have used a machine at some previous period—perhaps in college. To say that the letter relieved me would be only fair, yet beneath my relief lay a substratum of uneasiness. If Akeley had been sane in his terror, was he now sane in his deliverance? And the sort of "improved rapport" mentioned . . . what was it? The entire thing implied such a diametrical reversal of Akeley's previous attitude! But here is the substance of the text, carefully transcribed from a memory in which I take some pride.

Townshend, Vermont, Thursday, Sept. 6, 1928.

My dear Wilmarth:—

It gives me great pleasure to be able to set you at rest regarding all the silly things I've been writing you. I say "silly," although by

53. This theme is used to great effect in the charming 1950 tale "To Serve Man," by Damon Knight, later a *Twilight Zone* episode (1962), in which the title of an alien book thought to express means to aid humankind is revealed to be a cookbook.

that I mean my frightened attitude rather than my descriptions of certain phenomena. Those phenomena are real and important enough; my mistake had been in establishing an anomalous attitude toward them.

I think I mentioned that my strange visitors were beginning to communicate with me, and to attempt such communication. Last night this exchange of speech became actual. In response to certain signals I admitted to the house a messenger from those outside—a fellow-human, let me hasten to say. He told me much that neither you nor I had even begun to guess, and shewed clearly how totally we had misjudged and misinterpreted the purpose of the Outer Ones in maintaining their secret colony on this planet.

It seems that the evil legends about what they have offered to men, and what they wish in connexion with the earth, are wholly the result of an ignorant misconception of allegorical speech—speech, of course, moulded by cultural backgrounds and thought-habits vastly different from anything we dream of.[53] My own conjectures, I freely own, shot as widely past the mark as any of the guesses of illiterate farmers and savage Indians. What I had thought morbid and shameful and ignominious is in reality awesome and mind-expanding and even glorious—my previous estimate being merely a phase of man's eternal tendency to hate and fear and shrink from the utterly different.

Now I regret the harm I have inflicted upon these alien and incredible beings in the course of our nightly skirmishes. If only I had consented to talk peacefully and reasonably with them in the first place! But they bear me no grudge, their emotions being organised very differently from ours. It is their misfortune to have had as their human agents in Vermont some very inferior specimens—the late Walter Brown, for example. He prejudiced me vastly against them. Actually, they have never knowingly harmed men, but have often been cruelly wronged and spied upon by our species. There is a whole secret cult of evil men (a man of your mystical erudition will understand me when I link them with Hastur and the Yellow Sign) devoted to the purpose of tracking them down and injuring them on behalf of monstrous powers from other dimensions. It is against these aggressors—not against normal humanity—that the drastic precautions of the Outer Ones are directed. Incidentally, I learned that many of our lost letters were stolen not by the Outer Ones but by the emissaries of this malign cult.

All that the Outer Ones wish of man is peace and non-molestation and an increasing intellectual rapport. This latter is absolutely necessary now that our inventions and devices are expanding our knowledge and motions, and making it more and more impossible for the Outer Ones' necessary outposts to exist secretly on this planet. The alien beings desire to know mankind more fully, and to have a few of mankind's philosophic and scientific leaders know more about them. With such an exchange of knowledge all perils will pass, and a satisfactory modus vivendi be established. The very idea of any attempt to enslave or degrade mankind is ridiculous.

As a beginning of this improved rapport, the Outer Ones have naturally chosen me—whose knowledge of them is already so considerable—as their primary interpreter on earth. Much was told me last night—facts of the most stupendous and vista-opening nature—and more will be subsequently communicated to me both orally and in writing. I shall not be called upon to make any trip outside just yet, though I shall probably wish to do so later on— employing special means and transcending everything which we have hitherto been accustomed to regard as human experience. My house will be besieged no longer. Everything has reverted to normal, and the dogs will have no further occupation. In place of terror I have been given a rich boon of knowledge and intellectual adventure which few other mortals have ever shared.

The Outer Beings are perhaps the most marvellous organic things in or beyond all space and time—members of a cosmos-wide race of which all other life-forms are merely degenerate variants. They are more vegetable than animal, if these terms can be applied to the sort of matter composing them, and have a somewhat fungoid structure; though the presence of a chlorophyll-like substance and a very singular nutritive system differentiate them altogether from true cormophytic fungi.[54] Indeed, the type is composed of a form of matter totally alien to our part of space—with electrons having a wholly different vibration-rate. That is why the beings cannot be photographed on the ordinary camera films and plates of our known universe, even though our eyes can see them.

54. That is, fungi with an axis containing vascular tissue and foliage. There are estimated to be over 1.5 million species of fungi, and the classifications have changed markedly since the 1930s. Indeed, the division of plants into cormophytes (mosses, ferns, seed plants) and thallophytes (algae, fungi, lichens), established by the Austrian botanist, writer, literary scholar, and linguist Stephan Endlicher (1804–1849), is obsolete.

With proper knowledge, however, any good chemist could make a photographic emulsion which would record their images.

The genus is unique in its ability to traverse the heatless and airless interstellar void in full corporeal form, and some of its variants cannot do this without mechanical aid or curious surgical transpositions. Only a few species have the ether-resisting wings characteristic of the Vermont variety. Those inhabiting certain remote peaks in the Old World were brought in other ways. Their external resemblance to animal life, and to the sort of structure we understand as material, is a matter of parallel evolution rather than of close kinship. Their brain-capacity exceeds that of any other surviving life-form, although the winged types of our hill country are by no means the most highly developed. Telepathy is their usual means of discourse, though they have rudimentary vocal organs which, after a slight operation (for surgery is an incredibly expert and every-day thing among them), can roughly duplicate the speech of such types of organism as still use speech.

Their main immediate abode is a still undiscovered and almost lightless planet at the very edge of our solar system—beyond Neptune, and the ninth in distance from the sun. It is, as we have inferred, the object mystically hinted at as "Yuggoth" in certain ancient and forbidden writings; and it will soon be the scene of a strange focussing of thought upon our world in an effort to facilitate mental rapport. I would not be surprised if astronomers became sufficiently sensitive to these thought-currents to discover Yuggoth when the Outer Ones wish them to do so. But Yuggoth, of course, is only the stepping-stone. The main body of the beings inhabits strangely organised abysses wholly beyond the utmost reach of any human imagination. The space-time globule which we recognise as the totality of all cosmic entity is only an atom in the genuine infinity which is theirs. And as much of this infinity as any human brain can hold is eventually to be opened up to me, as it has been to not more than fifty other men since the human race has existed.

You will probably call this raving at first, Wilmarth, but in time you will appreciate the titanic opportunity I have stumbled upon. I want you to share as much of it as is possible, and to that end must tell you thousands of things that won't go on paper. In the past I have warned you not to come to see me. Now that all is safe, I take pleasure in rescinding that warning and inviting you.

Can't you make a trip up here before your college term opens? It would be marvellously delightful if you could. Bring along the phonograph record and all my letters to you as consultative data—we shall need them in piecing together the whole tremendous story. You might bring the kodak prints, too, since I seem to have mislaid the negatives and my own prints in all this recent excitement. But what a wealth of facts I have to add to all this groping and tentative material—and what a stupendous device I have to supplement my additions!

Don't hesitate—I am free from espionage now, and you will not meet anything unnatural or disturbing. Just come along and let my car meet you at the Brattleboro station—prepare to stay as long as you can, and expect many an evening of discussion of things beyond all human conjecture. Don't tell anyone about it, of course—for this matter must not get to the promiscuous public.

The train service to Brattleboro is not bad—you can get a time-table in Boston. Take the B. & M. to Greenfield, and then change for the brief remainder of the way. I suggest your taking the convenient 4:10 p.m.—standard—from Boston. This gets into Greenfield at 7:35, and at 9:19 a train leaves there which reaches Brattleboro at 10:01. That is week-days. Let me know the date and I'll have my car on hand at the station.

Pardon this typed letter, but my handwriting has grown shaky of late, as you know, and I don't feel equal to long stretches of script. I got this new Corona in Brattleboro yesterday—it seems to work very well.

Awaiting word, and hoping to see you shortly with the phonograph record and all my letters—and the kodak prints—

> I am
> Yours in anticipation,
> HENRY W. AKELEY

To Albert N. Wilmarth, Esq.,
Miskatonic University,
Arkham, Mass.

The complexity of my emotions upon reading, re-reading, and pondering over this strange and unlooked-for letter is past adequate description. I have said that I was at once relieved and made uneasy, but this expresses only crudely the overtones of diverse and largely subconscious feelings which comprised both the relief and the uneasiness. To begin with, the thing was so antipodally at variance with the whole chain of horrors preceding it—the change of mood from stark terror to cool complacency and even exultation was so unheralded, lightning-like, and complete! I could scarcely believe that a single day could so alter the psychological perspective of one who had written that final frenzied bulletin of Wednesday, no matter what relieving disclosures that day might have brought. At certain moments a sense of conflicting unrealities made me wonder whether this whole distantly reported drama of fantastic forces were not a kind of half-illusory dream created largely within my own mind. Then I thought of the phonograph record and gave way to still greater bewilderment.

The letter seemed so unlike anything which could have been expected! As I analysed my impression, I saw that it consisted of two distinct phases. First, granting that Akeley had been sane before and was still sane, the indicated change in the situation itself was so swift and unthinkable. And secondly, the change in Akeley's own manner, attitude, and language was so vastly beyond the normal or the predictable. The man's whole personality seemed to have undergone an insidious mutation—a mutation so deep that one could scarcely reconcile his two aspects with the supposition that both represented equal sanity. Word-choice, spelling—all were subtly different. And with my academic sensitiveness to prose style, I could trace profound divergences in his commonest reactions and rhythm-responses. Certainly, the emotional cataclysm or revelation which could produce so radical an overturn must be an extreme one indeed! Yet in another way the letter seemed quite characteristic of Akeley. The same old passion for infinity—the same old scholarly inquisitiveness. I could not a moment—or more than a moment—credit the idea of spuriousness or malign substitution. Did not the invitation—the willingness to have me test the truth of the letter in person—prove its genuineness?

I did not retire Saturday night, but sat up thinking of the

shadows and marvels behind the letter I had received. My mind, aching from the quick succession of monstrous conceptions it had been forced to confront during the last four months, worked upon this startling new material in a cycle of doubt and acceptance which repeated most of the steps experienced in facing the earlier wonders; till long before dawn a burning interest and curiosity had begun to replace the original storm of perplexity and uneasiness. Mad or sane, metamorphosed or merely relieved, the chances were that Akeley had actually encountered some stupendous change of perspective in his hazardous research; some change at once diminishing his danger—real or fancied—and opening dizzy new vistas of cosmic and superhuman knowledge. My own zeal for the unknown flared up to meet his, and I felt myself touched by the contagion of the morbid barrier-breaking. To shake off the maddening and wearying limitations of time and space and natural law—to be linked with the vast outside— to come close to the nighted and abysmal secrets of the infinite and the ultimate—surely such a thing was worth the risk of one's life, soul, and sanity! And Akeley had said there was no longer any peril—he had invited me to visit him instead of warning me away as before. I tingled at the thought of what he might now have to tell me—there was an almost paralysing fascination in the thought of sitting in that lonely and lately beleaguered farmhouse with a man who had talked with actual emissaries from outer space; sitting there with the terrible record and the pile of letters in which Akeley had summarised his earlier conclusions.

So late Sunday morning I telegraphed Akeley that I would meet him in Brattleboro on the following Wednesday—September 12th—if that date were convenient for him. In only one respect did I depart from his suggestions, and that concerned the choice of a train. Frankly, I did not feel like arriving in that haunted Vermont region late at night; so instead of accepting the train he chose I telephoned the station and devised another arrangement. By rising early and taking the 8:07 A.M. (standard) into Boston, I could catch the 9:25 for Greenfield; arriving there at 12:22 noon. This connected exactly with a train reaching Brattleboro at 1:08 P.M.—a much more comfortable hour than 10:01 for meeting Akeley and riding with him into the close-packed, secret-guarding hills.

I mentioned this choice in my telegram, and was glad to learn in the reply which came toward evening that it had met with my prospective host's endorsement. His wire ran thus:

ARRANGEMENT SATISFACTORY. WILL MEET 1:08 TRAIN WEDNES-
DAY. DON'T FORGET RECORD AND LETTERS AND PRINTS. KEEP
DESTINATION QUIET. EXPECT GREAT REVELATIONS.

AKELEY.

Receipt of this message in direct response to one sent to Akeley—and necessarily delivered to his house from the Townshend station either by official messenger or by a restored telephone service—removed any lingering subconscious doubts I may have had about the authorship of the perplexing letter. My relief was marked—indeed, it was greater than I could account for at that time; since all such doubts had been rather deeply buried. But I slept soundly and long that night, and was eagerly busy with preparations during the ensuing two days.

VI.

ON WEDNESDAY I started as agreed, taking with me a valise full of simple necessities and scientific data, including the hideous phonograph record, the kodak prints, and the entire file of Akeley's correspondence. As requested, I had told no one where I was going; for I could see that the matter demanded utmost privacy, even allowing for its most favourable turns. The thought of actual mental contact with alien, outside entities was stupefying enough to my trained and somewhat prepared mind; and this being so, what might one think of its effect on the vast masses of uninformed laymen? I do not know whether dread or adventurous expectancy was uppermost in me as I changed trains in Boston and began the long westward run out of familiar regions into those I knew less thoroughly. Waltham—Concord—Ayer—Fitchburg—Gardner—Athol—

My train reached Greenfield seven minutes late, but the northbound connecting express had been held. Transferring in haste, I felt a curious breathlessness as the cars rumbled on through the early afternoon sunlight into territories I had always read of but had never before visited. I knew I was entering an altogether older-fashioned and more primitive New England than the mechanised, urbanised coastal and southern areas where all my life had been spent; an unspoiled, ancestral New England without the foreigners and factory-smoke, billboards and concrete roads, of the sections which modernity has touched. There would be odd survivals of that continuous native life whose deep roots make it the one authentic outgrowth of the landscape—the continuous native life which keeps alive strange ancient memories, and fertilises the soil for shadowy, marvellous, and seldom-mentioned beliefs.

Now and then I saw the blue Connecticut River gleaming in the sun, and after leaving Northfield we crossed it. Ahead loomed green and cryptical hills, and when the conductor came around I learned that I was at last in Vermont. He told me to set my watch back an hour, since the northern hill country will have no dealings with new-fangled daylight time schemes.[55] As I did so it seemed to me that I was likewise turning the calendar back a century.

The train kept close to the river, and across in New Hampshire I could see the approaching slope of steep Wantastiquet, about which singular old legends cluster.[56] Then streets appeared on my left, and a green island shewed in the stream on my right. People rose and filed to the door, and I followed them. The car stopped, and I alighted beneath the long train-shed of the Brattleboro station.

Looking over the line of waiting motors I hesitated a moment to see which one might turn out to be the Akeley Ford, but my identity was divined before I could take the initiative. And yet it was clearly not Akeley himself who advanced to meet me with an outstretched hand and a mellowly phrased query as to whether I was indeed Mr. Albert N. Wilmarth of Arkham. This man bore no resemblance to the bearded, grizzled Akeley of the snapshot; but was a younger and more urban person, fashionably dressed, and wearing only a small, dark moustache. His cultivated voice held an odd and almost disturbing hint of vague familiarity, though I could not definitely place it in my memory.

As I surveyed him I heard him explaining that he was a friend

55. Daylight saving time, now a matter of federal legislation, was in 1927 still a matter of some controversy and largely local option. Farmers generally opposed the idea as antithetical to their natural work schedule.

56. The principal "legend" relating to Wantastiquet (the Indian name for West River, as the mountain was originally called by white settlers) is that the mountain is a dormant volcano, with activity reported in the 1870s. Investigations by geologists have demonstrated that this is not so; that the loud "explosions" heard by local residents from time to time are the sound of large chunks of the mountain breaking off and falling, and that the detritus identified as material put forth by the "volcano" is in fact Umbilicaria (a lichen) and brown hematite (a mineral), not matter ejected by a volcanic explosion. While Wantastiquet may be an extinct volcano, there is no evidence of any activity in more than two hundred years.

57. The Sacred Cod is a memorial to the importance of the cod fisheries of Massachusetts and hangs in the Hall of Representatives, where it was transferred from the Old State House. The sign is of pine and was made in 1784 to replace one destroyed by fire in the Old State House.

of my prospective host's who had come down from Townshend in his stead. Akeley, he declared, had suffered a sudden attack of some asthmatic trouble, and did not feel equal to making a trip in the outdoor air. It was not serious, however, and there was to be no change in plans regarding my visit. I could not make out just how much this Mr. Noyes—as he announced himself—knew of Akeley's researches and discoveries, though it seemed to me that his casual manner stamped him as a comparative outsider. Remembering what a hermit Akeley had been, I was a trifle surprised at the ready availability of such a friend; but did not let my puzzlement deter me from entering the motor to which he gestured me. It was not the small ancient car I had expected from Akeley's descriptions, but a large and immaculate specimen of recent pattern—apparently Noyes's own, and bearing Massachusetts licence plates with the amusing "sacred codfish" device of that year.[57] My guide, I concluded, must be a summer transient in the Townshend region.

Noyes climbed into the car beside me and started it at once. I was glad that he did not overflow with conversation, for some peculiar atmospheric tensity made me feel disinclined to talk. The town seemed very attractive in the afternoon sunlight as we swept up an incline and turned to the right into the main street. It drowsed like the older New England cities which one remembers from boyhood, and something in the collocation of roofs and steeples and chimneys and brick walls formed contours touching deep viol-strings of ancestral emotion. I could tell that I was at the gateway of a region half-bewitched through the piling-up of unbroken time-accumulations; a region where old, strange things have had a chance to grow and linger because they have never been stirred up.

As we passed out of Brattleboro my sense of constraint and foreboding increased, for a vague quality in the hill-crowded countryside with its towering, threatening, close-pressing green and granite slopes hinted at obscure secrets and immemorial survivals which might or might not be hostile to mankind. For a time our course followed a broad, shallow river which flowed down from unknown hills in the north, and I shivered when my companion told me it was the West River. It was in this stream,

I recalled from newspaper items, that one of the morbid crab-like beings had been seen floating after the floods.

Gradually the country around us grew wilder and more deserted. Archaic covered bridges lingered fearsomely out of the past in pockets of the hills, and the half-abandoned railway track paralleling the river seemed to exhale a nebulously visible air of desolation. There were awesome sweeps of vivid valley where great cliffs rose, New England's virgin granite shewing grey and austere through the verdure that scaled the crests. There were gorges where untamed streams leaped, bearing down toward the river the unimagined secrets of a thousand pathless peaks. Branching away now and then were narrow, half-concealed roads that bored their way through solid, luxuriant masses of forest among whose primal trees whole armies of elemental spirits might well lurk. As I saw these I thought of how Akeley had been molested by unseen agencies on his drives along this very route, and did not wonder that such things could be.

The quaint, sightly village of Newfane,[58] reached in less than an hour, was our last link with that world which man can definitely call his own by virtue of conquest and complete occupancy. After that we cast off all allegiance to immediate, tangible, and time-touched things, and entered a fantastic world of hushed unreality in which the narrow, ribbon-like road rose and fell and curved with an almost sentient and purposeful caprice amidst the tenantless green peaks and half-deserted valleys. Except for the sound of the motor, and the faint stir of the few lonely farms we passed at infrequent intervals, the only thing that reached my ears was the gurgling, insidious trickle of strange waters from numberless hidden fountains in the shadowy woods.

The nearness and intimacy of the dwarfed, domed hills now became veritably breath-taking. Their steepness and abruptness were even greater than I had imagined from hearsay, and suggested nothing in common with the prosaic objective world we know. The dense, unvisited woods on those inaccessible slopes seemed to harbour alien and incredible things, and I felt that the very outline of the hills themselves held some strange and æon-forgotten meaning, as if they were vast hieroglyphs left by a rumoured titan race whose glories live only in rare, deep dreams.

58. Population in the 1930 census was 662.

All the legends of the past, and all the stupefying imputations of Henry Akeley's letters and exhibits, welled up in my memory to heighten the atmosphere of tension and growing menace. The purpose of my visit, and the frightful abnormalities it postulated struck at me all at once with a chill sensation that nearly overbalanced my ardour for strange delvings.

My guide must have noticed my disturbed attitude; for as the road grew wilder and more irregular, and our motion slower and more jolting, his occasional pleasant comments expanded into a steadier flow of discourse. He spoke of the beauty and weirdness of the country, and revealed some acquaintance with the folklore studies of my prospective host. From his polite questions it was obvious that he knew I had come for a scientific purpose, and that I was bringing data of some importance; but he gave no sign of appreciating the depth and awfulness of the knowledge which Akeley had finally reached.

His manner was so cheerful, normal, and urbane that his remarks ought to have calmed and reassured me; but oddly enough, I felt only the more disturbed as we bumped and veered onward into the unknown wilderness of hills and woods. At times it seemed as if he were pumping me to see what I knew of the monstrous secrets of the place, and with every fresh utterance that vague, teasing, baffling *familiarity* in his voice increased. It was not an ordinary or healthy familiarity despite the thoroughly wholesome and cultivated nature of the voice. I somehow linked it with forgotten nightmares, and felt that I might go mad if I recognised it. If any good excuse had existed, I think I would have turned back from my visit. As it was, I could not well do so—and it occurred to me that a cool, scientific conversation with Akeley himself after my arrival would help greatly to pull me together.

Besides, there was a strangely calming element of cosmic beauty in the hypnotic landscape through which we climbed and plunged fantastically. Time had lost itself in the labyrinths behind, and around us stretched only the flowering waves of færy and the recaptured loveliness of vanished centuries—the hoary groves, the untainted pastures edged with gay autumnal blossoms, and at vast intervals the small brown farmsteads nestling amidst huge trees beneath vertical precipices of fragrant brier and meadow-grass. Even the sunlight assumed a supernal glamour, as if some special atmosphere or exhalation mantled the whole region. I had seen nothing like it before save in the magic vistas that sometimes form the backgrounds of Italian primitives. Sodoma[59] and Leonardo conceived such expanses, but only in the distance, and through the vaultings of Renaissance arcades. We were now burrowing bodily through the midst of the picture, and I seemed to find in its necromancy a thing I had innately known or inherited and for which I had always been vainly searching.

Suddenly, after rounding an obtuse angle at the top of a sharp ascent, the car came to a standstill. On my left, across a well-kept lawn which stretched to the road and flaunted a border of whitewashed stones, rose a white, two-and-a-half-story house of unusual size and elegance for the region, with a congeries[60] of contiguous or arcade-linked barns, sheds, and windmill behind and to the right. I recognised it at once from the snapshot I had received, and was not surprised to see the name of Henry Akeley on the galvanised-iron mail-box near the road. For some distance back of the house a level stretch of marshy and sparsely wooded land extended, beyond which soared a steep, thickly forested hillside ending in a jagged leafy crest. This latter, I knew, was the summit of Dark Mountain, half way up which we must have climbed already.

Alighting from the car and taking my valise, Noyes asked me to wait while he went in and notified Akeley of my advent. He himself, he added, had important business elsewhere, and could not stop for more than a moment. As he briskly walked up the path to the house I climbed out of the car myself, wishing to stretch my legs a little before settling down to a sedentary conversation. My feeling of nervousness and tension had risen to a maximum again now that I was on the actual scene of the morbid beleaguering described so hauntingly in Akeley's letters, and I honestly dreaded the coming discussions which were to link me with such alien and forbidden worlds.

Close contact with the utterly bizarre is often more terrifying than inspiring, and it did not cheer me to think that this very bit of dusty road was the place where those monstrous tracks and that fœtid green ichor had been found after moonless nights of fear and death. Idly I noticed that none of Akeley's dogs seemed to be about. Had he sold them all as soon as the Outer Ones made

59. Il Sodoma (1477–1549), more formally the Italian Renaissance painter Giovanni Antonio Bazzi (or Razzi). Some scholars assert that his family name was Sodona (as some of his paintings are signed) or Sodoma. The judgment of the British National Gallery on his art is that it has a "slightly provincial but vigorous air." Sodoma's work was grounded in that of the thirteenth- and fourteenth-century Italian tempera painters who broke away from medieval techniques and subjects and the paintings of Leonardo da Vinci (1452–1519).

St. Sebastian by Il Sodoma (1525).

60. A collection or aggregation.

peace with him? Try as I might, I could not have the same confidence in the depth and sincerity of that peace which appeared in Akeley's final and queerly different letter. After all, he was a man of much simplicity and with little worldly experience. Was there not, perhaps, some deep and sinister undercurrent beneath the surface of the new alliance?

Led by my thoughts, my eyes turned downward to the powdery road surface which had held such hideous testimonies. The last few days had been dry, and tracks of all sorts cluttered the rutted, irregular highway despite the unfrequented nature of the district. With a vague curiosity I began to trace the outline of some of the heterogeneous impressions, trying meanwhile to curb the flights of macabre fancy which the place and its memories suggested. There was something menacing and uncomfortable in the funereal stillness, in the muffled, subtle trickle of distant brooks, and in the crowding green peaks and black-wooded precipices that choked the narrow horizon.

And then an image shot into my consciousness which made those vague menaces and flights of fancy seem mild and insignificant indeed. I have said that I was scanning the miscellaneous prints in the road with a kind of idle curiosity—but all at once that curiosity was shockingly snuffed out by a sudden and paralysing gust of active terror. For though the dust tracks were in general confused and overlapping, and unlikely to arrest any casual gaze, my restless vision had caught certain details near the spot where the path to the house joined the highway; and had recognised beyond doubt or hope the frightful significance of those details. It was not for nothing, alas, that I had pored for hours over the kodak views of the Outer Ones' claw-prints which Akeley had sent. Too well did I know the marks of those loathsome nippers, and that hint of ambiguous direction which stamped the horrors as no creatures of this planet. No chance had been left me for merciful mistake. Here, indeed, in objective form before my own eyes, and surely made not many hours ago, were at least three marks which stood out blasphemously among the surprising plethora of blurred footprints leading to and from the Akeley farmhouse. *They were the hellish tracks of the living fungi from Yuggoth.*

I pulled myself together in time to stifle a scream. After all, what more was there than I might have expected, assuming that I had really believed Akeley's letters? He had spoken of making peace with the things. Why, then, was it strange that some of them had visited his house? But the terror was stronger than the reassurance. Could any man be expected to look unmoved for the first time upon the claw-marks of animate beings from outer depths of space? Just then I saw Noyes emerge from the door and approach with a brisk step. I must, I reflected, keep command of myself, for the chances were this genial friend knew nothing of Akeley's profoundest and most stupendous probings into the forbidden.

Akeley, Noyes hastened to inform me, was glad and ready to see me; although his sudden attack of asthma would prevent him from being a very competent host for a day or two. These spells hit him hard when they came, and were always accompanied by a debilitating fever and general weakness. He never was good for much while they lasted—had to talk in a whisper, and was very clumsy and feeble in getting about. His feet and ankles swelled, too, so that he had to bandage them like a gouty old beef-eater.[61] Today he was in rather bad shape, so that I would have to attend very largely to my own needs; but he was none the less eager for conversation. I would find him in the study at the left of the front hall—the room where the blinds were shut. He had to keep the sunlight out when he was ill, for his eyes were very sensitive.

As Noyes bade me adieu and rode off northward in his car I began to walk slowly toward the house. The door had been left ajar for me; but before approaching and entering I cast a searching glance around the whole place, trying to decide what had struck me as so intangibly queer about it. The barns and sheds looked trimly prosaic enough, and I noticed Akeley's battered Ford in its capacious, unguarded shelter. Then the secret of the queerness reached me. It was the total silence. Ordinarily a farm is at least moderately murmurous from its various kinds of livestock, but here all signs of life were missing. What of the hens and the hogs? The cows, of which Akeley had said he possessed several, might conceivably be out to pasture, and the dogs might possibly have been sold; but the absence of any trace of cackling or grunting was truly singular.

I did not pause long on the path, but resolutely entered the

61. By "beef-eater," the narrator here simply means an Englishman, not necessarily one of the yeomen of the traditional queen's guards. He conjures the stereotypical image of an old English clubman who suffers from gout, a painful arthritic disease that creates severe swelling of joints, once thought to be the result of eating too much red meat (the "rich man's disease").

open house door and closed it behind me. It had cost me a distinct psychological effort to do so, and now that I was shut inside I had a momentary longing for precipitate retreat. Not that the place was in the least sinister in visual suggestion; on the contrary, I thought the graceful late-colonial hallway very tasteful and wholesome, and admired the evident breeding of the man who had furnished it. What made me wish to flee was something very attenuated and indefinable. Perhaps it was a certain odd odour which I thought I noticed—though I well knew how common musty odours are in even the best of ancient farmhouses.

VII.

REFUSING TO LET these cloudy qualms overmaster me, I recalled Noyes's instructions and pushed open the six-panelled, brass-latched white door on my left. The room beyond was darkened, as I had known before; and as I entered it I noticed that the queer odour was stronger there. There likewise appeared to be some faint, half-imaginary rhythm or vibration in the air. For a moment the closed blinds allowed me to see very little, but then a kind of apologetic hacking or whispering sound drew my attention to a great easy-chair in the farther, darker corner of the room. Within its shadowy depths I saw the white blur of a man's face and hands; and in a moment I had crossed to greet the figure who had tried to speak. Dim though the light was, I perceived that this was indeed my host. I had studied the kodak picture repeatedly, and there could be no mistake about this firm, weather-beaten face with the cropped, grizzled beard.

But as I looked again my recognition was mixed with sadness and anxiety; for certainly, this face was that of a very sick man. I felt that there must be something more than asthma behind that strained, rigid, immobile expression and unwinking glassy stare; and realised how terribly the strain of his frightful experiences must have told on him. Was it not enough to break any human being—even a younger man than this intrepid delver into the forbidden? The strange and sudden relief, I feared, had come too late to save him from something like a general breakdown. There was a touch of the pitiful in the limp, lifeless way his lean hands rested in his lap. He had on a loose dressing-gown, and was swathed around the head and high around the neck with a vivid yellow scarf or hood.

And then I saw that he was trying to talk in the same hacking whisper with which he had greeted me. It was a hard whisper to catch at first, since the grey moustache concealed all movements of the lips, and something in its timbre disturbed me greatly; but by concentrating my attention I could soon make out its purport surprisingly well. The accent was by no means a rustic one, and the language was even more polished than correspondence had led me to expect.

"Mr. Wilmarth, I presume? You must pardon my not rising. I am quite ill, as Mr. Noyes must have told you; but I could not resist having you come just the same. You know what I wrote in my last letter—there is so much to tell you tomorrow when I shall feel better. I can't say how glad I am to see you in person after all our many letters. You have the file with you, of course? And the kodak prints and record? Noyes put your valise in the hall—I suppose you saw it. For tonight I fear you'll have to wait on yourself to a great extent. Your room is upstairs—the one over this—and you'll see the bathroom door open at the head of the staircase. There's a meal spread for you in the dining-room—right through this door at your right—which you can take whenever you feel like it. I'll be a better host tomorrow—but just now weakness leaves me helpless.

"Make yourself at home—you might take out the letters and pictures and record and put them on the table here before you go upstairs with your bag. It is here that we shall discuss them—you can see my phonograph on that corner stand.

"No, thanks—there's nothing you can do for me. I know these spells of old. Just come back for a little quiet visiting before night, and then go to bed when you please. I'll rest right here—perhaps sleep here all night as I often do. In the morning I'll be far better able to go into the things we must go into. You realise, of course, the utterly stupendous nature of the matter before us. To us, as to only a few men on this earth, there will be opened up gulfs of time and space and knowledge beyond anything within the conception of human science and philosophy.

"Do you know that Einstein is wrong, and that certain objects

62. These underground lands are described in detail in Zealia Bishop's "The Mound," which was extensively revised by Lovecraft in 1929–1930—almost to the point of ghostwriting—but not published until 1940 (in an abbreviated version) and finally published in its full version in 1989. The realm is actually located under Oklahoma.

63. The Manuscripts (also referred to as the Pnakotic Fragments) are mentioned in a number of other tales by Lovecraft: *The Dream-Quest of Unknown Kadath*, *At the Mountains of Madness* (1936; pp. 457–572, below), "Polaris" (1920), "The Other Gods" (1933), and "The Shadow Out of Time" (1936; pp. 711–78, below). These sacred texts predate the *Necronomicon*, written in the eighth century. In a letter to William Lumley (May 12, 1931, *Selected Letters*, III, 372–73), Lovecraft described them as "the work of the 'Elder Ones,' preceding the human race on this planet, and handed down through an early human civilisation which once existed around the north pole. . . ." In another letter, this one in 1936, Lovecraft wrote,

> Exact data regarding the Pnakotic Mss. are lacking. They were brought down from Hyperborea by a secret cult (allied to that which preserved the *Book of Eibon*), & are in the secret Hyperborean language, but there is a rumour that they are a translation of something hellishly older—brought from the land of Lomar & of fabulous antiquity even there. That they antedate the human race is freely whispered. Curious parallelisms betwixt them & the Eltdown Shards [see "The Shadow Out of Time," note 40, below] have been pointed out—as if both were remote derivatives of some immeasurably anterior source, on this or some other planet (Lovecraft

and forces can move with a velocity greater than that of light? With proper aid I expect to go backward and forward in time, and actually *see* and *feel* the earth of remote past and future epochs. You can't imagine the degree to which those beings have carried science. There is nothing they can't do with the mind and body of living organisms. I expect to visit other planets, and even other stars and galaxies. The first trip will be to Yuggoth, the nearest world fully peopled by the beings. It is a strange dark orb at the very rim of our solar system—unknown to earthly astronomers as yet. But I must have written you about this. At the proper time, you know, the beings there will direct thought-currents toward us and cause it to be discovered—or perhaps let one of their human allies give the scientists a hint.

"There are mighty cities on Yuggoth—great tiers of terraced towers built of black stone like the specimen I tried to send you. That came from Yuggoth. The sun shines there no brighter than a star, but the beings need no light. They have other, subtler senses, and put no windows in their great houses and temples. Light even hurts and hampers and confuses them, for it does not exist at all in the black cosmos outside time and space where they came from originally. To visit Yuggoth would drive any weak man mad—yet I am going there. The black rivers of pitch that flow under those mysterious Cyclopean bridges—things built by some elder race extinct and forgotten before the beings came to Yuggoth from the ultimate voids—ought to be enough to make any man a Dante or Poe if he can keep sane long enough to tell what he has seen.

"But remember—that dark world of fungoid gardens and windowless cities isn't really terrible. It is only to us that it would seem so. Probably this world seemed just as terrible to the beings when they first explored it in the primal age. You know they were here long before the fabulous epoch of Cthulhu was over, and remember all about sunken R'lyeh when it was above the waters. They've been inside the earth, too—there are openings which human beings know nothing of—some of them in these very Vermont hills—and great worlds of unknown life down there; blue-litten K'n-yan, red-litten Yoth, and black, lightless N'kai.[62] It's from N'kai that frightful Tsathoggua came—you know, the amorphous, toad-like god-creature mentioned in the Pnakotic Manuscripts[63] and the *Necronomicon* and the Commoriom[64] myth-cycle preserved by the Atlantean high-priest Klarkash-Ton.[65]

"But we will talk of all this later on. It must be four or five o'clock by this time. Better bring the stuff from your bag, take a bite, and then come back for a comfortable chat."

Very slowly I turned and began to obey my host; fetching my valise, extracting and depositing the desired articles, and finally ascending to the room designated as mine. With the memory of that roadside claw-print fresh in my mind, Akeley's whispered paragraphs had affected me queerly; and the hints of familiarity with this unknown world of fungous life—forbidden Yuggoth— made my flesh creep more than I cared to own. I was tremendously sorry about Akeley's illness, but had to confess that his hoarse whisper had a hateful as well as pitiful quality. If only he wouldn't *gloat* so about Yuggoth and its black secrets!

My room proved a very pleasant and well-furnished one, devoid alike of the musty odour and disturbing sense of vibration; and after leaving my valise there I descended again to greet Akeley and take the lunch he had set out for me. The dining-room was just beyond the study, and I saw that a kitchen ell extended still farther in the same direction. On the dining-table an ample array of sandwiches, cake, and cheese awaited me, and a Thermos-bottle beside a cup and saucer testified that hot coffee had not been forgotten. After a well-relished meal I poured myself a liberal cup of coffee, but found that the culinary standard had suffered a lapse in this one detail. My first spoonful revealed a faintly unpleasant acrid taste, so that I did not take more. Throughout the lunch I thought of Akeley sitting silently in the great chair in the darkened next room. Once I went in to beg him to share the repast, but he whispered that he could eat nothing as yet. Later on, just before he slept, he would take some malted milk—all he ought to have that day.

After lunch I insisted on clearing the dishes away and washing them in the kitchen sink—incidentally emptying the coffee which I had not been able to appreciate. Then returning to the darkened study I drew up a chair near my host's corner and prepared for such conversation as he might feel inclined to conduct. The letters, pictures, and record were still on the large centre-table, but for the nonce we did not have to draw upon them.

to Richard F. Searight, February 13, 1936, *Selected Letters*, V, 225).

64. The first capital of the Hyperborean continent, described in the stories of Clark Ashton Smith (see "The Call of Cthulhu," note 55, above).

65. Get it?

66. Dwarf galaxies visible in the Southern Hemisphere. Richard H. Allen, in his 1899 *Star Names: Their Lore and Meaning*, notes that the major Magellanic Cloud was known to the early Persian astronomer Al Sufi, who named it al-Bakr (the Sheep) and pointed out that it was only visible from the southernmost tip of Arabia.

67. The Tao, the "way," is the central allegory of Taoism and is by definition unknowable.

68. Called "Dholes" or "Bholes" elsewhere, they seem to be large, slimy, worm-like creatures from the description in *The Dream-Quest of Unknown Kadath*. Machen's "The White People" (see "The Dunwich Horror," note 44, above) mentions "Dôls" but without description. "Dholes" are also wild dogs that inhabit South and Southeast Asia.

69. They first appeared in Frank Belknap Long's 1931 story "The Hounds of Tindalos" and are said to live in the angles of time; that is, they cannot enter curved time, where humans are believed to live. In this formulation, time is tangible, like fabric, with billows and creases, as it were. See "The Dunwich Horror," note 25, above.

70. "The Curse of Yig," another story by Zealia Bishop almost completely rewritten by Lovecraft, introduces this figure. Lovecraft worked on the story in 1928, and it appeared in *Weird Tales* in November 1929. Yig is described there as a snake-god, half-man, half-snake, but little other information is provided.

71. In other words, points out Robert M. Price, in "Demythologizing Cthulhu," "the gibbering dæmon-sultan of the

Before long I forgot even the bizarre odour and curious suggestions of vibration.

I have said that there were things in some of Akeley's letters—especially the second and most voluminous one—which I would not dare to quote or even form into words on paper. This hesitancy applies with still greater force to the things I heard whispered that evening in the darkened room among the lonely haunted hills. Of the extent of the cosmic horrors unfolded by that raucous voice I cannot even hint. He had known hideous things before, but what he had learned since making his pact with the Outside Things was almost too much for sanity to bear. Even now I absolutely refuse to believe what he implied about the constitution of ultimate infinity, the juxtaposition of dimensions, and the frightful position of our known cosmos of space and time in the unending chain of linked cosmos-atoms which makes up the immediate super-cosmos of curves, angles, and material and semi-material electronic organisation.

Never was a sane man more dangerously close to the arcana of basic entity—never was an organic brain nearer to utter annihilation in the chaos that transcends form and force and symmetry. I learned whence Cthulhu *first* came, and why half the great temporary stars of history had flared forth. I guessed—from hints which made even my informant pause timidly—the secret behind the Magellanic Clouds[66] and globular nebulæ, and the black truth veiled by the immemorial allegory of Tao.[67] The nature of the Doels[68] was plainly revealed, and I was told the essence (though not the source) of the Hounds of Tindalos.[69] The legend of Yig, Father of Serpents,[70] remained figurative no longer, and I started with loathing when told of the monstrous nuclear chaos beyond angled space which the *Necronomicon* had mercifully cloaked under the name of Azathoth.[71] It was shocking to have the foulest nightmares of secret myth cleared up in concrete terms whose stark, morbid hatefulness exceeded the boldest hints of ancient and mediæval mystics. Ineluctably I was led to believe that the first whisperers of these accursed tales must have had discourse with Akeley's Outer Ones, and perhaps have visited outer cosmic realms as Akeley now proposed visiting them.

I was told of the Black Stone and what it implied, and was glad that it had not reached me. My guesses about those hieroglyphics had been all too correct! And yet Akeley now seemed reconciled to the whole fiendish system he had stumbled upon; reconciled and eager to probe farther into the monstrous abyss. I wondered what beings he had talked with since his last letter to me, and whether many of them had been as human as that first emissary he had mentioned. The tension in my head grew insufferable, and I built up all sorts of wild theories about the queer, persistent odour and those insidious hints of vibration in the darkened room.

Night was falling now, and as I recalled what Akeley had written me about those earlier nights I shuddered to think there would be no moon. Nor did I like the way the farmhouse nestled in the lee of that colossal forested slope leading up to Dark Mountain's unvisited crest. With Akeley's permission I lighted a small oil lamp, turned it low, and set it on a distant bookcase beside the ghostly bust of Milton; but afterward I was sorry I had done so, for it made my host's strained, immobile face and listless hands look damnably abnormal and corpse-like. He seemed half-incapable of motion, though I saw him nod stiffly once in a while.

After what he had told, I could scarcely imagine what profounder secrets he was saving for the morrow; but at last it developed that his trip to Yuggoth and beyond—*and my own possible participation in it*—was to be the next day's topic. He must have been amused by the start of horror I gave at hearing a cosmic voyage on my part proposed, for his head wabbled violently when I shewed my fear. Subsequently he spoke very gently of how human beings might accomplish—and several times had accomplished—the seemingly impossible flight across the interstellar void. *It seemed that complete human bodies did not indeed make the trip,* but that the prodigious surgical, biological, chemical, and mechanical skill of the Outer Ones had found a way to convey human brains without their concomitant physical structure.

There was a harmless way to extract a brain, and a way to keep the organic residue alive during its absence. The bare, compact cerebral matter was then immersed in an occasionally replenished fluid within an ether-tight cylinder of a metal mined in Yuggoth, certain electrodes reaching through and connecting at will with elaborate instruments capable of duplicating the three vital faculties of sight, hearing, and speech. For the winged

Necronomicon was merely a cipher for the much more frightening revelations of science" (8).

72. Fritz Leiber Jr., an early enthusiast of Lovecraft's work and a highly regarded critic of the genre as well as a renowned science-fiction author, in his highly appreciative essay entitled "Through Hyperspace with Brown Jenkin: Lovecraft's Contribution to Speculative Fiction" found the idea amusing, calling this "the charmingly friendly touch of the Mi-Go carrying about with them through space in small cannisters—tucked under their wings or clutched in their maternal pincers—the living brains of beings so unfortunate as not to be able to travel space embodied. In the story this is effectively presented as horror, but on second thought such immortality has great appeal" (169).

73. A Victorian term for a malarial or intermittent fever, in which successive fits of hot, cold, and shaking occur. Edgar Allan Poe's characters, such as the narrator of "The Pit and the Pendulum," frequently shook or shivered with fright "as with a fit of the ague."

fungus-beings to carry the brain-cylinders intact through space was an easy matter.[72] Then, on every planet covered by their civilisation, they would find plenty of adjustable faculty-instruments capable of being connected with the encased brains; so that after a little fitting these travelling intelligences could be given a full sensory and articulate life—albeit a bodiless and mechanical one—at each stage of their journeying through and beyond the space-time continuum. It was as simple as carrying a phonograph record about and playing it wherever a phonograph of the corresponding make exists. Of its success there could be no question. Akeley was not afraid. Had it not been brilliantly accomplished again and again?

For the first time one of the inert, wasted hands raised itself and pointed stiffly to a high shelf on the farther side of the room. There, in a neat row, stood more than a dozen cylinders of a metal I had never seen before—cylinders about a foot high and somewhat less in diameter, with three curious sockets set in an isosceles triangle over the front convex surface of each. One of them was linked at two of the sockets to a pair of singular-looking machines that stood in the background. Of their purport I did not need to be told, and I shivered as with ague.[73] Then I saw the hand point to a much nearer corner where some intricate instruments with attached cords and plugs, several of them much like the two devices on the shelf behind the cylinders, were huddled together.

"There are four kinds of instruments here, Wilmarth," whispered the voice. "Four kinds—three faculties each—makes twelve pieces in all. You see there are four different sorts of beings presented in those cylinders up there. Three humans, six fungoid beings who can't navigate space corporeally, two beings from Neptune (God! if you could see the body this type has on its own planet!), and the rest entities from the central caverns of an especially interesting dark star beyond the galaxy. In the principal outpost inside Round Hill you'll now and then find more cylinders and machines—cylinders of extra-cosmic brains with different senses from any we know—allies and explorers from the uttermost Outside—and special machines for giving them impressions and expression in the several ways suited at once to them and to the comprehensions of different types of listeners. Round Hill, like most of the beings' main outposts all through the various universes, is a very cosmopolitan place! Of course, only the more common types have been lent to me for experiment.

"Here—take the three machines I point to and set them on the table. That tall one with the two glass lenses in front—then the box with the vacuum tubes and sounding-board—and now the one with the metal disc on top. Now for the cylinder with the label 'B-67' pasted on it. Just stand in that Windsor chair to reach the shelf. Heavy? Never mind! Be sure of the number—B-67. Don't bother that fresh, shiny cylinder joined to the two testing instruments—the one with my name on it. Set B-67 on the table near where you've put the machines—and see that the dial switch on all three machines is jammed over to the extreme left.

"Now connect the cord of the lens machine with the upper socket on the cylinder—there! Join the tube machine to the lower left-hand socket, and the disc apparatus to the outer socket. Now move all the dial switches on the machines over to the extreme right—first the lens one, then the disc one, and then the tube one. That's right. I might as well tell you that this is a human being—just like any of us. I'll give you a taste of some of the others tomorrow."

To this day I do not know why I obeyed those whispers so slavishly, or whether I thought Akeley was mad or sane. After what had gone before, I ought to have been prepared for anything; but this mechanical mummery seemed so like the typical vagaries of crazed inventors and scientists that it struck a chord of doubt which even the preceding discourse had not excited. What the whisperer implied was beyond all human belief—yet were not the other things still farther beyond, and less preposterous only because of their remoteness from tangible concrete proof?

As my mind reeled amidst this chaos, I became conscious of a mixed grating and whirring from all three of the machines lately linked to the cylinder—a grating and whirring which soon subsided into a virtual noiselessness. What was about to happen? Was I to hear a voice? And if so, what proof would I have that it was not some cleverly concocted radio device talked into by a concealed but closely watching speaker? Even now I am unwilling to swear just what I heard, or just what phenomenon really took place before me. But something certainly seemed to take place.

To be brief and plain, the machine with the tubes and sound-box began to speak, and with a point and intelligence which left no doubt that the speaker was actually present and observing us. The voice was loud, metallic, lifeless, and plainly mechanical in every detail of its production. It was incapable of inflection or expressiveness, but scraped and rattled on with a deadly precision and deliberation.

"Mr. Wilmarth," it said, "I hope I do not startle you. I am a human being like yourself, though my body is now resting safely under proper vitalising treatment inside Round Hill, about a mile and a half east of here. I myself am here with you—my brain is in that cylinder and I see, hear, and speak through these electronic vibrators. In a week I am going across the void as I have been many times before, and I expect to have the pleasure of Mr. Akeley's company. I wish I might have yours as well; for I know you by sight and reputation, and have kept close track of your correspondence with our friend. I am, of course, one of the men who have become allied with the outside beings visiting our planet. I met them first in the Himalayas, and have helped them in various ways. In return they have given me experiences such as few men have ever had.

"Do you realise what it means when I say I have been on thirty-seven different celestial bodies—planets, dark stars, and less definable objects—including eight outside our galaxy and two outside the curved cosmos of space and time? All this has not harmed me in the least. My brain has been removed from my body by fissions so adroit that it would be crude to call the operation surgery. The visiting beings have methods which make these extractions easy and almost normal—and one's body never ages when the brain is out of it. The brain, I may add, is virtually immortal with its mechanical faculties and a limited nourishment supplied by occasional changes of the preserving fluid.

"Altogether, I hope most heartily that you will decide to come with Mr. Akeley and me. The visitors are eager to know men of knowledge like yourself, and to shew them the great abysses that most of us have had to dream about in fanciful ignorance. It may seem strange at first to meet them, but I know you will be above minding that. I think Mr. Noyes will go along, too—the man who doubtless brought you up here in his car. He has been one of us for years—I suppose you recognised his voice as one of those on the record Mr. Akeley sent you."

At my violent start the speaker paused a moment before concluding. "So Mr. Wilmarth, I will leave the matter to you; merely adding that a man with your love of strangeness and folklore ought never to miss such a chance as this. There is nothing to fear. All transitions are painless, and there is much to enjoy in a wholly mechanised state of sensation. When the electrodes are disconnected, one merely drops off into a sleep of especially vivid and fantastic dreams.

"And now, if you don't mind, we might adjourn our session till tomorrow. Good night—just turn all the switches back to the left; never mind the exact order, though you might let the lens machine be last. Good night, Mr. Akeley—treat our guest well! Ready now with those switches?"

That was all. I obeyed mechanically and shut off all three switches, though dazed with doubt of everything that had occurred. My head was still reeling as I heard Akeley's whispering voice telling me that I might leave all the apparatus on the table just as it was. He did not essay any comment on what had happened, and indeed no comment could have conveyed much to my burdened faculties. I heard him telling me I could take the lamp to use in my room, and deduced that he wished to rest alone in the dark. It was surely time he rested, for his discourse of the afternoon and evening had been such as to exhaust even a vigorous man. Still dazed, I bade my host good night and went upstairs with the lamp, although I had an excellent pocket flashlight with me.

I was glad to be out of that downstairs study with the queer odour and vague suggestions of vibration, yet could not of course escape a hideous sense of dread and peril and cosmic abnormality as I thought of the place I was in and the forces I was meeting. The wild, lonely region, the black, mysteriously forested slope towering so close behind the house, the footprints in the road, the sick, motionless whisperer in the dark, the hellish cylinders and machines, and above all the invitations to strange surgery and stranger voyagings—these things, all so new and in such sudden succession, rushed in on me with a cumulative force which sapped my will and almost undermined my physical strength.

To discover that my guide Noyes was the human celebrant in that monstrous bygone Sabbat-ritual on the phonograph record was a particular shock, though I had previously sensed a dim, repellent familiarity in his voice. Another special shock came from my own attitude toward my host whenever I paused to analyse it; for much as I had instinctively liked Akeley as revealed in his correspondence, I now found that he filled me with a distinct repulsion. His illness ought to have excited my pity; but instead, it gave me a kind of shudder. He was so rigid and inert and corpse-like—and that incessant whispering was so hateful and unhuman!

It occurred to me that this whispering was different from anything else of the kind I had ever heard; that, despite the curious motionlessness of the speaker's moustache-screened lips, it had a latent strength and carrying-power remarkable for the wheezings of an asthmatic. I had been able to understand the speaker when wholly across the room, and once or twice it had seemed to me that the faint but penetrant sounds represented not so much weakness as deliberate repression—for what reason I could not guess. From the first I had felt a disturbing quality in their timbre. Now, when I tried to weigh the matter, I thought I could trace this impression to a kind of subconscious familiarity like that which had made Noyes's voice so hazily ominous. But when or where I had encountered the thing it hinted at, was more than I could tell.

One thing was certain—I would not spend another night here. My scientific zeal had vanished amidst fear and loathing, and I felt nothing now but a wish to escape from this net of morbidity and unnatural revelation. I knew enough now. It must indeed be true that cosmic linkages do exist—but such things are surely not meant for normal human beings to meddle with.

Blasphemous influences seemed to surround me and press chokingly upon my senses. Sleep, I decided, would be out of the question; so I merely extinguished the lamp and threw myself on the bed fully dressed. No doubt it was absurd, but I kept ready for some unknown emergency; gripping in my right hand the revolver I had brought along, and holding the pocket flashlight in my left. Not a sound came from below, and I could imagine how my host was sitting there with cadaverous stiffness in the dark.

Somewhere I heard a clock ticking, and was vaguely grateful for the normality of the sound. It reminded me, though, of another thing about the region which disturbed me—the total absence of animal life. There were certainly no farm beasts about, and now I realised that even the accustomed night-noises of wild living things were absent. Except for the sinister trickle of distant unseen waters, that stillness was anomalous—interplanetary— and I wondered what star-spawned, intangible blight could be hanging over the region. I recalled from old legends that dogs and other beasts had always hated the Outer Ones, and thought of what those tracks in the road might mean.

VIII.

DO NOT ASK me how long my unexpected lapse into slumber lasted, or how much of what ensued was sheer dream. If I tell you that I awaked at a certain time, and heard and saw certain things, you will merely answer that I did not wake then; and that everything was a dream until the moment when I rushed out of the house, stumbled to the shed where I had seen the old Ford, and seized that ancient vehicle for a mad, aimless race over the haunted hills which at last landed me—after hours of jolting and winding through forest-threatened labyrinths—in a village which turned out to be Townshend.

You will also, of course, discount everything else in my report; and declare that all the pictures, record-sounds, cylinder-and-machine sounds, and kindred evidences were bits of pure deception practiced on me by the missing Henry Akeley. You will even hint that he conspired with other eccentrics to carry out a silly and elaborate hoax—that he had the express shipment removed at Keene, and that he had Noyes make that terrifying wax record. It is odd, though, that Noyes has not even yet been identified; that he was unknown at any of the villages near Akeley's place, though he must have been frequently in the region. I wish I had stopped to memorise the licence-number of his car—or perhaps it is better after all that I did not. For I, despite all you can say, and despite all I sometimes try to say to myself, know that loathsome outside influences must be lurking there in the half-unknown hills—and that those influences have spies and emissaries in the world of men. To keep as far as possible from such influences and such emissaries is all that I ask of life in future.

When my frantic story sent a sheriff's posse out to the farmhouse, Akeley was gone without leaving a trace. His loose dressing gown, yellow scarf, and foot-bandages lay on the study floor near his corner easy-chair, and it could not be decided whether any of his other apparel had vanished with him. The dogs and livestock were indeed missing, and there were some curious bullet-holes both on the house's exterior and on some of the walls within; but beyond this nothing unusual could be detected. No cylinders or machines, none of the evidences I had brought in my valise, no queer odour or vibration-sense, no footprints in the road, and none of the problematical things I glimpsed at the very last.

I stayed a week in Brattleboro after my escape, making inquiries among people of every kind who had known Akeley; and the results convince me that the matter is no figment of dream or delusion. Akeley's queer purchases of dogs and ammunition and chemicals, and the cutting of his telephone wires, are matters of record; while all who knew him—including his son in California—concede that his occasional remarks on strange studies had a certain consistency. Solid citizens believe he was mad, and unhesitatingly pronounce all reported evidences mere hoaxes devised with insane cunning and perhaps abetted by eccentric associates; but the lowlier country folk sustain his statements in every detail. He had shewed some of these rustics his photographs and black stone, and had played the hideous record for them; and they all said the footprints and buzzing voice were like those described in ancestral legends.

They said, too, that suspicious sights and sounds had been noticed increasingly around Akeley's house after he found the black stone, and that the place was now avoided by everybody except the mail man and other casual, tough-minded people. Dark Mountain and Round Hill were both notoriously haunted spots, and I could find no one who had ever closely explored either. Occasional disappearances of natives throughout the district's history were well attested, and these now included the semi-vagabond Walter Brown, whom Akeley's letters had mentioned. I even came upon one farmer who thought he had personally glimpsed one of the queer bodies at flood-time in the swollen West River, but his tale was too confused to be really valuable.

When I left Brattleboro I resolved never to go back to Vermont, and I feel quite certain I shall keep my resolution. Those wild hills are surely the outpost of a frightful cosmic race—as I doubt all the less since reading that a new ninth planet has been glimpsed beyond Neptune, just as those influences had said it would be glimpsed. Astronomers, with a hideous appropriateness they little suspect, have named this thing "Pluto." I feel, beyond question, that it is nothing less than nighted Yuggoth—and I shiver when I try to figure out the real reason *why* its monstrous denizens wish it to be known in this way at this especial time. I vainly try to assure myself that these dæmoniac creatures are not gradually leading up to some new policy hurtful to the earth and its normal inhabitants.

But I have still to tell of the ending of that terrible night in the farmhouse. As I have said, I did finally drop into a troubled doze; a doze filled with bits of dream which involved monstrous landscape-glimpses. Just what awaked me I cannot yet say, but that I did indeed awake at this given point I feel very certain. My first confused impression was of stealthily creaking floor-boards in the hall outside my door, and of a clumsy, muffled fumbling at the latch. This, however, ceased almost at once; so that my really clear impressions began with the voices heard from the study below. There seemed to be several speakers, and I judged that they were controversially engaged.

By the time I had listened a few seconds I was broad awake, for the nature of the voices was such as to make all thought of sleep ridiculous. The tones were curiously varied, and no one who had listened to that accursed phonograph record could harbour any doubts about the nature of at least two of them. Hideous though the idea was, I knew that I was under the same roof with nameless things from abysmal space; for those two voices were unmistakably the blasphemous buzzings which the Outside Beings used in their communication with men. The two were individually different—different in pitch, accent, and tempo— but they were both of the same damnable general kind.

A third voice was indubitably that of a mechanical utterance-machine connected with one of the detached brains in the cylinders. There was as little doubt about that as about the buzzings; for the loud, metallic, lifeless voice of the previous evening, with its inflectionless, expressionless scraping and rattling, and its impersonal precision and deliberation, had been utterly unforgettable. For a time I did not pause to question whether the intelligence behind the scraping was the identical one which had formerly talked to me; but shortly afterward I reflected that any brain would emit vocal sounds of the same quality if linked to the same mechanical speech-producer; the only possible differences being in language, rhythm, speed, and pronunciation. To complete the eldritch colloquy there were two actually human voices—one the crude speech of an unknown and evidently rustic man, and the other the suave Bostonian tones of my erstwhile guide Noyes.

As I tried to catch the words which the stoutly-fashioned floor so bafflingly intercepted, I was also conscious of a great deal of stirring and scratching and shuffling in the room below; so that I could not escape the impression that it was full of living beings—many more than the few whose speech I could single out. The exact nature of this stirring is extremely hard to describe, for very few good bases of comparison exist. Objects seemed now and then to move across the room like conscious entities; the sound of their footfalls having something about it like a loose, hard-surfaced clattering—as of the contact of ill-coördinated surfaces of horn or hard rubber. It was, to use a more concrete but less accurate comparison, as if people with loose, splintery wooden shoes were shambling and rattling about on the polished board floor. Of the nature and appearance of those responsible for the sounds, I did not care to speculate.

Before long I saw that it would be impossible to distinguish any connected discourse. Isolated words—including the names of Akeley and myself—now and then floated up, especially when uttered by the mechanical speech-producer; but their true significance was lost for want of continuous context. Today I refuse to form any definite deductions from them, and even their frightful effect on me was one of *suggestion* rather than of *revelation*. A terrible and abnormal conclave, I felt certain, was assembled below me; but for what shocking deliberations I could not tell. It was curious how this unquestioned sense of the malign and the blasphemous pervaded me despite Akeley's assurances of the Outsiders' friendliness.

With patient listening I began to distinguish clearly between voices, even though I could not grasp much of what any of the voices said. I seemed to catch certain typical emotions behind some of the speakers. One of the buzzing voices, for example, held an unmistakable note of authority; whilst the mechanical voice, notwithstanding its artificial loudness and regularity, seemed to be in a position of subordination and pleading. Noyes's tones exuded a kind of conciliatory atmosphere. The others I could make no attempt to interpret. I did not hear the familiar whisper of Akeley, but well knew that such a sound could never penetrate the solid flooring of my room.

I will try to set down some of the few disjointed words and other sounds I caught, labelling the speakers of the words as best I know how. It was from the speech-machine that I first picked up a few recognisable phrases.

(THE SPEECH-MACHINE)

". . . brought it on myself . . . sent back the letters and the record . . . end on it . . . taken in . . . seeing and hearing . . . damn you . . . impersonal force, after all . . . fresh, shiny cylinder . . . great God . . ."[74]

(FIRST BUZZING VOICE)

". . . time we stopped . . . small and human . . . Akeley . . . brain . . . saying . . ."

(SECOND BUZZING VOICE)

"Nyarlathotep . . . Wilmarth . . . records and letters . . . cheap imposture. . . ."[75]

(NOYES)

". . . (an unpronounceable word or name, possibly *N'gah-Kthun*) . . . harmless . . . peace . . . couple of weeks . . . theatrical . . . told you that before. . . ."

(FIRST BUZZING VOICE)

". . . no reason . . . original plan . . . effects . . . Noyes can watch . . . Round Hill . . . fresh cylinder . . . Noyes's car. . . ."

74. Of course, this is the voice of the disembodied Akeley.

75. Some have suggested that the first buzzing voice is that of Nyarlathotep, the dominant leader of the creatures and an object of worship, here spoken to by another of the alien visitors. See "Nyarlathotep" (pp. 30–34, above).

(NOYES)

". . . well . . . all yours . . . down here . . . rest . . . place. . . ."

(SEVERAL VOICES AT ONCE IN INDISTINGUISH-
ABLE SPEECH)

(MANY FOOTSTEPS, INCLUDING THE PECULIAR
LOOSE STIRRING OR CLATTERING)

(A CURIOUS SORT OF FLAPPING SOUND)

(THE SOUND OF AN AUTOMOBILE STARTING
AND RECEDING)

(SILENCE)

That is the substance of what my ears brought me as I lay rigid upon that strange upstairs bed in the haunted farmhouse among the dæmoniac hills—lay there fully dressed, with a revolver clenched in my right hand and a pocket flashlight gripped in my left. I became, as I have said, broad awake; but a kind of obscure paralysis nevertheless kept me inert till long after the last echoes of the sounds had died away. I heard the wooden, deliberate ticking of the ancient Connecticut clock somewhere far below, and at last made out the irregular snoring of a sleeper. Akeley must have dozed off after the strange session, and I could well believe that he needed to do so.

Just what to think or what to do was more than I could decide. After all, what *had* I heard beyond things which previous information might have led me to expect? Had I not known that the nameless Outsiders were now freely admitted to the farm-house? No doubt Akeley had been surprised by an unexpected visit from them. Yet something in that fragmentary discourse had chilled me immeasurably, raised the most grotesque and horrible doubts, and made me wish fervently that I might wake up and prove everything a dream. I think my subconscious mind must have caught something which my consciousness has not yet recognised. But what of Akeley? Was he not my friend, and would he not have protested if any harm were meant me? The peaceful snoring below seemed to cast ridicule on all my suddenly intensified fears.

Was it possible that Akeley had been imposed upon and used as a lure to draw me into the hills with the letters and pictures and phonograph record? Did those beings mean to engulf us both in a common destruction because we had come to know too much? Again I thought of the abruptness and unnaturalness of that change in the situation which must have occurred between Akeley's penultimate and final letters. Something, my instinct told me, was terribly wrong. All was not as it seemed. That acrid coffee which I refused—had there not been an attempt by some hidden, unknown entity to drug it? I must talk to Akeley at once, and restore his sense of proportion. They had hypnotised him with their promises of cosmic revelations, but now he must listen to reason. We must get out of this before it would be too late. If he lacked the will power to make the break for liberty, I would supply it. Or if I could not persuade him to go, I could at least go myself. Surely he would let me take his Ford and leave it in a garage at Brattleboro. I had noticed it in the shed—the door being left unlocked and open now that peril was deemed past— and I believed there was a good chance of its being ready for instant use. That momentary dislike of Akeley which I had felt during and after the evening's conversation was all gone now. He was in a position much like my own, and we must stick together. Knowing his indisposed condition, I hated to wake him at this juncture, but I knew that I must. I could not stay in this place till morning as matters stood.

At last I felt able to act, and stretched myself vigorously to regain command of my muscles. Arising with a caution more impulsive than deliberate, I found and donned my hat, took my valise, and started downstairs with the flashlight's aid. In my nervousness I kept the revolver clutched in my right hand, being able to take care of both valise and flashlight with my left. Why I exerted these precautions I do not really know, since I was even then on my way to awaken the only other occupant of the house.

As I half tiptoed down the creaking stairs to the lower hall I could hear the sleeper more plainly, and noticed that he must be in the room on my left—the living-room I had not entered. On my right was the gaping blackness of the study in which I had heard the voices. Pushing open the unlatched door of the living-room I traced a path with the flashlight toward the source of the snoring, and finally turned the beams on the sleeper's face. But in the next second I hastily turned them away and commenced a cat-like retreat to the hall, my caution this time springing from reason as well as from instinct. For the sleeper on the couch was not Akeley at all, but my quondam guide Noyes.

Just what the real situation was, I could not guess; but common sense told me that the safest thing was to find out as much as possible before arousing anybody. Regaining the hall, I silently closed and latched the living-room door after me; thereby lessening the chances of awaking Noyes. I now cautiously entered the dark study, where I expected to find Akeley, whether asleep or awake, in the great corner chair which was evidently his favourite resting-place. As I advanced, the beams of my flashlight caught the great centre-table, revealing one of the hellish cylinders with sight and hearing machines attached, and with a speech-machine standing close by, ready to be connected at any moment. This, I reflected, must be the encased brain I had heard talking during the frightful conference; and for a second I had a perverse impulse to attach the speech machine and see what it would say.

It must, I thought, be conscious of my presence even now; since the sight and hearing attachments could not fail to disclose the rays of my flashlight and the faint creaking of the floor beneath my feet. But in the end I did not dare meddle with the thing. I idly saw that it was the fresh, shiny cylinder with Akeley's name on it, which I had noticed on the shelf earlier in the evening and which my host had told me not to bother. Looking back at that moment, I can only regret my timidity and wish that I had boldly caused the apparatus to speak. God knows what mysteries and horrible doubts and questions of identity it might have cleared up! But then, it may be merciful that I let it alone.

From the table I turned my flashlight to the corner where I thought Akeley was, but found to my perplexity that the great easy-chair was empty of any human occupant asleep or awake. From the seat to the floor there trailed voluminously the familiar old dressing-gown, and near it on the floor lay the yellow scarf and the huge foot-bandages I had thought so odd. As I hesitated, striving to conjecture where Akeley might be, and why he had so suddenly discarded his necessary sick-room garments, I observed that the queer odour and sense of vibration were no longer in the room. What had been their cause? Curiously it

"I let my flashlight return to the vacant easy-chair, then noticed for the first time the presence of certain objects in the seat." *Weird Tales* 18, no. 1 (August 1931) (artist: Curtis C. Senf)

occurred to me that I had noticed them only in Akeley's vicinity. They had been strongest where he sat, and wholly absent except in the room with him or just outside the doors of that room. I paused, letting the flashlight wander about the dark study and racking my brain for explanations of the turn affairs had taken.

Would to heaven I had quietly left the place before allowing that light to rest again on the vacant chair. As it turned out, I did not leave quietly; but with a muffled shriek which must have disturbed, though it did not quite awake, the sleeping sentinel across the hall. That shriek, and Noyes's still-unbroken snore, are the last sounds I ever heard in that morbidity-choked farmhouse beneath the black-wooded crest of a haunted mountain—that focus of trans-cosmic horror amidst the lonely green hills and curse-muttering brooks of a spectral rustic land.

It is a wonder that I did not drop flashlight, valise, and revolver in my wild scramble, but somehow I failed to lose any of

76. Why was Wilmarth allowed to escape? Perhaps to spread the word of the coming of the Mi-Go, which seems on the verge of disclosure? If so, something must have subsequently occurred that delayed the public revelation.

77. See note 46, above, for the suggestion that this is the "mask" of Nyarlathotep. However, as Steven J. Mariconda points out in "Tightening the Coil: The Revision of 'The Whisperer in Darkness,'" the allusions to "prodigious surgical . . . skill" and the use of the word "identity" here suggest that the mask is a representation of Akeley's actual face.

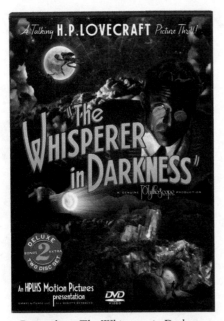

Poster from *The Whisperer in Darkness* (GraveHill Productions, 2007).

these. I actually managed to get out of that room and that house without making any further noise, to drag myself and my belongings safely into the old Ford in the shed, and to set that archaic vehicle in motion toward some unknown point of safety in the black, moonless night. The ride that followed was a piece of delirium out of Poe or Rimbaud or the drawings of Doré, but finally I reached Townshend. That is all. If my sanity is still unshaken, I am lucky. Sometimes I fear what the years will bring, especially since that new planet Pluto has been so curiously discovered.[76]

As I have implied, I let my flashlight return to the vacant easy-chair after its circuit of the room; then noticing for the first time the presence of certain objects in the seat, made inconspicuous by the adjacent loose folds of the empty dressing-gown. These are the objects, three in number, which the investigators did not find when they came later on. As I said at the outset, there was nothing of actual visual horror about them. The trouble was in what they led one to infer. Even now I have my moments of half-doubt—moments in which I half-accept the scepticism of those who attribute my whole experience to dream and nerves and delusion.

The three things were damnably clever constructions of their kind, and were furnished with ingenious metallic clamps to attach them to organic developments of which I dare not form any conjecture. I hope—devoutly hope—that they were the waxen products of a master artist, despite what my inmost fears tell me. Great God! That whisperer in darkness with its morbid odour and vibrations! Sorcerer, emissary, changeling, outsider . . . that hideous repressed buzzing . . . and all the time in that fresh, shiny cylinder on the shelf . . . poor devil . . . "Prodigious surgical, biological, chemical, and mechanical skill . . ."

For the things in the chair, perfect to the last, subtle detail of microscopic resemblance—or identity—were the face and hands of Henry Wentworth Akeley.[77]

At the Mountains of Madness[1]

There can be little doubt that in this short novel, Lovecraft's work reached its zenith. Cinematic in its sweep, epic in the scope of the story and the weight of its revelations about the place of humankind in the universe, it is no wonder that S. T. Joshi, in his masterful biography of Lovecraft, calls it "a triumph in every way." Lovecraft termed it an attempt at "non-supernatural cosmic art," and the meticulous scientific records kept by Professor Dyer and Dyer's cautious, measured tone lend utter credibility to the tale. Lovecraft was a student of many sciences and had a special fondness for polar expeditions; such knowledge is used to great effect here. Sadly, the story was rejected several times before finally being published near the end of Lovecraft's life and then by Astounding Stories, *which paid him a pittance.*

I.

I am forced into speech because men of science have refused to follow my advice without knowing why.[2] It is altogether against my will that I tell my reasons for opposing this contemplated invasion of the antarctic[3]—with its vast fossil-hunt and its wholesale boring and melting of the ancient ice-cap—and I am the more reluctant because my warning may be in vain.

Doubt of the real facts, as I must reveal them, is inevitable; yet if I suppressed what will seem extravagant and incredible there would be nothing left. The hitherto withheld photographs, both ordinary and ærial, will count in my favor, for they are damnably vivid and graphic. Still, they will be doubted because of the great lengths to which clever fakery can be carried.[4] The ink drawings, of course, will be jeered at as obvious impostures, notwithstanding a strangeness of technique which art experts ought to remark and puzzle over.

1. Written during February and March 1931, the story first appeared in three installments, in *Astounding Stories* 16, no. 6 (February 1936), 8–32; 17, no. 1 (March 1936), 125–55; and 17, no. 2 (April 1936), 132–50. The following is the restored, corrected text prepared by S. T. Joshi. The original published text had many different paragraph breaks and cut a considerable amount of Lovecraft's manuscript; the changes are indicated below.

2. The narrator, referred to only as "Dyer" here, is fully identified in "The Shadow Out of Time" as Professor William Dyer of the geology department of Miskatonic University. See text accompanying note 51 in "The Shadow Out of Time," below.

3. Lovecraft, ever the antiquarian, never refers in this story to Antarctica or the Antarctic, with a capital A (except as

First page of the manuscript of *At the Mountains of Madness*.

In the end I must rely on the judgment and standing of the few scientific leaders who have, on the one hand, sufficient independence of thought to weigh my data on its own hideously convincing merits or in the light of certain primordial and highly baffling myth-cycles; and on the other hand, sufficient influence to deter the exploring world in general from any rash and overambitious programme in the region of those mountains of madness. It is an unfortunate fact that relatively obscure men like myself and my associates, connected only with a small university, have little chance of making an impression where matters of a wildly bizarre or highly controversial nature are concerned.

It is further against us that we are not, in the strictest sense, specialists in the fields which came primarily to be concerned. As a geologist my object in leading the Miskatonic University Expedition was wholly that of securing deep-level specimens of rock and soil from various parts of the antarctic continent, aided by the remarkable drill devised by Professor Frank H. Pabodie of our engineering department. I had no wish to be a pioneer in any other field than this, but I did hope that the use of this new mechanical appliance at different points along previously explored paths would bring to light materials of a sort hitherto unreached by the ordinary methods of collection. Pabodie's drilling apparatus, as the public already knows from our reports, was unique and radical in its lightness, portability, and capacity to combine the ordinary artesian drill principle with the principle of the small circular rock drill in such a way as to cope quickly with strata of varying hardness. Steel head, jointed rods, gasoline motor, collapsible wooden derrick, dynamiting paraphernalia, cording, rubbish-removal auger, and sectional piping for bores five inches wide and up to 1000 feet deep all formed, with needed accessories, no greater load than three seven-dog sledges could carry; this being made possible by the clever aluminum alloy of which most of the metal objects were fashioned.[5] Four large Dornier[6] aëroplanes, designed especially for the tremendous altitude flying necessary on the antarctic plateau and with added fuel-warming and quick-starting devices worked out by Pabodie, could transport our entire expedition from a base at the edge of the great ice barrier to various suitable inland points, and from these points a sufficient quota of dogs would serve us.

part of the formal names of the "Antarctic Ocean" or "Antarctic Circle"). The name Antarctica, based on the Greek word *antarktos* (meaning "the opposite of the Bear," a constellation in the Northern Hemisphere) and its English usage "antarctic," was adopted by Scottish cartographer John George Bartholomew, who in 1887 was the first to publish a chart with that name applied to the land mass. See "John George Bartholomew and the naming of Antarctica." Maps and atlases published in the 1850s had referred to the Antarctic Ocean or Antarctic Circle but usually termed the land the "South Polar" continent.

4. Dyer may well have had in mind the 1920–1921 controversy surrounding the photographs of the Cottingley fairies that so blemished the reputation of Sir Arthur Conan Doyle. Conan Doyle died in July 1930, about when Dyer was writing up his notes, and some of the obituaries rehashed the controversy over the photographs. Conan Doyle's version of the tale is told in his book *The Coming of the Fairies* (1921); a more balanced overview is found in magician James Randi's *Flim-Flam! The Truth About Unicorns, Parapsychology, and Other Delusions*.

5. Professor Pabodie's work has been developed further since the 1930s. In the first decade of the twenty-first century, the ANDRILL (Antarctic geological drilling) program introduced new instruments permitting the operator to go deeper and bring up material at a faster rate. This has been accomplished by introducing hot water into the drill hole so that the machinery essentially melts the ice and drills simultaneously.

6. A German aircraft manufacturer founded in 1914 by Claudius Dornier. Dornier became known in the 1920s

and 1930s as a quality manufacturer of large, all-metal flying boats—seaplanes that come equipped with a hull, enabling them to land on water—including the 1924 Wal (Whale) and the Do X, which had twelve engines. In 1924, when Roald Amundsen and Lincoln Ellsworth prepared to fly over the North Pole, they chose a pair of Dornier Do-J Wals, particularly for their ability to handle rough ice and snow.

7. There was a significant hiatus in South Polar exploration during the 1930s and 1940s, in large part because of World War II. Byrd flew over the Pole in 1929; no one was to return to it until 1956. For a detailed study of the many similarities between Byrd's 1930 expedition and the Miskatonic expedition, see "Behind the Mountains of Madness: Lovecraft and the Antarctic in 1930," by Jason C. Eckhardt.

8. The continent known now as Antarctica was once part of the supercontinent called Gondwana, which likely had a temperate or even tropical climate. The breakup of Gondwana and separation of Antarctica, after which Antarctica cooled and the first ice appeared, probably occurred about 40 million years ago. The concepts of a supercontinent and of continental drift were forcefully put forward by Alfred Wegener (1880–1930), a German meteorologist and polar explorer, in 1912. (Although he formed his theories independently, Wegener later credited earlier scientists as proposing parts of his overall theory.) He posited a single gigantic landmass, or *Urkontinent*. Others later named it Pangaea, for the Greek "All Lands" or "All Earth," and described it as being composed of Gondwana and a second supercontinent, Laurasia.

9. Now known to be almost three miles in depth near the Pole.

The Dornier aeroplane. Artist: Jason C. Eckhardt, copyright © Jason C. Eckhardt 1989, reprinted with permission

We planned to cover as great an area as one antarctic season—or longer, if absolutely necessary—would permit, operating mostly in the mountain ranges and on the plateau south of Ross Sea; regions explored in varying degree by Shackleton, Amundsen, Scott, and Byrd.[7] With frequent changes of camp, made by aëroplane and involving distances great enough to be of geological significance, we expected to unearth a quite unprecedented amount of material; especially in the pre-Cambrian strata of which so narrow a range of antarctic specimens had previously been secured. We wished also to obtain as great as possible a variety of the upper fossiliferous rocks, since the primal life-history of this bleak realm of ice and death is of the highest importance to our knowledge of the earth's past. That the antarctic continent was once temperate and even tropical, with a teeming vegetable and animal life of which the lichens, marine fauna, arachnida, and penguins of the northern edge are the only survivals, is a matter of common information;[8] and we hoped to expand that information in variety, accuracy, and detail. When a simple boring revealed fossiliferous signs, we should enlarge the aperture by blasting in order to get specimens of suitable size and condition.

Our borings, of varying depth according to the promise held out by the upper soil or rock, were to be confined to exposed or nearly exposed land surfaces—these inevitably being slopes and ridges because of the mile or two-mile thickness of solid ice overlying the lower levels.[9] We could not afford to waste drilling depth on any considerable amount of mere glaciation, though Pabodie had worked out a plan for sinking copper electrodes in thick clusters of borings and melting off limited areas of ice with current from a gasoline-driven dynamo. It is this plan—which we could not put into effect except experimentally on an expedition such as ours—that the coming Starkweather-Moore Expedition proposes to follow despite the warnings I have issued since our return from the antarctic.

The public knows of the Miskatonic Expedition through our frequent wireless reports to the *Arkham Advertiser* and Associated Press, and through the later articles of Pabodie and myself. We consisted of four men from the University—Pabodie, Lake of the biology department, Atwood of the physics department (also a meteorologist), and I, representing geology and having nominal command—besides sixteen assistants: seven graduate students from Miskatonic and nine skilled mechanics. Of these sixteen, twelve were qualified aëroplane pilots, all but two of whom were competent wireless operators. Eight of them understood navigation with compass and sextant, as did Pabodie, Atwood, and I. In addition, of course, our two ships—wooden ex-whalers, reinforced for ice conditions and having auxiliary steam—were fully manned.[10] The Nathaniel Derby Pickman Foundation,[11] aided by a few special contributions, financed the expedition; hence our preparations were extremely thorough despite the absence of great publicity. The dogs, sledges, machines, camp materials, and unassembled parts of our five planes were delivered in Boston, and there our ships were loaded. We were marvellously well-equipped for our specific purposes, and in all matters pertaining to supplies, regimen, transportation, and camp construction we profited by the excellent example of our many recent and exceptionally brilliant predecessors. It was the unusual number and

10. In Lovecraft's notes for the tale, reproduced in *Something About Cats and Other Pieces*, he provides the following personnel lists:

Party of 12

Lake +	Atwood *
# Gedney	Orrendorf
Carroll+	Watkins #
# Moulton +&	Brennar #&
# Fowler +	Aiello
# Mills +	Boudrean #

Party of Seven	* Professor
Prof. Byer *	+ Student
Pabodie *	# Pilot
Allen	& Wireless Op.
# & Williamson	The Students
McTighe	(Lake's Party)
& # Ropes +	Gedney
	Carroll
Relief Plane	Moulton
Sherman # &	Fowler
Gunnarson	Mills
Larsen	
	(Dyer's Party)
	Danforth
	Ropes

Qualified Pilots

Gedney	Sherman
Carroll	Danforth
Moulton	McTighe
Fowler	Ropes
Mills	
Brennan	
Watkins (non op)	
Boudrean (non op)	

11. Derby and Pickman are prominent Arkham names that reappear in other Lovecraft tales, notably "The Thing on the Doorstep" and "Pickman's Model."

12. Line-crossing ceremonies (principally of the Equator) are found in records of English voyages as early as 1823. Those records suggest that the ceremonies were based on earlier Spanish, Portuguese, and Italian rituals performed upon the passing of certain headlands. Members of the U.S. Navy who cross that line are initiated into the Order of the Red Nose.

Technically, the Antarctic Circle is the northern extreme of the Southern Hemisphere, the point at which the Sun remains above or below the horizon for twenty-four hours (on the respective winter or summer solstice). Because of the tilting of the Earth's axis over time, the exact latitude changes over the years. In 2012, the exact latitude was 66°33'44" South, and the line moves closer to the South Pole at about 1,100 meters per year.

fame of these predecessors which made our own expedition—ample though it was—so little noticed by the world at large.

As the newspapers told, we sailed from Boston Harbour on September 2nd, 1930; taking a leisurely course down the coast and through the Panama Canal, and stopping at Samoa and Hobart, Tasmania, at which latter place we took on final supplies. None of our exploring party had ever been in the polar regions before, hence we all relied greatly on our ship captains—J. B. Douglas, commanding the brig *Arkham*, and serving as commander of the sea party, and Georg Thorfinnssen, commanding the barque *Miskatonic*—both veteran whalers in antarctic waters. As we left the inhabited world behind, the sun sank lower and lower in the north, and stayed longer and longer above the horizon each day. At about 62° South Latitude we sighted our first icebergs—table-like objects with vertical sides—and just before reaching the Antarctic Circle, which we crossed on October 20 with appropriately quaint ceremonies,[12] we were considerably troubled with field ice. The falling temperature bothered me considerably after our long voyage through the tropics, but I tried to brace up for the worse rigours to come. On many occasions the curious atmospheric effects enchanted me vastly; these including a strikingly vivid mirage—the first I had ever seen—in which distant bergs became the battlements of unimaginable cosmic castles.

Pushing through the ice, which was fortunately neither extensive nor thickly packed, we regained open water at South Latitude 67°, East Longitude 175°. On the morning of October 26 a strong land "blink" appeared on the south, and before noon we all felt a thrill of excitement at beholding a vast, lofty, and snow-clad mountain chain which opened out and covered the whole vista ahead. At last we had encountered an outpost of the great unknown continent and its cryptic world of frozen death. These peaks were obviously the Admiralty Range discovered by Ross, and it would now be our task to round Cape Adare and sail down the east coast of Victoria Land to our contemplated base on the shore of McMurdo Sound, at the foot of the volcano Erebus in South Latitude 77°9'.

The last lap of the voyage was vivid and fancy-stirring, great barren peaks of mystery looming up constantly against the west as the low northern sun of noon or the still lower horizon-grazing southern sun of midnight poured its hazy reddish rays over the white snow, bluish ice and water lanes, and black bits of exposed granite slope. Through the desolate summits swept raging intermittent gusts of the terrible antarctic wind; whose cadences sometimes held vague suggestions of a wild and half-sentient musical piping, with notes extending over a wide range, and which for some subconscious mnemonic reason seemed to me disquieting and even dimly terrible. Something about the scene reminded me of the strange and disturbing Asian paintings of Nicholas Roerich,[13] and of the still stranger and more disturbing descriptions of the evilly fabled plateau of Leng which occur in the dreaded *Necronomicon* of the mad Arab Abdul Alhazred. I was rather sorry, later on, that I had ever looked into that monstrous book at the college library.

On the seventh of November, sight of the westward range having been temporarily lost, we passed Franklin Island; and the next day descried the cones of Mts. Erebus and Terror on Ross Island ahead, with the long line of the Parry Mountains beyond. There now stretched off to the east the low, white line of the great ice barrier; rising perpendicularly to a height of 200 feet like the rocky cliffs of Quebec, and marking the end of southward navigation. In the afternoon we entered McMurdo Sound and stood off the coast in the lee of smoking Mt. Erebus. The scoriac[14] peak towered up some 12,700 feet against the eastern sky, like a Japanese print of the sacred Fujiyama, while beyond it rose the white, ghost-like height of Mt. Terror, 10,900 feet in altitude, and now extinct as a volcano. Puffs of smoke from Erebus came intermittently,[15] and one of the graduate assistants—a brilliant young fellow named Danforth—pointed out what looked like lava on the snowy slope; remarking that this mountain, discovered in 1840, had undoubtedly been the source of Poe's image when he wrote seven years later:

> —the lavas that restlessly roll
> Their sulphurous currents down Yaanek
> In the ultimate climes of the pole—
> That groan as they roll down Mount Yaanek
> In the realms of the boreal pole.[16]

13. Nicholas Roerich (1874–1947) was a Russian mystic, philosopher, scientist, and writer who traveled extensively in the Himalayas. He also created thousands of paintings. Lovecraft was extremely impressed by Roerich's work when he saw it in New York in 1930. Commenting in his last, unfinished letter (addressed to James F. Morton and probably written on March 15, 1937 [*Selected Letters*, V, 422–436]) on an exhibition of surrealist work at the Museum of Modern Art that he hoped would travel to Providence, Lovecraft wrote, "Better than the surrealists, though, is good old Nick Roerich, whose joint at Riverside Drive and 103rd Street is one of my shrines in the pest zone. There is something in his handling of perspective and atmosphere which to me, suggests other dimensions and alien orders of being—or at least, the gateways leading to such. Those fantastic carven stones in lonely upland deserts—those ominous, almost sentient, lines of jagged pinnacles—and above all, those curious cubical edifices clinging to precipitous slopes and edging upward to forbidden needle-like peaks!"

A Himalayan range, painted by
Nicholas Roerich in 1924.

14. Scoriæ are dense chunks of lava resembling coral or sponges, pierced with holes caused by gases forming bubbles in the lava.

15. Erebrus has been continuously active since 1972. It remains the most active of all of the Antarctic's volcanoes. Terror, on the other hand, has been inactive for over eight hundred thousand years.

16. Although some associate the fictitious Mount Yaanek with Erebrus, discovered in 1841, it should be noted that Poe specifically refers to the *boreal* pole—that is, the North Pole.

17. *The Narrative of Arthur Gordon Pym of Nantucket* (1838), Poe's only novel, deals with the voyage of young Pym on a whaling ship. In the end, the protagonist encounters black natives, from whom he and a companion escape in a boat, but although they find "white" water (presumably based on the freezing water of the Antarctic region, although Poe describes it as becoming warmer and warmer), the story ends before they reach the Antarctic. Little was known of the polar region when Poe wrote this, and so he was free to imagine a subtropical climate. After its publication, in a letter, Poe dismissed it as a "very silly book" (Poe to William E. Burton, June 1, 1840, http://www.eapoe.org/works/letters/p4006010.htm).

Some scholars have termed *At the Mountains of Madness* a "loose sequel" to *Pym*. See, for example, Jules Zanger's "Poe's "Endless Voyage: *The Narrative of Arthur Gordon Pym*." Others have shown, however, that at most Lovecraft was *inspired* by *Pym* and drew very few specific elements from the tale. Marc A. Cerasini, in "Thematic Links in *Arthur Gordon Pym*, *At the Mountains of Madness*, and *Moby Dick*," writes that while *Madness* is not "a literal sequel to the events described in Poe's *Pym*, [it] is surely a thematic sequel—with more than merely incidental tributes to the source novel" (17). In particular, Cerasini comments on the shared themes of "whiteness," racial harmony, and the

Danforth was a great reader of bizarre material, and had talked a good deal of Poe. I was interested myself because of the antarctic scene of Poe's only long story—the disturbing and enigmatical Arthur Gordon Pym.[17] On the barren shore, and on the lofty ice barrier in the background, myriads of grotesque penguins squawked and flapped their fins, while many fat seals were visible on the water, swimming or sprawling across large cakes of slowly drifting ice.

Using small boats, we effected a difficult landing on Ross Island shortly after midnight on the morning of the 9th, carrying a line of cable from each of the ships and preparing to unload supplies by means of a breeches-buoy arrangement.[18] Our sensations on first treading antarctic soil were poignant and complex, even though at this particular point the Scott and Shackleton expeditions had preceded us.[19] Our camp on the frozen shore below the volcano's slope was only a provisional one; headquarters being kept aboard the *Arkham*. We landed all our drilling apparatus, dogs,[20] sledges, tents, provisions, gasoline tanks, experimental ice-melting outfit, cameras both ordinary and aërial, aëroplane parts, and other accessories, including three small portable wireless outfits (besides those in the planes) capable of communicating with the *Arkham*'s large outfit from any part of the antarctic continent that we would be likely to visit. The ship's outfit, communicating with the outside world, was to convey press reports to the *Arkham Advertiser*'s powerful wireless station on Kingsport Head, Mass. We hoped to complete our work during a single antarctic summer; but if this proved impossible we would winter on the *Arkham*, sending the *Miskatonic* north before the freezing of the ice[21] for another summer's supplies.

I need not repeat what the newspapers have already published about our early work: of our ascent of Mt. Erebus; our successful mineral borings at several points on Ross Island and the singular speed with which Pabodie's apparatus accomplished them, even through solid rock layers; our provisional test of the small ice-melting equipment; our perilous ascent of the great barrier with sledges and supplies; and our final assembling of five huge aëroplanes at the camp atop the barrier. The health of our land party—twenty men and 55 Alaskan sledge dogs—was remarkable, though of course we had so far encountered no really destructive temperatures or windstorms. For the most part, the thermometer varied between zero and 20° or 25° above, and our experience with New England winters had accustomed us to rigours of this sort.[22] The barrier camp was semi-permanent, and destined to be a storage cache for gasoline, provisions, dynamite, and other supplies.

Only four of our planes were needed to carry the actual exploring material, the fifth being left with a pilot and two men from the ships at the storage cache to form a means of reaching us from the *Arkham* in case all our exploring planes were lost. Later, when not using all the other planes for moving apparatus, we would employ one or two in a shuttle transportation service between this cache and another permanent base on the great plateau from 600 to 700 miles southward, beyond Beardmore Glacier. Despite the almost unanimous accounts of appalling winds and tempests that pour down from the plateau, we determined to dispense with intermediate bases, taking our chances in the interest of economy and probable efficiency.

Wireless reports have spoken of the breath-taking, four-hour non-stop flight of our squadron on November 21 over the lofty shelf ice, with vast peaks rising on the west, and the unfathomed silences echoing to the sound of our engines. Wind troubled us only moderately, and our radio compasses helped us through the one opaque fog we encountered. When the vast rise loomed ahead, between Latitudes 83° and 84°, we knew we had reached Beardmore Glacier, the largest valley glacier in the world, and that the frozen sea was now giving place to a frowning and mountainous coastline. At last we were truly entering the white, æon-dead world of the ultimate south, and even as we realised it we saw the peak of Mt. Nansen in the eastern distance, towering up to its height of almost 15,000 feet.[23]

The successful establishment of the southern base above the glacier in Latitude 86°7', East Longitude 174°23', and the phenomenally rapid and effective borings and blastings made at various points reached by our sledge trips and short aëroplane flights, are matters of history; as is the arduous and triumphant ascent of Mt. Nansen by Pabodie and two of the graduate students— Gedney and Carroll—on December 13–15. We were some 8500 feet above sea-level, and when experimental drillings revealed

spiritual journey. See also Peter Cannon's "*At the Mountains of Madness* as a Sequel to *Arthur Gordon Pym*," in which he terms Lovecraft's story an "incidental tribute to Poe," and his subsequent remarks on a panel on *At the Mountains of Madness*, reported in *Lovecraft Studies*; and Ben P. Indick's "Lovecraft's POEtical Adventure," in which Indick calls Lovecraft's tale a "sequel (but not a *continuation*) of Poe's novel" (25).

There were in fact sequels to Poe's book, notably Jules Verne's *Le Sphinx des Glaces* (The Ice Sphinx) (1897) and Charles Romyn Dake's *A Strange Discovery* (1899).

18. A breeches buoy is a lifesaving device rigged from one ship to another or from ship to shore. It consists of a line that is shot aboard a disabled vessel by a line-throwing gun. Effectively, the device functions as a huge vintage clothesline on a continuous reel, along which the rescued party is ferried on a canvas "seat" attached to a cork-filled life preserver, shaped like a pair of breeches or pants (hence the name).

A breeches buoy in use.

19. Scott in 1911 and Shackleton in 1909 and again in 1914.

20. Famously, the use of dogs in the Antarctic was pioneered by the Amundsen expedition and shunned by the doomed Scott expedition. The latter used ineffective tractors and man-hauled sledges.

21. Otherwise, the expedition risked the ship's becoming frozen in the ice. Shackleton's *Endeavour* suffered that fate. Anchored in the polar waters, it became trapped when the water froze, and the explorers could not return home. The ice did not thaw, and the ship could not get free, for more than eight months, during which time the ice floes surrounding the ship drifted almost fifteen hundred miles. When the weather warmed sufficiently for the ice to begin to break apart, the released blocks of ice crushed the ship, and it sank.

22. This is of course summer in the Southern Hemisphere, and temperatures on the western side of the continent, where the expedition was based at this point, have been recorded as being as high as 59° on the western coast. However, interior temperatures in the winter can drop to −100° or lower. The narrator seems to have no appreciation of what he could be in for.

23. This is technically Mount Fridtjof Nansen, in the Queen Maud Mountains; there is another Mount Nansen in Antarctica, elevation only 8,990 feet, in the Eisenhower Range.

24. Byrd's exploratory flights in 1934 demonstrated that Antarctica was a single continent—not two, as previously believed. However, not until the first coast-to-coast air crossing of Antarctica took place, in November 1935, when Lincoln Ellsworth and his pilot, Herbert Hollick-Kenyon, flew from the Weddell Sea to the Ross Sea, could this be stated

solid ground only twelve feet down through the snow and ice at certain points, we made considerable use of the small melting apparatus and sunk bores and performed dynamiting at many places where no previous explorer had ever thought of securing mineral specimens. The pre-Cambrian granites and beacon sandstones thus obtained confirmed our belief that this plateau was homogeneous, with the great bulk of the continent to the west, but somewhat different from the parts lying eastward below South America—which we then thought to form a separate and smaller continent divided from the larger one by a frozen junction of Ross and Weddell Seas, though Byrd has since disproved the hypothesis.[24]

In certain of the sandstones, dynamited and chiselled after boring revealed their nature, we found some highly interesting fossil markings and fragments; notably ferns, seaweeds, trilobites, crinoids, and such molluscs as linguellæ and gasteropods—all of which seemed of real significance in connexion with the region's primordial history. There was also a queer triangular, striated marking about a foot in greatest diameter which Lake pieced together from three fragments of slate brought up from a deep-blasted aperture. These fragments came from a point to the westward, near the Queen Alexandra Range; and Lake, as a biologist, seemed to find their curious marking unusually puzzling and provocative, though to my geological eye it looked not unlike some of the ripple effects reasonably common in the sedimentary rocks. Since slate is no more than a metamorphic formation into which a sedimentary stratum is pressed, and since the pressure itself produces odd distorting effects on any markings which may exist, I saw no reason for extreme wonder over the striated depression.

On January 6, 1931, Lake, Pabodie, Daniels,[25] all six of the students, four mechanics, and I flew directly over the south pole in two of the great planes, being forced down once by a sudden high wind which fortunately did not develop into a typical storm. This was, as the papers have stated, one of several observation flights; during others of which we tried to discern new topographical features in areas unreached by previous explorers. Our early flights were disappointing in this latter respect; though they afforded us some magnificent examples of the richly fantastic and deceptive mirages of the polar regions, of which our sea voyage had given us some brief foretastes. Distant mountains floated in the sky as enchanted cities, and often the whole white world would dissolve into a gold, silver, and scarlet land of Dunsanian dreams and adventurous expectancy under the magic of the low midnight sun. On cloudy days we had considerable trouble in flying owing to the tendency of snowy earth and sky to merge into one mystical opalescent void with no visible horizon to mark the junction of the two.

At length we resolved to carry out our original plan of flying 500 miles eastward with all four exploring planes and establishing a fresh sub-base at a point which would probably be on the smaller continental division, as we mistakenly conceived it. Geological specimens obtained there would be desirable for purposes of comparison. Our health so far had remained excellent—limejuice well offsetting the steady diet of tinned and salted food, and temperatures generally above zero enabling us to do without our thickest furs. It was now midsummer, and with haste and care we might be able to conclude work by March and avoid a tedious wintering through the long antarctic night. Several savage windstorms had burst upon us from the west, but we had escaped damage through the skill of Atwood in devising rudimentary aëroplane shelters and windbreaks of heavy snow blocks, and reinforcing the principal camp buildings with snow. Our good luck and efficiency had indeed been almost uncanny.

The outside world knew, of course, of our programme, and was told also of Lake's strange and dogged insistence on a westward—or rather, northwestward—prospecting trip before our radical shift to the new base. It seems he had pondered a great deal, and with alarmingly radical daring, over that triangular striated marking in the slate; reading into it certain contradictions in Nature and geological period which whetted his curiosity to the utmost, and made him avid to sink more borings and blastings in the west-stretching formation to which the exhumed fragments evidently belonged. He was strangely convinced that the marking was the print of some bulky, unknown, and radically unclassifiable organism of considerably advanced evolution, notwithstanding that the rock which bore it was of so vastly ancient a date—Cambrian if not actually pre-Cambrian—as to preclude

definitively. The information must have been added in the editorial process prior to publication of the story in 1936.

25. No "Daniels" appears on the personnel list; this is evidently Dyer's slip of the pen for "Danforth."

26. In 2012, an American expedition, the Whillans Ice Stream Subglacial Access Research Drilling (WISSARD) project, found bacteria a half-mile below the ice. (The discovery was made in Lake Whillans, for which the expedition had been named.) Like Lake Vostok, Whillans is one of the hundreds of interconnected subglacial lakes between the continent of Antarctica itself and the ice surrounding it. A Russian expedition, plumbing two miles below the icy surface of Lake Vostok for microbial life, found bacteria in 2013.

27. Archæan, a term that is used a good deal in the following narrative, refers to the Archæozoic era, roughly 3.8 million to 2.5 million years before today—part of the Precambrian period. The oldest rocks discovered to date are said to have been formed or to have existed in this period.

the probable existence not only of all highly evolved life, but of any life at all above the unicellular or at most the trilobite stage.[26] These fragments, with their odd marking, must have been 500 million to a thousand million years old.

II.

POPULAR IMAGINATION, I judge, responded actively to our wireless bulletins of Lake's start northwestward into regions never trodden by human foot or penetrated by human imagination, though we did not mention his wild hopes of revolutionising the entire sciences of biology and geology. His preliminary sledging and boring journey of January 11–18 with Pabodie and five others—marred by the loss of two dogs in an upset when crossing one of the great pressure ridges in the ice—had brought up more and more of the Archæan[27] slate; and even I was interested by the singular profusion of evident fossil markings in that unbelievably ancient stratum. These markings, however, were of very primitive life-forms involving no great paradox except that any life-forms should occur in rock as definitely pre-Cambrian as this seemed to be; hence I still failed to see the good sense of Lake's demand for an interlude in our time-saving programme—an interlude requiring the use of all four planes, many men, and the whole of the expedition's mechanical apparatus. I did not, in the end, veto the plan; though I decided not to accompany the northwestward party despite Lake's plea for my geological advice. While they were gone, I would remain at the base with Pabodie and five men and work out final plans for the eastward shift. In preparation for this transfer, one of the planes had begun to move up a good gasoline supply from McMurdo Sound; but this could wait temporarily. I kept with me one sledge and nine dogs, since it is unwise to be at any time without possible transportation in an utterly tenantless world of æon-long death.

Lake's sub-expedition into the unknown, as everyone will recall, sent out its own reports from the short-wave transmitters on the planes; these being simultaneously picked up by our apparatus at the southern base and by the *Arkham* at McMurdo Sound, whence they were relayed to the outside world on wave lengths up to fifty metres.[28] The start was made January 22 at 4 a.m., and the first wireless message we received came only two hours later, when Lake spoke of descending and starting a small-scale ice-melting and bore at a point some 300 miles away from us. Six hours after that a second and very excited message told of the frantic, beaver-like work whereby a shallow shaft had been sunk and blasted; culminating in the discovery of slate fragments with several markings approximately like the one which had caused the original puzzlement.

Three hours later a brief bulletin announced the resumption of the flight in the teeth of a raw and piercing gale; and when I despatched a message of protest against further hazards, Lake replied curtly that his new specimens made any hazard worth taking. I saw that his excitement had reached the point of mutiny, and that I could do nothing to check this headlong risk of the whole expedition's success; but it was appalling to think of his plunging deeper and deeper into that treacherous and sinister white immensity of tempests and unfathomed mysteries which stretched off for some 1500 miles to the half-known, half-suspected coast line of Queen Mary and Knox Lands.

Then, in about an hour and a half more, came that doubly excited message from Lake's moving plane which almost reversed my sentiments and made me wish I had accompanied the party:

"10:05 P.M. On the wing. After snowstorm, have spied mountain range ahead higher than any hitherto seen. May equal Himalayas allowing for height of plateau. Probable Latitude 76°15', Longitude 11°10' E.[29] Reaches far as can see to right and left. Suspicion of two smoking cones. All peaks black and bare of snow. Gale blowing off them impedes navigation."

After that Pabodie, the men and I hung breathlessly over the receiver. Thought of this titanic mountain rampart 700 miles away inflamed our deepest sense of adventure; and we rejoiced that our expedition, if not ourselves personally, had been its discoverers. In half an hour Lake called us again.

"Moulton's plane forced down on plateau in foothills, but nobody hurt and perhaps can repair. Shall transfer essentials

28. While Sir Douglas Mawson had pioneered the use of shortwave radio on his Antarctic voyage of 1911–12 (see note 77, below), it wasn't until Byrd's expedition in 1928–29 that public radio broadcasts became part of the program. Byrd was accompanied by Russell Owen, a reporter for the *New York Times*, who sent daily dispatches, and Byrd himself made frequent radio broadcasts.

29. This is a distance of 864 miles from the base camp.

30. In 2010, scientists revealed radar data of the Gamburtsev Mountains, discovered in 1958, the so-called ghost mountains of Antarctica and the last remaining unexplored mountain range on the planet. The data reveal that the subglacial range, believed to have formed a billion years ago, includes rocky summits, deep river valleys, and liquid, not frozen, lakes, all hidden beneath three miles of ice. The range approximates the Alps in size and covers an area that is roughly the size of the state of New York. Further exploration has revealed, however, that the ghost mountains do not begin to approach Everest in height. The highest mountain on the continent of Antarctica, at 16,050 feet, is Mount Vinson, in the Ellsworth Range. Everest, by comparison, is over 29,000 feet.

to other three for return or further moves if necessary, but no more heavy plane travel needed just now. Mountains surpass anything in imagination. Am going up scouting in Carroll's plane, with all weight out.

"You can't imagine anything like this. Highest peaks must go over 35,000 feet. Everest out of the running.[30] Atwood to work out height with theodolite while Carroll and I go up. Probably wrong about cones, for formations look stratified. Possibly pre-Cambrian slate with other strata mixed in. Queer skyline effects—regular sections of cubes clinging to highest peaks. Whole thing marvellous in red-gold light of low sun. Like land of mystery in a dream or gateway to forbidden world of untrodden wonder. Wish you were here to study."

Though it was technically sleeping-time, not one of us listeners thought for a moment of retiring. It must have been a good deal the same at McMurdo Sound, where the supply cache and the *Arkham* were also getting the messages; for Capt. Douglas gave out a call congratulating everybody on the important find, and Sherman, the cache operator, seconded his sentiments. We were sorry, of course, about the damaged aëroplane; but hoped it could be easily mended. Then, at 11 P.M., came another call from Lake.

"Up with Carroll over highest foothills. Don't dare try really tall peaks in present weather, but shall later. Frightful work climbing, and hard going at this altitude, but worth it. Great range fairly solid, hence can't get any glimpses beyond. Main summits exceed Himalayas, and very queer. Range looks like pre-Cambrian slate, with plain signs of many other upheaved strata. Was wrong about volcanism. Goes farther in either direction than we can see. Swept clear of snow above about 21,000 feet.

"Odd formations on slopes of highest mountains. Great low square blocks with exactly vertical sides, and rectangular lines of low vertical ramparts, like the old Asian castles clinging to steep mountains in Roerich's paintings. Impressive from distance. Flew close to some, and Carroll thought they were formed of smaller separate pieces, but that is probably weathering. Most edges crumbled and rounded off as if exposed to storms and climate changes for millions of years.

"Parts, especially upper parts, seem to be of lighter-coloured rock than any visible strata on slopes proper, hence an evidently crystalline origin. Close flying shews many cave-mouths, some unusually regular in outline, square or semicircular. You must come and investigate. Think I saw rampart squarely on top of one peak. Height seems about 30,000 to 35,000 feet. Am up 21,500 myself, in devilish gnawing cold. Wind whistles and pipes through passes and in and out of caves, but no flying danger so far."

From then on for another half-hour Lake kept up a running fire of comment, and expressed his intention of climbing some of the peaks on foot. I replied that I would join him as soon as he could send a plane, and that Pabodie and I would work out the best gasoline plan—just where and how to concentrate our supply in view of the expedition's altered character. Obviously, Lake's boring operations, as well as his aëroplane activities, would need a great deal delivered for the new base which he was to establish at the foot of the mountains; and it was possible that the eastward flight might not be made after all this season. In connexion with this business I called Capt. Douglas and asked him to get as much as possible out of the ships and up the barrier with the single dog team we had left there. A direct route across the unknown region between Lake and McMurdo Sound was what we really ought to establish.

Lake called me later to say that he had decided to let the camp stay where Moulton's plane had been forced down, and where repairs had already progressed somewhat. The ice sheet was very thin, with dark ground here and there visible, and he would sink some borings and blasts at that very point before making any sledge trips or climbing expeditions. He spoke of the ineffable majesty of the whole scene, and the queer state of his sensations at being in the lee of vast, silent pinnacles whose ranks shot up like a wall reaching the sky at the world's rim. Atwood's theodolite observations had placed the height of the five tallest peaks at from 30,000 to 34,000 feet. The windswept nature of the terrain clearly disturbed Lake, for it argued the occasional existence of

31. Antarctica has indeed the worst winds on Earth, brought on by intense high pressure over the cold interior, which pushes the atmosphere outward toward the warmer surrounding seas. A strong slope toward the seas draws air downhill, and it picks up speed from gravity, creating katabatic winds. The windiest known location is in the Cape Denison/Commonwealth Bay area, on the coast south of Australia. Its annual average wind speed is 50 mph. A twenty-four-hour average of 108 mph was recorded on one occasion; peak gusts top 200 mph.

"It was a queer state of sensations—being in the lee of vast, silent pinnacles, where ranks shot up like a wall reaching the sky at the world's rim." *Astounding Stories* 16, no. 6 (February 1936) (artist: Howard V. Brown)

prodigious gales, violent beyond anything we had so far encountered.[31] His camp lay a little more than five miles from where the higher foothills abruptly rose. I could almost trace a note of subconscious alarm in his words—flashed across a glacial void of 700 miles—as he urged that we all hasten with the matter and get the strange, new region disposed of as soon as possible. He was about to rest now, after a continuous day's work of almost unparalleled speed, strenuousness, and results.

In the morning I had a three-cornered wireless talk with Lake and Capt. Douglas at their widely separated bases; and it was agreed that one of Lake's planes would come to my base for Pabodie, the five men, and myself, as well as for all the fuel it could carry. The rest of the fuel question, depending on our decision about an easterly trip, could wait for a few days; since Lake had enough for immediate camp heat and borings. Eventually the old southern base ought to be restocked; but if we postponed the easterly trip we would not use it till the next summer, and meanwhile Lake must send a plane to explore a direct route between his new mountains and McMurdo Sound.

Pabodie and I prepared to close our base for a short or long period, as the case might be. If we wintered in the antarctic we would probably fly straight from Lake's base to the *Arkham* without returning to this spot. Some of our conical tents had already been reinforced by blocks of hard snow, and now we decided to complete the job of making a permanent Esquimau village. Owing to a very liberal tent supply, Lake had with him all that his base would need even after our arrival. I wirelessed that Pabodie and I would be ready for the northwestward move after one day's work and one night's rest.

Our labours, however, were not very steady after 4 P.M., for about that time Lake began sending in the most extraordinary and excited messages. His working day had started unpropitiously; since an aëroplane survey of the nearly-exposed rock surfaces shewed an entire absence of those Archæan and primordial strata for which he was looking, and which formed so great a part of the colossal peaks that loomed up at a tantalising distance from the camp. Most of the rocks glimpsed were apparently Jurassic and Comanchian sandstones and Permian and Triassic schists, with now and then a glossy black outcropping suggesting a hard and slaty coal. This rather discouraged Lake, whose plans all hinged on unearthing specimens more than 500 million years older. It was clear to him that in order to recover the Archæan slate vein in which he had found the odd markings, he would have to make a long sledge trip from these foothills to the steep slopes of the gigantic mountains themselves.

He had resolved, nevertheless, to do some local boring as part of the expedition's general programme; hence set up the drill and

32. The Mesozoic era is the span of the Triassic, Jurassic, and Cretaceous periods, from 225 million to 65 million years ago.

put five men to work with it while the rest finished settling the camp and repairing the damaged aëroplane. The softest visible rock—a sandstone about a quarter of a mile from the camp—had been chosen for the first sampling; and the drill made excellent progress without much supplementary blasting. It was about three hours afterward, following the first really heavy blast of the operation, that the shouting of the drill crew was heard; and that young Gedney—the acting foreman—rushed into the camp with the startling news.

They had struck a cave. Early in the boring the sandstone had given place to a vein of Comanchian limestone, full of minute fossil cephalopods, corals, echini, and spirifera, and with occasional suggestions of siliceous sponges and marine vertebrate bones—the latter probably of teliosts, sharks, and ganoids. This in itself was important enough, as affording the first vertebrate fossils the expedition had yet secured; but when shortly afterward the drill-head dropped through the stratum into apparent vacancy, a wholly new and doubly intense wave of excitement spread among the excavators. A good-sized blast had laid open the subterrene secret; and now, through a jagged aperture perhaps five feet across and three feet thick, there yawned before the avid searchers a section of shallow limestone hollowing worn more than fifty million years ago by the trickling ground waters of a bygone tropic world.

The hollowed layer was not more than seven or eight feet deep, but extended off indefinitely in all directions and had a fresh, slightly moving air which suggested its membership in an extensive subterranean system. Its roof and floor were abundantly equipped with large stalactites and stalagmites, some of which met in columnar form; but important above all else was the vast deposit of shells and bones which in places nearly choked the passage. Washed down from unknown jungles of Mesozoic[32] tree-ferns and fungi, and forests of Tertiary cycads, fan-palms, and primitive angiosperms, this osseous medley contained representatives of more Cretaceous, Eocene, and other animal species than the greatest palæontologist could have counted or classified in a year. Molluscs, crustacean armour, fishes, amphibians, reptiles, birds, and early mammals—great and small, known and unknown. No wonder Gedney ran back to the camp shouting, and no wonder everyone else dropped work and rushed headlong through the biting cold to where the tall derrick marked a new-found gateway to secrets of inner earth and vanished æons.

When Lake had satisfied the first keen edge of his curiosity he scribbled a message in his notebook and had young Moulton run back to the camp to despatch it by wireless. This was my first word of the discovery, and it told of the identification of early shells, bones of ganoids and placoderms,[33] remnants of labyrintho-donts and thecodonts, great mososaur skull fragments, dinosaur vertebræ and armour-plates, pterodactyl teeth and wing-bones, Archæopteryx debris, Miocene sharks' teeth, primitive bird-skulls, and skulls, vertebræ, and other bones of archaic mammals such as palæotheres, xiphodons, dinocerases, eohippi, oreodons, and titanotheres. There was nothing as recent as a mastodon, elephant, true camel, deer, or bovine animal; hence Lake con-cluded that the last deposits had occurred during the Oligocene age, and that the hollowed stratum had lain in its present dried, dead, and inaccessible state for at least thirty million years.

On the other hand, the prevalence of very early life-forms was singular in the highest degree. Though the limestone formation was, on the evidence of such typical imbedded fossils as ventricu-lites, positively and unmistakably Comanchian and not a particle earlier; the free fragments in the hollow space included a surpris-ing proportion from organisms hitherto considered as peculiar to far older periods—even rudimentary fishes, molluscs, and corals as remote as the Silurian or Ordovician. The inevitable inference was that in this part of the world there had been a remarkable and unique degree of continuity between the life of over 300 mil-lion years ago and that of only thirty million years ago. How far this continuity had extended beyond the Oligocene age when the cavern was closed, was of course past all speculation. In any event, the coming of the frightful ice in the Pleistocene some 500,000 years ago—a mere yesterday as compared with the age of this cavity—must have put an end to any of the primal forms which had locally managed to outlive their common terms.

Lake was not content to let his first message stand, but had another bulletin written and despatched across the snow to the camp before Moulton could get back. After that Moulton stayed at the wireless in one of the planes; transmitting to me—and to

33. Placodermi flourished between 450 to 250 million years ago, and so finding their remains with organisms depos-ited between 150 million to 50 million years ago should have alerted Lake that something was "wrong," according to Bert Atama (in "An Autopsy on the Old Ones").

the *Arkham*, for relaying to the outside world—the frequent postscripts which Lake sent him by a succession of messengers. Those who followed the newspapers will remember the excitement created among men of science by that afternoon's reports—reports which have finally led, after all these years, to the organisation of that very Starkweather-Moore Expedition which I am so anxious to dissuade from its purposes. I had better give the messages literally as Lake sent them, and as our base operator McTighe translated them from his pencil shorthand.

"Fowler makes discovery of highest importance in sandstone and limestone fragments from blasts. Several distinct triangular striated prints like those in Archæan slate, proving that source survived from over 600 million years ago to Comanchian times without more than moderate morphological changes and decrease in average size. Comanchian prints apparently more primitive or decadent, if anything, than older ones. Emphasise importance of discovery in press. Will mean to biology what Einstein has meant to mathematics and physics. Joins up with my previous work and amplifies conclusions. Appears to indicate, as I suspected, that earth has seen whole cycle or cycles of organic life before known one that begins with Archæozoic cells. Was evolved and specialised not later than a thousand million years ago, when planet was young and recently uninhabitable for any life-forms or normal protoplasmic structure. Question arises when, where, and how development took place."

"Later. Examining certain skeletal fragments of large land and marine saurians and primitive mammals, find singular local wounds or injuries to bony structure not attributable to any known predatory or carnivorous animal of any period. Of two sorts—straight, penetrant bores, and apparently hacking incisions. One or two cases of cleanly severed bone. Not many specimens affected. Am sending to camp for electric torches. Will extend search area underground by hacking away stalactites."

"Still later. Have found peculiar soapstone fragment about six inches across and an inch and a half thick, wholly unlike any visible local formation. Greenish, but no evidences to place its period. Has curious smoothness and regularity. Shaped like five-pointed star with tips broken off, and signs of other cleavage at inward angles and in centre of surface. Small, smooth depression in centre of unbroken surface. Arouses much curiosity as to source and weathering. Probably some freak of water action. Carroll, with magnifier, thinks he can make out additional markings of geologic significance. Groups of tiny dots in regular patterns. Dogs growing uneasy as we work, and seem to hate this soapstone. Must see if it has any peculiar odour. Will report again when Mills gets back with light and we start on underground area."

"10:15 P.M. Important discovery. Orrendorf and Watkins, working underground at 9:45 with light, found monstrous barrel-shaped fossil of wholly unknown nature; probably vegetable unless overgrown specimen of unknown marine radiata. Tissue evidently preserved by mineral salts. Tough as leather, but astonishing flexibility retained in places. Marks of broken-off parts at ends and around sides. Six feet end to end, 3.5 feet central diameter, tapering to 1 foot at each end. Like a barrel with five bulging ridges in place of staves. Lateral breakages, as of thinnish stalks, are at equator in middle of these ridges. In furrows between ridges are curious growths. Combs or wings that fold up and spread out like fans. All greatly damaged but one, which gives almost seven-foot wing spread. Arrangement reminds one of certain monsters of primal myth, especially fabled Elder Things in *Necronomicon*. These wings seem to be membraneous, stretched on framework of glandular tubing. Apparent minute orifices in frame tubing at wing tips. Ends of body shrivelled, giving no clue to interior or to what has been broken off there. Must dissect when we get back to camp. Can't decide whether vegetable or animal. Many features obviously of almost incredible primitiveness. Have set all hands cutting stalactites and looking for further specimens. Additional scarred bones found, but these must wait. Having trouble with dogs. They can't endure the new specimen, and would probably tear it to pieces if we didn't keep it at a distance from them."

"11:30 P.M. Attention, Dyer, Pabodie, Douglas. Matter of highest—I might say transcendent—importance. *Arkham* must relay to Kingsport Head Station at once. Strange barrel growth is the Archæan thing that left prints in rocks. Mills, Boudreau, and Fowler discover cluster of thirteen more at underground point forty feet from aperture. Mixed with curiously rounded and configured soapstone fragments smaller than one previously found—star-shaped, but no marks of breakage except at some of the points.

"Of organic specimens, eight apparently perfect, with all appendages. Have brought all to surface, leading off dogs to distance. They cannot stand the things. Give close attention to description and repeat back for accuracy Papers must get this right.

"Objects are eight feet long all over. Six-foot, five-ridged barrel torso 3.5 feet central diameter, one foot end diameters. Dark grey, flexible, and infinitely tough. Seven-foot membraneous wings of same colour, found folded, spread out of furrows between ridges. Wing framework tubular or glandular, of lighter grey, with orifices at wing tips. Spread wings have serrated edge. Around equator, one at central apex of each of the five vertical, stave-like ridges, are five systems of light grey flexible arms or tentacles found tightly folded to torso but expansible to maximum length of over 3 feet. Like arms of primitive crinoid. Single stalks 3 inches diameter branch after 6 inches into five sub-stalks, each of which branches after 8 inches into five small, tapering tentacles or tendrils, giving each stalk a total of 25 tentacles.

"At top of torso blunt bulbous neck of lighter grey with gill-like suggestions holds yellowish five-pointed starfish-shaped apparent head covered with three-inch wiry cilia of various prismatic colours.

"Head thick and puffy, about 2 feet point to point, with three-inch flexible yellowish tubes projecting from each point. Slit in exact centre of top probably breathing aperture. At end of each tube is spherical expansion where yellowish membrane rolls back on handling to reveal glassy, red-irised globe, evidently an eye.

"Five slightly longer reddish tubes start from inner angles of starfish-shaped head and end in sac-like swellings of same colour which upon pressure open to bell-shaped orifices 2 inches maximum diameter and lined with sharp white tooth-like projections. Probable mouths. All these tubes, cilia, and points of starfish head, found folded tightly down; tubes and points clinging to bulbous neck and torso. Flexibility surprising despite vast toughness.

"At bottom of torso, rough but dissimilarly functioning counterparts of head arrangements exist. Bulbous light-grey pseudo-neck, without gill suggestions, holds greenish five-pointed starfish-arrangement. Tough, muscular arms 4 feet long and tapering from 7 inches diameter at base to about 2.5 at point. To each point is attached small end of a greenish five-veined membraneous triangle 8 inches long and 6 wide at farther end. This is the paddle, fin, or pseudo-foot which has made prints in rocks from a thousand million to fifty or sixty million years old. From inner angles of starfish-arrangement project two-foot reddish tubes tapering from 3 inches diameter at base to 1 at tip. Orifices at tips. All these parts infinitely tough and leathery, but extremely flexible. Four-foot arms with paddles undoubtedly used for locomotion of some sort, marine or otherwise. When moved, display suggestions of exaggerated muscularity. As found, all these projections tightly folded over pseudo-neck and end of torso, corresponding to projections at other end.

"Cannot yet assign positively to animal or vegetable kingdom, but odds now favour animal. Probably represents incredibly advanced evolution of radiata without loss of certain primitive features. Echinoderm resemblances unmistakable despite local contradictory evidences.

"Wing structure puzzles in view of probable marine habitat, but may have use in water navigation. Symmetry is curiously vegetable-like, suggesting vegetable's essentially up-and-down structure rather than animal's fore-and-aft structure. Fabulously early date of evolution, preceding even simplest Archæan protozoa hitherto known, baffles all conjecture as to origin.

"Complete specimens have such uncanny resemblance to certain creatures of primal myth that suggestion of ancient existence outside antarctic becomes inevitable. Dyer and Pabodie have read *Necronomicon* and seen Clark Ashton Smith's nightmare paintings based on text, and will under-

The narrator of "The Whisperer in Darkness" (pp. 388–456, above), who, it will be recalled, was also on the faculty of Miskatonic University.

stand when I speak of Elder Things supposed to have created all earth-life as jest or mistake. Students have always thought conception formed from morbid imaginative treatment of very ancient tropical radiata. Also like prehistoric folklore things Wilmarth[34] has spoken of—Cthulhu cult appendages, *etc.*

"Vast field of study opened. Deposits probably of late Cretaceous or early Eocene period, judging from associated specimens. Massive stalagmites deposited above them. Hard work hewing out, but toughness prevented damage. State of preservation miraculous, evidently owing to limestone action. No more found so far, but will resume search later. Job now to get fourteen huge specimens to camp without dogs, which bark furiously and can't be trusted near them.

"With nine men—three left to guard the dogs—we ought to manage the three sledges fairly well, though wind is bad. Must establish plane communication with McMurdo Sound and begin shipping material. But I've got to dissect one of these things before we take any rest. Wish I had a real laboratory here. Dyer better kick himself for having tried to stop my

"'I've got to dissect one of these things before—'" *Astounding Stories* 16, no. 6 (February 1936) (artist: Howard V. Brown)

[480]

westward trip. First the world's greatest mountains, and then this. If this last isn't the high spot of the expedition, I don't know what is. We're made scientifically. Congrats, Pabodie, on the drill that opened up the cave. Now will *Arkham*, please repeat description?"

The sensations of Pabodie and myself at receipt of this report were almost beyond description, nor were our companions much behind us in enthusiasm. McTighe, who had hastily translated a few high spots as they came from the droning receiving set, wrote out the entire message from his shorthand version as soon as Lake's operator signed off. All appreciated the epoch-making significance of the discovery, and I sent Lake congratulations as soon as the *Arkham*'s operator had repeated back the descriptive parts as requested; and my example was followed by Sherman from his station at the McMurdo Sound supply cache, as well as by Capt. Douglas of the *Arkham*. Later, as head of the expedition, I added some remarks to be relayed through the *Arkham* to the outside world. Of course, rest was an absurd thought amidst

"'First the world's greatest mountains—then this!'" *Astounding Stories* 16, no. 6 (February 1936) (artist: Howard V. Brown)

this excitement; and my only wish was to get to Lake's camp as quickly as I could. It disappointed me when he sent word that a rising mountain gale made early aërial travel impossible.

But within an hour and a half interest again rose to banish disappointment. Lake was sending more messages, and told of the completely successful transportation of the fourteen great specimens to the camp. It had been a hard pull, for the things were surprisingly heavy; but nine men had accomplished it very neatly. Now some of the party were hurriedly building a snow corral at a safe distance from the camp, to which the dogs could be brought for greater convenience in feeding. The specimens were laid out on the hard snow near the camp, save for one on which Lake was making crude attempts at dissection.

This dissection seemed to be a greater task than had been expected, for, despite the heat of a gasoline stove in the newly raised laboratory tent, the deceptively flexible tissues of the chosen specimen—a powerful and intact one—lost nothing of their more than leathery toughness. Lake was puzzled as to how he might make the requisite incisions without violence destructive enough to upset all the structural niceties he was looking for. He had, it is true, seven more perfect specimens; but these were too few to use up recklessly unless the cave might later yield an unlimited supply. Accordingly he removed the specimen and dragged in one which, though having remnants of the starfish-arrangements at both ends, was badly crushed and partly disrupted along one of the great torso furrows.

Results, quickly reported over the wireless, were baffling and provocative indeed. Nothing like delicacy or accuracy was possible with instruments hardly able to cut the anomalous tissue, but the little that was achieved left us all awed and bewildered. Existing biology would have to be wholly revised, for this thing was no product of any cell-growth science knows about. There had been scarcely any mineral replacement, and despite an age of perhaps forty million years the internal organs were wholly intact. The leathery, undeteriorative, and almost indestructible quality was an inherent attribute of the thing's form of organisation, and pertained to some paleogean cycle of invertebrate evolution utterly beyond our powers of speculation. At first all that Lake found was dry, but as the heated tent produced its thawing effect, organic moisture of pungent and offensive odour was encountered toward the thing's uninjured side. It was not blood, but a thick, dark-green fluid apparently answering the same purpose. By the time Lake reached this stage, all 37 dogs had been brought to the still uncompleted corral near the camp; and even at that distance set up a savage barking and show of restlessness at the acrid, diffusive smell.

Far from helping to place the strange entity, this provisional dissection merely deepened its mystery. All guesses about its external members had been correct, and on the evidence of these one could hardly hesitate to call the thing animal; but internal inspection brought up so many vegetable evidences that Lake was left hopelessly at sea. It had digestion and circulation, and eliminated waste matter through the reddish tubes of its starfish-shaped base. Cursorily, one would say that its respiratory apparatus handled oxygen rather than carbon dioxide, and there were odd evidences of air-storage chambers and methods of shifting respiration from the external orifice to at least two other fully developed breathing-systems—gills and pores. Clearly, it was amphibian and probably adapted to long airless hibernation-periods as well. Vocal organs seemed present in connexion with the main respiratory system, but they presented anomalies beyond immediate solution. Articulate speech, in the sense of syllable-utterance, seemed barely conceivable; but musical piping notes covering a wide range were highly probable. The muscular system was almost preternaturally developed.

The nervous system was so complex and highly developed as to leave Lake aghast. Though excessively primitive and archaic in some respects, the thing had a set of ganglial centres and connectives arguing the very extremes of specialised development. Its five-lobed brain was surprisingly advanced, and there were signs of a sensory equipment, served in part through the wiry cilia of the head, involving factors alien to any other terrestrial organism. Probably it had more than five senses, so that its habits could not be predicted from any existing analogy. It must, Lake thought, have been a creature of keen sensitiveness and delicately differentiated functions in its primal world; much like the ants and bees of today. It reproduced like the vegetable cryptogams, especially the pteridophytes;[35] having spore-cases at the tips of

35. The narrator here confuses the terminology; although "pterodactyls" have wings, "pteridophytes" are ferns with roots, stems, and leaves (but no flowers or seeds). The name has nothing to do with wings.

36. Another reference to Wilmarth of "The Whisperer in Darkness," above.

the wings and evidently developing from a thallus or prothallus.

But to give it a name at this stage was mere folly. It looked like a radiate, but was clearly something more. It was partly vegetable, but had three-fourths of the essentials of animal structure. That it was marine in origin, its symmetrical contour and certain other attributes clearly indicated; yet one could not be exact as to the limit of its later adaptations. The wings, after all, held a persistent suggestion of the aërial. How it could have undergone its tremendously complex evolution on a new-born earth in time to leave prints in Archæan rocks was so far beyond conception as to make Lake whimsically recall the primal myths about Great Old Ones who filtered down from the stars and concocted earth-life as a joke or mistake; and the wild tales of cosmic hill things from Outside told by a folklorist colleague in Miskatonic's English department.[36]

Naturally, he considered the possibility of the pre-Cambrian prints' having been made by a less evolved ancestor of the present specimens; but quickly rejected this too-facile theory upon considering the advanced structural qualities of the older fossils.

Lovecraft's drawing of an Old One, from the manuscript of *At the Mountains of Madness*.

If anything, the later contours shewed decadence rather than higher evolution. The size of the pseudo-feet had decreased, and the whole morphology seemed coarsened and simplified. Moreover, the nerves and organs just examined held singular suggestions of retrogression from forms still more complex. Atrophied and vestigial parts were surprisingly prevalent. Altogether, little could be said to have been solved; and Lake fell back on mythology for a provisional name—jocosely dubbing his finds "The Elder Ones."

At about 2:30 A.M., having decided to postpone further work and get a little rest, he covered the dissected organism with a tarpaulin, emerged from the laboratory tent, and studied the intact specimens with renewed interest. The ceaseless antarctic sun had begun to limber up their tissues a trifle, so that the head-points and tubes of two or three shewed signs of unfolding; but Lake did not believe there was any danger of immediate decomposition in the almost sub-zero air. He did, however, move all the undissected specimens closer together and throw a spare tent over them in order to keep off the direct solar rays. That would also help to keep their possible scent away from the dogs, whose hostile unrest was really becoming a problem even at their substantial distance and behind the higher and higher snow walls which an increased quota of the men were hastening to raise around their quarters. He had to weight down the corners of the tent cloth with heavy blocks of snow to hold it in place amidst the rising gale, for the titan mountains seemed about to deliver some gravely severe blasts. Early apprehensions about sudden antarctic winds were revived, and under Atwood's supervision precautions were taken to bank the tents, new dog corral, and crude aëroplane shelters with snow on the mountainward side. These latter shelters, begun with hard snow blocks during odd moments, were by no means as high as they should have been; and Lake finally detached all hands from other tasks to work on them.

It was after four when Lake at last prepared to sign off and advised us all to share the rest period his outfit would take when the shelter walls were a little higher. He held some friendly chat with Pabodie over the ether, and repeated his praise of the really marvellous drills that had helped him make his discovery. Atwood also sent greetings and praises. I gave Lake a warm word of congratulation, owning up that he was right about the western trip; and we all agreed to get in touch by wireless at ten in the morning. If the gale was then over, Lake would send a plane for the party at my base. Just before retiring I despatched a final message to the *Arkham* with instructions about toning down the day's news for the outside world, since the full details seemed radical enough to rouse a wave of incredulity until further substantiated.

III.

NONE OF US, I imagine, slept very heavily or continuously that morning; for both the excitement of Lake's discovery and the mounting fury of the wind were against such a thing. So savage was the blast, even where we were, that we could not help wondering how much worse it was at Lake's camp, directly under the vast unknown peaks that bred and delivered it. McTighe was awake at ten o'clock and tried to get Lake on the wireless, as agreed, but some electrical condition in the disturbed air to the westward seemed to prevent communication. We did, however, get the *Arkham*, and Douglas told me that he had likewise been vainly trying to reach Lake. He had not known about the wind, for very little was blowing at McMurdo Sound, despite its persistent rage where we were.

Throughout the day we all listened anxiously and tried to get Lake at intervals, but invariably without results. About noon a positive frenzy of wind stampeded out of the west, causing us to fear for the safety of our camp; but it eventually died down, with only a moderate relapse at 2 P.M. After three o'clock it was very quiet, and we redoubled our efforts to get Lake. Reflecting that he had four planes, each provided with an excellent short-wave outfit, we could not imagine any ordinary accident capable of crippling all his wireless equipment at once. Nevertheless the stony silence continued, and when we thought of the delirious force the wind must have had in his locality we could not help making the most direful conjectures.

By six o'clock our fears had become intense and definite, and after a wireless consultation with Douglas and Thorfinnssen I resolved to take steps toward investigation. The fifth aëroplane, which we had left at the McMurdo Sound supply cache with Sherman and two sailors, was in good shape and ready for instant use, and it seemed that the very emergency for which it had been saved was now upon us. I got Sherman by wireless and ordered him to join me with the plane and the two sailors at the southern base as quickly as possible, the air conditions being apparently highly favourable. We then talked over the personnel of the coming investigation party; and decided that we would include all hands, together with the sledge and dogs which I had kept with me. Even so great a load would not be too much for one of the huge planes built to our especial orders for heavy machinery transportation. At intervals I still tried to reach Lake with the wireless, but all to no purpose.

Sherman, with the sailors Gunnarsson and Larsen, took off at 7:30; and reported a quiet flight from several points on the wing. They arrived at our base at midnight, and all hands at once discussed the next move. It was risky business sailing over the antarctic in a single aëroplane without any line of bases, but no one drew back from what seemed like the plainest necessity. We turned in at two o'clock for a brief rest after some preliminary loading of the plane, but were up again in four hours to finish the loading and packing.

At 7:15 A.M., January 25th, we started flying northwestward under McTighe's pilotage with ten men, seven dogs, a sledge, a fuel and food supply, and other items including the plane's wireless outfit. The atmosphere was clear, fairly quiet, and relatively mild in temperature; and we anticipated very little trouble in reaching the latitude and longitude designated by Lake as the site of his camp. Our apprehensions were over what we might find, or fail to find, at the end of our journey, for silence continued to answer all calls despatched to the camp.

Every incident of that four-and-a-half-hour flight is burned into my recollection because of its crucial position in my life. It marked my loss, at the age of fifty-four, of all that peace and balance which the normal mind possesses through its accustomed conception of external Nature and Nature's laws. Thenceforward the ten of us—but the student Danforth and myself above all others—were to face a hideously amplified world of lurking horrors which nothing can erase from our emotions, and which

37. Roald Amundsen, in *The South Pole* (1913), recorded:

> With the low temperatures we experienced on this trip, we noticed a curious snow-formation that I had never seen before. Fine—extremely fine—drift-snow collected, and formed small cylindrical bodies of an average diameter of 1¼ inches, and about the same height; they were, however, of various sizes. They generally rolled over the surface like a wheel, and now and then collected into large heaps, from which again, one by one, or several together, they continued their rolling (I, 287).

Such "cylinders," also known as snow bales, snow rollers, or snow doughnuts, form when tubelike drifts are lifted by the wind and blown around like tumbleweed. They have been spotted in many cold, windy places around the world, including North America and England.

These snow rollers were photographed in Czechoslovakia.

we would refrain from sharing with mankind in general if we could. The newspapers have printed the bulletins we sent from the moving plane; telling of our non-stop course, our two battles with treacherous upper-air gales, our glimpse of the broken surface where Lake had sunk his mid-journey shaft three days before, and our sight of a group of those strange fluffy snow-cylinders noted by Amundsen and Byrd as rolling in the wind across the endless leagues of frozen plateau.[37] There came a point, though, when our sensations could not be conveyed in any words the press would understand, and a later point when we had to adopt an actual rule of strict censorship.

The sailor Larsen was first to spy the jagged line of witch-like cones and pinnacles ahead, and his shouts sent everyone to the windows of the great cabined plane. Despite our speed, they were very slow in gaining prominence; hence we knew that they must be infinitely far off, and visible only because of their abnormal height. Little by little, however, they rose grimly into the western sky; allowing us to distinguish various bare, bleak, blackish summits, and to catch the curious sense of phantasy which they inspired as seen in the reddish antarctic light against the provocative background of iridescent ice-dust clouds. In the whole spectacle there was a persistent, pervasive hint of stupendous secrecy and potential revelation; as if these stark, nightmare spires marked the pylons of a frightful gateway into forbidden spheres of dream, and complex gulfs of remote time, space, and ultra-dimensionality. I could not help feeling that they were evil things—mountains of madness whose farther slopes looked out over some accursed ultimate abyss. That seething, half-luminous cloud background held ineffable suggestions of a vague, ethereal *beyondness* far more than terrestrially spatial, and gave appalling reminders of the utter remoteness, separateness, desolation, and æon-long death of this untrodden and unfathomed austral world.

It was young Danforth who drew our notice to the curious regularities of the higher mountain skyline—regularities like clinging fragments of perfect cubes, which Lake had mentioned in his messages, and which indeed justified his comparison with the dream-like suggestions of primordial temple ruins, on cloudy Asian mountain-tops so subtly and strangely painted by Roerich. There was indeed something hauntingly Roerich-like about this whole unearthly continent of mountainous mystery. I had felt it in October when we first caught sight of Victoria Land, and I felt it afresh now. I felt, too, another wave of uneasy consciousness of Archæan mythical resemblances; of how disturbingly this lethal realm corresponded to the evilly famed plateau of Leng in the primal writings. Mythologists have placed Leng in Central Asia; but the racial memory of man—or of his predecessors—is long, and it may well be that certain tales have come down from lands and mountains and temples of horror earlier than Asia and earlier than any human world we know. A few daring mystics have hinted at a pre-Pleistocene origin for the fragmentary Pnakotic Manuscripts, and have suggested that the devotees of Tsathoggua were as alien to mankind as Tsathoggua itself. Leng, wherever in space or time it might brood, was not a region I would care to be in or near, nor did I relish the proximity of a world that had ever bred such ambiguous and Archæan monstrosities as those Lake had just mentioned. At the moment I felt sorry that I had ever read the abhorred *Necronomicon*, or talked so much with that unpleasantly erudite folklorist Wilmarth at the university.

This mood undoubtedly served to aggravate my reaction to the bizarre mirage which burst upon us from the increasingly opalescent zenith as we drew near the mountains and began to make out the cumulative undulations of the foothills. I had seen dozens of polar mirages during the preceding weeks, some of them quite as uncanny and fantastically vivid as the present sample; but this one had a wholly novel and obscure quality of menacing symbolism, and I shuddered as the seething labyrinth of fabulous walls and towers and minarets loomed out of the troubled ice vapours above our heads.

The effect was that of a Cyclopean city of no architecture known to man or to human imagination, with vast aggregations of night-black masonry embodying monstrous perversions of geometrical laws and attaining the most grotesque extremes of sinister bizarrerie. There were truncated cones, sometimes terraced or fluted, surmounted by tall cylindrical shafts here and there bulbously enlarged and often capped with tiers of thinnish scalloped discs; and strange beetling, table-like constructions suggesting piles of multitudinous rectangular slabs or circular plates or five-pointed stars with each one overlapping the one

38. William Scoresby (1789–1857), an English scientist, curate, and explorer, published in 1820 *An Account of the Arctic Regions and Northern Whale-Fishery*, a narrative of his own voyages as well as those of previous navigators. It was read by Melville, who referred to Scoresby in *Moby-Dick*. Scoresby also wrote a memoir, *Memorials of the Sea* (London: Longman, 1851), primarily about his father, who took him to sea at the age of eleven.

beneath. There were composite cones and pyramids either alone or surmounting cylinders or cubes or flatter truncated cones and pyramids and occasional needle-like spires in curious clusters of five. All of these febrile structures seemed knit together by tubular bridges crossing from one to the other at various dizzy heights, and the implied scale of the whole was terrifying and oppressive in its sheer giganticism. The general type of mirage was not unlike some of the wilder forms observed and drawn by the Arctic whaler Scoresby in 1820;[38] but at this time and place, with those dark, unknown mountain peaks soaring stupendously ahead, that anomalous elder-world discovery in our minds, and the pall of probable disaster enveloping the greater part of our expedition, we all seemed to find in it a taint of latent malignity and infinitely evil portent.

I was glad when the mirage began to break up, though in the process the various nightmare turrets and cones assumed distorted, temporary forms of even vaster hideousness. As the whole illusion dissolved to churning opalescence we began to look earthward again, and saw that our journey's end was not far off. The unknown mountains ahead rose dizzyingly up like a fearsome rampart of giants, their curious regularities shewing with startling clearness even without a field-glass. We were over the lowest foothills now, and could see amidst the snow, ice, and bare patches of their main plateau a couple of darkish spots which we took to be Lake's camp and boring. The higher foothills shot up between five and six miles away, forming a range almost distinct from the terrifying line of more than Himalayan peaks beyond them. At length Ropes—the student who had relieved McTighe at the controls—began to head downward toward the left-hand dark spot whose size marked it as the camp. As he did so, McTighe sent out the last uncensored wireless message the world was to receive from our expedition.

Everyone, of course, has read the brief and unsatisfying bulletins of the rest of our antarctic sojourn. Some hours after our landing we sent a guarded report of the tragedy we found, and reluctantly announced the wiping out of the whole Lake party by the frightful wind of the preceding day, or of the night before that. Eleven known dead, young Gedney missing. People pardoned our hazy lack of details through realisation of the shock the sad event must have caused us, and believed us when we explained that the mangling action of the wind had rendered all eleven bodies unsuitable for transportation outside. Indeed, I flatter myself that even in the midst of our distress, utter bewilderment, and soul-clutching horror, we scarcely went beyond the truth in any specific instance. The tremendous significance lies in what we dared not tell—what I would not tell now but for the need of warning others off from nameless terrors.

It is a fact that the wind had wrought dreadful havoc. Whether all could have lived through it, even without the other thing, is gravely open to doubt. The storm, with its fury of madly driven ice particles, must have been beyond anything our expedition had encountered before. One aëroplane shelter—all, it seems, had been left in a far too flimsy and inadequate state—was nearly pulverised; and the derrick at the distant boring was entirely shaken to pieces. The exposed metal of the grounded planes and drilling machinery was bruised into a high polish, and two of the small tents were flattened despite their snow banking. Wooden surfaces left out in the blast were pitted and denuded of paint, and all signs of tracks in the snow were completely obliterated. It is also true that we found none of the Archæan biological objects in a condition to take outside as a whole. We did gather some minerals from a vast tumbled pile, including several of the greenish soapstone fragments whose odd five-pointed rounding and faint patterns of grouped dots caused so many doubtful comparisons; and some fossil bones, among which were the most typical of the curiously injured specimens.

None of the dogs survived, their hurriedly built snow enclosure near the camp being almost wholly destroyed. The wind may have done that, though the greater breakage on the side next the camp, which was not the windward one, suggests an outward leap or break of the frantic beasts themselves. All three sledges were gone, and we have tried to explain that the wind may have blown them off into the unknown. The drill and ice-melting machinery at the boring were too badly damaged to warrant salvage, so we used them to choke up that subtly disturbing gateway to the past which Lake had blasted. We likewise left at the camp the two most shaken-up of the planes; since our surviving party had only four real pilots—Sherman, Danforth, McTighe, and Ropes—

in all, with Danforth in a poor nervous shape to navigate. We brought back all the books, scientific equipment, and other incidentals we could find, though much was rather unaccountably blown away. Spare tents and furs were either missing or badly out of condition.

It was approximately 4 P.M., after wide plane cruising had forced us to give Gedney up for lost, that we sent our guarded message to the *Arkham* for relaying; and I think we did well to keep it as calm and non-committal as we succeeded in doing. The most we said about agitation concerned our dogs, whose frantic uneasiness near the biological specimens was to be expected from poor Lake's accounts. We did not mention, I think, their display of the same uneasiness when sniffing around the queer greenish soapstones and certain other objects in the disordered region; objects including scientific instruments, aëroplanes, and machinery both at the camp and at the boring, whose parts had been loosened, moved, or otherwise tampered with by winds that must have harboured singular curiosity and investigativeness.

About the fourteen biological specimens we were pardonably indefinite. We said that the only ones we discovered were damaged, but that enough was left of them to prove Lake's description wholly and impressively accurate. It was hard work keeping our personal emotions out of this matter—and we did not mention numbers or say exactly how we had found those which we did find. We had by that time agreed not to transmit anything suggesting madness on the part of Lake's men, and it surely looked like madness to find six imperfect monstrosities carefully buried upright in nine-foot snow graves under five-pointed mounds punched over with groups of dots in patterns exactly like those on the queer greenish soapstones dug up from Mesozoic or Tertiary times. The eight perfect specimens mentioned by Lake seemed to have been completely blown away.

We were careful, too, about the public's general peace of mind; hence Danforth and I said little about that frightful trip over the mountains the next day. It was the fact that only a radically lightened plane could possibly cross a range of such height which mercifully limited that scouting tour to the two of us. On our return at 1 a.m. Danforth was close to hysterics, but kept an admirably stiff upper lip. It took no persuasion to make him promise not

to shew our sketches and the other things we brought away in
our pockets, not to say anything more to the others than what
we had agreed to relay outside, and to hide our camera films for
private development later on; so that part of my present story will
be as new to Pabodie, McTighe, Ropes, Sherman, and the rest
as it will be to the world in general. Indeed—Danforth is closer
mouthed than I; for he saw—or thinks he saw—one thing he will
not tell even me.

As all know, our report included a tale of a hard ascent; a confirmation of Lake's opinion that the great peaks are of Archæan
slate and other very primal crumpled strata unchanged since at
least middle Comanchian times; a conventional comment on the
regularity of the clinging cube and rampart formations; a decision that the cave-mouths indicate dissolved calcareous veins;
a conjecture that certain slopes and passes would permit of the
scaling and crossing of the entire range by seasoned mountaineers; and a remark that the mysterious other side holds a lofty
and immense super-plateau as ancient and unchanging as the
mountains themselves—20,000 feet in elevation, with grotesque
rock formations protruding through a thin glacial layer and with
low gradual foothills between the general plateau surface and the
sheer precipices of the highest peaks.

This body of data is in every respect true so far as it goes, and
it completely satisfied the men at the camp. We laid our absence
of sixteen hours—a longer time than our announced flying, landing, reconnoitring, and rock-collecting programme called for—to
a long mythical spell of adverse wind conditions; and told truly of
our landing on the farther foothills. Fortunately our tale sounded
realistic and prosaic enough not to tempt any of the others into
emulating our flight. Had any tried to do that, I would have used
every ounce of my persuasion to stop them—and I do not know
what Danforth would have done. While we were gone, Pabodie,
Sherman, Ropes, McTighe, and Williamson had worked like
beavers over Lake's two best planes; fitting them again for use
despite the altogether unaccountable juggling of their operative
mechanism.

We decided to load all the planes the next morning and start
back for our old base as soon as possible. Even though indirect,
that was the safest way to work toward McMurdo Sound; for a

straight-line flight across the most utterly unknown stretches of the æon-dead continent would involve many additional hazards. Further exploration was hardly feasible in view of our tragic decimation and the ruin of our drilling machinery; and the doubts and horrors around us—which we did not reveal—made us wish only to escape from this austral world of desolation and brooding madness as swiftly as we could.

As the public knows, our return to the world was accomplished without further disasters. All planes reached the old base on the evening of the next day—January 27th—after a swift non-stop flight; and on the 28th we made McMurdo Sound in two laps, the one pause being very brief, and occasioned by a faulty rudder in the furious wind over the ice-shelf after we had cleared the great plateau. In five days more the *Arkham* and *Miskatonic*, with all hands and equipment on board, were shaking clear of the thickening field ice and working up Ross Sea with the mocking mountains of Victoria Land looming westward against a troubled antarctic sky and twisting the wind's wails into a wide-ranged musical piping which chilled my soul to the quick. Less than a fortnight later we left the last hint of polar land behind us and thanked heaven that we were clear of a haunted, accursed realm where life and death, space and time, have made black and blasphemous alliances in the unknown epochs since matter first writhed and swam on the planet's scarce-cooled crust.

Since our return we have all constantly worked to discourage antarctic exploration, and have kept certain doubts and guesses to ourselves with splendid unity and faithfulness. Even young Danforth, with his nervous breakdown, has not flinched or babbled to his doctors—indeed, as I have said, there is one thing he thinks he alone saw which he will not tell even me, though I think it would help his psychological state if he would consent to do so. It might explain and relieve much, though perhaps the thing was no more than the delusive aftermath of an earlier shock. That is the impression I gather after those rare irresponsible moments when he whispers disjointed things to me—things which he repudiates vehemently as soon as he gets a grip on himself again.

It will be hard work deterring others from the great white south, and some of our efforts may directly harm our cause by drawing inquiring notice. We might have known from the first that human curiosity is undying, and that the results we announced would be enough to spur others ahead on the same age-long pursuit of the unknown. Lake's reports of those biological monstrosities had aroused naturalists and paleontologists to the highest pitch; though we were sensible enough not to shew the detached parts we had taken from the actual buried specimens, or our photographs of those specimens as they were found. We also refrained from shewing the more puzzling of the scarred bones and greenish soapstones; while Danforth and I have closely guarded the pictures we took or drew on the super-plateau across the range, and the crumpled things we smoothed, studied in terror, and brought away in our pockets. But now that Starkweather-Moore party is organising, and with a thoroughness far beyond anything our outfit attempted. If not dissuaded, they will get to the innermost nucleus of the antarctic and melt and bore till they bring up that which may end the world we know. So I must break through all reticences at last—even about that ultimate nameless thing beyond the mountains of madness.[39]

IV.

IT IS ONLY with vast hesitancy and repugnance that I let my mind go back to Lake's camp and what we really found there— and to that other thing beyond the frightful mountain wall. I am constantly tempted to shirk the details, and to let hints stand for actual facts and ineluctable deductions. I hope I have said enough already to let me glide briefly over the rest; the rest, that is, of the horror at the camp. I have told of the wind-ravaged terrain, the damaged shelters, the disarranged machinery, the varied uneasinesses of our dogs, the missing sledges and other items, the deaths of men and dogs, the absence of Gedney, and the six insanely buried biological specimens, strangely sound in texture for all their structural injuries, from a world forty million years dead. I do not recall whether I mentioned that upon checking up the canine bodies we found one dog missing. We did not think much about that till later—indeed, only Danforth and I have thought of it at all.

39. Here ends the first installment in *Astounding Stories.*

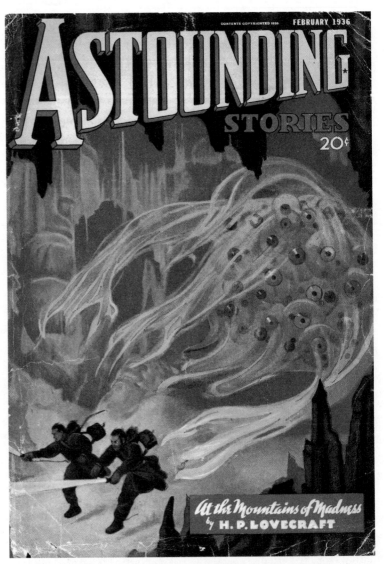

Astounding Stories 16, no. 6 (February 1936) (artist: Howard V. Brown)

The principal things I have been keeping back relate to the bodies, and to certain subtle points which may or may not lend a hideous and incredible kind of rationale to the apparent chaos. At the time, I tried to keep the men's minds off those points; for it was so much simpler—so much more normal—to lay everything to an outbreak of madness on the part of some of Lake's party. From the look of things, that dæmon mountain wind must have been enough to drive any man mad in the midst of this centre of all earthly mystery and desolation.

The crowning abnormality, of course, was the condition of

the bodies—men and dogs alike. They had all been in some terrible kind of conflict, and were torn and mangled in fiendish and altogether inexplicable ways. Death, so far as we could judge, had in each case come from strangulation or laceration. The dogs had evidently started the trouble, for the state of their ill-built corral bore witness to its forcible breakage from within. It had been set some distance from the camp because of the hatred of the animals for those hellish Archæan organisms, but the precaution seemed to have been taken in vain. When left alone in that monstrous wind behind flimsy walls of insufficient height, they must have stampeded—whether from the wind itself, or from some subtle, increasing odour emitted by the nightmare specimens, one could not say.[40] Those specimens, of course, had been covered with a tent-cloth; yet the low antarctic sun had beat steadily upon that cloth, and Lake had mentioned that solar heat tended to make the strangely sound and tough tissues of the things relax and expand. Perhaps the wind had whipped the cloth from over them and jostled them about in such a way that their more pungent olfactory qualities became manifest despite their unbelievable antiquity.

But whatever had happened, it was hideous and revolting enough. Perhaps I had better put squeamishness aside and tell the worst at last—though with a categorical statement of opinion, based on the first-hand observations and most rigid deductions of both Danforth and myself, that the then missing Gedney was in no way responsible for the loathsome horrors we found. I have said that the bodies were frightfully mangled. Now I must add that some were incised and subtracted from in the most curious, cold-blooded, and inhuman fashion. It was the same with dogs and men. All the healthier, fatter bodies, quadrupedal or bipedal, had had their most solid masses of tissue cut out and removed, as by a careful butcher; and around them was a strange sprinkling of salt—taken from the ravaged provision chests on the planes—which conjured up the most horrible associations.[41] The thing had occurred in one of the crude aëroplane shelters from which the plane had been dragged out, and subsequent winds had effaced all tracks which could have supplied any plausible theory. Scattered bits of clothing, roughly slashed from the human incision-subjects, hinted no clues. It is useless to bring up

40. The two sentences following have been restored to the text by S. T. Joshi; they did not appear in the original publication.

41. It is ironic that Dyer refers to the autopsy work performed by the Elder Ones as "inhuman," similar as it is to the work done by Lake himself on the "specimens" he discovered.

42. Strewn.

the half-impression of certain faint snow-prints in one shielded corner of the ruined enclosure—because that impression did not concern human prints at all, but was clearly mixed up with all the talk of fossil prints which poor Lake had been giving throughout the preceding weeks. One had to be careful of one's imagination in the lee of those overshadowing mountains of madness.

As I have indicated, Gedney and one dog turned out to be missing in the end. When we came on that terrible shelter we had missed two dogs and two men; but the fairly unharmed dissecting tent, which we entered after investigating the monstrous graves, had something to reveal. It was not as Lake had left it, for the covered parts of the primal monstrosity had been removed from the improvised table. Indeed, we had already realised that one of the six imperfect and insanely buried things we had found—the one with the trace of a peculiarly hateful odour—must represent the collected sections of the entity which Lake had tried to analyse. On and around that laboratory table were strown[42] other things, and it did not take long for us to guess that those things were the carefully though oddly and inexpertly dissected parts of one man and one dog. I shall spare the feelings of survivors by omitting mention of the man's identity. Lake's anatomical instruments were missing, but there were evidences of their careful cleansing. The gasoline stove was also gone, though around it we found a curious litter of matches. We buried the human parts beside the other ten men, and the canine parts with the other 35 dogs. Concerning the bizarre smudges on the laboratory table, and on the jumble of roughly handled illustrated books scattered near it, we were much too bewildered to speculate.

This formed the worst of the camp horror, but other things were equally perplexing. The disappearance of Gedney, the one dog, the eight uninjured biological specimens, the three sledges, and certain instruments, illustrated technical and scientific books, writing materials, electric torches and batteries, food and fuel, heating apparatus, spare tents, fur suits, and the like, was utterly beyond sane conjecture; as were likewise the spatter-fringed ink blots on certain pieces of paper, and the evidences of curious alien fumbling and experimentation around the planes and all other mechanical devices both at the camp and at the boring. The dogs seemed to abhor this oddly disordered machinery. Then, too, there was the upsetting of the larder, the disappearance of certain staples, and the jarringly comical heap of tin cans pried open in the most unlikely ways and at the most unlikely places. The profusion of scattered matches, intact, broken, or spent, formed another minor enigma—as did the two or three tent cloths and fur suits which we found lying about with peculiar and unorthodox slashings conceivably due to clumsy efforts at unimaginable adaptations. The maltreatment of the human and canine bodies, and the crazy burial of the damaged Archæan specimens, were all of a piece with this apparent disintegrative madness. In view of just such an eventuality as the present one, we carefully photographed all the main evidences of insane disorder at the camp; and shall use the prints to buttress our pleas against the departure of the proposed Starkweather-Moore Expedition.

Our first act after finding the bodies in the shelter was to photograph and open the row of insane graves with the five-pointed snow mounds. We could not help noticing the resemblance of these monstrous mounds, with their clusters of grouped dots, to poor Lake's descriptions of the strange greenish soapstones; and when we came on some of the soapstones themselves in the great mineral pile we found the likeness very close indeed. The whole general formation, it must be made clear, seemed abominably suggestive of the starfish-head of the Archæan entities; and we agreed that the suggestion must have worked potently upon the sensitised minds of Lake's overwrought party.[43] Our own first sight of the actual buried entities formed a horrible moment, and sent the imaginations of Pabodie and myself back to some of the shocking primal myths we had read and heard. We all agreed that the mere sight and continued presence of the things must have coöperated with the oppressive polar solitude and dæmon mountain wind in driving Lake's party mad.

For madness—centring in Gedney as the only possible surviving agent—was the explanation spontaneously adopted by everybody so far as spoken utterance was concerned; though I will not be so naive as to deny that each of us may have harboured wild guesses which sanity forbade him to formulate completely. Sherman, Pabodie, and McTighe made an exhaustive aëroplane cruise over all the surrounding territory in the afternoon, sweeping the horizon with field-glasses in quest of Gedney and of the various

43. The two sentences following have been restored to the text by S. T. Joshi; they did not appear in the original publication.

missing things; but nothing came to light. The party reported that the titan barrier range extended endlessly to right and left alike, without any diminution in height or essential structure. On some of the peaks, though, the regular cube and rampart formations were bolder and plainer; having doubly fantastic similitudes to Roerich-painted Asian hill ruins. The distribution of cryptical cave-mouths on the black snow-denuded summits seemed roughly even as far as the range could be traced.

In spite of all the prevailing horrors we were left with enough sheer scientific zeal and adventurousness to wonder about the unknown realm beyond those mysterious mountains. As our guarded messages stated, we rested at midnight after our day of terror and bafflement; but not without a tentative plan for one or more range-crossing altitude flights in a lightened plane with aërial camera and geologist's outfit, beginning the following morning. It was decided that Danforth and I try it first, and we awaked at 7 A.M. intending an early trip; though heavy winds—mentioned in our brief bulletin to the outside world—delayed our start till nearly nine o'clock.

I have already repeated the non-committal story we told the men at camp—and relayed outside—after our return sixteen hours later. It is now my terrible duty to amplify this account by filling in the merciful blanks with hints of what we really saw in the hidden trans-montane world—hints of the revelations which have finally driven Danforth to a nervous collapse. I wish he would add a really frank word about the thing which he thinks he alone saw—even though it was probably a nervous delusion—and which was perhaps the last straw that put him where he is; but he is firm against that. All I can do is to repeat his later disjointed whispers about what set him shrieking as the plane soared back through the wind-tortured mountain pass after that real and tangible shock which I shared. This will form my last word. If the plain signs of surviving elder horrors in what I disclose be not enough to keep others from meddling with the inner antarctic—or at least from prying too deeply beneath the surface of that ultimate waste of forbidden secrets and unhuman, æon-cursed desolation—the responsibility for unnamable and perhaps immensurable evils will not be mine.

Danforth and I, studying the notes made by Pabodie in his

afternoon flight and checking up with a sextant, had calculated that the lowest available pass in the range lay somewhat to the right of us, within sight of camp, and about 23,000 or 24,000 feet above sea-level. For this point, then, we first headed in the lightened plane as we embarked on our flight of discovery. The camp itself, on foothills which sprang from a high continental plateau, was some 12,000 feet in altitude; hence the actual height increase necessary was not so vast as it might seem. Nevertheless we were acutely conscious of the rarefied air and intense cold as we rose; for, on account of visibility conditions, we had to leave the cabin windows open.[44] We were dressed, of course, in our heaviest furs.

As we drew near the forbidding peaks, dark and sinister above the line of crevasse-riven snow and interstitial glaciers, we noticed more and more the curiously regular formations clinging to the slopes; and thought again of the strange Asian paintings of Nicholas Roerich. The ancient and wind-weathered rock strata fully verified all of Lake's bulletins, and proved that these hoary pinnacles had been towering up in exactly the same way since a surprisingly early time in earth's history—perhaps over fifty million years. How much higher they had once been, it was futile to guess; but everything about this strange region pointed to obscure atmospheric influences unfavourable to change, and calculated to retard the usual climatic processes of rock disintegration.

But it was the mountainside tangle of regular cubes, ramparts, and cave-mouths which fascinated and disturbed us most. I studied them with a field-glass and took aërial photographs whilst Danforth drove; and at times relieved him at the controls—though my aviation knowledge was purely an amateur's—in order to let him use the binoculars. We could easily see that much of the material of the things was a lightish Archæan quartzite, unlike any formation visible over broad areas of the general surface; and that their regularity was extreme and uncanny to an extent which poor Lake had scarcely hinted.

As he had said, their edges were crumbled and rounded from untold æons of savage weathering; but their preternatural solidity and tough material had saved them from obliteration. Many parts, especially those closest to the slopes, seemed identical in

44. They were very lucky not to pass out: In 1804, the French chemist Joseph Gay-Lussac ascended in a balloon to 23,000 feet. At that height, he experienced quickened pulse, shortness of breath, and finally unconsciousness—symptoms of oxygen deprivation—until the balloon began to descend. Gay-Lussac's measurements demonstrated that the *quantity* of oxygen in the atmosphere remained constant at different heights; it was not then understood that the reduced air pressure at this great height affected the diffusion of the gas, producing oxygen starvation.

45. An Inca site in the eastern Andes, dating from the fifteenth century. Set in a range of tropical forests in the Amazon Basin and incomparably beautiful, it is considered an apotheosis of urban civilization.

46. From 1923 to 1933, the Field Museum of Natural History of Chicago and the Ashmolean Museum of Oxford University conducted excavations at the site of the ancient city of Kish, fifty miles south of modern Baghdad. Unfortunately, no final site report was ever published. Kish was an important Mesopotamian city, occupied from 3200 BCE.

substance with the surrounding rock surface. The whole arrangement looked like the ruins of Machu Picchu in the Andes,[45] or the primal foundation-walls of Kish as dug up by the Oxford Field Museum Expedition in 1929;[46] and both Danforth and I obtained that occasional impression of *separate Cyclopean blocks* which Lake had attributed to his flight-companion Carroll. How to account for such things in this place was frankly beyond me, and I felt queerly humbled as a geologist. Igneous formations often have strange regularities—like the famous Giants' Causeway in Ireland—but this stupendous range, despite Lake's original suspicion of smoking cones, was above all else non-volcanic in evident structure.

The curious cave-mouths, near which the odd formations seemed most abundant, presented another albeit a lesser puzzle because of their regularity of outline. They were, as Lake's bulletin had said, often approximately square or semicircular; as

In County Antrim, on the northeast coast of Ireland, lie these 40,000-plus naturally formed basalt columns, referred to colloquially as the "Giants' Causeway."

if the natural orifices had been shaped to greater symmetry by some magic hand. Their numerousness and wide distribution were remarkable, and suggested that the whole region was honeycombed with tunnels dissolved out of limestone strata. Such glimpses as we secured did not extend far within the caverns, but we saw that they were apparently clear of stalactites and stalagmites. Outside, those parts of the mountain slopes adjoining the apertures seemed invariably smooth and regular; and Danforth thought that the slight cracks and pittings of the weathering tended toward unusual patterns. Filled as he was with the horrors and strangenesses discovered at the camp, he hinted that the pittings vaguely resembled those baffling groups of dots sprinkled over the primeval greenish soapstones, so hideously duplicated on the madly conceived snow mounds above those six buried monstrosities.

We had risen gradually in flying over the higher foothills and along toward the relatively low pass we had selected. As we advanced we occasionally looked down at the snow and ice of the land route, wondering whether we could have attempted the trip with the simpler equipment of earlier days. Somewhat to our surprise we saw that the terrain was far from difficult as such things go; and that despite the crevasses and other bad spots it would not have been likely to deter the sledges of a Scott, a Shackleton, or an Amundsen. Some of the glaciers appeared to lead up to wind-bared passes with unusual continuity, and upon reaching our chosen pass we found that its case formed no exception.

Our sensations of tense expectancy as we prepared to round the crest and peer out over an untrodden world can hardly be described on paper; even though we had no cause to think the regions beyond the range essentially different from those already seen and traversed. The touch of evil mystery in these barrier mountains, and in the beckoning sea of opalescent sky glimpsed betwixt their summits, was a highly subtle and attenuated matter not to be explained in literal words. Rather was it an affair of vague psychological symbolism and æsthetic association—a thing mixed up with exotic poetry and paintings, and with archaic myths lurking in shunned and forbidden volumes. Even the wind's burden held a peculiar strain of conscious malignity; and for a second it seemed that the composite sound included a bizarre musical whistling or piping over a wide range as the blast swept in and out of the omnipresent and resonant cave-mouths. There was a cloudy note of reminiscent repulsion in this sound, as complex and unplaceable as any of the other dark impressions.

We were now, after a slow ascent, at a height of 23,570 feet according to the aneroid; and had left the region of clinging snow definitely below us. Up here were only dark, bare rock slopes and the start of rough-ribbed glaciers—but with those provocative cubes, ramparts, and echoing cave-mouths to add a portent of the unnatural, the fantastic, and the dream-like. Looking along the line of high peaks, I thought I could see the one mentioned by poor Lake, with a rampart exactly on top. It seemed to be half-lost in a queer antarctic haze; such a haze, perhaps, as had been responsible for Lake's early notion of volcanism. The pass loomed directly before us, smooth and windswept between its jagged and malignly frowning pylons. Beyond it was a sky fretted with swirling vapours and lighted by the low polar sun—the sky of that mysterious farther realm upon which we felt no human eye had ever gazed.

A few more feet of altitude and we would behold that realm. Danforth and I, unable to speak except in shouts amidst the howling, piping wind that raced through the pass and added to the noise of the unmuffled engines, exchanged eloquent glances. And then, having gained those last few feet, we did indeed stare across the momentous divide and over the unsampled secrets of an elder and utterly alien earth.

V.

I THINK THAT both of us simultaneously cried out in mixed awe, wonder, terror, and disbelief in our own senses as we finally cleared the pass and saw what lay beyond. Of course, we must have had some natural theory in the back of our heads to steady our faculties for the moment. Probably we thought of such things as the grotesquely weathered stones of the Garden of the Gods in Colorado, or the fantastically symmetrical wind-carved rocks of the Arizona desert. Perhaps we even half thought the sight a mirage like that we had seen the morning before on first approach-

47. Harmoniously proportioned.

The so-called Garden of the Gods, a National Natural Landmark near Colorado Springs, Colorado.

This sandstone formation is known as "The Wave" and lies near the Utah-Arizona border.

ing those mountains of madness. We must have had some such normal notions to fall back upon as our eyes swept that limitless, tempest-scarred plateau and grasped the almost endless labyrinth of colossal, regular, and geometrically eurhythmic[47] stone masses which reared their crumbled and pitted crests above a glacial sheet not more than forty or fifty feet deep at its thickest, and in places obviously thinner.

The effect of the monstrous sight was indescribable, for some fiendish violation of known natural law seemed certain at the outset. Here, on a hellishly ancient table-land fully 20,000 feet high, and in a climate deadly to habitation since a pre-human age not less than 500,000 years ago, there stretched nearly to the vision's limit a tangle of orderly stone which only the desperation of mental self-defence could possibly attribute to any but a conscious and artificial cause. We had previously dismissed, so far as serious thought was concerned, any theory that the cubes and ramparts of the mountainsides were other than natural in origin. How could they be otherwise, when man himself could scarcely have been differentiated from the great apes at the time when this region succumbed to the present unbroken reign of glacial death?

Yet now the sway of reason seemed irrefutably shaken, for this Cyclopean maze of squared, curved, and angled blocks had fea-

"The effect of the monstrous sight was indescribable!
Some fiendish violation of natural law!"
Astounding Stories 16, no. 7 (March 1936) (artist: Howard V. Brown)

tures which cut off all comfortable refuge. It was, very clearly, the blasphemous city of the mirage in stark, objective, and ineluctable reality. That damnable portent had had a material basis after all—there had been some horizontal stratum of ice-dust in the upper air, and this shocking stone survival had projected its image across the mountains according to the simple laws of reflection. Of course the phantom had been twisted and exaggerated, and had contained things which the real source did not contain; yet now, as we saw that real source, we thought it even more hideous and menacing than its distant image.

Only the incredible, unhuman massiveness of these vast stone towers and ramparts had saved the frightful thing from utter annihilation in the hundreds of thousands—perhaps millions—of years it had brooded there amidst the blasts of a bleak upland. "Corona Mundi . . . Roof of the World . . ."[48] All sorts of fantastic phrases sprang to our lips as we looked dizzily down at the unbelievable spectacle. I thought again of the eldritch primal myths that had so persistently haunted me since my first sight of this dead antarctic world—of the dæmoniac plateau of Leng, of the Mi-Go, or Abominable Snow-Men of the Himalayas, of the Pnakotic Manuscripts with their pre-human implications, of the Cthulhu cult, of the *Necronomicon*, and of the Hyperborean legends of formless Tsathoggua and the worse than formless star spawn associated with that semi-entity.

For boundless miles in every direction the thing stretched off with very little thinning; indeed, as our eyes followed it to the right and left along the base of the low, gradual foothills which separated it from the actual mountain rim, we decided that we could see no thinning at all except for an interruption at the left of the pass through which we had come. We had merely struck, at random, a limited part of something of incalculable extent. The foothills were more sparsely sprinkled with grotesque stone structures, linking the terrible city to the already familiar cubes and ramparts which evidently formed its mountain outposts. These latter, as well as the queer cave-mouths, were as thick on the inner as on the outer sides of the mountains.

The nameless stone labyrinth consisted, for the most part, of walls from 10 to 150 feet in ice-clear height, and of a thickness

48. These phrases (the former means "crown of the world") are associated with the region known as "high Asia," the mountainous interior, and in particular the Pamirs and the Himalayas. Nicholas Roerich, who traveled extensively in the region, established the Corona Mundi International Arts Center in 1922 with his wife, the Russian philosopher, writer, photographer, and art restorer Helena Roerich (1879–1955). See note 13, above.

"It was, very clearly, the blasphemous city of the mirage—in stark, objective, reality!" *Astounding Stories* 17, no. 1 (March 1936) (artist: Howard V. Brown)

varying from five to ten feet. It was composed mostly of prodigious blocks of dark primordial slate, schist, and sandstone—blocks in many cases as large as 4 x 6 x 8 feet—though in several places it seemed to be carved out of a solid, uneven bed-rock of pre-Cambrian slate. The buildings were far from equal in size; there being innumerable honeycomb arrangements of enormous extent as well as smaller separate structures. The general shape of these things tended to be conical, pyramidal, or terraced; though there were many perfect cylinders, perfect cubes, clusters of cubes, and other rectangular forms, and a peculiar sprinkling of angled edifices whose five-pointed ground plan roughly suggested modern fortifications. The builders had made constant and expert use of the principle of the arch, and domes had probably existed in the city's heyday.

The whole tangle was monstrously weathered, and the glacial surface from which the towers projected was strown with fallen blocks and immemorial debris. Where the glaciation was transparent we could see the lower parts of the gigantic piles, and noticed the ice-preserved stone bridges which connected the different towers at varying distances above the ground. On the exposed walls we could detect the scarred places where other and higher bridges of the same sort had existed. Closer inspection revealed countless largish windows; some of which were closed with shutters of a petrified material originally wood, though most gaped open in a sinister and menacing fashion. Many of the ruins, of course, were roofless, and with uneven though wind-rounded upper edges; whilst others, of a more sharply conical or pyramidal model or else protected by higher surrounding structures, preserved intact outlines despite the omnipresent crumbling and pitting. With the field-glass we could barely make out what seemed to be sculptural decorations in horizontal bands—decorations including those curious groups of dots whose presence on the ancient soapstones now assumed a vastly larger significance.

In many places the buildings were totally ruined and the ice-sheet deeply riven from various geologic causes. In other places the stonework was worn down to the very level of the glaciation. One broad swath, extending from the plateau's interior to a cleft in the foothills about a mile to the left of the pass we had traversed, was wholly free from buildings; and it probably represented, we concluded, the course of some great river which in Tertiary times—millions of years ago—had poured through the city and into some prodigious subterranean abyss of the great barrier range. Certainly, this was above all a region of caves, gulfs, and underground secrets beyond human penetration.

Looking back to our sensations, and recalling our dazedness at viewing this monstrous survival from æons we had thought pre-human, I can only wonder that we preserved the semblance of equilibrium which we did. Of course we knew that something—chronology, scientific theory, or our own consciousness—was woefully awry; yet we kept enough poise to guide the plane, observe many things quite minutely, and take a careful series of photographs which may yet serve both us and the world in good stead. In my case, ingrained scientific habit may have helped; for above all my bewilderment and sense of menace there burned

49. Lemuria was proposed in 1864 by the English zoologist Philip Sclater as a land bridge joining the islands Madagascar, Ceylon, and Sumatra. The theories of plate tectonics that emerged in the early twentieth century largely eliminated Lemuria from scientific thought. However, in *The Secret Doctrine* (1888), the Theosophist Madame Blavatsky announced that Lemuria was the home of what she termed a "root race" of humanity (in this case, egg-laying hermaphrodites), and others embraced the concept, most notably the investment banker and Theosophist William Scott-Elliot, in his *The Lost Lemuria* (1904). See also "The Call of Cthulhu," note 16, above.

50. Another capital of Hyperborea, succeeding Commoriom, described in numerous tales by Robert E. Howard (see "The Whisperer in Darkness," note 64, above).

51. In "The Mound," a story cowritten by Lovecraft with Zealia Bishop in late 1929 and early 1930 (but not published until 1940), the land is said to be near the North Pole. Olathoë and Lomar are first mentioned in Lovecraft's "Polaris" (1920).

52. Another Robert E. Howard–referenced land, filled with serpent-men, identified later as coextensive with modern (that is, post-Archæan) Europe.

53. See, of course, "The Nameless City" (pp. 80–93, above).

a dominant curiosity to fathom more of this age-old secret—to know what sort of beings had built and lived in this incalculably gigantic place, and what relation to the general world of its time or of other times so unique a concentration of life could have had.

For this place could be no ordinary city. It must have formed the primary nucleus and centre of some archaic and unbelievable chapter of earth's history whose outward ramifications, recalled only dimly in the most obscure and distorted myths, had vanished utterly amidst the chaos of terrene convulsions long before any human race we know had shambled out of apedom. Here sprawled a palæogæan megalopolis compared with which the fabled Atlantis and Lemuria,[49] Commoriom and Uzuldaroum,[50] and Olathoë in the land of Lomar,[51] are recent things of today— not even of yesterday; a megalopolis ranking with such whispered pre-human blasphemies as Valusia,[52] R'lyeh, Ib in the land of Mnar, and the Nameless City of Arabia Deserta.[53] As we flew above that tangle of stark titan towers my imagination sometimes escaped all bounds and roved aimlessly in realms of fantastic associations—even weaving links betwixt this lost world and some of my own wildest dreams concerning the mad horror at the camp.

The plane's fuel-tank, in the interest of greater lightness, had been only partly filled; hence we now had to exert caution in our explorations. Even so, however, we covered an enormous extent of ground—or, rather, air—after swooping down to a level where the wind became virtually negligible. There seemed to be no limit to the mountain-range, or to the length of the frightful stone city which bordered its inner foothills. Fifty miles of flight in each direction shewed no major change in the labyrinth of rock and masonry that clawed up corpse-like through the eternal ice. There were, though, some highly absorbing diversifications; such as the carvings on the canyon where that broad river had once pierced the foothills and approached its sinking-place in the great range. The headlands at the stream's entrance had been boldly carved into Cyclopean pylons; and something about the ridgy, barrel-shaped designs stirred up oddly vague, hateful, and confusing semi-remembrances in both Danforth and me.

We also came upon several star-shaped open spaces, evidently public squares; and noted various undulations in the terrain. Where a sharp hill rose, it was generally hollowed out into some sort of rambling stone edifice; but there were at least two exceptions. Of these latter, one was too badly weathered to disclose what had been on the jutting eminence, while the other still bore a fantastic conical monument carved out of the solid rock and roughly resembling such things as the well-known Snake Tomb in the ancient valley of Petra.

Flying inland from the mountains, we discovered that the city was not of infinite width, even though its length along the foothills seemed endless. After about thirty miles the grotesque stone buildings began to thin out, and in ten more miles we came to an unbroken waste virtually without signs of sentient artifice. The course of the river beyond the city seemed marked by a broad depressed line; while the land assumed a somewhat greater ruggedness, seeming to slope slightly upward as it receded in the mist-hazed west.

So far we had made no landing, yet to leave the plateau without an attempt at entering some of the monstrous structures would have been inconceivable. Accordingly we decided to find a smooth place on the foothills near our navigable pass, there grounding the plane and preparing to do some exploration on foot. Though these gradual slopes were partly covered with a scattering of ruins, low flying soon disclosed an ample number of possible landing-places. Selecting that nearest to the pass, since our next flight would be across the great range and back to camp, we succeeded about 12:30 P.M. in coming down on a smooth, hard snowfield wholly devoid of obstacles and well adapted to a swift and favourable takeoff later on.

It did not seem necessary to protect the plane with a snow banking for so brief a time and in so comfortable an absence of high winds at this level; hence we merely saw that the landing skis were safely lodged, and that the vital parts of the mechanism were guarded against the cold. For our foot journey we discarded the heaviest of our flying furs, and took with us a small outfit consisting of pocket compass, hand camera, light provisions, voluminous notebooks and paper, geologist's hammer and chisel, specimen-bags, coil of climbing rope, and powerful electric torches with extra batteries; this equipment having been carried in the plane on the chance that we might be able to effect a landing, take ground pictures, make drawings and topographical sketches, and obtain rock specimens from some bare slope, outcropping, or mountain cave. Fortunately we had a supply of extra paper to tear up, place in a spare specimen-bag, and use on the ancient principle of hare-and-hounds for marking our course in any interior mazes we might be able to penetrate. This had been brought in case we found some cave system with air quiet enough to allow such a rapid and easy method in place of the usual rock-chipping method of trail-blazing.

Walking cautiously downhill over the crusted snow toward the stupendous stone labyrinth that loomed against the opalescent west, we felt almost as keen a sense of imminent marvels as we had felt on approaching the unfathomed mountain pass four hours previously. True, we had become visually familiar with the incredible secret concealed by the barrier peaks; yet the prospect of actually entering primordial walls reared by conscious beings perhaps millions of years ago—before any known race of men could have existed—was none the less awesome and potentially terrible in its implications of cosmic abnormality. Though the thinness of the air at this prodigious altitude made exertion somewhat more difficult than usual; both Danforth and I found ourselves bearing up very well, and felt equal to almost any task which might fall to our lot. It took only a few steps to bring us to a shapeless ruin worn level with the snow, while ten or fifteen rods farther on there was a huge roofless rampart still complete in its gigantic five-pointed outline and rising to an irregular height of ten or eleven feet. For this latter we headed; and when at last we were able actually to touch its weathered Cyclopean blocks, we felt that we had established an unprecedented and almost blasphemous link with forgotten æons normally closed to our species.

This rampart, shaped like a star and perhaps 300 feet from point to point, was built of Jurassic sandstone blocks of irregular size, averaging 6 x 8 feet in surface. There was a row of arched loopholes or windows about four feet wide and five feet high; spaced quite symmetrically along the points of the star and at its inner angles, and with the bottoms about four feet from the glaciated surface. Looking through these, we could see that the masonry was fully five feet thick, that there were no partitions remaining within, and that there were traces of banded carvings or bas-reliefs on the interior walls; facts we had indeed guessed before, when flying low over this rampart and others like it. Though lower parts must have originally existed, all traces of such things were now wholly obscured by the deep layer of ice and snow at this point.

We crawled through one of the windows and vainly tried to decipher the nearly effaced mural designs, but did not attempt to disturb the glaciated floor. Our orientation flights had indicated that many buildings in the city proper were less ice-choked, and that we might perhaps find wholly clear interiors leading down to the true ground level if we entered those structures still roofed at the top. Before we left the rampart we photographed it carefully, and studied its mortarless Cyclopean masonry with complete bewilderment. We wished that Pabodie were present, for his engineering knowledge might have helped us guess how such titanic blocks could have been handled in that unbelievably remote age when the city and its outskirts were built up.

The half-mile walk downhill to the actual city, with the upper wind shrieking vainly and savagely through the skyward peaks in the background, was something whose smallest details will always remain engraved on my mind. Only in fantastic nightmares could any human beings but Danforth and me conceive such optical effects. Between us and the churning vapours of the west lay that monstrous tangle of dark stone towers; its outré and incredible forms impressing us afresh at every new angle of vision. It was a mirage in solid stone, and were it not for the photographs I would still doubt that such a thing could be. The general type of masonry was identical with that of the rampart we had examined; but the extravagant shapes which this masonry took in its urban manifestations were past all description.

Even the pictures illustrate only one or two phases of its infinite bizarrerie, endless variety, preternatural massiveness, and utterly alien exoticism. There were geometrical forms for which an Euclid could scarcely find a name—cones of all degrees of irregularity and truncation; terraces of every sort of provocative disproportion; shafts with odd bulbous enlargements; broken columns in curious groups; and five-pointed or five-ridged arrangements of mad grotesqueness. As we drew nearer we could see beneath certain transparent parts of the ice-sheet, and detect some of the tubular stone bridges that connected the crazily sprinkled structures at various heights. Of orderly streets there seemed to be none, the only broad open swath being a mile to the left, where the ancient river had doubtless flowed through the town into the mountains.

Our field-glasses shewed the external horizontal bands of nearly effaced sculptures and dot-groups to be very prevalent, and we could half-imagine what the city must once have looked like—even though most of the roofs and tower-tops had necessarily perished. As a whole, it had been a complex tangle of twisted lanes and alleys; all of them deep canyons, and some little better than tunnels because of the overhanging masonry or overarching bridges. Now, outspread below us, it loomed like a dream phantasy against a westward mist through whose northern end the low, reddish antarctic sun of early afternoon was struggling to shine; and when for a moment that sun encountered a denser obstruction and plunged the scene into temporary shadow, the effect was subtly menacing in a way I can never hope to depict. Even the faint howling and piping of the unfelt wind in the great mountain passes behind us took on a wilder note of purposeful malignity. The last stage of our descent to the town was unusually steep and abrupt, and a rock outcropping at the edge where the grade changed led us to think that an artificial terrace had once existed there. Under the glaciation, we believed, there must be a flight of steps or its equivalent.

When at last we plunged into the labyrinthine town itself, clambering over fallen masonry and shrinking from the oppressive nearness and dwarfing height of omnipresent crumbling and pitted walls, our sensations again became such that I marvel at the amount of self-control we retained. Danforth was frankly jumpy, and began making some offensively irrelevant speculations about the horror at the camp—which I resented all the more because I could not help sharing certain conclusions forced upon us by many features of this morbid survival from nightmare antiquity. The speculations worked on his imagination, too; for in one place—where a debris-littered alley turned a sharp corner—he insisted that he saw faint traces of ground markings which he did not like; whilst elsewhere he stopped to listen to a subtle imaginary sound from some undefined point—a muffled musical piping, he said, not unlike that of the wind in the mountain caves yet somehow disturbingly different. The ceaseless *five-pointedness* of the surrounding architecture and of the few distinguishable mural arabesques had a dimly sinister suggestiveness we could not escape; and gave us a touch of terrible subconscious certainty concerning the primal entities which had reared and dwelt in this unhallowed place.

Nevertheless our scientific and adventurous souls were not wholly dead; and we mechanically carried out our programme of chipping specimens from all the different rock types represented in the masonry. We wished a rather full set in order to draw better conclusions regarding the age of the place. Nothing in the great outer walls seemed to date from later than the Jurassic and Comanchian[54] periods, nor was any piece of stone in the entire place of a greater recency than the Pliocene age. In stark certainty, we were wandering amidst a death which had reigned at least 500,000 years, and in all probability even longer.

As we proceeded through this maze of stone-shadowed twilight we stopped at all available apertures to study interiors and investigate entrance possibilities. Some were above our reach, whilst others led only into ice-choked ruins as unroofed and barren as the rampart on the hill. One, though spacious and inviting, opened on a seemingly bottomless abyss without visible means of descent. Now and then we had a chance to study the petrified wood of a surviving shutter, and were impressed by the fabulous antiquity implied in the still discernible grain. These things had come from Mesozoic gymnosperms and conifers—especially Cretaceous cycads—and from fan palms and early angiosperms of plainly Tertiary date. Nothing definitely later than the Pliocene could be discovered. In the placing of these shutters—whose edges shewed the former presence of queer and long-vanished hinges—usage seemed to be varied; some being on the outer and some on the inner side of the deep embrasures. They seemed to have become wedged in place, thus surviving the rusting of their former and probably metallic fixtures and fastenings.

After a time we came across a row of windows—in the bulges of a colossal five-ridged cone of undamaged apex—which led into

54. The Comanchian or Commanchean period was an American usage, coined by geologist Robert T. Hill, to designate a portion of what in Europe was termed the Lower Cretaceous period. This was perhaps 100 million years ago, as contrasted with the Upper Cretaceous period of a mere 70 to 80 million years ago. The name was derived from the location of the rock strata examined, which were in the Comanche territories in Texas. It was a time when sauropods, giant dinosaurs with tiny heads and long necks, proliferated.

a vast, well-preserved room with stone flooring; but these were too high in the room to permit descent without a rope. We had a rope with us, but did not wish to bother with this twenty-foot drop unless obliged to—especially in this thin plateau air where great demands were made upon the heart action. This enormous room was probably a hall or concourse of some sort, and our electric torches shewed bold, distinct, and potentially startling sculptures arranged round the walls in broad, horizontal bands separated by equally broad strips of conventional arabesques. We took careful note of this spot, planning to enter here unless a more easily gained interior were encountered.

Finally, though, we did encounter exactly the opening we wished; an archway about six feet wide and ten feet high, marking the former end of an aërial bridge which had spanned an alley about five feet above the present level of glaciation. These archways, of course, were flush with upper-story floors; and in this case one of the floors still existed. The building thus accessible was a series of rectangular terraces on our left facing westward. That across the alley, where the other archway yawned, was a decrepit cylinder with no windows and with a curious bulge about ten feet above the aperture. It was totally dark inside, and the archway seemed to open on a well of illimitable emptiness.

Heaped debris made the entrance to the vast left-hand building doubly easy, yet for a moment we hesitated before taking advantage of the long-wished chance. For though we had penetrated into this tangle of archaic mystery, it required fresh resolution to carry us actually inside a complete and surviving building of a fabulous elder world whose nature was becoming more and more hideously plain to us. In the end, however, we made the plunge; and scrambled up over the rubble into the gaping embrasure. The floor beyond was of great slate slabs, and seemed to form the outlet of a long, high corridor with sculptured walls.

Observing the many inner archways which led off from it, and realising the probable complexity of the nest of apartments within, we decided that we must begin our system of hare-and-hound trail-blazing. Hitherto our compasses, together with frequent glimpses of the vast mountain-range between the towers in our rear, had been enough to prevent our losing our way; but from now on, the artificial substitute would be necessary. Accordingly we reduced our extra paper to shreds of suitable size, placed these in a bag to be carried by Danforth, and prepared to use them as economically as safety would allow. This method would probably gain us immunity from straying, since there did not appear to be any strong air-currents inside the primordial masonry. If such should develop, or if our paper supply should give out, we could of course fall back on the more secure though more tedious and retarding method of rock-chipping.

Just how extensive a territory we had opened up, it was impossible to guess without a trial. The close and frequent connexion of the different buildings made it likely that we might cross from one to another on bridges underneath the ice except where impeded by local collapses and geologic rifts, for very little glaciation seemed to have entered the massive constructions. Almost all the areas of transparent ice had revealed the submerged windows as tightly shuttered, as if the town had been left in that uniform state until the glacial sheet came to crystallise the lower part for all succeeding time. Indeed, one gained a curious impression that this place had been deliberately closed and deserted in some dim, bygone æon, rather than overwhelmed by any sudden calamity or even gradual decay. Had the coming of the ice been foreseen, and had a nameless population left en masse to seek a less doomed abode? The precise physiographic conditions attending the formation of the ice-sheet at this point would have to wait for later solution. It had not, very plainly, been a grinding drive. Perhaps the pressure of accumulated snows had been responsible; and perhaps some flood from the river, or from the bursting of some ancient glacial dam in the great range, had helped to create the special state now observable. Imagination could conceive almost anything in connexion with this place.

VI.

IT WOULD BE cumbrous to give a detailed, consecutive account of our wanderings inside that cavernous, æon-dead honeycomb of primal masonry; that monstrous lair of elder secrets which now echoed for the first time, after uncounted epochs, to the tread of human feet. This is especially true

55. The commercial flashbulb, patented on September 23, 1930, in Germany. Put in production under the trade name Vacublitz by the Hauser Company, which used a model invented by Johannes Ostermeier, they were soon sold in America by General Electric under the brand name Sashalite. French and Austrian versions of the technology, by Louis Bouton (in 1895) and Paul Vierkötter (in 1925), preceded Ostermeier's.

Early Sashalite flashbulbs.

because so much of the horrible drama and revelation came from a mere study of the omnipresent mural carvings. Our flashlight[55] photographs of those carvings will do much toward proving the truth of what we are now disclosing, and it is lamentable that we had not a larger film supply with us. As it was, we made crude notebook sketches of certain salient features after all our films were used up.

The building which we had entered was one of great size and elaborateness, and gave us an impressive notion of the architecture of that nameless geologic past. The inner partitions were less massive than the outer walls, but on the lower levels were excellently preserved. Labyrinthine complexity, involving curiously irregular differences in floor levels, characterised the entire arrangement; and we should certainly have been lost at the very outset but for the trail of torn paper left behind us. We decided to explore the more decrepit upper parts first of all, hence climbed aloft in the maze for a distance of some 100 feet, to where the topmost tier of chambers yawned snowily and ruinously open to the polar sky. Ascent was effected over the steep, transversely ribbed stone ramps or inclined planes which everywhere served in lieu of stairs. The rooms we encountered were of all imaginable shapes and proportions, ranging from five-pointed stars to triangles and perfect cubes. It might be safe to say that their general average was about 30 x 30 feet in floor area, and 20 feet in height; though many larger apartments existed. After thoroughly examining the upper regions and the glacial level we descended story by story into the submerged part, where indeed we soon saw we were in a continuous maze of connected chambers and passages probably leading over unlimited areas outside this particular building. The Cyclopean massiveness and giganticism of everything about us became curiously oppressive; and there was something vaguely but deeply unhuman in all the contours, dimensions, proportions, decorations, and constructional nuances of the blasphemously archaic stonework. We soon realised, from what the carvings revealed, that this monstrous city was many million years old.

We cannot yet explain the engineering principles used in the anomalous balancing and adjustment of the vast rock masses, though the function of the arch was clearly much relied on. The rooms we visited were wholly bare of all portable contents, a circumstance which sustained our belief in the city's deliberate desertion. The prime decorative feature was the almost universal system of mural sculpture, which tended to run in continuous horizontal bands three feet wide and arranged from floor to ceiling in alternation with bands of equal width given over to geometrical arabesques. There were exceptions to this rule of arrangement, but its preponderance was overwhelming. Often, however, a series of smooth cartouches containing oddly patterned groups of dots would be sunk along one of the arabesque bands.

The technique, we soon saw, was mature, accomplished, and æsthetically evolved to the highest degree of civilised mastery; though utterly alien in every detail to any known art tradition of the human race. In delicacy of execution no sculpture I have ever seen could approach it. The minutest details of elaborate vegetation, or of animal life, were rendered with astonishing vividness despite the bold scale of the carvings; whilst the conventional designs were marvels of skilful intricacy. The arabesques displayed a profound use of mathematical principles, and were made up of obscurely symmetrical curves and angles based on the quantity of five. The pictorial bands followed a highly formalised tradition, and involved a peculiar treatment of perspective; but had an artistic force that moved us profoundly notwithstanding the intervening gulf of vast geologic periods. Their method of design hinged on a singular juxtaposition of the cross-section with the two-dimensional silhouette, and embodied an analytical psychology beyond that of any known race of antiquity. It is useless to try to compare this art with any represented in our museums. Those who see our photographs will probably find its closest analogue in certain grotesque conceptions of the most daring futurists.[56]

The arabesque tracery consisted altogether of depressed lines, whose depth on unweathered walls varied from one to two inches. When cartouches with dot-groups appeared—evidently as inscriptions in some unknown and primordial language and alphabet—the depression of the smooth surface was perhaps an inch and a half, and of the dots perhaps a half inch more. The pictorial bands were in counter-sunk low relief, their background being depressed about two inches from the original wall sur-

56. See "The Call of Cthulhu," note 11, above, for a discussion of Futurism and other art movements.

face. In some specimens marks of a former colouration could be detected, though for the most part the untold æons had disintegrated and banished any pigments which may have been applied. The more one studied the marvellous technique, the more one admired the things. Beneath their strict conventionalisation one could grasp the minute and accurate observation and graphic skill of the artists; and indeed, the very conventions themselves served to symbolise and accentuate the real essence or vital differentiation of every object delineated. We felt, too, that besides these recognisable excellences there were others lurking beyond the reach of our perceptions. Certain touches here and there gave vague hints of latent symbols and stimuli which another mental and emotional background, and a fuller or different sensory equipment, might have made of profound and poignant significance to us.

The subject-matter of the sculptures obviously came from the life of the vanished epoch of their creation, and contained a large proportion of evident history. It is this abnormal historic-mindedness of the primal race—a chance circumstance operating, through coincidence, miraculously in our favour—which made the carvings so awesomely informative to us, and which caused us to place their photography and transcription above all other considerations. In certain rooms the dominant arrangement was varied by the presence of maps, astronomical charts, and other scientific designs on an enlarged scale—these things giving a naive and terrible corroboration to what we gathered from the pictorial friezes and dadoes. In hinting at what the whole revealed, I can only hope that my account will not arouse a curiosity greater than sane caution on the part of those who believe me at all. It would be tragic if any were to be allured to that realm of death and horror by the very warning meant to discourage them.

Interrupting these sculptured walls were high windows and massive twelve-foot doorways; both now and then retaining the petrified wooden planks—elaborately carved and polished—of the actual shutters and doors. All metal fixtures had long ago vanished, but some of the doors remained in place and had to be forced aside as we progressed from room to room. Window frames with odd transparent panes—mostly elliptical—survived here and there, though in no considerable quantity. There were also frequent niches of great magnitude, generally empty, but once in a while containing some bizarre object carved from green soapstone which was either broken or perhaps held too inferior to warrant removal. Other apertures were undoubtedly connected with bygone mechanical facilities—heating, lighting, and the like—of a sort suggested in many of the carvings. Ceilings tended to be plain, but had sometimes been inlaid with green soapstone or other tiles, mostly fallen now. Floors were also paved with such tiles, though plain stonework predominated.

As I have said, all furniture and other moveables were absent; but the sculptures gave a clear idea of the strange devices which had once filled these tomb-like, echoing rooms. Above the glacial sheet the floors were generally thick with detritus, litter, and debris; but farther down this condition decreased. In some of the lower chambers and corridors there was little more than gritty dust or ancient incrustations, while occasional areas had an uncanny air of newly swept immaculateness. Of course, where rifts or collapses had occurred, the lower levels were as littered as the upper ones. A central court—as in other structures we had seen from the air—saved the inner regions from total darkness; so that we seldom had to use our electric torches in the upper rooms except when studying sculptured details. Below the ice-cap, however, the twilight deepened; and in many parts of the tangled ground level there was an approach to absolute blackness.

To form even a rudimentary idea of our thoughts and feelings as we penetrated this æon-silent maze of unhuman masonry, one must correlate a hopelessly bewildering chaos of fugitive moods, memories, and impressions. The sheer appalling antiquity and lethal desolation of the place were enough to overwhelm almost any sensitive person, but added to these elements were the recent unexplained horror at the camp, and the revelations all too soon effected by the terrible mural sculptures around us. The moment we came upon a perfect section of carving, where no ambiguity of interpretation could exist, it took only a brief study to give us the hideous truth—a truth which it would be naive to claim Danforth and I had not independently suspected before, though we had carefully refrained from even hinting it to each other. There could now be no further merciful doubt about the nature

57. That is, *Scarabaeus sacer*, the dung beetle revered in ancient Egypt as a sacred symbol of the sun god Ra. The beetle is often depicted rolling a ball of dung across the sand; this symbolizes the rolling of the sun across the sky.

58. In other words, points out Robert M. Price, in "Demythologizing Cthulhu," the "occult and transcendent Great Old Ones . . . were simply a race of space aliens," still horrifying, but horrifying because they underline the cosmic insignificance of humankind (9).

of the beings which had built and inhabited this monstrous dead city millions of years ago, when man's ancestors were primitive archaic mammals, and vast dinosaurs roamed the tropical steppes of Europe and Asia.

We had previously clung to a desperate alternative and insisted—each to himself—that the omnipresence of the five-pointed motif meant only some cultural or religious exaltation of the Archæan natural object which had so patently embodied the quality of five-pointedness; as the decorative motifs of Minoan Crete exalted the sacred bull, those of Egypt the scarabæus,[57] those of Rome the wolf and the eagle, and those of various savage tribes some chosen totem-animal. But this lone refuge was now stripped from us, and we were forced to face definitely the reason-shaking realisation which the reader of these pages has doubtless long ago anticipated. I can scarcely bear to write it down in black and white even now, but perhaps that will not be necessary.

The things once rearing and dwelling in this frightful masonry in the age of dinosaurs were not indeed dinosaurs, but far worse. Mere dinosaurs were new and almost brainless objects—but the builders of the city were wise and old, and had left certain traces in rocks even then laid down well-nigh a thousand million years . . . rocks laid down before the true life of earth had advanced beyond plastic groups of cells . . . rocks laid down before the true life of earth had existed at all. They were the makers and enslavers of that life, and above all doubt the originals of the fiendish elder myths which things like the Pnakotic Manuscripts and the *Necronomicon* affrightedly hint about.[58] They were the Great Old Ones that had filtered down from the stars when earth was young—the beings whose substance an alien evolution had shaped, and whose powers were such as this planet had never bred. And to think that only the day before, Danforth and I had actually looked upon fragments of their millennially fossilised substance . . . and that poor Lake and his party had seen their complete outlines. . . . It is of course impossible for me to relate in proper order the stages by which we picked up what we know of that monstrous chapter of pre-human life. After the first shock of the certain revelation we had to pause a while to recuperate, and it was fully three o'clock before we got started on our actual tour of systematic research. The sculptures in the building we entered were of relatively late date—perhaps two million years ago—as checked up by geological, biological, and astronomical features; and embodied an art which would be called decadent in comparison with that of specimens we found in older buildings after crossing bridges under the glacial sheet. One edifice hewn from the solid rock seemed to go back forty or possibly fifty million years—to the lower Eocene or upper Cretaceous—and contained bas-reliefs of an artistry surpassing anything else, with one tremendous exception, that we encountered. That was, we have since agreed, the oldest domestic structure we traversed.

Were it not for the support of those snapshots[59] soon to be made public, I would refrain from telling what I found and inferred, lest I be confined as a madman. Of course, the infinitely early parts of the patchwork tale—representing the pre-terrestrial life of the star-headed beings on other planets, and in other galaxies, and in other universes—can readily be interpreted as the fantastic mythology of those beings themselves; yet such parts sometimes involved designs and diagrams so uncannily close to the latest findings of mathematics and astrophysics that I scarcely know what to think. Let others judge when they see the photographs I shall publish.

Naturally, no one set of carvings which we encountered told more than a fraction of any connected story; nor did we even begin to come upon the various stages of that story in their proper order. Some of the vast rooms were independent units so far as their designs were concerned, whilst in other cases a continuous chronicle would be carried through a series of rooms and corridors. The best of the maps and diagrams were on the walls of a frightful abyss below even the ancient ground level—a cavern perhaps 200 feet square and sixty feet high, which had almost undoubtedly been an educational centre of some sort. There were many provoking repetitions of the same material in different rooms and buildings, since certain chapters of experience, and certain summaries or phases of racial history, had evidently been favourites with different decorators or dwellers. Sometimes, though, variant versions of the same theme proved useful in settling debatable points and filling in gaps.

I still wonder that we deduced so much in the short time at our disposal. Of course, we even now have only the barest out-

59. "Flashlights" in the original published version—that is, flash photos.

60. See "Beyond the Wall of Sleep," note 7, above, for a discussion of the ether.

61. Again, a reference to Wilmarth, in "The Whisperer in Darkness," above.

line; and much of that was obtained later on from a study of the photographs and sketches we made. It may be the effect of this later study—the revived memories and vague impressions acting in conjunction with his general sensitiveness and with that final supposed horror-glimpse whose essence he will not reveal even to me—which has been the immediate source of Danforth's present breakdown. But it had to be; for we could not issue our warning intelligently without the fullest possible information, and the issuance of that warning is a prime necessity. Certain lingering influences in that unknown antarctic world of disordered time and alien natural law make it imperative that further exploration be discouraged.

VII.

THE FULL STORY, so far as deciphered, will shortly appear in an official bulletin of Miskatonic University. Here I shall sketch only the salient high lights in a formless, rambling way. Myth or otherwise, the sculptures told of the coming of those star-headed things to the nascent, lifeless earth out of cosmic space—their coming, and the coming of many other alien entities such as at certain times embark upon spatial pioneering. They seemed able to traverse the interstellar ether[60] on their vast membraneous wings—thus oddly confirming some curious hill folklore long ago told me by an antiquarian colleague.[61] They had lived under the sea a good deal, building fantastic cities and fighting terrific battles with nameless adversaries by means of intricate devices employing unknown principles of energy. Evidently their scientific and mechanical knowledge far surpassed man's today, though they made use of its more widespread and elaborate forms only when obliged to. Some of the sculptures suggested that they had passed through a stage of mechanised life on other planets, but had receded upon finding its effects emotionally unsatisfying. Their preternatural toughness of organisation and simplicity of natural wants made them peculiarly able to live on a high plane without the more specialised fruits of artificial manufacture, and even without garments, except for occasional protection against the elements.

It was under the sea, at first for food and later for other purposes, that they first created earth-life—using available substances according to long-known methods. The more elaborate experiments came after the annihilation of various cosmic enemies. They had done the same thing on other planets; having manufactured not only necessary foods, but certain multicellular protoplasmic masses capable of moulding their tissues into all sorts of temporary organs under hypnotic influence and thereby forming ideal slaves to perform the heavy work of the community. These viscous masses were without doubt what Abdul Alhazred whispered about as the "shoggoths" in his frightful *Necronomicon*, though even that mad Arab had not hinted that any existed on earth except in the dreams of those who had chewed a certain alkaloidal herb.[62] When the star-headed Old Ones on this planet had synthesised their simple food forms and bred a good supply of shoggoths, they allowed other cell groups to develop into other forms of animal and vegetable life for sundry purposes, extirpating any whose presence became troublesome.

With the aid of the shoggoths, whose expansions could be made to lift prodigious weights, the small, low cities under the sea grew to vast and imposing labyrinths of stone not unlike those which later rose on land. Indeed, the highly adaptable Old Ones had lived much on land in other parts of the universe, and probably retained many traditions of land construction. As we studied the architecture of all these sculptured palæogean[63] cities, including that whose æon-dead corridors we were even then traversing, we were impressed by a curious coincidence which we have not yet tried to explain, even to ourselves. The tops of the buildings, which in the actual city around us had of course been weathered into shapeless ruins ages ago, were clearly displayed in the bas-reliefs; and shewed vast clusters of needle-like spires, delicate finials on certain cone and pyramid apexes, and tiers of thin, horizontal scalloped discs capping cylindrical shafts. This was exactly what we had seen in that monstrous and portentous mirage, cast by a dead city whence such skyline features had been absent for thousands and tens of thousands of years, which loomed on our ignorant eyes across the unfathomed mountains of madness as we first approached poor Lake's ill-fated camp.

Of the life of the Old Ones, both under the sea and after

62. Shoggoths are also mentioned in "The Shadow over Innsmouth" (pp. 573–643, below) and "The Thing on the Doorstep" (pp. 681–710, below). In his notes for *At the Mountains of Madness*, Lovecraft explicitly describes shoggoths (without identifying them as such) as "hideous giant luminous savagely intelligent protoplasm masses composed of plastic jet-black—reflective iridescent bubbles & capable of forming temporary organs adaptable to any medium—air, water, nether spawn of inner earth. Mimic piping voices. 15 ft. diameter as sphere, but viscous like Tsathoggua" (*Something About Cats and Other Pieces*, 188).

63. A Byzantine dynasty from the eleventh century to the seventeenth century CE. Lovecraft evidently means simply "old"—palaeology is the study of antiquities.

64. Crinoids are marine animals, with a mouth on top and feeding arms around the mouth.

65. Heart-shaped structures, like twigs, that form as a pteridophyte grows.

part of them migrated to land, volumes could be written. Those in shallow water had continued the fullest use of the eyes at the ends of their five main head tentacles, and had practiced the arts of sculpture and of writing in quite the usual way—the writing accomplished with a stylus on waterproof waxen surfaces. Those lower down in the ocean depths, though they used a curious phosphorescent organism to furnish light, pieced out their vision with obscure special senses operating through the prismatic cilia on their heads—senses which rendered all the Old Ones partly independent of light in emergencies. Their forms of sculpture and writing had changed curiously during the descent, embodying certain apparently chemical coating processes—probably to secure phosphorescence—which the bas-reliefs could not make clear to us. The beings moved in the sea partly by swimming— using the lateral crinoid[64] arms—and partly by wriggling with the lower tier of tentacles containing the pseudo-feet. Occasionally they accomplished long swoops with the auxiliary use of two or more sets of their fan-like folding wings. On land they locally used the pseudo-feet, but now and then flew to great heights or over long distances with their wings. The many slender tentacles into which the crinoid arms branched were infinitely delicate, flexible, strong, and accurate in muscular-nervous coördination; ensuring the utmost skill and dexterity in all artistic and other manual operations.

The toughness of the things was almost incredible. Even the terrific pressures of the deepest sea-bottoms appeared powerless to harm them. Very few seemed to die at all except by violence, and their burial-places were very limited. The fact that they covered their vertically inhumed dead with five-pointed inscribed mounds set up thoughts in Danforth and me which made a fresh pause and recuperation necessary after the sculptures revealed it. The beings multiplied by means of spores—like vegetable pteridophytes as Lake had suspected—but owing to their prodigious toughness and longevity, and consequent lack of replacement needs, they did not encourage the large-scale development of new prothalli[65] except when they had new regions to colonise. The young matured swiftly, and received an education evidently beyond any standard we can imagine. The prevailing intellectual

"The toughness of the things was almost incredible. Even terrific
pressures were powerless to harm them!" *Astounding Stories* 16, no. 7
(March 1936) (artist: Howard V. Brown)

and æsthetic life was highly evolved, and produced a tenaciously
enduring set of customs and institutions which I shall describe
more fully in my coming monograph. These varied slightly
according to sea or land residence, but had the same foundations
and essentials.

Though able, like vegetables, to derive nourishment from
inorganic substances; they vastly preferred organic and especially

animal food. They ate uncooked marine life under the sea, but cooked their viands on land. They hunted game and raised meat herds—slaughtering with sharp weapons whose odd marks on certain fossil bones our expedition had noted. They resisted all ordinary temperatures marvellously, and in their natural state could live in water down to freezing. When the great chill of the Pleistocene drew on, however—nearly a million years ago—the land dwellers had to resort to special measures including artificial heating; until at last the deadly cold appears to have driven them back into the sea. For their prehistoric flights through cosmic space, legend said, they had absorbed certain chemicals and became almost independent of eating, breathing, or heat conditions; but by the time of the great cold they had lost track of the method. In any case they could not have prolonged the artificial state indefinitely without harm.

Being non-pairing and semi-vegetable in structure, the Old Ones had no biological basis for the family phase of mammal life; but seemed to organise large households on the principles of comfortable space-utility and—as we deduced from the pictured occupations and diversions of co-dwellers—congenial mental association. In furnishing their homes they kept everything in the centre of the huge rooms, leaving all the wall spaces free for decorative treatment. Lighting, in the case of the land inhabitants, was accomplished by a device probably electro-chemical in nature. Both on land and under water they used curious tables, chairs, and couches like cylindrical frames—for they rested and slept upright with folded-down tentacles—and racks for the hinged sets of dotted surfaces forming their books.

Government was evidently complex and probably socialistic, though no certainties in this regard could be deduced from the sculptures we saw. There was extensive commerce, both local and between different cities; certain small, flat counters, five-pointed and inscribed, serving as money. Probably the smaller of the various greenish soapstones found by our expedition were pieces of such currency. Though the culture was mainly urban, some agriculture and much stock-raising existed. Mining and a limited amount of manufacturing were also practiced. Travel was very frequent, but permanent migration seemed relatively rare except for the vast colonising movements by which the race expanded.

For personal locomotion no external aid was used; since in land, air, and water movement alike the Old Ones seemed to possess excessively vast capacities for speed. Loads, however, were drawn by beasts of burden—shoggoths under the sea, and a curious variety of primitive vertebrates in the later years of land existence.

These vertebrates, as well as an infinity of other life forms—animal and vegetable, marine, terrestrial, and aërial—were the products of unguided evolution acting on life-cells made by the Old Ones but escaping beyond their radius of attention. They had been suffered to develop unchecked because they had not come in conflict with the dominant beings. Bothersome forms, of course, were mechanically exterminated.[66] It interested us to see in some of the very last and most decadent sculptures a shambling primitive mammal, used sometimes for food and sometimes as an amusing buffoon by the land dwellers, whose vaguely simian and human foreshadowings were unmistakable. In the building of land cities the huge stone blocks of the high towers were generally lifted by vast-winged pterodactyls of a species heretofore unknown to paleontology.

The persistence with which the Old Ones survived various geologic changes and convulsions of the earth's crust was little short of miraculous. Though few or none of their first cities seem to have remained beyond the Archæan age, there was no interruption in their civilisation or in the transmission of their records. Their original place of advent to the planet was the Antarctic Ocean, and it is likely that they came not long after the matter forming the moon was wrenched from the neighbouring South Pacific.[67] According to one of the sculptured maps, the whole globe was then under water, with stone cities scattered farther and farther from the antarctic as æons passed. Another map shews a vast bulk of dry land around the south pole, where it is evident that some of the beings made experimental settlements, though their main centres were transferred to the nearest sea-bottom. Later maps, which display this land mass as cracking and drifting, and sending certain detached parts northward, uphold in a striking way the theories of continental drift lately advanced by Taylor,[68] Wegener,[69] and Joly.[70]

With the upheaval of new land in the South Pacific tremendous events began. Some of the marine cities were hopelessly

66. Cf. the similar views on eugenics expressed by another alien race in "The Shadow Out of Time," note 38, below. In the late nineteenth century and early twentieth century, Darwin's theories had been transmuted by scientists and some political leaders into the idea that the genetic composition of human populations should be managed. Darwin's cousin Sir Francis Galton (1822–1911), credited with the first modern use of the term "eugenics," in 1883 (to replace "viriculture," which he'd suggested earlier but which he had come to feel was clumsy), reported to the British government in 1909 that one of every 118 persons was "mad, feeble-minded, or idiotic" and recommended "colonies" to separate them from the remainder of the populace. In 1910, Winston Churchill advocated sterilization of these "moral degenerates," and as late as 1934, the Brock Committee, in the so-called Brock Report, recommended voluntary sterilization of mental defectives. (The report's chief signatory, Sir Lawrence Brock, was chairman of Britain's Board of Control for Lunacy and Mental Deficiency.) Lovecraft sympathized with such views (see in particular "The Lurking Fear," written in 1923, for its example of moral degeneracy and suggestions that sterilization could have avoided the problem), and his support of Hitler's eugenics programs, including the "racial cleansing" advocated by Ernst Rüdin and others, is well known. Yet Lovecraft's views, extreme as they may sound today, must be regarded in the context of prevailing cultural attitudes. See, for example, Martin S. Pernick's *The Black Stork: Eugenics and the Death of "Defective" Babies in American Medicine and Motion Pictures Since 1915*. By the 1930s, many American states required the sterilization of "defective" individuals who failed to meet "standards" based on IQ tests, income, education, criminal behavior, and even physical appearance.

The adoption of the eugenicists' viewpoint by Nazi Germany led to its eventual rejection. See generally Elof Axel Carlson's *The Unfit: A History of a Bad Idea* (2001).

67. This theory of the origin of the moon is known as "fission" theory and has been rejected. The first to develop the theory was George H. Darwin, the son of Charles Darwin. In 1878, he postulated that the earth and moon consisted of a common, molten, viscous mass. The sun's tidal action, he argued, triggered "fission," and a mass approximately equal to that of the moon spun off from the rapidly rotating earth. Others later proposed that the basin of the Pacific Ocean was the scar left over from the separation. As late as 1936, the "fission" theory still had widespread popularity (as evidenced by a 1936 U.S. Department of Education script for a radio program on the subject of the moon), and, in the words of Stephen G. Brush, in "Early History of Selenogony" (1986), it had become "translated into popular mythology." In scientific circles, British astronomer Harold Jeffreys announced in 1930 that he had discovered what he considered to be a fatal objection to the theory, and his views were subsequently adopted. Having set sail in September 1930, however, the narrator Dyer may not have had time to catch up on his reading of British scientific journals. Today scientists still have not agreed on a theory of the moon's creation, even with the data provided by lunar exploration.

68. American geologist Frank Bursley Taylor (1869–1938), who proposed the idea of continental drift in 1910. In fact, there were several others who had independently formulated similar thoughts earlier than Taylor—Roberto Mantovani (1889), William H. Pickering (1907), and

shattered, yet that was not the worst misfortune. Another race—a land race of beings shaped like octopi and probably corresponding to fabulous pre-human spawn of Cthulhu—soon began filtering down from cosmic infinity and precipitated a monstrous war which for a time drove the Old Ones wholly back to the sea—a colossal blow in view of the increasing land settlements. Later peace was made, and the new lands were given to the Cthulhu spawn whilst the Old Ones held the sea and the older lands. New land cities were founded—the greatest of them in the antarctic, for this region of first arrival was sacred. From then on, as before, the antarctic remained the centre of the Old Ones' civilisation, and all the discoverable cities built there by the Cthulhu spawn were blotted out. Then suddenly the lands of the Pacific sank again, taking with them the frightful stone city of R'lyeh and all the cosmic octopi, so that the Old Ones were again supreme on the planet except for one shadowy fear about which they did not like to speak. At a rather later age their cities dotted all the land and water areas of the globe—hence the recommendation in my coming monograph that some archæologist make systematic borings with Pabodie's type of apparatus in certain widely separated regions.

The steady trend down the ages was from water to land; a movement encouraged by the rise of new land masses, though the ocean was never wholly deserted. Another cause of the landward movement was the new difficulty in breeding and managing the shoggoths upon which successful sea-life depended. With the march of time, as the sculptures sadly confessed, the art of creating new life from inorganic matter had been lost; so that the Old Ones had to depend on the moulding of forms already in existence. On land the great reptiles proved highly tractable; but the shoggoths of the sea, reproducing by fission and acquiring a dangerous degree of accidental intelligence, presented for a time a formidable problem.

They had always been controlled through the hypnotic suggestion of the Old Ones, and had modelled their tough plasticity into various useful temporary limbs and organs; but now their self-modelling powers were sometimes exercised independently, and in various imitative forms implanted by past suggestion. They had, it seems, developed a semi-stable brain whose separate and occasionally stubborn volition echoed the will of the Old Ones without always obeying it. Sculptured images of these shoggoths filled Danforth and me with horror and loathing. They were normally shapeless entities composed of a viscous jelly which looked like an agglutination of bubbles; and each averaged about fifteen feet in diameter when a sphere. They had, however, a constantly shifting shape and volume; throwing out temporary developments or forming apparent organs of sight, hearing, and speech in imitation of their masters, either spontaneously or according to suggestion.

They seem to have become peculiarly intractable toward the middle of the Permian age, perhaps 150 million years ago, when a veritable war of re-subjugation was waged upon them by the marine Old Ones. Pictures of this war, and of the headless, slime-coated fashion in which the shoggoths typically left their slain victims, held a marvellously fearsome quality despite the intervening abyss of untold ages. The Old Ones had used curious weapons of molecular disturbance against the rebel entities, and in the end had achieved a complete victory. Thereafter the sculptures shewed a period in which shoggoths were tamed and broken by armed Old Ones as the wild horses of the American west were tamed by cowboys. Though during the rebellion the shoggoths had shewn an ability to live out of water, this transition was not encouraged; since their usefulness on land would hardly have been commensurate with the trouble of their management.

During the Jurassic age the Old Ones met fresh adversity in the form of a new invasion from outer space—this time by half-fungous, half-crustacean creatures from a planet identifiable as the remote and recently discovered Pluto; creatures undoubtedly the same as those figuring in certain whispered hill legends of the north,[71] and remembered in the Himalayas as the Mi-Go, or Abominable Snow-Men. To fight these beings the Old Ones attempted, for the first time since their terrene advent, to sally forth again into the planetary ether; but despite all traditional preparations found it no longer possible to leave the earth's atmosphere. Whatever the old secret of interstellar travel had been, it was now definitely lost to the race. In the end the Mi-Go

even Franklin Coxworthy (perhaps as early as 1848).

69. See note 8, above.

70. John Joly (1857–1933) was an Irish physicist who studied methods of determining the length of geological ages. He proposed convection-driven drift, a notion unpopular among geologists. Among his other achievements was extracting radium to be used in the treatment of cancer (radiotherapy).

71. These creatures are described in detail in "The Whisperer in Darkness" (pp. 388–456, above).

drove the Old Ones out of all the northern lands, though they were powerless to disturb those in the sea. Little by little the slow retreat of the elder race to their original antarctic habitat was beginning.

It was curious to note from the pictured battles that both the Cthulhu spawn and the Mi-Go seem to have been composed of matter more widely different from that which we know than was the substance of the Old Ones. They were able to undergo transformations and reintegrations impossible for their adversaries, and seem therefore to have originally come from even remoter gulfs of cosmic space. The Old Ones, but for their abnormal toughness and peculiar vital properties, were strictly material, and must have had their absolute origin within the known space-time continuum; whereas the first sources of the other beings can only be guessed at with bated breath. All this, of course, assuming that the non-terrestrial linkages and the anomalies ascribed to the invading foes are not pure mythology. Conceivably, the Old Ones might have invented a cosmic framework to account for their occasional defeats; since historical interest and pride obviously formed their chief psychological element. It is significant that their annals failed to mention many advanced and potent races of beings whose mighty cultures and towering cities figure persistently in certain obscure legends.

The changing state of the world through long geologic ages appeared with startling vividness in many of the sculptured maps and scenes. In certain cases existing science will require revision, while in other cases its bold deductions are magnificently confirmed. As I have said, the hypothesis of Taylor, Wegener, and Joly that all the continents are fragments of an original antarctic land mass which cracked from centrifugal force and drifted apart over a technically viscous lower surface—an hypothesis suggested by such things as the complementary outlines of Africa and South America, and the way the great mountain chains are rolled and shoved up—receives striking support from this uncanny source.

Maps evidently shewing the Carboniferous world of an hundred million or more years ago displayed significant rifts and chasms destined later to separate Africa from the once continuous realms of Europe (then the Valusia of hellish primal legend),

Asia, the Americas, and the antarctic continent. Other charts—and most significantly one in connexion with the founding fifty million years ago of the vast dead city around us—shewed all the present continents well differentiated. And in the latest discoverable specimen—dating perhaps from the Pliocene age—the approximate world of today appeared quite clearly despite the linkage of Alaska with Siberia, of North America with Europe through Greenland, and of South America[72] with the antarctic continent through Graham Land.[73] In the Carboniferous[74] map the whole globe-ocean floor and rifted land mass alike—bore symbols of the Old Ones' vast stone cities, but in the later charts the gradual recession toward the antarctic became very plain. The final Pliocene specimen shewed no land cities except on the antarctic continent and the tip of South America, nor any ocean cities north of the fiftieth parallel of South Latitude. Knowledge and interest in the northern world, save for a study of coast-lines probably made during long exploration flights on those fan-like membraneous wings, had evidently declined to zero among the Old Ones.

Destruction of cities through the upthrust of mountains, the centrifugal rending of continents, the seismic convulsions of land or sea bottom, and other natural causes was a matter of common record; and it was curious to observe how fewer and fewer replace-

72. There is a legendary lost South American city of Patagonia, known as Ciudad de los Césares or Lin Lin or Trapananda. It was thought to have been occupied by Patagonian giants (or, less interestingly, by lost Spanish explorers).

73. A peninsula on the northern edge of the continent, and the closest part of the continent to South America. This sixteenth-century map made by the Flemish cartographer Abraham Ortelius clearly shows the linkage of South America and Terra Australis ("Land of the South").

74. A geologic period between the Devonian and Permian periods, extending from about 360 million to 300 million years ago. The Earth then was heavily forested (so that many coal beds were formed during this period, providing the name), and it was widely populated by amphibians and arthropods.

This map by Abraham Ortelius, the first map of the Americas, was published in 1589.

[533]

75. Known in German as Prinzregent-Luitpold-Land, it was named by its discoverer in 1911 for the Bavarian prince-regent.

ments were made as the ages wore on. The vast dead megalopolis that yawned around us seemed to be the last general centre of the race; built early in the Cretaceous age after a titanic earth-buckling had obliterated a still vaster predecessor not far distant. It appeared that this general region was the most sacred spot of all, where reputedly the first Old Ones had settled on a primal sea bottom. In the new city—many of whose features we could recognise in the sculptures, but which stretched fully an hundred miles along the mountain-range in each direction beyond the farthest limits of our aërial survey—there were reputed to be pre-served certain sacred stones forming part of the first sea-bottom city, which were thrust up to light after long epochs in the course of the general crumpling of strata.

VIII.

NATURALLY, DANFORTH AND I studied with especial interest and a peculiarly personal sense of awe everything pertaining to the immediate district in which we were. Of this local material there was naturally a vast abundance; and on the tangled ground level of the city we were lucky enough to find a house of very late date whose walls, though somewhat damaged by a neighbouring rift, contained sculptures of decadent workmanship carrying the story of the region much beyond the period of the Pliocene map whence we derived our last general glimpse of the pre-human world. This was the last place we examined in detail, since what we found there gave us a fresh immediate objective.

Certainly, we were in one of the strangest, weirdest, and most terrible of all the corners of earth's globe. Of all existing lands it was infinitely the most ancient; and the conviction grew upon us that this hideous upland must indeed be the fabled nightmare plateau of Leng which even the mad author of the *Necronomicon* was reluctant to discuss. The great mountain chain was tremen-dously long—starting as a low range at Luitpold Land[75] on the coast of Weddell Sea and virtually crossing the entire continent. The really high part stretched in a mighty arc from about Lati-tude 82°, E. Longitude 60° to Latitude 70°, E. Longitude 115°, with its concave side toward our camp and its seaward end in the region of that long, ice-locked coast whose hills were glimpsed by Wilkes[76] and Mawson[77] at the Antarctic Circle.

Yet even more monstrous exaggerations of Nature seemed disturbingly close at hand. I have said that these peaks are higher than the Himalayas, but the sculptures forbid me to say that they are earth's highest. That grim honour is beyond doubt reserved for something which half the sculptures hesitated to record at all, whilst others approached it with obvious repugnance and trepidation. It seems that there was one part of the ancient land— the first part that ever rose from the waters after the earth had flung off the moon and the Old Ones had seeped down from the stars—which had come to be shunned as vaguely and namelessly evil. Cities built there had crumbled before their time, and had been found suddenly deserted. Then when the first great earth-buckling had convulsed the region in the Comanchian age, a frightful line of peaks had shot suddenly up amidst the most appalling din and chaos—and earth had received her loftiest and most terrible mountains.[78]

If the scale of the carvings was correct, these abhorred things must have been much over 40,000 feet high—radically vaster than even the shocking mountains of madness we had crossed. They extended, it appeared, from about Latitude 77°, E. Longitude 70° to Latitude 70°, E. Longitude 100°—less than 300 miles away from the dead city, so that we would have spied their dreaded summits in the dim western distance had it not been for that vague, opalescent haze. Their northern end must likewise be visible from the long Antarctic Circle coast-line at Queen Mary Land.

Some of the Old Ones, in the decadent days, had made strange prayers to those mountains; but none ever went near them or dared to guess what lay beyond. No human eye had ever seen them, and as I studied the emotions conveyed in the carvings, I prayed that none ever might. There are protecting hills along the coast beyond them—Queen Mary and Kaiser Wilhelm Lands—and I thank heaven no one has been able to land and climb those hills. I am not as sceptical about old tales and fears as I used to be, and I do not laugh now at the pre-human sculptor's notion that lightning paused meaningfully now and then at each of the brooding crests, and that an unexplained glow shone from one of those terrible pinnacles all through the long polar night.

76. Charles Wilkes (1798–1877), whose eccentricities and rigidity were said to have been borrowed by Melville in his characterization of Captain Ahab in *Moby-Dick* (see, for instance, Nathaniel Philbrick's *Sea of Glory*), was an American naval officer who led the United States Exploring Expedition from 1838 to 1842. In December 1839, he sailed into the Antarctic Ocean and reported sighting the coast of "an Antarctic continent." It is generally agreed that the continent was first sighted by explorers in 1820, and that the first landing occurred in 1821.

77. Sir Douglas Mawson (1882–1958), Australian geologist. He turned down the opportunity to join Scott's 1910 expedition, choosing instead to lead his own, the so-called Australasian Antarctic Expedition, in 1911 and 1912 to King George V Land and Adélie Land— due south of Australia and then almost completely unexplored. The expedition included a visit to the South Magnetic Pole. Mawson returned to Antarctica in 1929 to 1931 with a joint British, Australian, and New Zealand expedition, the first since Ernest Shackleton's 1922 expedition. (Shackleton's trip was his third and final, during which he suffered a heart attack and died.)

78. Subsequent explorers have failed to find these awesome peaks, and they are invisible to satellite photography. See note 30, above.

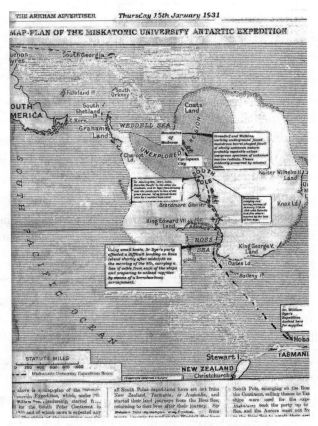

A map of Antarctica showing the location of the Mountains of Madness.
Artist: Karl Beech, copyright © Karl Beech 2012, reprinted with permission

There may be a very real and very monstrous meaning in the old Pnakotic whispers about Kadath in the Cold Waste.

But the terrain close at hand was hardly less strange, even if less namelessly accursed. Soon after the founding of the city the great mountain range became the seat of the principal temples, and many carvings shewed what grotesque and fantastic towers had pierced the sky where now we saw only the curiously clinging cubes and ramparts. In the course of ages the caves had appeared, and had been shaped into adjuncts of the temples. With the advance of still later epochs, all the limestone veins of the region were hollowed out by ground waters, so that the mountains, the foothills, and the plains below them were a veritable network of connected caverns and galleries. Many graphic sculptures told of explorations deep underground, and of the final discovery of the Stygian sunless sea that lurked at earth's bowels.

This vast nighted gulf had undoubtedly been worn by the great river which flowed down from the nameless and horrible westward mountains, and which had formerly turned at the base of the Old Ones' range and flowed beside that chain into the Indian Ocean between Budd and Totten Lands on Wilkes's coast-line. Little by little it had eaten away the limestone hill base at its turning, till at last its sapping currents reached the caverns of the ground waters and joined with them in digging a deeper abyss. Finally its whole bulk emptied into the hollow hills and left the old bed toward the ocean dry. Much of the later city as we now found it had been built over that former bed. The Old Ones, understanding what had happened, and exercising their always keen artistic sense, had carved into ornate pylons those head-lands of the foothills where the great stream began its descent into eternal darkness.

This river, once crossed by scores of noble stone bridges, was plainly the one whose extinct course we had seen in our aëro-plane survey. Its position in different carvings of the city helped us to orient ourselves to the scene as it had been at various stages of the region's age-long, æon-dead history; so that we were able to sketch a hasty but careful map of the salient features—squares, important buildings, and the like—for guidance in further explo-rations. We could soon reconstruct in fancy the whole stupen-dous thing as it was a million or ten million or fifty million years ago, for the sculptures told us exactly what the buildings and mountains and squares and suburbs and landscape setting and luxuriant Tertiary vegetation had looked like. It must have had a marvellous and mystic beauty, and as I thought of it I almost forgot the clammy sense of sinister oppression with which the city's inhuman age and massiveness and deadness and remoteness and glacial twilight had choked and weighed on my spirit. Yet accord-ing to certain carvings the denizens of that city had themselves known the clutch of oppressive terror; for there was a sombre and recurrent type of scene in which the Old Ones were shewn in the act of recoiling affrightedly from some object—never allowed to appear in the design—found in the great river and indicated as having been washed down through waving, vine-draped cycad-forests from those horrible westward mountains.

It was only in the one late-built house with the decadent

carvings that we obtained any foreshadowing of the final calamity leading to the city's desertion. Undoubtedly there must have been many sculptures of the same age elsewhere, even allowing for the slackened energies and aspirations of a stressful and uncertain period; indeed, very certain evidence of the existence of others came to us shortly afterward. But this was the first and only set we directly encountered. We meant to look farther later on; but as I have said, immediate conditions dictated another present objective. There would, though, have been a limit—for after all hope of a long future occupancy of the place had perished among the Old Ones, there could not but have been a complete cessation of mural decoration. The ultimate blow, of course, was the coming of the great cold which once held most of the earth in thrall, and which has never departed from the ill-fated poles—the great cold that, at the world's other extremity, put an end to the fabled lands of Lomar and Hyperborea.

Just when this tendency began in the antarctic, it would be hard to say in terms of exact years. Nowadays we set the beginning of the general glacial periods at a distance of about 500,000 years from the present, but at the poles the terrible scourge must have commenced much earlier. All quantitative estimates are partly guesswork; but it is quite likely that the decadent sculptures were made considerably less than a million years ago, and that the actual desertion of the city was complete long before the conventional opening of the Pleistocene—500,000 years ago—as reckoned in terms of the earth's whole surface.

In the decadent sculptures there were signs of thinner vegetation everywhere, and of a decreased country life on the part of the Old Ones. Heating devices were shewn in the houses, and winter travellers were represented as muffled in protective fabrics. Then we saw a series of cartouches (the continuous band arrangement being frequently interrupted in these late carvings) depicting a constantly growing migration to the nearest refuges of greater warmth—some fleeing to cities under the sea off the far-away coast, and some clambering down through networks of limestone caverns in the hollow hills to the neighbouring black abyss of subterrene waters.

In the end it seems to have been the neighbouring abyss

which received the greatest colonisation. This was partly due, no doubt, to the traditional sacredness of this especial region; but may have been more conclusively determined by the opportunities it gave for continuing the use of the great temples on the honeycombed mountains, and for retaining the vast land city as a place of summer residence and base of communication with various mines. The linkage of old and new abodes was made more effective by means of several gradings and improvements along the connecting routes, including the chiselling of numerous direct tunnels from the ancient metropolis to the black abyss—sharply down-pointing tunnels whose mouths we carefully drew, according to our most thoughtful estimates, on the guide map we were compiling. It was obvious that at least two of these tunnels lay within a reasonable exploring distance of where we were; both being on the mountainward edge of the city, one less than a quarter-mile toward the ancient river-course, and the other perhaps twice that distance in the opposite direction.

The abyss, it seems, had shelving shores of dry land at certain places; but the Old Ones built their new city under water—no doubt because of its greater certainty of uniform warmth. The depth of the hidden sea appears to have been very great, so that the earth's internal heat could ensure its habitability for an indefinite period. The beings seem to have had no trouble in adapting themselves to part-time—and eventually, of course, whole-time—residence under water; since they had never allowed their gill systems to atrophy. There were many sculptures which shewed how they had always frequently visited their submarine kinsfolk elsewhere, and how they had habitually bathed on the deep bottom of their great river. The darkness of inner earth could likewise have been no deterrent to a race accustomed to long antarctic nights.

Decadent though their style undoubtedly was, these latest carvings had a truly epic quality where they told of the building of the new city in the cavern sea. The Old Ones had gone about it scientifically; quarrying insoluble rocks from the heart of the honeycombed mountains, and employing expert workers from the nearest submarine city to perform the construction according to the best methods. These workers brought with them all that was necessary to establish the new venture—shoggoth-tissue

79. Constantine, the emperor of Rome from 306 to 337 CE, stripped the temples of pagan cities to decorate his new capital city of Constantinople, founded in 324 on the site of the former city of Byzantium.

from which to breed stone-lifters and subsequent beasts of burden for the cavern city, and other protoplasmic matter to mould into phosphorescent organisms for lighting purposes.

At last a mighty metropolis rose on the bottom of that Stygian sea; its architecture much like that of the city above, and its workmanship displaying relatively little decadence because of the precise mathematical element inherent in building operations. The newly bred shoggoths grew to enormous size and singular intelligence, and were represented as taking and executing orders with marvellous quickness. They seemed to converse with the Old Ones by mimicking their voices—a sort of musical piping over a wide range, if poor Lake's dissection had indicated aright—and to work more from spoken commands than from hypnotic suggestions as in earlier times. They were, however, kept in admirable control. The phosphorescent organisms supplied light with vast effectiveness, and doubtless atoned for the loss of the familiar polar auroras of the outer-world night.

Art and decoration were pursued, though of course with a certain decadence. The Old Ones seemed to realise this falling off themselves; and in many cases anticipated the policy of Constantine the Great[79] by transplanting especially fine blocks of ancient carving from their land city, just as the emperor, in a similar age of decline, stripped Greece and Asia of their finest art to give his new Byzantine capital greater splendours than its own people could create. That the transfer of sculptured blocks had not been more extensive, was doubtless owing to the fact that the land city was not at first wholly abandoned. By the time total abandonment did occur—and it surely must have occurred before the polar Pleistocene was far advanced—the Old Ones had perhaps become satisfied with their decadent art—or had ceased to recognise the superior merit of the older carvings. At any rate, the æon-silent ruins around us had certainly undergone no wholesale sculptural denudation, though all the best separate statues, like other moveables, had been taken away.

The decadent cartouches and dadoes telling this story were, as I have said, the latest we could find in our limited search. They left us with a picture of the Old Ones shuttling back and forth betwixt the land city in summer and the sea-cavern city in winter, and sometimes trading with the sea-bottom cities off the antarctic coast. By this time the ultimate doom of the land city must have been recognised, for the sculptures shewed many signs of the cold's malign encroachments. Vegetation was declining, and the terrible snows of the winter no longer melted completely even in midsummer. The saurian livestock were nearly all dead, and the mammals were standing it none too well. To keep on with the work of the upper world it had become necessary to adapt some of the amorphous and curiously cold-resistant shoggoths to land life; a thing the Old Ones had formerly been reluctant to do. The great river was now lifeless, and the upper sea had lost most of its denizens except the seals and whales. All the birds had flown away, save only the great, grotesque penguins.

What had happened afterward we could only guess. How long had the new sea-cavern city survived? Was it still down there, a stony corpse in eternal blackness? Had the subterranean waters frozen at last? To what fate had the ocean-bottom cities of the outer world been delivered? Had any of the Old Ones shifted north ahead of the creeping ice cap? Existing geology shews no trace of their presence. Had the frightful Mi-Go been still a menace in the outer land world of the north? Could one be sure of what might or might not linger even to this day in the lightless and unplumbed abysses of earth's deepest waters? Those things had seemingly been able to withstand any amount of pressure— and men of the sea have fished up curious objects at times. And has the killer-whale theory really explained the savage and mysterious scars on antarctic seals noticed a generation ago by Borchgrevingk?[80]

The specimens found by poor Lake did not enter into these guesses, for their geologic setting proved them to have lived at what must have been a very early date in the land city's history. They were, according to their location, certainly not less than thirty million years old; and we reflected that in their day the sea-cavern city, and indeed the cavern itself, had no existence. They would have remembered an older scene, with lush Tertiary vegetation everywhere, a younger land city of flourishing arts around them, and a great river sweeping northward along the base of the mighty mountains toward a far-away tropic ocean.

And yet we could not help thinking about these specimens— especially about the eight perfect ones that were missing from

80. Carsten Egeberg Borchgrevink (1864–1934) was an Anglo-Norwegian polar explorer and a pioneer of modern Antarctic travel. His great Southern Cross Expedition of 1898–1900 was largely sponsored by Sir George Newnes, the publisher of the Sherlock Holmes stories in the *Strand Magazine*. The newspaper the *Queenslander* reported, on February 27, 1897:

One remark that [Borchgrevink] let fall suggests an interesting query. He found that nearly all the seals which the party shot on Campbell Island and its vicinity had scars and scratches on their skin. Now, Sir John Ross had noticed the same fact. Ross explained it on the basis that they had been inflicted by the large, sharp tusks with which the sea leopards are provided, and that these wounds had been received in civil war among themselves. Borchgrevink's theory, on the other hand, is that these scars are due to some enemy of a different species than the seal. The wounds are not like the ordinary cuts inflicted by a tusk or tooth; they are of a straight, narrow shape, varying from 2in. to 20in. in length, and where several of these cuts appear on one animal they are too far from one another to have possibly been produced by the numerous sharp teeth of a seal. . . . That they were inflicted by some animal of a superior and more dangerous kind than the seals themselves is evident from the fact that the scars never appear about the head and neck, which undoubtedly would have been the case if any battles were fought among themselves. This may explain the strange scarcity of seals in this particular locality, though they abound elsewhere. But the query suggests itself—What like is this mysterious monster, and where is his habitat?

Borchgrevink went on to speculate that he might even find a new human race residing in the Antarctic. However, a study by Edward A. "Uncle Bill" Wilson, published as *Mammalia* in 1907, concluded that *Orcinus orca*, also known as *Orca gladiator*, or the killer whale, was responsible for the scarring. More recently, mammalogists think that leopard seals may be responsible, not orcas.

81. This is the end of the second installment published in *Astounding Stories*.

Lake's hideously ravaged camp. There was something abnormal about that whole business—the strange things we had tried so hard to lay to somebody's madness—those frightful graves—the amount *and nature* of the missing material—Gedney—the unearthly toughness of those archaic monstrosities, and the queer vital freaks the sculptures now shewed the race to have. . . . Danforth and I had seen a good deal in the last few hours, and were prepared to believe and keep silent about many appalling and incredible secrets of primal Nature.[81]

IX.

I HAVE SAID that our study of the decadent sculptures brought about a change in our immediate objective. This of course had to do with the chiselled avenues to the black inner world, of whose existence we had not known before, but which we were now eager to find and traverse. From the evident scale of the carvings we deduced that a steeply descending walk of about a mile through either of the neighbouring tunnels would bring us to the brink of the dizzy, sunless cliffs above the great abyss; down whose side adequate paths, improved by the Old Ones, led to the rocky shore of the hidden and nighted ocean. To behold this fabulous gulf in stark reality was a lure which seemed impossible of resistance once we knew of the thing—yet we realised we must begin the quest at once if we expected to include it on our present flight.

It was now 8 P.M., and we had not enough battery replacements to let our torches burn on forever. We had done so much of our studying and copying below the glacial level that our battery supply had had at least five hours of nearly continuous use; and despite the special dry cell formula would obviously be good for only about four more—though by keeping one torch unused, except for especially interesting or difficult places, we might manage to eke out a safe margin beyond that. It would not do to be without a light in these Cyclopean catacombs, hence in order to make the abyss trip we must give up all further mural deciphering. Of course we intended to revisit the place for days and

Cover of *At the Mountains of Madness: A Graphic Novel.*
Sterling Publishing, 2010 (artist: I. N. J. Culbard)

perhaps weeks of intensive study and photography—curiosity having long ago got the better of horror—but just now we must hasten.

Our supply of trail-blazing paper was far from unlimited, and we were reluctant to sacrifice spare notebooks or sketching paper to augment it; but we did let one large notebook go. If worse came to worst we could resort to rock-chipping—and of course it would be possible, even in case of really lost direction, to work up to full daylight by one channel or another if granted sufficient time for plentiful trial and error. So at last we set off eagerly in the indicated direction of the nearest tunnel.

According to the carvings from which we had made our map, the desired tunnel-mouth could not be much more than a quarter-mile from where we stood; the intervening space shewing solid-looking buildings quite likely to be penetrable still at a subglacial level. The opening itself would be in the basement—on the angle nearest the foothills—of a vast five-pointed structure of evidently public and perhaps ceremonial nature, which we tried to identify from our aërial survey of the ruins.

No such structure came to our minds as we recalled our flight, hence we concluded that its upper parts had been greatly damaged, or that it had been totally shattered in an ice-rift we had noticed. In the latter case the tunnel would probably turn out to be choked, so that we would have to try the next nearest one— the one less than a mile to the north. The intervening river-course prevented our trying any of the more southerly tunnels on this trip; and indeed, if both of the neighbouring ones were choked it was doubtful whether our batteries would warrant an attempt on the next northerly one—about a mile beyond our second choice.

As we threaded our dim way through the labyrinth with the aid of map and compass—traversing rooms and corridors in every stage of ruin or preservation, clambering up ramps, crossing upper floors and bridges and clambering down again, encountering choked doorways and piles of debris, hastening now and then along finely preserved and uncannily immaculate stretches, taking false leads and retracing our way (in such cases removing the blind paper trail we had left), and once in a while striking the bottom of an open shaft through which daylight poured or trickled down—we were repeatedly tantalised by the sculptured walls along our route. Many must have told tales of immense historical importance, and only the prospect of later visits reconciled us to the need of passing them by. As it was, we slowed down once in a while and turned on our second torch. If we had had more films we would certainly have paused briefly to photograph certain bas-reliefs, but time-consuming hand copying was clearly out of the question.

I come now once more to a place where the temptation to hesitate, or to hint rather than state, is very strong. It is necessary, however, to reveal the rest in order to justify my course in discouraging further exploration.[82] We had wormed our way very close to the computed site of the tunnel's mouth—having crossed a second-story bridge to what seemed plainly the tip of a pointed wall, and descended to a ruinous corridor especially rich in decadently elaborate and apparently ritualistic sculptures of late workmanship—when, about 8:30 P.M., Danforth's keen young nostrils gave us the first hint of something unusual. If we had had a dog with us, I suppose we would have been warned before. At first we could not precisely say what was wrong with the formerly crystal-pure air, but after a few seconds our memories reacted only too definitely. Let me try to state the thing without flinching. There was an odour—and that odour was vaguely, subtly, and unmistakably akin to what had nauseated us upon opening the insane grave of the horror poor Lake had dissected.

Of course the revelation was not as clearly cut at the time as it sounds now. There were several conceivable explanations, and we did a good deal of indecisive whispering. Most important of all, we did not retreat without further investigation; for having come this far, we were loath to be balked by anything short of certain disaster. Anyway, what we must have suspected was altogether too wild to believe. Such things did not happen in any normal world. It was probably sheer irrational instinct which made us dim our single torch—tempted no longer by the decadent and sinister sculptures that leered menacingly from the oppressive walls—and which softened our progress to a cautious tiptoeing and crawling over the increasingly littered floor and heaps of debris.

Danforth's eyes as well as nose proved better than mine, for it was likewise he who first noticed the queer aspect of the debris after we had passed many half-choked arches leading to chambers and corridors on the ground level. It did not look quite as it ought after countless thousands of years of desertion, and when we cautiously turned on more light we saw that a kind of swath seemed to have been lately tracked through it. The irregular nature of the litter precluded any definite marks, but in the smoother places there were suggestions of the dragging of heavy

82. The preceding four sentences were omitted from the *Astounding Stories* publication.

objects. Once we thought there was a hint of parallel tracks as if of runners. This was what made us pause again.

It was during that pause that we caught—simultaneously this time—the other odour ahead. Paradoxically, it was both a less frightful and a more frightful odour—less frightful intrinsically, but infinitely appalling in this place under the known circumstances . . . unless, of course, Gedney. . . . For the odour was the plain and familiar one of common petrol—every-day gasoline.

Our motivation after that is something I will leave to psychologists. We knew now that some terrible extension of the camp horrors must have crawled into this nighted burial place of the æons, hence could not doubt any longer the existence of nameless conditions—present or at least recent just ahead. Yet in the end we did let sheer burning curiosity—or anxiety—or auto-hypnotism—or vague thoughts of responsibility toward Gedney—or what not—drive us on. Danforth whispered again of the print he thought he had seen at the alley-turning in the ruins above; and of the faint musical piping—potentially of tremendous significance in the light of Lake's dissection report despite its close resemblance to the cave-mouth echoes of the windy peaks—which he thought he had shortly afterward half heard from unknown depths below. I, in my turn, whispered of how the camp was left—of what had disappeared, and of how the madness of a lone survivor might have conceived the inconceivable—a wild trip across the monstrous mountains and a descent into the unknown primal masonry—

But we could not convince each other, or even ourselves, of anything definite. We had turned off all light as we stood still, and vaguely noticed that a trace of deeply filtered upper day kept the blackness from being absolute. Having automatically begun to move ahead, we guided ourselves by occasional flashes from our torch. The disturbed debris formed an impression we could not shake off, and the smell of gasoline grew stronger. More and more ruin met our eyes and hampered our feet, until very soon we saw that the forward way was about to cease. We had been all too correct in our pessimistic guess about that rift glimpsed from the air. Our tunnel quest was a blind one, and we were not even going to be able to reach the basement out of which the abyss-ward aperture opened.

The torch, flashing over the grotesquely carven walls of the blocked corridor in which we stood, shewed several doorways in various states of obstruction; and from one of them the gasoline odour—quite submerging that other hint of odour—came with especial distinctness. As we looked more steadily, we saw that beyond a doubt there had been a slight and recent clearing away of debris from that particular opening. Whatever the lurking horror might be, we believed the direct avenue toward it was now plainly manifest. I do not think anyone will wonder that we waited an appreciable time before making any further motion.

And yet, when we did venture inside that black arch, our first impression was one of anticlimax. For amidst the littered expanse of that sculptured crypt—a perfect cube with sides of about twenty feet—there remained no recent object of instantly discernible size; so that we looked instinctively, though in vain, for a farther doorway. In another moment, however, Danforth's sharp vision had descried a place where the floor debris had been disturbed; and we turned on both torches full strength. Though what we saw in that light was actually simple and trifling, I am none the less reluctant to tell of it because of what it implied. It was a rough levelling of the debris, upon which several small objects lay carelessly scattered, and at one corner of which a considerable amount of gasoline must have been spilled lately enough to leave a strong odour even at this extreme super-plateau altitude. In other words, it could not be other than a sort of camp—a camp made by questing beings who like us had been turned back by the unexpectedly choked way to the abyss.

Let me be plain. The scattered objects were, so far as substance was concerned, all from Lake's camp; and consisted of tin cans as queerly opened as those we had seen at that ravaged place, many spent matches, three illustrated books more or less curiously smudged, an empty ink bottle with its pictorial and instructional carton, a broken fountain pen, some oddly snipped fragments of fur and tent-cloth, a used electric battery with circular of directions, a folder that came with our type of tent heater, and a sprinkling of crumpled papers. It was all bad enough, but when we smoothed out the papers and looked at what was on them we felt we had come to the worst. We had found certain inexplicably blotted papers at the camp which might have prepared us, yet the effect of the sight down there in the pre-human vaults of a nightmare city was almost too much to bear.

A mad Gedney might have made the groups of dots in imitation of those found on the greenish soapstones, just as the dots on those insane five-pointed grave-mounds might have been made; and he might conceivably have prepared rough, hasty sketches—varying in their accuracy or lack of it—which outlined the neighbouring parts of the city and traced the way from a circularly represented place outside our previous route—a place we identified as a great cylindrical tower in the carvings and as a vast circular gulf glimpsed in our aërial survey—to the present five-pointed structure and the tunnel-mouth therein. He might, I repeat, have prepared such sketches; for those before us were quite obviously compiled as our own had been from late sculptures somewhere in the glacial labyrinth, though not from the ones which we had seen and used. But what this art-blind bungler could never have done was to execute those sketches in a strange and assured technique perhaps superior, despite haste and carelessness, to any of the decadent carvings from which they were taken—the characteristic and unmistakable technique of the Old Ones themselves in the dead city's heyday.

There are those who will say Danforth and I were utterly mad not to flee for our lives after that; since our conclusions were now—notwithstanding their wildness—completely fixed, and of a nature I need not even mention to those who have read my account as far as this. Perhaps we were mad—for have I not said those horrible peaks were mountains of madness? But I think I can detect something of the same spirit—albeit in a less extreme form—in the men who stalk deadly beasts through African jungles to photograph them or study their habits. Half-paralysed with terror though we were, there was nevertheless fanned within us a blazing flame of awe and curiosity which triumphed in the end.

Of course we did not mean to face that—or those—which we knew had been there, but we felt that they must be gone by now. They would by this time have found the other neighbouring entrance to the abyss, and have passed within to whatever night-black fragments of the past might await them in the ultimate gulf—the ultimate gulf they had never seen. Or if that entrance, too, was blocked, they would have gone on to the north seeking another. They were, we remembered, partly independent of light.

Looking back to that moment, I can scarcely recall just what precise form our new emotions took—just what change of immediate objective it was that so sharpened our sense of expectancy. We certainly did not mean to face what we feared—yet I will not deny that we may have had a lurking, unconscious wish to spy certain things from some hidden vantage-point. Probably we had not given up our zeal to glimpse the abyss itself, though there was interposed a new goal in the form of that great circular place shewn on the crumpled sketches we had found. We had at once recognised it as a monstrous cylindrical tower figuring in the very earliest carvings, but appearing only as a prodigious round aperture from above. Something about the impressiveness of its rendering, even in these hasty diagrams, made us think that its sub-glacial levels must still form a feature of peculiar importance. Perhaps it embodied architectural marvels as yet unencountered by us. It was certainly of incredible age according to the sculptures in which it figured—being indeed among the first things built in the city. Its carvings, if preserved, could not but be highly significant. Moreover, it might form a good present link with the upper world—a shorter route than the one we were so carefully blazing, and probably that by which those others had descended.

At any rate, the thing we did was to study the terrible sketches—which quite perfectly confirmed our own—and start back over the indicated course to the circular place; the course which our nameless predecessors must have traversed twice before us. The other neighbouring gate to the abyss would lie beyond that. I need not speak of our journey—during which we continued to leave an economical trail of paper—for it was precisely the same in kind as that by which we had reached the cul de sac; except that it tended to adhere more closely to the ground level and even descend to basement corridors. Every now and then we could trace certain disturbing marks in the debris or litter under foot; and after we had passed outside the radius of the gasoline scent we were again faintly conscious—spasmodically—of that more hideous and more persistent scent. After the way had branched from our former course, we sometimes gave the rays of our single torch a furtive sweep along the walls; noting in almost every case the well-nigh omnipresent sculptures, which indeed seem to have formed a main æsthetic outlet for the Old Ones.

About 9:30 P.M., while traversing a vaulted corridor whose increasingly glaciated floor seemed somewhat below the ground level and whose roof grew lower as we advanced, we began to see strong daylight ahead and were able to turn off our torch. It appeared that we were coming to the vast circular place, and that our distance from the upper air could not be very great. The corridor ended in an arch surprisingly low for these megalithic ruins, but we could see much through it even before we emerged. Beyond there stretched a prodigious round space—fully 200 feet in diameter—strown with debris and containing many choked archways corresponding to the one we were about to cross. The walls were—in available spaces—boldly sculptured into a spiral band of heroic proportions; and displayed, despite the destructive weathering caused by the openness of the spot, an artistic splendour far beyond anything we had encountered before. The littered floor was quite heavily glaciated, and we fancied that the true bottom lay at a considerably lower depth.

But the salient object of the place was the titanic stone ramp which, eluding the archways by a sharp turn outward into the open floor, wound spirally up the stupendous cylindrical wall like an inside counterpart of those once climbing outside the monstrous towers or ziggurats of antique Babylon. Only the rapidity of our flight, and the perspective which confounded the descent with the tower's inner wall, had prevented our noticing this feature from the air, and thus caused us to seek another avenue to the sub-glacial level. Pabodie might have been able to tell what sort of engineering held it in place, but Danforth and I could merely admire and marvel. We could see mighty stone corbels and pillars here and there, but what we saw seemed inadequate to the function performed. The thing was excellently preserved up to the present top of the tower—a highly remarkable circumstance in view of its exposure—and its shelter had done much to protect the bizarre and disturbing cosmic sculptures on the walls.

As we stepped out into the awesome half-daylight of this monstrous cylinder-bottom—fifty million years old, and without doubt the most primally ancient structure ever to meet our eyes—we saw that the ramp-traversed sides stretched dizzily up to a height of fully sixty feet. This, we recalled from our aërial survey, meant an outside glaciation of some forty feet; since the yawning gulf we had seen from the plane had been at the top of an approximately twenty-foot mound of crumbled masonry, somewhat sheltered for three-fourths of its circumference by the massive curving walls of a line of higher ruins. According to the sculptures the original tower had stood in the centre of an immense circular plaza; and had been perhaps 500 or 600 feet high, with tiers of horizontal discs near the top, and a row of needle-like spires along the upper rim. Most of the masonry had obviously toppled outward rather than inward—a fortunate happening, since otherwise the ramp might have been shattered and the whole interior choked. As it was, the ramp shewed sad battering; whilst the choking was such that all the archways at the bottom seemed to have been recently half-cleared.

It took us only a moment to conclude that this was indeed the route by which those others had descended, and that this would be the logical route for our own ascent despite the long trail of paper we had left elsewhere. The tower's mouth was no farther from the foothills and our waiting plane than was the great terraced building we had entered, and any further sub-glacial exploration we might make on this trip would lie in this general region. Oddly, we were still thinking about possible later trips—even after all we had seen and guessed. Then as we picked our way cautiously over the debris of the great floor, there came a sight which for the time excluded all other matters.

It was the neatly huddled array of three sledges in that farther angle of the ramp's lower and outward-projecting course which had hitherto been screened from our view. There they were—the three sledges missing from Lake's camp—shaken by a hard usage which must have included forcible dragging along great reaches of snowless masonry and debris, as well as much hand portage over utterly unnavigable places. They were carefully and intelligently packed and strapped, and contained things memorably familiar enough—the gasoline stove, fuel cans, instrument cases, provision tins, tarpaulins obviously bulging with books, and some bulging with less obvious contents—everything derived from Lake's equipment.

After what we had found in that other room, we were in a

83. The *Astounding Stories* version reads, "a waste utterly and irrevocably void of every vestige of normal life."

measure prepared for this encounter. The really great shock came when we stepped over and undid one tarpaulin whose outlines had peculiarly disquieted us. It seems that others as well as Lake had been interested in collecting typical specimens; for there were two here, both stiffly frozen, perfectly preserved, patched with adhesive plaster where some wounds around the neck had occurred, and wrapped with patent care to prevent further damage. They were the bodies of young Gedney and the missing dog.

X.

MANY PEOPLE WILL probably judge us callous as well as mad for thinking about the northward tunnel and the abyss so soon after our sombre discovery, and I am not prepared to say that we would have immediately revived such thoughts but for a specific circumstance which broke in upon us and set up a whole new train of speculations. We had replaced the tarpaulin over poor Gedney and were standing in a kind of mute bewilderment when the sounds finally reached our consciousness—the first sounds we had heard since descending out of the open where the mountain wind whined faintly from its unearthly heights. Well-known and mundane though they were, their presence in this remote world of death was more unexpected and unnerving than any grotesque or fabulous tones could possibly have been—since they gave a fresh upsetting to all our notions of cosmic harmony.

Had it been some trace of that bizarre musical piping over a wide range which Lake's dissection report had led us to expect in those others—and which, indeed, our overwrought fancies had been reading into every wind-howl we had heard since coming on the camp horror—it would have had a kind of hellish congruity with the æon-dead region around us. A voice from other epochs belongs in a graveyard of other epochs. As it was, however, the noise shattered all our profoundly seated adjustments—all our tacit acceptance of the inner antarctic as a waste as utterly and irrevocably void of every vestige of normal life as the sterile disc of the moon.[83] What we heard was not the fabulous note of any buried blasphemy of elder earth from whose supernal toughness an age-denied polar sun had evoked a monstrous response.

Instead, it was a thing so mockingly normal and so unerringly familiarised by our sea days off Victoria Land and our camp days at McMurdo Sound that we shuddered to think of it here, where such things ought not to be. To be brief—it was simply the raucous squawking of a penguin.

The muffled sound floated from sub-glacial recesses nearly opposite to the corridor whence we had come—regions manifestly in the direction of that other tunnel to the vast abyss. The presence of a living water-bird in such a direction—in a world whose surface was one of age-long and uniform lifelessness—could lead to only one conclusion; hence our first thought was to verify the objective reality of the sound. It was, indeed, repeated; and seemed at times to come from more than one throat. Seeking its source, we entered an archway from which much debris had been cleared; resuming our trail-blazing—with an added paper-supply taken with curious repugnance from one of the tarpaulin bundles on the sledges—when we left daylight behind.

As the glaciated floor gave place to a litter of detritus we plainly discerned some curious, dragging tracks; and once Danforth found a distinct print of a sort whose description would be only too superfluous. The course indicated by the penguin cries was precisely what our map and compass prescribed as an approach to the more northerly tunnel-mouth, and we were glad to find that a bridgeless thoroughfare on the ground and basement levels seemed open. The tunnel, according to the chart, ought to start from the basement of a large pyramidal structure which we seemed vaguely to recall from our aërial survey as remarkably well preserved. Along our path the single torch shewed a customary profusion of carvings, but we did not pause to examine any of these.

Suddenly a bulky white shape loomed up ahead of us, and we flashed on the second torch. It is odd how wholly this new quest had turned our minds from earlier fears of what might lurk near. Those other ones, having left their supplies in the great circular place, must have planned to return after their scouting trip toward or into the abyss; yet we had now discarded all caution concerning them as completely as if they had never existed. This white, waddling thing was fully six feet high, yet we seemed to realise at once that it was not one of those others. They were larger and

84. Bones of a 25-million-year-old penguin, named Kairuku, four feet two in height, were discovered in New Zealand in 1977 and reconstructed in 2012, according to results published in the *Journal of Vertebrate Paleontology*. Of course, the skeletal remains did not display either albinism or virtual eyelessness.

dark, and according to the sculptures their motion over land surfaces was a swift, assured matter despite the queerness of their sea-born tentacle equipment. But to say that the white thing did not profoundly frighten us would be vain. We were indeed clutched for an instant by a primitive dread almost sharper than the worst of our reasoned fears regarding those others. Then came a flash of anticlimax as the white shape sidled into a lateral archway to our left to join two others of its kind which had summoned it in raucous tones. For it was only a penguin—albeit of a huge, unknown species larger than the greatest of the known king penguins, and monstrous in its combined albinism and virtual eyelessness.[84]

When we had followed the thing into the archway and turned both our torches on the indifferent and unheeding group of three we saw that they were all eyeless albinos of the same unknown and gigantic species. Their size reminded us of some of the archaic penguins depicted in the Old Ones' sculptures, and it did not take us long to conclude that they were descended from the same stock—undoubtedly surviving through a retreat to some warmer inner region whose perpetual blackness had destroyed their pigmentation and atrophied their eyes to mere useless slits. That their present habitat was the vast abyss we sought, was not for a moment to be doubted; and this evidence of the gulf's continued warmth and habitability filled us with the most curious and subtly perturbing fancies.

We wondered, too, what had caused these three birds to venture out of their usual domain. The state and silence of the great dead city made it clear that it had at no time been an habitual seasonal rookery, whilst the manifest indifference of the trio to our presence made it seem odd that any passing party of those others should have startled them. Was it possible that those others had taken some aggressive action or tried to increase their meat supply? We doubted whether that pungent odour which the dogs had hated could cause an equal antipathy in these penguins, since their ancestors had obviously lived on excellent terms with the Old Ones—an amicable relationship which must have survived in the abyss below as long as any of the Old Ones remained. Regretting—in a flareup of the old spirit of pure science—that we could not photograph these anomalous creatures, we shortly left them to their squawking and pushed on toward the abyss whose openness was now so positively proved to us, and whose exact direction occasional penguin tracks made clear.

Not long afterward a steep descent in a long, low, doorless, and peculiarly sculptureless corridor led us to believe that we were approaching the tunnel mouth at last. We had passed two more penguins, and heard others immediately ahead.[85] Then the corridor ended in a prodigious open space which made us gasp involuntarily—a perfect inverted hemisphere, obviously deep underground; fully an hundred feet in diameter and fifty feet high, with low archways opening around all parts of the circumference but one, and that one yawning cavernously with a black arched aperture which broke the symmetry of the vault to a height of nearly fifteen feet. It was the entrance to the great abyss.

In this vast hemisphere, whose concave roof was impressively though decadently carved to a likeness of the primordial celestial dome, a few albino penguins waddled—aliens there, but indifferent and unseeing. The black tunnel yawned indefinitely off at a steep, descending grade, its aperture adorned with grotesquely chiselled jambs and lintel. From that cryptical mouth we fancied a current of slightly warmer air, and perhaps even a suspicion of vapour proceeded; and we wondered what living entities other than penguins the limitless void below, and the contiguous honeycombings of the land and the titan mountains, might conceal. We wondered, too, whether the trace of mountain-top smoke at first suspected by poor Lake, as well as the odd haze we had ourselves perceived around the rampart-crowned peak, might not be caused by the tortuous-channelled rising of some such vapour from the unfathomed regions of earth's core.

Entering the tunnel, we saw that its outline was—at least at the start—about fifteen feet each way; sides, floor, and arched roof composed of the usual megalithic masonry. The sides were sparsely decorated with cartouches of conventional designs in a late, decadent style; and all the construction and carving were marvellously well preserved. The floor was quite clear, except for a slight detritus bearing outgoing penguin tracks and the inward tracks of those others. The farther one advanced, the warmer it became; so that we were soon unbuttoning our heavy garments. We wondered whether there were any actually igneous manifestations below, and whether the waters of that sunless sea were

85. In *Astounding Stories*, the sentence read, "We had heard two more penguins."

hot. After a short distance the masonry gave place to solid rock, though the tunnel kept the same proportions and presented the same aspect of carved regularity. Occasionally its varying grade became so steep that grooves were cut in the floor. Several times we noted the mouths of small lateral galleries not recorded in our diagrams; none of them such as to complicate the problem of our return, and all of them welcome as possible refuges in case we met unwelcome entities on their way back from the abyss. The nameless scent of such things was very distinct. Doubtless it was suicidally foolish to venture into that tunnel under the known conditions, but the lure of the unplumbed is stronger in certain persons than most suspect—indeed, it was just such a lure which had brought us to this unearthly polar waste in the first place. We saw several penguins as we passed along, and speculated on the distance we would have to traverse. The carvings had led us to expect a steep downhill walk of about a mile to the abyss, but our previous wanderings had shewn us that matters of scale were not wholly to be depended on.

After about a quarter of a mile that nameless scent became greatly accentuated, and we kept very careful track of the various lateral openings we passed. There was no visible vapour as at the mouth, but this was doubtless due to the lack of contrasting cooler air. The temperature was rapidly ascending, and we were not surprised to come upon a careless heap of material shudderingly familiar to us. It was composed of furs and tent-cloth taken from Lake's camp, and we did not pause to study the bizarre forms into which the fabrics had been slashed. Slightly beyond this point we noticed a decided increase in the size and number of the side galleries, and concluded that the densely honeycombed region beneath the higher foothills must now have been reached. The nameless scent was now curiously mixed with another and scarcely less offensive odour—of what nature we could not guess, though we thought of decaying organisms and perhaps unknown subterrene fungi. Then came a startling expansion of the tunnel for which the carvings had not prepared us—a broadening and rising into a lofty, natural-looking elliptical cavern with a level floor; some 75 feet long and 50 broad, and with many immense side-passages leading away into cryptical darkness.

Though this cavern was natural in appearance, an inspection

with both torches suggested that it had been formed by the artificial destruction of several walls between adjacent honeycombings. The walls were rough, and the high vaulted roof was thick
with stalactites; but the solid rock floor had been smoothed off,
and was free from all debris, detritus, or even dust to a positively
abnormal extent. Except for the avenue through which we had
come, this was true of the floors of all the great galleries opening off from it; and the singularity of the condition was such as
to set us vainly puzzling. The curious new fœtor which had supplemented the nameless scent was excessively pungent here; so
much so that it destroyed all trace of the other. Something about
this whole place, with its polished and almost glistening floor,
struck us as more vaguely baffling and horrible than any of the
monstrous things we had previously encountered.

The regularity of the passage immediately ahead, as well as
the larger proportion of penguin-droppings there, prevented all
confusion as to the right course amidst this plethora of equally
great cave-mouths. Nevertheless we resolved to resume our paper
trail-blazing if any further complexity should develop; for dust
tracks, of course, could no longer be expected. Upon resuming
our direct progress we cast a beam of torchlight over the tunnel
walls—and stopped short in amazement at the supremely radical change which had come over the carvings in this part of
the passage. We realised, of course, the great decadence of the
Old Ones' sculpture at the time of the tunnelling, and had
indeed noticed the inferior workmanship of the arabesques in
the stretches behind us. But now, in this deeper section beyond
the cavern, there was a sudden difference wholly transcending
explanation—a difference in basic nature as well as in mere quality, and involving so profound and calamitous a degradation of
skill that nothing in the hitherto observed rate of decline could
have led one to expect it.

This new and degenerate work was coarse, bold, and wholly
lacking in delicacy of detail. It was counter-sunk with exaggerated depth in bands following the same general line as the sparse
cartouches of the earlier sections, but the height of the reliefs
did not reach the level of the general surface. Danforth had the
idea that it was a second carving—a sort of palimpsest formed
after the obliteration of a previous design. In nature it was wholly

86. Palmyra (Tidmor or Tadmor) was an ancient city in Syria, northeast of Damascus, that flourished more than 3,000 years ago. Sometimes called "Syria's Stonehenge," its sculpture was distinctive. The Bible (2 Chronicles 8:4) credits Solomon (whose reign was probably 970 to 931 BCE) with "building" the city, but he may have merely fortified a preexisting city; Tadmor is also mentioned in older Sumerian archives.

87. This and the two preceding sentences do not appear in *Astounding Stories*.

88. In *Astounding Stories*, the sentence ends here, and the following sentence is omitted.

decorative and conventional; and consisted of crude spirals and angles roughly following the quintile mathematical tradition of the Old Ones, yet seeming more like a parody than a perpetuation of that tradition. We could not get it out of our minds that some subtly but profoundly alien element had been added to the æsthetic feeling behind the technique—an alien element, Danforth guessed, that was responsible for the manifestly laborious substitution. It was like, yet disturbingly unlike, what we had come to recognise as the Old Ones' art; and I was persistently reminded of such hybrid things as the ungainly Palmyrene sculptures[86] fashioned in the Roman manner. That others had recently noticed this belt of carving was hinted by the presence of a used torch battery on the floor in front of one of the most characteristic designs.[87]

Since we could not afford to spend any considerable time in study, we resumed our advance after a cursory look;[88] though frequently casting beams over the walls to see if any further decorative changes developed. Nothing of the sort was perceived, though the carvings were in places rather sparse because of the numerous mouths of smooth-floored lateral tunnels. We saw and heard fewer penguins, but thought we caught a vague suspicion of an infinitely distant chorus of them somewhere deep within the earth. The new and inexplicable odour was abominably strong, and we could detect scarcely a sign of that other nameless scent. Puffs of visible vapour ahead bespoke increasing contrasts in temperature, and the relative nearness of the sunless sea-cliffs of the great abyss. Then, quite unexpectedly, we saw certain obstructions on the polished floor ahead—obstructions which were quite definitely not penguins—and turned on our second torch after making sure that the objects were quite stationary.

XI.

STILL ANOTHER TIME have I come to a place where it is very difficult to proceed. I ought to be hardened by this stage; but there are some experiences and intimations which scar too deeply to permit of healing, and leave only such an added sensitiveness that memory reinspires all the original horror. We saw, as I have said, certain obstructions on the polished floor ahead; and I may add that our nostrils were assailed almost simultaneously by a very curious intensification of the strange prevailing fœtor, now quite plainly mixed with the nameless stench of those others which had gone before us. The light of the second torch left no doubt of what the obstructions were, and we dared approach them only because we could see, even from a distance, that they were quite as past all harming power as had been the six similar specimens unearthed from the monstrous star-mounded graves at poor Lake's camp.

They were, indeed, as lacking in completeness as most of those we had unearthed—though it grew plain from the thick, dark-green pool gathering around them that their incompleteness was of infinitely greater recency. There seemed to be only four of them, whereas Lake's bulletins would have suggested no less than eight as forming the group which had preceded us. To find them in this state was wholly unexpected, and we wondered what sort of monstrous struggle had occurred down here in the dark.

Penguins, attacked in a body, retaliate savagely with their beaks; and our ears now made certain the existence of a rookery far beyond. Had those others disturbed such a place and aroused murderous pursuit? The obstructions did not suggest it, for penguin beaks against the tough tissues Lake had dissected could hardly account for the terrible damage our approaching glance was beginning to make out. Besides, the huge blind birds we had seen appeared to be singularly peaceful.

Had there, then, been a struggle among those others, and were the absent four responsible? If so, where were they? Were they close at hand and likely to form an immediate menace to us? We glanced anxiously at some of the smooth-floored lateral passages as we continued our slow and frankly reluctant approach. Whatever the conflict was, it had clearly been that which had frightened the penguins into their unaccustomed wandering. It must, then, have arisen near that faintly heard rookery in the incalculable gulf beyond, since there were no signs that any birds had normally dwelt here. Perhaps, we reflected, there had been a hideous running fight, with the weaker party seeking to get back to the cached sledges when their pursuers finished them. One could picture the dæmoniac fray between namelessly monstrous entities as it surged out of the black abyss with great clouds of frantic penguins squawking and scurrying ahead.

I say that we approached those sprawling and incomplete obstructions slowly and reluctantly. Would to heaven we had never approached them at all, but had run back at top speed out of that blasphemous tunnel with the greasily smooth floors and the degenerate murals aping and mocking the things they had superseded—run back, before we had seen what we did see, and before our minds were burned with something which will never let us breathe easily again!

Both of our torches were turned on the prostrate objects, so that we soon realised the dominant factor in their incompleteness. Mauled, compressed, twisted, and ruptured as they were, their chief common injury was total decapitation. From each one the tentacled starfish-head had been removed; and as we drew near we saw that the manner of removal looked more like some hellish tearing or suction than like any ordinary form of cleavage. Their noisome dark-green ichor formed a large, spreading pool; but its stench was half overshadowed by that newer and stranger stench, here more pungent than at any other point along our route. Only when we had come very close to the sprawling obstructions could we trace that second, unexplainable fœtor to any immediate source—and the instant we did so Danforth, remembering certain very vivid sculptures of the Old Ones' history in the Permian age 150 million years ago, gave vent to a nerve-tortured cry which echoed hysterically through that vaulted and archaic passage with the evil palimpsest carvings.

I came only just short of echoing his cry myself; for I had seen those primal sculptures, too, and had shudderingly admired the way the nameless artist had suggested that hideous slime-coating found on certain incomplete and prostrate Old Ones—those whom the frightful shoggoths had characteristically slain and sucked to a ghastly headlessness in the great war of re-subjugation. They were infamous, nightmare sculptures even when telling of age-old, bygone things; for shoggoths and their work ought not to be seen by human beings or portrayed by any beings. The mad author of the *Necronomicon* had nervously tried to swear that none had been bred on this planet, and that only drugged dreamers had ever conceived them. Formless protoplasm able to mock and reflect all forms and organs and processes—viscous agglutinations of bubbling cells—rubbery fifteen-foot spheroids infinitely plastic and ductile—slaves of suggestion, builders of cities—more and more sullen, more and more intelligent, more and more amphibious, more and more imitative—Great God! What madness made even those blasphemous Old Ones willing to use and to carve such things?

And now, when Danforth and I saw the freshly glistening and reflectively iridescent black slime which clung thickly to those headless bodies and stank obscenely with that new unknown odour whose cause only a diseased fancy could envisage—clung to those bodies and sparkled less voluminously on a smooth part of the accursedly re-sculptured wall *in a series of grouped dots*—we understood the quality of cosmic fear to its uttermost depths. It was not fear of those four missing others—for all too well did we suspect they would do no harm again. Poor devils! After all, they were not evil things of their kind. They were the men of another age and another order of being. Nature had played a hellish jest on them—as it will on any others that human madness, callousness, or cruelty may hereafter drag up in that hideously dead or sleeping polar waste—and this was their tragic homecoming. They had not been even savages—for what indeed had they done? That awful awakening in the cold of an unknown epoch—perhaps an attack by the furry, frantically barking quadrupeds, and a dazed defence against them and the equally frantic white simians with the queer wrappings and paraphernalia . . . poor Lake, poor Gedney . . . and poor Old Ones! Scientists to the last—what had they done that we would not have done in their place? God, what intelligence and persistence! What a facing of the incredible, just as those carven kinsmen and forbears had faced things only a little less incredible! Radiates, vegetables, monstrosities, star-spawn—whatever they had been, they were men!

They had crossed the icy peaks on whose templed slopes they had once worshipped and roamed among the tree ferns. They had found their dead city brooding under its curse, and had read its carven latter days as we had done. They had tried to reach their living fellows in fabled depths of blackness they had

89. See note 17, above. Lovecraft thus implies that Poe may have had access to the truth about Antarctica. Poe was likely inspired by the 1828–29 American Antarctic Exploring Expedition led by Benjamin Pendleton and Nathaniel Palmer and the landing on the continent by John Davis, of New Haven, Connecticut, in 1831. Poe's story was also informed by his admiration for his contemporary Jeremiah N. Reynolds (1799–1858), an author, scientist, and explorer. In 1837, Poe favorably reviewed Reynolds's book *Address, on the Subject of a Surveying and Exploring Expedition to the Pacific Ocean and South Seas* (New York, 1836) first delivered to the House of Representatives on April 2, 1836, and he borrowed seven hundred words of the book for a chapter of *Pym*. (Poe also borrowed heavily from other travel writers.) Reynolds espoused the "hollow earth" theory outlined by John Cleves Symmes in his novel *Symzonia: A Voyage of Discovery* (1820).

never seen—and what had they found? All this flashed in unison through the thoughts of Danforth and me as we looked from those headless, slime-coated shapes to the loathsome palimpsest sculptures and the diabolical dot-groups of fresh slime on the wall beside them—looked and understood what must have triumphed and survived down there in the Cyclopean water-city of that nighted, penguin-fringed abyss, whence even now a sinister curling mist had begun to belch pallidly as if in answer to Danforth's hysterical scream.

The shock of recognising that monstrous slime and headlessness had frozen us into mute, motionless statues, and it is only through later conversations that we have learned of the complete identity of our thoughts at that moment. It seemed æons that we stood there, but actually it could not have been more than ten or fifteen seconds. That hateful, pallid mist curled forward as if veritably driven by some remoter advancing bulk—and then came a sound which upset much of what we had just decided, and in so doing broke the spell and enabled us to run like mad past squawking, confused penguins over our former trail back to the city, along ice-sunken megalithic corridors to the great open circle, and up that archaic spiral ramp in a frenzied automatic plunge for the sane outer air and light of day.

The new sound, as I have intimated, upset much that we had decided; because it was what poor Lake's dissection had led us to attribute to those we had just judged dead. It was, Danforth later told me, precisely what he had caught in infinitely muffled form when at that spot beyond the alley-corner above the glacial level; and it certainly had a shocking resemblance to the wind-pipings we had both heard around the lofty mountain caves. At the risk of seeming puerile I will add another thing, too; if only because of the surprising way Danforth's impression chimed with mine. Of course common reading is what prepared us both to make the interpretation, though Danforth has hinted at queer notions about unsuspected and forbidden sources to which Poe may have had access when writing his *Arthur Gordon Pym* a century ago.[89] It will be remembered that in that fantastic tale there is a word of unknown but terrible and prodigious significance connected with the antarctic and screamed eternally by the gigantic spec-

"And then came a sound—a horrible sound—which
enabled us to run like mad for the same outer air—"
Astounding Stories 17, no. 2 (April 1936)
(artist: Howard V. Brown)

90. In Pym's narrative, it is not only the
white birds that cry out "Tekeli-li!," it is
also the natives. The natives' calls are in
response to flapping white objects that
they may have confused with the birds.

trally snowy birds of that malign region's core. "*Tekeli-li! Tekeli-li!*"[90] That, I may admit, is exactly what we thought we heard conveyed by that sudden sound behind the advancing white mist—that insidious musical piping over a singularly wide range.

We were in full flight before three notes or syllables had been uttered, though we knew that the swiftness of the Old Ones would enable any scream-roused and pursuing survivor of the slaughter to overtake us in a moment if it really wished to do so. We had a vague hope, however, that non-aggressive conduct and a display of kindred reason might cause such a being to spare us in case of capture; if only from scientific curiosity. After all, if such an one had nothing to fear for itself it would have no motive in harming us. Concealment being futile at this juncture, we used our torch for a running glance behind, and perceived that the mist was thinning. Would we see, at last, a complete and living specimen of those others? Again came that insidious musical piping—"*Tekeli-li! Tekeli-li!*" Then, noting that we were actually gaining on our pursuer, it occurred to us that the entity might be wounded. We could take no chances, however, since it was very obviously approaching in answer to Danforth's scream rather than in flight from any other entity. The timing was too close to admit of doubt. Of the whereabouts of that less conceivable and less mentionable nightmare—that fœtid, unglimpsed mountain of slime-spewing protoplasm whose race had conquered the abyss and sent land pioneers to re-carve and squirm through the burrows of the hills—we could form no guess; and it cost us a genuine pang to leave this probably crippled Old One—perhaps a lone survivor—to the peril of recapture and a nameless fate.

Thank heaven we did not slacken our run. The curling mist had thickened again, and was driving ahead with increased speed; whilst the straying penguins in our rear were squawking and screaming and displaying signs of a panic really surprising in view of their relatively minor confusion when we had passed them. Once more came that sinister, wide-ranged piping—"*Tekeli-li! Tekeli-li!*" We had been wrong. The thing was not wounded, but had merely paused on encountering the bodies of its fallen kindred and the hellish slime inscription above them. We could never know what that dæmon message was—but those burials at Lake's camp had shewn how much importance the beings attached to their dead. Our recklessly used torch now revealed ahead of us the large open cavern where various ways converged, and we were glad to be leaving those morbid palimpsest sculptures—almost felt even when scarcely seen—behind.

Another thought which the advent of the cave inspired was the possibility of losing our pursuer at this bewildering focus of large galleries. There were several of the blind albino penguins in the open space, and it seemed clear that their fear of the oncoming entity was extreme to the point of unaccountability. If at that point we dimmed our torch to the very lowest limit of travelling need, keeping it strictly in front of us, the frightened squawking motions of the huge birds in the mist might muffle our footfalls, screen our true course, and somehow set up a false lead. Amidst the churning, spiralling fog the littered and unglistening floor of the main tunnel beyond this point, as differing from the other morbidly polished burrows, could hardly form a highly distinguishing feature; even, so far as we could conjecture, for those indicated special senses which made the Old Ones partly though imperfectly independent of light in emergencies. In fact, we were somewhat apprehensive lest we go astray ourselves in our haste. For we had, of course, decided to keep straight on toward the dead city; since the consequences of loss in those unknown foothill honeycombings would be unthinkable.

The fact that we survived and emerged is sufficient proof that the thing did take a wrong gallery whilst we providentially hit on the right one. The penguins alone could not have saved us, but in conjunction with the mist they seem to have done so. Only a benign fate kept the curling vapours thick enough at the right moment, for they were constantly shifting and threatening to vanish. Indeed, they did lift for a second just before we emerged from the nauseously re-sculptured tunnel into the cave; so that we actually caught one first and only half-glimpse of the oncoming entity as we cast a final, desperately fearful glance backward before dimming the torch and mixing with the penguins in the hope of dodging pursuit. If the fate which screened us was benign, that which gave us the half-glimpse was infinitely the opposite; for to that flash of semi-vision can be traced a full half of the horror which has ever since haunted us.

Our exact motive in looking back again was perhaps no more than the immemorial instinct of the pursued to gauge the nature and course of its pursuer; or perhaps it was an automatic attempt to answer a subconscious question raised by one of our senses. In the midst of our flight, with all our faculties centred on the problem of escape, we were in no condition to observe and analyse details; yet even so our latent brain-cells must have wondered at the message brought them by our nostrils. Afterward we realised what it was—that our retreat from the fœtid slime coating on those headless obstructions, and the coincident approach of the pursuing entity, had not brought us the exchange of stenches which logic called for. In the neighbourhood of the prostrate

91. Orpheus, according to Virgil, descended to the underworld to bring his wife, Eurydice, back to the living. When he won her release, Hades and Persephone instructed him not to look back even once during the ascent. When he did so, Eurydice was forever lost to death. According to the Bible, Lot and his family, on fleeing the destruction of Sodom, were told by angels not to look back, and when his wife did so in disobedience of these orders, she was turned to a pillar of salt (Genesis 19).

92. This and the four previous sentences are omitted from *Astounding Stories*.

things that new and lately unexplainable fœtor had been wholly dominant; but by this time it ought to have largely given place to the nameless stench associated with those others. This it had not done—for instead, the newer and less bearable smell was now virtually undiluted, and growing more and more poisonously insistent each second.

So we glanced back—simultaneously, it would appear; though no doubt the incipient motion of one prompted the imitation of the other. As we did so we flashed both torches full strength at the momentarily thinned mist; either from sheer primitive anxiety to see all we could, or in a less primitive but equally unconscious effort to dazzle the entity before we dimmed our light and dodged among the penguins of the labyrinth-centre ahead. Unhappy act! Not Orpheus himself, or Lot's wife,[91] paid much more dearly for a backward glance. And again came that shocking, wide-ranged piping—"*Tekeli-li! Tekeli-li!*"

I might as well be frank—even if I cannot bear to be quite direct—in stating what we saw; though at the time we felt that it was not to be admitted even to each other. The words reaching the reader can never even suggest the awfulness of the sight itself. It crippled our consciousness so completely that I wonder we had the residual sense to dim our torches as planned, and to strike the right tunnel toward the dead city. Instinct alone must have carried us through—perhaps better than reason could have done; though if that was what saved us, we paid a high price. Of reason we certainly had little enough left.[92]

Danforth was totally unstrung, and the first thing I remember of the rest of the journey was hearing him light-headedly chant an hysterical formula in which I alone of mankind could have found anything but insane irrelevance. It reverberated in falsetto echoes among the squawks of the penguins; reverberated through the vaultings ahead, and—thank God—through the now empty vaultings behind. He could not have begun it at once—else we would not have been alive and blindly racing. I shudder to think of what a shade of difference in his nervous reactions might have brought.

"South Station Under—Washington Under—Park Street Under—Kendall—Central—Harvard. . . ." The poor fellow was chanting the familiar stations of the Boston-Cambridge tunnel that burrowed through our peaceful native soil thousands of miles away in New England, yet to me the ritual had neither irrelevance nor home-feeling. It had only horror, because I knew unerringly the monstrous, nefandous[93] analogy that had suggested it. We had expected, upon looking back, to see a terrible and incredibly moving entity if the mists were thin enough; but of that entity we had formed a clear idea. What we did see—for the mists were indeed all too malignly thinned—was something altogether different, and immeasurably more hideous and detestable. It was the utter, objective embodiment of the fantastic novelist's "thing that should not be"; and its nearest comprehensible analogue is a vast, onrushing subway train as one sees it from a station platform—the great black front looming colossally out of infinite subterraneous distance, constellated with strangely coloured lights and filling the prodigious burrow as a piston fills a cylinder.

But we were not on a station platform. We were on the track ahead as the nightmare plastic column of fœtid black iridescence oozed tightly onward through its fifteen-foot sinus; gathering unholy speed and driving before it a spiral, re-thickening cloud of the pallid abyss-vapour. It was a terrible, indescribable thing vaster than any subway train—a shapeless congeries of protoplasmic bubbles, faintly self-luminous, and with myriads of temporary eyes forming and unforming as pustules of greenish light all over the tunnel-filling front that bore down upon us, crushing the frantic penguins and slithering over the glistening floor that it and its kind had swept so evilly free of all litter. Still came that eldritch, mocking cry—"*Tekeli-li! Tekeli-li!*" And at last we remembered that the dæmoniac shoggoths—given life, thought, and plastic organ patterns solely by the Old Ones, and having no language save that which the dot-groups expressed—*had likewise no voice save the imitated accents of their bygone masters.*

XII.

DANFORTH AND I have recollections of emerging into the great sculptured hemisphere and of threading our back trail through the Cyclopean rooms and corridors of the dead city; yet these are

93. Unfit to speak of; unmentionable.

94. This and the preceding three sentences are omitted from *Astounding Stories*.

95. This sentence does not appear in *Astounding Stories*.

96. This and the succeeding sentence are omitted from *Astounding Stories*.

purely dream-fragments involving no memory of volition, details, or physical exertion. It was as if we floated in a nebulous world or dimension without time, causation, or orientation. The grey half-daylight of the vast circular space sobered us somewhat; but we did not go near those cached sledges or look again at poor Gedney and the dog. They have a strange and titanic mausoleum, and I hope the end of this planet will find them still undisturbed.

It was while struggling up the colossal spiral incline that we first felt the terrible fatigue and short breath which our race through the thin plateau air had produced; but not even the fear of collapse could make us pause before reaching the normal outer realm of sun and sky.[94] There was something vaguely appropriate about our departure from those buried epochs; for as we wound our panting way up the sixty-foot cylinder of primal masonry we glimpsed beside us a continuous procession of heroic sculptures in the dead race's early and undecayed technique—a farewell from the Old Ones, written fifty million years ago.

Finally scrambling out at the top, we found ourselves on a great mound of tumbled blocks, with the curved walls of higher stonework rising westward, and the brooding peaks of the great mountains shewing beyond the more crumbled structures toward the east. The low antarctic sun of midnight peered redly from the southern horizon through rifts in the jagged ruins, and the terrible age and deadness of the nightmare city seemed all the starker by contrast with such relatively known and accustomed things as the features of the polar landscape.[95] The sky above was a churning and opalescent mass of tenuous ice-vapours, and the cold clutched at our vitals. Wearily resting the outfit-bags to which we had instinctively clung throughout our desperate flight, we rebuttoned our heavy garments for the stumbling climb down the mound and the walk through the æon-old stone maze to the foothills where our aëroplane waited.[96] Of what had set us fleeing from the darkness of earth's secret and archaic gulfs we said nothing at all.

In less than a quarter of an hour we had found the steep grade to the foothills—the probable ancient terrace—by which we had descended, and could see the dark bulk of our great plane amidst the sparse ruins on the rising slope ahead. Half way uphill toward our goal we paused for a momentary breathing spell, and turned to look again at the fantastic palæogean tangle of incredible stone shapes below us—once more outlined mystically against an unknown west. As we did so we saw that the sky beyond had lost its morning haziness; the restless ice-vapours having moved up to the zenith, where their mocking outlines seemed on the point of settling into some bizarre pattern which they feared to make quite definite or conclusive.

There now lay revealed on the ultimate white horizon behind the grotesque city a dim, elfin line of pinnacled violet whose needle-pointed heights loomed dream-like against the beckoning rose colour of the western sky. Up toward this shimmering rim sloped the ancient table-land, the depressed course of the bygone river traversing it as an irregular ribbon of shadow. For a second we gasped in admiration of the scene's unearthly cosmic beauty, and then vague horror began to creep into our souls. For this far violet line could be nothing else than the terrible mountains of the forbidden land—highest of earth's peaks and focus of earth's evil; harbourers of nameless horrors and Archæan secrets; shunned and prayed to by those who feared to carve their meaning; untrodden by any living thing of earth, but visited by the sinister lightnings and sending strange beams across the plains in the polar night—beyond doubt the unknown archetype of that dreaded Kadath in the Cold Waste beyond abhorrent Leng, whereof unholy primal legends hint evasively. We were the first human beings ever to see them—and I hope to God we may be the last.[97]

If the sculptured maps and pictures in that pre-human city had told truly, these cryptic violet mountains could not be much less than 300 miles away; yet none the less sharply did their dim elfin essence jut above that remote and snowy rim, like the serrated edge of a monstrous alien planet about to rise into unaccustomed heavens. Their height, then, must have been tremendous beyond all known comparison—carrying them up into tenuous atmospheric strata peopled by such gaseous wraiths as rash flyers have barely lived to whisper of after unexplainable falls.[98] Looking at them, I thought nervously of certain sculptured hints of what the great bygone river had washed down into the city from their accursed slopes—and wondered how much sense and how much folly had lain in the fears of those Old Ones who carved them so reticently. I recalled how their northerly end must come

97. This sentence does not appear in *Astounding Stories*.

98. Similar encounters are reported in Arthur Conan Doyle's "The Horror of the Heights," published in November 1913 in the *Strand Magazine* and, in the United States, *Everybody's Magazine*. Note that this sentence does not appear in *Astounding Stories*.

99. This sentence does not appear in *Astounding Stories*.

near the coast at Queen Mary Land, where even at that moment Sir Douglas Mawson's expedition was doubtless working less than a thousand miles away; and hoped that no evil fate would give Sir Douglas and his men a glimpse of what might lie beyond the protecting coastal range. Such thoughts formed a measure of my overwrought condition at the time—and Danforth seemed to be even worse.

Yet long before we had passed the great star-shaped ruin and reached our plane our fears had become transferred to the lesser but vast enough range whose re-crossing lay ahead of us. From these foothills the black, ruin-crusted slopes reared up starkly and hideously against the east, again reminding us of those strange Asian paintings of Nicholas Roerich; and when we thought of the damnable honeycombs inside them, and of the frightful amorphous entities that might have pushed their fœtidly squirming way even to the topmost hollow pinnacles, we could not face without panic the prospect of again sailing by those suggestive skyward cave-mouths where the wind made sounds like an evil musical piping over a wide range. To make matters worse, we saw distinct traces of local mist around several of the summits— as poor Lake must have done when he made that early mistake about volcanism—and thought shiveringly of that kindred mist from which we had just escaped; of that, and of the blasphemous, horror-fostering abyss whence all such vapours came.

All was well with the plane, and we clumsily hauled on our heavy flying furs. Danforth got the engine started without trouble, and we made a very smooth takeoff over the nightmare city. Below us the primal Cyclopean masonry spread out as it had done when first we saw it—so short, yet infinitely long, a time ago—and we began rising and turning to test the wind for our crossing through the pass.[99] At a very high level there must have been great disturbance, since the ice-dust clouds of the zenith were doing all sorts of fantastic things; but at 24,000 feet, the height we needed for the pass, we found navigation quite practicable. As we drew close to the jutting peaks the wind's strange piping again became manifest, and I could see Danforth's hands trembling at the controls. Rank amateur though I was, I thought at that moment that I might be a better navigator than he in effecting the dangerous crossing between pinnacles; and when I made motions to change seats and take over his duties he did not protest. I tried to keep all my skill and self-possession about me, and stared at the sector of reddish farther sky betwixt the walls of the pass[100]—resolutely refusing to pay attention to the puffs of mountain-top vapour, and wishing that I had wax-stopped ears like Ulysses' men off the Sirens' coast[101] to keep that disturbing wind-piping from my consciousness.

But Danforth, released from his piloting and keyed up to a dangerous nervous pitch, could not keep quiet. I felt him turning and wriggling about as he looked back at the terrible receding city, ahead at the cave-riddled, cube-barnacled peaks, sidewise at the bleak sea of snowy, rampart-strown foothills, and upward at the seething, grotesquely clouded sky. It was then, just as I was trying to steer safely through the pass, that his mad shrieking brought us so close to disaster by shattering my tight hold on myself and causing me to fumble helplessly with the controls for a moment. A second afterward my resolution triumphed and we made the crossing safely—yet I am afraid that Danforth will never be the same again.

I have said that Danforth refused to tell me what final horror made him scream out so insanely—a horror which, I feel sadly sure, is mainly responsible for his present breakdown. We had snatches of shouted conversation above the wind's piping and the engine's buzzing as we reached the safe side of the range and swooped slowly down toward the camp, but that had mostly to do with the pledges of secrecy we had made as we prepared to leave the nightmare city. Certain things, we had agreed, were not for people to know and discuss lightly—and I would not speak of them now but for the need of heading off that Starkweather-Moore Expedition, and others, at any cost. It is absolutely necessary, for the peace and safety of mankind, that some of earth's dark, dead corners and unplumbed depths be let alone; lest sleeping abnormalities wake to resurgent life, and blasphemously surviving nightmares squirm and splash out of their black lairs to newer and wider conquests.[102]

All that Danforth has ever hinted is that the final horror was a mirage. It was not, he declares, anything connected with the cubes and caves of echoing, vaporous, wormily-honeycombed mountains of madness which we crossed; but a single fantastic,

100. The sentence ends here in *Astounding Stories*.

101. Homer recounts this tale. The Sirens of legend could lure men to their deaths with their singing. Odysseus, who desired to sail near the coast of the Sirens, had his men stop their ears with wax to prevent them from falling under their spell. Desiring to hear their reputedly lovely voices for himself, Odysseus had his men tie him to the mast.

102. This and the previous sentence do not appear in *Astounding Stories*.

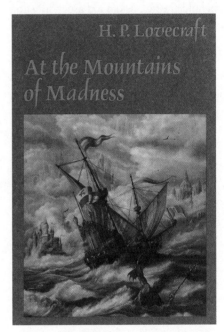

Cover of *At the Mountains of Madness*. Sauk City, WI: Arkham House Publishers, 1964 (artist: Raymond Bayless)

103. A *pharos* is a lighthouse; the Pharos of Alexandria was one of the seven wonders of the ancient world, according to tourist guidebooks of the age.

104. A little self-promotion: Lovecraft thought "The Colour Out of Space," published in 1927, quite the best of his longer tales.

105. In poetry and folklore, the moon-ladder is often identified as the staircase for angels. In the Bible, Jacob, son of Isaac and Rebekah, "dreamed, and behold, a ladder set up on the earth, and the top of it reached to heaven; and behold the angels of God ascending and descending on it" (Genesis 28:12, King James Version).

dæmoniac glimpse, among the churning zenith clouds, of what lay back of those other violet westward mountains which the Old Ones had shunned and feared. It is very probable that the thing was a sheer delusion born of the previous stresses we had passed through, and of the actual though unrecognised mirage of the dead transmontane city experienced near Lake's camp the day before; but it was so real to Danforth that he suffers from it still.

He has on rare occasions whispered disjointed and irresponsible things about "the black pit," "the carven rim," "the proto-shoggoths," "the windowless solids with five dimensions," "the nameless cylinder," "the elder pharos,"[103] "Yog-Sothoth," "the primal white jelly," "the colour out of space,"[104] "the wings," "the eyes in darkness," "the moon-ladder,"[105] "the original, the eternal, the undying," and other bizarre conceptions; but when he is fully himself he repudiates all this and attributes it to his curious and macabre reading of earlier years. Danforth, indeed, is known to be among the few who have ever dared go completely through that worm-riddled copy of the *Necronomicon* kept under lock and key in the college library.

The higher sky, as we crossed the range, was surely vaporous and disturbed enough; and although I did not see the zenith I can well imagine that its swirls of ice-dust may have taken strange forms. Imagination, knowing how vividly distant scenes can sometimes be reflected, refracted, and magnified by such layers of restless cloud, might easily have supplied the rest—and of course Danforth did not hint any of those specific horrors till after his memory had had a chance to draw on his bygone reading. He could never have seen so much in one instantaneous glance.

At the time his shrieks were confined to the repetition of a single mad word of all too obvious source: "*Tekeli-li! Tekeli-li!*"

The Shadow over Innsmouth[1]

Another of Lovecraft's masterpieces, "The Shadow over Innsmouth" explores a dark New England village that is home to an alien race, the Deep Ones. Lovecraft's notes for the story identify the otherwise unnamed narrator as one Robert Olmstead.[2] The tragic story of Olmstead and his very personal discovery of decay and degeneration includes both a long folkloric tale in dialect (much in fashion in the 1930s) and a narrative of nail-biting suspense. Although the theme of the danger of miscegenation may express Lovecraft's personal racist views, ultimately the evil depicted is less the result of mere miscegenation than the product of humans' greed and lust for immortality.

I.

During the winter of 1927–28 officials of the Federal government made a strange and secret investigation of certain conditions in the ancient Massachusetts seaport of Innsmouth. The public first learned of it in February, when a vast series of raids and arrests occurred, followed by the deliberate burning and dynamiting—under suitable precautions—of an enormous number of crumbling, worm-eaten, and supposedly empty houses along the abandoned waterfront. Uninquiring souls let this occurrence pass as one of the major clashes in a spasmodic war on liquor.[3]

Keener news-followers, however, wondered at the prodigious number of arrests, the abnormally large force of men used in making them, and the secrecy surrounding the disposal of the prisoners. No trials, or even definite charges were reported; nor were any of the captives seen thereafter in the regular gaols of the nation. There were vague statements about disease and concentration camps,[4] and later about dispersal in various naval and

1. Written in November–December 1931, the story first appeared in a small-press publication by Visionary Publishing Co. (Everett, PA) in 1936; it ran in abridged form, after Lovecraft's death, in *Weird Tales* 36, no. 3 (January 1942), 6–33, where it was introduced with this reading line: "Unspeakable monstrousness overhung the crumbling, stench-cursed town of Innsmouth . . . and folks there had somehow got out of the idea of dying. . . ."

2. Lovecraft's notes and an early draft of the story are found in the book *Something About Cats and Other Pieces*, a collection of writings by and about Lovecraft published by Arkham House in 1949. The book also includes a family tree for Olmstead, showing his descent from Captain Obed Marsh. See note 48, below.

3. Prohibition, as the U.S. antiliquor movement was eventually known, became federal law with ratification

of the Eighteenth Amendment to the United States Constitution, on January 16, 1919. The amendment prohibited the "manufacture, sale, or transportation of intoxicating liquors within, the importation thereof into, or the exportation thereof from the United States. . . ." The "great social and economic experiment," as it was called by President Herbert Hoover, lasted until December 5, 1933, when the Twenty-first Amendment to the Constitution was ratified, repealing the Eighteenth Amendment and leaving the regulation of intoxicating liquors to the individual states.

4. Not Nazi concentration camps, of course, but these horror chambers were not invented by them: In the Boer War at the end of the nineteenth century, Field Marshal Horatio Herbert Kitchener, 1st Earl Kitchener, known as Lord Kitchener and commonly called Herbert, commander in chief of the British forces, saw systematic cruelty as his most effective option. He set up corrugated stone-and-iron blockhouses along the railway lines as lookout posts, then cleared the land by burning farms, killing livestock, and herding women and children into "concentration camps" (a technique probably learned from the Spanish, who used the tactic of *reconcentrado* against Cuban guerrillas in 1895) that were watched over by the blockhouses. By the end of 1901, more than 100,000 Boers were living in the inadequately supplied camps; some 20,000 inmates, most of them children, died of disease brought on by unsanitary conditions. Kitchener's strategy, despite the international outrage it provoked, worked, and a new weapon entered the vocabulary of terror. Arthur Conan Doyle defended Britain's use of the tactics in *The War in South Africa: Its Cause and Conduct* (1902) and received a knighthood at least partially in reward for this propaganda.

military prisons, but nothing positive ever developed. Innsmouth itself was left almost depopulated, and is even now only beginning to shew signs of a sluggishly revived existence.

Complaints from many liberal organisations were met with long confidential discussions, and representatives were taken on trips to certain camps and prisons. As a result, these societies became surprisingly passive and reticent. Newspaper men were harder to manage, but seemed largely to coöperate with the government in the end. Only one paper—a tabloid always discounted because of its wild policy—mentioned the deep-diving submarine that discharged torpedoes downward in the marine abyss just beyond Devil Reef. That item, gathered by chance in a haunt of sailors, seemed indeed rather far-fetched; since the low, black reef lies a full mile and a half out from Innsmouth Harbour.

People around the country and in the nearby towns muttered a great deal among themselves, but said very little to the outer world. They had talked about dying and half-deserted Innsmouth for nearly a century, and nothing new could be wilder or more hideous than what they had whispered and hinted years before. Many things had taught them secretiveness, and there was now no need to exert pressure on them. Besides, they really knew very little; for wide salt marshes, desolate and unpeopled, keep neighbours off from Innsmouth on the landward side.

But at last I am going to defy the ban on speech about this thing. Results, I am certain, are so thorough that no public harm save a shock of repulsion could ever accrue from a hinting of what was found by those horrified raiders at Innsmouth. Besides, what was found might possibly have more than one explanation. I do not know just how much of the whole tale has been told even to me, and I have many reasons for not wishing to probe deeper. For my contact with this affair has been closer than that of any other layman, and I have carried away impressions which are yet to drive me to drastic measures.

It was I who fled frantically out of Innsmouth in the early morning hours of July 16, 1927, and whose frightened appeals for government inquiry and action brought on the whole reported episode. I was willing enough to stay mute while the affair was fresh and uncertain; but now that it is an old story, with public interest and curiosity gone, I have an odd craving to whisper about those few frightful hours in that ill-rumoured and evilly shadowed seaport of death and blasphemous abnormality. The mere telling helps me to restore confidence in my own faculties; to reassure myself that I was not simply the first to succumb to a contagious nightmare hallucination. It helps me, too, in making up my mind regarding a certain terrible step which lies ahead of me.

I never heard of Innsmouth till the day before I saw it for the first and—so far—last time. I was celebrating my coming of age by a tour of New England—sightseeing, antiquarian, and genealogical—and had planned to go directly from ancient Newburyport[5] to Arkham,[6] whence my mother's family was derived. I had no car, but was travelling by train, trolley and motor-coach, always seeking the cheapest possible route. In Newburyport they told me that the steam train was the thing to take to Arkham; and it was only at the station ticket-office, when I demurred at the high fare, that I learned about Innsmouth. The stout, shrewd-faced agent, whose speech shewed him to be no local man, seemed sympathetic toward my efforts at economy, and made a suggestion that none of my other informants had offered.

"You could take that old bus, I suppose," he said with a certain hesitation, "but it ain't thought much of hereabouts. It goes through Innsmouth—you may have heard about that—and so the people don't like it. Run by an Innsmouth fellow—Joe Sargent—but never gets any custom from here, or Arkham either, I guess. Wonder it keeps running at all. I s'pose it's cheap enough, but I never see more'n two or three people in it—nobody but those Innsmouth folks. Leaves the Square—front of Hammond's Drug Store—at 10 A.M. and 7 P.M. unless they've changed lately. Looks like a terrible rattletrap—I've never ben on it."

That was the first I ever heard of shadowed Innsmouth. Any reference to a town not shewn on common maps or listed in recent guide-books would have interested me, and the agent's odd manner of allusion roused something like real curiosity. A town able to inspire such dislike in its neighbours, I thought, must be at least rather unusual, and worthy of a tourist's attention. If it came before Arkham I would stop off there and so I asked the agent to tell me something about it. He was very deliberate, and spoke with an air of feeling slightly superior to what he said.

"Innsmouth? Well, it's a queer kind of a town down at the

5. A small coastal town in Massachusetts about thirty-five miles northeast of Boston.

6. If Arkham is to be identified with Salem (and this is far from certain—there is evidence in "The Dunwich Horror" that Arkham is in central Massachusetts), Newburyport is about twenty miles north. A bus that ran through "Innsmouth" would also likely run through the towns of Newbury (not to be confused with Newburyport), Ipswich, South Hamilton, and Beverly, none of which, however, is a harbor town. The closest harbor town in a straight line from Newburyport to Salem is Manchester-by-the-Sea. There are several small unnamed islands not far from Manchester-by-the-Sea that might be "Devil Reef." In an early draft of "The Shadow over Innsmouth," Lovecraft indicated that the narrator, after traveling to Arkham, planned to visit Gloucester. This is not inconsistent with the "Arkham is in reality Salem, and Manchester is Innsmouth" theory; Gloucester is about thirteen miles northeast of Salem, a few miles northeast of Manchester-by-the-Sea (Innsmouth?). Lovecraft's notes for the tale also indicate that Innsmouth is closer to Arkham than to Newburyport.

7. A fictional river. There are only three significant rivers in the immediate vicinity of "Innsmouth": the Merrimack, which flows into the Atlantic in Newburyport, the Ipswich (flowing into the Atlantic at Ipswich Bay), and the Rowley, a small river in the vicinity of Rowley. While Ipswich is in the right place, between Newburyport and Salem, and has a river that might be disguised as the Manuxet, it is clear that Ipswich is *not* Innsmouth, for it is mentioned shortly as an alternate destination for the narrator.

8. The Boston & Maine Railroad went bankrupt in the 1970s, selling off many lines, and in 1983, the company itself was sold; today its lines are part of the Massachusetts Bay Transit Authority network. It had stations in Newburyport, Rowley (another town on the line between Newburyport and Salem), and Salem.

9. A town in Addison County, on the western border of Vermont, with a current population of under 700 people. Vermonters have been heard to say, "I may be a fool, but I'm not a damned fool."

mouth of the Manuxet.[7] Used to be almost a city—quite a port before the War of 1812—but all gone to pieces in the last hundred years or so. No railroad now—B. & M.[8] never went through, and the branch line from Rowley was given up years ago.

"More empty houses than there are people, I guess, and no business to speak of except fishing and lobstering. Everybody trades mostly either here or in Arkham or Ipswich. Once they had quite a few mills, but nothing's left now except one gold refinery running on the leanest kind of part time.

"That refinery, though, used to be a big thing, and Old Man Marsh, who owns it, must be richer'n Croesus. Queer old duck, though, and sticks mighty close in his home. He's supposed to have developed some skin disease or deformity late in life that makes him keep out of sight. Grandson of Captain Obed Marsh, who founded the business. His mother seems to've ben some kind of foreigner—they say a South Sea islander—so everybody raised Cain when he married an Ipswich girl fifty years ago. They always do that about Innsmouth people, and folks here and hereabouts always try to cover up any Innsmouth blood they have in 'em. But Marsh's children and grandchildren look just like anyone else so far's I can see. I've had 'em pointed out to me here—though, come to think of it, the elder children don't seem to be around lately. Never saw the old man.

"And why is everybody so down on Innsmouth? Well, young fellow, you mustn't take too much stock in what people around here say. They're hard to get started, but once they do get started they never let up. They've ben telling things about Innsmouth—whispering 'em, mostly—for the last hundred years, I guess, and I gather they're more scared than anything else. Some of the stories would make you laugh—about old Captain Marsh driving bargains with the devil and bringing imps out of hell to live in Innsmouth, or about some kind of devil-worship and awful sacrifices in some place near the wharves that people stumbled on around 1845 or thereabouts—but I come from Panton, Vermont,[9] and that kind of story don't go down with me.

"You ought to hear, though, what some of the old-timers tell about the black reef off the coast—Devil Reef, they call it. It's well above water a good part of the time, and never much below it, but at that you could hardly call it an island. The story is that there's a whole legion of devils seen sometimes on that reef—sprawled about, or darting in and out of some kind of caves near the top. It's a rugged, uneven thing, a good bit over a mile out, and toward the end of shipping days sailors used to make big detours just to avoid it.

"That is, sailors that didn't hail from Innsmouth. One of the things they had against old Captain Marsh was that he was supposed to land on it sometimes at night when the tide was right. Maybe he did, for I dare say the rock formation was interesting, and it's just barely possible he was looking for pirate loot and maybe finding it; but there was talk of his dealing with dæmons there. Fact is, I guess on the whole it was really the Captain that gave the bad reputation to the reef.

"That was before the big epidemic of 1846, when over half the folks in Innsmouth was carried off.[10] They never did quite figure out what the trouble was, but it was probably some foreign kind of disease brought from China or somewhere by the shipping. It surely was bad enough—there was riots over it, and all sorts of ghastly doings that I don't believe ever got outside of town—and it left the place in awful shape. Never came back—there can't be more'n 300 or 400 people living there now.

"But the real thing behind the way folks feel is simply race prejudice—and I don't say I'm blaming those that hold it. I hate those Innsmouth folks myself, and I wouldn't care to go to their town. I s'pose you know—though I can see you're a Westerner by your talk[11]—what a lot our New England ships used to have to do with queer ports in Africa, Asia, the South Seas, and everywhere else, and what queer kinds of people they sometimes brought back with 'em. You've probably heard about the Salem man that came home with a Chinese wife, and maybe you know there's still a bunch of Fiji Islanders somewhere around Cape Cod.[12]

"Well, there must be something like that back of the Innsmouth people. The place always was badly cut off from the rest of the country by marshes and creeks, and we can't be sure about the ins and outs of the matter; but it's pretty clear that old Captain Marsh must have brought home some odd specimens when he had all three of his ships in commission back in the twenties and thirties. There certainly is a strange kind of streak in the Innsmouth folks today—I don't know how to explain it, but it

10. This was clearly a local epidemic; there is no recorded history of any epidemics in Massachusetts in 1846, although yellow fever was a severe problem nationwide five years earlier. According to Donald R. Burleson, in *H. P. Lovecraft: A Critical Study*, Newburyport had a smallpox epidemic in the late 1700s.

11. The narrator, we learn later, is from Toledo, Ohio, hardly a westerner by the 1920s. Perhaps he spent summers out West.

12. Lovecraft apparently saw such a colony in 1930 on a drive to Onset, Massachusetts, a small summer resort for Bostonians, and mentioned it in a letter dated August 15–16, 1930, to his aunt Mrs. F. C. Clark.

13. Probably drawing its name from the Gilmans, mentioned later in the tale as one of Innsmouth's "gently bred" families—nonetheless, a terrible pun in light of later revelations about the "Innsmouth look" (each of the fishy-looking folk could be described as a "gill-man") and its origins.

sort of makes you crawl. You'll notice a little in Sargent if you take his bus. Some of 'em have queer narrow heads with flat noses and bulgy, stary eyes that never seem to shut, and their skin ain't quite right. Rough and scabby, and the sides of their necks are all shrivelled or creased up. Get bald, too, very young. The older fellows look the worst—fact is, I don't believe I've ever seen a very old chap of that kind. Guess they must die of looking in the glass! Animals hate 'em—they used to have lots of horse trouble before autos came in.

"Nobody around here or in Arkham or Ipswich will have anything to do with 'em, and they act kind of offish themselves when they come to town or when anyone tries to fish on their grounds. Queer how fish are always thick off Innsmouth Harbour when there ain't any anywhere else around—but just try to fish there yourself and see how the folks chase you off! Those people used to come here on the railroad—walking and taking the train at Rowley after the branch was dropped—but now they use that bus.

"Yes, there's a hotel in Innsmouth—called the Gilman House[13]—but I don't believe it can amount to much. I wouldn't advise you to try it. Better stay over here and take the ten o'clock bus tomorrow morning; then you can get an evening bus there for Arkham at eight o'clock. There was a factory inspector who stopped at the Gilman a couple of years ago, and he had a lot of unpleasant hints about the place. Seems they get a queer crowd there, for this fellow heard voices in other rooms—though most of 'em was empty—that gave him the shivers. It was foreign talk, he thought, but he said the bad thing about it was the kind of voice that sometimes spoke. It sounded so unnatural—sloppinglike, he said—that he didn't dare undress and go to sleep. Just waited up and lit out the first thing in the morning. The talk went on most all night.

"This fellow—Casey, his name was—had a lot to say about how the Innsmouth folks watched him and seemed kind of on guard. He found the Marsh refinery a queer place—it's in an old mill on the lower falls of the Manuxet. What he said tallied up with what I'd heard. Books in bad shape, and no clear account of any kind of dealings. You know it's always ben a kind of mystery where the Marshes get the gold they refine. They've never seemed to do much buying in that line, but years ago they shipped out an enormous lot of ingots.

"Used to be talk of a queer foreign kind of jewellery that the sailors and refinery men sometimes sold on the sly, or that was seen once or twice on some of the Marsh womenfolks. People allowed maybe old Captain Obed traded for it in some heathen port, especially since he was always ordering stacks of glass beads and trinkets such as seafaring men used to get for native trade. Others thought and still think he'd found an old pirate cache out on Devil Reef. But here's a funny thing. The old Captain's ben dead these sixty years, and there ain't ben a good-sized ship out of the place since the Civil War; but just the same the Marshes still keep on buying a few of those native trade things—mostly glass and rubber gewgaws, they tell me. Maybe the Innsmouth folks like 'em to look at themselves—Gawd knows they've gotten to be about as bad as South Sea cannibals and Guinea savages.

"That plague of '46 must have taken off the best blood in the place. Anyway, they're a doubtful lot now, and the Marshes and the other rich folks are as bad as any. As I told you, there probably ain't more'n 400 people in the whole town in spite of all the streets they say there are. I guess they're what they call 'white trash' down South—lawless and sly, and full of secret doings. They get a lot of fish and lobsters and do exporting by truck. Queer how the fish swarm right there and nowhere else.

"Nobody can ever keep track of these people, and state school officials and census men have a devil of a time. You can bet that prying strangers ain't welcome around Innsmouth. I've heard personally of more'n one business or government man that's disappeared there, and there's loose talk of one who went crazy and is out at Danvers[14] now. They must have fixed up some awful scare for that fellow.

"That's why I wouldn't go at night if I was you. I've never ben there and have no wish to go, but I guess a daytime trip couldn't hurt you—even though the people hereabouts will advise you not to make it. If you're just sightseeing, and looking for old-time stuff, Innsmouth ought to be quite a place for you."

And so I spent part of that evening at the Newburyport Public Library looking up data about Innsmouth. When I had tried to question the natives in the shops, the lunch room, the garages,

14. The Danvers State Hospital is said to have introduced the prefrontal lobotomy as a treatment for serious cases.

Like many such institutions, in the twentieth century Danvers stopped advertising itself by name as a psychiatric hospital. At its opening, in 1878, in Danvers, Massachusetts, and in subsequent transformations, it was clearly designated as such: the State Lunatic Hospital at Danvers, the Danvers Lunatic Asylum, and the Danvers State Insane Asylum. It is no longer thought to be politically correct, apparently, to refer to safe havens for mentally ill persons as "insane asylums." A similar comment is made by the admittedly crazy narrator of Caitlin Kiernan's award-winning novel *The Drowning Girl* (2012) about Butler Hospital, where both of Lovecraft's parents died (the institution was then known as Butler Hospital for the Insane—see the foreword, note 26, above).

Perhaps evidence of Lovecraft's abhorrence of asylums was his behavior when his mother was admitted to Butler in 1921 for her final illness: He would visit her frequently, meeting her on the grounds of the hospital, but he never entered the buildings, even when she was confined to her bed (Joshi, *I Am Providence*, 306). Lovecraft failed to visit his father when he was institutionalized, but this behavior is understandable: The boy was only eight when his father died, and it appears that he was told (falsely) that his father was completely paralyzed and comatose in his final years. See Kenneth W. Faig Jr.'s *The Parents of Howard Phillips Lovecraft* (50). In later years, Lovecraft never told anyone that his father had been confined as insane, in the final stages of neurosyphilis, only that he was "stricken with a complete paralysis resulting from a brain overtaxed with study & business cares" (Lovecraft to Reinhardt Kleiner, November 16, 1916, *Selected Letters*, I, 33).

15. Manchester was officially incorporated in 1645. It was a fishing village until 1845, when it became a summer residence for Boston's elite. It has never had any manufacturing.

The Danvers Asylum in 2010. Photograph copyright © Donovan K. Loucks 2010, reprinted with permission

and the fire station, I had found them even harder to get started than the ticket agent had predicted; and realised that I could not spare the time to overcome their first instinctive reticences. They had a kind of obscure suspiciousness, as if there were something amiss with anyone too much interested in Innsmouth. At the Y.M.C.A., where I was stopping, the clerk merely discouraged my going to such a dismal, decadent place; and the people at the library shewed much the same attitude. Clearly, in the eyes of the educated, Innsmouth was merely an exaggerated case of civic degeneration.

The Essex County histories on the library shelves had very little to say, except that the town was founded in 1643,[15] noted for shipbuilding before the Revolution, a seat of great marine prosperity in the early nineteenth century, and later a minor factory centre using the Manuxet as power. The epidemic and riots of 1846 were very sparsely treated, as if they formed a discredit to the county.

References to decline were few, though the significance of the later record was unmistakable. After the Civil War all industrial life was confined to the Marsh Refining Company, and the marketing of gold ingots formed the only remaining bit of major commerce aside from the eternal fishing. That fishing paid less and less as the price of the commodity fell and large-scale corporations offered competition, but there was never a dearth of fish around Innsmouth Harbour. Foreigners seldom settled there, and there was some discreetly veiled evidence that a number of Poles and Portuguese who had tried it had been scattered in a peculiarly drastic fashion.

Most interesting of all was a glancing reference to the strange jewellery vaguely associated with Innsmouth. It had evidently impressed the whole countryside more than a little, for mention was made of specimens in the museum of Miskatonic University at Arkham, and in the display room of the Newburyport Historical Society.[16] The fragmentary descriptions of these things were bald and prosaic, but they hinted to me an undercurrent of persistent strangeness. Something about them seemed so odd and provocative that I could not put them out of my mind, and despite the relative lateness of the hour I resolved to see the local sample—said to be a large, queerly proportioned thing evidently meant for a tiara—if it could possibly be arranged.

The librarian gave me a note of introduction to the curator of the Society, a Miss Anna Tilton,[17] who lived nearby, and after a brief explanation that ancient gentlewoman was kind enough to pilot me into the closed building, since the hour was not outrageously late. The collection was a notable one indeed, but in my present mood I had eyes for nothing but the bizarre object which glistened in a corner cupboard under the electric lights.

It took no excessive sensitiveness to beauty to make me literally gasp at the strange, unearthly splendour of the alien, opulent phantasy that rested there on a purple velvet cushion. Even now I can hardly describe what I saw, though it was clearly enough a sort of tiara, as the description had said. It was tall in front, and with a very large and curiously irregular periphery, as if designed for a head of almost freakishly elliptical outline. The material seemed to be predominantly gold, though a weird lighter lustrousness hinted at some strange alloy with an equally beautiful and scarcely identifiable metal. Its condition was almost perfect, and one could have spent hours in studying the striking and puzzlingly untraditional designs—some simply geometrical, and

16. Originally founded as the Antiquarian and Historical Society of Old Newbury, the Historical Society of Old Newbury was organized in 1877 and, in 1927, was located at the corner of High and Winter streets; it has since moved to 98 High Street.

17. Helen E. Tilton supervised the reading room of the Newburyport library beginning in 1905; it is likely that Anna was a close relative.

18. That is, half fish-like and half toad-like (Batrachia is the order of amphibians including frogs and toads).

some plainly marine—chased or moulded in high relief on its surface with a craftsmanship of incredible skill and grace.

The longer I looked, the more the thing fascinated me; and in this fascination there was a curiously disturbing element hardly to be classified or accounted for. At first I decided that it was the queer other-worldly quality of the art which made me uneasy. All other art objects I had ever seen either belonged to some known racial or national stream, or else were consciously modernistic defiances of every recognised stream. This tiara was neither. It clearly belonged to some settled technique of infinite maturity and perfection, yet that technique was utterly remote from any—Eastern or Western, ancient or modern—which I had ever heard of or seen exemplified. It was as if the workmanship were that of another planet.

However, I soon saw that my uneasiness had a second and perhaps equally potent source residing in the pictorial and mathematical suggestions of the strange designs. The patterns all hinted of remote secrets and unimaginable abysses in time and space, and the monotonously aquatic nature of the reliefs became almost sinister. Among these reliefs were fabulous monsters of abhorrent grotesqueness and malignity—half ichthyic and half batrachian[18] in suggestion—which one could not dissociate from a certain haunting and uncomfortable sense of pseudo-memory, as if they called up some image from deep cells and tissues whose retentive functions are wholly primal and awesomely ancestral. At times I fancied that every contour of these blasphemous fish-frogs was overflowing with the ultimate quintessence of unknown and inhuman evil.

In odd contrast to the tiara's aspect was its brief and prosy history as related by Miss Tilton. It had been pawned for a ridiculous sum at a shop in State Street in 1873, by a drunken Innsmouth man shortly afterward killed in a brawl. The Society had acquired it directly from the pawnbroker, at once giving it a display worthy of its quality. It was labelled as of probable East-Indian or Indo-Chinese provenance, though the attribution was frankly tentative.

Miss Tilton, comparing all possible hypotheses regarding its origin and its presence in New England, was inclined to believe that it formed part of some exotic pirate hoard discovered by old

Captain Obed Marsh. This view was surely not weakened by the insistent offers of purchase at a high price which the Marshes began to make as soon as they knew of its presence, and which they repeated to this day despite the Society's unvarying determination not to sell.

As the good lady shewed me out of the building she made it clear that the pirate theory of the Marsh fortune was a popular one among the intelligent people of the region. Her own attitude toward shadowed Innsmouth—which she had never seen—was one of disgust at a community slipping far down the cultural scale, and she assured me that the rumours of devil-worship were partly justified by a peculiar secret cult which had gained force there and engulfed all the orthodox churches.

It was called, she said, "The Esoteric Order of Dagon," and was undoubtedly a debased, quasi-pagan thing imported from the East a century before, at a time when the Innsmouth fisheries seemed to be going barren. Its persistence among a simple people was quite natural in view of the sudden and permanent return of abundantly fine fishing, and it soon came to be the greatest influence on the town, replacing Freemasonry altogether and taking up headquarters in the old Masonic Hall on New Church Green.

All this, to the pious Miss Tilton, formed an excellent reason for shunning the ancient town of decay and desolation; but to me it was merely a fresh incentive. To my architectural and historical anticipations was now added an acute anthropological zeal, and I could scarcely sleep in my small room at the "Y" as the night wore away.

II.

SHORTLY BEFORE TEN the next morning I stood with one small valise in front of Hammond's Drug Store in old Market Square waiting for the Innsmouth bus. As the hour for its arrival drew near I noticed a general drift of the loungers to other places up the street, or to the Ideal Lunch across the square. Evidently the ticket-agent had not exaggerated the dislike which local people bore toward Innsmouth and its denizens. In a few moments a small motor-coach of extreme decrepitude and dirty grey colour rattled down State Street, made a turn, and drew up at the curb beside me. I felt immediately that it was the right one; a guess which the half-illegible sign on the windshield—*"Arkham-Innsmouth-Newb'port"*—soon verified.

There were only three passengers—dark, unkempt men of sullen visage and somewhat youthful cast—and when the vehicle stopped they clumsily shambled out and began walking up State Street in a silent, almost furtive fashion. The driver also alighted, and I watched him as he went into the drug store to make some purchase. This, I reflected, must be the Joe Sargent mentioned by the ticket-agent; and even before I noticed any details there spread over me a wave of spontaneous aversion which could be neither checked nor explained. It suddenly struck me as very natural that the local people should not wish to ride on a bus owned and driven by this man, or to visit any oftener than possible the habitat of such a man and his kinsfolk.

When the driver came out of the store I looked at him more carefully and tried to determine the source of my evil impression. He was a thin, stoop-shouldered man not much under six feet tall, dressed in shabby blue civilian clothes and wearing a frayed grey golf cap. His age was perhaps thirty-five, but the odd, deep creases in the sides of his neck made him seem older when one did not study his dull, expressionless face. He had a narrow head, bulging, watery blue eyes that seemed never to wink, a flat nose, a receding forehead and chin, and singularly undeveloped ears. His long thick lip and coarse-pored, greyish cheeks seemed almost beardless except for some sparse yellow hairs that straggled and curled in irregular patches; and in places the surface seemed queerly irregular, as if peeling from some cutaneous disease. His hands were large and heavily veined, and had a very unusual greyish-blue tinge. The fingers were strikingly short in proportion to the rest of the structure, and seemed to have a tendency to curl closely into the huge palm. As he walked toward the bus I observed his peculiarly shambling gait and saw that his feet were inordinately immense. The more I studied them the more I wondered how he could buy any shoes to fit them.

A certain greasiness about the fellow increased my dislike. He was evidently given to working or lounging around the fish docks, and carried with him much of their characteristic smell. Just what foreign blood was in him I could not even guess. His oddities certainly did not look Asiatic, Polynesian, Levantine, or negroid, yet I could see why the people found him alien. I myself would have thought of biological degeneration rather than alienage.

I was sorry when I saw that there would be no other passengers on the bus. Somehow I did not like the idea of riding alone with this driver. But as leaving time obviously approached I conquered my qualms and followed the man aboard, extending him a dollar bill and murmuring the single word "Innsmouth." He looked curiously at me for a second as he returned forty cents change without speaking. I took a seat far behind him, but on the same side of the bus, since I wished to watch the shore during the journey.

At length the decrepit vehicle started with a jerk, and rattled noisily past the old brick buildings of State Street amidst a cloud of vapour from the exhaust. Glancing at the people on the sidewalks, I thought I detected in them a curious wish to avoid looking at the bus—or at least a wish to avoid seeming to look at it. Then we turned to the left into High Street, where the going was smoother; flying by stately old mansions of the early republic and still older colonial farmhouses, passing the Lower Green and Parker River, and finally emerging into a long, monotonous stretch of open shore country.

The day was warm and sunny, but the landscape of sand, sedge-grass, and stunted shrubbery became more and more desolate as we proceeded. Out the window I could see the blue water and the sandy line of Plum Island, and we presently drew very near the beach as our narrow road veered off from the main highway to Rowley and Ipswich. There were no visible houses, and I could tell by the state of the road that traffic was very light hereabouts. The small, weather-worn telephone poles carried only two wires. Now and then we crossed crude wooden bridges over tidal creeks that wound far inland and promoted the general isolation of the region.

Once in a while I noticed dead stumps and crumbling foundation-walls above the drifting sand, and recalled the old tradition quoted in one of the histories I had read, that this was once a fertile and thickly-settled countryside. The change, it was said, came simultaneously with the Innsmouth epidemic of 1846, and was thought by simple folk to have a dark connexion with hidden

19. Kingsport, it will be recalled, may be identified with Marblehead, Massachusetts, but may also be identified as Salem. See "The Festival," note 7, above. Both would be visible from Manchester.

20. The house is investigated further by Lovecraft in "The Strange High House in the Mist," written in 1926 and first published in *Weird Tales* 18, no. 3 (October 1931), 394–400.

forces of evil. Actually, it was caused by the unwise cutting of woodlands near the shore, which robbed the soil of its best protection and opened the way for waves of wind-blown sand.

At last we lost sight of Plum Island and saw the vast expanse of the open Atlantic on our left. Our narrow course began to climb steeply, and I felt a singular sense of disquiet in looking at the lonely crest ahead where the rutted roadway met the sky. It was as if the bus were about to keep on in its ascent, leaving the sane earth altogether and merging with the unknown arcana of upper air and cryptical sky. The smell of the sea took on ominous implications, and the silent driver's bent, rigid back and narrow head became more and more hateful. As I looked at him I saw that the back of his head was almost as hairless as his face, having only a few straggling yellow strands upon a grey scabrous surface.

Then we reached the crest and beheld the outspread valley beyond, where the Manuxet joins the sea just north of the long line of cliffs that culminate in Kingsport Head[19] and veer off toward Cape Ann. On the far misty horizon I could just make out the dizzy profile of the Head, topped by the queer ancient house of which so many legends are told;[20] but for the moment all my attention was captured by the nearer panorama just below me. I had, I realised, come face to face with rumour-shadowed Innsmouth.

It was a town of wide extent and dense construction, yet one with a portentous dearth of visible life. From the tangle of chimney-pots scarcely a wisp of smoke came, and the three tall steeples loomed stark and unpainted against the seaward horizon. One of them was crumbling down at the top, and in that and another there were only black gaping holes where clock-dials should have been. The vast huddle of sagging gambrel roofs and peaked gables conveyed with offensive clearness the idea of wormy decay, and as we approached along the now descending road I could see that many roofs had wholly caved in. There were some large square Georgian houses, too, with hipped roofs, cupolas, and railed "widow's walks." These were mostly well back from the water, and one or two seemed to be in moderately sound condition. Stretching inland from among them I saw the rusted, grass-grown line of the abandoned railway, with leaning telegraph-poles now devoid of wires, and the half-obscured lines of the old carriage roads to Rowley and Ipswich.

The decay was worst close to the waterfront, though in its very midst I could spy the white belfry of a fairly well-preserved brick structure which looked like a small factory. The harbour, long clogged with sand, was enclosed by an ancient stone breakwater; on which I could begin to discern the minute forms of a few seated fishermen, and at whose end were what looked like the foundations of a bygone lighthouse. A sandy tongue had formed inside this barrier, and upon it I saw a few decrepit cabins, moored dories, and scattered lobster-pots. The only deep water seemed to be where the river poured out past the belfried structure and turned southward to join the ocean at the breakwater's end.

Here and there the ruins of wharves jutted out from the shore to end in indeterminate rottenness, those farthest south seeming the most decayed. And far out at sea, despite a high tide, I glimpsed a long, black line scarcely rising above the water yet carrying a suggestion of odd latent malignancy. This, I knew, must be Devil Reef. As I looked, a subtle, curious sense of beckoning seemed superadded to the grim repulsion; and oddly enough, I found this overtone more disturbing than the primary impression.

We met no one on the road, but presently began to pass deserted farms in varying stages of ruin. Then I noticed a few inhabited houses with rags stuffed in the broken windows and shells and dead fish lying about the littered yards. Once or twice I saw listless-looking people working in barren gardens or digging clams on the fishy-smelling beach below, and groups of dirty, simian-visaged children playing around weed-grown doorsteps. Somehow these people seemed more disquieting than the dismal buildings, for almost every one had certain peculiarities of face and motions which I instinctively disliked without being able to define or comprehend them. For a second I thought this typical physique suggested some picture I had seen, perhaps in a book, under circumstances of particular horror or melancholy; but this pseudo-recollection passed very quickly.

As the bus reached a lower level I began to catch the steady note of a waterfall through the unnatural stillness. The leaning, unpainted houses grew thicker, lined both sides of the road, and displayed more urban tendencies than did those we were leaving behind. The panorama ahead had contracted to a street scene, and in spots I could see where a cobblestone pavement and stretches of brick sidewalk had formerly existed. All the houses were apparently deserted, and there were occasional gaps where tumbledown chimneys and cellar walls told of buildings that had collapsed. Pervading everything was the most nauseous fishy odour imaginable.

Soon cross streets and junctions began to appear; those on the left leading to shoreward realms of unpaved squalor and decay, while those on the right shewed vistas of departed grandeur. So far I had seen no people in the town, but there now came signs of a sparse habitation—curtained windows here and there, and an occasional battered motor-car at the curb. Pavement and sidewalks were increasingly well defined, and though most of the houses were quite old—wood and brick structures of the early nineteenth century—they were obviously kept fit for habitation. As an amateur antiquarian I almost lost my olfactory disgust and my feeling of menace and repulsion amidst this rich, unaltered survival from the past.

But I was not to reach my destination without one very strong impression of poignantly disagreeable quality. The bus had come to a sort of open concourse or radial point with churches on two sides and the bedraggled remains of a circular green in the centre, and I was looking at a large pillared hall on the right-hand junction ahead. The structure's once white paint was now grey and peeling, and the black and gold sign on the pediment was so faded that I could only with difficulty make out the words "Esoteric Order of Dagon." This, then, was the former Masonic Hall now given over to a degraded cult. As I strained to decipher this inscription my notice was distracted by the raucous tones of a cracked bell across the street, and I quickly turned to look out the window on my side of the coach.

The sound came from a squat-towered stone church of manifestly later date than most of the houses, built in a clumsy Gothic fashion and having a disproportionately high basement with shuttered windows. Though the hands of its clock were missing on the side I glimpsed, I knew that those hoarse strokes were telling the hour of eleven. Then suddenly all thoughts of time were blotted out by an onrushing image of sharp intensity and unaccountable horror which had seized me before I knew what it really was. The door of the church basement was open, revealing a rectangle of blackness inside. And as I looked, a certain object crossed or seemed to cross that dark rectangle; burning into my brain a momentary conception of nightmare which was all the more maddening because analysis could not shew a single nightmarish quality in it.

It was a living object—the first except the driver that I had seen since entering the compact part of the town—and had I been in a steadier mood I would have found nothing whatever of terror in it. Clearly, as I realised a moment later, it was the pastor; clad in some peculiar vestments doubtless introduced since the Order of Dagon had modified the ritual of the local churches. The thing which had probably caught my first subconscious glance and supplied the touch of bizarre horror was the tall tiara he wore; an almost exact duplicate of the one Miss Tilton had shewn me the previous evening. This, acting on my imagination, had supplied namelessly sinister qualities to the indeterminate face and robed, shambling form beneath it. There was not, I soon decided, any reason why I should have felt that shuddering touch of evil pseudo-memory. Was it not natural that a local mystery cult should adopt among its regimentals an unique type of head-dress made familiar to the community in some strange way—perhaps as treasure-trove?

A very thin sprinkling of repellent-looking youngish people now became visible on the sidewalks—lone individuals, and silent knots of two or three. The lower floors of the crumbling houses sometimes harboured small shops with dingy signs, and I noticed a parked truck or two as we rattled along. The sound of waterfalls became more and more distinct, and presently I saw a fairly deep river-gorge ahead, spanned by a wide, iron-railed highway bridge beyond which a large square opened out. As we clanked over the bridge I looked out on both sides and observed some factory buildings on the edge of the grassy bluff or part way down. The water far below was very abundant, and I could see two vigorous sets of falls upstream on my right and at least one downstream on my left. From this point the noise was quite deafening. Then we rolled into the large semicircular square across the river and drew up on the right-hand side in front of a tall, cupola-crowned building with remnants of yellow paint and with a half-effaced sign proclaiming it to be the Gilman House.

21. The dominant Northeast grocery chain for many years, the company incorporated in 1917, changing its corporate name from the Ginter Company to First National Stores, Inc., in 1925. Its stores were later branded as Finast. The names of the stores were changed again when the company disappeared in the 1990s through mergers.

I was glad to get out of that bus, and at once proceeded to check my valise in the shabby hotel lobby. There was only one person in sight—an elderly man without what I had come to call the "Innsmouth look"—and I decided not to ask him any of the questions which bothered me; remembering that odd things had been noticed in this hotel. Instead, I strolled out on the square, from which the bus had already gone, and studied the scene minutely and appraisingly.

One side of the cobblestoned open space was the straight line of the river; the other was a semicircle of slant-roofed brick buildings of about the 1800 period, from which several streets radiated away to the southeast, south, and southwest. Lamps were depressingly few and small—all low-powered incandescents—and I was glad that my plans called for departure before dark, even though I knew the moon would be bright. The buildings were all in fair condition, and included perhaps a dozen shops in current operation; of which one was a grocery of the First National chain,[21] others a dismal restaurant, a drug store, and a wholesale fish-dealer's office, and still another, at the eastern extremity of the square near the river an office of the town's only industry—the Marsh Refining Company. There were perhaps ten people visible, and four or five automobiles and motor trucks stood scattered about. I did not need to be told that this was the civic centre of Innsmouth. Eastward I could catch blue glimpses of the harbour, against which rose the decaying remains of three once beautiful Georgian steeples. And toward the shore on the opposite bank of the river I saw the white belfry surmounting what I took to be the Marsh refinery.

For some reason or other I chose to make my first inquiries at the chain grocery, whose personnel was not likely to be native to Innsmouth. I found a solitary boy of about seventeen in charge, and was pleased to note the brightness and affability which promised cheerful information. He seemed exceptionally eager to talk, and I soon gathered that he did not like the place, its fishy smell, or its furtive people. A word with any outsider was a relief to him. He hailed from Arkham, boarded with a family who came from Ipswich, and went back home whenever he got a moment off. His family did not like him to work in Innsmouth, but the chain had transferred him there and he did not wish to give up his job.

There was, he said, no public library or chamber of commerce in Innsmouth, but I could probably find my way about. The street I had come down was Federal. West of that were the fine old residence streets—Broad, Washington, Lafayette, and Adams—and east of it were the shoreward slums. It was in these slums—along Main Street—that I would find the old Georgian churches, but they were all long abandoned. It would be well not to make oneself too conspicuous in such neighbourhoods—especially north of the river since the people were sullen and hostile. Some strangers had even disappeared.

Certain spots were almost forbidden territory, as he had learned at considerable cost. One must not, for example, linger much around the Marsh refinery, or around any of the still used churches, or around the pillared Order of Dagon Hall at New Church Green. Those churches were very odd—all violently disavowed by their respective denominations elsewhere, and apparently using the queerest kind of ceremonials and clerical vestments. Their creeds were heterodox and mysterious, involving hints of certain marvellous transformations leading to bodily immortality—of a sort—on this earth. The youth's own pastor— Dr. Wallace of Asbury M. E. Church in Arkham—had gravely urged him not to join any church in Innsmouth.

As for the Innsmouth people—the youth hardly knew what to make of them. They were as furtive and seldom seen as animals that live in burrows, and one could hardly imagine how they passed the time apart from their desultory fishing. Perhaps—judging from the quantities of bootleg liquor they consumed—they lay for most of the daylight hours in an alcoholic stupor. They seemed sullenly banded together in some sort of fellowship and understanding—despising the world as if they had access to other and preferable spheres of entity. Their appearance—especially those staring, unwinking eyes which one never saw shut—was certainly shocking enough; and their voices were disgusting. It was awful to hear them chanting in their churches at night, and especially during their main festivals or revivals, which fell twice a year on April 30th and October 31st.[22]

They were very fond of the water, and swam a great deal in both river and harbour. Swimming races out to Devil Reef were very common, and everyone in sight seemed well able to share in

22. Of course, Walpurgisnacht and All Hallows' Eve. See *The Case of Charles Dexter Ward*, note 138, above.

this arduous sport. When one came to think of it, it was generally only rather young people who were seen about in public, and of these the oldest were apt to be the most tainted-looking. When exceptions did occur, they were mostly persons with no trace of aberrancy, like the old clerk at the hotel. One wondered what became of the bulk of the older folk, and whether the "Innsmouth look" were not a strange and insidious disease-phenomenon which increased its hold as years advanced.

Only a very rare affliction, of course, could bring about such vast and radical anatomical changes in a single individual after maturity—changes involving osseous factors as basic as the shape of the skull—but then, even this aspect was no more baffling and unheard-of than the visible features of the malady as a whole. It would be hard, the youth implied, to form any real conclusions regarding such a matter; since one never came to know the natives personally no matter how long one might live in Innsmouth.

The youth was certain that many specimens even worse than the worst visible ones were kept locked indoors in some places. People sometimes heard the queerest kind of sounds. The tottering waterfront hovels north of the river were reputedly connected by hidden tunnels, being thus a veritable warren of unseen abnormalities. What kind of foreign blood—if any—these beings had, it was impossible to tell. They sometimes kept certain especially repulsive characters out of sight when government agents and others from the outside world came to town.

It would be of no use, my informant said, to ask the natives anything about the place. The only one who would talk was a very aged but normal-looking man who lived at the poorhouse on the north rim of the town and spent his time walking about or lounging around the fire station. This hoary character, Zadok Allen, was ninety-six years old and somewhat touched in the head, besides being the town drunkard. He was a strange, furtive creature who constantly looked over his shoulder as if afraid of something, and when sober could not be persuaded to talk at all with strangers. He was, however, unable to resist any offer of his favourite poison; and once drunk would furnish the most astonishing fragments of whispered reminiscence.

After all, though, little useful data could be gained from him;

since his stories were all insane, incomplete hints of impossible marvels and horrors which could have no source save in his own disordered fancy. Nobody believed him, but the natives did not like him to drink and talk with strangers; and it was not always safe to be seen questioning him. It was probably from him that some of the wildest popular whispers and delusions were derived.

Several non-native residents had reported monstrous glimpses from time to time, but between old Zadok's tales and the malformed denizens it was no wonder such illusions were current. None of the non-natives ever stayed out late at night, there being a widespread impression that it was not wise to do so. Besides, the streets were loathsomely dark.

As for business—the abundance of fish was certainly almost uncanny, but the natives were taking less and less advantage of it. Moreover, prices were falling and competition was growing. Of course the town's real business was the refinery, whose commercial office was on the square only a few doors east of where we stood. Old Man Marsh was never seen, but sometimes went to the works in a closed, curtained car.

There were all sorts of rumours about how Marsh had come to look. He had once been a great dandy, and people said he still wore the frock-coated finery of the Edwardian age,[23] curiously adapted to certain deformities. His sons had formerly conducted the office in the square, but latterly they had been keeping out of sight a good deal and leaving the brunt of affairs to the younger generation. The sons and their sisters had come to look very queer, especially the elder ones; and it was said that their health was failing.

One of the Marsh daughters was a repellent, reptilian-looking woman who wore an excess of weird jewellery clearly of the same exotic tradition as that to which the strange tiara belonged. My informant had noticed it many times, and had heard it spoken of as coming from some secret hoard, either of pirates or of dæmons. The clergymen—or priests, or whatever they were called nowadays—also wore this kind of ornament as a head-dress; but one seldom caught glimpses of them. Other specimens the youth had not seen, though many were rumoured to exist around Innsmouth.

The Marshes, together with the other three gently bred families of the town—the Waites, the Gilmans, and the Eliots—were

23. That is, the reign of King Edward VII, from 1901 to 1910.

24. Lovecraft drew a partial map of Innsmouth, reproduced (along with his notes) in *Something About Cats and Other Pieces.* In 1972, artist Eric Carlson produced a larger version, and in 2006, Joseph Morales redrew it for better legibility.

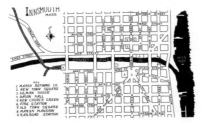

Map of Innsmouth, drawn by Eric Carlson, 1972, appearing in *Nyctalops* 6 (February 1972).

all very retiring. They lived in immense houses along Washington Street, and several were reputed to harbour in concealment certain living kinsfolk whose personal aspect forbade public view, and whose deaths had been reported and recorded.

Warning me that many of the street signs were down, the youth drew for my benefit a rough but ample and painstaking sketch map of the town's salient features. After a moment's study I felt sure that it would be of great help, and pocketed it with profuse thanks. Disliking the dinginess of the single restaurant I had seen, I bought a fair supply of cheese crackers and ginger wafers to serve as a lunch later on. My programme, I decided, would be to thread the principal streets, talk with any non-natives I might encounter, and catch the eight o'clock coach for Arkham. The town, I could see, formed a significant and exaggerated example of communal decay; but being no sociologist I would limit my serious observations to the field of architecture.

Thus I began my systematic though half-bewildered tour of Innsmouth's narrow, shadow-blighted ways.[24] Crossing the bridge and turning toward the roar of the lower falls, I passed close to the Marsh refinery, which seemed oddly free from the noise of industry. This building stood on the steep river bluff near a bridge and an open confluence of streets which I took to be the earliest

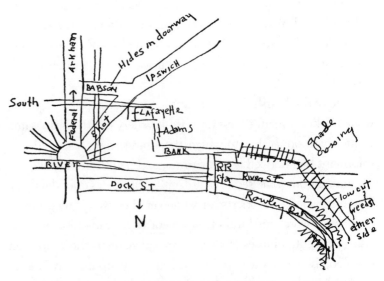

Map of Innsmouth, drawn by Lovecraft and reproduced in *Something About Cats* (p. 174).

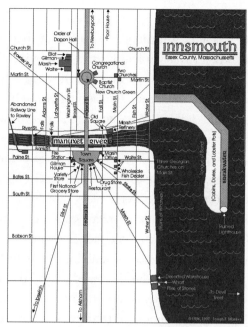

Map of Innsmouth. Copyright © 1996, 1997
Joseph Morales, reprinted with permission

civic centre, displaced after the Revolution by the present Town Square.

Re-crossing the gorge on the Main Street bridge, I struck a region of utter desertion which somehow made me shudder. Collapsing huddles of gambrel roofs formed a jagged and fantastic skyline, above which rose the ghoulish, decapitated steeple of an ancient church. Some houses along Main Street were tenanted, but most were tightly boarded up. Down unpaved side streets I saw the black, gaping windows of deserted hovels, many of which leaned at perilous and incredible angles through the sinking of part of the foundations. Those windows stared so spectrally that it took courage to turn eastward toward the waterfront. Certainly, the terror of a deserted house swells in geometrical rather than arithmetical progression as houses multiply to form a city of stark desolation. The sight of such endless avenues of fishy-eyed vacancy and death, and the thought of such linked infinities of black, brooding compartments given over to cobwebs and memories and the conqueror worm, start up vestigial fears and aversions that not even the stoutest philosophy can disperse.

Fish Street was as deserted as Main, though it differed in

having many brick and stone warehouses still in excellent shape. Water Street was almost its duplicate, save that there were great seaward gaps where wharves had been. Not a living thing did I see, except for the scattered fishermen on the distant breakwater, and not a sound did I hear save the lapping of the harbour tides and the roar of the falls in the Manuxet. The town was getting more and more on my nerves, and I looked behind me furtively as I picked my way back over the tottering Water Street bridge. The Fish Street bridge, according to the sketch, was in ruins.

North of the river there were traces of squalid life—active fish-packing houses in Water Street, smoking chimneys and patched roofs here and there, occasional sounds from indeterminate sources, and infrequent shambling forms in the dismal streets and unpaved lanes—but I seemed to find this even more oppressive than the southerly desertion. For one thing, the people were more hideous and abnormal than those near the centre of the town; so that I was several times evilly reminded of something utterly fantastic which I could not quite place. Undoubtedly the alien strain in the Innsmouth folk was stronger here than farther inland—unless, indeed, the "Innsmouth look" were a disease rather than a blood strain, in which case this district might be held to harbour the more advanced cases.

One detail that annoyed me was the *distribution* of the few faint sounds I heard. They ought naturally to have come wholly from the visibly inhabited houses, yet in reality were often strongest inside the most rigidly boarded-up facades. There were creakings, scurryings, and hoarse doubtful noises; and I thought uncomfortably about the hidden tunnels suggested by the grocery boy. Suddenly I found myself wondering what the voices of those denizens would be like. I had heard no speech so far in this quarter, and was unaccountably anxious not to do so.

Pausing only long enough to look at two fine but ruinous old churches at Main and Church Streets, I hastened out of that vile waterfront slum. My next logical goal was New Church Green, but somehow or other I could not bear to repass the church in whose basement I had glimpsed the inexplicably frightening form of that strangely diademed priest or pastor. Besides, the grocery youth had told me that the churches, as well as the Order of Dagon Hall, were not advisable neighbourhoods for strangers.

Accordingly I kept north along Main to Martin, then turning inland, crossing Federal Street safely north of the Green, and entering the decayed patrician neighbourhood of northern Broad, Washington, Lafayette, and Adams Streets. Though these stately old avenues were ill-surfaced and unkempt, their elm-shaded dignity had not entirely departed. Mansion after mansion claimed my gaze, most of them decrepit and boarded up amidst neglected grounds, but one or two in each street shewing signs of occupancy. In Washington Street there was a row of four or five in excellent repair and with finely tended lawns and gardens. The most sumptuous of these—with wide terraced parterres[25] extending back the whole way to Lafayette Street—I took to be the home of Old Man Marsh, the afflicted refinery owner.

In all these streets no living thing was visible, and I wondered at the complete absence of cats and dogs from Innsmouth. Another thing which puzzled and disturbed me, even in some of the best-preserved mansions, was the tightly shuttered condition of many third-story and attic windows. Furtiveness and secretiveness seemed universal in this hushed city of alienage and death, and I could not escape the sensation of being watched from ambush on every hand by sly, staring eyes that never shut.

I shivered as the cracked stroke of three sounded from a belfry on my left. Too well did I recall the squat church from which those notes came. Following Washington Street toward the river, I now faced a new zone of former industry and commerce; noting the ruins of a factory ahead, and seeing others, with the traces of an old railway station and covered railway bridge beyond, up the gorge on my right.

The uncertain bridge now before me was posted with a warning sign, but I took the risk and crossed again to the south bank where traces of life reappeared. Furtive, shambling creatures stared cryptically in my direction, and more normal faces eyed me coldly and curiously. Innsmouth was rapidly becoming intolerable, and I turned down Paine Street toward the Square in the hope of getting some vehicle to take me to Arkham before the still-distant starting-time of that sinister bus.

It was then that I saw the tumbledown fire station on my left, and noticed the red-faced, bushy-bearded, watery-eyed old man in nondescript rags who sat on a bench in front of it talking with

25. Ornamental patterned flower gardens.

26. The phrase was popularized through publication of Edgar Allan Poe's story "The Imp of the Perverse" (which first appeared in *Graham's American Monthly* in 1845), and it means that urge to do nothing—or the wrong thing—when crises arise:

> Again:—We have a task before us which must be speedily performed. We know that it will be ruinous to make delay. The most important crisis of our life calls, trumpet-tongued, for immediate energy and action. . . . It must—it shall be undertaken to-day—and yet we put it off until to-morrow. And why? There is no answer, except that we feel *perverse*, using the word with no comprehension of the principle. . . . The clock strikes and is the knell of our welfare, but at the same time is the chanticleer-note to the Thing that has so long overawed us. It flies. It disappears. We are free. The old energy returns. We will labor *now*. Alas, it is *too late!*

a pair of unkempt but not abnormal-looking firemen. This, of course, must be Zadok Allen, the half-crazed, liquorish nonagenarian whose tales of old Innsmouth and its shadow were so hideous and incredible.

III.

IT MUST HAVE been some imp of the perverse[26]—or some sardonic pull from dark, hidden sources—which made me change my plans as I did. I had long before resolved to limit my observations to architecture alone, and I was even then hurrying toward the Square in an effort to get quick transportation out of this festering city of death and decay; but the sight of old Zadok Allen set up new currents in my mind and made me slacken my pace uncertainly.

I had been assured that the old man could do nothing but hint at wild, disjointed, and incredible legends, and I had been warned that the natives made it unsafe to be seen talking to him; yet the thought of this aged witness to the town's decay, with memories going back to the early days of ships and factories, was a lure that no amount of reason could make me resist. After all, the strangest and maddest of myths are often merely symbols or allegories based upon truth—and old Zadok must have seen everything which went on around Innsmouth for the last ninety years. Curiosity flared up beyond sense and caution, and in my youthful egotism I fancied I might be able to sift a nucleus of real history from the confused, extravagant outpouring I would probably extract with the aid of raw whiskey.

I knew that I could not accost him then and there, for the firemen would surely notice and object. Instead, I reflected, I would prepare by getting some bootleg liquor at a place where the grocery boy had told me it was plentiful. Then I would loaf near the fire station in apparent casualness, and fall in with old Zadok after he had started on one of his frequent rambles. The youth said that he was very restless, seldom sitting around the station for more than an hour or two at a time.

A quart bottle of whiskey was easily, though not cheaply, obtained in the rear of a dingy variety-store just off the Square in Eliot Street. The dirty-looking fellow who waited on me had a touch of the staring "Innsmouth look," but was quite civil in his way; being perhaps used to the custom of such convivial strangers—truckmen, gold-buyers, and the like—as were occasionally in town.

Reëntering the Square I saw that luck was with me; for—shuffling out of Paine Street around the corner of the Gilman House—I glimpsed nothing less than the tall, lean, tattered form of old Zadok Allen himself. In accordance with my plan, I attracted his attention by brandishing my newly purchased bottle; and soon realised that he had begun to shuffle wistfully after me as I turned into Waite Street on my way to the most deserted region I could think of.

I was steering my course by the map the grocery boy had prepared, and was aiming for the wholly abandoned stretch of southern waterfront which I had previously visited. The only people in sight there had been the fishermen on the distant breakwater; and by going a few squares south I could get beyond the range of these, finding a pair of seats on some abandoned wharf and being free to question old Zadok unobserved for an indefinite time. Before I reached Main Street I could hear a faint and wheezy "Hey, Mister!" behind me, and I presently allowed the old man to catch up and take copious pulls from the quart bottle.

I began putting out feelers as we walked along to Water Street and turned southward amidst the omnipresent desolation and crazily tilted ruins, but found that the aged tongue did not loosen as quickly as I had expected. At length I saw a grass-grown opening toward the sea between crumbling brick walls, with the weedy length of an earth-and-masonry wharf projecting beyond. Piles of moss-covered stones near the water promised tolerable seats, and the scene was sheltered from all possible view by a ruined warehouse on the north. Here, I thought, was the ideal place for a long secret colloquy; so I guided my companion down the lane and picked out spots to sit in among the mossy stones. The air of death and desertion was ghoulish, and the smell of fish almost insufferable; but I was resolved to let nothing deter me.

About four hours remained for conversation if I were to catch the eight o'clock coach for Arkham, and I began to dole out more

27. Robert H. Waugh, in "The Weird Historical Novel: *Jonathan Strange & Mr. Norell, The Case of Charles Dexter Ward,* and Other Historical Ventures," from his collection *A Monster of Voices: Speaking for H. P. Lovecraft,* points out that the description that follows is inaccurate with respect to the economic cycles of nineteenth-century New England but accurate regarding the cycles of the early twentieth century (152).

28. A snow (pronounced "snoo") or snaw was a small three-masted sailing vessel similar to a brig, used as a merchant ship and as a warship. The *Oxford English Dictionary* records usage of the term as early as 1676 and as recent as 1881.

29. Although *Eliza* (which Zadok corrupts into "Elizy") and *Hetty* may sound like odd names for ships, there was an American ship named *Eliza* sailing in 1799 under Captain Rowan (the first American ship to sail into San Francisco Bay); and in 1802, a schooner named *Hetty* sailed out of Philadelphia, under Captain Jona Briggs.

liquor to the ancient tippler; meanwhile eating my own frugal lunch. In my donations I was careful not to overshoot the mark, for I did not wish Zadok's vinous garrulousness to pass into a stupor. After an hour his furtive taciturnity shewed signs of disappearing, but much to my disappointment he still sidetracked my questions about Innsmouth and its shadow-haunted past. He would babble of current topics, revealing a wide acquaintance with newspapers and a great tendency to philosophise in a sententious village fashion.

Toward the end of the second hour I feared my quart of whiskey would not be enough to produce results, and was wondering whether I had better leave old Zadok and go back for more. Just then, however, chance made the opening which my questions had been unable to make; and the wheezing ancient's rambling took a turn that caused me to lean forward and listen alertly. My back was toward the fishy-smelling sea, but he was facing it, and something or other had caused his wandering gaze to light on the low, distant line of Devil Reef, then shewing plainly and almost fascinatingly above the waves. The sight seemed to displease him, for he began a series of weak curses which ended in a confidential whisper and a knowing leer. He bent toward me, took hold of my coat lapel, and hissed out some hints that could not be mistaken.

"Thar's whar it all begun—that cursed place of all wickedness whar the deep water starts. Gate o' hell—sheer drop daown to a bottom no saoundin'-line kin tech. Ol' Cap'n Obed done it—him that faound aout more'n was good fer him in the Saouth Sea islands.

"Everybody was in a bad way them days.[27] Trade fallin' off, mills losin' business—even the new ones—an' the best of our menfolks kilt a-privateerin' in the War of 1812 or lost with the *Elizy* brig an' the *Ranger* snow[28]—both on 'em Gilman venters. Obed Marsh he had three ships afloat—brigantine *Columby,* brig *Hetty,*[29] an' barque *Sumatry Queen.* He was the only one as kep' on with the East-Injy an' Pacific trade, though Esdras Martin's barkentine *Malay Pride* made a venter as late as 'twenty-eight.

"Never was nobody like Cap'n Obed—old limb o' Satan! Heh, heh! I kin mind him a-tellin' abaout furren parts, an' callin' all the folks stupid fer goin' to Christian meetin' an' bearin' their burdens meek an' lowly. Says they'd orter git better gods like some o' the folks in the Injies—gods as ud bring 'em good fishin' in return for their sacrifices, an' ud reely answer folks's prayers.

"Matt Eliot, his fust mate, talked a lot too, only he was agin' folks's doin' any heathen things. Told abaout an island east of Otaheité[30] whar they was a lot o' stone ruins older'n anybody knew anything abaout, kind o' like them on Ponape,[31] in the Carolines, but with carvin's of faces that looked like the big statues on Easter Island.[32] They was a little volcanic island near thar, too, whar they was other ruins with diff'rent carvin's—ruins all wore away like they'd ben under the sea onct, an' with picters of awful monsters all over 'em.[33]

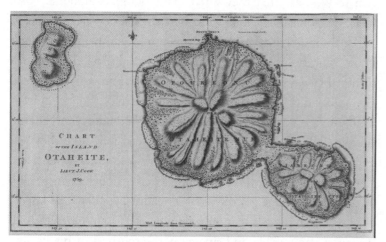

A chart of Otaheite made by Lieut. J. Clark in 1769.

These statues on Easter Island uniquely face the ocean.

30. Otaheite (more often rendered without the acute accent), visited by Captain Cook on an early voyage, is now known as Tahiti.

31. Now Pohnpei, an island in the Caroline Islands in the Pacific; one of four Federated States of Micronesia and home of the sovereign island nation's capital, Palikir.

32. The Easter Island heads (actually, they are whole-body statues, but the large heads dominate) were first discovered by Westerners in 1722 when Dutch explorer Jacob Roggeveen visited the island (now Rapa Nui). Called *moai* in the native Polynesian tongue, and measuring about thirteen feet high and five feet wide each, the statues appear to have been carved by native Polynesians between 1250 and 1500 CE and were transported using rollers made from trees to their coastal sites. The statues appear to be a mixture of memorials for deceased ancestors and commemorations of important local figures. Richard Huber, in "H. P. Lovecraft and Easter Island," points to the uncanny resemblance between Lovecraft and the statues! The statues are mentioned again in "The Haunter of the Dark" (pp. 779–806, below), where images resembling them—thought to be representations of aliens—populate the secret chapel of the Shining Trapezohedron.

33. See "Dagon" (pp. 3–10, above).

"Wal, Sir, Matt he says the natives araound thar had all the fish they cud ketch, an' sported bracelets an' armlets an' head rigs made aout of a queer kind o' gold an' covered with picters o' monsters jest like the ones carved over the ruins on the little island—sorter fish-like frogs or frog-like fishes that was drawed in all kinds o' positions like they was human bein's. Nobody cud git aout o' them whar they got all the stuff, an' all the other natives wondered haow they managed to find fish in plenty even when the very next islands had lean pickin's. Matt he got to wonderin' too, an' so did Cap'n Obed. Obed he notices, besides, that lots of the han'some young folks ud drop aout o' sight fer good from year to year, an' that they wa'n't many old folks araound. Also, he thinks some of the folks looks durned queer even fer Kanakys.

"It took Obed to git the truth aout o' them heathen. I dun't know haow he done it, but he begun by tradin' fer the gold-like things they wore. Ast 'em whar they come from, an' ef they cud git more, an' finally wormed the story aout o' the old chief—Walakea, they called him. Nobody but Obed ud ever a believed the old yeller devil, but the Cap'n cud read folks like they was books. Heh, heh! Nobody never believes me naow when I tell 'em, an' I dun't s'pose you will, young feller—though come to look at ye, ye hev kind o' got them sharp-readin' eyes like Obed had."

The old man's whisper grew fainter, and I found myself shuddering at the terrible and sincere portentousness of his intonation, even though I knew his tale could be nothing but drunken phantasy.

"Wal, Sir, Obed he larnt that they's things on this arth as most folks never heerd abaout—an' wouldn't believe ef they did hear. It seems these Kanakys was sacrificin' heaps o' their young men an' maidens to some kind o' god-things that lived under the sea, an' gittin' all kinds o' favour in return. They met the things on the little islet with the queer ruins, an' it seems them awful picters o' frog-fish monsters was supposed to be picters o' these things. Mebbe they was the kind o' critters as got all the mermaid stories an' sech started.

"They had all kinds o' cities on the sea-bottom, an' this island was heaved up from thar. Seems they was some of the things alive in the stone buildin's when the island come up sudden to the surface. That's haow the Kanakys got wind they was down thar.

Made sign-talk as soon as they got over bein' skeert, an' pieced up a bargain afore long.

"Them things liked human sacrifices. Had had 'em ages afore, but lost track o' the upper world arter a time. What they done to the victims it ain't fer me to say, an' I guess Obed wa'n't none too sharp abaout askin'. But it was all right with the heathens, because they'd ben havin' a hard time an' was desp'rate abaout everything. They give a sarten number o' young folks to the sea-things twict every year—May-Eve an' Hallowe'en—reg'lar as cud be. Also give some o' the carved knick-knacks they made. What the things agreed to give in return was plenty o' fish—they druv 'em in from all over the sea—an' a few gold-like things naow an' then.

"Wal, as I says, the natives met the things on the little volcanic islet—goin' thar in canoes with the sacrifices et cet'ry, and bringin' back any of the gold-like jools as was comin' to 'em. At fust the things didn't never go onto the main island, but arter a time they come to want to. Seems they hankered arter mixin' with the folks, an' havin' j'int ceremonies on the big days—May-Eve an' Hallowe'en. Ye see, they was able to live both in an' aout o' water—what they call amphibians, I guess. The Kanakys told 'em as haow folks from the other islands might wanta wipe 'em aout ef they got wind o' their bein' thar, but they says they dun't keer much, because they cud wipe aout the hull brood o' humans ef they was willin' to bother—that is, any as didn't hev sarten signs sech as was used onct by the lost Old Ones, whoever they was. But not wantin' to bother, they'd lay low when anybody visited the island.

"When it come to matin' with them toad-lookin' fishes, the Kanakys kind o' balked, but finally they larnt something as put a new face on the matter. Seems that human folks has got a kind o' relation to sech water-beasts—that everything alive come aout o' the water onct an' only needs a little change to go back agin. Them things told the Kanakys that ef they mixed bloods there'd be children as ud look human at fust, but later turn more'n more like the things, till finally they'd take to the water an' jine the main lot o' things daown thar. An' this is the important part, young feller—them as turned into fish things an' went into the water *wouldn't never die*. Them things never died excep' they was kilt violent.

"Wal, Sir, it seems by the time Obed knowed them islanders they was all full o' fish blood from them deep-water things. When they got old an' begun to shew it, they was kep' hid until they felt like takin' to the water an' quittin' the place. Some was more teched than others, an' some never did change quite enough to take to the water; but mostly they turned aout jest the way them things said. Them as was born more like the things changed arly, but them as was nearly human sometimes stayed on the island till they was past seventy, though they'd usually go daown under fer trial trips afore that. Folks as had took to the water gen'rally come back a good deal to visit, so's a man ud often be a-talkin' to his own five-times-great-grandfather, who'd left the dry land a couple o' hundred years or so afore.

"Everybody got aout o' the idee o' dyin'—excep' in canoe wars with the other islanders, or as sacrifices to the sea-gods daown below, or from snake-bite or plague or sharp gallopin' ailments or somethin' afore they cud take to the water—but simply looked forrad to a kind o' change that wa'n't a bit horrible arter a while. They thought what they'd got was well wuth all they'd had to give up—an' I guess Obed kind o' come to think the same hisself when he'd chewed over old Walakea's story a bit. Walakea, though, was one of the few as hadn't got none of the fish blood— bein' of a royal line that intermarried with royal lines on other islands.

"Walakea he shewed Obed a lot o' rites an' incantations as had to do with the sea-things, an' let him see some o' the folks in the village as had changed a lot from human shape. Somehaow or other, though, he never would let him see one of the reg'lar things from right aout o' the water. In the end he give him a funny kind o' thingumajig made aout o' lead or something, that he said ud bring up the fish things from any place in the water whar they might be a nest of 'em. The idee was to drop it daown with the right kind o' prayers an' sech. Walakea allaowed as the things was scattered all over the world, so's anybody that looked abaout cud find a nest an' bring 'em up ef they was wanted.

"Matt he didn't like this business at all, an' wanted Obed shud keep away from the island; but the Cap'n was sharp fer gain, an' faound he cud git them gold-like things so cheap it ud pay him to make a specialty of 'em. Things went on that way fer years an'

Obed got enough o' that gold-like stuff to make him start the refinery in Waite's old run-daown fullin' mill. He didn't dass sell the pieces like they was, fer folks ud be all the time askin' questions. All the same his crews ud git a piece an' dispose of it naow and then, even though they was swore to keep quiet; an' he let his women-folks wear some o' the pieces as was more human-like than most.

"Wal, come abaout 'thutty-eight—when I was seven year' old—Obed he faound the island people all wiped aout between v'yages. Seems the other islanders had got wind o' what was goin' on, an' had took matters into their own hands. S'pose they musta had, arter all, them old magic signs as the sea-things says was the only things they was afeard of. No tellin' what any o' them Kanakys will chance to git a holt of when the sea-bottom throws up some island with ruins older'n the deluge. Pious cusses, these was—they didn't leave nothin' standin' on either the main island or the little volcanic islet excep' what parts of the ruins was too big to knock daown. In some places they was little stones strewed abaout—like charms—with somethin' on 'em like what ye call a swastika[34] naowadays. Prob'ly them was the Old Ones' signs. Folks all wiped aout no trace o' no gold-like things, an' none o' the nearby Kanakys ud breathe a word abaout the matter. Wouldn't even admit they'd ever ben any people on that island.

"That naturally hit Obed pretty hard, seein' as his normal trade was doin' very poor. It hit the whole of Innsmouth, too, because in seafarin' days what profited the master of a ship gen'lly profited the crew proportionate. Most o' the folks araound the taown took the hard times kind o' sheep-like an' resigned, but they was in bad shape because the fishin' was peterin' aout an' the mills wa'n't doin' none too well.

"Then's the time Obed he begun a-cursin' at the folks fer bein' dull sheep an' prayin' to a Christian heaven as didn't help 'em none. He told 'em he'd knowed of folks as prayed to gods that give somethin' ye reely need, an' says ef a good bunch o' men ud stand by him, he cud mebbe git a holt o' sarten paowers as ud bring plenty o' fish an' quite a bit o' gold. O' course them as sarved on the *Sumatry Queen* an' seed the island knowed what he meant, an' wa'n't none too anxious to git clost to sea-things

34. The symbol has been traced to ancient civilizations in the Indus Valley and elsewhere and remains a powerful icon in various Eastern religions. In 1920, the Nazi Party adopted the swastika to link the party leaders to the Aryans (Indo-Europeans), viewed by the Nazis as the true and direct ancestors of the German people. Bennett Lovett-Graff, in "Shadows over Lovecraft: Reactionary Fantasy and Immigrant Eugenics," asserts that it is no coincidence that the Nazi symbol appears in Lovecraft's tale of the dangers of racial impurity. Note that after exposure by the narrator and capture by federal agents, the Deep Ones, like the victims of the Nazis, end up in "camps and prisons." See note 4, above.

"... odd how he could stand so much whiskey." *Shadow over Innsmouth.*
Visionary Publishing Co., 1936
(artist: Frank Utpatel)

35. Astarte or Ishtar, a goddess of sexuality and fertility, found in several cultures, including the Canaanite.

36. The phrase itself, referring to several ancient coins (essentially the equivalent of saying "nickel, nickel, dime, and some pennies"), has no literal significance, but the prophet Daniel explains to King Belshazzar that the phrase is a portent of the doom and division of his kingdom (Daniel 5:25–28). Here it is merely an example of the "wrath of Jehovah" that Zadok recalls being threatened.

like they'd heerd tell on, but them as didn't know what 'twas all abaout got kind o' swayed by what Obed had to say, an' begun to ast him what he cud do to set 'em on the way to the faith as ud bring 'em results."

Here the old man faltered, mumbled, and lapsed into a moody and apprehensive silence; glancing nervously over his shoulder and then turning back to stare fascinatedly at the distant black reef. When I spoke to him he did not answer, so I knew I would have to let him finish the bottle. The insane yarn I was hearing interested me profoundly, for I fancied there was contained within it a sort of crude allegory based upon the strangenesses of Innsmouth and elaborated by an imagination at once creative and full of scraps of exotic legend. Not for a moment did I believe that the tale had any really substantial foundation; but none the less the account held a hint of genuine terror if only because it brought in references to strange jewels clearly akin to the malign tiara I had seen at Newburyport. Perhaps the ornaments had, after all, come from some strange island; and possibly the wild stories were lies of the bygone Obed himself rather than of this antique toper.

I handed Zadok the bottle, and he drained it to the last drop. It was curious how he could stand so much whiskey, for not even a trace of thickness had come into his high, wheezy voice. He licked the nose of the bottle and slipped it into his pocket, then beginning to nod and whisper softly to himself. I bent close to catch any articulate words he might utter, and thought I saw a sardonic smile behind the stained, bushy whiskers. Yes—he was really forming words, and I could grasp a fair proportion of them.

"Poor Matt—Matt he allus was agin' it—tried to line up the folks on his side, an' had long talks with the preachers—no use—they run the Congregational parson aout o' taown, an' the Methodist feller quit—never did see Resolved Babcock, the Baptist parson, agin—Wrath o' Jehovy—I was a mighty little critter, but I heerd what I heerd an' seen what I seen—Dagon an' Ashtoreth[35]—Belial an' Beëlzebub—Golden Caff an' the idols o' Canaan an' the Philistines—Babylonish abominations—*Mene, mene, tekel, upharsin*—."[36]

He stopped again, and from the look in his watery blue eyes I feared he was close to a stupor after all. But when I gently shook his shoulder he turned on me with astonishing alertness and snapped out some more obscure phrases.

"Dun't believe me, hey? Heh, heh, heh—then jest tell me, young feller, why Cap'n Obed an' twenty odd other folks used to row aout to Devil Reef in the dead o' night an' chant things so laoud ye cud hear 'em all over taown when the wind was right? Tell me that, hey? An' tell me why Obed was allus droppin' heavy things daown into the deep water t'other side o' the reef whar the bottom shoots daown like a cliff lower'n ye kin saound? Tell me what he done with that funny-shaped lead thingumajig as Walakea give him? Hey, boy? An' what did they all haowl on May-Eve, an' agin the next Hallowe'en? An' why'd the new church parsons—fellers as used to be sailors—wear them queer robes an' cover theirselves with them gold-like things Obed brung? Hey?"

The watery blue eyes were almost savage and maniacal now, and the dirty white beard bristled electrically. Old Zadok probably saw me shrink back, for he began to cackle evilly.

"Heh, heh, heh, heh! Beginnin' to see, hey? Mebbe ye'd like to a ben me in them days, when I seed things at night aout to sea from the cupalo top o' my haouse. Oh, I kin tell ye, little pitchers hev big ears, an' I wa'n't missin' nothin' o' what was gossiped abaout Cap'n Obed an' the folks aout to the reef! Heh, heh, heh! Haow abaout the night I took my pa's ship's glass up to the cupalo an' seed the reef a-bristlin' thick with shapes that dove off quick soon's the moon riz? Obed an' the folks was in a dory, but them shapes dove off the far side into the deep water an' never come up. . . . Haow'd ye like to be a little shaver alone up in a cupalo a-watchin' shapes *as wa'n't human shapes?* . . . Hey? . . . Heh, heh, heh, heh. . . ."

The old man was getting hysterical, and I began to shiver with a nameless alarm. He laid a gnarled claw on my shoulder, and it seemed to me that its shaking was not altogether that of mirth.

"S'pose one night ye seed somethin' heavy heaved offen Obed's dory beyond the reef, an' then larned nex' day a young feller was missin' from home? Hey? Did anybody ever see hide or hair o' Hiram Gilman agin? Did they? An' Nick Pierce, an' Luelly Waite, an' Adoniram Saouthwick, an' Henry Garrison? Hey? Heh, heh, heh, heh. . . . Shapes talkin' sign language with their hands . . . them as had reel hands . . .

"Wal, Sir, that was the time Obed begun to git on his feet

37. An administrative division of the Knights Templar, a fraternal order.

38. This mirrors an era of the history of Freemasonry in America. In 1826, William Morgan disappeared after threatening to reveal the secrets of the Masons, with the result that some accused the Masons of having murdered Morgan. A period of public disrepute for the Masons followed, leading to the founding of an anti-Masonic political party (Andrew Jackson was a Mason, and so the new party was also anti-Jacksonian). By 1850, however, interest in the order had rebounded, and by the time of the American Civil War, Freemasonry was more popular than ever.

agin. Folks see his three darters a-wearin' gold-like things as nobody'd never see on 'em afore, an' smoke started comin' aout o' the refin'ry chimbly. Other folks wer prosp'rin', too—fish begun to swarm into the harbour fit to kill, an' heaven knows what sized cargoes we begun to ship aout to Newb'ryport, Arkham, an' Boston. 'Twas then Obed got the ol' branch railrud put through. Some Kingsport fishermen heerd abaout the ketch an' come up in sloops, but they was all lost. Nobody never see 'em agin. An' jest then our folks organised the Esoteric Order o' Dagon, an' bought Masonic Hall offen Calvary Commandery[37] for it . . . heh, heh, heh! Matt Eliot was a Mason an' agin' the sellin', but he dropped aout o' sight jest then.[38]

"Remember, I ain't sayin' Obed was set on hevin' things jest like they was on that Kanaky isle. I dun't think he aimed at fust to do no mixin', nor raise no younguns to take to the water an' turn into fishes with eternal life. He wanted them gold things, an' was willin' to pay heavy, an' I guess the *others* was satisfied fer a while. . . .

"Come in 'forty-six the taown done some lookin' an' thinkin' fer itself. Too many folks missin'—too much wild preachin' at meetin' of a Sunday—too much talk abaout that reef. I guess I done a bit by tellin' Selectman Mowry what I see from the cupalo. They was a party one night as follered Obed's craowd aout to the reef, an' I heerd shots betwixt the dories. Nex' day Obed an' thutty-two others was in gaol, with everbody a-wonderin' jest what was afoot an' jest what charge agin' 'em cud be got to holt. God, ef anybody'd look'd ahead . . . a couple o' weeks later, when nothin' had ben throwed into the sea fer that long. . . ."

Zadok was shewing signs of fright and exhaustion, and I let him keep silence for a while, though glancing apprehensively at my watch. The tide had turned and was coming in now, and the sound of the waves seemed to arouse him. I was glad of that tide, for at high water the fishy smell might not be so bad. Again I strained to catch his whispers.

"That awful night . . . I seed 'em . . . I was up in the cupalo . . . hordes of 'em . . . swarms of 'em . . . all over the reef an' swimmin' up the harbour into the Manuxet . . . God, what happened in the streets of Innsmouth that night . . . they rattled our door, but pa wouldn't open . . . then he clumb aout the kitchen winder

with his musket to find Selectman Mowry an' see what he cud do.
. . . Maounds o' the dead an' the dyin' . . . shots an' screams . . .
shaoutin' in Ol' Squar an' Taown Squar an' New Church Green
. . . gaol throwed open . . . proclamation . . . treason . . . called it
the plague when folks come in an' faound haff our people missin'
. . . nobody left but them as ud jine in with Obed an' them things
or else keep quiet . . . never heerd o' my pa no more . . ."

The old man was panting, and perspiring profusely. His grip
on my shoulder tightened.

"Everything cleaned up in the mornin'—but they was *traces*.
. . . Obed he kinder takes charge an' says things is goin' to be
changed . . . *others'll* worship with us at meetin'-time, an' sarten
haouses hez got to entertain *guests* . . . *they* wanted to mix like
they done with the Kanakys, an' he fer one didn't feel baound
to stop 'em. Far gone, was Obed . . . jest like a crazy man on the
subjeck. He says they brung us fish an' treasure, an' shud hev what
they hankered arter. . . .

"Nothin' was to be diff'runt on the aoutside, only we was to
keep shy o' strangers ef we knowed what was good fer us.

"We all hed to take the Oath o' Dagon, an' later on they was
secon' an' third oaths that some on us took. Them as ud help
special, ud git special rewards—gold an' sech—No use balkin', fer
they was millions of 'em daown thar. They'd ruther not start risin'
an' wipin' aout humankind, but ef they was gave away an' forced
to, they cud do a lot toward jest that. We didn't hev them old
charms to cut 'em off like folks in the Saouth Sea did, an' them
Kanakys wudn't never give away their secrets.

"Yield up enough sacrifices an' savage knick-knacks an' harbourage in the taown when they wanted it, an' they'd let well
enough alone. Wudn't bother no strangers as might bear tales
aoutside—that is, withaout they got pryin'. All in the band of
the faithful—Order o' Dagon—an' the children shud never die,
but go back to the Mother Hydra[39] an' Father Dagon what we
all come from onct—*Iä! Iä! Cthulhu fhtagn! Ph'nglui mglw'nafh
Cthulhu R'lyeh wgah-nagl fhtagn*—"

Old Zadok was fast lapsing into stark raving, and I held my
breath. Poor old soul—to what pitiful depths of hallucination
had his liquor, plus his hatred of the decay, alienage, and disease
around him, brought that fertile, imaginative brain! He began to

39. In Greek mythology, the hydra is a
serpentlike, many-headed water beast,
slain by Hercules as part of his labors.
This is the first and only mention of the
female leader of the Deep Ones.

moan now, and tears were coursing down his channelled cheeks into the depths of his beard.

"God, what I seen senct I was fifteen year' *old—Mene, mene, tekel, upharsin!—*the folks as was missin', an' them as kilt theirselves—them as told things in Arkham or Ipswich or sech places was all called crazy, like you're a-callin' me right naow—but God, what I seen—They'd a kilt me long ago fer what I know, only I'd took the fust an' secon' Oaths o' Dagon offen Obed, so was pertected unlessen a jury of 'em proved I told things knowin' an' delib'rit . . . but I wudn't take the third Oath—I'd a died ruther'n take that—

"It got wuss araound Civil War time, *when children born senct 'forty-six begun to grow up—*some of 'em, that is. I was afeard—never did no pryin' arter that awful night, an' never see one of—*them—*clost to in all my life. That is, never no full-blooded one. I went to the war, an' ef I'd a had any guts or sense I'd a never come back, but settled away from here. But folks wrote me things wa'n't so bad. That, I s'pose, was because gov'munt draft men was in taown arter 'sixty-three. Arter the war it was jest as bad agin. People begun to fall off—mills an' shops shet daown—shippin' stopped an' the harbour choked up—railrud give up—but they . . . they never stopped swimmin' in an' aout o' the river from that cursed reef o' Satan—an' more an' more attic winders got a-boarded up, an' more an' more noises was heerd in haouses as wa'n't s'posed to hev nobody in 'em . . .

"Folks aoutside hev their stories abaout us—s'pose you've heerd a plenty on 'em, seein' what questions ye ast—stories abaout things they've seed naow an' then, an' abaout that queer joolry as still comes in from somewhars an' ain't quite all melted up—but nothin' never gits def'nite. Nobody'll believe nothin'. They call them gold-like things pirate loot, an' allaow the Innsmouth folks hez furren blood or is distempered or somethin'. Besides, them that lives here shoo off as many strangers as they kin, an' encourage the rest not to git very cur'ous, specially raound night time. Beasts balk at the critters—hosses wuss'n mules—but when they got autos that was all right.

"In 'forty-six Cap'n Obed took a second wife *that nobody in the taown never see—*some says he didn't want to, but was made to by them as he'd called in—had three children by her—two as disappeared young, but one gal as looked like anybody else an' was eddicated in Europe. Obed finally got her married off by a trick to an Arkham feller as didn't suspect nothin'. But nobody aoutside'll hev nothin' to do with Innsmouth folks naow. Barnabas Marsh that runs the refin'ry naow is Obed's grandson by his fust wife—son of Onesiphorus, his eldest son, *but his mother was another o' them as wa'n't never seed aoutdoors.*

"Right naow Barnabas is abaout changed. Can't shet his eyes no more, an' is all aout o' shape. They say he still wears clothes, but he'll take to the water soon. Mebbe he's tried it already— they do sometimes go daown fer little spells afore they go fer good. Ain't ben seed abaout in public fer nigh on ten year'. Dun't know haow his poor wife kin feel—she come from Ipswich, an' they nigh lynched Barnabas when he courted her fifty odd year' ago. Obed he died in 'seventy-eight an' all the next gen'ration is gone naow— the fust wife's children dead, an' the rest . . . God knows. . . ."

The sound of the incoming tide was now very insistent, and little by little it seemed to change the old man's mood from maudlin tearfulness to watchful fear. He would pause now and then to renew those nervous glances over his shoulder or out toward the reef, and despite the wild absurdity of his tale, I could not help beginning to share his vague apprehensiveness. Zadok now grew shriller, and seemed to be trying to whip up his courage with louder speech.

"Hey, yew, why dun't ye say somethin'? Haow'd ye like to be livin' in a taown like this, with everything a-rottin' an' a-dyin', an' boarded-up monsters crawlin' an' bleatin' an' barkin' an' hoppin' araoun' black cellars an' attics every way ye turn? Hey? Haow'd ye like to hear the haowlin' night arter night from the churches an' Order o' Dagon Hall, *an' know what's doin' part o' the haowlin'?* Haow'd ye like to hear what comes from that awful reef every May-Eve an' Hallowmass? Hey? Think the old man's crazy, eh? Wal, Sir, *let me tell ye that ain't the wust!*"

Zadok was really screaming now, and the mad frenzy of his voice disturbed me more than I care to own.

"Curse ye, dun't set thar a-starin' at me with them eyes—I tell Obed Marsh he's in hell, an' hez got to stay thar! Heh, heh . . . in hell, I says! Can't git me—I hain't done nothin' nor told nobody nothin'—

"Oh, you, young feller? Wal, even ef I hain't told nobody nothin' yet, I'm a-goin' to naow! You jest set still an' listen to me, boy—this is what I ain't never told nobody. . . . I says I didn't do no pryin' arter that night—*but I faound things aout jest the same!*

"Yew want to know what the reel horror is, hey? Wal, it's this—it ain't what them fish devils *hez done, but what they're a-goin' to do!* They're a-bringin' things up aout o' whar they come from into the taown—ben doin' it fer years, an' slackenin' up lately. Them haouses north o' the river betwixt Water an' Main Streets is full of 'em—them devils *an' what they brung*—an' when they git ready. . . . I say, *when they git ready* . . . ever hear tell of a *shoggoth?* . . .

"Hey, d'ye hear me? *I tell ye I know what them things be—I seen 'em one night when . . . EH-AHHH-AH! E'YAAHHHH. . . .*"

The hideous suddenness and inhuman frightfulness of the old man's shriek almost made me faint. His eyes, looking past me toward the malodorous sea, were positively starting from his head; while his face was a mask of fear worthy of Greek tragedy. His bony claw dug monstrously into my shoulder, and he made no motion as I turned my head to look at whatever he had glimpsed.

There was nothing that I could see. Only the incoming tide, with perhaps one set of ripples more local than the long-flung line of breakers. But now Zadok was shaking me, and I turned back to watch the melting of that fear-frozen face into a chaos of twitching eyelids and mumbling gums. Presently his voice came back—albeit as a trembling whisper.

"*Git aout o' here! Git aout o' here! They seen us*—git aout fer your life! Dun't wait fer nothin'—*they know naow*— Run fer it— quick—*aout o' this taown*—"

Another heavy wave dashed against the loosening masonry of the bygone wharf, and changed the mad ancient's whisper to another inhuman and blood-curdling scream.

"E-YAAHHHH! . . . YHAAAAAA! . . ."

Before I could recover my scattered wits he had relaxed his clutch on my shoulder, and dashed wildly inland toward the street, reeling northward around the ruined warehouse wall.

I glanced back at the sea, but there was nothing there. And when I reached Water Street and looked along it toward the north there was no remaining trace of Zadok Allen.

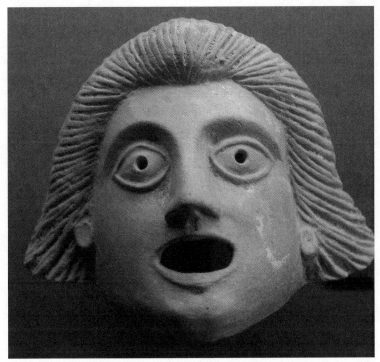

This mask is from approximately the first century BCE.

IV.

I CAN HARDLY describe the mood in which I was left by this harrowing episode—an episode at once mad and pitiful, grotesque and terrifying. The grocery boy had prepared me for it, yet the reality left me none the less bewildered and disturbed. Puerile though the story was, old Zadok's insane earnestness and horror had communicated to me a mounting unrest which joined with my earlier sense of loathing for the town and its blight of intangible shadow.

Later I might sift the tale and extract some nucleus of historic allegory; just now I wished to put it out of my head. The hour had grown perilously late—my watch said 7:15, and the Arkham bus left Town Square at eight—so I tried to give my thoughts as neutral and practical a cast as possible, meanwhile walking rapidly through the deserted streets of gaping roofs and leaning houses toward the hotel where I had checked my valise and would find my bus.

Though the golden light of late afternoon gave the ancient

40. In Lovecraft's notes, it is clear that the driver has been *instructed* that the bus is unable to go farther.

roofs and decrepit chimneys an air of mystic loveliness and peace, I could not help glancing over my shoulder now and then. I would surely be very glad to get out of malodorous and fear-shadowed Innsmouth, and wished there were some other vehicle than the bus driven by that sinister-looking fellow Sargent. Yet I did not hurry too precipitately, for there were architectural details worth viewing at every silent corner; and I could easily, I calculated, cover the necessary distance in a half-hour.

Studying the grocery youth's map and seeking a route I had not traversed before, I chose Marsh Street instead of State for my approach to Town Square. Near the corner of Fall Street I began to see scattered groups of furtive whisperers, and when I finally reached the Square I saw that almost all the loiterers were congregated around the door of the Gilman House. It seemed as if many bulging, watery, unwinking eyes looked oddly at me as I claimed my valise in the lobby, and I hoped that none of these unpleasant creatures would be my fellow-passengers on the coach.

The bus, rather early, rattled in with three passengers somewhat before eight, and an evil-looking fellow on the sidewalk muttered a few indistinguishable words to the driver.[40] Sargent threw out a mail-bag and a roll of newspapers, and entered the hotel; while the passengers—the same men whom I had seen arriving in Newburyport that morning—shambled to the sidewalk and exchanged some faint guttural words with a loafer in a language I could have sworn was not English. I boarded the empty coach and took the same seat I had taken before, but was hardly settled before Sargent reappeared and began mumbling in a throaty voice of peculiar repulsiveness.

I was, it appeared, in very bad luck. There had been something wrong with the engine, despite the excellent time made from Newburyport, and the bus could not complete the journey to Arkham. No, it could not possibly be repaired that night, nor was there any other way of getting transportation out of Innsmouth either to Arkham or elsewhere. Sargent was sorry, but I would have to stop over at the Gilman. Probably the clerk would make the price easy for me, but there was nothing else to do. Almost dazed by this sudden obstacle, and violently dreading the fall of night in this decaying and half-unlighted town, I left the bus and reëntered the hotel lobby; where the sullen queer-looking night clerk told me I could have Room 428 on next the top floor—large, but without running water—for a dollar.

Despite what I had heard of this hotel in Newburyport, I signed the register, paid my dollar, let the clerk take my valise, and followed that sour, solitary attendant up three creaking flights of stairs past dusty corridors which seemed wholly devoid of life. My room, a dismal rear one with two windows and bare, cheap furnishings, overlooked a dingy courtyard otherwise hemmed in by low, deserted brick blocks, and commanded a view of decrepit westward-stretching roofs with a marshy countryside beyond. At the end of the corridor was a bathroom—a discouraging relique with ancient marble bowl, tin tub, faint electric light, and musty wooden panelling around all the plumbing fixtures.

It being still daylight, I descended to the Square and looked around for a dinner of some sort; noticing as I did so the strange glances I received from the unwholesome loafers. Since the grocery was closed, I was forced to patronise the restaurant I had shunned before; a stooped, narrow-headed man with staring, unwinking eyes, and a flat-nosed wench with unbelievably thick, clumsy hands being in attendance. The service was all of the counter type, and it relieved me to find that much was evidently served from cans and packages. A bowl of vegetable soup with crackers was enough for me, and I soon headed back for my cheerless room at the Gilman; getting an evening paper and a flyspecked magazine from the evil-visaged clerk at the rickety stand beside his desk.

As twilight deepened I turned on the one feeble electric bulb over the cheap, iron-framed bed, and tried as best I could to continue the reading I had begun. I felt it advisable to keep my mind wholesomely occupied, for it would not do to brood over the abnormalities of this ancient, blight-shadowed town while I was still within its borders. The insane yarn I had heard from the aged drunkard did not promise very pleasant dreams, and I felt I must keep the image of his wild, watery eyes as far as possible from my imagination.

Also, I must not dwell on what that factory inspector had told the Newburyport ticket-agent about the Gilman House and the voices of its nocturnal tenants—not on that, nor on the face beneath the tiara in the black church doorway; the face for whose

The narrator may have had a device something like this screwdriver made for gun sights.

horror my conscious mind could not account. It would perhaps have been easier to keep my thoughts from disturbing topics had the room not been so gruesomely musty. As it was, the lethal mustiness blended hideously with the town's general fishy odour and persistently focussed one's fancy on death and decay.

Another thing that disturbed me was the absence of a bolt on the door of my room. One had been there, as marks clearly shewed, but there were signs of recent removal. No doubt it had become out of order, like so many other things in this decrepit edifice. In my nervousness I looked around and discovered a bolt on the clothes-press which seemed to be of the same size, judging from the marks, as the one formerly on the door. To gain a partial relief from the general tension I busied myself by transferring this hardware to the vacant place with the aid of a handy three-in-one device including a screw-driver which I kept on my key-ring. The bolt fitted perfectly, and I was somewhat relieved when I knew that I could shoot it firmly upon retiring. Not that I had any real apprehension of its need, but that any symbol of security was welcome in an environment of this kind. There were adequate bolts on the two lateral doors to connecting rooms, and these I proceeded to fasten.

I did not undress, but decided to read till I was sleepy and then lie down with only my coat, collar, and shoes off. Taking a pocket flashlight from my valise, I placed it in my trousers, so that I could read my watch if I woke up later in the dark. Drowsiness, however, did not come; and when I stopped to analyse my thoughts I found to my disquiet that I was really unconsciously listening for something—listening for something which I dreaded but could not name. That inspector's story must have worked on my imagination more deeply than I had suspected. Again I tried to read, but found that I made no progress.

After a time I seemed to hear the stairs and corridors creak at intervals as if with footsteps, and wondered if the other rooms were beginning to fill up. There were no voices, however, and it struck me that there was something subtly furtive about the creaking. I did not like it, and debated whether I had better try to sleep at all. This town had some queer people, and there had undoubtedly been several disappearances. Was this one of those inns where travellers were slain for their money? Surely I had no look of excessive prosperity. Or were the townsfolk really so resentful about curious visitors? Had my obvious sightseeing, with its frequent map-consultations, aroused unfavourable notice? It occurred to me that I must be in a highly nervous state to let a few random creakings set me off speculating in this fashion—but I regretted none the less that I was unarmed.

At length, feeling a fatigue which had nothing of drowsiness in it, I bolted the newly outfitted hall door, turned off the light, and threw myself down on the hard, uneven bed—coat, collar, shoes, and all. In the darkness every faint noise of the night seemed magnified, and a flood of doubly unpleasant thoughts swept over me. I was sorry I had put out the light, yet was too tired to rise and turn it on again. Then, after a long, dreary interval, and prefaced by a fresh creaking of stairs and corridor, there came that soft, damnably unmistakable sound which seemed like a malign fulfilment of all my apprehensions. Without the least shadow of a doubt, the lock on my hall door was being tried—cautiously, furtively, tentatively—with a key.

My sensations upon recognising this sign of actual peril were perhaps less rather than more tumultuous because of my previous vague fears. I had been, albeit without definite reason, instinctively on my guard—and that was to my advantage in the new and real crisis, whatever it might turn out to be. Nevertheless the change in the menace from vague premonition to immediate reality was a profound shock, and fell upon me with the force of a genuine blow. It never once occurred to me that the fumbling might be a mere mistake. Malign purpose was all I could think of, and I kept deathly quiet, awaiting the would-be intruder's next move.

After a time the cautious rattling ceased, and I heard the room to the north entered with a pass-key. Then the lock of the connecting door to my room was softly tried. The bolt held, of course, and I heard the floor creak as the prowler left the room. After a moment there came another soft rattling, and I knew that the room to the south of me was being entered. Again a furtive trying of a bolted connecting door, and again a receding creaking. This time the creaking went along the hall and down the stairs, so I knew that the prowler had realised the bolted condition of my doors and was giving up his attempt for a greater or lesser time, as the future would shew.

The readiness with which I fell into a plan of action proves that I must have been subconsciously fearing some menace and considering possible avenues of escape for hours. From the first I felt that the unseen fumbler meant a danger not to be met or dealt with, but only to be fled from as precipitately as possible. The one thing to do was to get out of that hotel alive as quickly as I could, and through some channel other than the front stairs and lobby.

Rising softly and throwing my flashlight on the switch, I sought to light the bulb over my bed in order to choose and pocket some belongings for a swift, valiseless flight. Nothing, however, happened; and I saw that the power had been cut off. Clearly, some cryptic, evil movement was afoot on a large scale—just what, I could not say. As I stood pondering with my hand on the now useless switch I heard a muffled creaking on the floor below, and thought I could barely distinguish voices in conversation. A moment later I felt less sure that the deeper sounds were voices, since the apparent hoarse barkings and loose-syllabled croakings bore so little resemblance to recognised human speech. Then I thought with renewed force of what the factory inspector had heard in the night in this mouldering and pestilential building.

Having filled my pockets with the flashlight's aid, I put on my hat and tiptoed to the windows to consider chances of descent. Despite the state's safety regulations there was no fire escape on this side of the hotel, and I saw that my windows commanded only a sheer three story drop to the cobbled courtyard. On the right and left, however, some ancient brick business blocks abutted on the hotel; their slant roofs coming up to a reasonable jumping distance from my fourth-story level. To reach either of these lines of buildings I would have to be in a room two doors from my own—in one case on the north and in the other case on the south—and my mind instantly set to work calculating what chances I had of making the transfer.

I could not, I decided, risk an emergence into the corridor; where my footsteps would surely be heard, and where the difficulties of entering the desired room would be insuperable. My progress, if it was to be made at all, would have to be through the less solidly built connecting doors of the rooms; the locks and bolts of which I would have to force violently, using my shoulder as a battering-ram whenever they were set against me. This, I thought, would be possible owing to the rickety nature of the house and its fixtures; but I realised I could not do it noiselessly. I would have to count on sheer speed, and the chance of getting to a window before any hostile forces became coördinated enough to open the right door toward me with a pass-key. My own outer door I reinforced by pushing the bureau against it—little by little, in order to make a minimum of sound.

I perceived that my chances were very slender, and was fully prepared for any calamity. Even getting to another roof would not solve the problem for there would then remain the task of reaching the ground and escaping from the town. One thing in my favour was the deserted and ruinous state of the abutting buildings and the number of skylights gaping blackly open in each row.

Gathering from the grocery boy's map that the best route out of town was southward, I glanced first at the connecting door on the south side of the room. It was designed to open in my direction, hence I saw—after drawing the bolt and finding other fastenings in place—it was not a favourable one for forcing. Accordingly abandoning it as a route, I cautiously moved the bedstead against it to hamper any attack which might be made on it later from the next room. The door on the north was hung to open away from me, and this—though a test proved it to be locked or bolted from the other side—I knew must be my route. If I could gain the roofs of the buildings in Paine Street and descend successfully to the ground level, I might perhaps dart through the courtyard and the adjacent or opposite buildings to Washington or Bates—or else emerge in Paine and edge around southward into Washington. In any case, I would aim to strike Washington somehow and get quickly out of the Town Square region. My preference would be to avoid Paine, since the fire station there might be open all night.

As I thought of these things I looked out over the squalid sea of decaying roofs below me, now brightened by the beams of a moon not much past full.[41] On the right the black gash of the river-gorge clove the panorama; abandoned factories and railway station clinging barnacle-like to its sides. Beyond it the rusted railway and the Rowley road led off through a flat, marshy terrain dotted with islets of higher and dryer scrub-grown land. On the left the creek-threaded countryside was nearer, the narrow road

"'I looked over the squalid sea of roofs below me.'" *Shadow over Innsmouth.*
Visionary Publishing Co., 1936
(artist: Frank Utpatel)

41. This is in accord with the records of the U.S. Naval Observatory, which show that the full moon occurred on July 14, 1927.

to Ipswich gleaming white in the moonlight. I could not see from my side of the hotel the southward route toward Arkham which I had determined to take.

I was irresolutely speculating on when I had better attack the northward door, and on how I could least audibly manage it, when I noticed that the vague noises underfoot had given place to a fresh and heavier creaking of the stairs. A wavering flicker of light shewed through my transom, and the boards of the corridor began to groan with a ponderous load. Muffled sounds of possible vocal origin approached, and at length a firm knock came at my outer door.

For a moment I simply held my breath and waited. Eternities seemed to elapse, and the nauseous fishy odour of my environment seemed to mount suddenly and spectacularly. Then the knocking was repeated—continuously, and with growing insistence. I knew that the time for action had come, and forthwith drew the bolt of the northward connecting door, bracing myself for the task of battering it open. The knocking waxed louder, and I hoped that its volume would cover the sound of my efforts. At last beginning my attempt, I lunged again and again at the thin panelling with my left shoulder, heedless of shock or pain. The door resisted even more than I had expected, but I did not give in. And all the while the clamour at the outer door increased.

Finally the connecting door gave, but with such a crash that I knew those outside must have heard. Instantly the outside knocking became a violent battering, while keys sounded ominously in the hall doors of the rooms on both sides of me. Rushing through the newly opened connexion, I succeeded in bolting the northerly hall door before the lock could be turned; but even as I did so I heard the hall door of the third room—the one from whose window I had hoped to reach the roof below—being tried with a pass-key.

For an instant I felt absolute despair, since my trapping in a chamber with no window egress seemed complete. A wave of almost abnormal horror swept over me, and invested with a terrible but unexplainable singularity the flashlight-glimpsed dust prints made by the intruder who had lately tried my door from this room. Then, with a dazed automatism which persisted despite hopelessness, I made for the next connecting door and performed the blind motion of pushing at it in an effort to get through and—granting that fastenings might be as providentially intact as in this second room—bolt the hall door beyond before the lock could be turned from outside.

Sheer fortunate chance gave me my reprieve—for the connecting door before me was not only unlocked but actually ajar. In a second I was through, and had my right knee and shoulder against a hall door which was visibly opening inward. My pressure took the opener off guard, for the thing shut as I pushed, so that I could slip the well-conditioned bolt as I had done with the other door. As I gained this respite I heard the battering at the two other doors abate, while a confused clatter came from the connecting door I had shielded with the bedstead. Evidently the bulk of my assailants had entered the southerly room and were massing in a lateral attack. But at the same moment a pass-key sounded in the next door to the north, and I knew that a nearer peril was at hand.

The northward connecting door was wide open, but there was no time to think about checking the already turning lock in the hall. All I could do was to shut and bolt the open connecting door, as well as its mate on the opposite side—pushing a bedstead against the one and a bureau against the other, and moving a washstand in front of the hall door. I must, I saw, trust to such makeshift barriers to shield me till I could get out the window and on the roof of the Paine Street block. But even in this acute moment my chief horror was something apart from the immediate weakness of my defences. I was shuddering because not one of my pursuers, despite some hideous pantings, gruntings, and subdued barkings at odd intervals, was uttering an unmuffled or intelligible vocal sound.

As I moved the furniture and rushed toward the windows I heard a frightful scurrying along the corridor toward the room north of me, and perceived that the southward battering had ceased. Plainly, most of my opponents were about to concentrate against the feeble connecting door which they knew must open directly on me. Outside, the moon played on the ridgepole of the block below, and I saw that the jump would be desperately hazardous because of the steep surface on which I must land.

Surveying the conditions, I chose the more southerly of the

two windows as my avenue of escape; planning to land on the inner slope of the roof and make for the nearest skylight. Once inside one of the decrepit brick structures I would have to reckon with pursuit; but I hoped to descend and dodge in and out of yawning doorways along the shadowed courtyard, eventually getting to Washington Street and slipping out of town toward the south.

The clatter at the northerly connecting door was now terrific, and I saw that the weak panelling was beginning to splinter. Obviously, the besiegers had brought some ponderous object into play as a battering-ram. The bedstead, however, still held firm; so that I had at least a faint chance of making good my escape. As I opened the window I noticed that it was flanked by heavy velour draperies suspended from a pole by brass rings, and also that there was a large projecting catch for the shutters on the exterior. Seeing a possible means of avoiding the dangerous jump, I yanked at the hangings and brought them down, pole and all; then quickly hooking two of the rings in the shutter catch and flinging the drapery outside. The heavy folds reached fully to the abutting roof, and I saw that the rings and catch would be likely to bear my weight. So, climbing out of the window and down the improvised rope ladder, I left behind me forever the morbid and horror-infested fabric of the Gilman House.

I landed safely on the loose slates of the steep roof, and succeeded in gaining the gaping black skylight without a slip. Glancing up at the window I had left, I observed it was still dark, though far across the crumbling chimneys to the north I could see lights ominously blazing in the Order of Dagon Hall, the Baptist church, and the Congregational church which I recalled so shiveringly. There had seemed to be no one in the courtyard below, and I hoped there would be a chance to get away before the spreading of a general alarm. Flashing my pocket lamp into the skylight, I saw that there were no steps down. The distance was slight, however, so I clambered over the brink and dropped; striking a dusty floor littered with crumbling boxes and barrels.

The place was ghoulish-looking, but I was past minding such impressions and made at once for the staircase revealed by my flashlight—after a hasty glance at my watch, which shewed the hour to be 2 a.m. The steps creaked, but seemed tolerably sound; and I raced down past a barn-like second story to the ground

The escape from the Gilman Hotel. Artist: Jason C. Eckhardt, copyright ©
Jason C. Eckhardt 2013, reprinted with permission

floor. The desolation was complete, and only echoes answered
my footfalls. At length I reached the lower hall at one end of
which I saw a faint luminous rectangle marking the ruined Paine
Street doorway. Heading the other way, I found the back door
also open; and darted out and down five stone steps to the grass-
grown cobblestones of the courtyard.

The moonbeams did not reach down here, but I could just see
my way about without using the flashlight. Some of the windows
on the Gilman House side were faintly glowing, and I thought
I heard confused sounds within. Walking softly over to the

42. Originally conceived as a cost-saving move, turning off streetlights on moonlit nights has become a "green" cause, not only for the resulting energy-saving but to reduce light pollution.

Washington Street side I perceived several open doorways, and chose the nearest as my route out. The hallway inside was black, and when I reached the opposite end I saw that the street door was wedged immovably shut. Resolved to try another building, I groped my way back toward the courtyard, but stopped short when close to the doorway.

For out of an opened door in the Gilman House a large crowd of doubtful shapes was pouring—lanterns bobbing in the darkness, and horrible croaking voices exchanging low cries in what was certainly not English. The figures moved uncertainly, and I realised to my relief that they did not know where I had gone; but for all that they sent a shiver of horror through my frame. Their features were indistinguishable, but their crouching, shambling gait was abominably repellent. And worst of all, I perceived that one figure was strangely robed, and unmistakably surmounted by a tall tiara of a design altogether too familiar. As the figures spread throughout the courtyard, I felt my fears increase. Suppose I could find no egress from this building on the street side? The fishy odour was detestable, and I wondered I could stand it without fainting. Again groping toward the street, I opened a door off the hall and came upon an empty room with closely shuttered but sashless windows. Fumbling in the rays of my flashlight, I found I could open the shutters; and in another moment had climbed outside and was carefully closing the aperture in its original manner.

I was now in Washington Street, and for the moment saw no living thing nor any light save that of the moon. From several directions in the distance, however, I could hear the sound of hoarse voices, of footsteps, and of a curious kind of pattering which did not sound quite like footsteps. Plainly I had no time to lose. The points of the compass were clear to me, and I was glad that all the street-lights were turned off, as is often the custom on strongly moonlit nights in unprosperous rural regions.[42] Some of the sounds came from the south, yet I retained my design of escaping in that direction. There would, I knew, be plenty of deserted doorways to shelter me in case I met any person or group who looked like pursuers.

I walked rapidly, softly, and close to the ruined houses. While hatless and dishevelled after my arduous climb, I did not look especially noticeable; and stood a good chance of passing unheeded if forced to encounter any casual wayfarer. At Bates Street I drew into a yawning vestibule while two shambling figures crossed in front of me, but was soon on my way again and approaching the open space where Eliot Street obliquely crosses Washington at the intersection of South. Though I had never seen this space, it had looked dangerous to me on the grocery youth's map; since the moonlight would have free play there. There was no use trying to evade it, for any alternative course would involve detours of possibly disastrous visibility and delaying effect. The only thing to do was to cross it boldly and openly; imitating the typical shamble of the Innsmouth folk as best I could, and trusting that no one—or at least no pursuer of mine—would be there.

Just how fully the pursuit was organised—and indeed, just what its purpose might be—I could form no idea. There seemed to be unusual activity in the town, but I judged that the news of my escape from the Gilman had not yet spread. I would, of course, soon have to shift from Washington to some other southward street; for that party from the hotel would doubtless be after me. I must have left dust prints in that last old building, revealing how I had gained the street.

The open space was, as I had expected, strongly moonlit; and I saw the remains of a park-like, iron-railed green in its centre. Fortunately no one was about, though a curious sort of buzz or roar seemed to be increasing in the direction of Town Square. South Street was very wide, leading directly down a slight declivity to the waterfront and commanding a long view out at sea; and I hoped that no one would be glancing up it from afar as I crossed in the bright moonlight.

My progress was unimpeded, and no fresh sound arose to hint that I had been spied. Glancing about me, I involuntarily let my pace slacken for a second to take in the sight of the sea, gorgeous in the burning moonlight at the street's end. Far out beyond the breakwater was the dim, dark line of Devil Reef, and as I glimpsed it I could not help thinking of all the hideous legends I had heard in the last thirty-four hours—legends which portrayed this ragged rock as a veritable gateway to realms of unfathomed horror and inconceivable abnormality.

Then, without warning, I saw the intermittent flashes of light

". . . The reef was alive with a teeming horde of alien shapes . . ." *The Shadow over Innsmouth.* Visionary Publishing Co., 1936 (artist: Frank Utpatel)

on the distant reef. They were definite and unmistakable, and awaked in my mind a blind horror beyond all rational proportion. My muscles tightened for panic flight, held in only by a certain unconscious caution and half-hypnotic fascination. And to make matters worse, there now flashed forth from the lofty cupola of the Gilman House, which loomed up to the northeast behind me, a series of analogous though differently spaced gleams which could be nothing less than an answering signal.

Controlling my muscles, and realising afresh how plainly visible I was, I resumed my brisker and feignedly shambling pace; though keeping my eyes on that hellish and ominous reef as long as the opening of South Street gave me a seaward view. What the whole proceeding meant, I could not imagine; unless it involved some strange rite connected with Devil Reef, or unless some party had landed from a ship on that sinister rock. I now bent to the left around the ruinous green; still gazing toward the ocean as it blazed in the spectral summer moonlight, and watching the cryptical flashing of those nameless, unexplainable beacons.

It was then that the most horrible impression of all was borne in upon me—the impression which destroyed my last vestige of self-control and set me running frantically southward past the yawning black doorways and fishily staring windows of that deserted nightmare street. For at a closer glance I saw that the moonlit waters between the reef and the shore were far from empty. They were alive with a teeming horde of shapes swimming inward toward the town; and even at my vast distance and in my single moment of perception I could tell that the bobbing heads and flailing arms were alien and aberrant in a way scarcely to be expressed or consciously formulated.

My frantic running ceased before I had covered a block, for at my left I began to hear something like the hue and cry of organised pursuit. There were footsteps and guttural sounds, and a rattling motor wheezed south along Federal Street. In a second all my plans were utterly changed—for if the southward highway were blocked ahead of me, I must clearly find another egress from Innsmouth. I paused and drew into a gaping doorway, reflecting how lucky I was to have left the moonlit open space before these pursuers came down the parallel street.

A second reflection was less comforting. Since the pursuit was down another street, it was plain that the party was not following me directly. It had not seen me, but was simply obeying a general plan of cutting off my escape. This, however, implied that all roads leading out of Innsmouth were similarly patrolled; for the denizens could not have known what route I intended to take. If this were so, I would have to make my retreat across country away from any road; but how could I do that in view of the marshy and creek-riddled nature of all the surrounding region? For a moment my brain reeled—both from sheer hopelessness and from a rapid increase in the omnipresent fishy odour.

Then I thought of the abandoned railway to Rowley, whose solid line of ballasted, weed-grown earth still stretched off to the northwest from the crumbling station on the edge of the river-gorge. There was just a chance that the townsfolk would not think of that; since its brier-choked desertion made it half-impassable, and the unlikeliest of all avenues for a fugitive to choose. I had seen it clearly from my hotel window and knew about how it lay. Most of its earlier length was uncomfortably visible from the Rowley road, and from high places in the town itself; but one could perhaps crawl inconspicuously through the undergrowth. At any rate, it would form my only chance of deliverance, and there was nothing to do but try it.

Drawing inside the hall of my deserted shelter, I once more consulted the grocery boy's map with the aid of the flashlight. The immediate problem was how to reach the ancient railway; and I now saw that the safest course was ahead to Babson Street; then west to Lafayette—there edging around but not crossing an open space homologous to the one I had traversed—and subsequently back northward and westward in a zigzagging line through Lafayette, Bates, Adams, and Bank Streets—the latter skirting the river-gorge—to the abandoned and dilapidated station I had seen from my window. My reason for going ahead to Babson was that I wished neither to re-cross the earlier open space nor to begin my westward course along a cross street as broad as South.

Starting once more, I crossed the street to the right-hand side in order to edge around into Babson as inconspicuously as possible. Noises still continued in Federal Street, and as I glanced behind me I thought I saw a gleam of light near the building through which I had escaped. Anxious to leave Washington

Street, I broke into a quiet dog-trot, trusting to luck not to encounter any observing eye. Next the corner of Babson Street I saw to my alarm that one of the houses was still inhabited, as attested by curtains at the window; but there were no lights within, and I passed it without disaster.

In Babson Street, which crossed Federal and might thus reveal me to the searchers, I clung as closely as possible to the sagging, uneven buildings; twice pausing in a doorway as the noises behind me momentarily increased. The open space ahead shone wide and desolate under the moon, but my route would not force me to cross it. During my second pause I began to detect a fresh distribution of the vague sounds; and upon looking cautiously out from cover beheld a motor car darting across the open space, bound outward along Eliot Street, which there intersects both Babson and Lafayette.

As I watched—choked by a sudden rise in the fishy odour after a short abatement—I saw a band of uncouth, crouching shapes loping and shambling in the same direction; and knew that this must be the party guarding the Ipswich road, since that highway forms an extension of Eliot Street. Two of the figures I glimpsed were in voluminous robes, and one wore a peaked diadem which glistened whitely in the moonlight. The gait of this figure was so odd that it sent a chill through me—for it seemed to me the creature was almost *hopping*.

When the last of the band was out of sight I resumed my progress; darting around the corner into Lafayette Street, and crossing Eliot very hurriedly lest stragglers of the party be still advancing along that thoroughfare. I did hear some croaking and clattering sounds far off toward Town Square, but accomplished the passage without disaster. My greatest dread was in re-crossing broad and moonlit South Street—with its seaward view—and I had to nerve myself for the ordeal. Someone might easily be looking, and possible Eliot Street stragglers could not fail to glimpse me from either of two points. At the last moment I decided I had better slacken my trot and make the crossing as before in the shambling gait of an average Innsmouth native.

When the view of the water again opened out—this time on my right—I was half-determined not to look at it at all. I could not, however, resist; but cast a sidelong glance as I carefully and imitatively shambled toward the protecting shadows ahead. There was no ship visible, as I had half expected there would be. Instead, the first thing which caught my eye was a small row-boat pulling in toward the abandoned wharves and laden with some bulky, tarpaulin-covered object. Its rowers, though distantly and indistinctly seen, were of an especially repellent aspect. Several swimmers were still discernible; while on the far black reef I could see a faint, steady glow unlike the winking beacon visible before, and of a curious colour which I could not precisely identify.[43] Above the slant roofs ahead and to the right there loomed the tall cupola of the Gilman House, but it was completely dark. The fishy odour, dispelled for a moment by some merciful breeze, now closed in again with maddening intensity.

I had not quite crossed the street when I heard a muttering band advancing along Washington from the north. As they reached the broad open space where I had had my first disquieting glimpse of the moonlit water I could see them plainly only a block away—and was horrified by the bestial abnormality of their faces and the dog-like sub-humanness of their crouching gait. One man moved in a positively simian way, with long arms frequently touching the ground; while another figure—robed and tiaraed—seemed to progress in an almost hopping fashion. I judged this party to be the one I had seen in the Gilman's court-yard—the one, therefore, most closely on my trail. As some of the figures turned to look in my direction I was transfixed with fright, yet managed to preserve the casual, shambling gait I had assumed. To this day I do not know whether they saw me or not. If they did, my stratagem must have deceived them, for they passed on across the moonlit space without varying their course—meanwhile croaking and jabbering in some hateful guttural patois I could not identify.

Once more in shadow, I resumed my former dog-trot past the leaning and decrepit houses that stared blankly into the night. Having crossed to the western sidewalk I rounded the nearest corner into Bates Street, where I kept close to the buildings on the southern side. I passed two houses shewing signs of habitation, one of which had faint lights in upper rooms, yet met with no obstacle. As I turned into Adams Street I felt measurably safer, but received a shock when a man reeled out of a black doorway

43. Just as in "The Colour Out of Space," there is the suggestion that true alienness involves physical attributes, such as color, that are not part of human perception.

directly in front of me. He proved, however, too hopelessly drunk to be a menace; so that I reached the dismal ruins of the Bank Street warehouses in safety.

No one was stirring in that dead street beside the river-gorge, and the roar of the waterfalls quite drowned my footsteps. It was a long dog-trot to the ruined station, and the great brick warehouse walls around me seemed somehow more terrifying than the fronts of private houses. At last I saw the ancient arcaded station—or what was left of it—and made directly for the tracks that started from its farther end.

The rails were rusty but mainly intact, and not more than half the ties had rotted away. Walking or running on such a surface was very difficult; but I did my best, and on the whole made very fair time. For some distance the line kept on along the gorge's brink, but at length I reached the long covered bridge where it crossed the chasm at a dizzy height. The condition of this bridge would determine my next step. If humanly possible, I would use it; if not, I would have to risk more street wandering and take the nearest intact highway bridge.

The vast, barn-like length of the old bridge gleamed spectrally in the moonlight, and I saw that the ties were safe for at least a few feet within. Entering, I began to use my flashlight, and was almost knocked down by the cloud of bats that flapped past me. About half way across there was a perilous gap in the ties which I feared for a moment would halt me; but in the end I risked a desperate jump which fortunately succeeded.

I was glad to see the moonlight again when I emerged from that macabre tunnel. The old tracks crossed River Street at grade, and at once veered off into a region increasingly rural and with less and less of Innsmouth's abhorrent fishy odour. Here the dense growth of weeds and briers hindered me and cruelly tore my clothes, but I was none the less glad that they were there to give me concealment in case of peril. I knew that much of my route must be visible from the Rowley road.

The marshy region began very shortly, with the single track on a low, grassy embankment where the weedy growth was somewhat thinner. Then came a sort of island of higher ground, where the line passed through a shallow open cut choked with bushes and brambles. I was very glad of this partial shelter, since at this point the Rowley road was uncomfortably near according to my window view. At the end of the cut it would cross the track and swerve off to a safer distance; but meanwhile I must be exceedingly careful. I was by this time thankfully certain that the railway itself was not patrolled.

Just before entering the cut I glanced behind me, but saw no pursuer. The ancient spires and roofs of decaying Innsmouth gleamed lovely and ethereal in the magic yellow moonlight, and I thought of how they must have looked in the old days before the shadow fell. Then, as my gaze circled inland from the town, something less tranquil arrested my notice and held me immobile for a second.

What I saw—or fancied I saw—was a disturbing suggestion of undulant motion far to the south; a suggestion which made me conclude that a very large horde must be pouring out of the city along the level Ipswich road. The distance was great, and I could distinguish nothing in detail; but I did not at all like the look of that moving column. It undulated too much, and glistened too brightly in the rays of the now westering moon. There was a suggestion of sound, too, though the wind was blowing the other way—a suggestion of bestial scraping and bellowing even worse than the muttering of the parties I had lately overheard.

All sorts of unpleasant conjectures crossed my mind. I thought of those very extreme Innsmouth types said to be hidden in crumbling, centuried warrens near the waterfront; I thought, too, of those nameless swimmers I had seen. Counting the parties so far glimpsed, as well as those presumably covering other roads, the number of my pursuers must be strangely large for a town as depopulated as Innsmouth.

Whence could come the dense personnel of such a column as I now beheld? Did those ancient, unplumbed warrens teem with a twisted, uncatalogued, and unsuspected life? Or had some unseen ship indeed landed a legion of unknown outsiders on that hellish reef? Who were they? Why were they there? And if such a column of them was scouring the Ipswich road, would the patrols on the other roads be likewise augmented?

I had entered the brush-grown cut and was struggling along at a very slow pace when that damnable fishy odour again waxed dominant. Had the wind suddenly changed eastward, so that it blew in from the sea and over the town? It must have, I concluded, since I now began to hear shocking guttural murmurs from that hitherto silent direction. There was another sound, too—a kind of wholesale, colossal flopping or pattering which somehow called up images of the most detestable sort. It made me think illogically of that unpleasantly undulating column on the far-off Ipswich road.

And then both stench and sounds grew stronger, so that I paused shivering and grateful for the cut's protection. It was here, I recalled, that the Rowley road drew so close to the old railway before crossing westward and diverging. Something was coming along that road, and I must lie low till its passage and vanishment in the distance. Thank heaven these creatures employed no dogs for tracking—though perhaps that would have been impossible amidst the omnipresent regional odour. Crouched in the bushes of that sandy cleft I felt reasonably safe, even though I knew the searchers would have to cross the track in front of me not much more than an hundred yards away. I would be able to see them, but they could not, except by a malign miracle, see me.

All at once I began dreading to look at them as they passed. I saw the close moonlit space where they would surge by, and had curious thoughts about the irredeemable pollution of that space. They would perhaps be the worst of all Innsmouth types—something one would not care to remember.

The stench waxed overpowering, and the noises swelled to a bestial babel of croaking, baying and barking without the least suggestion of human speech. Were these indeed the voices of my pursuers? Did they have dogs after all? So far I had seen none of the lower animals in Innsmouth. That flopping or pattering was monstrous—I could not look upon the degenerate creatures responsible for it. I would keep my eyes shut till the sounds receded toward the west. The horde was very close now—the air foul with their hoarse snarlings, and the ground almost shaking with their alien-rhythmed footfalls. My breath nearly ceased to come, and I put every ounce of will power into the task of holding my eyelids down.

I am not even yet willing to say whether what followed was a hideous actuality or only a nightmare hallucination. The later action of the government, after my frantic appeals, would tend to confirm it as a monstrous truth; but could not an hallucination have been repeated under the quasi-hypnotic spell of that ancient, haunted, and shadowed town? Such places have strange properties, and the legacy of insane legend might well have acted on more than one human imagination amidst those dead, stench-cursed streets and huddles of rotting roofs and crumbling steeples. Is it not possible that the germ of an actual contagious madness lurks in the depths of that shadow over Innsmouth? Who can be sure of reality after hearing things like the tale of old Zadok Allen? The government men never found poor Zadok, and have no conjectures to make as to what became of him. Where does madness leave off and reality begin? Is it possible that even my latest fear is sheer delusion?

But I must try to tell what I thought I saw that night under the mocking yellow moon—saw surging and hopping down the Rowley road in plain sight in front of me as I crouched among the wild brambles of that desolate railway cut. Of course my resolution to keep my eyes shut had failed. It was foredoomed to failure—for who could crouch blindly while a legion of croaking, baying entities of unknown source flopped noisomely past, scarcely more than a hundred yards away?

I thought I was prepared for the worst, and I really ought to have been prepared considering what I had seen before. My other pursuers had been accursedly abnormal—so should I not have been ready to face a *strengthening* of the abnormal element; to look upon forms in which there was no mixture of the normal at all? I did not open my eyes until the raucous clamour came loudly from a point obviously straight ahead. Then I knew that a long section of them must be plainly in sight where the sides of the cut flattened out and the road crossed the track—and I could no longer keep myself from sampling whatever horror that leering yellow moon might have to shew.

It was the end, for whatever remains to me of life on the surface of this earth, of every vestige of mental peace and confidence in the integrity of Nature and of the human mind. Nothing that I could have imagined—nothing, even, that I could have gathered had I credited old Zadok's crazy tale in the most literal

"... Flopping, hopping, surging inhumanly through the spectral moonlight ..." *The Shadow over Innsmouth.* Visionary Publishing Co., 1936 (artist: Frank Utpatel)

way—would be in any way comparable to the dæmoniac, blasphemous reality that I saw—or believe I saw. I have tried to hint what it was in order to postpone the horror of writing it down baldly. Can it be possible that this planet has actually spawned such things; that human eyes have truly seen, as objective flesh, what man has hitherto known only in febrile phantasy and tenuous legend?

And yet I saw them in a limitless stream—flopping, hopping, croaking, bleating—surging inhumanly through the spectral moonlight in a grotesque, malignant saraband of fantastic nightmare. And some of them had tall tiaras of that nameless whitish-gold metal ... and some were strangely robed ... and one, who led the way, was clad in a ghoulishly humped black coat and striped trousers, and had a man's felt hat perched on the shapeless thing that answered for a head. ...

I think their predominant colour was a greyish-green, though they had white bellies. They were mostly shiny and slippery, but the ridges of their backs were scaly. Their forms vaguely suggested the anthropoid, while their heads were the heads of fish, with prodigious bulging eyes that never closed. At the sides of their necks were palpitating gills, and their long paws were webbed. They hopped irregularly, sometimes on two legs and sometimes on four. I was somehow glad that they had no more than four limbs. Their croaking, baying voices, clearly used for articulate speech, held all the dark shades of expression which their staring faces lacked.

But for all of their monstrousness they were not unfamiliar to me. I knew too well what they must be—for was not the memory of that evil tiara at Newburyport still fresh? They were the blasphemous fish-frogs of the nameless design—living and horrible—and as I saw them I knew also of what that humped, tiaraed priest in the black church basement had so fearsomely reminded me. Their number was past guessing. It seemed to me that there were limitless swarms of them—and certainly my momentary glimpse could have shewn only the least fraction. In another instant everything was blotted out by a merciful fit of fainting; the first I had ever had.

V.

IT WAS A gentle daylight rain that awaked me from my stupor in the brush-grown railway cut, and when I staggered out to the roadway ahead I saw no trace of any prints in the fresh mud. The fishy odour, too, was gone. Innsmouth's ruined roofs and toppling steeples loomed up greyly toward the southeast, but not a living creature did I spy in all the desolate salt marshes around. My watch was still going, and told me that the hour was past noon.

The reality of what I had been through was highly uncertain in my mind, but I felt that something hideous lay in the background. I must get away from evil-shadowed Innsmouth—and accordingly I began to test my cramped, wearied powers of locomotion. Despite weakness, hunger, horror, and bewilderment I found myself after a time able to walk; so started slowly along the muddy road to Rowley. Before evening I was in the village, getting a meal and providing myself with presentable clothes. I caught the night train to Arkham, and the next day talked long and earnestly with government officials there; a process I later repeated in Boston. With the main result of these colloquies the public is now familiar—and I wish, for normality's sake, there were nothing more to tell. Perhaps it is madness that is overtaking me—yet perhaps a greater horror—or a greater marvel—is reaching out.

As may well be imagined, I gave up most of the foreplanned features of the rest of my tour—the scenic, architectural, and antiquarian diversions on which I had counted so heavily. Nor did I dare look for that piece of strange jewellery said to be in the Miskatonic University Museum. I did, however, improve my stay in Arkham by collecting some genealogical notes I had long wished to possess; very rough and hasty data, it is true, but capable of good use later on when I might have time to collate and codify them. The curator of the historical society there—Mr. E. Lapham Peabody—was very courteous about assisting me, and expressed unusual interest when I told him I was a grandson of Eliza Orne of Arkham, who was born in 1867 and had married James Williamson of Ohio at the age of seventeen.

It seemed that a maternal uncle of mine had been there many years before on a quest much like my own; and that my grandmoth-

44. Maumee is a suburb of Toledo. The narrator may be concealing a stay at the Toledo Asylum for the Insane, opened in 1888 and built on the "cottage" system (rather than the immense main buildings of an older period). In 1894, the institution changed its name to the more benign Toledo State Hospital. If the narrator told others of his observations in Innsmouth, he was likely deemed as crazy as his cousin Lawrence.

45. A small private liberal arts college located in Oberlin, Ohio, about ninety miles east of Toledo. Although Oberlin always embraced progressive causes and community activities, it is unlikely that the student body would have embraced the Innsmouth program of devil worship!

er's family was a topic of some local curiosity. There had, Mr. Peabody said, been considerable discussion about the marriage of her father, Benjamin Orne, just after the Civil War; since the ancestry of the bride was peculiarly puzzling. That bride was understood to have been an orphaned Marsh of New Hampshire—a cousin of the Essex County Marshes—but her education had been in France and she knew very little of her family. A guardian had deposited funds in a Boston bank to maintain her and her French governess; but that guardian's name was unfamiliar to Arkham people, and in time he dropped out of sight, so that the governess assumed his role by court appointment. The Frenchwoman—now long dead—was very taciturn, and there were those who said she could have told more than she did.

But the most baffling thing was the inability of anyone to place the recorded parents of the young woman—Enoch and Lydia (Meserve) Marsh—among the known families of New Hampshire. Possibly, many suggested, she was the natural daughter of some Marsh of prominence—she certainly had the true Marsh eyes. Most of the puzzling was done after her early death, which took place at the birth of my grandmother—her only child. Having formed some disagreeable impressions connected with the name of Marsh, I did not welcome the news that it belonged on my own ancestral tree; nor was I pleased by Mr. Peabody's suggestion that I had the true Marsh eyes myself. However, I was grateful for data which I knew would prove valuable; and took copious notes and lists of book references regarding the well-documented Orne family.

I went directly home to Toledo from Boston, and later spent a month at Maumee recuperating from my ordeal.[44] In September I entered Oberlin[45] for my final year, and from then till the next June was busy with studies and other wholesome activities—reminded of the bygone terror only by occasional official visits from government men in connexion with the campaign which my pleas and evidence had started. Around the middle of July—just a year after the Innsmouth experience—I spent a week with my late mother's family in Cleveland; checking some of my new genealogical data with the various notes, traditions, and bits of heirloom material in existence there, and seeing what kind of a connected chart I could construct.

I did not exactly relish this task, for the atmosphere of the Williamson home had always depressed me. There was a strain of morbidity there, and my mother had never encouraged my visiting her parents as a child, although she always welcomed her father when he came to Toledo. My Arkham-born grandmother had seemed strange and almost terrifying to me, and I do not think I grieved when she disappeared. I was eight years old then, and it was said that she had wandered off in grief after the suicide of my uncle Douglas, her eldest son. He had shot himself after a trip to New England—the same trip, no doubt, which had caused him to be recalled at the Arkham Historical Society.

This uncle had resembled her, and I had never liked him either. Something about the staring, unwinking expression of both of them had given me a vague, unaccountable uneasiness. My mother and uncle Walter had not looked like that. They were like their father, though poor little cousin Lawrence—Walter's son—had been an almost perfect duplicate of his grandmother before his condition took him to the permanent seclusion of a sanitarium at Canton.[46] I had not seen him in four years, but my uncle once implied that his state, both mental and physical, was very bad. This worry had probably been a major cause of his mother's death two years before.

My grandfather and his widowed son Walter now comprised the Cleveland household, but the memory of older times hung thickly over it. I still disliked the place, and tried to get my researches done as quickly as possible. Williamson records and traditions were supplied in abundance by my grandfather; though for Orne material I had to depend on my uncle Walter, who put

46. There was no insane asylum in Canton at the time, but about ten miles west, in Massillon, was the Massillon State Hospital for the Insane, opened in 1898.

Massillon is located in the northeastern portion of Ohio in Stark County, on the Tuscarawas River, fifty miles south of Cleveland, and departed from the style of earlier asylums, which had massive buildings to house inmates. The Athens Lunatic Asylum, in Athens, Ohio, about 170 miles distant, and Norwich State Hospital, in Preston, Connecticut, similarly adopted the cottage-style of architecture.

The main building at the Athens Lunatic Asylum, Athens, Ohio. There were seven smaller cottages on the 1,000-acre property.

Massillon State Hospital building, ca. 1914.

This aerial view of Norwich State Hospital, in Preston, Connecticut, taken in 1934, shows the cottage design still in use.

at my disposal the contents of all his files, including notes, letters, cuttings, heirlooms, photographs, and miniatures.

It was in going over the letters and pictures on the Orne side that I began to acquire a kind of terror of my own ancestry. As I have said, my grandmother and uncle Douglas had always disturbed me. Now, years after their passing, I gazed at their pictured faces with a measurably heightened feeling of repulsion and alienation. I could not at first understand the change, but gradually a horrible sort of *comparison* began to obtrude itself on my unconscious mind despite the steady refusal of my consciousness to admit even the least suspicion of it. It was clear that the typical expression of these faces now suggested something it had not suggested before—something which would bring stark panic if too openly thought of.

But the worst shock came when my uncle shewed me the Orne jewellery in a downtown safe-deposit vault. Some of the items were delicate and inspiring enough, but there was one box of strange old pieces descended from my mysterious great-grandmother which my uncle was almost reluctant to produce. They were, he said, of very grotesque and almost repulsive design, and had never to his knowledge been publicly worn; though my grandmother used to enjoy looking at them. Vague legends of bad luck clustered around them, and my great-grandmother's French governess had said they ought not to be worn in New England, though it would be quite safe to wear them in Europe.

As my uncle began slowly and grudgingly to unwrap the things he urged me not to be shocked by the strangeness and frequent hideousness of the designs. Artists and archæologists who had seen them pronounced the workmanship superlatively and exotically exquisite, though no one seemed able to define their exact material or assign them to any specific art tradition. There were two armlets, a tiara, and a kind of pectoral; the latter having in high relief certain figures of almost unbearable extravagance.

During this description I had kept a tight rein on my emotions, but my face must have betrayed my mounting fears. My uncle looked concerned, and paused in his unwrapping to study my countenance. I motioned to him to continue, which he did with renewed signs of reluctance. He seemed to expect some demonstration when the first piece—the tiara—became visible, but I doubt if he expected quite what actually happened. I did not expect it, either, for I thought I was thoroughly forewarned regarding what the jewellery would turn out to be. What I did was to faint silently away, just as I had done in that brier-choked railway cut a year before.

From that day on my life has been a nightmare of brooding and apprehension, nor do I know how much is hideous truth and how much madness. My great-grandmother had been a Marsh of unknown source whose husband lived in Arkham—and did not old Zadok say that the daughter of Obed Marsh by a monstrous mother was married to an Arkham man through a trick? What was it the ancient toper had muttered about the likeness of my eyes to Captain Obed's? In Arkham, too, the curator had told me I had the true Marsh eyes. Was Obed Marsh my own great-great-grandfather? Who—or *what*—then, was my great-great-grandmother? But perhaps this was all madness. Those whitish-gold ornaments might easily have been bought from some Innsmouth sailor by the father of my great-grandmother, whoever he was. And that look in the staring-eyed faces of my grandmother and self-slain uncle might be sheer fancy on my part—sheer fancy, bolstered up by the Innsmouth shadow which had so darkly coloured my imagination. But why had my uncle killed himself after an ancestral quest in New England?

For more than two years I fought off these reflections with partial success. My father secured me a place in an insurance office, and I buried myself in routine as deeply as possible. In the winter of 1930–31, however, the dreams began. They were very sparse and insidious at first, but increased in frequency and vividness as the weeks went by. Great watery spaces opened out before me, and I seemed to wander through titanic sunken porticos and labyrinths of weedy Cyclopean walls with grotesque fishes as my companions. Then the *other shapes* began to appear, filling me with nameless horror the moment I awoke. But during the dreams they did not horrify me at all—I was one with them; wearing their unhuman trappings, treading their aqueous ways, and praying monstrously at their evil sea-bottom temples.

There was much more than I could remember, but even what I did remember each morning would be enough to stamp me as a madman or a genius if ever I dared write it down.

"One night, in a frightful dream, I met two Ancient Ones under the
sea . . ." ". . . in a phosphorescent, many terraced palace surrounded
by gardens of strange, leprous corals."
Weird Tales 36, no. 3 (January 1942) (artist: Hannes Bok)

Some frightful influence, I felt, was seeking gradually to drag
me out of the sane world of wholesome life into unnamable
abysses of blackness and alienage; and the process told heavily on me. My health and appearance grew steadily worse, till
finally I was forced to give up my position and adopt the static,
secluded life of an invalid. Some odd nervous affliction had
me in its grip, and I found myself at times almost unable to
shut my eyes.

It was then that I began to study the mirror with mounting
alarm. The slow ravages of disease are not pleasant to watch,
but in my case there was something subtler and more puzzling
in the background. My father seemed to notice it, too, for he
began looking at me curiously and almost affrightedly. What was
taking place in me? Could it be that I was coming to resemble my
grandmother and uncle Douglas?

One night I had a frightful dream in which I met my grandmother under the sea. She lived in a phosphorescent palace of
many terraces, with gardens of strange leprous corals and gro-

tesque brachiate[47] efflorescences, and welcomed me with a warmth that may have been sardonic. She had changed—as those who take to the water change—and told me she had never died. Instead, she had gone to a spot her dead son had learned about, and had leaped to a realm whose wonders—destined for him as well—he had spurned with a smoking pistol. This was to be my realm, too—I could not escape it. I would never die, but would live with those who had lived since before man ever walked the earth.

I met also that which had been her grandmother. For eighty thousand years Pth'thya-l'yi had lived in Y'ha-nthlei, and thither she had gone back after Obed Marsh was dead. Y'ha-nthlei was not destroyed when the upper-earth men shot death into the sea. It was hurt, but not destroyed. The Deep Ones could never be destroyed, even though the palæogean magic of the forgotten Old Ones might sometimes check them. For the present they would rest; but some day, if they remembered, they would rise again for the tribute Great Cthulhu craved. It would be a city greater than Innsmouth next time. They had planned to spread, and had brought up that which would help them, but now they must wait once more. For bringing the upper-earth men's death I must do a penance, but that would not be heavy. This was the dream in which I saw a *shoggoth* for the first time, and the sight set me awake in a frenzy of screaming. That morning the mirror definitely told me I had acquired the *Innsmouth look.*[48]

So far I have not shot myself as my uncle Douglas did. I bought an automatic and almost took the step, but certain dreams deterred me. The tense extremes of horror are lessening, and I feel queerly drawn toward the unknown sea-deeps instead of fearing them. I hear and do strange things in sleep, and awake with a kind of exaltation instead of terror. I do not believe I need to wait for the full change as most have waited. If I did, my father would probably shut me up in a sanitarium as my poor little cousin is shut up. Stupendous and unheard-of splendours await me below, and I shall seek them soon. *Iä-R'lyeh! Cthulhu fhtagn! Iä! Iä!* No, I shall not shoot myself—I cannot be made to shoot myself!

I shall plan my cousin's escape from that Canton madhouse,

47. With armlike appendages or branches.

48. Lovecraft's notes (reproduced in *Something About Cats and Other Pieces*) lay out several versions of the family tree:

Obed—gt. gt. grandfather b. 1798–1878 Innsmouth.

Ft'thya-ly:—fish-thing—gt. gt. grandmother b. B.C. 78,000—returned to water after death of earthly husband.

Alice Marsh—gt. grandmother 1847–1867 Innsmouth. Aunt of Old Man marsh—half-sister of his father. Dau. of /Capt. Marsh's son Onesiphorus & Thing/m. Arkham man Joshua Orne 1840–1904. [An alternate verison adds Capt. Obed Marsh, born 1830, Ezekiel Marsh, also born 1830, and Alice Marsh, born 1847.] Henry Marsh, also known as Old Man Marsh, was born in 1862.

Eliza Orne—grandmother. Only child (John Marsh Orne b. 1870—Suicide 1903 after 1st child die—Charles Peckham Orne b. 1873 disappeared 1914—Rebecca Orne b. 1875 m. 1900, 2 children odd 1 dead other queer bachelor) 1869–19 Arkham d. 1899 m. Cleveland man James Wmson [an alternate version indicates he remarried Helen Crane in 1895]

Mary Williamson—mother 1885–1922 Cleveland d. 1922 m. Henry Olmstead of Akron ["strange illness" is noted in an alternate version]

Douglas Orne Williamson b. 1887 m. 1915 1 ch.b. 1917 queer [an alternate version indicates he committed suicide in 1913]

Walter Williamson—b. 1890 concealed 1900 in Canton sanitarium [an alternate version indicates that Walter had one child born in 1917, and adds "queer in sanit.," though whether this refers to Walter or the child is unclear].

Robert (Martin) Olmstead—narrator— b. 1906—? Akron

49. Donald R. Burleson, in *H. P. Love-craft: A Critical Study*, calls this final phrase a "delectable parody of the ending of the 23rd Psalm," which reads, "and I will dwell in the house of the Lord forever."

and together we shall go to marvel-shadowed Innsmouth. We shall swim out to that brooding reef in the sea and dive down through black abysses to Cyclopean and many-columned Y'ha-nthlei, and in that lair of the Deep Ones we shall dwell amidst wonder and glory for ever.[49]

The Dreams in the Witch House[1]

One scholar called this tale "Lovecraft's Magnificent Failure," and there are certainly parts of the narrative that are confused and difficult to understand. Yet it is in many ways Lovecraft's most cosmic tale, an effort to imagine the fourth dimension, or hyperspace—science-fictional concepts unexplored in fiction at the time he was writing. Lovecraft proffers a scientific explanation for seventeenth-century witchcraft as well, involving higher mathematics, and adds an air of "realism" with references to the Old Ones he describes in other tales.

1. The story was written in 1932 and first appeared in *Weird Tales* 22, no. 1 (July 1933), 86–111, where it was described by the editors as follows: "A story of mathematics, witchcraft and Walpurgis Night, in which the horror creeps and grows—a new tale by the author of 'The Rats in the Walls.'"

Whether the dreams brought on the fever or the fever brought on the dreams Walter Gilman did not know. Behind everything crouched the brooding, festering horror of the ancient town, and of the mouldy, unhallowed garret gable where he wrote and studied and wrestled with figures and formulæ when he was not tossing on the meagre iron bed. His ears were growing sensitive to a preternatural and intolerable degree, and he had long ago stopped the cheap mantel clock whose ticking had come to seem like a thunder of artillery. At night the subtle stirring of the black city outside, the sinister scurrying of rats in the wormy partitions, and the creaking of hidden timbers in the centuried house, were enough to give him a sense of strident pandæmonium. The darkness always teemed with unexplained sound—and yet he sometimes shook with fear lest the noises he heard should subside and allow him to hear certain other, fainter, noises which he suspected were lurking behind them.

He was in the changeless, legend-haunted city of Arkham, with its clustering gambrel roofs that sway and sag over attics where witches hid from the King's men in the dark, olden days of the Province. Nor was any spot in that city more steeped in

2. This is a fictitious name; no "Keziah" or "Mason" is to be found in the transcripts of the Salem Witch Trials of 1692–93.

3. A nonsensical term, as Robert Weinberg demonstrates in "H. P. Lovecraft and Pseudomathematics," because there is no real connection between geometry and calculus. Gilman speculates on four-dimensional objects, but necessarily, such an object *cannot* be constructed in a three-dimensional system. Donald R. Burleson disagrees, in "A Note on Lovecraft, Mathematics, and the Outer Spheres," arguing that Lovecraft merely imagined realms in which such common geometric notions as distances have no ready meaning. "For example," he argues, "a mathematician may work with the abstract structure called a 'locally compact topological group,' and in that context define an abstract 'measure' and what is called the Haar integral—so that even in this wholly abstract setting one may do a kind of 'calculus.'" These are deep waters indeed!

4. A notion that was gaining traction at the time, as architects tried to blend the mysticism of Theosophy with science and the Society for Psychical Research attracted many prominent members. Later, physicists would note the resemblances between the descriptions of the Zen Buddhist universe and the chaotic world of the atom (see, for example, *The Tao of Physics*, by Fritjof Capra).

5. A town in Essex County, Massachusetts, on the Merrimack River, about ten miles west of Newburyport.

macabre memory than the gable room which harboured him—for it was this house and this room which had likewise harboured old Keziah Mason,[2] whose flight from Salem Gaol at the last no one was ever able to explain. That was in 1692—the gaoler had gone mad and babbled of a small white-fanged furry thing which scuttled out of Keziah's cell, and not even Cotton Mather could explain the curves and angles smeared on the grey stone walls with some red, sticky fluid.

Possibly Gilman ought not to have studied so hard. Non-Euclidean calculus[3] and quantum physics are enough to stretch any brain, and when one mixes them with folklore,[4] and tries to trace a strange background of multi-dimensional reality behind the ghoulish hints of the Gothic tales and the wild whispers of the chimney-corner, one can hardly expect to be wholly free from mental tension. Gilman came from Haverhill,[5] but it was only after he had entered college in Arkham that he began to connect his mathematics with the fantastic legends of elder magic. Something in the air of the hoary town worked obscurely on his imagination. The professors at Miskatonic had urged him to slacken up, and had voluntarily cut down his course at several points. Moreover, they had stopped him from consulting the dubious old books on forbidden secrets that were kept under lock and key in a vault at the university library. But all these precautions came

The Jonathan Corwin "Witch House," 310½ Essex Street, Salem, Massachusetts, in 2013. The old gambrel roof was removed in the 1940s.
Photograph copyright © Donovan K. Loucks 2013, reprinted with permission

late in the day, so that Gilman had some terrible hints from the dreaded *Necronomicon* of Abdul Alhazred, the fragmentary *Book of Eibon*,[6] and the suppressed *Unaussprechlichen Kulten* of von Junzt[7] to correlate with his abstract formulæ on the properties of space and the linkage of dimensions known and unknown.

He knew his room was in the old Witch House—that, indeed, was why he had taken it. There was much in the Essex County records about Keziah Mason's trial,[8] and what she had admitted under pressure to the Court of Oyer and Terminer had fascinated Gilman beyond all reason. She had told Judge Hathorne of lines and curves that could be made to point out directions leading through the walls of space to other spaces beyond, and had implied that such lines and curves were frequently used at certain midnight meetings in the dark valley of the white stone beyond Meadow Hill and on the unpeopled island in the river. She had spoken also of the Black Man, of her oath, and of her new secret name of Nahab. Then she had drawn those devices on the walls of her cell and vanished.

Gilman believed strange things about Keziah, and had felt a queer thrill on learning that her dwelling was still standing after more than 235 years. When he heard the hushed Arkham whispers about Keziah's persistent presence in the old house and the narrow streets, about the irregular human tooth-marks left on certain sleepers in that and other houses, about the childish cries heard near May-Eve, and Hallowmass,[9] about the stench often noted in the old house's attic just after those dreaded seasons, and about the small, furry, sharp-toothed thing which haunted the mouldering structure and the town and nuzzled people curiously in the black hours before dawn, he resolved to live in the place at any cost. A room was easy to secure; for the house was unpopular, hard to rent, and long given over to cheap lodgings. Gilman could not have told what he expected to find there, but he knew he wanted to be in the building where some circumstance had more or less suddenly given a mediocre old woman of the seventeenth century an insight into mathematical depths perhaps beyond the utmost modern delvings of Planck, Heisenberg, Einstein, and de Sitter.[10]

He studied the timber and plaster walls for traces of cryptic designs at every accessible spot where the paper had peeled,

6. The book is first mentioned in Clark Ashton Smith's 1932 story "Ubbo-Sathla": "The Book of Eibon, that strangest and rarest of occult forgotten volumes . . . is said to have come down through a series of manifold translations from a prehistoric original written in the lost language of Hyperborea."

7. The book is first mentioned in Robert E. Howard's 1931 story "The Children of the Night," where it is titled *Nameless Cults*. Nothing is known of von Junzt.

8. See, in *The Case of Charles Dexter Ward*, notes 126 et seq., the discussion of the Salem witch trials and explanations of some of the words and phrases used here (such as "Oyer and Terminer").

9. That is, April 30 and October 31, prominent dates when spirits are abroad.

10. Willem de Sitter (1872–1934), a Dutch mathematician, physicist, and astronomer, cowrote a paper with Einstein on dark matter but is no longer as renowned as Planck, Heisenberg, or Einstein. Nonetheless, his contributions were considerable, including, as José Natário writes, in *General Relativity Without Calculus: A Concise Introduction to the Geometry of Relativity* (Berlin: Springer-Verlag, 2011), a cosmological model "representing a hyperspherical Universe without matter but with a positive cosmological constant" (97).

and within a week managed to get the eastern attic room where Keziah was held to have practiced her spells. It had been vacant from the first—for no one had ever been willing to stay there long—but the Polish landlord had grown wary about renting it. Yet nothing whatever happened to Gilman till about the time of the fever. No ghostly Keziah flitted through the sombre halls and chambers, no small furry thing crept into his dismal eyrie to nuzzle him, and no record of the witch's incantations rewarded his constant search. Sometimes he would take walks through shadowy tangles of unpaved musty-smelling lanes where eldritch brown houses of unknown age leaned and tottered and leered mockingly through narrow, small-paned windows. Here he knew strange things had happened once, and there was a faint suggestion behind the surface that everything of that monstrous past might not—at least in the darkest, narrowest, and most intricately crooked alleys—have utterly perished. He also rowed out twice to the ill-regarded island in the river, and made a sketch of the singular angles described by the moss-grown rows of grey standing stones whose origin was so obscure and immemorial.

Gilman's room was of good size but queerly irregular shape; the north wall slanting perceptibly inward from the outer to the inner end, while the low ceiling slanted gently downward in the same direction. Aside from an obvious rat-hole and the signs of other stopped-up ones, there was no access—nor any appearance of a former avenue of access—to the space which must have existed between the slanting wall and the straight outer wall on the house's north side, though a view from the exterior shewed where a window had been boarded up at a very remote date. The loft above the ceiling—which must have had a slanting floor—was likewise inaccessible. When Gilman climbed up a ladder to the cobwebbed level loft above the rest of the attic he found vestiges of a bygone aperture tightly and heavily covered with ancient planking and secured by the stout wooden pegs common in colonial carpentry. No amount of persuasion, however, could induce the stolid landlord to let him investigate either of these two closed spaces.

As time wore along, his absorption in the irregular wall and ceiling of his room increased; for he began to read into the odd angles a mathematical significance which seemed to offer vague clues regarding their purpose. Old Keziah, he reflected, might have had excellent reasons for living in a room with peculiar angles; for was it not through certain angles that she claimed to have gone outside the boundaries of the world of space we know? His interest gradually veered away from the unplumbed voids beyond the slanting surfaces, since it now appeared that the purpose of those surfaces concerned the side he was already on.

The touch of brain-fever and the dreams began early in February. For some time, apparently, the curious angles of Gilman's room had been having a strange, almost hypnotic effect on him; and as the bleak winter advanced he had found himself staring more and more intently at the corner where the down-slanting ceiling met the inward-slanting wall. About this period his inability to concentrate on his formal studies worried him considerably, his apprehensions about the mid-year examinations being very acute. But the exaggerated sense of hearing was scarcely less annoying. Life had become an insistent and almost unendurable cacophony, and there was that constant, terrifying impression of *other* sounds—perhaps from regions beyond life—trembling on the very brink of audibility. So far as concrete noises went, the rats in the ancient partitions were the worst. Sometimes their scratching seemed not only furtive but deliberate. When it came from beyond the slanting north wall it was mixed with a sort of dry rattling—and when it came from the century-closed loft above the slanting ceiling Gilman always braced himself as if expecting some horror which only bided its time before descending to engulf him utterly.

The dreams were wholly beyond the pale of sanity, and Gilman felt that they must be a result, jointly, of his studies in mathematics and in folklore. He had been thinking too much about the vague regions which his formulæ told him must lie beyond the three dimensions we know, and about the possibility that old Keziah Mason—guided by some influence past all conjecture—had actually found the gate to those regions. The yellowed county records containing her testimony and that of her accusers were so damnably suggestive of things beyond human experience—and the descriptions of the darting little furry object which served as her familiar were so painfully realistic despite their incredible details.

11. Their testimony has apparently been bodily removed from the transcripts of the trials. However, Rebecca Eames testified that the devil appeared to her in the form of a mouse or rat.

12. Fritz Leiber Jr., in "Through Hyperspace with Brown Jenkin," points out that this and other aspects of Gilman's experiences sound remarkably like modern suggestions of the effects of travel through hyperspace or wormholes. "Here," Leiber notes, "(1) a rational foundation for such travel is set up; (2) hyperspace is visualised; and (3) a trigger for such travel is devised."

That object—no larger than a good-sized rat and quaintly called by the townspeople "Brown Jenkin"—seemed to have been the fruit of a remarkable case of sympathetic herd-delusion, for in 1692 no less than eleven persons had testified to glimpsing it.[11] There were recent rumours, too, with a baffling and disconcerting amount of agreement. Witnesses said it had long hair and the shape of a rat, but that its sharp-toothed, bearded face was evilly human while its paws were like tiny human hands. It took messages betwixt old Keziah and the devil, and was nursed on the witch's blood, which it sucked like a vampire. Its voice was a kind of loathsome titter, and it could speak all languages. Of all the bizarre monstrosities in Gilman's dreams, nothing filled him with greater panic and nausea than this blasphemous and diminutive hybrid, whose image flitted across his vision in a form a thousandfold more hateful than anything his waking mind had deduced from the ancient records and the modern whispers.

Gilman's dreams consisted largely in plunges through limitless abysses of inexplicably coloured twilight and bafflingly disordered sound; abysses whose material and gravitational properties, and whose relation to his own entity, he could not even begin to explain. He did not walk or climb, fly or swim, crawl or wriggle; yet always experienced a mode of motion partly voluntary and partly involuntary. Of his own condition he could not well judge, for sight of his arms, legs, and torso seemed always cut off by some odd disarrangement of perspective; but he felt that his physical organisation and faculties were somehow marvellously transmuted and obliquely projected—though not without a certain grotesque relationship to his normal proportions and properties.[12]

The abysses were by no means vacant, being crowded with indescribably angled masses of alien-hued substance, some of which appeared to be organic while others seemed inorganic. A few of the organic objects tended to awake vague memories in the back of his mind, though he could form no conscious idea of what they mockingly resembled or suggested. In the later dreams he began to distinguish separate categories into which the organic objects appeared to be divided, and which seemed to involve in each case a radically different species of conduct-pattern and basic motivation. Of these categories one seemed to him to include objects slightly less illogical and irrelevant in their motions than the members of the other categories.

All the objects—organic and inorganic alike—were totally beyond description or even comprehension. Gilman sometimes compared the inorganic masses to prisms, labyrinths, clusters of cubes and planes, and Cyclopean buildings; and the organic things struck him variously as groups of bubbles, octopi, centipedes, living Hindoo idols, and intricate Arabesques roused into a kind of ophidian animation. Everything he saw was unspeakably menacing and horrible; and whenever one of the organic entities appeared by its motions to be noticing him, he felt a stark, hideous fright which generally jolted him awake. Of how the organic entities moved, he could tell no more than of how he moved himself. In time he observed a further mystery—the tendency of certain entities to appear suddenly out of empty space, or to disappear totally with equal suddenness. The shrieking, roaring confusion of sound which permeated the abysses was past all analysis as to pitch, timbre, or rhythm; but seemed to be synchronous with vague visual changes in all the indefinite objects, organic and inorganic alike. Gilman had a constant sense of dread that it might rise to some unbearable degree of intensity during one or another of its obscure, relentlessly inevitable fluctuations.

But it was not in these vortices of complete alienage that he saw Brown Jenkin. That shocking little horror was reserved for certain lighter, sharper dreams which assailed him just before he dropped into the fullest depths of sleep. He would be lying in the dark fighting to keep awake when a faint lambent glow would seem to shimmer around the centuried room, shewing in a violet mist the convergence of angled planes which had seized his brain so insidiously. The horror would appear to pop out of the rat-hole in the corner and patter toward him over the sagging, wide-planked floor with evil expectancy in its tiny, bearded human face—but mercifully, this dream always melted away before the object got close enough to nuzzle him. It had hellishly long, sharp, canine teeth. Gilman tried to stop up the rat-hole every day, but each night the real tenants of the partitions would gnaw away the obstruction, whatever it might be. Once he had the landlord nail tin over it, but the next night the rats gnawed

13. Georg Friedrich Bernhard Riemann (1826–1866), a German mathematician who essentially singlehandedly created the field known as Riemannian geometry, the study of higher dimensions and the extension of differential geometry in *n* dimensions. Riemann's work was vital to Einstein's theory of relativity. Thomas Pynchon's brilliant 2006 novel *Against the Day* explores in part the darkly co(s)mic aspects of the work of Riemann and his students.

a fresh hole—in making which they pushed or dragged out into the room a curious little fragment of bone.

Gilman did not report his fever to the doctor, for he knew he could not pass the examinations if ordered to the college infirmary when every moment was needed for cramming. As it was, he failed in Calculus D and Advanced General Psychology, though not without hope of making up lost ground before the end of the term. It was in March when the fresh element entered his lighter preliminary dreaming, and the nightmare shape of Brown Jenkin began to be companioned by the nebulous blur which grew more and more to resemble a bent old woman. This addition disturbed him more than he could account for, but finally he decided that it was like an ancient crone whom he had twice actually encountered in the dark tangle of lanes near the abandoned wharves. On those occasions the evil, sardonic, and seemingly unmotivated stare of the beldame had set him almost shivering—especially the first time, when an overgrown rat darting across the shadowed mouth of a neighbouring alley had made him think irrationally of Brown Jenkin. Now, he reflected, those nervous fears were being mirrored in his disordered dreams.

That the influence of the old house was unwholesome, he could not deny; but traces of his early morbid interest still held him there. He argued that the fever alone was responsible for his nightly phantasies, and that when the touch abated he would be free from the monstrous visions. Those visions, however, were of abhorrent vividness and convincingness, and whenever he awaked he retained a vague sense of having undergone much more than he remembered. He was hideously sure that in unrecalled dreams he had talked with both Brown Jenkin and the old woman, and that they had been urging him to go somewhere with them and to meet a third being of greater potency.

Toward the end of March he began to pick up in his mathematics, though other studies bothered him increasingly. He was getting an intuitive knack for solving Riemannian equations,[13] and astonished Professor Upham by his comprehension of fourth-dimensional and other problems which had floored all the rest of the class. One afternoon there was a discussion of possible freakish curvatures in space, and of theoretical points of approach or even contact between our part of the cosmos and various other regions as distant as the farthest stars or the trans-galactic gulfs themselves—or even as fabulously remote as the tentatively conceivable cosmic units beyond the whole Einsteinian space-time continuum. Gilman's handling of this theme filled everyone with admiration, even though some of his hypothetical illustrations caused an increase in the always plentiful gossip about his nervous and solitary eccentricity. What made the students shake their heads was his sober theory that a man might—given mathematical knowledge admittedly beyond all likelihood of human acquirement—step deliberately from the earth to any other celestial body which might lie at one of an infinity of specific points in the cosmic pattern.

Such a step, he said, would require only two stages; first, a passage out of the three-dimensional sphere we know, and second, a passage back to the three-dimensional sphere at another point, perhaps one of infinite remoteness. That this could be accomplished without loss of life was in many cases conceivable. Any being from any part of three-dimensional space could probably survive in the fourth dimension; and its survival of the second stage would depend upon what alien part of three-dimensional space it might select for its re-entry. Denizens of some planets might be able to live on certain others—even planets belonging to other galaxies, or to similar-dimensional phases of other space-time continua—though of course there must be vast numbers of mutually uninhabitable even though mathematically juxtaposed bodies or zones of space.

It was also possible that the inhabitants of a given dimensional realm could survive entry to many unknown and incomprehensible realms of additional or indefinitely multiplied dimensions—be they within or outside the given space-time continuum—and that the converse would be likewise true. This was a matter for speculation, though one could be fairly certain that the type of mutation involved in a passage from any given dimensional plane to the next higher plane would not be destructive of biological integrity as we understand it. Gilman could not be very clear about his reasons for this last assumption, but his haziness here was more than overbalanced by his clearness on other complex points. Professor Upham especially liked his demonstration of the kinship of higher mathematics to certain phases of magical lore

14. A loomfixer is a worker who adjusts or repairs looms in the textile industry. "It is better to be a successful loomfixer than an unsuccessful overseer," admonished Albert Ainley, in *Woolen and Worsted Loomfixing: A Book for Loomfixers and All Who Are Interested in the Production of Plain and Fancy Worsteds and Woolens* (Lawrence, MA: Privately printed, 1900). The profession continues today, although with unionization, the lot of the loomfixer has improved. A 1921 editorial in the *Shoe Workers' Journal* on the need for trade unions quoted from a Manchester, New Hampshire, newspaper that pointed out that a loomfixer in Lawrence, Massachusetts, might work 48 hours per week for $32, while a loomfixer at the Amoskeag company of Manchester, minding 20 looms more than the Lawrence loomfixer, worked a 54-hour week for only $25.

Loomfixers in New Market,
New Hampshire (probably 1903–7).

transmitted down the ages from an ineffable antiquity—human or pre-human—whose knowledge of the cosmos and its laws was greater than ours.

Around the first of April Gilman worried considerably because his slow fever did not abate. He was also troubled by what some of his fellow-lodgers said about his sleep-walking. It seemed that he was often absent from his bed, and that the creaking of his floor at certain hours of the night was remarked by the man in the room below. This fellow also spoke of hearing the tread of shod feet in the night; but Gilman was sure he must have been mistaken in this, since shoes as well as other apparel were always precisely in place in the morning. One could develop all sorts of aural delusions in this morbid old house—for did not Gilman himself, even in daylight, now feel certain that noises other than rat-scratchings came from the black voids beyond the slanting wall and above the slanting ceiling? His pathologically sensitive ears began to listen for faint footfalls in the immemorially sealed loft overhead, and sometimes the illusion of such things was agonisingly realistic.

However, he knew that he had actually become a somnambulist; for twice at night his room had been found vacant, though with all his clothing in place. Of this he had been assured by Frank Elwood, the one fellow-student whose poverty forced him to room in this squalid and unpopular house. Elwood had been studying in the small hours and had come up for help on a differential equation, only to find Gilman absent. It had been rather presumptuous of him to open the unlocked door after knocking had failed to rouse a response, but he had needed the help very badly and thought that his host would not mind a gentle prodding awake. On neither occasion, though, had Gilman been there—and when told of the matter he wondered where he could have been wandering, barefoot and with only his night-clothes on. He resolved to investigate the matter if reports of his sleep-walking continued, and thought of sprinkling flour on the floor of the corridor to see where his footsteps might lead. The door was the only conceivable egress, for there was no possible foothold outside the narrow window.

As April advanced, Gilman's fever-sharpened ears were disturbed by the whining prayers of a superstitious loomfixer,[14] named Joe Mazurewicz, who had a room on the ground floor. Mazurewicz had told long, rambling stories about the ghost of old Keziah and the furry sharp-fanged, nuzzling thing, and had said he was so badly haunted at times that only his silver crucifix—given him for the purpose by Father Iwanicki[15] of St. Stanislaus' Church—could bring him relief. Now he was praying because the Witches' Sabbath was drawing near. May-Eve was Walpurgis-Night, when hell's blackest evil roamed the earth and all the slaves of Satan gathered for nameless rites and deeds. It was always a very bad time in Arkham, even though the fine folks up in Miskatonic Avenue and High and Saltonstall Streets pretended to know nothing about it. There would be bad doings—and a child or two would probably be missing. Joe knew about such things, for his grandmother in the old country had heard tales from her grandmother. It was wise to pray and count one's beads at this season.[16] For three months Keziah and Brown Jenkin had not been near Joe's room, nor near Paul Choynski's room, nor anywhere else—and it meant no good when they held off like that. They must be up to something.

Gilman dropped in at a doctor's office on the 16th of the month, and was surprised to find his temperature was not as high as he had feared. The physician questioned him sharply, and advised him to see a nerve specialist. On reflection, he was glad he had not consulted the still more inquisitive college doctor. Old Waldron, who had curtailed his activities before, would have made him take a rest—an impossible thing now that he was so close to great results in his equations. He was certainly near the boundary between the known universe and the fourth dimension, and who could say how much farther he might go?

But even as these thoughts came to him he wondered at the source of his strange confidence. Did all of this perilous sense of imminence come from the formulæ on the sheets he covered day by day? The soft, stealthy, imaginary footsteps in the sealed loft above were unnerving. And now, too, there was a growing feeling that somebody was constantly persuading him to do something terrible which he could not do. How about the somnambulism? Where did he go sometimes in the night? And what was that faint suggestion of sound which once in a while seemed to trickle through the maddening confusion of identifiable sounds even in

15. The name appears also in Lovecraft's discarded draft of "The Shadow over Innsmouth."

16. That is, say the rosary.

broad daylight and full wakefulness? Its rhythm did not correspond to anything on earth, unless perhaps to the cadence of one or two unmentionable Sabbat-chants, and sometimes he feared it corresponded to certain attributes of the vague shrieking or roaring in those wholly alien abysses of dream.

The dreams were meanwhile getting to be atrocious. In the lighter preliminary phase the evil old woman was now of fiendish distinctness, and Gilman knew she was the one who had frightened him in the slums. Her bent back, long nose, and shrivelled chin were unmistakable, and her shapeless brown garments were like those he remembered. The expression on her face was one of hideous malevolence and exultation, and when he awaked he could recall a croaking voice that persuaded and threatened. He must meet the Black Man, and go with them all to the throne of Azathoth at the centre of ultimate Chaos. That was what she said. He must sign in his own blood the book of Azathoth and take a new secret name now that his independent delvings had gone so far. What kept him from going with her and Brown Jenkin and the other to the throne of Chaos where the thin flutes pipe mindlessly was the fact that he had seen the name "Azathoth" in the *Necronomicon* and knew it stood for a primal evil too horrible for description.

The old woman always appeared out of thin air near the corner where the downward slant met the inward slant. She seemed to crystallise at a point closer to the ceiling than to the floor, and every night she was a little nearer and more distinct before the dream shifted. Brown Jenkin, too was always a little nearer at the last, and its yellowish-white fangs glistened shockingly in that unearthly violet phosphorescence. Its shrill loathsome tittering stuck more and more in Gilman's head, and he could remember in the morning how it had pronounced the words "Azathoth" and "Nyarlathotep."

In the deeper dreams everything was likewise more distinct, and Gilman felt that the twilight abysses around him were those of the fourth dimension. Those organic entities whose motions seemed least flagrantly irrelevant and unmotivated were probably projections of life-forms from our own planet, including human beings. What the others were in their own dimensional sphere or spheres he dared not try to think. Two of the less irrelevantly moving things—a rather large congeries of iridescent, prolately spheroidal bubbles[17] and a very much smaller polyhedron of unknown colours and rapidly shifting surface angles—seemed to take notice of him and follow him about or float ahead as he changed position among the titan prisms, labyrinths, cube-and-plane clusters, and quasi-buildings; and all the while the vague shrieking and roaring waxed louder and louder, as if approaching some monstrous climax of utterly unendurable intensity.

During the night of April 19–20 the new development occurred. Gilman was half-involuntarily moving about in the twilight abysses with the bubble-mass and the small polyhedron floating ahead, when he noticed the peculiarly regular angles formed by the edges of some gigantic neighbouring prism-clusters. In another second he was out of the abyss and standing tremulously on a rocky hillside bathed in intense, diffused green light. He was barefooted and in his night-clothes and when he tried to walk discovered that he could scarcely lift his feet. A swirling vapour hid everything but the immediate sloping terrain from sight, and he shrank from the thought of the sounds that might surge out of that vapour.

Then he saw the two shapes laboriously crawling toward him—the old woman and the little furry thing. The crone strained up to her knees and managed to cross her arms in a singular fashion, while Brown Jenkin pointed in a certain direction with a horribly anthropoid fore paw which it raised with evident difficulty. Spurred by an impulse he did not originate, Gilman dragged himself forward along a course determined by the angle of the old woman's arms and the direction of the small monstrosity's paw, and before he had shuffled three steps he was back in the twilight abysses. Geometrical shapes seethed around him, and he fell dizzily and interminably. At last he woke in his bed in the crazily angled garret of the eldritch old house.

He was good for nothing that morning, and stayed away from all his classes. Some unknown attraction was pulling his eyes in a seemingly irrelevant direction, for he could not help staring at a certain vacant spot on the floor. As the day advanced the focus of his unseeing eyes changed position, and by noon he had conquered the impulse to stare at vacancy. About two o'clock he went out for lunch, and as he threaded the narrow lanes of the

17. A prolate spheroid is one in which the polar axis is longer than the diameter; that is, it is a sphere that's been "stretched" vertically to be more oval-shaped than round.

18. The water snake, also representing the dragon of Æëtes, slain by Jason and the Argonauts to capture the golden fleece. Hydra is the largest constellation in the sky.

19. Argo Navis, the ship *Argo* (Jason's ship), is a constellation that lies entirely in the Southern Hemisphere, east of Canis Major, and covers a great portion of the sky. Only a few of its numerous stars are visible over the East Coast. It includes Canopus, an extremely bright white star.

city he found himself turning always to the southeast. Only an effort halted him at a cafeteria in Church Street, and after the meal he felt the unknown pull still more strongly.

He would have to consult a nerve specialist after all—perhaps there was a connexion with his somnambulism—but meanwhile he might at least try to break the morbid spell himself. Undoubtedly he could still manage to walk away from the pull; so with great resolution he headed against it and dragged himself deliberately north along Garrison Street. By the time he had reached the bridge over the Miskatonic he was in a cold perspiration, and he clutched at the iron railing as he gazed upstream at the ill-regarded island whose regular lines of ancient standing stones brooded sullenly in the afternoon sunlight.

Then he gave a start. For there was a clearly visible living figure on that desolate island, and a second glance told him it was certainly the strange old woman whose sinister aspect had worked itself so disastrously into his dreams. The tall grass near her was moving, too, as if some other living thing were crawling close to the ground. When the old woman began to turn toward him he fled precipitately off the bridge and into the shelter of the town's labyrinthine waterfront alleys. Distant though the island was, he felt that a monstrous and invincible evil could flow from the sardonic stare of that bent, ancient figure in brown.

The southeastward pull still held, and only with tremendous resolution could Gilman drag himself into the old house and up the rickety stairs. For hours he sat silent and aimless, with his eyes shifting gradually westward. About six o'clock his sharpened ears caught the whining prayers of Joe Mazurewicz two floors below, and in desperation he seized his hat and walked out into the sunset-golden streets, letting the now directly southward pull carry him where it might. An hour later darkness found him in the open fields beyond Hangman's Brook, with the glimmering spring stars shining ahead. The urge to walk was gradually changing to an urge to leap mystically into space, and suddenly he realised just where the source of the pull lay.

It was in the sky. A definite point among the stars had a claim on him and was calling him. Apparently it was a point somewhere between Hydra[18] and Argo Navis,[19] and he knew that he had been urged toward it ever since he had awaked soon after dawn.[20] In the morning it had been underfoot; afternoon found it rising in the southeast, and now it was roughly south but wheeling toward the west. What was the meaning of this new thing? Was he going mad? How long would it last? Again mustering his resolution, Gilman turned and dragged himself back to the sinister old house.

Mazurewicz was waiting for him at the door, and seemed both anxious and reluctant to whisper some fresh bit of superstition. It was about the witch light. Joe had been out celebrating the night before—it was Patriots' Day in Massachusetts[21]—and had come home after midnight. Looking up at the house from outside, he had thought at first that Gilman's window was dark; but then he had seen the faint violet glow within. He wanted to warn the gentleman about that glow, for everybody in Arkham knew it was Keziah's witch light which played near Brown Jenkin and the ghost of the old crone herself. He had not mentioned this before, but now he must tell about it because it meant that Keziah and her long-toothed familiar were haunting the young gentleman. Sometimes he and Paul Choynski and Landlord Dombrowski thought they saw that light seeping out of cracks in the sealed loft above the young gentleman's room, but they had all agreed not to talk about that. However, it would be better for the gentleman to take another room and get a crucifix from some good priest like Father Iwanicki.

As the man rambled on Gilman felt a nameless panic clutch at his throat. He knew that Joe must have been half drunk when he came home the night before, yet this mention of a violet light in the garret window was of frightful import. It was a lambent glow of this sort which always played about the old woman and the small furry thing in those lighter, sharper dreams which prefaced his plunge into unknown abysses, and the thought that a wakeful second person could see the dream-luminance was utterly beyond sane harbourage. Yet where had the fellow got such an odd notion? Had he himself talked as well as walked around the house in his sleep? No, Joe said, he had not—but he must check up on this. Perhaps Frank Elwood could tell him something, though he hated to ask.

Fever—wild dreams—somnambulism—illusions of sounds— a pull toward a point in the sky—and now a suspicion of insane

20. T. R. Livesey points out, in "Dispatches from the Providence Observatory," that this "is one of the emptiest regions in the sky; no star brighter than third magnitude is found anywhere near Hydra's second magnitude Alphard" (40).

21. The third Monday in April, a holiday commemorating the beginning of the American War of Independence.

sleep-talking! He must stop studying, see a nerve specialist, and take himself in hand. When he climbed to the second story he paused at Elwood's door but saw that the other youth was out. Reluctantly he continued up to his garret room and sat down in the dark. His gaze was still pulled to the southwest, but he also found himself listening intently for some sound in the closed loft above, and half imagining that an evil violet light seeped down through an infinitesimal crack in the low, slanting ceiling.

That night as Gilman slept the violet light broke upon him with heightened intensity, and the old witch and small furry thing—getting closer than ever before—mocked him with inhuman squeals and devilish gestures. He was glad to sink into the vaguely roaring twilight abysses, though the pursuit of that iridescent bubble-congeries and that kaleidoscopic little polyhedron was menacing and irritating. Then came the shift as vast converging planes of a slippery-looking substance loomed above and below him—a shift which ended in a flash of delirium and a blaze of unknown, alien light in which yellow, carmine, and indigo were madly and inextricably blended.

He was half lying on a high, fantastically balustraded terrace above a boundless jungle of outlandish, incredible peaks, balanced planes, domes, minarets, horizontal discs poised on pinnacles, and numberless forms of still greater wildness—some of stone and some of metal—which glittered gorgeously in the mixed, almost blistering glare from a polychromatic sky. Looking upward he saw three stupendous discs of flame, each of a different hue, and at a different height above an infinitely distant curving horizon of low mountains. Behind him tiers of higher terraces towered aloft as far as he could see. The city below stretched away to the limits of vision, and he hoped that no sound would well up from it.

The pavement from which he easily raised himself was of a veined polished stone beyond his power to identify, and the tiles were cut in bizarre-angled shapes which struck him as less asymmetrical than based on some unearthly symmetry whose laws he could not comprehend. The balustrade was chest-high, delicate, and fantastically wrought, while along the rail were ranged at short intervals little figures of grotesque design and exquisite workmanship. They, like the whole balustrade, seemed to be made of some sort of shining metal whose colour could not be guessed in this chaos of mixed effulgences; and their nature utterly defied conjecture. They represented some ridged, barrel-shaped object with thin horizontal arms radiating spoke-like from a central ring, and with vertical knobs or bulbs projecting from the head and base of the barrel.[22] Each of these knobs was the hub of a system of five long, flat, triangularly tapering arms arranged around it like the arms of a starfish—nearly horizontal, but curving slightly away from the central barrel. The base of the bottom knob was fused to the long railing with so delicate a point of contact that several figures had been broken off and were missing. The figures were about four and a half inches in height, while the spiky arms gave them a maximum diameter of about two and a half inches.

When Gilman stood up the tiles felt hot to his bare feet. He was wholly alone, and his first act was to walk to the balustrade and look dizzily down at the endless, Cyclopean city almost two thousand feet below. As he listened he thought a rhythmic confusion of faint musical pipings covering a wide tonal range welled up from the narrow streets beneath, and he wished he might discern the denizens of the place. The sight turned him giddy after a while, so that he would have fallen to the pavement had he not clutched instinctively at the lustrous balustrade. His right hand fell on one of the projecting figures, the touch seeming to steady him slightly. It was too much, however, for the exotic delicacy of the metal-work, and the spiky figure snapped off under his grasp. Still half-dazed, he continued to clutch it as his other hand seized a vacant space on the smooth railing.

But now his oversensitive ears caught something behind him, and he looked back across the level terrace. Approaching him softly though without apparent furtiveness were five figures, two of which were the sinister old woman and the fanged, furry little animal. The other three were what sent him unconscious—for they were living entities about eight feet high, shaped precisely like the spiky images on the balustrade, and propelling themselves by a spider-like wriggling of their lower set of starfish-arms.

Gilman awaked in his bed, drenched by a cold perspiration and with a smarting sensation in his face, hands and feet. Springing to the floor, he washed and dressed in frantic haste, as if it

22. These creatures also appear in *At the Mountains of Madness* (pp. 457–572, above).

were necessary for him to get out of the house as quickly as possible. He did not know where he wished to go, but felt that once more he would have to sacrifice his classes. The odd pull toward that spot in the sky between Hydra and Argo had abated, but another of even greater strength had taken its place. Now he felt that he must go north—infinitely north. He dreaded to cross the bridge that gave a view of the desolate island in the Miskatonic, so went over the Peabody Avenue bridge. Very often he stumbled, for his eyes and ears were chained to an extremely lofty point in the blank blue sky.

After about an hour he got himself under better control, and saw that he was far from the city. All around him stretched the bleak emptiness of salt marshes, while the narrow road ahead led to Innsmouth—that ancient, half-deserted town which Arkham people were so curiously unwilling to visit. Though the northward pull had not diminished, he resisted it as he had resisted the other pull, and finally found that he could almost balance the one against the other. Plodding back to town and getting some coffee at a soda fountain, he dragged himself into the public library and browsed aimlessly among the lighter magazines. Once he met some friends who remarked how oddly sunburned he looked, but he did not tell them of his walk. At three o'clock he took some lunch at a restaurant, noting meanwhile that the pull had either lessened or divided itself. After that he killed the time at a cheap cinema show, seeing the inane performance over and over again without paying any attention to it.

About nine at night he drifted homeward and stumbled into the ancient house. Joe Mazurewicz was whining unintelligible prayers, and Gilman hastened up to his own garret chamber without pausing to see if Elwood was in. It was when he turned on the feeble electric light that the shock came. At once he saw there was something on the table which did not belong there, and a second look left no room for doubt. Lying on its side—for it could not stand up alone—was the exotic spiky figure which in his monstrous dream he had broken off the fantastic balustrade. No detail was missing. The ridged, barrel-shaped centre, the thin radiating arms, the knobs at each end, and the flat, slightly outward-curving starfish-arms spreading from those knobs—all were there. In the electric light the colour seemed to be a kind of iridescent grey veined with green; and Gilman could see amidst his horror and bewilderment that one of the knobs ended in a jagged break corresponding to its former point of attachment to the dream-railing.

Only his tendency toward a dazed stupor prevented him from screaming aloud. This fusion of dream and reality was too much to bear. Still dazed, he clutched at the spiky thing and staggered downstairs to Landlord Dombrowski's quarters. The whining prayers of the superstitious loomfixer were still sounding through the mouldy halls, but Gilman did not mind them now. The landlord was in, and greeted him pleasantly. No, he had not seen that thing before and did not know anything about it. But his wife had said she found a funny tin thing in one of the beds when she fixed the rooms at noon, and maybe that was it. Dombrowski called her, and she waddled in. Yes, that was the thing. She had found it in the young gentleman's bed—on the side next the wall. It had looked very queer to her, but of course the young gentleman had lots of queer things in his room—books and curios and pictures and markings on paper. She certainly knew nothing about it.

So Gilman climbed upstairs again in a mental turmoil, convinced that he was either still dreaming or that his somnambulism had run to incredible extremes and led him to depredations in unknown places. Where had he got this outré thing? He did not recall seeing it in any museum in Arkham. It must have been somewhere, though; and the sight of it as he snatched it in his sleep must have caused the odd dream-picture of the balustraded terrace. Next day he would make some very guarded inquiries— and perhaps see the nerve specialist.

Meanwhile he would try to keep track of his somnambulism. As he went upstairs and across the garret hall he sprinkled about some flour which he had borrowed—with a frank admission as to its purpose—from the landlord. He had stopped at Elwood's door on the way, but had found all dark within. Entering his room, he placed the spiky thing on the table, and lay down in complete mental and physical exhaustion without pausing to undress. From the closed loft above the slanting ceiling he thought he heard a faint scratching and padding, but he was too disorganised even to mind it. That cryptical pull from the north was getting

23. Evidently the sound of the Black Man's cloven hooves.

very strong again, though it seemed now to come from a lower place in the sky.

In the dazzling violet light of dream the old woman and the fanged, furry thing came again and with a greater distinctness than on any former occasion. This time they actually reached him, and he felt the crone's withered claws clutching at him. He was pulled out of bed and into empty space, and for a moment he heard a rhythmic roaring and saw the twilight amorphousness of the vague abysses seething around him. But that moment was very brief, for presently he was in a crude, windowless little space with rough beams and planks rising to a peak just above his head, and with a curious slanting floor underfoot. Propped level on that floor were low cases full of books of every degree of antiquity and disintegration, and in the centre were a table and bench, both apparently fastened in place. Small objects of unknown shape and nature were ranged on the tops of the cases, and in the flaming violet light Gilman thought he saw a counterpart of the spiky image which had puzzled him so horribly. On the left the floor fell abruptly away, leaving a black triangular gulf out of which, after a second's dry rattling, there presently climbed the hateful little furry thing with the yellow fangs and bearded human face.

The evilly grinning beldame still clutched him, and beyond the table stood a figure he had never seen before—a tall, lean man of dead black colouration but without the slightest sign of negroid features; wholly devoid of either hair or beard, and wearing as his only garment a shapeless robe of some heavy black fabric. His feet were indistinguishable because of the table and bench, but he must have been shod, since there was a clicking whenever he changed position.[23] The man did not speak, and bore no trace of expression on his small, regular features. He merely pointed to a book of prodigious size which lay open on the table, while the beldame thrust a huge grey quill into Gilman's right hand. Over everything was a pall of intensely maddening fear, and the climax was reached when the furry thing ran up the dreamer's clothing to his shoulders and then down his left arm, finally biting him sharply in the wrist just below his cuff. As the blood spurted from this wound Gilman lapsed into a faint.

He awaked on the morning of the 22nd with a pain in his left wrist, and saw that his cuff was brown with dried blood. His recollections were very confused, but the scene with the black man in the unknown space stood out vividly. The rats must have bitten him as he slept, giving rise to the climax of that frightful dream. Opening the door, he saw that the flour on the corridor floor was undisturbed except for the huge prints of the loutish fellow who roomed at the other end of the garret. So he had not been sleepwalking this time. But something would have to be done about those rats. He would speak to the landlord about them. Again he tried to stop up the hole at the base of the slanting wall, wedging in a candlestick which seemed of about the right size. His ears were ringing horribly, as if with the residual echoes of some horrible noise heard in dreams.

As he bathed and changed clothes he tried to recall what he had dreamed after the scene in the violet-litten space, but nothing definite would crystallise in his mind. That scene itself must have corresponded to the sealed loft overhead, which had begun to attack his imagination so violently, but later impressions were faint and hazy. There were suggestions of the vague, twilight abysses, and of still vaster, blacker abysses beyond them—abysses in which all fixed suggestions of form were absent. He had been taken there by the bubble-congeries and the little polyhedron which always dogged him; but they, like himself, had changed to wisps of milky, barely luminous mist in this farther void of ultimate blackness. Something else had gone on ahead—a larger wisp which now and then condensed into nameless approximations of form—and he thought that their progress had not been in a straight line, but rather along the alien curves and spirals of some ethereal vortex which obeyed laws unknown to the physics and mathematics of any conceivable cosmos. Eventually there had been a hint of vast, leaping shadows, of a monstrous, half-acoustic pulsing, and of the thin, monotonous piping of an unseen flute—but that was all. Gilman decided he had picked up that last conception from what he had read in the *Necronomicon*, about the mindless entity Azathoth, which rules all time and space from a curiously environed black throne at the centre of Chaos.

When the blood was washed away the wrist wound proved very slight, and Gilman puzzled over the location of the two tiny punctures. It occurred to him that there was no blood on the bedspread where he had lain—which was very curious in view of the amount on his skin and cuff. Had he been sleep-walking within his room, and had the rat bitten him as he sat in some chair or paused in some less rational position? He looked in every corner for brownish drops or stains, but did not find any. He had better, he thought, sprinkle flour within the room as well as outside the door—though after all no further proof of his sleep-walking was needed. He knew he did walk and the thing to do now was to stop it. He must ask Frank Elwood for help. This morning the strange pulls from space seemed lessened, though they were replaced by another sensation even more inexplicable. It was a vague, insistent impulse to fly away from his present situation, but held not a hint of the specific direction in which he wished to fly. As he picked up the strange spiky image on the table he thought the older northward pull grew a trifle stronger; but even so, it was wholly overruled by the newer and more bewildering urge.

He took the spiky image down to Elwood's room, steeling himself against the whines of the loomfixer which welled up from the ground floor. Elwood was in, thank heaven, and appeared to be stirring about. There was time for a little conversation before leaving for breakfast and college, so Gilman hurriedly poured forth an account of his recent dreams and fears. His host was very sympathetic, and agreed that something ought to be done. He was shocked by his guest's drawn, haggard aspect, and noticed the queer, abnormal-looking sunburn which others had remarked during the past week.

There was not much, though, that he could say. He had not seen Gilman on any sleep-walking expedition, and had no idea what the curious image could be. He had, though, heard the French-Canadian who lodged just under Gilman talking to Mazurewicz one evening. They were telling each other how badly they dreaded the coming of Walpurgis-Night, now only a few days off; and were exchanging pitying comments about the poor, doomed young gentleman. Desrochers, the fellow under Gilman's room, had spoken of nocturnal footsteps both shod and unshod, and of the violet light he saw one night when he had stolen fearfully up to peer through Gilman's keyhole. He had not dared to peer, he told Mazurewicz, after he had glimpsed that light through the cracks around the door. There had been soft talking, too—and as he began to describe it his voice had sunk to an inaudible whisper.

Elwood could not imagine what had set these superstitious creatures gossiping, but supposed their imaginations had been roused by Gilman's late hours and somnolent walking and talking on the one hand, and by the nearness of traditionally feared May-Eve on the other hand. That Gilman talked in his sleep was plain, and it was obviously from Desrochers' keyhole-listenings that the delusive notion of the violet dream-light had got abroad. These simple people were quick to imagine they had seen any odd thing they had heard about. As for a plan of action—Gilman had better move down to Elwood's room and avoid sleeping alone. Elwood would, if awake, rouse him whenever he began to talk or rise in his sleep. Very soon, too, he must see the specialist. Meanwhile they would take the spiky image around to the various museums and to certain professors; seeking identification and stating that it had been found in a public rubbish-can.[24] Also, Dombrowski must attend to the poisoning of those rats in the walls.

Braced up by Elwood's companionship, Gilman attended classes that day. Strange urges still tugged at him, but he could sidetrack them with considerable success. During a free period he shewed the queer image to several professors, all of whom were intensely interested, though none of them could shed any light upon its nature or origin. That night he slept on a couch which Elwood had had the landlord bring to the second-story room, and for the first time in weeks was wholly free from disquieting dreams. But the feverishness still hung on, and the whines of the loomfixer were an unnerving influence.

During the next few days Gilman enjoyed an almost perfect immunity from morbid manifestations. He had, Elwood said, shewed no tendency to talk or rise in his sleep; and meanwhile the landlord was putting rat-poison everywhere. The only disturbing element was the talk among the superstitious foreigners, whose imaginations had become highly excited. Mazurewicz was always trying to make him get a crucifix, and finally forced one upon him which he said had been blessed by the good Father Iwanicki. Desrochers, too, had something to say—in fact, he insisted that cautious steps had sounded in the now vacant room

24. Unfortunately for Gilman, no one at Miskatonic University had yet learned of the creature depicted. The story is set sometime between 1927 (235 years after the trial of Kizziah Brown) and 1931, when the building was demolished. Professor Dyer's expedition to the Antarctic (reported in *At the Mountains of Madness*), on which he would see creatures fitting this description, did not take place until 1930, and he did not return to Arkham until at least early 1931.

25. Around 1868, two men, working independently, observed the periodicity—that is, patterns in the properties—of the sixty-three elements then known. Dimitri Mendeleev (1834–1907) published his work first and is generally credited with having devised the periodic table, an arrangement of the known elements in a recurring pattern of those properties. Lothar Meyer's work, actually completed slightly earlier but unpublished, was soon forgotten. Mendeleev's table also proved *predictive*—that is, gaps in the recurring patterns were thought to be descriptions of elements not yet discovered; and this thesis proved correct when the table accurately predicted the discoveries of gallium, scandium, and germanium. The first table was adjusted and refined (most importantly, with the addition of the noble gases by Sir William Ramsay about thirty years later), but the fundamental structure of Mendeleev's periodic table is unchanged.

above him on the first and second nights of Gilman's absence from it. Paul Choynski thought he heard sounds in the halls and on the stairs at night, and claimed that his door had been softly tried, while Mrs. Dombrowski vowed she had seen Brown Jenkin for the first time since All-Hallows. But such naïve reports could mean very little, and Gilman let the cheap metal crucifix hang idly from a knob on his host's dresser.

For three days Gilman and Elwood canvassed the local museums in an effort to identify the strange spiky image, but always without success. In every quarter, however, interest was intense; for the utter alienage of the thing was a tremendous challenge to scientific curiosity. One of the small radiating arms was broken off and subjected to chemical analysis, and the result is still talked about in college circles. Professor Ellery found platinum, iron, and tellurium in the strange alloy; but mixed with these were at least three other apparent elements of high atomic weight which chemistry was absolutely powerless to classify. Not only did they fail to correspond with any known element, but they did not even fit the vacant places reserved for probable elements in the periodic system.[25] The mystery remains unsolved to this day, though the image is on exhibition at the museum of Miskatonic University.

On the morning of April 27 a fresh rat-hole appeared in the room where Gilman was a guest, but Dombrowski tinned it up during the day. The poison was not having much effect, for scratchings and scurryings in the walls were virtually undiminished. Elwood was out late that night, and Gilman waited up for him. He did not wish to go to sleep in a room alone—especially since he thought he had glimpsed in the evening twilight the repellent old woman whose image had become so horribly transferred to his dreams. He wondered who she was, and what had been near her rattling the tin can in a rubbish-heap at the mouth of a squalid courtyard. The crone had seemed to notice him and leer evilly at him—though perhaps this was merely his imagination.

The next day both youths felt very tired, and knew they would sleep like logs when night came. In the evening they drowsily discussed the mathematical studies which had so completely and perhaps harmfully engrossed Gilman, and speculated about the linkage with ancient magic and folklore which seemed so darkly probable. They spoke of old Keziah Mason, and Elwood agreed that Gilman had good scientific grounds for thinking she might have stumbled on strange and significant information. The hidden cults to which these witches belonged often guarded and handed down surprising secrets from elder, forgotten æons; and it was by no means impossible that Keziah had actually mastered the art of passing through dimensional gates. Tradition emphasises the uselessness of material barriers in halting a witch's motions; and who can say what underlies the old tales of broomstick rides through the night?

Whether a modern student could ever gain similar powers from mathematical research alone, was still to be seen. Success, Gilman added, might lead to dangerous and unthinkable situations; for who could foretell the conditions pervading an adjacent but normally inaccessible dimension? On the other hand, the picturesque possibilities were enormous. Time could not exist in certain belts of space, and by entering and remaining in such a belt one might preserve one's life and age indefinitely; never suffering organic metabolism or deterioration except for slight amounts incurred during visits to one's own or similar planes. One might, for example, pass into a timeless dimension and emerge at some remote period of the earth's history as young as before.

Whether anybody had ever managed to do this, one could hardly conjecture with any degree of authority. Old legends are hazy and ambiguous, and in historic times all attempts at crossing forbidden gaps seem complicated by strange and terrible alliances with beings and messengers from outside. There was the immemorial figure of the deputy or messenger of hidden and terrible powers—the "Black Man" of the witch-cult, and the "Nyarlathotep" of the *Necronomicon*. There was, too, the baffling problem of the lesser messengers or intermediaries—the quasi-animals and queer hybrids which legend depicts as witches' familiars. As Gilman and Elwood retired, too sleepy to argue further, they heard Joe Mazurewicz reel into the house half-drunk, and shuddered at the desperate wildness of his whining prayers.

That night Gilman saw the violet light again. In his dream he had heard a scratching and gnawing in the partitions, and thought that someone fumbled clumsily at the latch. Then he

"The hideous crone seized Gilman by the shoulder, yanking him out of bed and into empty space." *Weird Tales* 22, no. 1 (July 1933) (artist: Jayem Wilcox)

saw the old woman and the small furry thing advancing toward him over the carpeted floor. The beldame's face was alight with inhuman exultation, and the little yellow-toothed morbidity tittered mockingly as it pointed at the heavily sleeping form of Elwood on the other couch across the room. A paralysis of fear stifled all attempts to cry out. As once before, the hideous crone seized Gilman by the shoulders, yanking him out of bed and into empty space. Again the infinitude of the shrieking twilight abysses flashed past him, but in another second he thought he was in a dark, muddy, unknown alley of foetid odours with the rotting walls of ancient houses towering up on every hand.

Ahead was the robed black man he had seen in the peaked space in the other dream, while from a lesser distance the old woman was beckoning and grimacing imperiously. Brown Jenkin was rubbing itself with a kind of affectionate playfulness around the ankles of the black man, which the deep mud largely concealed. There was a dark open doorway on the right, to which the black man silently pointed. Into this the grimacing crone started, dragging Gilman after her by his pajama sleeve. There were evil-smelling staircases which creaked ominously, and on which the old woman seemed to radiate a faint violet light; and finally a door leading off a landing. The crone fumbled with the latch and pushed the door open, motioning to Gilman to wait, and disappearing inside the black aperture.

The youth's oversensitive ears caught a hideous strangled cry, and presently the beldame came out of the room bearing a small, senseless form which she thrust at the dreamer as if ordering him to carry it. The sight of this form, and the expression on its face, broke the spell. Still too dazed to cry out, he plunged recklessly down the noisome staircase and into the mud outside; halting only when seized and choked by the waiting black man. As consciousness departed he heard the faint, shrill tittering of the fanged, rat-like abnormality.

On the morning of the 29th Gilman awaked into a mælstrom of horror. The instant he opened his eyes he knew something was terribly wrong, for he was back in his old garret room with the slanting wall and ceiling, sprawled on the now unmade bed. His throat was aching inexplicably, and as he struggled to a sitting posture he saw with growing fright that his feet and pajama-bottoms were brown with caked mud. For the moment his recollections were hopelessly hazy, but he knew at least that he must have been sleep-walking. Elwood had been lost too deeply in slumber to hear and stop him. On the floor were confused muddy prints, but oddly enough they did not extend all the way to the door. The more Gilman looked at them, the more peculiar they seemed; for in addition to those he could recognise as his there were some smaller, almost round markings—such as the legs of a large chair or table might make, except that most of them tended to be divided into halves. There were also some curious muddy rat-tracks leading out of a fresh hole and back into it again. Utter bewilderment and the fear of madness racked Gilman as he staggered to the door and saw that there were no muddy prints outside. The more he remembered of his hideous dream the more terrified he felt, and it added to his desperation to hear Joe Mazurewicz chanting mournfully two floors below.

Descending to Elwood's room he roused his still-sleeping host and began telling of how he had found himself, but Elwood could form no idea of what might really have happened. Where Gilman could have been, how he got back to his room without making tracks in the hall, and how the muddy, furniture-like prints came to be mixed with his in the garret chamber, were wholly beyond conjecture. Then there were those dark, livid marks on his throat, as if he had tried to strangle himself. He put his hands up to them, but found that they did not even approximately fit. While they were talking Desrochers dropped in to say that he had heard a terrific clattering overhead in the dark small hours. No, there had been no one on the stairs after midnight—though just before midnight he had heard faint footfalls in the garret, and cautiously descending steps he did not like. It was, he added, a very bad time of year for Arkham. The young gentleman had better be sure to wear the crucifix Joe Mazurewicz had given him. Even the day-time was not safe, for after dawn there had been strange sounds in the house—especially a thin, childish wail hastily choked off.

Gilman mechanically attended classes that morning, but was wholly unable to fix his mind on his studies. A mood of hide-ous apprehension and expectancy had seized him, and he seemed to be awaiting the fall of some annihilating blow. At noon he lunched at the University Spa, picking up a paper from the next

26. The name Orne has appeared in several other tales, notably "The Shadow over Innsmouth," where the family dominates the town, and *The Case of Charles Dexter Ward*, in which the diabolical connections of the Salem branch of the family are revealed. The site mentioned here ties in to the shipping business conducted by the Innsmouth branch.

27. This suggestive remark probably reflects Lovecraft's low view of the morality of the foreign populations in New England.

seat as he waited for dessert. But he never ate that dessert; for an item on the paper's first page left him limp, wild-eyed, and able only to pay his check and stagger back to Elwood's room.

There had been a strange kidnapping the night before in Orne's Gangway,[26] and the two-year-old child of a clod-like laundry worker named Anastasia Wolejko had completely vanished from sight. The mother, it appeared, had feared the event for some time; but the reasons she assigned for her fear were so grotesque that no one took them seriously. She had, she said, seen Brown Jenkin about the place now and then ever since early in March, and knew from its grimaces and titterings that little Ladislas must be marked for sacrifice at the awful Sabbat on Walpurgis-Night. She had asked her neighbour Mary Czanek to sleep in the room and try to protect the child, but Mary had not dared. She could not tell the police, for they never believed such things. Children had been taken that way every year ever since she could remember. And her friend Pete Stowacki would not help because he wanted the child out of the way anyhow.[27]

But what threw Gilman into a cold perspiration was the report of a pair of revellers who had been walking past the mouth of the gangway just after midnight. They admitted they had been drunk, but both vowed they had seen a crazily dressed trio furtively entering the dark passageway. There had, they said, been a huge robed negro, a little old woman in rags, and a young white man in his night-clothes. The old woman had been dragging the youth, while around the feet of the negro a tame rat was rubbing and weaving in the brown mud.

Gilman sat in a daze all the afternoon, and Elwood—who had meanwhile seen the papers and formed terrible conjectures from them—found him thus when he came home. This time neither could doubt but that something hideously serious was closing in around them. Between the phantasms of nightmare and the realities of the objective world a monstrous and unthinkable relationship was crystallising, and only stupendous vigilance could avert still more direful developments. Gilman must see a specialist sooner or later, but not just now, when all the papers were full of this kidnapping business.

Just what had really happened was maddeningly obscure, and for a moment both Gilman and Elwood exchanged whispered theories of the wildest kind. Had Gilman unconsciously succeeded better than he knew in his studies of space and its dimensions? Had he actually slipped outside our sphere to points unguessed and unimaginable? Where—if anywhere—had he been on those nights of dæmoniac alienage? The roaring twilight abysses—the green hillside—the blistering terrace—the pulls from the stars—the ultimate black vortex—the black man—the muddy alley and the stairs—the old witch and the fanged, furry horror—the bubble-congeries and the little polyhedron—the strange sunburn—the wrist wound—the unexplained image—the muddy feet—the throat-marks—the tales and fears of the superstitious foreigners—what did all this mean? To what extent could the laws of sanity apply to such a case?

There was no sleep for either of them that night, but next day they both cut classes and drowsed. This was April 30th, and with the dusk would come the hellish Sabbat-time which all the foreigners and the superstitious old folk feared. Mazurewicz came home at six o'clock and said people at the mill were whispering that the Walpurgis revels would be held in the dark ravine beyond Meadow Hill where the old white stone stands in a place queerly void of all plant-life. Some of them had even told the police and advised them to look there for the missing Wolejko child, but they did not believe anything would be done. Joe insisted that the poor young gentleman wear his nickel-chained crucifix, and Gilman put it on and dropped it inside his shirt to humour the fellow.

Late at night the two youths sat drowsing in their chairs, lulled by the rhythmical praying of the loomfixer on the floor below. Gilman listened as he nodded, his preternaturally sharpened hearing seeming to strain for some subtle, dreaded murmur beyond the noises in the ancient house. Unwholesome recollections of things in the *Necronomicon* and the Black Book welled up, and he found himself swaying to infandous[28] rhythms said to pertain to the blackest ceremonies of the Sabbat and to have an origin outside the time and space we comprehend.

Presently he realised what he was listening for—the hellish chant of the celebrants in the distant black valley. How did he know so much about what they expected? How did he know the time when Nahab and her acolyte were due to bear the brimming

28. Too horrible to be described.

bowl which would follow the black cock and the black goat? He saw that Elwood had dropped asleep, and tried to call out and waken him. Something, however, closed his throat. He was not his own master. Had he signed the black man's book after all?

Then his fevered, abnormal hearing caught the distant, wind-borne notes. Over miles of hill and field and alley they came, but he recognised them none the less. The fires must be lit, and the dancers must be starting in. How could he keep himself from going? What was it that had enmeshed him? Mathematics—folklore—the house—old Keziah—Brown Jenkin . . . and now he saw that there was a fresh rat-hole in the wall near his couch. Above the distant chanting and the nearer praying of Joe Mazurewicz came another sound—a stealthy, determined scratching in the partitions. He hoped the electric lights would not go out. Then he saw the fanged, bearded little face in the rat-hole—the accursed little face which he at last realised bore such a shocking, mocking resemblance to old Keziah's—and heard the faint fumbling at the door.

The screaming twilight abysses flashed before him, and he felt himself helpless in the formless grasp of the iridescent bubble-congeries. Ahead raced the small, kaleidoscopic polyhedron and all through the churning void there was a heightening and acceleration of the vague tonal pattern which seemed to foreshadow some unutterable and unendurable climax. He seemed to know what was coming—the monstrous burst of Walpurgis-rhythm in whose cosmic timbre would be concentrated all the primal, ultimate space-time seethings which lie behind the massed spheres of matter and sometimes break forth in measured reverberations that penetrate faintly to every layer of entity and give hideous significance throughout the worlds to certain dreaded periods.

But all this vanished in a second. He was again in the cramped, violet-litten peaked space with the slanting floor, the low cases of ancient books, the bench and table, the queer objects, and the triangular gulf at one side. On the table lay a small white figure—an infant boy, unclothed and unconscious—while on the other side stood the monstrous, leering old woman with a gleaming, grotesque-hafted knife in her right hand, and a queerly proportioned pale metal bowl covered with curiously chased designs and having delicate lateral handles in her left. She was intoning some croaking ritual in a language which Gilman could not understand, but which seemed like something guardedly quoted in the *Necronomicon*.

As the scene grew clear he saw the ancient crone bend forward and extend the empty bowl across the table—and unable to control his own motions, he reached far forward and took it in both hands, noticing as he did so its comparative lightness. At the same moment the disgusting form of Brown Jenkin scrambled up over the brink of the triangular black gulf on his left. The crone now motioned him to hold the bowl in a certain position while she raised the huge, grotesque knife above the small white victim as high as her right hand could reach. The fanged, furry thing began tittering a continuation of the unknown ritual, while the witch croaked loathsome responses. Gilman felt a gnawing, poignant abhorrence shoot through his mental and emotional paralysis, and the light metal bowl shook in his grasp. A second later the downward motion of the knife broke the spell completely, and he dropped the bowl with a resounding bell-like clangour while his hands darted out frantically to stop the monstrous deed.

In an instant he had edged up the slanting floor around the end of the table and wrenched the knife from the old woman's claws; sending it clattering over the brink of the narrow triangular gulf. In another instant, however, matters were reversed; for those murderous claws had locked themselves tightly around his own throat, while the wrinkled face was twisted with insane fury. He felt the chain of the cheap crucifix grinding into his neck, and in his peril wondered how the sight of the object itself would affect the evil creature. Her strength was altogether superhuman, but as she continued her choking he reached feebly in his shirt and drew out the metal symbol, snapping the chain and pulling it free.[29]

At sight of the device the witch seemed struck with panic, and her grip relaxed long enough to give Gilman a chance to break it entirely. He pulled the steel-like claws from his neck, and would have dragged the beldame over the edge of the gulf had not the claws received a fresh access of strength and closed in again. This time he resolved to reply in kind, and his own hands reached out for the creature's throat. Before she saw what

29. This is the only suggestion in any of Lovecraft's stories that religious symbols might have some effect on the beings confronted by the various narrators. Perhaps Lovecraft means to show that Keziah was not a supernatural being but rather merely a human, with seventeenth-century superstitions.

he was doing he had the chain of the crucifix twisted about her neck, and a moment later he had tightened it enough to cut off her breath. During her last struggle he felt something bite at his ankle, and saw that Brown Jenkin had come to her aid. With one savage kick he sent the morbidity over the edge of the gulf and heard it whimper on some level far below.

Whether he had killed the ancient crone he did not know, but he let her rest on the floor where she had fallen. Then, as he turned away, he saw on the table a sight which nearly snapped the last thread of his reason. Brown Jenkin, tough of sinew and with four tiny hands of dæmoniac dexterity, had been busy while the witch was throttling him, and his efforts had been in vain. What he had prevented the knife from doing to the victim's chest, the yellow fangs of the furry blasphemy had done to a wrist—and the bowl so lately on the floor stood full beside the small lifeless body.

In his dream-delirium Gilman heard the hellish, alien-rhythmed chant of the Sabbat coming from an infinite distance, and knew the black man must be there. Confused memories mixed themselves with his mathematics, and he believed his sub-conscious mind held the *angles* which he needed to guide him back to the normal world—alone and unaided for the first time. He felt sure he was in the immemorially sealed loft above his own room, but whether he could ever escape through the slanting floor or the long-stopped egress he doubted greatly. Besides, would not an escape from a dream-loft bring him merely into a dream-house—an abnormal projection of the actual place he sought? He was wholly bewildered as to the relation betwixt dream and reality in all his experiences.

The passage through the vague abysses would be frightful, for the Walpurgis-rhythm would be vibrating, and at last he would have to hear that hitherto veiled cosmic pulsing which he so mortally dreaded. Even now he could detect a low, monstrous shaking whose tempo he suspected all too well. At Sabbat-time it always mounted and reached through to the worlds to summon the initiate to nameless rites. Half the chants of the Sabbat were patterned on this faintly overheard pulsing which no earthly ear could endure in its unveiled spatial fulness. Gilman wondered, too, whether he could trust his instinct to take him back to the right part of space. How could he be sure he would not land on that green-litten hillside of a far planet, on the tessellated terrace above the city of tentacled monsters somewhere beyond the galaxy or in the spiral black vortices of that ultimate void of Chaos wherein reigns the mindless dæmon-sultan Azathoth?

Just before he made the plunge the violet light went out and left him in utter blackness. The witch—old Keziah—Nahab—that must have meant her death. And mixed with the distant chant of the Sabbat and the whimpers of Brown Jenkin in the gulf below he thought he heard another and wilder whine from unknown depths. Joe Mazurewicz—the prayers against the Crawling Chaos now turning to an inexplicably triumphant shriek—worlds of sardonic actuality impinging on vortices of febrile dream—Iä! Shub-Niggurath! The Goat with a Thousand Young. . . .

They found Gilman on the floor of his queerly angled old garret room long before dawn, for the terrible cry had brought Desrochers and Choynski and Dombrowski and Mazurewicz at once, and had even wakened the soundly sleeping Elwood in his chair. He was alive, and with open, staring eyes, but seemed largely unconscious. On his throat were the marks of murderous hands, and on his left ankle was a distressing rat-bite. His clothing was badly rumpled and Joe's crucifix was missing, Elwood trembled, afraid even to speculate on what new form his friend's sleep-walking had taken. Mazurewicz seemed half-dazed because of a "sign" he said he had had in response to his prayers, and he crossed himself frantically when the squealing and whimpering of a rat sounded from beyond the slanting partition.

When the dreamer was settled on his couch in Elwood's room they sent for Dr. Malkowski—a local practitioner who would repeat no tales where they might prove embarrassing—and he gave Gilman two hypodermic injections which caused him to relax in something like natural drowsiness. During the day the patient regained consciousness at times and whispered his newest dream disjointedly to Elwood. It was a painful process, and at its very start brought out a fresh and disconcerting fact.

Gilman—whose ears had so lately possessed an abnormal sensitiveness—was now stone deaf. Dr. Malkowski, summoned again in haste, told Elwood that both ear-drums were ruptured, as if by the impact of some stupendous sound intense beyond all human conception or endurance. How such a sound could have been heard in the last few hours without arousing all the Miskatonic Valley was more than the honest physician could say.

Elwood wrote his part of the colloquy on paper, so that a fairly easy communication was maintained. Neither knew what to make of the whole chaotic business, and decided it would be better if they thought as little as possible about it. Both, though, agreed that they must leave this ancient and accursed house as soon as it could be arranged. Evening papers spoke of a police raid on some curious revellers in a ravine beyond Meadow Hill just before dawn, and mentioned that the white stone there was an object of age-long superstitious regard. Nobody had been caught, but among the scattering fugitives had been glimpsed a huge negro. In another column it was stated that no trace of the missing Ladislas Wolejko had been found.

The crowning horror came that very night. Elwood will never forget it, and was forced to stay out of college the rest of the term because of the resulting nervous breakdown. He had thought he heard rats in the partitions all the evening, but paid little attention to them. Then, long after both he and Gilman had retired, the atrocious shrieking began. Elwood jumped up, turned on the lights and rushed over to his guest's couch. The occupant was emitting sounds of veritably inhuman nature, as if racked by some torment beyond description. He was writhing under the bedclothes, and a great red stain was beginning to appear on the blankets.

Elwood scarcely dared to touch him, but gradually the screaming and writhing subsided. By this time Dombrowski, Choynski, Desrochers, Mazurewicz, and the top-floor lodger were all crowding into the doorway, and the landlord had sent his wife back to telephone for Dr. Malkowski. Everybody shrieked when a large rat-like form suddenly jumped out from beneath the ensanguined bedclothes and scuttled across the floor to a fresh, open hole close by. When the doctor arrived and began to pull down those frightful covers Walter Gilman was dead.

It would be barbarous to do more than suggest what had killed Gilman. There had been virtually a tunnel through his body—something had eaten his heart out. Dombrowski, frantic at the failure of his constant rat-poisoning efforts, cast aside all thought of his lease and within a week had moved with all his older lodgers to a dingy but less ancient house in Walnut Street. The worst thing for a while was keeping Joe Mazurewicz quiet; for the brooding loomfixer would never stay sober, and was constantly whining and muttering about spectral and terrible things.

It seems that on that last hideous night Joe had stooped to look at the crimson rat-tracks which led from Gilman's couch to the nearby hole. On the carpet they were very indistinct, but a piece of open flooring intervened between the carpet's edge and the base-board. There Mazurewicz had found something monstrous—or thought he had, for no one else could quite agree with him despite the undeniable queerness of the prints. The tracks on the flooring were certainly vastly unlike the average prints of a rat, but even Choynski and Desrochers would not admit that they were like the prints of four tiny human hands.[30]

The house was never rented again. As soon as Dombrowski left it the pall of its final desolation began to descend, for people shunned it both on account of its old reputation and because of the new foetid odour. Perhaps the ex-landlord's rat-poison had worked after all, for not long after his departure the place became a neighbourhood nuisance. Health officials traced the smell to the closed spaces above and beside the eastern garret room, and agreed that the number of dead rats must be enormous. They decided, however, that it was not worth their while to hew open and disinfect the long-sealed spaces; for the foetor would soon be over, and the locality was not one which encouraged fastidious standards. Indeed, there were always vague local tales of unexplained stenches upstairs in the Witch House just after May-Eve and Hallowmass. The neighbours grumblingly acquiesced in the inertia—but the foetor none the less formed an additional count against the place. Toward the last the house was condemned as an habitation by the building inspector.

Gilman's dreams and their attendant circumstances have never been explained. Elwood, whose thoughts on the entire episode are sometimes almost maddening, came back to college the next autumn and graduated in the following June. He found the spectral gossip of the town much diminished, and it is indeed a fact that—notwithstanding certain reports of a ghostly tittering in the deserted house which lasted almost as long as that edi-

30. Evidently, it is Brown Jenkin that killed Gilman. How did the fanged, furry thing get out of the abyss?

fice itself—no fresh appearances either of old Keziah or of Brown Jenkin have been muttered of since Gilman's death. It is rather fortunate that Elwood was not in Arkham in that later year when certain events abruptly renewed the local whispers about elder horrors. Of course he heard about the matter afterward and suffered untold torments of black and bewildered speculation; but even that was not as bad as actual nearness and several possible sights would have been.

In March 1931, a gale wrecked the roof and great chimney of the vacant Witch House, so that a chaos of crumbling bricks, blackened, moss-grown shingles, and rotting planks and timbers crashed down into the loft and broke through the floor beneath. The whole attic story was choked with debris from above, but no one took the trouble to touch the mess before the inevitable razing of the decrepit structure. That ultimate step came in the following December, and it was when Gilman's old room was cleared out by reluctant, apprehensive workmen that the gossip began.

Among the rubbish which had crashed through the ancient slanting ceiling were several things which made the workmen pause and call in the police. Later the police in turn called in the coroner and several professors from the university. There were bones—badly crushed and splintered, but clearly recognisable as human—whose manifestly modern date conflicted puzzlingly with the remote period at which their only possible lurking-place, the low, slant-floored loft overhead, had supposedly been sealed from all human access. The coroner's physician decided that some belonged to a small child, while certain others—found mixed with shreds of rotten brownish cloth—belonged to a rather undersized, bent female of advanced years. Careful sifting of debris also disclosed many tiny bones of rats caught in the collapse, as well as older rat-bones gnawed by small fangs in a fashion now and then highly productive of controversy and reflection.

Other objects found included the mingled fragments of many books and papers, together with a yellowish dust left from the total disintegration of still older books and papers. All, without exception, appeared to deal with black magic in its most advanced and horrible forms; and the evidently recent date of certain items is still a mystery as unsolved as that of the modern human bones. An even greater mystery is the absolute homogeneity of the crabbed, archaic writing found on a wide range of papers whose conditions and watermarks suggest age differences of at least 150 to 200 years. To some, though, the greatest mystery of all is the variety of utterly inexplicable objects—objects whose shapes, materials, types of workmanship, and purposes baffle all conjecture—found scattered amidst the wreckage in evidently diverse states of injury. One of these things—which excited several Miskatonic professors profoundly—is a badly damaged monstrosity plainly resembling the strange image which Gilman gave to the college museum, save that it is larger, wrought of some peculiar bluish stone instead of metal, and possessed of a singularly angled pedestal with undecipherable hieroglyphics.

Archæologists and anthropologists are still trying to explain the bizarre designs chased on a crushed bowl of light metal whose inner side bore ominous brownish stains when found. Foreigners and credulous grandmothers are equally garrulous about the modern nickel crucifix with broken chain mixed in the rubbish and shiveringly identified by Joe Mazurewicz as that which he had given poor Gilman many years before. Some believe this crucifix was dragged up to the sealed loft by rats, while others think it must have been on the floor in some corner of Gilman's old room all the time. Still others, including Joe himself, have theories too wild and fantastic for sober credence.

When the slanting wall of Gilman's room was torn out, the once sealed triangular space between that partition and the house's north wall was found to contain much less structural debris, even in proportion to its size, than the room itself; though it had a ghastly layer of older materials which paralysed the wreckers with horror. In brief, the floor was a veritable ossuary of the bones of small children—some fairly modern, but others extending back in infinite gradations to a period so remote that crumbling was almost complete. On this deep bony layer rested a knife of great size, obvious antiquity, and grotesque, ornate, and exotic design—above which the debris was piled.

In the midst of this debris, wedged between a fallen plank and a cluster of cemented bricks from the ruined chimney, was an object destined to cause more bafflement, veiled fright, and openly superstitious talk in Arkham than anything else discovered in the haunted and accursed building.

This object was the partly crushed skeleton of a huge, diseased rat, whose abnormalities of form are still a topic of debate and source of singular reticence among the members of Miskatonic's department of comparative anatomy. Very little concerning this skeleton has leaked out, but the workmen who found it whisper in shocked tones about the long, brownish hairs with which it was associated.

The bones of the tiny paws, it is rumoured, imply prehensile characteristics more typical of a diminutive monkey than of a rat; while the small skull with its savage yellow fangs is of the utmost anomalousness, appearing from certain angles like a miniature, monstrously degraded parody of a human skull. The workmen crossed themselves in fright when they came upon this blasphemy, but later burned candles of gratitude in St. Stanislaus' Church because of the shrill, ghostly tittering they felt they would never hear again.

The Thing on the Doorstep[1]

The transfer of minds is a theme that Lovecraft regularly visited (in "Beyond the Wall of Sleep" and The Case of Charles Dexter Ward*). Here, however, he experiments with the idea that the personalities alternate, as the "recipient" of the transferred mind puts up a struggle. The victim, Edward Derby, resembles Lovecraft's idol Edgar Allan Poe in his tastes in poetry and women (Poe also married a woman thirteen years his junior—his thirteen-year-old cousin). As in Charles Dexter Ward, the mind transfer appears to be the result of dark magic invoking Lovecraft's Cthulhulian deities. The tale also weaves in elements of "The Shadow over Innsmouth." While the outcome here is far less subtle than the conclusion of that tale, there is a deliciously ghoulish pleasure in the revelation of the "thing on the doorstep."*

1. Written in 1933, it first appeared in *Weird Tales* 29, no. 1 (January 1937), 52–70, with the following reading line: "A powerful tale by one of the supreme masters of weird fiction—a tale in which the horror creeps and grows, to spring at last upon the reader in all its hideous totality."

2. Asenath is named as the daughter of Potiphera, priest of On, in Genesis 41:45. Pharaoh gives her in marriage to Joseph. One of Asenath's sons is Ephraim (here the name of her father). These connections were first made by Robert M. Price, in "Two Biblical Curiosities in Lovecraft."

I.

It is true that I have sent six bullets through the head of my best friend, and yet I hope to shew by this statement that I am not his murderer. At first I shall be called a madman—madder than the man I shot in his cell at the Arkham Sanitarium. Later some of my readers will weigh each statement, correlate it with the known facts, and ask themselves how I could have believed otherwise than as I did after facing the evidence of that horror—that thing on the doorstep.

Until then I also saw nothing but madness in the wild tales I have acted on. Even now I ask myself whether I was misled—or whether I am not mad after all. I do not know—but others have strange things to tell of Edward and Asenath[2] Derby, and even the stolid police are at their wits' ends to account for that last terrible visit. They have tried weakly to concoct a theory of a ghastly jest or warning by discharged servants, yet they know in their hearts that the truth is something infinitely more terrible and incredible.

So I say that I have not murdered Edward Derby. Rather have I avenged him, and in so doing purged the earth of a horror whose survival might have loosed untold terrors on all mankind. There are black zones of shadow close to our daily paths, and now and then some evil soul breaks a passage through. When that happens, the man who knows must strike before reckoning the consequences.

I have known Edward Pickman Derby all his life. Eight years my junior, he was so precocious that we had much in common from the time he was eight and I sixteen. He was the most phenomenal child scholar I have ever known, and at seven was writing verse of a sombre, fantastic, almost morbid cast which astonished the tutors surrounding him. Perhaps his private education and coddled seclusion had something to do with his premature flowering. An only child, he had organic weaknesses which startled his doting parents and caused them to keep him closely chained to their side. He was never allowed out without his nurse, and seldom had a chance to play unconstrainedly with other children. All this doubtless fostered a strange secretive inner life in the boy, with imagination as his one avenue of freedom.

At any rate, his juvenile learning was prodigious and bizarre; and his facile writings such as to captivate me despite my greater age. About that time I had leanings toward art of a somewhat grotesque cast, and I found in this younger child a rare kindred spirit. What lay behind our joint love of shadows and marvels was, no doubt, the ancient, mouldering, and subtly fearsome town in which we lived—witch-cursed, legend-haunted Arkham, whose huddled, sagging gambrel roofs and crumbling Georgian balustrades brood out the centuries beside the darkly muttering Miskatonic.

As time went by I turned to architecture and gave up my design of illustrating a book of Edward's dæmoniac poems, yet our comradeship suffered no lessening. Young Derby's odd genius developed remarkably, and in his eighteenth year his collected nightmare-lyrics made a real sensation when issued under the title *Azathoth and Other Horrors*. He was a close correspondent of the notorious Baudelairean poet Justin Geoffrey, who wrote *The*

People of the Monolith and died screaming in a madhouse in 1926 after a visit to a sinister, ill-regarded village in Hungary.[3]

In self-reliance and practical affairs, however, Derby was greatly retarded because of his coddled existence. His health had improved, but his habits of childish dependence were fostered by overcareful parents, so that he never travelled alone, made independent decisions, or assumed responsibilities. It was early seen that he would not be equal to a struggle in the business or professional arena, but the family fortune was so ample that this formed no tragedy. As he grew to years of manhood he retained a deceptive aspect of boyishness. Blond and blue-eyed, he had the fresh complexion of a child; and his attempts to raise a moustache were discernible only with difficulty. His voice was soft and light, and his pampered, unexercised life gave him a juvenile chubbiness rather than the paunchiness of premature middle age. He was of good height, and his handsome face would have made him a notable gallant had not his shyness held him to seclusion and bookishness.

Derby's parents took him abroad every summer, and he was quick to seize on the surface aspects of European thought and expression. His Poe-like talents turned more and more toward the decadent, and other artistic sensitivenesses and yearnings were half-aroused in him. We had great discussions in those days. I had been through Harvard, had studied in a Boston architect's office, had married, and had finally returned to Arkham to practice my profession—settling in the family homestead in Saltonstall St. since my father had moved to Florida for his health. Edward used to call almost every evening, till I came to regard him as one of the household. He had a characteristic way of ringing the doorbell or sounding the knocker that grew to be a veritable code signal, so that after dinner I always listened for the familiar three brisk strokes followed by two more after a pause. Less frequently I would visit at his house and note with envy the obscure volumes in his constantly growing library.

Derby went through Miskatonic University in Arkham since his parents would not let him board away from them. He entered at sixteen and completed his course in three years, majoring in English and French literature and receiving high marks in everything but mathematics and the sciences. He mingled very little

3. The first mention of the fictional poet Justin Geoffrey is to be found in Robert E. Howard's 1931 story "The Black Stone." The tale begins with the following sample of Geoffrey's verse:

> They say foul things of Old Times still lurk
> In dark forgotten corners of the world.
> And Gates still gape to loose, on certain nights.
> Shapes pent in Hell.

Howard's "The Thing on the Roof" (1932) begins with the following excerpt from another of Geoffrey's works, *Out of the Old Land*:

> They lumber through the night
> With their elephantine tread;
> I shudder in affright
> As I cower in my bed.
> They lift colossal wings
> On the high gable roofs
> Which tremble to the trample
> Of their mastodonic hoofs.

4. Volunteerism swept the United States at the outbreak of the Great War in 1914, but there was little military preparedness. "Summer camps" were established to train volunteers at several locations, including, by late 1914, Plattsburg, New York (now spelled Plattsburgh). The official name of the Plattsburg camp was the Business Men's Camp; the press lampooned it as the "Tired Businessmen's Camp." Many of its first graduates went on to the newly formed Military Training Camps Association (MTCA), which gained sufficient political clout to influence Congress's approval of a full appropriation for the 1917 camps. In April, however, the United States declared war against Germany, and the civilian camps were converted into officers' training camps. The narrator's mention of a "commission" suggests that he was at Plattsburg in this later phase.

with the other students, though looking enviously at the "daring" or "Bohemian" set—whose superficially "smart" language and meaninglessly ironic pose he aped, and whose dubious conduct he wished he dared adopt.

What he did do was to become an almost fanatical devotee of subterranean magical lore, for which Miskatonic's library was and is famous. Always a dweller on the surface of phantasy and strangeness, he now delved deep into the actual runes and riddles left by a fabulous past for the guidance or puzzlement of posterity. He read things like the frightful *Book of Eibon*, the *Unaussprechlichen Kulten* of von Junzt, and the forbidden *Necronomicon* of the mad Arab Abdul Alhazred, though he did not tell his parents he had seen them. Edward was twenty when my son and only child was born, and seemed pleased when I named the newcomer Edward Derby Upton after him.

By the time he was twenty-five Edward Derby was a prodigiously learned man and a fairly well-known poet and fantaisiste, though his lack of contacts and responsibilities had slowed down his literary growth by making his products derivative and over-bookish. I was perhaps his closest friend—finding him an inexhaustible mine of vital theoretical topics, while he relied on me for advice in whatever matters he did not wish to refer to his parents. He remained single—more through shyness, inertia, and parental protectiveness than through inclination—and moved in society only to the slightest and most perfunctory extent. When the war came both health and ingrained timidity kept him at home. I went to Plattsburg for a commission but never got overseas.[4]

So the years wore on. Edward's mother died when he was thirty-four, and for months he was incapacitated by some odd psychological malady. His father took him to Europe, however, and he managed to pull out of his trouble without visible effects. Afterward he seemed to feel a sort of grotesque exhilaration, as if of partial escape from some unseen bondage. He began to mingle in the more "advanced" college set despite his middle age, and was present at some extremely wild doings—on one occasion paying heavy blackmail (which he borrowed of me) to keep his presence at a certain affair from his father's notice. Some of the whispered rumours about the wild Miskatonic set were extremely singular. There was even talk of black magic and of happenings utterly beyond credibility.

II.

EDWARD WAS THIRTY-EIGHT when he met Asenath Waite. She was, I judge, about twenty-three at the time; and was taking a special course in mediæval metaphysics at Miskatonic. The daughter of a friend of mine had met her before—in the Hall School at Kingsport[5]—and had been inclined to shun her because of her odd reputation. She was dark, smallish, and very good-looking except for overprotuberant eyes; but something in her expression alienated extremely sensitive people. It was, however, largely her origin and conversation which caused average folk to avoid her. She was one of the Innsmouth Waites, and dark legends have clustered for generations about crumbling, half-deserted Innsmouth and its people.[6] There are tales of horrible bargains about the year 1850, and of a strange element "not quite human" in the ancient families of the run-down fishing port—tales such as only old-time Yankees can devise and repeat with proper awesomeness.

Asenath's case was aggravated by the fact that she was Ephraim Waite's daughter—the child of his old age by an unknown wife who always went veiled. Ephraim lived in a half-decayed mansion in Washington Street, Innsmouth, and those who had seen the place (Arkham folk avoid going to Innsmouth whenever they can) declared that the attic windows were always boarded, and that strange sounds sometimes floated from within as evening drew on. The old man was known to have been a prodigious magical student in his day, and legend averred that he could raise or quell storms at sea according to his whim. I had seen him once or twice in my youth as he came to Arkham to consult forbidden tomes at the college library, and had hated his wolfish, saturnine face with its tangle of iron-grey beard. He had died insane—under rather queer circumstances—just before his daughter (by his will made a nominal ward of the principal)[7] entered the Hall School, but she had been his morbidly avid pupil and looked fiendishly like him at times.

5. The Hall School in Bridgeport, Connecticut, founded in 1914 and named after the American Revolutionary War hero Lyman Hall, is a possible but unlikely identification of this school.

6. The Waites are mentioned, along with the Gilmans, the Eliots, and the Marshes (in "The Shadow over Innsmouth"), as one of the four "gently bred" families of Innsmouth.

7. The principal of the Hall School, presumably.

The friend whose daughter had gone to school with Asenath Waite repeated many curious things when the news of Edward's acquaintance with her began to spread about. Asenath, it seemed, had posed as a kind of magician at school; and had really seemed able to accomplish some highly baffling marvels. She professed to be able to raise thunderstorms, though her seeming success was generally laid to some uncanny knack at prediction. All animals markedly disliked her, and she could make any dog howl by certain motions of her right hand. There were times when she displayed snatches of knowledge and language very singular—and very shocking—for a young girl; when she would frighten her schoolmates with leers and winks of an inexplicable kind, and would seem to extract an obscene and zestful irony from her present situation.

Most unusual, though, were the well-attested cases of her influence over other persons. She was, beyond question, a genuine hypnotist. By gazing peculiarly at a fellow-student she would often give the latter a distinct feeling of *exchanged personality*—as if the subject were placed momentarily in the magician's body and able to stare half across the room at her real body, whose eyes blazed and protruded with an alien expression. Asenath often made wild claims about the nature of consciousness and about its independence of the physical frame—or at least from the life-processes of the physical frame. Her crowning rage, however, was that she was not a man; since she believed a male brain had certain unique and far-reaching cosmic powers. Given a man's brain, she declared, she could not only equal but surpass her father in mastery of unknown forces.

Edward met Asenath at a gathering of "intelligentsia" held in one of the students' rooms, and could talk of nothing else when he came to see me the next day. He had found her full of the interests and erudition which engrossed him most, and was in addition wildly taken with her appearance. I had never seen the young woman, and recalled casual references only faintly, but I knew who she was. It seemed rather regrettable that Derby should become so upheaved about her; but I said nothing to discourage him, since infatuation thrives on opposition. He was not, he said, mentioning her to his father.

In the next few weeks I heard of very little but Asenath from young Derby. Others now remarked Edward's autumnal gallantry, though they agreed that he did not look even nearly his actual age, or seem at all inappropriate as an escort for his bizarre divinity. He was only a trifle paunchy despite his indolence and self-indulgence, and his face was absolutely without lines. Asenath, on the other hand, had the premature crow's feet which come from the exercise of an intense will.

About this time Edward brought the girl to call on me, and I at once saw that his interest was by no means one-sided. She eyed him continually with an almost predatory air, and I perceived that their intimacy was beyond untangling. Soon afterward I had a visit from old Mr. Derby, whom I had always admired and respected. He had heard the tales of his son's new friendship, and had wormed the whole truth out of "the boy." Edward meant to marry Asenath, and had even been looking at houses in the suburbs. Knowing my usually great influence with his son, the father wondered if I could help to break the ill-advised affair off; but I regretfully expressed my doubts. This time it was not a question of Edward's weak will but of the woman's strong will. The perennial child had transferred his dependence from the parental image to a new and stronger image, and nothing could be done about it.

The wedding was performed a month later—by a justice of the peace, according to the bride's request. Mr. Derby, at my advice, offered no opposition; and he, my wife, my son, and I attended the brief ceremony—the other guests being wild young people from the college. Asenath had bought the old Crowninshield place in the country at the end of High Street,[8] and they proposed to settle there after a short trip to Innsmouth, whence three servants and some books and household goods were to be brought. It was probably not so much consideration for Edward and his father as a personal wish to be near the college, its library, and its crowd of "sophisticates," that made Asenath settle in Arkham instead of returning permanently home.

When Edward called on me after the honeymoon I thought he looked slightly changed. Asenath had made him get rid of the undeveloped moustache, but there was more than that. He

8. There is a Crowninshield-Bentley House in Salem, Massachusetts, listed in the National Register of Historic Places. Frank Crowninshield edited *Vanity Fair* magazine in the early twentieth century, and the family, Boston Brahmins, were prominent in seafaring, government, the military, publishing, and the arts. Lovecraft revered class status, devoting much energy to tracing his own lineage, and his Anglophilia was at times obsessive. His 1916 poem "An American to Mother England" includes these embarrassingly racist lines:

> What man that springs from thy untainted line
> But sees Columbia's virtues all as thine?
> Whilst nameless multitudes upon our shore
> From the dim corners of creation pour,
> Whilst mongrel slaves crawl hither to partake
> Of Saxon liberty they could not make,
> From such an alien crew in grief I turn,
> And for the mother's voice of Britain burn.

The Crowninshield-Bentley House, Salem, Massachusetts, built in 1727, shown here in 2013. Photograph copyright © Donovan K. Loucks 2013, reprinted with permission

looked soberer and more thoughtful, his habitual pout of childish rebelliousness being exchanged for a look almost of genuine sadness. I was puzzled to decide whether I liked or disliked the change. Certainly he seemed for the moment more normally adult than ever before. Perhaps the marriage was a good thing— might not the change of dependence form a start toward actual *neutralisation*, leading ultimately to responsible independence? He came alone, for Asenath was very busy. She had brought a vast store of books and apparatus from Innsmouth (Derby shuddered as he spoke the name), and was finishing the restoration of the Crowninshield house and grounds.

Her home in—that town—was a rather disquieting place, but certain objects in it had taught him some surprising things. He was progressing fast in esoteric lore now that he had Asenath's guidance. Some of the experiments she proposed were very daring and radical—he did not feel at liberty to describe them—but he had confidence in her powers and intentions. The three servants were very queer—an incredibly aged couple who had been with old Ephraim and referred occasionally to him and to Asenath's dead mother in a cryptic way, and a swarthy young wench who had marked anomalies of feature and seemed to exude a perpetual odour of fish.

III.

FOR THE NEXT two years I saw less and less of Derby. A fortnight would sometimes slip by without the familiar three-and-two strokes at the front door; and when he did call—or when, as happened with increasing infrequency, I called on him—he was very little disposed to converse on vital topics. He had become secretive about those occult studies which he used to describe and discuss so minutely, and preferred not to talk of his wife. She had aged tremendously since her marriage, till now—oddly enough—she seemed the elder of the two. Her face held the most concentratedly determined expression I had ever seen, and her whole aspect seemed to gain a vague, unplaceable repulsiveness. My wife and son noticed it as much as I, and we all ceased gradually to call on her—for which, Edward admitted in one of his boyishly tactless moments, she was unmitigatedly grateful. Occasionally the Derbys would go on long trips—ostensibly to Europe, though Edward sometimes hinted at obscurer destinations.

It was after the first year that people began talking about the change in Edward Derby. It was very casual talk, for the change was purely psychological; but it brought up some interesting points. Now and then, it seemed Edward was observed to wear an expression and to do things wholly incompatible with his usual flabby nature. For example—although in the old days he could not drive a car, he was now seen occasionally to dash into or out of the old Crowninshield driveway with Asenath's powerful Packard, handling it like a master, and meeting traffic entanglements with skill and determination utterly alien to his accustomed nature. In such cases he seemed always to be just back from some trip or just starting on one—what sort of trip, no one could guess, although he mostly favoured the Innsmouth road.

Oddly, the metamorphosis did not seem altogether pleasing. People said he looked too much like his wife, or like old Ephraim Waite himself, in these moments—or perhaps these moments seemed unnatural because they were so rare. Sometimes, hours after starting out in this way, he would return listlessly sprawled on the rear seat of his car while an obviously hired chauffeur or mechanic drove. Also, his preponderant aspect on the streets during his decreasing round of social contacts (including, I may say, his calls on me) was the old-time indecisive one—its irresponsible childishness even more marked than in the past. While Asenath's face aged, Edward's—aside from those exceptional occasions—actually relaxed into a kind of exaggerated immaturity, save when a trace of the new sadness or understanding would flash across it. It was really very puzzling. Meanwhile the Derbys almost dropped out of the gay college circle—not through their own disgust, we heard, but because something about their present studies shocked even the most callous of the other decadents.

It was in the third year of the marriage that Edward began to hint openly to me of a certain fear and dissatisfaction. He would let fall remarks about things "going too far," and would talk darkly about the need of "saving his identity." At first I ignored such references, but in time I began to question him guardedly, remembering what my friend's daughter had said about Asenath's hypnotic influence over the other girls at school—the cases where students had thought they were in her body looking across the room at themselves. This questioning seemed to make him at once alarmed and grateful, and once he mumbled something about having a serious talk with me later. About this time old Mr. Derby died, for which I was afterward very thankful. Edward was badly upset, though by no means disorganised. He had seen astonishingly little of his parent since his marriage, for Asenath had concentrated in herself all his vital sense of family linkage. Some called him callous in his loss—especially since those jaunty and confident moods in the car began to increase. He now wished to move back into the old Derby mansion, but Asenath insisted on staying in the Crowninshield house, to which she had become well adjusted.

Not long afterward my wife heard a curious thing from a friend—one of the few who had not dropped the Derbys. She had been out to the end of High St. to call on the couple, and had seen a car shoot briskly out of the drive with Edward's oddly confident and almost sneering face above the wheel. Ringing the bell, she had been told by the repulsive wench that Asenath was also out; but had chanced to look up at the house in leaving. There, at one of Edward's library windows, she had glimpsed a hastily withdrawn face—a face whose expression of pain, defeat,

The Derby House, Salem, Massachusetts, built in 1762, shown here in 2013.
Photograph copyright © Donovan K. Loucks 2013, reprinted with permission

9. This concept is explored in depth in "The Dreams in the Witch House" (pp. 643–80, above).

and wistful hopelessness was poignant beyond description. It was—incredibly enough in view of its usual domineering cast—Asenath's; yet the caller had vowed that in that instant the sad, muddled eyes of poor Edward were gazing out from it.

Edward's calls now grew a trifle more frequent, and his hints occasionally became concrete. What he said was not to be believed, even in centuried and legend-haunted Arkham; but he threw out his dark lore with a sincerity and convincingness which made one fear for his sanity. He talked about terrible meetings in lonely places, of Cyclopean ruins in the heart of the Maine woods beneath which vast staircases lead down to abysses of nighted secrets, of complex angles that lead through invisible walls to other regions of space and time,[9] and of hideous exchanges of personality that permitted explorations in remote and forbidden places, on other worlds, and in different space-time continua.

He would now and then back up certain crazy hints by exhibiting objects which utterly nonplussed me—elusively coloured and bafflingly textured objects like nothing ever heard of on earth, whose insane curves and surfaces answered no conceivable purpose, and followed no conceivable geometry. These things, he said, came "from outside"; and his wife knew how to get them. Sometimes—but always in frightened and ambiguous whispers—

10. Chesuncook Lake is in the middle of Piscataquis County, today still the least populous county in Maine. The tiny village on the northeast shore has a year-round population of only ten people.

he would suggest things about old Ephraim Waite, whom he had seen occasionally at the college library in the old days. These adumbrations were never specific, but seemed to revolve around some especially horrible doubt as to whether the old wizard were really dead—in a spiritual as well as corporeal sense.

At times Derby would halt abruptly in his revelations, and I wondered whether Asenath could possibly have divined his speech at a distance and cut him off through some unknown sort of telepathic mesmerism—some power of the kind she had displayed at school. Certainly, she suspected that he told me things, for as the weeks passed she tried to stop his visits with words and glances of a most inexplicable potency. Only with difficulty could he get to see me, for although he would pretend to be going somewhere else, some invisible force would generally clog his motions or make him forget his destination for the time being. His visits usually came when Asenath was away—"away in her own body," as he once oddly put it. She always found out later—the servants watched his goings and comings—but evidently she thought it inexpedient to do anything drastic.

IV.

DERBY HAD BEEN married more than three years on that August day when I got the telegram from Maine. I had not seen him for two months, but had heard he was away "on business." Asenath was supposed to be with him, though watchful gossips declared there was someone upstairs in the house behind the doubly curtained windows. They had watched the purchases made by the servants. And now the town marshal of Chesuncook had wired of the draggled madman who stumbled out of the woods with delirious ravings and screamed to me for protection. It was Edward—and he had been just able to recall his own name and my name and address.

Chesuncook is close to the wildest, deepest, and least explored forest belt in Maine,[10] and it took a whole day of feverish jolting through fantastic and forbidding scenery to get there in a car. I found Derby in a cell at the town farm, vacillating between frenzy and apathy. He knew me at once, and began pouring out a meaningless, half-incoherent torrent of words in my direction.

"Dan—for God's sake! The pit of the shoggoths! Down the six thousand steps . . . the abomination of abominations . . . I never would let her take me, and then I found myself there . . . Iä! Shub-Niggurath! . . . The shape rose up from the altar, and there were 500 that howled . . . The Hooded Thing bleated 'Kamog! Kamog!'—that was old Ephraim's secret name in the coven. . . . I was there, where she promised she wouldn't take me. . . . A minute before I was locked in the library, and then I was there where she had gone with my body—in the place of utter blasphemy, the unholy pit where the black realm begins and the watcher guards the gate. . . . I saw a shoggoth—it changed shape. . . . I can't stand it. . . . I won't stand it. . . . I'll kill her if she ever sends me there again. . . . I'll kill that entity . . . her, him, it . . . I'll kill it! I'll kill it with my own hands!"

"The pit of the shoggoths! Down the six thousand steps . . . the abomination of abominations." *Weird Tales* 29, no. 1 (January 1937) (artist: Virgil Finlay)

It took me an hour to quiet him, but he subsided at last. The next day I got him decent clothes in the village, and set out with him for Arkham. His fury of hysteria was spent, and he was inclined to be silent, though he began muttering darkly to himself when the car passed through Augusta—as if the sight of a city aroused unpleasant memories. It was clear that he did not wish to go home; and considering the fantastic delusions he seemed to have about his wife—delusions undoubtedly springing from some actual hypnotic ordeal to which he had been subjected—I thought it would be better if he did not. I would, I resolved, put him up myself for a time; no matter what unpleasantness it would make with Asenath. Later I would help him get a divorce, for most assuredly there were mental factors which made this marriage suicidal for him. When we struck open country again Derby's muttering faded away, and I let him nod and drowse on the seat beside me as I drove.

During our sunset dash through Portland the muttering commenced again, more distinctly than before, and as I listened I caught a stream of utterly insane drivel about Asenath. The extent to which she had preyed on Edward's nerves was plain, for he had woven a whole set of hallucinations around her. His present predicament, he mumbled furtively, was only one of a long series. She was getting hold of him, and he knew that some day she would never let go. Even now she probably let him go only when she had to, because she couldn't hold on long at a time. She constantly took his body and went to nameless places for nameless rites, leaving him in her body and locking him upstairs—but sometimes she couldn't hold on, and he would find himself suddenly in his own body again in some far-off, horrible, and perhaps unknown place. Sometimes she'd get hold of him again and sometimes she couldn't. Often he was left stranded somewhere as I had found him . . . time and again he had to find his way home from frightful distances, getting somebody to drive the car after he found it.

The worst thing was that she was holding on to him longer and longer at a time. She wanted to be a man—to be fully human—that was why she got hold of him. She had sensed the mixture of fine-wrought brain and weak will in him. Some day she would crowd him out and disappear with his body—disappear to become a great magician like her father and leave him marooned in that female shell that wasn't even quite human.[11] Yes, he knew about the Innsmouth blood now. There had been traffick with things from the sea—it was horrible. . . . And old Ephraim—he had known the secret, and when he grew old did a hideous thing to keep alive . . . he wanted to live forever . . . Asenath would succeed—one successful demonstration had taken place already.

As Derby muttered on I turned to look at him closely, verifying the impression of change which an earlier scrutiny had given me. Paradoxically, he seemed in better shape than usual—harder, more normally developed, and without the trace of sickly flabbiness caused by his indolent habits. It was as if he had been really active and properly exercised for the first time in his coddled life, and I judged that Asenath's force must have pushed him into unwonted channels of motion and alertness. But just now his mind was in a pitiable state; for he was mumbling wild extravagances about his wife, about black magic, about old Ephraim, and about some revelation which would convince even me. He repeated names which I recognised from bygone browsings in forbidden volumes, and at times made me shudder with a certain thread of mythological consistency—of convincing coherence—which ran through his maundering. Again and again he would pause, as if to gather courage for some final and terrible disclosure.

"Dan, Dan, don't you remember him—the wild eyes and the unkempt beard that never turned white? He glared at me once, and I never forgot it. Now *she* glares that way. *And I know why!* He found it in the *Necronomicon*—the formula. I don't dare tell you the page yet, but when I do you can read and understand. Then you will know what has engulfed me. On, on, on, on—body to body to body—he means never to die. The life-glow—he knows how to break the link . . . it can flicker on a while even when the body is dead. I'll give you hints, and maybe you'll guess. Listen, Dan—do you know why my wife always takes such pains with that silly backhand writing? Have you ever seen a manuscript of old Ephraim's? Do you want to know why I shivered when I saw some hasty notes Asenath had jotted down?

"Asenath—*is there such a person?* Why did they half think

11. Ephraim-Asenath's plan is obscure. We learned in "The Shadow over Innsmouth" that those who had congress with the Deep Ones would achieve immortality. What did it profit Ephraim-Asenath to trade Asenath's immortal body for a mortal one? Edward was no physical prize, although he was in "better shape than usual." The only possible explanation, and there are hints that this is the correct one, is that Ephraim wanted—perhaps required—a male body in order for his personality to persist.

12. See note 6, above. The Gilmans and the other leading families of Innsmouth appear to have been closely tied.

there was poison in old Ephraim's stomach? Why do the Gilmans[12] whisper about the way he shrieked—like a frightened child—when he went mad and Asenath locked him up in the padded attic room where—the other—had been? Was it *old Ephraim's soul* that was locked in? *Who locked in whom?* Why had he been looking for months for someone with a fine mind and a weak will? Why did he curse that his daughter wasn't a son? Tell me, Daniel Upton—*what devilish exchange was perpetrated in the house of horror where that blasphemous monster had his trusting, weak-willed half-human child at his mercy?* Didn't he make it permanent—as she'll do in the end with me? Tell me why that thing that calls itself Asenath writes differently when off guard, *so that you can't tell its script from. . . ."*

Then the thing happened. Derby's voice was rising to a thin treble scream as he raved, when suddenly it was shut off with an almost mechanical click. I thought of those other occasions at my home when his confidences had abruptly ceased—when I had half-fancied that some obscure telepathic wave of Asenath's mental force was intervening to keep him silent. This, though, was something altogether different—and, I felt, infinitely more horrible. The face beside me was twisted almost unrecognisably for a moment, while through the whole body there passed a shivering motion—as if all the bones, organs, muscles, nerves, and glands were readjusting themselves to a radically different posture, set of stresses, and general personality.

Just where the supreme horror lay, I could not for my life tell; yet there swept over me such a swamping wave of sickness and repulsion—such a freezing, petrifying sense of utter alienage and abnormality—that my grasp of the wheel grew feeble and uncertain. The figure beside me seemed less like a lifelong friend than like some monstrous intrusion from outer space—some damnable, utterly accursed focus of unknown and malign cosmic forces.

I had faltered only a moment, but before another moment was over my companion had seized the wheel and forced me to change places with him. The dusk was now very thick, and the lights of Portland far behind, so I could not see much of his face. The blaze of his eyes, though, was phenomenal; and I knew that he must now be in that queerly energised state—so unlike his usual self—which so many people had noticed. It seemed odd and incredible that listless Edward Derby—he who could never assert himself, and who had never learned to drive—should be ordering me about and taking the wheel of my own car, yet that was precisely what had happened. He did not speak for some time, and in my inexplicable horror I was glad he did not.

In the lights of Biddeford and Saco I saw his firmly set mouth, and shivered at the blaze of his eyes. The people were right—he did look damnably like his wife and like old Ephraim when in these moods. I did not wonder that the moods were disliked—there was certainly something unnatural and diabolic in them, and I felt the sinister element all the more because of the wild ravings I had been hearing. This man, for all my lifelong knowledge of Edward Pickman Derby, was a stranger—an intrusion of some sort from the black abyss.

He did not speak until we were on a dark stretch of road, and when he did his voice seemed utterly unfamiliar. It was deeper, firmer, and more decisive than I had ever known it to be; while its accent and pronunciation were altogether changed—though vaguely, remotely, and rather disturbingly recalling something I could not quite place. There was, I thought, a trace of very profound and very genuine irony in the timbre—not the flashy, meaninglessly jaunty pseudo-irony of the callow "sophisticate," which Derby had habitually affected, but something grim, basic, pervasive, and potentially evil. I marvelled at the self-possession so soon following the spell of panic-struck muttering.

"I hope you'll forget my attack back there, Upton," he was saying. "You know what my nerves are, and I guess you can excuse such things. I'm enormously grateful, of course, for this lift home.

"And you must forget, too, any crazy things I may have been saying about my wife—and about things in general. That's what comes from overstudy in a field like mine. My philosophy is full of bizarre concepts, and when the mind gets worn out it cooks up all sorts of imaginary concrete applications. I shall take a rest from now on—you probably won't see me for some time, and you needn't blame Asenath for it.

"This trip was a bit queer, but it's really very simple. There are certain Indian relics in the north woods—standing stones, and all that—which mean a good deal in folklore, and Asenath and I are following that stuff up. It was a hard search, so I seem to have

13. In 1932, a year before Lovecraft wrote this story, the occultist Aleister Crowley, head of the London-based A∴A∴, a magical fraternity centered around a pantheon of Crowley's own devising, parted company with his secretary, Israel Regardie. Regardie would go on to write several important histories of occult orders. While he did not move to New York until 1937, at some earlier date he may have temporarily taken up residence there to explore his options. (Crowley was expelled from France in 1929; after living in New York during the war years, from 1914 to 1919, he returned to England.)

gone off my head. I must send somebody for the car when I get home. A month's relaxation will put me back on my feet."

I do not recall just what my own part of the conversation was, for the baffling alienage of my seatmate filled all my consciousness. With every moment my feeling of elusive cosmic horror increased, till at length I was in a virtual delirium of longing for the end of the drive. Derby did not offer to relinquish the wheel, and I was glad of the speed with which Portsmouth and Newburyport flashed by.

At the junction where the main highway runs inland and avoids Innsmouth I was half afraid my driver would take the bleak shore road that goes through that damnable place. He did not, however, but darted rapidly past Rowley and Ipswich toward our destination. We reached Arkham before midnight, and found the lights still on at the old Crowninshield house. Derby left the car with a hasty repetition of his thanks, and I drove home alone with a curious feeling of relief. It had been a terrible drive—all the more terrible because I could not quite tell why—and I did not regret Derby's forecast of a long absence from my company.

V.

THE NEXT TWO months were full of rumours. People spoke of seeing Derby more and more in his new energised state, and Asenath was scarcely ever in to her few callers. I had only one visit from Edward, when he called briefly in Asenath's car—duly reclaimed from wherever he had left it in Maine—to get some books he had lent me. He was in his new state, and paused only long enough for some evasively polite remarks. It was plain that he had nothing to discuss with me when in this condition—and I noticed that he did not even trouble to give the old three-and-two signal when ringing the doorbell. As on that evening in the car, I felt a faint, infinitely deep horror which I could not explain; so that his swift departure was a prodigious relief.

In mid-September Derby was away for a week, and some of the decadent college set talked knowingly of the matter—hinting at a meeting with a notorious cult-leader, lately expelled from England, who had established headquarters in New York.[13] For my part I could not get that strange ride from Maine out of my head. The transformation I had witnessed had affected me profoundly, and I caught myself again and again trying to account for the thing—and for the extreme horror it had inspired in me.

But the oddest rumours were those about the sobbing in the old Crowninshield house. The voice seemed to be a woman's, and some of the younger people thought it sounded like Asenath's. It was heard only at rare intervals, and would sometimes be choked off as if by force. There was talk of an investigation, but this was dispelled one day when Asenath appeared in the streets and chatted in a sprightly way with a large number of acquaintances—apologising for her recent absences and speaking incidentally about the nervous breakdown and hysteria of a guest from Boston. The guest was never seen, but Asenath's appearance left nothing to be said. And then someone complicated matters by whispering that the sobs had once or twice been in a man's voice.

One evening in mid-October I heard the familiar three-and-two ring at the front door. Answering it myself, I found Edward on the steps, and saw in a moment that his personality was the old one which I had not encountered since the day of his ravings on that terrible ride from Chesuncook. His face was twitching with a mixture of odd emotions in which fear and triumph seemed to share dominion, and he looked furtively over his shoulder as I closed the door behind him.

Following me clumsily to the study, he asked for some whiskey to steady his nerves. I forbore to question him, but waited till he felt like beginning whatever he wanted to say. At length he ventured some information in a choking voice.

"Asenath has gone, Dan. We had a long talk last night while the servants were out, and I made her promise to stop preying on me. Of course I had certain—certain occult defences I never told you about. She had to give in, but got frightfully angry. Just packed up and started for New York—walked right out to catch the 8:20 in to Boston. I suppose people will talk, but I can't help that. You needn't mention that there was any trouble—just say she's gone on a long research trip.

"She's probably going to stay with one of her horrible groups of devotees. I hope she'll go west and get a divorce—anyhow, I've made her promise to keep away and let me alone. It was horrible, Dan—she was stealing my body—crowding me out—making a prisoner of me. I laid low and pretended to let her do it, but I had to be on the watch. I could plan if I was careful, for she can't read my mind literally, or in detail. All she could read of my planning was a sort of general mood of rebellion—and she always thought I was helpless. Never thought I could get the best of her . . . but I had a spell or two that worked."

Derby looked over his shoulder and took some more whiskey.

"I paid off those damned servants this morning when they got back. They were ugly about it, and asked questions, but they went. They're her kind—Innsmouth people—and were hand and glove with her. I hope they'll let me alone—I didn't like the way they laughed when they walked away. I must get as many of Dad's old servants again as I can. I'll move back home now.

"I suppose you think I'm crazy, Dan—but Arkham history ought to hint at things that back up what I've told you—and what I'm going to tell you. You've seen one of the changes, too—in your car after I told you about Asenath that day coming home from Maine. That was when she got me—drove me out of my body. The last thing of the ride I remember was when I was all worked up trying to tell you *what that she-devil is*. Then she got me, and in a flash I was back at the house—in the library where those damned servants had me locked up—and in that cursed fiend's body . . . that isn't even human. . . . You know it was she you must have ridden home with . . . that preying wolf in my body. . . . You ought to have known the difference!"

I shuddered as Derby paused. Surely, I *had* known the difference—yet could I accept an explanation as insane as this? But my distracted caller was growing even wilder.

"I had to save myself—I had to, Dan! She'd have got me for good at Hallowmass—they hold a Sabbat up there beyond Chesuncook, and the sacrifice would have clinched things. She'd have got me for good . . . she'd have been I, and I'd have been she . . . forever . . . too late. . . . My body'd have been hers for good. . . . She'd have been a man, and fully human, just as she wanted to be. . . . I suppose she'd have put me out of the way—killed her own ex-body with me in it, damn her, *just as she did before*—just as she, he, or it did before. . . ." Edward's face was now atrociously distorted, and he bent it uncomfortably close to mine as his voice fell to a whisper.

"You must know what I hinted in the car—*that she isn't Asenath at all, but really old Ephraim himself.* I suspected it a year and a half ago, but I know it now. Her handwriting shews it when he's off guard—sometimes she jots down a note in writing that's just like her father's manuscripts, stroke for stroke—and sometimes she says things that nobody but an old man like Ephraim could say. He changed forms with her when he felt death coming—she was the only one he could find with the right kind of brain and a weak enough will—he got her body permanently, just as she almost got mine, and then poisoned the old body he'd put her into. Haven't you seen old Ephraim's soul glaring out of that she-devil's eyes *dozens* of times . . . and out of mine when she had control of my body?"

The whisperer was panting, and paused for breath. I said nothing, and when he resumed his voice was nearer normal. This, I reflected, was a case for the asylum, but I would not be the one to send him there. Perhaps time and freedom from Asenath would do its work. I could see that he would never wish to dabble in morbid occultism again.

"I'll tell you more later—I must have a long rest now. I'll tell you something of the forbidden horrors she led me into—something of the age-old horrors that even now are festering in out-of-the-way corners with a few monstrous priests to keep them alive. Some people know things about the universe that nobody ought to know, and can do things that nobody ought to be able to do. I've been in it up to my neck, but that's the end. Today I'd burn that damned *Necronomicon* and all the rest if I were librarian at Miskatonic.

"But she can't get me now. I must get out of that accursed house as soon as I can, and settle down at home. You'll help me, I know, if I need help. Those devilish servants, you know . . . and if people should get too inquisitive about Asenath. You see, I can't give them her address. . . . Then there are certain groups of searchers—certain cults, you know—that might misunderstand our breaking up . . . some of them have damnably curious ideas and methods. I know you'll stand by me if anything happens—even if I have to tell you a lot that will shock you. . . ."

I had Edward stay and sleep in one of the guest-chambers that night, and in the morning he seemed calmer. We discussed certain possible arrangements for his moving back into the Derby mansion, and I hoped he would lose no time in making the change. He did not call the next evening, but I saw him frequently during the ensuing weeks. We talked as little as possible about strange and unpleasant things, but discussed the renovation of the old Derby house, and the travels which Edward promised to take with my son and me the following summer.

Of Asenath we said almost nothing, for I saw that the subject was a peculiarly disturbing one. Gossip, of course, was rife; but that was no novelty in connexion with the strange ménage at the old Crowninshield house. One thing I did not like was what Derby's banker let fall in an overexpansive mood at the Miskatonic Club—about the cheques Edward was sending regularly to a Moses and Abigail Sargent and a Eunice Babson in Innsmouth. That looked as if those evil-faced servants were extorting some kind of tribute from him—yet he had not mentioned the matter to me.

I wished that the summer—and my son's Harvard vacation—would come, so that we could get Edward to Europe. He was not, I soon saw, mending as rapidly as I had hoped he would; for there was something a bit hysterical in his occasional exhilaration, while his moods of fright and depression were altogether too frequent. The old Derby house was ready by December, yet Edward constantly put off moving. Though he hated and seemed to fear the Crowninshield place, he was at the same time queerly enslaved by it. He could not seem to begin dismantling things, and invented every kind of excuse to postpone action. When I pointed this out to him he appeared unaccountably frightened. His father's old butler—who was there with other reacquired family servants—told me one day that Edward's occasional prowlings about the house, and especially down cellar, looked odd and unwholesome to him. I wondered if Asenath had been writing disturbing letters, but the butler said there was no mail which could have come from her.

VI.

IT WAS ABOUT Christmas that Derby broke down one evening while calling on me. I was steering the conversation toward next summer's travels when he suddenly shrieked and leaped up from his chair with a look of shocking, uncontrollable fright—a cosmic panic and loathing such as only the nether gulfs of nightmare could bring to any sane mind.

"My brain! My brain! God, Dan—it's tugging—from beyond—knocking—clawing—that she-devil—even now—Ephraim—Kamog! Kamog!—The pit of the shoggoths—Iä! Shub-Niggurath! The Goat with a Thousand Young! . . .

"The flame—the flame . . . beyond body, beyond life . . . in the earth—oh, God! . . ."

I pulled him back to his chair and poured some wine down his throat as his frenzy sank to a dull apathy. He did not resist, but kept his lips moving as if talking to himself. Presently I realised that he was trying to talk to me, and bent my ear to his mouth to catch the feeble words.

". . . again, again . . . she's trying . . . I might have known . . . nothing can stop that force; not distance nor magic, nor death . . . it comes and comes, mostly in the night . . . I can't leave . . . it's horrible . . . oh, God, Dan, *if you only knew as I do just how horrible it is. . . .*"

When he had slumped down into a stupor I propped him with pillows and let normal sleep overtake him. I did not call a doctor, for I knew what would be said of his sanity, and wished to give nature a chance if I possibly could. He waked at midnight, and I put him to bed upstairs, but he was gone by morning. He had let himself quietly out of the house—and his butler, when called on the wire, said he was at home pacing restlessly about the library.

Edward went to pieces rapidly after that. He did not call again, but I went daily to see him. He would always be sitting in his library, staring at nothing and having an air of abnormal listening. Sometimes he talked rationally, but always on trivial topics. Any mention of his trouble, of future plans, or of Asenath would send him into a frenzy. His butler said he had frightful seizures at night, during which he might eventually do himself harm.

I had a long talk with his doctor, banker, and lawyer, and finally took the physician with two specialist colleagues to visit him. The spasms that resulted from the first questions were violent and pitiable—and that evening a closed car took his poor struggling body to the Arkham Sanitarium. I was made his guardian and called on him twice weekly—almost weeping to hear his wild shrieks, awesome whispers, and dreadful, droning repetitions of such phrases as "I had to do it . . . I had to do it . . . it'll get me . . . it'll get me . . . down there . . . down there in the dark. . . . Mother, mother! Dan! Save me . . . save me . . ."

How much hope of recovery there was, no one could say, but I tried my best to be optimistic. Edward must have a home if he emerged, so I transferred his servants to the Derby mansion, which would surely be his sane choice. What to do about the Crowninshield place with its complex arrangements and collections of utterly inexplicable objects I could not decide, so left it momentarily untouched—telling the Derby housemaid to go over and dust the chief rooms once a week, and ordering the furnace man to have a fire on those days.

The final nightmare came before Candlemas—heralded, in cruel irony, by a false gleam of hope. One morning late in January the sanitarium telephoned to report that Edward's reason had suddenly come back. His continuous memory, they said, was badly impaired; but sanity itself was certain. Of course he must remain some time for observation, but there could be little doubt of the outcome. All going well, he would surely be free in a week.

I hastened over in a flood of delight, but stood bewildered when a nurse took me to Edward's room. The patient rose to greet me, extending his hand with a polite smile; but I saw in an instant that he bore the strangely energised personality which had seemed so foreign to his own nature—the competent personality I had found so vaguely horrible, and which Edward himself had once vowed was the intruding soul of his wife. There was the same blazing vision—so like Asenath's and old Ephraim's—and the same firm mouth; and when he spoke I could sense the same grim, pervasive irony in his voice—the deep irony so redolent of potential evil. This was the person who had driven my car through the night five months before—the person I had not seen since that brief call when he had forgotten the old-time doorbell signal and stirred such nebulous fears in me—and now he filled me with the same dim feeling of blasphemous alienage and ineffable cosmic hideousness.

He spoke affably of arrangements for release—and there was nothing for me to do but assent, despite some remarkable gaps in his recent memories. Yet I felt that something was terribly, inexplicably wrong and abnormal. There were horrors in this thing that I could not reach. This was a sane person—but was it indeed the Edward Derby I had known? If not, who or what was it—and where *was* Edward? Ought it to be free or confined . . . or ought it to be extirpated from the face of the earth? There was a hint of the abysmally sardonic in everything the creature said—the Asenath-like eyes lent a special and baffling mockery to certain words about the "early liberty earned by *an especially close confinement!*" I must have behaved very awkwardly, and was glad to beat a retreat.

All that day and the next I racked my brain over the problem. What had happened? What sort of mind looked out through those alien eyes in Edward's face? I could think of nothing but this dimly terrible enigma, and gave up all efforts to perform my usual work. The second morning the hospital called up to say that the recovered patient was unchanged, and by evening I was close to a nervous collapse—a state I admit, though others will vow it coloured my subsequent vision. I have nothing to say on this point except that no madness of mine could account for *all* the evidence.

VII.

IT WAS IN the night—after that second evening—that stark, utter horror burst over me and weighted my spirit with a black, clutching panic from which it can never shake free. It began with a telephone call just before midnight. I was the only one up, and sleepily took down the receiver in the library. No one seemed to be on the wire, and I was about to hang up and go to bed when my ear caught a very faint suspicion of sound at the other end. Was someone trying under great difficulties to talk? As I listened I thought I heard a sort of half-liquid bubbling noise—"*glub . . .*

glub . . . glub"—which had an odd suggestion of inarticulate, unintelligible word and syllable divisions. I called "Who is it?" But the only answer was "*glub-glub* . . . glub-glub." I could only assume that the noise was mechanical; but fancying that it might be a case of a broken instrument able to receive but not to send, I added, "I can't hear you. Better hang up and try Information." Immediately I heard the receiver go on the hook at the other end.

This, I say, was just before midnight. When that call was traced afterward it was found to come from the old Crownin-shield house, though it was fully half a week from the house-maid's day to be there. I shall only hint what was found at that house—the upheaval in a remote cellar storeroom, the tracks, the dirt, the hastily rifled wardrobe, the baffling marks on the telephone, the clumsily used stationery, and the detestable stench lingering over everything. The police, poor fools, have their smug little theories, and are still searching for those sinister discharged servants—who have dropped out of sight amidst the present furore. They speak of a ghoulish revenge for things that were done, and say I was included because I was Edward's best friend and adviser.

Idiots!—do they fancy those brutish clowns could have forged that handwriting? Do they fancy they could have brought what later came? Are they blind to the changes in that body that was Edward's? As for me, *I now believe all that Edward Derby ever told me.* There are horrors beyond life's edge that we do not suspect, and once in a while man's evil prying calls them just within our range.

Ephraim—Asenath—that devil called them in, and they engulfed Edward as they are engulfing me.

Can I be sure that I am safe? Those powers survive the life of the physical form. The next day—in the afternoon, when I pulled out of my prostration and was able to walk and talk coherently—I went to the madhouse and shot him dead for Edward's and the world's sake, but can I be sure till he is cremated? They are keep-ing the body for some silly autopsies by different doctors—but I say he must be cremated. *He must be cremated—he who was not Edward Derby when I shot him.* I shall go mad if he is not, for I may be the next. But my will is not weak—and I shall not let it be undermined by the terrors I know are seething around it. One life—Ephraim, Asenath, and Edward—who now? I will not be driven out of my body . . . I *will not* change souls with that bullet-ridden lich[14] in the madhouse!

But let me try to tell coherently of that final horror. I will not speak of what the police persistently ignored—the tales of that dwarfed, grotesque, malodorous thing met by at least three wayfarers in High St. just before two o'clock, and the nature of the single footprints in certain places. I will say only that just about two the doorbell and knocker waked me—doorbell and knocker both, applied alternately and uncertainly in a kind of weak desperation, and *each trying to keep to Edward's old signal of three-and-two strokes.*

Roused from sound sleep, my mind leaped into a turmoil. Derby at the door—and remembering the old code! That new personality had not remembered it . . . was Edward suddenly back in his rightful state? Why was he here in such evident stress and haste? Had he been released ahead of time, or had he escaped? Perhaps, I thought as I flung on a robe and bounded downstairs, his return to his own self had brought raving and violence, revoking his discharge and driving him to a desperate dash for freedom. Whatever had happened, he was good old Edward again, and I would help him!

When I opened the door into the elm-arched blackness a gust of insufferably fœtid wind almost flung me prostrate. I choked in nausea, and for a second scarcely saw the dwarfed, humped figure on the steps. The summons had been Edward's, but who was this foul, stunted parody? Where had Edward had time to go? His ring had sounded only a second before the door opened.

The caller had on one of Edward's overcoats—its bottom almost touching the ground, and its sleeves rolled back yet still covering the hands. On the head was a slouch hat pulled low, while a black silk muffler concealed the face. As I stepped unsteadily forward, the figure made a semi-liquid sound like that I had heard over the telephone—"*glub . . . glub . . .*"—and thrust at me a large, closely written paper impaled on the end of a long pencil. Still reeling from the morbid and unaccountable fœtor, I seized this paper and tried to read it in the light from the doorway.

Beyond question, it was in Edward's script. But why had he written when he was close enough to ring—and why was the

14. Ambrose Bierce, in "The Death of Halpin Frayser" (an 1893 tale almost surely familiar to Lovecraft, who ranked Bierce's work highly—see pp. xxiv–xxv, above), quotes the fictional source Hali on liches as follows: "For by death is wrought greater change than hath been shown. Whereas in general the spirit that removed cometh back upon occasion, and is sometimes seen of those in flesh (appearing in the form of the body it bore) yet it hath happened that the veritable body without the spirit hath walked. And it is attested of those encountering who have lived to speak thereon that a lich so raised up hath no natural affection, nor remembrance thereof, but only hate. Also, it is known that some spirits which in life were benign become by death evil altogether." (*The Complete Short Stories of Ambrose Bierce*, edited by Ernest Jerome Hopkins [Lincoln: University of Nebraska Press, 1984], 58–59.) Hali is also quoted in Bierce's 1891 story "An Inhabitant of Carcosa," and a Lake Hali is mentioned in Robert Chambers's 1895 collection *The King in Yellow*, though it is unclear who Hali is meant to be. In Bierce's story, the lich is the victim's mother, returned from the dead. In modern fantasy-gaming parlance, a lich is an undead wizard of great power.

script so awkward, coarse and shaky? I could make out nothing in the dim half light, so edged back into the hall, the dwarf figure clumping mechanically after but pausing on the inner door's threshold. The odour of this singular messenger was really appalling, and I hoped (not in vain, thank God!) that my wife would not wake and confront it.

Then, as I read the paper, I felt my knees give under me and my vision go black. I was lying on the floor when I came to, that accursed sheet still clutched in my fear-rigid hand. This is what it said.

Dan—go to the sanitarium and kill it. Exterminate it. It isn't Edward Derby any more. She got me—it's Asenath—and she has been dead three months and a half. I lied when I said she had gone away. I killed her. I had to. It was sudden, but we were alone and I was in my right body. I saw a candlestick and smashed her head in. She would have got me for good at Hallowmass.

I buried her in the farther cellar storeroom under some old boxes and cleaned up all the traces. The servants suspected next morning, but they have such secrets that they dare not tell the police. I sent them off, but God knows what they—and others of the cult—will do.

I thought for a while I was all right, and then I felt the tugging at my brain. I knew what it was—I ought to have remembered. A soul like hers—or Ephraim's—is half detached, and keeps right on after death as long as the body lasts. She was getting me—making me change bodies with her—seizing my body and putting me in that corpse of hers buried in the cellar.

I knew what was coming—that's why I snapped and had to go to the asylum. Then it came—I found myself choked in the dark—in Asenath's rotting carcass down there in the cellar under the boxes where I put it. And I knew she must be in my body at the sanitarium—permanently, for it was after Hallowmass, and the sacrifice would work even without her being there—sane, and ready for release as a menace to the world. I was desperate, and in spite of everything I clawed my way out.

I'm too far gone to talk—I couldn't manage to telephone—but I can still write. I'll get fixed up somehow and bring you this last word and warning. Kill that fiend if you value the peace and

comfort of the world. See that it is cremated. If you don't, it will
live on and on, body to body forever, and I can't tell you what it
will do. Keep clear of black magic, Dan, it's the devil's business.
Goodbye—you've been a great friend. Tell the police whatever
they'll believe—and I'm damnably sorry to drag all this on you. I'll
be at peace before long—this thing won't hold together much more.
Hope you can read this. And kill that thing—kill it.

Yours—Ed.

It was only afterward that I read the last half of this paper, for
I had fainted at the end of the third paragraph. I fainted again
when I saw and smelled what cluttered up the threshold where

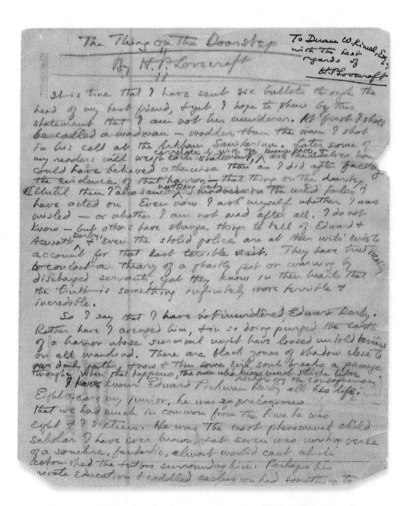

First page of the handwritten manuscript of "The Thing on the
Doorstep."

the warm air had struck it. The messenger would not move or have consciousness any more.

The butler, tougher-fibred than I, did not faint at what met him in the hall in the morning. Instead, he telephoned the police. When they came I had been taken upstairs to bed, but the—other mass—lay where it had collapsed in the night. The men put handkerchiefs to their noses.

What they finally found inside Edward's oddly assorted clothes was mostly liquescent horror. There were bones, too—and a crushed-in skull. Some dental work positively identified the skull as Asenath's.

The Shadow Out of Time[1]

Although it is easy to dismiss this tale—one of Lovecraft's last efforts at fiction—as just another "mind-exchange" story, it displays a scope and craft rivaled only by At the Mountains of Madness. *Building slowly, and meticulously recording Peaslee's strange experiences, it allows us to share the narrator's struggle to avoid the obvious conclusion—that he has been possessed by another mind and has himself traveled into the far distant past. The stunning ending conveys both horror and awe, confirming humankind's relatively minor role on the cosmic stage.*

I.

fter twenty-two years of nightmare and terror, saved only by a desperate conviction of the mythical source of certain impressions, I am unwilling to vouch for the truth of that which I think I found in Western Australia on the night of July 17–18, 1935. There is reason to hope that my experience was wholly or partly an hallucination—for which, indeed, abundant causes existed. And yet, its realism was so hideous that I sometimes find hope impossible.

If the thing did happen, then man must be prepared to accept notions of the cosmos, and of his own place in the seething vortex of time, whose merest mention is paralysing. He must, too, be placed on guard against a specific lurking peril which, though it will never engulf the whole race, may impose monstrous and unguessable horrors upon certain venturesome members of it.

It is for this latter reason that I urge, with all the force of my being, final abandonment of all attempts at unearthing those fragments of unknown, primordial masonry which my expedition set out to investigate.

1. Written during 1934 and 1935, this first appeared in *Astounding Stories* 17, no. 4 (June 1936), 110–54.

Astounding Stories 17, no. 4 (June 1936) (artist: Howard V. Brown)

Assuming that I was sane and awake, my experience on that night was such as has befallen no man before. It was, moreover, a frightful confirmation of all I had sought to dismiss as myth and dream. Mercifully there is no proof, for in my fright I lost the awesome object which would—if real and brought out of that noxious abyss—have formed irrefutable evidence. When I came upon the horror I was alone—and I have up to now told no one about it. I could not stop the others from digging in its direction, but chance and the shifting sand have so far saved them from finding it. Now I must formulate some definitive statement—not only for the sake of my own mental balance, but to warn such others as may read it seriously.

These pages—much in whose earlier parts will be familiar to close readers of the general and scientific press—are written in the cabin of the ship that is bringing me home. I shall give them to my son, Prof. Wingate Peaslee of Miskatonic University—the only member of my family who stuck to me after my queer amnesia of long ago, and the man best informed on the inner facts of my case. Of all living persons, he is least likely to ridicule what I shall tell of that fateful night.

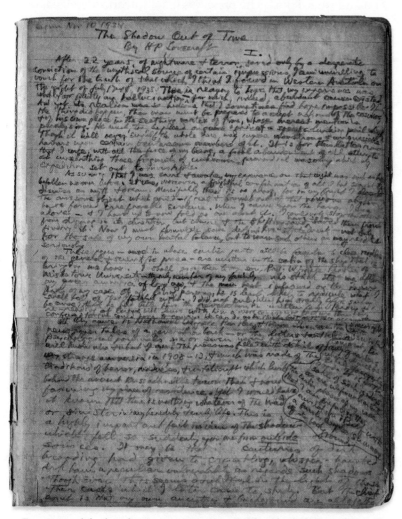

First page of the handwritten manuscript of "The Shadow Out of Time."

2. Lovecraft's notes, reproduced in *Something About Cats and Other Pieces*, gives the following brief biography:

> Nathaniel Wingate Peaslee b. Haverhill 1871 son of Jonathan & Hannah (Wingate) Peaslee. :: att. Miskatonic U. 1889–1893. Harvard 1893–5. Instructor Pol. Econ. Miskatonic 1895–1898. M. Alice Keezar of Harvard 1896. Robert K. B. 1898. Wingate b. 1900. Hannah b. 1903. Assc. Prof. 1898–1902. Prof. 1902–1908. ::: Amnesia Thurs. May 14, 1908 (age 37) 1913 (age 42). Work on strange dreams and Amnesia—studies in psychology 1915 onward. Instr. Psych. Miskatonic 1922+ (age 51). Hear of Australian legends from Perth 1934. Visit Australia—June (equin. Dec.) 1935. Climax July 1935. Age 64. . . .

I did not enlighten him orally before sailing, because I think he had better have the revelation in written form. Reading and re-reading at leisure will leave with him a more convincing picture than my confused tongue could hope to convey. He can do as he thinks best with this account—shewing it, with suitable comment, in any quarters where it will be likely to accomplish good. It is for the sake of such readers as are unfamiliar with the earlier phases of my case that I am prefacing the revelation itself with a fairly ample summary of its background.

My name is Nathaniel Wingate Peaslee, and those who recall the newspaper tales of a generation back—or the letters and articles in psychological journals six or seven years ago—will know who and what I am.[2] The press was filled with the details of my strange amnesia in 1908–13, and much was made of the traditions of horror, madness, and witchcraft which lurk behind the ancient Massachusetts town then and now forming my place of residence. Yet I would have it known that there is nothing whatever of the mad or sinister in my heredity and early life. This is a highly important fact in view of the shadow which fell so suddenly upon me from *outside* sources. It may be that centuries of dark brooding had given to crumbling, whisper-haunted Arkham a peculiar vulnerability as regards such shadows—though even this seems doubtful in the light of those other cases which I later came to study. But the chief point is that my own ancestry and background are altogether normal. What came, came from *somewhere else*—where, I even now hesitate to assert in plain words.

I am the son of Jonathan and Hannah (Wingate) Peaslee, both of wholesome old Haverhill stock. I was born and reared in Haverhill—at the old homestead in Boardman Street near Golden Hill—and did not go to Arkham till I entered Miskatonic University at the age of eighteen. That was in 1889. After my graduation, I studied economics at Harvard and came back to Miskatonic as Instructor of Political Economy in 1895. For thirteen years more my life ran smoothly and happily. I married Alice Keezar of Haverhill in 1896, and my three children, Robert K., Wingate, and Hannah, were born in 1898, 1900, and 1903, respectively. In 1898 I became an associate professor, and in 1902 a full professor. At no time had I the least interest in either occultism or abnormal psychology.

It was on Thursday, May 14, 1908, that the queer amnesia came. The thing was quite sudden, though later I realised that certain brief, glimmering visions of several hours previous—chaotic visions which disturbed me greatly because they were so unprecedented—must have formed premonitory symptoms. My head was aching, and I had a singular feeling—altogether new to me—that someone else was trying to get possession of my thoughts.

The collapse occurred about 10:20 a.m., while I was conducting a class in Political Economy VI—history and present tendencies of economics—for juniors and a few sophomores. I began to see strange shapes before my eyes, and to feel that I was in a grotesque room other than the classroom. My thoughts and speech wandered from my subject, and the students saw that something was gravely amiss. Then I slumped down, unconscious in my chair, in a stupor from which no one could arouse me. Nor did my rightful faculties again look out upon the daylight of our normal world for five years, four months, and thirteen days.

It is, of course, from others that I have learned what followed. I shewed no sign of consciousness for sixteen and a half hours, though removed to my home at 27 Crane St. and given the best of medical attention.

At 3 A.M. May 15 my eyes opened and I began to speak, but before long the doctors and my family were thoroughly frightened by the trend of my expression and language. It was clear that I had no remembrance of my identity or of my past, though for some reason I seemed anxious to conceal this lack of knowledge. My eyes gazed strangely at the persons around me, and the flexions of my facial muscles were altogether unfamiliar.

Even my speech seemed awkward and foreign. I used my vocal organs clumsily and gropingly, and my diction had a curiously stilted quality, as if I had laboriously learned the English language from books. The pronunciation was barbarously alien, whilst the idiom seemed to include both scraps of curious archaism and expressions of a wholly incomprehensible cast. Of the latter one in particular was very potently—even terrifiedly—recalled by the youngest of the physicians twenty years afterward. For at that late period such a phrase began to have an actual currency—first in England and then in the United States—and though of much complexity and indisputable newness, it reproduced in every least particular the mystifying words of the strange Arkham patient of 1908.

Physical strength returned at once, although I required an odd amount of re-education in the use of my hands, legs, and bodily apparatus in general. Because of this and other handicaps inherent in the mnemonic lapse, I was for some time kept under strict medical care. When I saw that my attempts to conceal the lapse had failed, I admitted it openly, and became eager for information of all sorts. Indeed, it seemed to the doctors that I had lost interest in my proper personality as soon as I found the case of amnesia accepted as a natural thing. They noticed that my chief efforts were to master certain points in history, science, art, language, and folklore—some of them tremendously abstruse, and some childishly simple—which remained, very oddly in many cases, outside my consciousness.

At the same time they noticed that I had an inexplicable command of many almost unknown sorts of knowledge—a command which I seemed to wish to hide rather than display. I would inadvertently refer, with casual assurance, to specific events in dim ages outside the range of accepted history—passing off such references as a jest when I saw the surprise they created. And I had a way of speaking of the future which two or three times caused actual fright. These uncanny flashes soon ceased to appear, though some observers laid their vanishment more to a certain furtive caution on my part than to any waning of the strange knowledge behind them. Indeed, I seemed anomalously avid to absorb the speech, customs, and perspectives of the age around me; as if I were a studious traveller from a far, foreign land.

As soon as permitted, I haunted the college library at all hours; and shortly began to arrange for those odd travels, and special courses at American and European universities, which evoked so much comment during the next few years. I did not at any time suffer from a lack of learned contacts, for my case had a mild celebrity among the psychologists of the period. I was lectured upon as a typical example of secondary personality—even though I seemed to puzzle the lecturers now and then with some bizarre symptom or some queer trace of carefully veiled mockery.

Of real friendliness, however, I encountered little. Something in my aspect and speech seemed to excite vague fears and aversions in everyone I met, as if I were a being infinitely removed from all that is normal and healthful. This idea of a black, hidden horror connected with incalculable gulfs of some sort of *distance* was oddly widespread and persistent. My own family formed no exception. From the moment of my strange waking my wife had regarded me with extreme horror and loathing, vowing that I was some utter alien usurping the body of her husband.[3] In 1910 she obtained a legal divorce, nor would she ever consent to see me even after my return to normalcy in 1913. These feelings were shared by my elder son and my small daughter, neither of whom I have ever seen since.

Only my second son Wingate seemed able to conquer the terror and repulsion which my change aroused. He indeed felt that I was a stranger, but though only eight years old held fast to a faith that my proper self would return. When it did return he sought me out, and the courts gave me his custody. In succeeding years he helped me with the studies to which I was driven, and today at thirty-five he is a professor of psychology at Miskatonic. But I do not wonder at the horror I caused—for certainly, the mind, voice, and facial expression of the being that awaked on May 15, 1908, were not those of Nathaniel Wingate Peaslee.

I will not attempt to tell much of my life from 1908 to 1913, since readers may glean all the outward essentials—as I largely had to do—from files of old newspapers and scientific journals. I was given charge of my funds, and spent them slowly and on the whole wisely, in travel and in study at various centres of learning. My travels, however, were singular in the extreme; involving long visits to remote and desolate places. In 1909 I spent a month in the Himalayas, and in 1911 aroused much attention through a camel trip into the unknown deserts of Arabia.[4] What happened on those journeys I have never been able to learn. During the summer of 1912 I chartered a ship and sailed in the Arctic; north of Spitzbergen,[5] afterward shewing signs of disappointment. Later in that year I spent weeks alone beyond the limits of previous or subsequent exploration in the vast limestone cavern systems of western Virginia—black labyrinths so complex that no retracing of my steps could even be considered.[6]

My sojourns at the universities were marked by abnormally rapid assimilation, as if the secondary personality had an intelli-

3. A similar reaction is recorded in Walter de la Mare's *The Return* (1910), in which the wife of a man possessed by the spirit of an eighteenth-century suicide rejects him.

4. This may be the incident recorded in "The Nameless City" (pp. 80–93, above).

5. An island, beyond 80° north latitude, 600 miles east of northern Greenland.

6. These are likely the "Endless Caverns" of New Market, Virginia, approximately six miles in length. Only the eighteenth-longest caves in Virginia, they have been promoted widely since 1920 as a tourist destination.

7. High priests.

8. The book is mentioned again in "The Haunter of the Dark," below. D'Erlette is said to have been the family name of Lovecraft's friend and apostle August Derleth, but this is likely a fiction.

9. *Mysteries of the Worm*, a fictional text or grimoire known mainly by the Latin title Lovecraft provides here, and its author, Ludvig Prinn, are the creation of Robert Bloch. The text appears in Bloch's short story "The Shambler from the Stars" (1935). He wrote to Lovecraft about "Shambler," and Lovecraft provided a Latin incantation that appears in the story: "*Tibi, magnum Innominandum, signa stellarum nigrarum et bufaniformis Sadoquae sigillum*" (To you, the great Not-to-Be-Named, signs of the black stars, and the seal of the toad-shaped Tsathoggua). References to the Bloch text also appear in "The Haunter of the Dark," below, and in Lovecraft's story "The Diary of Alonzo Typer."

gence enormously superior to my own. I have found, also, that my rate of reading and solitary study was phenomenal. I could master every detail of a book merely by glancing over it as fast as I could turn the leaves; while my skill at interpreting complex figures in an instant was veritably awesome. At times there appeared almost ugly reports of my power to influence the thoughts and acts of others, though I seemed to have taken care to minimise displays of this faculty.

Other ugly reports concerned my intimacy with leaders of occultist groups, and scholars suspected of connexion with nameless bands of abhorrent elder-world hierophants.[7] These rumours, though never proved at the time, were doubtless stimulated by the known tenor of some of my reading—for the consultation of rare books at libraries cannot be effected secretly. There is tangible proof—in the form of marginal notes—that I went minutely through such things as the Comte d'Erlette's *Cultes des Goules*,[8] Ludvig Prinn's *De Vermis Mysteriis*,[9] the *Unaussprechlichen Kulten* of von Junzt, the surviving fragments of the puzzling *Book of Eibon*, and the dreaded *Necronomicon* of the mad Arab Abdul Alhazred. Then, too, it is undeniable that a fresh and evil wave of underground cult activity set in about the time of my odd mutation.

In the summer of 1913 I began to display signs of ennui and flagging interest, and to hint to various associates that a change might soon be expected in me. I spoke of returning memories of my earlier life—though most auditors judged me insincere, since all the recollections I gave were casual, and such as might have been learned from my old private papers. About the middle of August I returned to Arkham and reopened my long-closed house in Crane St. Here I installed a mechanism of the most curious aspect, constructed piecemeal by different makers of scientific apparatus in Europe and America, and guarded carefully from the sight of anyone intelligent enough to analyse it. Those who did see it—a workman, a servant, and the new housekeeper—say that it was a queer mixture of rods, wheels, and mirrors, though only about two feet tall, one foot wide, and one foot thick. The central mirror was circular and convex. All this is borne out by such makers of parts as can be located.

On the evening of Friday, Sept. 26, I dismissed the house-keeper and the maid till noon of the next day. Lights burned in the house till late, and a lean, dark, curiously foreign-looking man called in an automobile. It was about 1 A.M. that the lights were last seen. At 2:15 A.M. a policeman observed the place in darkness, but with the stranger's motor still at the curb. By four o'clock the motor was certainly gone. It was at six that a hesitant, foreign voice on the telephone asked Dr. Wilson to call at my house and bring me out of a peculiar faint. This call—a long-distance one—was later traced to a public booth in the North Station[10] in Boston, but no sign of the lean foreigner was ever unearthed.

When the doctor reached my house he found me unconscious in the sitting-room—in an easy-chair with a table drawn up before it. On the polished table-top were scratches shewing where some heavy object had rested. The queer machine was gone, nor was anything afterward heard of it. Undoubtedly the dark, lean foreigner had taken it away. In the library grate were abundant ashes evidently left from the burning of every remaining scrap of paper on which I had written since the advent of the amnesia. Dr. Wilson found my breathing very peculiar, but after an hypodermic injection it became more regular.

At 11.15 A.M., Sept. 27, I stirred vigorously, and my hitherto mask-like face began to shew signs of expression. Dr. Wilson remarked that the expression was not that of my secondary personality, but seemed much like that of my normal self. About 11:30 I muttered some very curious syllables—syllables which seemed unrelated to any human speech. I appeared, too, to struggle against something. Then, just after noon—the housekeeper and the maid having meanwhile returned—I began to mutter in English.

" . . . of the orthodox economists of that period, Jevons[11] typi-fies the prevailing trend toward scientific correlation. His attempt to link the commercial cycle of prosperity and depression with the physical cycle of the solar spots forms perhaps the apex of . . ."

Nathaniel Wingate Peaslee had come back—a spirit in whose time-scale it was still that Thursday morning in 1908, with the economics class gazing up at the battered desk on the platform.

10. Located at 120 Causeway Street in Boston, serving the Boston & Maine Railroad.

11. A Liverpudlian who trained in chemistry and botany at University College London and in logic and philosophy at the University of London, William Stanley Jevons (1835–1882) first demonstrated that economics was a science concerned with mathematical quantities. He helped to develop the theory of utility and was prolific in his writings on economics and logic equally. This particular lecture by Peaslee seems to be a discussion of Jevons's empirical study of economic upturns and downturns coincident with meteorological conditions influenced by sunspots, outlined in his essay "The Solar Period and the Price of Corn," first read at a conference in 1875 and published posthumously in *Investigations in Currency and Finance* (1884). Jevons died in an accidental drowning while swimming recreationally.

II.

MY REABSORPTION INTO normal life was a painful and difficult process. The loss of over five years creates more complications than can be imagined, and in my case there were countless matters to be adjusted. What I heard of my actions since 1908 astonished and disturbed me, but I tried to view the matter as philosophically as I could. At last regaining custody of my second son Wingate, I settled down with him in the Crane Street house and endeavoured to resume teaching—my old professorship having been kindly offered me by the college.

I began work with the February, 1914, term, and kept at it just a year. By that time I realised how badly my experience had shaken me. Though perfectly sane—I hoped—and with no flaw in my original personality, I had not the nervous energy of the old days. Vague dreams and queer ideas continually haunted me, and when the outbreak of the world war turned my mind to history I found myself thinking of periods and events in the oddest possible fashion. My conception of *time*, my ability to distinguish between consecutiveness and simultaneousness—seemed subtly disordered; so that I formed chimerical notions about living in one age and casting one's mind all over eternity for knowledge of past and future ages.

The war gave me strange impressions of *remembering* some of its far-off *consequences*—as if I knew how it was coming out and could look back upon it in the light of future information. All such quasi-memories were attended with much pain, and with a feeling that some artificial psychological barrier was set against them. When I diffidently hinted to others about my impressions I met with varied responses. Some persons looked uncomfortably at me, but men in the mathematics department spoke of new developments in those theories of relativity—then discussed only in learned circles—which were later to become so famous. Dr. Albert Einstein, they said, was rapidly reducing *time* to the status of a mere dimension.

But the dreams and disturbed feelings gained on me, so that I had to drop my regular work in 1915. Certain of the impressions were taking an annoying shape—giving me the persistent notion that my amnesia had formed some unholy sort of *exchange*; that the secondary personality had indeed been an intruding force from unknown regions, and that my own personality had suffered displacement. Thus I was driven to vague and frightful speculations concerning the whereabouts of my true self during the years that another had held my body. The curious knowledge and strange conduct of my body's late tenant troubled me more and more as I learned further details from persons, papers, and magazines. Queernesses that had baffled others seemed to harmonise terribly with some background of black knowledge which festered in the chasms of my subconscious. I began to search feverishly for every scrap of information bearing on the studies and travels of *that other one* during the dark years.

Not all of my troubles were as semi-abstract as this. There were the dreams—and these seemed to grow in vividness and concreteness. Knowing how most would regard them, I seldom mentioned them to anyone but my son or certain trusted psychologists, but eventually I commenced a scientific study of other cases in order to see how typical or non-typical such visions might be among amnesia victims. My results, aided by psychologists, historians, anthropologists, and mental specialists of wide experience, and by a study that included all records of split personalities from the days of dæmonic-possession legends to the medically realistic present, at first bothered me more than they consoled me.

I soon found that my dreams had indeed no counterpart in the overwhelming bulk of true amnesia cases. There remained, however, a tiny residue of accounts which for years baffled and shocked me with their parallelism to my own experience. Some of them were bits of ancient folklore; others were case-histories in the annals of medicine; one or two were anecdotes obscurely buried in standard histories. It thus appeared that, while my special kind of affliction was prodigiously rare, instances of it had occurred at long intervals ever since the beginning of man's annals. Some centuries might contain one, two, or three cases; others none—or at least none whose record survived.

The essence was always the same—a person of keen thoughtfulness seized a strange secondary life and leading for a greater or lesser period an utterly alien existence typified at first by

12. This being the incidents recorded in "Beyond the Wall of Sleep" (pp. 18–29, above).

vocal and bodily awkwardness, and later by a wholesale acquisition of scientific, historic, artistic, and anthropological knowledge; an acquisition carried on with feverish zest and with a wholly abnormal absorptive power. Then a sudden return of the rightful consciousness, intermittently plagued ever after with vague unplaceable dreams suggesting fragments of some hideous memory elaborately blotted out. And the close resemblance of those nightmares to my own—even in some of the smallest particulars—left no doubt in my mind of their significantly typical nature. One or two of the cases had an added ring of faint, blasphemous familiarity, as if I had heard of them before through some cosmic channel too morbid and frightful to contemplate. In three instances there was specific mention of such an unknown machine as had been in my house before the second change.

Another thing that cloudily worried me during my investigation was the somewhat greater frequency of cases where a brief, elusive glimpse of the typical nightmares was afforded to persons not visited with well-defined amnesia. These persons were largely of mediocre mind or less—some so primitive that they could scarcely be thought of as vehicles for abnormal scholarship and preternatural mental acquisitions. For a second they would be fired with alien force—then a backward lapse and a thin, swift-fading memory of un-human horrors.

There had been at least three such cases during the past half century—one only fifteen years before.[12] Had something been *groping blindly through time* from some unsuspected abyss in Nature? Were these faint cases monstrous, sinister *experiments* of a kind and authorship utterly beyond sane belief? Such were a few of the formless speculations of my weaker hours—fancies abetted by myths which my studies uncovered. For I could not doubt but that certain persistent legends of immemorial antiquity, apparently unknown to the victims and physicians connected with recent amnesia cases, formed a striking and awesome elaboration of memory lapses such as mine.

Of the nature of the dreams and impressions which were growing so clamorous I still almost fear to speak. They seemed to savour of madness, and at times I believed I was indeed going mad. Was there a special type of delusion afflicting those who had suffered lapses of memory? Conceivably, the efforts of the subconscious mind to fill up a perplexing blank with pseudo-memories might give rise to strange imaginative vagaries. This, indeed (though an alternative folklore theory finally seemed to me more plausible), was the belief of many of the alienists who helped me in my search for parallel cases, and who shared my puzzlement at the exact resemblances sometimes discovered. They did not call the condition true insanity, but classed it rather among neurotic disorders. My course in trying to track it down and analyse it, instead of vainly seeking to dismiss or forget it, they heartily endorsed as correct according to the best psychological principles. I especially valued the advice of such physicians as had studied me during my possession by the other personality.

My first disturbances were not visual at all, but concerned the more abstract matters which I have mentioned. There was, too, a feeling of profound and inexplicable horror concerning *myself*. I developed a queer fear of seeing my own form, as if my eyes would find it something utterly alien and inconceivably abhorrent. When I did glance down and behold the familiar human shape in quiet grey or blue clothing I always felt a curious relief, though in order to gain this relief I had to conquer an infinite dread. I shunned mirrors as much as possible, and was always shaved at the barber's. It was a long time before I correlated any of these disappointed feelings with the fleeting visual impressions which began to develop. The first such correlation had to do with the odd sensation of an external, artificial restraint on my memory. I felt that the snatches of sight I experienced had a profound and terrible meaning, and a frightful connexion with myself, but that some purposeful influence held me from grasping that meaning and that connexion. Then came that queerness about the element of *time*, and with it desperate efforts to place the fragmentary dream-glimpses in the chronological and spatial pattern.

The glimpses themselves were at first merely strange rather than horrible. I would seem to be in an enormous vaulted chamber whose lofty stone groinings were well-nigh lost in the shadows overhead. In whatever time or place the scene might be, the principle of the arch was known as fully and used as extensively as by the Romans. There were colossal round windows and high arched doors, and pedestals or tables each as tall as the height of an ordinary room. Vast shelves of dark wood lined the walls, holding what seemed to be volumes of immense size with strange hieroglyphs on their backs. The exposed stonework held curious carvings, always in curvilinear mathematical designs, and there were chiselled inscriptions in the same characters that the huge books bore. The dark granite masonry was of a monstrous megalithic type, with lines of convex-topped blocks fitting the concave-bottomed courses which rested upon them. There were no chairs, but the tops of the vast pedestals were littered with books, papers, and what seemed to be writing materials—oddly figured jars of a purplish metal, and rods with stained tips. Tall as the pedestals were, I seemed at times able to view them from above. On some of them were great globes of luminous crystal serving as lamps, and inexplicable machines formed of vitreous tubes and metal rods. The windows were glazed, and latticed with stout-looking bars. Though I dared not approach and peer out them, I could see from where I was the waving tops of singular fern-like growths. The floor was of massive octagonal flagstones, while rugs and hangings were entirely lacking.

Later I had visions of sweeping through Cyclopean corridors of stone, and up and down gigantic inclined planes of the same monstrous masonry. There were no stairs anywhere, nor was any passageway less than thirty feet wide. Some of the structures through which I floated must have towered into the sky for thousands of feet. There were multiple levels of black vaults below, and never-opened trap-doors, sealed down with metal bands and holding dim suggestions of some special peril. I seemed to be a prisoner, and horror hung broodingly over everything I saw. I felt that the mocking curvilinear hieroglyphs on the walls would blast my soul with their message were I not guarded by a merciful ignorance.

Still later my dreams included vistas from the great round windows, and from the titanic flat roof, with its curious gardens, wide barren area, and high, scalloped parapet of stone, to which the topmost of the inclined planes led. There were almost endless leagues of giant buildings, each in its garden, and ranged along paved roads fully two hundred feet wide. They differed greatly in aspect, but few were less than five hundred feet square or a thousand feet high. Many seemed so limitless that they must have had a frontage of several thousand feet, while some shot up to mountainous altitudes in the grey, steamy heavens. They seemed to be mainly of stone or concrete, and most of them embodied the oddly curvilinear type of masonry noticeable in the building that held me. Roofs were flat and garden-covered, and tended to have scalloped parapets. Sometimes there were terraces and higher levels, and wide, cleared spaces amidst the gardens. The great roads held hints of motion, but in the earlier visions I could not resolve this impression into details.

In certain places I beheld enormous dark cylindrical towers which climbed far above any of the other structures. These appeared to be of a totally unique nature, and shewed signs of prodigious age and dilapidation. They were built of a bizarre type of square-cut basalt masonry, and tapered slightly toward their rounded tops. Nowhere in any of them could the least traces of windows or other apertures save huge doors be found. I noticed also some lower buildings—all crumbling with the weathering of æons—which resembled these dark cylindrical towers in basic architecture. Around all these aberrant piles of square-cut masonry there hovered an inexplicable aura of menace and concentrated fear, like that bred by the sealed trap-doors.

The omnipresent gardens were almost terrifying in their strangeness, with bizarre and unfamiliar forms of vegetation nodding over broad paths lined with curiously carven monoliths. Abnormally vast fern-like growths predominated; some green, and some of a ghastly, fungoid pallor. Among them rose great spectral things resembling calamites,[13] whose bamboo-like trunks towered to fabulous heights. Then there were tufted forms like fabulous cycads, and grotesque dark-green shrubs and trees of coniferous aspect. Flowers were small, colourless, and unrecognisable, blooming in geometrical beds and at large among the greenery. In a few of the terrace and roof-top gardens were larger and more vivid blossoms of almost offensive contours and seeming to suggest artificial breeding. Fungi of inconceivable size, outlines, and colours speckled the scene in patterns bespeaking some unknown but well-established horticultural tradition. In the larger gardens on the ground there seemed to be some attempt to preserve the irregularities of Nature, but on the roofs there was more selectiveness, and more evidences of the topiary art.

13. Extinct horsetail plants, typically growing as high as 100 feet.

14. Note that the astronomical observations—150 million years in the past—are consistent with astronomical theories of the nineteenth century, including a contracting sun (because of its consumption of solar fuel), lesser evidence of volcanic action on the lunar surface, and the shifting positions of stars because of "star streams." See generally T. R. Livesey's "Dispatches from the Providence Observatory" for a discussion of Lovecraft's knowledge of astronomy. Livesey points out that, in the scientific community, these theories had been largely discounted by the 1930s. Peaslee made his observations, it must be noted, under highly unreliable conditions. Not a man of science, more than twenty years after the events, he recorded what he *thought* he should have seen, based on his out-of-date knowledge of astronomy.

15. Vegetation of the Carboniferous age, from about 360 million years ago to 300 million years ago.

The skies were almost always moist and cloudy, and sometimes I would seem to witness tremendous rains. Once in a while, though, there would be glimpses of the sun—which looked abnormally large—and of the moon, whose markings held a touch of difference from the normal that I could never quite fathom. When—very rarely—the night sky was clear to any extent, I beheld constellations which were nearly beyond recognition.[14] Known outlines were sometimes approximated, but seldom duplicated; and from the position of the few groups I could recognise, I felt I must be in the earth's southern hemisphere, near the Tropic of Capricorn. The far horizon was always steamy and indistinct, but I could see that great jungles of unknown tree-ferns, calamites, lepidodendra, and sigillaria[15] lay outside the city, their fantastic frondage waving mockingly in the shifting vapours. Now and then there would be suggestions of motion in the sky, but these my early visions never resolved.

By the autumn of 1914 I began to have infrequent dreams of strange floatings over the city and through the regions around it. I saw interminable roads through forests of fearsome growths with mottled, fluted, and banded trunks, and past other cities as strange as the one which persistently haunted me. I saw monstrous constructions of black or iridescent stone in glades and clearings where perpetual twilight reigned, and traversed long causeways over swamps so dark that I could tell but little of their moist, towering vegetation. Once I saw an area of countless miles strown with age-blasted basaltic ruins whose architecture had been like that of the few windowless, round-topped towers in the haunting city. And once I saw the sea—a boundless steamy expanse beyond the colossal stone piers of an enormous town of domes and arches. Great shapeless suggestions of shadow moved over it, and here and there its surface was vexed with anomalous spoutings.

III.

AS I HAVE said, it was not immediately that these wild visions began to hold their terrifying quality. Certainly, many persons have dreamed intrinsically stranger things—things compounded of unrelated scraps of daily life, pictures, and reading, and arranged in fantastically novel forms by the unchecked caprices of sleep. For some time I accepted the visions as natural, even though I had never before been an extravagant dreamer. Many of the vague anomalies, I argued, must have come from trivial sources too numerous to track down; while others seemed to reflect a common text-book knowledge of the plants and other conditions of the primitive world of a hundred and fifty million years ago—the world of the Permian or Triassic age.[16] In the course of some months, however, the element of terror did figure with accumulating force. This was when the dreams began so unfailingly to have the aspect of *memories*, and when my mind began to link them with my growing abstract disturbances—the feeling of mnemonic restraint, the curious impressions regarding *time*, the sense of a loathsome exchange with my secondary personality of 1908–13, and, considerably later, the inexplicable loathing of my own person.

As certain definite details began to enter the dreams, their horror increased a thousandfold—until by October, 1915, I felt I must do something. It was then that I began an intensive study of other cases of amnesia and visions, feeling that I might thereby objectivise my trouble and shake clear of its emotional grip. However, as before mentioned, the result was at first almost exactly opposite. It disturbed me vastly to find that my dreams had been so closely duplicated; especially since some of the accounts were too early to admit of any geological knowledge—and therefore of any idea of primitive landscapes—on the subjects' part. What is more, many of these accounts supplied very horrible details and explanations in connexion with the visions of great buildings and jungle gardens—and other things. The actual sights and vague impressions were bad enough, but what was hinted or asserted by some of the other dreamers savoured of madness and blasphemy. Worst of all, my own pseudo-memory was aroused to wilder dreams and hints of coming revelations. And yet most doctors deemed my course, on the whole, an advisable one.

I studied psychology systematically, and under the prevailing stimulus my son Wingate did the same—his studies leading eventually to his present professorship. In 1917 and 1918 I took special courses at Miskatonic. Meanwhile, my examination of medical,

16. The Permian period followed the Carboniferous and was in turn succeeded by the Triassic age. The latter saw the breakup of the supercontinent Pangaea.

historical, and anthropological records became indefatigable; involving travels to distant libraries, and finally including even a reading of the hideous books of forbidden elder lore in which my secondary personality had been so disturbingly interested. Some of the latter were the actual copies I had consulted in my altered state, and I was greatly disturbed by certain marginal notations and ostensible *corrections* of the hideous text in a script and idiom which somehow seemed oddly un-human.

These markings were mostly in the respective languages of the various books, all of which the writer seemed to know with equal though obviously academic facility. One note appended to von Junzt's *Unaussprechlichen Kulten*, however, was alarmingly otherwise. It consisted of certain curvilinear hieroglyphs in the same ink as that of the German corrections, but following no recognised human pattern. And these hieroglyphs were closely and unmistakably akin to the characters constantly met with in my dreams—characters whose meaning I would sometimes momentarily fancy I knew or was just on the brink of recalling. To complete my black confusion, my librarians assured me that, in view of previous examinations and records of consultation of the volumes in question, all of these notations must have been made by myself in my secondary state. This despite the fact that I was and still am ignorant of three of the languages involved.

Piecing together the scattered records, ancient and modern, anthropological and medical, I found a fairly consistent mixture of myth and hallucination whose scope and wildness left me utterly dazed. Only one thing consoled me—the fact that the myths were of such early existence. What lost knowledge could have brought pictures of the Palæozoic or Mesozoic landscape into these primitive fables, I could not even guess, but the pictures had been there. Thus, a basis existed for the formation of a fixed type of delusion. Cases of amnesia no doubt created the general myth-pattern—but afterward the fanciful accretions of the myths must have reacted on amnesia sufferers and coloured their pseudo-memories. I myself had read and heard all the early tales during my memory lapse—my quest had amply proved that. Was it not natural, then, for my subsequent dreams and emotional impressions to become coloured and moulded by what my memory subtly held over from my secondary state? A few of the myths had significant connexions with other cloudy legends of the pre-human world, especially those Hindoo tales involving stupefying gulfs of time and forming part of the lore of modern theosophists.

Primal myth and modern delusion joined in their assumption that mankind is only one—perhaps the least—of the highly evolved and dominant races of this planet's long and largely unknown career. Things of inconceivable shape, they implied, had reared towers to the sky and delved into every secret of Nature before the first amphibian forbear of man had crawled out of the hot sea three hundred million years ago. Some had come down from the stars; a few were as old as the cosmos itself, others had arisen swiftly from terrene germs as far behind the first germs of our life-cycle as those germs are behind ourselves. Spans of thousands of millions of years, and linkages with other galaxies and universes, were freely spoken of. Indeed, there was no such thing as time in its humanly accepted sense.

But most of the tales and impressions concerned a relatively late race, of a queer and intricate shape resembling no life-form known to science, which had lived till only fifty million years before the advent of man. This, they indicated, was the greatest race of all; because it alone had conquered the secret of time. It had learned all things that ever were known *or ever would be known* on the earth, through the power of its keener minds to project themselves into the past and future, even through gulfs of millions of years, and study the lore of every age. From the accomplishments of this race arose all legends of *prophets*, including those in human mythology.

In its vast libraries were volumes of texts and pictures holding the whole of earth's annals—histories and descriptions of every species that had ever been or that ever would be, with full records of their arts, their achievements, their languages, and their psychologies. With this æon-embracing knowledge, the Great Race chose from every era and life-form such thoughts, arts, and processes as might suit its own nature and situation. Knowledge of the past, secured through a kind of mind-casting outside the recognised senses, was harder to glean than knowledge of the future.

In the latter case the course was easier and more material. With suitable mechanical aid a mind would project itself forward

17. Wrinkled.

18. That is, capable of being distended.

in time, feeling its dim, extra-sensory way till it approached the desired period. Then, after preliminary trials, it would seize on the best discoverable representative of the highest of that period's life-forms; entering the organism's brain and setting up therein its own vibrations while the displaced mind would strike back to the period of the displacer, remaining in the latter's body till a reverse process was set up. The projected mind, in the body of the organism of the future, would then pose as a member of the race whose outward form it wore; learning as quickly as possible all that could be learned of the chosen age and its massed information and techniques.

Meanwhile the displaced mind, thrown back to the displacer's age and body, would be carefully guarded. It would be kept from harming the body it occupied, and would be drained of all its knowledge by trained questioners. Often it could be questioned in its own language, when previous quests into the future had brought back records of that language. If the mind came from a body whose language the Great Race could not physically reproduce, clever machines would be made, on which the alien speech could be played as on a musical instrument. The Great Race's members were immense rugose[17] cones ten feet high, and with head and other organs attached to foot-thick, distensible[18] limbs spreading from the apexes. They spoke by the clicking or scraping of huge paws or claws attached to the end of two of their four limbs, and walked by the expansion and contraction of a viscous layer attached to their vast ten-foot bases.

When the captive mind's amazement and resentment had worn off, and when (assuming that it came from a body vastly different from the Great Race's) it had lost its horror at its unfamiliar temporary form, it was permitted to study its new environment and experience a wonder and wisdom approximating that of its displacer. With suitable precautions, and in exchange for suitable services, it was allowed to rove all over the habitable world in titan airships or on the huge boat-like atomic-engined vehicles which traversed the great roads, and to delve freely into the libraries containing the records of the planet's past and future. This reconciled many captive minds to their lot; since none were other than keen, and to such minds the unveiling of hidden mysteries of earth—closed chapters of inconceivable

OUT OF TIME

They spoke by the clicking or scraping of huge paws!

"They spoke by the clicking or scraping of huge paws!" *Astounding Stories* 17, no. 4 (June 1936) (artist: Howard V. Brown)

pasts and dizzying vortices of future time which include the years ahead of their own natural ages—forms always, despite the abysmal horrors often unveiled, the supreme experience of life.

Now and then certain captives were permitted to meet other captive minds seized from the future—to exchange thoughts with consciousnesses living a hundred or a thousand or a million years before or after their own ages. And all were urged to write copi-

The Great Race, as depicted for the cover
of *Dreams and Fancies* (Sauk City, WI:
Arkham House Publishers, 1962).
(artist: Richard Taylor)

ously in their own languages of themselves and their respective periods; such documents to be filed in the great central archives.

It may be added that there was one sad special type of captive whose privileges were far greater than those of the majority. These were the dying *permanent* exiles, whose bodies in the future had been seized by keen-minded members of the Great Race who, faced with death, sought to escape mental extinction. Such melancholy exiles were not as common as might be expected, since the longevity of the Great Race lessened its love of life—especially among those superior minds capable of projection. From cases of the permanent projection of elder minds arose many of those lasting changes of personality noticed in later history—including mankind's.

As for the ordinary cases of exploration—when the displacing mind had learned what it wished in the future, it would build an apparatus like that which had started its flight and reverse the process of projection. Once more it would be in its own body in its own age, while the lately captive mind would return to that body of the future to which it properly belonged. Only when one or the other of the bodies had died during the exchange was this restoration impossible. In such cases, of course, the exploring mind had—like those of the death-escapers—to live out an alien-bodied life in the future; or else the captive mind—like the dying permanent exiles—had to end its days in the form and past age of the Great Race.

This fate was least horrible when the captive mind was also of the Great Race—a not infrequent occurrence, since in all its periods that race was intensely concerned with its own future. The number of dying permanent exiles of the Great Race was very slight—largely because of the tremendous penalties attached to displacements of future Great Race minds by the moribund. Through projection, arrangements were made to inflict these penalties on the offending minds in their new future bodies—and sometimes forced re-exchanges were effected. Complex cases of the displacement of exploring or already captive minds by minds in various regions of the past had been known and carefully rectified. In every age since the discovery of mind projection, a minute but well-recognised element of the population consisted of Great Race minds from past ages, sojourning for a longer or shorter while.

When a captive mind of alien origin was returned to its own body in the future, it was purged by an intricate mechanical hypnosis of all it had learned in the Great Race's age—this because of certain troublesome consequences inherent in the general carrying forward of knowledge in large quantities. The few existing instances of clear transmission had caused, and would cause at known future times, great disasters. And it was largely in consequence of two cases of the kind (said the old myths) that mankind had learned what it had concerning the Great Race. Of all things surviving *physically* and *directly* from that æon-distant world, there remained only certain ruins of great stones in far places and under the sea, and parts of the text of the frightful Pnakotic Manuscripts.

Thus the returning mind reached its own age with only the faintest and most fragmentary visions of what it had undergone since its seizure. All memories that could be eradicated were eradicated, so that in most cases only a dream-shadowed blank stretched back to the time of the first exchange. Some minds recalled more than others, and the chance joining of memories had at rare times brought hints of the forbidden past to future ages. There probably never was a time when groups or cults did not secretly cherish certain of these hints. In the *Necronomicon* the presence of such a cult among human beings was suggested— a cult that sometimes gave aid to minds voyaging down the æons from the days of the Great Race.

And meanwhile the Great Race itself waxed well-nigh omniscient, and turned to the task of setting up exchanges with the minds of other planets, and of exploring their pasts and futures. It sought likewise to fathom the past years and origin of that black, æon-dead orb in far space whence its own mental heritage had come—for the mind of the Great Race was older than its bodily form. The beings of a dying elder world, wise with the ultimate secrets, had looked ahead for a new world and species wherein they might have long life; and had sent their minds en masse into that future race best adapted to house them—the cone-shaped things that peopled our earth a billion years ago. Thus the Great

Race came to be, while the myriad minds sent backward were left to die in the horror of strange shapes. Later the race would again face death, yet would live through another forward migration of its best minds into the bodies of others who had a longer physical span ahead of them.

Such was the background of intertwined legend and hallucination. When, around 1920, I had my researches in coherent shape, I felt a slight lessening of the tension which their earlier stages had increased. After all, and in spite of the fancies prompted by blind emotions, were not most of my phenomena readily explainable? Any chance might have turned my mind to dark studies during the amnesia—and then I read the forbidden legends and met the members of ancient and ill-regarded cults. That, plainly, supplied the material for the dreams and disturbed feelings which came after the return of memory. As for the marginal notes in dream-hieroglyphs and languages unknown to me, but laid at my door by librarians—I might easily have picked up a smattering of the tongues during my secondary state, while the hieroglyphs were doubtless coined by my fancy from descriptions in old legends, and *afterward* woven into my dreams. I tried to verify certain points through conversation with known cult-leaders, but never succeeded in establishing the right connexions.

At times the parallelism of so many cases in so many distant ages continued to worry me as it had at first, but on the other hand I reflected that the excitant folklore was undoubtedly more universal in the past than in the present. Probably all the other victims whose cases were like mine had had a long and familiar knowledge of the tales I had learned only when in my secondary state. When these victims had lost their memory, they had associated themselves with the creatures of their household myths—the fabulous invaders supposed to displace men's minds—and had thus embarked upon quests for knowledge which they thought they could take back to a fancied, non-human past. Then when their memory returned, they reversed the associative process and thought of themselves as the former captive minds instead of as the displacers. Hence the dreams and pseudo-memories following the conventional myth-pattern.

Despite the seeming cumbrousness of these explanations, they came finally to supersede all others in my mind—largely because of the greater weakness of any rival theory. And a substantial number of eminent psychologists and anthropologists gradually agreed with me. The more I reflected, the more convincing did my reasoning seem; till in the end I had a really effective bulwark against the visions and impressions which still assailed me. Suppose I did see strange things at night? These were only what I had heard and read of. Suppose I did have odd loathings and perspectives and pseudo-memories? These, too, were only echoes of myths absorbed in my secondary state. Nothing that I might dream, nothing that I might feel, could be of any actual significance.

Fortified by this philosophy, I greatly improved in nervous equilibrium, even though the visions (rather than the abstract impressions) steadily became more frequent and more disturbingly detailed. In 1922 I felt able to undertake regular work again, and put my newly gained knowledge to practical use by accepting an instructorship in psychology at the university. My old chair of political economy had long been adequately filled—besides which, methods of teaching economics had changed greatly since my heyday. My son was at this time just entering on the post-graduate studies leading to his present professorship, and we worked together a great deal.

IV.

I CONTINUED, HOWEVER, to keep a careful record of the outré dreams which crowded upon me so thickly and vividly. Such a record, I argued, was of genuine value as a psychological document. The glimpses still seemed damnably like *memories*, though I fought off this impression with a goodly measure of success. In writing, I treated the phantasmata as things seen; but at all other times I brushed them aside like any gossamer illusions of the night. I had never mentioned such matters in common conversation; though reports of them, filtering out as such things will, had aroused sundry rumours regarding my mental health. It is amusing to reflect that these rumours were confined wholly to laymen, without a single champion among physicians or psychologists.

Of my visions after 1914 I will here mention only a few, since fuller accounts and records are at the disposal of the serious student. It is evident that with time the curious inhibitions somewhat waned, for the scope of my visions vastly increased. They have never, though, become other than disjointed fragments seemingly without clear motivation. Within the dreams I seemed gradually to acquire a greater and greater freedom of wandering. I floated through many strange buildings of stone, going from one to the other along mammoth underground passages which seemed to form the common avenues of transit. Sometimes I encountered those gigantic sealed trap-doors in the lowest level, around which such an aura of fear and forbiddenness clung. I saw tremendous tessellated pools, and rooms of curious and inexplicable utensils of myriad sorts. Then there were colossal caverns of intricate machinery whose outlines and purpose were wholly strange to me, and whose *sound* manifested itself only after many years of dreaming. I may here remark that sight and sound are the only senses I have ever exercised in the visionary world.

The real horror began in May, 1915, when I first saw the *living things*. This was before my studies had taught me what, in view of the myths and case histories, to expect. As mental barriers wore down, I beheld great masses of thin vapour in various parts of the building and in the streets below. These steadily grew more solid and distinct, till at last I could trace their monstrous outlines with uncomfortable ease. They seemed to be enormous iridescent cones, about ten feet high and ten feet wide at the base, and made up of some ridgy, scaly, semi-elastic matter. From their apexes projected four flexible, cylindrical members, each a foot thick, and of a ridgy substance like that of the cones themselves. These members were sometimes contracted almost to nothing, and sometimes extended to any distance up to about ten feet. Terminating two of them were enormous claws or nippers. At the end of a third were four red, trumpet-like appendages. The fourth terminated in an irregular yellowish globe some two feet in diameter and having three great dark eyes ranged along its central circumference. Surmounting this head were four slender grey stalks bearing flower-like appendages, whilst from its nether side dangled eight greenish antennæ or tentacles. The great base of the central cone was fringed with a rubbery, grey substance which moved the whole entity through expansion and contraction.

Their actions, though harmless, horrified me even more than their appearance—for it is not wholesome to watch monstrous objects doing what one has known only human beings to do. These objects moved intelligently around the great rooms, getting books from the shelves and taking them to the great tables, or vice versa, and sometimes writing diligently with a peculiar rod gripped in the greenish head-tentacles. The huge nippers were used in carrying books and in conversation-speech consisting of a kind of clicking and scraping. The objects had no clothing, but wore satchels or knapsacks suspended from the top of the conical trunk. They commonly carried their head and its supporting member at the level of the cone top, although it was frequently raised or lowered. The other three great members tended to rest downward on the sides of the cone, contracted to about five feet each, when not in use. From their rate of reading, writing, and operating their machines (those on the tables seemed somehow connected with thought) I concluded that their intelligence was enormously greater than man's.

Afterward I saw them everywhere; swarming in all the great chambers and corridors, tending monstrous machines in vaulted crypts, and racing along the vast roads in gigantic boat-shaped cars. I ceased to be afraid of them, for they seemed to form supremely natural parts of their environment. Individual differences amongst them began to be manifest, and a few appeared to be under some kind of restraint. These latter, though shewing no physical variation, had a diversity of gestures and habits which marked them off not only from the majority, but very largely from one another. They wrote a great deal in what seemed to my cloudy vision a vast variety of characters—never the typical curvilinear hieroglyphs of the majority. A few, I fancied, used our own familiar alphabet. Most of them worked much more slowly than the general mass of the entities.

All this time *my own part* in the dreams seemed to be that of a disembodied consciousness with a range of vision wider than the normal; floating freely about, yet confined to the ordinary avenues and speeds of travel. Not until August, 1915, did any suggestions of bodily existence begin to harass me. I say *harass*, because the first phase was a purely abstract though infinitely terrible association of my previously noted body-loathing with the

19. "Agglutinative speech" is a feature of languages (such as Turkish, Sanskrit, and Bengali, among many others) in which compound words are formed that contain the meaning of short sentences In Bantu, for instance, the word "*yu-le m-tu m-moja m-refu a-li y-e ki-soma ki-le ki-tabu ki-refu*" means "that tall person who read the long book," and in Japanese, the word "*tabetakunakatta*" (食べたくなかった) means that the subject did not want to eat.

scenes of my visions. For a while my chief concern during dreams was to avoid looking down at myself, and I recall how grateful I was for the total absence of large mirrors in the strange rooms. I was mightily troubled by the fact that I always saw the great tables—whose height could not be under ten feet—from a level not below that of their surfaces.

And then the morbid temptation to look down at myself became greater and greater, till one night I could not resist it. At first my downward glance revealed nothing whatever. A moment later I perceived that this was because my head lay at the end of a flexible neck of enormous length. Retracting this neck and gazing down very sharply, I saw the scaly, rugose, iridescent bulk of a vast cone ten feet tall and ten feet wide at the base. That was when I waked half of Arkham with my screaming as I plunged madly up from the abyss of sleep.

Only after weeks of hideous repetition did I grow half-reconciled to these visions of myself in monstrous form. In the dreams I now moved bodily among the other unknown entities, reading terrible books from the endless shelves and writing for hours at the great tables with a stylus managed by the green tentacles that hung down from my head. Snatches of what I read and wrote would linger in my memory. There were horrible annals of other worlds and other universes, and of stirrings of formless life outside of all universes. There were records of strange orders of beings which had peopled the world in forgotten pasts, and frightful chronicles of grotesque-bodied intelligences which would people it millions of years after the death of the last human being. And I learned of chapters in human history whose existence no scholar of today has ever suspected. Most of these writings were in the language of the hieroglyphs; which I studied in a queer way with the aid of droning machines, and which was evidently an agglutinative speech[19] with root systems utterly unlike any found in human languages. Other volumes were in other unknown tongues learned in the same queer way. A very few were in languages I knew. Extremely clever pictures, both inserted in the records and forming separate collections, aided me immensely. And all the time I seemed to be setting down a history of my own age in English. On waking, I could recall only minute and meaningless scraps of the unknown tongues which my dream-self had mastered, though whole phrases of the history stayed with me.

I learned—even before my waking self had studied the parallel cases or the old myths from which the dreams doubtless sprang—that the entities around me were of the world's greatest race, which had conquered time and had sent exploring minds into every age. I knew, too, that I had been snatched from my age while *another* used my body in that age, and that a few of the other strange forms housed similarly captured minds. I seemed to talk, in some odd language of claw-clickings, with exiled intellects from every corner of the solar system. There was a mind from the planet we know as Venus, which would live incalculable epochs to come, and one from an outer moon of Jupiter[20] six million years in the past. Of earthly minds there were some from the winged, star-headed, half-vegetable race of palæogean Antarctica;[21] one from the reptile people of fabled Valusia;[22] three from the furry pre-human Hyperborean worshippers of Tsathoggua;[23] one from the wholly abominable Tcho-Tchos;[24] two from the arachnid denizens of earth's last age; five from the hardy coleopterous species immediately following mankind, to which the Great Race was some day to transfer its keenest minds en masse in the face of horrible peril; and several from different branches of humanity.

I talked with the mind of Yiang-Li, a philosopher from the cruel empire of Tsan-Chan,[25] which is to come in A.D. 5000; with that of a general of the great-headed brown people who held South Africa in B.C. 50,000; with that of a twelfth-century Florentine monk named Bartolomeo Corsi; with that of a king of Lomar who had ruled that terrible polar land 100,000 years before the squat, yellow Inutos came from the west to engulf it;[26] with that of Nug-Soth, a magician of the dark conquerors of A.D. 16,000; with that of a Roman named Titus Sempronius Blæsus, who had been a quæstor in Sulla's time[27]; with that of Khephnes, an Egyptian of the 14th Dynasty[28] who told me the hideous secret of Nyarlathotep; with that of a priest of Atlantis' middle kingdom; with that of a Suffolk gentleman of Cromwell's day,[29] James Woodville; with that of a court astronomer of pre-Inca Peru;[30] with that of the Australian physicist Nevil Kingston-

20. Possibly the beings referred to in "Beyond the Wall of Sleep" (pp. 18–29, above).

21. That is, the race of Old Ones described in *At the Mountains of Madness*.

22. See *At the Mountains of Madness*, note 52, above.

23. Mentioned in Clark Ashton Smith's "The Tale of Satampra Zeiros" (1931; written in 1929), in the northern realm of Hyperborea.

24. The Tcho-Tchos appear in "The Lair of the Star-Spawn," by August Derleth and Mark Schorer (1932).

25. Referred to in "Beyond the Wall of Sleep" (pp. 18–29, above).

26. The story of this invasion is told in part in "Polaris," probably written in the late spring or early summer of 1918 and first appearing in *The Philosopher* (December 1920).

27. Lucius Cornelius Sulla (138–78 BCE) was a Roman tyrant and reformer. The quaestors were appointed financial officials.

28. From the year 1705 BCE to the year 1690 BCE. Historians are uncertain about who ruled during this period. Kephren ruled Egypt from 2558 to 2535 BCE.

29. Oliver Cromwell lived from 1599 to 1658 and took his seat on the Council of State of England immediately following the execution of Charles I in 1649; he held more and more powerful positions until he eventually became lord protector in 1653, supreme governor of England; he held this post until his death.

30. That is, prior to the thirteenth century.

31. The Greco-Bactrian kingdom held sway from 250 to 125 BCE in Bactria and Sogdiana. These regions are referred to as the easternmost portion of the Hellenistic world.

32. Louis XIII, known as Louis the Just, lived from 1601 to 1643. Counseled by Cardinal Richelieu, who served as his prime minister, he ended the role of the great feudal lords (in part by ordering the destruction of all of their castles), consolidating royal power and leading France toward becoming a centralized state. His reign was also marked by struggles with the Huguenots, which had a sizable military force and were a leading religious power, and the Habsburg Empire, which had dominion over Austria and Spain.

33. Cimmeria was the name of a continent in the Hyperborean age, home to Conan the Barbarian (see "The Whisperer in Darkness," note 37, above).

Brown, who will die in A.D. 2518; with that of an archimage of vanished Yhe in the Pacific; with that of Theodotides, a Græco-Bactrian official of B.C. 200;[31] with that of an aged Frenchman of Louis XIII's time[32] named Pierre-Louis Montmagny; with that of Crom-Ya, a Cimmerian chieftain of B.C. 15,000;[33] and with so many others that my brain cannot hold the shocking secrets and dizzying marvels I learned from them.

I awaked each morning in a fever, sometimes frantically trying to verify or discredit such information as fell within the range of modern human knowledge. Traditional facts took on new and doubtful aspects, and I marvelled at the dream-fancy which could invent such surprising addenda to history and science. I shivered at the mysteries the past may conceal, and trembled at the menaces the future may bring forth. What was hinted in the speech of post-human entities of the fate of mankind produced such an effect on me that I will not set it down here. After man there would be the mighty beetle civilisation, the bodies of whose members the cream of the Great Race would seize when the monstrous doom overtook the elder world. Later, as the earth's span closed, the transferred minds would again migrate through time and space—to another stopping-place in the bodies of the bulbous vegetable entities of Mercury. But there would be races after them, clinging pathetically to the cold planet and burrowing to its horror-filled core, before the utter end.

Meanwhile, in my dreams, I wrote endlessly in that history of my own age which I was preparing—half voluntarily and half through promises of increased library and travel opportunities—for the Great Race's central archives. The archives were in a colossal subterranean structure near the city's centre, which I came to know well through frequent labours and consultations. Meant to last as long as the race, and to withstand the fiercest of earth's convulsions, this titan repository surpassed all other buildings in the massive, mountain-like firmness of its construction.

The records, written or printed on great sheets of a curiously tenacious cellulose fabric, were bound into books that opened from the top, and were kept in individual cases of a strange, extremely light rustless metal of greyish hue, decorated with mathematical designs and bearing the title in the Great Race's curvilinear hieroglyphs. These cases were stored in tiers of rectangular vaults—like closed, locked shelves—wrought of the same rustless metal and fastened by knobs with intricate turnings. My own history was assigned a specific place in the vaults of the lowest or vertebrate level—the section devoted to the culture of mankind and of the furry and reptilian races immediately preceding it in terrestrial dominance.

But none of the dreams ever gave me a full picture of daily life. All were the merest misty, disconnected fragments, and it is certain that these fragments were not unfolded in their rightful sequence. I have, for example, a very imperfect idea of my own living arrangements in the dream-world; though I seem to have possessed a great stone room of my own. My restrictions as a prisoner gradually disappeared, so that some of the visions included vivid travels over the mighty jungle roads, sojourns in strange cities, and explorations of some of the vast dark windowless ruins from which the Great Race shrank in curious fear. There were also long sea-voyages in enormous, many-decked boats of incredible swiftness, and trips over wild regions in closed, projectile-like airships lifted and moved by electrical repulsion. Beyond the wide, warm ocean were other cities of the Great Race, and on one far continent I saw the crude villages of the black-snouted, winged creatures who would evolve as a dominant stock after the Great Race had sent its foremost minds into the future to escape the creeping horror. Flatness and exuberant green life were always the keynote of the scene. Hills were low and sparse, and usually displayed signs of volcanic forces.

Of the animals I saw, I could write volumes. All were wild; for the Great Race's mechanised culture had long since done away with domestic beasts, while food was wholly vegetable or synthetic. Clumsy reptiles of great bulk floundered in steaming morasses, fluttered in the heavy air, or spouted in the seas and lakes; and among these I fancied I could vaguely recognise lesser, archaic prototypes of many forms—dinosaurs, pterodactyls, ichthyosaurs, labyrinthodonts,[34] rhamphorhynci,[35] plesiosaurs,[36] and the like—made familiar through palæontology. Of birds or mammals there were none that I could discern.

The ground and swamps were constantly alive with snakes, lizards, and crocodiles while insects buzzed incessantly amidst the lush vegetation. And far out at sea, unspied and unknown

34. Amphibians with a complicated (hence the name, after *labyrinthine*) set of infolded teeth and massive skull roofs.

35. Long-tailed winged pterosaurs (Jurassic period).

36. Marine reptiles (Mesozoic era).

"Of the animals I saw I could write volumes!" *Astounding Stories* 17,
no. 4 (June 1936) (artist: Howard V. Brown)

Astounding Stories, 17, no. 4 (June 1936) (artist: Howard V. Brown)

monsters spouted mountainous columns of foam into the vaporous sky. Once I was taken under the ocean in a gigantic submarine vessel with searchlights, and glimpsed some living horrors of awesome magnitude. I saw also the ruins of incredible sunken cities, and the wealth of crinoid, brachiopod, coral, and ichthyic life[37] which everywhere abounded.

Of the physiology, psychology, folkways, and detailed history of the Great Race my visions preserved but little information, and many of the scattered points I here set down were gleaned from my study of old legends and other cases rather than from my own dreaming. For in time, of course, my reading and research caught up with and passed the dreams in many phases; so that certain dream-fragments were explained in advance, and formed verifications of what I had learned. This consolingly established my belief that similar reading and research, accomplished by my secondary self, had formed the source of the whole terrible fabric of pseudo-memories.

The period of my dreams, apparently, was one somewhat less than 150,000,000 years ago, when the Palæozoic age was giving place to the Mesozoic. The bodies occupied by the Great Race represented no surviving—or even scientifically known—line of terrestrial evolution, but were of a peculiar, closely homogeneous, and highly specialised organic type inclining as much to the vegetable as to the animal state. Cell-action was of an unique sort almost precluding fatigue, and wholly eliminating the need of sleep. Nourishment, assimilated through the red trumpet-like appendages on one of the great flexible limbs, was always semi-fluid and in many aspects wholly unlike the food of existing animals. The beings had but two of the senses which we recognise—sight and hearing, the latter accomplished through the flower-like appendages on the grey stalks above their heads—but of other and incomprehensible senses (not, however, well utilisable by alien captive minds inhabiting their bodies) they possessed many. Their three eyes were so situated as to give them a range of vision wider than the normal. Their blood was a sort of deep-greenish ichor of great thickness. They had no sex, but reproduced through seeds or spores which clustered on their bases and could be developed only under water. Great, shallow tanks were used for the growth of their young—which were,

37. All classes of deep-sea life.

38. See *At the Mountains of Madness*, note 66, for a discussion of Lovecraft's own views on eugenics and the sterilization of the unfit.

however, reared only in small numbers on account of the longevity of individuals; four or five thousand years being the common life span.

Markedly defective individuals were quietly disposed of as soon as their defects were noticed.[38] Disease and the approach of death were, in the absence of a sense of touch or of physical pain, recognised by purely visual symptoms. The dead were incinerated with dignified ceremonies. Once in a while, as before mentioned, a keen mind would escape death by forward projection in time; but such cases were not numerous. When one did occur, the exiled mind from the future was treated with the utmost kindness till the dissolution of its unfamiliar tenement.

The Great Race seemed to form a single loosely knit nation or league, with major institutions in common, though there were four definite divisions. The political and economic system of each unit was a sort of fascistic socialism, with major resources rationally distributed, and power delegated to a small governing board elected by the votes of all able to pass certain educational and psychological tests. Family organisation was not overstressed, though ties among persons of common descent were recognised, and the young were generally reared by their parents.

Resemblances to human attitudes and institutions were, of course, most marked in those fields where on the one hand highly abstract elements were concerned, or where on the other hand there was a dominance of the basic, unspecialised urges common to all organic life. A few added likenesses came through conscious adoption as the Great Race probed the future and copied what it liked. Industry, highly mechanised, demanded but little time from each citizen; and the abundant leisure was filled with intellectual and æsthetic activities of various sorts. The sciences were carried to an unbelievable height of development, and art was a vital part of life, though at the period of my dreams it had passed its crest and meridian. Technology was enormously stimulated through the constant struggle to survive, and to keep in existence the physical fabric of great cities, imposed by the prodigious geologic upheavals of those primal days.

Crime was surprisingly scanty, and was dealt with through highly efficient policing. Punishments ranged from privilege deprivation and imprisonment to death or major emotion wrenching, and were never administered without a careful study of the criminal's motivations. Warfare, largely civil for the last few millennia though sometimes waged against reptilian and octopodic invaders, or against the winged, star-headed Old Ones who centred in the Antarctic,[39] was infrequent though infinitely devastating. An enormous army, using camera-like weapons which produced tremendous electrical effects, was kept on hand for purposes seldom mentioned, but obviously connected with the ceaseless fear of the dark, windowless elder ruins and of the great sealed trap-doors in the lowest subterrene levels.

This fear of the basalt ruins and trap-doors was largely a matter of unspoken suggestion—or, at most, of furtive quasi-whispers. Everything specific which bore on it was significantly absent from such books as were on the common shelves. It was the one subject lying altogether under a taboo among the Great Race, and seemed to be connected alike with horrible bygone struggles, and with that future peril which would some day force the race to send its keener minds ahead en masse in time. Imperfect and fragmentary as were the other things presented by dreams and legends, this matter was still more bafflingly shrouded. The vague old myths avoided it—or perhaps all allusions had for some reason been excised. And in the dreams of myself and others, the hints were peculiarly few. Members of the Great Race never intentionally referred to the matter, and what could be gleaned came only from some of the more sharply observant captive minds.

According to these scraps of information, the basis of the fear was a horrible elder race of half-polypous, utterly alien entities which had come through space from immeasurably distant universes and had dominated the earth and three other solar planets about six hundred million years ago. They were only partly material—as we understand matter—and their type of consciousness and media of perception differed wholly from those of terrestrial organisms. For example, their senses did not include that of sight; their mental world being a strange, non-visual pattern of impressions. They were, however, sufficiently material to use implements of normal matter when in cosmic areas containing it; and they required housing—albeit of a peculiar kind. Though their *senses* could penetrate all material barriers, their *substance* could not; and certain forms of electrical

39. As described in *At the Mountains of Madness* (pp. 457–572, above).

40. First mentioned by Richard F. Searight in "The Sealed Casket," published in *Weird Tales* in March 1935. Reportedly, Lovecraft himself contributed this fragment that was intended to head the story but was omitted from publication:

> . . . And it is recorded that in the Elder Times, Om Oris, mightiest of the wizards, laid crafty snare for the dæmon Avaloth, and pitted dark magic against him; for Avaloth plagued the earth with a strange growth of ice and snow that crept as if alive, ever southward, and swallowed up the forests and the mountains. And the outcome of the contest with the dæmon is not known; but wizards of that day maintained that Avaloth, who was not easily discernable, could not be destroyed save by a great heat, the means whereof was not then known, although certain of the wizards foresaw that one day it should be. Yet, at this time the ice fields began to shrink and dwindle and finally vanished; and the earth bloomed forth afresh.

Lovecraft wrote to Searight on January 15, 1934 (quoted in Edward P. Berglund's "Lovecraft on Eldritch Tomes"):

> I like the fragment from the Eltdown Shards, too. These cryptic & terrible records of man's earliest struggles with the survivors of the pre-human world—related as they are to the abhorred paragraphs of the Book of Eibon & the later (& purely human) sections of the Pnakotic Manuscripts—have always fascinated me . . . especially in view of those tantalising & subtly disquieting references in the dreaded *Necronomicon* of the mad Arab Abdul Alhazred, the more obscure (& often disputed)

energy could wholly destroy them. They had the power of aërial motion, despite the absence of wings or any other visible means of levitation. Their minds were of such texture that no exchange with them could be effected by the Great Race.

When these things had come to the earth they had built mighty basalt cities of windowless towers, and had preyed horribly upon the beings they found. Thus it was when the minds of the Great Race sped across the void from that obscure, transgalactic world known in the disturbing and debatable Eltdown Shards[40] as Yith. The newcomers, with the instruments they created, had found it easy to subdue the predatory entities and drive them down to those caverns of inner earth which they had already joined to their abodes and begun to inhabit. Then they had sealed the entrances and left them to their fate, afterward occupying most of their great cities and preserving certain important buildings for reasons connected more with superstition than with indifference, boldness, or scientific and historical zeal.

But as the æons passed, there came vague, evil signs that the Elder Things were growing strong and numerous in the inner world. There were sporadic irruptions of a particularly hideous character in certain small and remote cities of the Great Race, and in some of the deserted elder cities which the Great Race had not peopled—places where the paths to the gulfs below had not been properly sealed or guarded.[41] After that greater precautions were taken, and many of the paths were closed for ever—though a few were left with sealed trap-doors for strategic use in fighting the Elder Things if ever they broke forth in unexpected places; fresh rifts caused by that selfsame geologic change which had choked some of the paths and had slowly lessened the number of outer-word structures and ruins surviving from the conquered entities.

The irruptions of the Elder Things must have been shocking beyond all description, since they had permanently coloured the psychology of the Great Race. Such was the fixed mood of horror that the very aspect of the creatures was left unmentioned. At no time was I able to gain a clear hint of what they looked like. There were veiled suggestions of a monstrous *plasticity*, and of temporary *lapses of visibility*, while other fragmentary whispers referred to their control and military use of *great winds*. Singular *whistling* noises, and colossal footprints made up of five circular toe-marks, seemed also to be associated with them.[42]

It was evident that the coming doom so desperately feared by the Great Race—the doom that was one day to send millions of keen minds across the chasm of time to strange bodies in the safer future—had to do with a final successful irruption of the Elder Beings. Mental projections down the ages had clearly foretold such a horror, and the Great Race had resolved that none who could escape should face it. That the foray would be a matter of vengeance, rather than an attempt to reoccupy the outer world, they knew from the planet's later history—for their projections shewed the coming and going of subsequent races untroubled by the monstrous entities. Perhaps these entities had come to prefer earth's inner abysses to the variable, storm-ravaged surface, since light meant nothing to them. Perhaps, too, they were slowly weakening with the æons. Indeed, it was known that they would be quite dead in the time of the post-human beetle race which the fleeing minds would tenant. Meanwhile the Great Race maintained its cautious vigilance, with potent weapons ceaselessly ready despite the horrified banishing of the subject from common speech and visible records. And always the shadow of nameless fear hung about the sealed trap-doors and the dark, windowless elder towers.

V.

THAT IS THE world of which my dreams brought me dim, scattered echoes every night. I cannot hope to give any true idea of the horror and dread contained in such echoes, for it was upon a wholly intangible quality—the sharp sense of *pseudo-memory*—that such feelings mainly depended. As I have said, my studies gradually gave me a defence against these feelings, in the form of rational psychological explanations; and this saving influence was augmented by the subtle touch of accustomedness which comes with the passage of time. Yet in spite of everything the

single allusion in the monstrous *Unaussprechlichen Kulten* of the ill-fated Friedrich-Wilhelm von Junzt.

41. This may be a reference to the vaults beneath the Nameless City (see "The Nameless City," pp. 80–93, above).

42. All of these characteristics are described in detail in *At the Mountains of Madness* (pp. 457–572, above).

43. In 1894 the American Psychological Association began publishing a journal, *Psychological Review*, which continues today.

44. The Pilbara, in the northwest of Australia, though sparsely populated, boasts a huge minerals and energy industry, described by the University of Western Australia as "the heaving heart of the resources economy" (*UWA News* 31, no. 19 [November 26, 2012], 1). Known for its gas, mineral, and iron ore deposits, it has some of the oldest known rock formations on Earth.

vague, creeping terror would return momentarily now and then. It did not, however, engulf me as it had before; and after 1922 I lived a very normal life of work and recreation.

In the course of years I began to feel that my experience—together with the kindred cases and the related folklore—ought to be definitely summarised and published for the benefit of serious students; hence I prepared a series of articles briefly covering the whole ground and illustrated with crude sketches of some of the shapes, scenes, decorative motifs, and hieroglyphs remembered from the dreams. These appeared at various times during 1928 and 1929 in the *Journal of the American Psychological Society*,[43] but did not attract much attention. Meanwhile I continued to record my dreams with the minutest care, even though the growing stack of reports attained troublesomely vast proportions. On July 10, 1934, there was forwarded to me by the Psychological Society the letter which opened the culminating and most horrible phase of the whole mad ordeal. It was postmarked Pilbarra, Western Australia,[44] and bore the signature of one whom I found, upon inquiry, to be a mining engineer of considerable prominence. Enclosed were some very curious snapshots. I will reproduce the text in its entirety, and no reader can fail to understand how tremendous an effect it and the photographs had upon me.

I was, for a time, almost stunned and incredulous; for although I had often thought that some basis of fact must underlie certain phases of the legends which had coloured my dreams, I was none the less unprepared for anything like a tangible survival from a lost world remote beyond all imagination. Most devastating of all were the photographs—for here, in cold, incontrovertible realism, there stood out against a background of sand certain worn-down, water-ridged, storm-weathered blocks of stone whose slightly convex tops and slightly concave bottoms told their own story.

And when I studied them with a magnifying glass I could see all too plainly, amidst the batterings and pittings, the traces of those vast curvilinear designs and occasional hieroglyphs whose significance had become so hideous to me. But here is the letter, which speaks for itself.

49, Dampier Str.,[45]
Pilbarra, W. Australia,
18 May 1934.

Prof. N. W Peaslee,
c/o Am. Psychological Society,
30 E. 41st Str.,
N. Y. City, U.S.A.

My dear Sir:—

A recent conversation with Dr. E. M. Boyle of Perth, and some papers with your articles which he has just sent me, make it advisable for me to tell you about certain things I have seen in the Great Sandy Desert east of our gold field here. It would seem, in view of the peculiar legends about old cities with huge stonework and strange designs and hieroglyphs which you describe, that I have come upon something very important.

The blackfellows[46] *have always been full of talk about "great stones with marks on them," and seem to have a terrible fear of such things. They connect them in some way with their common racial legends about Buddai, the gigantic old man who lies asleep for ages underground with his head on his arm, and who will some day awake and eat up the world.*[47]

There are some very old and half-forgotten tales of enormous underground huts of great stones, where passages lead down and down, and where horrible things have happened. The blackfellows claim that once some warriors, fleeing in battle, went down into one and never came back, but that frightful winds began to blow from the place soon after they went down. However, there usually isn't much in what these natives say.

But what I have to tell is more than this. Two years ago, when I was prospecting about 500 miles east in the desert, I came on a lot of queer pieces of dressed stone perhaps 3 x 2 x 2 feet in size, and weathered and pitted to the very limit. At first I couldn't find any of the marks the blackfellows told about, but when I looked close enough I could make out some deeply carved lines in spite of the weathering. They were peculiar curves, just like what the

45. Dampier Street is in the very small town of Dampier, a major industrial port on the eponymous archipelago (on the coast of the Pilbara). William Dampier (1652–1715) was an early British explorer of northwestern Australia.

46. That is, Australian Aborigines.

47. Buddai is described in the *Encyclopædia Britannica* (9th ed.): "The only idea of a god known to be entertained by these people [the native Australians], is that of Buddai, a gigantic old man lying asleep for ages, with his head resting upon his arm, which is deep in the sand. He is expected one day to awake and eat up the world. They have no religion beyond those gloomy dreams."

blacks had tried to describe. I imagine there must have been 30 or 40 blocks, some nearly buried in the sand, and all within a circle perhaps a quarter of a mile's diameter.

When I saw some, I looked around closely for more, and made a careful reckoning of the place with my instruments. I also took pictures of 10 or 12 of the most typical blocks, and will enclose the prints for you to see. I turned my information and pictures over to the government at Perth, but they have done nothing with them. Then I met Dr. Boyle, who had read your articles in the Journal of the American Psychological Society, and in time happened to mention the stones. He was enormously interested, and became quite excited when I shewed him my snapshots, saying that the stones and markings were just like those of the masonry you had dreamed about and seen described in legends.

He meant to write you, but was delayed. Meanwhile he sent me most of the magazines with your articles, and I saw at once from your drawings and descriptions, that my stones are certainly the kind you mean. You can appreciate this from the enclosed prints. Later on you will hear directly from Dr. Boyle.

Now I can understand how important all this will be to you. Without question we are faced with the remains of an unknown civilisation older than any dreamed of before, and forming a basis for your legends.

As a mining engineer, I have some knowledge of geology, and can tell you that these blocks are so ancient they frighten me. They are mostly sandstone and granite, though one is almost certainly made of a queer sort of cement or concrete. They bear evidence of water action, as if this part of the world had been submerged and come up again after long ages—all since these blocks were made and used. It is a matter of hundreds of thousands of years—or heaven knows how much more. I don't like to think about it.

In view of your previous diligent work in tracking down the legends and everything connected with them, I cannot doubt but that you will want to lead an expedition to the desert and make some archæological excavations. Both Dr. Boyle and I are prepared to coöperate in such work if you—or organisations known to you—can furnish the funds. I can get together a dozen miners for the heavy digging—the blacks would be of no use, for I've found that *they have an almost maniacal fear of this particular spot. Boyle and I are saying nothing to others, for you very obviously ought to have precedence in any discoveries or credit.*

The place can be reached from Pilbarra in about 4 days by motor tractor—which we'd need for our apparatus. It is somewhat west and south of Warburton's path of 1873,[48] and 100 miles southeast of Joanna Spring. We could float things up the De Grey River instead of starting from Pilbarra—but all that can be talked over later.[49] Roughly the stones lie at a point about 22°3'14" South Latitude, 125°0'39" East Longitude.[50] The climate is tropical, and the desert conditions are trying. Any expedition had better be made in winter—June or July or August. I shall welcome further correspondence upon this subject, and am keenly eager to assist in any plan you may devise. After studying your articles I am deeply impressed with the profound significance of the whole matter. Dr. Boyle will write later. When rapid communication is needed, a cable to Perth can be relayed by wireless.

Hoping profoundly for an early message,

Believe me,
Most faithfully yours,
Robert B. F. Mackenzie

Of the immediate aftermath of this letter, much can be learned from the press. My good fortune in securing the backing of Miskatonic University was great, and both Mr. Mackenzie and Dr. Boyle proved invaluable in arranging matters at the Australian end. We were not too specific with the public about our objects, since the whole matter would have lent itself unpleasantly to sensational and jocose treatment by the cheaper newspapers. As a result, printed reports were sparing; but enough appeared to tell of our quest for reported Australian ruins and to chronicle our various preparatory steps.

Professors William Dyer of the college's geology department (leader of the Miskatonic Antarctic Expedition of 1930–31),[51] Ferdinand C. Ashley of the department of ancient history, and Tyler M. Freeborn of the department of anthropology—together with my son Wingate—accompanied me. My correspondent Mackenzie came to Arkham early in 1935 and assisted in our final preparations. He proved to be a tremendously competent and affable

48. Peter Egerton Warburton (1813–1889) explored Western Australia and the Great Sandy Desert from 1872 to 1874, becoming the first Briton or European to do so. An expedition from South Australia—its purpose was to establish a trail—presented almost insurmountable obstacles. Although the travelers reached Alice Springs in early 1873 without hardship, after their departure in April they experienced extreme heat and a scarcity of water. As with Roald Amundsen's South Pole expedition of 1910–12, the men survived only by eating their transportation—Warburton his camels, Amundsen his dogs. Eventually, Warburton, prostrate with heat and thirst, was strapped to a camel and arrived, thus transported, at the Oakover River. On January 11, 1874, the expedition pulled in to Charles Harper's De Grey station—an 883,000-acre outpost—in northern Western Australia. Warburton is said to have credited his Aboriginal companion Charley with his survival and success. Lovecraft's notes for the tale, reproduced in *Something About Cats and Other Pieces*, also reveal that the location is "East of Mr. Macpherson & Gregory's path of 1861." "Gregory" refers to Francis Thomas Gregory (1821–1888), brother of the explorer Sir Augustus George Gregory; Frank, as he was known, led a party of nine in the Pilbara in 1861. Macpherson is unidentified.

49. The nearest body of water to the digsite is the seasonal (or, in the language of unique seawater environments, "impermanent") Percival Lakes, which is described in the singular, despite the final *s*.

50. The spot is about four hundred miles south of Dampier. Lovecraft's notes describe it further as "N. of Dry Salt Lake & Amgas Range. S. of St. George Range, Fitzroy R. & Kimberly goldfield. East of De Grey R. & Pilbarra goldfield."

51. As recounted in *At the Mountains of Madness*, above. Donald R. Burleson comments, in *H. P. Lovecraft: A Critical Study*, "One has to wonder about Dyer's frame of mind, after the Antarctic experience, embarking on this second unearthing of primal secrets . . ." (201).

man of about fifty, admirably well-read, and deeply familiar with all the conditions of Australian travel. He had tractors waiting at Pilbarra, and we chartered a tramp steamer of sufficiently light draught to get up the river to that point. We were prepared to excavate in the most careful and scientific fashion, sifting every particle of sand, and disturbing nothing which might seem to be in or near its original situation.

Sailing from Boston aboard the wheezy *Lexington* on March 28, 1935, we had a leisurely trip across the Atlantic and Mediterranean, through the Suez Canal, down the Red Sea, and across the Indian Ocean to our goal. I need not tell how the sight of the low, sandy West Australian coast depressed me, and how I detested the crude mining town and dreary gold fields where the tractors were given their last loads. Dr. Boyle, who met us, proved to be elderly, pleasant, and intelligent—and his knowledge of psychology led him into many long discussions with my son and me.

Discomfort and expectancy were oddly mingled in most of us when at length our party of eighteen rattled forth over the arid leagues of sand and rock. On Friday, May 31st, we forded a branch of the De Grey and entered the realm of utter desolation. A certain positive terror grew on me as we advanced to this actual site of the elder world behind the legends—a terror of course abetted by the fact that my disturbing dreams and pseudo-memories still beset me with unabated force.

It was on Monday, June 3, that we saw the first of the half-buried blocks. I cannot describe the emotions with which I actually touched—in objective reality—a fragment of Cyclopean masonry in every respect like the blocks in the walls of my dream-buildings. There was a distinct trace of carving—and my hands trembled as I recognised part of a curvilinear decorative scheme made hellish to me through years of tormenting nightmare and baffling research.

A month of digging brought a total of some 1250 blocks in varying stages of wear and disintegration. Most of these were carven megaliths with curved tops and bottoms. A minority were smaller, flatter, plain-surfaced, and square or octagonally cut— like those of the floors and pavements in my dreams—while a few were singularly massive and curved or slanted in such a manner as to suggest use in vaulting or groining, or as parts of arches or round window casings. The deeper—and the farther north and east—we dug, the more blocks we found; though we still failed to discover any trace of arrangement among them. Professor Dyer was appalled at the measureless age of the fragments, and Freeborn found traces of symbols which fitted darkly into certain Papuan and Polynesian legends of infinite antiquity. The condition and scattering of the blocks told mutely of vertiginous cycles of time and geologic upheavals of cosmic savagery.

We had an aëroplane with us, and my son Wingate would often go up to different heights and scan the sand-and-rock waste for signs of dim, large-scale outlines—either differences of level or trails of scattered blocks. His results were virtually negative; for whenever he would one day think he had glimpsed some significant trend, he would on his next trip find the impression replaced by another equally insubstantial—a result of the shifting, wind-blown sand. One or two of these ephemeral suggestions, though, affected me queerly and disagreeably. They seemed, after a fashion, to dovetail horribly with something I had dreamed or read, but which I could no longer remember. There was a terrible *pseudo-familiarity* about them—which somehow made me look furtively and apprehensively over the abominable, sterile terrain toward the north and northeast.

Around the first week in July I developed an unaccountable set of mixed emotions about that general northeasterly region. There was horror, and there was curiosity—but more than that, there was a persistent and perplexing illusion of *memory*. I tried all sorts of psychological expedients to get these notions out of my head, but met with no success. Sleeplessness also gained upon me, but I almost welcomed this because of the resultant shortening of my dream-periods. I acquired the habit of taking long, lone walks in the desert late at night—usually to the north or northeast, whither the sum of my strange new impulses seemed subtly to pull me.

Sometimes, on these walks, I would stumble over nearly buried fragments of the ancient masonry. Though there were fewer visible blocks here than where we had started, I felt sure that there must be a vast abundance beneath the surface. The ground was less level than at our camp, and the prevailing high winds now and then piled the sand into fantastic temporary

52. The full moon occurred five days later, on July 16, 1935, consistent with Peaslee's record.

hillocks—exposing some traces of the elder stones while it covered other traces. I was queerly anxious to have the excavations extend to this territory, yet at the same time dreaded what might be revealed. Obviously, I was getting into a rather bad state—all the worse because I could not account for it.

An indication of my poor nervous health can be gained from my response to an odd discovery which I made on one of my nocturnal rambles. It was on the evening of July 11th, when a gibbous moon flooded the mysterious hillocks with a curious pallor.[52] Wandering somewhat beyond my usual limits, I came upon a great stone which seemed to differ markedly from any we had yet encountered. It was almost wholly covered, but I stooped and cleared away the sand with my hands, later studying the object carefully and supplementing the moonlight with my electric torch. Unlike the other very large rocks, this one was perfectly square-cut, with no convex or concave surface. It seemed, too, to be of a dark basaltic substance wholly dissimilar to the granite and sandstone and occasional concrete of the now familiar fragments.

Suddenly I rose, turned, and ran for the camp at top speed. It was a wholly unconscious and irrational flight, and only when I was close to my tent did I fully realise why I had run. Then it came to me. The queer dark stone was something which I had dreamed and read about, and which was linked with the uttermost horrors of the æon-old legendry. It was one of the blocks of that basaltic elder masonry which the fabled Great Race held in such fear—the tall, windowless ruins left by those brooding, half-material, alien Things that festered in earth's nether abysses and against whose wind-like, invisible forces the trap-doors were sealed and the sleepless sentinels posted.

I remained awake all that night, but by dawn realised how silly I had been to let the shadow of a myth upset me. Instead of being frightened, I should have had a discoverer's enthusiasm. The next forenoon I told the others about my find, and Dyer, Freeborn, Boyle, my son, and I set out to view the anomalous block. Failure, however, confronted us. I had formed no clear idea of the stone's location, and a late wind had wholly altered the hillocks of shifting sand.

VI.

I COME NOW to the crucial and most difficult part of my narrative—all the more difficult because I cannot be quite certain of its reality. At times I feel uncomfortably sure that I was not dreaming or deluded; and it is this feeling—in view of the stupendous implications which the objective truth of my experience would raise—which impels me to make this record. My son—a trained psychologist with the fullest and most sympathetic knowledge of my whole case—shall be the primary judge of what I have to tell.

First let me outline the externals of the matter, as those at the camp know them. On the night of July 17–18, after a windy day, I retired early but could not sleep. Rising shortly before eleven, and afflicted as usual with that strange feeling regarding the northeastward terrain, I set out on one of my typical nocturnal walks; seeing and greeting only one person—an Australian miner named Tupper—as I left our precincts. The moon, slightly past full, shone from a clear sky and drenched the ancient sands with a white, leprous radiance which seemed to me somehow infinitely evil. There was no longer any wind, nor did any return for nearly five hours, as amply attested by Tupper and others who did not sleep through the night. The Australian last saw me walking rapidly across the pallid, secret-guarding hillocks toward the northeast.

About 3:30 A.M. a violent wind blew up, waking everyone in camp and felling three of the tents. The sky was unclouded, and the desert still blazed with that leprous moonlight. As the party saw to the tents my absence was noted, but in view of my previous walks this circumstance gave no one alarm. And yet, as many as three men—all Australians—seemed to feel something sinister in the air. Mackenzie explained to Prof. Freeborn that this was a fear picked up from blackfellow folklore—the natives having woven a curious fabric of malignant myth about the high winds which at long intervals sweep across the sands under a clear sky. Such winds, it is whispered, blow out of the great stone huts under the ground where terrible things have happened—and are never felt except near places where the big marked stones are scattered.

Close to four the gale subsided as suddenly as it had begun, leaving the sand hills in new and unfamiliar shapes.

It was just past five, with the bloated, fungoid moon sinking in the west, when I staggered into camp—hatless, tattered, features scratched and ensanguined, and without my electric torch. Most of the men had returned to bed, but Prof. Dyer was smoking a pipe in front of his tent. Seeing my winded and almost frenzied state, he called Dr. Boyle, and the two of them got me on my cot and made me comfortable. My son, roused by the stir, soon joined them, and they all tried to force me to lie still and attempt sleep.

But there was no sleep for me. My psychological state was very extraordinary—different from anything I had previously suffered. After a time I insisted upon talking—nervously and elaborately explaining my condition. I told them I had become fatigued, and had lain down in the sand for a nap. There had, I said, been dreams even more frightful than usual—and when I was awaked by the sudden high wind my overwrought nerves had snapped. I had fled in panic, frequently falling over half-buried stones and thus gaining my tattered and bedraggled aspect. I must have slept long—hence the hours of my absence.

Of anything strange either seen or experienced I hinted absolutely nothing—exercising the greatest self-control in that respect. But I spoke of a change of mind regarding the whole work of the expedition, and earnestly urged a halt in all digging toward the northeast. My reasoning was patently weak—for I mentioned a dearth of blocks, a wish not to offend the superstitious miners, a possible shortage of funds from the college, and other things either untrue or irrelevant. Naturally, no one paid the least attention to my new wishes—not even my son, whose concern for my health was very obvious.

The next day I was up and around the camp, but took no part in the excavations. Seeing that I could not stop the work, I decided to return home as soon as possible for the sake of my nerves, and made my son promise to fly me in the plane to Perth—a thousand miles to the southwest—as soon as he had surveyed the region I wished let alone. If, I reflected, the thing I had seen was still visible, I might decide to attempt a specific warning even at the cost of ridicule. It was just conceivable that the miners who knew the local folklore might back me up. Humouring me, my son made the survey that very afternoon; flying over all the terrain my walk could possibly have covered. Yet nothing of what I had found remained in sight. It was the case of the anomalous basalt block all over again—the shifting sand had wiped out every trace. For an instant I half regretted having lost a certain awesome object in my stark fright—but now I know that the loss was merciful. I can still believe my whole experience an illusion—especially if, as I devoutly hope, that hellish abyss is never found.

Wingate took me to Perth July 20, though declining to abandon the expedition and return home. He stayed with me until the 25th, when the steamer for Liverpool sailed. Now, in the cabin of the *Empress*, I am pondering long and frantically on the entire matter, and have decided that my son at least must be informed. It shall rest with him whether to diffuse the matter more widely. In order to meet any eventuality I have prepared this summary of my background—as already known in a scattered way to others—and will now tell as briefly as possible what seemed to happen during my absence from the camp that hideous night.

Nerves on edge, and whipped into a kind of perverse eagerness by that inexplicable, dread-mingled, pseudo-mnemonic urge toward the northeast, I plodded on beneath the evil, burning moon. Here and there I saw, half-shrouded by the sand, those primal Cyclopean blocks left from nameless and forgotten æons. The incalculable age and brooding horror of this monstrous waste began to oppress me as never before, and I could not keep from thinking of my maddening dreams, of the frightful legends which lay behind them, and of the present fears of natives and miners concerning the desert and its carven stones.

And yet I plodded on as if to some eldritch rendezvous—more and more assailed by bewildering fancies, compulsions, and pseudo-memories. I thought of some of the possible contours of the lines of stones as seen by my son from the air, and wondered why they seemed at once so ominous and so familiar. Something was fumbling and rattling at the latch of my recollection, while another unknown force sought to keep the portal barred.

The night was windless, and the pallid sand curved upward and downward like frozen waves of the sea. I had no goal, but somehow ploughed along as if with fate-bound assurance. My dreams welled up into the waking world, so that each sand-embedded megalith seemed part of endless rooms and corridors of pre-human masonry, carved and hieroglyphed with symbols that I knew too well from years of custom as a captive mind of the Great Race. At moments I fancied I saw those omniscient, conical horrors moving about at their accustomed tasks, and I feared to look down lest I find myself one with them in aspect. Yet all the while I saw the sand-covered blocks as well as the rooms and corridors; the evil, burning moon as well as the lamps of luminous crystal; the endless desert as well as the waving ferns and cycads beyond the windows. I was awake and dreaming at the same time.

I do not know how long or how far—or indeed, in just what direction—I had walked when I first spied the heap of blocks bared by the day's wind. It was the largest group in one place that I had so far seen, and so sharply did it impress me that the visions of fabulous æons faded suddenly away. Again there were only the desert and the evil moon and the shards of an unguessed past. I drew close and paused, and cast the added light of my electric torch over the tumbled pile. A hillock had blown away, leaving a low, irregularly round mass of megaliths and smaller fragments some forty feet across and from two to eight feet high.

From the very outset I realised that there was some utterly unprecedented quality about these stones. Not only was the mere number of them quite without parallel, but something in the sand-worn traces of design arrested me as I scanned them under the mingled beams of the moon and my torch. Not that any one differed essentially from the earlier specimens we had found. It was something subtler than that. The impression did not come when I looked at one block alone, but only when I ran my eye over several almost simultaneously. Then, at last, the truth dawned upon me. The curvilinear patterns on many of these blocks were *closely related*—parts of one vast decorative conception. For the first time in this æon-shaken waste I had come upon a mass of masonry in its old position—tumbled and fragmentary, it is true, but none the less existing in a very definite sense.

Mounting at a low place, I clambered laboriously over the heap; here and there clearing away the sand with my fingers, and constantly striving to interpret varieties of size, shape, and style, and relationships of design. After a while I could vaguely guess at the nature of the bygone structure, and at the designs which had once stretched over the vast surfaces of the primal masonry. The perfect identity of the whole with some of my dream-glimpses appalled and unnerved me. This was once a Cyclopean corridor thirty feet tall, paved with octagonal blocks and solidly vaulted overhead. There would have been rooms opening off on the right, and at the farther end one of those strange inclined planes would have wound down to still lower depths.

I started violently as these conceptions occurred to me, for there was more in them than the blocks themselves had supplied. How did I know that this level should have been far underground? How did I know that the plane leading upward should have been behind me? How did I know that the long subterrene passage to the Square of Pillars ought to lie on the left one level above me? How did I know that the room of machines, and the rightward-leading tunnel to the central archives, ought to lie two levels below? How did I know that there would be one of those horrible, metal-banded trap-doors at the very bottom, four levels down? Bewildered by this intrusion from the dream-world, I found myself shaking and bathed in a cold perspiration.

Then, as a last, intolerable touch, I felt that faint, insidious stream of cool air trickling upward from a depressed place near the centre of the huge heap. Instantly, as once before, my visions faded, and I saw again only the evil moonlight, the brooding desert, and the spreading tumulus of palæogean masonry. Something real and tangible, yet fraught with infinite suggestions of nighted mystery, now confronted me. For that stream of air could argue but one thing—a hidden gulf of great size beneath the disordered blocks on the surface. My first thought was of the sinister blackfellow legends of vast underground huts among the megaliths where horrors happen and great winds are born. Then thoughts of my own dreams came back, and I felt dim pseudo-memories tugging at my mind. What manner of place lay below me? What primal, inconceivable source of age-old myth-cycles and haunting nightmares might I be on the brink of uncovering? It was only for a moment that I hesitated, for more than curiosity and scientific zeal was driving me on and working against my growing fear.

I seemed to move almost automatically, as if in the clutch of some compelling fate. Pocketing my torch, and struggling with a strength that I had not thought I possessed, I wrenched aside first one titan fragment of stone and then another, till there welled up a strong draught whose dampness contrasted oddly with the desert's dry air. A black rift began to yawn, and at length—when I had pushed away every fragment small enough to budge—the leprous moonlight blazed on an aperture of ample width to admit me.

I drew out my torch and cast a brilliant beam into the opening. Below me was a chaos of tumbled masonry, sloping roughly down toward the north at an angle of about forty-five degrees, and evidently the result of some bygone collapse from above. Between its surface and the ground level was a gulf of impenetrable blackness at whose upper edge were signs of gigantic, stress-heaved vaulting. At this point, it appeared, the desert's sands lay directly upon a floor of some titan structure of earth's youth—how preserved through æons of geologic convulsion I could not then and cannot now even attempt to guess.

In retrospect, the barest idea of a sudden, lone descent into such a doubtful abyss—and at a time when one's whereabouts were unknown to any living soul—seems like the utter apex of insanity. Perhaps it was—yet that night I embarked without hesitancy upon such a descent. Again there was manifest that lure and driving of fatality which had all along seemed to direct my course. With torch flashing intermittently to save the battery, I commenced a mad scramble down the sinister, Cyclopean incline below the opening—sometimes facing forward as I found good hand and foot holds, and at other times turning to face the heap of megaliths as I clung and fumbled more precariously. In two directions beside me, distant walls of carven, crumbling masonry loomed dimly under the direct beams of my torch. Ahead, however, was only unbroken blackness.

I kept no track of time during my downward scramble. So seething with baffling hints and images was my mind, that all objective matters seemed withdrawn into incalculable distances. Physical sensation was dead, and even fear remained as a wraith-like, inactive gargoyle leering impotently at me. Eventually I reached a level floor strown with fallen blocks, shapeless fragments of stone, and sand and detritus of every kind. On either side—perhaps thirty feet apart—rose massive walls culminating in huge groinings. That they were carved I could just discern, but the nature of the carvings was beyond my perception. What held me the most was the vaulting overhead. The beam from my torch could not reach the roof, but the lower parts of the monstrous arches stood out distinctly. And so perfect was their identity with what I had seen in countless dreams of the elder world, that I trembled actively for the first time.

Behind and high above, a faint luminous blur told of the distant moonlit world outside. Some vague shred of caution warned me that I should not let it out of my sight, lest I have no guide for my return. I now advanced toward the wall on my left, where the traces of carving were plainest. The littered floor was nearly as hard to traverse as the downward heap had been, but I managed to pick my difficult way. At one place I heaved aside some blocks and kicked away the detritus to see what the pavement was like, and shuddered at the utter, fateful familiarity of the great octagonal stones whose buckled surface still held roughly together.

Reaching a convenient distance from the wall, I cast the torchlight slowly and carefully over its worn remnants of carving. Some bygone influx of water seemed to have acted on the sandstone surface, while there were curious incrustations which I could not explain. In places the masonry was very loose and distorted, and I wondered how many æons more this primal, hidden edifice could keep its remaining traces of form amidst earth's heavings.

But it was the carvings themselves that excited me most. Despite their time-crumbled state, they were relatively easy to trace at close range; and the complete, intimate familiarity of every detail almost stunned my imagination. That the major attributes of this hoary masonry should be familiar, was not beyond normal credibility. Powerfully impressing the weavers of certain myths, they had become embodied in a stream of cryptic lore which, somehow coming to my notice during the amnesic period, had evoked vivid images in my subconscious mind. But how could I explain the exact and minute fashion in which each line and spiral of these strange designs tallied with what I had dreamt for more than a score of years? What obscure, forgotten iconography could have reproduced each subtle shading and

53. See "The Haunter of the Dark," note 25, below, for a discussion of trans-Neptunian objects, a subject about which Lovecraft himself published a paper.

nuance which so persistently, exactly, and unvaryingly besieged my sleeping vision night after night?

For this was no chance or remote resemblance. Definitely and absolutely, the millennially ancient, æon-hidden corridor in which I stood was the original of something I knew in sleep as intimately as I knew my own house in Crane Street, Arkham. True, my dreams shewed the place in its undecayed prime; but the identity was no less real on that account. I was wholly and horribly oriented. The particular structure I was in was known to me. Known, too, was its place in that terrible elder city of dreams. That I could visit unerringly any point in that structure or in that city which had escaped the changes and devastations of uncounted ages, I realised with hideous and instinctive certainty. What in God's name could all this mean? How had I come to know what I knew? And what awful reality could lie behind those antique tales of the beings who had dwelt in this labyrinth of primordial stone?

Words can convey only fractionally the welter of dread and bewilderment which ate at my spirit. I knew this place. I knew what lay before me, and what had lain overhead before the myriad towering stories had fallen to dust and debris and the desert. No need now, I thought with a shudder, to keep that faint blur of moonlight in view. I was torn betwixt a longing to flee and a feverish mixture of burning curiosity and driving fatality. What had happened to this monstrous megalopolis of eld in the millions of years since the time of my dreams? Of the subterrene mazes which had underlain the city and linked all its titan towers, how much had still survived the writhings of earth's crust?

Had I come upon a whole buried world of unholy archaism? Could I still find the house of the writing-master, and the tower where S'gg'ha, a captive mind from the star-headed vegetable carnivores of Antarctica, had chiselled certain pictures on the blank spaces of the walls? Would the passage at the second level down, to the hall of the alien minds, be still unchoked and traversable? In that hall the captive mind of an incredible entity—a half-plastic denizen of the hollow interior of an unknown trans-Plutonian planet[53] eighteen million years in the future—had kept a certain thing which it had modelled from clay.

I shut my eyes and put my hand to my head in a vain, pitiful effort to drive these insane dream-fragments from my consciousness. Then, for the first time, I felt acutely the coolness, motion, and dampness of the surrounding air. Shuddering, I realised that a vast chain of æon-dead black gulfs must indeed be yawning somewhere beyond and below me. I thought of the frightful chambers and corridors and inclines as I recalled them from my dreams. Would the way to the central archives still be open? Again that driving fatality tugged insistently at my brain as I recalled the awesome records that once lay cased in those rectangular vaults of rustless metal.

There, said the dreams and legends, had reposed the whole history, past and future, of the cosmic space-time continuum—written by captive minds from every orb and every age in the solar system. Madness, of course—but had I not now stumbled into a nighted world as mad as I? I thought of the locked metal shelves, and of the curious knob-twistings needed to open each one. My own came vividly into my consciousness. How often had I gone through that intricate routine of varied turns and pressures in the terrestrial vertebrate section on the lowest level! Every detail was fresh and familiar. If there were such a vault as I had dreamed of, I could open it in a moment. It was then that madness took me utterly. An instant later, and I was leaping and stumbling over the rocky debris toward the well-remembered incline to the depths below.

VII.

FROM THAT POINT forward my impressions are scarcely to be relied on—indeed, I still possess a final, desperate hope that they all form parts of some dæmonic dream—or illusion born of delirium. A fever raged in my brain, and everything came to me through a kind of haze—sometimes only intermittently. The rays of my torch shot feebly into the engulfing blackness, bringing phantasmal flashes of hideously familiar walls and carvings, all blighted with the decay of ages. In one place a tremendous mass of vaulting had fallen, so that I had to clamber over a mighty mound of stones reaching almost to the ragged, grotesquely stalactited roof. It was all the ultimate apex of nightmare, made worse by the blasphemous tug of pseudo-memory. One thing only was unfamiliar, and that was my own size in relation to the monstrous masonry. I felt oppressed by a sense of unwonted smallness, as if the sight of these towering walls from a mere human body was something wholly new and abnormal. Again and again I looked nervously down at myself, vaguely disturbed by the human form I possessed.

Onward through the blackness of the abyss I leaped, plunged, and staggered—often falling and bruising myself, and once nearly shattering my torch. Every stone and corner of that dæmonic gulf was known to me, and at many points I stopped to cast beams of light through choked and crumbling yet familiar archways. Some rooms had totally collapsed; others were bare or debris-filled. In a few I saw masses of metal—some fairly intact, some broken, and some crushed or battered—which I recognised as the colossal pedestals or tables of my dreams. What they could in truth have been, I dared not guess.

I found the downward incline and began its descent—though after a time halted by a gaping, ragged chasm whose narrowest point could not be much less than four feet across. Here the stonework had fallen through, revealing incalculable inky depths beneath. I knew there were two more cellar levels in this titan edifice, and trembled with fresh panic as I recalled the metal-clamped trap-door on the lowest one. There could be no guards now—for what had lurked beneath had long since done its hideous work and sunk into its long decline. By the time of the post-human beetle race it would be quite dead. And yet, as I thought of the native legends, I trembled anew.

It cost me a terrible effort to vault that yawning chasm, since the littered floor prevented a running start—but madness drove me on. I chose a place close to the left-hand wall—where the rift was least wide and the landing-spot reasonably clear of dangerous debris—and after one frantic moment reached the other side in safety. At last gaining the lower level, I stumbled on past the archway of the room of machines, within which were fantastic ruins of metal half-buried beneath fallen vaulting. Everything was where I knew it would be, and I climbed confidently over the heaps which barred the entrance of a vast transverse corridor. This, I realised, would take me under the city to the central archives.

Endless ages seemed to unroll as I stumbled, leaped, and crawled along that debris-cluttered corridor. Now and then I could make out carvings on the age-stained walls—some familiar, others seemingly added since the period of my dreams. Since this was a subterrene house-connecting highway, there were no archways save when the route led through the lower levels of various buildings. At some of these intersections I turned aside long enough to look down well-remembered corridors and into well-remembered rooms. Twice only did I find any radical changes from what I had dreamed of—and in one of these cases I could trace the sealed-up outlines of the archway I remembered.

I shook violently, and felt a curious surge of retarding weakness, as I steered a hurried and reluctant course through the crypt of one of those great windowless, ruined towers whose alien basalt masonry bespoke a whispered and horrible origin. This primal vault was round and fully two hundred feet across, with nothing carved upon the dark-hued stonework. The floor was here free from anything save dust and sand, and I could see the apertures leading upward and downward. There were no stairs or inclines—indeed, my dreams had pictured those elder towers as wholly untouched by the fabulous Great Race. Those who had built them had not needed stairs or inclines. In the dreams, the downward aperture had been tightly sealed and nervously guarded. Now it lay open—black and yawning, and giving forth a current of cool, damp air. Of what limitless caverns of eternal night might brood below, I would not permit myself to think.

Later, clawing my way along a badly heaped section of the corridor, I reached a place where the roof had wholly caved in. The debris rose like a mountain, and I climbed up over it, passing through a vast empty space where my torchlight could reveal neither walls nor vaulting. This, I reflected, must be the cellar of the house of the metal-purveyors, fronting on the third square not far from the archives. What had happened to it I could not conjecture.

I found the corridor again beyond the mountain of detritus and stones, but after a short distance encountered a wholly choked place where the fallen vaulting almost touched the perilously sagging ceiling. How I managed to wrench and tear aside enough blocks to afford a passage, and how I dared disturb the tightly packed fragments when the least shift of equilibrium might have brought down all the tons of superincumbent masonry to crush me to nothingness, I do not know. It was sheer madness that impelled and guided me—if, indeed, my whole underground adventure was not—as I hope—a hellish delusion or phase of dreaming. But I did make—or dream that I made—a passage that I could squirm through. As I wriggled over the mound of debris—my torch, switched continuously on, thrust deeply within my mouth—I felt myself torn by the fantastic stalactites of the jagged floor above me.

I was now close to the great underground archival structure which seemed to form my goal. Sliding and clambering down the farther side of the barrier, and picking my way along the remaining stretch of corridor with hand-held, intermittently flashing torch, I came at last to a low, circular crypt with arches—still in a marvellous state of preservation—opening off on every side. The walls, or such parts of them as lay within reach of my torchlight, were densely hieroglyphed and chiselled with typical curvilinear symbols—some added since the period of my dreams.

This, I realised, was my fated destination, and I turned at once through a familiar archway on my left. That I could find a clear passage up and down the incline to all the surviving levels, I had oddly little doubt. This vast, earth-protected pile, housing the annals of all the solar system, had been built with supernal skill and strength to last as long as that system itself. Blocks of stupendous size, poised with mathematical genius and bound with cements of incredible toughness, had combined to form a mass as firm as the planet's rocky core. Here, after ages more prodigious than I could sanely grasp, its buried bulk stood in all its essential contours; the vast, dust-drifted floors scarce sprinkled with the litter elsewhere so dominant.

The relatively easy walking from this point onward went curiously to my head. All the frantic eagerness hitherto frustrated by obstacles now took itself out in a kind of febrile speed, and I literally raced along the low-roofed, monstrously well-remembered aisles beyond the archway. I was past being astonished by the familiarity of what I saw. On every hand the great hieroglyphed metal shelf-doors loomed monstrously; some yet in place, others sprung open, and still others bent and buckled under bygone geological stresses not quite strong enough to shatter the titan masonry. Here and there a dust-covered heap below a gaping empty shelf seemed to indicate where cases had been shaken down by earth-tremors. On occasional pillars were great symbols or letters proclaiming classes and sub-classes of volumes.

Once I paused before an open vault where I saw some of the accustomed metal cases still in position amidst the omnipresent gritty dust. Reaching up, I dislodged one of the thinner specimens with some difficulty, and rested it on the floor for inspection. It was titled in the prevailing curvilinear hieroglyphs, though something in the arrangement of the characters seemed subtly unusual. The odd mechanism of the hooked fastener was perfectly well known to me, and I snapped up the still rustless and workable lid and drew out the book within. The latter, as expected, was some twenty by fifteen inches in area, and two inches thick; the thin metal covers opening at the top. Its tough cellulose pages seemed unaffected by the myriad cycles of time they had lived through, and I studied the queerly pigmented, brush-drawn letters of the text—symbols utterly unlike either the usual curved hieroglyphs or any alphabet known to human scholarship—with a haunting, half-aroused memory. It came to me that this was the language used by a captive mind I had known slightly in my dreams—a mind from a large asteroid on which had survived much of the archaic life and lore of the primal planet whereof it formed a fragment.[54] At the same time I recalled that this level of the archives was devoted to volumes dealing with the non-terrestrial planets.

As I ceased poring over this incredible document I saw that the light of my torch was beginning to fail, hence quickly inserted the extra battery I always had with me. Then, armed with the stronger radiance, I resumed my feverish racing through unending tangles of aisles and corridors—recognising now and then some familiar shelf, and vaguely annoyed by the acoustic conditions which made my footfalls echo incongruously in these catacombs of æon-long death and silence. The very prints of my shoes behind me in the millennially untrodden dust made me shudder. Never before, if my mad dreams held anything of truth, had human feet pressed upon those immemorial pavements. Of the particular goal of my insane racing, my conscious mind held

54. "The asteroids," Lovecraft observed, "are a numerous group of tiny planets which lie between the orbits of Mars and Jupiter, and whose discovery was prompted by the belief that, according to the law of proportion of planetary distances, some body ought to exist in that region" ("The March Sky," *Providence Evening News*, March 2, 1914, 8). Ceres was the first planetoid or asteroid discovered in the predicted space. It was observed by Giuseppe Piazzi (1746–1826) on January 1, 1801, at the "shoulder" of the constellation Taurus; Piazzi was unsure whether it was a star or a comet. Others, however, among them the brilliant German mathematician Carl Friedrich Gauss, recognized it as the missing "planet" foretold by the theories of Johannes Kepler, Johann Elert Bode, and Johann Daniel Titius.

Giuseppe Piazzi and Ceres, probably painted by Giuseppe Velasco (ca. 1803).

In 1802, the asteroid Pallas was observed; by 1807, two more, Juno and Vesta, had joined what would become, within a century, a long list. H. W. M. Olbers (1758–1840), upon discovering Pallas, formulated a hypothesis about the origin of these small bodies, described in the *Encyclopædia Britannica* (11th ed.):

They were "fragments of a larger planet which had been shattered by an internal convulsion; and [Olbers] proposed that search should be made near the common node of the two orbits to see whether other fragments could be found." By 1910, more than six hundred had been found, and by the time of Lovecraft's essay, he said that over one thousand had been tallied.

Today the "explosion" theory has been replaced with the idea of astronomer Daniel Kirkwood, first propounded in 1867, that asteroids are the result of formations from a ring of matter inside the orbit of Jupiter, left over from the original solar nebula, that failed to reach planet size because of the disruptive gravitational pull of Jupiter.

no hint. There was, however, some force of evil potency pulling at my dazed will and buried recollections, so that I vaguely felt I was not running at random.

I came to a downward incline and followed it to profounder depths. Floors flashed by me as I raced, but I did not pause to explore them. In my whirling brain there had begun to beat a certain rhythm which set my right hand twitching in unison. I wanted to unlock something, and felt that I knew all the intricate twists and pressures needed to do it. It would be like a modern safe with a combination lock. Dream or not, I had once known and still knew. How any dream—or scrap of unconsciously absorbed legend—could have taught me a detail so minute, so intricate, and so complex, I did not attempt to explain to myself. I was beyond all coherent thought. For was not this whole experience— this shocking familiarity with a set of unknown ruins, and this monstrously exact identity of everything before me with what

Never before had human feet pressed upon those immemorial pavements!

"Never before had human feet pressed upon those immemorial pavements!" *Astounding Stories* 17, no. 4 (June 1936) (artist: Howard V. Brown)

only dreams and scraps of myth could have suggested—a horror beyond all reason? Probably it was my basic conviction then—as it is now during my saner moments—that I was not awake at all, and that the entire buried city was a fragment of febrile hallucination.

Eventually I reached the lowest level and struck off to the right of the incline. For some shadowy reason I tried to soften my steps, even though I lost speed thereby. There was a space I was afraid to cross on this last, deeply buried floor; and as I drew near it I recalled what thing in that space I feared. It was merely one of the metal-barred and closely guarded trap-doors. There would be no guards now, and on that account I trembled and tiptoed as I had done in passing through that black basalt vault where a similar trap-door had yawned. I felt a current of cool, damp air, as I had felt there, and wished that my course led in another direction. Why I had to take the particular course I was taking, I did not know.

When I came to the space I saw that the trap-door yawned widely open. Ahead the shelves began again, and I glimpsed on the floor before one of them a heap very thinly covered with dust, where a number of cases had recently fallen. At the same moment a fresh wave of panic clutched me, though for some time I could not discover why. Heaps of fallen cases were not uncommon, for all through the æons this lightless labyrinth had been racked by the heavings of earth and had echoed at intervals to the deafening clatter of toppling objects. It was only when I was nearly across the space that I realised why I shook so violently.

Not the heap, but something about the dust of the level floor was troubling me. In the light of my torch it seemed as if that dust were not as even as it ought to be—there were places where it looked thinner, as if it had been disturbed not many months before. I could not be sure, for even the apparently thinner places were dusty enough; yet a certain suspicion of regularity in the fancied unevenness was highly disquieting. When I brought the torchlight close to one of the queer places I did not like what I saw—for the illusion of regularity became very great. It was as if there were regular lines of composite impressions—impressions that went in threes, each slightly over a foot square, and consisting of five nearly circular three-inch prints, one in advance of the other four.

These possible lines of foot-square impressions appeared to lead in two directions, as if something had gone somewhere and returned. They were of course very faint, and may have been illusions or accidents; but there was an element of dim, fumbling terror about the way I thought they ran. For at one end of them was the heap of cases which must have clattered down not long before, while at the other end was the ominous trap-door with the cool, damp wind, yawning unguarded down to abysses past imagination.

VIII.

THAT MY STRANGE sense of compulsion was deep and overwhelming is shewn by its conquest of my fear. No rational motive could have drawn me on after that hideous suspicion of prints and the creeping dream-memories it excited. Yet my right hand, even as it shook with fright, still twitched rhythmically in its eagerness to turn a lock it hoped to find. Before I knew it I was past the heap of lately fallen cases and running on tiptoe through aisles of utterly unbroken dust toward a point which I seemed to know morbidly, horribly well. My mind was asking itself questions whose origin and relevancy I was only beginning to guess. Would the shelf be reachable by a human body? Could my human hand master all the æon-remembered motions of the lock? Would the lock be undamaged and workable? And what would I do—what dare I do—with what (as I now commenced to realise) I both hoped and feared to find? Would it prove the awesome, brain-shattering truth of something past normal conception, or shew only that I was dreaming?

The next I knew I had ceased my tiptoe racing and was standing still, staring at a row of maddeningly familiar hieroglyphed shelves. They were in a state of almost perfect preservation, and only three of the doors in this vicinity had sprung open. My feelings toward these shelves cannot be described—so utter and insistent was the sense of old acquaintance. I was looking high up, at a row near the top and wholly out of my reach, and wondering how I could climb to best advantage. An open door four rows from the bottom would help, and the locks of the closed doors formed possible holds for hands and feet. I would grip the torch between my teeth, as I had in other places where both hands were needed. Above all, I must make no noise. How to get down what I wished to remove would be difficult, but I could probably hook its movable fastener in my coat collar and carry it like a knapsack. Again I wondered whether the lock would be undamaged. That I could repeat each familiar motion I had not the least doubt. But I hoped the thing would not scrape or creak—and that my hand could work it properly.

Even as I thought these things I had taken the torch in my mouth and begun to climb. The projecting locks were poor supports; but as I had expected, the opened shelf helped greatly. I used both the difficultly swinging door and the edge of the aperture itself in my ascent, and managed to avoid any loud creaking. Balanced on the upper edge of the door, and leaning far to my right, I could just reach the lock I sought. My fingers, half-numb from climbing, were very clumsy at first; but I soon saw that they were anatomically adequate. And the memory-rhythm was strong in them. Out of unknown gulfs of time the intricate secret motions had somehow reached my brain correctly in every detail—for after less than five minutes of trying there came a click whose familiarity was all the more startling because I had not consciously anticipated it. In another instant the metal door was slowly swinging open with only the faintest grating sound.

Dazedly I looked over the row of greyish case-ends thus exposed, and felt a tremendous surge of some wholly inexplicable emotion. Just within reach of my right hand was a case whose curving hieroglyphs made me shake with a pang infinitely more complex than one of mere fright. Still shaking, I managed to dislodge it amidst a shower of gritty flakes, and ease it over toward myself without any violent noise. Like the other case I had handled, it was slightly more than twenty by fifteen inches in size, with curved mathematical designs in low relief. In thickness it just exceeded three inches. Crudely wedging it between myself and the surface I was climbing, I fumbled with the fastener and finally got the hook free. Lifting the cover, I shifted the heavy object to my back, and let the hook catch hold of my collar. Hands now free, I awkwardly clambered down to the dusty floor, and prepared to inspect my prize.

Kneeling in the gritty dust, I swung the case around and rested it in front of me. My hands shook, and I dreaded to draw out the book within almost as much as I longed—and felt compelled—to do so. It had very gradually become clear to me what I ought to find, and this realisation nearly paralysed my faculties. If the thing were there—and if I were not dreaming—the implications would be quite beyond the power of the human spirit to bear. What tormented me most was my momentary inability to feel that my surroundings were a dream. The sense of reality was hideous—and again becomes so as I recall the scene.

At length I tremblingly pulled the book from its container and stared fascinatedly at the well-known hieroglyphs on the cover. It seemed to be in prime condition, and the curvilinear letters of the title held me in almost as hypnotised a state as if I could read them. Indeed, I cannot swear that I did not actually read them in some transient and terrible access of abnormal memory. I do not know how long it was before I dared to lift that thin metal cover. I temporised and made excuses to myself. I took the torch from my mouth and shut it off to save the battery. Then, in the dark, I screwed up my courage—finally lifting the cover without turning on the light. Last of all I did indeed flash the torch upon the exposed page—steeling myself in advance to suppress any sound no matter what I should find.

I looked for an instant, then almost collapsed. Clenching my teeth, however, I kept silence. I sank wholly to the floor and put a hand to my forehead amidst the engulfing blackness. What I dreaded and expected was there. Either I was dreaming, or time and space had become a mockery. I must be dreaming—but I would test the horror by carrying this thing back and shewing it to my son if it were indeed a reality. My head swam frightfully, even though there were no visible objects in the unbroken gloom to swirl around me. Ideas and images of the starkest terror—excited by vistas which my glimpse had opened up—began to throng in upon me and cloud my senses.

I thought of those possible prints in the dust, and trembled at the sound of my own breathing as I did so. Once again I flashed on the light and looked at the page as a serpent's victim may look at his destroyer's eyes and fangs. Then, with clumsy fingers in the dark, I closed the book, put it in its container, and snapped the lid and the curious hooked fastener. This was what I must carry back to the outer world if it truly existed—if the whole abyss truly existed—if I, and the world itself, truly existed.

Just when I tottered to my feet and commenced my return I cannot be certain. It comes to me oddly—as a measure of my sense of separation from the normal world—that I did not even once look at my watch during those hideous hours underground. Torch in hand, and with the ominous case under one arm, I eventually found myself tiptoeing in a kind of silent panic past the draught-giving abyss and those lurking suggestions of prints. I lessened my precautions as I climbed up the endless inclines, but could not shake off a shadow of apprehension which I had not felt on the downward journey.

I dreaded having to re-pass through that black basalt crypt that was older than the city itself, where cold draughts welled up from unguarded depths. I thought of that which the Great Race had feared, and of what might still be lurking—be it ever so weak and dying—down there. I thought of those possible five-circle prints and of what my dreams had told me of such prints—and of strange winds and whistling noises associated with them. And I thought of the tales of the modern blacks, wherein the horror of great winds and nameless subterrene ruins was dwelt upon.

I knew from a carven wall symbol the right floor to enter, and came at last—after passing that other book I had examined—to the great circular space with the branching archways. On my right, and at once recognisable, was the arch through which I had arrived. This I now entered, conscious that the rest of my course would be harder because of the tumbled state of the masonry outside the archive building. My new metal-cased burden weighed upon me, and I found it harder and harder to be quiet as I stumbled among debris and fragments of every sort.

Then I came to the ceiling-high mound of debris through which I had wrenched a scanty passage. My dread at wriggling through again was infinite; for my first passage had made some noise, and I now—after seeing those possible prints—dreaded sound above all things. The case, too, doubled the problem of traversing the narrow crevice. But I clambered up the barrier as best I could, and pushed the case through the aperture ahead of me. Then, torch in mouth, I scrambled through myself—my back torn as before by stalactites. As I tried to grasp the case again, it fell some distance ahead of me down the slope of the debris, making a disturbing clatter and arousing echoes which sent me into a cold perspiration. I lunged for it at once, and regained it without further noise—but a moment afterward the slipping of blocks under my feet raised a sudden and unprecedented din.

The din was my undoing. For, falsely or not, I thought I heard it answered in a terrible way from spaces far behind me. I thought I heard a shrill, whistling sound, like nothing else on earth, and beyond any adequate verbal description. It may have been only my imagination. If so, what followed has a grim irony—since, save for the panic of this thing, the second thing might never have happened.

As it was, my frenzy was absolute and unrelieved. Taking my torch in my hand and clutching feebly at the case, I leaped and bounded wildly ahead with no idea in my brain beyond a mad desire to race out of these nightmare ruins to the waking world of desert and moonlight which lay so far above. I hardly knew it when I reached the mountain of debris which towered into the vast blackness beyond the caved-in roof, and bruised and cut myself repeatedly in scrambling up its steep slope of jagged blocks and fragments. Then came the great disaster. Just as I blindly crossed the summit, unprepared for the sudden dip ahead, my feet slipped utterly and I found myself involved in a mangling avalanche of sliding masonry whose cannon-loud uproar split the black cavern air in a deafening series of earth-shaking reverberations.

I have no recollection of emerging from this chaos, but a momentary fragment of consciousness shews me as plunging and tripping and scrambling along the corridor amidst the clangour—case and torch still with me. Then, just as I approached that primal basalt crypt I had so dreaded, utter madness came. For as the echoes of the avalanche died down, there became audible a repetition of that frightful, alien whistling I thought I had heard before. This time there was no doubt about it—and what was worse, it came from a point not behind but *ahead of me.*

Probably I shrieked aloud then. I have a dim picture of myself as flying through the hellish basalt vault of the Elder Things, and hearing that damnable alien sound piping up from the open, unguarded door of limitless nether blacknesses. There was a wind, too—not merely a cool, damp draught, but a violent, purposeful blast belching savagely and frigidly from that abominable gulf whence the obscene whistling came.

There are memories of leaping and lurching over obstacles of every sort, with that torrent of wind and shrieking sound growing moment by moment, and seeming to curl and twist purposefully around me as it struck out wickedly from the spaces behind and beneath. Though in my rear, that wind had the odd effect of hindering instead of aiding my progress; as if it acted like a noose or lasso thrown around me. Heedless of the noise I made, I clattered over a great barrier of blocks and was again in the structure that led to the surface. I recall glimpsing the archway to the room of machines and almost crying out as I saw the incline leading down to where one of those blasphemous trap-doors must be yawning two levels below. But instead of crying out I muttered over and over to myself that this was all a dream from which I must soon awake. Perhaps I was in camp—perhaps I was at home in Arkham. As these hopes bolstered up my sanity I began to mount the incline to the higher level.

I knew, of course, that I had the four-foot cleft to re-cross, yet was too racked by other fears to realise the full horror until I came almost upon it. On my descent, the leap across had been easy—but could I clear the gap as readily when going uphill, and hampered by fright, exhaustion, the weight of the metal case, and the anomalous backward tug of that dæmon wind? I thought of these things at the last moment, and thought also of the nameless entities which might be lurking in the black abysses below the chasm.

My wavering torch was growing feeble, but I could tell by some obscure memory when I neared the cleft. The chill blasts of wind and the nauseous whistling shrieks behind me were for the moment like a merciful opiate, dulling my imagination to the horror of the yawning gulf ahead. And then I became aware of the added blasts and whistling *in front of me*—tides of abomination surging up through the cleft itself from depths unimagined and unimaginable.

Now, indeed, the essence of pure nightmare was upon me.

Sanity departed—and, ignoring everything except the animal impulse of flight, I merely struggled and plunged upward over the incline's debris as if no gulf had existed. Then I saw the chasm's edge, leaped frenziedly with every ounce of strength I possessed, and was instantly engulfed in a pandæmoniac vortex of loathsome sound and utter, materially tangible blackness.

This is the end of my experience, so far as I can recall. Any further impressions belong wholly to the domain of phantasmagoric delirium. Dream, madness, and memory merged wildly together in a series of fantastic, fragmentary delusions which can have no relation to anything real. There was a hideous fall through incalculable leagues of viscous, sentient darkness, and a babel of noises utterly alien to all that we know of the earth and its organic life. Dormant, rudimentary senses seemed to start into vitality within me, telling of pits and voids peopled by floating horrors and leading to sunless crags and oceans and teeming cities of windowless basalt towers upon which no light ever shone.

Secrets of the primal planet and its immemorial æons flashed through my brain without the aid of sight or sound, and there were known to me things which not even the wildest of my former dreams had ever suggested. And all the while cold fingers of damp vapour clutched and picked at me, and that eldritch, damnable whistling shrieked fiendishly above all the alternations of babel and silence in the whirlpools of darkness around.

Afterward there were visions of the Cyclopean city of my dreams—not in ruins, but just as I had dreamed of it. I was in my conical, non-human body again, and mingled with crowds of the Great Race and the captive minds who carried books up and down the lofty corridors and vast inclines. Then, superimposed upon these pictures, were frightful momentary flashes of a non-visual consciousness involving desperate struggles, a writhing free from clutching tentacles of whistling wind, an insane, bat-like flight through half-solid air, a feverish burrowing through the cyclone-whipped dark, and a wild stumbling and scrambling over fallen masonry.

Once there was a curious, intrusive flash of half-sight—a faint, diffuse suspicion of bluish radiance far overhead. Then there came a dream of wind-pursued climbing and crawling—of wriggling into a blaze of sardonic moonlight through a jumble of debris which slid and collapsed after me amidst a morbid hurricane. It was the evil, monotonous beating of that maddening moonlight which at last told me of the return of what I had once known as the objective, waking world.

I was clawing prone through the sands of the Australian desert, and around me shrieked such a tumult of wind as I had never before known on our planet's surface. My clothing was in rags, and my whole body was a mass of bruises and scratches. Full consciousness returned very slowly, and at no time could I tell just where true memory left off and delirious began. There had seemed to be a mound of titan blocks, an abyss beneath it, a monstrous revelation from the past, and a nightmare horror at the end—but how much of this was real? My flashlight was gone, and likewise any metal case I may have discovered. Had there been such a case—or any abyss—or any mound? Raising my head, I looked behind me, and saw only the sterile, undulant sands of the waste.

The dæmon wind died down, and the bloated, fungoid moon sank reddeningly in the west. I lurched to my feet and began to stagger southwestward toward the camp. What in truth had happened to me? Had I merely collapsed in the desert and dragged a dream-racked body over miles of sand and buried blocks? If not, how could I bear to live any longer? For in this new doubt all my faith in the myth-born unreality of my visions dissolved once more into the hellish older doubting. If that abyss was real, then the Great Race was real—and its blasphemous reachings and seizures in the cosmos-wide vortex of time were no myths or nightmares, but a terrible, soul-shattering actuality.

Had I, in full hideous fact, been drawn back to a pre-human world of a hundred and fifty million years ago in those dark, baffling days of the amnesia? Had my present body been the vehicle of a frightful alien consciousness from palæogean gulfs of time? Had I, as the captive mind of those shambling horrors, indeed known that accursed city of stone in its primordial heyday, and wriggled down those familiar corridors in the loathsome shape of my captor? Were those tormenting dreams of more than twenty years the offspring of stark, monstrous *memories*? Had I once veritably talked with minds from reachless corners of time and space, learned the universe's secrets past and to come, and written the annals of my own world for the metal cases of those titan archives? And were those others—those shocking Elder Things of the mad winds and dæmon pipings—in truth a lingering, lurking menace, waiting and slowly weakening in black abysses while varied shapes of life drag out their multimillennial courses on the planet's age-racked surface?

I do not know. If that abyss and what it held were real, there is no hope. Then, all too truly, there lies upon this world of man a mocking and incredible shadow out of time. But mercifully, there is no proof that these things are other than fresh phases of my myth-born dreams. I did not bring back the metal case that would have been a proof, and so far those subterrene corridors have not been found. If the laws of the universe are kind, they will never be found. But I must tell my son what I saw or thought I saw, and let him use his judgment as a psychologist in gauging the reality of my experience, and communicating this account to others.

I have said that the awful truth behind my tortured years of dreaming hinges absolutely upon the actuality of what I thought I saw in those Cyclopean, buried ruins. It has been hard for me literally to set down the crucial revelation, though no reader can have failed to guess it. Of course, it lay in that book within the metal case—the case which I pried out of its forgotten lair amidst the undisturbed dust of a million centuries. No eye had seen, no hand had touched that book since the advent of man to this planet. And yet, when I flashed my torch upon it in that frightful megalithic abyss, I saw that the queerly pigmented letters on the brittle, æon-browned cellulose pages were not indeed any nameless hieroglyphs of earth's youth. They were, instead, the letters of our familiar alphabet, spelling out the words of the English language in my own handwriting.

The Haunter of the Dark[1]

Lovecraft wrote only one more original story after "The Shadow Out of Time," and it is a tale that in many ways uses the standard Lovecraftian recipe. It combines a specific New England setting—this time, the actual geography of Lovecraft's beloved Providence—with his trademark fear of the unknown. Although superficially similar to his German contemporary Hanns Heinz Ewers's "The Spider," which Lovecraft had read, this story adds the history of an ancient cult, much like the Esoteric Order of Dagon described in "The Shadow over Innsmouth," and an element of cosmicism, with hints that the extraterrestrial stone the Shining Trapezohedron, "a window on all time and space," is the vehicle for one more alien visitor. While hardly the best of Lovecraft's work, it is exemplary of the originality he brought to the realm of supernatural fiction.

[Dedicated to Robert Bloch][2]

I have seen the dark universe yawning
Where the black planets roll without aim,
Where they roll in their horror unheeded,
Without knowledge or lustre or name.[3]

C autious investigators will hesitate to challenge the common belief that Robert Blake was killed by lightning, or by some profound nervous shock derived from an electrical discharge. It is true that the window he faced was unbroken, but Nature has shewn herself capable of many freakish performances. The expression on his face may easily have arisen from some obscure muscular source unrelated to anything he saw, while the entries in his diary are clearly the result of a fantastic imagination aroused by certain local superstitions and by certain old matters he had uncovered. As for the anomalous conditions at

1. The story was written in November 1935 and first appeared in *Weird Tales* 28, no. 5 (December 1936), 538–53, where it was summarized and introduced as follows: "A powerful story about an old church in Providence, Rhode Island, that was shunned and feared by all who knew it."

2. Bloch (1917–1994) was then a young writer in Lovecraft's circle. The author of countless mystery, horror, and science-

fiction stories and screenplays, he is best remembered today for his chilling novel *Psycho* (1959), the basis for the 1960 film by Alfred Hitchcock. "The Haunter of the Dark" apparently was written in response to a reader's letter to *Weird Tales* about Bloch's 1935 story "The Shambler from the Stars." Bloch's tale includes the death of a character easily identified as Lovecraft. The reader suggested that Lovecraft "return the compliment" and dedicate a story to Bloch—which he did.

3. From "Nemesis," a poem by Lovecraft published in 1917.

4. These events were never recorded by Lovecraft.

the deserted church on Federal Hill—the shrewd analyst is not slow in attributing them to some charlatanry, conscious or unconscious, with at least some of which Blake was secretly connected.

For after all, the victim was a writer and painter wholly devoted to the field of myth, dream, terror, and superstition, and avid in his quest for scenes and effects of a bizarre, spectral sort. His earlier stay in the city—a visit to a strange old man as deeply given to occult and forbidden lore as he—had ended amidst death and flame, and it must have been some morbid instinct which drew him back from his home in Milwaukee.[4] He may have known of the old stories despite his statements to the contrary in the diary, and his death may have nipped in the bud some stupendous hoax destined to have a literary reflection.

Among those, however, who have examined and correlated all this evidence, there remain several who cling to less rational and commonplace theories. They are inclined to take much of Blake's diary at its face value, and point significantly to certain facts such as the undoubted genuineness of the old church record, the verified existence of the disliked and unorthodox Starry Wisdom sect prior to 1877, the recorded disappearance of an inquisitive reporter named Edwin M. Lillibridge in 1893, and—above all—the look of monstrous, transfiguring fear on the face of the young writer when he died. It was one of these believers who, moved to fanatical extremes, threw into the bay the curiously angled stone and its strangely adorned metal box found in the old church steeple—the black windowless steeple, and not the tower where Blake's diary said those things originally were. Though widely censured both officially and unofficially, this man—a reputable physician with a taste for odd folklore—averred that he had rid the earth of something too dangerous to rest upon it.

Between these two schools of opinion the reader must judge for himself. The papers have given the tangible details from a sceptical angle, leaving for others the drawing of the picture as Robert Blake saw it—or thought he saw it—or pretended to see it. Now, studying the diary closely, dispassionately, and at leisure, let us summarise the dark chain of events from the expressed point of view of their chief actor.

Young Blake returned to Providence in the winter of 1934–5, taking the upper floor of a venerable dwelling in a grassy court off College Street—on the crest of the great eastward hill near the Brown University campus and behind the marble John Hay Library.[5] It was a cosy and fascinating place, in a little garden oasis of village-like antiquity where huge, friendly cats sunned themselves atop a convenient shed. The square Georgian house had a monitor roof, classic doorway with fan carving, small-paned windows, and all the other earmarks of early nineteenth-century workmanship. Inside were six-panelled doors, wide floor-boards, a curving colonial staircase, white Adam-period mantels, and a rear set of rooms three steps below the general level.

Blake's study, a large southwest chamber, overlooked the front garden on one side, while its west windows—before one of which he had his desk—faced off from the brow of the hill and commanded a splendid view of the lower town's outspread roofs and of the mystical sunsets that flamed behind them. On the far horizon were the open countryside's purple slopes. Against these, some two miles away, rose the spectral hump of Federal Hill, bristling with huddled roofs and steeples whose remote outlines wavered mysteriously, taking fantastic forms as the smoke of the city swirled up and enmeshed them. Blake had a curious sense that he was looking upon some unknown, ethereal world which might or might not vanish in dream if ever he tried to seek it out and enter it in person.

Having sent home for most of his books, Blake bought some

5. Donovan Loucks identifies this as the Samuel B. Mumford House, originally built in 1825 at 66 College Street. In 1959 it was moved to 65 Prospect Street. Lovecraft lived in the room described as Blake's.

The Samuel D. Mumford House, in 1990. Photograph courtesy of Will Hart

6. A principal building on the campus of the Rhode Island School of Design, built in 1902–3.

7. This being the Providence County Courthouse, at 250 Benefit Street, built in 1932.

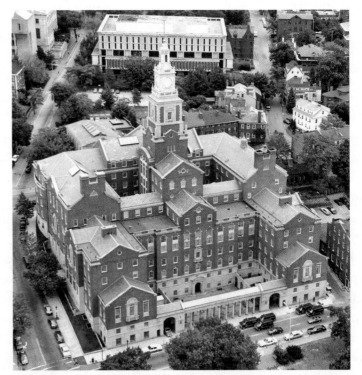

Providence County Courthouse, 250 Benefit Street, in 1990.
Photograph courtesy of Will Hart

antique furniture suitable to his quarters and settled down to write and paint—living alone, and attending to the simple housework himself. His studio was in a north attic room, where the panes of the monitor roof furnished admirable lighting. During that first winter he produced five of his best-known short stories—"The Burrower Beneath," "The Stairs in the Crypt," "Shaggai," "In the Vale of Pnath," and "The Feaster from the Stars"—and painted seven canvases; studies of nameless, unhuman monsters, and profoundly alien, non-terrestrial landscapes.

At sunset he would often sit at his desk and gaze dreamily off at the outspread west—the dark towers of Memorial Hall[6] just below, the Georgian court-house belfry,[7] the lofty pinnacles of the downtown section, and that shimmering, spire-crowned mound in the distance whose unknown streets and labyrinthine gables so potently provoked his fancy. From his few local acquaintances he learned that the far-off slope was a vast Italian quarter, though most of the houses were remnants of older Yankee and Irish days. Now and then he would train his field-glasses on that spectral, unreachable world beyond the curling smoke; picking out individual roofs and chimneys and steeples, and speculating upon the bizarre and curious mysteries they might house. Even with optical aid Federal Hill seemed somehow alien, half fabulous, and linked to the unreal, intangible marvels of Blake's own tales and pictures. The feeling would persist long after the hill had faded into the violet, lamp-starred twilight, and the court-house floodlights and the red Industrial Trust beacon[8] had blazed up to make the night grotesque.

Of all the distant objects on Federal Hill, a certain huge, dark church most fascinated Blake. It stood out with especial distinctness at certain hours of the day, and at sunset the great tower and tapering steeple loomed blackly against the flaming sky. It seemed to rest on especially high ground; for the grimy façade, and the obliquely seen north side with sloping roof and the tops of great pointed windows, rose boldly above the tangle of surrounding ridgepoles and chimney-pots. Peculiarly grim and austere, it appeared to be built of stone, stained and weathered with the smoke and storms of a century and more. The style, so far as the glass could shew, was that earliest experimental form of Gothic revival which preceded the stately Upjohn period[9] and held over some of the outlines and proportions of the Georgian age. Perhaps it was reared around 1810 or 1815.[10]

As months passed, Blake watched the far-off, forbidding structure with an oddly mounting interest. Since the vast windows were never lighted, he knew that it must be vacant. The longer he watched, the more his imagination worked, till at length he began to fancy curious things. He believed that a vague, singular aura of desolation hovered over the place, so that even the pigeons and swallows shunned its smoky eaves. Around other towers and belfries his glass would reveal great flocks of birds, but here they never rested. At least, that is what he thought and set down in his diary. He pointed the place out to several friends, but none of them had even been on Federal Hill or possessed the faintest notion of what the church was or had been.

In the spring a deep restlessness gripped Blake. He had begun his long-planned novel—based on a supposed survival of the witch-cult in Maine—but was strangely unable to make progress with it. More and more he would sit at his westward window and

8. Built in 1927 at 111 Westminster Street, the Industrial Trust Tower, later the Bank of America Building, is now vacant and dark. It was rumored to have been the model for the home of the *Daily Planet*, the newspaper that employed Clark Kent (Superman).

The beacon atop the Bank of America Building (formerly Industrial Trust), in 1990. Photograph courtesy of Will Hart

9. Richard Upjohn (1802–1878) was an English-born architect who designed numerous Gothic Revival churches in America.

10. The church in question is certainly St. John's Catholic Church, which was located on Atwells Avenue, the main thoroughfare of Federal Hill. Erected in 1871, it was demolished in 1992. The steeple was destroyed in a storm in 1935.

The St. John's Roman Catholic Church
(1871), in 1990.
Photograph courtesy of Will Hart

An enlargement of the view from
Prospect Terrace in 1990, showing the
church tower in the center.
Photograph courtesy of Will Hart

gaze at the distant hill and the black, frowning steeple shunned by the birds. When the delicate leaves came out on the garden boughs the world was filled with a new beauty, but Blake's restlessness was merely increased. It was then that he first thought of crossing the city and climbing bodily up that fabulous slope into the smoke-wreathed world of dream.

Late in April, just before the æon-shadowed Walpurgis time, Blake made his first trip into the unknown. Plodding through the endless downtown streets and the bleak, decayed squares beyond, he came finally upon the ascending avenue of century-worn steps, sagging Doric porches, and blear-paned cupolas which he felt must lead up to the long-known, unreachable world beyond the mists. There were dingy blue-and-white street signs which meant nothing to him, and presently he noted the strange, dark faces of the drifting crowds, and the foreign signs over curious shops in brown, decade-weathered buildings. Nowhere could he find any of the objects he had seen from afar; so that once more he half fancied that the Federal Hill of that distant view was a dream-world never to be trod by living human feet.

Now and then a battered church façade or crumbling spire came in sight, but never the blackened pile that he sought. When he asked a shopkeeper about a great stone church the man smiled and shook his head, though he spoke English freely. As Blake climbed higher, the region seemed stranger and stranger, with bewildering mazes of brooding brown alleys leading eternally off to the south. He crossed two or three broad avenues, and once thought he glimpsed a familiar tower. Again he asked a merchant about the massive church of stone, and this time he could have sworn that the plea of ignorance was feigned. The dark man's face had a look of fear which he tried to hide, and Blake saw him make a curious sign with his right hand.

Then suddenly a black spire stood out against the cloudy sky on his left, above the tiers of brown roofs lining the tangled southerly alleys. Blake knew at once what it was, and plunged toward it through the squalid, unpaved lanes that climbed from the avenue. Twice he lost his way, but he somehow dared not ask any of the patriarchs or housewives who sat on their doorsteps, or any of the children who shouted and played in the mud of the shadowy lanes.

Closeup of the church tower in 1990
Photograph courtesy of Will Hart

At last he saw the tower plain against the southwest, and a
huge stone bulk rose darkly at the end of an alley. Presently he
stood in a windswept open square, quaintly cobblestoned, with a
high bank wall on the farther side.[11] This was the end of his quest;
for upon the wide, iron-railed, weed-grown plateau which the wall
supported—a separate, lesser world raised fully six feet above the
surrounding streets—there stood a grim, titan bulk whose identity, despite Blake's new perspective, was beyond dispute.

The vacant church was in a state of great decrepitude. Some
of the high stone buttresses had fallen, and several delicate finials lay half lost among the brown, neglected weeds and grasses.
The sooty Gothic windows were largely unbroken, though many
of the stone mullions were missing. Blake wondered how the
obscurely painted panes could have survived so well, in view
of the known habits of small boys the world over. The massive
doors were intact and tightly closed. Around the top of the bank
wall, fully enclosing the grounds, was a rusty iron fence whose
gate—at the head of a flight of steps from the square—was vis-

St. John's Church, the model for the Starry Wisdom Church. Artist: Jason
C. Eckhardt, copyright © Jason C. Eckhardt 2013, reprinted with permission

ibly padlocked. The path from the gate to the building was completely overgrown. Desolation and decay hung like a pall above
the place, and in the birdless eaves and black, ivyless walls Blake
felt a touch of the dimly sinister beyond his power to define.

There were very few people in the square, but Blake saw a
policeman at the northerly end and approached him with questions about the church. He was a great wholesome Irishman, and
it seemed odd that he would do little more than make the sign
of the cross and mutter that people never spoke of that building.

When Blake pressed him he said very hurriedly that the Italian priests warned everybody against it, vowing that a monstrous evil had once dwelt there and left its mark. He himself had heard dark whispers of it from his father, who recalled certain sounds and rumours from his boyhood.

There had been a bad sect there in the ould days—an outlaw sect that called up awful things from some unknown gulf of night. It had taken a good priest to exorcise what had come, though there did be those who said that merely the light could do it. If Father O'Malley were alive there would be many the thing he could tell. But now there was nothing to do but let it alone. It hurt nobody now, and those that owned it were dead or far away. They had run away like rats after the threatening talk in '77, when people began to mind the way folks vanished now and then in the neighbourhood. Some day the city would step in and take the property for lack of heirs, but little good would come of anybody's touching it. Better it be left alone for the years to topple, lest things be stirred that ought to rest forever in their black abyss.

After the policeman had gone Blake stood staring at the sullen steepled pile. It excited him to find that the structure seemed as sinister to others as to him, and he wondered what grain of truth might lie behind the old tales the bluecoat had repeated. Probably they were mere legends evoked by the evil look of the place, but even so, they were like a strange coming to life of one of his own stories.

The afternoon sun came out from behind dispersing clouds, but seemed unable to light up the stained, sooty walls of the old temple that towered on its high plateau. It was odd that the green of spring had not touched the brown, withered growths in the raised, iron-fenced yard. Blake found himself edging nearer the raised area and examining the bank wall and rusted fence for possible avenues of ingress. There was a terrible lure about the blackened fane[12] which was not to be resisted. The fence had no opening near the steps, but around on the north side were some missing bars. He could go up the steps and walk around on the narrow coping outside the fence till he came to the gap. If the people feared the place so wildly, he would encounter no interference.

12. A temple or church; a place dedicated to a deity.

He was on the embankment and almost inside the fence before anyone noticed him. Then, looking down, he saw the few people in the square edging away and making the same sign with their right hands that the shopkeeper in the avenue had made. Several windows were slammed down, and a fat woman darted into the street and pulled some small children inside a rickety, unpainted house. The gap in the fence was very easy to pass through, and before long Blake found himself wading amidst the rotting, tangled growths of the deserted yard. Here and there the worn stump of a headstone told him that there had once been burials in this field; but that, he saw, must have been very long ago. The sheer bulk of the church was oppressive now that he was close to it, but he conquered his mood and approached to try the three great doors in the façade. All were securely locked, so he began a circuit of the Cyclopean building in quest of some minor and more penetrable opening. Even then he could not be sure that he wished to enter that haunt of desertion and shadow, yet the pull of its strangeness dragged him on automatically.

A yawning and unprotected cellar window in the rear furnished the needed aperture. Peering in, Blake saw a subterrene gulf of cobwebs and dust faintly litten by the western sun's filtered rays. Debris, old barrels, and ruined boxes and furniture of numerous sorts met his eye, though over everything lay a shroud of dust which softened all sharp outlines. The rusted remains of a hot-air furnace shewed that the building had been used and kept in shape as late as mid-Victorian times.

Acting almost without conscious initiative, Blake crawled through the window and let himself down to the dust-carpeted and debris-strown concrete floor. The vaulted cellar was a vast one, without partitions; and in a corner far to the right, amid dense shadows, he saw a black archway evidently leading upstairs. He felt a peculiar sense of oppression at being actually within the great spectral building, but kept it in check as he cautiously scouted about—finding a still-intact barrel amid the dust, and rolling it over to the open window to provide for his exit. Then, bracing himself, he crossed the wide, cobweb-festooned space toward the arch. Half choked with the omnipresent dust, and covered with ghostly gossamer fibres, he reached and began to climb the worn stone steps which rose into the darkness. He had no light, but groped carefully with his hands. After a sharp turn he felt a closed door ahead, and a little fumbling revealed its ancient latch. It opened inward, and beyond it he saw a dimly illumined corridor lined with worm-eaten panelling.

Once on the ground floor, Blake began exploring in a rapid fashion. All the inner doors were unlocked, so that he freely passed from room to room. The colossal nave was an almost eldritch place with its drifts and mountains of dust over box pews, altar, hourglass pulpit, and sounding-board and its titanic ropes of cobweb stretching among the pointed arches of the gallery and entwining the clustered Gothic columns. Over all this hushed desolation played a hideous leaden light as the declining afternoon sun sent its rays through the strange, half-blackened panes of the great apsidal windows.

The paintings on those windows were so obscured by soot that Blake could scarcely decipher what they had represented, but from the little he could make out he did not like them. The designs were largely conventional, and his knowledge of obscure symbolism told him much concerning some of the ancient patterns. The few saints depicted bore expressions distinctly open to criticism, while one of the windows seemed to shew merely a dark space with spirals of curious luminosity scattered about in it. Turning away from the windows, Blake noticed that the cobwebbed cross above the altar was not of the ordinary kind, but resembled the primordial ankh or crux ansata of shadowy Egypt.[13]

In a rear vestry room beside the apse Blake found a rotting desk and ceiling-high shelves of mildewed, disintegrating books. Here for the first time he received a positive shock of objective horror, for the titles of those books told him much. They were the black, forbidden things which most sane people have never even heard of, or have heard of only in furtive, timorous whispers; the banned and dreaded repositories of equivocal secrets and immemorial formulæ which have trickled down the stream of time from the days of man's youth, and the dim, fabulous days before man was. He had himself read many of them—a Latin version of the abhorred *Necronomicon*, the sinister *Liber Ivonis*, the infamous *Cultes des Goules* of Comte d'Erlette, the *Unaussprechlichen Kulten* of von Junzt, and old Ludvig Prinn's hellish *De Vermis Mysteriis*. But there were others he had known merely by reputa-

13. The "key of life," as it is popularly known (the symbol is also a hieroglyph meaning "life"), is used by pagan cults as well as those that aspire to Egyptian origins. Its significance in Egyptian tomb art, where it is frequently found, is unclear, although an obvious possible point of reference is the afterlife. In 1869, Thomas Inman, in *Ancient Pagan and Modern Christian Symbolism*, made the suggestion that the symbol "represents the male triad and the female unit, under a decent form. . . . In some remarkable sculptures, where the sun's rays are represented as terminating in hands, the offerings which these bring are many a crux ansata, emblematic of the truth that a fruitful union is a gift from the deity." However, there are numerous other theories of the meaning of the "handed cross." Ironically, the symbol adorns the favorite necklace of Death, elder sister of Dream of the Endless, the subject of Neil Gaiman's *Sandman* series.

14. The Book of Dzyan (comprising the Stanzas of Dzyan) is a reputedly ancient text of Tibetan origin, the basis for Helena Petrovna Blavatsky's 1875 mystical book *The Secret Doctrine*. Blavatsky, the founder of the Theosophical movement, claimed to have seen the work while studying in Tibet and to have extracted texts in the original language of Senzar, "the secret sacerdotal tongue" (Blavatsky, *The Secret Doctrine* [New York: Tarcher, 2009], xliii), also working with existing Tibetan and Sanskrit translations. She described the work as "not in the possession of European Libraries" and "utterly unknown to our Philologists" (xxii).

tion or not at all—the Pnakotic Manuscripts, the *Book of Dzyan*,[14] and a crumbling volume in wholly unidentifiable characters yet with certain symbols and diagrams shudderingly recognisable to the occult student. Clearly, the lingering local rumours had not lied. This place had once been the seat of an evil older than mankind and wider than the known universe.

In the ruined desk was a small leather-bound record-book filled with entries in some odd cryptographic medium. The manuscript writing consisted of the common traditional symbols used today in astronomy and anciently in alchemy, astrology, and other dubious arts—the devices of the sun, moon, planets, aspects, and zodiacal signs—here massed in solid pages of text, with divisions and paragraphings suggesting that each symbol answered to some alphabetical letter.

In the hope of later solving the cryptogram, Blake bore off this volume in his coat pocket. Many of the great tomes on the shelves fascinated him unutterably, and he felt tempted to borrow them at some later time. He wondered how they could have remained undisturbed so long. Was he the first to conquer the clutching, pervasive fear which had for nearly sixty years protected this deserted place from visitors?

Having now thoroughly explored the ground floor, Blake ploughed again through the dust of the spectral nave to the front vestibule, where he had seen a door and staircase presumably leading up to the blackened tower and steeple—objects so long familiar to him at a distance. The ascent was a choking experience, for dust lay thick, while the spiders had done their worst in this constricted place. The staircase was a spiral with high, narrow wooden treads, and now and then Blake passed a clouded window looking dizzily out over the city. Though he had seen no ropes below, he expected to find a bell or peal of bells in the tower whose narrow, louver-boarded lancet windows his field-glass had studied so often. Here he was doomed to disappointment; for when he attained the top of the stairs he found the tower chamber vacant of chimes, and clearly devoted to vastly different purposes.

The room, about fifteen feet square, was faintly lighted by four lancet windows, one on each side, which were glazed within their screening of decayed louver-boards. These had been further fitted with tight, opaque screens, but the latter were now largely rotted away. In the centre of the dust-laden floor rose a curiously angled stone pillar some four feet in height and two in average diameter, covered on each side with bizarre, crudely incised, and wholly unrecognisable hieroglyphs. On this pillar rested a metal box of peculiarly asymmetrical form; its hinged lid thrown back, and its interior holding what looked beneath the decade-deep dust to be an egg-shaped or irregularly spherical object some four inches through. Around the pillar in a rough circle were seven high-backed Gothic chairs still largely intact, while behind them, ranging along the dark-panelled walls, were seven colossal images of crumbling, black-painted plaster, resembling more than anything else the cryptic carven megaliths of mysterious Easter Island.[15] In one corner of the cobwebbed chamber a ladder was built into the wall, leading up to the closed trap-door of the windowless steeple above.

As Blake grew accustomed to the feeble light he noticed odd bas-reliefs on the strange open box of yellowish metal. Approaching, he tried to clear the dust away with his hands and handkerchief, and saw that the figurings were of a monstrous and utterly alien kind; depicting entities which, though seemingly alive, resembled no known life-form ever evolved on this planet. The four-inch seeming sphere turned out to be a nearly black, red-striated polyhedron with many irregular flat surfaces; either a very remarkable crystal of some sort, or an artificial object of carved and highly polished mineral matter. It did not touch the bottom of the box, but was held suspended by means of a metal band around its centre, with seven queerly designed supports extending horizontally to angles of the box's inner wall near the top. This stone, once exposed, exerted upon Blake an almost alarming fascination. He could scarcely tear his eyes from it, and as he looked at its glistening surfaces he almost fancied it was transparent, with half-formed worlds of wonder within. Into his mind floated pictures of alien orbs with great stone towers, and other orbs with titan mountains and no mark of life, and still remoter spaces where only a stirring in vague blacknesses told of the presence of consciousness and will.

15. See "The Shadow over Innsmouth," note 32, above.

16. The *Providence Evening Telegram* was founded in 1880; the *Sunday Telegram* was its companion newspaper. In 1906, the *Telegram* became the *Evening Tribune and Telegram*, and eventually the *Telegram* portion of the name was dropped.

17. David Haden has suggested that "Bowen" is modeled on Charles Edwin Wilbour (1833–1896), a Rhode Island–born graduate of Brown University who became a leading Egyptologist (http://tentaclii .wordpress.com/2013/05/03/looking-into-the-shining-trapezohedron/). However, Wilbour did not travel to Egypt until after 1874. A more likely candidate to have discovered the Shining Trapezohedron is the Prussian archaeologist Carl Richard Lepsius (1810–1884), called the father of modern Egyptology. Lepsius traveled through Egypt in 1843. The report of his travels, *Discoveries in Egypt, Ethiopia, and the Peninsula of Sinai, in the Years 1842–45* (London: Richard Bentley, 1852), makes no mention of the find, however, and there is no known connection between Lepsius and Providence, Rhode Island. Lepsius is also remembered as the first to translate *The Egyptian Book of the Dead*, an ancient funerary text, in 1842; Lovecraft owned a 1923 edition of the first English translation, by E. A. Wallis Budge. According to S. T. Joshi's *I Am Providence*, Lovecraft may have studied and written about Egyptian myths as early as age six.

When he did look away, it was to notice a somewhat singular mound of dust in the far corner near the ladder to the steeple. Just why it took his attention he could not tell, but something in its contours carried a message to his unconscious mind. Ploughing toward it, and brushing aside the hanging cobwebs as he went, he began to discern something grim about it. Hand and handkerchief soon revealed the truth, and Blake gasped with a baffling mixture of emotions. It was a human skeleton, and it must have been there for a very long time. The clothing was in shreds, but some buttons and fragments of cloth bespoke a man's grey suit. There were other bits of evidence—shoes, metal clasps, huge buttons for round cuffs, a stickpin of bygone pattern, a reporter's badge with the name of the old *Providence Telegram*,[16] and a crumbling leather pocketbook. Blake examined the latter with care, finding within it several bills of antiquated issue, a celluloid advertising calendar for 1893, some cards with the name "Edwin M. Lillibridge," and a paper covered with pencilled memoranda.

This paper held much of a puzzling nature, and Blake read it carefully at the dim westward window. Its disjointed text included such phrases as the following:

Prof. Enoch Bowen home from Egypt May 1844—buys old Free-Will Church in July—his archæological work & studies in occult well known.[17]

Dr. Drowne of 4th Baptist warns against Starry Wisdom in sermon Dec. 29, 1844.

Congregation 97 by end of '45.

1846—3 disappearances—first mention of Shining Trapezohedron.

7 disappearances 1848—stories of blood sacrifice begin.

Investigation 1853 comes to nothing—stories of sounds.

Fr O'Malley tells of devil-worship with box found in great Egyptian ruins—says they call up something that can't exist in light. Flees a little light, and banished by strong light. Then has to be summoned again. Probably got this from death-bed confession of Francis X. Feeney, who had joined Starry

Wisdom in '49. These people say the Shining Trapezohedron shews them heaven & other worlds, & that the Haunter of the Dark tells them secrets in some way.

Story of Orrin B. Eddy 1857. They call it up by gazing at the crystal, & have a secret language of their own.

200 or more in cong. 1863, exclusive of men at front.

Irish boys mob church in 1869 after Patrick Regan's disappearance.

Veiled article in J. March 14, '72, but people don't talk about it.

6 disappearances 1876—secret committee calls on Mayor Doyle.[18]

Action promised Feb. 1877—church closes in April.

Gang—Federal Hill Boys—threaten Dr.—and vestrymen in May.

181 persons leave city before end of '77—mention no names.

Ghost stories begin around 1880—try to ascertain truth of report that no human being has entered church since 1877.

Ask Lanigan for photograph of place taken 1851 . . .

Restoring the paper to the pocketbook and placing the latter in his coat, Blake turned to look down at the skeleton in the dust. The implications of the notes were clear, and there could be no doubt but that this man had come to the deserted edifice forty-two years before in quest of a newspaper sensation which no one else had been bold enough to attempt. Perhaps no one else had known of his plan—who could tell? But he had never returned to his paper. Had some bravely-suppressed fear risen to overcome him and bring on sudden heart-failure? Blake stooped over the gleaming bones and noted their peculiar state. Some of them were badly scattered, and a few seemed oddly *dissolved* at the ends. Others were strangely yellowed, with vague suggestions of charring. This charring extended to some of the fragments of clothing. The skull was in a very peculiar state—stained yellow,

18. The Republican mayor of Providence in 1876 was Thomas A. Doyle. He served for eighteen years and made many civic improvements to the town as its population doubled during his terms of office.

"He had come to the deserted edifice in quest of a newspaper sensation."
Weird Tales 28, no. 5 (December 1936) (artist: Virgil Finlay)

and with a charred aperture in the top as if some powerful acid had eaten through the solid bone. What had happened to the skeleton during its four decades of silent entombment here Blake could not imagine.

Before he realised it, he was looking at the stone again, and letting its curious influence call up a nebulous pageantry in his mind. He saw processions of robed, hooded figures whose outlines were not human, and looked on endless leagues of desert lined with carved, sky-reaching monoliths. He saw towers and walls in nighted depths under the sea, and vortices of space where wisps of black mist floated before thin shimmerings of cold purple haze. And beyond all else he glimpsed an infinite gulf of darkness, where solid and semi-solid forms were known only by their windy stirrings, and cloudy patterns of force seemed to superimpose order on chaos and hold forth a key to all the paradoxes and arcana of the worlds we know.

Then all at once the spell was broken by an access of gnawing, indeterminate panic fear. Blake choked and turned away from the stone, conscious of some formless alien presence close to him and watching him with horrible intentness. He felt entangled with something—something which was not in the stone, but which had looked through it at him—something which would ceaselessly follow him with a cognition that was not physical sight. Plainly, the place was getting on his nerves—as well it might in view of his gruesome find. The light was waning, too, and since he had no illuminant with him he knew he would have to be leaving soon.

It was then, in the gathering twilight, that he thought he saw a faint trace of luminosity in the crazily angled stone. He had tried to look away from it, but some obscure compulsion drew his eyes back. Was there a subtle phosphorescence of radioactivity about the thing? What was it that the dead man's notes had said concerning a *Shining Trapezohedron*? What, anyway, was this abandoned lair of cosmic evil? What had been done here, and what might still be lurking in the bird-shunned shadows? It seemed now as if an elusive touch of fœtor had arisen somewhere close by, though its source was not apparent. Blake seized the cover of the long-open box and snapped it down. It moved easily on its alien hinges, and closed completely over the unmistakably glowing stone.

At the sharp click of that closing a soft stirring sound seemed to come from the steeple's eternal blackness overhead, beyond the trap-door. Rats, without question—the only living things to reveal their presence in this accursed pile since he had entered it. And yet that stirring in the steeple frightened him horribly, so that he plunged almost wildly down the spiral stairs, across the ghoulish nave, into the vaulted basement, out amidst the gathering dusk of the deserted square, and down through the teeming, fear-haunted alleys and avenues of Federal Hill toward the sane central streets and the home-like brick sidewalks of the college district.

During the days which followed, Blake told no one of his expedition. Instead, he read much in certain books, examined long years of newspaper files downtown, and worked feverishly at the cryptogram in that leather volume from the cobwebbed vestry room. The cipher, he soon saw, was no simple one; and

19. See *At the Mountains of Madness* (pp. 457–572, above).

20. See *The Case of Charles Dexter Ward*, note 185, above.

after a long period of endeavour he felt sure that its language could not be English, Latin, Greek, French, Spanish, Italian, or German. Evidently he would have to draw upon the deepest wells of his strange erudition.

Every evening the old impulse to gaze westward returned, and he saw the black steeple as of yore amongst the bristling roofs of a distant and half-fabulous world. But now it held a fresh note of terror for him. He knew the heritage of evil lore it masked, and with the knowledge his vision ran riot in queer new ways. The birds of spring were returning, and as he watched their sunset flights he fancied they avoided the gaunt, lone spire as never before. When a flock of them approached it, he thought, they would wheel and scatter in panic confusion—and he could guess at the wild twitterings which failed to reach him across the intervening miles.

It was in June that Blake's diary told of his victory over the cryptogram. The text was, he found, in the dark Aklo language used by certain cults of evil antiquity, and known to him in a halting way through previous researches. The diary is strangely reticent about what Blake deciphered, but he was patently awed and disconcerted by his results. There are references to a Haunter of the Dark awaked by gazing into the Shining Trapezohedron, and insane conjectures about the black gulfs of chaos from which it was called. The being is spoken of as holding all knowledge, and demanding monstrous sacrifices. Some of Blake's entries shew fear lest the thing, which he seemed to regard as summoned, stalk abroad; though he adds that the street-lights form a bulwark which cannot be crossed.

Of the Shining Trapezohedron he speaks often, calling it a window on all time and space, and tracing its history from the days it was fashioned on dark Yuggoth, before ever the Old Ones brought it to earth. It was treasured and placed in its curious box by the crinoid things of Antarctica,[19] salvaged from their ruins by the serpent-men of Valusia, and peered at æons later in Lemuria by the first human beings. It crossed strange lands and stranger seas, and sank with Atlantis before a Minoan fisher meshed it in his net and sold it to swarthy merchants from nighted Khem. The Pharaoh Nephren-Ka[20] built around it a temple with a windowless crypt, and did that which caused his name to be stricken from all monuments and records. Then it slept in the ruins of that evil fane which the priests and the new Pharaoh destroyed, till the delver's spade once more brought it forth to curse mankind.

Early in July the newspapers oddly supplement Blake's entries, though in so brief and casual a way that only the diary has called general attention to their contribution. It appears that a new fear had been growing on Federal Hill since a stranger had entered the dreaded church. The Italians whispered of unaccustomed stirrings and bumpings and scrapings in the dark windowless steeple, and called on their priests to banish an entity which haunted their dreams. Something, they said, was constantly watching at a door to see if it were dark enough to venture forth. Press items mentioned the long-standing local superstitions, but failed to shed much light on the earlier background of the horror. It was obvious that the young reporters of today are no antiquarians. In writing of these things in his diary, Blake expresses a curious kind of remorse, and talks of the duty of burying the Shining Trapezohedron and of banishing what he had evoked by letting daylight into the hideous jutting spire. At the same time, however, he displays the dangerous extent of his fascination, and admits a morbid longing—pervading even his dreams—to visit the accursed tower and gaze again into the cosmic secrets of the glowing stone.

Then something in the *Journal* on the morning of July 17 threw the diarist into a veritable fever of horror. It was only a variant of the other half-humorous items about the Federal Hill restlessness, but to Blake it was somehow very terrible indeed. In the night a thunderstorm had put the city's lighting-system out of commission for a full hour, and in that black interval the Italians had nearly gone mad with fright. Those living near the dreaded church had sworn that the thing in the steeple had taken advantage of the street-lamps' absence and gone down into the body of the church, flopping and bumping around in a viscous, altogether dreadful way. Toward the last it had bumped up to the tower, where there were sounds of the shattering of glass. It could go wherever the darkness reached, but light would always send it fleeing.

When the current blazed on again there had been a shocking commotion in the tower, for even the feeble light trickling through the grime-blackened, louver-boarded windows was too

21. In 1863, the publishers of the *Providence Journal* began publication of the *Providence Evening Bulletin*. The newspaper continued in existence until June 2, 1995; the name, if not the paper, continued when, a week later, it was combined with the *Journal* into the *Providence Journal-Bulletin*. All traces of the *Bulletin* disappeared in 1998 when the name was shortened to the *Providence Journal*.

much for the thing. It had bumped and slithered up into its tenebrous steeple just in time—for a long dose of light would have sent it back into the abyss whence the crazy stranger had called it. During the dark hour praying crowds had clustered round the church in the rain with lighted candles and lamps somehow shielded with folded paper and umbrellas—a guard of light to save the city from the nightmare that stalks in darkness. Once, those nearest the church declared, the outer door had rattled hideously.

But even this was not the worst. That evening in the *Bulletin*[21] Blake read of what the reporters had found. Aroused at last to the whimsical news value of the scare, a pair of them had defied the frantic crowds of Italians and crawled into the church through the cellar window after trying the doors in vain. They found the dust of the vestibule and of the spectral nave ploughed up in a singular way, with bits of rotted cushions and satin pew-linings scattered curiously around. There was a bad odour everywhere, and here and there were bits of yellow stain and patches of what looked like charring. Opening the door to the tower, and pausing a moment at the suspicion of a scraping sound above, they found the narrow spiral stairs wiped roughly clean.

In the tower itself a similarly half-swept condition existed. They spoke of the heptagonal stone pillar, the overturned Gothic chairs, and the bizarre plaster images; though strangely enough the metal box and the old mutilated skeleton were not mentioned. What disturbed Blake the most—except for the hints of stains and charring and bad odours—was the final detail that explained the crashing glass. Every one of the tower's lancet windows was broken, and two of them had been darkened in a crude and hurried way by the stuffing of satin pew-linings and cushion-horsehair into the spaces between the slanting exterior louver-boards. More satin fragments and bunches of horsehair lay scattered around the newly swept floor, as if someone had been interrupted in the act of restoring the tower to the absolute blackness of its tightly curtained days.

Yellowish stains and charred patches were found on the ladder to the windowless spire, but when a reporter climbed up, opened the horizontally sliding trap-door and shot a feeble flashlight beam into the black and strangely fœtid space, he saw nothing but darkness, and an heterogeneous litter of shapeless fragments near the aperture. The verdict, of course, was charlatanry. Somebody had played a joke on the superstitious hill-dwellers, or else some fanatic had striven to bolster up their fears for their own supposed good. Or perhaps some of the younger and more sophisticated dwellers had staged an elaborate hoax on the outside world. There was an amusing aftermath when the police sent an officer to verify the reports. Three men in succession found ways of evading the assignment, and the fourth went very reluctantly and returned very soon without adding to the account given by the reporters.

From this point onward Blake's diary shews a mounting tide of insidious horror and nervous apprehension. He upbraids himself for not doing something, and speculates wildly on the consequences of another electrical breakdown. It has been verified that on three occasions—during thunderstorms—he telephoned the electric light company in a frantic vein and asked that desperate precautions against a lapse of power be taken. Now and then his entries shew concern over the failure of the reporters to find the metal box and stone, and the strangely marred old skeleton, when they explored the shadowy tower room. He assumed that these things had been removed—whither, and by whom or what, he could only guess. But his worst fears concerned himself, and the kind of unholy rapport he felt to exist between his mind and that lurking horror in the distant steeple—that monstrous thing of night which his rashness had called out of the ultimate black spaces. He seemed to feel a constant tugging at his will, and callers of that period remember how he would sit abstractedly at his desk and stare out of the west window at that far-off, spire-bristling mound beyond the swirling smoke of the city. His entries dwell monotonously on certain terrible dreams, and of a strengthening of the unholy rapport in his sleep. There is mention of a night when he awaked to find himself fully dressed, outdoors, and headed automatically down College Hill toward the west. Again and again he dwells on the fact that the thing in the steeple knows where to find him.

The week following July 30 is recalled as the time of Blake's partial breakdown. He did not dress, and ordered all his food by telephone. Visitors remarked the cords he kept near his bed, and he said that sleep-walking had forced him to bind his ankles every night with knots which would probably hold or else waken him with the labour of untying. In his diary he told of the hideous experience which had brought the collapse. After retiring on the night of the 30th, he had suddenly found himself groping about in an almost black space. All he could see were short, faint, horizontal streaks of bluish light, but he could smell an overpowering fœtor and hear a curious jumble of soft, furtive sounds above him. Whenever he moved he stumbled over something, and at each noise there would come a sort of answering sound from above—a vague stirring, mixed with the cautious sliding of wood on wood.

Once his groping hands encountered a pillar of stone with a vacant top, whilst later he found himself clutching the rungs of a ladder built into the wall, and fumbling his uncertain way upward toward some region of intenser stench where a hot, searing blast beat down against him. Before his eyes a kaleidoscopic range of phantasmal images played, all of them dissolving at intervals into the picture of a vast, unplumbed abyss of night wherein whirled suns and worlds of an even profounder blackness. He thought of the ancient legends of Ultimate Chaos, at whose centre sprawls the blind idiot god Azathoth, Lord of All Things, encircled by his flopping horde of mindless and amorphous dancers, and lulled by the thin monotonous piping of a dæmoniac flute held in nameless paws.

Then a sharp report from the outer world broke through his stupor and roused him to the unutterable horror of his position. What it was, he never knew—perhaps it was some belated peal from the fireworks heard all summer on Federal Hill as the dwellers hail their various patron saints, or the saints of their native villages in Italy. In any event he shrieked aloud, dropped frantically from the ladder, and stumbled blindly across the obstructed floor of the almost lightless chamber that encompassed him.

He knew instantly where he was, and plunged recklessly down the narrow spiral staircase, tripping and bruising himself at every turn. There was a nightmare flight through a vast cobwebbed nave whose ghostly arches reached up to realms of leering shadow, a sightless scramble through a littered basement, a climb to regions of air and street-lights outside, and a mad racing down a spectral hill of gibbering gables, across a grim, silent city of tall black towers, and up the steep eastward precipice to his own ancient door.

On regaining consciousness in the morning he found himself lying on his study floor fully dressed. Dirt and cobwebs covered him, and every inch of his body seemed sore and bruised. When he faced the mirror he saw that his hair was badly scorched while a trace of strange, evil odour seemed to cling to his upper outer clothing. It was then that his nerves broke down. Thereafter, lounging exhaustedly about in a dressing-gown, he did little but stare from his west window, shiver at the threat of thunder, and make wild entries in his diary.

The great storm broke just before midnight on August 8th. Lightning struck repeatedly in all parts of the city, and two remarkable fireballs were reported. The rain was torrential, while a constant fusillade of thunder brought sleeplessness to thousands. Blake was utterly frantic in his fear for the lighting system, and tried to telephone the company around 1 a.m. though by that time service had been temporarily cut off in the interest of safety. He recorded everything in his diary—the large, nervous, and often undecipherable hieroglyphs telling their own story of growing frenzy and despair, and of entries scrawled blindly in the dark.

He had to keep the house dark in order to see out the window, and it appears that most of his time was spent at his desk, peering anxiously through the rain across the glistening miles of downtown roofs at the constellation of distant lights marking Federal Hill. Now and then he would fumblingly make an entry in his diary, so that detached phrases such as "The lights must not go"; "It knows where I am"; "I must destroy it"; and "It is calling to me, but perhaps it means no injury this time"; are found scattered down two of the pages.

Then the lights went out all over the city. It happened at 2:12 A.M. according to power-house records, but Blake's diary gives no indication of the time. The entry is merely, "Lights out—God help me." On Federal Hill there were watchers as anxious as he, and rain-soaked knots of men paraded the square and alleys around the evil church with umbrella-shaded candles, electric flashlights, oil lanterns, crucifixes, and obscure charms of the many sorts common to southern Italy. They blessed each flash of lightning, and made cryptical signs of fear with their right hands

22. Foul-smelling, as of decomposition.

when a turn in the storm caused the flashes to lessen and finally to cease altogether. A rising wind blew out most of the candles, so that the scene grew threateningly dark. Someone roused Father Merluzzo of Spirito Santo Church, and he hastened to the dismal square to pronounce whatever helpful syllables he could. Of the restless and curious sounds in the blackened tower, there could be no doubt whatever.

For what happened at 2:35 we have the testimony of the priest, a young, intelligent, and well-educated person; of Patrolman William J. Monahan of the Central Station, an officer of the highest reliability who had paused at that part of his beat to inspect the crowd; and of most of the seventy-eight men who had gathered around the church's high bank wall—especially those in the square where the eastward façade was visible. Of course there was nothing which can be proved as being outside the order of Nature. The possible causes of such an event are many. No one can speak with certainty of the obscure chemical processes arising in a vast, ancient, ill-aired, and long-deserted building of heterogeneous contents. Mephitic vapours[22]—spontaneous combustion—pressure of gases born of long decay—any one of numberless phenomena might be responsible. And then, of course, the factor of conscious charlatanry can by no means be excluded. The thing was really quite simple in itself, and covered less than three minutes of actual time. Father Merluzzo, always a precise man, looked at his watch repeatedly.

It started with a definite swelling of the dull fumbling sounds inside the black tower. There had for some time been a vague exhalation of strange, evil odours from the church, and this had now become emphatic and offensive. Then at last there was a sound of splintering wood, and a large, heavy object crashed down in the yard beneath the frowning easterly façade. The tower was invisible now that the candles would not burn, but as the object neared the ground the people knew that it was the smoke-grimed louver-boarding of that tower's east window.

Immediately afterward an utterly unbearable fœtor welled forth from the unseen heights, choking and sickening the trembling watchers, and almost prostrating those in the square. At the same time the air trembled with a vibration as of flapping wings, and a sudden east-blowing wind more violent than any previous blast snatched off the hats and wrenched the dripping umbrellas of the crowd. Nothing definite could be seen in the candleless night, though some upward-looking spectators thought they glimpsed a great spreading blur of denser blackness against the inky sky—something like a formless cloud of smoke that shot with meteorlike speed toward the east.

That was all. The watchers were half numbed with fright, awe, and discomfort, and scarcely knew what to do, or whether to do anything at all. Not knowing what had happened, they did not relax their vigil; and a moment later they sent up a prayer as a sharp flash of belated lightning, followed by an earsplitting crash of sound, rent the flooded heavens. Half an hour later the rain stopped, and in fifteen minutes more the street-lights sprang on again, sending the weary, bedraggled watchers relievedly back to their homes.

The next day's papers gave these matters minor mention in connexion with the general storm reports. It seems that the great lightning flash and deafening explosion which followed the Federal Hill occurrence were even more tremendous farther east, where a burst of the singular fœtor was likewise noticed. The phenomenon was most marked over College Hill, where the crash awaked all the sleeping inhabitants and led to a bewildered round of speculations. Of those who were already awake only a few saw the anomalous blaze of light near the top of the hill, or noticed the inexplicable upward rush of air which almost stripped the leaves from the trees and blasted the plants in the gardens. It was agreed that the lone, sudden lightning-bolt must have struck somewhere in this neighbourhood, though no trace of its striking could afterward be found. A youth in the Tau Omega[23] fraternity house thought he saw a grotesque and hideous mass of smoke in the air just as the preliminary flash burst, but his observation has not been verified. All of the few observers, however, agree as to the violent gust from the west and the flood of intolerable stench which preceded the belated stroke; whilst evidence concerning the momentary burned odour after the stroke is equally general.

These points were discussed very carefully because of their probable connexion with the death of Robert Blake. Students in the Psi Delta[24] house, whose upper rear windows looked into

23. A fictional fraternity. There is an *Alpha* Tau Omega fraternity founded in 1865 that may be the intended reference; the chapter at the University of Rhode Island was not founded, however, until 1994. The fraternity had no chapter at Brown University.

24. Psi Delta Omega was formed in 1922 but had no chapter in Providence.

Blake's study, noticed the blurred white face at the westward window on the morning of the 9th, and wondered what was wrong with the expression. When they saw the same face in the same position that evening, they felt worried, and watched for the lights to come up in his apartment. Later they rang the bell of the darkened flat, and finally had a policeman force the door.

The rigid body sat bolt upright at the desk by the window, and when the intruders saw the glassy, bulging eyes, and the marks of stark, convulsive fright on the twisted features, they turned away in sickened dismay. Shortly afterward the coroner's physician made an examination, and despite the unbroken window reported electrical shock, or nervous tension induced by electrical discharge, as the cause of death. The hideous expression he ignored altogether, deeming it a not improbable result of the profound shock as experienced by a person of such abnormal imagination and unbalanced emotions. He deduced these latter qualities from the books, paintings, and manuscripts found in the apartment, and from the blindly scrawled entries in the diary on the desk. Blake had prolonged his frenzied jottings to the last, and the broken-pointed pencil was found clutched in his spasmodically contracted right hand.

The entries after the failure of the lights were highly disjointed, and legible only in part. From them certain investigators have drawn conclusions differing greatly from the materialistic official verdict, but such speculations have little chance for belief among the conservative. The case of these imaginative theorists has not been helped by the action of superstitious Dr. Dexter, who threw the curious box and angled stone—an object certainly self-luminous as seen in the black windowless steeple where it was found—into the deepest channel of Narragansett Bay. Excessive imagination and neurotic unbalance on Blake's part, aggravated by knowledge of the evil bygone cult whose startling traces he had uncovered, form the dominant interpretation given those final frenzied jottings. These are the entries—or all that can be made of them.

Lights still out—must be five minutes now. Everything depends on lightning. Yaddith grant it will keep up! . . . Some influence seems beating through it. . . . Rain and thunder and wind deafen. . . .

The thing is taking hold of my mind. . . . Trouble with memory. I see things I never knew before. Other worlds and other galaxies . . . Dark . . . The lightning seems dark and the darkness seems light. . . .

It cannot be the real hill and church that I see in the pitch-darkness. Must be retinal impression left by flashes. Heaven grant the Italians are out with their candles if the lightning stops!

What am I afraid of? Is it not an avatar of Nyarlathotep, who in antique and shadowy Khem even took the form of man? I remember Yuggoth, and more distant Shaggai,[25] and the ultimate void of the black planets. . . .

The long, winging flight through the void . . . cannot cross the universe of light . . . re-created by the thoughts caught in the Shining Trapezohedron . . . send it through the horrible abysses of radiance. . . .

My name is Blake—Robert Harrison Blake of 620 East Knapp Street, Milwaukee, Wisconsin[26]. . . . .I am on this planet. . . .

Azathoth have mercy!—the lightning no longer flashes—horrible—I can see everything with a monstrous sense that is not sight—light is dark and dark is light . . . those people on the hill . . . guard . . . candles and charms . . . their priests. . . .

Sense of distance gone—far is near and near is far. No light—no glass—see that steeple—that tower—window—can hear—Roderick Usher[27]—am mad or going mad—the thing is stirring and fumbling in the tower—I am it and it is I—I want to get out . . . must get out and unify the forces. . . . It knows where I am. . . .

I am Robert Blake, but I see the tower in the dark. There is a monstrous odour . . . senses transfigured . . . boarding at that tower window cracking and giving way. . . . Iä . . . ngai . . . ygg. . . .

I see it—coming here—hell-wind—titan blur—black wings—Yog-Sothoth save me—the three-lobed burning eye . . .[28]

25. If Yuggoth is to be understood as Pluto (see "The Whisperer in Darkness," note 28), then Shaggai is another trans-Neptunian object (TNO), past the orbit of Pluto. At the time of Blake's notes, Percival Lowell had posited the existence of Planet X, a tenth large, planet-like object in the solar system. While the existence of a large unknown object was disproved definitively by the *Voyager 2* flyby of Neptune in 1989, other smaller objects, known as dwarf planets, have been discovered in that realm of space, the first in 1992. In fact, the TNO known as Eris, discovered in 2005, is larger than Pluto but farther out. This may well be Shaggai.

An image of Eris and its moon Dysnomia taken by the Hubble Space Telescope.

26. This was the actual address of Robert Bloch. The Bloch-Blake identification is examined in detail in Robert H. Waugh's "Bloch and Leiber: The Siblings at War with Lovecraft."

27. Roderick Usher is the victim in Edgar Allan Poe's "The Fall of the House of Usher" (1839)—killed by the apparition of his sister, a corpse. His death is witnessed by the narrator, who then escapes the House of Usher. As he does so, he sees a gleam of "wild light" from a blood-red moon as the house is rent in two.

Here, Blake refers to Usher's hypersensitivity to distant sounds.

28. Lovecraft explains Blake's helplessness in a letter dated February 20, 1937, to Arthur Widner (*Selected Letters*, II, 413–414): ". . . the night-monster has secured a hold upon Blake's brain, partly penetrating it, almost effecting an exchange of personalities. Blake could not think for himself or protect himself . . . With a clear head something might have been done—but the Thing had already seized his brain."

Cover of *H. P. Lovecraft's The Dream-Quest of Unknown Kadath*, no. 3 (Mock Man Press, Summer 1998).

(artist: Jason Thompson)

Appendix 1

CHRONOLOGICAL TABLE

(Partial)[1]

Likely Date of Occurrence	Work by Lovecraft
1771	Death of Joseph Curwen (*The Case of Charles Dexter Ward*)
1882, June	A meteor falls near Arkham ("The Colour Out of Space")
1896, November	Events of "The Picture in the House"
1901, February 21	Events of "Beyond the Wall of Sleep"
1903, Autumn	Events of "Herbert West: Reanimator" (Pt. I, From the Dark)
1904	"Herbert West: Reanimator" begins
1905, Autumn	"Herbert West: Reanimator" (Pt. II, The Plague-Daemon)
1907, November 1	Inspector Legrasse leads a police raid of the swamps south of New Orleans ("The Call of Cthulhu")
1908, May 14	Nathaniel Wingate Peaslee begins his five-year amnesia ("The Shadow Out of Time")
1909	Peaselee spends a month in the Himalayas ("The Shadow Out of Time")
1910, July	"Herbert West: Reanimator" (Pt. IV, The Scream of the Dead)
1911	Peaslee makes a trip by camel into the unknown deserts of Arabia ("The Shadow Out of Time")
1912, May 1	Wilbur Whateley is conceived ("The Dunwich Horror")
1912, Summer	Peaslee sails to the Arctic ("The Shadow Out of Time")
1913, February 2	Wilbur Whateley is born ("The Dunwich Horror")

1. For a more detailed record, covering ca. 700 CE to 1935, see Peter Cannon's *The Chronology Out of Time: Dates in the Fiction of H. P. Lovecraft*. Speculative dates have been omitted.

Likely Date of Occurrence	Work by Lovecraft
1914, February	Peaslee's memories have apparently returned ("The Shadow Out of Time")
1914, Autumn	"Dagon"
1915	"Herbert West: Reanimator" (Pt. V, The Horror from the Shadows)
1915, May 1	Akeley makes a recording near Dark Mountain ("The Whisperer in Darkness")
1915, May 1	Tremors in Aylesbury ("The Dunwich Horror")
1915, May	Peaslee sees the Great Race in his dreams ("The Shadow Out of Time")
1918 (?)	Statement of Randolph Carter
1918	Charles Dexter Ward learns he is descended from Joseph Curwen (*The Case of Charles Dexter Ward*)
1919, early August	Charles Dexter Ward discovers the portrait and journal of Curwen (*The Case of Charles Dexter Ward*)
1919, Autumn	Nyarlathotep
1920 (?)	"The Festival"
1921	Herbert West: Reanimator (Pt. VI, The Tomb-Legions)
1925, March 1	Professor Angell first learns of the disturbances caused by Cthulhu ("The Call of Cthulhu")
1925, March 22	The *Emma* meets the *Alert* ("The Call of Cthulhu"), landing on a small island the following day
1925, April 12	The *Vigilant* comes upon the derelict *Alert*
1926, May	Charles Dexter Ward returns to Providence from abroad (*The Case of Charles Dexter Ward*)
1927, April 1	Probable resurrection of Joseph Curwen (*The Case of Charles Dexter Ward*)
1927, July 15	Robert Olmstead arrives in Innsmouth, departing the next day ("The Shadow over Innsmouth")
1927, November 3	Vermont floods ("The Whisperer in Darkness")
1927	Walter Gilman consults *Necronomicon* at Miskatonic University ("The Dreams in the Witch House")
1927	Wilbur Whateley consults the *Necronomicon* at Miskatonic University ("The Dunwich Horror")

Likely Date of Occurrence	Work by Lovecraft
1927	Surveying is under way for new reservoir near Arkham ("The Colour Out of Space")
1928, April 13	Charles Dexter Ward vanishes, never to be seen again (*The Case of Charles Dexter Ward*)
1928, May 1	Walter Gilman dies ("The Dreams in the Witch House")
1928, May 5	Akeley alerts Wilmarth of the presence of creatures in the woods ("The Whisperer in Darkness")
1928, August 3	Wilbur Whately tries to steal the *Necronomicon* ("The Dunwich Horror")
1928, September 9	Wilbur Whatley's brother breaks loose ("The Dunwich Horror")
1928, September 12	Wilmarth leaves for Vermont, departing from Vermont the following day ("The Whisperer in Darkness"); Dr. Armitage learns of Wilbur Whatley's brother ("The Dunwich Horror")
1928, September 15	Wilbur Whatley's brother departs ("The Dunwich Horror")
1928	Asenath takes course in medieval metaphysics at Miskatonic ("The Thing on the Doorstep")
1930, September 2	Miskatonic Antarctic Expedition departs from Boston Harbor (*At the Mountains of Madness*)
1930, November 9	The Miskatonic Antarctic Expedition lands on Ross Island (*At the Mountains of Madness*)
1931, January 22	Professor Lake travels into the unknown (*At the Mountains of Madness*)
1931, January 25	Professor Dyer discovers the Lake expedition's fate; the following day, Dyer flies into the unknown (*At the Mountains of Madness*)
1931, November	Gilman's old rooms are opened and strange matters are discovered ("Dreams in the Witch House")
1934, July 10	Peaslee learns of discoveries in Australia ("The Shadow Out of Time")
1935, July 17	Peaslee makes a nocturnal discovery in Australia ("The Shadow Out of Time")
1935, August 8	A great storm breaks over Providence; at 2:12 the following morning, Robert Blake dies ("The Haunter of the Dark")

Appendix 2

FACULTY OF MISKATONIC UNIVERSITY

(Partial List)

Name	Position/Discipline	Mentioned In
Dr. Henry Armitage	Chief librarian	"The Dunwich Horror"
Professor Ferdinand C. Ashley	Ancient history	"The Shadow Out of Time"
Professor Atwood	Physics	*At the Mountains of Madness*
Professor Dexter	Zoology	"The Whisperer in Darkness"
Professor William Dyer	Geology	*At the Mountains of Madness*, "The Shadow Out of Time"
Professor Ellery	Chemistry	"The Dreams in the Witch House"
Professor Tyler M. Freeborn	Anthropology	"The Shadow Out of Time"
Dr. Allen Halsey	Dean of the Medical School	"Herbert West: Reanimator"
Professor Lake	Biology	*At the Mountains of Madness*
Dr. Francis Morgan	Archaeology	"The Dunwich Horror"
Professor Frank H. Pabodie	Engineering	*At the Mountains of Madness*
Professor Nathaniel Wingate Peaslee	Political economy	"The Shadow Out of Time"
Professor Wingate Peaslee	Psychology	"The Shadow Out of Time"
Professor Warren Rice	Languages	"The Dunwich Horror"
Professor Upham	Mathematics	"The Dreams in the Witch House"
Dr. Waldron ("Old Waldron")	College physician	"The Dreams in the Witch House"
Albert N. Wilmarth	English	*At the Mountains of Madness*, "The Whisperer in Darkness"

Appendix 3

HISTORY OF THE NECRONOMICON

(An Outline)

BY H. P. LOVECRAFT[1]

Original title *Al Azif*—*azif* being the word used by Arabs to designate that noctur-nal sound (made by insects) suppos'd to be the howling of daemons.[2]

Composed by Abdul Alhazred, a mad poet of Sanaá,[3] in Yemen, who is said to have flourished during the period of the Ommiade caliphs, circa 700 A.D. He visited the ruins of Babylon and the subterranean secrets of Memphis[4] and spent ten years alone in the great southern desert of Arabia—the Roba el Khaliyeh[5] or "Empty Space" of the ancients—and "Dahna" or "Crimson" desert of the modern Arabs,[6] which is held to be inhabited by protective evil spirits and monsters of death. Of this desert many strange and unbelievable marvels are told by those who pretend to have penetrated it. In his last years Alhazred dwelt in Damascus, where the *Necronomicon* (*Al Azif*) was written, and of his final death or disappearance

1. First published in 1938 as a pamphlet by Rebel Press (Oakman, AL). Probably written in Novem-ber 1927; Lovecraft mentioned the history in a letter to Clark Ashton Smith dated November 27, 1927 (*Selected Letters*, II, 201).

2. Lovecraft told Clark Ashton Smith in a letter dated November 27, 1927, that he learned this from the notes of Samuel Henley to his 1786 English translation of William Beckford's *The History of the Caliph Vathek* (1782), an early but important French work of fantasy and a favorite of Lovecraft's (letter of November 27, 1927, in *Selected Letters*, II, 201).

3. The chief settlement of Yemen.

4. See text accompanying note 184 in *The Case of Charles Dexter Ward*.

5. Properly, Rub' al Khali, located in the southern part of the Arabian peninsula.

6. Cf. the *Encyclopædia Britannica* (9th ed., II, 240): "[T]he 'Roba el Khaliyeh' or 'Empty Space' of geographers—the 'Dahna' or 'Crimson' of modern Arabs, so called from the prevailing colour of its heated sands . . . is never traversed in its full width, not even by Bedouins; and little or no credit can be attached to the relations of those who pretend to have explored it, and to have found wonders in its recesses."

(738 A.D.) many terrible and conflicting things are told. He is said by Ebn Khallikan (12th cent. biographer)[7] to have been seized by an invisible monster in broad daylight and devoured horribly before a large number of fright-frozen witnesses.[8] Of his madness many things are told. He claimed to have seen fabulous Irem, or City of Pillars,[9] and to have found beneath the ruins of a certain nameless desert town the shocking annals and secrets of a race older than mankind. He was only an indifferent Moslem, worshipping unknown entities whom he called Yog-Sothoth and Cthulhu.

In A.D. 950 the *Azif*, which had gained a considerable tho' surreptitious circulation amongst the philosophers of the age, was secretly translated into Greek by Theodorus Philetas of Constantinople under the title *Necronomicon*. For a century it impelled certain experimenters to terrible attempts, when it was suppressed and burnt by the patriarch Michael.[10] After this it is only heard of furtively, but (1228) Olaus Wormius made a Latin translation later in the Middle Ages, and the Latin text was printed twice—once in the fifteenth century in black-letter (evidently in Germany) and once in the seventeenth (prob. Spanish)—both editions being without identifying marks, and located as to time and place by internal typographical evidence only. The work both Latin and Greek was banned by Pope Gregory IX in 1232, shortly after its Latin translation,[11] which called attention to it. The Arabic original was lost as early as Wormius' time, as indicated by his prefatory note; and no sight of the Greek copy—which was printed in Italy between 1500 and 1550—has been reported since the burning of a certain Salem man's library in 1692.[12] An English translation made by Dr. Dee[13] was never printed, and exists only in fragments recovered from the original manuscript. Of the Latin texts now existing one (15th cent.) is known to be in the British Museum under lock and

---

7. Ibn Khallikan (1211–1282 CE), born in Iraq, was a judge and a scholar and the author of *Wafayāt al-a ā 'yān wa-anbā' abnā' az-zamān* (Deaths of Eminent Men and History of the Sons of the Epoch), a biographical dictionary that also served as an important work of civil and literary history.

8. There is reason to question whether Alhazred actually died. In "The Last Test," a tale cowritten by Lovecraft that appeared in *Weird Tales* in November 1928, Clarendon claims to have met an "old man" who may well have been the poet himself. See "Is Abdul Alhazred Still Alive?," by Robert M. Price.

9. See "The Nameless City," note 24, above.

10. The Greek Orthodox patriarch at Constantinople from 1043 to 1059 CE.

11. Gregory also banned the Talmud and declared that black cats were satanic beings.

12. Joseph Curwen fled Salem in 1692. See *The Case of Charles Dexter Ward*, above.

13. Most likely Doctor John Dee (1527–1608), an astrologer and a confidant of Queen Elizabeth I, who had an extensive occult library.

key,[14] while another (17th cent.) is in the Bibliothèque Nationale at Paris. A seventeenth-century edition is in the Widener Library at Harvard, and in the library of Miskatonic University at Arkham. Also in the library of the University of Buenos Ayres. Numerous other copies probably exist in secret, and a fifteenth-century one is persistently rumoured to form part of the collection of a celebrated American millionaire. A still vaguer rumour credits the preservation of a sixteenth-century Greek text in the Salem family of Pickman; but if it was so preserved, it vanished with the artist R. U. Pickman, who disappeared early in 1926.[15] The book is rigidly suppressed by the authorities of most countries, and by all branches of organised ecclesiasticism. Reading leads to terrible consequences. It was from rumours of this book (of which relatively few of the general public know) that R. W. Chambers is said to have derived the idea of his early novel *The King in Yellow*.[16]

Chronology

Al Azif written circa 730 A.D. at Damascus by Abdul Alhazred

Tr. to Greek 950 A.D. as *Necronomicon* by Theodorus Philetas

Burnt by Patriarch Michael 1050 (*i.e.*, Greek text). Arabic text now lost.

Olaus translates Gr. to Latin 1228

1232 Latin ed. (and Gr.) suppr. by Pope Gregory IX

14 . . . Black-letter printed edition (Germany)

15 . . . Gr. text printed in Italy

16 . . . Spanish reprint of Latin text

---

14. The Private Case was the select collection of pornographic and other "forbidden" books held by the British Museum. It was formally established in 1857, but the collection grew significantly upon receipt of the bequest of the prominent Victorian pornographer-bibliophile Henry Spencer Ashbee in 1900. The collection has now been dispersed into the general catalog.

15. See Lovecraft's tale "Pickman's Model" (1926).

16. Published in 1894. See "The Whisperer in Darkness," note 36, above.

History of the Necronomicon

Original title __Al Azif__ — azif being the word used by the Arabs to designate that nocturnal sound (made by insects) suppos'd to be the howling of daemons.

Composed by Abdul Alhazred, a mad poet of Sanaá, in Yemen, who is said to have flourished during the period of the Ommiade caliphs, circa 700 A.D. He visited the ruins of Babylon & the subterranean secrets of Memphis & spent ten years alone in the great southern desert of Arabia — the Roba El Khaliyeh or "Empty Space" of the ancients — & "Dahna" or "Crimson" desert of the modern Arabs, which is held to be inhabited by protective evil spirits & monsters of death. Of this desert many strange & unbelievable marvels are told by those who pretend to have penetrated it. In his last years Alhazred dwelt in Damascus, where the Necronomicon (Al Azif) was written, & of his final death or disappearance (738 A.D.) many terrible & conflicting things are told. He is said by Ebn Khallikan (12th cent. biographer) to have been seized by an invisible monster in broad daylight & devoured horribly before a large number of fright-frozen witnesses. Of his madness many things are told. He claimed to have seen the fabulous Irem, or City of Pillars, & to have found beneath the ruins of a certain nameless desert town the shocking annals & secrets of a race older than mankind. He was only an indifferent Moslem, worshipping unknown Entities whom he called Yog-Sothoth & Cthulhu.

In A.D. 950 the __Azif__, which had gained a considerable tho' surreptitious circulation amongst the philosophers of the age, was secretly translated into Greek by Theodorus Philetas of Constantinople under the title Necronomicon. For a century it impelled certain experimenters to terrible attempts, when it was suppressed & burnt by the patriarch Michael. After this it is only heard of furtively, but (1228) Olaus Wormius made a Latin translation later in the Middle Ages, & the Latin text was printed twice — once in the 15th century (evidently in Germany) & once in the 17th — (prob. Spanish) both in black-letter

(over)

editions being without identifying marks, & located as to time & place by internal typographical evidence only.) The Arabic original was lost as early as Wormius' time, as indicated by his prefatory note; & no sight of the Greek copy —which was printed in Italy bet. 1500 & 1550— has been reported since the burning of a certain Salem man's library in 1692. A translation made by Dr. Dee was never printed, & exists only in fragments recovered from the original M.S. Of the Latin texts now existing one (15th cent.) is known to be in the British Museum under lock & key, while another (17th cent.) is in the Bibliotheque Nationale at Paris. A 17th cent. edition is in the Widener Library at Harvard, & in the library of Miskatonic University at Arkham. Also in the library of the Univ. of Buenos Ayres. Numerous other copies probably exist in secret, & a 15th cent. one is persistently rumoured to form part of the collection of a celebrated American millionaire. A still vague rumour credits the preservation of a 16th cent. Greek text in the Salem family of Pickman; but if it was so preserved, it vanished with the artist R.U. Pickman, who disappeared early in 1926. The book is rigidly suppressed by the authorities of most countries, & by all branches of organised ecclesiasticism. Reading leads to terrible consequences. It was from rumours of this book (of which relatively few of the general public know) that R.W. Chambers is said to have derived the idea of his early novel "The King in Yellow."

— H.P. Lovecraft

[marginal annotations:]

both Latin & Gr.

The work was banned by Pope Gregory IX in 1232, shortly after its Latin translation, which called attention to it. N.

CHRONOLOGY

Al Azif written circa 730 A.D. at Damascus by Abdul Alhazred
Tr. to Greek 950 A.D. as *Necronomicon* by Theodorus Philetas
Burnt by Patriarch Michael 1050 (i.e. Greek text)
Arabic text now lost
Olaus translates gr. to Latin 1228
1232 Latin (& gr.?) ed. supp. by Pope Gregory IX
14.... black-letter edition (Germany)
15.... gr. text printed in Italy
16.... Spanish reprint of Latin text

Mr. H. P. Lovecraft
10 Barn Street
Providence, Rhode Island

My Dear Mr. Lovecraft:

I have inclosed your questionnaire with the letter to Dr. Fisher of Brown University with a request that he fill it out and return it to me. As soon as I get it, I will send it to you.

Dr. Fisher no doubt has all the information you wish as he has told me he has been visiting most of the localities and knows far more about them than I do as yet. I have only lived here two years and have not had a chance to see many of the outcrops.

With kind regards
Yours very truly
William L. Bryant
Director of the Museum.

April 27, 1927

PARK MUSEUM
ROGER WILLIAMS PARK
PROVIDENCE, R. I.
CITY OF PROVIDENCE

PARK COMMISSIONERS
EDWARD R. HOUGH, Chairman
JOSEPH E. C. FARNHAM
FREDERIC P. GORHAM

WILLIAM L. BRYANT
Director

Appendix 4

GENEALOGY OF THE ELDER RACES

*Drawn from a letter from H. P. Lovecraft to James F. Morton
(April 27, 1933, Selected Letters, IV, 183)*

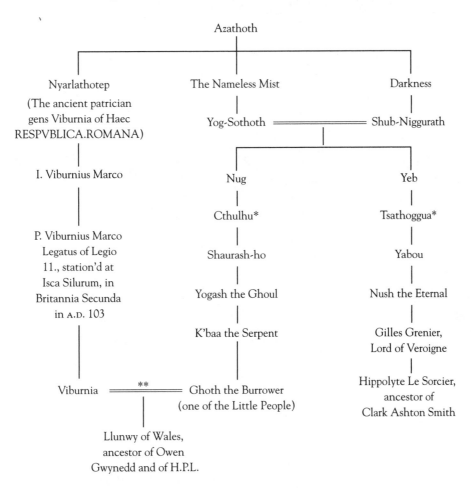

Azathoth

Nyarlathotep
(The ancient patrician
gens Viburnia of Haec
RESPVBLICA.ROMANA)

The Nameless Mist

Darkness

Yog-Sothoth ═══════ Shub-Niggurath

I. Viburnius Marco

Nug

Yeb

P. Viburnius Marco
Legatus of Legio
11., station'd at
Isca Silurum, in
Britannia Secunda
in A.D. 103

Cthulhu*

Tsathoggua*

Shaurash-ho

Yabou

Yogash the Ghoul

Nush the Eternal

K'baa the Serpent

Gilles Grenier,
Lord of Veroigne

Viburnia ═══**═══ Ghoth the Burrower
(one of the Little People)

Hippolyte Le Sorcier,
ancestor of
Clark Ashton Smith

Llunwy of Wales,
ancestor of Owen
Gwynedd and of H.P.L.

* First of their respective lines to inhabit this planet.

** This union was an hellish and nameless tragedy.

Appendix 5

THE WORKS OF H. P. LOVECRAFT[1]

Title	Year Written	Year First Published
"The Alchemist"	1908	1916
At the Mountains of Madness	1931	1936
"Azathoth" (fragment)	1922	1938
"The Beast in the Cave"	1905	1918
"Beyond the Wall of Sleep"	1919	1919
"The Book" (fragment)	1933 (?)	1938
"The Call of Cthulhu"	1926	1928
The Case of Charles Dexter Ward	1927	1941
"The Cats of Ulthar"	1920	1920
"Celephaïs"	1920	1922
"The Colour Out of Space"	1927	1927
"Cool Air"	1926 (?)	1928
"Dagon"	1917	1919
"The Descendants" (fragment)	1926 or 1927	1938
"The Doom That Came to Sarnath"	1919	1920
The Dream-Quest of Unknown Kadath	1926–27	1943
"The Dreams in the Witch House"	1932	1933
"The Dunwich Horror"	1928	1929
"The Evil Clergyman" (dream account)	1933	1939
"Ex Oblivione"	1920 or 1921	1921
"Facts Concerning the Late Arthur Jermyn and His Family"	1920	1921

1. Based on *H. P. Lovecraft: A Comprehensive Bibliography*, by S. T. Joshi. The list omits fiction that Lovecraft wrote in collaboration with other authors or revisions of their work.

Title	Year Written	Year First Published
"The Festival"	1923	1925
"From Beyond"	1920	1934
"The Haunter of the Dark"	1935	1936
"He"	1925	1926
"Herbert West: Reanimator"	1921–22	1922
"History of the *Necronomicon*"	1927	1937
"The Horror at Red Hook"	1925	1927
"The Hound"	1922	1924
"Hypnos"	1922	1923
"Ibid."	1928 (?)	1938
"In the Vault"	1925	1925
"The Little Glass Bottle"	1897	1959
"The Lurking Fear"	1922	1923
"Memory"	1919 (?)	1919
"The Moon-Bog"	1921	1926
"The Music of Erich Zann"	1921 (?)	1922
"The Mysterious Ship"	1921	1959
"The Mystery of the Grave-Yard"	1898	1959
"The Nameless City"	1921	1921
"Nyarlathotep"	1920	1921
"Of Evill Sorceries Done in New England, of Daemons in No Humane Shape" (frag.)	Unknown	1945
"Old Bugs"	1919	1959
"The Other Gods"	1921	1933
"The Outsider"	1921	1926
"Pickman's Model"	1926	1927
"The Picture in the House"	1920	1921
"Polaris"	1918	1920
"The Quest of Iranon"	1921	1935
"The Rats in the Walls"	1923	1924
"A Reminiscence of Dr. Samuel Johnson"	1917 (?)	1917
"The Secret Cave"	1898	1959
"The Shadow Out of Time"	1934–35	1936

Title	Year Written	Year First Published
"The Shadow over Innsmouth"	1931	1936
"The Shunned House"	1924	1928
"The Silver Key"	1926	1929
"The Statement of Randolph Carter"	1919	1920
"The Strange High House in the Mist"	1926	1931
"The Street"	1919	1920
"Sweet Ermengarde; or, The Heart of a Country Girl"	Unknown	1943
"The Temple"	1920	1925
"The Terrible Old Man"	1920	1921
"The Thing on the Doorstep"	1933	1937
"The Tomb"	1917	1922
"The Transition of Juan Romero"	1919	1944
"The Tree"	1920	1921
"The Unnamable"	1923	1925
"What the Moon Brings"	1922	1923
"The Whisperer in Darkness"	1930	1931
"The White Ship"	1919	1919

HPL's own list of his stories, compiled in 1936 for Willis Conover.
Note the touching blanks for the years 1937–48!

Appendix 6

THE "REVISIONS" OF H. P. LOVECRAFT

(Stories Cowritten or Ghostwritten by Lovecraft)[1]

Title	Author (or Coauthor)	Year Written	Year Published
"Ashes"	C. M. Eddy Jr.	1923	1924
"The Battle That Ended the Century"	R. H. Barlow	1934	1934
"The Challenge from Beyond"	C. L. Moore, A. Merritt, Robert E. Howard, and Frank Belknap Long	1935	1935
"Collapsing Cosmoses"	R. H. Barlow	1938	1938
"The Crawling Chaos"	Winifred V. Jackson	1920	1921
"The Curse of Yig"	Zealia Bishop	1928	1929
"Deaf, Dumb and Blind"	C. M. Eddy Jr.	1924	1925
"The Diary of Alonzo Typer"	William Lumley	1935	1938
"The Disinterment"	Duane W. Rimel	1935	1937
"The Electric Executioner"	Adolphe de Castro	1929	1930
"The Ghost-Eater"	C. M. Eddy Jr.	1923	1924
"The Green Meadow"	Winifred V. Jackson	1918–19	1927

1. "Bothon," a story nominally by Henry S. Whitehead, appeared in 1946, and there have been suggestions that Lovecraft may have had a hand in its creation. S. T. Joshi, in *I Am Providence*, concludes "from internal evidence" that none of the writing is Lovecraft's. "The Thing in the Moonlight" is an edited account of several dreams of Lovecraft's worked up by J. Chapman Miske and passed off as a story by Lovecraft in 1940. August Derleth subsequently reprinted it at face value. The scholarship of David E. Schultz (in "'The Thing in the Moonlight': A Hoax Revealed") has since clarified its true authorship.

Title	Author (or Coauthor)	Year Written	Year Published
"The Hoard of the Wizard-Beast"	R. H. Barlow	1933	1933
"The Horror at Martin's Beach"	Sonia Greene (later Sonia Greene Lovecraft)	1922	1923
"The Horror in the Burying-Ground"	Hazel Heald	1933–34	1937
"The Horror in the Museum"	Hazel Heald	1932	1933
"In the Walls of Eryx"	Kenneth Sterling	1936	1939
"The Last Test"	Adolphe de Castro	1927	1928
"The Loved Dead"	C. M. Eddy Jr.	1923	1924
"The Man of Stone"	Hazel Heald	1932	1932
"Medusa's Coil"	Zealia Bishop	1930	1939
"The Mound"	Zealia Bishop	1929–30	1940
"The Night Ocean"	R. H. Barlow	1936	1939
"Out of the Aeons"	Hazel Heald	1933	1935
"Poetry and the Gods"	Anna Helen Crofts	1920	1920
"The Slaying of the Monster"	R. H. Barlow	1933	1933
"The Sorcery of Aphlar"	Duane W. Rimel	1934	1934
"Through the Gates of the Silver Key"	E. H. Price	1932–33	1934
"Till A' the Seas"	R. H. Barlow	1935	1935
"The Trap"	Henry S. Whitehead	1931	1932
"The Tree on the Hill"	Duane W. Rimel	1934	1940
"Two Black Bottles"	Wilfred Blanch Talman	1926	1927
"Under the Pyramids"	Harry Houdini	1924	1924
"Winged Death"	Hazel Heald	1932	1934

Appendix 7

H. P. LOVECRAFT IN POPULAR CULTURE

In the preface to the second French edition of his *H. P. Lovecraft: Against the World, Against Life*, Michel Houellebecq noted: "At book signings, once in a while, young people come to see me and ask me to sign this book. They have discovered Lovecraft through role-playing games [in which players assume the personae of characters] or CD-ROMs. They have not read his work and don't even intend to do so. None the less, oddly, they want to find out more—beyond the texts—about the individual and about how he constructed his world." Unsurprisingly, this is not a phenomenon limited to Lovecraft. Houellebecq drew parallels with the work of Conan Doyle, who, notwithstanding Conan Doyle's disdain for the popularity of his Sherlock Holmes tales, created an essential mythology for the iconic detective. Just as for a century Sherlockians have pretended—or pretended to pretend—that Holmes and Watson really lived,[1] H. P. Lovecraft fans have breathed life into his creations and pretended that Cthulhu and its spawn exist.

Lovecraft T-shirt, sold by Zazzle.

Although Lovecraft did not find motion pictures compelling,[2] filmmakers have found his stories to be rich material for the screen. An incomplete list of films based on Lovecraft's stories is set forth below. It would be pleasant to report that many are sensitive, caring adaptations, but such is not the case. Most are blatant appropriations of characters and titles, with little regard for the subtleties of Lovecraft's plots or characterizations, and many have simply borrowed character names or vague concepts of tentacled creatures. Only those by the H. P. Lovecraft Historical Society—two so far, careful adaptations of "The Call of Cthulhu" and "The Whisperer in Darkness"—have been true to the source material. Existing television adaptations have no greater merit. Audio adaptations have been far more successful; these

"Hello Cthulhu" T-shirt, sold by Studio Tees.

---

1. In his sonnet "1895," Vincent Starrett wrote of Holmes and Watson as "two men of note who never lived and so can never die." He admonished, "Only those things the heart believes are true."

2. With rare exceptions, according to S. T. Joshi, Lovecraft "did not care for the surprising number of films he saw in the course of his life" (*I Am Providence*, 236). One that stood out was *Barclay Square*, a time-travel movie made in 1933, which loosely inspired "The Shadow Out of Time."

are dominated by the H. P. Lovecraft Historical Society and another producer, the Atlanta Radio Theatre Company.

The H. P. Lovecraft band, pictured in 1967.

Musicians and bands influenced by Lovecraft's stories, including the 1970s band H. P. Lovecraft, are too numerous to mention. A more pervasive influence—mentioned by Houellebecq, above—is in the world of gaming. In the 1980s, Chaosium introduced a role-playing game (RPG), Call of Cthulhu (currently in its sixth major edition), which drew many new fans to Lovecraft's books. The RPG spawned the board game Arkham Horror and a dice game, Elder Sign, and other spinoffs are the collectible card games Mythos and Call of Cthulhu, the Living Card Game (both similar to Magic: The Gathering). Several video (computer-derived) games are based on or influenced heavily by Lovecraft, such as Call of Cthulhu: Dark Corners of the Earth, Shadow of the Comet, Prisoner of Ice, Shadowman, the successful Alone in the Dark series, Chzo Mythos, Eternal Darkness: Sanity's Requiem, Cthulhu Saves the World, Amnesia: The Dark Descent, Dead Space, Splatterhouse, Darkness Within: In Pursuit of Loath Nolder, Penumbra, Blood, and Quake. Sherlock Holmes: The Awakened, from Frogwares Games, is an important crossover. The massively multiplayer online role-playing game The Secret World draws directly from Lovecraft's work.

Cover by Gene Day of first edition of *Call of Cthulhu* role-playing game (1981).

Call of Cthulhu card game.

Another essential medium for Lovecraft interpretations is visual—comic books and graphic novels. There are far too many to list, although some noteworthy covers are reproduced throughout this volume. The earliest seem to be "Experiment . . . In Death," loosely based on "Herbert West: Reanimator" (*Weird Science* 12, May–June 1950, published by EC Comics and written by Al Feldstein, with art by Jack Kamen), "Fitting Punishment," based on "In the Vault" (*The Vault of Horror* 1, no. 16, December 1950–January 1951, 9–15, from the same publisher and written by Al Feldstein, with art by Graham Ingels) and "Baby . . . It's Cold Inside!," based on "Cool Air" (*The Vault of Horror* 1, no. 17, February–March 1951, 9–15 (from the same publisher and creative team). For more detailed listings, see Donovan K. Loucks's page (http://www.hplovecraft.com/popcult/comics.aspx), as well as the catalogue of Miskatonic University (http://www.yankeeclassic.com/miskatonic/library/ stacks/periodicals/comics/lovecraft/comics1.htm) and Brian Lingard's page, H. P. Lovecraft in the Comics (http://darktreepress.50megs.com/hplcomics/ index.html). For an excellent overview of the history of Lovecraft in comics, see "Co(s)mic Horror," by Chris Murray and Kevin Corstorphine.

Vault of Horror 1, no. 16 (December 1950–January 1951).

Vault of Horror 1, no. 17 (February–
March 1951).

The following tabulates the feature-length theatrical films that have been based (very loosely, in some cases) on stories by H. P. Lovecraft.[3]

Title	Production Company	Year Released	Work by Lovecraft	Notes
The Haunted Palace	American International Pictures	1963	*The Case of Charles Dexter Ward*	With Vincent Price and Lon Chaney Jr.
Die, Monster, Die!, aka Monster of Terror	American International Pictures	1965	"The Colour out of Space"	With Boris Karloff
The Shuttered Room, aka Blood Island	Seven Arts Productions	1967	Id.	With Gig Young, Carol Lynley, and Oliver Reed
Curse of the Crimson Altar, aka The Crimson Cult	Tigon British Film Productions	1968	"The Dreams in the Witch House"	With Boris Karloff, Christopher Lee, and Barbara Steele
The Dunwich Horror	American International Pictures	1970	Id.	With Dean Stockwell, Sam Jaffe, and Sandra Dee
Screamers, aka Island of the Fishmen	Dania Film	1979	"The Shadow over Innsmouth"	With Barbara Bach and Richard Johnson
Re-Animator	Empire Pictures	1985	"Herbert West: Reanimator"	Stuart Gordon directs
From Beyond	Empire Pictures	1986	Id.	Another Stuart Gordon film
The Curse	Trans World Entertainment	1987	"The Colour out of Space"	With Claude Akin and Wil Wheaton
Pulse Pounders	Empire Pictures	1988	"The Evil Clergyman"	With David Warner; directed by Charles Band
The Unnamable	Distributed by Image Entertainment	1988	Id.	With Mark Kinsey Stephenson

3. "Id." signifies that the story mentioned in the title is the basis of the film.

Title	Production Company	Year Released	Work by Lovecraft	Notes
Dark Heritage	Cornerstone Films	1989	"The Lurking Fear"	
Bride of Re-Animator	Wild Street	1990	"Herbert West: Reanimator"	Directed by Brian Yuzna, with much of the original cast
Shatterbrain, aka *The Resurrected*	Scotti Brothers Pictures	1991	*The Case of Charles Dexter Ward*	With Chris Sarandon; directed by Dan O'Bannon
The Unnamable II: The State-ment of Randolph Carter	Yankee Classic	1992	Id.	A direct sequel to the 1988 film *The Unnamable*
Necronomicon: Book of Dead	Davis-Films	1994	"The Rats in the Wall"; "Cool Air"; "The Whisperer in Darkness"	Some of the cast of *Re-Animator* returns, in dif-ferent roles. Lovecraft is portrayed in the framing story.
Lurking Fear	Full Moon Productions	1994	"The Lurking Fear"	
Bleeders, aka *Hemoglobin*	Fries/Schultz Film Group	1997	"The Lurking Fear"	Written by Dan O'Bannon
Chilean Gothic	Kaos Producciones	2000	"Pickman's Model"	
Dagon	Fantastic Factory	2001	"Dagon"; "The Shadow over Innsmouth"	Another Stuart Gordon film
The Thing on the Doorstep	Maelstrom Productions	2003	Id.	
The Dream-Quest of Unknown Kaddath	Guerrilla Productions	2003	Id.	
The Call of Cthulhu	H. P. Lovecraft Historical Society	2005	Id.	Silent film
Beyond the Wall of Sleep	El Globo Films	2006	Id.	

Title	Production Company	Year Released	Work by Lovecraft	Notes
The Rats in the Walls	n/a	2006	Id.	A live performance from the Minnesota Film Festival
The Whisperer in Darkness	GraveHill Productions	2007	Id.	
Cthulhu	Arkham Northwest Productions	2007	"The Call of Cthulhu"	
H. P. Lovecraft's Dunwich Horror and Other Stories	Distributed by Toei Animation Company	2007	Id.	A Japanese production
Beyond the Dunwich Horror	Scorpio Film Releasing	2008	Id.	
Colour from the Dark	Studio Interzona	2008	"The Colour out of Space"	
Die Farbe (The Colour out of Space)	Sphärentor Filmproduktionen	2010	Id.	
The Whisperer in Darkness	HPLHS Motion Pictures	2011	Id.	

The following are noteworthy audio adaptations of Lovecraft's work:[4]

At the Mountains of Madness
> Performed by Dark Adventure Radio Theatre. Compact disc (1:15). The H. P. Lovecraft Historical Society. 2006.

At the Mountains of Madness
> Performed by the Atlanta Radio Theatre Company. Compact disc and audio cassette (0:45). Centauri Express. 1995.

At the Mountains of Madness/Hour of the Wolf
> Performed by the Atlanta Radio Theatre Company. Compact disc and audio cassette (0:45). Atlanta Radio Theater Company. 1997.

At the Mountains of Madness and *The Competitor*
> By H. P. Lovecraft and Brad Linaweaver. Performed by the Atlanta Radio Theatre Company. Audiocassette. Sunset Productions. 1995.

Beyond the Wall of Sleep
> *Mind Webs* radio drama. April 16, 1983.

---

4. Compiled by Donovan K. Loucks.

The Call of Cthulhu
> Performed by the Middlebury Radio Theater of Thrills and Suspense. 2008.

The Colour Out of Space
> Performed by the Atlanta Radio Theatre Company. Atlanta Radio Theater Company. 2006.

The Dunwich Horror
> Performed by Dark Adventure Radio Theatre. Compact disc (1:15). The H. P. Lovecraft Historical Society. 2008.

The Dunwich Horror
> *Suspense* radio drama. With Ronald Colman and William Johnstone. November 1, 1945.

The Dunwich Horror
> Performed by the Atlanta Radio Theatre Company. Compact disc and audio cassette (1:14). Atlanta Radio Theatre Company. 1988.

The Dunwich Horror and *The Happy Man*
> By H. P. Lovecraft and Gerald R. Page. Performed by the Atlanta Radio Theatre Company. Audiocassette. Sunset Productions. 1995, 1996, 1997.

The Lovecraft Tapes: The Dunwich Horror and Pickman's Model
> Performed by the Atlanta Radio Theatre Company. Audiocassette. Centauri Express. 1990.

The Outsider
> *Black Mass* radio drama. October 1965.

The Rats in the Walls
> Performed by the Atlanta Radio Theatre Company. Compact disc and audiocassette (1:00). Centauri Express. 1990.

The Rats in the Walls
> *Black Mass* radio drama. July 1964.

The Shadow out of Time
> Performed by Dark Adventure Radio Theatre. Compact disc (1:18). The H. P. Lovecraft Historical Society. 2008.

The Shadow over Innsmouth
> Performed by Dark Adventure Radio Theatre. Compact disc. The H. P. Lovecraft Historical Society. 2008.

The Shadow over Innsmouth
> Performed by the Atlanta Radio Theatre Company. Compact disc and audio cassette (1:00). Atlanta Radio Theatre Company. 1989.

The Shadow over Innsmouth and *Ghost Dance*
> By H. P. Lovecraft and Thomas E. Fuller. Performed by the Atlanta Radio Theatre Company. Audiocassette (1:30). Sunset Productions. 1995.

Cover of H. P. Lovecraft's *The Dream-Quest of Unknown Kadath*, no. 2
(Mock Man Press, Spring 1998).

(artist: Jason Thompson)

Bibliography[1]

WORKS BY H. P. LOVECRAFT

The Ancient Track: Complete Poetical Works. 2nd ed. Edited by S. T. Joshi. New York: Hippocampus Press, 2013.

The Annotated H. P. Lovecraft. Edited by S. T. Joshi. New York: Dell, 1997.

The Annotated Supernatural Horror in Literature. Edited by S. T. Joshi. New York: Hippocampus Press, 2000.

At the Mountains of Madness and Other Novels. Edited by August Derleth. Sauk City, WI: Arkham House Publishers, 1964.

Beyond the Wall of Sleep. Edited by August Derleth and Donald Wandrei. Sauk City, WI: Arkham House Publishers, 1943.

The Call of Cthulhu and Other Weird Stories. Edited by S. T. Joshi. New York: Penguin Classics, 1999.

The Case of Charles Dexter Ward. Edited by S. T. Joshi. Tampa, FL: University of Tampa Press, 2010.

The Classic Horror Stories. Edited by Roger Luckhurst. New York: Oxford University Press, 2013.

Collected Essays. Edited by S. T. Joshi. New York: Hippocampus Press, 2004–6. 5 vols.

Collected Poems. Edited by August Derleth. Sauk City, WI: Arkham House Publishers, 1963.

The Complete Fiction. Edited with an introduction by S. T. Joshi. New York: Barnes & Noble, 2011.

Dagon and Other Macabre Tales. Edited by August Derleth, S. T. Joshi, and T. E. Klein. Sauk City, WI: Arkham House Publishers, 1986.

In Defence of Dagon. Edited by S. T. Joshi. West Warwick, RI: Necronomicon Press, 1985.

The Dreams in the Witch House and Other Weird Stories. Edited by S. T. Joshi. New York: Penguin Classics, 2004.

---

1. This is a bibliography of works consulted in connection with preparation of this volume. It is by no means a complete bibliography of the important material regarding Lovecraft, and the reader is directed to S. T. Joshi's *H. P. Lovecraft: A Comprehensive Bibliography* (2009) for further information.

The Dunwich Horror and Others. Edited by August Derleth. Sauk City, WI: Arkham House Publishers, 1963.

Letters from New York. Edited by S. T. Joshi and David E. Schultz. San Francisco: Night Shade Books, 2005. (*The Lovecraft Letters*, II).

Lord of a Visible World: An Autobiography in Letters. Edited by S. T. Joshi and David E. Schultz. Athens: Ohio University Press, 2000.

Marginalia. Edited by August Derleth. Sauk City, WI: Arkham House Publishers, 1944.

Miscellaneous Writings. Edited by S. T. Joshi. Sauk City, WI: Arkham House Publishers, 1995.

More Annotated H. P. Lovecraft. Edited by S. T. Joshi and Peter Cannon. New York: Dell, 1999.

Mysteries of Time and Spirit: The Letters of H. P. Lovecraft and Donald Wandrei. Edited by S. T. Joshi and David E. Schultz. San Francisco: Night Shade Books, 2002.

The Outsider and Others. Edited by August Derleth and Donald Wandrei. Sauk City, WI: Arkham House Publishers, 1939.

Selected Letters, 1911–1924. Edited by S. T. Joshi. Sauk City, WI: Arkham House Publishers, 1965. (*Selected Letters*, I.)

Selected Letters, 1925–1929. Edited by S. T. Joshi. Sauk City, WI: Arkham House Publishers, 1968. (*Selected Letters*, II.)

Selected Letters, 1929–1931. Edited by S. T. Joshi. Sauk City, WI: Arkham House Publishers, 1969. (*Selected Letters*, III.)

Selected Letters, 1932–1934. Edited by S. T. Joshi. Sauk City, WI: Arkham House Publishers, 1971. (*Selected Letters*, IV.)

Selected Letters 1934–1937. Edited by S. T. Joshi. Sauk City, WI: Arkham House Publishers, 1976. (*Selected Letters*, V.)

The Shadow Out of Time. Edited by S. T. Joshi and David E. Schultz. New York: Hippocampus Press, 2003.

The Shadow over Innsmouth. Edited by S. T. Joshi and David E. Schultz. West Warwick, RI: Necronomicon Press, 1994.

The Shuttered Room and Other Pieces. Edited by August Derleth. Sauk City, WI: Arkham House Publishers, 1959.

"Some Notes on Interplanetary Fiction." *The Californian* 3, no. 3 (Winter 1935), 39–42.

Something About Cats and Other Pieces. Edited by August Derleth. Sauk City, WI: Arkham House Publishers, 1949.

Tales. Edited by Peter Straub. New York: Library of America, 2005.

Tales of H. P. Lovecraft. Selected and edited by Joyce Carol Oates. New York: Ecco Press, 2000.

The Thing on the Doorstep and Other Weird Stories. Edited by S. T. Joshi. New York: Penguin Classics, 2001.

"The Vermont Horror." Edited by Robert M. Price. *Call of Cthulhu* 101 (Eastertide, 1999), 3–39.

A Winter Wish. Edited by Tom Collins. Chapel Hill, NC: Whispers Press, 1977.

Lovecraft, H. P., and Divers Hands. *The Dark Brotherhood and Other Pieces.* Sauk City, WI: Arkham House Publishers, 1966.

Lovecraft, H. P., and Willis Conover. *Lovecraft at Last.* Arlington, VA: Carrollton Clark, 1975.

SECONDARY SOURCES (CRITICAL/BIOGRAPHICAL)

Airaksinen, Timo. *The Philosophy of H. P. Lovecraft: The Route to Horror.* New York: Peter Lang, 1999. New Studies in Aesthetics, vol. 29.

Anderson, James Arthur. *Out of the Shadows: A Structuralist Approach to Understanding the Fiction of H. P. Lovecraft.* Holicong, PA: Borgo Press, 2011.

Atama, Bert. "An Autopsy on the Old Ones." *Crypt of Cthulhu* 32 (St. John's Eve, 1985), 3–7.

Beckwith, Henry L. P., Jr. *Lovecraft's Providence & Adjacent Parts.* West Kingston, RI: Donald M. Grant Publishers, 1990.

Beherec, Marc A. "The Devil, the Terror, and the Horror: The Whateley Twins' Further Debts to Folklore and Fiction." *Lovecraft Studies* 44 (2004), 23–25.

Berglund, Edward P. "Lovecraft on Eldritch Tomes." *Crypt of Cthulhu* 35 (Hallowmas, 1985), 26–27.

Bloch, Robert. "Out of the Ivory Tower." In *The Shuttered Room and Other Pieces.* Sauk City, WI: Arkham House Publishers, 1949.

Bouchard, Alexandre, and Louis-Pierre Smith Lacroix. "*Necronomicon:* A Note." *Lovecraft Studies* 44 (2004), 107–12.

Bryant, Roger. "The Alchemist and the Scientist." *Nyctalops* 2, no. 3 (Issue 10, January–February 1975), 26–29, 43.

Burke, Rusty, S. T. Joshi, and David E. Schultz, eds. *A Means to Freedom: The Letters of H. P. Lovecraft and Robert E. Howard.* New York: Hippocampus Press, 2011. 2 vols.

Burleson, Donald R. *H. P. Lovecraft, A Critical Study.* Westport, CT: Greenwood Press, 1983.

———. "Humour Beneath Horror: Some Sources for 'The Dunwich Horror' and 'The Whisperer in Darkness,'" *Lovecraft Studies* 1, no. 2 (Spring 1980), 5–15.

———. "A Note on Lovecraft, Mathematics, and the Outer Spheres." *Crypt of Cthulhu* 1, no. 4 (Eastertide, 1982), 23–24.

Callaghan, Gavin. *H. P. Lovecraft's Dark Arcadia: The Satire, Symbology and Contradiction.* Jefferson, NC, and London: McFarland & Company, 2013.

————. "Elementary, My Dear Lovecraft: H. P. Lovecraft and Sherlock Holmes." *Love-craft Annual*, 6 (2012), 199–229.

————. "A Reprehensible Habit: H. P. Lovecraft and the Munsey Magazines." In *Lovecraft and Influence: His Predecessors and Successors*. Edited by Robert H. Waugh, 69–82. Lanham, MD, Toronto, and Plymouth, UK: The Scarecrow Press, 2013.

Cannon, Peter. "*At the Mountains of Madness* as a Sequel to *Arthur Gordon Pym*." *Crypt of Cthulhu* 32 (St. John's Eve, 1985), 33–34.

————. *H. P. Lovecraft*. Twayne's United States Authors Series. Boston: Twayne, 1989.

————. *The Chronology Out of Time: Dates in the Fiction of H. P. Lovecraft*. West Warwick, RI: Necronomicon Press, 1986.

————. "The Late Francis Wayland Thurston of Boston: Lovecraft's Last Dilettante." *Lovecraft Studies* 19/20 (Fall 1989), 32, 39.

————. "Parallel Passages in 'The Adventure of the Copper Beeches' and 'The Picture in the House.'" *Lovecraft Studies* 1, no. 1 (1979), 3–6.

————. "The Return of Sherlock Holmes and H. P. Lovecraft." *Baker Street Journal* 34, no. 4 (December 1984), 217–20.

————. "Some Thoughts on the State of Lovecraft Studies." *Books at Brown* 38–39 (1991–92), 1–5.

————. "You Have Been in Providence, I Perceive." *Nyctalops* 14 (March, 1978), 45–46.

Cannon, Peter, Jason C. Eckhardt, Steven J. Mariconda, and Hubert Van Calenbergh. "On *At The Mountains of Madness*: A Panel Discussion." *Lovecraft Studies* 34 (Spring 1996), 2–10.

Carlson, Eric. "Map of Innsmouth." *Nyctalops* 6 (February 1972), 9.

Cerasini, Marc A. "Thematic Links in *Arthur Gordon Pym*, *At the Mountains of Madness*, and *Moby Dick*." *Crypt of Cthulhu* 49 (Lammas, 1987), 3–20.

Clore, Dan. *Weird Words*. New York: Hippocampus Press, 2009.

Cockroft, T. G. L. Letter to the editor of *Nyctalops* 2, no. 2 (July 1974), 45 (Pnakotic Manuscripts).

————. "Some Notes on 'The Shadow over Innsmouth.'" *Lovecraft Studies* 1, no. 3 (Fall 1980), 3–4.

Colavito, Jason. *The Cult of Alien Gods: H. P. Lovecraft and Extraterrestrial Pop Culture*. Amherst, NY: Prometheus Books, 2005.

Connors, Scott, ed. *A Century Less a Dream: Selected Criticism on H. P. Lovecraft*. Holicong, PA: Wildside Press , 2002.

Cook, W. Paul. "A Plea for Lovecraft." *The Ghost* 3 (May 1945), 55–56. Reprinted in *Lovecraft Studies* 19–20 (Fall 1989), 26–27.

Cooke, Jon B., ed. *H. P. Lovecraft Centennial Guidebook*. Providence: Mantilla Publications, 1990.

Cuppy, Will. Review of *Beyond the Wall of Sleep*. *New York Herald Tribune Book Review*, January 2, 1944, 10.

————. Review of *The Outsider and Others*. *New York Herald Tribune Book Review*, December 17, 1939, 14.

Davis, Sonia H. [Greene]. *The Private Life of H. P. Lovecraft*. Edited by S. T. Joshi. West Warwick, RI: Necronomicon Press, 1985, rev. ed. 1992.

De Camp, L. Sprague. *Lovecraft: A Biography*. Garden City, NY: Doubleday, 1975.

Derleth, August. *H. P. L: A Memoir*. New York: Ben Abramson, Publisher, 1945.

————. *Some Notes on H. P. Lovecraft*. Sauk City, WI: Arkham House, 1959.

De Vries, Peter. Review of *Beyond the Wall of Sleep*. *Chicago Sun Book Week*, December 26, 1943, 4.

Eckhardt, Jason C. "Behind the Mountains of Madness: Lovecraft and the Antarctic in 1930." *Lovecraft Studies* 14 (Spring 1987), 31–38.

————. "Cthulhu's Scald: Lovecraft and the Nordic Tradition." *Lovecraft Studies* 3, no. 1 (Spring 1984), 25–29.

————. *Off the Ancient Track: A Lovecraftian Guide to New England & Adjacent New York*. Privately printed, 2013.

Ellison, Harlan, and Stuart Gordon, eds. *A Lovecraft Retrospective: Artists Inspired by H. P. Lovecraft*. Lakewood, CO: Centipede Press, 2008.

Everts, R. Alain. *The Death of a Gentleman: The Last Days of Howard Phillips Lovecraft*. Madison, WI: The Strange Company, 1987.

Faig, Kenneth W., Jr. *The Parents of Howard Phillips Lovecraft*. West Warwick, RI: Necronomicon Press, 1990. Reprinted in slightly revised and updated form in *Epicure in the Terrible: A Centennial Anthology of Essays in Honor of H. P. Lovecraft*, edited by David E. Schultz and S. T. Joshi. New York: Hippocampus Press, 2011.

————. "'The Silver Key' and Lovecraft's Childhood." *Crypt of Cthulhu* 81 (St. John's Eve, 1992), 11–47.

————. *The Site of Joseph Curwen's Home in H. P. Lovecraft's The Case of Charles Dexter Ward*. Glenview, IL: Moshassuck Press, 2013.

————. *The Unknown Lovecraft*. New York: Hippocampus Press, 2009.

Ferraresi, Rodolfo A. "The Question of Shub-Niggurath." *Crypt of Cthulhu* 35 (Hallowmas, 1985), 17–18, 22.

Frenschkowski, Marco. "Hali." *Crypt of Cthulhu* 92 (Eastertide, 1966), 8–11.

————. "The Secret of Leng." *Crypt of Cthulhu* 14, no. 1 (Hallowmas, 1994), 6–7.

Gaiman, Neil. *Only the End of the World Again*. Portland, OR: Oni Press, 2000.

Goho, James. "The Shape of Darkness: Origins for H. P. Lovecraft within the American Gothic Tradition." In *Lovecraft and Influence: His Predecessors and Successors*, edited by Robert H. Waugh, 21–34. Lanham, MD, Toronto, and Plymouth, UK: The Scarecrow Press, 2013.

Goodenough, Arthur H. Correspondence with H. P. Lovecraft (approximately August 30, 1931). http://revelatormagazine.com/from-the-vaults/brattleboro-days-yuggoth-nights/.

Haden, David. *Lovecraft in Historical Context: Essays*. Privately printed, 2011.

———. *Lovecraft in Historical Context: Further Essays and Notes*. Privately printed, 2011.

———. *Lovecraft in Historical Context: A Third Collection of Essays and Notes*. Privately printed, 2012.

———. *Walking with Cthulhu: H. P. Lovecraft as Psychogeographer, New York City, 1924–1926*. Privately printed, 2012.

Haefele, John D. *A Look Behind the Derleth Mythos: Origins of the Cthulhu Mythos*. Odense, Denmark: H. Harksen Productions, 2012.

Harman, Gregory. *Weird Realism: Lovecraft and Philosophy*. Alresford, UK: Zeno Books, 2012.

Harms, Daniel. *Encyclopedia Cthulhiana (Call of Cthulhu Fiction)*. Hayward, CA: Chaosium, 1994.

Hay, George. *The Necronomicon*. London: Corgi, 1980.

Hoefler, Eric. "Lovecraft Rising: Tracing the Growth of Scholarship on Howard Phillips Lovecraft, 1990-2004. " Unpublished thesis, George Mason University (Fairfax, VA). http://erichoefler.com/uploads/research/Lovecraft_Rising.pdf.

Houellebecq, Michel. *H. P. Lovecraft: Against the World, Against Life*. Translated by Dorna Khazeni. London: Gollancz, 2008.

Houston, Alex. *The Language of Lovecraft & Other Essays*. Privately printed, 2013.

Huber, Richard. "H. P. Lovecraft and Easter Island." *Nyctalops* 4, no. 1 (Issue 19, April 1991), 60–61.

Indick, Ben P. "Lovecraft's POEtical Adventure." *Crypt of Cthulhu* 32 (St. John's Eve, 1985), 25–32.

Jeffery, Peter F. "Who Killed St. John?" *Crypt of Cthulhu* 48 (St. John's Eve, 1987), 6–8.

Joshi, S. T. *Dissecting Cthulhu*. Lakeland, FL: Miskatonic River Press, 2011.

———. *The Evolution of the Weird Tale*. New York: Hippocampus Press, 2004.

———. *H. P. Lovecraft: A Comprehensive Bibliography*. Tampa, FL: University of Tampa Press, 2009.

———. *H. P. Lovecraft: The Decline of the West*. Berkeley Heights, NJ: Wildside Press, 1990.

———. *H. P. Lovecraft: Nightmare Countries, the Master of Cosmic Horror*. New York: Metro Books, 2012.

———. *I Am Providence: The Life and Times of H. P. Lovecraft*. New York: Hippocampus Press (2010). 2 vols.

———. *An Index to the Fiction & Poetry of H. P. Lovecraft*. West Warwick, RI: Necronomicon Press, 1992.

———. Introduction to *H. P. Lovecraft in the Argosy: Collected Correspondence from the Munsey Magazines*, by H. P. Lovecraft. West Warwick, RI: Necronomicon Press, 1994.

———. *Lovecraft's Library: A Catalogue (Revised and Enlarged)*. New York: Hippocampus Press, 2002.

———. *The Modern Weird Tale*. Jefferson, NC, and London: McFarland & Co., 2001.

———. *The Rise and Fall of the Cthulhu Mythos*. Poplar Bluff, MO: Mythos Books, 2008.

———. *A Subtler Magick: The Writings and Philosophy of H. P. Lovecraft*. Gillette, NJ: Wildside Press, 1999.

Joshi, S. T., ed. *H. P. Lovecraft: Four Decades of Criticism*. Athens, OH: Ohio University Press, 1980.

———. *Primal Sources: Essays on H. P. Lovecraft*. New York: Hippocampus Press, 2003.

———. *A Weird Writer in Our Midst: Early Criticism of H. P. Lovecraft*. New York: Hippocampus Press, 2010.

Joshi, S. T., and David E. Schultz, eds. *An H. P. Lovecraft Encyclopedia*. New York: Hippocampus Press, 2004.

———. *H. P. Lovecraft: Letters to Alfred Galpin*. New York: Hippocampus Press, 2003.

———. *H. P. Lovecraft: Letters to Rheinhart Kleiner*. New York: Hippocampus Press, 2005.

———. *Lord of a Visible World, An Autobiography in Letters: H. P. Lovecraft*. Athens: Ohio University Press, 2000.

———. *O Fortunate Floridian: H. P. Lovecraft's Letters to R. H. Barlow*. Tampa, FL: University of Tampa Press, 2007.

King, Stephen. "Lovecraft's Pillow." Introduction to Michel Houellebecq, *H. P. Lovecraft: Against the World, Against Life*. London: Weidenfeld & Nicholson, 2006.

Leiber, Fritz, Jr. "A Literary Copernicus." In *Something About Cats and Other Pieces*, edited by August Derleth, 290–303. Sauk City, WI: Arkham House Publishers, 1949.

———. "Through Hyperspace with Brown Jenkin: Lovecraft's Contribution to Speculative Fiction." In *The Dark Brotherhood and Other Pieces*, by H. P. Lovecraft and Divers Hands, 164–78. Sauk City, WI: Arkham House Publishers, 1966.

Levy, Maurice. *Lovecraft A Study in the Fantastic*. Translated by S. T. Joshi. Detroit: Wayne State University Press, 1988.

Livesey, T. R. "Dispatches from the Providence Observatory: Astronomical Motifs and Sources in the Writings of H. P. Lovecraft." *Lovecraft Annual* 2 (2008), 3–87.

———. "Green Storm Rising: Lovecraft's Roots in Invasion Literature." In *Lovecraft and Influence: His Predecessors and Successors*, edited by Robert H. Waugh, 83–94. Lanham, MD, Toronto, and Plymouth, UK: Scarecrow Press, 2013.

Lord, Bruce. "The Genetics of Horror: Sex and Racism in H. P. Lovecraft's Fiction." http://www.contrasoma.com/writing/lovecraft.html.

Loucks, Donovan K. "Antique Dreams: Marblehead and Lovecraft's Kingsport." *Lovecraft Studies* 42/43 (Autumn 2001), 45–51.

Lovecraft: A Symposium. Panelists: Fritz Leiber, Robert Bloch, Sam Russell, Arthur Jean Cox, Leland Sapiro. Annotations by August Derleth. Privately printed: Riverside Quarterly, 1963.

Lovett-Graff, Bennett. "Shadows over Lovecraft: Reactionary Fantasy and Immigrant Eugenics." *Extrapolation* 38, no. 3 (Fall 1997), 175–92.

Mabbott, Thomas Ollive. Review of *The Outsider and Others*. *American Literature* 12, no. 1 (March 1940), 136.

Mariconda, Steven J. "Tightening the Coil: The Revision of 'The Whisperer in Darkness.'" *Lovecraft Studies* 32 (Spring 1995), 12–17.

Marten, Robert D. "Arkham Country: In Rescue of Lost Searchers." *Lovecraft Studies* 39 (Summer 1998), 1–20.

Martin, Sean Elliot. *H. P. Lovecraft and the Modernist Grotesque*. Privately printed, 2008.

Migliore, Andrew, and John Strysik. *Lurker in the Lobby: A Guide to the Cinema of H. P. Lovecraft*. Portland and San Francisco: Night Shade Books, 2006.

Mosig, Dirk W. "H. P. Lovecraft: Myth-Maker." *Whispers* 3, no. 1 (December 1976), 48–55.

Mosig, Yōzan Dirk W. *Mosig At Last: A Psychologist Looks at H. P. Lovecraft*. West Warwick, RI: Necronomicon Press, 1997.

Murray, Chris, and Kevin Corstorphine. "Co(s)mic Horror." In *New Critical Essays on H. P. Lovecraft*, edited by David Simmons, 57–92. New York: Palgrave Macmillan, 2013.

Murray, Will. "Behind the Mask of Nyarlathotep." *Lovecraft Studies* 25 (Fall 1991), 25–29.

———. "The Dunwich Chimera and Others: Correlating the Cthulhu Mythos." *Lovecraft Studies* 3, no. 1 (Spring 1984), 10–24.

———. "In Search of Arkham Country." *Lovecraft Studies* 5, no. 2 (Fall 1986), 54–67.

———. "In Search of Arkham Country Revisited." *Lovecraft Studies* 19/20 (Fall 1989), 65–69.

Oates, Joyce Carol. "The King of Weird." *New York Review of Books*, October 31, 1996.

Owens, P. S. "The Mirror in the House: Looking at the Horror of Looking at the Horror." *Lovecraft Studies* 42/43 (Autumn 2001), 70–73.

Pearsall, Anthony Brainard. *The Lovecraft Lexicon: A Reader's Guide to Persons, Places, and Things in the Tales of H. P. Lovecraft*. Tempe, AZ: New Falcon Publications, 2005.

Petersen, Sandy. *S. Petersen's Field Guide to Cthulhu Monsters: A Field Observer's Handbook of Preternatural Entities*. Hayward, CA: Chaosium, 1988.

Pohl, Frederick. *Necronomicon (Call of Cthulhu)*. Hayward, CA: Chaosium, 2002.

Price, Robert M. "A Critical Commentary on the *Necronomicon*," *Crypt of Cthulhu* 58 (Lammas, 1988), 8.

———. "Demythologizing Cthulhu." *Lovecraft Studies* 3, no. 1 (Spring 1984), 3–9, 24.

———. "Is Abdul Alhazred Still Alive?" *Crypt of Cthulhu* 7 (Lammas, 1982), 31–32.

———. "Lovecraft's 'Artificial Mythology.'" In *An Epicure in the Terrible: A Centennial Anthology of Essays in Honor of H. P. Lovecraft*, edited by David E. Schultz and S. T. Joshi, 259–68. New York: Hippocampus Press, 2011.

———. "The Old Ones' Promise of Eternal Life." *Nyctalops* 3, no. 3 (Issue 17, June 1982), 4–11.

———. "Two Biblical Curiosities in Lovecraft." *Lovecraft Studies* 7, no. 1 (Spring 1988), 12–13, 18.

———. "You Fool! Loveman Is Dead!" *Crypt of Cthulhu* 98 (Eastertide, 1998), 16–21.

Quinn, Dennis. "Endless Bacchanal: Rome, Livy, and Lovecraft's Cthulhu Cult." *Lovecraft Annual* 5 (2011), 188–215.

Rawlik. "History of the Miskatonic Valley, Part One." *Crypt of Cthulhu* 19, no. 2 (Eastertide, 2000), 21–28.

Rodionoff, Hans. *Lovecraft*. New York: Vertigo, 2004.

St. Armand, Barton Levi. *The Roots of Horror in the Fiction of H. P. Lovecraft*. Elizabethtown, NY: Dragon Press, 1977.

———. "Facts in the Case of H. P. Lovecraft." *Rhode Island History* 31, no. 1 (February 1972), 3–19.

———. "The Source for Lovecraft's Knowledge of Borellus in *The Case of Charles Dexter Ward*." *Nyctalops* 13 (May 1977), 16–17.

Schultz, David E. "'The Thing in the Moonlight': A Hoax Revealed." *Crypt of Cthulhu* 53 (Candlemas, 1988), 12–13.

———. "Who Needs the 'Cthulhu Mythos'?" In *A Century Less a Dream: Selected Criticism on H. P. Lovecraft*, edited by Scott Connors. Holicong, PA: Wildside Press, 2002. The essay originally appeared in *Lovecraft Studies* 5, no. 2 (Fall 1986), 43–53, in slightly different form.

Schultz, David E., and S. T. Joshi, eds. *An Epicure in the Terrible: A Centennial Anthology of Essays in Honor of H. P. Lovecraft*. New York: Hippocampus Press, 2011.

———. *Essential Solitude: The Letters of H. P. Lovecraft and August Derleth*. New York: Hippocampus Press, 2013. 2 vols.

———. *Lovecraft*. New York: Hippocampus Press, 2011.

Schweitzer, Darrell. *The Dream Quest of H. P. Lovecraft*. San Bernardino, CA: Borgo Press, 1978.

———. *Lovecraft in the Cinema*. Privately printed, 1975.

———. "Lovecraft's Debt to Lord Dunsany." In *Lovecraft and Influence: His Predecessors and Successors*, edited by Robert H. Waugh, 55–68. Lanham, Toronto, and Plymouth, UK: The Scarecrow Press, 2013.

———. *Windows of the Imagination*. Berkley Heights, NJ: Wildside Press, 1999.

Schweitzer, Darrell, ed. *Essays Lovecraftian*. Baltimore: T-K Graphics, 1976.

Shea, J. Vernon. *H. P. Lovecraft: The House and the Shadows*. New York: Necronomicon Press, 1982.

Shreffler, Philip A. *The H. P. Lovecraft Companion*. Westport, CT, and London: Greenwood Press, 1977.

Smith, Don G. *H. P. Lovecraft in Popular Culture: The Works and Their Adaptations in Film, Television, Comics, Music and Games*. Jefferson, NC, and London: McFarland & Co., 2006.

Spence, Lewis. *Encyclopedia of the Occult*. London: Bracken Books, 1994.

Stefans, Brian Kim. "Let's Get Weird: On Graham Harman's H. P. Lovecraft." *Los Angeles Review of Books*, April 13, 2013. http://lareviewofbooks.org/article.php?type=&id=1556&fulltext=1&media=#article-text-cutpoint.

Szumskyj, Ben S. J., and S. T. Joshi, eds. *Fritz Leiber and H. P. Lovecraft: Writers of the Dark*. Holicong, PA: Wildside Press, 2003.

Taylor, Justin. "'A Mountain Walked or Stumbled': Madness, Apocalypse, and H. P. Lovecraft's 'The Call of Cthulhu.'" *The Modern Word*, 2004. http://www.themodernword.com/scriptorium/lovecraft_taylor.pdf.

Tierney, Richard L. "The Derleth Mythos." In *HPL: A Tribute to Howard Phillips Lovecraft*, edited by Meade Frierson III and Penny Frierson, 53. Birmingham, AL: The Editors, 1972, 1975.

———. "When the Stars Are Right." In *Discovering H. P. Lovecraft*, edited by Darrell Schweitzer, 67–71. Holicong, PA: Wildside Press, 2001.

Tyson, Donald. *The Dream World of H. P. Lovecraft*. Woodbury, MN: Llewellyn Publications, 2010.

———. *The 13 Gates of the Necronomicon*. Woodbury, MN: Llewellyn Publications, 2010.

Wallace, Bill. "The Untravelled Road 'Round Arkham." In *Essays Lovecraftian*, edited by Darrell Schweitzer, 76–79. Baltimore: T-K Graphics, 1976.

Waugh, Robert H. "Lovecraft's Rats and Doyle's Hound: A Study in Reason and Madness." *Lovecraft Annual, no. 7* (2013), 60–74.

———. *The Monster in the Mirror: Looking for H. P. Lovecraft*. New York: Hippocampus Press, 2006.

———. *A Monster of Voices: Speaking for H. P. Lovecraft*. New York: Hippocampus Press, 2011.

Weinberg, Robert. "H. P. Lovecraft and Pseudomathematics." In *Discovering H. P. Lovecraft*, edited by Darrell Schweitzer, 88–91. Holicong, PA: Wildside Press, 2001.

———. *The Weird Tales Story*. Berkeley Heights, NJ: Wildside Press, 1999.

Wetzel, George T. "The Cthulhu Mythos: A Study." In *H. P. Lovecraft: Four Decades of Criticism*, edited by S. T. Joshi, 79–95. Athens, OH: Ohio University Press, 1980.

Wilson, Edmund. "Mr. Holmes, They Were the Footprints of a Gigantic Hound!" *The New Yorker*, February 17, 1945.

———. "Oo, Those Awful Orcs." *The Nation*, April 14, 1956.

———. "Tales of the Marvelous and the Ridiculous." *The New Yorker*, November 24, 1945. Reprinted in Wilson's *Classics and Commercials: A Literary Chronicle of the Forties*. New York: Farrar, Straus, 1950.

Zanger, Jules. "Poe's "Endless Voyage: *The Narrative of Arthur Gordon Pym*." *Papers on Language and Literature 22, no. 3* (Summer 1986): 276–83.

GENERAL

Allen, Richard H. *Star Names: Their Lore and Meaning.* Mineola, NY: Dover Publications, 1963.

Amundsen, Roald. *The South Pole.* Translated by A. G. Chater. London: John Murray, 1913. 2 vols.

Arenstein, Joseph. *Austria at the International Exhibition of 1862.* Vienna: Imperial Court and State Printing-Office, 1862.

Beck, Jane C. *Vermont Recollections.* Maine Folklife Center, Department of Anthropology, University of Maine, 1995.

Belcher, Hillary, and Erica Swale. "To Catch a Falling Star." *Folklore* 95, no. 2 (1984): 210–20.

Birkhead, Edith. *The Tale of Terror: A Study of the Gothic Romance.* London: Constable & Co., 1921.

Brewer, E. Cobham. *Dictionary of Phrase and Fable.* Philadelphia: Henry Altemus, 1894.

Brush, Stephen G. "Early History of Selenogony." In *Origin of the Moon,* edited by W. K. Hartmann, R. J. Phillips, and G. J. Taylor, 3–15. Houston: Lunar & Planetary Institute, 1986.

Calmet, Augustine. *The Phantom World; or, the Philosophy of Spirits, Apparitions, &c.* Translated by the Rev. Henry Christmas. London: Richard Bentley, 1850. 2 vols.

Campbell, Joseph. *The Masks of God.* Vol. 4: *Creative Mythology.* New York: Penguin, 1991.

Carlson, Elof Axel. *The Unfit: A History of a Bad Idea.* Cold Spring Harbor, NY: Cold Spring Harbor Laboratory Press, 2001.

Chace, Henry R. *Owners and Occupants of the Houses, Lots, and Shops in the Town of Providence Rhode Island in 1798.* Providence: Privately printed, 1914.

Clauson, J. Earl. *These Plantations.* Providence: Roger Williams Press, 1937.

Cohen, Charles Lloyd. *God's Caress: The Psychology of Puritan Religious Experience.* New York: American Council of Learned Societies E-book Project, 2001.

Coleridge, Samuel Taylor. Review of *The Monk.* Reproduced in *The Norton Anthology of English Literature,* 8th Ed., edited by Stephen Greenblatt and M. H. Abrams, 603–6. New York: W. W. Norton, 2006.

Collections of the Rhode Island Historical Society. Providence: Printed by John Miller, 1827.

Crane, Charles Edward. *Pendrift.* Brattleboro, VT: Stephen Daye Press, 1931.

Dalley, Stephanie. *The Mystery of the Hanging Garden of Babylon: An Elusive World Wonder Traced.* New York: Oxford University Press, 2013.

Daniels, Les. *Living in Fear: A History of Horror in the Mass Media.* New York: Scribner, 1975.

Dunlap, William. *History of the Rise and Progress of the Arts of Design in the United States.* New York: George P. Scott & Co., 1834.

Dunsany, Lord. *Patches of Sunlight.* London: William Heinemann, 1938.

———. *Tales of War.* Boston: Little, Brown, 1919.

Encyclopædia Britannica. 11th ed. New York: The Encyclopædia Britannica Company, 1910.

Encyclopædia Britannica. 9th ed. The R. S. Peale Reprint. Chicago: The Werner Company, 1893.

Fell-Smith, Charlotte. *John Dee.* London: Constable & Co., 1909.

Field, Edward. *Manual of the Rhode Island Society of the Sons of the American Revolution.* Central Falls, RI: E. L. Freeman & Sons, 1800.

Field, Edward, ed. *State of Rhode Island and Providence Plantations at the End of the Century.* Boston and Syracuse: Mason Publishing Company, 1902. 2 vols.

Finger, Stanley. *Origins of Neuroscience.* New York: Oxford University Press, 1994.

Flint, R. W., ed. *Let's Murder the Machine: Selected Writings/F. T. Martinetti.* Translated by R. W. Flint and Arthur A. Coppotelli. Los Angeles: Sun & Moon Press, 1991.

Forbes, B. C. "Edison Working on How to Communicate with the Next World." *American Magazine,* October 1920.

Fort, Charles. *The Complete Books of Charles Fort.* New York: Dover Publications, 1974. Contains *Book of the Damned, Lo!, Wild Talents,* and *New Lands.*

Gardner, Martin. *Did Adam and Eve Have Navels? Debunking Pseudoscience.* New York: W. W. Norton, 2001.

Gibbon, Edward. *The History of the Decline and Fall of the Roman Empire.* Edited by H. H. Milman. New York: Harper & Bros., 1879. 6 vols.

Ginzburg, Carlo. *Ecstasies: Deciphering the Witches' Sabbath.* Translated by Raymond Rosenthal. Chicago: University of Chicago Press, 2004.

Goodwin, Joscelyn. *Arktos: The Polar Myth in Science, Symbolism, and Nazi Survival.* Kempton, IL: Adventures Unlimited Press, 1996.

Goulart, Ron. *An Informal History of the Pulp Magazines.* New York: Ace Books, 1973.

Greene, Welcome Arnold. *The Providence Plantations for Two Hundred and Fifty Years: An Historical Review of the Foundation, Rise, and Progress of the City of Providence.* Providence: J. A. & R. A. Reid, 1886.

Haefele, John D. *August Derleth Redux: The Weird Tale, 1930–1971.* Odense, Denmark: H. Harksen Productions, 2009.

Henderson, Susan R., "Architecture and Theosophy: An Introduction." *Architronic* 7, no. 2 (1998). http://corbu2.caed.kent.edu/architronic/v8n1/v8n102.pdf.

Heschel, Abraham Joshua. *The Prophets.* New York: Harper Perennial, 2001.

Homer. *The Iliad.* Translated by Robert Fagles. New York: Penguin, 1991.

———. *The Odyssey.* Translated by A. T. Murray. Cambridge, MA: Harvard/Loeb Classical Library, 1919.

Hornig, Charles D. *The Fantasy Fan, The Fans' Own Magazine: September 1933–February 1935*. Facsimile by Lance Thingmaker, 2010.

Howard-Bury, Charles K. *Mount Everest: The Reconnaissance, 1921*. New York: Longmans, Green & Co., 1922.

James, Edward, and Farah Mendelsohn, eds. *The Cambridge Companion to Fantasy Literature*. Cambridge: Cambridge University Press, 2012.

Jeans, James Hopwood. *The Universe Around Us*. New York: Macmillan, 1929.

"John George Bartholomew and the Naming of Antarctica." *Cairt*, Newsletter of the Scottish Maps Forum, Issue 13. National Library of Scotland, July 2008. http://www.nls .uk/media/1008031/cairt13.pdf.

Johnson, P. R. *Johnson's Business and Professional Directory of Providence, etc*. P. R. Johnson, 1901.

Joshi, S. T. *Unutterable Horror: A History of Supernatural Fiction*. Hornsea, England: PS Publishing, 2012. 2 vols.

———. *The Weird Tale*. 1990; reprint, Holicong, PA: Wildside Press, 2003.

Kimball, Gertrude S. *Pictures of Rhode Island in the Past, 1642–1833*. Providence: Preston & Rounds Co., 1900.

———. Kimball, Gertrude S. *Providence in Colonial Times*. New York: Houghton Mifflin, 1912.

King, Stephen. *Just After Sunset*. New York: Pocket Books, 2009.

Lepsius, Richard. *Discoveries in Egypt, Ethiopia and the Peninsula of Sinai in the Years 1842–1845*. Cambridge: Cambridge University Press, 2010.

Lescarboura, Austin C. "Edison's Views on Life After Death." *Scientific American*, October 1920.

Lévi, Eliphas. *The Mysteries of Magic: A Digest of the Writings of Eliphas Lévi*. Translated and edited by Arthur Edward Waite. London: George Redway, 1886.

———. *The Ritual of Transcendantal Magic*. Translated by Arthur Edward Waite. London: Rider & Company, 1896.

Lichauco, Marcial P., and Moorfield Storey. *The Conquest of the Philippines by the United States, 1898–1925*. New York: Putnam, 1926.

Macdonald, D. L., and Kathleen Scherf, eds. *The Vampyre and Ernestus Berchtold; or, The Modern Oedipus: Collected Fiction of John William Polidori*. Toronto: University of Toronto Press, 1994.

McGhee, Robert. *The Last Imaginary Place: A Human History of the Arctic World*. Chicago: University of Chicago Press, 2007.

McNamara, Patrick H. *Nightmares: The Science and Solution of Those Frightening Visions During Sleep (Brain, Behaviour, and Evolution)*. Westport, CT: Praeger, 2008.

Montgomery, Michelle C. "The Modernization of the Salon of the Société Nationale." *Apollo: The International Magazine for Collectors*, October 2003.

Munger, F. M. "A Jack in the Box: An Account of the Strange Performances of the Most Wonderful Island in the World." *National Geographic*, February 1909.

Nash, Henry Sylvester. *Genesis of the Social Conscience: The Relation Between the Establishment of Christianity in Europe and the Social Question.* New York: Macmillan, 1897.

Pernick, Martin S. *The Black Stork: Eugenics and the Death of "Defective" Babies in American Medicine and Motion Pictures Since 1915.* New York: Oxford University Press, 1999.

Philbrick, Nathaniel. *Sea of Glory.* New York: Penguin, 2004.

Pigafetta, Filippo. *Vera Descriptio Regni Africani, Quod Tam Ab incolis Quam I Vistanis Congus appellatur.* http://books.google.com/books?id=JM5—2AuRFoC&printsec=frontcover&dq=pigafetta+regni+africani&hl=en&sa=X&ei=SuLVUZj4F6iQigKI8oHoDg&ved=0CC0Q6AEwAA.

Pliny the Elder. *Naturalis Historia.* Translated by Philemon Holland, 1601. London: Privately printed for the Wernerian Club, 1847–48. 37 vols.

Prerau, David. *Seize the Daylight: The Curious and Contentious Story of Daylight Saving Time.* New York: Thunder's Mouth Press, 2005.

Punter, David. *The Literature of Terror: A History of Gothic Fictions from 1765 to the Present Day.* London: Longman, 1996. 2 vols.

Putnam, George R., "Hidden Perils of the Deep," *National Geographic*, September 1909.

Radford, Edwin, and Mona A. Radford. *Encyclopædia of Superstitions.* New York: Philosophical Library, 1949.

Railo, Eino. *The Haunted Castle: A Study of the Elements of English Romanticism.* London: George Routledge & Sons, 1927.

Randi, James. *Flim-Flam! The Truth About Unicorns, Parapsychology, and Other Delusions.* New York: Lippincott & Crowell, 1980.

Rice, Patty Jo. "Beginning with Candle Making: A History of the Whaling Museum" *Historic Nantucket*, Summer 1998.

Röhl, John C. G. *Wilhelm II: The Kaiser's Personal Monarchy, 1888–1900.* Translated by Sheila de Bellaique. Cambridge: Cambridge University Press, 2004.

Scarborough, Dorothy. *The Supernatural in Modern English Fiction.* New York and London: Putnam, 1917.

Scoresby, William. *An Account of the Arctic Regions and Northern Whale-Fishery.* London: Archibald Constable & Co., 1820.

Simmons, William S. *Spirit of the New England Tribes: Indian History and Folklore, 1620–1984.* Hanover, NH: University Press of New England, 1986.

Slafter, Edmund F. *John Checkley; or, the Evolution of Religious Tolerance in Massachusetts Bay.* Boston, 1897. http://www.archive.org/stream/johncheckleyorev01slaf#page/n9/mode/2up.

Spence, Lewis. *Encyclopedia of the Occult.* London: Bracken Books, 1994.

Spoto, Donald. *The Kindness of Strangers: The Life of Tennessee Williams.* New York: Da Capo Press, 1985.

Staples, William Read. *Annals of the Town of Providence*. Providence: Knowles & Vose, 1843.

Thoreau, Henry David. *The Maine Woods*. Introduction by Edward Hoagland. New York: Penguin, 1988.

Upham, Charles W. *Salem Witchcraft*. Boston: Wiggin & Lunt, 1867. 2 vols.

Waite, Arthur Edward. *Lives of Alchemystical Philosophers Based on Materials Collected in 1815*. London: George Redway, 1888.

Weinberg, Robert E. *The* Weird Tales *Story*. Berkeley Heights, NJ: Wildside Press, 1999.

Wilkinson, William. *An Account of the Principalities of Wallachia and Moldavia, with Various Political Observations Relating to Them*. London: Longman, Hurst, Rees, Orme & Brown, 1820.

Wolf, Norbert. *The Art of the Salon: The Triumph of 19th-Century Painting*. Munich, London, New York: Prestel, 2012.

Woodward, Walter W. *Prospero's America: John Winthrop, Jr., Alchemy, and the Creation of New England Culture (1606–1676)*. Chapel Hill: University of North Carolina Press, 2010.

Wright, Marion I., and Robert J. Sullivan. *The Rhode Island Atlas*. Providence: Rhode Island Publications Society, 1982.

Acknowledgements

PREPARATION OF A book such as this requires two kinds of assistance: research and inspiration. The breadth of the research reflected here would not have been possible in pre-Internet days, but, as always, I have relied heavily upon the kindness of strangers in obtaining books, journals, pictures, and other material. The staff of the Malibu Public Library was essential, as usual, and a multitude of booksellers put up with my inquiries about obscure editions, lost issues, and missing pictures. Jason Eckhardt and Stefan Dziemianowicz kindly made copies of various materials for me. Peter Horrocks, a longtime friend and now curator of the essential John Hay Collection at Brown University, was also very supportive. Will Hart and Donovan K. Loucks went far out of their way to provide me with photographs used throughout the book; Donovan even took new ones when he found the old photos unsatisfactory. S. T. Joshi's work deserves special mention: His indices and guides to Lovecraft's output, collection of HPL's *Selected Letters*, and monumental biography *I Am Providence*, as well as numerous essays and books on Lovecraft's life and writings, were crucial to the undertaking. In addition, he kindly provided me with the latest version of the definitive text of the stories, adopted throughout except where noted, and patiently answered many questions about the text. Peter Cannon not only went out of his way to track down missing material for me, he provided wise and helpful comments on the foreword. Pals Leah Moore and John Reppion got excited about the project and sold Leah's father, Alan, on joining the team, to my great delight.

Inspiration came from my usual sources: my editor, Bob Weil, and the wonderful team at Liveright/W. W. Norton, including Will Menaker, Phil Marino, Jo Anne Metsch, Anna Oler, Peter Miller, and Albert Tang; my consulting editor-researcher, Janet Byrne; my agent, Don Maass; my lawyer and friend Jonathan Kirsch; my longtime Sherlockian friends Andy Peck, Jerry Margolin, and Mike Whelan, constant cheerleaders; my various amazing and generous writer friends, including Laurie R. King, Nancy Holder, Cornelia Funke, and horror scholars Rocky Wood and Lisa Morton; my friend and colleague Neil Gaiman, who always reaches for the stars and shows us how to follow; my dear friend Laura Caldwell, who has read and criticized more of my work than I ever had any right to expect; my children, Matt, Wendy, Stacy, Evan, and Amanda, and especially, as always, *the* woman, my wife, Sharon, who never quite understood why I wanted to write about Lovecraft but who dauntlessly proofread every story and never flagged in her support and enthusiasm for the project.

—LESLIE S. KLINGER
Malibu, Spring 2013